THE TUBA
Source Book

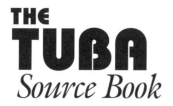

THE TUBA
Source Book

Compiled and Edited by
R. Winston Morris and
Edward R. Goldstein

Indiana University Press
Bloomington • Indianapolis

The paper used in this publication meets the minimum
requirements of American National Standard for Information Sciences—Permanence of Paper for Printed Library
Materials, ANSI Z39.48–1984.

(∞)™

Manufactured in the United States of America

Library of Congress Cataloging-in-Publication Data

The tuba source book / compiled and edited by R.
Winston Morris and Edward R. Goldstein.
    p.   cm.
    Includes bibliographical references, discographies, and
indexes.
    ISBN 0–253–32889–6
    1. Tuba. 2. Tuba—Bibliography. 3. Tuba music—Bibli-
ography. 4. Tuba music—Discography. I. Morris, R.
Winston. II. Goldstein, Edward R.
ML970.T83 1995
788.9'8—dc20   94-48097
1 2 3 4 5 00 99 98 97 96   MN

CONTENTS

FOREWORD

Harvey G. Phillips

Information contained in *The Tuba Source Book* (*TSB*) is thorough and definitive. It will be greeted with grateful enthusiasm by everyone interested in the tuba, most especially by professional performers, teachers, serious students, composers/orchestrators/arrangers, and enthusiasts of every age. The cliché "everything you ever wanted to know about the tuba" applies to this collection of facts about the instrument—its evolution and heritage; those who play it, teach it, study it, and compose for it; and those who just plain love it in all its myriad forms and configurations. Serious researchers and inquisitive laypersons alike will surely find that which they seek about the tuba in this text.

As one whose life has been rapturously and professionally dedicated to music and devoted to the tuba family of instruments, I join countless others of the present and future generations who share deepest gratitude to R. Winston Morris, the mentor of this project. He possessed the vision to conceptualize, structure, implement, and supervise the enormous undertaking of collecting, compiling, editing, and finalizing all materials important to a complete accounting of information about the tuba. As senior editor, he spearheaded the effort to select, assign, supervise, and inspire a staff of outstanding editors, contributors, and consultants for every chapter and topic.

In my many years of association with Winston, my admiration for his strength, professional and personal integrity, patience and understanding, knowledge and wisdom has never diminished. More than any other, he has tenaciously maintained commitment, dignity, and purpose for the cause of the tuba and its rightful place in the art of music performance. From the beginnings of Tubists Universal Brotherhood Association (T.U.B.A.), he was a force in formalizing that organization with a charter, by-laws, and a constitution. He championed the policy that membership is open to everyone interested in the tuba family of instruments. He was founder and first editor of the *T.U.B.A. Journal,* the organization's official publication. No one has so consistently and selflessly given of his or her time and expertise to shepherd T.U.B.A. to its present preeminence among peer organizations representing brass instruments.

Given that all prejudice is born of ignorance, *The Tuba Source Book* promises to be an important influence in tempering and ultimately eradicating long-suffering prejudice and misunderstanding imposed on the tuba by a heretofore uninformed public audience.

The Tuba Source Book is a monument to the personal and professional expertise of R. Winston Morris and the most recent of his many efforts to benefit his colleagues and the world of music.

PREFACE

The *Tuba Source Book* (*TSB*) has been 158 years in the making. The purpose of the project is to define the current status of the tuba and document its growth from its original 1835 conception by Prussian instrument maker Wilhelm Wieprecht to July 1993, the closing date for the research for *TSB*.

Two earlier publications that provide a relatively recent basis for comparison, primarily in the area of literature available for the tuba, are *Encyclopedia of Literature for the Tuba* by William J. Bell and R. Winston Morris (New York: Colin, 1967) and *Tuba Music Guide* by R. Winston Morris (Evanston, IL: The Instrumentalist Company, 1973). References will be found throughout *TSB* relating the extraordinary growth in the tuba repertoire since the publication of *Tuba Music Guide*.

However, *TSB* goes much further in documenting the status of the tuba than either of these books, which were primarily devoted to literature. Although the heart of the present publication is the identification of tuba literature, the editors have an equal commitment to documenting other aspects, such as discography, bibliography, biography, history, usage, and equipment.

After twenty years of contemplating and one year of structuring the content of *TSB*, eight editors were assembled to oversee various sections of the project. Twenty-three contributors recognized as having expertise in specific categories were solicited. To ensure as much international participation as possible, forty international consultants (mostly professional tuba artists native to the countries they represented) from thirty-five countries were selected. They supplied information from their countries on all areas of *TSB* consideration; and this information was distributed to the appropriate editors or contributors for incorporation in their final reports.

Most of *TSB* is of a reference nature and provides factual information on the tuba. Several sections, which warrant careful reading, provide a historical perspective that will significantly enhance the understanding of this material. They include the chapters by Clifford Bevan on the history of the tuba, Robert E. Eliason on instru-

ment collections, and James Self on doubling and free-lancing on the tuba. The chapter compiled by Harvey G. Phillips, presenting the thinking on writing for the tuba by twenty-two outstanding composers and arrangers of successful tuba materials, should also be considered required reading for all students of the tuba.

The editors established the cut-off date of July 1993, and later information is generally not included here. In the areas of literature and discography, our major objective was to document materials that have been created and to one degree or another "published." The current availability of these materials was not a primary consideration. Therefore, some of the literature and recordings listed may not be currently available through normal channels, and in such cases, the best source of information concerning the acquisition of such materials is given. Some of these items may be available through large music and record dealers that have accumulated extensive inventories over the years. Other sources for such materials are library systems and the libraries of private individuals who might be willing to share information on out-of-print items.

Music listed in *TSB* generally falls into one of the following categories:

1. Published: includes all music that is currently available through commercial outlets (from large established publishers to smaller private-based publishers).

2. Out of print: includes music that was previously published (distributed) but is now listed as out of print or not listed at all. If the work possibly exists in the holdings of a large music retail dealer or might be accessed through libraries (such as the T.U.B.A. Resource Library or other major private, university, or municipal libraries), it has been included.

3. Manuscript: includes music in manuscript form that is generally being made available by professional composers/arrangers. If the music was ever copyrighted and distributed but is cur-

rently unavailable, it would, for *TSB* purposes, be considered "published" but out of print.

For the most part, manuscripts by students and relatively unknown composers/arrangers that have never been generally available are not included. Only works specifically designated for tuba are listed. Music published for media other than tuba (vocal music, string bass music, trombone, etc.), while perhaps quite useful and appropriate for study on the tuba, has not been included here. The astute reader will notice a major omission in the area of literature. An editorial decision was made very early in the planning stages of *TSB* not to include brass quintet literature. The standard brass quintet utilizing tuba is certainly one of the most important developments in the history of the tuba, but it was felt that this literature could not be dealt with in the comprehensive manner required. This also applies to the discography section.

To the extent that information was available, the following order and format have been utilized in the entries annotating music for the tuba.

1. Composer's name (last name first).

2. Complete title (as it appears on the music).

3. Arranger (arr.)/Transcriber (tr.)/Editor (ed.) (last name first).

4. Publisher/Source (see Appendix E, "Publishers' and Composers' Addresses" for the complete address for all sources).

5. Instrumentation (in the sections "Music for Tuba in Mixed Ensemble" and "Music for Multiple Tubas").

6. Date (copyright date for published works, date of composition for manuscript works, when available).

7. Price (publisher's recommended/suggested retail price, generally expressed in dollars; when possible, as of July 1993).

8. Duration (solos, expressed in minutes as indicated on the printed music or actually timed; collections/compilations, etc., expressed in number of pages).

9. Level (These are general guidelines and are recognized as subjective. Level indications describe attributes and requirements of the music more so than the expected skills of the player.)

Level I: Beginner, up to one year. Limited range, approximately one octave: Bb_1–B(d). Limited rhythmic/technical requirements. No note values shorter than eighth notes, no syncopated rhythms. Music of a tonal nature.

Level II: Intermediate, two–three years of instruction. Range approximately A_1–e(f). Rhythmic/technical requirements involve simple sixteenth-note patterns. Simple, limited syncopated patterns.

Level III: High school, secondary school, pre-college. Range approximately F_1–b(c'). Moderate tessitura. More rhythmic complexity. Extended syncopations, sixteenth-note patterns, triplets, etc. Moderate amount of multiple tonguing.

Level IV: University/college. Range approximately $(Bb_2)C_1$–f'(g'). Higher advanced tessitura. Increased rhythmic complexity/multimetric. Angular melodic lines. Dissonant harmonies/contemporary harmonies. Endurance factors. Introduction to avant-garde techniques (flutter tongue, multiphonics, etc.). Multiple tonguing. Dynamic control and extremes.

Level V: Professional. Total range: (C_3) D_2–b' (c"+). Extended high tessitura. Rhythmic/technical complexity of highest order. Angular lines, large skips in melody. Advanced twentieth-century techniques. Extreme dynamic contrasts.

Combinations: I–II, II–III, III–IV, IV–V.

10. Range. Every note starting with and including C_1 downward may be referred to as a "pedal tone" (obviously relating to the CC tuba). To the extent that optional pitches (as encountered in ossia parts) impact the overall range of a composition, such pitches are presented in parentheses (see staff).

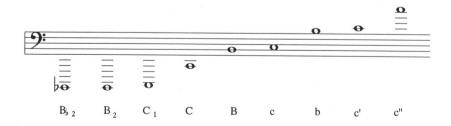

Bb_2 B_2 C_1 C   B   c   b   c'   c"

11. Movements (specific names and/or numbers).

12. Commission (name of commissioning party).

13. Dedication (name of dedicatee).

14. Annotation (short, concise, annotative comments concerning the general nature and style of a composition. Outstanding technical problems and other pertinent information are noted.)

15. Recordings (reference is made to the artist[s] responsible for the recording, and the reader should refer to the main Discography listing "Tuba Recordings by Artist" for complete information).

16. Tape accompaniments. (A few works have taped accompaniments. The reader should also refer to the Discography section on "Recorded Accompaniments.")

17. See: Thompson/Lemke, *French Music for Low Brass Instruments*. Refers the reader to additional information contained in J. Mark Thompson and Jeffrey Jon Lemke, *French Music for Low Brass Instruments: An Annotated Bibliography* (Bloomington: Indiana University Press, 1994). This publication presents a complete listing and short description of French solo and pedagogical materials for various low brass instruments, including the French tuba, which is pitched one octave higher, in C (ut) or Bb (Sib), than the more commonly encountered contrabass tubas (CC or BBb). Note that the solo parts designated for tuba in Sib are transposed. Tubists accustomed to performing music in concert pitch should always utilize the part designated as "Tuba in ut."

18. See: Bird, Gary, ed., *Program Notes for the Solo Tuba* (Bloomington: Indiana University Press, 1994). This book contains extensive program notes, mostly written by the composers, for 88 important works that feature the tuba in a solo capacity.

19. A cross-reference is made when a particular entry is included in more than one chapter of

TSB. For example, works for solo tuba and orchestra are almost always available with piano reduction. Since some works for multiple tubas can be performed by tuba and other low brass instruments, there are cross-references between "Music for Multiple Tubas" and "Music for Tuba in Mixed Ensemble."

When no information is available in a particular category, that "field" is omitted. For the reader who does not know the composer/arranger of a particular composition in the "Music for Tuba and Keyboard" or "Music for Multiple Tubas" sections, there are also listings by title. The literature chapters are not primarily concerned with identifying currently available materials but with documenting all literature that has been generated for the tuba. The chapter entitled "Recommended Basic Repertoire," however, provides a highly selected listing of recommended literature.

The biographical section of *TSB* presents information on as many professional tubists as it was possible to identify within the time frame of the project. Every attempt was made to contact professional tubists internationally and to acquire information on their activities. Unfortunately, some individuals who have made significant contributions to the advancement of the tuba are not listed because they could not be reached or because they failed to return requests for information. The bibliographical entries provide a starting point for future research efforts on the tuba; and the equipment sections document the availability of materials and services of interest to the tubist.

The editors, contributors, and consultants for *TSB* take great pride in presenting this publication, which represents the most comprehensive and definitive research effort ever undertaken on a single musical instrument. The tuba is, after all, an equal partner with all other instruments in the art of making music.

ACKNOWLEDGMENTS

The two major influences in my professional life have been my teacher, the late William J. Bell, and that indefatigable spirit of tubadom, the great Harvey G. Phillips. According to Bill Bell, it is not what you do but how you do it; and I learned from him an immense love and respect for the art of making music. Bill Bell never *played* tuba; he *performed* every time he put the horn on his face. I once wrote that he could make you cry with a C-major scale. My relationship with Harvey, a fellow Bell student, began about twenty-five years ago, when we first met in Chicago and discussed the organization of the Tubists Universal Brotherhood Association. We have been working together on numerous projects since the late 1960s, and his total dedication and enthusiasm have served as a source of inspiration and example for everyone who has had the privilege of knowing and working with him.

To start naming professional colleagues who over the years have provided encouragement and inspiration to keep on keeping on would be dangerous because inevitably someone would be temporarily overlooked, but I must acknowledge the influence of two of my best friends, Daniel T. Perantoni and James Self. Mere words cannot describe the degree of respect and admiration I have for these two long-time colleagues. We have seen many dreams become reality, and this publication documents some of them.

Then there is the "team," the *TSB* team, that is. Put this down as a major labor of love for the most dedicated group of individuals I have ever had the honor of being associated with. This is not a profit-making venture. The editors will never come close to being reimbursed for their efforts and expenses; the contributors generously gave of their time and expertise; and the consultants made themselves available to everyone involved in the venture. There are no egos here, no hidden personal agendas, no great individual acclaim, and no funds exchanging hands. Everyone said yes and spent a year fulfilling a personal and professional commitment to the tuba and to future students of the instrument.

It has been a pleasure and an honor getting to know and work with Edward R. Goldstein. Ed has worked tirelessly and unselfishly on this volume, and he became known as the "good cop" on this project. He was tenacious and unrelenting in pursuing every aspect of *TSB* to its final conclusion. In the twenty years since the publication of *Tuba Music Guide*, many individuals suggested that I bring out a new edition or an update; and I had steadfastly refused to consider it, as the job had grown too big for one person. But Ed was persistent, and we would periodically discuss the possibilities of a new volume. I started formulating the "team" approach, which seemed feasible and practical, and we drew up a tentative table of contents. Then we proceeded to identify individuals who would be not only the most appropriate editors for particular sections but also willing to dedicate the necessary time and effort.

Those individuals are our assistant editors. They each made a total commitment to the entire project, not just to their individual areas of responsibility. Actually, their individual contributions are of such a magnitude as to be considered separate publications. These six talented experts—Ronald Davis, Jeffrey L. Funderburk, Skip Gray, Charles A. McAdams, Mark A. Nelson, and Jerry Young—were on call virtually twenty-four hours a day for over a year. I hereby express my extreme gratitude and profound thanks for the work of these wonderful friends.

To the twenty-six dedicated contributors, who conducted research on specific subjects, go my sincerest gratitude and admiration for a job well done. For the forty international consultants from thirty-five different countries, there were major language problems, 3 a.m. FAX transmissions, and sometimes expensive air mail packages, yet these world leaders persevered and contributed greatly to the ultimate success of *TSB*. I am sincerely indebted to them.

I am grateful to Joseph Skillen, who provided all the musical examples for *TSB* through his talents on the computer; to the English euphoniumist Steven Mead, for information on music distributors in the UK; to Dennis Avey, of Robert King Music Sales, for his cooperation in identifying music publishers and supplying numerous publications for review purposes; to Bert Wiley, of Bernel Music, for assistance in gathering information on recordings and music representative of the British brass band repertoire; to Raoul R. Ronson, president of Seesaw Music Corporation, for supplying a large number of compositions for review purposes; and to my good friend Robert Tucci at the Horn and Tuba Center in Munich for his valuable assistance. I would like to express appreciation to the German euphoniumist Manfred Heidler for helping to identify military musicians in his country. Also, I am appreciative of the cooperation of a number of international music centers, especially the Canadian Music Centre, the Swedish Music Information Centre, and the Scottish Music Information Centre.

I am indebted and gratefully acknowledge the early support and encouragement we received from everyone involved with Tubists Universal Brotherhood Association. Karen Cotton, David Lewis, and then T.U.B.A. president Marty Erickson were behind this project from the first, as were all the other members of the T.U.B.A. Executive Committee.

TSB is a product of electronic technology, and to those who assisted in this regard, we owe a debt of gratitude. On my own campus, Tennessee Technological University, I wish to thank Barbara Goodson and Frank Bush of Academic Computing Support for their assistance in utilizing Internet, the international computer network. This publication was essentially written on Internet. The final manuscript of *TSB* accounted for five megabytes of information on disk. This information was handled flawlessly by my trusty Macintosh SE/30 running System 7 with a total of ten megabytes of combined built-in and virtual memory. My 80-megabyte hard disk drive started getting very pushed toward the end. To the rescue came Jan M. Bodeux, Educational Associate Sales Representative for Microsoft Corporation, who graciously supplied the latest version (5.1a) of Microsoft Word for the Macintosh. The disks I received from the contributors were produced on many types of computer operating systems and with every imaginable word processing program. Thanks are extended to Bonnie L. Orsini of DataViz, Inc., which supplied its MacLinkPlus/Translators™, a program which allows for more than 700 translations from PC to Mac, Mac to PC, and Mac to Mac. The tremendous software incompatibilities encountered in this project could not have been resolved without this program. Finally, as my hard drive was reaching overload status, Fifth Generation Systems, Inc., provided demonstration copies of its AutoDoubler and DiskDoubler programs, which automatically compress information so that one can store twice as much information on floppies or on a hard disk. These programs work in tandem, invisibly, and expertly. I am deeply grateful to these software publishers for their contributions to our project.

I am grateful to Dr. John E. Taylor, chairperson of the Department of Music and Art at Tennessee Tech during the time of this research, for his strong support and encouragement. I am also immensely grateful to my wife, Barbara, for all the support and help on this project and all the others I have engaged in over the past thirty years. Not only has she provided complete moral support and understanding but she has been the best of all possible English teachers. I only wish I could say that I have learned at least half of everything she has tried to teach me about the English language. She really should be listed as an Editorial Assistant, as she has spent an immense amount of time helping with editorial considerations and proofreading. Her red ink and support have been crucial.

Finally, but certainly not least, as this publication would not exist without their commitment, I would like to express my profound gratitude to everyone at Indiana University Press for their interest in this project. It is perhaps almost too logical that Indiana University Press would be the publisher of this document. It was thirty years ago at Indiana University that Bill Bell and I originally conceived and ultimately compiled *Encyclopedia of Literature for the Tuba*.

R. Winston Morris

When I was a student at Peabody Conservatory in the 1970s, my teacher David Bragunier suggested that I pick up a copy of *Tuba Music Guide* by R. Winston Morris. It quickly became a constant companion, for it was one of the few sources of literature for the tuba. I started collecting as much of the music as I could find and used the book as my primary resource. Unfortunately, its listings did not go beyond 1972, and it contained such outdated information as a price of seventy-five cents for the Bach/Bell arrangement of *Air and Bourrée.*

In the mid-1970s I wrote to R. Winston Morris, encouraging him to update his book. He sent back a long and generous note, thanking me for my kind words, but saying that it was doubtful that he would ever continue the research in a formal way. In the early 1980s I finally met Winston at a United States Army Tuba-Euphonium Conference at Ft. Myer, Virginia. I reminded him of our correspondence and again suggested that he update the book. Almost ten years had passed, and the literature had grown exponentially. He again said, "No way," and recommended that I do it myself. A seed was planted.

We saw each other again at the International Brass Congress at Indiana University in 1984. I told Winston that I was indeed interested in pursuing the project myself. He told me enthusiastically to "go for it." Good intentions notwithstanding, the years passed and my schedule continued to get busier and busier. In 1991 I decided that enough was enough. I called Winston and declared that the time had come. I think that my timing was just right. He had mellowed a bit about getting involved with another project and suggested a meeting. We got together in January 1992 and brainstormed for hours. We listed everything imaginable that would be necessary, practical, and impractical to include. We decided that this project should not be an update of *Tuba Music Guide* but a completely new source of information on the tuba. Everything from recordings to repair services to music to symposia was on our initial list. To this day, nothing has been deleted from it.

Winston soon convinced me that no one person could do the job. The amount of information had grown in volume, diversity, and especially in international scope. A second brainstorming session began with names being attached to the various proposed topics. Virtually everyone we asked to work on the proposed book said yes. The talent and creative abilities among the editors were formidable indeed. In May 1992 Winston and I met at the International Tuba-Euphonium Symposium in Lexington, Kentucky, and established a timetable. The editors started assembling information that very afternoon.

Several friends have made my work smoother and more complete. Thanks are extended to Becky Gutin for key-stroking thousands of entries; to Edith Stark, Blanche Stark, and Sylvia Goldstein for stuffing hundreds of envelopes; and to Maurice the mailman for delivering tons of letters and packages. For translation help, I must thank Paul Maillet, Lisa Schultze, and Buddy Wachter. Thanks also go to David Sager and Jim Gregory, two excellent jazz musicians and historians, who helped to fill in the holes from a firsthand viewpoint. Michael Marks suggested early on that a history of the tuba be included—it took a clarinetist to figure that out. Thanks to the hundreds of publishers and composers who responded to our pleas for information, catalogs, and review copies. Of the more than a thousand requests sent out, there was only one refusal of help. That is a real tribute to the industry. Without the support of Towson State University, both the Music Department and the Computer Department, my participation in this project would have been next to impossible.

A special expression of gratitude goes to my wife, Ruthie, and to our daughter, Leah, who day after day asked, "Can you play with me?" Even when she realized that it was going to be another *Tuba Source Book* day, she did not give up. I hope that I can make up for that lost time.

The editors owe it to future generations of performers and composers to document their work on an on-going basis and to make that material available. Although we do not know what form these updates will take, we hope that readers will inform us about new compositions, recordings, festivals, etc. Please send this information to me, at Music Department, Towson State University, Towson, MD 21204-7097.

Edward R. Goldstein

1. A Brief History of the Tuba

Clifford Bevan

The true nature of the tubist, and therefore of the tuba, has tended to be controversial. In the English newspaper *The Observer*, the Sunday edition of April 27, 1980 discussed the results of a National Essay Award for children. A favorite subject had been big business versus small. "It must be boring [it was suggested], spending your whole life playing two notes on a tuba when you can't hear what tune the rest of the orchestra is playing . . . " reported the judges of one teenager's thoughts about being part of a large company. *The Musical Times* of July 1890 reported this incident: "The collector of customs at New York has sent back an English tuba player, whom Barnum had engaged, on the ground of his being a contract laborer. It was held by the authority in question that the mere playing of an E♭ tuba does not make an artist. The collector got pretty near a truth capable of wide application." So, is the tuba the equivalent of a hod, a shovel, or a screwdriver? Is its function essential, irrelevant, or ambivalent? And *why* is the tuba?

The Need for the Tuba

About the year 1600, attention became focused on the lower part of the harmonic structure. With the introduction of *basso continuo* as the favored foundation of instrumental and often other compositions, the provision of a bass line written out in at least as much detail as the parts to be played by the treble melodic instruments became essential if those providing the improvised filling were to conform to a common harmonic pattern. As for the harmonies themselves, now elevated to a position of much greater importance with the decline of the hitherto all-important polyphony, the intervals were calculated from the bass note, which, in its relationship to the root of the chord, also dictated whether that chord was in root position or an inversion.

By the end of the seventeenth century, composers usually specified the instruments they wished to play upper parts, but they remained far more flexible in relation to the bass. From a practical performance point of view, this was fairly reasonable. The average listener tends to concentrate on the melody but is only subliminally aware of the supporting harmonies. So long as the bass part was present, the tone color of the instrument(s) providing it was relatively unimportant. It is much more difficult to differentiate between a quiet bassoon and a quiet cello than between a quiet violin and a quiet flute.

With the decline in the use of *continuo* by the end of the eighteenth century and the gradual establishment of the symphony orchestra, the ear became increasingly accustomed to hearing the orchestral bass line provided by cellos with double basses an octave below and (even in Haydn's earlier symphonies) violas an octave above. The bass part was thus arguably given greater prominence than would have seemed necessary for orchestral balance. As the Classical period approached its zenith and the woodwind section of the orchestra in the years after Mozart's death in 1791 adopted a versatile and complete instrumentation of pairs of flutes, oboes, clarinets, and bassoons, composers found the idea of contrasting the string and woodwind groups increasingly attractive. Meanwhile, the recently introduced horn had already assumed its somewhat ambiguous free association with either woodwind or trumpets, and the latter retained their traditional association with the timpani.

It is often pointed out that developments in orchestration tend to take place outside the concert room: particularly in the theater. Already, Classical composers had found problems with the provision of a sufficiently strong bass wind in works for voices with orchestra. When Haydn, for instance, composed his oratorio *The Creation* in 1798, he included a double bassoon in the score, positioning it below the three trombones commonly found in sacred music of the time in German-speaking countries. This instrument was regularly used in Austrian and German military bands, and it was, of course, precisely in these developing ensembles that the need of an effective bass wind instrument was most severely felt.

There is much evidence that, in pursuit of a strength of bass tone capable of balancing the increasing number of higher wind instruments, directors crammed together a variety of assorted instruments that were more or less capable of playing notes of the appropriate pitch. There are descriptions of bass sections including two serpents and one *buccin* (probably a trombone with a dragon's head) and two contrabassoons. As late as 1835, the year in which the bass tuba was invented, a correspondent of the *American Musical Journal* recommended that the bass section for a "full band" should consist of a serpent and a bass horn. If the bass trombone and bassoon represented the bass part, then (depending on the country of origin) double bassoon and serpent were often expected to provide the sixteen-foot tone, an octave below the true bass. That alone can strengthen the foundation of any ensemble. (Simply doubling, trebling, or quadrupling instruments at any given pitch is an extremely ineffective method of increasing the power of the resultant sound in comparison with the addition of an instrument an octave higher or lower.)

Of the bass instruments, the serpent, since it utilized a lip-reed system of sound production (with a mouthpiece something like that of a tenor trombone, but usually deeper), might lay claim to being the earliest ancestor of the tuba. It is generally accepted that the serpent was invented by Canon Edmé Guillaume of the cathedral at Auxerre, France, around the end of the sixteenth century. As in his probable source of inspiration, the cornett (known since the fifteenth century), the tube was more than 200 centimeters long, and changes of pitch were effected by opening or closing finger holes in the side of the instrument. Its initial use was the accompaniment of plainsong, where its distinctive vocal tone ensured that it played a suitably inferior role to the singers and their liturgical text. However, toward the end of the eighteenth century, the serpent began to find its way into military bands in both Western Europe and North America. Played in a more aggressive style, it was capable of producing a strong rhythmic bass line in the marching band. The portability of this tortuously bent instrument was improved by various developments toward 1800, when types of upright (bassoon-shaped) serpents such as the French serpent basson, basson russe, and English bass horn became common. With or without the addition of keys (most frequently three), the instrument remained in wide use throughout much of the nineteenth

century (although rarely in bands after about 1830), and while composers as eminent as Mendelssohn, Verdi, and Wagner specified serpent in their scores, the last orchestral part composed for it appears to have been Friedrich Klose's symphonic poem *Das Leben ein Traum* (1899).

The ophicleide, a type of brass keyed serpent in bassoon shape, was invented by Halary of Paris in 1817. It was a scaled-up version of the widely popular and effective keyed bugle (of cornet pitch) invented by Joseph Halliday in 1810, with intonation and tone qualities considerably improved by covering every side hole with a key. In consequence, it was possible to position them in far more acoustically correct positions than on the mainly finger-operated serpent. The ophicleide gained favor rapidly in Mediterranean countries, the British Isles, North America, and particularly France, especially through the advocacy of Berlioz, whose considerable numbers of high woodwind and brass were often set against as many as four ophicleides.

Neither the serpent nor the ophicleide was a contrabass instrument. The former, built in C, had as its lowest note C (although it is possible for an expert player to bend the lowest note down through several semitones). C or B♭ ophicleides had lowest notes of B_1 and A_1 respectively. Paradoxically, the intonation, tone quality, and ease of fingering of both instruments show marked improvement as one progresses upward through the range of the instrument(s).

Many mid-nineteenth century composers still found it difficult to decide on the most appropriate instrument to take the role of the bass of the brass. Perhaps Mendelssohn showed the most frustration and (unexpectedly, for a relatively conservative composer) the most inclination to experiment. The ophicleide part in his incidental music to *A Midsummer Night's Dream* is the most renowned in the repertoire; he also used this instrument in *Elijah* and *Lobgesang*. In *Meerestille* and *St. Paul*, he specified serpent; in the *Ouverture für Harmoniemusik*, corno basso; and in the *Trauer-Marsch* for wind band, corno di basso.

Performing musicians were also exercising their minds over this problem. In 1835 Wilhelm Wieprecht, who had overall charge of Prussian military bands, wrote:

> For 10 years now I have been working with
> military bands, and have felt, I suppose, most sorely
> the need of a true contrabass wind instrument.

None of the bass wind instruments, such as: 1) the English bass horn, 2) the serpent (both with an effective compass of at the most two and one half octaves, viz. from treble G down to contrabass C) and 3) the bass trombones (with a compass of 3 octaves from second octave C to contrabass C), could fill the place of the needed contrabass which wind band music demanded.

 . . . The wish, indeed, the burning desire for such a contrabass instrument spurred me on to all kinds of researches, and my reflections at last led me to compare the natural notes which may be found in every brass instrument without resort to artificial means to the segments of a stretched catgut string on any stringed instrument.

This brought me close to my goal, and I owe the invention of the Bass-Tuba to this idea, and this idea alone, for the entire contrivance is built hereupon as to both its compass and its harmonic arrangement. . . .

Wieprecht patented his bass-tuba in Prussia (Patent 9121) on September 12, 1835. (A full translation of the document by Veronica Lawson appears in *The Tuba Family* [London: Faber and Faber, 1978], Appendix A.) Like many a tuba in current use, it was pitched in F and C and had five valves. However, in bore, bell size, and general outline, it looked rather more like an ophicleide than a modern tuba.

Although Wieprecht's was the first instrument to bear the name bass-tuba, it was probably not the first valved brass instrument capable of producing contrabass register notes (i.e., able to play in a range below the established bass instruments, cello and bassoon). The introduction of these bass brass instruments stemmed directly from the invention of the first practical valve, announced on May 3, 1815, in the *Allgemeine Musikalische Zeitung* under the heading "New Discovery." While the mechanism was applied initially to existing instruments (at least one of its two probable inventors, Heinrich Stölzel, was a professional horn player), it allowed the development of a brass instrument utilizing a much longer overall length of tubing—in other words, with the potential to play much lower notes—than any in existence at the time. There is evidence that following the application of the valve to various pitches of horn, trumpet, and alto bugle-horn instruments, a brass instrument called bombardon of lower pitch still (possibly F) may have been in use by some German military bands as early as 1831.

The First Tuba

Details of Wieprecht's bass-tuba are known not only through the patent document but also through the existence of a number of instruments built around the time of its introduction. There are examples, for instance, in the Musik-Instrumenten Museum, Berlin (4456, by Johann Gottfried Moritz), and the University of Oxford Bate Collection (663, by Johann Heinrich Zetsche). Both of these—like the prototype—have Berliner-Pumpe valves. It was the invention of this valve by Wieprecht in conjunction with the Berlin musical instrument maker Johann Gottfried Moritz earlier in 1835 that allowed the construction of the bass-tuba.

Previously existing valves were capable only of controlling a tube of relatively narrow bore. An instrument utilizing the longer length of tubing required to produce lower frequencies needs a relatively wide bore if it is to be viable. (Quite simply, this is to reduce the amount of friction produced by a longer vibrating column of air; a constricted tube makes it impossible for the column to vibrate with sufficient freedom for the practical production of the required low note.) The Berliner-Pumpe, a piston valve, adopted the novel concept of all the piston-passages positioned in one plane, totally avoiding the tortuous twists and turns of the widely used Stölzel valve. In addition, the piston moved the minimum distance and was capable of coping with tubing of a bore sufficiently wide for the requirements of an instrument with a potential lowest note of C_1.

Wieprecht also worked with Moritz in his experiments to determine the dimensions of the new instrument, and it was Moritz who made the prototype. Wieprecht writes in the patent document:

> After numerous experiments very difficult to devise, the aforementioned Moritz succeeded in making me a tube in the prescribed key (F), which despite its extraordinary length and the bulk of its tubing and bell not only was very pure in intonation and very responsive, but also established the exceedingly beautiful timbre of this instrument.
>
> After I had confirmed by testing this tube that all the notes hypothesized . . . were truly present in this tube, I had an attachment made for it which pitched the F tube . . . down to pedal C, and at this pitch, also, the notes computed . . . were exhibited.

F: Open (first *Mutter-Töne*)   B: 5th and 4th valves
E: 1st valve   B♭: 5th and 3rd valves
E♭: 2nd valve   A: 5th, 4th, and 3rd valves
D: 1st and 2nd valves   A♭: 5th, 4th, 3rd, and 2nd valves
D♭: 1st and 4th valves   G: 5th, 4th, 3rd, and 1st valves
C: 3rd valve (as 2nd *Mutter-Töne*)   G♭: 5th, 4th, 3rd, 2nd, and 1st valves

A contrabass instrument with two differently-pitched *Mutter-Töne* [fundamentals of the open instrument] had now been created.

He then describes how he calculated the additional tube lengths to be given by each of the five valves in order "that all major keys found in music, of which there are twelve, could be produced on this instrument." He finished with the above fingering. Wieprecht described the bass-tuba as having "a height of three feet when upright, and a weight of seven to eight pounds; the manner of playing it is as the English bass horn or bassoon, that is, the top two valves with the left hand, the bottom three with the right."

There are a number of similarities with instruments in use today. The very first tubists also had to face the problems encountered by the need to produce some notes with all the valves depressed. Nonetheless, Wieprecht had achieved a historic breakthrough. Perhaps his only real error was to name his instrument *tuba*. The previous instrument with this name was the straight military trumpet used by the Romans. This was a mere 125 centimeters or so in length, and as a trumpet, the profile of its tubing was essentially parallel; whereas Wieprecht's instrument, like modern tubas, was a descendant of the bugle horn, of which the main characteristic is a widely conical profile. Organologists have sometimes been confused, and even more frequently dismayed, by Wieprecht's casual adoption of the name—presumably in an attempt to confer respectability through Classical connotations.

Early Developments

Prototypes of anything are rarely perfect, and there is no doubt that Wieprecht's tubists (of whom there were twelve in the massed band which performed for Berlioz during his visit to Berlin) would have found the lower notes, in particular, not very free-blowing. However, Berlioz himself instantly formed a high opinion of the instrument, declaring the tone "impressively noble, not at all flat like the ophicleide's" and maintaining that it served as a "true bass" to the trombones and trumpets. On returning to Paris, he gave a practical demonstration of his enthusiasm by altering virtually every indication of "ophicleide" in his scores to "tuba."

Inevitably, in a period of expansion in band and orchestral activity, there was no shortage of inventors and craftsmen seeking ways to overcome the instrument's imperfections. The most significant improvements were made by Adolphe Sax, the Belgian who spent virtually all his working life in Paris, where he was actively supported by Berlioz, among others. His greatest achievement in the area of the tuba was to demonstrate the musical advantages of building the various sizes and pitches to carefully calculated matching proportions in order to produce a consistent blend of timbre; through his fine craftsmanship (Sax instruments are always beautifully made) and constant experiment, he calculated the optimum proportions and turned the tuba into an instrument much more like the tuba of today.

It is interesting to note that while Wieprecht stated that he invented the bass-tuba for use in bands, the pitches of his instrument (F and C) came to be associated with the orchestral tuba. Precisely why he chose these two pitches is obvious from his patent document. He was aware that the lowest note available should be an octave below that of the English bass horn and serpent: C_1. Once having established this as his aim, the rest followed.

Sax's normal pitches (from sopranino to contrabass) alternated in E♭ and B♭, a pattern that came to be associated with bands. The British brass band, in particular, conforms totally to these pitches in an instrumentation which, apart from cornets and trombones, consists exclusively of Saxhorns.

Like any self-respecting nineteenth-century inventor, Sax made sure that his own name was permanently enshrined in his innovations, so the tuba, via the bombardon, became *saxhorn*, a name by which it is scarcely ever called, although from time to time publishers (particularly of band music) have printed it on their instrumental parts. Wisely, Sax adopted the Berliner-Pumpe on many of his instruments, at least until the modern Périnet piston valve (invented by the Frenchman Étienne Périnet in 1838) became available. The rotary valve had been invented by the Austrian Josef Riedl in 1835, that most magical of years for tubists, and Sax did from time to time utilize this pattern also. Sax took out his first saxhorn patent in 1843, but it was not until 1855 that his family was complete. However, by 1845 even brass bands in rural England were using "Sax basses" and they were rapidly spreading throughout Western Europe and beyond.

Other makers built and marketed similar instruments under different names, and Sax was constantly involved in costly litigation, but he was not helped by the relatively ineffective patent laws of the time. A limited number of makers did, however, introduce more or less significant developments. Among these were the "Kaiser" instruments (apparently first developed by Cerveny of Hradek Králóve, Czechoslovakia), which maintained a conical profile through the valves and were of significantly larger bore than other instruments of the time. They were subsequently imitated by other makers of many nationalities.

The Establishment of Form

The range of shapes in which the tuba has been built is vast. The original instrument by Wieprecht adopted the approximate form of the Russian bassoon, English bass horn, and (although he possibly did not realize this) ophicleide (substantially that of the bassoon). The reason is easy to understand, particularly when Wieprecht and subsequent instrument manufacturers caused a loop of main tubing to stand away at some distance from the bell tube, thus forming a space in which the valve tubing and tuning slides could be accommodated. It is clear from illustrations of tubas made prior to the 1850s that this was sometimes done in a very arbitrary way. Wieprecht's own tubing conformation appears to be messy but, in fact, manages to avoid too many sharp bends, a highly desirable aim, particularly in brass instruments with longer tubing. Today, however, the overall form is dictated more by choice of valve type than by any other single factor.

In his patent document, Wieprecht was careful to refer to the playing position of the five Berliner-Pumpen: "the top two valves with the left hand, the bottom three with the right." In the bass horn and the bassoon before it, the same requirement for operation by fingers of both hands dictated "the pleasing form" adopted for the new instrument by Moritz. The valves were a type of piston valve, but because they faced away from the player and were mounted on the front of the instrument horizontally, the player's arms encircled the instrument itself, conveniently cradling it and giving it both support and adjustment to the individual player's physique. The bell, viewed from the player's side, therefore, had to face to the left.

When Adolphe Sax decided to adopt the same type of valve for his earlier saxhorns, he used only three, relying on the purchaser to cover the required compass by providing perhaps two players in the band, one on E♭ and one on B♭ bass saxhorn. The valves were therefore mounted vertically to extend above the large branch at the top by the bell. The player normally used the fingers of the right hand to operate these valves and the left hand simply for supporting the instrument. This became the standard format for French instruments adopted in the neighboring countries of Britain and Spain and is still in common use in those parts of Europe. The bell of these instruments had to face the player's right. With the addition of a fourth valve, the left hand was available for its operation, and it was therefore positioned more or less horizontally across the lower end of the branch opposite the bell.

The rotary valve, which was already being used on smaller valved bugle horns during the 1840s, was mounted on the side of the instrument away from the player, whose arm position was therefore identical to that necessitated by the front-facing Berliner-Pumpe on the Wieprecht model tuba. For the same reason, the bell of the rotary-valve tuba also faces left, and additional (up to three) valves can be mounted conveniently for the left hand, facing inward toward the player or outward at will. (When facing inward there is normally only one valve, and it is conveniently placed for operation by the thumb.) The main tubing of the instrument is usually built in parallel branches, but in the smaller sizes (rarely smaller than euphonium) the tubing may be in the familiar European oval form.

When the bell faces left, it is customary to arrange a number of valve tuning slides in such a way that they may be manipulated by the player to assist intonation. This is not possible with right-facing tubas, and, consequently, better-quality instruments normally incorporate an automatic compensating system generally based on that developed by David Blaikley of Boosey in 1874.

There is no strong evidence that tubists in German-speaking countries favored the rotary valve while those in French- and English-speaking Europe preferred the piston valve. It was simply the availability of these particular models that made them familiar to players in these particular countries. While in modern times there has been a wide choice in, for example, Germany and the United States, the United Kingdom still persists in assuming that the upward-facing piston valve is the norm, and rotary valves are only to be used for certain pitches of orchestral tuba, despite occasional experiments earlier in the twentieth century by British manufacturers with rotary valves and front-facing piston valves. Characteristic tuba forms for various ethnic regions have thus been established and continue, in general, to be favored.

Since tubas exist in more commonly recognized shapes and pitches than most other modern instruments, the problems of identifying mutant forms are relatively difficult. However, accepting that the shapes described above constitute the basic forms, the variants remain to be considered. These can be generally classed under two headings: pure tubas built in unusual shapes; and combinations of tuba and other instrument.

Tubas in Unusual Forms

In view of the weight of a tuba (and even a three-valve single E♭ tuba can weigh five kilograms), it is not surprising that at an early stage in the development of this (primarily) band instrument, methods of managing the weight, especially for the marching tubist, were investigated. The helicon, in which the tubing of the instrument is built in circular form, allowing it to rest on the player's shoulder while the bell faces forward, beside, or above the head, first appeared in Russia about 1845 and was built in Western Europe by the Viennese company of Ignaz Stowasser about four years later. The shape was not new; in fact, the Roman buccina featured a bell which rested on the left shoulder and main tubing which passed below the right arm. However, from the 1850s the helicon proliferated throughout Europe, with major brass instrument companies introducing models under trade names like Pelittone (Pelitti, Milan), Sonorophone (Metzler, London), and Jumbo (Higham, Manchester).

The saxtuba was patented by Adolphe Sax in 1849 and was based on the "tuba curva," as depicted on Trajan's Column in Rome. In this, also, the bell faced forward above the player's head. The design was such that the Berliner-Pumpe valves were not readily visible by the viewer, so the impression of a Classical instrument was enhanced. Apart from the use of twelve of the instruments in a massed military band of 1,500 in a Paris ceremony of 1852, their only other appearance was in the stage band of an ill-fated opera by Halévy, *Le Juif errant*, premiered at the Paris Opéra the same year. It is possible that models in E♭ and B♭ existed. (Only one, probably in E♭, remains extant: Metropolitan Museum of Art, New York, No. 89.4.1109.)

The last, and most familiar, instrument in this shape was the sousaphone, designed by Ted Pounder of Conn for Sousa's United States Marine Band in 1898. Although the outstanding characteristic of this model was the relatively large bell diameter, even more startling was the fact that it faced upward; whereas previous helicons had featured forward-facing bells. The upward-facing bell was introduced at Sousa's specific request to diffuse the sound "over the entire band," but for practical reasons it had to be redesigned, and ten years later the familiar form with forward-facing bell appeared. There are examples of the original model in a number of collections in the United States, however (notably the Streitwieser Trumpet Museum in Pottstown, Pennsylvania).

Since the 1960s and the publication of a report detailing the injurious effects of the concentration of weight on the player's left collar bone (the Holton 130 model of the 1930s weighed fourteen and one half kilograms), sousaphones have generally been made with much lighter Fibreglas bells.

Variant forms have, for obvious reasons, been much more popular in the smaller instruments, euphonium pitch and higher, but the snail-shell configuration of the antoniophone was an exception. This instrument, thought to have been pitched in Eb, had its three valves in the center and a detachable bell, which could face either upward or under the arm. It was invented by Antoine Courtois but also manufactured by Sax, and it appeared from time to time toward the end of the nineteenth century. (The Gilmore band featured an Antoniophone quintet in 1889.)

Tubas in Conjunction

Higher pitches of valved bugle horn have regularly been paired with other brass in various types of duplex (for example, euphonium and valve trombone). Practical reasons prevent this approach with the true tuba, as by definition the tuba is generally the only brass instrument of its pitch. However, the possibility of moderating timbre by introducing an unusual element into the sound-generation system was investigated in 1892, when François Sudre patented the sudrephones. This family was made in a range of pitches, including BBb and CC, both with four valves. The instruments were built in ophicleide shape with the valves and branches on one side, along with a cylinder containing a vibrating membrane which could be brought into action at will. The instrument was, in effect, a combination of tuba and kazoo, but with the serious intention of increasing the range of instrumental color available in wind bands.

Adolphe Sax invented at least two types of instrument which were, in effect, modified tubas. The saxotromba's bore was midway between the profile of bugle and French horn and, like the latter, used a funnel mouthpiece rather than the cup mouthpiece of the tuba. The range of instruments covered sopranino to Bb₁ contrabass, each with three Berliner-Pumpe valves. Patented in 1845, they were used for some twenty years, particularly in French cavalry bands, where the player was free to use his left hand to control his mount. A model made later in the century, specifically for performances of Wagner's *Ring* in Paris, had a bell which could be positioned either facing forward (by the player's head) or downward at floor level.

Another instrument with roughly tuba bore but using a funnel mouthpiece was the Cornon, built by Cerveny in both oval and helicon shapes. Instruments in Eb and Bb₁ were produced. These may have inspired the Wagner tuba, another instrument with bore midway between horn and tuba and using a funnel mouthpiece. The *Tuben* are traditionally built in two sizes: tenor in Bb (euphonium pitch) and bass in F (tuba pitch), but more recently models in Bb/F have been introduced. They are consistently oval in shape, always used in sets of four, and played by horn players.

The Establishment of Pitch

The reasons for Wieprecht's choice of the two fundamentals of F and C have been given above; they are explained in his patent document. The F tuba soon became established as the primary pitch for orchestral use in Germany, and there is no doubt that contemporary composers considered this to be the "normal" instrument. Many of Wagner's tuba parts composed prior to the mid-1850s, for example, lie relatively high (though none so high as in the Overture to *The Mastersingers* of 1867). However, following the introduction of the contrabass tuba in C (probably by Cerveny in 1845), Wagner was careful to specify either "tuba" or "contrabass tuba"; he asks for the latter, for example, throughout *The Ring*. With the additional nobility of tone conferred by the large bore, the deeper instrument tended to become standard, while the F was used as players felt appropriate.

The situation differed in other countries. In France, the ophicleide was difficult to oust, despite Berlioz's advocacy of the tuba and his practical support of Adolphe Sax. By the time the tuba became generally available, most of the Berlioz scores requiring a pair of low brass instruments (ophicleides) had already been completed, and it was difficult to substitute a tuba, particularly for the higher of the two parts, which often lies consistently above the bass staff.

A tuba pitched in c (one tone above the Bb euphonium) thus became standard in France by the mid-1840s. Its high fundamental allowed ophicleide parts to be played with ease, and its relatively narrow bore tubing accorded well with French tendencies in the design of other brass (and woodwind) of the time. At the Paris Opéra, a c tuba with a fourth valve, giving a much more useful lower register—which could cope even with Wagner's contrabass tuba parts—was introduced about 1874, and a five-valve c tuba appeared in 1880. Finally, about 1892 Courtois marketed the six-valve c tuba, which was to remain standard in France until after the Second World War. In comparison with the type of tuba favored in other countries, the bore was narrow (the whole instrument was no bigger than a euphonium, although much heavier), the tone could be "stuffy," and the intonation was frequently suspect. Yet, alongside the three narrow-bore tenor trombones expected by French composers up to the middle of the twentieth century, the timbre was not inappropriate. It was really only since the 1960s, when a more universal concept of tuba tone and orchestral sound, generally, was established through the widespread availability of international recordings and equally widespread proliferation of jet-setting conductors, that the French gave up their very individual tuba.

In most parts of the United Kingdom during the nineteenth century, brass instrument practice followed the French lead. Some French companies (e.g., Besson) even set up operations across the English Channel. Certainly, in brass and woodwind generally, the narrow-bore French-style instruments were favored in comparison with the wider-bore German models. Yet the small c tuba did not migrate. Apart from the occasional use of a brass band Eb bass, an instrument built in F with up to five piston valves became standard in the United Kingdom from the early 1860s, when the ophicleide generally disappeared from the orchestra. Alternatively (and here at least lip-service was paid to French practice), the euphonium was used, particularly in lighter music.

The British style of F tuba was not, however, the relatively massive German model, but something much more like a large euphonium with (certainly in the case of the twentieth-century Besson model designed by Harry Barlow of the Hallé Orchestra) quite a large bore. The combination of relatively high fundamental and relatively wide bore resulted in an instrument that could cope with the agile parts which British composers from Elgar onward gave their tubists to play and also the extremes of range which equally characterized their works. The 1960s were a time of change in the United Kingdom, and the larger four-valve EEb tuba was imported

from the brass band. Given an appropriately larger mouthpiece and appropriately adjusted attitude, this still remains the standard professional orchestral instrument, despite a limited number of players favoring imported F, CC, or BBb models.

In addition to the French influence (which is always strongly denied in any connection in Britain), another reason for players' preferring a smaller, lighter instrument was the fact that the majority of professional orchestral tubists had been army euphoniumists. In the United States, on the other hand, the more rational situation was that professional orchestral tubists were more often recruited from among tuba players who had learned their craft in the military. As a result (and also stemming from the strong influence of German-speaking immigrants in the formation of the major symphony orchestras of the United States during the early twentieth century), the large-bore instrument of deep pitch (CC or BBb) became standard. Nonetheless, the immense variety of cultures represented by immigrants resulted in a wider range of tuba patterns in normal use in the United States than in any single European country. It still remains noticeable, however, that the top-facing piston valve instrument (probably in Eb) tends to be restricted to the school and amateur band, while the serious player prefers either the rotary-valve in CC or BBb or its equivalent with forward-facing piston valves (in effect, an identical instrument except for the type of valve). The result is that the typical American composer conceives of the tuba as being a deep instrument with a large sound, and this has been the most universal influence on styles of tuba playing in past decades. There are now only isolated corners of a limited number of countries where this is no longer the case, regardless of the precise pitch or model of instrument used.

Where do we Go from Here in Instrument Design?

The short answer is "Probably not very far." It is true that each month a clutch of new inventions applicable to the tuba is patented. The developments may apply to forms, mechanisms, materials, or accessories. With the exception of utilizing new materials, there has usually been a predecessor. It has all been done before—perhaps not so well, perhaps with less ingenuity, perhaps with no commercial success. Each tiny improvement may make the instrument more acceptable to another few players, enable the standards of performance to improve, or make life more comfortable for the tubist. But in an era when the very nature of the musical material is changing, minds and resources tend to be concentrated elsewhere.

Although Wieprecht may appear to have invented the instrument for altruistic reasons, in reality it was the returns represented by commercial success which encouraged Wieprecht, Adolphe Sax, and a myriad of other inventors since 1835 to spend time and energy investigating the possibilities of improving the tuba. The tuba of today looks remarkably like the tuba of a hundred years ago, and there is a good likelihood that it resembles the tuba of a hundred years hence. Tubists know the differences and similarities, although they may not be obvious to the casual observer. The tuba will not need to change unless the present repertoire of band and orchestra is no longer performed.

2. Music for Tuba and Keyboard
Edward R. Goldstein

There is, as they say, good news and bad news regarding a tuba performing with a keyboard instrument. The good news is that the keyboard adds an infinite palette of colors. The ensemble can take a unison sound on the tuba on a harmonic journey that could be quite limited alone. It is fun to add that extra bit of musical spontaneity, collaborating with another creative mind to create something more than just the sum of both performers' musical contributions. The bad news is that it might not be possible to choose a more unlikely marriage.

The harmonic and acoustical structures of the two instruments are fundamentally different. The tuba is based on the natural overtone system. For the most part, these overtones lie in readiness, waiting for the performer's lips to vibrate sympathetically at the natural acoustical core of each note. Bending them from that core in order to accommodate the acoustical structure of the keyboard instrument means sacrificing a bit of tone quality. It demands a flexibility and a degree of musical integrity that is only learned through frequent collaborations with instruments constructed acoustically unlike the tuba. The temperament of the modern keyboard instrument is an acoustical compromise that spreads the natural intonation discrepancies over the total range of the keyboard, thus allowing the instrument to be as in tune as possible, but ultimately placing every note in a different place from the natural acoustics of a perfect harmonic series instrument such as the tuba.

The two instruments are not meant to come together. The tubist, the only one of the pair that can truly alter the pitch (modern synthesizers notwithstanding), has to take the role of the superior musician and must bear the brunt of making the pair sound in tune. This can, of course, be accomplished by using different valve combinations, adjusting valve slides, or adjusting the aperture, but in the end it needs to be controlled by the ears and the heart, processing the musical stimulus of the collaboration, converting that into a constantly evolving process, and anticipating the eventual combination of tones. The more one plays tuba with a keyboard instrument, the more one will have the flexibility of intonation needed for such a collaboration.

That qualification aside, the state of tuba and keyboard is very good indeed. When William Bell and Winston Morris compiled *Encyclopedia of Literature for the Tuba* in 1967, they listed 388 pieces for "Tuba and Keyboard Collections." In 1973, *Tuba Music Guide* listed 572 pieces. Compare that to the listing in *The Tuba Source Book*—almost 1,900 pieces for tuba and keyboard with new additions arriving daily. They include works by world-class composers like Paul Hindemith, John Williams, Alec Wilder, and Ralph Vaughan Williams. There has been quite an evolution from the time when tubists were limited to arrangements of "Asleep in the Deep" for public performance. In addition to pieces written specifically for tuba and keyboard, this chapter lists works for solo tuba and band or orchestra or for tuba in mixed ensemble if a piano accompaniment is also available. These entries are cross-referenced to the appropriate chapters.

My thanks go to the hundreds of publishers and composers who responded to requests for information about their offerings. Specific thanks go to the international consultants and contacts, particularly Bob Tucci and David LeClair, who provided much information.

Works Listed by Composer

Abt, Franz. *Dear Old Songs of Home*. arr. de Ville, Paul. Carl Fischer Inc. 1906. Out of print. See: de Ville, Paul, *Pleasant Hours,* under "Tuba and Keyboard Collections."

Abt, Franz. *Oh, My Home*. arr. de Ville, Paul. Carl Fischer Inc. 1906. Out of print. See: de Ville, Paul, *Pleasant Hours,* under "Tuba and Keyboard Collections."

Adams. *Holy City*. Neil A. Kjos Music Company. 1958. Out of print. 2:00. II–III. (A_1) D–e♭. No technical problems.

Alary, G. *Morceau de Concours*. Voxman, Himie, ed. Rubank, Inc. 1972. 4:00. III–IV. B♭$_1$–b♭. Opus 57. "For E♭ Bass." Arpeggios, triplets, technical and lyrical playing with bravura. See: Voxman, Himie, *Concert and Contest Collection,* under "Tuba and Keyboard Collections."

Albeniz, I. *Mallorca Barcarola*. arr. Amaz, J. Union Musical Espanola. 1970. 4:00. IV–V. d–b♭' (c"). For "Trombon, Bombardino and Tuba."

Albeniz, I. *Puerta de Tierra Bolero*. arr. Amaz, J. Union Musical Espanola. 1970. 3:30. IV–V. D–a'. For "Fagot, Bombardino, Trombon and Tuba." High tessitura.

Albinoni, [Tommaso]. *Sonate en fa majeur*. arr. Goudenhooft, André. Gérard Billaudot. III.

Albinoni, [Tommaso]. *Sonate en ré majeur*. arr. Goudenhooft, André. Gérard Billaudot.

Alletter, Wilhelm, and Knight, Joseph Philip. *Deep Sea Stories*. Carl Fischer Inc. 1938. $3.50. 1:35. II. A♭₁–e♭. "E♭ or BB♭ Tuba." Easy, accessible solo for the younger player. Uses the tune *Rocked in the Cradle of the Deep*. Would stretch the range of the very beginning BB♭ player.

Ameller, André. *Bamboola*. Gérard Billaudot. 1983.

Ameller, André. *Bassutecy*. Alphonse Leduc Editions Paris. 1984. $5.45. 1:30. II–III. B♭–f'. "Pour Tuba Basse en ut ou Saxhorn Basse Si♭ avec accompagnement de Piano." For French tuba. Melodic writing with a few rhythmic challenges. Includes syncopation, some 32nd notes, and a few eighth-note abbreviations. See review in *T.U.B.A. Journal*, Vol. 18, no. 3, p. 17.

Ameller, André. *Batifol*. Éditions M. Combre. 1983. 1:15. II–III. E–e♭'. "Pour tuba en ut ou saxhorns en Si♭ et piano." For French tuba. Espressivo lyrical section and not too technical playful Allegro section with some syncopations.

Ameller, André. *Belle Province: Hauterive*. Alphonse Leduc Editions Paris. 1973. $8.60. 2:30. II. E♭–e♭'. Cordialement à Jean Arnoult. Andante espressivo. "Pour Tuba en ut ou Trombone Basse ou Saxhorns Si♭ ou Mi♭ et Piano." For French tuba. Moderate tempo, 3/4 time, expressive melody. No rhythms faster than eighth notes. See: Thompson/Lemke, *French Music for Low Brass Instruments*. Also see review in *T.U.B.A. Journal*, Vol. 1, no. 3, p. 6.

Ameller, André. *Dolce Espressivo*. Gérard Billaudot. 1983.

Ameller, André. *Irish-Cante*. Alphonse Leduc Editions Paris. 1977. $11.50. 5:15. IV–V. E♭₁–g'. Cordialement à Paul Bernard Professeur au Conservatoire National Superiéur de Musique. "Pour Tuba ut ou Saxhorn basse Si♭ ou Trombone basse et Piano." For French tuba. Very wide range. See: Thompson/Lemke, *French Music for Low Brass Instruments*. See review in *T.U.B.A. Journal*, Vol. 7, no. 2, p. 20.

Ameller, André. *Ive*. Gérard Billaudot. 1981. 1:45. II–III. G–g'. Andante expressivo. "Pour Bugle et pour Baryton-Tuba ténor Si♭-Basse Si♭ et Piano." French tuba tessitura. Lyrical, mostly scalewise solo.

Ameller, André. *Kryptos*. Hinrichsen Edition. 1958. 5:00. V. G♭₁–c'. En Hommage à Paul Bernard, professeur au Conservatoire National Supérieur de Musique de Paris; Rene Poinsard, professeur au Conservatoire National de Musique Dijon; Maurice Smith, trombone Professor at the Royal College of Music, London. "Etude pour tous les Trombones, ou Tuba, le Saxhorn-basse en Si♭ (B♭) et piano." Wide Range. Muted passages. Includes passages in both bass and tenor clefs. Cadenza passages with complex rhythms. See: Thompson/Lemke, *French Music for Low Brass Instruments*.

Ameller, André. *Logos*. Alphonse Leduc Editions Paris. 1982. $18.25. 6:50. V. E₁–a♭'. "Pour tuba basse ou tuba en Fa ou Saxhorn basse Si♭ et Piano." Very wide range—has ottava basso notes for lower tubas throughout. Strong technique required: double tonguing, wide interval skips, plenty of notes! See: Thompson/Lemke, *French Music for Low Brass Instruments*.

Ameller, André. *Philae*. Gérard Billaudot. 1991. For French tuba.

Ameller, André. *Tuba-Abut*. Éditions Max Eschig. 1975. 5:30. V. (E♭₁) E₁–g'. Cordialement à Paul Bernard Professeur au Conservatoire National de Musique de Paris. "Pour Tuba ut ou saxhorn Si♭ et Piano." Strong technique required: wide interval jumps, wide range, quick tempos.

Ameller, André. *Tuba-Concert*. Éditions Max Eschig. 1952. 4:40. V. D♯₁–c". Cordialement à Paul Bernard Professeur au Conservatoire National de Musique de Paris. Opus 69. "Pour Tuba ut ou Saxhorn basse Si♭." Piano reduction. Written for French tuba. Was published for tuba and orchestra. Very wide range—good showcase. See: Thompson/Lemke, *French Music for Low Brass Instruments*.

Amos, K. *Tuba Compositae*. Boosey and Hawkes, Inc. $13.50.

Anderson, Eugene D. *Concert Piece for Tuba and Piano*. Anderson's Arizona Originals. 1971. See listing under "Music for Tuba and Band." Also see: Bird, Gary, ed., *Program Notes for the Solo Tuba*.

Anderson, Eugene D. *Tuba Concerto No. 1 in B Minor*. Anderson's Arizona Originals. 1971. $25.00. See listing under "Music for Tuba and Band." Also see: Bird, Gary, ed., *Program Notes for the Solo Tuba*.

Anderson, Garland. *Sonata*. Southern Music Company. 1985. $10.00. 12:53 (5:52, 3:26, 3:35). IV–V. A₁–c♯'. In Memoriam Ralph Allen Anderson (the composer's brother). First performed April 25, 1984 at Ball State University by Jeffrey Rideout, tuba, and Garland Anderson, piano. Three movements: Molto Sostenuto/Allegro con brio—Andante Sostenuto—Allegro Amabile. Major work. Good technique required; slurring, sustained playing. Conservative range. Good recital material.

Aranyi, Gyorgy. *Kis Humoreszk*. Hungarian Publication; available from the Tuba Center.

Arban, Jean Baptiste. *Arban's Fantaisie Brillante*. arr. Weber, Carl. J. W. Pepper and Son. 1914. Out of print. See: Weber, Carl, *Nineteen Solos For E♭ Bass with Piano Accompaniment*, under "Tuba and Keyboard Collections."

Arban, Jean Baptiste. *Carnival of Venice in F Major*. arr. Le Clair. Reift. 1993. IV. In preparation.

Arban, Jean Baptiste. *The Carnival of Venice* (*Variations*). arr. Wekselblatt, Herbert. G. Schirmer Inc. 1972. 1:53. III–IV. B♭₁–f. Flowingly. Theme and (two) variations. Chorus and two variations based on Arban's variations, but with notes left out for breathing. Good introduction to the heritage of the tune. See: Wekselblatt, Herbert, *First Solos for the Tuba Player,* under "Tuba and Keyboard Collections."

Arban, Jean Baptiste. *Variations on the "Carnival of Venice."* arr. Domek, Richard. Available from the arranger. 1981. For Skip Gray. See listing under "Music for Tuba and Orchestra" and "Music for Tuba in Mixed Ensemble."

Arban, Jean Baptiste. *Variations on the "Carnival of Venice."* arr. Schmidt and Davis. Western International Music. In preparation.

Arbel, Chaya. *Roundarounds.* Kibutz Movement League of Composers. Recorded by Adi Herschko.

Arensky, A. *Ballade.* Mitegin, V., ed. Moscow: Muzyka. 1969. See: Mitegin, V., *Pieces for Tuba and Piano,* in "Tuba and Keyboard Collections."

Armand, Migani. *Tuba Mosaique.*

Arne, Thomas A. *Air from "Comus."* arr. Little, Donald C. CPP/Belwin, Inc. 1978. $4.00. 2:04. II. B♭₁–e♭. Allegro. Stately air in 3/4 time. A few eighth notes, a few slurs, a few accidentals, otherwise no technical problems. See review in *T.U.B.A. Journal,* Vol. 7, no. 4, p. 31. See also Lamb, Jack, *Solo Sounds for Tuba Levels 1–3, Volume 1,* under "Tuba and Keyboard Collections."

Arutiunian, Alexandre. *Expromt.* arr. Lebedev, A. Military Band Masters Faculty of Moscow Conservatiore. 1971. See: Lebedev, A., *Collection of Pieces for Tuba "Es" and Piano,* under "Tuba and Keyboard Collections."

Ascher, Alice. *Where Art Thou?* arr. Weber, Carl. J. W. Pepper and Son. 1914. Out of print. See: Weber, Carl, *Nineteen Solos for E♭ Bass with Piano Accompaniment,* under "Tuba and Keyboard Collections."

Assafyev, B. *Scherzo.* ed. Melnikov, S. Moskow: Military Band Masters Institute. 1957. See: Melnikov, S., *Pieces for Tuba and piano,* under "Tuba and Keyboard Collections."

Aubain, Jean Emmanuel. *Thème et Variations.* Amphion. 1975. 9:25. V. F₁–b♭'. For French tuba. See: Thompson/Lemke, *French Music for Low Brass Instruments.*

Autran, Alphonse. *Quadrille en Forme de Ronds d'Eau.* Gérard Billaudot. 1990. 3:00. III. E–c'. "Pour tuba et piano." For French tuba. Cute tune with no big technical problems. See: Daniel-Lesur, *Collection Panorama,* under "Tuba and Keyboard Collections."

Baader-Nobs, Heidi. *Bifurcation.* Éditions BIM. 1991. $22.50. 3:53. V. B₁–a♯'. Morceau imposé du Concours International d'Exécution Musicale-Genève 1991. Modern notation, score needed for performance. Wide range. Contemporary performance requirements: flutter tongue, glissandos, improvise timing with given pitches. Recorded by Oystein Baadsvik; Jens Bjorn-Larsen.

Bach, E. *Spring's Awakening* (*Frühlings Erwachen*). Carl Fischer Inc. Out of print. 3:02. III. (F₁) C–c' (d'). Written with E♭ tuba in mind. Typical old-style melodic solo.

Bach, Johann Sebastian. *Adagio.* arr. Hilgers, Walter. Editions Marc Reift. 1990. $7.50. 3:18. IV. A₁–d'. "Für Tuba und Klavier/Orgel." Good transcription with ornamentation included. Some mordents, trills, etc. Good recital material.

Bach, Johann Sebastian. *Air and Bourée.* arr. Bell, William J. Carl Fischer Inc. 1937. $4.50. 3:25. III–IV. G₁–b♭. A standard solo. Two movements: Air *Komm, süsser Tod* (Come, Sweet Death), a very lyrical chorale and bourée (from *Second Violin Sonata*), scalewise, very musical transcription. A couple of harmonic seconds will challenge the young ear. Excellent recital material. See listing under "Music for Tuba and Band." Recorded by Rex Conner; Ronald Davis; Harvey Phillips; Peter Popiel. *Komm süsser Tod* recorded by Karl Megules.

Bach, Johann Sebastian. *Bourée.* ed. Melnikov, S. Moscow: Military Band Masters Institute. 1957. See: Melnikov, S., *Pieces for Tuba and Piano,* under "Tuba and Keyboard Collections."

Bach, Johann Sebastian. *Gavotte.* arr. Swanson, Ken. CPP/Belwin, Inc. 1970. $4.00. 1:27. II. A₁–e. Moderato. In cut time. Fastest rhythm is eighth note. All tongued; some accidentals. Good transcription of classic Baroque solo. Good advanced beginner recital material. See: *CPP/Belwin, Tuba Solos, Level Two,* under "Tuba and Keyboard Collections."

Bach, Johann Sebastian. *Musette.* trans. Dishinger, Ronald Christian. Medici Music Press. 1982. $3.50. 1:36. II. A₁–c. From *Anna Magdalena Bach Notebook.* Transcription of popular Bach melody. Some syncopation, some sixteenth notes, no big technical problems.

Bach, Johann Sebastian. *Musette.* arr. Wekselblatt, Herbert. G. Schirmer Inc. 1972. 1:25. III. B♭₁–f. Allegretto. A few wide leaps both articulated and slurred. Fun, musical tune. See: Wekselblatt, Herbert, *First Solos for the Tuba Player,* under "Tuba and Keyboard Collections."

Bach, Johann Sebastian. *O Mensch, bewein' dein' Sünde gross.* arr. Hilgers, Walter. Editions Marc Reift. 1990. $12.50. 5:33. IV. b♭–g'. "Für Tuba und Orgel." BMV 622. Transcribed part includes ornamentation: mordents, grace notes, trills. Best on E♭/F tuba because of high tessitura. Some 32nd notes should not be a problem if played at a musical (not too fast) tempo. Recorded by Walter Hilgers.

Bach, Johann Sebastian. *Patron of the Wind from "Phoebus and Pan."* arr. Ostrander, Allen. Editions Musicus. 1959. $2.75. 2:20. III. C–g. Allegro giocoso. Good transcription. A few scalewise eighth notes. No technical problems.

Bach, Johann Sebastian. *Rondo from Suite in B minor for Flute.* tr. Howe, Marvin C. Lawson-Gould Music Publishers Inc. 1965. 1:35. III. (A_1) D–g (a). Mostly scalewise motion in this transcription. Some optional ottava basso. See: Howe, M., *Three Tuba Solos,* under "Tuba and Keyboard Collections."

Bach, Johann Sebastian. *Second Part from Capriccio.* ed. Melnikov, S. Moscow: Military Band Masters Institute. 1957. See: Melnikov, S., *Pieces for Tuba and Piano,* under "Tuba and Keyboard Collections."

Bach, Johann Sebastian. *Siciliano.* arr. Maganini, Quinto. Editions Musicus. 1950. 3:54. III–IV. D–db'. In 6/8 time with eighth note as pulse. Sustained lyrical playing. See: Ostrander, Allen, *Concert Album for Tuba,* under "Tuba and Keyboard Collections."

Bach, Johann Sebastian. *Siciliano and Chorale.* arr. Perantoni, Daniel. Hal Leonard Publishing Corp. 1976. See: Perantoni, Daniel, *Master Solos Intermediate Level,* under "Tuba and Keyboard Collections."

Bach, Johann Sebastian. *Siciliano from Sonata No. II.* arr. Hall, Harry H. Brodt Music Company. 1962. $1.50. 2:49. II–III. C–a. Lovely melody in slow 6/8 time. Requires very lyrical approach. Some flexible slurring involved. Good recital material.

Bach, Johann Sebastian. *Sicilienne d'apres la 1re Sonate en Sol mineur (BMV 1001) pour Violin seul.* ed. Rougeron, Philippe. Alphonse Leduc Editions Paris. 1983. $3.55. 3:30. F–f'. For French tuba. See: Thompson/Lemke, *French Music for Low Brass Instruments.*

Bach, Johann Sebastian. *Sonata II.* arr. Hilgers. Editions Marc Reift. 1990. $18.00. 6:00. IV. ($Eb_1$) D–db'. Allegro moderato, Siciliano, Allegro. "Für Tuba und Klavier/Orgel." An excellent transcription with some ornamentation and dynamics included.

Bach, Johann Sebastian. *Sonate II for Tuba and Piano.* arr. Jacobs, Wesley. Encore Music Publishers. 1992. $10.50. 10:12 (3:40, 2:23, 4:09). IV. D–d'. Allegro Moderato, Siciliano, Allegro. Part provided has no expression/dynamic marks. Mostly scalewise baroque writing. Requires good technique, fun transcription. Last movement requires some breathing planning.

Baeyens, H. *Introduction et Cantabile.* Edition Andel Uitgaven. 1958. $7.25. 3:00. III. Bb–f'. Upper tessitura; better on F tuba.

Bak, Mikhail Abromovich. *A Joke.* ed. Lebedev, A. Moscow: Muzyka. 1986. Second piece in next listing. See: Lebedev, A., *Tuba Tutor Vol. 2,* under "Tuba and Keyboard Collections."

Bak, Mikhail Abromovich. *Two Pieces.* 1969. 3:56 (2:02, 1:54). IV. Gb_1–cb'. *Melody* (Andantino cantabile); *Joke* (Allegretto scherzando). *Melody*: lush, lyrical lullaby in Db major; some slurring; some

accidentals; warm vocal approach required. *Joke*: requires some flexibility and style. Good recital material.

Baker, Claude. *Omaggi e Fantasie for Tuba and Piano (1981/87).* MMB Music, Inc. 1990. 16:00. V. For David Randolph. Intended for F tuba, but playable on C tuba. Very modern writing for both tuba and piano. Tuba: complex rhythms, using the instrument and mouthpiece percussively, whispering through horn, muted passages. Piano: striking soundboard, strings, beams. Composer suggests amplifying the piano to enhance the more delicate effects. Score needed for performance. Recorded by David Randolph.

Bales, Kenton. *Fantasy on a Lakota Theme for Tuba and Piano.* Southern Music Company. 1993. $6.50. 4:14. IV–V. F_1–bb (eb'). For Craig Fuller. Completed 1992. Some mixed meter. Requires good flexibility, good technique, a good ear, and a strong accompanist.

Ball, Eric. *In the Army.* Salvationist Publishing and Supplies, Ltd. n. d. 3:10. III–IV. Bb_1–bb. "Solo for Bombardon in Eb—Advanced Level Test Item." Solo part in treble clef. Traditional showcase solo with a martial flavor: dotted rhythms, octave jumps, theme and variation "feel." Good intermediate solo.

Balthazar, J. L. *Poème,* Op. 10. Edition Andel Uitgaven.

Barat, J. Edouard. *Introduction and Dance.* arr. Smith, Glenn. Southern Music Company. 1973. $5.50. 3:54. IV. ($C_2$) E_1–g. Baritone part also included. See following listing. This arrangement is ottava basso from original. See: Thompson/Lemke, *French Music for Low Brass Instruments;* and review in *T.U.B.A. Journal,* Vol. 1, no. 1, p. 7.

Barat, J. Edouard. *Introduction et Danse.* Alphonse Leduc Editions Paris. n. d. $11.50. 3:54. IV–V. C–f. À mon excellent ami Paul Achard, Administrateur de la Sirène. "Pour Saxhorn-Basse Sib avec Accompagnement de Piano." See listing under "Music for Tuba and Band." Also see: Thompson/Lemke, *French Music for Low Brass Instruments.* Recorded by Roger Bobo.

Barat, J. Edouard. *Introduction et Sérénade.* Alphonse Leduc Editions Paris. 1963. $11.50. 4:02. IV–V. F_1–f'. "Pour Tuba ut ou saxhorn basse Sib ou saxhorn baryton Sib avec accompagnement de piano." For French tuba. Originally published in 1957. Stately opening section followed by a technical serenade section with scales, arpeggios, and typical French harmonies. See: Thompson/Lemke, *French Music for Low Brass Instruments.*

Barat, J. Edouard. *Morceau de Concours (Contest Piece).* Alphonse Leduc Editions Paris. n. d. $12.80. 6:10. IV–V. C–ab'. À l'artiste et Ami J. Balay ex-soliste de la Musique de la Garde et de l'Opéra (de la Garde Républicaine). Lent/Moderato. "Pour Baryton ou Basse Sib avec Accompagnement de Piano." For French tuba. Requires facility. Good recital material. See: Thompson/ Lemke, *French Music for Low Brass Instruments.*

Barat, J. Edouard. *Reminiscences de Navarre.* Alphonse Leduc Editions Paris. 1950. $12.80. 4:00. IV–V. F_1–g'. À mon Ami Paul Bernard Professeur au Conservatoire National de Musique. "Pour Tuba en ut ou Saxhorn basse Sib et piano." See: Thompson/Lemke, *French Music for Low Brass Instruments.*

Baratto, Paolo. *Jumbo-Baby.* Available from the composer. See: Baratto, Paolo, *Jumbo-Baby,* under "Music for Tuba and Band." Also written for bassoon or bass trombone with piano.

Barber, S. *Adagio and Scherzo from Sonata in C Minor.* ed. Lebedev, A. Moscow: Muzyka. 1986. 4:02. III–IV. F_1–bb. Some very slow, easy playing combined with Presto articulations in 12/8 time. Some 3 against 4 in Presto section. See: Lebedev, A., *Tuba Tutor Vol. 2,* under "Tuba and Keyboard Collections."

Barboteu, Georges. *Prélude et cadence.* Editions Choudens. 1977. IV–V. E_1–c". For French tuba. See: Thompson/Lemke, *French Music for Low Brass Instruments.*

Barcos, George. *Preludes.* Editions Marc Reift. In preparation.

Bardwell, William. *Sonata for Tuba and Piano.* Robert King Music Co. and Alphonse Leduc Editions Paris. 1974. $5.85. 10:15. V. E_1–e'. To John Fletcher. Written in 1968. Dialogue, Scherzo, Passacaglia. Dialogue is a series of cadenza-like speeches between soloist and accompanist (4:45). Scherzo is based on appoggiaturas; in 5/8 time with some (unmarked) 2/8. Passacaglia has mixed meter and will take some coordinating with piano part.

Bariller, Robert. *Hans de Schnokeloch.* Alphonse Leduc Editions Paris. 1961. $11.50. 5:00. II–III. C#–a'. For French tuba. See: Thompson/Lemke, *French Music for Low Brass Instruments.*

Bariller, Robert. *L'Enterrement de Saint-Jean (The Funeral of St. John)* Alphonse Leduc Editions Paris. 1960. $8.60. 5:00. II. A_1 (A)–f'. À Paul Bernard, très amicalement. "Pour Tuba ut ou Trombone basse ou Saxhorn basse Sib et Piano." Based on A. de Musset's play *Fantasio,* Act I, Scene II. Easy rhythms, no technical problems. See: Thompson/ Lemke, *French Music for Low Brass Instruments.*

Barnby, Sir Joseph. *Sweet And Low.* arr. Ostling, Acton. CPP/Belwin, Inc. 1969. 0:59. I. D–c. Middle range solo in 6/8 time. Good introduction to 6/8. See: Ostling, Acton, *Tuba (Bass) Soloist, Level One,* under "Tuba and Keyboard Collections."

Barnby, Sir Joseph. *Sweet And Low.* arr. Kinyon, John. M. Witmark and Sons. 1958. I. See: Kinyon, John, *Breeze-Easy Recital Pieces,* under "Tuba and Keyboard Collections."

Barnes, Clifford P. *Arioso and Caprice.* Robbins Music. 1961. $4.00. 2:37. II–III. Bb$_1$–f. Lyrical an-

dante section followed by an advanced beginner technical Allegretto section. A few sixteenth-note scales and a few arpeggios.

Barnes, Clifford P. *Valse Impromptu.* Robbins Music. 1961. 2:08. III. C–eb. Allegro. Dotted half note = 64. Some eighth-note scalewise runs. Depending on tempo, very accessible and challenging to advanced beginner.

Barnes, James. *In a Modal Mood.* Belwin Mills Publishing. 1980. 2:07. I–II. A_1–c. Slowly and Sadly. Easy introduction to modes (Dorian mode). Mostly quarter and eighth notes at a slow tempo, making this solo very accessible to the beginning player. See review in *T.U.B.A. Journal,* Vol. 9, no. 4, p. 33. See also: CPP/Belwin, *Tuba Solos, Level Two,* under "Tuba and Keyboard Collections."

Barnes, James. *Marching Right Along.* CPP/Belwin, Inc. 1980. $4.00. 1:20. I. Bb$_1$–d. Steady march tempo. Mostly stepwise motion with quarter note as fastest rhythm. Some accents, no technical problems. See: CPP/Belwin, *Tuba Solos, Level One,* under "Tuba and Keyboard Collections."

Barnes, James. *The Nervous Turkey Rag* (November Is Here Again). Medici Music Press. 1982. $4.50. 1:15. II. Bb$_1$–c. Very comical ragtime feeling. Cute novelty (with a few other tunes thrown in). Tempo chosen will determine difficulty. Solo in cut time; a few eighth notes (optional quarter notes). See review in *T.U.B.A. Journal,* Vol. 11, no. 4, p. 22.

Barnes, James. *Old Time Theme and Variations.* Medici Music Press. 1982. $4.50. 1:49. II. C–e (f). Allegro moderato. Good introduction to theme and variations. Limited range. Sixteen-measure theme and three variations. Contains some slurring and staccato passages. In 3/4; can be played "in one" for more advanced players.

Barnes, James. *Whistlin' Tune.* CPP/Belwin, Inc. 1980. $4.00. 0:51. I. Bb$_1$–c. Lightly and with humor. Cut time. Short introduction, eight-measure motifs repeated. Limited range. Contains only quarter and half notes. Also has accents, fermatas, ritards, and crescendos; makes a nice introduction to these musical devices. See: CPP/Belwin, Inc., *Tuba Solos, Level One,* under "Tuba and Keyboard Collections."

Barnes, James. *Work Song, a "Blues Song" for the Young Tubist.* Belwin Mills, Inc. 1980. Out of print, was published separately. 1:35. I–II. Bb$_1$–c. Not too fast; very deliberate. Some eighth notes, accents, use of Gb as a blues note. Blues/rock feel. Good beginner solo. See: Lamb, Jack, *Classic Festival Solos,* and CPP/Belwin, *Tuba Solos, Level Two,* under "Tuba and Keyboard Collections."

Barnes, James, arr. *Sometimes I Feel Like a Motherless Child.* CPP/Belwin, Inc. 1980. $4.00. 1:30. I. A_1–A. Published individually as well as included in collections. Sad spiritual feel. One octave range. Ideal for early ability. After piano introduction, eight-measure phrase repeated twice, with five-measure coda. Some slurring of eighth notes. Eighth note is fastest rhythm. See: Lamb, Jack, *Classic Festival Solos,* and CPP/Belwin, *Tuba Solos, Level Two,* under "Tuba and Keyboard Collections."

Barnet, Richard D. *Four Segments.* Fema Music Publications. 1974. $3.75. 4:04 (0:50, 1:47, 0:45, 0:42). IV. F_1c'. To Edward Livingston. Four Movements: March (Briskly); Ballad (Tempo rubato); Waltz (Lightly); Dance. Short musical vignettes with plenty of opportunity for expression. Advanced intermediate technique needed; one glissando in first movement.

Barnhouse, Charles Lloyd. *Barbarossa—Air Varie.* arr. Buchtel, Forrest L. C. L. Barnhouse. 1935. $3.50. 5:30. Composed in 1897. Solo for BB♭ tuba or BB♭ bass saxophone. See listing under "Music for Tuba and Band."

Barraine, Elsa Jacqueline. *Andante et Allegro.* Éditions Salabert. 1958. B♭₁–b♭'. For French tuba. See: Thompson/Lemke, *French Music for Low Brass Instruments.*

Barraine, Elsa Jacqueline. *Chiens de Paille (Straw Dogs).* Jobert. 1966. V. G_1–b♭'. For French tuba. See: Thompson/Lemke, *French Music for Low Brass Instruments.*

Bartles, Alfred. *Scherzo for Tuba and Wind Ensemble.* Sam Fox Publishing Co. Inc. 1970. 4:30. To Harvey G. Phillips. Out of print. Piano reduction by the composer. See listing under "Music for Tuba and Band."

Bartók, Béla. *Adagio.* ed. Lebedev, A. Moscow: Muzyka. 1984. 0:50. II. A_1–e. Lyrical folk song in A minor; 2/4 time. See: Lebedev, A., *Tuba Tutor Vol. 1,* under "Tuba and Keyboard Collections."

Bartók, Béla. *Dance.* ed. Lebedev, A. Moscow: Muzyka. 1984. 0:32. II. F_1–d♭. In 2/4 time; with exception of last three notes on F_1s, range is very limited. See: Lebedev, A., *Tuba Tutor Vol. 1,* under "Tuba and Keyboard Collections."

Bartók, Béla. *Dance of the Bear.* arr. Lebedev, A. Military Band Masters Faculty of Moscow Conservatoire. 1971. See: Lebedev, A., *Collection of Pieces for Tuba "Es" and Piano,* under "Tuba and Keyboard Collections."

Bartók, Béla. *Dance of the Slovaks.* trans. Dishinger, Ronald Christian. Studio 224/CPP/Belwin, Inc. 1979. 1:15. II. B♭₁–c. Solo in 2/4 time with a variety of articulations: staccatos, tenutos, accents. Modal in nature with limited range. Eighth note is fastest rhythm. Mostly stepwise motion; no technical problems. See: Lamb, Jack, *Classic Festival Solos,* under "Tuba and Keyboard Collections."

Bartók, Béla. *Dirge No. 4.* arr. Davis, Sharon. Western International Music. 1991. $5.00. 2:37. III–IV. E_1 (B_1)–b♭. Assai andante. Sustained, lyrical Bartók melody. Some dissonant jumps of sevenths and ninths; requires a good ear. Easy rhythmically; a few eighth notes at a very reasonable tempo. Good intermediate twentieth-century writing.

Bartók, Béla. *Hungarian Folk Song.* ed. Lebedev, A. Moscow: Muzyka. 1984. 0:55. II–III. B♭₁–g♭. Simple rhythms in 2/4 time; in B♭ minor. See: Lebedev, A., *Tuba Tutor Vol. 1,* under "Tuba and Keyboard Collections."

Bartók, Béla. *A Song.* ed. Lebedev, A. Moscow: Muzyka. 1984. 1:00. II–III. C–d. In C minor and 4/4 time, with all phrases slurred. No technical problems. See: Lebedev, A., *Tuba Tutor Vol. 1,* under "Tuba and Keyboard Collections."

Bartsch, Ch. *Adagio and Allegro.* J. Maurer Editions Musicales. 1971. $5.95. 5:20 (1:53, 3:27). IV. F_1–c'. À Norbert Van Ser Jeught. Adagio—Allegro moderato. "Pour Bastuba en ut ou pour Contrebasse et Piano." Lyrical Adagio movement followed by a comfortably, musical Allegro section. Good recital material.

Baseler, J. *Happy Thoughts.* Carl Fischer Inc. 1887. Out of print.

Bassett, Leslie. *Song and Dance for Tuba and Piano.* C. F. Peters Corporation. 1993. 5:10 (3:10, 2:00). IV. E_1–d♭'. To Fritz Kaenzig. Song: some meter changes; meditative quality. Dance: quick with mostly stepwise writing.

Baudrier, Émile. *Relax.* Gérard Billaudot. 1977. 1:57. II–III. F–e'. Moderato. "Pour Trombone Tenor, Trombone Basse, Tuba ut et Piano." For French tuba. Relaxed tempo, relaxed rhythms, relaxed range. Tenuto and slurred notes throughout; lyrical solo. No technical problems.

Bauer, Guilherme. *Três miniaturas.* Fundação Nacional De Arte. 4:08 (1:30, 1:18, 1:20). IV–V. (D_1) E♯₁–d'. Three movements. Mixed meter, modern (tonal) melody, glissando, flutter tongue, and technical passages (last movement has quick articulations) make this a worthwhile challenge.

Bayley, Thomas Haynes. *Faith of Our Fathers.* arr. Kinyon, John. M. Witmark and Sons. 1958. I. See: Kinyon, John, *Breeze-Easy Recital Pieces,* under "Tuba and Keyboard Collections."

Bayley, Thomas Haynes. *Long, Long Ago.* arr. Kinyon, John. M. Witmark and Sons. 1958. I. See: Kinyon, John, *Breeze-Easy Recital Pieces,* under "Tuba and Keyboard Collections."

Bayly [sic], T. H. *Long, Long Ago.* arr. Feldstein, Sandy. CPP/Belwin, Inc. 1990. I. B♭₁–G. See: Feldstein, Sandy, *First Solo Songbook,* under "Tuba and Keyboard Collections."

Beach, Bennie. *Lamento.* Southern Music Company. 1961. $2.50. Out of print. 4:20. Reflective lament in 5/4 time. Slow tempo makes this accessible to the player not used to 5/4. Only a few sixteenth notes. Plenty of room for expression. Recorded by Rex Conner; Robert LeBlanc.

Beaucamp, Albert. *Cortège.* Alphonse Leduc Editions Paris. 1953. Out of print. 2:25. II–III. C–g'. À Armand François. Grave. "Pour Tuba ut ou Contrebasse à Cordes ou Saxhorn basse Si♭ ou Trombone basse et Piano." For French tuba. Very melodic (mostly slurred) melody at a slow reflective tempo makes this very accessible to the advanced beginner. See: Thompson/Lemke, *French Music for Low Brass Instruments.*

Beeler, Walter. *The Virtuoso.* Out of print. 2:18. II–III. F$_1$–d. Typical theme and (three) variations solo. First variation has some sixteenth notes, second variation has low tessitura, third variation is based on triplets.

Beethoven, Ludwig van. *Beloved from Afar (An die ferne Geliebte),* Op. 98, no. 6. trans. Dishinger, Ronald Christian. Medici Music Press. 1990. $3.50. 2:52. II–III. B♭$_1$–f. A few tempo changes. Some easy slurs, no difficult rhythm or technical problems.

Beethoven, Ludwig van. *Country Dance.* arr. Wekselblatt, Herbert. G. Schirmer Inc. 1972. 0:48. III. C–g. Short, quick 2/4 dance with some accidentals and quick sixteenth-note articulations. See: Wekselblatt, Herbert, *First Solos for the Tuba Player,* under "Tuba and Keyboard Collections."

Beethoven, Ludwig van. *Danse villageoise (Rustic Dance).* arr. Goudenhooft, André, and Maillard, Augustin (piano realization). Gérard Billaudot. 1989. $6.50. 3:00. II–III. C–c'. "Extraite de thèmes variés pour violon; adaptation pour le trombone basse et le tuba basse." Wide range for beginning player. Some flexibility needed for slurred arpeggios. See: Thompson/Lemke, *French Music for Low Brass Instruments.*

Beethoven, Ludwig van. *Hymn to Joy.* arr. Jacobs, Wesley. Encore Music Publishers. 0:33. I. C–c. Strict time. Short solo with easy rhythms, limited range, some stepwise slurs. See: Jacobs, Wesley, *Solos from the Classics,* under "Tuba and Keyboard Collections."

Beethoven, Ludwig van. *Le Désir.* tr. Bilbaut, J. Editions Salabert. n. d. Out of print.

Beethoven, Ludwig van. *May Song (Mailied),* Op. 52, no. 4. trans. Dishinger, Ronald Christian. Medici Music Press. 1990. $3.50. 2:29. II–III. E♭–e♭. Classical solo in 2/4 time; in E♭ major within one octave. Some easy slurring; tenutos, staccatos; no technical problems.

Beethoven, Ludwig van. *Menuet.* arr. Maganini, Quinto. Editions Musicus. 1954. 2:00. III. G$_1$–a♭. Light articulation and flexibility needed. See: Ostrander, Allen, *Concert Album for Tuba,* under "Tuba and Keyboard Collections." Recorded by Rex Conner.

Beethoven, Ludwig van. *Nature's Adoration.* arr. Ostrander, Allen. Editions Musicus. 1954. 1:36. II. B♭$_1$–f. Maestoso. Well-transcribed advanced-beginner solo. Very easy rhythms (one eighth note in entire piece); easy accompaniment. See: Ostrander, Allen, *Concert Album for Tuba,* under "Tuba and Keyboard Collections."

Beethoven, Ludwig van. *Ode to Joy.* arr. Boyd, Bill; and ed. Daellenbach, Charles. Hal Leonard Publishing Corp. 1992. 0:45. I. B♭$_1$–B♭. Adapted from *Symphony No. 9.* A couple of eighth notes; easy

rhythms. Comes with practice/performance cassette. See: Daellenbach, Charles, *Book of Beginning Tuba Solos,* under "Tuba and Keyboard Collections."

Beethoven, Ludwig van. *Ode to Joy.* arr. Feldstein, Sandy. CPP/Belwin, Inc. 1990. I. B♭$_1$–F. See: Feldstein, Sandy, *First Solo Songbook,* under "Tuba and Keyboard Collections."

Beethoven, Ludwig van. *Sonata in G Major for Tuba and Piano.* trans. Frank Proto. Liben Music Publishers. 1981. $6.00. 9:15 (4:58, 1:00, 3:17). V. G$_1$–g'. From the Horn Sonata in F major, Op. 17. Three movements: Allegro Moderato; Poco Adagio Quasi Andante; Rondo. Takes a player with great flexibility combined with a French horn "lightness." Mostly upper tessitura and mostly staccato and slurred passages. Recorded by Michael Thornton. See review in *T.U.B.A. Journal,* Vol. 10, no. 4, p. 36.

Beethoven, Ludwig van. *Variations on the Theme of "Judas Maccabeus" by G. F. Handel.* tr. Bell, William J. Carl Fischer Inc. 1937. $5.00. 4:45. III–IV. (F$_1$) A$_1$–b♭. Theme and (four) variations. First variation is piano solo. Second variation is entirely triplets. Third variation introduces sixteenth notes. Fourth variation is in cut time with mostly eighth notes. Good intermediate solo. Recorded by William Bell.

Belden, George R. *Black Holes in Space.* ed. Little, Donald C. CPP/Belwin, Inc. 1978. $4.00. 2:17. II. Allegro. A few accidentals and a chance of rushing are the only black holes to avoid. Good beginning solo. See review in *T.U.B.A. Journal,* Vol. 8, no. 1, p. 34. See: Lamb, Jack, *Solo Sounds for Tuba Levels 1–3,* under "Tuba and Keyboard Collections."

Belden, George R. *Neutron Stars.* arr. Little, Donald C. CPP/Belwin, Inc. 1978. $4.00. 3:45. III. G♭$_1$–g♭. Dramatic; Allegro. Tubist blows air through instrument twice for dramatic effect. Some easy 4/4, 3/4 meter changes, some syncopation, otherwise good pre-intermediate solo. Plenty of opportunity for dramatic expression (*sfp, sfz,* etc.). See review in *T.U.B.A. Journal,* Vol. 4, no. 3, p. 35.

Bell, J. H. *Sans Pareil.* arr. Weber, Carl. J. W. Pepper and Son. 1914. Out of print. See listing under "Music for Tuba and Band," and Weber, Carl, *Nineteen Solos for E♭ Bass with Piano Accompaniment,* under "Tuba and Keyboard Collections."

Bell, William J. *Chief John.* CPP/Belwin, Inc. 1963. $4.00. 1:13. I. C–e. Dedicated to the late John Kuhn, famous Indian tuba player. Solo in cut time; in D minor. Includes comments by Bell, setting the mood for the piece. Quarter note is the fastest rhythm. One upper e, otherwise medium tessitura. A few slurs, a few accents, no technical problems. See: CPP/Belwin, *Tuba Solos, Level Two,* under "Tuba and Keyboard Collections."

Bell, William J., arr. *Folksong Medley.* CPP/Belwin, Inc. 1965. $4.00. 1:39. II. B♭$_1$–f. Three folksongs:

Allegro (Irish Washerwoman); Meno mosso (Scotch); Allegretto (Russian). Optional notes to leave out for breathing; well-arranged solo.

Bell, William J. *Gavotte*. Carl Fischer Inc. 1935. $2.50. 1:47. I. A₁–c. Tempo di Gavotte. "E♭ or BB♭ tuba." A few eighth notes; no technical problems.

Bell, William J. *Jig Elephantine*. Carl Fischer Inc. 1935. Out of print. 1:00. II. b♭₁–g. At moderate speed. "E♭ or B♭ Tuba." In cut time. A few grace notes and arpeggios. Half-valve glissando explained very well by Bell.

Bell, William J. *Jolly Jumbo*. CPP/Belwin, Inc. 1963. $4.00. 1:01. I–II. (A♭₁) D–e♭. Good descriptive comments by Bell. Elephants dancing with a jolly 6/8 feel. No technical problems. See: CPP/Belwin, *Tuba Solos, Level Two*, under "Tuba and Keyboard Collections."

Bell, William J. *Low Down Bass*. Carl Fischer Inc. 1935. Out of print. 1:11. I. B♭₁–b♭. With animation and spirit. "E♭ or BB♭ Tuba." Solo in 12/8 for the beginner. Great dynamic range. No technical problems.

Bell, William J. *Melodious Etude*. CPP/Belwin, Inc. 1962. $4.00. 1:32. I. D–c. Moderately. Very limited range, limited rhythms—quarter note is the fastest rhythm. Good beginners introduction to slurring. See: CPP/Belwin, Inc., *Tuba Solos, Level One*, under "Tuba and Keyboard Collections."

Bell, William J. *Nautical John Medley*. Carl Fischer Inc. 1935. $3.25. 3:50. III. (E♭₁) A♭₁–c'. Based on *Blow the Man Down* and *Rocked in the Cradle of the Deep*. Trills, optional glissando, a couple of cadenzas. Plenty of opportunity for expression.

Bell, William J., arr. *Russian Medley*. CPP/Belwin, Inc. 1964. $4.00. 2:11. I–II. B♭₁–d. A majestic 4/4 section (*1812 Overture* and a theme from Tchaikovsky's Fourth Symphony) and a slow 3/4 rhythmic waltz. A few scalewise eighth-note runs in waltz; otherwise no technical problems for slightly advanced beginners. See: Lamb, Jack, *Solo Sounds for Tuba Levels 1–3, Vol. 1*, under "Tuba and Keyboard Collections."

Bell, William J. *Sousaphone Polka*. Waterloo Music. 1950. 4:20. III–IV. B♭₁–b♭. Written at the request of John Philip Sousa, this was the first composition (originally copyrighted in 1924) to show off the sousaphone. Optional triple tonguing, traditional polka style with two cadenzas.

Bell, William J. *The Spartan*. CPP/Belwin, Inc. 1963. $4.00. 1:16. I–II. (B♭₁) C–f. March tempo. Good descriptive comments by Bell, including an encouragement to "sniff breathe." Slightly high range for beginner, otherwise easy rhythms and no technical problems. See: CPP/Belwin, *Tuba Solos, Level Two*, under "Tuba and Keyboard Collections."

Bell, William J. *The Tubaman*. Piano arr., L. S. CPP/Belwin, Inc. 1962. $4.00. 1:05. I. (B♭₁ E♭–c. Based on *Blow the Man Down*. Very easy beginning solo. Quarter note is fastest rhythm. No technical prob-

lems. See: CPP/Belwin, Inc., *Tuba Solos, Level One*, under "Tuba and Keyboard Collections."

Bell, William J. *The Tubateer Polka* . CPP/Belwin, Inc. 1964. $4.00. 1:24. II–III. (A♭₁) C–e♭. Tempo di Polka. Incorrect rhythm in first measure of coda. Traditional easy polka in A♭ and D♭ major. A few sharps, no technical problems.

Bellini, [Vincenzo]. *Come Brave the Sea*. arr. de Ville, Paul. Carl Fischer Inc. 1906. Out of print. See: de Ville, Paul, *Pleasant Hours*, under "Tuba and Keyboard Collections."

Bencriscutto, Frank. *Concertino for Tuba and Band*. Shawnee Press Inc. 1971. $7.50. Written for and dedicated to Stanford Freese. See: Bencriscutto, Frank, *Concertino for Tuba and Band*, under "Music for Tuba and Band." Some cuts needed in solo (band) part to work with piano (listed in composer's notes). Recorded by Stanford Freese. See review in *T.U.B.A. Journal*, Vol. 4, no. 4, p. 25.

Benedict, Julius. *Carnival of Venice*. arr. Boyd, Bill. Hal Leonard Publishing Corp. 1992. 0:41. I. B♭₁– G. Melody only; in 3/4 time; no variations. Quarter note is fastest rhythm. Limited range. Comes with practice/performance cassette. See: Daellenbach, Charles, *Book of Beginning Tuba Solos*, under "Tuba and Keyboard Collections."

Benedict, Julius. *Carnival of Venice*. arr. Kinyon, John. M. Witmark and Sons. 1958. I. See: Kinyon, John, *Breeze-Easy Recital Pieces*, under "Tuba and Keyboard Collections."

Benjamin, Thomas. *Sonata*. Southern Music Company. 1991. $12.00. 12:00. IV–V. G₁–f'. Composed June, 1986, at Clearwater Pond, Maine. Three movements. Flutter tongue; cadenza in second movement. Will take some work to prepare, but well worth it. Good recital material. See review in *T.U.B.A. Journal*, Vol. 18, no. 4, p. 15.

Benker, Heinz. *Miniaturen-Suite*. Zinneberg Musikverlag. 1986. 10:42 (1:14, 3:16, 1:32, 1:16, 1:50, 1:34. IV. F₁–e♭'. Für Tuba und Klavier. Lebhaft; Nachdenklich; Heiter; Gemütlich; Feierlich; Tänzerisch. Very fine modern tonal writing for tuba and piano. Third movement has a few glissandos. Tempos notated are very playable and accessible to strong high school player. Highly recommended.

Bennet, David. *Voice of the Viking*. Carl Fischer Inc. 1938. $3.25. 4:50. III–IV. F₁–a. Typical solo from the period. Moderate technique required. Slow, fast, loud, soft, slurred, staccato etc.—it's all there.

Bennett, Malcolm, arr. *Luzerne Song*. 1988. 0:58. III. (A♭₁) E♭–a♭. Leggiero. Part for treble (E♭ bass) included. See: Bennett, Malcolm, *Five Solos for Tuba*, under "Tuba and Keyboard Collections." Traditional tune with a "yodeling feel." For a real treat, listen to the recording of John Fletcher playing this tune with the Phillip Jones Brass Ensemble.

Bennett, Malcolm, arr. *McLeods Reel*. 1988. 1:24. III. B♭–c'. Gioviale. Part for treble (E♭ bass) included. Fun reel in cut time. Some octave jumps, some eighth-note runs. Pretend that you are a piper! See: Bennett, Malcolm, *Five Solos for Tuba,* under "Tuba and Keyboard Collections."

Bennett, Malcolm, arr. *Shenandoah.* 1988. 2:01. II–III. C–a. Semplice. Parts for bass clef and treble (E♭ Bass) included. Very lyrical traditional melody repeated with a piano interlude. Great opportunity for making beautiful music. See: Bennett, Malcolm, *Five Solos for Tuba,* under "Tuba and Keyboard Collections."

Benson, Warren. *Arioso.* Hal Leonard Publishing Corp. 1959. $3.95. 1:29. III. D$_1$–f. To Dirk. Originally published by Piedmont Music. Slowly, in 3/2 time. Very lyrical minor tune. Plenty of room for extreme expression. With the exception of the last four dotted whole notes on D$_1$, not a very difficult piece. Recorded by Peter Popiel.

Benson, Warren. *Helix* (Concerto for Solo Tuba and Concert Band). Carl Fischer Inc. 1976. $7.50. 14:00. Commissioned by Harvey Phillips; premiered February 12, 1967 at the 50th Anniversary Eastern Division M. E. N. C. Conference, Boston, by Harvey Phillips, soloist, and the Ithaca High School Band, Frank L. Battisti, conductor. See listing under "Music for Tuba and Band." Recorded by Harvey Phillips; Jack Robinson; John Turk.

Bentzon, Niels Viggo. *Fett und Filtz,* Op. 403d. Wilhelm Hansen Musikforlag. 1977. Part four of an homage to Joseph Beuys in seven parts.

Bentzon, Niels Viggo. *Sonata for Tuba,* Op. 393. Manuscript. 1976. Work in progress.

Bentzon, Niels Viggo. *Sonata for Tuba and Piano,* Op. 277. Wilhelm Hansen Musikforlag. 1971.

Beresford, Arnold. *The Smuggler.* arr. Rubin, Elsa. JTL Publications/G. Scott Music Publishing Co. 1989. $3.50. 3:00. III. D–b♭. Slurred phrases. Spirited 4/4 section and slower 6/8 section. Upper tessitura.

Berlin, A. *Ballade.* ed. Voronov, G. Moscow: Muzyka. 1984. See: Voronov, G., *Works for Tuba and Piano by Russian Composers,* under "Tuba and Keyboard Collections."

Berlioz, G. P. *Air Gai.* ed. Voxman, Himie. Rubank, Inc. 1972. 3:00. III. (A♭$_1$) C–g. "For E♭ or BB♭ Bass." Solo in 2/4 time with few technical problems. See: Voxman, Himie, *Concert and Contest Collection,* under "Tuba and Keyboard Collections."

Berlioz, Hector. *Bolero.* (Zaide, 1845). trans. Dishinger, Ronald Christian. Medici Music Press. 1989. $3.50. 3:10. III. C–f. Bolero in 3/4 time requiring a good stylistic sense. Aria style. Accessible accompaniment.

Berlioz, Hector. *Sanctus.* arr. Fletcher, John. Chester Music Ltd. London. 1982. 2:25. II. E♭–f. Adagio. From *Grande Messe des Morts.* Slow, sustained playing. Listen to *Sanctus* in Berlioz's *Mass* for conception. See: Fletcher, John, *Tuba Solos (Tuba in C), Volume One,* under "Tuba and Keyboard Collections."

Bernaud, Alain. *Humoresque.* Éditions Max Eschig. 1964. 9:10. V. F$_1$–b♭. À Paul Bernard, Professeur au Conservatoire de Paris. "Pour Tuba ou Saxhorn-Basse en Si♭ et Piano." For French tuba. Mixed meter; requires great flexibility, full range. See: Thompson/Lemke, *French Music for Low Brass Instruments.*

Bernstein, Leonard. *Waltz for Mippy.* ed. Larin, J. Moscow: Muzyka. 1979. See: Larin, J., *Pieces for Tuba and Piano,* under "Tuba and Keyboard Collections."

Bernstein, Leonard. *Waltz For Mippy III.* arr. Wekselblatt, Herbert. G. Schirmer Inc. 1950. 2:00. III. A$_1$–g♯. See: Wekselblatt, H., *Solos for the Tuba Player,* under "Tuba and Keyboard Collections." "As gracefully as possible under the circumstances." Some passages one octave lower than original, making it more accessible to the intermediate player. Some double sharps; leaps of tenths. Muted passage. Feeling of one (3/4) and some mixed meter; trills. Piano uses middle pedal. See other listing in this section.

Bernstein, Leonard. *Waltz for Mippy III for Tuba and Piano.* Jalni Publications. 1977. $6.00. 2:00. IV. B$_1$–e^1. For my brother Burtie. Published by G. Schirmer in 1950. "Mippy III was a mongrel belonging to my brother Burtie." Upper tessitura. See above listing.

Beugniot, Jean-Pierre. *Légende.* ed. Lelong, Fernand. Gérard Billaudot. 1981. $8.75. 2:15. II. E–f^1. "Pour Tuba ut ou trombone basse, Saxhorn-Basse Si♭ et piano." For French tuba. No technical problems; only a few sixteenth notes. See: Thompson/Lemke, *French Music for Low Brass Instruments.*

Bevan, Clifford. *G. F. Handel's Third Tuba Concerto.* Piccolo Press. 1990. 5:00 (1:30, 1:50, 1:40). IV. F$_1$–f^1. Courante; Sarabande; Gigue. First performance given by Robert Steadman in Wantage Civic Hall, Oxfordshire, November 28, 1987. Orchestral version available for hire from Piccolo Press. In a Baroque style, complete with *Pop Goes the Weasel* interpolated at the end.

Beversdorf, Thomas G. *Sonata for Bass Tuba and Piano.* Southern Music Company. 1962. $14.95. 18:00. IV–V. F$_1$–a. Three movements. Allegro con moto; Allegretto con grazioso e espressivo; Allegro con brio. Well-written major work for the tuba. Comfortable range; no overwhelming technique needed. Good recital piece. Recorded by Robert LeBlanc. See review in *T.U.B.A. Journal,* Vol. 9, no. 1, p. 11. Also see: Bird, Gary, ed., *Program Notes for the Solo Tuba.*

Bigelow, Albert. *Winter Carousel.* Kendor Music, Inc. 1986. $4.50. 1:35. I. A$_1$–B♭. Good beginning solo in 3/4 time. Has dotted quarter notes, first and second endings, ritards, fermatas, and some slurring. Limited range.

Bigot, Eugène. *Carillon et Bourdon (Carillon and Great Bell).* Alphonse Leduc Editions Paris. 1951.

$12.80. 4:00. V. E_1–ab'. À Monsieur Paul Bernard Professeur au Conservatoire National de Musique. "Pour Tuba en ut ou Saxhorn basse Sib et Piano." For French tuba. Some very wide interval jumps, very large range, some quick technical passages. See: Thompson/Lemke, *French Music for Low Brass Instruments.*

Bigot, Pierre. *Cortège (Procession).* Éditions M. Combre. 1983. $6.00. 1:23. I–II. F–c'. "Pour Tuba en ut (ou Saxhorn basse in Sib) et Piano." Maestoso. Stately beginning solo. Presents no difficult technical challenges for French tuba. Fastest rhythm is eighth note. Good high-range practice for BBb (CC) tubas. Easy accompaniment. See: Thompson/Lemke, *French Music for Low Brass Instruments.*

Bigot, Pierre. *Tubaria.* Gérard Billaudot. 1991. For French tuba.

Bilbaut, J. *Le Carnaval de Venise.* Éditions Salabert. n. d. Out of print. Theme and variations.

Bilik, Jerry H. *Introduction and Dance.* RBC Publications. 1969. Was published by Samuel French. See listing under "Music for Tuba and Band."

Billings, William. *Old American Patriotic Song* (Chester). arr. Barnes, James. CPP/Belwin, Inc. 1980. $4.00. 1:30. I–II. Bb–eb. Very deliberate. Mostly stepwise motion. Except for a few upper notes (for the beginning player), presents no difficult technical challenges and would be a good confidence builder for the younger student. Fastest rhythm is an eighth note. See review in *T.U.B.A. Journal,* Vol. 9, no. 2, p. 29. See also: CPP/Belwin, Inc., *Tuba Solos, Level One,* under "Tuba and Keyboard Collections."

Bitsch, Marcel. *Impromptu.* Alphonse Leduc Editions Paris. 1957. $11.50. 4:15. V. F_1–bb'. À Paul Bernard, Professeur au Conservatoire National de Musique. "Pour Saxhorn basse Sib ou Tuba ut ou Trombone basse et Piano." Written for French tuba. Requires strong technique. Some tenor clef in part. Cadenza, quick tempos, 5/8 section. See: Thompson/Lemke, *French Music for Low Brass Instruments.*

Bitsch, Marcel. *Intermezzo.* Alphonse Leduc Editions Paris. 1968. $12.80. 5:00. IV. G_1–bb'. À Paul Bernard, professeur au Conservatoire National Supérieur de Musique. "Pour Tuba en ut ou Saxhorn basse Sib et Piano." Introductory lyrical section, cadenza, then a technical Allegro moderato section. See: Thompson/Lemke, *French Music for Low Brass Instruments.*

Bitsch, Marcel. *Ritcherkar.* ed. Guzii, V. Moscow: Muzyka. 1978. See: Guzii, V., *Pieces for Tuba and Piano,* under "Tuba and Keyboard Collections."

Bizet, Georges. *Adagietto from L'Arlésienne.* arr. Maganini, Quinto. Editions Musicus. 1949. 1:48. IV. C–f'. Adagio. Some quintuplets; grace notes. Easier on F tuba; playable on lower instrument. All slurred and vocally oriented. See: Ostrander, Allen, *Con-*

cert Album for Tuba, under "Tuba and Keyboard Collections."

Bizet, Georges. *Carmen Excerpts.* arr. Bell, William J. CPP/Belwin, Inc. 1965. $4.00. 2:05. III. Bb_1–f. Not as faithful to the original as *Toreador's Song,* arr. G. E. Holmes, but easier rhythms. See: Lamb, Jack, *Solo Sounds for Tuba Levels 3–5, Vol. 1,* under "Tuba and Keyboard Collections."

Bizet, Georges. *Habanera from "Carmen."* arr. Yasumoto, Hiroyuki. Toa Music International Co. 1986. 3:15. III. F–a. Allegretto quasi Andantino. Good transcription for opera aria. See: Yasumoto, Hiroyuki, *Tuba Volume #1,* under "Tuba and Keyboard Collections."

Bizet, Georges. *Toreador's Song.* arr. Holmes, G. E. and Voxman, H. Rubank, Inc. 1966. 2:07. III. Bb_1–f. "Solo Tuba—Eb or BBb tuba." Allegro Moderato. Stately transcription in original keys of F minor/F major of famous Bizet aria. Some syncopation, triplets, grace notes. Good opportunity for musical operatic expression. Wide dynamic range. See: Rubank, *Soloist Folio for Bass (Eb or BBb),* under "Tuba and Keyboard Collections." Also arr. Holmes, G. E. Rubank, Inc. 1939. Published separately.

Bjorn, Frank. *Alley Cat.* arr. Polansky, David. Kendor Music, Inc. 1961. $5.50. 2:25. I–II. Bb_1–c. Dotted rhythms and syncopations throughout. Limited range. Almost all stepwise intervals. Makes for a cute novelty recital piece for an advanced beginning player.

Bland, J. *Carry Me Back to Old Virginny.* arr. Yasumoto, Hiroyuki. Toa Music International Co. 1986. 1:08. II. F–f. Moderato. Some syncopations, all slurs, otherwise no technical problems. See: Yasumoto, Hiroyuki, *Tuba Volume #1,* under "Tuba and Keyboard Collections."

Blank, Hans. *Variationen über ein Volkslied.* Musikverlag Rundel GmbH. See listing under "Music for Tuba and Band."

Blanquer, Amando. *L'os Hispánic.* Sociedad General de Autores de Espana. 1976. See listing under "Music for Tuba and Orchestra."

Blazhevich, Vladislav. *Concert Etude.* See: Krotov and Blazhevich, *Concert Etude,* in this section.

Blazhevich, Vladislav. *Concerto No. 2, Part 3.* ed. Melnikov, S. Moscow: Military Band Masters Institute. 1957. See: Melnikov, S., *Pieces for Tuba and Piano,* under "Tuba and Keyboard Collections."

Blazhevich, Vladislav. *Miniature No. 7.* ed. Melnikov, S. Moscow: Military Band Masters Institute. 1957. See: Melnikov, S., *Pieces for Tuba and Piano,* under "Tuba and Keyboard Collections."

Blazhevich, Vladislav. *Sonatas for Tuba and Piano.* Manuscript. According to A. Lebedev, Vladislav Blazhevich composed fifteen sonatas for tuba and piano. Of these, seven exist in manuscript form and eight have been lost.

Bliss, P. P. *Dare to Be a Daniel.* arr. Smith, David E. David E. Smith Publications. 1985. $2.50. 3:00. I.

$B_1\flat$–$b\flat$. Alla Den (Adagio). Very easy beginning solo with limited range. Fastest rhythm is quarter note. Modulation with essentially the same musical material.

Blodek, Vilém. *Arie Janeks aus der Oper "Im Brunnen."* ed. Hoza, Václav. Editio Supraphon. 1982. 1:56. IV. E♭–e♭'. Allegretto. Technical aria: scales, triplets alternating with duplets, arpeggios. Would lie well on E♭ tuba. See: Hoza, Václav, *Schule für Tuba in F und in B,* under "Methods and Studies."

Blumenfeld, Aaron. *Sonata for Tuba and Piano.* Trombone Association Publishing. 1989. $14.00. 12:11 (5:28, 4:06, 2:37). V. Three movements. With the exception of a few eighth note rests in the last movement, there are no rests in this piece! This presents endurance challenges. Technical challenges are everywhere: quintuplets, sextuplets, septuplets; slurring out of "Arban's Method," dissonant interval skips. Unmarked meter changes in lyrical second movement. Third movement has a surprising fun jazz flavor, interpolating *Way Down upon the Swanee River* and *Toot Toot Tootsie Goodbye.* Has tricky syncopation. Very challenging piano accompaniment requiring left-hand stride playing in last movement.

Boccherini, L. *Menuette.* arr. Yasumoto, Hiroyuki. Toa Music International Co. 1986. 3:10. III–IV. B♭₁–c'. Tempo di Menuett. Has trills, grace notes, syncopation. Requires lightness and flexibility. See: Yasumoto, Hiroyuki, *Tuba Volume #1,* under "Tuba and Keyboard Collections." A different version has been recorded by Zdizislaw Piernik.

Boda, John. *Sonatina.* Robert King Music Co. and Alphonse Leduc Editions Paris. 1968. $4.05. 6:29 (2:56/3:53). IV. G₁–b. Written in 1967. First movement: most complex rhythm are triplets; moderate tempo. Second movement: mixed meter; a recitative-like cadenza. Very playable by strong high school student. Was published by W. D. Stuart Music. See: Bird, Gary, ed., *Program Notes for the Solo Tuba.*

Bogár, István. *Quick Dance.* arr. Wastall, Peter. Boosey and Hawkes, Inc. 1979. 0:48. I–II. E♭–f. See: Wastall, Peter, *Learn As You Play Tuba,* under "Tuba and Keyboard Collections." Vivace. Hungarian flavor. Some sixteenth notes and one octave F jump in last measure; otherwise not too demanding.

Bonheur, Theodore. *The Lancer.* arr. Walters, Harold L. Rubank, Inc. 1954. $1.50. 2:30. II. B♭₁–d. "Solo for E♭ or BB♭ Bass." In 4/4 time with no technical problems.

Bononcini, Giovanni. *Per la Gloria d'Adorarri from "Griselda."* Phillips, Harry I. (compiled and edited). Shawnee Press Inc. 1967. 1:32. II. C–e♭. Lyrical, slurred 3/4 transcription. Mostly scalewise motion. No big technical challenges. See: Phillips, Harry I., *Eight Bel Canto Songs,* in this section.

Bordogni, G. M. *24 Easy Vocalises.* arr. Yasumoto, Hiroyuki. Toa Music International Co. 1989. No.

4: 2:29. III. C–f. All slurred phrases. (Same as Rochut/Bordogni No. 4.) No. 9: 2:05. III. C–a. All slurred phrases. (Same as Rochut/Bordogni No. 9.) Some trills, grace notes. No. 10: 2:33. III. G₁–g. All slurred phrases. (Same as Rochut/Bordogni #10.) Some grace notes. See: Yasumoto, Hiroyuki, *Tuba Volume #3,* under "Tuba and Keyboard Collections."

Bordogni, Marco. *Bordogni Medley.* arr. Bowles, Richard W. CPP/Belwin, Inc. 1973. 2:20. II. C–e (f). Two contrasting melodious etudes, one in 3/4, the other in 2/4 time. Some slurring, syncopation. Good introduction to Bordogni's works. See: Lamb, Jack, *Solo Sounds for Tuba Levels 1–3, Vol. 1;* and Lamb, Jack, *Classic Festival Solos,* under "Tuba and Keyboard Collections."

Borg, Kim. *Finnish Rhapsody.* Finnish Music Information Centre. 1980. Three Scetches [*sic*] for tuba and piano. See listing under "Music for Tuba and Orchestra."

Bottesini, [Giovanni]. *Bombardon Polka.* arr. Weber, Carl. J. W. Pepper and Son. 1914. Out of print. See: Weber, Carl, *Nineteen Solos for E♭ Bass with Piano Accompaniment,* under "Tuba and Keyboard Collections."

Bottje, Will Gay. *Concerto.* American Composers Edition, Inc. 1973. $21.70. 15:00. See listing under "Music for Tuba and Orchestra.". See review in *T.U.B.A. Journal,* Vol. 1, no. 2, p. 10 and Vol. 1, no. 2, p. 6.

Bottje, Will Gay. *Prelude and Fugue.* Composers Facsimile Edition. 1959. 5:43 (3:23, 2:20). IV. b♭₁–e'. Two movements: Slowly; Moderato. First movement is lyrical with some more modern intervals; tonal. Second movement has some sixteenth-note runs but no overwhelming technical requirements.

Bourassa, Richard. *A Time, a Season.* 1982. Commissioned by Rodger Vaughan.

Bourgeois, Derek. *Air and Galumph.,* in *Two Pieces for Tuba and Piano,* Op. 53. Vanderbeek and Imrie Ltd. 1985. 1:56 (1:00, 0:56). IV. F₁–d♭'. Treble and bass clef parts included. Air has some slurred arpeggios and lyrical passages. Galumph in 6/8 time. Light accessible tonal modern writing requiring good stylistic sense.

Bourgeois, Derek. *Romance,* Op. 77. Vanderbeek and Imrie Ltd. 1985. 8:11. IV. E♭₁–f'. Treble and bass clef parts included. Intended for CC or E♭ tuba. Lovely lyrical solo mostly in slow 6/8 time with some mixed meter. Good showcase for moderate flexibility, expressiveness. Good recital material.

Bourgeois, Derek. *Tuba Concerto,* Op. 38. R. Smith and Co. 1972. For John Fletcher. See listing under "Music for Tuba and Orchestra."

Bourgeois, Louis, and Ken, Thomas. *Doxology.* arr. Boyd, Bill; and ed. Daellenbach, Charles. Hal Leonard Publishing Corp. 1992. 0:32. I. B♭₁–B♭. Chorale style with fermatas. All quarter notes (except last note). Comes with practice/performance cassette. See: Daellenbach, Charles, *Book of Beginning Tuba Solos,* under "Tuba and Keyboard Collections."

Boutry, Roger. *Tubacchanale.* Alphonse Leduc Editions Paris. 1956. $14.45. 7:32. V. E$_1$–b'. Á mon ami Paul Bernard, Professeur au Conservatoire National de Musique. "Pour tuba en ut ou Saxhorn basse Si♭ et Piano." Exploits the full range of the tuba; designed for French tuba. Double tonguing, fast tempi, mixed meter, strong technique required. See: Thompson/Lemke, *French Music for Low Brass Instruments.*

Boutry, Roger. *Tubaroque.* Alphonse Leduc Editions Paris. 1955. $11.50. À mon ami Paul Bernard . "Pièce pour Tuba ut ou Saxhorn basse Si♭ ou Trombone basse et Piano." See listing under "Music for Tuba and Orchestra." Also see: Thompson/Lemke, *French Music for Low Brass Instruments.*

Bowles, Richard W. *Changing Scene.* CPP/Belwin, Inc. 1973. $4.00. 2:55. III. F$_1$–f. Good solid intermediate solo using mixed meter (3/4, 4/5, 5/4) to give a spacious feeling. Andante rubato quasi cadenza passages as well as faster allegro passages. Eighth note is fastest rhythm. See: Lamb, Jack, *Solo Sounds for Tuba Levels 3–5, Vol. 1,* under "Tuba and Keyboard Collections."

Bowles, Richard W. *Deep Rock.* CPP/Belwin, Inc. 1973. $4.00. 2:43. II. A♭$_1$–e♭. Easy rock tempo; Slow waltz; Tempo 1. Fun light rock feel with few technical challenges. Some infrequently used notes for beginning level (c♭, g♭, etc.). Some slurring. See: Lamb, Jack, *Solo Sounds for Tuba Levels 1–3, Vol. 1,* under "Tuba and Keyboard Collections."

Bowles, Richard W. *Venetian Carnival.* CPP/Belwin, Inc. 1973. $4.00. 2:08. II–III. B$_1$♭–e♭. Intermediate theme and variations based on the "classic" *Carnival of Venice.* Includes a simple cadenza. See listing under "Music for Tuba and Band"; and Lamb, Jack, *Solo Sounds for Tuba Levels 1–3, Vol. 1* under "Tuba and Keyboard Collections."

Boyce, William. *Gavotte from Symphony No. 4.* arr. Vedesky, Anton. Medici Music Press. 1982. $3.50. 2:36. III. C–f. Good transcription of Baroque work in cut time. A few eighth-note runs, otherwise no technical problems.

Boyd, Bill. *Canadian Brass Blues.* ed. Daellenbach, Charles. Hal Leonard Publishing Corp. 1992. 0:32. I. E♭–B♭. Very limited range, repetitive blues figure. Some eighth notes. Comes with practice/performance cassette. See: Daellenbach, Charles, *Book of Beginning Tuba Solos,* under "Tuba and Keyboard Collections."

Boyd, Bill, arr. *Come, Thou Fount of Every Blessing.* Hal Leonard Publishing Corp. 1992. 1:02. II. B♭$_1$–c. American folk hymn. See: Daellenbach, Charles, *Book of Easy Tuba Solos,* under "Tuba and Keyboard Collections."

Boyd, Bill, arr. *The Cruel War Is Raging.* ed. Daellenbach, Charles. Hal Leonard Publishing Corp. 1992. 0:53. I. C–a. American folk song. Two dot-

ted-quarter and eighth-note rhythms; otherwise very simple rhythms. Comes with practice/performance cassette. See: Daellenbach, Charles, *Book of Beginning Tuba Solos,* under "Tuba and Keyboard Collections."

Boyd, Bill, arr. *The Erie Canal.* Hal Leonard Publishing Corp. 1992. 0:53. II. D–c. Moderately. American folk song. A few syncopations and dotted rhythms. See: Daellenbach, Charles, *Book of Easy Tuba Solos,* under "Tuba and Keyboard Collections."

Boyd, Bill, arr. *Hey, Ho! Nobody Home.* Hal Leonard Publishing Corp. 1992. 0:43. II. C–d. Moderately (not too fast). English folk song. Twice through in F minor, once in G minor. See: Daellenbach, Charles, *Book of Easy Tuba Solos,* under "Tuba and Keyboard Collections."

Boyd, Bill, arr. *Loch Lomond.* Hal Leonard Publishing Corp. 1992. 0:48. I. C–d. Moderately. Scottish folk song. See: Daellenbach, Charles, *Book of Easy Tuba Solos,* under "Tuba and Keyboard Collections."

Boyd, Bill, arr. *The Riddle Song.* ed. Daellenbach, Charles. Hal Leonard Publishing Corp. 1992. 0:46. I. B♭$_1$–c. Moderately. English ballad. Quarter note is fastest rhythm. Comes with practice/performance cassette. See: Daellenbach, Charles, *Book of Beginning Tuba Solos,* under "Tuba and Keyboard Collections."

Boyd, Bill, arr. *Song of the Volga Boatman.* ed. Daellenbach, Charles. Hal Leonard Publishing Corp. 1992. 0:58. I. D–B♭. Russian folk song. Very limited range. A couple of sixteenth notes included. Comes with practice/performance cassette. See: Daellenbach, Charles, *Book of Beginning Tuba Solos,* under "Tuba and Keyboard Collections."

Boyd, Bill, arr. *Streets of Laredo.* ed. Daellenbach, Charles. Hal Leonard Publishing Corp. 1992. 0:35. I. B♭$_1$–B♭. American folk song (adapted from old Irish air). In 3/4 time with no technical problems. Comes with practice/performance cassette. See: Daellenbach, Charles, *Book of Beginning Tuba Solos,* under "Tuba and Keyboard Collections."

Boyd, Bill, arr. *The Wayfaring Stranger.* Hal Leonard Publishing Corp. 1992. 0:45. I–II. C–d. Slowly. American folk song. See: Daellenbach, Charles, *Book of Easy Tuba Solos,* under "Tuba and Keyboard Collections."

Boyd, Bill, arr. *Yankee Doodle.* ed. Daellenbach, Charles. Hal Leonard Publishing Corp. 1992. 0:27. I. B♭$_1$a. Traditional American. Once through the tune, complete with *Shave and a Haircut* at the end. Two dotted-eighth, sixteenth patterns; otherwise eighth and quarter notes. Comes with practice/performance cassette. See: Daellenbach, Charles, *Book of Beginning Tuba Solos,* under "Tuba and Keyboard Collections."

Bozza, Eugène. *Allegro et Finale.* Alphonse Leduc Editions Paris. 1953. $11.50. 5:35. IV–V. E–a' (b'). "Pour Contrebasse à Cordes ou Tuba ut ou Saxhorn basse Si♭ ou Trombone basse et piano."

For French tuba. Neo-Baroque writing. Mostly scalewise writing; a few large interval skips. Good recital material. See: Thompson/Lemke, *French Music for Low Brass Instruments.* Recorded by Gerhard Georgie.

Bozza, Eugène. *Allegro and Finale.* ed. Larin, J. Moscow: Muzyka. 1979. See: Larin, J., *Pieces for Tuba and Piano,* under "Tuba and Keyboard Collections."

Bozza, Eugène. *Concertino.* Alphonse Leduc Editions Paris. 1967. $19.05. 17:00. Written for Harvey Phillips. "Pour Tuba en ut ou Saxhorn basse en Sib et orchestre ou piano." See listing under "Music for Tuba and Orchestra." Also see: Thompson/Lemke, *French Music for Low Brass Instruments.* Recorded by Steven Seward.

Bozza, Eugène. *New Orleans.* Alphonse Leduc Editions Paris. 1962. $14.45. 4:30. V. F_1–bb'. "Pour Saxhorn basse Sib ou Tuba ut ou Trombone basse et Piano." Cadenzalike passages. Impressionistic tonal colors throughout combined with pseudo-jazz/ragtime syncopation. Wide skips; wide range. See: Thompson/Lemke, *French Music for Low Brass Instruments.*

Bozza, Eugène. *Prélude et Allegro.* Alphonse Leduc Editions Paris. 1953. $11.50. IV. (A_1) E–a'. À Monsieur Moulard, Professeur de Contrebasse au Conservatoire National de Valenciennes. "Pour contrebasse à Cordes ou Tuba ut ou saxhorn basse Sib ou Trombone basse et Piano." For French tuba. One-movement work with several moods, including a cadenza in the middle. Primarily conceived as a solo for string bass, still makes a nice addition to the repertoire. See: Thompson/Lemke, *French Music for Low Brass Instruments.* See next two listings.

Bozza, Eugène. *Prélude and Allegro.* ed. Larin, J. Moscow: Muzyka. 1979. See: Larin, J., *Pieces for Tuba and Piano,* under "Tuba and Keyboard Collections."

Bozza, Eugène. *Prélude et Allegro.* arr. Yasumoto, Hiroyuki. Toa Music International Co. 1989. Transposed a major third down from original. Also see: Yasumoto, Hiroyuki, *Tuba Volume #3,* under "Tuba and Keyboard Collections."

Bozza, Eugène. *Thème Varié.* Alphonse Leduc Editions Paris. 1957. $11.50. 4:00. IV–V. G_1(f')–g. "Pour Tuba ut ou Saxhorn basse Sib ou Trombone basse et Piano." Theme and (four) variations with cadenza. Fun piece to play; good recital material. (A variation of the *Elephant* from Saint-Saëns, *Carnival of the Animals?*) See: Thompson/Lemke, *French Music for Low Brass Instruments.*

Brahms, Johannes. *Cradle Song.* arr. Kinyon, John. M. Witmark and Sons. 1958. I. See: Kinyon, John, *Breeze-Easy Recital Pieces,* under "Tuba and Keyboard Collections."

Brahms, Johannes. *Five Songs.* arr. Little, Donald C. Southern Music Company. $6.50. 8:22 (1:32, 1:28, 1:55, 2:01, 1:26). III–IV. F–b. 1. *Ständchen,* Op. 106, 1889; 2. *O kühler Wald,* Op. 72, 1877; 3.

Minnelied, Op. 71, 1877; 4. *Sonntag,* Op. 47, 1868; 5. *Vergebliches Ständchen,* Op. 84, 1882. For tuba and piano or bass trombone and piano. Very lyrical transcriptions retaining the wonderful vocal quality of the songs. Good recital material.

Brahms, J. *Lullaby.* arr. Jacobs, Wesley. Encore Music Publishers. 0:41. I–II. D–d. Slowly. In D major. With exception of key, level I. Some slurring; some D–d octave jumps. See: Jacobs, Wesley, *Solos from the Classics,* under "Tuba and Keyboard Collections."

Brahms, Johannes. *On the Lake (Auf dem See),* Op. 59. arr. Dishinger, Ronald Christian. Medici Music Press. 1990. $3.50. 3:05. II–III. D–f. Limited range. Lyrical solo in 3/4 time with some slurring. No technical problems.

Brahms, Johannes. *Sandman.* arr. Jacobs, Wesley. Encore Music Publishers. 0:42. I. C–d. Quietly. Some easy slurring, a couple of dotted quarter notes; no other technical problems. See: Jacobs, Wesley, *Solos from the Classics,* under "Tuba and Keyboard Collections."

Brahms, Johannes. *Sunday, (Sonntag),* Op. 47, 1868. CPP/Belwin, Inc. Published separately. Out of print. ed. Little, Don. CPP/Belwin, Inc. 1991. Also see: Little, Don, *Solo-Pak for Tuba, Part Two,* under "Tuba and Keyboard Collections."

Brahms, Johannes. *Two Lieder.* arr. Perantoni, Daniel. Hal Leonard Publishing Corp. 1976. See: Perantoni, Daniel, *Master Solos, Intermediate Level,* under "Tuba and Keyboard Collections."

Brahms, Johannes. *Waltz.* arr. Graham, James. TUBA Press. 1991. 2:02. III. G–a. Moderato. Good recital material. See: Graham, James, *Concert Music for Tuba,* under "Tuba and Keyboard Collections."

Brahms, Johannes. *Waltz.* arr. Jacobs, Wesley. Encore Music Publishers. 1:14. I–II. B_1–d. Slow Waltz. Slurring throughout. In 3/4 time; in C major. See: Jacobs, Wesley, *Solos from the Classics,* under "Tuba and Keyboard Collections."

Brahms, S. [*sic*]. *Waltz.* ed. Lebedev, A. Moscow: Muzyka. 1986. 1:15. III. G–bb. Grazioso. Same as two preceding listings. See: Lebedev, A., *Tuba Tutor, Vol. 2,* under "Tuba and Keyboard Collections."

Brahmstedt, N. K. *Stupendo.* Voxman, Himie (compiled and edited). Rubank, Inc. 1937. Pubished separately, $1.50. "Solo Tuba—Eb or BBb tuba." See: Rubank, *Soloist Folio for Bass (Eb or BBb),* under "Tuba and Keyboard Collections." Also see listing under "Music for Tuba and Band."

Brandon, Sy. *Designs and Patterns for Tuba and Grand Piano.* TUBA Press. 1973. $7.00. 4:37 (0:51, 0:41, 1:16, 0:57, 1:32). V. C_2–e'. To Barton Cummings. Honorable Mention in 1973 NACWPI Composition Contest. Five movements, fourth movement unaccompanied. Very contemporary writing, especially for piano. Pianist must snap strings, rap knuckles on wood, move pedals up and down, roll mallets on strings. Tuba has wide skips, mixed meter, trills etc. Takes two mature players. Two copies needed for performance. Written November 28, 1973, Boise, Idaho. See review in *T.U.B.A. Journal,* Vol. 1, no. 3, p. 6.

Brandon, Sy. *Sonata for Tuba and Piano.* TUBA Press. 1981. $12.00. 15:10 (4:06, 3:20, 7:44). IV–V. F₁–f'. To Harvey Phillips. Three movements. Allegretto; Andante; Allegro Moderato (Rondo—Passacaglia). Contemporary writing with quite a bit of lyricism. Requires a good repetitive tongue. Wide range, mixed meter, well within the ability of an advanced player.

Brandon, Sy. *Three Episodes.* Co-Op Press. 1988. $5.00. 6:40 (2:34, 2:40, 1:26) . IV. G₁–bb. To Amy. Three movements: Frolic; Song; March. Very lyrical. Each movement has a slight modal quality and some easy meter changes. Frequent imitation between tuba and piano.

Brass Wind Publications. See listings under "Tuba and Keyboard Collections."

Bratton, John W. *The Teddy Bears' Picnic.* arr. MacLean, Douglas. M. Witmark and Sons. 1942. 3:00. II–III. (F₁) Bb₁–f (bb). Complete version of the classic solo associated with the tuba. Makes for a nice recital piece or novelty encore piece for an advanced player.

Braun, Yehezkel. *Three Traditional Tunes for Sabbath* (1974). Israel Music Institute. 1975. III. G–c'. *Adon Olom* (*Lord of the Universe*), Andante; *Yom Ze Meecoubad* (*This Day Is Honored*), Larghetto; *Yigdal* (*Growing*), Maestoso. Three traditional songs presented in a simple musical way. No technical problems; easy accompaniment. Upper tessitura—best on F tuba or euphonium.

Braun, Yehezkel. *Three Traditional Tunes for Sabbath Eve* (1974). Israel Music Institute. 1975. III. C–eb'. *Lecha Dodi* (*Come My Beloved*), Andante cantabile; *Sholom Alechem* (*Peace Unto You*), Largo e festivo; *Ya Reebom* (*The Master*), Andantino. Three traditional songs presented in a simple musical way. No technical problems; easy accompaniment. Upper tessitura—best on F tuba or euphonium.

Briegel, George F. *Basso Profundo.* Available from the composer. 1952. See listing under "Music for Tuba and Band."

Briegel, George F. *Mulberry Street Tarantella.* Was available from the composer. 1963. 2:00. II. C–eb (g). Good intermediate solo.

Brink, Daniel S. *Three Movements.* Sound Ideas Publications. 1989. $16.00. 10:35 (2:57, 4:38, 3:00). IV. F₁–e'. Tuba Pomposa; Tuba Lirica; Tuba Gioconda. Lyrical and technical passages throughout. Last movement has quick articulations and 7/8 interspersed. See review in *T.U.B.A. Journal,* Vol. 18, no. 3, p. 17.

Britten, Benjamin. *The Sentimental Sarabande from the "Simple Symphony" for String Orchestra.* ed. Lebedev, A. Moscow: Muzyka. 1984. 1:05. III. Ab₁–ab. In 3/2 time. No technical problems. See:

Lebedev, A., *Tuba Tutor, Vol. 1,* under "Tuba and Keyboard Collections."

Brizzi, Aldo. *Carnival Time.*

Brooks, E. *The Message.* arr. Buchtel, Forrest L. Neil A. Kjos Music Company. 1952 (renewed 1980). $2.00. 3:19. III. Ab₁–f. "Tuba (Eb or BBb)." Allegretto; Andante sostenuto; Allegretto. Melodic 3/4 section followed by a 2/4 "polka-like" technical section. Well within intermediate player's grasp.

Brothern, Hartman. *Tuba Sonata in A.* See review in *T.U.B.A. Journal,* Vol. 1, no. 2, p. 10.

Broughton, Bruce. *Sonata* (*Concerto*). Masters Music Publications, Inc. 1976. $7.95. To Tommy Johnson. See listing under "Music for Tuba and Band." Also see: Bird, Gary, ed., *Program Notes for the Solo Tuba.*

Brouquières, Jean. *Au Temps de la Coeur* (*At the Time of the Heart*). Éditions Robert Martin. 1982. $4.25. 2:00. I–II. F–bb. "Pour basse Sib ou Tuba ut et piano." For French tuba. Stately early solo with mostly stepwise motion. See: Thompson/Lemke, *French Music for Low Brass Instruments.* Also see review in *T.U.B.A. Journal,* Vol. 11, no. 4, p. 26.

Brouquières, Jean. *Tubaria.* Éditions Robert Martin. 1983. $4.25. 2:15. II. F–f '. À Jean-Paul Dambacher, amicalement. J.B. "Pour Tuba ut (in C) ou Basse Sib (in Bb et Piano." Concours de Composition 1983 de la Confédération Musicale de France. Prix Robert Martin. For French tuba. Some sixteenth notes. See: Thompson/Lemke, *French Music for Low Brass Instruments.*

Brown, Charles. *Récitatif, Lied et Final.* Alphonse Leduc Editions Paris. 1961. Out of print. 7:00. E₁ (C)–(a') bb'. Á mon ami Paul Bernard, Professeur au Conservatoire National Supérieur de Musique. "Pour Saxhorn basse Sib ou Tuba ut ou Trombone Basse et Piano." Some passages in tenor clef. See: Thompson/Lemke, *French Music for Low Brass Instruments.*

Brown, Newel Kay. *And Then There Were Six* (*Variations for Tuba and Piano*). Seesaw Music Corporation Publishers. 1978. $14.00. 9:05. V. A₁b–e'. For Gary Bird. Contemporary writing. Takes a soloist with a good technique and a good ear. Good rhythmical dialogue between instruments. Strong accompanist required. Completed January 31, 1975 in Denton, TX. See: Bird, Gary, ed., *Program Notes for the Solo Tuba.*

Brown, Newel Kay. *Prelude and Scherzo.* Seesaw Music Corporation Publishers. 1969. $12.00. 5:00. IV–V. Bb₁–d'. Some large interval skips. See review in *T.U.B.A. Journal,* Vol. 7, no. 2, p. 24.

Brown, Rayner. *Diptych.* Western International Music. 1970. $4.00. 5:10 (2:49, 2:21). IV. E₁–e'. Prelude–Fugue. Prelude, in 3/2 time, has a dialogue going with accompanist; nothing faster than quarter notes at a slow tempo. Fugue in 6/8, with a jump from f to e' and some low articulations. No big technical problems for the suggested level.

Browning, Zack. *For the Funk of It.* Brixton Publications. 1992. $10.00. 5:00. IV–V. E♭₁–f'. To Fritz Kaenzig. Multi-styles: funk and off-beat reggae, contrasted with lyrical passages developed from a twelve-tone set. Needs a strong accompanist and a soloist with a strong stylistic and rhythmic sense.

Bruniau, Aug. *Sur la Montagne (Pastorale).* Gérard Billaudot. 4:25. III–IV. B♭–g (b♭'). Andantino; Allegretto. "Baryton Solo ou Basse Si♭ ou Trombone Si♭" For French tuba. Lovely lyrical opening section; moderately technical allegro section follows.

Buchtel, Forrest Lawrence. *Adonis.* Neil A. Kjos Music Company. 1948. Out of print. 1:58. I. E♭– (c) e♭. Moderato. Very easy beginning solo in 3/4 time at a reasonable tempo. Quarter note is fastest rhythm.

Buchtel, Forrest Lawrence. *Ajax.* Neil A. Kjos Music Company. 1975. $1.75. 1:44. I. D–d. Andante. Original copyright 1948. Good beginning solo in 4/4 time. Quarter note is fastest rhythm at reasonable tempo. Mostly stepwise motion.

Buchtel, Forrest Lawrence. *Apollo.* Mills Music. 1945. Out of print. 3:03. II–III. B♭₁–f. Andante/Allegretto. Advanced beginner level polka solo. Stately Andante section in 4/4, Allegretto section in 2/4.

Buchtel, Forrest Lawrence. *The Archer.* M. M. Cole Publishing Co. 1938. Out of print. 3:33. II. B♭₁d–(f). Andante; Allegretto. Some repeated sixteenth notes in Allegretto section. See listing under "Tuba and Keyboard Collections."

Buchtel, Forrest Lawrence. *At the Ball.* Neil A. Kjos Music Company. 1954. Out of print. 2:00. I. B♭₁–c. Good beginning solo.

Buchtel, Forrest Lawrence. *Attila.* Neil A. Kjos Music Company. 1948. Out of print. 1:55. I–II. (D) E♭–e♭. Andante—mostly stepwise solo in 4/4 time; followed by faster (Con Moto) section.

Buchtel, Forrest Lawrence. *The Ballerina.* M. M. Cole Publishing Co. 1938. Out of print. 3:08. II–III. G₁–f. Waltz. In 3/4 time with some eighth-note runs. See listing under "Tuba and Keyboard Collections."

Buchtel, Forrest Lawrence. *The Cavalier.* M. M. Cole Publishing Co. 1938. Out of print. 2:38. II. C–f. Andante and Waltz. A few accidentals; otherwise no technical problems. See listing under "Tuba and Keyboard Collections."

Buchtel, Forrest Lawrence. *The Courier.* M. M. Cole Publishing Co. 1938. Out of print. 3:05. I–II. A♭₁–d♭. Andante and Waltz. Theme and variation. See listing under "Tuba and Keyboard Collections."

Buchtel, Forrest Lawrence. *The Flatterer.* Mills Music. 1958. Out of print. 2:00. II. B♭₁–f. No major problems.

Buchtel, Forrest Lawrence. *Gladiator.* Neil A. Kjos Music Company. 1945. Out of print. 2:00. I. B♭₁–B♭. Very limited range. Good introduction to legato and staccato.

Buchtel, Forrest Lawrence. *Golden Dreams Waltz.* Neil A. Kjos Music Company. 1957. Out of print. 2:00. I. B♭₁–B♭. Good beginning solo in 3/4 time.

Buchtel, Forrest Lawrence. *Golden Glow.* Mills Music. 1958. 1:00. I. C–B♭. Good beginning solo in 3/4 time.

Buchtel, Forrest Lawrence. *The Grenadier.* M. M. Cole Publishing Co. 1938. Out of print. 2:23. II. C–f. Andantino section in 6/8. Allegretto section in cut time with syncopation throughout. See listing under "Tuba and Keyboard Collections."

Buchtel, Forrest Lawrence. *Harlequin.* Neil A. Kjos Music Company. 1957. Out of print. 1:55. II. (A♭₁ D–c. "E♭ or BB♭ Tuba." Andante 4/4 section is stately with optional octave choices for ease of range. Difficulty of Allegro 2/2 section depends on choice of tempo.

Buchtel, Forrest Lawrence. *Hercules.* Neil A. Kjos Music Company. 1948. Out of print. 1:31. I. D–e♭. Con Moto. Mostly stepwise solo in quick 4/4 time. Fastest rhythm is quarter note. Repeated material with eight measures in the middle.

Buchtel, Forrest Lawrence. *Hermes.* Mills Music. 1945. 2:52. III. B♭₁–e♭. Stately opening Andante; polka style Allegretto section with cadenza. Minor technical considerations include interval jumps of sixths and octaves, and, depending on tempo of the Allegretto section, articulations.

Buchtel, Forrest Lawrence. *How Can I Leave Thee.* M. M. Cole Publishing Co. 1938. Out of print. 2:56. II–III. E♭–g. "In different rhythms." In 4/4, 2/4, and cut time. Short cadenza. Last Allegro section is all syncopated. See listing under "Tuba and Keyboard Collections."

Buchtel, Forrest Lawrence. *The Hussar.* M. M. Cole Publishing Co. 1938. Out of print. 3:29. II. G₁–d♭. Andante; Tempo di Polonaise. Solo in 3/4 time. No technical problems except for three quick articulated lower notes. See listing under "Tuba and Keyboard Collections."

Buchtel, Forrest Lawrence. *Introduction and Rondo.* C. L. Barnhouse Company. 1937. $3.50. 4:30. III. G₁–g. Andantino; Allegretto; Andantino; Presto. Andantino section in 6/8 followed by a cut time Allegretto section with some technical work to master; depending on the tempo chosen could be challenging to the early intermediate player.

Buchtel, Forrest Lawrence. *Jolly Sailor.* Mills Music. 1945. 1:13. II. B♭₁–f. Cut time Allegretto, depending on the tempo chosen, could present eighth-note articulation challenges. Mostly stepwise motion with a nautical flavor.

Buchtel, Forrest Lawrence. *The Juggler.* M. M. Cole Publishing Co. 1938. Out of print. 2:36. II–III. G₁–c. Allegretto. Cut time or 4/4 time. Repeated and stepwise eighth notes. Short cadenza. See listing under "Tuba and Keyboard Collections."

Buchtel, Forrest Lawrence. *King Mydas.* Fillmore. 1935. Out of print. 4:32. II–III. G₁–e♭. Maestoso; Faster. "Solo for BB♭ Bass." Short cadenza, smooth

26 THE TUBA SOURCE BOOK

Maestoso-like section and a series of optional cut-time polka sections.

Buchtel, Forrest Lawrence, arr. *Londonderry Air.* Neil A. Kjos Music Company. 1978. $2.00. 2:29. II–III. A₁–f. Andante. Written for a variety of solo instruments. Traditional melody in D♭ major. Great opportunity for lyricism. Key is the only technical consideration.

Buchtel, Forrest Lawrence. *The Mannequin.* M. M. Cole Publishing Co. 1938. Out of print. 2:21. II. C–d. Tempo di Valse. Some slurs, some repeated eighth notes. Short cadenza. See listing under "Tuba and Keyboard Collections."

Buchtel, Forrest Lawrence. *The Mariner.* M. M. Cole Publishing Co. 1938. Out of print. 2:35. II. A♭₁–e♭. Andante section majestic, "In a pompous manner." Allegretto section has repeated and stepwise sixteenth notes with a short cadenza. See listing under "Tuba and Keyboard Collections."

Buchtel, Forrest Lawrence. *Il Penseroso e L'Allegro.* Carl Fischer Inc. 1939. $3.25. 3:50. III. (A♭₁) B♭₁–f. Andante con moto; Allegro. "Solo for Baritone or Tuba; Tuba E♭-BB♭." Originally published by The Fillmore Bros. Co. Andante section has a lyrical (mostly slurred) vocal quality. Allegro section in 3/4 time has triplets and at tempo given will require some flexibility.

Buchtel, Forrest Lawrence. *Pied Piper.* Neil A. Kjos Music Company. 1957. Out of print. 2:30. I. B♭₁–d. Good beginning solo.

Buchtel, Forrest Lawrence. *The Ranger.* M. M. Cole Publishing Co. 1938. Out of print. 3:04. II. D–d (f). Andantino; Allegro. Some repeated eighth notes in cut-time Allegro section; otherwise no technical problems. See listing under "Tuba and Keyboard Collections."

Buchtel, Forrest Lawrence. *The Reluctant Clown.* Mills Music. 1945. Out of print. 1:13. II. D–f. Andantino. Light solo in cut time. Arpeggios and D octave jumps; otherwise no technical problems for the young player.

Buchtel, Forrest Lawrence. *The Salamander.* C. L. Barnhouse Company. 1937. $3.50. 3:44. III. F₁–e♭. Andante; Allegro moderato; Tempo di Bolero. Theme-and-variation form. Some articulation considerations depending on tempo. Some grace note "rips" and a short cadenza.

Buchtel, Forrest Lawrence. *Song of the Sea.* Neil A. Kjos Music Company. 1971. $2.00. 2:10. II–III. B♭₁–e♭. Original copyright date 1944. Andante section in 12/8; Allegretto in 2/4. Mostly stepwise motion throughout. No technical problems. Is part of the *First Soloist Band Book* and was also published for tuba and band.

Buchtel, Forrest Lawrence. *Song of the Viking.* M. M. Cole Publishing Co. 1938. Out of print. 1:43. II. G₁–d. Moderato; Maestoso. G minor and G major. No technical problems. See listing under "Tuba and Keyboard Collections."

Buchtel, Forrest Lawrence. *The Spartan.* M. M. Cole Publishing Co. 1938. Out of print. 4:27. III. A♭₁–f. Andante and Allegretto. Theme and variations. Last variation in D♭ major. See listing under "Tuba and Keyboard Collections."

Buchtel, Forrest Lawrence. *The Troubadour.* M. M. Cole Publishing Co. 1938. Out of print. 3:14. III. F₁–f. Moderato and Bolero. See listing under "Tuba and Keyboard Collections."

Buchtel, Forrest Lawrence. *The Volunteer.* M. M. Cole Publishing Co. 1938. Out of print. 4:00. II. B♭₁–f. Tempo de Valse. Solo in 3/4 time. Some eighth notes, otherwise no technical problems. See listing under "Tuba and Keyboard Collections."

Buchtel, Forrest Lawrence. *The Voyageur.* M. M. Cole Publishing Co. 1938. Out of print. 3:25. II–III. A♭₁–d♭. Andantino section in 6/8, Waltz in 3/4. Last section in D♭ major. See listing under "Tuba and Keyboard Collections."

Buchtel, Forrest Lawrence, arr. *When the Saints Go Marching In.* Neil A. Kjos Music Company. 1966. Out of print. 1:25. I. B♭₁–B♭. March tempo. Familiar solo in cut time. Some eighth notes. No technical problems. Written for a variety of solo instruments.

Buchtel, Forrest Lawrence. *Wotan.* Neil A. Kjos Music Company. 1975. $1.75. 1:25. I–II. (B♭₁) E♭–e♭. Andante; Waltz Tempo. Original copyright 1948. Stately theme in 4/4 time followed by a Waltz variation in one. No technical problems.

Buchtel, Forrest Lawrence. See listing under "Tuba and Keyboard Collections."

Buononcini, Giovanni. *Pupille Nere (Dark Eyes).* tr. Gershenfeld, Mitchell. Medici Music Press. 1985. 1:50. II. C–d. In 3/4 time; some slurring. See: Gershenfeld, Mitchell, *Medici Masterworks Solos, Volume 1,* under "Tuba and Keyboard Collections."

Burgstahler, Elton E. *Chansonnoir.* Pro Art Publications. 1974. Out of print. 4:52. III. G₁–a♭. Andante maestoso; Andante sostenuto. Stately passages combined with lyrical phrases throughout. Cadenza included.

Burgstahler, Elton E. *Tuba Caper.* Pro Art Publications. 1974. Out of print. 2:31. II. G₁ (C)–f. Easy rhythms, a few octave jumps; good advanced beginner material. Cadenza (with bar lines) included.

Burgstahler, Elton E. *Tubalow.* Pro Art Publications. 1974. Out of print. 3:04. III. B♭₁–g. Theme-and-variation feel to this piece. Some technical passages, some lyrical ones. Cadenza included (third note from end of cadenza should be E♮).

Burshtin, M. *Legend.* ed. Voronov, G. Moscow: Muzyka. 1984. See: Voronov, G., *Works for Tuba and Piano by Russian Composers,* under "Tuba and Keyboard Collections."

Büsser, Henri P. *Récit et Thème Variations,* Op. 37.

Butterfield, Don. *Journal of Days.* DB Publishing Co. In preparation. For tuba and harpsichord or piano.

Butts, Carrol M. *Suite for Tuba and Piano*. Neil A. Kjos Music Company. 1978. $5.00. 6:21 (3:35, 2:46). IV. C–d'. Dedicated to Barton Cummings. Andante; Andante Meno Mosso. Middle-upper tessitura. Good opportunity for great lyricism. Not overwhelming technique for Level IV player. Recorded by Barton Cummings. See review in *T.U.B.A. Journal*, Vol. 8, no. 3, p. 31.

Byrd, William. *The Earle of Oxford's Marche*, from *Fitzwilliam Virginal Book*. tr. Dishinger, Ronald Christian. Medici Music Press. 1990. $3.50. 2:20. III. B♭₁–f. Printed tempo may be a bit fast. A few sixteenth notes; no big technical problems.

Cabus. *Alla Cacia*. Edition Andel Uitgaven.

Caccini, Giulio. *Amarilli, Mia Bella*. arr. Little, Don. CPP/Belwin, Inc. 1991. 2:50. II. C–d. Lyrical solo in F minor. Good opportunity for musical expression. See: Little, Don, *Solo-Pak for Tuba, Part Two*, under "Tuba and Keyboard Collections."

Caccini, Giulio. *Amarilli, Mia Bella*. Phillips, Harry I. (compiled and edited). Shawnee Press Inc. 1967. 2:14. II–III. E–e. Moderato affetuoso. Lyrical, slurred 4/4 transcription in a minor key. See: Phillips, Harry I., *Eight Bel Canto Songs*, in this section.

Calabro, Louis. *Sonata-Fantasia for Tuba and Piano*. TUBA Press. 1993. 23:00 (10:57, 3:11, 8:44). V. F₁–ab'. Slow/Fast/Slow; B major Paradox; Quasi Rondo. Soon to be published. Original copyright 1987 by Louis Calabro. Several melodies heard over a repeating ostinato by the pianist. Some jazz elements. Recorded by Mark Nelson. See review in *T.U.B.A. Journal*, Vol. 15, no. 3, p. 39.

Caldara, Antonio. *Sebben, Crudele*. Phillips, Harry I. (compiled and edited). Shawnee Press Inc. 1967. 2:07. II. D–e. Allegretto grazioso. Lyrical, slurred 3/4 transcription in a minor key. A couple of grace notes; no difficult technical challenges. See: Phillips, Harry I., *Eight Bel Canto Songs*, in this section.

Callahan, Charles. *In the Beginning, Biblical Poem for Tuba (Cello) and Organ*. Morning Star Music Publishers. 1993. 4:10. III–IV. In preparation. A–eb'. Genesis I:1–5. Upper tessitura throughout; easy rhythms. Very lyrical and reflective writing.

Cals, Michel. *Pièce Prève*. Alphonse Leduc Editions Paris. $18.25.

Capuzzi, Antonio. *Andante and Rondo from Concerto for Double Bass*. arr. Catelinet, Philip. Hinrichsen Edition. 1967. $8.95. 8:00. IV–V. (F₁) Bb₁–g (eb'). "For tuba (bass clef), Euphonium/Trombone (treble and bass clef), Bass Eb and Bb (treble-clef) and Piano." The Andante cantabile is a lovely lyrical section containing some legato sixteenth-note passages. Rondo contains many sixteenth-note runs with optional octave ranges. Middle section of Rondo in Eb minor. Excellent recital material. A different version recorded by James Self.

Carey, Henry, and Smith, Samuel. *America*. arr. Boyd, Bill. Hal Leonard Publishing Corp. 1992. 0:37. I.

D–c. Once through the melody in 3/4 time. A couple of eighth notes; easy rhythms. Comes with practice/performance cassette. See: Daellenbach, Charles, *Book of Beginning Tuba Solos*, under "Tuba and Keyboard Collections."

Carion, M. *Jumbo*. Edition Andel Uitgaven.

Carissimi, Gian Giacomo. *Heart Victorious (Cantata)*. arr. Barnes, Clifford P. Jack Spratt Music Co. 1965. $3.00. 1:15. II–III. Bb₁–eb. Allegro con brio. Dotted-half note = 60; some eighth-note runs; depending on tempo, requires lightness of articulation. No other technical problems.

Carles, Marc. *Introduction et Toccata*. Alphonse Leduc Editions Paris. 1961. $16.85. 6:25. V. B₁–a'. À Paul Bernard, Professeur au Conservatoire National de Musique. "Pour Trombone Basse ou Tuba ut ou Saxhorn Basse Sib et Piano." For French tuba. Wide range, mixed meter, strong technique required. See: Thompson/Lemke, *French Music for Low Brass Instruments*.

Carrier, Loran F. *Tuba Concerto*. Available from the composer. 1969. 12:00. V. Db₁–f'. Composed for and dedicated to Arthur Green. Two movements. Twelve-tone writing with some improvisation. Difficult accompaniment.

Casas, Bartolomé Perez. *Concierto para Tuba y Piano*. arr. Mas, Vicente Navarro. Very musical. IV–V. D₁–c'. Andante maestoso. Major work by this Spanish composer. Strong articulation and flexible technique required. Recorded by Vicente Navarro Mas.

Casey. *Honeysuckle Polka*. arr. Buchtel, Forrest L. Neil A. Kjos Music Company. 1957. Out of print. 4:00. III–IV. A₁–g. Traditional polka with cadenzas. Triple tonguing.

Casey. *Remembrance of Liberati*. arr. Buchtel, Forrest L. Neil A. Kjos Music Company. 1957. Out of print. 4:30. III–IV. Bb₁–ab. Based on melodies associated with the cornetist Liberati. Triple tonguing throughout.

Castellucci, Louis. *Intermezzo Capriccioso*. Mills Music. 1953. Out of print. 4:30. IV. F₁–d'. Allegretto grazioso. "Tuba or Bassoon Solo." Polka style, requiring flexibility from the tubist.

Castérède, Jacques. *Fantaisie Concertante*. Alphonse Leduc Editions Paris. 1960. $16.85. 7:30. V. B₁–a'. À Paul Bernard, Professeur au Conservatoire National Supérieur de Musique. "Pour Trombone basse ou Tuba ut ou Saxhorn basse Sib et Piano." Very wide range and technique required. For French tuba. Mixed meter, crisp articulation, endurance required. See: Thompson/Lemke, *French Music for Low Brass Instruments*. Also Moscow: Muzyka. 1976. See: Guzii, V., *Pieces for Tuba and Piano*, under "Tuba and Keyboard Collections."

Castérède, Jacques. *Sonatine*. Alphonse Leduc Editions Paris. 1963. $16.85. 7:15. V. E₁–a'. À Paul Bernard, Professeur au Conservatoire National Supérieur de Musique. *Défilé; Sérénade; Final*. "Pour Tuba ut ou Saxhorn basse Sib, et Piano." Wide

range, strong technique required. For French Tuba. Good recital material. Recorded by Gene Pokorny. See: Thompson/Lemke, *French Music for
Low Brass Instruments.*

Catelinet, Philip. *The Dith.* Obrasso Verlag AG. III.

Catelinet, Philip. *Legend.*

Catelinet, Philip. *Valse Gentile.* Obrasso Verlag AG.
III. Written for tuba and brass band. Piano reduction.

Catozzi, A. *Beelzebub.* arr. Seredy, Julius S. Carl Fischer
Inc. 1932. $5.00. 5:30. "Dedicated to my Friend
G. Marquardt, Tuba Soloist." See listing under
"Music for Tuba and Band."

Cecconi, Monic. *Tuba—I.* Éditions Rideau Rouge.
1971. $5.50. 4:30. V. F_1–g'. Morceau de Concours
du Conservatoire National Supérieur de Musique
de Paris 1971. For French tuba. Modern writing:
very free playing, glissandos, wide range. See: Th-
ompson/Lemke, *French Music for Low Brass Instruments.*

Censhu, Jiro. *Hikari-Aru Sora-Wa Shiazukani (Bright
and Early under the Silent Sky. Prelude for Tuba and
Piano).* Available from the composer. 1990. IV–V.
G_1–eb. To Shuzo Karakawa. Very free cadenza/
recitative playing; combined with traditional 6/8
feel. Good recital material.

Censhu, Jiro. *Verdurous Aubade for Tuba and Piano.*
Toa Music International Co. 1989. 3:39. IV. G_1–f'.
For Hiroyuki Yasumoto. Dramatic piece with many
quartal intervals. Lyrical and technical sections.
Good recital piece. See: Yasumoto, Hiroyuki, *Tuba
Volume #3,* under "Tuba and Keyboard Collec-
tions." Recorded by Hiroyuki Yasumoto.

Challan, Henri. *Intermezzo.* Alphonse Leduc Editions
Paris. 1970. $14.95. 6:40. IV–V. A_1–b'. "Pour
Tuba en ut ou Saxhorn basse en Sib et Piano." For
French tuba. Strong lyrical, technical playing equal-
ly needed. Cadenza, 15/8, other compound and
complex meters. See: Thompson/Lemke, *French
Music for Low Brass Instruments.*

Chambers, W. Paris. *The Commodore.* arr. Buchtel,
Forrest Lawrence. Neil A. Kjos Music Company.
1985. $2.50. 3:35. III. A_1–f(g). Original copyright
1959. Published for a variety of instruments with
piano. Cadenza, Andante section, then an Allegretto polka section. Depending on tempo, triple
tonguing involved.

Charles, C. *Cortège et Danse.* Éditions Musicales
Transatlantiques. See: Thompson/Lemke, *French
Music for Low Brass Instruments.*

Charpentier, Jacques. *Prélude et Allegro.* Alphonse
Leduc Editions Paris. 1959. $12.80. 6:00. V. E_1–
bb' (c"). "Pour Saxhorn basse Sib ou Tuba ut ou
Contrebasse à Cordes et Piano." Some tenor clef,
with optional ottava basso in bass clef. Wide range,
strong technique required. For French tuba. See:
Thompson/Lemke, *French Music for Low Brass
Instruments.*

Childs, Barney. *Mary's Idea.* Seesaw Music Corporation Publishers. 1972. 7:20. V. Gb$_1$–eb'. For Lewis

Waldeck. Composed in Deep Springs, September–
June 1972. For tuba and harpsichord: "tuba and
piano are hardly this reviewer's vision of the Prom-
ised Land. How about tuba and harpsichord?"
(Mary Rasmussen in *Brass Quarterly,* Spring 1963
[VI, 3] p. 140.) The composer says "under no
circumstances is piano to be substituted for harpsichord!" Contemporary writing. Score required for
performance; tuba and harpsichord in different
meters at times. See: Bird, Gary, ed., *Program Notes
for the Solo Tuba.*

Childs, Barney. *Seaview for Tuba and Piano.* M. M.
Cole Publishing Co. 1971. Out of print. 8:00. IV.
E_1–eb. For Ray Weisling. "Orchestral tuba; upright
bell." Contemporary writing. Includes mixed meters; free playing using given pitches, with performer's own rhythms, dynamics, durations, pauses;
playing fragments in random order; speaking, combined with more structured playing. Pianist must
improvise given established pitches. See: Bird,
Gary, ed., *Program Notes for the Solo Tuba.*

Choen, Michael. *Diversita Continua.* Kibutz Movement League of Composers. Recorded by Adi
Hershko.

Chopin, Frederick. *Etude,* no. 3 from *27 Etudes,* Op.
10. trans. Dishinger, Ronald Christian. Medici
Music Press. 1989. $3.50. 3:00. II–III. C-f. Lyrical
transcription of familiar Chopin melody presenting
no major techical problems. Quarter note is fastest
rhythm.

Chopin, Frederick. *Nocturne.* Hudadoff, Igor, and
Westcott, William (piano arr.). Pro Art Publica-
tions. 1967. Out of print. See: Hudadoff, Igor,
Fifteen Intermediate Tuba Solos, under "Tuba and
Keyboard Collections."

Chopin, Frederick. *Op. 28—Preludes Nos. 3, 2, and 24.*
arr. Davis, Sharon. Western International Music.
1975. $5.00. 3:49 (1:05, 1:07, 1:36). IV. C–c'
(c#'). Allegro con moto; Lento e legato; Allegro
appassionato. Very lyrical transcriptions. Requires a
good stylistic sense with good flexibility.

Chopin, Frederick. *Prelude No. 6.* ed. Melnikov, S.
Moscow: Military Band Masters Institute. 1957.
See: Melnikov, S., *Pieces for Tuba and Piano,* under
"Tuba and Keyboard Collections."

Chopin, Frederick. *Three Chopin Preludes for Tuba
and Piano.* arr. Frackenpohl, Arthur. TUBA Press.
1993. $6.00. 3:27 (1:20, 1:03, 1:04). IV. (E_1) G_1–
c'. Lento assai (Op. 28, no. 6); Molto agitato (Op.
28, no. 22); Maestoso (Op. 28, no. 9). Very musical transcriptions. Large melodic leaps, flexibility
required. Good recital material.

Christensen, James. *Ballad for Tuba.* Kendor Music,
Inc. 1963. $4.50. 2:00. III. F–a (c'). Dedicated to
Donald Heeren. Upper tessitura with simple
rhythms. All slurred phrases. Pretty melody. Comes
with flexible Songsheet record with Barton Cummings, tuba.

Cioffari, Richard J. *Rhapsody for Tuba and Orchestra.*
Trombone Association Publishing. 1975. For Ivan

Hammond. See listing under "Music for Tuba and Orchestra.".

Clais, Tristan. *Tub' 88.* Gérard Billaudot. 1990. 2:00. III. c–c'. "Pour tuba et piano." For French tuba. Modern notation; three blocks to use with improvised rhythm durations. Composed in 1988. See: Daniel-Lesur, *Collection Panorama,* under "Tuba and Keyboard Collections."

Clarke, Herbert L. *Twilight Dreams.* arr. Jacobs, Wesley. Encore Music Publishers. 1991. $5.00. 2:42. IV. E♭–d♭'. "Waltz Intermezzo for Tuba." Enjoy a dreamy ride through these very accessible Clarke transcriptions. Much lyricism. Requires strong melodic sense and technical strength. Good recital material on any pitch of tuba!

Clarke, Jeremiah. *Trumpet Voluntary.* arr. Lillya, Clifford, and Lillya, Merle. Carl Fischer Inc. 1960. Out of print. 2:30. II–III. F–g. Allegro moderato. Formerly attributed to Henry Purcell. As in the trumpet solo, trill from c to d is included. Eight measures on, eight measures off, also per Jeremiah Clarke's conception.

Cleemput, Werner Van. *Caribbean Flush.* J. Maurer Editions Musicales. 1982. $6.35. 5:33. IV. B♭–a'. Tranquillo, voluttuoso, un poco mesto. "Voor Bastuba Of: Tuba Bariton Euphonium Trombone En Harmonieorkest Of Piano." Upper tessitura; better on F tuba. In cut time with a Caribbean/ Latin flavor. Good recital material.

Clérisse, Robert. *Andante and Allegro.* ed. Voxman, Himie. Rubank, Inc. 1972. 3:00. II–III. B♭₁–f. "For E♭ or BB♭ Bass. Typical French tuba piece with many fermatas and tempo changes in Andante section. Depending on tempo, Allegro section in 2/4 time has no big technical problems. See: Voxman, Himie, *Concert and Contest Collection,* under "Tuba and Keyboard Collections."

Clérisse, Robert. *Chant d'Amour.* Gérard Billaudot. n. d. $5.75. 5:52. IV. D♭–g'. Modéré, sans lenteur. "Pour Saxhorn-Baryton ou Basse avec accompagnement de Piano." French tuba tessitura. Lyrical song. Tempo is slow enough to make technical passages accessible. Depending on instrument chosen, tessitura could be a challenge. See: Thompson/Lemke, *French Music for Low Brass Instruments.*

Clérisse, Robert. *Idylle.* Alphonse Leduc Editions Paris. n. d. $8.60. 1:56. III. B♭–e♭'. "Basse Si♭." Easy intermediate musical solo starting in 3/4 and ending with a 2/4 section with some sixteenth-note scales. For French tuba.

Clérisse, Robert. *Marine.* Éditions M. Combre. 1962. 1:19. III. C–g'. Allargando. "Pour Tuba en ut ou Saxhorn Basse Si♭ avec accompagnement de piano." Requires a good ear: Intervals of a minor ninth, tenth, tritones. Good recital material. See: Thompson/Lemke, *French Music for Low Brass Instruments.*

Clérisse, Robert. *Pièce Lyrique.* Alphonse Leduc Editions Paris. 1957. $11.50. 6:40. III–IV. B₁ (F)–(f') f♯'. À mon ami D. Candelle, Soliste des Concerts Colonne et de la Musique de L'Air. "Pour Tuba ut ou contrebasse à cordes ou Saxhorn basse Si♭ ou trombone basse et Piano." Lyrical writing interspersed with a few technical challenges. For French tuba. See: Thompson/Lemke, French Music for Low Brass Instruments.

Clérisse, Robert. *Prélude et divertissement.* Gérard Billaudot. n. d. $9.50. III–IV. G♭–g'. "Pour Trombone Ut-Basson ou Tuba ou Contrebasse Mi♭ ou Baryton Si♭ ou Saxophone Ténor Si♭ avec accompagnement de Piano." For French tuba. Intermediate flexibility and spirit required.

Clérisse, Robert. *Romance.* Alphonse Leduc Editions Paris. 1957. $8.60. 2:31. II–III. c–f'. Andante con moto. "Basse Si♭." Stately advanced beginner solo. For French tuba.

Clérisse, Robert. *Soir.* Gérard Billaudot. 1953.

Clérisse, Robert. *Voce Nobile (Noble Voice).* Alphonse Leduc Editions Paris. 1953. $7.95. 2:44. III. C–f'. Moderato. "Pour Tuba ut ou contrebasse à Cordes ou Saxhorn basse Si♭ ou Trombone basse et Piano." For French tuba. See: Thompson/Lemke, *French Music for Low Brass Instruments.*

Clews, Eileen. *Quintessence.* Novello and Company.

Clews, Eileen. *Tango.* Novello and Company.

Cody, Robert O. *Theater Piece for Tuba and Piano.* See review in *T.U.B.A. Journal,* Vol. 1, no. 1, p. 37.

Coeck, Louis Jan Alfons Leopold. *Promenade.* de haske muziekuitgave bv. 5:30. IV–V. (C₁) E♭–d'. Good contemporary writing. Combination of textures: glissandos, cadenzas, etc., along with tonal melody.

Cohan, George M. *George M. Cohan Medley.* Hudadoff, Igor, and Westcott, William (piano arr.). Pro Art Publications. 1967. Out of print. See: Hudadoff, Igor, *Fifteen Intermediate Tuba Solos,* under "Tuba and Keyboard Collections."

Cohan, George M. *Give My Regards to Broadway.* arr. Boyd, Bill; ed. Daellenbach, Charles. Hal Leonard Publishing Corp. 1992. 0:38. I. C–B♭. Moderately. In cut time. Quarter note is fastest rhythm. Comes with practice/performance cassette. See: Daellenbach, Charles, *Book of Beginning Tuba Solos,* under "Tuba and Keyboard Collections."

Cohen, Sol B. *Romance and Scherzo.* CPP/Belwin, Inc. 1941. $6.50. 4:22. III. G₁–f. "BB♭ Bass (Tuba) solo with Piano accompaniment." Lyrical Andantino section in 12/8 followed by Scherzo in 2/4. No technical problems.

Cohn, James. *Sonata Romantica for Tuba and Piano.* Liben Music Publishers. 1981. $6.00. 10:10 (2:20, 6:30, 1:20). E₁–e'. For Arthur Bialas. *Ballade* (Allegretto); *Theme and Variations* (Moderato); *Capriccio* (Presto). Requires a flexible technique and solid upper range. Good recital material.

Cole, Keith Ramon. *Romance "Homage to Peter Ilyich."* ed. Wastall, Peter. Boosey and Hawkes, Inc. 1981. 1:11. I–II. C–e♭. See: Wastall, Peter, *Learn As You Play Tuba,* under "Tuba and Keyboard

Collections." Lovely lyrical solo in 3/4 time. Some slurred passages; one leap of a major sixth. Good challenging solo for beginning player.

Cole, Keith Ramon. *Solstice*. ed. Wastall, Peter. Boosey and Hawkes, Inc. 1980. 1:05. II. F–f. See: Wastall, Peter, *Learn As You Play Tuba*, under "Tuba and Keyboard Collections." Misterioso. Easier on E♭ tuba versus BB♭ for younger player.

Compello, Joseph. *Theme and Variations for Tuba*. Joseph Compello Publications. 1987. 3:29 (1:11, 1:24, 1:04). II. F₁–d. Written for Zachary A. Kaminsky. Theme: Ponderous Polka—Lugubrious Ländler—Helicon Hyperdrive. "For B♭ tuba or Baritone 8va." Good advanced-beginner theme and variations with a cadenza that descends chromatically from B♭₁ to F₁. Otherwise range is very comfortable for the level.

Concone, Giuseppe. *Allegretto animato*. arr. Schwotzer, Stephan. Hofmeister. 1993. 3:01. II–III. B♭₁–e♭. In 3/4 time. Some easy arpeggios. See: Meschke, Dieter, *Zum Üben und Vorspielen/B-Tuba*, under "Tuba and Keyboard Collections."

Concone, G. *Etude*, (Op. 10, no. 11). arr. Ostrander, Allen. Editions Musicus. 1954. 3:14. II–III. G₁–e. Andante Cantabile. Very lyrical etude in 3/4 time. Slurring for four bars at a time. Some grace notes. Good advanced-beginner material. See: Ostrander, Allen, *Concert Album for Tuba*, under "Tuba and Keyboard Collections."

Conley, Lloyd, arr. *The First Noel*. Kendor Music, Inc. 1985. 2:20. II. C–e. Melody and some accompaniment by the soloist. Cut for shorter version possible. See listing under "Tuba and Keyboard Collections."

Conley, Lloyd, arr. *Joy to the World*. Kendor Music, Inc. 1985. 1:13. II–III. C–e. Cut for shorter version possible. See listing under "Tuba and Keyboard Collections."

Conley, Lloyd, arr. *O Come, All Ye Faithful*. Kendor Music, Inc. 1985. 2:16. II–III. D–e♭. Nice arrangement of the melody and some accompaniment by the soloist. Cut for shorter version possible. See listing under "Tuba and Keyboard Collections."

Conley, Lloyd, arr. *O Little Town of Bethlehem*. Kendor Music, Inc. 1985. 1:29. II. D–d. Cut for shorter version possible. A few accidentals, otherwise no technical problems. See listing under "Tuba and Keyboard Collections."

Conley, Lloyd, arr. *Silent Night*. Kendor Music, Inc. 1985. 2:22. II. D–e♭. Cut for shorter version possible. Slurring throughout, some temporary shifting of key, otherwise no technical problems. See listing under "Tuba and Keyboard Collections."

Connor, Eddie. *McCluskeys Rag*. arr. Bennett, Malcolm. 1988. 2:36. III. B♭₁–b♭. Ragtime. Part for treble (E♭ Bass) included. Playful ragtime feel complete with syncopations and a few glissandos. Good recital material. See: Bennett, Malcolm, *Five Solos for Tuba*, under "Tuba and Keyboard Collections."

Constantinides, Dinos. *Mutability Fantasy*. Trombone Association Publishing. 1979. $6.00. 4:29. IV–V. D–d' (g'). "For Euphonium or Tuba and Piano." Lyrical and rhythmical textures. Some very quick articulations required. One octave lower for tuba in spots. See review in *T.U.B.A. Journal*, Vol. 8, no. 4, p. 27.

Constantino, Joseph G. *Bill's Tune*. Kendor Music, Inc. 1985. $7.00. 4:25. III–IV. (C₁) G₁–c'. Dedicated to Bill Troiano. Lyrical tune in a waltz and rock setting. See review in *T.U.B.A. Journal*, Vol. 14, no. 2, p. 40.

Corelli, Arcangelo. *Gigue*. arr. Maganini, Quinto. Editions Musicus. 1949. 2:15. III–IV. B♭₁–b♭. Allegro con delicatezza, in 12/8. One rest in entire transcription. Requires flexibility, endurance, and a good ear. See: Ostrander, Allen, *Concert Album for Tuba*, under "Tuba and Keyboard Collections." Recorded by Harvey Phillips.

Corelli, Arcangelo. *Petit pièce en fa*. arr. Goudenhooft, André. Gérard Billaudot. III.

Corelli, Arcangelo. *Preludio and Allemanda*, from *Sonata No. X for Violin*. arr. Hall, Harry H. Brodt Music Company. 1962. $2.00. 4:49 (1:29, 3:10). II–III. G₁–e. Good transcription at conservative tempos with no big technical problems.

Corelli, Arcangelo. *Sarabanda and Gavotta*. ed. Voxman, Himie. Rubank, Inc. 1972. 3:00. II–III. D–e♭. "For E♭ or BB♭ Bass." Legato Largo section in 3/4 time followed by an Allegro 4/4 section with mostly stepwise motion. See: Voxman, Himie, *Concert and Contest Collection*, under "Tuba and Keyboard Collections."

Corelli, Arcangelo. *Sarabande*. ed. Lebedev, A. Moscow: Muzyka. 1986. 1:30. II–III. D–a. Largo. Lyrical transcription utilizing some slurring; no big technical problems but strong musical demands. See: Lebedev, A., *Tuba Tutor, Vol. 2*, under "Tuba and Keyboard Collections."

Corelli, Arcangelo. *Sonata No. 9, Op. 5*. arr. Graham, James. TUBA Press. 1991. IV. (A₁) B₁–c♯'. Largo; *Giga* (Allegro—poco moderato); *Tempo de Gavotta* (Allegro). From violin sonata. See: Graham, James, *Concert Music for Tuba*, under "Tuba and Keyboard Collections."

Corelli, Arcangelo. *Sonata No. 10, Op. 5*. arr. Graham, James. TUBA Press. 1991. IV. G₁–c'. *Preludio* (Adagio); *Allemanda* (Allegro moderato); *Sarabanda* (Largo); *Gavotta* (Moderato); *Giga* (Allegro). From violin sonata. See: Graham, James, *Concert Music for Tuba*, under "Tuba and Keyboard Collections."

Coriolis, Emmanuel de. *Fantaisie Italienne*. Éditions Musicales Transatlantiques. 1969. 3:12. IV. F–f'. "Pour Contrebasse ou Saxhorn Basse avec accompagnement de Piano." "Pseudo" theme and variations in a pseudo neo-Classical feel. High tessitura with growing intensity throughout. Strong technique required: trills, scales with strong, clean articulation; and the flexibility of a contrabass player. Octave basso would be the sounding pitch of a contrabasse and more in the range of a good intermediate tubist.

Costa Ciscar, Francisco Javier. *Ambitos.*

Couperin, F. *Concertpièce.* arr. Yasumoto, Hiroyuki. Toa Music International Co. 1986. 8:42 (1:38, 2:00, 2:00, 0:55, 2:09). IV. C–eb'. Prélude; Siciliène; La Tromba; Plainte; Air de Diable. See: Yasumoto, Hiroyuki, *Tuba Volume #1,* under "Tuba and Keyboard Collections." CPP/Belwin, Inc. See listings under "Tuba and Keyboard Collections."

Crockett, Edgar. *Mystique.* TUBA Press. 1989. $8.00. 4:09. IV–V. D–f'. "Intense little ballad" with a Satie flavor, using the upper tessitura of the tubists' range. On F tuba, this piece is a cuddly toy; on CC, it is a lesson in how to relax and sing. "Quick pizzicato jazz bass" part in middle of composition. Requires a strong sensitive accompanist with a relaxed jazz feel. Good recital piece.

Croley, R. *Three Expressioni.* Philharmusica. 1968. $8.50. 2:43 (0:46, 0:33, 1:24). V. D_1–a'. For Robert Tucci. Lento ma non rigido; Adagio molto; Allegro engerico. Composed in 1967. Contemporary writing with strong musical and technical demands. Muted passages.

Cruft, Adrian. *Prelude and Scherzo,* Op. 65. Leeds Music Limited. 1981. 7:00 (5:31, 1:29). III–IV. Bb_1–g♯. For Eugene Cruft's pupils' pupils. Prelude (Andante/comodo); Scherzo (Ben ritmico, quasi allegro/comodo). Completed in Kent, June 1970. Suggested for tuba (for double bass or other bass-clef instrument and pianoforte) by the composer who also invites ottava basso playing. Harmonies not always traditional. Tubist should also adhere to the spirit of the articulation suggested for the bass part (pizzicato and arco). Bassoon/tuba part also included. Prelude has easy meter changes; Scherzo has meter changes and cluster harmonies.

Cui [César]. *Orientale.* Hudadoff, Igor, and Westcott, William (piano arr.). Pro Art Publications. 1967. Out of print. See: Hudadoff, Igor, *Fifteen Intermediate Tuba Solos,* under "Tuba and Keyboard Collections."

Cummings, Barton. *Cantilena for Tuba and Piano.* Editions Musicus. 1989. $4.50. 4:00. IV. E_1–e'. One-movement work requiring lyricism, creativity (two cadenza sections), and strong articulation (sixteenth-note scale runs in Allegro section). See review in *T.U.B.A. Journal,* Vol. 18, no. 2, p. 20.

Cummings, Barton. *Fantasia Breve for Tuba and Piano.* PRB Productions. 1989. $12.00. 11:49 (3:55, 5:22, 2:27). V. E_1–a'. Respectfully dedicated to Mark Nelson. Upper tessitura; best on F tuba. Some quick articulations and flexibility demands. Recorded by Mark Nelson. See review in *T.U.B.A. Journal,* Vol. 17, no. 3, p. 25.

Cummings, Barton. *Miniatures for Tuba and Piano.* PRB Productions. 1991. 4:46 (0:43, 0:43, 0:27, 0:24, 0:38, 1:51). IV–V. E–g♯'. Chorale; Day Dream; Tarentelle; Song Two; Declaration. Short vignettes incorporating upper tessitura, good modern stylistic sense, lyricism, and imagination. Two tacet movements for tuba.

Cummings, Barton. *Remembrance for Tuba and Piano.* TUBA Press. 1991. $7.00. 4:44. IV. D_1–d'. To the memory of Stuart Snyder. Reflective composition utilizing slow tempos with lyrical phrases, and cadenza. Peppy Allegro section in the middle requires a light articulation of staccato sixteenth notes at a brisk tempo.

Cummings, Barton. *Soliloquy for Tuba and Piano.* Whaling Music Publishers. 1988. $7.50. 3:36. IV. Db–c'. Andante. Lovely lyrical ballad interspersed with a cadenza. All legato and slurred playing. Solo lies in the "sweet" upper range of the tuba.

Cummings, Barton. *Thu Sau (Sad Autumn),* Vietnamese Song. Wimbledon Music Incorporated. 1983. $4.95. 2:05. III. G–c'. Andante—espressivo rubato. A song of strength and pathos; plenty of room for making a strong musical statement. Upper tessitura for CC tuba. Powerful recital piece.

Cunningham, Michael. *Sonata for Tuba,* Op. 55. Seesaw Music Corporation Publishers. 1974. $10.00. 9:29 (3:48, 2:40, 3:01). V. F♯–f♯'. Moderato/Allegro; (Bell Piece) Lento; Allegro. "Composed Aug.–Sept. 1972, Bloomington." Contemporary intervals and rhythms (4 against 3, etc.). Wide range and mature approach needed for successful performance. Strong accompanist needed.

Curnow, James. *Concertino.* Sainer, Paul (arr. piano accomp.). TUBA Press. 1988. $12.00. For Barton Cummings. See listing under "Music for Tuba and Band." Recorded by Charles McAdams; Daniel Perantoni.

Curnow, James. *Symphonic Variants for Euphonium and Band.* TUBA Press. $20.00. Dedicated to my teacher and friend, Harry Begian, and the University of Illinois Bands. For euphonium, tuba, or trombone and band. Piano reduction. Winner of the 1984 American Bandmasters Association–NABIM Band Composition Award.

Dacre, Harry. *Bicycle Built for Two.* arr. Little, Donald C. CPP/Belwin, Inc. 1977. $4.00. 0:58. I. ($Bb_1$) C–Bb (c). Moderato. Once through the limited range tune in 3/4 time. Quarter note is fastest rhythm in this beginning solo. Optional octaves for Bb and C further reduce (on stretches) range. See: Lamb, Jack, *Solo Sounds for Tuba Levels 1–3, Vol. 1,* under "Tuba and Keyboard Collections."

Daellenbach, Charles, arr. See listing under "Tuba and Keyboard Collections."

Damase, Jean-Michel. *Automne.* Gérard Billaudot. 1987. $4.25. 2:00. I. d–d'. "Pour saxhorn basse Sib ou tuba basse et piano." For French tuba. Very lyrical (no slurs) melody in the beginning F tuba/ euphonium range. Good recital material even for advanced player. See: Thompson/Lemke, *French Music for Low Brass Instruments*. See review in *T.U.B.A. Journal*, Vol. 18, no. 3, p. 18.

Damase, Jean-Michel. *Bourrée*. Gérard Billaudot. 1987. $8.75. 2:30. II–III. E♭–e♭'. À Fernand Lelong. "Pour saxhorn basse Si♭ ou tuba basse et piano." For French tuba. Solo in 3/4 time with some slurring, triplets, super triplets, sixteenth notes, tenutos, and hard accents. Good opportunity for stylistic character in playing. See: Thompson/Lemke, *French Music for Low Brass Instruments*. See review in *T.U.B.A. Journal*, Vol. 18, no. 4, p. 15.

Damase, Jean-Michel. *Menuet Éclaté*. Gérard Billaudot. 1987. $5.75. 2:20. III. G–d'. Allegretto Moderato. "Pour saxhorn basse Si♭ ou tuba basse et piano." For French tuba. Some 5/4 time; mostly 3/4. See: Thompson/Lemke, *French Music for Low Brass Instruments*.

Danburg, Russell. *Sonatina*. Wingert-Jones Music, Incorporated. 1989. $4.00. 5:06 (1:25, 2:01, 1:40). IV. A♭₁–c♯'/d♭'. Allegretto Moderato; Lento e Sostenuto (in a relaxed "Blues" style); Allegro Moderato. Mute optional. Very lyrical writing; good audience pleaser. Lyrical playing with a lot of style required. In the second movement (blues), the eighth notes should be "rolled" with a jazz/ blues "triplet" feel.

Daniel-Lesur, and Werner, Jean-Jacques. See listing under "Tuba and Keyboard Collections."

Danks, H. P., and Harris, A. E. *Silver Threads among the Gold* and *Deep River*. Cundy-Bettoney/Carl Fischer Inc. Out of print. 3:00 and 2:00. II. B♭₁–e♭. Two beginning solos.

Danmark, Max F. *Scène de Concert*. Ludwig Music Publishing Company. 1979. $4.50. 2:58. III. F₁– b♭. "Solo for Trombone or Baritone B. C., Cornet or Baritone T. C., and Tuba." Original copyright 1951. Old-style solo requiring moderate technique. Cadenza; some lyrical playing.

Daquin, Louis-Claude. *Rigaudon*. arr. Schwotzer, Stephan. Hofmeister. 1993. 0:49. II. B♭₁–c. In 4/ 4 time (misprinted time signature) with no technical problems. See: Meschke, Dieter, *Zum Üben und Vorspielen/B-Tuba*, under "Tuba and Keyboard Collections."

Dargomijsky, Aleksander S. *Nur Lieben!* tr. Gershenfeld, Mitchell. Medici Music Press. 1985. 0:51. II– III. E–e♭. In C minor in 6/8 time. No technical problems. See: Gershenfeld, Mitchell, *Medici Masterworks Solos, Volume 1,* under "Tuba and Keyboard Collections."

Daucé, Edouard. *Concertino*. Éditions M. Combre. 1961. 4:05. IV. G₁–a'. À Monsieur J. Demailly. "Pour Tuba en ut et Piano." For French tuba. Lyrical solo with upper tessitura; very wide range. Aside from range considerations, no technical problems. Good recital material. See: Thompson/ Lemke, *French Music for Low Brass Instruments*.

Davidson, Douglass. *Fantasy on a Theme of Scarlatti*. Douglass Davidson. 1968.

Davies, Kenneth. *Excursions for Tuba and Piano*. Kenvad Music, Inc. 1980. $6.00. 5:40. IV. F♯₁–b♭. Commissioned by Jay Mueller. Completed October 1980. Starts with rubato lyrical ballad and increases in intensity and tempo throughout to a rock feel. Some fingering patterns to look at, but well within reason at stated tempo. Keep rock eighth notes even. Conservative range. Short cadenza. See review in *T.U.B.A. Journal*, Vol. 9, no. 1, p. 13.

Davis, William. *Variations on a Theme of Robert Schumann*. Southern Music Company. 1983. $4.95. Also written for B♭ bass clarinet or E♭ baritone saxophone or baritone and piano. See listing under "Music for Tuba and Band."

de Grignon, Lamote. *Canço de Maria*. tr. Amaz, J. Union Musical Española. 1970. French tuba and piano.

de Grignon, Lamote. *Reverie (Schumanniana)*. tr. Amaz, J. Union Musical Española. 1970. For French tuba and piano.

de Jong, Marinus. *Concert Piece*, Op. 50. Henri Elkan Music Publishers Inc. For French tuba and piano.

de Jong, Marinus. *Morceau de Concert—Concertstuk*, Op. 50. Editions Musicales. Brogneaux. 1953. $7.50. 7:50. IV. B♭₁–b♭'. À Mr. P. Rouchcinsky, Professeur au Conservatoire Royal d'Anvers. Aan de Heer P. Roupcinsky, Leraar aan het Koninklijk Muziekconservatorium van Antwerpen. "Pour Trombone ou Tuba ut ou Basson avec accompagnement de piano voor Bazuin of Tuba ut of Fagot met klavierbegeleiding." Very wide range; upper tessitura. With the exception of a few B♭₁s, better suited for euphonium or trombone than bass tuba. Traditional bravura solo with intermediate technical requirements.

de Ville, Paul, arr. See listing under "Tuba and Keyboard Collections."

de Ville, Paul, arr. *Atlas, Grand Air varié*. Carl Fischer Inc. 1919. Out of print. 7:04. III–IV. (A♭₁) B♭₁–g. Good intermediate theme and variations within a very conservative range for this genre. Optional cuts for shorter length.

de Ville, Paul, arr. *Happy Be Thy Dreams*. Carl Fischer Inc. 1905. Out of print. 3:30. II–III. A₁–f. Good intermediate solo. No technical problems.

Deason, David. *Two Pieces*. Kiwi Music Press. 1984. $9.00. 2:44 (1:14, 1:30). IV. F♯₁–c. Mesto; Allegro. Tricky mixed meter. Strong sense of rhythmic ensemble needed between soloist and accompanist. Short, crisp, fast articulation required in second piece. See review in *T.U.B.A. Journal*, Vol. 7, no. 3, p. 30.

Debaar, M. *Legende et Caprice*. Henri Elkan Music Publishers Inc. $3.00. For French tuba and piano.

Debussy, Claude. *Golliwogg's Cake-walk*. tr. Frackenpohl, Arthur. TUBA Press. 1993. 2:12. IV. (E♭₁) G♭₁–b♭. Flexibility and good Debussy sense of style required. Good transcription with a bit of Wagner interpolated. Listen to piano original for conception. See: Debussy, Claude, *Two Pieces from "Children's Corner" for Tuba and Piano,* below.

Debussy, Claude. *Jimbo's Lullaby.* arr. Davis, Sharon. Western International Music. 1984. $6.00. 3:03. III. F₁–g. Moderato. "Sweetly and a little clumsy." Good transcription in cut time. Slurring throughout; impressionistic lyricism a must. Eight measures of low-range melody toward the end.

Debussy, Claude. *Jimbo's Lullaby.* tr. Frackenpohl, Arthur. TUBA Press. 1993. 2:35. IV. (B♭₂) F₁–b♭. Lyrical transcription in 2/2 time. See: Debussy, Claude, *Two Pieces from "Children's Corner" for Tuba and Piano,* below.

Debussy, Claude. *Jimbo's Lullaby from "Children's Corner."* arr. Wastall, Peter. Boosey and Hawkes, Inc. 1985. 0:52. I–II. B₁♭–e♭. See: Wastall, Peter, *Learn As You Play Tuba,* under "Tuba and Keyboard Collections." Impressionistic transcription. Some unaccompanied sections. Use of staccatos and tenutos. Cluster-like piano accompaniment will open younger ears.

Debussy, Claude. *Reverie.* Hudadoff, Igor, and Westcott, William (piano arr.). Pro Art Publications. 1967. Out of print. See: Hudadoff, Igor, *Fifteen Intermediate Tuba Solos,* under "Tuba and Keyboard Collections."

Debussy, Claude. *Two Pieces from "Children's Corner" for Tuba and Piano.* tr. Frackenpohl, Arthur. TUBA Press. 1993. $8.00. 4:47 (2:35, 2:12). IV. Includes: *Jimbo's Lullaby; Golliwogg's Cake-walk.* See individual listings above.

Dedrick, Art. *A Touch Of Tuba.* Kendor Music, Inc. 1954. $5.50. Dedicated to Harold L. Walters. See listing under "Music for Tuba and Band." Includes songsheet record with Peter Popiel, tuba.

Defaye, Jean-Michel. *Morceau de Concours I.* Alphonse Leduc Editions Paris. 1990. $7.95. 2:10. II–III. F♯–d'. For French tuba. Mostly stepwise writing with no major technical challenges. Some syncopations with the same rhythmic figure repeated. See: Thompson/Lemke, *French Music for Low Brass Instruments.*

Defaye, Jean-Michel. *Morceau de Concours II.* Alphonse Leduc Editions Paris. 1990. $9.15. 2:20. IV. C–g'. For French tuba. Contains lyrical and technical passages. See: Thompson/Lemke, *French Music for Low Brass Instruments.*

Defaye, Jean-Michel. *Morceau de Concours III.* Alphonse Leduc Editions Paris. 1990. $11.50. 4:50. IV–V. E♭₁–c". For French tuba. Strong flexibility, large range. Cadenza has no rhymic values. See: Thompson/Lemke, *French Music for Low Brass Instruments.*

Defaye, Jean-Michel. *Suite Marine.* Alphonse Leduc Editions Paris. 1989. $18.25. 7:58 (1:35, 1:30, 1:20, 1:20, 0:53, 1:20). III–IV. E♭–e♭'. For French tuba. *L'Otarie; Le Cachalot; Le Requin; L'Éléphant; Le Baleineau; Le Dauphin.* See: Thompson/Lemke, *French Music for Low Brass Instruments*

Del Negro, Luca. *Polka Graziosa.* Briegel. 1938. Out of print. 4:30. III. A₁–f. Typical polka solo with two cadenzas. Conservative range.

Del Negro, Luca. *The Sousaphone.* Manuscript in the Library of Congress. c. 1938. 5:40. III–IV. F₁–b♭ (e♭'). Excellent polka-style solo that really showcases the soloist. Two cadenzas include "advanced player" higher notes as well as optional lower possibilities.

DeLamater, E., arr. *Auld Lang Syne (Air and Variations).* Rubank, Inc. 1948. $3.00. "Solo for E♭ or BB♭ Bass." See listing under "Music for Tuba and Band."

DeLamater, E. *Rocked in the Cradle of the Deep.* ed. Voxman, Himie. Rubank, Inc. 1938. $3.00. "Solo Tuba—E♭ or BB♭ tuba." See listing under "Music for Tuba and Band." Also see: Rubank, *Soloist Folio for Bass (E♭ or BB♭),* under "Tuba and Keyboard Collections."

DeLamater, E., arr. *Tramp! Tramp! Tramp!* Rubank, Inc. 1948. Out of print. Also published for baritone or trombone and piano. See listing under "Music for Tuba and Band."

Delbecq, Laurent. *Bassette.* Éditions Robert Martin. 1972. 1:25. I. c–b♭. "Pour Basse Si♭ (bass clef) ou Baryton Si♭ (treble clef) et Piano." Beginning solo with limited range. A few eighth notes, otherwise very simple rhythm, no slurs, no technical problems (except for French tuba tessitura).

Delgiudice, Michel. *Abuto.* Alphonse Leduc Editions Paris. 1982. $5.85. 3:30. II. F–d'. "Pour Tuba en ut ou Basse Si♭ avec accompagnement de Piano." For French tuba. Mostly stepwise motion. Some eighth notes, otherwise no technical challenges (except for one syncopated measure).

Delgiudice, Michel. *Ali-Baba.* Gérard Billaudot. 1977. $4.50. I–II. B♭–d'. Prix de Composition de la Confédération Musicale de France 1977. "Pour Saxhorn Si♭ ou Ut et Piano ou Tuba en Ut ou Trombone basse." For French tuba. Stately solo. A few arpeggiated slurs, otherwise no technical problems. See: Thompson/Lemke, *French Music for Low Brass Instruments.* See review in *T.U.B.A. Journal,* Vol. 7, no. 2, p. 23.

Delgiudice, Michel. *Danse l'Éléphant.* Éditions Robert Martin. 1981. $13.50. 2:30. II. E♭–c'. Moderato. In 3/4 time, some triplets, some syncopation, dotted rhythms, otherwise no rhythmic problems. See review in *T.U.B.A. Journal,* Vol. 11, no. 2, p. 26. Also see: Thompson/Lemke, *French Music for Low Brass Instruments.*

Delgiudice, Michel. *Dix Petit Textes (10 Short Solos).* Éditions Max Eschig. 1954. 7:27 (0:55, 0:45, 0:52, 0:52, 0:42, 0:31, 0:39, 0:53, 0:48, 0:30) . IV–V. G₁–g♯'. À Monsieur P. Bernard, Professeur au Conservatoire de Paris. Moderato; Andante; Moderato; Andante; Mouvement de Java; Moderato; Moderato; Andante sostenuto; Moderato; Assez vite. For French tuba. Short movements with technical demands. Large interval jumps; mixed meter. Good challenging material. See: Thompson/Lemke, *French Music for Low Brass Instruments*.

Delgiudice, Michel. *Gargantua*. Éditions Robert Martin. 1991. $8.50. For French tuba.

Delgiudice, Michel. *L'Antre De Polypheme* (*The Lair of Polyphemus*). Éditions Robert Martin. 1981. $11.50. 4:20 (2:20, 2:00). II–III. C–f'. Andante; *Les astuces d'Ulysse*. For French tuba. Rhythmically easy; junior high level solo. See: Thompson/Lemke, *French Music for Low Brass Instruments*. See review in *T.U.B.A. Journal*, Vol. 11, no. 2, p. 26.

Delgiudice, Michel. *La baleine bleue*. Éditions Robert Martin. 1991. $4.75. For French tuba.

Delgiudice, Michel. *Le Petit Baobab*. Éditions Robert Martin. 1981. $12.00. 3:00. II. F–b♭. "Basse Si♭ ou Tuba ut (in C) et piano." A few dotted rhythms, otherwise no technical problems. For French tuba. See: Thompson/Lemke, *French Music for Low Brass Instruments*. See review in *T.U.B.A. Journal*, Vol. 11, no. 2, p. 26.

Delgiudice, Michel. *Le Petit Mamouth*. Éditions Robert Martin. 1981. $13.50. 2:30. II. G–d'. For French tuba. Solo in 6/8 with some slurring. Mostly stepwise motion with a few arpeggios. See: Thompson/Lemke, *French Music for Low Brass Instruments*. See review in *T.U.B.A. Journal*, Vol. 11, no. 2, p. 26.

Delgiudice, Michel. *Puissance 4*. Éditions Robert Martin. 1991. $4.75. For French tuba.

Delgiudice, Michel. *Superman*. Éditions Robert Martin. 1991. $4.75. For French tuba.

Demerssman, J. *Cavatina*, Op. 47. arr. Wilson, Don. Gamble Hinged Music Co. 1938. Out of print. 3:25. III. F_1–f. Traditional solo. Andantino in 9/8 followed by Allegro Maestoso in 4/4 with some triplets. No technical problems.

Demerssman, J. *Premier Solo de Concert*. tr. Watelle, Jules. Editions Salabert. n. d. 5:35. V. G–b'. "Transcription pour Saxhorn Basse Si♭; du Concerto pour Trombone." For French tuba. Technical solo; arpeggios, scales.

Denmark, Max F. *Scène de Concert*. Ludwig Music Publishing Company. 1984. $4.50. 2:54. III–IV. F_1–b♭. "Solo for Trombone or Baritone B. C., Cornet or Baritone T. C., and Tuba." Original copyright 1951. Older style technical showcase. Needs bravura style and strong intermediate level technique.

Depelsenaire, Jean-Marie. *Ce que chantait l'aede*. Éditions Choudens. 1975. 1:34. II–III. D–e' (f'). À Monsieur Oswald Dehaut. "Pour Trombone ou Basse Si♭ et piano." For French tuba. Sustained (tenuto and slurred) playing with upper tessitura for French instrument.

Depelsenaire, Jean-Marie. *Funambules* (*Tight-Rope Walkers*). Éditions Musicales Transatlantiques. 1961. $2.50. For French Tuba. See: Thompson/Lemke, *French Music for Low Brass Instruments*.

Depelsenaire, Jean-Marie. *Jeux Chromatiques* (*Chromatic Games*). Éditions M. Combre. 1960. 3:43. IV. E–g'. À Monsieur Moulard, Professeur au Conservatoire de Valenciennes. "Pour Trombone, Tuba ou Basse in Si♭." Much chromatic motion. Full range. For French tuba. See: Thompson/Lemke, *French Music for Low Brass Instruments*.

Depetris, C. *Concertino*. J. Maurer Editions Musicales. 1989. $5.50. 6:07 (2:46, 1:31, 1:50). IV–V. (C) E–c". À Dominique Lecomte. Maestoso (décidé); Andante; Décidé/Allegro. Better on euphonium or F tuba. Upper tessitura. Some lyrical and technical playing throughout. Very quick articulations; some triple tonguing.

Depetris, C. *Recitatif et Allegro*. Edition Andel Uitgaven.

Depetris, C. *Roghisness*. Edition Andel Uitgaven.

Désenclos, A. *Air*. ed. Larin, J. Moscow: Muzyka. 1979. See: Larin, J., *Pieces for Tuba and Piano*, under "Tuba and Keyboard Collections."

Désenclos, A. *Suite Brève dans le goût classique* (*Short suite in the Classical Style*). Alphonse Leduc Editions Paris. 1965. Out of print. 11:00. V. G_1–c". À Monsieur Paul Bernard, Professeur au Conservatoire National Supérieur de Musique. Prélude; Fuguette; Aria; Finale. "Pour Tuba et Piano." For French tuba. Strong flexibility, range, technique, musicality required. See: Thompson/Lemke, *French Music for Low Brass Instruments*.

Desmond, Walter. *The Sea Gong*. Belwin. 1942. Out of print. 2:55. III. Bb_1–b♭. Theme and (four) variations. Fun recital material for beginning intermediate player.

Desportes, Yvonne. *Un Souffle Profond* (*A Deep Breath*). ed. Douay, Jean. Gérard Billaudot. 1981. $6.00. 6:00. V. G_1–ab'. "Pour Trombone basse, ou Tuba et Piano." Requires strong technique: triple tonguing, glissando (optional for tuba), quadruplets, trills, and endurance (not many rests). Needs a strong accompanist. Good recital material. See: Thompson/Lemke, *French Music for Low Brass Instruments*.

Desprez, F. *Esquisse Concertante Concertschets*. Edition Andel Uitgaven.

Devos, Gérard. *Deux Mouvements Contrastés*. Alphonse Leduc Editions Paris. 1960. Out of print. 6:50. IV–V. D_1–bb'. "Pour Tuba ut ou Trombone basse ou Saxhorn basse Si♭ et Piano." For French tuba. See: Thompson/Lemke, *French Music for Low Brass Instruments*.

DeWitt, L. O. *Pride of America*, Op. 58. Carl Fischer Inc. 1895. Out of print. To Mr. Eldon Baker, Premier Tuba Soloist of America. See listing under "Music for Tuba and Band."

Dibdin. *Tom Bowling*. arr. de Ville, Paul. Carl Fischer Inc. 1906. Out of print. See: de Ville, Paul, *Pleasant Hours*, under "Tuba and Keyboard Collections."

Diehl, Louis. *The Water Mill*. arr. de Ville, Paul. Carl Fischer Inc. 1906. Out of print. See: de Ville, Paul,

Pleasant Hours, under "Tuba and Keyboard Collections."

Diercks, John. *Variations on a Theme of Gottschalk.* Theodore Presser Company. 1968. $4.00. 4:30. III–IV. A$_1$–c'. Theme (Le Bananier). No technical problems.

Dillon, Robert. *Concertpiece for Tuba and Piano.* Available from the composer. 1971. 6:00. IV. F$_1$–b. Contemporary writing: improvised passages on given pitches, mixed meter. Passage for pulling third valve out to flatten pitch on BB♭ tuba would have to be compensated for on CC tuba (lip down pitches), or pull out fourth valve.

Domazlicky, Frantisek. *Concerto for Tuba and Piano,* Op. 53. Artia, Foreign Trade Corp.

Donahue, Robert. *Bagatelles.* Tempo Music Publications. 1977. 3:24. III. C–f'. "Solo for trombone, baritone (B. C.), bassoon, cello, tuba with piano accompaniment." Not for contrabass tuba upper tessitura. Good intermediate piece for F tuba. Theme and (two) variations, second variation in a slow 5/8. No technical problems other than tessitura.

Donahue, Robert. *Two Impromptus.* Tempo Music Publications. 1976. 4:17 (2:01, 2:16). II–III. C–e♭. "Solo for tuba, string bass, bassoon, cello." Very conservative range and conservative rhythm patterns. Second impromptus is in an easy 5/4 time; no other technical problems.

Dondeyne, Désiré. *5 Études.* Gérard Billaudot. 1988. $9.25. 19:20 (3:00, 4:30, 2:00, 5:00, 4:30). V. F$_1$–e'. Written in 1987. "Pour tuba ou trombone basse ou saxhorn basse Si♭ et piano." Five etudes requiring flexibility and strong technique. Plenty of arpeggios and scales. See: Thompson/Lemke, *French Music for Low Brass Instruments.* See review in *T.U.B.A. Journal,* Vol. 18, no. 3, p. 18.

Dondeyne, Désiré. *5 "Pièces Courtes": Pour jeune tubistes.* Gérard Billaudot. 1987. $9.25. 7:15 (2:00, 0:30, 1:00, 1:45, 2:00). II–III. (G$_1$) C–c'. À Fernand Lelong, Professeur au C. N. S. M. de Paris. Andante expressivo; Tempo di Marcia; Modéré; Allegretto; Andante (sans lenteur). "Pour Tuba En ut ou Saxhorn basse Si♭ avec accompagnement de Piano." Very melodic little piece requiring some flexibility. See: Thompson/Lemke, *French Music for Low Brass Instruments.*

Dondeyne, Désiré. *Divertimento.* Lino Florenzo. 1978. V. (E$_1$) F$_1$–f♯'. "Pour Tuba et orchestre." Piano accompaniment available. See: Thompson/Lemke, *French Music for Low Brass Instruments.*

Dondeyne, Désiré. *Sonatine in C.* Éditions Musicales Transatlantiques. 1967. For bass saxhorn. See: Thompson/Lemke, *French Music for Low Brass Instruments.*

Dondeyne, Désiré. *Tubissimo.* ed. Lelong, Fernand. Gérard Billaudot. 1983. $7.50. 6:30. IV–V. F$_1$–e' (g'). À Fernand Lelong. "Pour Tuba Basse ou

Saxhorn Basse B♭ et Piano." For French tuba. Opens with a cadenza/recitative section, continues with a 4/8 expressivo lyrical section, and ends with a brisk Allegro section. Plenty of opportunity for expression. See: Thompson/Lemke, *French Music for Low Brass Instruments.*

Dondit, Dee Ann, arr. *Still Sweeter Every Day.* David E. Smith Publications. 1990. $3.50. 1:46. III. G$_1$–f. Theme and Variations. Some triplets, dotted rhythms; very accessible to player with advanced beginner/early intermediate technique.

Douliez, Victor. *Andante,* Op. 53. Editions Musicales Brogneaux. $2.40. For French tuba and piano.

Douliez, Victor. *Introduction et Andante.* Editions Musicales Brogneaux. $9.95. For French tuba and piano.

Dowland, John. *Come Again, Sweet Love Doth Now Invite.* arr. Perantoni, Daniel. Hal Leonard Publishing Corp. 1976. See: Perantoni, Daniel, *Master Solos, Intermediate Level,* under "Tuba and Keyboard Collections."

Dowland, John. *Dear If You Change.* arr. Perantoni, Daniel. Hal Leonard Publishing Corp. 1976. See: Perantoni, Daniel, *Master Solos, Intermediate Level,* under "Tuba and Keyboard Collections."

Dowland, John. *Now, O Now I Needs Must Part.* arr. Perantoni, Daniel. Hal Leonard Publishing Corp. 1976. See: Perantoni, Daniel, *Master Solos, Intermediate Level,* under "Tuba and Keyboard Collections."

Dowling, Robert. *His Majesty the Tuba.* CPP/Belwin, Inc. 1940. $4.00. 5:40. III. (B♭) F$_1$–c' (f'). Theme and (three) variations. Intermediate technique and flexibility required: scalewise sixteenths, octave jumps, triple tonguing, optional pedal B♭$_2$ for last note. See: Lamb, Jack, *Solo Sounds for Tuba Levels 3–5, Vol. 1,* under "Tuba and Keyboard Collections."

Downey, John. *Tabu for Tuba.* Mentor Music Inc. 1965. $4.00. 3:35. C$_1$–f♯'. To Daniel Neesley. Slow, reflective, lyrical playing throughout a wide range of the horn. Glissandos, trills, wide leaps, dissonant intervals require strong player. Recorded by Harvey G. Phillips. See: Bird, Gary, ed., *Program Notes for the Solo Tuba.*

Dragonetti, Domenico. *Kleiner Walzer.* arr. Schwotzer, Stephan. Hofmeister. 1993. 0:48. II. F–e♭. Some easy, slow slurring. No big technical problems. See: Meschke, Dieter, *Zum Uben und Vorspielen/B-Tuba,* under "Tuba and Keyboard Collections."

Dubois, Pierre Max. *Cornemuse.* Alphonse Leduc Editions Paris. 1961. $14.95. 3:30. III. E–a'. "Pour Tuba ut ou Trombone basse ou Saxhorn basse Si♭ ou Contrebasse à Cordes et Piano." Scales, phrases outlining triads, and a variety of (mostly short) articulations required. For French tuba. See: Thompson/Lemke, *French Music for Low Brass Instruments.*

Dubois, Pierre Max. *Fantaisie*. Editions Choudens. 1965. $12.50. IV–V. F_1–c". "Pour Tuba ut ou Saxhorn basse Si♭ ou Trombone bass et Piano." For French tuba. See: Thompson/Lemke, *French Music for Low Brass Instruments*.

Dubois, Pierre Max. *Histoires de Tuba, Vol. 1: Plantez les gars! (Plant Them Boys)*. Gérard Billaudot. 1984. $4.50. 2:09. II–III. F–(d') f. "Pour Saxhorn basse En Si♭, Tuba–Tenor en ut et Tuba-Basse." For French tuba. Good transition solo for F tuba starters. No big technical problems. See: Thompson/Lemke, *French Music for Low Brass Instruments*.

Dubois, Pierre Max. *Histoires de Tuba, Vol. 2: Le petit cinéma (The Little Theater)*. Gérard Billaudot. 1984. $4.50. 2:22. III. A_1–f. Andantino. "Pour Saxhorn basse en Si♭, Tuba-Tenor en ut et Tuba-Basse." For French tuba. Wide range required. Some flexibility and light articulations also needed. See: Thompson/Lemke, *French Music for Low Brass Instruments*.

Dubois, Pierre Max. *Histoires de Tuba, Vol. 3: Le grand cinéma (The Big Theater)*. Gérard Billaudot. 1984. $6.25. 4:08. III–IV. $G^{\sharp}_1$–(f♯') g'. "Pour Saxhorn basse en Si♭, Tuba-Tenor en ut et Tuba-Basse." For French tuba. The range is closer to Level IV. Flexibility required. See: Thompson/Lemke, *French Music for Low Brass Instruments*.

Dubois, Pierre Max. *Histoires de Tuba, Vol. 4: Concert Opéra*. Gérard Billaudot. 1988. $13.00. 9:00 (5:00, 4:00). IV–V. G_1–g♯'. "V" comme Verdi—"O" comme Offenbach. "Pour tuba basse ou saxhorn basse en Si♭ et piano." Composed 1987. For French tuba. Flexibility, lightness required. See: Thompson/Lemke, *French Music for Low Brass Instruments*. See review in *T.U.B.A. Journal*, Vol. 17, no. 2, p. 33.

Dubois, Pierre Max. *Piccolo Suite*. Alphonse Leduc Editions Paris. 1957. $14.95. 6:30. V. F_1–a♯'. À Monsieur Paul Bernard, Professeur au Conservatoire. Prelude; Air; Polka. "Pour Tuba ut ou Saxhorn basse Si♭ ou Trombone bass et Piano." For French tuba. Last movement (Polka) has accompaniment available for chamber orchestra (from Leduc). See: Thompson/Lemke, *French Music for Low Brass Instruments*.

Dubrovsky, I. *A Song and a Dance*. ed. Mitegin, V. Moscow: Muzyka. 1969. See: Mitegin, V., *Pieces for Tuba and Piano*, in "Tuba and Keyboard Collections."

Dumitru, Ionel. *Concerto for Tuba and Piano*. Available from the composer.

Dumitru, Ionel. *Fantezia nocturna*. Available from the composer. 1960. 5:00. Recorded by Ionel Dumitru.

Dumitru, Ionel. *Humoreska*. Available from the composer. 1960. 4:00.

Dumitru, Ionel. *Konzertstuk*. Available from the composer. 1961. 10:00.

Dumitru, Ionel. *Polka Funurenilor*. Available from the composer. 1961. 3:30.

Dumitru, Ionel. *Preludiu*. Available from the composer. 1947. 7:00.

Dumitru, Ionel. *Rumanian Dance No. 2*. Recorded by Roger Bobo.

Dumitru, Ionel. *Scherzo*. Available from the composer. 1961. 2:00.

Dumitru, Ionel. *Tuba Diobolica (Polka)*. Available from the composer.

Duntriev, G. *Ballada*. ed. Lebedev, A. Moscow: Muzyka. 1986. 2:22. IV. $F^{\sharp}_1$–g (c'). Lyrical tune with meter changes and modern melodic writing. See: Lebedev, A., *Tuba Tutor, Vol. 2*, under "Tuba and Keyboard Collections."

Dupriez, Christian. *Piccolo Capriccio pour tuba et piano*. Available from the composer. To Mr. Edward R. Goldstein. See listing under "Music for Tuba and Orchestra."

Durand-Audard, Pierre. *Dialogue*. Alphonse Leduc Editions Paris. 1970. Out of print. 7:20. V. $G^{\sharp}_1$–a'. À Monsieur Paul Bernard, Professeur au Conservatoire National Supérieur de Musique. "Pour Trombone bass ou Tuba en ut ou Saxhorn basse Si♭ et Piano." For French tuba and piano. Compound meters, wide range and flexibility required. See: Thompson/Lemke, *French Music for Low Brass Instruments*.

Durand-Audard, Pierre. *Tournevalse (Turning Valse)*. Gérard Billaudot. 1978. 6:30. IV–V. F_1–(g') b♭'. À Monsieur Paul Bernard Professeur au Conservatoire. "Pour Saxhorn basse (Tuba en ut ou Trombone basse) avec accompagnement de Piano." Flexibility required. See: Thompson/Lemke, *French Music for Low Brass Instruments*.

Durante, Francesco. *Preghiera*. Phillips, Harry I. (comp. and ed.). Shawnee Press Inc. 1967. 1:35. II–III. C–e♭. Largo. Lyrical, slurred 12/8 transcription in a minor key. A few trills. See: Phillips, Harry I., *Eight Bel Canto Songs*, in this section.

Durkó, Zsolt. *Five Pieces for Tuba and Piano*. Editio Musica Budapest. 1979. $9.25. 4:00. V. D_1–g. Szabó Vilmosnak és Schmidt Nórának. Completed in Budapest, January 20, 1978. Stretching of technique: very low and very high playing, mixed meters, complex meters, wide interval jumps, fast articulation, ensemble challenges for accurate performance. Needs an accomplished accompanist versed in modern technique. See review in *T.U.B.A. Journal*, Vol. 7, no. 2, p. 20.

Durkó, Zsolt. *Movements*. Editio Musica Budapest (Boosey and Hawkes). 1981. $12.00. 5:00. V. D_1f♯'. Szabó Vilmosnak és Schmidt Nórának. Completed in Budapest, July 22, 1980. Modern writing: Mixed meters, wide intervals, wide dynamic range, ensemble challenges. Needs two mature performers.

Dutillet, Jacques. *Big Bear Suite*.

Dutillet, Jacques. *Sonata*.

Dutton, Brent. *Rhapsody in Black and Blue*. Available from the composer. 1966. 3:30. IV–V. $E♭_1$–f'.

With the exception of high tessitura toward the end, this piece is accessible to the advanced high school player.

Dutton, Brent. *Virtuosity Study No. 1.* Available from the composer. 1967. 4'. V. F_1–g'. Very technical solo. Very wide range. Works better on F tuba.

Dvarionas, B. *Theme and Variations.* ed. Melnikov, S. Moscow: Military Band Masters Institute. 1957. See: Melnikov, S., *Pieces for Tuba and Piano,* under "Tuba and Keyboard Collections."

Dvořák, Antonin. *Gypsy Melody,* Op. 55. tr. Gershenfeld, Mitchell. Medici Music Press. 1985. 1:12. II–III. A_1–eb. Poco allegro (Bouncing). A few tempo changes; no technical problems. See: Gershenfeld, Mitchell, *Medici Masterworks, Solos Volume 1,* under "Tuba and Keyboard Collections."

Eccles, H. *First and Second Movements from Violin Sonata.* arr. Yasumoto, Hiroyuki. Toa Music International Co. 1986. IV. G_1–d'. Grave; Courente, Allegro con spiritoso. See: Yasumoto, Hiroyuki, *Tuba Volume #1,* under "Tuba and Keyboard Collections."

Eccles, John. *Minuet.* tr. Dishinger, Ronald Christian. Studio 224/Belwin, Inc. 1979. Separately published version out of print. 1:30. I. Bb_1–F. Very limited range for beginner's level. Solo in 3/4 time; a few slurs, tenuto marks; first and second endings, del segno, no technical problems. See: Lamb, Jack, *Classic Festival Solos,* under "Tuba and Keyboard Collections."

Edelson, Edward. *Tango Anyone?* 1986. 1:30. II–III. G_1–d. Tempo di Tango. Originally published as *Tuba Tango* by Pro Art Publications in 1966. Solo in cut time. Has slurs, super triplets, mostly stepwise motion; no technical problems. Keep eighth notes even for tango style. See review in *T.U.B.A. Journal,* Vol. 14, no. 4, p. 43.

Eerola, Lasse. *Music for Tuba and Orchestra.* Finnish Music Information Center. 1991. See listing under "Music for Tuba and Orchestra."

Eerola, Lasse. See listings under "Tuba and Keyboard Collections."

Ehmann, Heinrich. *Drei Stücke für Tuba und Orgel.* Moseler Verlag. 1982. 3:43 (1:00, 0:43, 2:00). IV. D_1–e. Modern tonality throughout. Second movement in 7/8 time. Third movement has some free rhythm passages. Will take some rehearsing as there are no organ cues in the tuba part.

Eitel, Butler. *Sting Ray.* Hal Leonard Publishing Corp. 1966. Out of print. 1:00. I. Bb_1–bb. Mostly an "ohm-pah" type of bass line for very beginning player; not very inspiring melody. From the Hal Leonard Elementary Solo Series.

Eitel, Butler. *Waltzing with a Whirlybird.* Hal Leonard Publishing Corp. 1966. Out of print. 2:00. I. Bb_1–d. Solo in 3/4 time. Fastest rhythm is quarter note. From the Hal Leonard Elementary Solo Series.

Ekkls, H. *Sonata.* ed. Melnikov, S. Moscow: Military Band Masters Institute. 1957. See: Melnikov, S., *Pieces for Tuba and Piano,* under "Tuba and Keyboard Collections."

Eklund, Hans. *Concerto per Tuba.* Manuscript available from the Tuba Center. 1982. See listing under "Music for Tuba and Band."

Elgar, Edward. *Two Songs for Tuba and Piano.* trans. Michael Thornton. Liben Music Publishers. 1981. $5.00. 6:00 (2:37, 3:23). IV. A_1–eb' (g'). *Chanson de Nuit,* Op. 15, No. 1; *Chanson de Matin,* Op. 15, No. 2. Well-transcribed songs. Good recital material. Requires strong lyrical sense, flexible technique, and endurance (no rests). Some mordents, grace notes, and trills. Recorded by John Fletcher; Michael Thornton (*Chanson de Matin*). See review in *T.U.B.A. Journal,* Vol. 10, no. 4, p. 36.

Elgar, Edward. *Two Songs from Sea Pictures.* arr. Friedman, Norman. Southern Music Company. 1983. $3.50. 5:43 (3:29, 2:04). III. Eb–bb. *Sea Slumber Song; Where Corals Lie.* Upper tessitura would lie perfectly on Eb or F tuba although very playable on lower instrument. Requires an expressive melodic approach. No technical problems but there are artistic musical conception considerations.

Enciña, Juan Del. *Triste España Sin Ventura (Lament).* tr. Buttery, Gary A. Whaling Music Publishers. 1978. $3.50. 0:50. IV. e–a'. "Presumably written on the occasion of Queen Isabella's death in the year 1504." Solo for F (or G) tuba or euphonium with harpsichord and optional cello. Solo in cut time with upper tessitura. All slurred and all stepwise motion; requires flexibility.

Endo, Masao. *Sculptured Tradition for Tuba and Piano.* The Japan Federation of Composers. 1983. V. E_1–f#'. À Hiroyuki Yasumoto. Very free playing; no bar lines. Score needed for performance. Flutter tonguing; extended E_1 section; good ear required.

Engelhardt, Ernst. *Tuba-Sepp'l.* Musikverlag Wilhelm Halter. n. d. 2:20. III. (F_1) C–f. Fun polka style solo in 2/4 time with some triplet sixteenth notes.

Epstein, Marti. *White Stones.* Encore Music Publishers. 1991. $10.00. V. A_2–gb'. Written for and dedicated to Sam Pilafian. Modern writing for both instruments. At one point the pianist is instructed to cover bottom strings with "Tic-Tacs™." Mixed meter, extreme dynamics, extreme range.

Everson, Dana F., arr. *Lead on O King Eternal.* David E. Smith Publications. 1992. $3.75. 3:00. II–III. (F_1) G_1–f. Strong martial style. March in 6/8 time with staccatos, slurs, and a lot of spirit. 4/4 legato section in middle of piece requires slurring in the lower range.

Everson, Dana F., arr. *My Anchor Holds.* David E. Smith Publications. 1992. $4.00. 2:40. III. G_1–f. Strong march style. March in 4/4 time with a lot of spirit. Middle legato section exploits the lower range.

Faillenot, Maurice. *Introduction et Rigaudon.* Gérard Billaudot. 1985. $5.50. 2:00. II. G–e' (g'). "Pour Saxophone tenor en Sib ou Saxhorn Baryton en Sib ou saxhorn basse en Sib ou tuba en ut et piano."

Lyrical playing combined with some easy technical playing. Some syncopation. For French tuba. See: Thompson/Lemke, *French Music for Low Brass Instruments.*

Faust, Randall E. *Fantasy for Tuba and Piano.* Manuscript available from Robert King Music Sales. 1985. 4:24. IV–V. G–e♭'. For Mark Moore. Requires two performers with strong rhythmical sense. Shifting mixed meter throughout. Well worth the effort! Very tonal and very good recital material.

Fayeulle, Roger. *Bravaccio.* Alphonse Leduc Editions Paris. 1958. $14.95. 5:30. IV–V. A₁–(f ') a'. À B. Mari, Tuba solo de l'orchestre du Théâtre National de L'Opéra. "Pour Tuba ut ou Saxhorn Basse Si♭ ou Trombone Basse et Piano." For French tuba. Includes some opera quotes. Requires flexible, dramatic players. See: Thompson/Lemke, *French Music for Low Brass Instruments.*

Featherstone, W. R., and Gordon, A. J. *My Jesus I Love Thee.* arr. Smith, David E. David E. Smith Publications. 1985. $2.50. 2:05. I. C–B♭. Very limited range and rhythm (fastest rhythm is quarter note). Some slurring, mostly stepwise motion, otherwise no technical problems. Good beginners' solo.

Feldman, Enrique C. *Fantasia.* 1994. V. In Progress; written for E♭ tuba. Range 3 1/2 octaves; extremely difficult, for advanced and professional performers.

Feldstein, Sandy. *Rainy Day Rock.* CPP/Belwin, Inc. 1990. I. B♭₁–G. See listing under "Tuba and Keyboard Collections."

Feldstein, Sandy, arr. *A-Tisket, A-Tasket.* CPP/Belwin, Inc. 1990. I. B♭₁–G. See listing under "Tuba and Keyboard Collections."

Feldstein, Sandy, arr. *Aura Lee.* CPP/Belwin, Inc. 1990. I. B♭₁–F. See listing under "Tuba and Keyboard Collections."

Feldstein, Sandy, arr. *Baa, Baa Black Sheep.* CPP/Belwin, Inc. 1990. I. B♭₁–G. See listing under "Tuba and Keyboard Collections."

Feldstein, Sandy, arr. *Beautiful Brown Eyes.* CPP/Belwin, Inc. 1990. I. B♭₁–E♭. See listing under "Tuba and Keyboard Collections."

Feldstein, Sandy, arr. *Caisson Song.* CPP/Belwin, Inc. 1990. I. B♭₁–G. See listing under "Tuba and Keyboard Collections."

Feldstein, Sandy, arr. *Erie Canal.* CPP/Belwin, Inc. 1990. I. C–G. See listing under "Tuba and Keyboard Collections."

Feldstein, Sandy, arr. *For He's a Jolly Good Fellow.* CPP/Belwin, Inc. 1990. I. B♭₁–G. See listing under "Tuba and Keyboard Collections."

Feldstein, Sandy, arr. *French Folk Song.* CPP/Belwin, Inc. 1990. I. B♭₁–D. *Au Claire de la Lune.* See listing under "Tuba and Keyboard Collections."

Feldstein, Sandy, arr. *Frère Jacques.* CPP/Belwin, Inc. 1990. I. B♭₁–G. Round. See listing under "Tuba and Keyboard Collections."

Feldstein, Sandy, arr. *Good King Wenceslas.* CPP/Belwin, Inc. 1990. I. B♭₁–F. See listing under "Tuba and Keyboard Collections."

Feldstein, Sandy, arr. *Hot Cross Buns.* CPP/Belwin, Inc. 1990. I. B♭₁–D. See listing under "Tuba and Keyboard Collections."

Feldstein, Sandy, arr. *Jolly Old St. Nicholas.* CPP/Belwin, Inc. 1990. I. B♭₁–G. See listing under "Tuba and Keyboard Collections."

Feldstein, Sandy, arr. *London Bridge.* CPP/Belwin, Inc. 1990. I. B♭₁–G. See listing under "Tuba and Keyboard Collections."

Feldstein, Sandy, arr. *Love Somebody.* CPP/Belwin, Inc. 1990. I. B♭₁–F. See listing under "Tuba and Keyboard Collections."

Feldstein, Sandy, arr. *Lovely Evening.* CPP/Belwin, Inc. 1990. I. B♭₁–G. Round. See listing under "Tuba and Keyboard Collections."

Feldstein, Sandy, arr. *Old McDonald.* CPP/Belwin, Inc. 1990. I. B♭₁–G. See listing under "Tuba and Keyboard Collections."

Feldstein, Sandy, arr. *There's a Hole in the Bucket.* CPP/Belwin, Inc. 1990. I. B♭₁–G. See listing under "Tuba and Keyboard Collections."

Feldstein, Sandy, arr. *This Old Man.* CPP/Belwin, Inc. 1990. I. B♭₁–G. See listing under "Tuba and Keyboard Collections."

Feldstein, Sandy, arr. *Tom Dooley.* CPP/Belwin, Inc. 1990. I. B♭₁–G. See listing under "Tuba and Keyboard Collections."

Feldstein, Sandy, arr. *Twinkle, Twinkle Little Star.* CPP/Belwin, Inc. 1990. I. B♭₁–G. See listing under "Tuba and Keyboard Collections."

Feldstein, Sandy, arr. *The Victors' March.* CPP/Belwin, Inc. 1990. I. B♭₁–G. See listing under "Tuba and Keyboard Collections."

Feldstein, Sandy, arr. *When the Saints Go Marching In.* CPP/Belwin, Inc. 1990. I. B♭₁–F. See listing under "Tuba and Keyboard Collections."

Fesh, D. *Prelude.* arr. Lebedev, A. Military Band Masters Faculty of Moscow Conservatiore. 1971. See. Lebedev, A., *Collection of Pieces for Tuba "Es" and Piano,* under "Tuba and Keyboard Collections."

Fiche, Michel. *Monsieur Tuba.* Éditions M. Combre. 1977. 1:38. II. F–d'. "Pour Saxhorn Si♭ ou Tuba ut et Piano." For French tuba. Cute advanced beginner solo that contains a portion of the *Bydlo* solo. Some slurring and tenuto, easy rhythms (fastest note is eighth note), otherwise no technical problems.

Fillmore, Henry. *Deep Bass.* Fillmore Bros. 1927. Out of print. See listing under "Music for Tuba and Band."

Fischer, Ludwig. *Down Deep within the Cellar.* arr. de Ville, Paul. Carl Fischer Inc. 1906. Out of print. See: de Ville, Paul, *Pleasant Hours,* under "Tuba and Keyboard Collections."

Fischer, Ludwig. *Down in the Deep Deep Cellar.* arr. Wekselblatt, Herbert. G. Schirmer Inc. 1972. 1:29. III–IV. B♭₁–g. Classic old tuba tune in a theme-and-variations format. Some wide interval jumps, some arpeggios. Intermediate technique required.

See: Wekselblatt, Herbert, *First Solos for the Tuba Player,* under "Tuba and Keyboard Collections."

Fischer, Ludwig. *Here I Sit in the Deep Cellar.* arr. Conley, Lloyd. Kendor Music, Inc. 1981. 4:00. II–III. F_1–f. Novelty theme and (a couple of) variations with cadenza. Novelty based on playing low F's for effect.

Fleming, Robert. *Concerto for Tuba.* Canadian Music Centre. 1966. Dedicated to Robert Ryker. See listing under "Music for Tuba and Orchestra."

Fletcher, John, arr. and ed. See listings under "Tuba and Keyboard Collections."

Flowers, Herbie. *Tuba Smarties.* arr. Stephens, Denzil. Obrasso Verlag AG. III.

Foley, Red. *Just a Closer Walk.* arr. Boyd, Bill; ed. Daellenbach, Charles. Hal Leonard Publishing Corp. 1992. 1:03. I. Bb_1–c. Arrangement cleverly switches octaves from original to preserve beginning level. Some accidentals, easy syncopation. Comes with practice/performance cassette. See: Daellenbach, Charles, *Book of Beginning Tuba Solos,* under "Tuba and Keyboard Collections."

Follas, Ronald W. *Concert Piece for "Music for Tuba and Band."* TUBA Press. 1982. $8.00. 11:30. Suggested by Sherman Botts, of Des Moines, and David Lewis, Principal Tuba of the North Carolina Symphony. First performed by David Lewis with the East Carolina University Symphonic Wind Ensemble on April 18, 1982 with Herbert L. Carter conducting. Very accessible piano reduction. See listing under "Music for Tuba and Band." See review in *T.U.B.A. Journal,* Vol. 10, no. 4, p. 31.

Foremny, Stephan. *Sonatine für Tuba und Klavier.* Manuscript. 1983. 4:57 (2:09, 1:46, 1:02). III. (G_1) Bb_1–c'. Gemachlich; Langsam und ausdrucksvoll; Lustig. Completed September 1983. Very musical solo with no major technical problems. Some counting with eighth note as the beat; some leaps of a sixth. Good recital material.

Foremny, Stephan. *Zwei Charakterstücke.* Manuscript. 1992. 2:41 (1:33, 1:08). III. A_1–b. Dolente; Allegretto. Conservative modern melodic language. Some accidentals, syncopation; no technical problems.

Forez, Henri. *Opus Open.* For tuba and harpsichord.

Foster, Stephen. *Camptown Races.* arr. Feldstein, Sandy. CPP/Belwin, Inc. 1990. I. Bb_1–G. See: Feldstein, Sandy, *First Solo Songbook,* under "Tuba and Keyboard Collections."

Foster, Stephen C. *Foster Medley.* arr. Yasumoto, Hiroyuki. Toa Music International Co. 1986. 4:06. III. D–g. Andante; Allegretto; Andante. Includes *Old Black Joe, Nelly Bly,* and *My Old Kentucky Home.* Very lyrical transcription. No technical problems. See: Yasumoto, Hiroyuki, *Tuba Volume #1,* under "Tuba and Keyboard Collections."

Fote, Richard. *Tubadour.* Kendor Music, Inc. 1971. $4.50. 1:13. I. Bb_1–Bb. Moderato. A few eighth notes, a few accidentals. Good slightly advanced beginning solo. Comes with songsheet.

Fotek, Jan. *Sonata Romantica per tuba e pianoforte.* Wspolczesna Muzyka Polska. 1985. 20:00. V. Eb_1–ab. Zdzislawowi Piernikowi. Largo Dramatico; Andante Tranquillo; Presto. Big piece; endurance required. Wide interval skips, quickness of articulation, wide range.

Frackenpohl, Arthur. *Basso Tomaso.* TUBA Press. 1992. In preparation.

Frackenpohl, Arthur. *Concertino for Tuba and String Orchestra.* Robert King Music Co. and Alphonse Leduc Editions Paris. 1967. $5.85. Written for Abe Torchinsky. See listing under "Music for Tuba and Orchestra."

Frackenpohl, Arthur. *Sonata for Tuba and Piano.* Kendor Music, Inc. 1982. $10.50. 13:20 (4:30/4:50/4:00). IV–V. G_1b–c'. For Harvey Phillips. Three movements: Fast; Slowly; Lively. First movement: some mixed meter, syncopation. Second movement: legato, lyrical modal/pentatonic feel; very expressive opportunities. Third movement: some mixed meter, syncopation. Good recital piece. See review in *T.U.B.A. Journal,* Vol. 11, no. 2, p. 21. Also see: Bird, Gary, ed., *Program Notes for the Solo Tuba.*

Frackenpohl, Arthur. *Variations for Tuba and Piano (The Cobblers Bench).* Shawnee Press, Inc. 1973. $6.00. 5:30. For Peter Popiel. See listing under "Music for Tuba and Band." Recorded by Ronald Davis; Peter Popiel. See review in *T.U.B.A. Journal,* Vol. 1, no. 2, p. 10 and Vol. 7, no. 4, p. 25.

Françaix, Jean. *Petite Valse Européene.* Schott's Söhne. 1980. $11.95. "Pour tuba et double quintette a vents." Piano reduction. Composed in 1979. See listing under "Music for Tuba in Mixed Ensemble."

Franck, Maurice. *Prélude, arioso et rondo.* Éditions Musicales Transatlantiques. 1969. 6:00. V. Ab_1–bb'. À Paul Bernard, professeur au Conservatoire National Supérieur de Musique. "Pour Saxhorn en Sib, et Trombone Basse ou Tuba et Piano; Concours du Conservatoire National Supérieur de Musique de Paris (1969)." Requires great flexibility and great range. Mixed meter. For French tuba. See: Thompson/Lemke, *French Music for Low Brass Instruments.*

Franck, Melchior. *Allemande.* arr. Schwotzer, Stephan. Hofmeister. 1993. 1:12. II. D–c. In cut time with no technical problems. See: Meschke, Dieter, *Zum Uben und Vorspielen/B-Tuba,* under "Tuba and Keyboard Collections."

Franck, Melchior. *Galliarde.* arr. Schwotzer, Stephan. Hofmeister. 1993. 1:04. II. C–d. Allegro. In 3/4 time. See: Meschke, Dieter, *Zum Uben und Vorspielen/B-Tuba,* under "Tuba and Keyboard Collections."

Frangkiser, Carl. *A Cavern Impression.* Belwin. 1941. Out of print. 4:00. III. F_1–g. Theme and variations utilizing much stepwise motion.

Frangkiser, Carl. *Melodie Romanza.* Belwin. 1946. Out of print. 2:55. III. A_1–f. Typical theme and variations; uses turns, triplets, and scales.

Frank, Marcel. *Scherzo*. Available from the composer. 1972. 3:30. IV. E♭–d♭'. Light solo, accessible to the strong high school player.

Fredrickson, Thomas. *Tubalied for Tuba and Contemporary Wind Ensemble or Piano*. 1975. Commissioned by T.U.B.A. and premiered in Carnegie Hall, October 29, 1975 by Daniel Perantoni, tuba. See listing under "Music for Tuba and Mixed Ensemble." Recorded by Daniel Perantoni.

Frid, G. *A Little Birch Tree*. ed. Lebedev, A. Moscow: Muzyka. 1984. 0:40. II–III. D–d. Mostly unaccompanied entrances. Meter is 3/4, 3/4, 2/4. See: Lebedev, A., *Tuba Tutor, Vol. 1,* under "Tuba and Keyboard Collections."

Friedman, Norman. *Sonare per Tuba e Piano*. Southern Music Company. 1974. $2.50. 2:55 (0:46, 1:14, 0:55). IV–V. G–e'. Allegro; Andantino; Moderato. Modern melodic writing. Some glissandos, large dissonant leaps. Flexibility required.

Fritze, Gregory. *Basso Concertino*. Manuscript. 1987. Synthesizer reduction (or piano). See listing under "Music for Tuba and Mixed Ensemble." Recorded by Gregory Fritze. Also see: Bird, Gary, ed., *Program Notes for the Solo Tuba*.

Fritze, Gregory. *Sonata for Tuba and Piano*. Manuscript. 1976. 12:43 (3:20, 2:28, 6:55). V. C♯₁–b♭'. To Chester Roberts, for all those train rides to Boston. Three numbered movements. Very wide glissandos, mixed meter, tricky rhythms, quick dissonant articulation patterns. Requires a mature approach, lyrically and rhythmically. Multiphonics, cadenzas for both players. See: Bird, Gary, ed., *Program Notes for the Solo Tuba*.

Fucik, Julius. *Der Alte Brummbär*. arr. Studnitzky, Norbert. Musikverlag Wilhelm Halter. 1987. "Polka comique für Solo-Tuba (od. Bariton) Op. 210." Piano reduction. Published by Molenaar in 1964.

Fux, Johann Joseph. *Allegro*. arr. Philipp, Gerd. Hofmeister. 1993. 1:25. II. D–e♭. A little dance in 3/4 time. One F–e♭ leap; no other technical problems. See: Meschke, Dieter, *Zum Uben und Vorspielen/B-Tuba*, under "Tuba and Keyboard Collections."

Gabaye, Pierre. *Tubabillage*. Alphonse Leduc Editions Paris. 1959. $12.80. 3:10. III. C–e'. "Pour Tuba ut ou Contrebasse à Cordes ou Saxhorn basse Si♭ ou Trombone basse et Piano." For French tuba. Some duples in 6/8 section; plenty of slurring and staccato; good intermediate solo. See: Thompson/Lemke, *French Music for Low Brass Instruments*.

Galán, Carlos. *Tuba Mirum*, Op. 35.

Galliard, John Ernest. *Sonata No. 5*. arr. Jacobs, Wesley. Encore Music Publishers. 1991. $15.00. IV. B♭₁–e♭'. Adagio; Allegro e spiritoso; Alla Siciliana; Allegro assai. Good transcription of standard brass work. Recorded by Roger Bobo.

Galliard, John Ernest. *Sonata No. 6*. arr. Jacobs, Wesley. Encore Music Publishers. 1989. $15.00. III–

IV. G₁–g. Larghetto; Alla breve; Sarabanda; Menuett. Good transcription of standard brass work.

Garbarino, Giuseppe. *Sonata per Tuba (Contrabasso) and Piano*.

Garlick, Antony. *Fantasia*. Seesaw Music Corporation Publishers. 1974. $6.00. 7:00. IV. (E₁) G♯₁–c'. For Carter Leeka. Andante. Has two improvised sections using given pitches. Short multiphonic section. Chromatic glissando. Conservative modern writing.

Garrett, James. *Sonata for Tuba and Piano*. 1970. Manuscript. See review in *T.U.B.A. Journal*, Vol. 1, no. 1, p. 7.

Gartenlaub, Odette. *Essai*. Éditions Rideau Rouge. 1970. F₁–g♯'. For bass saxhorn/(French) tuba/bass trombone and piano. See: Thompson/Lemke, *French Music for Low Brass Instruments*.

Garth, J. *Concerto for Tuba*. Henri Elkan Music Publishers Inc. 1960. For French tuba and piano.

Gasner, Moshe. *Science Fiction*. Kibutz Movement League of Composers. Recorded by Adi Hershko.

Gastinelle, Gerard. *Méloman*.

Gatty, A. S. *Lights Far Out at Sea*. arr. de Ville, Paul. Carl Fischer Inc. 1906. Out of print. See: de Ville, Paul, *Pleasant Hours*, under "Tuba and Keyboard Collections."

Gaucet, Charles. *Adagio and Finale from Concertino*. ed. Voxman, Himie. Rubank, Inc. 1972. 4:30. III–IV. F₁–f. "For BB♭ Bass." Adagio in 12/8 time. Allegro has several technical scale passages. Very expressive transcription of French tuba piece. See: Voxman, Himie, *Concert and Contest Collection*, under "Tuba and Keyboard Collections."

Geib, Fred. *Caprice*, Op. 4. Mills Music. 1941. Out of print. 3:10. III. A₁–a. Dramatic solo in D♭ major/B minor with cadenza. Triplets, scales, dotted rhythms; intermediate level technique required.

Geib, Fred. *Cavatina,* Op 6. arr. Forst, R. Mills Music. 1940. Out of print. 2:30. III. F₁–f. Composed for and dedicated to The Pennsylvania Forensic and Music League. Andante maestoso. Crisp, light articulation required; some octave jumps; no big technical problems.

Geib, Fred. *A Heroic Tale,* Op. 25. arr. Forst. Carl Fischer Inc. 1942. $3.25. 3:30. III. G₁–a. "Tuba E♭–C–BB♭." Slow tempo, no outstanding technical problems.

Geib, Fred. *In the Deep Forest,* Op. 20. Briegel. 1941. Out of print. 3:00. III. B♭₁–a♭. Theme and variations with cadenza.

Geib, Fred. *Introduction and Polka Piquante,* Op. 27. Mills Music. 1946. Out of print. 5:05. III. B₁–e♭'. A good polka style solo using mostly stepwise motion. Cadenza uses full range of piece.

Geib, Fred. *A Joyous Dialogue,* Op. 11. Mills Music. 1941. Out of print. "Tuba Solo or Duet." See listing under "Music for Multiple Tubas: Two Parts."

Geib, Fred. *Melody,* Op. 9. arr. Morse, Frank. Carl Fischer Inc. 1940. $4.00. 9:00. III–IV. G₁–b♭.

Long theme and (five) variations. See review in *T.U.B.A. Journal*, Vol. 9, no. 3, p. 25.

Geib, Fred. *Nocturne,* Op. 7. arr. Forst, R. Mills Music. 1941. Out of print. 2:00. II–III. A♮₁–g. Some sixteenth notes.

Geib, Fred. *Serenade,* Op. 10. arr. Forst, R. Mills Music. 1941. Out of print. 2:35. II–III. (F₁) A₁–g. Some sixteenth-note runs using scales and outlining triads; intermediate technique required.

Geib, Fred. *Song Without Words: Air with Variations.* Carl Fischer Inc. 1939. $4.00. 5:00. III–IV. C–b♭ (f'). "Tuba E♭ or BB♭." Theme and (four) variations. High range for the time period (optional). Intermediate technique required.

Geier, Oskar. *Concertstück für Tuba in F und Klavierbegleitung.* Musikverlag Barbara Evans. 1989. 12:52. IV–V. F₁–g'. Composed in 1954. Technical challenge involving quick articulations and flexibility. Neo-Romantic feel throughout.

George, Thom Ritter. *Concertino for Tuba.* Manuscript available from composer. 1984. See listing under "Music for Tuba and Band" and "Music for Tuba and Orchestra." Also see: Bird, Gary, ed., *Program Notes for the Solo Tuba.*

George, Thom Ritter. *Sonata for Tuba and Piano.* Manuscript available from the composer. 1980. 13:57 (2:46, 4:20, 3:18, 3:33). IV–V. E♭₁–g'. Vivace e con brio; Vivace assai; Ballad: Mesto (Molto cantabile); Ben ritmato. Major work for tuba and piano. Large tonal jumps and quick articulations will test technique. Well worth the effort! Good recital material. Very lyrical, hypnotic muted second movement. Mixed meter not always notated. Strong accompanist required. Recorded by Daniel Perantoni; David Randolph. See review in *T.U.B.A. Journal*, Vol. 9, no. 2, p. 24. Also see: Bird, Gary, ed., *Program Notes for the Solo Tuba.*

Gerschefski, Edwin. *"America" Variations for Winds,* Op. 45, no. 1. American Composers Edition, Inc. 1963. $3.15. 1:30. III–IV. A♭₁–b♭. Maestoso. Op. 45, no. 1. Solo in 12/8 time; a disjointed, interesting impression of *America.*

Gershenfeld, Mitchell, ed. See listing under "Tuba and Keyboard Collections."

Giordani, Giuseppe. *Arietta.* arr. Schwotzer, Stephan. Hofmeister. 1993. 1:51. II. E♭–e♭. Slow tempo; no technical problems. See: Meschke, Dieter, *Zum Uben und Vorspielen/B-Tuba,* under "Tuba and Keyboard Collections."

Giordani, Giuseppe. *Caro mio ben.* arr. Yasumoto, Hiroyuki. Toa Music International Co. 1986. 2:15. II. E♭–e♭. Larghetto. All tenuto or slurred. Very vocal approach needed. No technical problems. See: Yasumoto, Hiroyuki, *Tuba Volume #1,* under "Tuba and Keyboard Collections."

Giordani, Giuseppe. *Love Song (Caro mio ben).* ed. Daellenbach, Charles. Hal Leonard Publishing Corp. 1992. 1:55. II. B♭₁–d. Larghetto. C major, 4/4 time. A few dotted-eighth-and-sixteenth rhythms

and some grace notes and accidentals. See: Daellenbach, Charles, *Book of Easy Tuba Solos,* under "Tuba and Keyboard Collections."

Giordani, Giuseppe. *My Dearest Love (Caro mio ben) .* arr. Henderson, Luther; ed. Daellenbach, Charles. Hal Leonard Publishing Corp. 1989. $14.95. 3:10. III. E♭–g. Commercial/popular version of this aria in a rock ballade style. Some syncopation. Includes performance cassette. See review in *T.U.B.A. Journal*, Vol. 18, no. 2, p. 19.

Giovanini, J. *Challenge Concert Polka.* arr. Weber, Carl. J. W. Pepper and Son. 1914. Out of print. See listing under "Music for Tuba and Band"; and Weber, Carl, *Nineteen Solos for E♭ Bass with Piano Accompaniment,* under "Tuba and Keyboard Collections."

Gistelinck, E. *Koan II.* Edition Andel Uitgaven.

Glass, Jennifer. *Sonatina for Tuba and Piano.* Emerson Edition Limited. 1979. $18.75. 8:00. IV. E₁–f'. To John Fletcher. Allegro non troppo; Lento; Tempo di valse; Presto. Composed in 1963. Wonderful solo that allows for many musical moods; a good tuba showcase. Some mixed meter, glissandos. Strong technique required. Recorded by John Fletcher. See: Bird, Gary, ed., *Program Notes for the Solo Tuba.*

Gliere, Reinhold. *Intermezzo,* Op. 35, no. 11. arr. Graham, James. TUBA Press. 1991. IV. B♭₁–c'. Originally for horn. Andante cantabile. See: Graham, James, *Concert Music for Tuba,* under "Tuba and Keyboard Collections."

Gliere, Reinhold. *Nocturne,* Op. 35, no. 10. arr. Graham, James. TUBA Press. 1991. III–IV. G–d♭'. Originally for horn. Andante. In 9/8 time. See: Graham, James, *Concert Music for Tuba,* under "Tuba and Keyboard Collections."

Glinka, M. *Romance.* ed. Melnikov, S. Moscow: Military Band Masters Institute. 1957. See: Melnikov, S., *Pieces for Tuba and Piano,* under "Tuba and Keyboard Collections."

Glover, S. *Faith.* arr. de Ville, Paul. Carl Fischer Inc. 1906. Out of print. See: de Ville, Paul, *Pleasant Hours,* under "Tuba and Keyboard Collections."

Glover, S. *The Melodies of Many Lands.* arr. de Ville, Paul. Carl Fischer Inc. 1906. Out of print. See: de Ville, Paul, *Pleasant Hours,* under "Tuba and Keyboard Collections."

Gluck, Chr. *Air* from *Orpheus.* arr. Maganini, Quinto. Editions Musicus. 1954. 2:20. III. E–c'. In slow 3/4 time. See: Ostrander, Allen, *Concert Album for Tuba,* under "Tuba and Keyboard Collections."

Gluck, Christoph W. von. *Melody from "Orpheus and Euridice."* arr. Winter, Denis W. Whaling Music Publishers. $7.00. Originally for flute and strings.

Gluck, K. [*sic*]. *Gavotte.* ed. Lebedev, A. Moscow: Muzyka. 1984. 1:59. III. E–c'. In cut time; in A major and A minor. No technical problems. See: Lebedev, A., *Tuba Tutor, Vol. 1,* under "Tuba and Keyboard Collections."

Godel, Didier. *Concerto pour Tuba et Orchestre.* Editions Marc Reift. 1992. Piano reduction.

Godfrey, Fred. *Lucy Long.* arr. Harris, A. E. Cundy–Bettoney/Carl Fischer Inc. 1934. Out of print. 6:00. III–IV. B$_1$–c'. Theme and variations. High tessitura, large leaps.

Goedicke, A. *Dance.* ed. Lebedev, A. Moscow: Muzyka. 1984. 0:52. II. D–e♭. In 4/4 time and in D minor. A few eighth notes; no technical problems. See: Lebedev, A., *Tuba Tutor, Vol. 1,* under "Tuba and Keyboard Collections."

Goedicke, A. *Improvisation.* ed. Mitjagina, V. Moscow: Muzyka. 1969. 1:22. IV. D$_1$–a♭ (c'). Adagio sostenuto. Melodic writing utilizing middle and lower range. Other than range, no big technical problems. See: Mitjagina, V. ed., *Pieces for Tuba and Piano,* under "Tuba and Keyboard Collections."

Goeyens, A. *All 'Antica.* arr. Buchtel, Forrest Lawrence. Neil A. Kjos Music Company. 1975. $5.00. 3:47. III. A$_1$–g. "Tuba E♭ or BB♭." Baroque style; sixteenth-note scalewise movement, some octave jumps, trills, one mordent. Otherwise intermediate technique required. See review in *T.U.B.A. Journal,* Vol. 7, no. 1, p. 9.

Goldsmith, James J. *Pastorale.* arr. Werden, David R. Whaling Music Publishers. 1980. $9.50. 6:07. IV–V. D–e'. For Tucker Jolly. "For tuba or euphonium." Upper tessitura—would lie better on E♭/F tuba although it is possible on the lower instrument. Almost a "new age" feel to this lovely piece. Requires endurance, musicality and flexibility (some sextuplets). Good recital material.

Golland, J. *Scherzo for Tuba.* Hallamshire. Recorded by Stephen Sykes.

Goltermann, Georg Edvard. *Concerto No. 4,* Op. 65 arr. Bell, William J. Carl Fischer Inc. 1937. $5.00. 4:40. III–IV. F$_1$–b♭. Classic tuba transcription of excerpts from cello concerto. Differentiation between triplets and dotted rhythms a consideration. R. Winston Morris suggests putting a dot on the third note of each slurred triplet to separate.

Goode, Jack C. *Tune for Tuba (Sonatina for Tuba and Piano).* Pro Art Publications. 1969. Out of print. 3:50. III. G$_1$–b♭. To Bob Danner. Good flowing, lyrical solo with plenty of opportunity for expression. Some slurred and staccato passages. No technical problems.

Goodwin, Gordon. *Alborada (Spanish Dawn Song).* Southern Music Company. 1976. $2.50. 3:26. III. C♯–f♯. For Heather Leigh Caffey, 1974. Lovely little legato, flowing ballad. Requires a flexible tempo combined with bravura and lyricism. Some dissonant intervals, but manageable. Good recital material, even for the advanced player.

Gotkovsky, Ida. *Baladins.* Éditions Robert Martin. 1983. $4.25. 0:57. IV. D–a'. Upper tessitura throughout. Arpeggios and other technical demands.

Gotkovsky, Ida. *Suite.* Éditions Salabert. 1959. 7:05. V. G$_1$–b♭'. À Monsieur Paul Bernard Professeur au Conservatoire National Supérieur de Musique de Paris. Introduction; Andante; Finale. "Pour Tuba in ut et Piano." For French tuba. Some septuplets, many arpeggios, much scalewise motion.

Gounod, Charles. *Calf of Gold from "Faust."* arr. Ostrander, Allen. Editions Musicus. 1965. $2.75. 2:30. II–III. C–e♭. Allegro Maestoso. For trombone, baritone, or tuba with piano. Stately solo in 6/8 time.

Gounod, Charles. *Funeral March of a Marionette.* Hudadoff, Igor, and Westcott, William (piano arr.). Pro Art Publications. 1967. Out of print. See: Hudadoff, Igor, *Fifteen Intermediate Tuba Solos,* under "Tuba and Keyboard Collections."

Gounod, Charles. *March of a Marionette.* arr. Walters, Harold L. Rubank, Inc. 1965. $2.50. II–III. G$_1$–a. "Solo E♭ or BB♭ Bass." Very characteristic solo (think Alfred Hitchcock) in 6/8 time. No technical problems.

Gounod, Charles. *March of a Marionette.* arr. Wekselblatt, Herbert. G. Schirmer Inc. 1972. 1:23. III. C–g. Allegretto. Twice through the tune in 6/8 time. See: Wekselblatt, Herbert, *First Solos for the Tuba Player,* under "Tuba and Keyboard Collections."

Gounod, Charles. *Valentine's Song from "Faust."* arr. Bell, William J. CPP/Belwin, Inc. 1970. Separate publication out of print. See: CPP/Belwin, *Tuba Solos, Level Two,* under "Tuba and Keyboard Collections."

Gower, Albert. *Sonata.* The Brass Press. 1979. $4.00. 8:57 (3:00, 2:00, 1:56, 2:01). IV. F$_1$–f♯'. T. U. B. A. Series. Four numbered movements. Was published by Brass Music Ltd. Conservative modern writing. Some improvising based on given pitches with optional mute in second movement. See review in *T.U.B.A. Journal,* Vol. 1, no. 2, p. 10.

Gower, William. *Sonata for Tuba and Piano.* See review in *T.U.B.A. Journal,* Vol. 7, no. 2, p. 20.

Graetsch, Hans. *Tuba Kapriolen.* Regina Verlag. Piano reduction of tuba and band piece.

Graham, James, arr. See listing under "Tuba and Keyboard Collections."

Granados, E. *Playera.* Hudadoff, Igor, and Westcott, William (piano arr.). Pro Art Publications. 1967. Out of print. See: Hudadoff, Igor, *Fifteen Intermediate Tuba Solos,* under "Tuba and Keyboard Collections."

Granados, E. *Spanish Dance No. 2 (Oriental).* tr. Amaz, J. Union Musical Española. 1970.

Granados, E. *Spanish Dance No. 5 (Andaluza).* tr. Amaz, J. Union Musical Española. 1970.

Grant, Parks. *Concert Duo,* Op 48. American Composers Edition, Inc. 1954. $8.20. 4:50. V. D$_1$–e'. "For Tuba and Piano." Conservative contemporary writing. Double tonguing, mixed meter, dissonant intervals, wide range.

Gray, Louis Robert. *Impromptu in G,* Op. 7 no. 1. Boosey and Hawkes, Inc. 1954. Out of print. 4:45.

III. F$_1$–g. BB♭ bombardon solo. Typical technical solo with cadenza. Conservative intermediate range and technique required. Solo part in treble clef.

Gregor, František. *Konzertetüde.* ed. Hoza, Václav. Editio Supraphon. 1982. 3:17. IV. G$_1$–c'. Allegro moderato. Good technical solo. Arpeggios, scales, accents; very playable. See: Hoza, Václav, *Schule für Tuba in F und in B,* in "Methods and Studies."

Gregson, Edward. *Tuba Concerto.* Novello and Company. 1976. $22.00. For John Fletcher. See: Gregson, Edward, *Tuba Concerto,* under "Music for Tuba and Band" and "Music for Tuba and Orchestra." Also see: Bird, Gary, ed., *Program Notes for the Solo Tuba.* Recorded by John Fletcher; James Gourlay; Michael Lind; Josef Maierhofer; Lennart Nord; Michael Wagner. See review in *T.U.B.A. Journal,* Vol. 6, no. 2, p. 9.

Gregson, Edward, and Ridgeon, John. *Nine Miniatures.* Brass Wind Publications. I–II. For E♭ Bass/E♭ tuba. Solos with easy piano accompaniments. Treble and bass clef versions available.

Gretchaninoff, A. *Slumber Song.* arr. Swanson, Ken. CPP/Belwin, Inc. 1971. $4.00. 2:20. II–III. B♭$_1$–g. Andantino. Relaxed tempo solo in 4/4 time. A couple of octave jumps from G to g, otherwise no technical problems. See: Lamb, Jack, *Solo Sounds for Tuba Levels 3–5, Vol. 1,* under "Tuba and Keyboard Collections."

Grétry, André. *Air from "Richard Coeur de Lion."* arr. Wastall, Peter. Boosey and Hawkes, Inc. 1980. 1:06. I. E♭–e♭. Stately beginning solo that would be easier on E♭ rather than BB♭ for the beginning student. Easy accompaniment. See: Wastall, Peter, *Learn As You Play Tuba,* under "Tuba and Keyboard Collections."

Grieg, Edvard. *In the Hall of the Mountain King.* arr. Weber, Fred. CPP/Belwin, Inc. 1973. $4.00. 2:00. II. D–f. Published separately. Good scene-setting instructions from Fred Weber. An accelerando occurs throughout entire piece. Some grace notes, some accidentals. See also Lamb, Jack, *Solo Sounds for Tuba Levels 3–5, Vol. 1,* under "Tuba and Keyboard Collections."

Grieg, Edvard. *In the Hall of the Mountain King.* arr. Holmes, G. E. Rubank, Inc. 1939. "Solo Tuba—E♭ or BB♭ tuba." See: Grieg, Edvard, *In the Hall of the Mountain King,* under "Music for Tuba and Band." Also see: Rubank, *Soloist Folio for Bass (E♭ or BB♭),* under "Tuba and Keyboard Collections."

Grieg, Edvard. *In the Hall of the Mountain King (from "Peer Gynt").* arr. Wekselblatt, Herbert G. Schirmer Inc. 1972. 2:13. II–III. D–f♯. Slowly at first then faster. Classic solo with accelerando and some grace notes. See: Wekselblatt, Herbert, *First Solos for the Tuba Player,* under "Tuba and Keyboard Collections."

Grieg, E. *In Spring Time.* ed. Lebedev, A. Moscow: Muzyka. 1986. 2:26. IV. C♯–c♯'. Very melodic solo

in 6/4 time. See: Lebedev, A., *Tuba Tutor, Vol. 2,* under "Tuba and Keyboard Collections."

Grieg, Edvard. *The Last Saturday Evening.* ed. Daellenbach, Charles. Hal Leonard Publishing Corp. 1992. 1:16. II. (g$_1$) B♭$_1$–d. Andantino. In 6/8 time; in G minor. Some accidentals. See: Daellenbach, Charles, *Book of Easy Tuba Solos,* under "Tuba and Keyboard Collections."

Grieg, Edvard. *My Johann.* arr. Corwell, Neal. Kendor Music, Inc. 1988. $5.00. 2:00. II–III. C–g. Allegretto tranquilla e grazioso. Fun transcription for advanced beginner. Liberties with tempos and articulations (including grace notes) will enhance performance. Good recital material.

Gross, Eric. *Thoughts of Sunraysia,* Op. 172, no. 1. Manuscript. 1990. 4:00.

Gross, Eric. *Tubism,* Op.172, no. 2. Manuscript. 1990. 5:15.

Gruber, [Franz]. *Silent Night.* arr. Ostling, Acton. CPP/Belwin, Inc. 1969. 1:03. I–II. (A♭$_1$) C–d♭. Adagio cantabile. Melody in A♭ major with a five-bar tag. A few slurs, no technical problems. See: CPP/Belwin, Inc., *Tuba Solos, Level One,* and Ostling, Acton, *Tuba (Bass) Soloist, Level One,* under "Tuba and Keyboard Collections."

Grudzinski, Czeskaw. *Contraste per tuba e pianoforte.* Polskie Wydawnictwo Muzyczne. 7:12. IV. G♯$_1$–e'. Solid, very musical modern writing with few technical challenges. Conservative tempos. Good introduction to modern melody.

Grundman, Clare. *Tuba Rhapsody.* Boosey and Hawkes, Inc. 1976. $15.50. To Martin D. Erickson, Tuba Soloist, and the U. S. Navy Band. Optional cut lowers duration to 6:50. See listing under "Music for Tuba and Band." Recorded by Lesley Varner.

Gruner, Joachim. *Konzert für Tuba und Orchester.* Bensheimer Verlag. 1977. Recorded by Dietrich Unkrodt.

Gudmen, S. *Dance.* arr. Lebedev, A. Military Band Masters Faculty Of Moscow Conservatiore. 1971. See: Lebedev, A., *Collection of Pieces for Tuba "Es" and Piano,* under "Tuba and Keyboard Collections."

Guentzel, Gus. *Mastodon.* Mills Music. 1945. 5:00. II–III. A♭$_1$–f. "For tuba or B♭ Bass Saxophone." Very repetitive polka style solo for advanced beginner. Conservative range and mostly stepwise motion. Cadenza and lyrical Andante section. Running sixteenth-note passages in 2/4 time. Good confidence builder.

Guinot, Georges-Léonce. *Simplex pour tuba et piano.* Gérard Billaudot. 1990. 1:25 or 2:00. II. c–c'. For French tuba. Lyrical playing; no big technical problems. Two durations depending on optional cuts. See: Daniel-Lesur, *Collection Panorama,* under "Tuba and Keyboard Collections."

Guion, David M. *Sonata for Tuba.* Available from the composer. Completed San Diego, CA, September

14, 1972. 8:00. IV. A♭₁–b. Lento; Misterioso; Allegro. Some flutter tonguing. Conservative modern melodic language. Conservative range. Solid writing for tuba and piano.

Gully, Michel. *Recit.* Éditions M. Combre. 1988. 2:15. II. A♭–c'. "Pour Tuba ou Saxhorn Basse Si♭ et Piano." For French tuba. Easy rhythms, a few eighth notes at a medium tempo. No technical problems. Good recital material.

Gurlitt, Cornelius. *Andante from "First Steps,"* Op. 82. arr. Wastall, Peter. Boosey and Hawkes, Inc. 1980. 0:51. I. D–B♭. As the title indicates, good melodic, "carefully nurturing," first solo in 3/4 time. Very limited range—fastest rhythm is quarter note. Some stepwise slurring; appropriate to difficulty level. See: Wastall, Peter, *Learn As You Play Tuba,* under "Tuba and Keyboard Collections."

Guy, Earl. *Carry Me Back to Old Virginny.* arr. Holmes, G. E. Rubank, Inc. 1935. Out of print. 5:00. III. G♭₁–f. "BB♭ Bass (Sousaphone)." Theme, Variation, Obligato, two cadenzas, a finale. Intermediate technique. Planning ahead for breath required. Fun solo to play.

Haddad, Don. *Scherzino.* Southern Music Company. 1990. $3.50. 1:20. IV. F–c'. Allegro. Would lie well on F tuba; very playable on lower instrument. Needs lightness of articulation with drive at printed tempo. Resembles a quick Irish jig.

Haddad, Don. *Suite for Tuba.* Shawnee Press Inc. 1966. $10.00. See listing under "Music for Tuba and Band." Recorded by Ronald Davis; Rex Conner.

Haddad, Don. *Two Pieces.* Southern Music Company. 1990. $4.00. 2:49 (1:32, 1:17). III. D♭–c'. Andantino; Allegretto. Lyrical and easy rhythmic playing. Good recital material.

Hailstork, Adolphus C. *Duo.* Fema Music Publications. 1981. $5.00. 7:00. V. E₁–c". For John Turk. Demanding piece from both a technical and a musical point of view. Very wide range, mixed meters, quick articulations, flutter tonguing, tricky rhythms. Takes a strong player.

Haines, Edmund. *Modules.* GunMar Music, Incorporated. 1982. $20.00. 10:00. V. B♭₁–f'. For Charles English. Slow; Quite Fast; Very Slow; Dialogue; Fast. Original copyright 1972. Composers Facsimile Edition. Movements may be played in any order. Very free, unmeasured playing combined with traditional notation. Improvised and random-order passages. Flutter tonguing, compound meters, trills; strong technique required. Upper tessitura; best on F tuba.

Halévy, Jacques. *The Cardinal's Air from "La Juive."* arr. Clark, Frank. Editions Musicus. 1965. $2.75. 1:55. III. G₁–e. Andante. For trombone, baritone or tuba and piano. Slow solo in 2/4. A few eighth-note triplets, short cadenza; no technical problems.

Hall, Harry H., arr. *Menuet.* Brodt Music Company. 1962. 1:12. II. D–e♭. "German Folk Song." Simple

24-measure tune in 3/4 time with repeats. A few eighth notes; no technical problems.

Hanby, B. R. *Up on the Housetop.* arr. Feldstein, Sandy. CPP/Belwin, Inc. 1990. I. B♭₁–G. See: Feldstein, Sandy, *First Solo Songbook,* under "Tuba and Keyboard Collections."

Handel, George Frederick. *Adagio and Allegro from Sonata No. 7.* ed. Voxman, Himie. Rubank, Inc. 1972. 4:30. III. B♭₁–f. "For E♭ or BB♭ Bass." Adagio in 8 with trills. Attacca Allegro section in 4/4 time with trills, with melody based on inverted triads. See: Voxman, Himie, *Concert and Contest Collection,* under "Tuba and Keyboard Collections."

Handel, George Frederick. *Air.* arr. Lebedev, A. Military Band Masters Faculty of Moscow Conservatiore. 1971. See: Lebedev, A., *Collection of Pieces for Tuba "Es" and Piano,* under "Tuba and Keyboard Collections."

Handel, George Frederick. *Allegro from Concerto Grosso,* Op. 3, no. 4. trans. Dishinger, Ronald C. Medici Music Press. 1982. $4.50. 2:26. II. B♭₁–e♭. Distinction between staccato and tenuto marks as well as dynamics needs to be made. Some eighth-note scalelike figures, otherwise no technical problems.

Handel, George Frederick. *Allegro from Concerto in F minor.* arr. Barr, Robert M. Ludwig Music Publishing Company. 1968. $4.00. 2:10. IV. C–b♭. Allegro. Very good transcription. Mostly contains sixteenth-note scalewise runs. Planning breaths will help. Good recital material.

Handel, George Frederick. *Andante.* arr. Ostrander, Allen. Editions Musicus. 1954. 3:20. II–III. C–g. Andante Sostenuto. Well-transcribed solo with eighth note as the beat. Good continuo accompaniment. Good recital material (even for an advanced player). See: Ostrander, Allen, *Concert Album for Tuba,* under "Tuba and Keyboard Collections."

Handel, George Frederick. *Aria from "Judas Maccabeus."* arr. Hall, Harry H. Brodt Music Company. 1962. 3:57. II–III. G₁–e♭. Larghetto. Slow sustained lyrical playing. A few slow octave jumps, a few "low" tones, otherwise very accessible to the advanced beginner.

Handel, George Frederick. *Arioso.* arr. de Rooij, Piet. Molenaar N. V. 1966. 1:30. III–IV. d–f'. Works well on F tuba. High tessitura for lower instruments. No other technical challenges.

Handel, George Frederick. *Arm, Arm, Ye Brave, from "Judas Maccabeus."* arr. Ostrander, Allen. Editions Musicus. 1959. $3.00. 3:20. II–III. B₁–e. Andante and Allegro sections use a very conservative range. Attention should be paid to articulation: slurred dotted rhythms, staccato notes within slurs. Good transcription.

Handel, George Frederick. *Bourée.* ed. Lebedev, A. Moscow: Muzyka. 1984. 1:23. III. D–b. Same as other arrangements listed but with a few changed notes. In G major. See: Lebedev, A., *Tuba Tutor, Vol. 1,* under "Tuba and Keyboard Collections."

Handel, George Frederick. *Bourée* from *Flute Sonata No. 6.* arr. Maganini, Quinto. Editions Musicus. 1954. 1:20. III. F♯–c¹. Flexibility required. See: Ostrander, Allen, *Concert Album for Tuba,* under "Tuba and Keyboard Collections." Recorded by Rex Conner; Peter Popiel.

Handel, George Frederick. *Bourée.* ed. Melnikov, S. Moscow: Military Band Masters Institute. 1957. See: Melnikov, S., *Pieces for Tuba and Piano,* under "Tuba and Keyboard Collections."

Handel, George Frederick. *Bourrée.* arr. Swanson, Ken. CPP/Belwin, Inc. 1970. $4.00. 1:36. II. B♭₁– f. Moderato. Cut-time Baroque solo using eighth notes as fastest rhythm. A variety of articulations (staccato, tenuto, slurs) should not be overlooked. See: Lamb, Jack, *Classic Festival Solos,* and CPP/ Belwin, *Tuba Solos, Level Two,* under "Tuba and Keyboard Collections."

Handel, George Frederick. *Chorus from Judas Maccabaeus.* arr. Graham, James. TUBA Press. 1991. II–III. G–g. Maestoso. See: Graham, James, *Concert Music for Tuba,* under "Tuba and Keyboard Collections."

Handel, George Frederick. *Concerto No. 3 for Tuba and String Orchestra.* arr. Yasumoto, Hiroyuki. Toa Music International Co. 1946. III–IV. D–c¹. Grave; Allegro; Largo; Allegro. See: Yasumoto, Hiroyuki, *Tuba Volume #2,* under "Tuba and Keyboard Collections."

Handel, George Frederick. *Dove Sei from "Rodelinda."* arr. Little, Donald C. See review in *T.U.B.A. Journal,* Vol. 7, no. 4, p. 27.

Handel, George Frederick. *The Harmonious Blacksmith.* arr. de Ville, Paul. Carl Fischer Inc. 1906. Out of print. See: de Ville, Paul, *Pleasant Hours,* under "Tuba and Keyboard Collections."

Handel, George Frederick. *Honor and Arms.* arr. Bell, William J. CPP/Belwin, Inc. 1965. $4.00. 1:56. II–III. (G₁) B♭₁–e♭. Plenty of unison with piano for self-confidence in this arrangement. Stately transcription; some slurring. As Bell notes: "played in a very forceful style just as a fine basso would sing it." See: Lamb, Jack, *Solo Sounds for Tuba Levels 3–5, Vol. 1,* under "Tuba and Keyboard Collections." See following listing.

Handel, George Frederick. *Honor and Arms* from *Samson.* arr. Harvey, Russell. G. Schirmer Inc. 1940. $3.00. 4:45. III. (G₁) A₁–e♭. More slurring, tenutos and repeats in this arrangement than in Bell's (above). It also has an additional section.

Handel, George Frederick. *Konzert G-Moll.* arr. Mark Evans. Musikverlag Barbara Evans.

Handel, George Frederick. *Larghetto and Allegro.* arr. Little, Donald C. Figured bass realization by George R. Belden. CPP/Belwin, Inc. 1978. $4.00. 4:44. II–III. B♭₁–e♭. Larghetto (3/4 time) section followed by an extended Allegro in 3/8 time. Many

sixteenth notes, mostly in stepwise motion. Requires flexibility and facility. Good advanced beginner/early intermediate work. See: Lamb, Jack, *Classic Festival Solos,* under "Tuba and Keyboard Collections." Also see other listing in this section. Also see review in *T.U.B.A. Journal,* Vol. 7, no. 3, p. 35.

Handel, George Frederick. *Lento.* ed. Daellenbach, Charles. Hal Leonard Publishing Corp. 1992. 1:16. II. C♯–c. Good introduction to 3/2 time. Quarter note is fastest rhythm. A few accidentals. See: Daellenbach, Charles, *Book of Easy Tuba Solos,* under "Tuba and Keyboard Collections."

Handel, George Frederick. *Love That's True Will Live Forever* (*Si, Tra I Ceppi, from "Berenice"*). arr. Hume, James Ord. Boosey and Co. 1906. Out of print. See: Hume, J. Ord, *Boosey's Bombardon Solo Album,* under "Tuba and Keyboard Collections."

Handel, George Frederick. *Menuet from "Alcina."* arr. Hall, Harry H. Brodt Music Company. 1962. $1.50. 2:30. II. G₁–d. Gracefully. Some slurring, eighth note is fastest rhythm; no technical problems.

Handel, George Frederick. *Recitative and Air from "The Messiah."* arr. O'Neill, Charles. Waterloo Music Co. 1948. Out of print. 4:30. III. D♭–b♭. Sustained aria.

Handel, George Frederick. *Repentance* (*Chi sprezzando*) from *The Passion.* ed. Daellenbach, Charles. Hal Leonard Publishing Corp. 1992. 1:37. II. C–d♭. Adagio. Some large leaps; some accidentals. In 3/4 time with a feeling of 6 throughout. See: Daellenbach, Charles, *Book of Easy Tuba Solos,* under "Tuba and Keyboard Collections."

Handel, George Frederick. *Revenge! Timotheus Cries!* from *Alexander's Feast.* arr. Morris, R. Winston. Ludwig Music Publishing Company. 1970. $3.50. 1:35. III. C♯–e. Allegretto. Requires lightness of articulation and attention paid to dynamic contrast. Key of D♯ major; conservative range. Good transcription by a fine arranger.

Handel, George Frederick. *Sarabande from Concerto in F minor.* arr. Barr, Robert. Ludwig Music Publishing Company. 1968. $4.00. 2:20. II–III. (F₁) A♭₁–a♭. Largo. Slow solo in 3/4 time with a some dotted-eighth and sixteenth notes. A few slurs, some optional F₁'s. Probably closer to Level II, but requires musical intensity.

Handel, George Frederick. *See, the Conquering Hero Comes.* arr. de Ville, Paul. Carl Fischer Inc. 1906. Out of print. See: de Ville, Paul, *Pleasant Hours,* under "Tuba and Keyboard Collections."

Handel, George Frederick. *Sonata No. 6.* tr. Morris, R. Winston. Shawnee Press Inc. 1982. $8.00. 8:30. IV. D–e¹. Adagio; Allegro; Largo; Allegro. Composed for violin in E major; transposed to F. Very playable transcription. Adagio is in 8, with the eighth note getting the beat. Some trills. Requires flexibility and good Baroque conception. Four contrasting movements; good opportunity for conceptual variety.

Handel, George Frederick. *Sonate C-Dur für Tuba and Klavier/Orgel.* adapted by Hilgers, Walter. Editions Marc Reift. 1990. $20.25. 10:54 (2:17, 2:41, 2:24, 1:35, 1:45). IV–V. G–d'. Larghetto; Allegro; Larghetto; Tempo di Gavotte; Allegro. Good transcription from the sonata for recorder and basso continuo, Op. no. 7. Very full transcription; almost no rests. Challenging musically and technically. Quick articulations, flexibility, and endurance are required. Conservative range. Recorded by Walter Hilgers.

Handel, George Frederick. *Sound an Alarm from "Judas Maccabeus."* arr. Barnes, Clifford P. Jack Spratt Music Co. 1965. $3.00. 1:59. III. B♭₁–f. Allegro. Sprightly transcription in 6/8 time. Depending on tempo chosen, slurred sixteenth notes could present a challenge; otherwise no big technical problems.

Handel, George Frederick. *Suite in A–flat.* arr. Little, Donald C. See review in *T.U.B.A. Journal,* Vol. 7, no. 4, p. 27.

Handel, George Frederick. *Thrice Happy the Monarch from "Alexander Balus."* arr. Morris, R. Winston. Ludwig Music Publishing Company. 1970. $5.00. 2:50. III. G₁–f. Allegro. Composed in 1748. Also arranged for trombone, baritone (T. C. and B. C.), cornet, and piano. Transcribed solo in 3/8 time (felt in 1). Some sixteenth-note runs; some moving in thirds; otherwise this flowing solo has no technical problems.

Handel, George Frederick. *Two Short Pieces.* ed. Voxman, Himie. Rubank, Inc. 1972. 3:00. II–III. (A₁) B♭₁–f. *Aria; Bourée.* "For E♭ or BB♭ Bass. *Aria* from *Rinaldo* in 3/2 time. *Bourée* in cut-time. Both very recognizable. See: Voxman, Himie, *Concert and Contest Collection,* under "Tuba and Keyboard Collections."

Handel, George Frederick. *Variations.* arr. Lebedev, A. Military Band Masters Faculty Of Moscow Conservatiore. 1971. See: Lebedev, A., *Collection of Pieces for Tuba "Es" and Piano,* under "Tuba and Keyboard Collections."

Handel, George Frederick. *Where'er You Walk (from Semele).* arr. Swanson, Ken. Belwin Mills, Inc. 1971. Published separately. Out of print. 3:35. II. C–d. Moderato. A few accidentals; a few tonal jumps of a sixth and a seventh; mostly scalewise movement. See: Lamb, Jack, *Solo Sounds for Tuba Levels 1–3, Vol. 1,* under "Tuba and Keyboard Collections."

Hanmer, Ronald. *Tuba Tunes.* Emerson Edition Limited. 1979. $10.75. 3:49 (0:50, 1:03, 1:11, 0:45). II. E♭–a♭. Sostenuto (Allegro moderato); Staccato (Allegretto); Cantabile (Andante espressivo); Scherzando (Allegro). Advanced beginner level for E♭ tuba; more difficult for BB♭ because of tessitura.

Four contrasting cute vignettes, fun musically and good opportunity for expression. No technical problems. See review in *T.U.B.A. Journal,* Vol. 8, no. 4, p. 28.

Hanson, Raymond. *Romance.* Australian Music Centre.

Hanson, Ronald D. *Variations on a Theme for Tuba and Piano.* Editions Musicus. 1980. $6.00. 8:30. V. E♭₁–b♭'. Dedicated to Barton Cummings. One movement. Extreme range; high tessitura. Glissandos, very wide interval jumps. Complex time signatures. Requires a good ear and strong technique.

Harlow. *Old Home Down on the Farm.* arr. Buchtel, Forrest L. Neil A. Kjos Music Company. 1958. Out of print. 7:30. III–IV. F₁–g (b♭). Theme and variations.

Harris, Floyd O. *Dancing Silhouettes.* Ludwig Music Publishing Company. 1980. $4.00. 3:49. III. B♭–f. To my son, Dean A. Harris. For trombone, bassoon, baritone (B. C.), or tuba and piano. Old-style characteristic waltz. Some slurring, some grace notes, cadenza; no technical problems.

Harris, Floyd O. *The King's Jester.* Ludwig Music Publishing Company. 1950. $3.50. 2:07. II. D–e♭. Allegro. "Solo for E♭, BB♭ Bass." For trombone, baritone (B. C.) or tuba and piano. Solo in 6/8 time with short cadenza. Mostly stepwise motion; no technical problems.

Harris, Floyd O. *Little Caesar.* Ludwig Music Publishing Company. 1982. $3.50. 2:23. II. (E♭₁) C–d (e♭). Marcato. Original copyright 1955. "Solo for E♭, BB♭ Bass, Trombone or Baritone." A 6/8 march using mostly stepwise motion. No technical problems.

Harris, Floyd O. *Little Fiesta.* Ludwig Music Publishing Company. 1950. $3.50. 2:31. II. D–e♭. "E♭, BB♭ Bass." "Polka-Tango, Spanish rhythm." Simple polka-style solo in 2/4 time with a cadenza. Conservative range; no technical problems. Good advanced beginner solo.

Harris, John H. *Tempesta Polka.* Carl Fischer Inc. 1896. $3.25. See listing under "Music for Tuba and Band." See review in *T.U.B.A. Journal,* Vol. 9, no. 3, p. 25.

Hart, Lorenz, and Rodgers, Richard. *Blue Moon.* arr. Feldstein, Sandy. CPP/Belwin, Inc. 1990. I. B♭₁–G. See: Feldstein, Sandy, *First Solo Songbook,* under "Tuba and Keyboard Collections."

Hartley, V [sic]. *Concertino.* ed. Guzii, V. Moscow: Muzyka. 1978. See: Guzii, V., *Pieces for Tuba and Piano,* under "Tuba and Keyboard Collections."

Hartley, Walter S. *Aria for Tuba And Piano.* Elkan-Vogel, Inc. 1968. $3.95. 2:27. III–IV. b♭–b♭. Allegretto. "Tuba Part may be played by bassoon or euphonium." Composed in 1967. Lyrical modern writing. Part should be harmonically analyzed for greater understanding. Some sixteenth-note runs will need work; no other big technical problems.

Hartley, Walter S. *Concertino for Tuba and Wind Ensemble.* Theodore Presser Company. 1969. $21.00. See listing under "Music for Tuba and Band." Recorded by John Turk.

Hartley, Walter S. *Fantasia for Tuba and Chamber Orchestra.* Wingert-Jones Music, Incorporated. 1991. $8.00. Commissioned by Scott Watson with a General Research Grant from the University of Kansas. Composed in 1989. Piano reduction. See listing under "Music for Tuba and Orchestra."

Hartley, Walter S. *Largo for Tuba and Piano.* Philharmusica. 1974. $7.50. 3:40. IV–V. F_1–$f\sharp^1$. Dedicated to Michael Lind. Lyrical solo in 6/8 time with a pulse of 6. Wide range; some high and low tessitura with subtle dynamics.

Hartley, Walter S. *Sonata for Tuba and Piano.* Theodore Presser Company. 1967. $9.50. 6:00. IV. G_1–a. Andante; Allegretto grazioso; Adagio sostenuto; Allegro moderato, con anima. Modern melodic writing. Conservative range for the level. Recorded by Robert LeBlanc. See: Bird, Gary, ed., *Program Notes for the Solo Tuba.*

Hartley, Walter S. *Sonatina.* Fema Music Publications. 1970. $5.00. 6:00. IV. G_1–a. Allegretto; Largo Maestoso; Allegro Moderato. Composed in 1957. Originally published by Tenuto Press in 1958; Interlochen Press in 1961; Fema in 1970. Modern (tonal) writing. Requires flexibility. Recorded by Peter Popiel. See review in *T.U.B.A. Journal*, Vol. 1, no. 1, p. 7. Also see: Bird, Gary, ed., *Program Notes for the Solo Tuba.*

Hartley, Walter S. *Sonatina Giocosa.* 1988.

Hartley, Walter S. *Sonorities for Tuba and Piano.* Philharmusica. 1973. $8.50. C_1–g^1. For Rudy Emilson. Adagio. Composed in 1972. Musical textures. Requires solid rhythm control (at a slow speed, some syncopation, quintuplets), wide range, and good modern melodic sense.

Hartley, Walter S. *Tuba Rose (Polka).* Theodore Presser Company. 1977. $2.50. 2:53. IV. $E\flat_1$–b. For Eric Abis. Allegro molto. Sixteenth-note ascending and descending chromatic scales throughout at a quick tempo. Traditional polka feel with a modern harmonic and melodic approach. Good recital piece.

Hartzell, Doug. *The Egotistical Elephant.* Shawnee Press Inc. 1967. $5.00. Optional solo instruments include bass clarinet, contrabass clarinet, baritone saxophone, bassoon, bass trombone. See listing under "Music for Tuba and Band."

Hasse, Johann, and William Gower. *Menuet and Bourrée.* Rubank, Inc. Out of print. II.

Hastings, Ross. *Prelude and Faràndola.* TUBA Press. 1987. $8.00. See listing under "Music for Tuba and Band." Accompaniment also available for piano with tambour obbligato.

Hatton, J. L. *Simon the Cellarer.* arr. Hume, James Ord. Boosey and Co. 1906. Out of print. See: Hume, J. Ord, *Boosey's Bombardon Solo Album,* under "Tuba and Keyboard Collections."

Hatton, J. L. *Simon the Cellarer.* arr. Prendiville, Harry. A. Squire. 1888. Out of print. 1:12. II–III. ($B\flat_1$) C–f. In 6/8 time. "E♭ Bass; or, tuba with piano or organ Accompaniment, (ad lib)." See: Prendiville, Harry, *Six Popular Solos,* under "Tuba and Keyboard Collections."

Havens, Daniel. *Cançao.* Available from the composer. IV. Manuscript.

Haydn, Franz Joseph. *Allegro and Minuet.* Hudadoff, Igor, and Westcott, William (piano arr.). Pro Art Publications. 1967. Out of print. See: Hudadoff, Igor, *Fifteen Intermediate Tuba Solos,* under "Tuba and Keyboard Collections."

Haydn, Franz Joseph. *Andante.* arr. Scherzer. Musikverlag Johann Kliment KG.

Haydn, Franz Joseph. *Haydn Medley, from Symphony No. 94.* arr. Bell, William J. CPP/Belwin, Inc. 1970. $4.00. 3:00. I. $B\flat_1$–e♭. Three short selections from the *Surprise Symphony,* and *String Quartets* Op. 3, no. 5 and Op. 76, no. 5. Suggested tempo is very slow, allowing for beginning level. Some sixteenth notes; at this tempo not a problem. See: CPP/Belwin, *Tuba Solos, Level Two,* under "Tuba and Keyboard Collections." Also see other listing in this section.

Haydn, Franz Joseph. *Papa Haydn's Tune.* arr. Kinyon, John. M. Witmark and Sons. 1958. I. See: Kinyon, John, *Breeze-Easy Recital Pieces,* under "Tuba and Keyboard Collections."

Haydn, Franz Joseph. *Sonata No. 7.* arr. Bowles, Richard W. CPP/Belwin, Inc. 1973. $4.00. 5:23 (3:50 without repeat in exposition). II–III. $F\sharp_1$–g. Allegro. First movement of Haydn's *Sonata* in sonata form. Good transcription in E♭ major in 4/4 time. Some sixteenth-note stepwise runs, some slurs, no big technical problems. See: Lamb, Jack, *Solo Sounds for Tuba Levels 3–5, Vol. 1,* under "Tuba and Keyboard Collections."

Haydn, Franz Joseph. *The Spacious Firmament on High.* arr. Little, Don. CPP/Belwin, Inc. 1989. 1:55. I. ($B\flat_1$) C–B♭. Limited range, easy rhythms (only a few eighth notes). See: Little, Don, *Solo-Pak for Tuba, Part One,* under "Tuba and Keyboard Collections."

Haydn, J. *The Spacious Firmament.* arr. Jacobs, Wesley. Encore Music Publishers. 1:11. I. D–d. With vigor. In G major. A few eighth notes; some slurring; aside from key, no technical problems. See: Jacobs, Wesley, *Solos from the Classics,* under "Tuba and Keyboard Collections."

Haydn, Franz Joseph. *Trio 48.* tr. Greenstone, Paul. PP Music. 1987. $10.00. 9:30 (4:02, 2:06, 3:22). III. $B\flat_1$–b♭. Allegro; Menuet; Finale. Originally for baryton, viola and cello in D major. Some sixteenth-note (mostly stepwise) runs; no other technical problems. Good recital material, even for advanced player.

Haydn, Franz Joseph. *Two Classical Themes.* arr. Perantoni, Daniel. Hal Leonard Publishing Corp. 1976.

See: Perantoni, Daniel, *Master Solos, Intermediate Level,* under "Tuba and Keyboard Collections."

Haydn, J. *Hymn.* arr. Jacobs, Wesley. Encore Music Publishers. 0:47. I–II. Bb$_1$–eb. Singing style. Some slurring and dotted rhythms. Eighth note is fastest rhythm. See: Jacobs, Wesley, *Solos from the Classics,* under "Tuba and Keyboard Collections."

Hayes, Al. *Solo Pomposo.* Carl Fischer Inc. 1911. $3.00. Was published by The Fillmore Bros. See listing under "Music for Tuba and Band."

Heiden, Bernard. *Concerto for Tuba and Orchestra.* Peer-Southern Organization. 1979. For Harvey Phillips. Composed under a grant from the National Endowment for the Arts. Piano reduction by the composer. Composed in 1976. See listing under "Music for Tuba and Orchestra." See review in *T.U.B.A. Journal,* Vol. 9, no. 3, p. 23. Also see: Bird, Gary, ed., *Program Notes for the Solo Tuba.*

Heinl, Otto. *Bärentanz.* Musikverlag Wilhelm Halter. See listing under "Music for Tuba and Band."

Henry, Jean-Claude. *Mouvement.* Alphonse Leduc Editions Paris. 1972. $14.95. 5:45. V. F$_1$–b'. À Paul Bernard. "Pour Tuba, Saxhorn-basse Sib ou Trombone-basse et Piano." For French tuba. Very wide range required. Mixed and complex meters; cadenzas. Performer needs strong technique See: Thompson/Lemke, *French Music for Low Brass Instruments.*

Herbert, Victor. *Gypsy Love Song.* arr. Ostling, Acton. CPP/Belwin, Inc. 1969. 1:02. I. Bb$_1$–c. Once through the tune with a big finish. See: Ostling, Acton, *Tuba (Bass) Soloist, Level One,* under "Tuba and Keyboard Collections."

Herbert, Victor. *Victor Herbert Medley.* arr. Ostling, Acton. CPP/Belwin, Inc. 1969. 1:28. I. Bb$_1$–d. *Toyland; Because You're You.* Once through each tune. Includes 3/4 and 4/4 time. See: Ostling, Acton, *Tuba (Bass) Soloist, Level One,* under "Tuba and Keyboard Collections."

Hewitt, Harry. *Prelude No. 1,* Op.376B. CSI Publication. IV. G$_1$–a. Part of *Six Preludes.* Available separately.

Hewitt, Harry. *Prelude No. 6,* Op. 376C, no. 6. CSI Publication. 1973. 1:45. V. E$_1$–f#'. Very low and very high playing, 4/4, 5/4, 2/4 sections, modern melody. Composed in 1970. Part of *Twelve Preludes;* available separately.

Hewitt, Harry. *Six Preludes for Tuba and Piano,* Op.376B. CSI Publication. 1950–1970. 14:00. III–IV. G$_1$–f#'. Rhythmic solos that can be performed individually or as a suite. Accompaniment not difficult. See review in *T.U.B.A. Journal,* Vol. 7, no. 2, p. 21.

Hewitt, Harry. *Sonata No. 1 for Tuba and Piano.* CSI Publication. 1941–1950. 23:30. IV–V. Ab$_1$–bb. Long one-movement work.

Hewitt, Harry. *Sonata No. 2 for Tuba and Piano,* Op. 169, no. 2. CSI Publication. 1972. 15:00. IV–V. F$_1$–f'. Four movements. Some high-and low-range playing; mostly in middle range. Some 5/8, 5/4

meters involved. Reviewed in *T.U.B.A. Journal,* Vol. 7, no. 2, p. 21.

Hewitt, Harry. *Twelve Preludes Tuba and Piano,* Op. 376C. TUBA Press. 1973. $13.00. V. D$_1$–a'. Very wide range required. Differing styles, meters, modern harmony and melody. Requires mature performers.

Hill, William H. *Conquistadores.* Neil A. Kjos Music Company. 1978. $1.75. 1:32. I. Bb$_1$–c. Moderately. Simple melody with some dotted quarters, some eighths, some slurs, limited range. See review in *T.U.B.A. Journal,* Vol. 7, no. 1, p. 8.

Hindemith, Paul. *Sonate (Sonata for Bass Tuba and Piano).* European American—Schott. 1955. $14.95. 10:20. IV. G$_1$–c'. A major piece by a master composer. First movement: main theme uses a major ninth (adds decay to notes; like a long bell tone); requires fire and lyricism by both players; differing meters between piano and tuba require different emphasis to eighths in 6/4 and 9/4 sections. Second movement: practice with a metronome, especially last line; work on tightness of ensemble. Third movement: tempo will ultimately be decided by accompanist's technique; stress vocal quality of the lines; cadenza should be analyzed beat by beat initially, then add flexible pace. Listen to recordings for different conceptions of this major work. Familiarize yourself with the piano part as well as your own part. Recorded by Rudiger Augustin; Oystein Baadsvik; Roger Bobo; John Fletcher; Gerhard Georgie; Michael Lind; Daniel Perantoni; Gene Pokorny; Abe Torchinsky; John Turk. See: Bird, Gary, ed., *Program Notes for the Solo Tuba.*

Hogg, Merle E. *Etude 1 for Tuba and Piano.* Music Graphics Press. 1978. $8.50. 7:08. IV–V. (C#$_1$/ Db$_1$) E$_1$–d'. Composed in 1974. Fine contemporary writing. One-movement work with a lot of sevenths and ninths. Two cadenzas offer improvisitory possibilities. Optional multiphonic section; flutter tonguing. Some mixed and compound meters; some quintuplets and septuplets. Will take work, but worth it. Strong accompanist required. Good recital material. See review in *T.U.B.A. Journal,* Vol. 7, no. 3, p. 38.

Hogg, Merle E. *Sonatina for Tuba and Piano.* Lyceum Music Press. 1967. 8:45. IV–V. F$_1$–db'. Allegro; Larghetto; Allegro marcato. Solid piece for tuba and piano. Some possible double tonguing. See: Bird, Gary, ed., *Program Notes for the Solo Tuba.*

Holliday, Kent. *Sonata for Tuba in F and Piano.* Available from the composer. 1991. 15:04 (5:23, 4:18, 5:59). IV–V. F$_1$–f#'. For Skip Gray and Caryl Conger. Allegro Moderato; Andante Cantabile; Allegro con brio. Major work for tuba and piano. Requires two strong, musical players. Tubist has lyrical playing, dissonant and consonant large jumps. Strong technique and rhythmic sense needed. Good recital material.

Holmboe, Vagn. *Sonate for Tuba and Piano,* Op 162. Wilhelm Hansen Musikforlag. 1985.

Holmes, G. E. *Carnival of Venice (Fantasia).* Rubank, Inc. 1937. $2.50. 5:00. III. F_1–g. "BB♭ Bass (Sousaphone)." Written for cornet, trumpet, or tuba and piano. Theme and original technical variations on the classical tune. Good intermediate solo. See review in *T.U.B.A. Journal,* Vol. 9, no. 3, p. 25.

Holmes, G. E. *Emmett's Lullaby.* Rubank, Inc. 1933. $2.50. 5:30. III. F_1–f. Featured by William Bell, Bass Soloist with Armco Band and Cincinnati Symphony Orchestra. Was published for tuba and band. Good theme-and-variations solo. See review in *T.U.B.A. Journal,* Vol. 9, no. 3, p. 25.

Holmes, Paul. *Lento.* Shawnee Press Inc. 1961. $4.00. IV. E_1–d. Composed March 1958. Very lyrical legato composition with two contrasting sections: Lento and Allegro non troppo. Lento section mostly slurred; Allegro section has gentle shifting meters (3/4, 4/4) and easy syncopations. Good recital material. Recorded by Robert LeBlanc; Ronald Davis; Rex Conner.

Holstein, Jean Paul. *Triade.* Éditions Choudens. 1973. C–g♯'. For French tuba. See: Thompson/Lemke, *French Music for Low Brass Instruments.*

Hopkinson, Michael E. *Concerto for Tuba ("Concerto Euphonique").* Kirklees Music. 1978. 14:14 (5:05, 5:16, 3:53). E♭₁–e♭'. IV. Published for the Alexander Owen Memorial Fund Scholarship 1990. Allegro moderato; Adagio; Allegro giocoso. "For B♭ Soloist–B♭ Bass or Euphonium." Solo part in treble clef. Tonal technical and lyrical showcase. Flexibility for arpeggios needed. Optional lip slurs. Mixed meter. Good recital material.

Hopkinson, Michael E. *In Lively Spirits.* Kirklees Music. 1978. 4:30. IV. C–d'. A reworking of Senaillé's *Andante and Allegro Spiritoso* for E♭ bass. Solo part in treble clef in C minor. A bit updated from the original with different jazzed-up rhythms and melodic twists.

Horovitz, Joseph. *Tuba Concerto.* Manuscript available from the composer. 1989. See listing under "Music for Tuba and Band." Recorded by James Gourlay.

Howe, Marvin C., arr. *Three Tuba Solos.* Plymouth Music Co. Inc. 1965. $4.00. 6:08. III. G_1–g (a). Bach, *Rondo from Suite in B minor for Flute*; Pergolesi, *Spiritoso*; Purcell, *Next, Winter Comes Slowly.*

Hoza, Václav. *Ländler für Tuba und Klavier.* Editio Supraphon. 1982. 2:42. III. F_1–g. Moderato. Ländler style in a broad feeling of one. Fun to play. Eighth note is fastest rhythm. See: Hoza, Václav, *Schule für Tuba in F und in B,* under "Methods and Studies."

Hoza, Václav, and Hála, Jan. *Mosaik.* Editio Supraphon. 1982. c. 6:00. V. B♭₁–d' (f'). Appasionato. Very modern writing: free rhythms, flutter tonguing, multiphonics, trills, modern notation with explanations. See: Hoza, Václav, *Schule für Tuba in F und in B,* under "Methods and Studies."

Hrdina, Eman. *Slow-Fox-Medium.* ed. Hoza, Václav. Editio Supraphon. 1982. 1:14. III. F_1–b♭. Slow. Fox trot with syncopation. "Big band" accents. See: Hoza, Václav, *Schule für Tuba in F und in B,* under "Methods and Studies."

Hrdina, Eman. *Walzer.* ed. Hoza, Václav. Editio Supraphon. 1982. 0:55. II–III. E♭₁–B. Tempo di waltz. Low-middle tessitura. Pretty waltz. A couple of very low pitches, otherwise no big technical problems. See: Hoza, Václav, *Schule für Tuba in F und in B,* under "Methods and Studies."

Hrdina, Eman. *Westernstil.* ed. Hoza, Václav. Editio Supraphon. 1982. 1:35. II–III. F_1–g. Simple fox-trot tune. Some syncopation. Fastest rhythm is eighth-note. See: Hoza, Václav, *Schule für Tuba in F und in B,* under "Methods and Studies."

Huber, Adolf. *Theme from Concertino No. IV,* Op. 8. arr. Price, J. S. Carl Fischer Inc. 1938. $4.00. 1:35. II. B♭₁–d. Moderato. Good interpretive solo for an advanced beginning student. Musically satisfying and obtainable. Eighth note is fastest rhythm. Utilize ritard in last line.

Hubert, P. *Dans les pins.* Thomi-Berg. For French tuba.

Hudadoff, Igor, ed. *Marches, Marches, Marches.* Pro Art Publications. 1974. Out of print.

Hudadoff, Igor, ed., and Wescott, William. See listing under "Tuba and Keyboard Collections."

Hume, James Ord. *Giralda.* Boosey and Hawkes, Inc. Out of print. For E♭ bombardon. In bass and treble clef.

Hume, James Ord. *In the Deep, Deep Depths.* Boosey and Hawkes, Inc. 1941. Out of print. 5:00. III. E_1–f. Playing takes place mostly in the lower range of the instrument.

Hume, James Ord. *Qui Tollis.* Boosey and Hawkes, Inc. Out of print. For B♭ bombardon. In treble clef.

Hume, James Ord. *Romance Espagnuolo.* Boosey and Hawkes, Inc. Out of print. For E♭ bombardon. In bass and treble clef.

Hume, James Ord. *Soliloquy.* Boosey and Hawkes, Inc. Out of print. For E♭ bombardon. In bass and treble clef.

Hume, James Ord. *"Te Anau" Fantasia.* Boosey and Hawkes, Inc. 1960. Out of print. 6:00. III. E_1–f. Several cadenzas, several styles and tempos. Plenty of opportunity for many musical colors within a traditional solo style.

Hume, James Ord. *Wakatipu (Fantasia).* Boosey and Hawkes, Inc. Out of print. For E♭ bombardon. In bass and treble clef.

Hume, James Ord. *Whangaroa.* Boosey and Hawkes, Inc. 1913. Out of print. 5:07. III. F_1–f. For B♭ bombardon. Traditional style combining lyrical playing with moderate technical work. Three cadenzas.

Hume, James Ord, arr. See listing under "Tuba and Keyboard Collections."

Hummel, Bertold. *Sonatine für Basstuba und Klavier,* Op. 81a. Hofmeister. 1989. 13:35 (4:08, 5:17,

4:10). IV–V. E₁–f'. Allegro; Andante; Rondo Vivace. Utilizes a wide range of the tuba. Lyrical playing throughout; meter changes in last movement. Good recital material.

Humperdinck, Engelbert. *Children's Prayer*, from *Hansel and Gretel*. tr. Gershenfeld, Mitchell. Medici Music Press. 1985. 1:24. II–III. Bb₁–eb. Lyrical, legato transcription. See: Gershenfeld, Mitchell, *Medici Masterworks Solos, Volume 1,* under "Tuba and Keyboard Collections."

Hupfield, Herman. *When Yuba Plays the Rumba on the Tuba*. arr. McLean, Douglas. Harms. 1946. 2:10. II–III. G₁–e. Tempo de Rumba. Original copyright 1931. Classic tuba solo in G minor/major. Different versions of this recorded by William Bell; Harvey Phillips; Joe Tarto; Joe "Country" Washburn.

Hutchison, Warner. *Deep Calls to Deep*. Seesaw Music Corporation Publishers. 1992. $10.00. 8:28 (4:34, 3:54). V. Gb₁–f' (a'). For James Shearer. *Deep Calls to Deep; At The Thunder of Your Waterspouts*. Completed in Las Cruces, NM, April 1988. Based on Psalm 42:7. Requires strong technique: complex rhythms, wide dissonant leaps, wide range, glissandos. Requires tight ensemble with piano.

Huuck, Reinhard. *Ariette*. Gérard Billaudot. 1990. 2':30. III. F–e'. À Jean-Jacques Werner. "Pour tuba et piano." For French tuba. Composed in 1989. Impressionistic feel with a French tonality. See: Daniel-Lesur, *Collection Panorama*, under "Tuba and Keyboard Collections."

Hyde, Derek. *Promenade*. ed. Wastall, Peter. Boosey and Hawkes, Inc. 1980. 0:27. I–II. C–d. Conventional melody with slightly dissonant accompaniment. See: Wastall, Peter, *Learn As You Play Tuba,* under "Tuba and Keyboard Collections."

Hyde, Derek. *Tuba-Talk*. ed. Wastall, Peter. Boosey and Hawkes, Inc. 1985. 1:13. I–II. C–eb. Good introductory solo for beginning player, especially on Eb tuba. Limited range; mostly quarter and eighth notes. Some staccato allows for musical expression. See: Wastall, Peter, *Learn As You Play Tuba,* under "Tuba and Keyboard Collections."

Hyman, Dick. *Requiem for Pee Wee Ervin*. Manuscript. 1981. 2:46. IV. G₁–eb'. Dedicated to Harvey Phillips. Largo (thoughtfully). Lovely tribute to Pee Wee; very melodic reflective writing. Good recital material. Meter changes throughout. Requires great lyricism, flexibility. Some left-hand stride playing by pianist.

Ideta, Keizo. *Himatsuri*. Kumato Music Junior College.

Ilvea. *Impromptu*. Manuscript. 1975. 4:20. IV. F♯₁–db'. Russian composition in 6/8 time. Very musical and fun to play. Some flexibility required. One-movement sonata form with very tonal phrases. Good recital material.

Inagaki, Takuzo. *Piece of Tuba*, Op. 6. Academia Music Limited. 1976. 1:52. III–IV. Bb–d'. "For Tuba (or Euphonium) and piano." Cute short solo utiliz-

ing some 7/8 meter sections as well as 3/4 and 4/4. Upper tessitura; would lie best on F tuba or euphonium. Some flexibility required.

Innes, F. N. *La Coquette Concert Polka*. arr. Weber, Carl. J. W. Pepper and Son. 1914. Out of print. See: Weber, Carl, *Nineteen Solos for Eb Bass with Piano Accompaniment,* under "Tuba and Keyboard Collections."

Irons, Earl D. *Cedar Vale*. The Fillmore Bros. Co./Carl Fischer, Inc. 1941. Out of print. 4:00. II–III. A₁–d (eb). "Polka. Solo for Bb Cornet, Trombone, Baritone and BBb Bass, with Piano Accompaniment." Typical polka-style solo in an easier level than most in this genre.

Irons, Earl D. *Fleur de Lis*. The Fillmore Bros. Co./Carl Fischer, Inc. 1951. Out of print. 4:20. III. (G₁) A₁–f. "Solo for Cornet, Trumpet, Baritone, (Bass or Treble clef) Tuba with Piano Acc." "Bass Solo (Eb—BBb)." Polka style solo through a variety of tempos and styles. Short cadenza.

Israel, Brian. *Serenade for Tuba and Piano*. Theodore Presser Company. 1980. $4.00. For Jim Martin. March; Waltz; Galop. See review in *T.U.B.A. Journal*, Vol. 8, no. 3, p. 32.

Israel, Brian. *Sonata No. 2*. Theodore Presser Company. 1977. $3.00.

Issac, Merle J., arr. *The Jolly Dutchman*. Carl Fischer Inc. 1939. $2.50. 2:18. I–II. Bb₁–eb. Adapted from folk tunes by this renowned music educator. Would be Level I if not for slightly high tessitura. Some slurring, accents, staccato.

Istvàn, Bogar. *Tubaverseny*.

Jackman, Andrew. *Three Tuba Rags*. Novello and Company. 1989. $10.95. 8:35 (3:40, 3:25, 1:30). IV–V. C₁–f♯'. *Swing Rag; Music Box Rag; Gravy Train Rag*. Both treble and bass-clef parts included. Eighth notes are swung in first piece, "straight" (as written) in last two. Muted passages in second rag. Wide range and flexibility required. Glissando and multiphonics present. Good "showy" recital material. See review in *T.U.B.A. Journal*, Vol. 17, no. 1, p. 42.

Jacob, Gordon. *Bagatelles for Tuba*. Emerson Edition Limited. 1980. $11.00. 4:23 (1:13, 0:59, 0:57, 1:13). III. bb₁–f. To my Godson, Daniel Emerson. *In Tranquil Mood* (Andante); *The Corsair Bold* (Moderato); *A Sprightly Dance* (Allegro Moderato); *After Dinner Speech* (Andante poco pomposo). Both treble and bass-clef parts included. Very musical, short, contrasting pieces. Some slurring, dotted rhythms; no big technical problems—just very playable music. Good recital material. See review in *T.U.B.A. Journal*, Vol. 9, no. 1, p. 14.

Jacob, Gordon. *Six Little Tuba Pieces*. Emerson Edition Limited. 1978. $13.75. 7:36 (1:11, 1:00, 1:18, 1:01, 1:19, 1:47). III–IV. Bb₁–eb'. To Emma P. [Parkinson]. *Restful Prelude* (Andante tranquillo); *Marching Tune* (Alla marcia); *Minuet* (Alla menuetto grazioso); *Hungarian* (Allegro vivace);

In Folk Song Style (Andante moderato); *Scottish* (Vivace). Very musical suite of intermediate solos with a British (except fourth tune) flavor. Look out for 3/2 and 5/4 meters. One movement in E♭ minor. A few spots require upper range, otherwise no big technical problems. Level III except for range. Good recital material. See review in *T.U.B.A. Journal,* Vol. 9, no. 1, p. 14.

Jacob, Gordon. *Tuba Suite.* Boosey and Hawkes, Inc. 1973. $15.00. 17:03 (2:20, 1:39, 3:11, 1:00, 0:48, 1:43, 2:21, 4:06). IV. (D₁) F₁–d' (g'). To Ian King. *Prelude* (Largo); *Hornpipe* (Allegro); *Saraband* (Adagio); *Bourrée* (Allegro giojoso [*sic*]); *Brief Interlude* (Andante sostenuto); *Mazurka* (Allegro moderato); *Ground* (Jacob's Dream); *Grave*; *Galop* (Presto), with cadenza. Written in 1972. Originally called *Jacob's Suite for Tuba and Strings.* Eight short pieces with a British band feel; eight different moods with great opportunity for musical expression. Includes fast technical playing, slow lyrical playing. Good recital material. Recorded by Eugene Dowling. See review in *T.U.B.A. Journal,* Vol. 1, no. 2, p. 10.

Jacobs, Wesley. *Carnival of Venice.* Encore Music Publishers. 1989. $11.00. 5:30. IV–V. C–a♭'. Upper tessitura theme and (three) variations with cadenza. Strong technique required.

Jacobs, Wesley, arr. *Coventry Carole.* Encore Music Publishers. 1:06. I. F♯–d. English Carole. Limited range; a few accidentals, some stepwise slurs. Quarter note is fastest rhythm in 3/4 time. See listing under "Tuba and Keyboard Collections."

Jacobs, Wesley, arr. *Dona Nobis Pacem.* Encore Music Publishers. 0:50. I–II. C–d. Latin round. In 3/4 time. Some slurring, a couple of C–c octave jumps. See listing under "Tuba and Keyboard Collections."

Jacobs, Wesley, arr. *German Waltz.* Encore Music Publishers. 0:39. I–II. D–e♭. German folk song. Waltz in one. Some stepwise slurring; quarter note is fastest rhythm. See listing under "Tuba and Keyboard Collections."

Jacobs, Wesley, arr. *Go Down, Moses.* Encore Music Publishers. 1:35. I. D–d. With feeling. Spiritual. Some syncopation. See listing under "Tuba and Keyboard Collections."

Jacobs, Wesley, arr. *Greensleeves.* Encore Music Publishers. 0:34. II. A₁–c. Moderato. Old English air. In 6/8 and D minor. Once through the tune. Some slurring, accidentals and dotted rhythms. See listing under "Tuba and Keyboard Collections."

Jacobs, Wesley, arr. *Harvest Dance.* Encore Music Publishers. 0:27. I. B♭₁–d. Lightly. Czech folk song. Some syncopation. Mostly stepwise motion. In 2/4 time. See listing under "Tuba and Keyboard Collections."

Jacobs, Wesley, arr. *In Olden Times.* Encore Music Publishers. 0:47. II. B₁–c. Broadly. German folk song. In G major. Some slurring; flexibility required. Eighth note is fastest rhythm. See listing under "Tuba and Keyboard Collections."

Jacobs, Wesley, arr. *In Springtime.* Encore Music Publishers. 1:02. I–II. C–d. Gaily. German folk song. Flexibility required for interval jumps. Eighth note is fastest rhythm. See listing under "Tuba and Keyboard Collections."

Jacobs, Wesley, arr. *Little Maiden.* Encore Music Publishers. 0:27. I–II. E–d. Lightly. Moravian folk song. Some slurring; easy rhythms. One jump from d to E; otherwise no technical problems. See listing under "Tuba and Keyboard Collections."

Jacobs, Wesley, arr. *A Mighty Fortress.* Encore Music Publishers. 1:02. I. C–c. Broadly. Typical chorale style; (unwritten) ritards and fermatas. Quarter note is fastest rhythm. See listing under "Tuba and Keyboard Collections."

Jacobs, Wesley, arr. *Nightingale.* Encore Music Publishers. 1:17. II. D–c. Moderato. German folk song. In 2/4 with a pulse of 4 (eighth note gets the beat). A couple of written out turns (32nd notes) and some slurring. In A minor. See listing under "Tuba and Keyboard Collections."

Jacobs, Wesley, arr. *Solos from the Classics.* See listing under "Tuba and Keyboard Collections."

Jacobs, Wesley, arr. *Steal Away.* Encore Music Publishers. 1:01. II. F–d. Quietly. Spiritual. Some syncopation; limited range. See listing under "Tuba and Keyboard Collections."

Jacobs, Wesley, arr. *The Steeple.* Encore Music Publishers. 1:08. I. C–d. Moderately fast. English Folk Song. Quarter note is fastest rhythm. A few C–c octave jumps. See listing under "Tuba and Keyboard Collections."

Jacobs, Wesley, arr. *Thanksgiving.* Encore Music Publishers. 1:01. I. B♭₁–c. Lively. Netherlands air. Solo in 3/4 time. Some slurring, mostly stepwise motion. See listing under "Tuba and Keyboard Collections."

Jacobs, Wesley, arr. *Village Dance.* Encore Music Publishers. 0:32. I. E♭–b♭. Playfully. French folk song. Limited range. In 2/4 time with a few eighth notes as fastest rhythm. No technical problems. See listing under "Tuba and Keyboard Collections."

Jacobsen, Julius. *Humoresk.* Swedish Music Information Center. 1976.

Jacobsen, Julius. *Tuba Buffo.* Swedish Music Information Center. 1977. 7:00. Band accompaniment available. Modest range requirements; also possible on euphonium. Recorded by Michael Lind.

Jacobsen, Julius. *Twenty-Four Preludes for Tuba and Piano.* Swedish Music Information Center.

Jaffe, Gerard. *Centone Buffo Concertante.* Southern Music Company. 1973. $5.00. 5:10. III–IV. G₁–b♭. Allegro Moderato. Solo in cut time utilizing technical, lyrical, and two "after-beat" passages (for those who are tired of ohm-pahs). Some quintuplets in cadenza. Fun piece. See review in *T.U.B.A. Journal,* Vol. 1, no. 1, p. 7.

Jager, Robert. *Concerto for Bass Tuba.* Hal Leonard Publishing Corp. 1978. $7.50. Commissioned by the University of Illinois Band, Harry Begian, director for Dan Perantoni. See listing under "Music for Tuba and Band" and under "Music for Tuba and Orchestra." Also see: Bird, Gary, ed., *Program Notes for the Solo Tuba.* Recorded by R. Winston Morris; Daniel Perantoni. See review in *T.U.B.A. Journal,* Vol. 9, no. 2, p. 24.

Jager, Robert. *Reflections.* Neil A. Kjos Music Company. 1983. $6.00. 6:15. IV. B♭₁–b. Commissioned by Tubists Universal Brotherhood Association. Premiered by R. Winston Morris, tuba, and Barbara Young, piano, May 21, 1980, at the Second National Tuba-Euphonium Symposium Workshop; University of North Texas, Denton. Shifting meters throughout, for musical reasons, not for just academic sakes. Good recital material.

Jakma, Frits, Sr. *Dans der Teddyberen* (*Dance of the Teddy Bears*). Tierolff-Muziekcentrale. 4:38. III. A♭–e♭'. Allegro. "Solo voor Trombone, Tuba, Bes-Bas of Es-Bas met Begeleiding van Piano." Polka-style solo in cut time with cadenza. Best on F tuba or euphonium.

Jakma, Frits, Sr. *Herfstbloemen* (Autumn Flowers). Tierolff-Muziekcentrale. 4:00. c–f'. "Intermezzo voor Bugel Piston Trompet Baryton Trombone Tuba Bas in Es–Bes and C met Begeleiding van Piano." Polka-style solo in cut-time with short cadenza. Best on F tuba or euphonium.

Jakma, Henk. *Bassenparade* (*Parade of the Basses*). Tierolff-Muziekcentrale. 1965. 3:34. III. B♭–f'. High tessitura; best on F tuba or euphonium. Novelty polka-style work in 4/4 time with cadenza. Intermediate technique required.

Jeanneau, François. *Mini Suite.* For piano, four hands, and tuba.

Jenkins, Cyril. *Chanson Triste.* Boosey and Hawkes, Inc. 1922. Out of print. 3:27. III–IV. C♭–e♭'. "E♭ Bass." Solo part in treble clef. Romantic lyricism throughout. Some triplet arpeggios.

Jenkins, Cyril. *Rondelay.* Boosey and Hawkes, Inc. 1922. Out of print. 1:49. IV. B♭₁–f'. "B♭ Bass." Solo part in treble clef. Playful French-sounding theme in D♭ major that repeats and gets faster and faster throughout the piece until it reaches prestissimo. Good showcase and good recital material.

Jenne, Glenn. *Rondo.* Theodore Presser Company. 1968. $2.00. 3:50. IV. F₁–b♭. Some mixed meter; quick tempo. Not a technique buster but a solid, challenging piece.

Jennings. *Pomposo Polka.* arr. Weber, Carl. J. W. Pepper and Son. 1914. Out of print. 5:18. III. (F₁) B♭₁–g. Traditional polka style with no big technical problems. See: Weber, Carl, *Nineteen Solos for E♭ Bass with Piano Accompaniment,* under "Tuba and Keyboard Collections."

Jevtic, Ivan. *Concerto for Tuba and Symphony Orchestra.* Éditions BIM. 1992. See: Jevtic, Ivan, *Con-

certo for Tuba and Symphony Orchestra,* under "Music for Tuba and Orchestra."

Johnston, Richard. *Three Pieces for Tuba and Piano.* Canadian Music Centre. 1987. 5:50 (1:35, 2:45, 2:30). III. A₁–g. *Conversation; Barcarolle; Quick March.* Very well written suite for intermediate level. In a neo-romantic style, lyrical throughout. Good recital material.

Jolas, Betsy. *Trois Duos pour Tuba et Piano.* Alphonse Leduc Editions Paris. 1985. $12.80. 5:40 (2:30, 1:10, 2:00). IV–V. C₁–g'. "Pour les quatre-vingts ans de Francis Bott." Composed in 1983. Mixed meter. Wide range. See: Thompson/Lemke, *French Music for Low Brass Instruments.* See review in *T.U.B.A. Journal,* Vol. 14, no. 4, p. 42 and Vol. 15, no. 1, p. 28.

Jones, Roger. *Andante and Allegro for Tuba and Piano.* Manuscript. 3:14 (1:28, 1:46). IV. F₁–c' (d'). At indicated metronome markings, will take great flexibility. Many articulated eighth-note triplets and sixteenths to fit into quick cut-time tempo. See review in *T.U.B.A. Journal,* Vol. 1, no. 3, p. 6.

Jones, Roger. *Manta for Tuba and Piano.* TUBA Press. 1992. $8.00. 5:34. III–IV. F₁–a♭. Completed 1981. One-movement work with two tempos: a cut-time articulated feel and a 4/4 relaxed lyrical one. Some mixed meter, some syncopation. Good recital material.

Joubert, Claude-Henry. *Ballade du Moigne Que Nostre Dame Delivera Dou Dyable.* Éditions Robert Martin. 1991. $5.75.

Joubert, Claude-Henry. *Rudéral.* Gérard Billaudot. 1980. $4.50. 3:30. II–III. B₁–c♯'. "Pour Tuba en ut ou Si♭ et Piano (à une ou deux mains)." Very easy piano accompaniment. No major technical problems. See: Thompson/Lemke, *French Music for Low Brass Instruments.* See review in *T.U.B.A. Journal,* Vol. 9, no. 4, p. 36.

Joubert, Claude-Henry. *Tunuva Tuba.* Éditions M. Combre. 1985. 5:10 (0:45, 0:40, 0:45, 0:20, 0:45, 0:30, 0:20, 0:20, 0:45). III. A₁–d'. *Complainte; Marche; Variation 2; Valse; Polanaise; Variation 5; Scherzo; Variations 7 et 8.* "Pour Tuba (Ut ou Si♭) et Piano." For French tuba. Theme and (eight) variations. Theme is in 7/8, as is last variation. Others are in 4/4, 3/4, 3/8 time. Theme in stepwise motion, making it suitable for advanced beginner/intermediate player.

Jude, W. H. *The Mighty Deep.* arr. de Ville, Paul. Carl Fischer Inc. 1898. $2.50. See listing under "Music for Tuba and Band."

Jurovsky, V. *March.* arr. Lebedev, A. Military Band Masters Faculty of Moscow Conservatiore. 1971. See: Lebedev, A., *Collection of Pieces for Tuba "Es" and Piano,* under "Tuba and Keyboard Collections."

Kabalevsky, D. *Waltz and Galop from Petite Suite.* ed. Voxman, Himie. Rubank, Inc. 1972. 2:00. II–III. D–f. "For E♭ or BB♭ Bass. Moderato in 3/4 time with some slurs. Allegro in 2/4 time with mostly stepwise motion. See: Voxman, Himie, *Concert and Contest Collection,* under "Tuba and Keyboard Collections."

Kagan, Susan. *Oxford Gavotte.* arr. Wekselblatt, Herbert. G. Schirmer Inc. 1972. 1:47. II–III. A_1–f. Tempo di Gavotte. Good introduction to Baroque ornamentation: trills and mordent. Solo in cut time. See: Wekselblatt, Herbert, *First Solos for the Tuba Player,* under "Tuba and Keyboard Collections."

Kaï, Naohiko. *Légende.* Alphonse Leduc Editions Paris. 1962. $16.85. 6:35 (2:20, 4:15). V. F$\sharp_1$ (B_1)– (a$\flat$'/g$\sharp$') b$\flat$'. A Piacere; Allegro. "Pour Tuba ut ou Trombone basse ou Saxhorn basse Si$\flat$ et Piano." For French tuba. Very wide range. Strong technique and lyricism required. See: Thompson/ Lemke, *French Music for Low Brass Instruments.*

Kalinikov, V. *The Sad Song.* ed. Melnikov, S. Moscow: Military Band Masters Institute. 1957. See: Melnikov, S., *Pieces for Tuba and Piano,* under "Tuba and Keyboard Collections."

Kaneda, B. *Long, Long Ago.* arr. Lebedev, A. Military Band Masters Faculty of Moscow Conservatiore. 1971. See: Lebedev, A., *Collection of Pieces for Tuba "Es" and Piano,* under "Tuba and Keyboard Collections."

Kappey. *Introduction and Allegretto.* Boosey and Hawkes, Inc. Out of print. For B$\flat$ bombardon. In treble clef.

Kappey. *O Ruddier than the Cherry.* Boosey and Hawkes, Inc. Out of print. For E$\flat$ bombardon. In bass and treble clef.

Karaev, V. *Dance from the Ballet "Seven Beauties."* arr. Lebedev, A. Military Band Masters Faculty of Moscow Conservatiore. 1971. See: Lebedev, A., *Collection of Pieces for Tuba "Es" and Piano,* under "Tuba and Keyboard Collections."

Kardos, Istvan. *Poem and Burlesque for Double Bass (Tuba) and Piano.* General Music Publishing Co. 1969. Written for string bass primarily; double stops, extremely high range. Transposed solo part.

Karlsen, Kjell Mork. *Sonata for Tuba and Piano,* Op. 74. Norsk Musikforlag Oslo. 1988. 19:38 (6:26, 6:20, 6:52). V. A_1–f (b$\flat$'). *Lamento; Hommage à Sjostakovitsj; Tuba mirum.* Major work for tuba and piano. Three very different textures. *Lamento* is very lyrical, *Hommage* is very technical, and *Tuba mirum* is very dynamic, pesante, dissonant, and strong. Requires endurance, imagination, sharp technique, wide range, and a very strong accompanist. Good recital material.

Kazadezins, R. *Spanish Dance.* arr. Lebedev, A. Military Band Masters Faculty of Moscow Conservatiore. 1971. See: Lebedev, A., *Collection of Pieces for Tuba "Es" and Piano,* under "Tuba and Keyboard Collections."

Kellaway, Roger. *Arcades I.* Manuscript. 1984.

Kellaway, Roger. *For Harvey.* Manuscript. c. 1984. For Harvey Phillips. In the collection of Harvey G. Phillips.

Kellaway, Roger. *Morning Song.* Éditions BIM. 1980. $16.00. 7:00. IV–V. F_1–b$\flat$'. For Roger Bobo. Composed in 1978. Almost commercial sounding, this solo is a great crowd pleaser. Originally written for the Roger Kellaway Cello Quartet as a cello solo, *Morning Song* has a "new age/country" feel to it with an extremely lyrical solo part. Requires strong, flexible technique and a strong, flexible accompanist. Good recital material. Very wide range. Best on F tuba. Recorded by Jørgen Voight Arnsted; Roger Bobo.

Kellaway, Roger. *Songs of Ascent* (Concerto). Éditions BIM. 1986/89. Piano reduction in preparation (1993). See listing under "Music for Tuba and Orchestra." Also see: Bird, Gary, ed., *Program Notes for the Solo Tuba.*

Kellaway, Roger. *Westwood Song.* Éditions BIM. 1975, rev 1982 and 1989. 11:30. IV–V. One of five movements for brass quintet each featuring a different member. Very lyrical reflective solo. Piano part was initially improvised; this is a realization of that improvisation. Good recital material. Recorded by Roger Bobo.

Kesnar, Maurits. *Prelude.* Carl Fischer Inc. 1954. $3.50. 2:30. III. F_1–g. for Melvin Siener. Was published by Cundy-Bettoney. Maestoso. Regal feel followed by a lyrical section. Some slurred triplets, some low articulations, no major technical problems.

Khachaturian, A. *Dance from Ballet "Spartak."* arr. Lebedev, A. Military Band Masters Faculty of Moscow Conservatiore. 1971. See: Lebedev, A., *Collection of Pieces for Tuba "Es" and Piano,* under "Tuba and Keyboard Collections."

Kiefer, Bruno. *Interrogaçoes.* Fundação Nacional De Arte. 1985. 3:40. IV. A_1–c'. Quick (or triple) tonguing, dissonant phrases, mixed meter, upper tessitura.

Kikta, V. *Concerto for Tuba and Orchestra.* ed. Guzii, V. Moscow: Muzyka. 1978. Piano reduction. See: Guzii, V., *Pieces for Tuba and Piano,* under "Tuba and Keyboard Collections."

Kikta, V. *Epic Tale and Procession of the People in Costumes (Festival).* ed. Lebedev, A. Moscow: Muzyka. 1986. 4:30 (2:22, 2:08). IV. E_1–e$\flat$'. Very dramatic modern writing with an old feel. *Epic Tale* is reminiscent of a Gregorian chant. *Procession* has mixed meter combined with a Maestoso dramatic flair. See: Lebedev, A., *Tuba Tutor Vol. 2,* under "Tuba and Keyboard Collections."

Kilon, Moshe. *Sine Nomine.* Kibutz Movement League of Composers. Recorded by Adi Hershko.

King, Karl L. *The Octopus and the Mermaid.* C. L. Barnhouse Company. 1923. Out of print. 4:00. III. B$\flat_1$–a. Very melodic solo for the intermediate player.

Kinyon, John, arr. *All through the Night*. M. Witmark and Sons. 1958. I. Welsh. See listing under "Tuba and Keyboard Collections."

Kinyon, John, arr. *The Ash Grove*. M. Witmark and Sons. 1958. I. Welsh. See listing under "Tuba and Keyboard Collections."

Kinyon, John, arr. *Auld Lang Syne*. M. Witmark and Sons. 1958. I. Scottish. See listing under "Tuba and Keyboard Collections."

Kinyon, John, arr. *Bendemeer's Stream*. M. Witmark and Sons. 1958. I. Irish. See listing under "Tuba and Keyboard Collections."

Kinyon, John, arr. *The Blue Bells of Scotland*. M. Witmark and Sons. 1958. I. Scottish. See listing under "Tuba and Keyboard Collections."

Kinyon, John, arr. *Breeze-Easy Recital Pieces for Tuba*. See listing under "Tuba and Keyboard Collections."

Kinyon, John, arr. *Cockles and Mussels*. M. Witmark and Sons. 1958. I. Irish. See listing under "Tuba and Keyboard Collections."

Kinyon, John, arr. *Crusaders' Hymn*. M. Witmark and Sons. 1958. I. German. See listing under "Tuba and Keyboard Collections."

Kinyon, John, arr. *Drink to Me Only with Thine Eyes*. M. Witmark and Sons. 1958. I. English folk song. See listing under "Tuba and Keyboard Collections."

Kinyon, John, arr. *The Erie Canal*. M. Witmark and Sons. 1958. I. American work song. See listing under "Tuba and Keyboard Collections."

Kinyon, John, arr. *German Waltz*. M. Witmark and Sons. 1958. I. See listing under "Tuba and Keyboard Collections."

Kinyon, John, arr. *Home on the Range*. M. Witmark and Sons. 1958. I. American cowboy song. See listing under "Tuba and Keyboard Collections."

Kinyon, John, arr. *Instant Band Ensembles (Tuba)*. Alfred Music. 1969. Out of print. For any solo instrument and band or piano accompaniment. Sixteen popular songs, Christmas songs, etc.

Kinyon, John, arr. *John Peel*. M. Witmark and Sons. 1958. I. English. See listing under "Tuba and Keyboard Collections."

Kinyon, John, arr. *Loch Lomond*. M. Witmark and Sons. 1958. I. Scottish. See listing under "Tuba and Keyboard Collections."

Kinyon, John, arr. *Londonderry Air*. M. Witmark and Sons. 1958. I–II. Irish. See listing under "Tuba and Keyboard Collections."

Kinyon, John, arr. *Minstrel Boy*. M. Witmark and Sons. 1958. I–II. Irish. See listing under "Tuba and Keyboard Collections."

Kinyon, John, arr. *Red River Valley*. M. Witmark and Sons. 1958. I. American cowboy song. See listing under "Tuba and Keyboard Collections."

Kinyon, John, arr. *Steal Away*. M. Witmark and Sons. 1958. I. Negro spiritual. See listing under "Tuba and Keyboard Collections."

Kinyon, John, arr. *Sweet Betsy from Pike*. M. Witmark and Sons. 1958. I. English melody. See listing under "Tuba and Keyboard Collections."

Kinyon, John, arr. *When Love Is Kind*. M. Witmark and Sons. 1958. I. Old English. See listing under "Tuba and Keyboard Collections."

Kinyon, John, arr. *Ye Banks and Braes of Bonny Doon*. M. Witmark and Sons. 1958. I. Scottish. See listing under "Tuba and Keyboard Collections."

Kistetenyi, Melinda. *Kis Eloeadasi Darab Tubara*. Hungarian Edition. Available from the Tuba Center.

Kitsz, Dennis Bathory. *Sonata for Tuba and Piano*. Westleaf Edition. 1970. IV–V. F#$_1$–g'. For Stanley Michalowski. (Corrections 1988). Contemporary melodic writing. Muted passages, complex time signatures.

Kladnitzki, W. *Sonate für Tuba und Klavier*. Istazelstwo Musika Moskau. III.

Kling, G., and Neuling, G. *Grand Cadence*. ed. Guzii, V. Moscow: Muzyka. 1978. See: Guzii, V., *Pieces for Tuba and Piano*, under "Tuba and Keyboard Collections."

Klohr. *Billboard*. Hudadoff, Igor, and Westcott, William (piano arr.). Pro Art Publications. 1967. Out of print. See: Hudadoff, Igor, *Fifteen Intermediate Tuba Solos*, under "Tuba and Keyboard Collections."

Knight, Joseph Phillip. *Rock'd in the Cradle of the Deep*. arr. Prendiville, Harry. A. Squire. 1888. Out of print. 0:50. II–III. (Bb$_1$) F–f. No technical problems. "Eb Bass; or, tuba With Piano or Organ Accompaniment, (ad lib.)." See: Prendiville, Harry, *Six Popular Solos*, under "Tuba and Keyboard Collections."

Knight, Joseph Phillip. *Rocked in the Cradle of the Deep*. arr. Hume, James Ord. Boosey and Co. 1906. Out of print. See: Hume, J. Ord, *Boosey's Bombardon Solo Album*, under "Tuba and Keyboard Collections."

Knight, Joseph Phillip. *Rocked in the Cradle of the Deep*. arr. Ostling, Acton. CPP/Belwin, Inc. 1969. 1:23. I. (Ab$_1$) D–eb. Good introduction to slur two-tongue two. Add plenty of spirit to last two measures! See: Ostling, Acton, *Tuba (Bass) Soloist, Level One*, under "Tuba and Keyboard Collections."

Knight, Morris. *Exchange for Tuba and Piano*. Woodsum Music, Ltd. 1976. $8.00. 2:40. III–IV. F$_1$–c'. Lyrical solo in 6/8 time in a moderate tempo. Good introduction on an intermediate level to modern melodic writing. See review in *T.U.B.A. Journal*, Vol. 4, no. 2, p. 22.

Knight, Morris. *Tuba and Piano Sonata: Three Movements*. Woodsum Music, Ltd. 1989. $12.00. 12:26 (4:26, 4:00, 4:00). IV. E$_1$–c#'. For the artistry of John Jones. Energetically; Lyrically; Burlesquely. First movement alternates between 4/4 and 3/4. Second movement is a modern melodic work in 3/4 time. The third movement is in 6/8 time utilizing flexibility at a reasonable tempo.

Koch, Erland von. *Concerto for Tuba.* AB Carl Gehrmans Musikforlag. 1979. $20.25. Dedicated to Michael Lind. Completed in 1978. See listing under "Music for Tuba and Orchestra." See review in *T.U.B.A. Journal,* Vol. 10, no. 2, p. 23.

Koch, Erland von. *Tubania for Tuba and Piano.* AB Carl Gehrmans Musikforlag. 1983. Extreme high register for tuba; lies well on euphonium.

Koch, Frederick. *Introduction, Aria and Rondo.* Southern Music Company. 1992. $4.95. 4:33 (0:56, 1:39, 1:58). IV. F_1–f'. *Introduction* (Majestic) has a melodic regal feel. *Aria* (Slowly Moving) has lyrical modern lines. Rondo (Vivace) is pentatonic. Upper tessitura. A few trills.

Koch, Johannes H. E. *Sonatine für Tuba (Posaune) und Klavier.* Möseler Verlag. 1988. 6:19 (2:56, 1:46, 1:37). III. E_1–f. Breit; Lebhaft; Fugato. "For Tuba (Trombone) and Piano." Some modern, some conventional melodic language. Conservative range; no big technical problems.

Koepke, Paul. *Persiflage.* ed. Voxman, Himie. Rubank, Inc. 1972. 4:30. III. (A_1) B♭₁–f. "For E♭ or BB♭ Bass." Lyrical Andante cantabile section followed by a moderately technical Allegro section and a cadenza. See: Voxman, Himie, *Concert and Contest Collection,* under "Tuba and Keyboard Collections."

Koetsier, Jan. *Choralfantasie über "Es ist ein Schnitter, Der Heisst Tod,"* Op. 93. Donemus Publishing House Amsterdam. 1984. 10:00. IV. G_1–f'. For tuba and organ. Choral writing interspersed with technical arpeggios. Written with F tuba in mind. Upper tessitura

Koetsier, Jan. *Concertino,* Op. 77. Éditions BIM. 1990. $17.00. Dedicated to Manfred Hoppert. Composed 1978, revised 1982. See listing under "Music for Tuba and Orchestra."

Koetsier, Jan. *Sonatina.* Éditions Marc Reift. 1970. $14.50. 6:25 (2:45, 1:40, 2:00). IV–V. G_1–e♭'. See following entry.

Koetsier, Jan. *Sonatina Tuba e Pianoforte,* Op. 57. Donemus Publishing House Amsterdam. 1970. $17.50. 6:25 (2:45, 1:40, 2:00). IV–V. G_1–e♭'. Allegro: Romantic feel; very tonal, majestic lyrical style; some jumps of a tenth. Tempo di minuetto: arpeggios, leaps of a tenth. Allegro moderato: shifting meters (2/4, 5/8, 3/8). Suited for F tuba; very playable on lower instrument. Solid recital material. Fun to play and listen to. Recorded by Jan Z Duga; Manfred Hoppert. See review in *T.U.B.A. Journal,* Vol. 9, no. 3, p. 24.

Kolodub, L. *Humorous Dance.* ed. Voronov, G. Moscow: Muzyka. 1984. See: Voronov, G, *Works for Tuba and Piano by Russian Composers,* under "Tuba and Keyboard Collections."

Konagaya, Soichi. *Celebration for Tuba and Piano.* Toa Music International Co. 1989. 9:07. IV. E♭₁–

f'. For Hiroyuki Yasumoto. Big piece with a popular feel. Audience pleaser. See: Yasumoto, Hiroyuki, *Tuba Volume #3,* under "Tuba and Keyboard Collections."

Konagaya, Soichi. *Fantasy for Tuba and Piano.* Toa Music International Co. 1979. 7:20. IV–V. C–f'. For Mr. Yasumoto. Was published by TUBA Press. Optional mute. Some contemporary techniques: improvising in cadenza with predetermined pitches, compound meters, double tonguing. See: Yasumoto, Hiroyuki, arr., *Tuba Volume #2,* under "Tuba and Keyboard Collections." Recorded by Hiroyuki Yasumoto.

Konko, Iwao. *Sonata No. 1 for Tuba and Piano.* Teruo Miyagawa. 1968. 9:00. IV. F_1–b♭'. Three movements. One of the first pieces composed for tuba in Japan. Contemporary writing; pitch bends, etc.

Konko, Iwao. *Sonata No. 2 for Tuba and Piano.* Teruo Miyagawa. 1968.

Köper, Karl-Heinz. *Sonata.* Trombone Association Publishing. 1975. $14.00. 6:57 (3:32, 3:15, 3:10). IV. F_1–f'. Some mixed meter, trills, wide range. Good recital material.

Köper, Karl-Heinz. *Tuba-Tabu.* Musikverlag K. H. Köper. 1967. See listing under "Music for Tuba and Orchestra." Recorded by Michael Lind.

Kopprasch, C. No. 15, from *Etüden für Tuba.* arr. Yasumoto, Hiroyuki. Toa Music International Co. 1989. 4:02. IV. (D_1) A_1–a. Adagio. Good orchestration of this classic etude for French horn. Solo should have a feeling of relaxed 6 (subdivide). Last dynamic on first line should be "piano" not "forte." Requires great dynamic contrast and strong musical sense. See: Yasumoto, Hiroyuki, arr., *Tuba Volume #2,* under "Tuba and Keyboard Collections."

Kopprasch, C. No. 19, from *Etüden für Tuba.* arr. Yasumoto, Hiroyuki. Toa Music International Co. 1989. 4:25. IV. E–a. Feeling of 6 (subdividing) recommended. Extremely lyrical etude; aria quality. Some rhythmic deciphering involved. See: Yasumoto, Hiroyuki, arr., *Tuba Volume #2,* under "Tuba and Keyboard Collections."

Kosteck, Gregory. *The Enchanted Island.* Available from the composer. 1981. See listing under "Music for Tuba and Orchestra."

Kotshetov, V. *Adagio from the Ballet "Till Eulenspiegel."* arr. Lebedev, A. Military Band Masters Faculty of Moscow Conservatiore. 1971. See: Lebedev, A., *Collection of Pieces for Tuba "Es" and Piano,* under "Tuba and Keyboard Collections."

Kottaun, Celian. *Billy Blowhard.* Carl Fischer Inc. 1909. Out of print. See listing under "Music for Tuba and Band."

Krebs, Johann Ludwig. *Bourrée.* arr. Schwotzer, Stephan. Hofmeister. 1993. 2:08. II. C–d♭. In cut time. See: Meschke, Dieter, *Zum Uben und Vorspielen/B-Tuba,* under "Tuba and Keyboard Collections."

Kreisler, Alexander von. *Allegretto Grazioso.* Southern Music Company. 1964. $2.50. 2:00. III. B₁–f. In

6/8 time. Some slurring, no big technical problems.

Kreisler, Alexander von. *Rondo.* Southern Music Company. 1965. $1.50. 3:20. II–III. G_1–e. In cut time. Some slurring, no big technical problems.

Kreisler, Fritz. *Liebesfreud.* arr. Yasumoto, Hiroyuki. Toa Music International Co. 1989. 2:58. III. Bb_1–c'. Player is encouraged to listen to Heifeitz's recording of this for conception. Must have a joyous, flexible, rubato feel in one. Requires strong flexibility as well as musicality. See: Yasumoto, Hiroyuki, arr., *Tuba Volume No. 2,* under "Tuba and Keyboard Collections." Recorded by Hiroyuki Yasumoto.

Kreisler, Fritz. *Schön Rosmarin.* arr. Yasumoto, Hiroyuki. Toa Music International Co. 1989. 2:07. IV. Bb_1–d'. Violin showpiece. Requires flexibility for arpeggios. Excellent recital encore piece. See: Yasumoto, Hiroyuki, *Tuba Volume No. 3,* under "Tuba and Keyboard Collections."

Kroepsch, F. *Down in the Deep Cellar (Grand Fantasia).* Carl Fischer Inc. 1898. Out of print. "For Bb Clarinet, Bb Cornet, Trombone or Baritone, Bassoon." See listing under "Music for Tuba and Band." See review in *T.U.B.A. Journal,* Vol. 9, no. 3, p. 26.

Krol, Bernhard. *Falstaff Concerto,* Op. 119. Éditions BIM. 1990. $17.00. Commissioned by Éditions BIM. See listing under "Music for Tuba and Orchestra."

Krol, Bernhard. *Minuetto Profondo,* Op. 83, no. 1. Hofmeister. 1983. 3:27. IV. $F\#_1/Gb_1$–c'. À Mark Evans. Some flexibility and swiftness of articulation needed; technique not overwhelming. Good recital material.

Krol, Bernhard. *Recitativ and Burla,* Op. 83, no. 2. Hofmeister. 1987. 4:51 (0:51, 4:00). IV. G_1–c'. Some changing of meters. Conservative metronome markings make this accessible with intermediate technique. A few trills and mordents.

Krotov, and Blazhevich, Vladislav. *Concert Etude.* arr. Voxman, Himie, and Block, Robert Paul. Southern Music Company. 1989. $3.75. 3:00. IV. Eb_1–eb'. Technical solo consisting of mainly staccato sixteenth notes and large leaps. Fun and musical way to sharpen technique.

Krotov, and Blazhevich, Vladislav. *Concert Etude.* Moscow: Muzyka. 1962.

Krush, Jay. *Sonata for Tuba and Piano,* Op. 6. 1972. 12:18 (4:20, 1:51, 2:45, 3:22). V. E_1–g' (c''). For Michael Sanders. Contemporary techniques including muted passages, half tones, flutter tonguing, improvised passages, bending of pitches. First movement, *Contemplative ,* is very lyrical. Second, *Distraught,* is quick, and requires quick articulations. Third, *Melancholy,* is lyrical and requires some improvisation. Fourth, *Exuberant,* requires very fast articulation and optional very high tessitura. See review in *T.U.B.A. Journal,* Vol. 1, no. 2, p. 10.

Krzywicki, Jan. *Ballade.* Heilman Music. 1984. $6.00. 4:30. III–IV. E–e'. For Paul. First performed by Paul Krzywicki at the 1983 International Tuba-Euphonium Conference, University of Maryland, College Park. "For Baritone or Tuba and Piano." Would lie best on Eb/F tuba or euphonium, for advanced player with stamina in upper tessitura. Very accessible musically; simple, nice tune. See review in *T.U.B.A. Journal,* Vol. 12, no. 3, p. 22.

Kubes, Ladislav. *Alte Bekannte.* ed. Hoza, Václav. Editio Supraphon. 1982. 1:47. II–III. Bb_1–g. Polka. Typical polka style in two parts. See: Hoza, Václav, *Schule für Tuba in F und in B,* under "Methods and Studies."

Kulesha, Gary Alan. *Burlesque for Tuba and Piano.* Sonante Publications. 1984. $4.50. 1:51. IV. Gb_1–d'. Some changing of meter from 2/4 to 3/8. A few very large leaps and a couple of fast or double-tongued articulations; otherwise no big technical problems. Good recital material. See review in *T.U.B.A. Journal,* Vol. 13, no. 1, p. 20.

Kulesha, Gary Alan. *Concerto for Tuba.* Canadian Music Centre. 1979. Piano accompaniment 4 hands. See listings under "Music for Tuba and Band" and "Music for Tuba and Orchestra."

Kulesha, Gary Alan. *The Green Apple Two-Step.* Sonante Publications. 1993. $5.25. 1:53. III–IV. F_1–bb (f '). Written for Scott Irvine. Fast. "For Bass Tuba and Piano." Includes instructions to "blat" on C and F_1 for comedic effect. Polka-style solo with a few large interval jumps. Good novelty recital piece. Played on CBC's "Mr. Dressup" by Kent Mason.

Kulesha, Gary Alan. *Humoreske in F.* Sonante Publications. 1978. $5.25. 2:20. IV. C_1–c'. Written for Scott Irvine. "For Bass Tuba and Piano." Cute solo with a snappy feel to it; some syncopations and octave jumps. Good recital piece.

Kulesha, Gary Alan. *Sonata for Tuba and Organ.* Canadian Music Centre. 1976. 10:00. IV. C_1–d'. For Scott Irvine. Three numbered movements. Very lyrical addition to the pairing of tuba and organ. Quite a role reversal for the tuba to be playing the "organ pedal point" for a change. Good recital material.

Kulesha, Gary Alan. *Sonatina (1972) for Tuba and Piano.* Canadian Music Centre. 1972. 6:00. Written for and dedicated to Scott Irvine. Dance; Song; Dance. Sherburne G. McCurdy Festival Series. *Dance* has mixed meter: 5/8, 3/4, 3/8 and is marked "Distinctly bizarre." *Song* is very lyrical, has an optional muted section, and is marked "Passionately brooding." The second *Dance* is very quick; marked "Absolutely lunatic," it includes 9/8, 4/4, 5/8, 3/4, and 5/4 time and requires flexibility and strong rhythmic sense.

Kulesha, Gary Alan. *Two Little Leprechauns.* Sonante Publications. 1993. $5.25. 1:46. III–IV. Bb_1–g. For J. M. Moderately Slowly; Very Unsteadily. "For Drunken Tubist and Piano." Shifting mixed meter and slurring (flexibility required). Good novelty recital piece.

Kulesha, Gary Alan. *Visions for Jane.* Canadian Music Centre. 1975. 5:00. IV. G_1–c'. Completed October 30, 1975, 12:05 AM–1:20 AM. Very lyrical solo requiring some flexibility; no big technical problems for the level.

Laburda, Jiří. *Sonate.* Gérard Billaudot. 1987. $9.75. 12:40. IV. $F\sharp_1$–f'. Allegro moderato; Larghetto caloroso; Allegro assai. "Pour Tuba et Piano." For French tuba. Range is the only technical problem. See: Thompson/Lemke, *French Music for Low Brass Instruments.*

Lackey, Jerry. *Concertpiece for 3 Tubas and Band.* Available from the composer. 1963. See listing under "Music for Tuba and Band."

Lackey, Jerry. *Jazz Concerto for Tuba and Band.* Available from the composer. 1984. Piano Reduction. Solo tuba and band, drum set, piano, and electric bass. Same as *Jazz Concerto for Tuba and Orchestra.* See listing under "Music for Tuba and Band."

Lackey, Jerry. *Jazz Concerto for Tuba and Orchestra.* Available from the composer. 1984. $35.00. See listing under "Music for Tuba and Orchestra."

Lackey, Jerry. *Short Stuff.* Available from the composer. 1964. $15.00. See listing under "Music for Tuba and Band."

Lafont. *Invincible.* Boosey and Hawkes, Inc. Out of print.

Lamb, Jack, ed. See listings under "Tuba and Keyboard Collections."

Lancen, S. *Grave.* Alphonse Leduc Editions Paris. $16.85. For tuba/baritone or saxhorn and piano. For French tuba.

Lange. *Heather Rose Caprice.* arr. Weber, Carl. J. W. Pepper and Son. 1914. Out of print. See: Weber, Carl, *Nineteen Solos for E♭ Bass with Piano Accompaniment,* under "Tuba and Keyboard Collections."

Langgaard, Rued. *Dies Irae.* Danish Brass Publishing. 1986. DKR 77,05. 2:17. III. G♯–d. Completed 1948. Upper tessitura, best on F tuba, playable on lower instrument. Piano part harder than tuba part. Recorded by Jørgen Voight Arnsted.

Lannoy, J. B. de. *Souvenir de Paris.* Schott Frères. Out of print.

Lantier, Pierre. *Andante et Allegro.* Henri Lemoine and Cie. 1964. $11.00. IV–V. F_1 (A_1)–a'. À Paul Bernard, professeur au Conservatoire National Supérieur de Musique de Paris. "Pour Tuba et Piano." For French tuba. See: Thompson/Lemke, *French Music for Low Brass Instruments.*

LaPresti, Ronald. *Sonata for Tuba and Piano.* Manuscript. 1984. 5:00. IV–V. G_1–a'. Written for Daniel Perantoni. Adagio; Allegretto Grazioso; Allegro con Fuoco. Very tonal writing requiring strong technique. In the collection of Daniel Perantoni.

Largent, Edward. *Four Shorts for Tuba and Piano.* Seesaw Music Corporation Publishers. 1986. $11.50. 5:30. IV–V. G_1–g♭'. *Rhythms; Spots; Turns; Burlesque.* Completed 1984. Flutter tonguing,

multiphonics, glissandos, mixed meter, quintuplets, etc. Requires wide range and strong technique. Recorded by John Turk.

Larin, J., ed. See listing under "Tuba and Keyboard Collections."

Larsen, Libby. *Concert Piece for Tuba and Piano.* Manuscript. 1993. 3:19. IV–V. G_1–g'. For Mark Nelson. Quick tempo—feeling of one with 2/4 marked. Wide range and some flexibility required. Strong accompanist needed.

Lavalle, Paul, and Tarto, Joe. *Big Joe, the Tuba.* arr. Klickmann, F. Henri. Stargen Music Corp/Sam Fox Company. 1955. Out of print. 3:35. III. A♭$_1$–f. March feel in 6/8 time. Keys of A♭ and D♭ major. No technical problems.

Lawrance, Peter. *Six Modern Pieces.* Brass Wind Publications. II. For E♭ Bass/E♭ tuba. Solos with easy accompaniments. Treble and bass-clef versions available.

Lawrence, Lucinda. *Piece for Tuba and Piano.* Hal Leonard Publishing Corp. 1976. F_1–a. In the style of Bartók. Mixed meter. See: Perantoni, Daniel, *Master Solos, Intermediate Level,* under "Tuba and Keyboard Collections."

Layens, C. G. *Intermede.* Edition Andel Uitgaven.

Lebedev, A., arr. *Adagio.* Military Band Masters Faculty of Moscow Conservatiore. 1971. See: Lebedev, A., *Collection of Pieces for Tuba "Es" and Piano,* under "Tuba and Keyboard Collections."

Lebedev, A. *Concerto Allegro.* arr. Smith, Glenn P. University Music Press. 1962. Out of print. 5:00. IV. (E_1) F_1–c' (e♭'). Neo-romantic feel to this through-composed work. Very lyrical writing, intermediate flexibility and technique required. Good recital material.

Lebedev, A. *Concerto in One Movement.* arr. Ostrander, Allen. Editions Musicus. 1960. $6.75. 6:00. IV. $(E♭_1)$ E_1–c' (e♭'). Very lyrical, dramatic material. Good recital material. Recorded by Jeffrey Arwood; Manfred Hoppert.

Lebedev, A. *A Cradle Song.* Moscow: Muzyka. 1986. 0:55. III. A_1–a. Tempo di Valse. Andantino. Very musical way of practicing slurs between a sixth and an octave. See: Lebedev, A., *Tuba Tutor, Vol. 2,* under "Tuba and Keyboard Collections."

Lebedev, A. *Gavotte.* Moscow: Muzyka. 1986. 1:21. III. F_1–b♭. Alla Breve; Pesante. Playful little tune that shows the composer's ballet roots. See: Lebedev, A., *Tuba Tutor, Vol. 2,* under "Tuba and Keyboard Collections."

Lebedev, A. (Title Unknown). Manuscript. 1987. Third major composition for tuba and piano by this Russian master performer and teacher.

Lebedev, A., arr. *Estonian Folk Dance.* Moscow: Muzyka. 1974. 0:50. II. E–e. Allegretto. Pretty tune in 3/4 time with no technical problems. See: Lebedev, A., *Tuba Tutor, Vol. 1,* under "Tuba and Keyboard Collections."

Lebedev, A., arr. *On the Steep High Mountain.* Moscow: Muzyka. 1984. 1:14. III. F–a♭ (b♭). Russian folk song. In 4/4 time in B♭ minor. Some slurring; no technical problems beyond key. See: Lebedev, A., *Tuba Tutor, Vol. 1,* under "Tuba and Keyboard Collections."

Lebedev, A. arr. *A Ring.* Moscow: Muzyka. 1984. 0:20. II. C–f. Russian folk song. Short lyrical piece in F minor. See: Lebedev, A., *Tuba Tutor, Vol. 1,* under "Tuba and Keyboard Collections."

Lebedjew, A. *Konzert für Tuba und Klavier.* Hofmeister. 1954. $13.95. (E♭$_1$) E$_1$–e♭'. Same as Lebedev, A., *Concerto in One Movement,* above.

Leclair, Jean-Marie. *Sarabande.* arr. Goudenhooft, André piano realizations Maillard, Augustin. Gérard Billaudot. 1989. $9.50. 2:30. IV. C–f'. "Pour le trombone basse et le tuba basse. Extraite de la 3e Sonate pour violon." Packaged with *Courante* by Senaillé, Jean Baptiste. See: Thompson/Lemke, *French Music for Low Brass Instruments.*

LeClerc, E. *Concertino.* ed. Larin, J. Moscow: Muzyka. 1979. See: Larin, J., *Pieces for Tuba and Piano,* under "Tuba and Keyboard Collections."

Ledov, A. *Prelude.* arr. Lebedev, A. Military Band Masters Faculty of Moscow Conservatiore. 1971. See: Lebedev, A., *Collection of Pieces for Tuba "Es" and Piano,* under "Tuba and Keyboard Collections."

Legendre. *Souvenir du Poitou.* arr. Weber, Carl. J. W. Pepper and Son. 1914. Out of print. See: Weber, Carl, *Nineteen Solos for E♭ Bass with Piano Accompaniment,* under "Tuba and Keyboard Collections."

Legrady, Thomas. *Tubantella.* Molenaar. 1987. Piano reduction. See: Legrady, Thomas, *Tubantella,* under "Music for Tuba and Band."

Lehar, Franz. *Merry Widow Waltz.* arr. Ostling, Acton. CPP/Belwin, Inc. 1969. 1:23. I. B♭$_1$–d. Once through the tune with a tag. No technical problems. See: Ostling, Acton, *Tuba (Bass) Soloist, Level One,* under "Tuba and Keyboard Collections."

Lejet, Edith. *Méandres.* Gérard Billaudot. 1985. $7.00. 5:30. V. G$_1$–g♯'. A Fernand Lelong, professeur au CNSMP. "Pour Saxhorn Basse en Si♭ et Piano." Extreme flexibility required. Double tonguing, trills, rhythmic challenges, wide range. See: Thompson/Lemke, *French Music for Low Brass Instruments.*

Lemaire, Jean. *Trois Exercises de Style.* Alphonse Leduc Editions Paris. 1971. Out of print. 5:45. V. E$_1$–b♭'. For French tuba. See: Thompson/Lemke, *French Music for Low Brass Instruments.*

Lemaire, Jean. *Variations sur un Thème de Purcell.* Éditions Rideau Rouge. 1976. 4:45. IV. F$_1$–g'. "Concours du Conservatoire National Supérieur de Musique de Paris 1976." "Pour Tuba Et Piano." For French tuba. Wide range. Technical considerations consist mostly of sixteenth-note scalelike passages. Requires light articulation and flexibility.

Lennon, John, and McCartney, Paul. *Hey Jude!* arr. Yasumoto, Hiroyuki. Toa Music International Co. 1989. 4:10. IV. F$_1$–f' (g'). Nice transcription of classic Beatles tune. Some syncopation. Wide range.

See: Yasumoto, Hiroyuki, *Tuba Volume #3,* under "Tuba and Keyboard Collections."

Lennon, John, and McCartney, Paul. *Yesterday.* arr. Yasumoto, Hiroyuki. Toa Music International Co. 1989. 3:08. III. F$_1$–g. Good arrangement of the Beatles classic ballad. Strong lyric sense required when tubist plays the melody as well as when accompanying. See: Yasumoto, Hiroyuki, arr., *Tuba Volume #2,* under "Tuba and Keyboard Collections." Recorded by Hiroyuki Yasumoto.

Leonov, I. *Etude de concert.* ed. Melnikov, S. Moscow: Military Band Masters Institute. 1957. See: Melnikov, S., *Pieces for Tuba and Piano,* under "Tuba and Keyboard Collections."

Lesaffre, Charles. *En Glissant (Upon Sliding).* ed. Lelong, Fernand. Gérard Billaudot. 1984. $4.50. 2:00. II. (B♭) c–d' (e♭'). À mon frère Directeur de l'école de Musique de Dammarie. "Pour saxhorn basse Si♭ ou tuba ténor ou trombone en ut et piano." For French tuba. Eighth note is fastest rhythm. Mostly stepwise motion; no technical problems. See: Thompson/Lemke, *French Music for Low Brass Instruments.*

Lesaffre, Charles. *Petite Chanson pour Marion. (Little Song for Marion).* Gérard Billaudot. 1988. $5.75. 2:15. II. B♭–e♭' (f'). A ma mère. "Pour tuba en ut ou trombone ou baryton ou trompette ou cornet et piano." "Happy is the man who can make a living by his hobby!" G. B. Shaw. For French tuba. Pretty tune with a bit of rhythmic variation. A few arpeggios, no big technical problems. See: Thompson/Lemke, *French Music for Low Brass Instruments.*

Levy, Yehuda. *Mediterranean Rondo.* Kibutz Movement League of Composers. Recorded by Adi Hershko.

Liadov, Anatol. *Dancing Song* from *Eight Russian Folksongs,* Op 58. trans. Dishinger, Ronald Christian. Medici Music Press. 1989. 1:24. II. B♭$_1$–c. Repetitive spirited song with articulation contrasts: accents, slurs, tenutos, and staccatos. No big technical problems.

Liagré, Dartagnan. *Souvenir de Calais.* Andrieu Freres/Gérard Billaudot. 1951. $3.50. 4:35. III–IV. B♭$_1$–a'. À mon petit fils Jean-Marie (Liagré: soliste a la Musique de la Garde Republicaine). "Baryton en Si♭ ou Basse Si♭." For French tuba. Theme and variations. Mostly scalewise motion. Good intermediate solo.

Lincoln. *College March.* arr. Ostling, Acton. CPP/Belwin, Inc. 1969. 0:47. I. B♭$_1$–A♭. In 2/4 time. Introduces F♯. See: Ostling, Acton, *Tuba (Bass) Soloist, Level One,* under "Tuba and Keyboard Collections."

Link, I. *Sonatina Movement IV.* ed. Lebedev, A. Moscow: Muzyka. 1986. 1:11. III–IV. G$_1$–g. In 7/8 time with some flexibility requirements. See: Lebedev, A., *Tuba Tutor, Vol. 2,* under "Tuba and Keyboard Collections."

Link, Joachim-Dietrich. *Sonatine.* Hofmeister. 1951. Out of print. 6:00. IV–V. B$_1$–a'. Herrn Kammervirtuos Hans Lachmann. Allegro molto; Adagio improvvisato; Prestissimo. For F tuba. Upper tessitura. Last movement is in 7/8 time.

Linke, Paul. *The Glow Worm.* arr. Ostling, Acton. CPP/Belwin, Inc. 1969. 1:43. I. E♭–c. Very limited range. A few eighth notes; no technical problems. See: Ostling, Acton, *Tuba (Bass) Soloist, Level One,* under "Tuba and Keyboard Collections."

Linke, Paul, and Waldteufel, [Emil]. *Waltz Themes.* arr. Ostling, Acton. CPP/Belwin, Inc. 1969. 2:03. I. B♭₁–B♭. *Chimes of Spring; Très Jolie.* In 3/4 time with no technical problems. See: Ostling, Acton, *Tuba (Bass) Soloist, Level One,* under "Tuba and Keyboard Collections."

Lischka, Rainer. *Drei Skizzen.* Hofmeister. 1969. 5:55 (1:22, 3:13, 1:20). IV–V. B♭₁–f¹. "Für Basstuba oder Bassposaune und Klavier." Three movements. Middle to upper tessitura; best on F tuba, but very playable on lower tubas. Rhythmic and lyrical playing throughout. Good recital material.

Little, Don, arr. *Flow Gently, Sweet Afton.* CPP/Belwin, Inc. 1989. I–II. C–d. Traditional. In 3/4 time, some slurring of eighth notes. Mostly stepwise motion with a few jumps no larger than a sixth. See: Little, Don, *Solo-Pak for Tuba, Part One,* under "Tuba and Keyboard Collections."

Little, Donald C. *Lazy Lullaby.* CPP/Belwin, Inc. 1977. $4.00. 2:06. I. C–c. Slowly and expressively. Solo in slow 4/4 time with a few eighth notes. A few slurs covering a third, otherwise no technical problems. Limited range and technique. Recorded by Ronald Davis.

Little, Donald C. *Lazy Lullaby.* CPP/Belwin, Inc. 1977. See: Lamb, Jack, *Solo Sounds for Tuba Levels 1–3, Vol. 1,* under "Tuba and Keyboard Collections."

Little, Donald C., arr. *Military March.* CPP/Belwin, Inc. 1977. $4.00. 1:35. I. (B♭₁) C–c. Two patriotic songs with an eight-measure piano interlude. Solo in cut time with no technical problems. See: Lamb, Jack, *Solo Sounds for Tuba Levels 1–3, Vol. 1;* and Lamb, *Festival Solos,* under "Tuba and Keyboard Collections."

Little, Donald C., arr. See listings under "Tuba and Keyboard Collections."

Livingston, J., and Evans, R. *To Each His Own.* arr. Yasumoto, Hiroyuki. Toa Music International Co. 1989. 4:15. III–IV. F₁–e♭. With jazz feeling. A 4/4 ballad with a 12/8 feel. See: Yasumoto, Hiroyuki, *Tuba Volume #3,* under "Tuba and Keyboard Collections." Recorded by Hiroyuki Yasumoto.

Lloyd, Gerald. *Three Sketches.* Theodore Presser Company. 1968. $3.00. 4:00 (1:00, 1:10, 1:50). IV. G₁–a. Allegro; Recitativo; Allegro. Intermediate technique required.

Lockwood, Harry. *Sonata for Tuba and Piano.* Available from the composer. 1966. IV. For Robert LeBlanc. Four movements.

Lodéon, André. *Campagnarde (Country Woman).* Alphonse Leduc Editions Paris. 1964. $9.15. 2:00.

II. c–d¹. "Pour Tuba en ut ou Saxhorn basse en Si♭ et Piano." For French tuba. Easy rhythms. Can be played as upper tessitura for lower tubas. See: Thompson/Lemke, *French Music for Low Brass Instruments.*

Lodéon, André. *Tuba Show.* Alphonse Leduc Editions Paris. 1968. $12.80. 4:45. IV–V. A₁–a¹ (b♭¹). "Pour Tuba en ut ou Saxhorn Basse Si♭ et Piano." For French tuba. Flexibility and strong technique required. Wide range, some mixed meter, cadenza. See: Thompson/Lemke, *French Music for Low Brass Instruments.*

Loelliet, Jean-Baptiste. *Vivace, from Sonata in E minor.* arr. Buttery, Gary. Whaling Music Publishers. 1978. $5.00. 3:15. IV. E–d¹. "For Blöckflote and Continuo; Solo Tuba or Euphonium." Continuo part for harpsichord and cello or bassoon. Contains mordents and trills. Brisk cut time. Good recital material.

Löffler, Willi. *Der Herr Tubist.* arr. Cosmar, Harald. Available from The Tuba Center.

Lohr, Frederic N. *Out on the Deep.* arr. Holmes, G. E. Rubank, Inc. 1939. 1:10. II. b♭₁–f. "Solo Tuba—E♭ or BB♭." Allegro Moderato. Traditional sea chantey feel in 6/8. A few repeating sixteenth notes; no technical problems. See: Rubank, *Soloist Folio for Bass (E♭ or BB♭),* under "Tuba and Keyboard Collections."

Long, Lela. *Jesus Is the Sweetest Name.* arr. Moss, Alan. David E. Smith Publications. 1990. $3.50. 2:40. II–III. F–g. Lyrical solo with high tessitura for the level. Much slurring and many tenutos.

Lotzenhiser, G. W. *A Hornpipe.* Belwin. 1957. Out of print. 2:00. II. B♭₁–b♭. To W. J. L. Almost all in octaves, making the above range deceptive. In cut time with no hard rhythms. Some slurring involved.

Lotzenhiser, G. W. *Solitude.* Belwin. 1958. Out of print. 3:00. I–II. (G₁) A₁–B♭. To B. K. Some accidentals, no technical problems.

Louel, Jean. *Ritmico ed Arioso.* Centre Belge de Documentation Musicale. 1980. 4:52. IV–V. A♭₁–e♭¹. Muted passages. Complex and compound meters. Contemporary melodic writing. Will take swift articulations (possibly some double tonguing) and imaginative lyricism.

Louvier, Alain. *Cromagnon.* Alphonse Leduc Editions Paris. 1973. $12.20. 4:50. V. D₁–d♭". For French tuba. Strong technique required. Wide interval skips, wide range, flutter tonguing, trills, glissandos. Celeste accompaniment preferred, optional piano with some octave modifications. See: Thompson/Lemke; *French Music for Low Brass Instruments.*

Lovec, Vladimir. *Requiem for Euphonium or Basstuba and Piano.* ed. by Boswell, W., and Boswell, J. Philharmusica. 1974. $3.95. 1:59. IV. E–g¹. Lento espressivo. "For Euphonium or Basstuba and Accompaniment." Upper tessitura; better on F tuba or euphonium. Lyrical expressive solo that is mostly slurred. Good opportunity to show off high range and vocal approach.

Lovelock, William. *Concerto for "Music for Tuba and Orchestra."* Allans Publishing. c. 1965. For John Woods. Piano reduction by the composer. See listing under "Music for Tuba and Orchestra."

Luedeke, Raymond. *Fancies and Interludes I.* American Composers Edition, Inc. 1977. Score: $17.95; parts: $10.30. 14:00. V. B_2–f#'. Dedicated to Fritz Kaenzig. Commissioned by the University of Northern Iowa. Modern writing with some modern notation (explained). Very strong technique required. Multiphonics, bending of pitches, improvising, etc. See review in *T.U.B.A. Journal,* Vol. 7, no. 1, p. 5.

Lully, Jean-Baptiste. *Gavotte.* arr. Wekselblatt, Herbert. G. Schirmer Inc. 1972. 1:30. II–III. C–f. Tempo di Gavotte. Stately Baroque transcription. See: Wekselblatt, Herbert, *First Solos for the Tuba Player,* under "Tuba and Keyboard Collections."

Lully, Jean-Baptiste. *Gavotte en Rondeau.* tr. Post, Susan. Medici Music Press. 1981. $4.50. 2:30. II–III. C–c. In F minor and in 4/4 time. Lyrical solo with a limited range. Good introduction to late Renaissance/early Baroque style.

Lully, Jean-Baptiste. *The Lonely Forest (Bois Épais).* ed. Daellenbach, Charles. Hal Leonard Publishing Corp. 1992. 2:12. II. C–eb. Largo. A few dotted-eighth and sixteenth rhythms; otherwise rhythmically easy. Sustained feel. See: Daellenbach, Charles, *Book of Easy Tuba Solos,* under "Tuba and Keyboard Collections."

Lunde, Ivar, Jr. *Designs,* Variations for Tuba and Piano Op. 92. Norsk Musikforlag Oslo. 1987. 9:52 (1:41, 2:50, 3:32, 1:49). IV. F#₁–d#'. For Jerry and Barbara Young. *Interrupted lines; Continuous lines; Expressive lines; Dancing lines.* Modern melodic writing. Mixed meter, contemporary lyricism. Second movement is entirely muted. At end of third movement, tubist is instructed to blow across the open end of a tuba straight mute, producing a BBb (with option of playing it on tuba). Last movement has a modern ragtime feel with plenty of syncopation and some mixed meter.

Lundquist, Torbjorn Iwan. *Landskap.* 1978. Piano reduction. Recorded by Michael Lind.

Lyte, H., and Monk, W. *Abide with Me.* arr. Smith, David E. David E. Smith Publications. 1985. $2.50. 2:06. I. C–Bb. Beginning solo with limited range and easy rhythms—quarter note is fastest rhythm. Some stepwise slurring.

Macbeth, Allan. *Forget Me Not.* arr. Holmes, G. E. Rubank, Inc. 1939. 2:27. II–III. D–f (g). "Solo Tuba—Eb or BBb tuba." Allegretto. Traditional solo in cut time. Some simple arpeggios. Depending on tempo, not too difficult. See: Rubank, *Soloist Folio for Bass (Eb or BBb),* under "Tuba and Keyboard Collections."

MacDowell, Edward. *A Deserted Farm,* Op. 15. arr. Masso, George. Providence Music Press. 1966.

Out of print. 4:30. III. A₁–a. Woodland Sketches. Also for trombone or baritone (T. C.) and piano. Very lyrical transcription containing all slurred phrases. Good recital material.

Madsen, Trygve. *Introduction and Allegro.* Musikk-Huset Forlag. IV. See listing under "Music for Tuba and Band."

Madsen, Trygve. *Konzert,* Op. 35. Musikk-Huset Forlag. 1986. $26.00. See listing under "Music for Tuba and Orchestra."

Madsen, Trygve. *Sonata for (F) Tuba and Piano,* Op. 34. Musikk-Huset Forlag. 1980. $24.95. IV–V. Bb₁–f#'. To Roger Bobo. Andante sostenuto; Allegro energico; Allegro moderato. Flexibility required. As suggested by composer, for F tuba. Recorded by Oystein Baadsvik; Roger Bobo. See review in *T.U.B.A. Journal,* Vol. 9, no. 2, p. 25.

Maertens, J. *Cadenza e Allegro Scherzando.* Edition Andel Uitgaven.

Maes, J. *Concertstuk* (1944). Editions Musicales Brogneaux. 1953. 5:00. E–c". Dedicated to P. Roupcinsky. Written for trombone/tuba ut/ bassoon and piano. For French tuba and piano.

Maganini, Quinto. *An Ancient Greek Melody.* Editions Musicus. 1946. 1:37. II–III. C–ab. Lento. Melody believed to be that used by Aeschylus in *The House of Atreus.* Modal Greek feel; many augmented seconds. Easy accompaniment. See: Ostrander, Allen, *Concert Album for Tuba,* under "Tuba and Keyboard Collections."

Maganini, Quinto. *L'Après-Midi d'une Crocodille, (The Afternoon of a Female Crocodile).* Editions Musicus. 1969. $2.25. III–IV. E₁–ab. For bassoon and piano (tuba and piano). Material interpolated from Debussy, Claude, *L'après-midi d'un faune* and Wagner, Richard, *Liebestod* from *Tristan und Isolde.*

Mahler, Gustav. *Lieder eines Fahrenden Gesellen.* arr. Perantoni, Dan, and Yutzy, Miriam. Encore Music Publishers. 1992. $12.50. IV. F#–f'. Allegro; Gemächlich; Schnell und wild; Alla Marcia. Upper tessitura; best suited for F tuba. Good vocal transcriptions.

Manas, Franz. *Lustiger Bassist Konzertpolka.* Johann Kliment. 1970. See listing under "Music for Tuba and Band."

Mancini, Henry. *The Pink Panther.* arr. Frackenpohl, Arthur. Kendor Music, Inc. 1983. $5.00. 2:35. III–IV. C#–bb. Groovy misterioso. Contains an "improvise or play as written section" for those who feel comfortable stretching out. Has grace notes, falls, and a commercial feel. Listen to original composition for conception. Good recital piece.

Manen, Christian. *Grave et Scherzo,* Op. 107. Gérard Billaudot. 1978. $9.75. IV–V. F₁–a'. À Paul Bernard, en toute amitié. "Pour trombone basse et piano (tuba ou saxhorn)." Primarily for bass trombone (or French tuba). Scherzo section has changing meter section (7/8, 3/4, 6/8, 7/8) and a cadenza. Very wide range. See: Thompson/Lemke, *French Music for Low Brass Instruments.*

Maniet, René. *Piece in C.* Henri Elkan Music Publishers Inc. 1954. For French tuba and piano.

Maniet, René. *Poco Allegro.* Editions Musicales Brogneaux. 1955. $1.20. For French tuba and piano.

Maniet, René. *Premier Solo de Concours.* ed. Voxman, Himie. Rubank, Inc. 1972. 2:30. II–III. B♭₁–e♭. "For E♭ or BB♭ Bass. Very majestic French etude with no big technical problems. See: Voxman, Himie, *Concert and Contest Collection,* under "Tuba and Keyboard Collections."

Marcello, Benedetto. *Adagio from Sonata C-Dur.* arr. Buttery, Gary A. Whaling Music Publishers. 1978. $3.50. 4:00. IV. G–c'. Harpsichord and cello or bassoon continuo. For tuba or euphonium. With Baroque ornamentation. In 8 and in C major. Upper tessitura, mostly crisp dotted rhythms.

Marcello, Benedetto. *Il Mio Bel Foco.* Phillips, Harry I. (compiled and edited). Shawnee Press Inc. 1967. 2:30. III. C–g. Lyrical, slurred transcription in a minor key. In two sections, a 4/4 Recitative (felt in 8), and an Allegretto affettuoso in 3/4. See: Phillips, Harry I., *Eight Bel Canto Songs,* in this section.

Marcello, Benedetto. *Largo and Allegro.* ed. Melnikov, S. Moscow: Military Band Masters Institute. 1957. See: Melnikov, S., *Pieces for Tuba and Piano,* under "Tuba and Keyboard Collections."

Marcello, Benedetto. *Largo and Allegro.* ed. Voxman, Himie. Rubank, Inc. 1972. 3:30. II–III. (A♭₁) B♭₁–f. "For E♭ or BB♭ Bass." Easier transcription of original. Largo in 3/4 time; Allegro in 12/8. See: Voxman, Himie, *Concert and Contest Collection,* under "Tuba and Keyboard Collections."

Marcello, Benedetto. *Largo and Presto.* arr. Little, Donald C., figured bass realization by George R. Belden. CPP/Belwin, Inc. 1978. $4.00. 2:45. III. A♭₁–f(g). Well-transcribed arrangement with a melodic Largo section in 3/4 followed by a spirited Presto in 2/4 time. Detail should be paid to marked articulations and dynamics. A few trills, intermediate level technique should be adequate. See: Lamb, Jack, *Solo Sounds for Tuba Levels 3–5, Vol. 1,* under "Tuba and Keyboard Collections."

Marcello, Benedetto. *Sonata.* arr. Joosen. Henri Elkan Music Publishers Inc.

Marcello, Benedetto. *Sonata I, from 6 Solos for a Violoncello.* arr. Yasumoto, Hiroyuki. Toa Music International Co. 1989. IV. C–f'. Largo; Allegro; Largo; Allegro. Well-transcribed version of a very popular solo. Trills, scales, flexibility, and Baroque conception required. See: Yasumoto, Hiroyuki, arr., *Tuba Volume No. 2,* under "Tuba and Keyboard Collections."

Marcello, Benedetto. *Sonata No. 1 in F major.* arr. Little, Donald C., and Nelson, Richard B. Southern Music Company. 1984. $4.95. 9:30 (3.20, 3:16, 0:56, 1:58). IV. A₁–g. Largo; Allegro; Largo; Allegro. Accompaniment for piano or harpsichord. Many trills. Light, quick articulation required. Notes in parentheses for optional breaths. Good

recital material. Recorded in different arrangement by Michael Lind. See review in *T.U.B.A. Journal,* Vol. 12, no. 3, p. 23.

Marcello, Benedetto. *Sonata No. 5 in C Major.* arr. Little, Donald C., and Nelson, Richard B. Southern Music Company. 1983. $4.00. 9:53 (3:03, 3:20, 1:05, 2:26). IV. G₁–a. Adagio; Allegro; Largo; Allegro. Accompaniment for piano or harpsichord. Many trills. Light, quick articulation required. See review in *T.U.B.A. Journal,* Vol. 11, no. 2, p. 23.

Margoni, Alain. *Après une Lecture de Goldoni: Fantaisie dans le style du XVIII siècle (After a Lecture of Goldoni: Fantasy in the Style of the 18th Century).* Alphonse Leduc Editions Paris. 1964. $11.50. G♯₁–f♯'. For French tuba. See: Thompson/Lemke, *French Music for Low Brass Instruments.*

Markl, Max. *Concertino.* Available from the composer. See: Markl, Max, *Concertino,* under "Music for Tuba and Orchestra."

Marteau, Marcel. *Morceau Vivant.* arr. Barnes, Clifford P. Jack Spratt Music Co. 1958. $3.50. 3:09. IV. B♭₁–b♭. Old-style theme-and-variation-type solo in 4/4 time with some chromatic, slurred sextuplets. Triplet passages, slurred sixteenth-note stepwise patterns, crisp staccato passages; fun piece to play. Not overly demanding technically.

Martelli, Henri. *Dialogue,* Op. 100. Éditions Max Eschig. 1966. IV–V. B₁–f'. For bass trombone/tuba/saxhorn and piano. For French tuba. See: Thompson/Lemke, *French Music for Low Brass Instruments.*

Martelli, Henri. *Suite pour Tuba,* Op. 83. Éditions Max Eschig. 1954. 7:30. IV–V. G₁–ab'. À Monsieur Paul Bernard, professeur au Conservatoire National de Musique. "Pour saxhorn-basse en Si♭ ou trombone-basse et piano." For French tuba. Very wide range. Extended Lento sections combined with articulated Allegro sections.

Martin, Carroll. *Aeola.* Carl Fischer Inc. 1939. $3.25. 2:48. III. C–f. To John Kuhn. Moderato. "Tuba BB♭–E♭." Melodic solo with slurring, eighth-note triplets (in 4/4 time), and parts in A♭ major (still marked F major).

Martin, Carroll. *Pompola.* Carl Fischer Inc. 1939. Out of print. 2:00. II–III. B♭₁–d. Legato and slurred passages throughout in 4/4 time. Some accidentals, a few sixteenth notes. Recorded by Ronald Davis.

Martin, Easthope. *Hey-Ho, Come to the Fair.* arr. Fletcher, John. Chester Music Ltd. London. 1982. 1:30. III. (E♭₁) D–b♭. Allegro (But Don't Be Silly). In one (3/4 time), with spirit. See: Fletcher, John, *Tuba Solos (Tuba in C), Volume One,* under "Tuba and Keyboard Collections."

Martin, Hugh, and Blaine, Ralph. *The Trolley Song.* arr. Feldstein, Sandy. CPP/Belwin, Inc. 1990. I. B♭₁–D. See: Feldstein, Sandy, *First Solo Songbook,* under "Tuba and Keyboard Collections."

Martin, Vernon. *Concerto for Tuba and Strings.* Composers Autograph Publications. 1956. Out of print. See listing under "Music for Tuba and Orchestra."

Martini, J. P. A. *Plaisir d'Amour.* arr. Yasumoto, Hiroyuki. Toa Music International Co. 1986. 2:43. III. C–f. Very vocal approach needed. See: Yasumoto, Hiroyuki, *Tuba Volume #1,* under "Tuba and Keyboard Collections." Recorded by Hiroyuki Yasumoto.

Martini, Padre [*sic*]. *Plaisir d'Amour.* arr. Maganini, Quinto. Editions Musicus. 1954. 2:17. II. C–f (g). Molto Lento. Lyrical (slurred) 6/8 transcription. Good advanced beginner solo. See: Ostrander, Allen, *Concert Album for Tuba,* under "Tuba and Keyboard Collections."

Marttinen, Taune. *An Elephant and a Mouse.* SMOL.

Marzials. *The Fairy Jane.* arr. de Ville, Paul. Carl Fischer Inc. 1906. Out of print. See: de Ville, Paul, *Pleasant Hours,* under "Tuba and Keyboard Collections."

Masne, D. *Elegia.* ed. Melnikov, S. Moscow: Military Band Masters Institute. 1957. See: Melnikov, S., *Pieces for Tuba and Piano,* under "Tuba and Keyboard Collections."

Massenet, Jules. *Herod's Air from "Herodiade."* arr. Ostrander, Allen. Editions Musicus. 1965. $2.75. 2:30. II–III. B♭₁–e♭. In 9/8 time. Many accidentals, some slurring.

Masso, George. *Suite for Louise.* Kendor Music, Inc. 1966. $6.00. See listing under "Music for Tuba and Band." Comes with flexible Songsheet record, with Barton Cummings, tuba.

Matchett, Steve. *Walkabout.* RBC Publications. $5.00.

Mattei, Tito. *The Mariner.* arr. Walters, Harold L. Rubank, Inc. 1954. $1.75. 3:00. II. A₁–e♭. "Solo for E♭ or BB♭ Bass." Waltz in 3/4 time with no technical problems.

McCurdy, Gary L. *Four Faces of Tubby.* Tuba Materials Center. 1971. Out of print. 4:00. IV–V. E♭₁–b. In four movements with optional narrator.

McFarland, Michael. *Sketches for Tuba and Piano.* Theodore Presser Company. 1979. $3.50. 7:54. IV. F♭₁–b♭. To Fritz Kaenzig. Spirited; Slow and expressive; Marcato. Completed 1970. Conservative modern melodic writing. Mixed meter. Some glissandos on overtone series. Requires crisp articulations. See review in *T.U.B.A. Journal,* Vol. 7, no. 2, p. 23.

McHugh, Jim, and Fields, Dorothy. *On the Sunny Side of the Street.* arr. Yasumoto, Hiroyuki. Toa Music International Co. 1989. 1:57. III. (C₁) G₁–e. Swing. Soloist plays the melody as well as a "pizzicato" bass line for accompaniment. Player is encouraged to listen to "Fats" Waller's version of this piece for conception. See: Yasumoto, Hiroyuki, arr., *Tuba Volume #2,* under "Tuba and Keyboard Collections."

McKay, George Frederick. *Suite for Bass Clef Instruments.* University Music Press. 1958. Out of print. 9:00. IV. D₁–b. *Sea Spell; Barbaric Dance.* Baritone

and tuba parts supplied. Prize Composition, 1957-58, National Association of College Wind and Percussion Instructors. Low tessitura work in first movement. Major work for the instrument. Strong accompanist required.

McKimm, Barry. *Tuba Concerto.* Yarra Yarra Music Services. 1983. Commissioned by Peter Sykes. See listing under "Music for Tuba and Band."

McLin, Edward, arr. *With Melody for All.* Pro Art Publications. 1963. Out of print. "20 all-time favorite melodies for band, orchestra, ensemble, unison or solo performance."

McQuaide, George. *Samsonian Polka.* arr. Barnes, W. E. Ludwig Music Publishing Company. 1933. $3.00. 2:30. III. (B♭₁) D♭–g♭. Was published for "Music for Tuba and Band." Polka style solo in A♭/D♭ major with few technical challenges other than key. Short cadenza.

Meier, Jost. *Eclipse Finale?* (*Fantasia über "Der Mond ist aufgegangen"*). Éditions BIM. 1991. $22.50. See listing under "Music for Tuba and Orchestra" and "Music for Tuba and Band." Recorded by Oystein Baadsvik; Jens Bjorn-Larsen.

Mellilo, Peter. *Solo for Tuba and String Quartet.* DB Publishing Co. Out of print. Piano reduction.

Melnikov, S., ed. See listing under "Tuba and Keyboard Collections."

Mendelssohn, F. *Nocturne.* arr. Jacobs, Wesley. Encore Music Publishers. 1:27. I–II. D–d. Softly. Repetitive solo in G major. Some slurring, G♯ fermata. No big technical problems other than the key. See listing under "Tuba and Keyboard Collections."

Mendelssohn, Felix. *Aria from "Elijah."* arr. Blaauw, L. Molenaar N. V. 1959. 2:34. IV. c♯–e♭'. Good F tuba solo and also makes for a good study on lower tubas.

Mendelssohn, Felix. *It Is Enough from "Elijah."* arr. Ostrander, Allen. Editions Musicus. 1965. $3.00. 4:26. II. A♭₁–e♭. Very musical, expressive solo. Recorded by Peter Popiel.

Mendelssohn, Felix. *On Wings of Song.* arr. de Ville, Paul. Carl Fischer Inc. 1906. Out of print. See: de Ville, Paul, *Pleasant Hours,* under "Tuba and Keyboard Collections."

Mendelssohn, [Felix]. *On Wings of Song.* arr. Ostling, Acton. CPP/Belwin, Inc. 1969. 1:41. I. B♭₁–c. Andante cantabile. In 3/4 time. Some easy slurring. See: Ostling, Acton, *Tuba (Bass) Soloist, Level One,* under "Tuba and Keyboard Collections."

Mendelssohn, Felix. *Reverie,* Op. 85, no. 1 (1851). arr. Dishinger, Ronald Christian. Medici Music Press. 1990. $2.50. 2:08. II–III. D–f. Andante espressivo. Requires lyrical expressive playing. Limited range.

Mercadante, [Giuseppe]. *Solitude Caprice.* arr. Weber, Carl. J. W. Pepper and Son. 1914. Out of print. See: Weber, Carl, *Nineteen Solos for E♭ Bass with Piano Accompaniment,* under "Tuba and Keyboard Collections."

Merle, John. *Demetrius*. Carl Fischer Inc. 1939. Out of print. 2:00. II. B♭₁–e♭. "Tuba BB♭–E♭." In cut time; quarter note is fastest rhythm. No technical problems.

Merle, John. *Mummers—Danse Grotesque*. Carl Fischer Inc. 1938. Out of print. See listing under "Music for Tuba and Band." Recorded by William Bell.

Merle, John. *Quintero —The Farmer*. Carl Fischer Inc. 1940. Out of print. 2:22. I–II. D–e♭. "Tuba BB♭–E♭." In cut-time; quarter note is fastest rhythm. No technical problems.

Meschke, Dieter. *Musizierbuch für Basstuba*. Pro Musica Verlag Leipzig. II.

Meschke, Dieter, ed. See listing under "Tuba and Keyboard Collections."

Meunier, Gérard. *Anapausis (Repose)*. Gérard Billaudot. 1987. $11.50. 9:45. V. D₁–(g') a♭'. A mon cher ami l'incomparable musicien Fernand Lelong, professeur au C. N. S. M. de Paris. Très lent; Agité; Très lent. "Pour tuba et piano." For French tuba. Some mixed meter: 7/8, 5/8, 3/4 in second movement. Wide range. See: Thompson/Lemke, *French Music for Low Brass Instruments*. See review in *T.U.B.A. Journal*, Vol. 16, no. 3, p. 47.

Meunier, Gérard. *Tubabil*. Henri Lemoine and Cie. 1987. $4.75. 2:00. II. F–d'. "Pour tuba ou saxhorn (ut ou si bémol) et piano." Mournful little ballad with no technical problems. Easy rhythms. See review in *T.U.B.A. Journal*, Vol. 18, no. 3, p. 19.

Meunier, Gérard. *Une nuit d'harmonie*. Thomi-Berg Verlag. For French Tuba.

Meyerbeer, [Giacomo]. *Coronation March*. Huďadoff, Igor, and Westcott, William (piano arr.). Pro Art Publications. 1967. Out of print. See: Hudadoff, Igor, *Fifteen Intermediate Tuba Solos,* under "Tuba and Keyboard Collections."

Meyerbeer, [Giacomo]. *On Heaven's Just Cause Relying* and *Rataplan Chorus (from "Les Huguenots")*. arr. Hume, James Ord. Boosey and Co. 1906. Out of print. See: Hume, J. Ord, *Boosey's Bombardon Solo Album*, under "Tuba and Keyboard Collections."

Meyerbeer, [Giacomo]. *Piff, Paff (from Les Huguenots)*. arr. Hume, James Ord. Boosey and Co. 1906. Out of print. See: Hume, J. Ord, *Boosey's Bombardon Solo Album*, under "Tuba and Keyboard Collections."

Meyerbeer, [Giacomo]. *Veni Creator*. arr. Ostrander, Allen. Editions Musicus. 1954. 1:28. II–III. F–g. In 3/4 time; no big technical problems. See: Ostrander, Allen, *Concert Album for Tuba*, under "Tuba and Keyboard Collections."

Miaskovskii, N. *Song of the Field*. ed. Lebedev, A. Moscow: Muzyka. 1984. 0:31. II. G₁–g. One-octave range except for last note. All slurred phrases. Lyrical solo in 2/2 time in G minor. See: Lebedev, A., *Tuba Tutor, Vol. 1,* under "Tuba and Keyboard Collections."

Mignone, Francisco. *Divertimento*. Fundação Nacional de Arte. 1985. 6:31 (1:27, 1:30, 0:45, 1:10,

1:05, 0:34). IV–V. E₁–f '. Moderato; Decidido e amolecado; Moderato—Molto Allegro; Valsa Seresteira; Cançao de Roda; Brejeiro. Six canons, each with a different feel. Requires some flexibility and style. Good recital material.

Mihalovici, M. *Serioso*. Alphonse Leduc Editions Paris. $12.50. "Saxhorn Si♭ et Piano." See: Thompson/Lemke, *French Music for Low Brass Instruments*.

Miller, Vernon R. *Tuba Tantrum*. Pro Art Publications. 1962. Out of print. 2:10. II. B♭₁–B♭. Theme and variations. One-octave range with many sixteenth notes.

Mitegin, V., ed. See listing under "Tuba and Keyboard Collections."

Mitjagina, V., ed. See listing under "Tuba and Keyboard Collections."

Molloy, J. L. *The Kerry Dance*. arr. Bennett, Malcolm. 1988. 0:54. II–III. F–b♭. Moderato. Parts for bass clef and treble (E♭ bass) included. Sprightly 6/8 jig with a couple of piano interludes for endurance's sake make this a good advanced beginner solo. Slurring throughout, a couple of F octave jumps, no technical problems. See: Bennett, Malcolm, *Five Solos for Tuba*, under "Tuba and Keyboard Collections."

Moniushko, S. *An Air from the Opera "Halka."* ed. Melnikov, S. Moscow: Military Band Masters Institute. 1957. See: Melnikov, S., *Pieces for Tuba and Piano*, under "Tuba and Keyboard Collections."

Monk, W. H. *Abide with Me*. arr. Kinyon, John. M. Witmark and Sons. 1958. I. See Kinyon, John, *Breese-Easy Recital Pieces*, under "Tuba and Keyboard Collections."

Monroe, Margrethe. *In the Garden*. arr. Isaac, Merle J. Carl Fischer Inc. 1939. Out of print. I–II. F–e♭. Tempo di Valse. "Tuba (BB♭-E♭)." Lyrical 3/4 waltz with quarter note as fastest rhythm. Some slurring; a couple of F–d and F–e♭ slurs, otherwise no technical problems.

Monushko, S. *A Fairy Tale*. ed. Lebedev, A. Moscow: Muzyka. 1984. 0:41. II–III. C–f. Very imaginative little piece in F minor. See: Lebedev, A., *Tuba Tutor, Vol. 1,* under "Tuba and Keyboard Collections."

Moquin, Al. *King of the Deep*. The Fillmore Bros. Co. 1948. Out of print. 3:30. III. A₁–f. "Solo for Tuba (E♭ or BB♭) or Baritone." Introductory section in 12/8, then a 2/4 polka with cadenza.

Moquin, Al. *Sailing the Mighty Deep*. The Fillmore Bros. Co. 1948. Out of print. 3:00. III. F₁–b♭. "Solo for Tuba (E♭ or BB♭) or Baritone." Polka style solo utilizing a wide range. Cadenza included.

Moquin, Al. *Sousaphonium*. The Fillmore Bros. Co. 1948. Out of print. 3:00. III. A♭₁–g. "Solo for Tuba (E♭ or BB♭) or Baritone." Polka-style solo with short cadenza. Good intermediate technique required.

Morawetz, Oskar. *Sonata for Tuba*. Aeneas Music. 1984. 12:46 (3:31, 4:25, 4:50). IV–V. E♯₁–e'.

Allegro; Adagio; Allegro non troppo. Big piece requiring flexibility of technique and strong accompanist.

Moreau, J. *Piece from Suite "Colours in Movement."* ed. Larin, J. Moscow: Muzyka. 1979. See: Larin, J., *Pieces for Tuba and Piano,* under "Tuba and Keyboard Collections."

Moreau, James. *Couleurs En Mouvements (Moving Colours).* Alphonse Leduc Editions Paris. 1969. $20.95. 7:10. V. A_1–c". À ma mère, affectueusement. *Jaune Cuivre; Bleu Azur; Rouge Flamboyant* (Copper Yellow; Sky Blue; Flaming Red). "Pour Tuba en ut ou Saxhorn basse Si♭ et Piano." For French tuba. See: Thompson/Lemke, *French Music for Low Brass Instruments.*

Moreau, James. *Poursuites.* Éditions M. Combre. 1972. 1:54. IV–V. E–a'. "Pour basson (ou tuba) et piano." For French tuba. Allegretto section requires flexibility and swift articulations. Lyrical Adagio section in F♯ major.

Morra, Gene. *Nocturnal Serenade.* Carl Fischer Inc. 1964. $2.50. 2:00. II–III. D♭–g♭. Written for a variety of solo instruments with piano. Very lyrical 3/4 solo utilizing slurs and tenutos in D♭ major.

Mortimer, John Glenesk. *Tuba Concerto für Tuba and Klavier.* Editions Marc Reift. 1983. $20.25. For David LeClair. See listing under "Music for Tuba and Orchestra."

Moss, Alan. *Jesus/Sweetest Name I Know.* David E. Smith Publications. $3.50.

Moussorgsky, M. *Bydlo, from Pictures at an Exhibition.* arr. Mitjagina, V. Moscow: Muzyka. 1969. 2:17. IV. c♯–g♯'. Mostly straight from the orchestral part. High tessitura. See: Mitjagina, V. ed., *Pieces For Tuba and Piano,* under "Tuba and Keyboard Collections."

Moussorgsky, M. *Gopak.* Hudadoff, Igor, and Westcott, William (piano arr.). Pro Art Publications. 1967. Out of print. See: Hudadoff, Igor, *Fifteen Intermediate Tuba Solos,* under "Tuba and Keyboard Collections."

Moussorgsky, M. *Song of the Flea.* arr. Ostrander, Allen. Editions Musicus. 1959. $2.75. 2:50. III. C♯–a (b♭). Transcription; listen to recording of aria for conception. A version of this recorded by John Fletcher.

Mowery, Carl D. *Sonata No. 1 for Tuba and Piano.* See review in *T.U.B.A. Journal,* Vol. 1, no. 3, p. 6.

Mowery, Carl D. *Sonata No. 2 for Tuba and Piano.* See review in *T.U.B.A. Journal,* Vol. 1, no. 3, p. 6.

Moylan, William. *Solo and Duo for Tuba and Piano.* Seesaw Music Corporation Publishers. 1983. $10.00. 11:00. IV–V. A_1–e. Commissioned by the Ball State University Student Chapter of the Tubists Universal Brotherhood Association (T.U.B.A.) for Octubafest IX, 1982, Muncie, IN. Designed to be performed as a solo work (6 minutes), as a duo (5 minutes), or "Solo and Duo" (11 minutes). Flutter tonguing. Strong technique and strong accompanist required.

Mozart, Leopold. *Bourrée.* arr. Philipp, Gerd. Hofmeister. 1993. 2:04. II–III. F–f. In B♭ minor. See: Meschke, Dieter, *Zum Uben und Vorspielen/B-Tuba,* under "Tuba and Keyboard Collections."

Mozart, V. [*sic*]. *Leporello's Aria from Don Juan (Don Giovanni).* arr. Mitjagina, V. Moscow: Muzyka. 1969. 2:23. II–III. (F_1) D♭–f. Allegro molto. Easy transcription in 4/4 time (B♭ major) with no technical problems. See: Mitjagina, V. ed., *Pieces for Tuba and Piano,* under "Tuba and Keyboard Collections."

Mozart, Wolfgang Amadeus. *Allegro.* arr. Lebedev, A. Military Band Masters Faculty of Moscow Conservatiore. 1971. See: Lebedev, A., *Collection of Pieces for Tuba "Es" and Piano,* under "Tuba and Keyboard Collections."

Mozart, Wolfgang Amadeus. *All the World Is Full of Lovers.* arr. Frackenpohl, Arthur, and ed. Daellenbach, Charles. Hal Leonard Publishing Corp. 1989. 1:30. III–IV. C–c'. Light vocal approach necessary. See: Mozart, Wolfgang Amadeus, *Suite No. 1 from The Magic Flute,* under "Tuba and Keyboard Collections."

Mozart, Wolfgang Amadeus. *Alleluja, Exultate.* ed. Mathews, Donald Edward. Wingert-Jones Music, Incorporated. 1989. $5.00. 3:40. III. E♭–g (b♭). K. 165. Transcription of famous Mozart melody. Some stepwise sixteenth notes. Light Classical approach required.

Mozart, Wolfgang Amadeus. *Aria from La Clemenza di Tito.* arr. Little, Don. CPP/Belwin, Inc. 1992. 1:39. II–III. A_1–d. Allegretto. In 3/4 time, contains some sixteenth notes. See: Little, Don, *Solo-Pak for Tuba, Part Three,* under "Tuba and Keyboard Collections."

Mozart, Wolfgang Amadeus. *Aria "O Isis and Osiris."* arr. Wastall, Peter. Boosey and Hawkes, Inc. 1983. 2:28. II–III. B♭–f. Often transcribed aria in the key of B♭ major. See: Wastall, Peter, *Learn As You Play Tuba,* under "Tuba and Keyboard Collections."

Mozart, Wolfgang Amadeus. *Concert Rondo.* arr. Graham, James. TUBA Press. 1991. IV. (E♭₁) B♭₁–b♭. Allegro. K. 371. See: Graham, James, *Concert Music for Tuba,* under "Tuba and Keyboard Collections."

Mozart, Wolfgang Amadeus. *Concerto in D* (K. 412). arr. Graham, James. TUBA Press. 1991. III–IV. A–a. Allegro; Rondo (Allegro). From Horn Concerto No. 1. One-octave range. See: Graham, James, *Concert Music for Tuba,* under "Tuba and Keyboard Collections."

Mozart, Wolfgang Amadeus. *Concerto in E flat* (K.417). arr. Graham, James. TUBA Press. 1991. IV. B♭₁–c' (e♭'). Allegro maestoso; Andante; Rondo (Allegro). From Horn Concerto No. 2. See: Graham, James, *Concert Music for Tuba,* under "Tuba and Keyboard Collections." Recorded by Zdizislaw Piernik.

Mozart, Wolfgang Amadeus. *Concerto in E flat* (K.447). arr. Graham, James. TUBA Press. 1991.

IV. B♭₁–c'. Allegro; Romanze (Larghetto); Rondo (Allegro). From Horn Concerto No. 3. See: Graham, James, *Concert Music for Tuba,* under "Tuba and Keyboard Collections."

Mozart, Wolfgang Amadeus. *Concerto in E flat* (K.495). arr. Graham, James. TUBA Press. 1991. IV. B♭₁–e♭'. Allegro moderato; Romanza (Andante); Rondo (Allegro vivace). From Horn Concerto No. 4. See: Graham, James, *Concert Music for Tuba,* under "Tuba and Keyboard Collections."

Mozart, Wolfgang Amadeus. *Concerto No. 2 Part One.* ed. Melnikov, S. Moscow: Military Band Masters Institute. 1957. See: Melnikov, S., *Pieces for Tuba and Piano,* under "Tuba and Keyboard Collections."

Mozart, Wolfgang Amadeus. *Concerto No. 4 Part One.* ed. Melnikov, S. Moscow: Military Band Masters Institute. 1957. See: Melnikov, S., *Pieces for Tuba and Piano,* under "Tuba and Keyboard Collections."

Mozart, Wolfgang Amadeus. *First Movement from Concerto for Horn.* ed. Voxman, Himie. Rubank, Inc. 1972. 4:00. III. F–f. "For E♭ or BB♭ Bass." Trills, slurred and mixed articulation passages. Listen to horn recordings for conception. One octave range. See: Voxman, Himie, *Concert and Contest Collection,* under "Tuba and Keyboard Collections."

Mozart, Wolfgang Amadeus. *Ha! Just in the Nick of Time!* arr. Frackenpohl, Arthur, and ed. Daellenbach, Charles. Hal Leonard Publishing Corp. 1989. 1:44. III–IV. C–c'. See: Mozart, Wolfgang Amadeus, *Suite No. 2 from The Magic Flute,* under "Tuba and Keyboard Collections."

Mozart, Wolfgang Amadeus. *How Strong Your Tone with Magic Spell.* arr. Frackenpohl, Arthur; ed. Daellenbach, Charles. Hal Leonard Publishing Corp. 1989. 2:06. III–IV. C–a♭. Vocal approach necessary. See: Mozart, Wolfgang Amadeus, *Suite No. 1 from The Magic Flute,* under "Tuba and Keyboard Collections."

Mozart, Wolfgang Amadeus. *I'd Give My Finest Feather.* arr. Frackenpohl, Arthur; ed. Daellenbach, Charles. Hal Leonard Publishing Corp. 1989. 1:25. III–IV. D–b♭. See: Mozart, Wolfgang Amadeus, *Suite No. 2 from The Magic Flute,* under "Tuba and Keyboard Collections."

Mozart, Wolfgang Amadeus. *Marche* (from *"Les Petits Riens"*). arr. Wekselblatt, Herbert. G. Schirmer Inc. 1972. 0:36. III. B♭₁–e♭. Suggested tempo is a bit quick; would require much flexibility. In cut time. Some grace notes and one trill. See: Wekselblatt, Herbert, *First Solos for the Tuba Player,* under "Tuba and Keyboard Collections."

Mozart, Wolfgang Amadeus. *Menuetto.* arr. Swanson, Ken. CPP/Belwin, Inc. 1971. $4.00. 2:15. II–III. E♭–f. Allegretto. Melodic solo in 3/4 time. Some slurring, mostly stepwise movement. See: Lamb, Jack, *Solo Sounds for Tuba Levels 3–5, Vol. 1,* under "Tuba and Keyboard Collections."

Mozart, Wolfgang Amadeus. *O Isis and Osiris.* arr. Frackenpohl, Arthur; ed. Daellenbach, Charles. Hal Leonard Publishing Corp. 1989. 2:25. III–IV. (F₁) G₁–c'. Version in F major. See: Mozart, Wolfgang Amadeus, *Suite No. 1 from The Magic Flute,* under "Tuba and Keyboard Collections."

Mozart, Wolfgang Amadeus. *O Isis and Osiris from "The Magic Flute."* ed. Morris, R. Winston. The Brass Press. 1974. $3.00. 3:00. III–IV. F₁–c'. For Mr. B. [William J. Bell]. Adagio. Originally published by Manuscripts For Tubas, 1971. This version in F major. Very musical transcription utilizing the "sweet" range of the instrument. Recorded by William Bell; Harvey Phillips.

Mozart, Wolfgang Amadeus. *O Isis and Osiris (from The Magic Flute).* arr. Wekselblatt, Herbert. G. Schirmer Inc. 1964. 2:23. II–III. B♭₁–f. Adagio. Very lyrical accessible solo; a nice encore for advanced players. Fastest note is eighth-note. Version in B♭ major. See: Wekselblatt, H., *Solos for the Tuba Player,* under "Tuba and Keyboard Collections."

Mozart, Wolfgang Amadeus. *Per Questa Bella Mano,* K.612. arr. Barnes, Clifford P. Jack Spratt Music Co. 1965. $3.00. 4:00. III. G₁–e♭. Several different tempos, good opportunity for musical expression. No big technical problems.

Mozart, Wolfgang Amadeus. *Presto* from *Divertimento No. 12.* trans. Dishinger, Ronald Christian. Medici Music Press. 1989. $3.50. 1:35. III. B♭₁–f. Fun transcription with a few interval jumps to take a look at. Otherwise no big technical problems.

Mozart, Wolfgang Amadeus. *Priester-Aria aus die Zauberflöt (Aria of the Priests from The Magic Flute).* arr. Evertse, Jan. Tierolff-Muziekcentrale. 1952. 4:30. III. (F) G–d'. Includes *O Isis and Osiris* in F major.

Mozart, Wolfgang Amadeus. *Romanze and Rondo.* arr. Wekselblatt, Herbert. G. Schirmer Inc. 1964. 6:26 (2:37, 3:49). IV. B♭₁–c'. Romanze (Larghetto); Rondo (Allegro). Good transcriptions of two movements from Mozart, *Horn Concerto No. 3.* See: Wekselblatt, H., *Solos for the Tuba Player,* under "Tuba and Keyboard Collections."

Mozart, Wolfgang Amadeus. *Rondo de Concerto.* ed. Melnikov, S. Moscow: Military Band Masters Institute. 1957. See: Melnikov, S., *Pieces for Tuba and Piano,* under "Tuba and Keyboard Collections."

Mozart, Wolfgang Amadeus. *Rondo* from *Divertimento* No. 11. trans. Dishinger, Ronald Christian. Medici Music Press. 1989. $3.50. 3:30. II. A₁–e♭. Sprightly transcription requiring contrasting articulations: staccatos, tenutos, accents, and slurs.

Mozart, Wolfgang Amadeus. *Serenade.* trans. Morris, R. Winston. Shawnee Press Inc. 1982. $7.50. 9:30. IV. D–c'. Allegro; Menuetto; Adagio; Rondo. Composed for alto recorder. Well-transcribed solo requiring a light Mozart approach. Intermediate technique required. Good recital material.

Mozart, Wolfgang Amadeus. *Serenade from "Don Giovanni."* arr. Ostrander, Allen. Editions Musicus.

1965. $2.75. 1:10. II. D–e. In 6/8 time and in D major. No big technical problems.

Mozart, Wolfgang Amadeus. *Within These Holy Portals*. arr. Frackenpohl, Arthur; ed. Daellenbach, Charles. Hal Leonard Publishing Corp. 1989. 1:40. III–IV. (G$_1$) C–a. See: Mozart, Wolfgang Amadeus, *Suite No. 2 from The Magic Flute*, under "Tuba and Keyboard Collections."

Mueller, Florian. *Concert Music for Bass Tuba*. University Music Press. 1961. Out of print. To Arnold Jacobs. See: Mueller, Florian, *Concert Music for Bass Tuba*, under "Music for Tuba and Orchestra." Recorded by Rex Conner.

Mueller, Frederick A. *Variations on a Theme of Samuel Barber*. Available from the composer. 1972. To Bob Tucci. See listing under "Music for Tuba and Orchestra."

Mueller, J. I. *Praeludium, Chorale, Variations and Fugue*. arr. Ostrander, Allen. Editions Musicus. 1959. $5.50. 7:00. III–IV. F$_1$–bb. "From a manuscript dated 1839 for bass (or tenor) trombone and piano (or organ)." Some sixteenth-note broken arpeggios. Recorded on trombone by Mogens Andressen.

Murgier, Jacques. *Concertstück*. Éditions Musicales Transatlantiques. 1961. $15.50. 8:30. V. F$_1$–cb". For French tuba. Some mixed meter. Strong flexibility required. See: Thompson/Lemke, *French Music for Low Brass Instruments*.

Murphy, Bower. *Solo Miniature*. ed. Weldon, Constance. Charles Colin. 1969. Out of print. 4:30. III. Bb$_1$–bb. Also written for cornet or trumpet. Allegro marcato; Andante con moto; Allegro. No big technical problems.

Muscroft, Fred. *Carnival for Bass*. Studio Music Company. 1981. See listing under "Music for Tuba and Band."

Myers, Theldon. *Daydreams*. Lake State Publications. 1979. $1.25. 1:20. I. D–Bb. Moderato. Beginning solo using a very limited range. Quarter note is fastest rhythm in 4/4 time.

Myers, Theldon. *Just Foolin' Around*. Lake State Publications. 1982. $1.50. 1:10. I. C–Bb. Andante. Beginning solo using a very limited range. Quarter note is fastest rhythm in 4/4 time.

Myers, Theldon. *Lazy Day*. Lake State Publications. 1978. $1.25. 1:15. I. Bb$_1$–Bb. In 3/4 time. Beginning solo using a very limited range. Quarter note is fastest rhythm with a few slurs.

Myers, Theldon. *Waltzing Wind*. Lake State Publications. 1981. $1.50. 1:14. I. Bb$_1$–db. Moderate waltz tempo. In Ab major and 3/4 time. Quarter note is fastest rhythm. Some accidentals.

Nagel, Paul. *Design for Bass*. DB Publishing Co. c. 1973. For Don Butterfield. Piano reduction. Composed for tuba and band and for tuba and orchestra.

Nelhybel, Vaclav. *Concert Piece*. E. C. Kerby LTD. 1973. $3.50. See listing under "Music for Tuba and Band." See review in *T.U.B.A. Journal*, Vol. 1, no. 3, p. 6.

Nelhybel, Vaclav. *Suite for Tuba and Piano*. General Music Publishing Co. 1966. $7.95. 6:00. III–IV. F$_1$–g. Allegro marcato; Quasi improvisando; Allegretto. Some syncopation, mixed meters. Not overwhelming technically.

Nelson, [S.]. *The Hour of Prayer*. arr. de Ville, Paul. Carl Fischer Inc. 1906. Out of print. See: de Ville, Paul, *Pleasant Hours*, under "Tuba and Keyboard Collections."

Nelson, S. *The Pilot*. arr. Prendiville, Harry. A. Squire. 1888. Out of print. 1:38. II. Eb–db (eb). "Eb Bass; or, tuba with Piano or Organ Accompaniment (ad lib.)" No technical problems. See: Prendiville, Harry, *Six Popular Solos*, under "Tuba and Keyboard Collections."

Nelson, S. *The Pilot*. arr. de Ville, Paul. Carl Fischer Inc. 1906. Out of print. See: de Ville, Paul, *Pleasant Hours*, under "Tuba and Keyboard Collections."

Neuling, Hermann. *Konzert-Cadenz*. Pro Musica Verlag. 1954. $1.50. 2:00. IV. E$_1$–d. Recitativelike writing; in the form of a cadenza throughout.

Newsome, Roy. *The Bass in the Ballroom*. Studio Music Company. 1972. $14.00. "Solo for Eb Bass." See listing under "Music for Tuba and Band." Recorded by Stephen Sykes.

Newsome, Roy. *Swiss Air*. Studio Music Company. See listing under "Music for Tuba and Band." Recorded by Shaun Crowther.

Newton, John (lyrics). *Amazing Grace*. arr. Boyd, Bill; ed. Daellenbach, Charles. Hal Leonard Publishing Corp. 1992. 0:47. I. Bb$_1$–Bb. Traditional American melody in 3/4 time. A few eighth notes; no technical problems. Comes with practice/performance cassette. See: Daellenbach, Charles, *Book of Beginning Tuba Solos*, under "Tuba and Keyboard Collections."

Newton, Leonard G. *A Modern Lullaby*. Boosey and Hawkes, Inc. 1937. Out of print. 2:30. III. F$_1$–f. To Henry Cook. "Solo BBb Bass." Melodramatic, lyrical writing. Utilizes low range.

Newton, Rodney. *Capriccio*. Rosehill Music. 1990. $14.50. For James Gourlay. See listing under "Music for Tuba and Band." Recorded by James Gourlay.

Nicolai, Otto. *Falstaff's Drinking Song*, from *The Merry Wives of Windsor*. arr. Wekselblatt, Herbert. G. Schirmer Inc. 1972. 1:28. III. Bb$_1$–bb. Andante commode. Some mixed meter with eighth note getting the beat. Will take some interpretive thought. See: Wekselblatt, Herbert, *First Solos for the Tuba Player*, under "Tuba and Keyboard Collections."

Nicolai, W. F. G. *Minstrel's Song*. arr. de Ville, Paul. Carl Fischer Inc. 1906. Out of print. See: de Ville, Paul, *Pleasant Hours*, under "Tuba and Keyboard Collections."

Nilovic, Janko. *Chain*.

Nilovic, Janko. *Concerto*.

Nilovic, Janko. *Optima*.

Nissim, Mico. *Miroir et L'Eau.*

Niverd, Lucien. *Chant Mélancolique.* Gérard Billaudot/ Andrieu Frères. 1939. $2.50. 1:51. II–III. F–d'. Moderato, Cantabile. "For Saxhorn-basse en Si♭ ou Trombone en Si♭." F tuba tessitura. Mostly scalewise motion. A few triplets; no technical problems. See listing under "Tuba and Keyboard Collections."

Niverd, Lucien. *Complainte.* Gérard Billaudot/Andrieu Frères. 1939. $2.50. 1:17. II–III. D♯–b. Andantino. "For Saxhorn-basse en Si♭ ou Trombone en Si♭." F tuba tessitura. Mostly scalewise motion in 3/4 time. No technical problems. See listing under "Tuba and Keyboard Collections."

Niverd, Lucien. *Historiette Dramatique.* Gérard Billaudot/ Andrieu Frères. 1939. $2.00. 1:15. III. D–c' (f'). Modéré; Mélancolique. "For Saxhorn-basse en Si♭ ou Trombone en Si♭." F tuba tessitura. Lyrical dramatic melody. Good early intermediate solo. See listing under "Tuba and Keyboard Collections."

Niverd, Lucien. *Hymne.* Gérard Billaudot/ Andrieu Frères. 1939. $2.00. 1:38. II–III. G–d♭'. Moderato. "For Saxhorn-basse en Si♭ ou Trombone en Si♭." F tuba tessitura. A few sixteenth notes; a few triplets; syncopations. Lyrical hymn with a stately flavor. No technical problems. See listing under "Tuba and Keyboard Collections."

Niverd, Lucien. *Légende.* Gérard Billaudot/ Andrieu Frères. 1939. $9.50. V. E–c". "Pour Trombone ou Basse et Piano." Primarily composed with trombone in mind; "Trombone" is written on solo part. Written in tenor clef.

Niverd, Lucien. *Romance Sentimentale.* Gérard Billaudot/ Andrieu Frères. 1939. $1.95. 1:54. II–III. G–c'. Moderato. "For Saxhorn-basse en Si♭ ou Trombone en Si♭." F tuba tessitura. Lyrical writing. Some syncopation; some accidentals. No technical problems. See listing under "Tuba and Keyboard Collections."

Niverd, Lucien. *Scherzetto.* Gérard Billaudot/Andrieu Frères. 1939. $1.95. 0:45. III. G–d♭'. Vif et léger. "For Saxhorn-Basse en Si♭ ou Trombone en Si♭." F tuba tessitura. Quick tempo turns an easy piece into a technical challenge. Quarter note = 200 in 3/4 time. Mostly scalewise motion and repeated notes. See listing under "Tuba and Keyboard Collections."

Nodaïra, Ichiro. *Arabesque V.* Henri Lemoine and Cie. 1989. $20.75. V. F₁–a'. À Mel Culbertson. Difficult modern writing. Detailed remarks to both performers in French. Quite a bit of flutter tonguing and glissandos. Very wide interval jumps. Tricky rhythms. Muted passages. Will require two strong players with modern conceptions.

Nordel, Marius. *Toccata.* Manuscript. 1969. 7:00. IV. G♭₁–e'. Conservative contemporary writing. Mixed meter.

Norton, Christopher. *Make Mine a Tuba.* ed. Wastall, Peter. Boosey and Hawkes, Inc. 1985. 0:38. I–II.

E♭–e♭. Tuba part is doubled in the left hand of the piano for the most part. The right hand has colorful harmonies. The young player will greet the support of the unison accompaniment. See: Wastall, Peter, *Learn As You Play Tuba,* under "Tuba and Keyboard Collections."

Offenbach, Jacques. *Marine's Hymn.* arr. Boyd, Bill; ed. Daellenbach, Charles. Hal Leonard Publishing Corp. 1992. 0:40. I. B♭₁–B♭. Once through the melody in 2/4 time. No technical problems. Comes with practice/performance cassette. See: Daellenbach, Charles, *Book of Beginning Tuba Solos,* under "Tuba and Keyboard Collections."

Olcott, Chauncey. *My Wild Irish Rose.* arr. Ostling, Acton. CPP/Belwin, Inc. 1969. 1:43. I. C–c. See: Ostling, Acton, *Tuba (Bass) Soloist, Level One,* under "Tuba and Keyboard Collections."

O'Neill, Charles. *Spring Fancy.* Carl Fischer Inc. 1939. Out of print. 4:40. III. F₁–f. No big technical problems.

Orthel, L. *Prelude.* arr. Lebedev, A. Military Band Masters Faculty of Moscow Conservatiore. 1971. See: Lebedev, A., *Collection of Pieces for Tuba "Es" and Piano,* under "Tuba and Keyboard Collections."

Ortiz, Diego. *Recercada on the "Passamezzo Moderno"* (1553). arr. Kinney, Gordon J. Queen City Brass. 1981. $7.50. 1:43. III–IV. F–f'. For Rex Conner. In 3/2 and 6/4 time. Upper tessitura; good F tuba piece. Requires light articulations. Mostly stepwise motion.

Osborne, Chester. *Lowlands.* Pro Art Publications. c. 1981. Out of print. II. (E₁) A₁–e♭. Toward the end, soloist has the option of singing through the instrument or playing the portion. See review in *T.U.B.A. Journal,* Vol. 8, no. 4, p. 28.

Ostling, Acton. *Aurora.* CPP/Belwin, Inc. 1970. $4.00. 1:35. I. F–c. Moderato. Very limited range for beginners. Quarter note is fastest rhythm in 4/4 time. Mostly stepwise motion. A few simple slurs.

Ostling, Acton. *Aurora.* CPP/Belwin, Inc. 1970. See: Lamb, Jack, *Classic Festival Solos,* and CPP/Belwin, Inc., *Tuba Solos, Level One,* under "Tuba and Keyboard Collections."

Ostling, Acton. *Deep Cavern.* CPP/Belwin, Inc. 1970. $4.00. 1:36. I. D–d. Misterioso. Solo in G minor in 4/4 time with a few eighth notes. One-octave range with mostly stepwise motion. No technical problems. See: CPP/Belwin, Inc., *Tuba Solos, Level One,* under "Tuba and Keyboard Collections."

Ostling, Acton. *King Neptune.* CPP/Belwin, Inc. 1970. $4.00. 1:35. I. (B♭₁) D–c. Pomposo. Limited range in this nautical solo in 3/4 time. Quarter note is fastest rhythm, no technical problems. See: CPP/Belwin, Inc., *Tuba Solos, Level One,* under "Tuba and Keyboard Collections."

Ostling, Acton, arr. *All through the Night.* CPP/ Belwin, Inc. 1969. 1:10. I. B♭₁–d. Welsh air. A few dotted rhythms and slurs of a third. See listing under "Tuba and Keyboard Collections."

Ostling, Acton, arr. *Blow the Man Down.* CPP/Belwin, Inc. 1969. 1:40. I–II. C–d. Moderato. Traditional melody in 3/4 time with some light variations on that theme. A few eighth notes; no big technical problems. See: CPP/Belwin, Inc., *Tuba Solos, Level One,* and Ostling, Acton, *Tuba (Bass) Soloist, Level One,* under "Tuba and Keyboard Collections."

Ostling, Acton, arr. *Folk Song Melodies.* CPP/Belwin, Inc. 1969. 1:58. I. B♭₁–B♭. *Sweet Betsy from Pike; On Top of Old Smoky.* Once through each tune. A few simple stepwise slurs. See listing under "Tuba and Keyboard Collections."

Ostling, Acton, arr. *French Song.* CPP/Belwin, Inc. 1969. 0:38. I. B♭₁–G. Very easy familiar French tune. Quarter note is fastest rhythm; limited range. See listing under "Tuba and Keyboard Collections."

Ostling, Acton, arr. *Gallant Captain.* CPP/Belwin, Inc. 1970. $4.00. 1:39. I–II. (A♭₁) E♭–c (e♭). Moderato. Sea chantey. "Proud" solo in 4/4 time. Fastest rhythm is eighth note. No technical problems. Published separately. See: Lamb, Jack, *Classic Festival Solos,* and CPP/Belwin, *Tuba Solos, Level Two,* under "Tuba and Keyboard Collections."

Ostling, Acton, arr. *Military Marches Melodies.* CPP/Belwin, Inc. 1969. 1:00. I. B♭₁–c. *Marines; Army.* Once through each tune (with an abbreviated Army tune) in cut time. See lisiting under "Tuba and Keyboard Collections."

Ostling, Acton, arr. *Three Famous Melodies.* CPP/Belwin, Inc. 1969. 0:56. I. B♭₁–A♭. *Yankee Doodle; Old Mac Donald Had a Farm; The Daring Young Man on the Flying Trapeze.* Eight measures of first two tunes in 4/4 time, sixteen measures of last tune in 3/4 time with short piano interludes. A few easy slurs. Quarter note is fastest rhythm, no technical problems. See: CPP/Belwin, Inc., *Tuba Solos, Level One,* and Ostling, Acton, *Tuba (Bass) Soloist, Level One,* under "Tuba and Keyboard Collections."

Ostling, Acton, arr. *When the Saints Go Marching In.* CPP/Belwin, Inc. 1969. 1:09. I–II. E♭–c. Moderate march tempo. Melody and accompaniment section. One slur, some accidentals and accents. Accompaniment might take some rhythmic clarification for very beginning students; otherwise no technical problems. See: CPP/Belwin, Inc., *Tuba Solos, Level One,* and Ostling, Acton, *Tuba (Bass) Soloist, Level One,* under "Tuba and Keyboard Collections."

Ostrander, Allen. *Concert Piece in Fugal Style.* Editions Musicus. 1960. $3.75. 4:00. III–IV. (F₁) G₁–b♭. No technical problems.

Ostrander, Allen, ed. See listing under "Tuba and Keyboard Collections."

Ostransky, Leroy. *Serenade and Scherzo.* ed. Voxman, Himie. Rubank, Inc. 1972. 4:30. III–IV. A₁–a♭. "For E♭ or BB♭ Bass." Will require flexibility. See: Voxman, Himie, *Concert and Contest Collection,* under "Tuba and Keyboard Collections."

Owen, J. A. *Serenade.* arr. Weber, Carl. J. W. Pepper and Son. 1914. Out of print. See: Weber, Carl, *Nineteen Solos for E♭ Bass with Piano Accompaniment,* under "Tuba and Keyboard Collections."

Pachelbel, Johann. *Gavotte.* arr. Schwotzer, Stephan. Hofmeister. 1993. 0:29. II. A₁–c. In cut-time with a bit of syncopation. See: Meschke, Dieter, *Zum Uben und Vorspielen/B-Tuba,* under "Tuba and Keyboard Collections."

Paganini, N. *Perpetual Motion.* arr. Buttery, Gary. Whaling Music Publishers. 1978. $10.00. Piano reduction. See listing under "Music for Multiple Tubas, Seven or More Parts." Other arrangements of this piece have been recorded.

Painparé, H. *Concertpiece.* rev. Voxman, Himie. Rubank, Inc. $3.50. 7:00. III. (A♭₁) B♭₁–a♭. Theme and variations type solo. Lyrical and technical passages included. Good recital material.

Pascal, Claude. *Sonate in 6 Minutes 30.* Éditions Durand and Cie. 1958. $29.00. 6:30. IV–V. E₁–b¹. À Paul Bernard Professeur au Conservatoire National Supérieur de Musique de Paris. Anime; Lent et calme. "Pour Tuba, ou Trombone-Basse, ou Saxhorn en Si♭ et Piano." For French tuba. Very wide range; quick articulations required. See: Thompson/Lemke, *French Music for Low Brass Instruments.*

Pauer, Jirí. *Tubonetta.* Éditions BIM. 1991. $20.00. 10:00. V. B♭₂–b♭¹. Intráda; Arie; Rondo. Written in 1976. Quick playing in compound meters in first and third movements. Second movement is a lyrical cantabile. Very wide range; multiphonics.

Payne, Frank Lynn. *Sonata for Tuba and Piano.* Shawnee Press Inc. 1979. $5.00. 8:20 (2:00, 3:20, 1:00, 2:00). IV–V. C♯₁–f♯¹. For Mark Mordue, tubist with the Oklahoma Symphony Orchestra. Some mixed meter. Wide range, good ear and sharp technique required. See review in *T.U.B.A. Journal,* Vol. 7, no. 4, p. 27. Also see: Bird, Gary, ed., *Program Notes for the Solo Tuba.*

Perantoni, Daniel, ed. See listing under "Tuba and Keyboard Collections."

Pergolesi, Giovanni Battista. *Air.* arr. Lebedev, A. Military Band Masters Faculty of Moscow Conservatiore. 1971. See: Lebedev, A., *Collection of Pieces for Tuba "Es" and Piano,* under "Tuba and Keyboard Collections."

Pergolesi, Giovanni Battista. *Arie.* arr. Schwotzer, Stephan. Hofmeister. 1993. 1:43. II. E♭–f. See: Meschke, Dieter, *Zum Uben und Vorspielen/B-Tuba,* under "Tuba and Keyboard Collections."

Pergolesi, Giovanni Battista. *Canzona.* arr. Barnes, Clifford P. Jack Spratt Music Co. 1965. $3.00. 3:00. III. G₁–f (a♭). Transcription in 2/4 time. Some repeated slurred patterns, no big technical problems. Good recital material.

Pergolesi, Giovanni Battista. *Lied.* arr. Schwotzer, Stephan. Hofmeister. 1993. 1:13. II. F♯–e♭. No technical problems. See: Meschke, Dieter, *Zum*

Uben und Vorspielen/B-Tuba, under "Tuba and Keyboard Collections."

Pergolesi, Giovanni Battista. *Nina.* Phillips, Harry I. (compiled and edited). Shawnee Press Inc. 1967. 1:41. II–III. C♯–d. Andante. Lyrical, slurred transcription in minor key. A few 32nd notes and a few sixteenth-note triplets (turns), otherwise not too difficult technically. See: Phillips, Harry I., *Eight Bel Canto Songs,* in this section.

Pergolesi, Giovanni Battista. *Spiritoso.* tr. Howe, Marvin C. Lawson-Gould Music Publishers Inc. 1965. 2:39. III. C–g. Fun transcription. Mostly scalewise Baroque writing. Good recital material. See: Howe, M., *Three Tuba Solos,* under "Tuba and Keyboard Collections."

Perrie [*sic*], H.W. See Petrie, H.W., below.

Peter, C. *The Jolly Coppersmith.* arr. Bell, William J. CPP/Belwin, Inc. 1968. Originally copyright 1964. $4.00. 1:03. I. D–d. Lively. Solo in 2/4 with a few sixteenth notes. Some F–d jumps; otherwise no technical problems. See: Lamb, Jack, *Solo Sounds for Tuba Levels 1–3, Vol. 1,* under "Tuba and Keyboard Collections."

Peterson, Lawrence. *Sonata for BB♭ Bass and Piano.* Schmidt Publications. 1975. 7:16 (2:34, 1:58, 2:44). III–IV. G₁–g♭ First movement is lyrical movement and in 7/4. Second movement has low rhythmical writing with quartal intervals. Third movement has mixed meter (12/8, 9/8, 6/8). Lyrical writing with shifting tonal center. Good advanced-intermediate solo containing (not too) modern compositional material. Includes copy for competition.

Pethel, James. *Brass Talk.* Kendor Music, Inc. 1992. $5.00. 3:25. III. B₁–a. Dedicated to Joe Ray. Slowly and freely. Mostly slurred ballad. Strong flexibility and good ear required. Good recital material.

Pethel, Stan. *Essay for Tuba.* Kendor Music, Inc. 1980. $5.00. 2:42. III. G₁–f. Moderately. Intermediate level solo in 6/8. No big technical challenges; lyrical writing. See review in *T.U.B.A. Journal,* Vol. 8, no. 4, p. 26.

Petit, Alexandre. *Première Étude de Concours.* Gérard Billaudot. $5.25. 4:00. IV. F–d'. À mon ami Gabriel Pares, Chef de musique de la Garde Republicaine. Also written for "trompette ou cornet; clarinette Si; saxophone alto avec piano." Technical etude: dotted rhythms with 32nd notes, cadenza, trill. Requires comfortable technique with creative interpretation.

Petit, Pierre. *Fantaisie.* Alphonse Leduc Editions Paris. 1953. $12.80. 4:00. V. F₁–a'. À mon cher Maître et ami Paul Bernard. "Pour Tuba ou Trombone basse en ut ou Saxhorn basse Si♭ et Piano." For French tuba. Some tenor clef. See: Thompson/Lemke, *French Music for Low Brass Instruments.*

Petit, Pierre. *Grave.* Alphonse Leduc Editions Paris. 1952. $8.60. 2:00. IV. A♭₁–a'. À Paul Bernard. "Pour Tuba ut ou Trombone basse ou Contrebasse à Cordes ou Saxhorn basse Si♭ et Piano." For French tuba. Some tenor clef. See: Thompson/Lemke, *French Music for Low Brass Instruments.*

Petit, Pierre. *Thème Varié.* Alphonse Leduc Editions Paris. 1965. $16.00. 7:30. V. E₁–c". "Pour Saxhorn basse Si♭ ou Tuba ut et Piano." Theme and (eight) variations. For French tuba. See: Thompson/Lemke, *French Music for Low Brass Instruments.*

Petit, Pierre. *Wagenia.* Alphonse Leduc Editions Paris. 1957. $16.85. 5:30. IV. A♭₁–d'. "Pour Trombone basse ou Tuba ut ou Saxhorn basse Si♭ et Piano." See: Thompson/Lemke, *French Music for Low Brass Instruments.*

Petrie, H. W. *Asleep in the Deep.* arr. Buchtel, Forrest L. Neil A. Kjos Music Company. 1958. $2.00. 2:00. I–II. G₁–c. Verse and chorus in 6/8 time in E♭ major. A version of this recorded by William Bell; Barney Mallon.

Petrie, H. W. *Asleep in the Deep.* arr. Teague, William. Witmark. 1942. 2:00. II. B♭₁–g. Verse and chorus in 12/8 time and in B♭ major. A version of this recorded by William Bell; Barney Mallon.

Petrie, H. W. *Asleep in the Deep.* arr. Walters, Harold L. Rubank, Inc. 1954. $2.50. "Solo E♭ or BB♭ Bass." See: Petrie, H. W., *Asleep in the Deep,* under "Music for Tuba and Band." A version of this recorded by William Bell; Barney Mallon.

Petrie, H. W. *Asleep in the Deep.* arr. Wekselblatt, Herbert. G. Schirmer Inc. 1972. 1:48. II–III. B♭₁–g. Moderato. Erroneously attributed to H. W. Perrie. Classic solo (verse and chorus) in 12/8. See: Wekselblatt, Herbert, *First Solos for the Tuba Player,* under "Tuba and Keyboard Collections."

Pezel, Johann. *Intrade.* arr. Philipp, Gerd. Hofmeister. 1993. 1:08. II. E♭–e♭. In A♭ major and in 4/4 time. Quarter note is fastest rhythm; no technical problems. See: Meschke, Dieter, *Zum Uben und Vorspielen/B-Tuba,* under "Tuba and Keyboard Collections."

Phillips, Harry I., ed. *Eight Bel Canto Songs.* Shawnee Press Inc. 1967. $11.00. II–III. Written for a variety of solo instruments with piano. This collection of Italian songs from the seventeenth and eighteenth centuries includes Bononcini, Giovanni, *Per la Gloria d'Adorarri from "Griselda"*; Caccini, Giulio, *Amarilli, Mia Bella*; Caldara, Antonio, *Sebben, Crudele*; Durante, Francesco, *Preghiera*; Marcello, Benedetto, *Il mio bel Foco*; Pergolesi, Giovanni Battista, *Nina*; Scarlatti, Allessandro, *Sento Nel Core*; Stradella, Alessandro, *Pietà, Signore!*

Phillips, L. Z. *The Marines' Hymn March.* arr. Holmes, G. E. Rubank, Inc. 1939. Out of print. 1:30. II–III. E♭–e♭. "Solo Tuba—E♭ or BB♭ tuba." "Air Varie." Traditional theme and variations based on the United States Marine Corps Hymn. Mostly sixteenth-note scale motion for technical section. Limited range. See: Rubank, *Soloist Folio for Bass (E♭ or BB♭),* under "Tuba and Keyboard Collections."

Pierpont, J. *Jingle Bells.* arr. Feldstein, Sandy. CPP/ Belwin, Inc. 1990. I. B♭₁–F. See: Feldstein, Sandy, *First Solo Songbook,* under "Tuba and Keyboard Collections."

Pinsuti, Ciro. *Bedouin Love Song.* arr. Holmes, G. E. Rubank, Inc. 1939. 1:56. II. (G₁) B♭₁–e♭. "Solo Tuba — E♭ or BB♭ tuba." Allegretto moderato. A "middle eastern bolero" feel with some syncopation. Optional lower octaves for BB♭ players. Minor section, slower major section with entire piece repeating. See: Rubank, *Soloist Folio for Bass (E♭ or BB♭),* under "Tuba and Keyboard Collections."

Pisciotta, Louis V. *Sonata.* Sound Ideas Publications. 1989. $16.00. 9:50 (3:52, 2:02, 3:56). IV–V. C₁–f'. Allegro; Sostenuto; Vivace. Composed in 1961. Strong technique and rhythm required. Lyrical passages, meter changes, and some tricky interval jumps. Modern tonal writing

Planel, Robert. *Air et Final.* Alphonse Leduc Editions Paris. 1968. $13.35. 6:45. V. C♭–g'. For French tuba.

Plog, Anthony. *Three Miniatures.* Éditions BIM. 1991. $16.00. Commissioned by Custom Music Coimpany [*sic*] and written for Daniel Perantoni. See listing under "Music for Tuba and Band." Recorded by Roger Bobo.

Poot, Marcel. *Impromptu.* Éditions Max Eschig. 1933. 4:30. IV–V. G–b'. À E. Dax. "Pour Trombone et Piano ou Tuba ou Saxhorn baryton." "Morceau imposé au Concours Du Conservatiore Royal De Bruxelles Année 1931." Includes passages in tenor clef.

Popper, David. *Gavotte.* arr. Bell, William J. CPP/ Belwin, Inc. 1962. $4.00. 1:33. I. (B♭₁) F–e♭. Allegretto. Optional 4/4 or cut time. Optional low notes gives leeway for beginners to choose their level of difficulty. Fastest rhythm is quarter note. Very repetitive eight-measure phrase. A couple of articulated jumps from F to d; otherwise no technical problems. See: CPP/Belwin, Inc., *Tuba Solos, Level One,* under "Tuba and Keyboard Collections."

Porret, Julien. *Fifteenth Solo de Concours.* Molenaar N. V. 1963. 2:30. III. c–e'. Good F tuba solo or high study on lower instrument.

Porret, Julien. *Premier Pièce de Concours.* Gérard Billaudot. 1963. 4:51. IV. G₁–d'. "Pour Saxhorn Basse en Si♭ et piano." Technical solo. For French tuba. See: Thompson/Lemke, *French Music for Low Brass Instruments.*

Poullot, F. *L'installation au moulin.*

Poulton, George R. *Andantino.* arr. Ostling, Acton. CPP/Belwin, Inc. 1969. 1:00. I. C–d. In cut time. See: Ostling, Acton, *Tuba (Bass) Soloist, Level One,* under "Tuba and Keyboard Collections."

Poulton, George R. *Aura Lee.* arr. Ostling, Acton. CPP/Belwin, Inc. 1969. 1:17. I. B♭₁–A♭. Limited range; no technical problems. See: Ostling, Acton, *Tuba (Bass) Soloist, Level One,* under "Tuba and Keyboard Collections."

Poutoire, Patrick. *Petit Air.* Éditions M. Combre. 1983. 2:15. II. G–c'. Majestueux. Regal solo with few technical problems.

Powell, Morgan. *Introduction and Blues.* Hal Leonard Publishing Corp. 1976. See: Perantoni, Daniel, *Master Solos, Intermediate Level,* under "Tuba and Keyboard Collections."

Pozzoli, E. *The Sad Minute.* ed. Lebedev, A. Moscow: Muzyka. 1984. 1:00. II. B♭–f. Mostly half notes with limited range. Slow, lyrical, reflective tome. See: Lebedev, A., *Tuba Tutor, Vol. 1,* under "Tuba and Keyboard Collections."

Premru, Raymond. *Concerto for Tuba and Orchestra.* TUBA Press. Dedicated to the memory of John Fletcher. Piano reduction in preparation. See listing under "Music for Tuba and Orchestra."

Prendiville, Harry. *The Approach of the Lion.* arr. Weber, Carl. J. W. Pepper and Son. 1914. Out of print. See: Weber, Carl, *Nineteen Solos for E♭ Bass with Piano Accompaniment,* under "Tuba and Keyboard Collections."

Prendiville, Harry, arr. *Down among the Dead Men.* A. Squire. 1888. Out of print. 1:20. II. C–e♭. "E♭ Bass; or, tuba With Piano or Organ Accompaniment (ad lib.)." See listing under "Tuba and Keyboard Collections."

Prescott, John. *Sonata for Tuba and Piano,* Op. 23. TUBA Press. $15.00. 16:16 (5:00, 4:37, 6:29). IV–V. E♭₁–ab'. Commissioned by Scott Watson with a grant from the General Research Fund, University of Kansas. Three movements. Solid writing for tuba and piano. Takes flexibility, wide range, and a strong accompanist. See review in *T.U.B.A. Journal,* Vol. 18, no. 2, p. 19.

Presser, William. *Capriccio for Tuba and Band.* Theodore Presser Company. 1969. $7.00. For Rex Conner. See listing under "Music for Tuba and Band." Also see: Bird, Gary, ed., *Program Notes for the Solo Tuba.* Recorded by Michael Astwood.

Presser, William. *Concerto for Tuba and Strings.* Theodore Presser Company. 1970. $8.50. See listing under "Music for Tuba and Orchestra." Also see: Bird, Gary, ed., *Program Notes for the Solo Tuba.*

Presser, William. *Minute Sketches.* Autograph Editions. 1967. $5.95. 5:04 (1:02, 1:02, 1:00, 1:00, 1:00). IV. E₁–f♯' (g). *Trumgo; Song; Waltz; March; Scherzo.* Five contrasting movements, approximately one minute each. Requires quick articulations. Modern tonal writing.

Presser, William. *Rondo.* C. L. Barnhouse Company. 1966. $3.50. 2:13. III. (F₁) B♭₁–f (b♭). Conservative range; one phrase up to b♭. "Ohm-Pah" section repeats rhythmical motive.

Presser, William. *Second Sonatina for Tuba and Piano.* Theodore Presser Company. 1974. $8.00. 8:30 (3:52, 2:45, 1:44). IV. E♯₁–b♭. Completed 1973. Some lovely lyrical and technical modern melodic lines. See review in *T.U.B.A. Journal,* Vol. 1, no. 3, p. 6. Also see: Bird, Gary, ed., *Program Notes for the Solo Tuba.*

Presser, William. *Sonatina for Tuba and Piano.* Theodore Presser Company. 1973. $4.00. 10:35 (4:38, 3:23, 1:08, 1:26). IV. D_1–c'. For William Keck. Allegretto; Allegro; Adagio; Presto. Completed 1972. Third movement based on Robert Herrick's poem "Another Grace for A Child." Tonal modern writing. Quick articulations, both slurred and tongued . See: Bird, Gary, ed., *Program Notes for the Solo Tuba.*

Presser, William. *Suite for Tuba.* Lyceum Press (Ensemble Publications). 1967. $4.00. 8:10. For Rex Conner. See: Bird, Gary, ed., *Program Notes for the Solo Tuba.*

Price, Joseph. *The Search for the Missing Marble.* Version with piano accompaniment. See listing under "Music for Tuba and Tape."

Pro Art (publisher). See listing under "Tuba and Keyboard Collections."

Prokofiev, Sergei. *Recitative and Kutuzov's Air from the Opera "War and Peace."* arr. Lebedev, A. Military Band Masters Faculty of Moscow Conservatiore. 1971. See: Lebedev, A., *Collection of Pieces for Tuba "Es" and Piano,* under "Tuba and Keyboard Collections."

Proust, Pascal. *Élégie.* Gérard Billaudot. 1991. $4.00. 3:00. II–III. D–c'. "Pour Tuba en ut (ou saxhorn basse en Si♭ ou euphonium) et piano." Very lyrical section; articulated section has some arpeggios. For French tuba.

Pruyn, William. *Rocked in the Cradle of the Deep.* DB Publishing Co. For Don Butterfield. In manuscript.

Pryor, Arthur. *Exposition Echoes Polka.* arr. Weber, Carl. J. W. Pepper and Son. 1914. Out of print. See: Weber, Carl, *Nineteen Solos for E♭ Bass with Piano Accompaniment,* under "Tuba and Keyboard Collections."

Purcell, Henry. *Arise Ye Subterranean Winds.* arr. Ostrander, Allen. Editions Musicus. 1959. $2.75. 2:30. III. G_1–f. Some slurred technical passages (sixteenth notes in 4/4 time) in this fine transcription. Good recital material.

Purcell, Henry. *Gavotte,* from *Harpsichord Suite No. 5.* arr. Vedeski, Anton. Medici Music Press. 1986. $4.50. 1:42. II–III. B♭₁–e♭. A variety of marked articulations included. No technical problems. Good recital material.

Purcell, Henry. *Gavotte and Hornpipe.* trans. Dishinger, Ronald Christian. Medici Music Press. 1986. $2.50. 2:20. III. A_1–d. Difficulty of technical challenges depends on final tempo, otherwise manageable. Sections in 2/2 and 3/2.

Purcell, Henry. *March* from *Suite No. 5.* trans. Dishinger, Ronald Christian. Medici Music Press. 1989. $3.50. 2:23. II. C–d. Very accessible transcription utilizing simple technique. Regal march with some slurs and tenutos.

Purcell, Henry. *Next, Winter Comes Slowly.* tr. Howe, Marvin C. Lawson-Gould Music Publishers Inc. 1965. 1:54. II–III. (G_1) C–g. See: Howe, M.,

Three Tuba Solos, under "Tuba and Keyboard Collections."

Purcell, Henry. *Recitative, Song and Chorus,* from *Dido and Aeneas.* arr. Morris, R. Winston. Southern Music Company. 1972. $2.50. 4:30. III. C–g. Section in 3/2 time. Very lyrical transcription.

Purcell, Henry. *Song from Timon of Athens.* arr. Little, Don. CPP/Belwin, Inc. 1992. 2:16. II–III. (G_1) B♭₁–e♭. Solo in 3/4 time at a brisk tempo. Eighth note is fastest rhythm. Some slurring. See: Little, Don, *Solo-Pak for Tuba, Part Three,* under "Tuba and Keyboard Collections."

Quate, Amy. *The Feel Good Blues.* CPP/Belwin, Inc. 1992. 2:30. II–III. C–e. Blues style. "Swung" eighth notes, accidentals, and syncopations throughout. See: Little, Don, *Solo-Pak for Tuba, Part Three,* under "Tuba and Keyboard Collections."

Quate, Amy. *Los Cocos Locos, (Crazy Coconuts).* ed. Little, Don. CPP/Belwin, Inc. 1991. 2:02. II. (B♭₁) D–e♭. Latin flavor. "After-beat" rhythms. Various articulations: tenuto, staccato, accents. See: Little, Don, *Solo-Pak for Tuba, Part Two,* under "Tuba and Keyboard Collections."

Quate, Amy, and Little, Don. *Texas Horizons.* CPP/Belwin, Inc. 1989. 3:05. I–II. B♭₁–d (f). Some slurring of eighth notes at a conservative tempo. No other technical problems. See: Little, Don, *Solo-Pak for Tuba, Part One,* under "Tuba and Keyboard Collections."

Quérat, Marcel. *Allegretto Comodo.* Éditions M. Combre. 1971. 2:40. III. G–f'. "Pour Saxhorn-Basse et Piano." For French tuba. See: Thompson/Lemke, *French Music for Low Brass Instruments.*

Quérat, Marcel. *Moderation.* Éditions M. Combre. 1991. 2:23. III–IV. A♭₁–d'. À Bernard Lienard. "Pour Tuba Basse et Piano." Mostly lyrical solo with a French flavor.

Quérat, Marcel. *Relation.* Éditions M. Combre. 1971. 1:47. II. B♭–d'. "Pour Basse Si♭ et Piano." No technical problems. For French tuba. See: Thompson/Lemke, *French Music for Low Brass Instruments.*

Rachmaninoff, Sergei. *Elegia.* ed. Melnikov, S. Moscow: Military Band Masters Institute. 1957. See: Melnikov, S., *Pieces for Tuba and Piano,* under "Tuba and Keyboard Collections."

Rachmaninoff, Sergei. *Russian Song.* arr. Lebedev, A. Military Band Masters Faculty of Moscow Conservatiore. 1971. See: Lebedev, A., *Collection of Pieces for Tuba "Es" and Piano,* under "Tuba and Keyboard Collections."

Rachmaninoff, Sergei. *Vocalise,* Op. 34, no. 14. arr. Allen, Virginia. Ludwig Music Publishing Company. 1992. $5.00. 2:32. III–IV. C–c' (e♭'). Transcription of an incredibly lovely melody. Good recital material. A version of this recorded by Robert LeBlanc.

Radolt, Wenzel Ludwig Freiherr von. *Menuett im Kanon.* arr. Philipp, Gerd. Hofmeister. 1993. 1:06.

I–II. D–c. No technical problems; in E♭ major and 3/4 time. See: Meschke, Dieter, *Zum Uben und Vorspielen/B-Tuba,* under "Tuba and Keyboard Collections."

Rae, Allan. *Serenade for Tuba and Piano.* Canadian Music Centre. 1991. 4:00. IV. A₁–c♯'. Sherburne G. McCurdy Festival Series. Has both free-time duration section and more conventional notation. Nice textural solo. Good recital material. Requires very strong accompanist.

Raich, Heribert. *Bassistengruss.* Adler Musikverlag. Piano Reduction. See: Raich, *Bassistengruss,* under "Music for Tuba and Band."

Rakov, N. *Air.* ed. Mitegin, V., ed. Moscow: Muzyka. 1969. See: Mitegin, V., *Pieces for Tuba and Piano,* under "Tuba and Keyboard Collections."

Rakov, N. *Romance.* arr. Lebedev, A. Military Band Masters Faculty of Moscow Conservatiore. 1971. See: Lebedev, A., *Collection of Pieces for Tuba "Es" and Piano,* under "Tuba and Keyboard Collections."

Rakov, N. *Sonatina.* ed. Voronov, G. Moscow: Muzyka. 1984. See: Voronov, G, *Works for Tuba and Piano by Russian Composers,* under "Tuba and Keyboard Collections." Also see other listing.

Rakov, N. *Sonatina.* ed. Lebedev, A. Moscow: Muzyka. 1986. 1:51. III. E₁–b♭. Allegro. First seven pitches of this piece based on the name Lebedev. Composed in 1973. Fun piece with a lot of character. Lyrical and peasante playing. See: Lebedev, A., *Tuba Tutor, Vol. 2,* under "Tuba and Keyboard Collections."

Rameau, J. Ph. *Rigaudon.* arr. Maganini, Quinto. Editions Musicus. 1954. 1:20. III. E♭–a♭. Alternating slur two, tongue two (eighth note) articulation throughout in cut time. See: Ostrander, Allen, *Concert Album for Tuba,* under "Tuba and Keyboard Collections."

Rameau, Jean Philippe. *La Villageoise.* arr. Wekselblatt, Herbert. G. Schirmer Inc. 1972. 0:48. II. B♭₁–e♭. Cute 2/4 dance with no technical problems. See: Wekselblatt, Herbert, *First Solos for the Tuba Player,* under "Tuba and Keyboard Collections."

Rameau, Jean Philippe. *Rigaudon from Pièces de Clavecin,* 1724. trans. Dishinger, Ronald Christian. Medici Music Press. 1986. $4.50. 2:27. I. A₁–c. Good beginning solo with no major technical problems. Staccatos, tenutos, and some easy slurring.

Ramovš, Primož. *Koncert za Kontrabasovsko Tubo* (Concerto for Contrabass Tuba). Piano reduction. Available from Igor Krlvokapic.

Rance, E. (Adjutant). *Rocked in the Cradle of the Deep.* Salvationist Publishing and Supplies, Ltd. 3:00. III. B♭₁–b♭. "Solo for Bombardon in E♭." Solo part in treble clef.

Rappoldt, Lawrence I. *Concertpiece for Tuba and Piano.* Shawnee Press Inc. 1979. $6.00. 6:20. IV. A₁–d'. Mixed meter. Solid writing for tuba and piano. Takes some rhythmic (meter) inspection. See review in *T.U.B.A. Journal,* Vol. 10, no. 2, p. 24.

Ravel, Maurice. *Pavane.* arr. Lebedev, A. Military Band Masters Faculty of Moscow Conservatiore. 1971. See: Lebedev, A., *Collection of Pieces for Tuba "Es" and Piano,* under "Tuba and Keyboard Collections."

Reed, Alfred. *Fantasia a Due.* Edward B. Marks Music Co. 1979. 5:00. IV–V. G₁–e' (c"). Commissioned by and dedicated to T.U.B.A., for the Third International Tuba-Euphonium Symposium-Workshop, 1978. First T.U.B.A. commissioned work. Solid writing for tuba and piano. Requires strong technique. Good recital material. See review in *T.U.B.A. Journal,* Vol. 7, no. 3, p. 31. Recorded by William D. Porter.

Reiche, E. *Adagio from Concerto No. 2.* arr. Yasumoto, Hiroyuki. Toa Music International Co. 1989. 3:58. IV. (B₁) D–f. Would lie better on F tuba, although playable on lower instrument. Strong lyrical sense combined with flexibility. Subdivide in 6. See: Yasumoto, Hiroyuki, arr., *Tuba Volume #2,* under "Tuba and Keyboard Collections."

Rekhin, Igor. *Sonata for Tuba and Piano.* TUBA Press. $12.00. 9:30 (4:30, 2:00, 3:00). IV–V. D₁–f'. For Scott Watson. Three attacca movements. Neo-romantic feel. Major work for tuba and piano. Solid writing. Requires flexibility and vocal sense. Good recital material.

Renaud, Manuel. *Ton Coeur (Tuba).* Gérard Billaudot. 1990. 4:00. II–III. D♭–g♭. A Mon père. "Pour tuba basse en ut et piano." For French tuba. Extensive use of tritones. Modern melodic writing. Some slurring involved. See: Daniel-Lesur, *Collection Panorama,* under "Tuba and Keyboard Collections."

Reynaud, J. *Ah! vous dirai-je maman.* Editions Salabert. n. d. Out of print. Theme and variations.

Reynolds, Verne. *Sonata for Tuba and Piano.* Carl Fischer Inc. 1969. $8.50. 13:00. V. (A₂) D₁–a'. For Cherry Beauregard. Moderately fast; Slow; Variations. Difficult work for tuba and piano by this virtuoso French horn teacher and performer. Requires very strong technique and strong musicality.

Richardson, Alan. *In the Lowlands.* Braydeston Press. 1975. $9.95. 5:00 (1:15, 1:15, 1:15, 1:15). III. C–b♭. For Christine and Henry Erskine-Hill. Alla Marcia; Allegro; In folksong style; Lento moderato—espressivo, ma semplice; Vivace ritmico. Four movements with same duration. Very tonal, descriptive musical settings. Lyrical, vocal writing. Technical demands not outstanding. Good recital piece.

Rideout, Alan. *Concertino for Tuba and Strings.* Emerson Edition Limited. 1985. $9.50. See listing under "Music for Tuba and Orchestra."

Rimsky-Korsakov, N. *Andante Cantabile from Concerto.* ed. Voxman, Himie. Rubank, Inc. 1972. 3:00. III. C–g♭. "For E♭ or BB♭ Bass." Second movement from Trombone Concerto, including cadenza. As with original, in G♭ major. Very lyrical writing. See: Voxman, Himie, *Concert and Contest*

Collection, under "Tuba and Keyboard Collections."

Rimsky-Korsakov, N. *Song from the opera "Snow Maiden."* ed. Melnikov, S. Moscow: Military Band Masters Institute. 1957. See: Melnikov, S., *Pieces for Tuba and Piano,* under "Tuba and Keyboard Collections."

Rimsky-Korsakov, N. *Song of India.* Hudadoff, Igor, and Westcott, William (piano arr.). Pro Art Publications. 1967. Out of print. See: Hudadoff, Igor, *Fifteen Intermediate Tuba Solos,* under "Tuba and Keyboard Collections."

Rimsky-Korsakov, N. *Song of the East.* arr. Agounoff, M. Editions Musicus. 1950. 1:33. II–III. C♯–g. Andante. Quasi cadenza section followed by typical Rimsky-Korsakov recitative-like melody. Some 32nd notes (slow tempo); triplets and dotted rhythms (to be differentiated). Middle tessitura throughout. See: Ostrander, Allen, *Concert Album for Tuba,* under "Tuba and Keyboard Collections."

Ringleben, J. *The Storm King.* Carl Fischer Inc. 1897. $3.25. "Grand Fantasia." See listing under "Music for Tuba and Band." Also see review in *T.U.B.A. Journal,* Vol. 9, no. 3, p. 25.

Rivière, Jean-Pierre. *Ré mineur.* Éditions Max Eschig. 1979. 5:25. IV–V. G₁–g♯'. À Paul Bernard. For French tuba. Great flexibility required. Wide dissonant jumps, wide range, glissandos in cadenza.

Roberts, Sue. *Chanson and Divertissement.* 1982. Commissioned by Rodger Vaughan.

Rodgers, Thomas. *Chaconne.* The Brass Press. 1974. $3.50. 3:45. IV. A₁–b. Originally *Manuscripts for Tuba,* 1968. Two legato, lyrical sections separated by a marcato, staccato section. Some sixteenth-note triplets; optional mute in last variation. Would take an advanced high school or college player.

Roeckel, J. *Unforgotten Days.* arr. de Ville, Paul. Carl Fischer Inc. 1906. Out of print. See: de Ville, Paul, *Pleasant Hours,* under "Tuba and Keyboard Collections."

Roikjer, Kjell. *Andante,* Op 65. Imudico Musikforlaget. $14.00. 3:36. IV–V. F₁–f'. Dedicated to Michael Lind. Andante sostenuto. Premiered in 1974. Lyrical ballad in 3/2 using the full range of the horn. Depending on tempo, requires flexibility. Good recital material.

Roikjer, Kjell. *Capriccio for Tuba and Orchestra,* Op 66. Imudico Musikforlaget. 1974. $18.00. See listing under "Music for Tuba and Orchestra." See review in *T.U.B.A. Journal,* Vol. 6, no. 2, p. 10.

Roikjer, Kjell. *Koncert med orkester,* Op. 61. Imudico Musikforlaget. $16.00. See listing under "Music for Tuba and Orchestra."

Roikjer, Kjell. *Sonate for Tuba og Klaver,* Op. 68. Imudico Musikforlaget. 1981. 17:10 (6:30, 6:30, 4:10). IV. A₁–e♭'. Dedicated to Michael Lind. Premiered in 1976. Allegro moderato ed energico; Molto lento e pesante; Allegro energico e con agevolezza. Not too technical. Great on F tuba, playable on lower instruments. Good recital material. See: Bird, Gary, ed., *Program Notes for the Solo Tuba.*

Roikjer, Kjell. *Tonal Miniature Pieces,* Op. 75. Edition Edtved. 1983. $8.80. 25.00 IV–V. F₁–e'. Dedicated to Michael Lind. Composed 1981. Fourteen pieces, each in a different major key and its relative minor. Very musical and fun to play. Strong technique required.

Roikjer, Kjell. *Twenty-Four Pieces for Tuba and Piano.* Edition Edtved. 1981. Dedicated to Michael Lind. Twenty-four pieces in all major and minor keys.

Roitershteny. *Concertiya Sonatina.* 1986. 4:38. III–IV. F₁–d♭'. Except for some higher tessitura, level III. Cut time throughout. Light, very tonal melody; no hard rhythms. Good introduction to higher range for intermediate student.

Rollé. *Concerto brillant.* Éditions Salabert. n. d. Out of print.

Rollin, Robert. *Sonatina for Tuba and Piano.* Seesaw Music Corporation Publishers. 1986. $15.00. 6:33 (2:26, 4:07). IV–V. D₁–a♯. Commissioned by John Turk. Modern writing. Strong technique, modern melodic concept, and strong accompanist required. Low-range work. Second movement in 3/2 time.

Rollinson, T. H. *Columbia.* arr. Buchtel, Forrest L. Neil A. Kjos Music Company. 1958. Out of print. III. B₁–g. Theme and variations on *Columbia, the Gem of the Ocean.* Much triple tonguing. Traditional polka style.

Rollinson, T. H. *Hear Our Prayer—Paraphrase.* arr. Weber, Carl. J. W. Pepper and Son. 1914. Out of print. See: Weber, Carl, *Nineteen Solos For E♭ Bass with Piano Accompaniment,* under "Tuba and Keyboard Collections."

Rollinson, T. H. *Rocked in the Cradle of the Deep.* Cundy-Bettoney/Carl Fischer Inc. 1881 (oldest copyright date in this section). Out of print. 7:55. III–IV. B♭₁–c' (e'). Theme and variations intended for E♭ tuba. Recorded by Tim Lawhern.

Ronnes, Robert. *Adventure for Tuba and Piano.*

Rose, Phil. S. *Chromatic Concert Polka.* arr. Weber, Carl. J. W. Pepper and Son. 1914. Out of print. See: Weber, Carl, *Nineteen Solos for E♭ Bass with Piano Accompaniment,* under "Tuba and Keyboard Collections."

Ross, Walter. *Azure Etudes.* Mark Tezak. 1982. $6.00. 3:56. IV. G₁–d'. With the exception of last note (G₁), all middle to upper tessitura. Melodic, reflective tune. Mostly slurred phrases. Requires vocal approach.

Ross, Walter. *Tuba Concerto.* Boosey and Hawkes, Inc. 1975. $18.50. For R. Winston Morris. Composed in 1973. See listing under "Music for Tuba and Band." Also see: Bird, Gary, ed., *Program Notes for the Solo Tuba.* Recorded by Harvey Phillips.

Ross, Walter. *Villanella.* TUBA Press. 1992. $8.00. IV. C–b♭. For Mark Nelson. Two contrasting section: Lento affettuoso, a very lyrical 4/4 introduction; and Allegro burlesco in 6/8, which requires flexibility and lightness. Conservative range.

Rossini, Gioacchino. *Lord Preserve Me,* (*Stabat Mater*). arr. Ostrander, Allen. Editions Musicus. 1959. $3.00. 2:00. II–III. A_1–e. Dotted eighth-and-sixteenth-note slurred passages must be crisp, especially to contrast with triplets near the end.

Rossini, Gioacchino. *Two Rossini Pieces.* arr. Lethbridge, Lionel. Bernel/ R. Smith and Co Ltd. 1991. $16.75. 4:15 (2:56, 1:19). III. Bb_1–bb. *Softly, Softly,* from *The Barber of Seville,* has a light bouncing feel to it in 4/4 time. *The Dance* , from *Soirées Musicales,* is a quick-spirited Allegro con brio movement in 6/8 in Bb major and minor. Good recital material.

Rossini, Gioacchino. *Una Voce M'Ha Colpito,* from *L'inganno Fortunato.* arr. Hume, Lieut. J. Ord. L. F. Boosey and Hawkes, Inc. 1913. Out of print. 5:00. III. Bb_1–f. Andante: sixteenth-note triplets and 32nd-note figures need to be treated in a recitativo way. Allegro vivace: has cadenza-like, recitativo passages and triplet passages.

Rothgarber, Herbert. *Dialogue for Tuba and Piano.* Theodore Presser Company. 1971. $4.00. 7:30. IV–V. F_1–e'. Dedicated to David Winograd. Contemporary dissonant melodic language. Mixed meter.

Rottler, Werner. *Konzert für Tuba und Orchestra.* Available from Tuba Center. 1980. For Robert Tucci. See listing under "Music for Tuba and Orchestra."

Rottler, Werner. *Nachtstück.* Available from the composer. IV. Manuscript.

Rottler, Werner. *Sonatina für Tuba und Klavier,* Op. 14. Hofmeister. 1993. 7:46. IV–V. D_1–f'. Für Robert Tucci. Composed in 1983. Very musical piece requiring some quick articulations, flexibility, wide range, and playfulness. Good recital piece.

Rougeron, Philippe. *Valse Nostalgique.* Gérard Billaudot. 1979. $2.50. 1:48. II. (C) A–c'. "Pour Tuba (ou Trombone) et Piano." For French tuba. Cute waltz with no technical problems. Good recital material. See: Thompson/Lemke, *French Music for Low Brass Instruments.* Also see review in *T.U.B.A. Journal,* Vol. 9, no. 1, p. 14.

Rougnon, Paul. *Prière.* Alphonse Leduc Editions Paris. $6.75. Saxhorn Sib et Piano.

Rougnon, Paul. *Sicilienne.* Alphonse Leduc Editions Paris. $5.85. "Saxhorn Sib et Piano."

Rougnon, Paul. *Valse Lente.* Alphonse Leduc Editions Paris. $7.95. II. C (E)–c'. Instruments en Sib et Piano.

Rubank. See listing under "Tuba and Keyboard Collections."

Rubinstein, Anton. *Be Not Shy, My Pretty One,* Op. 34, no. 11. tr. Gershenfeld, Mitchell. Medici Music Press. 1985. 1:42. II–III. Eb–f. In Ab major in 3/4 time. A few sixteenth notes; no technical problems. See: Gershenfeld, Mitchell, *Medici Masterworks Solos, Volume 1,* under "Tuba and Keyboard Collections."

Rubinstein, A. *A Persian Song.* arr. Lebedev, A. Military Band Masters Faculty of Moscow Conservatiore. 1971. See: Lebedev, A., *Collection of Pieces for Tuba "Es" and Piano,* under "Tuba and Keyboard Collections."

Rubinstein, A. *Romance.* ed. Melnikov, S. Moscow: Military Band Masters Institute. 1957. See: Melnikov, S., *Pieces for Tuba and Piano,* under "Tuba and Keyboard Collections."

Rubinstein, A. *Romance.* arr. de Ville, Paul. Carl Fischer Inc. 1906. Out of print. See: de Ville, Paul, *Pleasant Hours,* under "Tuba and Keyboard Collections."

Rubinstein, A. *Song from the Cycle "Persian Songs."* ed. Melnikov, S. Moscow: Military Band Masters Institute. 1957. See: Melnikov, S., *Pieces for Tuba and Piano,* under "Tuba and Keyboard Collections."

Ruckauer, H. *Der fidele Bassist.* Rundel. II. Piano reduction. For tuba and band.

Rueff, Jeanine. *Concertstück.* Alphonse Leduc Editions Paris. 1960. $16.85. 6:45. V. Ab_1–a'. À Paul Bernard, Professeur au Conservatoire National Supérieur de Musique. "Pour Saxhorn basse Sib ou Tuba ut ou Trombone basse et Piano." For French tuba. Some tenor clef. See: Thompson/Lemke, *French Music for Low Brass Instruments.*

Ruelle, F. *Prélude et Danse Guerrière.* Edition Andel Uitgaven.

Rufeisen, Arie. *A Short Suspense Story.* Kibutz Movement League of Composers. Recorded by Adi Hershko.

Ruff, D. *Concert Piece.* Moscow: Muzyka. 1976. See: Guzii, V., *Pieces for Tuba and Piano,* under "Tuba and Keyboard Collections."

Russell, Armand. *Suite Concertante.* Accura Music. 1963. $20.50. See listing under "Music for Tuba in Mixed Ensemble." Also see: Bird, Gary, ed., *Program Notes for the Solo Tuba.* Recorded by Floyd Cooley.

Russell, H. *The Old Sexton.* arr. Prendiville, Harry. A. Squire. 1888. Out of print. 1:10. II. Db–f. "Eb Bass; or, tuba With Piano or Organ Accompaniment (ad lib.)." Some syncopation and sixteenth-eighth (reverse) type dotted rhythms. See: Prendiville, Harry, *Six Popular Solos,* under "Tuba and Keyboard Collections."

Sabathil, Ferd. *Divertissement,* Op. 54. arr. Wilson, Don. Gamble Hinged Music Co. 1938. Out of print. 8:45. III. G_1–f. Solo for BBb tuba. Long, old-style melodramatic solo. Intermediate technical requirements. Two cadenzas, scales.

Sacco, P. Peter. *Fantasy for Tuba and Piano.* Western International Music. 1972. Out of print. 4:42. IV–V. G_1–b. Modern melodic language. Meter changes; possible double tonguing, depending on tempo; muted passages. See review in *T.U.B.A. Journal,* Vol. 6, no. 2, p. 9.

Saglietti, Corrado Maria. *Concerto for Tuba and Four Horns.* Éditions BIM. 1985. Publication pending,

1993. See listing under "Music for Tuba in Mixed Ensemble."

Saint-Saëns, Camille. *Allegro.* trans. Dishinger, Ronald Christian. CPP/Belwin, Inc. 1981. 1:59. I. A_1–B♭. Limited range, just a few eighth notes. Some easy slurring, tenutos. Beginning solo; no technical problems. See: Lamb, Jack, *Classic Festival Solos,* under "Tuba and Keyboard Collections."

Saint-Saëns, Camille. *Cavatina.* arr. Mitjagina, V. Muzyka: Moscow. 1969. 4:53. III–IV. E_1–d♭'. Good transcription in D♭ and E major (3/4 time). Wide range but few outstanding technical problems. See: Mitjagina, V., ed., *Pieces for Tuba and Piano,* under "Tuba and Keyboard Collections."

Saint-Saëns, Camille. *Concert Piece.* ed. Melnikov, S. Moscow: Military Band Masters Institute. 1957. See: Melnikov, S., *Pieces for Tuba and Piano,* under "Tuba and Keyboard Collections."

Saint-Saëns, Camille. *Elephant from "Carnival of Animals."* arr. Yasumoto, Hiroyuki. Toa Music International Co. 1986. 0:51. III–IV. E_1–e. Allegretto pomposo. Listen to original bass solo for conception. Needs a light approach, with not too heavy an elephant. See: Yasumoto, Hiroyuki, *Tuba Volume #1,* under "Tuba and Keyboard Collections." Recorded by Hiroyuki Yasumoto. A different arrangement recorded by Zdzislaw Piernik.

Saint-Saëns, Camille. *L'Éléphant (Der Elefant),* aus *Der Karneval der Tiere.* Hofmeister. 1993. 1:25. III. G_1–e♭. Famous string bass solo. In E♭ major and in 3/8 time. See: Meschke, Dieter, *Zum Üben und Vorspielen/B-Tuba,* under "Tuba and Keyboard Collections."

Saint-Saëns, Camille. *Romance,* Op. 36. arr. Graham, James. TUBA Press. 1991. IV. E–c'. Moderato. Originally for horn. Very lyrical transcription. See: Graham, James, *Concert Music for Tuba,* under "Tuba and Keyboard Collections."

Salvationist Publishing & Supplies, Ltd. See listing under "Tuba and Keyboard Collections."

Salzedo, Leonard. *Sonata,* Op. 93. Chester Music Ltd. London. 1984. $13.95. 11:44 (3:46, 1:31, 2:09, 4:18. IV–V. E_1–g'. To John Fletcher. Allegro; Lentissimo; Allegretto; Vivace. First performed on December 7, 1980 by John Fletcher, tuba, and Robert Noble, piano, in "Music at the Green," at Southgate Music Club. Modern melodic language. Wide range. Large work requiring flexibility, strong technique, and musicality. A bit of tenor clef in part.

Samonov, A. *Good Night.* ed. Lebedev, A. Moscow: Muzyka. 1984. 0:57. II. F–f. Lyrical lullaby in 2/4 time. A few eighth notes, mostly half notes. See: Lebedev, A., *Tuba Tutor, Vol. 1,* under "Tuba and Keyboard Collections."

Samonov, A. *Grandfather Is Dancing.* ed. Lebedev, A. Moscow: Muzyka. 1984. 0:33. II–III. (A♭$_1$) E♭–a♭. Some accidentals and "dissonant" melody. See: Lebedev, A., *Tuba Tutor, Vol. 1,* under "Tuba and Keyboard Collections."

Saul, Walter B., III. *De Profundis.* TUBA Press. 1983. $5.00. 5:00. IV. F_1–a. Largo misterioso. Composed December 1983, Misenheimer, NC. From Psalm 130:1–4. Dark textural piece requiring some quick articulations. Conservative modern melodic language. Good recital piece.

Sauter, Eddie. *Conjectures.* Mentor Music Inc. 1968. $6.00. Written for Harvey Phillips. Piano accompaniment with optional percussion. Originally titled *Harvey Phillips—Tuba.* See listing under "Music for Tuba and Band." Recorded by Harvey Phillips.

Scarlatti, Alessandro. *Aria* from the opera *Tigraine.* arr. Barnes, Clifford P. Jack Spratt Music Co. 1965. $3.00. 2:30. II–III. B♭$_1$–f. No technical problems. Some slurring; vocal approach necessary.

Scarlatti, Allessandro. *Sento Nel Core.* Comp. and ed. Phillips, Harry I. Shawnee Press Inc. 1967. 4:17. II. C♯–d. Adagio. Lyrical, slurred transcription in 3/4 time. Good recital material. See: Phillips, Harry I., *Eight Bel Canto Songs,* in this section.

Scarmolin, A. Louis. *Introduction and Dance.* Ludwig Music Publishing Company. 1960. $4.50. 3:00. III. B♭$_1$–f. "For Tuba, Cello, String Bass and Piano." Good opportunity to show off advanced-beginner technique.

Scarmolin, A. Louis. *Polka Giocoso.* C. L. Barnhouse Company. 1953. $3.50. 3:30. III. C–f. Polka style solo with a somewhat tricky "road map" of D. S. al coda, etc. Mostly stepwise motion.

Scarmolin, A. Louis. *Pomp and Dignity.* Pro Art Publications. 1941. Out of print. 4:25. II–III. G_1–e. Maestoso. Some triplets in stepwise motion.

Schaefer, August H. *Gay Caballero.* The Fillmore Bros. Co. 1941. Out of print. 5:00. F♯$_1$–f. "Solo for Tuba, Baritone, (Bass or Treble) and B♭ Saxophones." Good opportunity to show off advanced-beginner/intermediate technique.

Schedrin, R. *Variations from the Ballet Konick-Gorbunoch.* ed. Lebedev, A. Moscow: Muzyka. 1986. 1:37. IV. (E♭$_1$) G_1–b♭. Requires flexibility and strong musical sense. See: Lebedev, A., *Tuba Tutor, Vol. 2,* under "Tuba and Keyboard Collections."

Schlemüller, Hugo. *Cradle Song.* arr. Price, J. S. Carl Fischer Inc. 1937. Out of print. 2:00. I. B♭$_1$–B♭. In 6/8 time with no technical problems.

Schlemüller, Hugo. *A Prayer.* arr. Price, J. S. Carl Fischer Inc. 1937. $2.50. 2:00. I. A_1–B♭. All half and whole notes. No technical problems. Ideal for beginner.

Schmidt, A. *Divertissement.* Edition Andel Uitgaven. 1974.

Schmidt, A. *Ostinato.* Edition Andel Uitgaven.

Schmidt, Ole. *Concerto for Tuba and Orchestra.* Chester Music Ltd. London. 1976. $26.95. See listing under "Music for Tuba and Orchestra.". Also see: Bird, Gary, ed., *Program Notes for the Solo Tuba.* Recorded by Michael Lind. See review in *T.U.B.A. Journal,* Vol. 7, no. 4, p. 26.

Schmidt, Ole. *Sonata for Tuba and Piano.* MS Publications.

Schmidt, William. *Serenade.* Western International Music. 1962. $7.00. 9:00. IV. F_1–c'. For Tommy Johnson. Romanza; Waltz; Dirge; March. Composed in 1958. Solid contemporary writing for tuba. See: Bird, Gary, ed., *Program Notes for the Solo Tuba.* Recorded by Rex Conner; John Thomas (Tommy) Johnson.

Schmidt, William. *Sonata.* Western International Music. 1984. $13.00. 17:19 (6:14, 5:15, 5:50). IV–V. F_1–g'. For Mel Culbertson. World premiere on May 24, 1982, by Mel Culbertson, tuba and Chantal de Buchy, piano, at the Paris Conservatory of Music. American premiere March 17, 1984 by Ron Davis, tuba, and Barbara Worsley, piano, at University of Southern California. Would rest best on F tuba. Meter changes, muted passages, glissandos. Flexibility and modern lyrical approach necessary. See review in *T.U.B.A. Journal,* Vol. 13, no. 2, p. 27. Also see: Bird, Gary, ed., *Program Notes for the Solo Tuba.*

Schmutz, Albert D. *Chorale Prelude.* Available from the composer. 1971. For tuba and organ.

Schneebiegl, Rolf. *Der Kellermeister.* Bosworth and Co. Ltd. 1979. See listing under "Music for Tuba and Band."

Scholtes, Walter. *My Tuba Solo.* Waterloo Music Company. 1950. 6:10. III. (A_1) Bb_1–ab. Traditional solo.

Scholtes, Walter, arr. *Rocked in the Cradle of the Deep.* Waterloo Music Company. 1950. Out of print. 5:00. II–III. (Ab_1) C–f. Theme and variations.

Schooley, John. *Serenata.* Heilman Music. 1976. $6.00. 6:36 (1:11, 2:03, 0:35, 1:39, 1:08). IV. (D_1) F_1–cb'. Dedicated to the Goals of T. U. B. A. *Intrada* (Allegro con spirito); *Air* (Andante e rubato); *Cabaletta* (Allegro); *Recitative* (Andante maestoso); *Paspy* (Allegretto e leggiero). First performed by Paul Kryzwicki at the 1970 Aspen Music Festival. Conservative contemporary melodic language. Lyrical and rhythmical playing. Some 5/8 and 7/8 meters. See review in *T.U.B.A. Journal,* Vol. 3, no. 3, p. 7.

Schoonenbeek, Kees. *Suite Concertante.* de haske muziekuitgave bv. 1990. 11:44. IV. Bb_1–bb. Four attacca movements: Allegretto; Allegro Giocoso; Valse lente; Allegro. Very lyrical, tonal, modern writing. Some meter changes. Last movement in 5/8 time. Requires quick articulations in spots. Good recital material.

Schrijver, Karel de. *Concertino.* Tierolff-Muziekcentrale. 1968. 8:40 (3:29, 2:19, 2:52). IV–V. F–bb'. "Voor Bariton-Trombone-Tuba Sib (Trombone-Euphonium Ut) met Piano Begeleiding" (not for contrabass tuba). Three movements. Very lyrical and technical solo for higher instrument. Strong technique and lyricism required.

Schrijver, Karel de. *Six Petits Morceaux.* Scherzando Editions Musicales.

Schroen, B. *Fantasie.* arr. Spencer, John. Cundy-Bettoney/Carl Fischer Inc. 1938. $4.00. 5:00. III. F_1–g. "Solo BBb Tuba." Several tempos and styles.

Schubert, Franz. *Ave Maria.* arr. Lebedev, A. Military Band Masters Faculty of Moscow Conservatiore. 1971. See: Lebedev, A., *Collection of Pieces for Tuba "Es" and Piano,* under "Tuba and Keyboard Collections."

Schubert, Franz. *By the Sea.* arr. de Ville, Paul. Carl Fischer Inc. 1906. Out of print. See: de Ville, Paul, *Pleasant Hours,* under "Tuba and Keyboard Collections."

Schubert, Franz. *Der Lindenbaum,* (*The Linden Tree*). arr. Fletcher, John. Chester Music Ltd. London. 1982. 3:10. II–III. D–g. Andante con moto. Expressive song in 3/4 time. Requires vocal approach. No technical problems. See: Fletcher, John, *Tuba Solos (Tuba in C), Volume One,* under "Tuba and Keyboard Collections."

Schubert, Franz. *Die böse Farbe.* tr. Feldman, Enrique C. Arizona University Music Press. 1987. 1:50. IV. B–eb'. Ziemlich geschwind (Allegro assai). Upper tessitura. Some flexibility required. See listing under "Tuba and Keyboard Collections."

Schubert, Franz. *Die liebe Farbe.* tr. Feldman, Enrique C. Arizona University Music Press. 1987. 1:55. III. d–d'. Etwas langsam (Poco Lento). Upper tessitura. No other technical problems. See listing under "Tuba and Keyboard Collections."

Schubert, Franz. *Entr'acte from "Rosamunde."* arr. Masso, George. Kendor Music, Inc. 1967. $5.50. 4:10. II. Eb–f. In 2/4 time. Some triplets, some slurring; no big technical problems. Good recital material.

Schubert, Franz. *Mein!* tr. Feldman, Enrique C. Arizona University Music Press. 1987. 4:58. IV. C–e'. Massig geschwind (Allegro moderato). Upper tessitura. Best on F tuba; endurance could be a factor with lower instrument. Some flexibility required. See listing under "Tuba and Keyboard Collections."

Schubert, Franz. *Moment Musical.* arr. Swanson, Ken. CPP/Belwin, Inc. 1970. See: CPP/Belwin, *Tuba Solos, Level Two,* under "Tuba and Keyboard Collections."

Schubert, Franz. *My Sweetheart's Eyes,* (*Geheimes*), Op. 14, no. 2, 1824. trans. Dishinger, Ronald Christian. Medici Music Press. 1990. $4.50. 1:53. II. C–e. In 2/4 time and in F major with no technical problems.

Schubert, Franz. *Ständchen.* arr. Yasumoto, Hiroyuki. Toa Music International Co. 1989. 3:10. IV. D–g'. Lovely transcription. High tessitura; best on F tuba. See: Yasumoto, Hiroyuki, *Tuba Volume #3,* under "Tuba and Keyboard Collections." Different arrangements recorded by Roger Bobo; The Contraband; Zdizislaw Piernik.

Schubert, Franz. *Swan Song,* (*My Last Abode*). arr. Ostrander, Allen. Editions Musicus. 1959. $3.00.

2:25. II. G_1–e♭. Several octave jumps and slurring; no other big technical problems.

Schubert, Franz. *Wohin?* tr. Feldman, Enrique C. Arizona University Music Press. 1987. 1:50. IV. B–e'. Maasig (Moderato). Upper tessitura. Some flexibility required. See listing under "Tuba and Keyboard Collections."

Schuller, Gunther. *Capriccio for Tuba and Small Orchestra.* Mentor Music Inc. 1969. See listing under "Music for Tuba and Orchestra." Also see: Bird, Gary, ed., *Program Notes for the Solo Tuba.* Recorded by Harvey Phillips.

Schumann, Robert. *Adagio and Allegro,* Op. 70. arr. Graham, James. TUBA Press. 1991. IV. B♭–e♭'. *Slow with expression; Quick, with animation.* Originally written for horn. See: Graham, James, *Concert Music for Tuba,* under "Tuba and Keyboard Collections." Recorded by Floyd Cooley; Eugene Dowling.

Schumann, Robert. *Fröhlicher Landmann.* arr. Schwotzer, Stephan. Hofmeister. 1993. 0:54. II–III. A_1–d. Frisch und munter. "Von der Arbeit zurückkehrend aus *Album für die Jugend,* Op. 68." Familiar tune in D major. See: Meschke, Dieter, *Zum Üben und Vorspielen/B-Tuba,* under "Tuba and Keyboard Collections."

Schumann, Robert. *The Happy Farmer (Variations from "Album for the Young").* arr. Wekselblatt, Herbert. G. Schirmer Inc. 1972. 1:30. III. C–f. Brisk and lively. Fun set of theme and (two) variations. Double tonguing possible, depending on tempo chosen. Some crisply articulated sixteenth-note repeated notes and stepwise passages. Good early intermediate material. See: Wekselblatt, Herbert, *First Solos for the Tuba Player,* under "Tuba and Keyboard Collections."

Schumann, Robert. *The Jolly Farmer Goes to Town.* arr. Bell, William J. Carl Fischer Inc. 1938. $3.50. 2:30. III–IV. G_1–a. Theme and variations. Optional triple tonguing passages. Recorded by William Bell.

Schumann, Robert. *The Jolly Peasant.* arr. Holmes, G. E. Rubank, Inc. 1939; published separately 1966, $2.00. 1:32. II–III. C–f. "Solo Tuba-E♭ or BB♭." Moderato. Short theme and variations. Mostly scalewise motion for sixteenth-note technical section. Very accessible to advanced beginner. See: Rubank, *Soloist Folio for Bass (E♭ or BB♭),* under "Tuba and Keyboard Collections."

Schumann, Robert. *The Merry Peasant, from "Album for the Young".* arr. Wastall, Peter. Boosey and Hawkes, Inc. 1985. 0:43. I–II. C–f. Nice arrangement of this classic tune. Good introduction to staccato and tenutos. Easy accompaniment. See: Wastall, Peter, *Learn As You Play Tuba,* under "Tuba and Keyboard Collections."

Schumann, Robert. *Romance No. 2.* arr. Werden, David R. Whaling Music Publishers. 1993. $8.00. 4:49. IV–V. C♯–c♯'. Arranged for euphonium, trombone, or tuba with piano. Lovely lyrical transcription. Mostly slurred; some skips of a tenth. Easy rhythms, some upper tessitura if played on lower tubas.

Schumann, Robert. *Romance No. 3.* arr. Perantoni, Daniel. Hal Leonard Publishing Corp. 1976. See: Perantoni, Daniel, *Master Solos, Intermediate Level,* under "Tuba and Keyboard Collections."

Schumann, Robert. *Sailors' Song,* from the *Album for the Young.* arr. Little, Donald C. CPP/Belwin, Inc. 1978. $4.00. 2:29. II. ($G_1$) A_1–e♭. Moderato. In 4/4 time and in G minor. Some eighth notes and some slurs. Variety of articulations: staccato, tenuto, accents. Lyrical approach very necessary. See review in *T.U.B.A. Journal,* Vol. 8, no. 1, p. 34. See: Lamb, Jack, *Solo Sounds for Tuba Levels 1–3, Vol. 1,* under "Tuba and Keyboard Collections."

Schumann, Robert. *Scenes from Childhood,* Op. 15. arr. Self, James. Bassett Hound Music. $15.00. 11:20 (1:35, 1:09, 0:55, 2:38, 1:03, 1:37, 2:23). IV–V. C♯–g'. *About Strange Lands and People; Curious Story; Important Event; The Poet Speaks; At the Fireside; Frightening; Reverie.* Composed in 1838. Very lyrical set of transcriptions utilizing a wide range. Recorded by James Self.

Schumann, Robert. *Träumerei.* arr. Yasumoto, Hiroyuki. Toa Music International Co. 1989. 1:44. III. F–e♭'. Beautiful lyrical transcription. Lies best on F tuba; playable on lower instrument. See: Yasumoto, Hiroyuki, arr., *Tuba Volume #2,* under "Tuba and Keyboard Collections." Different version recorded by Melton Tuba-Quartett ; Zdizislaw Piernik.

Schumann, Robert. *The Wild Horseman,* from *Album for the Young.* arr. Wekselblatt, Herbert. G. Schirmer Inc. 1972. 0:32. III. D–g. Fast. Short (even shorter depending on tempo chosen) romp in 6/8 time. Requires some flexibility. See: Wekselblatt, Herbert, *First Solos for the Tuba Player,* under "Tuba and Keyboard Collections."

Schumann, Robert. *Your Ring on my Finger, Frauenliebe und Leben,* Op. 42, no. 4. trans. Dishinger, Ronald Christian. Medici Music Press. 1990. $4.50. 2:01. II–III. C–f. Innig (Passionate). Well-transcribed solo with some slurring, some accidentals.

Schwartz, Elliott. *Flame.* American Composers Edition, Inc. 1988. 10:00. V. E♭–g♯'. Commissioned by Scott Watson, with the support of a University of Kansas research grant. Completed June 1988, Brunswick, ME. Modern writing and notation. Pitches based on the letters *FLAME, CHAR,* and *SEAR.* Spatial/proportional notation; each section fifteen seconds. Sung and spoken material for tubist. Piano also has contemporary techniques.

Schwartz, Jean, and Jerome, William. *Chinatown, My Chinatown.* arr. Boyd, Bill. Hal Leonard Publishing Corp. 1992. 0:34. I–II. B♭–D. Old jazz standard in cut time. Once through the melody in B♭

major. See: Daellenbach, Charles, *Book of Easy Tuba Solos,* under "Tuba and Keyboard Collections."

Schwotzer, Stephan, arr. *Altdeutscher Tanz (Narrentanz).* Hofmeister. 1993. 1:08. I–II. C–d. "Anonymus (um 1590)." No technical problems; quarter note is fastest rhythm. See: Meschke, Dieter, *Zum Üben und Vorspielen/B-Tuba,* under "Tuba and Keyboard Collections."

Scott, Kathleen. *Andante and Allegro.* Queen City Brass Publications/PP Music. 1984. $7.50. 5:13. IV. F_1–d'. Commissioned by Rodger Vaughan for his Fiftieth Birthday Tuba Recital. Composed 1981. Lyrical Andante section followed by moderately technical Allegro section. A few octave jumps; no big technical problems. Conventional tonal writing.

Scriabine, Alexander. *Etude.* arr. Lebedev, A. Military Band Masters Faculty of Moscow Conservatiore. 1971. See: Lebedev, A., *Collection of Pieces for Tuba "Es" and Piano,* under "Tuba and Keyboard Collections."

Scriabine, Alexander. *Romance.* arr. Graham, James. TUBA Press. 1991. III. E–a. Originally written for horn. See: Graham, James, *Concert Music for Tuba,* under "Tuba and Keyboard Collections."

Sear, Walter. *Sonatina for Tuba and Piano.* Cor Publishing Company. 1974. $5.00. 7:00. II–III. A_1–f. Original copyright date was 1969. Three movements. Major work for advanced beginner. Recorded by Ronald Davis; Karl Megules.

Séguin, Pierre. *Cortège, (Procession).* Alphonse Leduc Editions Paris. 1984. $5.45. D–f'. For French tuba. See: Thompson/Lemke, *French Music for Low Brass Instruments.*

Séguin, Pierre. *Tubavardage, (Tuba Chatter).* Alphonse Leduc Editions Paris. 1987. $5.45. C–e♭'. For French Tuba. See: Thompson/Lemke, *French Music for Low Brass Instruments.*

Semler-Collery, Jules. *Barcarolle et Chanson Bachique, (Barcarolle and Drinking Song).* Alphonse Leduc Editions Paris. 1953. $12.80. IV. $B♭_1$–g♭'. À Paul Bernard. "Pour Tuba ut ou Contrebasse à Cordes ou Saxhorn basse Si♭ ou Trombone basse et Piano." For French tuba. See: Thompson/Lemke, *French Music for Low Brass Instruments.*

Semler-Collery, Jules. *Cantabile et divertissement pour tuba et orchestre.* Éditions Max Eschig. 1963. V. $B♭_1$–f♯'. "Reduction pour tuba (ou saxhorn basse) et piano." See: Thompson/Lemke, *French Music for Low Brass Instruments.*

Semler-Collery, Jules. *Deux Pièces brèves.* Éditions Max Eschig. 1973. IV. F_1–f♯'. For French tuba. See: Thompson/Lemke, *French Music for Low Brass Instruments.*

Semler-Collery, Jules. *Saxhornia.* Alphonse Leduc Editions Paris. 1959. $14.45. V. F_1–a♭'. *Cantus Recitativo; Tarentella.* "Pour Saxhorn-basse Si♭ ou Tuba ut ou Trombone basse et Piano." For French tuba. See: Thompson/Lemke, *French Music for Low Brass Instruments.*

Semler-Collery, Jules. *Tubanova.* Éditions Max Eschig. 1967. 6:15. V. $A♭_1$ (E♭)–g'. À Paul Bernard, Professeur au Conservatoire National Supérieur de Musique de Paris en toute amitié. Andantino espressivo; Allegretto spiritoso. "Pour Tuba ou Saxhornbasse Si♭ ou Trombone-basse ou Contrebasse Si♭ ou Contrebasse à Cordes et Piano." "Solo de Concours." For French tuba. See: Thompson/Lemke, *French Music for Low Brass Instruments.*

Senaillé, Jean Baptiste. *Allegro Spiritoso.* arr. Jacobs, Wesley. Encore Music Publishers. 1990. $5.50. 2:49. IV. G_1–c'. Très vif. Similar to Catelinet arrangement (below) but in A minor. Some octave changes and a few notes left out to facilitate tuba breathing requirements. No ornamentation included.

Senaillé, Jean Baptiste. *Allegro Spiritoso.* arr. Thurston, Richard E. Southern Music Company. 1992. $4.50. 2:18. IV. C–a (a'). Third movement of Sonata in D minor. This arrangement in C minor. Some ornamentation included. Very quick indicated tempo (120) requiring quick articulations.

Senaillé, Jean Baptiste. *Courante.* arr. Goudenhooft, André, piano realizations Maillard, Augustin. Gérard Billaudot. 1989. $9.50. 2:30. IV. G_1–b. "Pour le trombone basse et le tuba basse. Extraite de la 8e Sonate, pour violon." Packaged with *Sarabande* by Leclair, Jean-Marie. Flexibility and quick articulations. See: Thompson/Lemke, *French Music for Low Brass Instruments.*

Senaillé, Jean Baptiste. *In Lively Spirits.* Hopkinson, Michael E. Kirklees Music. 1978. A reworking of J. B. Senaillé's *Andante and Allegro Spiritoso* for E♭ Bass. See: Hopkinson, Michael E., *In Lively Spirits,* in this section.

Senaillé, Jean Baptiste. *Introduction and Allegro Spiritoso.* arr. Catelinet, Philip. Hinrichsen Edition. 1964. $8.40. 2:49 (1:03, 1:46). IV. $B♭_1$–d'. Andante; Allegro Spiritoso . "For Tuba (B. C.), Euphonium/Trombone (T. C. and B. C.), Bass E♭ (T. C.) and Piano." Two attacca sections. Andante: very lyrical writing with several e♭ to f trills; all slurred phrases. Allegro spiritoso in B♭ minor; metronome marking quicker than other arrangements in this section (132) requires strong technique, both articulation and flexibility. Good recital material.

Senon, G. *Elementarité.*

Shaughnessy, Robert. *Concertino for Tuba and String Orchestra.* Peer-Southern Organization. 1969. $10.00. See listing under "Music for Tuba and Orchestra."

Shekov, Ivan. *Prelude und Scherzo für Tuba und Klavier.* Blasmusikverlag Fritz Schultz GmbH. 1986. 4:33 (2:48, 1:45). III. G_1–f. Prelude (Andante); Scherzo (Allegro). Treble and bass clef parts included. Some accidentals, otherwise no technical problems. Prelude is mostly lyrical with modern tonal writing. Scherzo is playful with mostly articulated passages.

Shield. *The Friar of Orders Gray*. arr. Prendiville, Harry. A. Squire. 1888. Out of print. 1:25. II–III. (Bb₁) C–f. "Eb Bass; or, tuba With Piano or Organ Accompaniment, (ad lib.)." In 6/8 time. Spirited solo with a nautical feel. One trill. See: Prendiville, Harry, *Six Popular Solos*, under "Tuba and Keyboard Collections."

Shostakovitch, Dimitri. *Adagio for Tuba and Piano*. Recorded by Roger Bobo.

Shostakovitch, Dimitri. *Polka from "The Age of Gold."* arr. Wekselblatt, Herbert. G. Schirmer Inc. 1964. 2:17. IV–V. G₁–f. Allegretto. Fun transcription. Wide range combined with "Shostakovitch intervals" (tritones, sevenths, ninths, etc.) make for some technical challenges. Good encore piece. See: Wekselblatt, H., *Solos for the Tuba Player*, under "Tuba and Keyboard Collections."

Shostakovitch, Dimitri. *Romance*. arr. Lebedev, A. Military Band Masters Faculty of Moscow Conservatiore. 1971. See: Lebedev, A., *Collection of Pieces for Tuba "Es" and Piano*, under "Tuba and Keyboard Collections."

Sibbing, Robert. *Sonata for Tuba and Piano*. Theodore Presser Company. 1973. $12.00. 10:30 (4:00, 3:50, 2:40). IV. F₁–c¹. For Kent Campbell. Written in Quincy, IL, November, 1963. Allegro Moderato; Larghetto; Allegro Giocoso. Very playable recital material. Good combination of lyricism and rhythm. Uses all ranges of the bass tuba. See: Bird, Gary, ed., *Program Notes for the Solo Tuba*. Recorded by Daniel Perantoni.

Sibelius, Jean. *Finlandia*. arr. Boyd, Bill, and ed. Daellenbach, Charles. Hal Leonard Publishing Corp. 1992. 1:06. I. Eb–c. In Eb major. Only one eighth-note; easy rhythms. Comes with practice/performance cassette. See: Daellenbach, Charles, *Book of Beginning Tuba Solos*, under "Tuba and Keyboard Collections."

Sibelius, Jean. *Finlandia*. arr. Jacobs, Wesley. Encore Music Publishers. 1:00. I–II. D–B. With dignity. In D major. With exception of key, level I. Limited range, some slurring. The main tune from *Finlandia*. See listing under "Tuba and Keyboard Collections."

Siebert, Edrich. *Bombastic Bombardon*. Molenaar. 1952. III. Piano Reduction. See listing under "Music for Tuba and Band."

Siebert, Edrich. *Dear to My Heart*. Studio Music Company. 1972. $14.00. See listing under "Music for Tuba and Band."

Siekmann, Frank H. *Parable for Tuba and Piano*. Manuscript. 1993. 3:51. III. Bb₁–g. Stately; not too demanding, limited range, intermediate solo. Good introduction to cadenzas, trill from A to Bb; brief passage in Db major.

Siennicki, Edmund J. *Happy Song*. Ludwig Music Publishing Company. 1990. $3.50. 1:52. I. Bb₁–Bb. Written for a variety of solo instruments. Easy piano accompaniment. Simple tune in Bb major (4/4 time)

with no technical problems. Quarter note is fastest rhythm.

Siennicki, Edmund J. *Harvest Waltz*. Ludwig Music Publishing Company. 1987. $2.95. 1:40. I. C–A. Written for a variety of solo instruments. Limited range. Waltz in C major in 3/4 time. Some dotted rhythms; some slurs. No other technical problems. Easy piano accompaniment. See review in *T.U.B.A. Journal*, Vol. 18, no. 4, p. 15.

Siennicki, Edmund J. *Memphis Ridge*. See review in *T.U.B.A. Journal*, Vol. 9, no. 4, p. 33.

Siennicki, Edmund J. *The Rooster*. Ludwig Music Publishing Company. 1990. $3.50. 2:07. I. Bb₁–Bb. Written for a variety of solo instruments. Beginning solo in 4/4 time with quarter note as fastest rhythm. A few slurs, a few tenutos; no technical problems.

Siennicki, Edmund J. *The Swan*. Ludwig Music Publishing Company. 1990. $3.50. 1:56. I. C–Bb. Limited-range solo in 3/4 time. Some slurring; a few dotted-quarter-and-eighth-note rhythms; no technical problems. Written for a variety of solo instruments.

Sikora, Elzbieta. *Il Viaggio 1 per tuba solo con pianoforte*. Recorded by Zdizislaw Piernik.

Simon, Frank. *Zillertal*. Rubank, Inc. 1974. Out of print. 4:13. III–IV. Bb₁–g (bb). To Harold Walters. Old-style technical solo involving several different meters and technical challenges, including triple tonguing.

Sivelov, Niklas. *Sonata for Tuba and Piano*. Recorded by Oystein Baadsvik.

Šivic, Pavle. *Pièce de Concerte*. Available from Igor Krlvokapic.

Skolnik, Walter. *Sonata*. Theodore Presser Company. 1985. $8.50. 10:00. IV. F♯₁–c¹. Pesante; Sostenuto; Allegretto. Conservative modern writing. Good introduction to contemporary tonal melody. Some meter changes.

Skolnik, Walter. *Valse Caprice*. Theodore Presser Company. 1973. $2.50. 2:32. III–IV. F₁–g. For tuba or string bass and piano. Completed August 1973, New York. Both solo parts included. One-movement work in 3/4 time. Fun tonal writing. Some flexibility needed; no big technical problems. See review in *T.U.B.A. Journal*, Vol. 1, no. 2, p. 10.

Smedvig, Egil. *Toga Virilis*. Saga Music Press. 1984. $5.50. 4:00. III. (Bb₁) C–g. To Samuel Pilafian. Written for tuba or bassoon and piano. Cut solo with optional cadenza. A few quartel moves in cadenza; no big technical problems.

Smironova, T. *A Joke*, Op. 18, no. 4. ed. Lebedev, A. Moscow: Muzyka. 1986. 1:47. III–IV. G₁–c¹. Alternating 2/4 and 3/4 time with some "joking" lines. See: Lebedev, A., *Tuba Tutor Vol. 2*, under "Tuba and Keyboard Collections."

Smironova, T. *Sonata*. ed. Voronov, G. Moscow: Muzyka. 1984. See: Voronov, G., *Works for Tuba and Piano by Russian Composers*, under "Tuba and Keyboard Collections."

Smironova, T. *A Tale.* ed. Voronov, G. Moscow: Muzyka. 1984. See: Voronov, G., *Works for Tuba and Piano by Russian Composers,* under "Tuba and Keyboard Collections."

Smith, Claude T. *Ballad and Presto Dance.* Wingert-Jones Music, Inc. 1988. $6.00. See listing under "Music for Tuba and Band." Recorded by Robert Daniel.

Smith, David E., arr. *Away in a Manger.* David E. Smith Publications. 1985. $2.50. 2:27. II. Bb$_1$–eb (f). Simple solo in 3/4 time with some slurring; no other technical problems.

Smith, David E., arr. *The Cross of Jesus.* David E. Smith Publications. 1987. $4.50. 3:59. III. Ab$_1$–bb. Several different keys, meters, and textures within this solo. A few flashy 32nd-note scales and possible triple tonguing near the end, depending on tempo. Good showcase solo for intermediate player.

Smith, David E., arr. *Hallelujah! What a Saviour!* David E. Smith Publications. 1988. $2.50. 1:46. II. D–d. Theme-and-variations style. Some slurring; no big technical problems.

Smith, David E., arr. *Praise Him, All Ye Little Children.* David E. Smith Publications. 1985. $2.50. 1:25. I. Bb$_1$–Bb. Anonymous. Solo in Bb major (4/4 time) with no technical problems. Quarter note is fastest rhythm.

Smith, David E., arr. *Stand Up, Stand Up Jesus.* David E. Smith Publications. 1985. $3.50. 3:24. II–III. (C) Eb–f (g). Optional octave change eases difficulty. Some technical articulations.

Smith, David E., arr. *'Tis So Sweet to Trust in Jesus.* David E. Smith Publications. 1988. $2.50. 2:09. I–II. Bb$_1$–c (e). Easy rhythms; one dotted rhythm. Some slurring. Modulates between F, Eb, and back to F major.

Smith, David E., arr. *We Gather Together.* David E. Smith Publications. 1984. $2.50. 1:58. I–II. A$_1$–d. Netherlands folk song. Simple rhythms in 3/4 time. Some slurring. No technical problems.

Smith, David E., arr. *Young Tuba Soloist.* See listing under "Tuba and Keyboard Collections."

Smith, Douglas, arr. *I Wonder As I Wander.* David E. Smith Publications. 1989. $3.50. 3:06. II. Bb$_1$–f. Solo in 3/4 time and Bb and Db major. Some slurring; no big technical problems.

Smith, Glenn. *Salicastrum.* Seesaw Music Corporation Publishers. 1992. $11.00. 8:23. V. Bb$_2$–a'. For John Turk. Completed Bloomington, IN, 1971. Modern writing. Very strong technique required. Multiphonics, muted passage, very quick articulations, optional circular breathing, rhythmic challenges. Difficult piano part.

Smith, Kile. *Sonata for Tuba and Piano.* Manuscript. 1986. 12:15 (4:25, 2:48, 5:02). IV–V. F$_1$–f'. For Brian Brown. Tonal modern melodic language. Strong technique required. Low slurred articulations as well as high melodic writing. Flexibility needed. Some meter shifting throughout. Good recital material.

Smolanoff, Michael. *Set of Three,* Op. 17. Southern Music Company. 1973. $2.50. 6:46 (3:27, 2:09, 1:10). IV. F#$_1$–c'. First movement in slow tempo with eighth note as beat; modern melody and harmony. Second movement in slow tempo again with lyrical modern writing. Third movement is a bit quicker, with syncopation and some easy meter changes. See review in *T.U.B.A. Journal,* Vol. 1, no. 1, p. 7.

Snyder, Randall. *Soundpiece.* Available from the composer. 1970. 3:00. V. C$_1$–f'. Contemporary writing with intricate rhythms and dissonant intervals. Slow tempo.

Solomon, Edward S. *One Tough Tuba.* Southern Music Company. 1991. $2.50. 2:07. II–III. Bb$_1$–e. Easy jazz/swing style. Eighth notes should be "swung" like triplets. Some syncopations; some accidentals. No big technical problems.

Soule, Edmund F. *Suite for Tuba and Piano.* TUBA Press. 1980. $12.00. 12:32 (4:19, 4:35, 3:38). IV–V. Eb$_1$–g'. Written for Eb tuba. Written for David Grosvenor. Molto moderato; Adagio; Marcia moderato, ma vigoroso. Completed modern writing. Technical challenges include wide range, meter changes, tricky rhythms.

Sousa, John Philip. *Stars and Stripes Forever.* arr. Ostling, Acton. CPP/Belwin, Inc. 1969. 0:35. I–II. Bb$_1$–bb. March tempo. In cut time, fastest rhythm is quarter note. Melody of last strain of march only (Trio section) with melody altered a bit to fit into conservative range. A few slurs, a few accidentals. No technical problems. See: CPP/Belwin, Inc., *Tuba Solos, Level One,* and Ostling, Acton, *Tuba (Bass) Soloist, Level One,* under "Tuba and Keyboard Collections."

Southwell, George. *My Tuba Solo.* arr. Di Ianni, Aldo. Volkwein Bros. 1954. See listing under "Music for Tuba and Band."

Sowerby, Leo. *Chaconne.* Carl Fischer Inc. 1938. $3.25. 4:47. III. Bb$_1$–bb. Continually metamorphosing set of variations. Lyrical playing combined with technical demands include slurring and some scalelike passages with quick articulations. Good intermediate solo. Recorded by Ron Davis.

Spaniola, Joseph. *Letters from a Friend.* TUBA Press. 1992. $8.00. 12:00 (3:37, 5:53, 2:40). IV. A$_1$–c#'. Sleepless Nights; The Journey; The Hope of Tomorrow. For euphonium or tuba and piano. Modern impressionistic writing. Meter changes, flexibility, and modern melodic appreciation required.

Spillman, James E. *Flow Gently, Sweet Afton.* arr. Kinyon, John. M. Witmark and Sons. 1958. I. See listing under "Tuba and Keyboard Collections."

Spillman, Robert. *Concerto.* Editions Musicus. 1962. $14.00. 8:00. IV. E$_1$–f'. High tessitura. Solid tonal contemporary writing. Requires strong technique.

Spillman, Robert. *Two Songs.* Editions Musicus. 1963. $8.50. 5:00. IV. Gb$_1$–e'. For Roger Bobo. Solid piece. Two numbered movements. Moderate range—only one section up to e'. Second song in

3/2 time. Good recital material. Recorded by Roger Bobo.

Spohr, Ludwig. *Adagio.* arr. Evans, Mark. Musikverlag Barbara Evans.

Sponholtz. *Peace of Mind.* arr. de Ville, Paul. Carl Fischer Inc. 1906. Out of print. See: de Ville, Paul, *Pleasant Hours,* under "Tuba and Keyboard Collections."

St. Clair, Floyd P. *Golden Days (Serenade).* J. E. Agnew. 1931. Out of print. 1:25. II. Bb₁–f. "Solo Tuba Eb or BBb." Sounds like an old school song. Simple rhythms, in 6/8 time.

Stabile, James. *Sonata for Tuba and Piano.* Western International Music. 1970. Out of print. III–IV. (C₁) G₁–db'. Allegro vivace; Moderato; Più mosso. Solid tonal writing for tuba and piano. Second and third movements attacca. Some quick articulations in first movement; second and third much less demanding.

Stamitz, Karl. *Rondo Alla Scherzo* (from *Clarinet Concerto in Eb*). arr. Wekselblatt, Herbert. G. Schirmer Inc. 1964. 4:34. IV. D–bb. Allegro Moderato. Generally higher tessitura—would be ideal on Eb (F) tuba, although very playable on lower instrument. Would develop steady mid-high range on BBb (CC) tuba. Some sixteenth-note runs. Could be challenging at fast tempo. Some grace notes. 6/8 time throughout. See: Wekselblatt, H., *Solos for the Tuba Player,* under "Tuba and Keyboard Collections."

Standford, Patric. *Invocation for Tuba and Piano.* Redcliffe. 1984. 5:19. IV. D₁–gb'. Also published for tuba and strings. Very melodic writing. Aside from full range, no major technical problems for the level.

Stanley, John. *Allegretto grazioso.* arr. Schwotzer, Stephan. Hofmeister. 1993. 1:35. II–III. C–d. In cut time and in F major. See: Meschke, Dieter, *Zum Uben und Vorspielen/B-Tuba,* under "Tuba and Keyboard Collections."

Staples, James. *Suite for Tuba and Piano.* Manuscript. 1989. 1:17, 3:16, 2:09, 3:06, 1:21. IV–V. E₁–g'. Commissioned by and dedicated to Gary Bird. Allegro scherzando; Adagio mesto; Moderato con moto; Adagio espressivo; Allegro vivace. Major work for tuba and piano requiring strong technique and endurance. Better on F tuba; high tessitura. Quick articulations throughout. One short muted passage. See: Bird, Gary, ed., *Program Notes for the Solo Tuba.*

Steckar, Franck. *Au Coeur de la Nuit.*

Steinquest, Eugene W. *Variations on a Theme of Roy Harris.* See review in *T.U.B.A. Journal,* Vol. 1, no. 3, p. 6.

Stekl, Konrad. *Sonate für Basstuba und Klavier (oder Bassposaune),* Op. 113a. Adler Musikverlag. 1976. 11:01 (4:08, 3:26, 3:27). IV–V. (B₁) C–eb' (g'). Three numbered movements. Contemporary technical and lyrical writing. Conventional melodic second movement. Upper tessitura; best on F tuba. See review in *T.U.B.A. Journal,* Vol. 8, no. 1, p. 28.

Stephens, Denzil. *The Dancing Tuba.* Obrasso Verlag AG. III. Piano reduction of tuba and brass band piece. See listing under "Music for Tuba and Band."

Stepovoi, J. *Cantabile.* arr. Lebedev, A. Military Band Masters Faculty of Moscow Conservatiore. 1971. See: Lebedev, A., *Collection of Pieces for Tuba "Es" and Piano,* under "Tuba and Keyboard Collections."

Steptoe, Roger. *Concerto for Tuba and Strings.* Stainer & Bell Ltd. London. 1983. $17.50. For James Gourlay. See listing under "Music for Tuba and Orchestra." See review in *T.U.B.A. Journal,* Vol. 18, no. 3, p. 19.

Stevens, Halsey. *Sonatina for Tuba and Piano.* Peer-Southern Organization. 1968. $6.50. 9:00. IV. G₁–f'. For Don Waldrop. Original copyright 1960. Originally called *Sonatina for Bass Tuba and Piano.* Mixed meter. "New Age" feel, lyrical solo with many colors. Opportunity for great expression. Part for trombone included. Upper tessitura; best on F tuba. Requires strong accompanist. See: Bird, Gary, ed., *Program Notes for the Solo Tuba.* Recorded by Donald Knaub; Daniel Perantoni; David Randolph; James Self.

Stevens, Thomas. *Variations in Olden Style (d'apres J. S. Bach).* Éditions BIM. 1990. "For Bozo the Great." Written in 1989 for Roger Bobo. See listing under "Music for Tuba and Orchestra." Recorded by Roger Bobo.

Stewart, Joseph. *Tuba.* Kendor Music, Inc. 1977. $6.50. Dedicated to Andy Peruzzini and the Maryvale High School Chorale. Comes with flexible Songsheet record with A. Peruzzini, tuba. See listing under "Music for Tuba and Band."

Stewart, Robert. *A Quiet Piece.* 1982. Commissioned by Rodger Vaughan.

Storm, Charles W. *Bold and Brave.* Lavell Publishing Co. 1961. Out of print. See listing under "Music for Tuba and Band."

Storm, Charles W. *Bouquet for Basses.* Volkwein Bros. 1954. Out of print. See listing under "Music for Tuba and Band."

Stoutamire, Albert L. *Legend.* Pro Art Publications/CPP/Belwin, Inc. 1970. Published separately. Out of print. 3:20. II–III. (G₁) A₁–f. Rather slow but with motion. In A minor and 4/4 time. Some triplets/duplets to be precise about. Some slurring, some optional low range. See: Lamb, Jack, *Classic Festival Solos,* under "Tuba and Keyboard Collections."

Stoutamire, Albert L. *Praeludium and Fughetta.* Ludwig Music Publishing Company. 1976. $4.00. 4:16. IV. (F₁) Bb₁–c'. Stately solo with lyrical Prelude section; "Pensively," in 4/4 time. Fugue, "Jocularly," is in cut time. No technical problems. See review in *T.U.B.A. Journal,* Vol. 1, no. 3, p. 3 and Vol. 7, no. 1, p. 9.

Stradella, Alessandro. *Pietà Signore!* comp. and ed. Phillips, Harry I. Shawnee Press Inc. 1967. 4:38.

II–III. (C) D–f. Andantino. Lyrical slurred transcription in 3/4 time. Minor key. Some trills and grace notes. See: Phillips, Harry I., *Eight Bel Canto Songs*, in this section. Recorded by Karl Megules.

Stradella, Alessandro. *Pietà, Signore!* tr. Felix, Clyde. Editions Musicus. 1960. $3.00. 4:00. III. F₁–g. No technical problems.

Stratton, Don. *In F.* Trombone Association Publishing. 1979. $7.00. 6:00. IV. F₁–d♭¹. For tuba and harpsichord. Completed 1979, Bangor, ME. Chance music. Six improvised sections lasting one minute each. Performers are requested not to rehearse or discuss the piece with anyone including each other before the performance. Muted passages. Harpsichordist must also improvise.

Strauss, Johann. *Artist's Life.* Hudadoff, Igor, and Westcott, William (piano arr.). Pro Art Publications. 1967. Out of print. See: Hudadoff, Igor, *Fifteen Intermediate Tuba Solos,* under "Tuba and Keyboard Collections."

Strauss, Johann. *Roses from the South.* arr. Kinyon, John. M. Witmark and Sons. 1958. I. See listing under "Tuba and Keyboard Collections."

Strauss, Richard. *Concerto,* Op. 11. arr. Graham, James. TUBA Press. 1991. IV. B♭₁–e♭¹. Allegro; Andante; Allegro. Originally written for horn. See: Graham, James, *Concert Music for Tuba,* under "Tuba and Keyboard Collections."

Strauss, Richard. *Second Horn Concerto,* (second movement only) arr. Graham, James. TUBA Press. 1991. IV. A♭₁–d♭¹. Andante con Moto. See: Graham, James, *Concert Music for Tuba,* under "Tuba and Keyboard Collections."

Stravinsky, Igor. *Berceuse,* from *The Firebird.* arr. Maganini, Quinto. Editions Musicus. 1948. 2:30. III. E–a. Legato (slurred) solo. See: Ostrander, Allen, *Concert Album for Tuba,* under "Tuba and Keyboard Collections."

Stravinsky, Igor. *Russian Song.* arr. Lebedev, A. Military Band Masters Faculty of Moscow Conservatiore. 1971. See: Lebedev, A., *Collection of Pieces for Tuba "Es" and Piano,* under "Tuba and Keyboard Collections."

Strebel, Neal. *Sonata for Bass Horn and Piano.* Available from the composer. 1962. 9:50. V. E₁–e¹. Complex rhythms; large dissonant intervals.

Strukov, V. *Lento Elegiaco.* ed. Voronov, G. Moscow: Muzyka. 1984. See: Voronov, G., *Works for Tuba and Piano by Russian Composers,* under "Tuba and Keyboard Collections."

Strukow, Valery. *Concerto for Tuba and Orchestra.* Éditions BIM. 1991. $19.00. Written in 1980. See listing under "Music for Tuba and Orchestra." Recorded by Jens Bjorn-Larsen.

Strukow, Valery. *Elegie.* Éditions BIM. 1991. $9.50.

Štuhec, Igor. *Groteskna Koračnica* (Grotesque March). Available from Igor Krivokapic.

Štuhec, Igor. *Menuet.* Available from Igor Krivokapic.

Sullivan, Arthur. *Oh, Is There Not One Maiden Breast?* from *Pirates of Penzance.* arr. Fletcher, John. Chester Music Ltd. London. 1982. 1:35. II–III. G–a♭. Andante. Some accidentals at a slow tempo, otherwise no technical problems. See: Fletcher, John, *Tuba Solos (Tuba in C), Volume One,* under "Tuba and Keyboard Collections."

Sullivan, Arthur. *The Policeman's Song,* from *Pirates of Penzance.* arr. Fletcher, John. Chester Music Ltd. London. 1982. 1:00. II. (B♭₁) F–f. Allegro non troppo. Mostly eighth notes with a quick tempo. Listen to aria in operetta for conception. See: Fletcher, John, *Tuba Solos (Tuba in C), Volume One,* under "Tuba and Keyboard Collections."

Sullivan, Arthur. *When Britain Really Ruled the Waves,* from *Iolanthe.* arr. Fletcher, John. Chester Music Ltd. London. 1982. 1:00. II–III. G–a. Maestoso. Listen to aria for conception. Song in 3/4 with dotted rhythms and plenty of spirit. See: Fletcher, John, *Tuba Solos (Tuba in C), Volume One,* under "Tuba and Keyboard Collections."

Sullivan, Arthur, and Gilbert, W. S. *Miya Sama from "The Mikado."* ed. Daellenbach, Charles. Hal Leonard Publishing Corp. 1992. 1:03. I. D–c. Allegro moderato. A few slurs, mostly quarter notes in 4/4 time with a Japanese flavor. See: Daellenbach, Charles, *Book of Easy Tuba Solos,* under "Tuba and Keyboard Collections."

Sviridov, G. *Iago's Song about King Stephen from the tragedy Othello.* ed. Lebedev, A. Moscow: Muzyka. 1986. 1:06. IV. G₁–c¹. Some quick articulations—possible double tonguing. See: Lebedev, A., *Tuba Tutor Vol. 2,* under "Tuba and Keyboard Collections."

Swann, Donald. *Two Moods for Tuba.* Chamber Music Library. 1961. $3.50. 5:00. IV. G♭₁–f¹. Dedicated to Gerard Hoffnung. Two attacca movements: *Elegy* (Affettuoso); *Scherzo* (Scherzando). Muted passages. Upper tessitura. Best on F tuba. Good recital material. See: Bird, Gary, ed., *Program Notes for the Solo Tuba.* Recorded by Harvey Phillips.

Swanson, Ken, arr. *Blue Bells of Scotland.* CPP/Belwin, Inc. 1970. $4.00. 1:58. II. B♭₁–f. Moderato. Theme and (one) variation of this traditional tune in 4/4 time. Eighth notes in variation; one scale and one arpeggio up to f, otherwise very comfortable tessitura. No technical problems. See review in *T.U.B.A. Journal,* Vol. 9, no. 2, p. 29. See: CPP/Belwin, *Tuba Solos, Level Two,* under "Tuba and Keyboard Collections."

Swinnen, Hans. *Grave and Allegro.* J. Maurer Editions Musicales. 1984. $2.10. 2:15. IV. G–g¹. "Voor Solo instrument En Piano: Viola Violoncello Fagotto Corno Sax—Tenore Flicorno (Saxhorn) Tuba Bariton." Fun solo best suited for F tuba. Upper tessitura. Lyrical Grave section followed by a Baroque-like Allegro section in a comfortable cut-time.

Tacuchian, Ricardo. *Os Mestres Cantores da Lapa.* Fundação Nacional De Arte. 1985. 5:06. IV. D♭₁–d♭¹. Moderato section has nationalistic rhythmical feel. Allegro section has repetitive patterns and requires intermediate technique. Some trills.

Takács, Jeno. *Sonata Capricciosa,* Op. 81. Ludwig Doblinger K. G. 1967. $21.00. 9:00. IV. A_1–d'. To Eva. Conservative contemporary writing. Strong technique required: double and triple tonguing, flutter tongue, half-valve pitches. Recorded by David Randolph. See review in *T.U.B.A. Journal,* Vol. 9, no. 3, p. 24.

Taktakishvili, O. *Aria from the Opera "Three Lives."* ed. Lebedev, A. Moscow: Muzyka. 1986. 1:28. III. E♭–b♭. No technical problems. See: Lebedev, A., *Tuba Tutor Vol. 2,* under "Tuba and Keyboard Collections."

Tal, Joseph. *Movement for Tuba and Piano* (1980). Israel Music Institute. 1981. 8:00. V. C–g'. To Michael Margulies. Modern feel—no barlines. Muted passages. High tessitura; best on F tuba. Strong technique required.

Tchaikovsky, Peter I. *Andante Cantabile.* Hudadoff, Igor, and Westcott, William (piano arr.). Pro Art Publications. 1967. Out of print. See: Hudadoff, Igor, *Fifteen Intermediate Tuba Solos,* under "Tuba and Keyboard Collections."

Tchaikovsky, Peter I. *Arioso from the opera "Jolanta."* ed. Mitegin, V. Moscow: Muzyka. 1969. See: Mitegin, V., *Pieces for Tuba and Piano,* under "Tuba and Keyboard Collections."

Tchaikovsky, Peter I. *At the Dance,* Op. 39. tr. Gershenfeld, Mitchell. Medici Music Press. 1985. 1:58. III. A_1–f. Moderato. In 3/8 time and in D minor. See: Gershenfeld, Mitchell, *Medici Masterworks Solos Volume 1,* under "Tuba and Keyboard Collections."

Tchaikovsky, Peter I. *None But the Lonely Heart,* Op. 6. arr. Wekselblatt, Herbert. G. Schirmer Inc. 1964. 2:22. II–III. D–g. Andante non tanto. Expressive lyrical solo. Some jumps of a sixth; otherwise not too technically challenging. See: Wekselblatt, H., *Solos for the Tuba Player,* under "Tuba and Keyboard Collections."

Tchaikovsky, Peter I. *The Sad Song.* ed. Melnikov, S. Moscow: Military Band Masters Institute. 1957. See: Melnikov, S., *Pieces for Tuba and Piano,* under "Tuba and Keyboard Collections."

Tchaikovsky, Peter I. *Tomsky's Song from the Opera "Queen Of Spades."* ed. Lebedev, A. Moscow: Muzyka. 1984. 0:55. II. D–f. Little aria in 2/4 with no technical problems. See: Lebedev, A., *Tuba Tutor, Vol. 1,* under "Tuba and Keyboard Collections."

Tchaikovsky, Peter I. *Waltz from Serenade for Strings.* Hudadoff, Igor, and Westcott, William (piano arr.). Pro Art Publications. 1967. Out of print. See: Hudadoff, Igor, *Fifteen Intermediate Tuba Solos,* under "Tuba and Keyboard Collections."

Tchebotarev, S. *Rondo.* ed. Larin, J. Moscow: Muzyka. 1979. See: Larin, J., *Pieces for Tuba and Piano,* under "Tuba and Keyboard Collections."

Tchérépnine, Alexandre. *Andante.* M. P. Belaieff. 1950. $8.00. 5:00. III–IV. $A\flat_1$–d'. À la memoire de mon chere père. "Pour Tuba ou Trombone et Piano." Alternative trombone part included. Theme and variations. Solid melodic writing. One passage in G♭ major. Recorded by Manfred Hoppert.

Telemann, Georg Philipp. *Adagio and Allegro,* from *Trumpet Concerto* in D major. arr. Friedman, Norman F. Southern Music Company. 1977. $3.00. 3:40 (2:02, 1:38). IV. B♭–c'. Adagio in 8; Allegro in 4/4 time. Typical Baroque transcription. Good recital material. See review in *T.U.B.A. Journal,* Vol. 5, no. 3, p. 22.

Telemann, Georg Philipp. *Andante and Allegro.* arr. Chidester, L. W. Southern Music Company. 1973. $3.50. 2:13 (1:01, 1:12). III. G_1–g♭. Andante in 3/2 time in D♭ major. Allegro in 2/4 time. No major technical problems.

Telemann, Georg Philipp. *Prelude and Allegretto.* arr. Chidester, L. W. Southern Music Company. 1966. $2.95. II–III. A♭–f. Prelude (Adagio) from Sonata in G minor; Allegretto (Tempo di minuetto) from Sonata in B♭ major. Solid Baroque transcriptions. Adagio has eighth-note pulse in 4/4 time (8/8). Allegretto is in a brisk 3/8 time.

Telemann, Georg Philipp. *Sonata in F major.* tr. Drobnak, Kenneth P. TUBA Press. 9:19 (2:22, 2:35, 2:07, 2:15). IV. D–d'. Harmonization by Frans Brügen. In preparation. Well-transcribed Baroque solo with four contrasting movements. Andante has a pulse of 8; Vivace is in 3/4 time with some syncopations; Grave is in 3/2 time; and Allegro has Baroque arpeggios and scales. Flexibility, good stylistic sense required. Good recital material.

Telemann, Georg Philipp. *Suite in A Minor for Flute and Strings.* arr. Davis, Ronald. Manuscript available from the arranger. 1982. 15:00. V. G–g'. Air à l'Italien; La Plaisir; Allegro/Ouverture; Réjouissance. Very high tessitura. Very agile flute transcription. Suggested ornamentation included. Solo part only.

Thompson, H. S. *Annie Lisle.* arr. Kinyon, John. M. Witmark and Sons. 1958. I. See Kinyon, John, *Breeze-Easy Recital Pieces,* under "Tuba and Keyboard Collections."

Thomson, Virgil. *Jay Rozen Portrait and Fugue.* Heilman Music. 1984 and 1985. $4.00. 1:52 (1:42, 1:10). IV. $G\flat_1$–f'. Commissioned by the Yale University Music Library by means of gifts from American and Canadian tubists. First performed by Jay Rozen and Newel Kay Brown at the National Conference of the American Society of University Composers, March 2, 1985, University of Missouri at Columbia. Portrait completed New York, April 1984. Fugue completed New York, February 1985. Requires full range and good ear. Tonal contemporary writing. Good recital material.

Tihomirov, A. *Concert Piece for Tuba and Piano.* (Russian publisher.) n. d. 4:26. IV. $E\flat_1$–f'. One-movement work with meter changes throughout. Melodic and technical challenges. Good ear, good rhythmic sense, and quick articulations required.

Tilzer, Albert von, and Norworth, Jack. *Take Me Out to the Ball Game.* arr. Boyd, Bill; ed. Daellenbach, Charles. Hal Leonard Publishing Corp. 1992. 0:39. I. B♭₁–c. Once through the melody in 3/4 time. Quarter note is the fastest rhythm. Comes with practice/performance cassette. See: Daellenbach, Charles, *Book of Beginning Tuba Solos,* under "Tuba and Keyboard Collections."

Toldra, Eduardo. *Ave Maria from "6 Sonnets."* tr. Amaz, J. Union Musical Espanola. 1970. 4:10. IV. G–g'. Good smaller tuba piece in E major.

Toldra, Eduardo. *Dels Quatre Vents from "6 Sonnets."* tr. Amaz, J. Union Musical Espanola. 1970. 2:00. III–IV. G♯–c♯'. Molto Lento. Easy intermediate solo in B major. Easy accompaniment.

Toldra, Eduardo. *Oracio al Main from "6 Sonnets."* tr. Amaz, J. Union Musical Española. 1970.

Toldra, Eduardo. *Serenada d'Hivern from "6 Sonnets."* tr. Amaz, J. Union Musical Española. 1970.

Tomasi, G. [*sic*]. *Hamlet's Monologue.* ed. Lebedev, A. Moscow: Muzyka. 1986. 4:23. IV. B₁–d'. Composed by Henri Tomasi. Recitative style with modern melodic lines. Imagination and dynamic contrast required. See: Lebedev, A., *Tuba Tutor Vol. 2,* under "Tuba and Keyboard Collections."

Tomasi, Henri. *Danse Sacrée.* Alphonse Leduc Editions Paris. 1960. $10.75. 3:00. (Ritual Dance) "No. 3 des Cinq profanes et sacreés." "Pour Tuba Ut ou Trombone ou Saxhorn basse Si♭ et Piano ou accompagnement d'Orchestre de Chambre." See listing under "Music for Tuba and Orchestra." Also see: Thompson/Lemke, *French Music for Low Brass Instruments.*

Tomasi, Henri. *Etre ou ne pas être.* Alphonse Leduc Editions Paris. 1963. $7.95. See listing under "Music for Tuba and Mixed Ensemble." Also see: Thompson/Lemke, *French Music for Low Brass Instruments.* Recorded by Arnold Jacobs and Toby Hanks; trombone quartet version recorded by the Leningrad Trombone Quartet.

Tomasi, Henri. *Etre ou ne pas être.* Moscow: Muzyka. 1976. See: Guzii, V., *Pieces for Tuba and Piano,* under "Tuba and Keyboard Collections." Also see above listing. Recorded by Arnold Jacobs and Toby Hanks.

Toulon, Jacques. *Trois caricatures.* Éditions Robert Martin. 1989. $4.00. G₁–b♭'. For French tuba. See: Thompson/Lemke, *French Music for Low Brass Instruments.*

Tournier, Franz. *Récit et Rondo.* Éditions Rideau Rouge. 1969. IV. F₁–b♭'. Concours du Conservatoire National Supérieur de Musique de Paris 1969. Récit; Rondo. "Pour Tuba ou Saxhorn Basse Si♭ et Piano." For French tuba. Great flexibility and wide range required. See: Thompson/Lemke, *French Music for Low Brass Instruments.*

Troje-Miller, N. *Sonatina Classica.* CPP/Belwin, Inc. 1941. $4.00. 6:00. III. B♭₁–a (b♭). Andante con moto; Andante grazioso; Allegro moderato. Challenging but approachable, solid work for intermediate level. No big technical problems.

Truillard, R. *Divertissement classique.* Truillard-Arpèges. For French Tuba.

Tuthill, Burnet. *Fantasia for Tuba or Bass Trombone with Band or Piano Accompaniment,* Op. 57. Lyceum Music Press. 1970. $5.00. For Rex Conner. Composed in 1968. See listing under "Music for Tuba and Band." See review in *T.U.B.A. Journal,* Vol. 1, no. 3, p. 6.

Uber, David. *Autumn Afternoon.* Kendor Music, Inc. 1992. $5.00. 2:35. III. G♯₁–f. Andante, molto espressivo. For solo trombone, baritone horn, or tuba with piano accompaniment. Lyrical piece with mostly slurred phrases. No technical problems. Good recital material.

Uber, David. *The Ballad of Enob Mort.* Southern Music Company. 1979. $5.00. 5:46 (2:29, 3:17). IV. G₁–c'. Allegretto agitato; Allegro. Allegro section is extremely lyrical and reflective. Allegro section requires flexibility. Good recital material.

Uber, David. *Bayou Legend for Solo Tuba and Piano,* Op. 297. Manuscript. 1992. 3:20. III. A♭₁–f. Melodic ballad section in 4/4 time and Più Mosso section in 2/4. No big technical problems.

Uber, David. *Danza Española.* Virgo Music Publishers. 1987. $6.95. In memory of Gordon Pulis. Allegro con fuoco. Written for trombone (euphonium, tuba) and piano. Opening tempo should be c. 100.

Uber, David. *A Delaware Rhapsody.* Kendor Music, Inc. 1981. $6.50. 5:45. III–IV. C–a♭ (d♭'). For solo trombone, baritone horn, or tuba with piano accompaniment. In 5/4 (3+2) time. Lyrical and moderately technical passages. See review in *T.U.B.A. Journal,* Vol. 10, no. 2, p. 26.

Uber, David. *Evensong,* Op. 64. Kendor Music, Inc. 1980. $7.00. 5:20. III–IV. C–b♭. Respectfully dedicated to the memory of Art Dedrick. Written for tuba or bass trombone. Conceived as a series of invocations with alternate responses by the piano. Reflective lyrical first half with occasional quintuplets. Middle section contains syncopated figures. Last section returns to the feeling of the beginning. Limited range; could be played by strong high school player. See review in *T.U.B.A. Journal,* Vol. 8, no. 4, p. 26.

Uber, David. *The Legend of Purple Hills,* Op. 137. Southern Music Company. 1980. $5.00. 7:10. IV. A₁–f '. For Scott Mendoker. Very lyrical ballad; mostly slurred phrases. Wide range, technical facility a must. See review in *T.U.B.A. Journal,* Vol. 7, no. 3, p. 31.

Uber, David. *Legend of The Sleeping Bear.* Kendor Music, Inc. 1986. $7.00. 6:10. IV. A₁–c'. Dedicated to Don Butterfield. Originally titled *Sound*

Sketches. Flexibility required. Lyrical writing. See review in *T.U.B.A. Journal,* Vol. 14, no. 4, p. 42.

Uber, David. *"Mr. Tuba" on Broadway.* Kendor Music, Inc. 1987. $7.50. 6:00. IV. E$_1$–b♭ (f'). Dedicated to my good friend, Harvey Phillips. Originally called *Caricatura* (1970). Flexibility required. See review in *T.U.B.A. Journal,* Vol. 16, no. 3, p. 48. Also see: Uber, David, *Caricatura,* under "Music for Tuba and Mixed Ensemble."

Uber, David. *Pantomime.* Charles Colin. 1967. $4.95. 6:00. III–IV. B♭$_1$–a♭ (b♭). Advanced-intermediate technique sufficient. Some "jazz rhythms" involved.

Uber, David. *Romance.* Kendor Music, Inc. 1986. $6.00. 6:00. III. A♭$_1$–f (g). Very lyrical solo requiring some flexibility. See review in *T.U.B.A. Journal,* Vol. 14, no. 4, p. 43.

Uber, David. *Skylines.* Hidalgo Music. 1992. $10.00. Composed for and dedicated to Douglas Yeo. Manhattan; Chicago; Boston. See listing under "Music for Tuba and Mixed Ensemble."

Uber, David. *Sonata di Bravura,* Op. 298. TUBA Press. 1992. 9:45 (3:30, 2:30, 3:45). IV. F$_1$–d'. Commissioned by Scott Mendoker, 1992. Allegro ma non troppo; Andantino espressione; Allegro assai. Publication pending. Lovely lyrical writing. Some technical demands involving flexibility and quick articulations. Good recital material.

Uber, David. *Sonata for Bass Tuba and Piano.* Editions Musicus. 1978. $9.50. 9:42 (5:15, 2:57, 1:40). IV. C–b♭ (d♭'). Commissioned by Frank H. Meredith. Allegro Moderato; Andante; Poco Agitato; Allegro. Also known as *Sonata for Euphonium or Bass Tuba and Piano.* Major work; lyrical and technical playing required. Technique involves mostly quick articulations and flexibility. Third movement in D♭ major.

Uber, David. *Sonatina.* Southern Music Company. 1985. $5.00. 6:45 (2:40, 1:47, 2:18). III–IV. A♭$_1$–a♭ (c'). Allegro moderato; Lento; Allegro moderato. Also for trombone, euphonium, and horn in F, and piano. Involves technical, flexible playing. Optional octave placement eases difficulty.

Uber, David. *Sonatine No. 1.* TUBA Press. 9:43 (3:39, 3:27, 2:37). IV. (G$_1$) A$_1$–c' (f '). Publication pending. Solid writing. Requires flexible technique and quick fingers. Fun to play.

Uber, David. *Sonatine No. 2.* TUBA Press. 4:39. IV. A$_1$–b♭. Publication pending. One-movement work requiring swift articulations, flexibility, and lyrical playing.

Uber, David. *Sonatuba.* TUBA Press. 1991. 7:45 (3:40, 1:40, 2:25). Completed summer 1991, Tinmouth, VT. See listing under "Music for Tuba and Mixed Ensemble."

Uber, David. *Summer Nocturne.* Southern Music Company. 1983. $6.00. 8:10. III–IV. A$_1$–b♭ (c'). Also for trombone or horn and piano. One-movement lyrical ballad requiring intermediate level flexibility.

Uber, David. *Theater Piece.* Encore Music Publishers. 1992. $9.00. 3:35. IV. C–c'. In preparation. For euphonium or tuba and piano. Cute solo utilizing syncopation; technical and lyrical playing. Good recital material.

Uga, Pierre. *Promenade.* ed. Douay, Jean. Gérard Billaudot. 1978. $9.50. 2:36. III. C–e'. Andantino/Allegretto. "Pour Trombone Ténor, Trombone Basse, Tuba ut ou Saxhorn Si♭." French tuba tessitura. Mostly scalewise motion. Some triplets; some sixteenth notes. Depending on instrument chosen, no technical problems. See: Thompson/Lemke, *French Music for Low Brass Instruments.*

Usher, Julia. *Venezia.* Primarera. 1982. 9:45 (1:39, 1:30, 1:40, 3:02, 0:33, 1:21). IV. (F$_1$) A$_1$)–d'. *Orient Express; Campanile; Piazza; San Marco; Emilio Panfido; Regatta Storica.* "Six Sketches for Tuba and Piano of Sights and Sounds of Venice." Musical portraits; conservative modern tonality. Some quick articulations.

Van Der Roost, J. *Obsessions.* Edition Andel Uitgaven.

Vander Cook, H. A. *Arbutus.* arr. Buchtel, Forrest L. Neil A. Kjos Music Company. 1954. Out of print. 2:55. III. A$_1$–g. Typical polka style.

Vander Cook, H. A. *Behemoth.* Rubank, Inc. 1941. $2.00. 4:00. III. F$_1$–f. "Solo for BB♭ Bass." Polka-style solo with cadenza.

Vander Cook, H. A. *Bombastoso.* Voxman, Himie (compiled and edited). Rubank, Inc. 1941. 3:01. II. B♭$_1$–f. "Solo Tuba—E♭ or BB♭ tuba." Caprice. Traditional theme and variations split up by solo piano interludes. Mostly sixteenth-note scalewise motion in technical section. Good advanced-beginner solo. Limited range. See: Rubank, *Soloist Folio for Bass (E♭ or BB♭),* under "Tuba and Keyboard Collections."

Vander Cook, H. A. *Bombastoso.* Voxman, Himie (compiled and edited). Rubank, Inc. 1941. Out of print. Published separately. See above listing.

Vander Cook, H. A. *Chrysanthemum.* arr. Buchtel, Forrest L. Neil A. Kjos Music Company. 1960. Out of print. 3:00. III. B♭$_1$–f. Tempo di Bolero. "Basses (E♭ or BB♭)." Traditional solo in two parts: Tempo di Bolero; Allegretto. Technical playing in a bolero and polka format. Triple tonguing or optional single notes. Cadenza.

Vander Cook, H. A. *Colossus.* Rubank, Inc. 1941. $3.50. 4:00. II–III. B♭$_1$–e♭. Theme and (three) variations.

Vander Cook, H. A. *Columbine.* arr. Buchtel, Forrest L. Neil A. Kjos Music Company. 1955. Out of print. 2:05. II. A$_1$–f. Easy advanced-beginner solo. A few sixteenth notes.

Vander Cook, H. A. *Daisies.* arr. Buchtel, Forrest L. Neil A. Kjos Music Company. 1957. Out of print. 3:05. II–III. B♭$_1$–f. Typical polka style.

Vander Cook, H. A. *Dewdrops.* arr. Buchtel, Forrest L. Neil A. Kjos Music Company. 1957. Out of print. 2:55. II–III. B♭$_1$–f. Typical polka style with a little triple tonguing.

Vander Cook, H. A. *Hyacinthe*. arr. Buchtel, Forrest L. Neil A. Kjos Music Company. 1952. Out of print. 3:04. II–III. B♭₁–f. Typical polka style. See review in *T.U.B.A. Journal*, Vol. 8, no. 4, p. 28.

Vander Cook, H. A. *Ivy*. arr. Buchtel, Forrest L. Neil A. Kjos Music Company. 1963. Out of print. 4:00. III. A₁–f♯. Lyrical 6/8 section, followed by a polka-style section.

Vander Cook, H. A. *Lily*. arr. Buchtel, Forrest L. Neil A. Kjos Music Company. 1952. Out of print. 3:00. II–III. A₁–f. "Tuba E♭ or BB♭." Lyrical section in 4/4 followed by a polka section.

Vander Cook, H. A. *Magnolia*. arr. Buchtel, Forrest L. Neil A. Kjos Music Company. 1980. $2.50. 4:00. III. G₁–a♭. Original copyright was 1952. Moderately technical lyrical section in 4/4 time followed by a polka. Tessitura a bit higher than others by Vander Cook.

Vander Cook, H. A. *Marigold*. arr. Buchtel, Forrest L. Neil A. Kjos Music Company. 1952. Out of print. 3:55. II. G₁–e♭. Typical polka style.

Vander Cook, H. A. *Morning Glory*. arr. Buchtel, Forrest L. Neil A. Kjos Music Company. 1952. Out of print. 4:00. II–III. G₁–e♭. "Tuba (E♭ or BB♭)." Andante section in 4/4 time followed by a polka.

Vander Cook, H. A. *Moss Rose*. arr. Buchtel, Forrest L. Neil A. Kjos Music Company. 1957. Out of print. 3:20. III–IV. G♯₁–f. Typical polka style with triple tonguing.

Vander Cook, H. A. *Pansies*. arr. Buchtel, Forrest L. Neil A. Kjos Music Company. 1957. Out of print. 3:20. II–III. B♭₁–f. Typical polka style.

Vander Cook, H. A. *Peony*. arr. Buchtel, Forrest L. Neil A. Kjos Music Company. 1952. Out of print. 3:20. II–III. G₁–f. Typical polka style.

Vander Cook, H. A. *Rosebuds*. arr. Buchtel, Forrest L. Neil A. Kjos Music Company. 1954. $2.50. 4:00. II. (A₁) C–f. "Tuba (E♭ and BB♭)." Andante section in 4/4, cadenza, polka. More limited in range than other Vander Cook pieces.

Vander Cook, H. A. *Tulip*. arr. Buchtel, Forrest L. Neil A. Kjos Music Company. 1980. $2.00. 3:00. II. B♭₁–e♭. "Tuba (E♭ or BB♭)." Original copyright 1952. Andante Cantabile section followed by an Allegretto Polka. Easier than other Vander Cook solos.

Vander Cook, H. A. *Wild Rose*. arr. Buchtel, Forrest L. Neil A. Kjos Music Company. 1952. Out of print. 3:45. III. A₁–g. Typical polka style.

Vanheel, L. *Tecnica In Aba*. Edition Andel Uitgaven. 1981.

Vansteenkiste, M. *Legende*. Edition Andel Uitgaven.

Vasconi, Eugene. *Shades of Tuba*. Southern Music Company. 1993. $3.95.

Vasilyev, V. *Melody*. arr. Lebedev, A. Military Band Masters Faculty of Moscow Conservatiore. 1971. See: Lebedev, A., *Collection of Pieces for Tuba "Es" and Piano*, under "Tuba and Keyboard Collections."

Vaughan, Rodger. *Concertpiece No. 1*. Fema Music Publications. 1970. $6.00. 5:00. IV. F♯₁–c'. Composed in 1959. Published by Interlochen Press in 1961. Conservative contemporary writing. Solid piece for tuba and piano. Recorded by Rex Conner; Ronald Davis.

Vaughan, Rodger. *Concertpiece No. 2*. Fema Music Publications. 1981. $6.00. 6:00. IV. f₁–c'. For Heidi Werth. Fine contemporary melodic writing. A few meter changes.

Vaughan, Rodger. *Elegy*. Available from the composer. 1986–87. See listing under "Music for Tuba and Band."

Vaughan, Rodger. *Manchester Parade (a British Slow-March)*. TUBA Press. 1981. $5.00. 2:05. III–IV. G₁–b♭. For Marianne Forster. Composed on a theme by H. K. Werth, December 1981. In cut time. Requires moderate flexibility. No big technical problems. Fun to play.

Vaughan Williams, Ralph. *Concerto for Bass Tuba*. Oxford University Press Inc. 1955. $18.95. See listing under "Music for Tuba and Orchestra." and "Music for Tuba and Band." Also see: Bird, Gary, ed., *Program Notes for the Solo Tuba*. Recorded by Jeffrey Arwood; Philip Catelinet; Floyd Cooley; Eugene Dowling; John Fletcher; Patrick Harrild; Manfred Hoppert; Arnold Jacobs; Ian King; Michael Lind; Richard Nahatzki; Daniel Perantoni; Harvey Phillips; Donald Strand.

Vaughan Williams, Ralph. *Six Studies in English Folk-Song*. tr. Wagner, Michael. Galaxy Music Corp/ ECS Publishing/ Stainer and Bell. 1927. $8.95. 8:36 (1:37, 1:25, 1:32, 1:51, 1:27, 0:44). IV. G₁– d. To May Mukle. Adagio; Andante Sostenuto; Larghetto; Lento; Andante tranquillo; Allegro vivace. For violoncello and pianoforte with alternate versions for violin, viola, clarinet, English horn, alto saxophone, bassoon, or tuba (and transposed versions by Paul Droste for euphonium, baritone, tenor saxophone, or bass clarinet). Very lyrical writing. With exception of last movement, mostly slurred phrases. Excellent recital material. Recorded by Eugene Dowling; Gene Pokorny.

Verdi, Giuseppe. *Aria from "Don Carlos."* arr. Ostrander, Allen. Editions Musicus. 1959. $2.75. 3:00. III. G₁–e. Listen to aria for conception. Vocal interpretation a must. Some sextuplets included.

Verdi, Giuseppe. *Aria from Falstaff*. arr. Weber, Carl. J. W. Pepper and Son. 1914. Out of print. See: Weber, Carl, *Nineteen Solos For E♭ Bass with Piano Accompaniment*, under "Tuba and Keyboard Collections."

Verdi, Giuseppe. *Grand Air from "The Masked Ball."* arr. Ostrander, Allen. Editions Musicus. 1965. $2.75. 2:50. III. A₁–g. Some dotted rhythms; very accessible, easy intermediate solo.

Vergauwen, A. *Ballade*. Edition Andel Uitgaven.

Villette, Pierre. *Fantaisie Contante*. Alphonse Leduc Editions Paris. 1962. $12.80. Au Maître Paul Bernard Professeur au Conservatoire National Su-périeur de Musique. See listing under "Music for Tuba and Orchestra.". Also see: Thompson/Lemke, *French Music for Low Brass Instruments.*

Villiams, V. R. [Vaughan Williams, Ralph]. *Concerto for Tuba and Orchestra.* Moscow: Muzyka. 1955. See above under Vaughan Williams, Ralph.

Vivaldi, Antonio. *Allegro* (from *Sonata No. 3*). arr. Swanson, Ken. CPP/Belwin, Inc. 1971. $4.00. 2:18. III. ($G_1$) C–f. Allegro. Crisp, light articulation is the biggest consideration in this quick 2/4 Baroque transcription. Syncopations throughout. Practice with metronome. See: Lamb, Jack, *Solo Sounds for Tuba Levels 3–5, Vol. 1,* under "Tuba and Keyboard Collections."

Vivaldi, Antonio. *Concerto in A minor.* arr. Ostrander, Allen. Editions Musicus. 1958. $11.00. 9:00. IV. B_1–d' (d♯'). Allegro molto; Andante molto; Allegro. Breathing can be tricky—plan ahead. Requires flexibility. Good transcription. Upper tessitura.

Vivaldi, Antonio. *Praeludium in C minor.* arr. Maganini, Quinto. Editions Musicus. 1965. $2.75. 3:00. III. G_1–a♭. Alternate baritone and trombone parts also included. In 3/2 time. Some flexibility required.

Vivaldi, Antonio. *Sonata.* ed. Melnikov, S. Moscow: Military Band Masters Institute. 1957. See: Melnikov, S., *Pieces for Tuba and Piano,* under "Tuba and Keyboard Collections."

Vivaldi, Antonio. *Sonata No. 3 in A minor.* arr. Morris, R. Winston. Shawnee Press Inc. 1982. $7.00. 17:45 (6:00, 4:15, 4:25, 3:05) . IV. G_1–c'. Largo; Allegro; Largo; Allegro. Large work; duration could be shortened by eliminating repeats. Combination of slow sustained playing and fast flexible passages. Good recital material.

Vogel, Roger C. *Temporal Landscape No. 1.* Shawnee Press Inc. 1978. $3.00. 5:00. IV–V. Lowest note possible–e♭'. For David Randolph. Modern writing. Contemporary techniques for both players. For tubist: tapping instrument with fingers, clicking valves, glissando, huge dissonant interval jumps. For pianist: stopping, vibrating, rubbing, and plucking strings. Muted passages. See review in *T.U.B.A. Journal,* Vol. 8, no. 1, p. 28.

Vogel, Roger C. *Temporal Landscape No. 4.* Theodore Presser Company. 1980. $3.50. 4:00. IV–V. E_1–e♭'. For David Randolph. Muted passages. Relatively more conventional than *Temporal Landscape No. 1.* Multiphonics, wide dissonant jumps. Will take a strong ear as well as a strong accompanist. See review in *T.U.B.A. Journal,* Vol. 8, no. 3, p. 27.

Volkmann, Rudy. *Suite Babu (Are You My).* William Grant Still Music. 1982. 3:30. III–IV. B♭₁–b♭. For Vicky Burke. Opus 6. Theme-and-variations style. Some cantabile as well as technical playing required. Some triple tonguing possible. Fun piece to play. Technical demands not overwhelming. See review in *T.U.B.A. Journal,* Vol. 10, no. 4, p. 37.

Volkov, K. *A Piece,.* ed. Lebedev, A. Moscow: Muzyka. 1986. 3:14. IV. E_1–c'. Beautiful lyrical modern dissonant and consonant lines presented in a very musical way. See: Lebedev, A., *Tuba Tutor Vol. 2,* under "Tuba and Keyboard Collections."

Vollrath, Carl. *Epode for Tuba and Piano.* Trombone Association Publishing. 1988. $9.00. 7:54. IV–V. $B♭_2$–f'. Very wide range only in a few passages. Modern tonal writing. Technique not overwhelming for the suggested level.

Voronov, G., ed. See listing under "Tuba and Keyboard Collections."

Voxman, Himie (comp. and ed.) See listing under "Tuba and Keyboard Collections."

Wadowick, James L., arr., and McCathren, Donald E., ed. *Christ the Lord Is Risen Today.* David E. Smith Publications. 1987. $4.50. 3:12. II–III. A_1–f. Theme and variations on traditional hymn melody. Last variation in D♭ major. A few sixteenth notes; otherwise no technical problems.

Wadowick, James L., arr., and McCathren, Donald E., ed. *Dona Nobis Pacem.* David E. Smith Publications. 1986. $4.00. 2:47. III. B♭₁–f. Theme and (five) variations.

Wadowick, James L., arr., and McCathren, Donald E., ed. *O Mighty God.* David E. Smith Publications. 1987. $3.50. 2:20. II–III. C–f. Some slurring; no big technical problems.

Wagner, Richard. *Die Meistersinger von Nürnberg.* arr. Yasumoto, Hiroyuki. Toa Music International Co. 1986. 2:40. IV. A_1–e'. Piano and tuba transcription of the most famous of tuba orchestral excerpts. Listen to orchestral version for conception. See: Yasumoto, Hiroyuki, *Tuba Volume #1,* under "Tuba and Keyboard Collections."

Wagner, Richard. *Die Meistersinger von Nürnberg* (from the *Prelude, Act One*). arr. Wekselblatt, Herbert. G. Schirmer Inc. 1964. 2:56. IV–V. A_1–e'. Tuba and piano transcription of perhaps the No. 1 tuba orchestral excerpt. See: Wekselblatt, H., *Solos for the Tuba Player,* under "Tuba and Keyboard Collections."

Wagner, Richard. *Die Walküre* (from Act III). arr. Wekselblatt, Herbert. G. Schirmer Inc. 1964. 1:57. IV–V. E_1–c♯. Two excerpts from Act III. Good opportunity to work on standard orchestral tuba excerpts with piano accompaniment. See: Wekselblatt, H., *Solos for the Tuba Player,* under "Tuba and Keyboard Collections."

Wagner, Richard. *Heav'n, in Pray'r, Thine Aid I Seek* and *Good Subjects of Brabant, 'Tis Well!* (From *Lohengrin*). arr. Hume, James Ord. Boosey & Co. 1906. Out of print. See: Hume, J. Ord, *Boosey's Bombardon Solo Album,* under "Tuba and Keyboard Collections."

Wagner, Richard. *O du mein holder Abendstern,* from *Tannhäuser.* arr. Yasumoto, Hiroyuki. Toa Music International Co. 1986. 1:11. III. D–g. Andante mosso. Very lyrical transcription. All slurred. See:

Yasumoto, Hiroyuki, *Tuba Volume #1,* under "Tuba and Keyboard Collections." A different version of this recorded by John Fletcher.

Wagner, Richard. *Siegfried* (from Act II, Prelude and First Scene). arr. Wekselblatt, Herbert. G. Schirmer Inc. 1964. 4:34. IV–V. F_1–a. Low, sustained, legato transcription. Good introduction to this excerpt as well as to Wagner's low tessitura writing for the tuba. See: Wekselblatt, H., *Solos for the Tuba Player,* under "Tuba and Keyboard Collections."

Wagner, Richard. *Walther's Prize Song,* from *Die Meistersinger.* arr. Masso, George. Kendor Music, Inc. 1966. 3:00. II. E–a. All slurred phrases. Upper tessitura for younger BB♭ player. Good, usable transcription.

Waignein, A. *First Contest.* Edition Andel Uitgaven.

Waignein, A. *Galejade.* Edition Andel Uitgaven.

Waldteufel, Emil. *The Skaters.* arr. Boyd, Bill; ed. Daellenbach, Charles. Hal Leonard Publishing Corp. 1992. 0:25. I. B♭$_1$–c. Traditional skating tune in 3/4 time. Easy rhythms. Comes with practice/performance cassette. See: Daellenbach, Charles, *Book of Beginning Tuba Solos,* under "Tuba and Keyboard Collections."

Waldteufel, [Emil]. *Skater's Waltz.* arr. Ostling, Acton. CPP/Belwin, Inc. 1969. 1:09. I. B♭$_1$,c. Simple version of the tune. Some slurring from F–B♭. See: Ostling, Acton, *Tuba (Bass) Soloist, Level One,* under "Tuba and Keyboard Collections."

Waldteufel, [Emil]. *Spanish Waltzes.* Hudadoff, Igor. and Westcott, William (piano arr.). Pro Art Publications. 1967. Out of print. See: Hudadoff, Igor, *Fifteen Intermediate Tuba Solos,* under "Tuba and Keyboard Collections."

Wallace. *Let Me Like a Soldier Fall,* from *Maritana.* arr. Weber, Carl. J. W. Pepper & Son. 1914. Out of print. 0:46. II–III. E–g. No technical problems. See: Weber, Carl, *Nineteen Solos for E♭ Bass with Piano Accompaniment,* under "Tuba and Keyboard Collections."

Walters, Harold L., arr. *Blow the Man Down.* Rubank, Inc. 1954. $2.50. 4:00. II–III. A♭$_1$–e♭. "Solo for E♭ or BB♭ Bass." Theme and variations with cadenza.

Walters, Harold L., arr. *Christmas Nocturne.* Rubank, Inc. 1954. Out of print. 1:55. I. E♭–c. Beginning solo. Includes *Lullaby, Thou Little Tiny Child* and *My Sheep Were Grazing.*

Walters, Harold L. *Concertante.* Rubank, Inc. 1960. $2.50. See listing under "Music for Tuba and Band."

Walters, Harold L. *Concertante.* Tierolff-Muziekcentrale.

Walters, Harold L., arr. *Down in the Valley.* Rubank, Inc. 1960. $2.95. 3:00. I. ($F_1$) C–c. "Fantasy on a Folk Song. Solo for E♭ or BB♭ and Piano." Nice solo for beginning student in 3/4 time. Easy rhythms. With the exception of last note (an optional F_1) this piece is within one octave.

Walters, Harold L. *Forty Fathoms.* Rubank, Inc. 1952. $3.50. "Solo for E♭ or BB♭ Bass." See listing under "Music for Tuba and Band."

Walters, Harold L. *Leprechauns Patrol.* Rubank, Inc. 1954. Out of print. 2:30. II. G_1–d. "Solo for E♭ or BB♭ Bass." In 6/8 time. No technical problems.

Walters, Harold L. *Scherzo Pomposo.* Rubank, Inc. 1958. $3.00. See listing under "Music for Tuba and Band."

Walters, Harold L. *Tarantelle.* Ludwig Music Publishing Company. 1946. $5.00. See listing under "Music for Tuba and Band."

Ward, Norman. *The Happy Hippo.* Kendor Music, Inc. 1967. $5.00. Comes with flexible Songsheet record with Barton Cummings, tuba. See listing under "Music for Tuba and Band."

Ward, S. A. *America the Beautiful.* arr. Jacobs, Wesley. Encore Music Publishers. 0:38. I. C–d. Moderato. Once through the tune. Some slurring, accidentals, one jump from F–d. See Jacobs, Wesley, *Solos from the Classics,* under "Tuba and Keyboard Collections."

Warner, Anna B., and Bradbury, William B. *Jesus Loves Me.* arr. Smith, David E. David E. Smith Publications. 1984. $3.00. 1:30. II. B♭$_1$–f. Some slurring; no technical problems.

Warren, David. *Mantis Dance.* Ludwig Music Publishing Company. 1987. $3.50. 2:00. II. B♭$_1$–e♭. Original copyright 1959. Lyrical playing and articulated sections with no technical problems.

Warren, Frank E. *Music for Tuba and Piano,* Op. 28a. ed. Roberts, Chester. Frank E. Warren Music Service. 1991. $5.00. 8:30. IV. ($D_1$) F_1–d♭^{1}. Conservative modern tonal writing. No major technical problems.

Warren, Frank E. *Sonata for Tuba and Piano,* Op. 1. Frank E. Warren Music Service. 1975. $12.00. 11:00. IV–V. C_1–f^1. For Rob Weller and Lucille Gaita. First performance April 22, 1976, Boston, with Rob Weller, tuba, and Lucille Gaita, piano. Three movements. Some multiphonics for tubist. Currently being revised.

Warren, Frank E. *Song for Tuba and Piano,* Op. 25. Frank E. Warren Music Service. 1989. $6.00. 8:30. IV. B♭$_1$–b♭. For Robert A. Orr. First performance given by Robert A. Orr and Hyeran Kim at Boston Conservatory of Music, April 21, 1990. Lyrical pentatonic main theme. Requires some quick articulations as well as lyrical playing.

Wastall, Peter, ed. See listing under "Tuba and Keyboard Collections."

Watelle, J. *Grand solo de concert.* Éditions Salabert.

Watz, Franz. *Concertino for Tuba and Klavier.* Rundel O.J.

Weber, Alain. *Soliloque.* Alphonse Leduc Editions Paris. 1969. $16.00. 6:45. V. G_1–a♯^{1}. À Monsieur Paul Bernard Professeur au Conservatoire National Supérieur de Musique. "Pour Trombone Basse, ou Tuba En Ut, ou Saxhorn En Si♭ et Piano." For French tuba. Strong technique required. See: Thompson/Lemke, *French Music for Low Brass Instruments.*

Weber, Carl, arr. See listings under "Tuba and Keyboard Collections."

Weber, Carl, arr. *The Old Sexton.* J. W. Pepper and Son. 1914. Out of print. 0:47. II–III. D♭–f. Old English. A few reverse dotted rhythms and syncopations. See: Weber, Carl, *Nineteen Solos For E♭ Bass with Piano Accompaniment,* under "Tuba and Keyboard Collections."

Weber, Carl, arr. *Pretty as a Butterfly.* J. W. Pepper and Son. 1914. Out of print. 2:05. III. E♭–b♭ (d♭'). Dotted rhythms and triplets. See: Weber, Carl, *Nineteen Solos for E♭ Bass with Piano Accompaniment,* under "Tuba and Keyboard Collections."

Weber, Carl Maria von. *Un Adagio.* arr. Goudenhooft, André; piano realizations Maillard, Augustin. Gérard Billaudot. 1986. $5.25. 2:00. III. G₁–e. "Pour trombone basse (ou tuba) et piano." Classical transcription with a few slurred sixteenth notes; no major technical problems. See: Thompson/Lemke, *French Music for Low Brass Instruments.*

Weber, Fred. *Big Boy.* Belwin. 1945. Out of print. See listing under "Music for Tuba and Band."

Weber, Fred. *Campus Queen.* arr. Ostling, Acton. CPP/Belwin, Inc. 1969. 2:05. I. C–c. A lot of music in a small solo. Lyrical, cantabile verse in B♭. Chorus (Allegro) has great opportunity for style. A couple of natural signs; no technical problems. See: Ostling, Acton, *Tuba (Bass) Soloist, Level One,* under "Tuba and Keyboard Collections."

Weber, Fred, and Garrett, Dorothy. *The Elephant Dance.* Belwin Mills, Inc. 1953. Published separately. Out of print. 1:11. I–II. D–e♭. Solo in G minor and in 6/8 time. Mostly stepwise motion with a couple of d–D jumps and a few accidentals. See: Lamb, Jack, *Classic Festival Solos,* and Lamb, Jack, *Solo Sounds for Tuba Levels 1–3, Vol. 1,* under "Tuba and Keyboard Collections."

Weber, Fred, arr. *Three Favorites.* Belwin, Inc. 1947. Out of print. 2:00. I. B♭₁–b♭. Includes *Massa's in the Cold, Cold Ground; Grandfathers Clock; Marines' Hymn.* Beginning solos.

Weber, K. M. [*sic*] *Adagio.* ed. Melnikov, S. Moscow: Military Band Masters Institute. 1957. See: Melnikov, S., *Pieces for Tuba and Piano,* under "Tuba and Keyboard Collections."

Weeks, Clifford M. *Triptych for Tuba and Piano.* Robert King Music Co. and Alphonse Leduc Editions Paris. 1964. $3.55. 6:00. C–d1. Adagio/Allegro; Lento; Allegro. Substitute parts for baritone/trombone included. Good dialogue between piano and tuba. Range and accompaniment not demanding. Recorded by Karl Megules.

Weiner, Lawrence. *Serenade.* Southern Music Company. 1989. $5.50. 6:22. IV. G₁–c♯'. Written for William Mayson. Conservative contemporary writing. Some lovely lyrical lines. Slow tempo makes any technical work very approachable. Some dissonant intervals requires sharp ear. Good recital material.

Weiss, W. H. *The Village Blacksmith.* arr. Prendiville, Harry. Carl Fischer Inc. 1898. Out of print. 3:35. II. B♭₁–d. Easy advanced-beginning solo.

Wekselblatt, Herbert, arr. *Civil War Medley.* G. Schirmer Inc. 1972. 1:41. II. D–d. *Battle Hymn of the Republic* and *When Johnny Comes Marching Home.* Piece consists of just playing through each tune. *Battle Hymn* is in a slow 4/4 with dotted rhythms. *Johnny* is in 6/8. See: Wekselblatt, Herbert, *First Solos for the Tuba Player,* under "Tuba and Keyboard Collections."

Wekselblatt, Herbert, arr. *Hornpipe.* G. Schirmer Inc. 1972. 1:52. III. B♭₁–g. Allegro. American folk dance. Show stopper—sounds harder than it really is. The sixteenth notes will take some practice, but are well worth it. Good recital material, even for advanced players. See: Wekselblatt, Herbert, *First Solos for the Tuba Player,* under "Tuba and Keyboard Collections."

Wekselblatt, Herbert, arr. *Military Suite.* G. Schirmer Inc. 1972. 1:59. II. E♭–g. March Tempo. Cut time medley includes *The Marines' Hymn; The Caisson Song; Anchors Aweigh.* Songs separated by eight-measure piano interludes. Slightly upper range for this level on BB♭ tuba. See: Wekselblatt, Herbert, *First Solos for the Tuba Player,* under "Tuba and Keyboard Collections."

Wenström-Lekare, Lennart. *Sonata for Tuba and Piano.* Available from the composer. 1991.

Werle, Floyd E. *Concertino for Three Brass and Band.* Bourne Company. 1970. See listing under "Music for Tuba and Band." Recorded by Ken Angerstein.

Werner, Jean-Jacques. *Libre-episode (Free Episode).* Éditions Musicales Transatlantiques. 1979. $6.75. F₁–a♭'. For French tuba. See: Thompson/Lemke, *French Music for Low Brass Instruments.* See review in *T.U.B.A. Journal,* Vol. 8, no. 3, p. 28.

Whatley, G. Larry. *Sonata for Tuba and Piano.* TUBA Press. 1991. $8.00. 12:56 (5:12, 3:44, 4:00). IV. B♭₁–c'. Contemporary melodic language. Some very lyrical playing in second movement. First and third movements have mixed meter throughout.

White, David Ashley. *Dance and Aria.* Shawnee Press Inc. 1978. $10.00. 6:24. IV–V. A♭₁–e♭'. To William Rose. "For Tuba, Tenor Trombone (Euphonium) or Bass Trombone and Piano." One-movement work with lyrical passages and mixed meters. Some quick articulations and tempos; a few glissandos. See review in *T.U.B.A. Journal,* Vol. 7, no. 4, p. 23.

White, Donald H. *Sonata for Tuba.* Ludwig Music Publishing Company. 1979. $16.00. 15:08 (5:25, 5:53, 4:00). V. F₁–a♭'. Commissioned by Custom Music Company, sole distributors of Hirsbrunner, Rudolf Meinl, and Sanders Tubas in cooperation with Tubists Universal Brotherhood Association. Premiered by Steven Bryant, tuba, and Jean Barr, piano, May 19, 1980, at the Second National Tuba-Euphonium Symposium-Workshop, Denton, TX. major work for tuba and piano. First movement:

syncopated, beat displacements, double tonguing, and large interval jumps. Second movement: lyrical writing. Third movement: very fast tempo markings; mixed meters: 7/8 and 2/4 time; very quick articulations. Requires strong technique and strong accompanist. Recorded by Fritz Kaenzig.

Widmer, Ernst. *Torre Alada.* Fundação Nacional de Arte. 1985. 4:30. IV. E_1–d'. Conservative tempos. No major technical problems. Optional glissandos. Conservative contemporary melodic language.

Wiegand, George. *The Leviathan,* Fantasia for E♭ Tuba. J. R. Lafleur and Son, and Harry Coleman. 1894. Out of print. 5:00. IV. Bb_1–e♭'. Old traditional-style solo with cadenza. See listing under "Music for Tuba and Band."

Wieschendorff, Heinrich. *Thema und Variationen und Tempo de Polonaise für Tuba und Klavier.* arr. Teuchert, Emil. C. F. Schmidt, Leipzig. 8:10. IV–V. Ab_1–f'. Technical theme and variations reminiscent of the Kopprasch Etudes. Some tricky tonal interval skips. Many arpeggio and scale passages.

Wilder, Alec. *Concerto for Tuba and Concert Band.* trans. Waddell, Robert George. Margun Music, Incorporated. 1965. $15.00. For Harvey Phillips. See listing under "Music for Tuba and Band." Also see review in *T.U.B.A. Journal,* Vol. 10, no. 3, p. 22.

Wilder, Alec. *Elegy for the Whale.* Margun Music, Incorporated. 1982. $6.00. See listing under "Music for Tuba and Orchestra." Also see review in *T.U.B.A. Journal,* Vol. 10, no. 3, p. 23.

Wilder, Alec. *Encore Piece for Tuba and Piano.* ed. Schuller, Gunther. Margun Music, Incorporated. 1981. $5.00. 0:55. V. A_1–ab'. A one-minute showcase of flexibility and technique. Arpeggios, fast articulations, trills, glissando, extreme range. Recorded by Roger Bobo.

Wilder, Alec. *Small Suite for Bass (Tuba) and Piano.* ed. Schuller, Gunther. Margun Music, Incorporated. 1981. Original copyright 1963. $9.00. 10:27 (2:31, 2:52, 2:18, 2:26). IV–V. $F\#_1$–f♯' (a'). For Gary Karr. Smoothly; Romantically; Flowingly; Quasi Jazz. Written with the breathing requirements of a string bass in mind; not many rests. Some sustained upper tessitura in second movement. Very playable, lyrical solo; no major technical problems other than wide range.

Wilder, Alec. *Sonata for Tuba and Piano.* Mentor Music Inc. 1963. $9.00. 10:31 (3:12, 2:11, 3:23, 1:45). IV. F_1–d'. For Harvey Phillips. Lovely solo. Lyrical playing. Demands flexibility and strong stylistic sense. Switches between a fast technical section and a swing section in second movement. Good recital material. See listing under "Music for Tuba and Orchestra." Also see: Bird, Gary, ed., *Program Notes for the Solo Tuba.* Recorded by Harvey Phillips.

Wilder, Alec. *Sonata No. 2 for Tuba and Piano.* Margun Music, Incorporated. 1976. $15.00. 17:27 (3:53, 2:37, 5:23, 3:14, 2:20). IV–V. G_1–ab'. For

Lottie Phillips [Harvey Phillips's mother]. Espressivo; Jazz Style; Slowly; Air; Energetically. Completed 1975. Big piece requires strong technique and mature sensitive lyrical playing.

Wilder, Alec. *Song for Carol.* Margun Music, Incorporated. 1981. $2.00. 2:15. IV. A_1–f'. Tenderly. Upper tessitura. All tenuto and slurred. Lovely lyrical tune. Recorded by Harvey Phillips.

Wilder, Alec. *Suite No. 1 for Tuba and Piano* (*"Effie Suite"*). Margun Music, Incorporated. 1968. $11.00. 11:00. IV. F_1–e'. *Effie Chases a Monkey; Effie Falls in Love; Effie Takes a Dancing Lesson; Effie Joins the Carnival; Effie Goes Folk Dancing; Effie Sings a Lullaby.* One of the most popular tuba and piano solos, for good musical reasons. Requires the entire spectrum from the tuba: very vocal, lyrical playing; quick articulations, slurred flexibility, and most important, an imaginative lyrical, approach. Great crowd pleaser; excellent recital material. See listings under "Music for Tuba and Orchestra" and "Music for Tuba and Mixed Ensemble." Also see: Bird, Gary, ed., *Program Notes for the Solo Tuba.* Recorded by Roger Bobo; Walter Hilgers; Michael Lind; Harvey Phillips.

Wilder, Alec. *Suite No. 2 for Tuba and Piano* (*Jesse Suite*). Margun Music, Incorporated. 1964. 4:25 (0:50, 1:18, 0:42, 1:35). IV. C–e'. Written on the occasion of the birth of Jesse Emmett Phillips, February 14, 1964. Four numbered movements. In preparation, available Fall 1993. Was published by Sam Fox Publishing. Playful solo requiring lyrical playing and quick articulations. Although it is titled "Suite No. 2," this is actually the third suite for tuba and piano composed by Alec Wilder. Recorded by Harvey Phillips.

Wilder, Alec. *Suite No. 3 for Tuba and Piano, "Suite for Little Harvey."* Margun Music, Incorporated. 1980. $6.50. 4:53 (1:32, 0:57, 1:34, 0:50). IV–V. C–ab'. Written on the occasion of the birth of Harvey Gene Phillips, Jr., Sept. 16, 1966. Andantino; II; Moderato; IV. Original copyright 1966. Some quick articulations and lyrical playing. Upper tessitura. Last movement in 5/4 time with flutter tonguing on gb'. Although it is titled "Suite No. 3," this is actually the fourth suite for tuba and piano composed by Alec Wilder. Recorded by Harvey Phillips.

Wilder, Alec. *Suite No. 4 for Tuba and Piano, "Thomas Suite."* Margun Music, Incorporated. 1982. $6.50. 2:20 (0:41, 1:10, 0:33, 0:26). IV. D_1–e'. Written on the occasion of the birth of Thomas Alexander Phillips, Sept. 23, 1968. Four movements. Upper tessitura (only one really low pitch—D_1). Very lyrical playing required in this short suite. Although it is titled "Suite No. 4," this is actually the fifth suite for tuba and piano composed by Alec Wilder. Recorded by Harvey Phillips.

Wilder, Alec. *Suite No. 5 for Tuba and Piano* (*Ethan Ayer*). Margun Music, Incorporated. 1964. $10.00. 5:00. IV–V. Ab_1–e♭'. Dedicated to a loyal friend. Written during a New York Brass Quintet tour in 1963. Ethan Ayer was an arts philanthropist. Although it is titled "Suite No. 5," this is actually the second suite for tuba and piano composed by Alec Wilder. Recorded by Harvey Phillips.

Wiley, Frank. *Caverns.* Ludwig Music Publishing Company. $7.95.

Wilhelm, Rolf. *Concertino for Tuba and Winds.* Available from Tuba Center. 1983. Written for Robert Tucci. See listing under "Music for Tuba and Band." Also see: Bird, Gary, ed., *Program Notes for the Solo Tuba.* Recorded by Michael Bunn, Jens Bjorn-Larsen.

Wilkenschildt, Georg. *Arie and Humuresque.* MS Publications.

Williams, Ernest. *Concerto No. 2.* Charles Colin. 1937. $5.95. IV. (E♭₁) A₁–c'. Allegro moderato; Adagio; Rondo. Transposed version of *Trumpet Concerto No. 2.* Technical challenges throughout. See listing under "Music for Tuba and Band."

Winteregg, Steven. *Three Movements for Tuba and Piano.* Pastiche Music. 1977. 6:02 (1:47, 2:46, 1:29). IV. F₁–e'. Meter changes. Quick articulations in last movement. Good recital material.

Witthauer, Johann Georg. *Allegretto und Gavotte.* arr. Philipp, Gerd. Hofmeister. 1993. 1:53 (1:00, 0:53). II. D♭–f. *Allegretto* in D♭ major, *Gavotte* in B♭ minor. See: Meschke, Dieter, *Zum Uben und Vorspielen/B-Tuba,* under "Tuba and Keyboard Collections."

Woestyne, David Van de. *Muziek (1976).* Centre Belge de Documentation Musicale. 1977. 6:30. IV. A₁–g♭'. "Voor tuba-saxhorn(c) en piano." Composed in 1976. Better on F tuba; upper tessitura throughout.

Woolf, Gregory. *Per Tuba ad Astram.* Previously available from the composer. For Daniel Perantoni. See listing under "Music for Tuba and Orchestra."

Worth, George E. *Serpent of the Brass.* Rubank, Inc. 1942. $2.00. 2:00. II–III. D–f. "Solo for E♭ or BB♭ Bass." Copyright 1941. Some optional triple tonguing. Not very demanding technically.

Wunder, Richard. *Song after Battle for Tuba and Piano.* Manuscript available from the composer. c. 1983. A₁–e'. Written for Gene Pokorny. See review in *T.U.B.A. Journal,* Vol. 10, no. 4, p. 34.

Wurmser, Lucien. *Solo de Concours.* Gérard Billaudot/Andrieu Frères. 1955. $3.50. 2:56. III. G–f'. À Mr Fernand Anne, President Fᵒⁿ Sᵗᵉˢ Mles de Normandie. Largement Quasi récitativo; Allegro. "Basse ou Baryton ou Saxo ténor, Basson ou Tuba ou Trombones." French tuba tessitura. Recitative-like passages combined with lyrical lines. Good recital material. Busy accompaniment part.

Wurmser, Lucien. *Tendres Mélodies.* Gérard Billaudot. 1956. $3.50. 1:48 (1:01, 0:47). III. F–f'. En hommage à Mr Adrien Maltête, President de la Féderation des sociétés musicales du Sud-Ouest. Lent; Andante. "Petites Pièces de Concours." "Pour Basse Si♭ ou Baryton ou saxo Si♭ ou trom-

bone, basson ou tuba." French tuba tessitura. Two lyrical songs. Depending on instrument chosen, only technical problem is that of tessitura.

Yarrow, Peter, and Lipton, Leonard. *Puff (The Magic Dragon).* arr. Maltby, Richard. Warner Brothers Music. 1967. See listing under "Music for Tuba and Band."

Yasumoto, Hiroyuki, arr. *Barcarolle for Tuba.* Toa Music International Co. 1986. 1:27. III. C–c'. Cantabile. Very lyrical solo requiring flexibility. See: Yasumoto, Hiroyuki, *Tuba Volume #1,* under "Tuba and Keyboard Collections."

Yasumoto, Hiroyuki, arr. *Londonderry Air.* Toa Music International Co. 1986. 2:14. II–III. C–g. Andante sostenuto. Irish tune. Very legato with a strong vocal sense. No technical problems. See: Yasumoto, Hiroyuki, *Tuba Volume #1,* under "Tuba and Keyboard Collections."

Yasumoto, Hiroyuki, arr. *Nobody Knows the Trouble I've Seen.* Toa Music International Co. 1986. 1:50. II. F–f. Religioso. Negro spiritual. All slurred with some syncopation. No technical problems. See: Yasumoto, Hiroyuki, *Tuba Volume #1,* under "Tuba and Keyboard Collections."

Yasumoto, Hiroyuki, arr. See listings under "Tuba and Keyboard Collections."

Yoffe, Shlomo. *Andante and Rondo.* Kibutz Movement League of Composers. Recorded by Adi Hershko.

Yuhas, D. *Three Miniatures for Tuba and Piano.* Manuscript. n. d. 2:38 (0:49, 1:17, 0:32). IV. B♭₁–a. Conservative contemporary melodic language. Some mixed meters.

Zajaczek, Roman. *Tema Cantabile con Piernicazioni per tuba universale e pianoforte.* Recorded by Zdizislaw Piernik.

Zaninelli, Luigi. *Peg Leg Pete.* Boosey and Hawkes, Inc. 1963. $7.00. "Burla for Tuba and Piano." See listing under "Music for Tuba and Band."

Zbar, [Michel]. *Jeu 3.* Alphonse Leduc Editions Paris. $12.80.

Zeman, Thomas. *Sonata.* Available from the composer. 1967. 12:00. IV–V. C₁–e'. For Winston Morris. Andante; Vivace; Allegro. Major piece; contemporary writing. Uses mute. Requires strong accompanist.

Zettler, Richard. *Alt und Neu für Zwei.* Thomi-Berg.

Zinos, Fredrick. *Elegy for Tuba and Piano.* Neil A. Kjos Music Company. 1968. $1.50. 6:35. III–IV. A₁–b (c♭'). Respectfully dedicated to Barton Cummings. One-movement work requiring flexibility and lyrical approach. Conservative contemporary melodic writing. Conservative range. Recorded by Barton Cummings.

Zverev, V. *Concertino.* ed. Voronov, G. Moscow: Muzyka. 1984. See: Voronov, G., *Works for Tuba and Piano by Russian Composers,* under "Tuba and Keyboard Collections."

Zverev, V. *Hungarian Melody.* ed. Mitjagina, V. Moscow: Muzyka. 1969. 1:23. III–IV. G₁–a. Mournful, lyrical tune with some syncopation. See: Mitjagina, V., ed., *Pieces for Tuba and Piano,* under "Tuba and Keyboard Collections."

Zverev, V. *Russian Dance.* ed. Mitjagina, V. Moscow: Muzyka. 1969. 2:19. II–III. G_1–g. Simple tune with easy melody and rhythms. See: Mitjagina, V., ed., *Pieces for Tuba and Piano,* under "Tuba and Keyboard Collections."

Zverev, V. *Song.* ed. Lebedev, A. Moscow: Muzyka. 1984. 0:52. III. Bb_1–g. A song of strength. In C minor and in 3/4 time. See: Lebedev, A., *Tuba Tutor, Vol. 1,* under "Tuba and Keyboard Collections."

Works Listed by Title

For annotations, see "Works Listed by Composer" and "Tuba and Keyboard Collections."

A

A-Tisket, A-Tasket, Feldstein, Sandy (arr.)
Abide with Me, Lyte, H., and Monk, W.
Abide with Me, Monk, W. H.
Abuto, Delgiudice, Michel
Adagietto from L'Arlésienne, Bizet, Georges
Adagio, Bach, Johann Sebastian
Adagio, Bartók, Bela
Adagio, Lebedev, A. (arr.)
Adagio, Spohr, Ludwig
Adagio, Weber, K. M. [*sic*]
Adagio, Un, Weber, Carl Maria von
Adagio and Allegro, Bartsch, Ch.
Adagio and Allegro, Schumann, Robert
Adagio and Allegro, Telemann, Georg Philipp
Adagio and Allegro from Sonata No. 7, Handel, George Frederick
Adagio and Finale from Concertino, Gaucet, Charles
Adagio and Scherzo from Sonata in C Minor, Barber, S.
Adagio for Tuba and Piano, Shostakovitch, Dimitri
Adagio from Concerto No. 2, Reiche, E.
Adagio from Sonata C, Dur, Marcello, Benedetto
Adagio from the Ballet "Till Eulenspigel," Kotshetov, V.
Adonis, Buchtel, Forrest Lawrence
Adventure for Tuba and Piano, Ronnes, Robert
Aeola, Martin, Carroll
Ah! vous dirai, je maman, Reynaud, J.
Air, Désenclos, A.
Air, Gluck, Chr.
Air, Handel, George Frederick
Air, Pergolesi, Giovanni Battista
Air, Rakov, N.
Air and Bourée, Bach, Johann Sebastian
Air and Galumph, Bourgeois, Derek
Air et Final, Planel, Robert
Air from "Comus," Arne, Thomas A.
Air from "Richard Coeur de Lion," Grétry, André
Air from the Opera "Halka," An, Moniushko, S.

Air Gai, Berlioz, G. P.
Ajax, Buchtel, Forrest Lawrence
Alborada, Goodwin, Gordon
Ali-Baba, Delgiudice, Michel
All 'Antica, Goeyens, A.
All the World is Full of Lovers, Mozart, Wolfgang Amadeus
All through the Night, Kinyon, John (arr.)
All through the Night, Ostling, Acton (arr.)
Alla Cacia, Cabus
Allegretto animato, Concone, Giuseppe
Allegretto Comodo, Quérat, Marcel
Allegretto Grazioso, Kreisler, Alexander von
Allegretto grazioso, Stanley, John
Allegretto und Gavotte, Witthauer, Johann Georg
Allegro, Fux, Johann Joseph
Allegro, Handel, George Frederick
Allegro, Mozart, Wolfgang Amadeus
Allegro, Saint-Saëns, Camille
Allegro and Finale, Bozza, Eugène
Allegro and Minuet, Haydn, Franz Joseph
Allegro et Finale, Bozza, Eugène
Allegro from Concerto in F Minor, Handel, George Frederick
Allegro (from Sonata No. 3), Vivaldi, Antonio
Allegro Spiritoso, Senaillé, Jean Baptiste
Alleluja, Exultate, Mozart, Wolfgang Amadeus
Allemande, Franck, Melchior
Alley Cat, Bjorn, Frank
Alt und Neu für Zwei, Zettler, Richard
Altdeutscher Tanz (Narrentanz), Schwotzer, Stephan (arr.)
Alte Bekannte, Kubes, Ladislav
Alte Brummbär, Der, Fucik, Julius
Amarilli, Mia Bella, Caccini, Giulio
Amazing Grace, Newton, John
Ambitos, Costa Ciscar, Francisco Javier
America, Carey, Henry, and Smith, Samuel
America the Beautiful, Ward, S. A.
"America" Variations for Winds, Gerschefski, Edwin
Anapausis, Meunier, Gérard
Ancient Greek Melody, An, Maganini, Quinto
And Then There Were Six, Brown, Newel Kay
Andante, Handel, George Frederick
Andante, Haydn, Franz Joseph
Andante, Roikjer, Kjell
Andante, Tchérépnine, Alexandre
Andante, Op. 53, Douliez, Victor
Andante and Allegro, Clérisse, Robert
Andante and Allegro, Scott, Kathleen
Andante and Allegro, Telemann, Georg Philipp
Andante and Allegro for Tuba and Piano, Jones, Roger
Andante and Rondo, Yoffe, Shlomo
Andante and Rondo from Concerto for Double Bass, Capuzzi, Antonio
Andante Cantabile, Tchaikovsky, Peter I.
Andante Cantabile from Concerto, Rimsky-Korsakov, N.

Andante et Allegro, Barraine, Elsa Jacqueline
Andante et Allegro, Lantier, Pierre
Andante from "First Steps," Op. 82, Gurlitt, Cornelius
Andantino, Poulton
Annie Lisle, Thompson, H. S.
Antre de Polypheme, L', Delgiudice, Michel
Apollo, Buchtel, Forrest Lawrence
Approach of the Lion, The, Prendiville
Après, Midi d'une Crocodille, L', Maganini, Quinto
Après une Lecture de Goldoni: Fantaisie dans le Style du XVIII Siècle, Margoni, Alain
Arabesque V, Nodaïra, Ichiro
Arban's Fantaisie Brillante, Arban, Jean Baptiste
Arbutus, Vander Cook, H. A.
Arcades I, Kellaway, Roger
Archer, The, Buchtel, Forrest Lawrence
Aria, Scarlatti, Alessandro
Aria for Tuba And Piano, Hartley, Walter S.
Aria from "Don Carlos," Verdi, Giuseppe
Aria from "Elijah," Mendelssohn, Felix
Aria from Falstaff, Verdi, Giuseppe
Aria from "Judas Maccabeus," Handel, George Frederick
Aria from La Clemenza di Tito, Mozart, Wolfgang Amadeus
Aria from the Opera "Three Lives," Taktakishvili, O.
Aria "O Isis and Osiris," Mozart, Wolfgang Amadeus
Arie, Pergolesi, Giovanni Battista
Arie and Humuresque, Wilkenschildt, Georg
Arie Janeks aus der Oper "Im Brunnen," Blodek, Vilém
Arietta, Giordani, Giuseppe
Ariette, Huuck, Reinhard
Arioso, Benson, Warren
Arioso, Handel, George Frederick
Arioso and Caprice, Barnes, Clifford P.
Arioso from the opera "Jolanta," Tchaikovsky, Peter I.
Arise Ye Subterranean Winds, Purcell, Henry
Arm, Arm, Ye Brave, from "Judas Maccabeus," Handel, George Frederick
Artist's Life, Strauss
Ash Grove, The, Kinyon, John (arr.)
Asleep in the Deep, Petrie, H. W.
At the Ball, Buchtel, Forrest Lawrence
At the Dance, Tchaikovsky, Peter I.
Atlas, Grand Air varié, de Ville, Paul (arr.)
Attila, Buchtel, Forrest Lawrence
Au Coeur de la Nuit, Steckar, Franck
Au Temps de la coeur, Brouquières, Jean
Auld Lang Syne, DeLamater, E. (arr.)
Auld Lang Syne, Kinyon, John (arr.)
Aura Lee, Feldstein, Sandy (arr.)
Aura Lee, Poulton
Aurora, Ostling, Acton
Automne, Damase, Jean-Michel
Autumn Afternoon, Uber, David
Ave Maria, Schubert, Franz
Ave Maria from "6 Sonnets," Toldra, Eduardo
Away in a Manger, Smith, David E. (arr.)

Azure Etudes, Ross, Walter

B

Baa, Baa Black Sheep, Feldstein, Sandy (arr.)
Bagatelles, Donahue, Robert
Bagatelles for Tuba, Jacob, Gordon
Baladins, Gotkovsky, Ida
Baleine bleue, La, Delgiudice, Michel
Ballad and Presto Dance, Smith, Claude T.
Ballad for Tuba, Christensen, James
Ballad of Enob Mort, The, Uber, David
Ballada, Duntriev, G.
Ballade, Arensky, A.
Ballade, Berlin, A.
Ballade, Krzywicki, Jan
Ballade, Vergauwen, A.
Ballade du Moigne Que Nostre Dame Delivera Dou Dyable, Joubert, Claude-Henry
Ballerina, The, Buchtel, Forrest Lawrence
Bamboola, Amellér, André
Barbarossa—Air Varie, Barnhouse, Charles Lloyd
Barcarolle et Chanson Bachique, Semler-Collery, Jules
Barcarolle for Tuba, Yasumoto, Hiroyuki (arr.)
Bärentanz, Heinl, Otto
Bass in the Ballroom, The, Newsome, Roy
Bass Solo Polka, Berg, Thomas
Bassenparade, Jakma, Henk
Basses Berserk, Bennet, David
Bassette, Delbecq, Laurent
Bassistengruss, Raich
Basso Concertino, Fritze, Gregory
Basso Profundo, Briegel, George F.
Basso Tomaso, Frackenpohl, Arthur
Bassutecy, Amellér, André
Batifol, Amellér, André
Bayou Legend for Solo Tuba and Piano, Uber, David
Be Not Shy, My Pretty One, Rubinstein, Anton
Beautiful Brown Eyes, Feldstein, Sandy (arr.)
Bedouin Love Song, Pinsuti, Ciro
Beelzebub, Catozzi, A.
Behemoth, Vander Cook, H. A.
Belle Province: Hauterive, Amellér, André
Beloved from Afar, Beethoven, Ludwig van
Bendemeer's Stream, Kinyon, John (arr.)
Berceuse, Stravinsky, Igor
Bicycle Built for Two, Dacre, Harry
Bifurcation, Baader-Nobs, Heidi
Big Bear Suite, Dutillet, Jacques
Big Boy, Weber, Fred
Big Joe, the Tuba, Lavalle, Paul, and Tarto, Joe
Bill's Tune, Constantino, Joseph G.
Billboard, Klohr
Billy Blowhard, Kottaun, Celian
Black Holes in Space, Belden, George R.
Blow the Man Down, Ostling, Acton (arr.)
Blow the Man Down, Walters, Harold L. (arr.)
Blue Bells of Scotland, The, Kinyon, John (arr.)
Blue Bells of Scotland, Swanson, Ken (arr.)

Blue Moon, Hart, Lorenz, and Rodgers, Richard
Bold and Brave, Storm, Charles W.
Bolero, Berlioz, Hector
Bombardon Polka, Bottesini, Giovanni
Bombastic Bombardon, Siebert, Edrich
Bombastoso, Vander Cook, H. A.
Book of Beginning Tuba Solos, Daellenbach, Charles
    (arr.)
Book of Easy Tuba Solos, Daellenbach, Charles (arr.)
Boosey's Bombardon Solo Album, Hume, James Ord
    (arr.)
Bordogni Medley, Bordogni, Marco
Bouquet for Basses, Storm, Charles W.
Bourée, Bach, Johann Sebastian
Bourrée, Damase, Jean-Michel
Bourrée, Handel, George Frederick
Bourrée, Krebs, Johann Ludwig
Bourrée, Mozart, Leopold
Brass Talk, Pethel, James
Bravaccio, Fayeulle, Roger
Breeze-Easy Recital Pieces for Tuba, Kinyon, John (arr.)
Burlesque for Tuba and Piano, Kulesha, Gary Alan
By the Sea, Schubert, Franz
Bydlo, from Pictures at an Exibition, Moussorgsky, M.

C

Cadenza e Allegro Scherzando, Maertens, J.
Caisson Song, Feldstein, Sandy (arr.)
Calf of Gold from "Faust," Gounod, Charles
Campagnarde, Lodéon, André
Camptown Races, Foster, Stephen
Campus Queen, Weber
Canadian Brass Blues, Boyd, Bill
Cançao, Havens, Daniel
Cançao de Maria, de Grignon, Lamote
Cantabile, Stepovoi, J.
Cantabile et divertissement pour tuba et orchestre, Sem-
    ler-Collery, Jules
Cantilena for Tuba and Piano, Cummings, Barton
Canzona, Pergolesi, G. B.
Capriccio, Newton, Rodney
Capriccio for Tuba and Band, Presser, William
Capriccio for Tuba and Orchestra, Roikjer, Kjell
Capriccio for Tuba and Small Orchestra, Schuller,
    Gunther
Caprice, Geib, Fred
Cardinal's Air from "La Juive," The, Halévy, Jacques
Caribbean Flush, Cleemput, Werner Van
Carillon et Bourdon, Bigot, Eugène
Carmen Excerpts, Bizet, Georges
Carnaval de Venise, Le, Bilbaut, J.
Carnival for Bass, Muscroft, Fred
Carnival of Venice, Benedict, Julius
Carnival of Venice, Jacobs, Wesley
Carnival of Venice (Fantasia), Holmes, G. E.
Carnival of Venice in F Major, Arban, Jean Baptiste
Carnival of Venice, The (Variations), Arban, Jean
    Baptiste
Carnival Time, Brizzi, Aldo

Caro mio ben, Giordani, Giuseppe
Carry Me Back to Old Virginny, Bland, J.
Carry Me Back to Old Virginny, Guy, Earl
Cavalier, The, Buchtel, Forrest Lawrence
Cavatina, Demerssman, J.
Cavatina, Geib, Fred
Cavatina, Saint-Saëns, Camille
Cavern Impression, A, Frangkiser, Carl
Caverns, Wiley, Frank
Ce que chantait l'aede, Depelsenaire, Jean-Marie
Cedar Vale, Irons, Earl D.
Celebration for Tuba and Piano, Konagaya, Soichi
Centone Buffo Concertante, Jaffe, Gerard
Chaconne, Rodgers, Thomas
Chaconne, Sowerby, Leo
Chain, Nilovic, Janko
Challenge Concert Polka, Giovanini, J.
Changing Scene, Bowles, Richard W.
Chanson and Divertissement, Roberts, Sue
Chanson Triste, Jenkins, Cyril
Chansonnoir, Burgstahler, Elton E.
Chant d'Amour, Clérisse, Robert
Chant Mélancolique, Niverd, Lucien
Chief John, Bell, William J.
Chiens de Paille, Barraine, Elsa Jacqueline
Children's Prayer, Humperdinck, Engelbert
Chinatown, My Chinatown, Schwartz, Jean, and Jer-
    ome, William
Chorale Prelude, Schmutz, Albert D.
*Choralfantasie über "Es ist ein Schnitter, Der Heisst
    Tod,"* Koetsier, Jan
Chorus from Judas Maccabaeus, Handel, George
    Frederick
Christ the Lord Is Risen Today, Wadowick, James L.,
    and McCathren, Donald E.
Christmas Cameos, Conley, Lloyd (arr.)
Christmas Nocturne, Walters, Harold L. (arr.)
Chromatic Concert Polka, Rose, Phil. S.
Chrysanthemum, Vander Cook, H. A.
Cinc (5) Études, Dondeyne, Désiré
Cinq (5) Pièces Courtes: Pour jeune tubistes, Dondeyne,
    Désiré
Civil War Medley, Wekselblatt, Herbert (arr.)
Classic Festival Solos, Lamb, Jack (ed.)
Cockles and Mussels, Kinyon, John (arr.)
Collection of Pieces for Tuba "Es" and Piano, Lebedev,
    A. (ed.)
Collection Panorama, Daniel-Lesur, and Werner, Jean-
    Jacques
College March, Lincoln
Colossus, Vander Cook, H. A.
Columbia, Rollinson, T. H.
Columbine, Vander Cook, H. A.
Come, Thou Fount of Every Blessing, Boyd, Bill (arr.)
Come Again, Sweet Love Doth Now Invite, Dowland,
    John
Come Brave the Sea, Bellini
Commodore, The, Chambers, W. Paris
Complainte, Niverd, Lucien
Concert Album for Tuba, Ostrander, Allen (ed.)

Concert and Contest Collection, Voxman, Himie (compiled and edited)

Concert Duo, Grant, Parks

Concert Etude, Krotov and Blazhevich, Vladislav

Concert Music for Bass Tuba, Mueller, Florian

Concert Music for Tuba, Graham, James (arr.)

Concert Piece, Nelhybel, Vaclav

Concert Piece, Ruff, D.

Concert Piece, Saint-Saëns, Camille

Concert Piece, Op. 50, De Jong, M.

Concert Piece for Tuba and Band, Follas, Ronald W.

Concert Piece for Tuba and Piano, Anderson, Eugene D.

Concert Piece for Tuba and Piano, Larsen, Libby

Concert Piece for Tuba and Piano, Tihomirov, A.

Concert Piece in Fugal Style, Ostrander, Allen

Concert Rondo, Mozart, Wolfgang Amadeus

Concertante, Walters, Harold L.

Concertino, Bozza, Eugène

Concertino, Curnow, James

Concertino, Daucé, Edouard

Concertino, Depetris, C.

Concertino, Hartley, V.

Concertino, Koetsier, Jan

Concertino, LeClerc, E

Concertino, Markl, Max

Concertino, Schrijver, Karel de

Concertino, Zverev, V.

Concertino for Three Brass and Band, Werle, Floyd E.

Concertino for Tuba, George, Thom Ritter

Concertino for Tuba and Band, Bencriscutto, Frank

Concertino for Tuba and Klavier, Watz, Franz

Concertino for Tuba and String Orchestra, Frackenpohl, Arthur

Concertino for Tuba and String Orchestra, Shaughnessy, Robert

Concertino for Tuba and Strings, Rideout, Alan

Concertino for Tuba and Wind Ensemble, Hartley, Walter S.

Concertino for Tuba and Winds, Wilhelm, Rolf

Concertino No. IV, Theme from, Huber, Adolf

Concertiya Sonatina, Roitershteny

Concerto, Bottje, Will Gay

Concerto, Nilovic, Janko

Concerto, Spillman, Robert

Concerto, Op. 11, Strauss, Richard

Concerto Allegro, Lebedev, A.

Concerto brillant, Rollé

Concerto for Bass Tuba, Jager, Robert

Concerto for Bass Tuba, Vaughan Williams, Ralph

Concerto for Tuba, Fleming, Robert

Concerto for Tuba, Garth, J.

Concerto for Tuba, Koch, Erland von

Concerto for Tuba, Kulesha, Gary Alan

Concerto for Tuba and Band, Beasley, Rule

Concerto for Tuba and Concert Band, Wilder, Alec

Concerto for Tuba and Four Horns, Saglietti, Corrado Maria

Concerto for Tuba and Orchestra, Arutiunian, Alexandre

Concerto for Tuba and Orchestra, Heiden, Bernard

Concerto for Tuba and Orchestra, Kikta, V.

Concerto for Tuba and Orchestra, Lovelock, William

Concerto for Tuba and Orchestra, Premru, Raymond

Concerto for Tuba and Orchestra, Schmidt, Ole

Concerto for Tuba and Orchestra, Strukow, Valery

Concerto for Tuba and Orchestra, Williams, V. R. (Vaughan Williams, Ralph)

Concerto for Tuba and Piano, Op. 53, Domazlicky, Frantisek

Concerto for Tuba and Piano, Dumitru, Ionel

Concerto for Tuba and Strings, Martin, Vernon

Concerto for Tuba and Strings, Presser, William

Concerto for Tuba and Strings, Steptoe, Roger

Concerto for Tuba and Symphony Orchestra, Jevtic, Ivan

Concerto for Tuba ("Concerto Euphonique"), Hopkinson, Michael E.

Concerto in A Minor, Vivaldi, Antonio

Concerto in D (K. 412), Mozart, Wolfgang Amadeus

Concerto in E flat (K.417), Mozart, Wolfgang Amadeus

Concerto in E flat (K.447), Mozart, Wolfgang Amadeus

Concerto in E flat (K.495), Mozart, Wolfgang Amadeus

Concerto in One Movement, Lebedev, A.

Concerto No. 2, Williams, Ernest

Concerto No. 2 Part 3, Blazhevich, Vladislav

Concerto No. 2, Part One, Mozart, Wolfgang Amadeus

Concerto No. 3 for Tuba and String Orchestra, Handel, George Frederick

Concerto No. 4, Opus 65 (Excerpts from), Goltermann, Georg Edvard

Concerto No. 4, Part One, Mozart, Wolfgang Amadeus

Concerto per Tuba, Eklund, Hans

Concerto pour Tuba et Orchestra, Godel, Didier

Concertpièce, Couperin, F.

Concertpiece, Painparé, H.

Concertpiece for 3 Tubas and Band, Lackey, Jerry

Concertpiece for Tuba and Piano, Dillon, Robert

Concertpiece for Tuba and Piano, Rappoldt, Lawrence I.

Concertpiece No. 1, Vaughan, Rodger

Concertpiece No. 2, Vaughan, Rodger

Concertstück, Murgier, Jacques

Concertstück, Rueff, Jeanine

Concertstück für Tuba in F und Klavierbegleitung, Geier, Oskar

Concertstuk (1944), Maes, J.

Concierto para Tuba y Piano, Casas, Bartolomé Perez

Conjectures, Sauter, Eddie

Conquistadores, Hill, William H.

Contraste per tuba e pianoforte, Grudzinski, Czeskaw

Conzertstuck für Tuba mit Klavierbegleitung, Geier, Oskar

Coquette, Concert Polka, La, Innes, F. N.

Cornemuse, Dubois, Pierre Max

Coronation March, Meyerbeer, Giacomo

Cortège, Beaucamp, Albert

Cortège, Bigot, Pierre
Cortège, Séguin, Pierre
Cortège et Danse, Charles, C.
Couleurs en Mouvements, Moreau, James
Country Dance, Beethoven, Ludwig van
Courante, Senaillé, Jean Baptiste
Courier, The, Buchtel, Forrest Lawrence
Coventry Carole, Jacobs, Wesley (arr.)
Cradle Song, Brahms, Johannes
Cradle Song, Schlemüller, Hugo
Cradle Song, A, Lebedev, A.
Cromagnon, Louvier, Alain
Cross of Jesus, The, Smith, David E. (arr.)
Cruel War Is Raging, The, Boyd, Bill (arr.)
Crusaders' Hymn, Kinyon, John (arr.)

D

Daisies, Vander Cook, H. A.
Dance, Bartók, Belá
Dance, Goedicke, A.
Dance, Gudmen, S.
Dance and Aria, White, David Ashley
Dance from the Ballet "Seven Beauties," Karaev, V.
Dance from the Ballet "Spartak," Khatchaturian, A.
Dance of the Bear, Bartók, Belá
Dance of the Slovaks, Bartók, Belá
Dance, The, Rossini, Gioacchino
Dancing Silhouettes, Harris, Floyd O.
Dancing Song, Liadov, Anatol
Dancing Tuba, The, Stephens, Denzil
Dans der Teddyberen, Jakma, Frits Sr.
Dans les pins, Hubert, P.
Danse l'Elephant, Delgiudice, Michel
Danse Sacrée, Tomasi, Henri
Danse villageoise, Beethoven, Ludwig van
Danza Española, Uber, David
Dare to Be a Daniel, Bliss, P. P.
Daydreams, Myers, Theldon
De Profundis, Saul, Walter B. III
Dear If You Change, Dowland, John
Dear Old Songs of Home, Abt, Fr.
Dear to My Heart, Siebert, Edrich
Deep Bass, Fillmore, Henry
Deep Calls to Deep, Hutchison, Warner
Deep Cavern, Ostling, Acton
Deep Rock, Bowles, Richard W.
Deep Sea Stories, Alletter, Wilhelm, and Knight, Joseph Philip
Delaware Rhapsody, A, Uber, David
Dels Quatre Vents from "6 Sonnets," Toldra, Eduardo
Demetrius, Merle, John
Deserted Farm, A, MacDowell, Edward
Design for Bass, Nagel, Paul
Designs, Lunde, Ivar Jr.
Designs and Patterns for Tuba and Grand Piano, Brandon, Sy
Désir, Le, Beethoven, Ludwig van
Deux Mouvements Contrastés, Devos, Gérard

Deux Pièces brèves, Semler-Collery, Jules
Dewdrops, Vander Cook, H. A.
Dialogue, Durand-Audard, Pierre
Dialogue, Martelli, Henri
Dialogue for Tuba and Piano, Rothgarber, Herbert
Dies Irae, Langgaard, Rued
Diptych, Brown, Rayner
Dirge No. 4, Bartók, Belá
Dith, The, Catelinet, Philip
Diversita Continua, Choen, Michael
Divertimento, Dondeyne, Désiré
Divertimento, Mignone, Francisco
Divertissement, Sabathil, Ferd.
Divertissement, Schmidt, A.
Divertissement classique, Truillard, R.
Dix Petit Textes, Delgiudice, Michel
Dolce Espressivo, Amellér, André
Dona Nobis Pacem, Jacobs, Wesley (arr.)
Dona Nobis Pacem, Wadowick, James L., and Mc-Cathren, Donald E.
Dove Sei from "Rodelinda," Handel, George Frederick
Down among the Dead Men, Prendiville, Harry (arr.)
Down Deep within the Cellar, Fischer, Ludwig
Down in the Deep Cellar, Kroepsch, F.
Down in the Deep Deep Cellar, Fischer, Ludwig
Down in the Valley, Walters, Harold L. (arr.)
Doxology, Bourgeois, Louis, and Ken, Thomas
Drei Skizzen, Lischka, Rainer
Drei Stücke für Tuba und Orgel, Ehmann, Heinrich
Drink to Me Only With Thine Eyes, Kinyon, John (arr.)
Duo, Hailstork, Adolphus C.

E

Earle of Oxford's Marche, The, Byrd, William
Eclipse Finale?, Meier, Jost
Egotistical Elephant, The, Hartzell, Doug
Eight Bel Canto Songs, Phillips, Harry I. (ed.)
Elegia, Masne, D.
Elegia, Rachmaninoff, Sergei
Élegié, Proust, Pascal
Elegie, Strukow, Valery
Elegy, Vaughan, Rodger
Elegy for the Whale, Wilder, Alec
Elegy for Tuba and Piano, Zinos, Fredrick
Elementarité, Senon, G.
Elephant and a Mouse, An, Marttinen, Taune
Elephant Dance, The, Weber, Fred, and Garrett, Dorothy
Elephant from "Carnival of Animals," Saint-Saëns, Camille
Éléphant (Der Elefant), L', Saint-Saëns, Camille
Emmett's Lullaby, Holmes, G. E.
En Glissant. . ., Lesaffre, Charles
Enchanted Island, The, Kosteck, Gregory
Encore Piece for Tuba and Piano, Wilder, Alec
Enterrement de Saint Jean, L', Bariller, Robert
Entr'acte from "Rosamunde," Schubert, Franz
Epic Tale and Procession of the People in Costumes

(Festival), Kikta, V.
Epode for Tuba and Piano, Vollrath, Carl
Erie Canal, Feldstein, Sandy (arr.)
Erie Canal, The, Boyd, Bill (arr.)
Erie Canal, The, Kinyon, John (arr.)
Esquisse Concertante Concertschets, Desprez, F.
Essai, Gartenlaub, Odette
Essay for Tuba, Pethel, Stan
Estonian Folk Dance, Lebedev, A. (arr.)
Etre ou ne pas être, Tomasi, Henri
Etude, Scriabine, Alexander
Etude de concert, Leonov, I.
Etude No.1 for Tuba and Piano, Hogg, Merle E.
Etude, Op.10, No. 3, Chopin, Frederick
Etude (Op. 10, No. 11), Concone, G.
Evensong, Uber, David
Exchange for Tuba and Piano, Knight, Morris
Excursions for Tuba and Piano, Davies, Kenneth
Exposition Echoes Polka, Pryor, Arthur
Expromt, Arutiunian, Alexandre

F

Fairy Jane, The, Marzials
Fairy Tail, A, Monushko, S.
Faith, Glover, S.
Faith of Our Fathers, Bayley, Thomas Haynes
Falstaff Concerto, Op. 119, Krol, Bernhard
Falstaff's Drinking Song, Nicolai, Otto
Fancies and Interludes I, Luedeke, Raymond
Fantaisie, Dubois, Pierre Max
Fantaisie, Petit, Pierre
Fantaisie Concertante, Castérède, Jacques
Fantaisie Contante, Villette, Pierre
Fantaisie Italienne, Coriolis, Emmanuel de
Fantasia, Feldman, Enrique C.
Fantasia, Garlick, Antony
Fantasia a Due, Reed, Alfred
Fantasia Breve for Tuba and Piano, Cummings, Barton
Fantasia for Tuba and Chamber Orchestra, Hartley, Walter S.
Fantasia for Tuba or Bass Trombone with Band or Piano Accompaniment, Op. 57, Tuthill, Burnet
Fantasie, Schroen, B.
Fantasy for Tuba and Piano, Faust, Randall E.
Fantasy for Tuba and Piano, Konagaya, Soichi
Fantasy for Tuba and Piano, Sacco, P. Peter
Fantasy on a Lakota Theme for Tuba and Piano, Bales, Kenton
Fantasy on a Theme of Scarlatti, Davidson, Douglass
Fantezia nocturna, Dumitru, Ionel
Feel Good Blues, The, Quate, Amy
Fett und Filtz, Op. 403d, Bentzon, Niels Viggo
Fidele Bassist, Der, Ruckauer, H.
Fifteen Intermediate Tuba Solos, Hudadoff, Igor, and Wescott, William
Fifteen Introductory Solos, Brass Wind Publications
Fifteenth Solo de Concours, Porret, Julien
Fifty Standard Solos, Pro Art

Finlandia, Sibelius, Jean
Finnish Rhapsody, Borg, Kim
First and Second Movements from Violin Sonata, Eccles, H.
First Contest, Waignein, A.
First Movement from Concerto for Horn, Mozart, Wolfgang Amadeus
First Noel, The, Conley, Lloyd (arr.)
First Solo Album, Weber, Carl (arr.)
First Solo Songbook, Feldstein, Sandy (arr.)
First Solos for the Tuba Player, Wekselblatt, Herbert
Five Pieces for Tuba and Piano, Durkó, Zsolt
Five Solos for Tuba, Bennett, Malcolm, and Connor, Eddie
Five Songs, Brahms, Johannes
Flame, Schwartz, Elliott
Flatterer, The, Buchtel, Forrest Lawrence
Fleur de Lis, Irons, Earl D.
Flow Gently, Sweet Afton, Little, Don (arr.)
Flow Gently, Sweet Afton, Spillman, James E.
Folk Song Melodies, Ostling, Acton (arr.)
Folksong Medley, Bell, William J. (arr.)
For Harvey, Kellaway, Roger
For He's a Jolly Good Fellow, Feldstein, Sandy (arr.)
For the Funk of It, Browning, Zack
Forget Me Not, Macbeth, Allan
Forty Fathoms, Walters, Harold L.
Foster Medley, Foster, Stephen C.
Four Faces of Tubby, McCurdy, Gary L.
Four Segments, Barnet, Richard D.
Four Shorts for Tuba and Piano, Largent, Edward
French Folk Song, Feldstein, Sandy (arr.)
French Song, Ostling, Acton (arr.)
Frère Jacques, Feldstein, Sandy (arr.)
Friar of Orders Gray, The, Shield
Fröhlicher Landmann, Schumann, Robert
Funambules, Depelsenaire, Jean-Marie
Funeral March of a Marionette, Gounod, Charles

G

G. F. Handel's Third Tuba Concerto, Bevan, Clifford
Galejade, Waignein, A.
Gallant Captain, Ostling, Acton (arr.)
Galliarde, Franck, Melchior
Gargantua, Delgiudice, Michel
Gavotte, Bach, Johann Sebastian
Gavotte, Bell, William J.
Gavotte, Gluck, K. [*sic*]
Gavotte, Lebedev, A.
Gavotte, Lully, Jean-Baptiste
Gavotte, Pachelbel, Johann
Gavotte, Popper, David
Gavotte, Purcell, Henry
Gavotte and Hornpipe, Purcell, Henry
Gavotte en Rondeau, Lully, Jean-Baptiste
Gavotte from Symphony No. 4, Boyce, William
Gay Caballero, Schaefer, August H.
George M. Cohan Medley, Cohan, George M.

German Waltz, Jacobs, Wesley (arr.)
German Waltz, Kinyon, John (arr.)
Gigue, Corelli, Arcangelo
Giralda, Hume, James Ord
Give My Regards to Broadway, Cohan, George M.
Gladiator, Buchtel, Forrest Lawrence
Glow Worm, The, Lincke
Go Down, Moses, Jacobs, Wesley (arr.)
Golden Days (Serenade), St. Clair, Floyd P.
Golden Dreams Waltz, Buchtel, Forrest Lawrence
Golden Glow, Buchtel, Forrest Lawrence
Golliwogg's Cake-walk, Debussy, Claude
Good King Wenceslas, Feldstein, Sandy (arr.)
Good Night, Samonov, A.
Gopak, Moussorgsky, M.
Grand Air from "The Masked Ball," Verdi, Giuseppe
Grand Cadence, Kling, G., and Neuling, G.
Grand solo de concert, Watelle, J.
Grandfather Is Dancing, Samonov, A.
Grave, Lancen, S.
Grave, Petit, Pierre
Grave and Allegro, Swinnen, Hans
Grave et Scherzo, Op. 107, Manen, Christian
Green Apple Two-Step, The, Kulesha, Gary Alan
Greensleeves, Jacobs, Wesley (arr.)
Grenadier, The, Buchtel, Forrest Lawrence
Groteskna Koračnica, Štuhec, Igor
Gypsy Love Song, Herbert, Victor
Gypsy Melody, Dvořák, Antonin

H

Ha! Just in the Nick of Time!, Mozart, Wolfgang Amadeus
Habanera from "Carmen," Bizet, Georges
Hallelujah! What a Saviour!, Smith, David E. (arr.)
Hamlet's Monologue, Tomasi, G. [*sic*]
Hans de Schnokeloch, Bariller, Robert
Happy Be Thy Dreams, de Ville, Paul (arr.)
Happy Farmer, The, Schumann, Robert
Happy Hippo, The, Ward, Norman
Happy Song, Siennicki, Edmund J.
Happy Thoughts, Baseler, J.
Harlequin, Buchtel, Forrest Lawrence
Harmonious Blacksmith, The, Handel, George Frederick
Harvest Dance, Jacobs, Wesley (arr.)
Harvest Waltz, Siennicki, Edmund J.
Haydn Medley, from Symphony No. 94, Haydn, Franz Joseph
Hear Our Prayer—Paraphrase, Rollinson, T. H.
Heart Victorious (Cantata), Carissimi, Gian Giacomo
Heather Rose Caprice, Lange
Heav'n, in Pray'r, Thine Aid I Seek and *Good Subjects of Brabant, 'tis well!* (from *Lohengrin*), Wagner, Richard
Helix (Concerto for Solo Tuba and Concert Band), Benson, Warren
Hercules, Buchtel, Forrest Lawrence
Here I Sit in the Deep Cellar, Fischer, Ludwig

Herfstbloemen, Jakma, Frits Sr.
Hermes, Buchtel, Forrest Lawrence
Herod's Air from "Herodiade," Massenet, Jules
Heroic Tale, A, Geib, Fred
Herr Tubist, Der, Löffler
Hey, Ho! Nobody Home, Boyd, Bill (arr.)
Hey Jude!, Lennon, John and McCartney, Paul
Hey-Ho, Come To The Fair, Martin, Easthope
Hikari, Aru Sora, Wa Shiazukani, Censhu, Jiro
Himatsuri, Ideta, Keizo
His Majesty the Tuba, Dowling, Robert
Histoires de Tuba Vol. 1: Plantez les gars!, Dubois, Pierre Max
Histoires de Tuba Vol. 2: Le petit cinéma, Dubois, Pierre Max
Histoires de Tuba Vol. 3: Le grand cinéma, Dubois, Pierre Max
Histoires de Tuba Vol. 4: Concert Opéra, Dubois, Pierre Max
Historiette Dramatique, Niverd, Lucien
Holy City, Adams
Home on the Range, Kinyon, John (arr.)
Honeysuckle Polka, Casey
Honor and Arms, Handel, George Frederick
Hornpipe, Wekselblatt, Herbert (arr.)
Hornpipe, A, Lotzenhiser, G. W.
Hot Cross Buns, Feldstein, Sandy (arr.)
Hour of Prayer, The, Nelson
How Can I Leave Thee, Buchtel, Forrest Lawrence
How Strong Your Tone with Magic Spell, Mozart, Wolfgang Amadeus
Humoreska, Dumitru, Ionel
Humoreske in F, Kulesha, Gary Alan
Humoresque, Bernaud, Alain
Humorous Dance, Kolodub, L
Humresque, Jacobsen, Julius
Hungarian Folk Song, Bartók, Belá
Hungarian Melody, Zverev, V.
Hussar, The, Buchtel, Forrest Lawrence
Hyacinthe, Vander Cook, H. A.
Hymn, Haydn, J.
Hymn to Joy, Beethoven, Ludwig van
Hymne, Niverd, Lucien

I

I Wonder As I Wander, Smith, Douglas (arr.)
Iago's Song about King Stephen from the Tragedy Othello, Sviridov, G.
I'd Give My Finest Feather, Mozart, Wolfgang Amadeus
Idylle, Clérisse, Robert
Il Mio Bel Foco, Marcello, Benedetto
Il Viaggio 1 per tuba solo con pianoforte, Sikora, Elzbieta
Impromptu, Bitsch, Marcel
Impromptu, Ilvea
Impromptu, Poot, Marcel
Impromptu in G, Op. 7 No. 1, Gray, Louis Robert
Improvisation, Goedicke, A.
In a Modal Mood, Barnes, James

In F, Stratton, Don
In Lively Spirits, Hopkinson, Michael E.
In Lively Spirits, Senaillé, Jean Baptiste
In Olden Times, Jacobs, Wesley (arr.)
In Spring Time, Grieg, E.
In Springtime, Jacobs, Wesley (arr.)
In the Army, Ball, Eric
In the Beginning, Biblical Poem for Tuba (Cello) and Organ, Callahan, Charles
In the Deep, Deep Depths, Hume, James Ord
In the Deep Forest, Geib, Fred
In the Garden, Monroe, Margrethe
In the Hall of The Mountain King, Grieg, Edvard
In the Lowlands, Richardson, Alan
Installation au moulin, L', Poullot, F.
Instant Band Ensembles (Tuba), Kinyon, John (arr.)
Instrumental Albums Number 14: Solos and Duets for Soprano Eb, Horn Eb, and Bass Eb with Pianoforte Accompaniment, Salvation Army Press
Intermede, Layens, C. G.
Intermezzo, Bitsch, Marcel
Intermezzo, Challan, Henri
Intermezzo, Gliere, Reinhold
Intermezzo Capriccioso, Castellucci, Louis
Interrogaçoes, Kiefer, Bruno
Intrade, Pezel, Johann
Introduction and Allegretto, Kappey
Introduction and Allegro, Madsen, Trygve
Introduction and Allegro Spiritoso, Senaillè, Jean-Baptiste
Introduction and Andante, Op. 54, Douliez, Victor
Introduction and Blues, Powell, Morgan
Introduction and Dance, Barat, J. Edouard
Introduction and Dance, Bilik, Jerry H.
Introduction and Dance, Scarmolin, A. Louis
Introduction and Polka Piquante, Geib, Fred
Introduction and Rondo, Buchtel, Forrest Lawrence
Introduction, Aria and Rondo, Koch, Frederick
Introduction et Cantabile, Baeyens, H.
Introduction et Danse, Barat, J. Edouard
Introduction et Rigaudon, Faillenot, Maurice
Introduction et Sérénade, Barat, J. Edouard
Introduction et Toccata, Carles, Marc
Invincible, Lafont
Invocation for Tuba and Piano, Standford, Patric
Irish, Cante, Amellér, André
It Is Enough from "Elijah," Mendelssohn, Felix
Ive, Amellér, André
Ivy, Vander Cook, H. A.

J

Jay Rozen Portrait and Fugue, Thomson, Virgil
Jazz Concerto for Tuba and Band, Lackey, Jerry
Jazz Concerto for Tuba and Orchestra, Lackey, Jerry
Jesus Is the Sweetest Name, Long, Lela
Jesus Loves Me, Warner and Bradbury
Jesus/Sweetest Name I Know, Moss, Alan
Jeu 3, Zbar, Michel
Jeux Chromatiques, Depelsenaire, Jean-Marie

Jig Elephantine, Bell, William J.
Jimbo's Lullaby, Debussy, Claude
Jingle Bells, Pierpont, J.
John Peel, Kinyon, John (arr.)
Joke, A, Bak, Mikhail Abromovich
Joke, A, Smironova, T.
Jolly Coppersmith, The, Peter, C.
Jolly Dutchman, The, Issac, Merle J. (arr.)
Jolly Farmer Goes to Town, The, Schumann, Robert
Jolly Jumbo, Bell, William J.
Jolly Old St. Nicholas, Feldstein, Sandy (arr.)
Jolly Peasant, The, Schumann, Robert
Jolly Sailor, Buchtel, Forrest Lawrence
Journal of Days, Butterfield, Don
Joy to the World, Conley, Lloyd (arr.)
Joyous Dialogue, A, Geib, Fred
Juggler, The, Buchtel, Forrest Lawrence
Jumbo, Carion, M.
Jumbo, Baby, Baratto, Paolo
Just a Closer Walk, Foley, Red
Just Foolin' Around, Myers, Theldon

K

Kellermeister, Der, Schneebiegl, Rolf
Kerry Dance, The, Molloy, J. L.
King Mydas, Buchtel, Forrest Lawrence
King Neptune, Ostling, Acton
King of the Deep, Moquin, Al
King's Jester, The, Harris, Floyd O.
Kis Eloeadasi Darab Tubara, Kistetenyi, Melinda
Kis Humoreszk, Aranyi, Gyorgy
Kleiner Walzer, Dragonetti, Domenico
Koan II, Gistelinck, E.
Koncert med orkester, Roikjer, Kjell
Koncert za Kontrabasovsko Tubo, Ramovš, Primož
Konzert für Tuba und Klavier, Lebedjew, A.
Konzert für Tuba und Orchester, Gruner, Joachim
Konzert für Tuba und Orchestra, Rottler, Werner
Konzert g, Moll, Handel, George Frederick
Konzert Op. 35, Madsen, Trygve
Konzert, Cadenz, Neuling, Hermann
Konzertetüde, Gregor, František
Konzertstuk, Dumitru, Ionel
Kryptos, Amellér, André

L

L'os hispánic, Blanquer, Amando
Lamento, Beach, Bennie
Lancer, The, Bonheur, Theodore
Ländler für Tuba und Klavier, Hoza, Václav
Landskap, Lundquist, Torbjorn Iwan
Larghetto and Allegro, Handel, George Frederick
Largo and Allegro, Marcello, Benedetto
Largo and Presto, Marcello, Benedetto
Largo for Tuba and Piano, Hartley, Walter S.
Last Saturday Evening, The, Grieg, Edvard
Lazy Day, Myers, Theldon
Lazy Lullaby, Little, Donald C.

Lead on O King Eternal, Everson, Dana F. (arr.)
Learn As You Play Tuba, Wastall, Peter (ed.)
Legend, Burshtin, M.
Legend, Catelinet, Philip
Legend, Stoutamire, Albert L.
Legend of Purple Hills, The, Uber, David
Legend of The Sleeping Bear, Uber, David
Légende, Beugniot, Jean-Pierre
Légende, Kaï, Naohiko
Légende, Niverd, Lucien
Legende, Vansteenkiste, M.
Legende et Caprice, Debaar, M.
Lento, Handel, George Frederick
Lento, Holmes, Paul
Lento Elegiaco, Strukov, V.
Leporello's Aria from Don Juan (Don Giovanni),
   Mozart, V. [*sic*]
Leprechauns Patrol, Walters, Harold L.
Let Me Like a Soldier Fall, Wallace
Letters from a Friend, Spaniola, Joseph
Leviathan, The, Wiegand, George
Libre-episode, Werner, Jean-Jacques
Liebe Farbe, Die, Schubert, Franz
Liebesfreud, Kreisler, Fritz
Lied, Pergolesi, Giovanni Battista
Lieder eines Fahrenden Gesellen, Mahler, Gustav
Lights Far Out at Sea, Gatty, A. S.
Lily, Vander Cook, H. A.
Lindenbaum, Der, Schubert, Franz
Little Birch Tree, A, Frid, G.
Little Caesar, Harris, Floyd O.
Little Fiesta, Harris, Floyd O.
Little Maiden, Jacobs, Wesley (arr.)
Loch Lomond, Boyd, Bill (arr.)
Loch Lomond, Kinyon, John (arr.)
Logos, Ameller, André
London Bridge, Feldstein, Sandy (arr.)
Londonderry Air, Buchtel, Forrest Lawrence (arr.)
Londonderry Air, Kinyon, John (arr.)
Londonderry Air, Yasumoto, Hiroyuki (arr.)
Lonely Forest, The, Lully, Jean-Baptiste
Long, Long Ago, Bayley, Thomas Haynes
Long, Long Ago, Kaneda, B.
Lord Preserve Me, Rossini, Gioacchino
Los Cocos Locos, Quate, Amy
Love Somebody, Feldstein, Sandy (arr.)
Love Song (Caro mio ben), Giordani, Giuseppe
Love That's True Will Live Forever (Si, Tra I Ceppi,
   from "Berenice"), Handel, George Frederick
Lovely Evening, Feldstein, Sandy (arr.)
Low Down Bass, Bell, William J.
Lowlands, Osborne, Chester
Lucy Long, Godfrey, Fred
Lullaby, Brahms, J.
Lustiger Bassist Konzertpolka, Manas, Franz
Luzerne Song, Bennett, Malcolm (arr.)

M

Magnolia, Vander Cook, H. A.

Make Mine a Tuba, Norton, Christopher
Mallorca (Barcarola), Albeniz, I.
Manchester Parade (a British Slow-March), Vaughan,
   Rodger
Mannequin, The, Buchtel, Forrest Lawrence
Manta for Tuba and Piano, Jones, Roger
Mantis Dance, Warren, David
March, Jurovsky, V.
March from *Suite No. 5*, Purcell, Henry
March of a Marionette, Gounod, Charles
Marche, Mozart, Wolfgang Amadeus
Marches, Marches, Marches, Hudadoff, Igor (ed.)
Marching Right Along, Barnes, James
Marigold, Vander Cook, H. A.
Marine, Clérisse, Robert
Mariner, The, Buchtel, Forrest Lawrence
Mariner, The, Mattei, Tito
Marines' Hymn, Offenbach, Jacques
Marines' Hymn March, The, Phillips, L. Z.
Mary's Idea, Childs, Barney
Master Solos Intermediate Level, Perantoni, Dan-
   iel (ed.)
Mastodon, Guentzel, Gus
May Song, Beethoven, Ludwig van
McCluskeys Rag, Connor, Eddie
McLeods Reel, Bennett, Malcolm (arr.)
Méandres, Lejet, Edith
Medici Masterworks Solos Volume 1, Gershenfeld,
   Mitchell (ed.)
Mediterranean Rondo, Levy, Yehuda
Mein!, Schubert, Franz
Meistersinger von Nürnberg, Die, Wagner, Richard
Melodie Romanza, Frangkiser, Carl
Melodies of Many Lands, The, Glover, S.
Melodious Etude, Bell, William J.
Melody, Geib, Fred
Melody, Vasilyev, V.
Melody from "Orpheus and Euridice," Gluck, Christoph
   W. von
Méloman, Gastinelle, Gerard
Memphis Ridge, Siennicki, Edmund J.
Menuet, Beethoven, Ludwig van
Menuet, Hall, Harry H. (arr.)
Menuet, Štuhec, Igor
Menuet and Bourrée, Hasse, Gower
Menuet Éclaté, Damase, Jean-Michel
Menuet from "Alcina," Handel, George Frederick
Menuett im Kanon, Radolt, Wenzel Ludwig Frei-
   herr von
Menuette, Boccherini, L.
Menuetto, Mozart, Wolfgang Amadeus
Merry Peasant, The, from "Album for the Young,"
   Schumann, Robert
Merry Widow Waltz, Lehar, Franz
Message, The, Brooks, E.
Mighty Deep, The, Jude, W. H.
Mighty Fortress, A, Jacobs, Wesley (arr.)
Military March, Little, Donald C. (arr.)
Military Marches Melodies, Ostling, Acton (arr.)
Military Suite, Wekselblatt, Herbert (arr.)

Mini Suite, Jeanneau, Francois
Miniature No. 7, Blazhevich, Vladislav
Miniaturen-Suite, Benker, Heinz
Miniatures for Tuba and Piano, Cummings, Barton
Minstrel Boy, Kinyon, John (arr.)
Minstrel's Song, Nicolai, W. F. G.
Minuet, Eccles, John
Minuetto Profondo, Op. 83, no. 1, Krol, Bernhard
Minute Sketches, Presser, William
Miroir et L'Eau, Nissim, Mico
Miya Sama from The Mikado, Sullivan, Arthur, and Gilbert, W. S.
Moderation, Quérat, Marcel
Modern Lullaby, A, Newton, Leonard G.
Modules, Haines, Edmund
Moment Musical, Schubert, Franz
Monsieur Tuba, Fiche, Michel
Morceau de Concert—Concertstuk, de Jong, Marinus
Morceau de Concours, Alary, G.
Morceau de Concours, Barat, J. Edouard
Morceau de Concours I, Defaye, Jean-Michel
Morceau de Concours II, Defaye, Jean-Michel
Morceau de Concours III, Defaye, Jean-Michel
Morceau Vivant, Marteau, Marcel
Morning Glory, Vander Cook, H. A.
Morning Song, Kellaway, Roger
Mosaik, Hoza, Václav, and Hála, Jan
Moss Rose, Vander Cook, H. A.
Mouvement, Henry, Jean-Claude
Movement for Tuba and Piano (1980), Tal, Joseph
Movements, Durkó, Zsolt
"Mr. Tuba" on Broadway, Uber, David
Mulberry Street Tarantella, Briegel, George F.
Mummers—Danse Grotesque, Merle, John
Musette, Bach, Johann Sebastian
Music for Tuba and Orchestra, Eerola, Lasse
Music for Tuba and Piano, Warren, Frank E.
Musizierbuch für Basstuba, Meschke, Dieter
Mutability Fantasy, Constantinides, Dinos
Muziek (1976), Woestyne, David Van de
My Anchor Holds, Everson, Dana F. (arr.)
My Dearest Love (Caro mio ben), Giordani, Giuseppe
My Jesus I Love Thee, Featherstone, W. R., and Gordon, A. J.
My Johann, Grieg, Edvard
My Sweetheart's Eyes, Schubert, Franz
My Tuba Solo, Scholtes, Walter
My Tuba Solo, Southwell, George
My Wild Irish Rose, Olcott
Mystique, Crockett, Edgar

N

N-sarja, Eerola, Lasse
Nachtstück, Rottler, Werner
Nature's Adoration, Beethoven, Ludwig van
Nautical John Medley, Bell, William J.
Nervous Turkey Rag, The (November Is Here Again), Barnes, James
Neutron Stars, Belden, George R.

New Orleans, Bozza, Eugène
Next, Winter Comes Slowly, Purcell, Henry
Nightingale, Jacobs, Wesley (arr.)
Nina, Pergolesi, Giovanni Battista
Nine Miniatures, Gregson, Edward, and Ridgeon, John
Nineteen Solos for Eb Bass with Piano Accompaniment, Weber, Carl (arr.)
No. 4 from 24 Easy Vocalises, Bordogni, G. M.
No. 9 from 24 Easy Vocalises, Bordogni, G. M.
No. 10 from 24 Easy Vocalises, Bordogni, G. M.
No. 15, from Etüden für Tuba, Kopprasch, C.
No. 19, from Etüden für Tuba, Kopprasch, C.
Nobody Knows the Trouble I've Seen, Yasumoto, Hiroyuki (arr.)
Nocturnal Serenade, Morra, Gene
Nocturne, Chopin, Frederick
Nocturne, Geib, Fred
Nocturne, Gliere, Reinhold
Nocturne, Mendelssohn, F.
None But The Lonely Heart, Op. 6, Tchaikovsky, Peter I.
Now, O Now I Needs Must Part, Dowland, John
Nuit d'harmonie, Une, Meunier, Gérard
Nur Lieben!, Dargomijsky, Aleksander S.

O

O Come, All Ye Faithful, Conley, Lloyd (arr.)
O du mein holder Abendstern, from "Tannhäuser," Wagner, Richard
O Isis and Osiris from "The Magic Flute," Mozart, Wolfgang Amadeus
O Little Town of Bethlehem, Conley, Lloyd (arr.)
O Mensch, bewein' dein' Sünde gross, Bach, Johann Sebastian
O Mighty God, Wadowick, James L., and McCathren, Donald E.
O Ruddier Than the Cherry, Kappey
Obsessions, Van Der Roost, J.
Octopus and the Mermaid, The, King, Karl L.
Ode to Joy, Beethoven, Ludwig van
Oh, Is There Not One Maiden Breast?, Sullivan, Arthur
Oh, My Home, Abt, Franz
Old American Patriotic Song (Chester), Billings, William
Old Home Down on the Farm, Harlow
Old McDonald, Feldstein, Sandy (arr.)
Old Sexton, The, Russell, H.
Old Sexton, The, Weber, Carl (arr.)
Old Time Theme and Variations, Barnes, James
Omaggi e Fantasie for Tuba and Piano (1981/87), Baker, Claude
On Heaven's Just Cause Relying and *Rataplan Chorus (from "Les Huguenots")*, Meyerbeer, G.
On the Lake, Brahms, Johannes
On the Steep High Mountain, Lebedev, A. (arr.)
On the Sunny Side of the Street, McHugh, Jim, and Fields, Dorothy
On Wings of Song, Mendelssohn, F.

One Tough Tuba, Solomon, Edward S.
Op. 28—Preludes Nos. 3, 2, and 24, Chopin, Frederick
Optima, Nilovic, Janko
Opus Open, Forez, Henri
Oracio al Main from "6 Sonnets," Toldra, Eduardo
Orientale, Cui, César
Os Mestres Cantores da Lapa, Tacuchian, Ricardo
Ostinato, Schmidt, A.
Out on the Deep, Lohr, Frederic N.
Oxford Gavotte, Kagan, Susan

P

Pansies, Vander Cook, H. A.
Pantomime, Uber, David
Papa Haydn's Tune, Haydn, Franz Joseph
Parable for Tuba and Piano, Siekmann, Frank H.
Pastorale, Goldsmith, James J.
Patron of the Wind from "Phoebus and Pan," Bach, Johann Sebastian
Pavane, Ravel, Maurice
Peace of Mind, Sponholtz
Peg Leg Pete, Zaninelli, Luigi
Penseroso e L'Allegro, Il, Buchtel, Forrest Lawrence
Peony, Vander Cook, H. A.
Per la Gloria d'Adorarri from "Griselda," Bononcini, Giovanni
Per Questa Bella Mano, Mozart, Wolfgang Amadeus
Per Tuba ad Astram, Woolf, Gregory
Perpetual Motion, Paganini
Persian Song, A, Rubinstein, A.
Persiflage, Koepke, Paul
Petit Air, Poutoire, Patrick
Petit Baobab, Le, Delgiudice, Michel
Petit Mamouth, Le, Delgiudice, Michel
Petit pièce en fa, Corelli, Arcangelo
Petite Chanson pour Marion, Lesaffre, Charles
Petite Valse Européene, Français, Jean
Philae, Amellér, André
Piccolo Capriccio pour tuba et piano, Dupriez, Christian
Piccolo Suite, Dubois, Pierre Max
Piece, A, Volkov, K.
Pièce de Concerte, Sivic, Pavle
Piece for Tuba and Piano, Lawrence, Lucinda
Piece from Suite "Colours in Movement," Moro, D.
Piece in C, Maniet, René
Pièce Lyrique, Clérisse, Robert
Piece of Tuba, Inagaki, Takuzo
Piece Preve, Cals
Pieces for Tuba and Piano, Guzii, V. (compiled)
Pieces for Tuba and Piano, Larin, J. (ed.)
Pieces for Tuba and Piano, Melnikov, S. (ed.)
Pieces for Tuba and Piano, Mitegin, V. (ed.)
Pieces for Tuba and Piano, Mitjagina, V. (ed.)
Pied Piper, Buchtel, Forrest Lawrence
Pietà, Signore!, Stradella, Alessandro
Piff, Paff (Les Huguenots), Meyerbeer, Giacomo
Pilot, The, Nelson, S.
Pink Panther, The, Mancini, Henry

Plaisir d'Amour, Martini, J. P. A.
Playera, Granados, E.
Pleasant Hours. A Collection of 20 Standard Melodies, de Ville, Paul (arr.)
Poco Allegro, Maniet, René
Poem and Burlesque for Double Bass (Tuba) and Piano, Kardos, Istvan
Poème, Op. 10, Balthazar, J. L.
Policeman's Song, The, Sullivan, Arthur
Polka from "The Age of Gold," Shostakovitch, Dimitri
Polka Funurenilor, Dumitru, Ionel
Polka Giocoso, Scarmolin, A. Louis
Polka Graziosa, Del Negro, Luca
Pomp and Dignity, Scarmolin, A. Louis
Pompola, Martin, Carroll
Pomposo Polka, Jennings
Popular Solos for the Young Bandsman, Edmunds, John (arr.)
Poursuites, Moreau, James
Praeludium and Fughetta, Stoutamire, Albert L.
Praeludium, Chorale, Variations and Fugue, Mueller, J. I.
Praeludium in C Minor, Vivaldi, Antonio
Praise Him, All Ye Little Children, Smith, David E. (arr.)
Prayer, A, Schlemüller, Hugo
Preghiera, Durante, Francesco
Prelude, Fesh, D.
Prelude, Kesnar, Maurits
Prelude, Ledov, A.
Prelude, Orthel, L
Prelude and Allegretto, Telemann, Georg Philipp
Prelude and Allegro, Bozza, Eugène
Prelude and Faràndola, Hastings, Ross
Prelude and Fugue, Bottje, Will Gay
Prelude and Scherzo, Brown, Newel Kay
Prelude and Scherzo, Cruft, Adrian
Prélude, arioso et rondo, Franck, Maurice
Prélude et Allegro, Bozza, Eugène
Prélude et Allegro, Charpentier, Jacques
Prélude et cadence, Barboteu, Georges
Prélude et Danse Guerrière, Ruelle, F.
Prélude et divertissement, Clérisse, Robert
Prelude No. 1, Op. 376B, Hewitt, Harry
Prelude No. 6, Chopin, Frederick
Prelude No. 6, Op. 376C, no. 6, Hewitt, Harry
Prelude und Scherzo für Tuba und Klavier, Shekov, Ivan
Preludes, Barcos, George
Preludio and Allemanda, Corelli, Arcangelo
Preludiu, Dumitru, Ionel
Premier Pièce de Concours, Porret, Julien
Premier Solo de Concert, Demerssman, J.
Premier Solo de Concours, Maniet, Rene
Première Étude de Concours, Petit, Alexandre
Presto from Divertimento No. 12, Mozart, Wolfgang Amadeus
Pretty as a Butterfly, Weber, Carl (arr.)
Pride of America, DeWitt, L. O.
Prière, Rougnon

Priester, Aria aus die Zauberflöte, Mozart, Wolfgang Amadeus
Promenade, Coeck, Louis Jan Alfons Leopold
Promenade, Hyde, Derek
Promenade, Uga, Pierre
Puerta de Tierra (Bolero), Albeniz, I.
Puff (The Magic Dragon), Yarrow, Peter, and Lipton, Leonard
Puissance 4, Delgiudice, Michel
Pupille Nere, Buononcini, Giovanni

Q

Quadrille en Forme de Ronds d'Eau, Autran, Alphonse
Qui Tollis, Hume, James Ord
Quick Dance, Bogár, István
Quiet Piece, A, Stewart, Robert
Quintero—The Farmer, Merle, John
Quintessence, Clews, Eileen

R

Rainy Day Rock, Feldstein, Sandy
Ranger, The, Buchtel, Forrest Lawrence
Ré mineur, Rivière, Jean-Pierre
Recercada on the "Passamezzo Moderno" (1553), Ortiz, Diego
Recit, Gully, Michel
Récit et Rondo, Tournier, Franz
Récit et Thème Variations,Op. 37, Büsser, P. Henri
Recitatif et Allegro, Depetris, C.
Récitatif, Lied et Final, Brown, Charles
Recitativ and Burla, Op.83, no. 2, Krol, Bernhard
Recitative and Air from "The Messiah," Handel, George Frederick
Recitative and Kutuzov's Air from the Opera "War and Peace," Prokofiev, Sergei
Recitative, Song and Chorus, Purcell, Henry
Red River Valley, Kinyon, John (arr.)
Reflections, Jager, Robert
Relation, Quérat, Marcel
Relax, Baudrier, Émile
Reluctant Clown, The, Buchtel, Forrest Lawrence
Remembrance for Tuba and Piano, Cummings, Barton
Remembrance of Liberati, Casey
Reminiscences de Navarre, Barat, J. Edouard
Repentance, Handel, George Frederick
Requiem for Euphonium or Basstuba and Piano, Lovec, Vladimir
Requiem for Pee Wee Ervin, Hyman, Dick
Revenge! Timotheus Cries!, Handel, George Frederick
Reverie, Debussy, Claude
Reverie, Mendelssohn, Felix
Reverie (Schumanniana), de Grignon, Lamote
Rhapsody for Tuba and Orchestra, Cioffari, Richard J.
Rhapsody in Black and Blue, Dutton, Brent
Riddle Song, The, Boyd, Bill (arr.)
Rigaudon, Daquin, Louis-Claude
Rigaudon, Rameau, J. Ph.
Rigaudon from Pièces de Clavecin, Rameau, Jean Philippe

Ring, A, Lebedev, A. (arr.)
Ritcherkar, Bitsch, Marcel
Ritmico ed Arioso, Louel, Jean
Rock'd in the Cradle of the Deep, Knight, J. P.
Rocked in the Cradle of the Deep, DeLamater, E.
Rocked in the Cradle of the Deep, Knight, J. P.
Rocked in the Cradle of the Deep, Pruyn, William
Rocked in the Cradle of the Deep, Rance, E. (Adjutant)
Rocked in the Cradle of the Deep, Rollinson, T. H.
Rocked in the Cradle of the Deep, Scholtes, Walter (arr.)
Roghisness, Depetris, C.
Rohtokokoelma, Eerola, Lasse
Romance, Clérisse, Robert
Romance, Glinka, M.
Romance, Hanson, Raymond
Romance, Rakov, N.
Romance, Rubinstein, A.
Romance, Saint-Saëns, Camille
Romance, Scriabine, Alexander
Romance, Shostakovitch, Dimitri
Romance, Uber, David
Romance and Scherzo, Cohen, Sol B.
Romance Espagnuolo, Hume, James Ord
Romance "Homage to Peter Ilyich," Cole, Keith Ramon
Romance No. 2, Schumann, Robert
Romance No. 3, Schumann, Robert
Romance, Op. 77, Bourgeois, Derek
Romance Sentimentale, Niverd, Lucien
Romanze and Rondo (from Horn Concerto No. 3), Mozart, Wolfgang Amadeus
Rondelay, Jenkins, Cyril
Rondo, Bach, Johann Sebastian
Rondo, Jenne, Glenn
Rondo, Kreisler, Alexander von
Rondo, Presser, William
Rondo, Tchebotarev, S.
Rondo Alla Scherzo (from Clarinet Concerto in E♭), Stamitz, Karl
Rondo de Concerto, Mozart, Wolfgang Amadeus
Rondo from Divertimento No. 11, Mozart, Wolfgang Amadeus
Rooster, The, Siennicki, Edmund J.
Rosebuds, Vander Cook, H. A.
Roses from the South, Strauss, Johann
Roundarounds, Arbel, Chaya
Rudéral, Joubert, Claude-Henry
Rumanian Dance No.2, Dumitru, Ionel
Russian Dance, Zverev, V.
Russian Medley, Bell, William J. (arr.)
Russian Song, Rachmaninoff, Sergei
Russian Song, Stravinsky, Igor

S

Sad Minute, The, Pozzoli, E.
Sad Song, The, Kalinikov, V.
Sad Song, The, Tchaikovsky, Peter I.
Sailing the Mighty Deep, Moquin, Al

Sailors' Song, Schumann, Robert
Salamander, The, Buchtel, Forrest Lawrence
Salicastrum, Smith, Glenn
Samsonian Polka, McQuaide, George
Sanctus, Berlioz, Hector
Sandman, Brahms, J.
Sans Pareil, Bell, J. H.
Sarabanda and Gavotta, Corelli, Arcangelo
Sarabande, Corelli, Arcangelo
Sarabande, Leclair, Jean-Marie
Sarabande from Concerto in F Minor, Handel, George
    Frederick
Saxhornia, Semler-Collery, Jules
Scène de Concert, Danmark, Max F.
Scenes from Childhood, Op. 15, Schumann, Robert
Scherzetto, Niverd, Lucien
Scherzino, Haddad, Don
Scherzo, Assafyev, B.
Scherzo, Dumitru, Ionel
Scherzo, Frank, Marcel
Scherzo for Tuba, Golland, J.
Scherzo for Tuba and Wind Ensemble, Bartles, Alfred
Scherzo Pomposo, Walters, Harold L.
Schön Rosmarin, Kreisler, Fritz
Schule für Tuba in F und in B, Hoza, Václav
Science Fiction, Gasner, Moshe
Sculptured Tradition for Tuba and Piano, En-
    do, Masao
Sea Gong, The, Desmond, Walter
Search for the Missing Marble, The, Price, Joseph
Seaview for Tuba and Piano, Childs, Barney
Sebben, Crudele, Caldara, Antonio
Second Horn Concerto, Strauss, Richard
Second Part from Capriccio, Bach, Johann Sebastian
Second Sonatina for Tuba and Piano, Presser, William
See, the Conquering Hero Comes, Handel, George
    Frederick
*Sentimental Sarabande, The, from the "Simple Sym-
    phony" for String Orchestra,* Britten, Benjamin
Sento Nel Core, Scarlatti, Allessandro
Serenada d'Hivern from "6 Sonnets," Toldra, Eduardo
Serenade, Geib, Fred
Serenade, Mozart, Wolfgang Amadeus
Serenade, Owen, J. A.
Serenade, Schmidt, William
Serenade, Weiner, Lawrence
Serenade and Scherzo, Ostransky, Leroy
Serenade for Tuba and Piano, Israel, Brian
Serenade for Tuba and Piano, Rae, Allan
Serenade from "Don Giovanni," Mozart, Wolfgang
    Amadeus
Serenata, Schooley, John
Serioso, Mihalovici, M.
Serpent of the Brass, Worth, George E.
Set of Three, Smolanoff, Michael
Shades of Tuba, Vasconi, Eugene
Shenandoah, Bennett, Malcolm (arr.)
Short Stuff, Lackey, Jerry
Short Suspense Story, A, Rufeisen, Arie

Siciliano, Bach, Johann Sebastian
Siciliano and Chorale, Bach, Johann Sebastian
Siciliano from Sonata No. II, Bach, Johann Sebastian
Sicilienne, Rougnon
*Sicilienne d'après la 1re Sonate en Sol mineur (BMV
    1001) pour Violin seul,* Bach, Johann Sebastian
Siegfried (from Act II, Prelude and First Scene), Wag-
    ner, Richard
Silent Night, Conley, Lloyd (arr.)
Silent Night, Gruber, Franz
Silver Threads Among the Gold and Deep River, Danks,
    H. P. and Harris, A. E.
Simon the Cellarer, Hatton, J. L.
Simplex pour tuba et piano, Guinot, Georges-Léonce
Sine Nomine, Kilon, Moshe
Six Little Tuba Pieces, Jacob, Gordon
Six Modern Pieces, Lawrance, Peter
Six Petites Pièces De Style, Niverd, Lucien
Six Petits Morceaux, Schrijver, Karel de
Six Popular Solos, Prendiville, Harry (arr.)
Six Preludes for Tuba and Piano, Op. 376B, Hew-
    itt, Harry
Six Studies in English Folk, Song, Vaughan Wil-
    liams, Ralph
Skaters, The, Waldteufel, Emil
Skater's Waltz, Waldteufel, Emil
Sketches for Tuba and Piano, McFarland, Michael
Skylines, Uber, David
Slow-Fox-Medium, Hrdina, Eman
Slumber Song, Gretchaninoff, A.
Small Suite for Bass (Tuba) and Piano, Wilder, Alec
Smuggler, The, Beresford, Arnold
Softly, Softly, Rossini, Gioacchino
Soir, Clérisse, Robert
Soliloque, Weber, Alain
Soliloquy for Tuba and Piano, Cummings, Barton
Soliloquy, Hume, James Ord
Solitude, Lotzenhiser, G. W.
Solitude Caprice, Mercadante, Giuseppe
Solo and Duo for Tuba and Piano, Moylan, William
Solo de Concours, Wurmser, Lucien
Solo for Tuba and String Quartet, Mellilo, Peter
Solo Miniature, Murphy, Bower
Solo Pomposo, Hayes, Al
Solo Sounds for Tuba, Level 1, 3, Vol. 1, Lamb, Jack (ed.)
Solo Sounds for Tuba, Level 3, 5, Vol. 1, Lamb, Jack (ed.)
Solo-Pak for Tuba, Part One, Little, Donald C. (arr.)
Solo-Pak for Tuba, Part Two, Little, Donald C. (arr.)
Solo-Pak for Tuba, Part Three, Little, Donald C. (arr.)
Soloist Folio for Bass (Eb or BBb), Rubank
Solos for the Tuba Player, Wekselblatt, Herbert (ed.)
Solos from the Classics, Jacobs, Wesley (arr.)
Solstice, Cole, Keith Ramon
Sometimes I Feel Like a Motherless Child, Barnes,
    James (arr.)
Sonare per Tuba e Piano, Friedman, Norman
Sonata, Anderson, Garland
Sonata, Benjamin, Thomas
Sonata, Dutillet, Jacques

Sonata, Ekkls, H.
Sonata, Gower, Albert
Sonata, Köper, Karl-Heinz
Sonata, Marcello, Benedetto
Sonata, Pisciotta, Louis V.
Sonata, Salzedo, Leonard
Sonata, Schmidt, William
Sonata, Skolnik, Walter
Sonata, Smironova, T.
Sonata, Vivaldi, Antonio
Sonata, Zeman, Thomas
Sonata Capricciosa, Takács, Jeno
Sonata (Concerto), Broughton, Bruce
Sonata di Bravura, Uber, David
Sonata for Bass Horn and Piano, Strebel, Neal
Sonata for Bass Tuba and Piano, Beversdorf, Thomas G.
Sonata for Bass Tuba and Piano, Uber, David
Sonata for BBb Bass and Piano, Peterson, Lawrence
Sonata for (F) Tuba and Piano Op. 34, Madsen, Trygve
Sonata for Tuba, Guion, David M.
Sonata for Tuba, Morawetz, Oskar
Sonata for Tuba, White, Donald H.
Sonata for Tuba, Op. 393, Bentzon, Niels Viggo
Sonata for Tuba, Op. 55, Cunningham, Michael
Sonata for Tuba and Organ, Kulesha, Gary Alan
Sonata for Tuba and Piano, Bardwell, William
Sonata for Tuba and Piano, Blumenfeld, Aaron
Sonata for Tuba and Piano, Brandon, Sy
Sonata for Tuba and Piano, Frackenpohl, Arthur
Sonata for Tuba and Piano, Fritze, Gregory
Sonata for Tuba and Piano, Garrett, James
Sonata for Tuba and Piano, George, Thom Ritter
Sonata for Tuba and Piano, Gower, William
Sonata for Tuba and Piano, Hartley, Walter S.
Sonata for Tuba and Piano, Kitsz, Dennis Bathory
Sonata for Tuba and Piano, Karlsen, Kjell Mork
Sonata for Tuba and Piano (Op. 6), Krush, Jay
Sonata for Tuba and Piano, LaPresti, Ronald
Sonata for Tuba and Piano, Lockwood, Harry
Sonata for Tuba and Piano, Payne, Frank Lynn
Sonata for Tuba and Piano, Prescott, John
Sonata for Tuba and Piano, Rekhin, Igor
Sonata for Tuba and Piano, Reynolds, Verne
Sonata for Tuba and Piano, Schmidt, Ole
Sonata for Tuba and Piano, Sibbing, Robert
Sonata for Tuba and Piano, Sivelov, Niklas
Sonata for Tuba and Piano, Smith, Kile
Sonata for Tuba and Piano, Stabile, James
Sonata for Tuba and Piano, Warren, Frank E.
Sonata for Tuba and Piano, Wenström-Lekare, Lennart
Sonata for Tuba and Piano, Whatley, G. Larry
Sonata for Tuba and Piano, Wilder, Alec
Sonata for Tuba and Piano, Op. 162, Holmboe, Vagn
Sonata for Tuba and Piano, Op. 277, Bentzon, Niels Viggo
Sonata for Tuba and Piano, Op. 393, Bentzon, Niels Viggo

Sonata for Tuba in F and Piano, Holliday, Kent
Sonata I, from 6 Solos for a Violoncello, Marcello, Benedetto
Sonata II, Bach, Johann Sebastian
Sonata in F Major, Telemann, Georg Philipp
Sonata in G Major for Tuba and Piano, Beethoven, Ludwig van
Sonata No. 1 for Tuba and Piano, Hewitt, Harry
Sonata No. 1 for Tuba and Piano, Konko, Iwao
Sonata No. 1 for Tuba and Piano, Mowery, Carl D.
Sonata No. 1 in F Major, Marcello, Benedetto
Sonata No. 2, Israel, Brian
Sonata No. 2 for Tuba and Piano, Hewitt, Harry
Sonata No. 2 for Tuba and Piano, Konko, Iwao
Sonata No. 2 for Tuba and Piano, Mowery, Carl D.
Sonata No. 2 for Tuba and Piano, Wilder, Alec
Sonata No. 3 in A Minor, Vivaldi, Antonio
Sonata No. 5, Galliard, John Ernest
Sonata No. 5 in C Major, Marcello, Benedetto
Sonata No. 6, Galliard, John Ernest
Sonata No. 6, Handel, George Frederick
Sonata No. 7, Haydn, Franz Joseph
Sonata No. 7, first movement, Haydn, Franz Joseph
Sonata No. 9, Op. 5, Corelli, Arcangelo
Sonata No. 10, Op. 5, Corelli, Arcangelo
Sonata per Tuba (Contrabasso) and Piano, Garbarino, Giuseppe
Sonata Romantica for Tuba and Piano, Cohn, James
Sonata Romantica per tuba e pianoforte, Fotek, Jan
Sonata-Fantasia for Tuba and Piano, Calabro, Louis
Sonatas for Tuba and Piano, Blazhevich, Vladislav
Sonate, Hindemith, Paul
Sonate, Laburda, Jirí
Sonate C, Dur für Tuba und Klavier/Orgel, Handel, George Frederick
Sonate en fa majeur, Albinoni, Tommaso
Sonate en ré majeur, Albinoni, Tommaso
Sonate for Tuba and Piano, Holmboe, Vagn
Sonate for Tuba og Klaver, Roikjer, Kjell
Sonate für Basstuba und Klavier, Stekl, Konrad
Sonate für Tuba und Klavier, Kladnitzki, W.
Sonate in 6 Minutes 30, Pascal, Claude
Sonate II for Tuba and Piano, Bach, Johann Sebastian
Sonatina, Boda, John
Sonatina, Danburg, Russell
Sonatina, Hartley, Walter S.
Sonatina, Koetsier, Jan
Sonatina, Rakov, N.
Sonatina, Uber, David
Sonatina (1972) for Tuba and Piano, Kulesha, Gary Alan
Sonatina Classica, Troje-Miller, N.
Sonatina for Tuba and Piano, Glass, Jennifer
Sonatina for Tuba and Piano, Hogg, Merle E.
Sonatina for Tuba and Piano, Presser, William
Sonatina for Tuba and Piano, Rollin, Robert
Sonatina for Tuba and Piano, Sear, Walter
Sonatina for Tuba and Piano, Stevens, Halsey
Sonatina für Tuba und Klavier, Rottler, Werner

Sonatina Giocosa, Hartley, Walter S.
Sonatina Movement IV, Link, I.
Sonatina Tuba e Pianoforte, Koetsier, Jan
Sonatine, Castérède, Jacques
Sonatine, Link, Joachim-Dietrich
Sonatine für Basstuba und Klavier, Hummel, Bertold
Sonatine für Tuba (Posaune) und Klavier, Koch, Johannes H. E.
Sonatine für Tuba und Klavier, Foremny, Stephan
Sonatine in C, Dondeyne, Désiré
Sonatine No. 1, Uber, David
Sonatine No. 2, Uber, David
Sonatuba, Uber, David
Song, Zverev, V.
Song, A, Bartók, Belá
Song after Battle for Tuba and Piano, Wunder, Richard
Song and a Dance, A, Dubrovsky, I.
Song and Dance for Tuba and Piano, Bassett, Leslie
Song for Carol, Wilder, Alec
Song for Tuba and Piano, Warren, Frank E.
Song from the Cycle "Persian Songs," Rubinstein, A.
Song from the Opera "Snow Maiden," Rimsky-Korsakov, N.
Song from Timon of Athens, Purcell, Henry
Song of India, Rimsky-Korsakov, N.
Song of the East, Rimsky-Korsakov, N.
Song of the Field, Miaskovskii, N.
Song of the Flea, Moussorgsky, M.
Song of the Sea, Buchtel, Forrest Lawrence
Song of the Viking, Buchtel, Forrest Lawrence
Song of the Volga Boatman, Boyd, Bill (arr.)
Song Without Words: Air with Variations, Geib, Fred
Songs from Die Schöne Müllerin, Schubert, Franz
Songs of Ascent (Concerto), Kellaway, Roger
Sonorities for Tuba and Piano, Hartley, Walter S.
Souffle Profond, Un, Desportes, Yvonne
Sound an Alarm from "Judas Maccabeus," Handel, George Frederick
Soundpiece, Snyder, Randall
Sousaphone Polka, Bell, William J.
Sousaphone, The, Del Negro, Luca
Sousaphonium, Moquin, Al
Souvenir de Calais, Liagré, Dartagnan
Souvenir de Paris, Lannoy, J. B. de
Souvenir du Poitou, Legendre
Spacious Firmament, The, Haydn, J.
Spacious Firmament on High, The, Haydn, Franz Joseph
Spanish Dance, Kazadezins, R.
Spanish Dance No. 2 (Oriental), Granados, E.
Spanish Dance No. 5 (Andaluza), Granados, E.
Spanish Waltzes, Waldteufel, Emil
Spartan, The, Bell, William J.
Spartan, The, Buchtel, Forrest Lawrence
Spiritoso, Pergolesi, Giovanni Battista
Spring Fancy, O'Neill, Charles
Spring's Awakening, Bach, E.
Stand Up, Stand Up Jesus, Smith, David E. (arr.)
Ständchen, Schubert, Franz
Stars and Stripes Forever, Sousa, John Philip

Steal Away, Jacobs, Wesley (arr.)
Steal Away, Kinyon, John (arr.)
Steeple, The, Jacobs, Wesley (arr.)
Still Sweeter Every Day, Dondit, Dee Ann (arr.)
Sting Ray, Eitel, Butler
Storm King, The, Ringleben, J.
Streets of Laredo, Boyd, Bill (arr.)
Stupendo, Brahmstedt, N. K.
Suite, Gotkovsky, Ida
Suite Babu (Are You My), Volkmann, Rudy
Suite Brève dans le goût classique, Désenclos, A.
Suite Concertante, Russell, Armand
Suite Concertante, Schoonenbeek, Kees
Suite for Bass Clef Instruments, McKay, George Frederick
Suite for Louise, Masso, George
Suite for Tuba, Haddad, Don
Suite for Tuba, Presser, William
Suite for Tuba and Piano, Butts, Carrol M.
Suite for Tuba and Piano, Nelhybel, Vaclav
Suite for Tuba and Piano, Soule, Edmund F.
Suite for Tuba and Piano, Staples, James
Suite in A-flat, Handel, George Frederick
Suite in A Minor for Flute and Strings, Telemann, Georg Philipp
Suite Marine, Defaye, Jean-Michel
Suite No. 1 for Tuba and Piano ("Effie Suite"), Wilder, Alec
Suite No. 1 from The Magic Flute, Mozart, Wolfgang Amadeus
Suite No. 2 for Tuba and Piano (Jesse Suite), Wilder, Alec
Suite No. 2 from The Magic Flute, Mozart, Wolfgang Amadeus
Suite No. 3 for Tuba and Piano "Suite for Little Harvey," Wilder, Alec
Suite No. 4 for Tuba and Piano "Thomas Suite," Wilder, Alec
Suite No. 5 for Tuba and Piano (Ethan Ayer), Wilder, Alec
Suite pour Tuba, Martelli, Henri
Summer Nocturne, Uber, David
Sunday, Brahms, Johannes
Sunday (Sonntag, Op. 47, 1868), Brahms, Johannes
Superman, Delgiudice, Michel
Sur la Montagne (Pastorale), Bruniau, Aug
Svensk Concerto, Sagvik, Stellan
Swan, The, Siennicki, Edmund J.
Swan Song, Schubert, Franz
Sweet and Low, Barnby, Sir Joseph
Sweet Betsy from Pike, Kinyon, John (arr.)
Swiss Air, Newsome, Roy
Symphonic Variants for Euphonium and Band, Curnow, James

T

Tabu for Tuba, Downey, John
Take Me Out to the Ball Game, Tilzer, Albert von, and Norworth, Jack

Tale, A, Smironova, T.
Tango, Clews, Eileen
Tango Anyone?, Edelson, Edward
Tarantelle, Walters, Harold L.
"Te Anau" Fantasia, Hume, James Ord
Tecnica In Aba, Vanheel, L.
Teddy Bears' Picnic, The, Bratton, John W.
Tema Cantabile con Piernicazioni per tuba universale e pianoforte, Zajaczek, Roman
Tempesta Polka, Harris, John H.
Temporal Landscape No. 1, Vogel, Roger C.
Temporal Landscape No. 4, Vogel, Roger C.
Tendres Mélodies, Wurmser, Lucien
Texas Horizons, Quate, Amy, and Little, Don
Thanksgiving, Jacobs, Wesley (arr.)
Theater Piece, Uber, David
Theater Piece for Tuba and Piano, Cody, Robert O.
Thema und Variationen und Tempo de Polonaise fur Tuba und Klavier, Wieschendorff, Heinrich
Theme and Variations, Dvarionas, B.
Theme and Variations for Tuba, Compello, Joseph
Thème et Variations, Aubain, Jean Emmanuel
Thème Varié, Bozza, Eugène
Thème Varié, Petit, Pierre
There's a Hole in the Bucket, Feldstein, Sandy (arr.)
This Old Man, Feldstein, Sandy (arr.)
Thoughts of Sunraysia, Gross, Eric
Three Chopin Preludes for Tuba and Piano, Chopin, Frederick
Three Episodes, Brandon, Sy
Three Expressioni, Croley, R.
Three Famous Melodies, Ostling, Acton (arr.)
Three Favorites, Weber, Fred (arr.)
Three Miniatures, Plog, Anthony
Three Miniatures for Tuba and Piano, Yuhas, D.
Three Movements (1988), Brink, Daniel S.
Three Movements for Tuba and Piano, Winteregg, Steven
Three Pieces for Tuba and Piano, Johnston, Richard
Three Sketches, Lloyd, Gerald
Three Traditional Tunes for Sabbath (1974), Braun, Yehezkel
Three Traditional Tunes for Sabbath Eve (1974), Braun, Yehezkel
Three Tuba Rags, Jackman, Andrew
Three Tuba Solos, Howe, Marvin C. (arr.)
Thrice Happy the Monarch from "Alexander Balus," Handel, George Frederick
Thu Sau, Cummings, Barton
Time, a Season, A, Bourassa, Richard
Tis So Sweet to Trust in Jesus, Smith, David E. (arr.)
(Title Unknown), Lebedev, A.
To Each His Own, Livingston, J., and Evans, R.
Toccata, Nordel, Marius
Toga Virilis, Smedvig, Egil
Tom Bowling, Dibdin
Tom Dooley, Feldstein, Sandy (arr.)
Tomsky's Song from the Opera "Queen of Spades," Tchaikovsky, Peter I.

Ton Coeur (Tuba), Renaud, Manuel
Tonal Miniature Pieces, Roikjer, Kjell
Toreador's Song, Bizet, Georges
Torre Alada, Widmer, Ernst
Touch of Tuba, A, Dedrick, Art
Tournevalse, Durand-Audard, Pierre
Tramp! Tramp! Tramp!, DeLamater, E. (arr.)
Träumerei, Schumann, Robert
Três miniaturas, Bauer, Guilherme
Triade, Holstein, Jean Paul
Trio 48, Haydn, Franz Joseph
Triptych for Tuba and Piano, Weeks, Clifford M.
Triste España Sin Ventura, Enciña, Juan Del
Trois caricatures, Toulon, Jacques
Trois Duos pour Tuba et Piano, Jolas, Betsy
Trois Exercises de Style, Lemaire, Jean
Trolley Song, The, Martin, Hugh, and Blaine, Ralph
Troubadour, The, Buchtel, Forrest Lawrence
Trumpet Voluntary, Clarke, Jeremiah
Tub' 88, Clais, Tristan
Tuba, Stewart, Joseph
Tuba and Piano Sonata: Three Movements, Knight, Morris
Tuba (Bass) Soloist, Book 1, Ostling, Acton, and Weber, Fred
Tuba Buffo, Jacobsen, Julius
Tuba Caper, Burgstahler, Elton E.
Tuba Compositae, Amos, K.
Tuba Concerto, Carrier, Loran F.
Tuba Concerto, Gregson, Edward
Tuba Concerto, Horovitz, Joseph
Tuba Concerto, McKimm, Barry
Tuba Concerto, Ross, Walter
Tuba Concerto für Tuba und Klavier, Mortimer, John Glenesk
Tuba Concerto No. 1 in B Minor, Anderson, Eugene D.
Tuba Concerto, Op. 38, Bourgeois, Derek
Tuba Diobolica (Polka), Dumitru, Ionel
Tuba—I, Cecconi, Monic
Tuba Kapriolen, Graetsch, Hans
Tuba Mirum, Op. 35, Galán, Carlos
Tuba Mosaique, Armand, Migani
Tuba Rhapsody, Grundman, Clare
Tuba Rose (Polka), Hartley, Walter S.
Tuba Show, Lodéon, André
Tuba Smarties, Flowers, Herbie
Tuba Solos (BB♭ Bass) Volume One, Fletcher, John (arr.)
Tuba Solos (E♭ Bass) Volume One, Fletcher, John (arr.)
Tuba Solos (Tuba in C) Volume One, Fletcher, John (arr.)
Tuba Solos, Level One, CPP/Belwin, Inc.
Tuba Solos, Level Two, CPP/Belwin, Inc.
Tuba Sonata in A, Brothern, Hartman
Tuba Suite, Jacob, Gordon
Tuba Tango, Edelson, Edward
Tuba Tantrum, Miller, Vernon R.
Tuba Tunes, Hanmer, Ronald
Tuba Tutor Vol. 1, Lebedev, A. (ed.)
Tuba Tutor Vol. 2, Lebedev, A. (ed.)

Tuba Volume #1, Yasumoto, Hiroyuki (arr.)
Tuba Volume #2, Yasumoto, Hiroyuki (arr.)
Tuba Volume #3, Yasumoto, Hiroyuki (arr.)
Tuba-Abut, Amellér, André
Tuba-Concert, Amellér, André
Tuba-Sepp'l, Engelhardt, Ernst
Tuba-Tabu, Köper, Karl-Heinz
Tuba-Talk, Hyde, Derek
Tubabil, Meunier, Gérard
Tubabillage, Gabaye, Pierre
Tubacchanale, Boutry, Roger
Tubadour, Fote, Richard
Tubalied for Tuba and Contemporary Wind Ensemble or Piano, Fredrickson, Thomas
Tubalow, Burgstahler, Elton E.
Tubaman, The, Bell, William J.
Tubania for Tuba and Piano, Koch, Erland von
Tubanova, Semler-Collery, Jules
Tubantella, Legrady, Thomas
Tubaria, Bigot, Pierre
Tubaria, Brouquières, Jean
Tubaroque, Boutry, Roger
Tubateer Polka, The, Bell, William J.
Tubavardage, Séguin, Pierre
Tubaverseny, Istvàn, Bogar
Tubism, Gross, Eric
Tubissimo, Dondeyne, Désiré
Tubonetta, Pauer, Jirí
Tulip, Vander Cook, H. A.
Tune for Tuba (Sonatina for Tuba and Piano), Goode, Jack C.
Tunuva Tuba, Joubert, Claude-Henry
Twelve Preludes for Tuba and Piano, Hewitt, Harry
Twenty-Four Pieces for Tuba and Piano, Roikjer, Kjell
Twenty-Four Preludes for Tuba and Piano, Jacobsen, Julius
Twenty-Four Preludes for Tuba and Piano, Roikjer, Kjell
Twilight Dreams, Clarke, Herbert L.
Twinkle, Twinkle Little Star, Feldstein, Sandy (arr.)
Two Classical Themes, Haydn, Franz Joseph
Two Impromptus, Donahue, Robert
Two Lieder, Brahms, Johannes
Two Little Leprechauns, Kulesha, Gary Alan
Two Moods for Tuba, Swann, Donald
Two Pieces, Bak, Mikhail Abromovich
Two Pieces, Deason, David
Two Pieces, Haddad, Don
Two Pieces from "Children's Corner" for Tuba and Piano, Debussy, Claude
Two Rossini Pieces, Rossini, Gioacchino
Two Short Pieces, Handel, George Frederick
Two Songs, Spillman, Robert
Two Songs for Tuba and Piano, Elgar, Edward
Two Songs from Sea Pictures, Elgar, Edward

U

Unforgotten Days, Roeckel, J.
Up Front Albums Book 1, Brass Wind Publications

Up Front Albums Book 2, Brass Wind Publications
Up on the Housetop, Hanby, B. R.

V

Valentine's Song from "Faust," Gounod, Charles
Valse Caprice, Skolnik, Walter
Valse Gentile, Catelinet, Philip
Valse Impromptu, Barnes, Clifford P.
Valse Lente, Rougnon
Valse Nostalgique, Rougeron, Philippe
Variationen über ein Volkslied, Blank, Hans
Variations, Handel, George Frederick
Variations for Tuba and Piano (The Cobblers Bench), Frackenpohl, Arthur
Variations from the Ballet Konick-Gorbunoch, Schedrin, R.
Variations in Olden Style (d'après J.S. Bach), Stevens, Thomas
Variations on a Theme for Tuba and Piano, Hanson, Ronald D.
Variations on a Theme of Gottschalk, Diercks, John
Variations on a Theme of Robert Schumann, Davis, William
Variations on a Theme of Roy Harris, Steinquest, Eugene W.
Variations on a Theme of Samuel Barber, Mueller, Frederick A.
Variations on the "Carnival of Venice," Arban, Jean Baptiste
Variations on the Theme of "Judas Maccabeus" by G. F. Handel, Beethoven, Ludwig van
Variations sur un Thème de Purcell, Lemaire, Jean
Venetian Carnival, Bowles, Richard W.
Venezia, Usher, Julia
Veni Creator, Meyerbeer, Giacomo
Verdurous Aubade for Tuba and Piano, Censhu, Jiro
Victor Herbert Medley, Herbert, Victor
Victors' March, The, Feldstein, Sandy (arr.)
Village Blacksmith, The, Weiss, W.H.
Village Dance, Jacobs, Wesley (arr.)
Villageoise, La, Rameau, Jean Philippe
Villanella, Ross, Walter
Virtuosity Study No. 1, Dutton, Brent
Virtuoso, The, Beeler, Walter
Visions for Jane, Kulesha, Gary Alan
Vivace, from Sonata in E minor, Loelliet, Jean-Baptiste
Vocalise, Rachmaninoff, Sergei
Voce M'Ha Colpito, Una, Rossini, Gioacchino
Voce Nobile, Clérisse, Robert
Voice of the Viking, Bennet, David
Volunteer, The, Buchtel, Forrest Lawrence
Voyageur, The, Buchtel, Forrest Lawrence

W

Wagenia, Petit, Pierre
Wakatipu, Hume, James Ord
Walkabout, Matchett, Steve

Walküre (from Act III), Die, Wagner, Richard

Walther's Prize Song, Wagner, Richard

Waltz, Brahms, J.

Waltz, Brahms, S. [*sic*]

Waltz and Galop from Petite Suite, Kabalevsky, D.

Waltz for Mippy III for Tuba and Piano, Bernstein, Leonard

Waltz from Serenade for Strings, Tchaikovsky, Peter I.

Waltz Themes, Lincke, and Waldteufel, Emil

Waltzing Wind, Myers, Theldon

Waltzing with a Whirlybird, Eitel, Butler

Walzer, Hrdina, Eman

Water Mill, The, Diehl, Louis

Wayfaring Stranger, The, Boyd, Bill (arr.)

We Gather Together, Smith, David E. (arr.)

Westernstil, Hrdina, Eman

Westwood Song, Kellaway, Roger

Whangaroa, Hume, James Ord

When Britain Really Ruled the Waves, Sullivan, Arthur

When Love Is Kind, Kinyon, John (arr.)

When the Saints Go Marching In, Buchtel, Forrest Lawrence (arr.)

When the Saints Go Marching In, Feldstein, Sandy (arr.)

When the Saints Go Marching In, Ostling, Acton (arr.)

When Yuba Plays the Rumba on the Tuba, Hupfield, Herman

Where'er You Walk (from Semele), Handel, George Frederick

Where Art Thou?, Ascher, Alice

Whistlin' Tune, Barnes, James

White Stones, Epstein, Marti

Wild Horseman, The, Schumann, Robert

Wild Rose, Vander Cook, H. A.

Winter Carousel, Bigelow, Albert

With Melody for All, McLin, Edward (arr.)

Within These Holy Portals, Mozart, Wolfgang Amadeus

Wohin?, Schubert, Franz

Work Song, A "Blues Song" for the Young Tubist, Barnes, James

Works for Tuba and Piano by Russian Composers, Voronov, G. (ed.)

Wotan, Buchtel, Forrest Lawrence

XYZ

Yankee Doodle, Boyd, Bill (arr.)

Ye Banks and Braes of Bonny Doon, Kinyon, John (arr.)

Yesterday, Lennon, John, and McCartney, Paul

Young Artists First Book of Solos for BBb Tuba, The, Buchtel, Forrest Lawrence

Young Tuba Soloist, Smith, David E. (arr.)

Your Ring on My Finger, Schumann, Robert

Zillertal, Simon, Frank

Zum Uben und Vorspielen/B-Tuba, Meschke, Dieter (ed.)

Zum Uben und Vorspielen/F-Tuba, Meschke, Dieter (ed.)

Zwei Charakterstücke, Foremny, Stephan

Tuba and Keyboard Collections

Many of the selections included in these collections were published separately. Acquiring them in the collections is a good way to build up a large library of tuba solos on a budget.

Bennett, Malcolm, arr. Connor, Eddie (selected). *Five Solos for Tuba*. Unlimited Music. 1988. $25.25. II–III. Contains: Connor, Eddie, *McCluskeys Rag*; Molloy, J. L., *The Kerry Dance*; traditional, *Luzerne Song*; traditional, *McLeods Reel*; traditional, *Shenandoah*.

Brass Wind Publications. *Fifteen Introductory Solos*. II. For Eb Bass/Tuba. Solos by Django Bates; Arthur Butterworth; Nigel Clarke; Douglas Coombes; Robert Ramskill. Treble and bass clef versions available.

Brass Wind Publications. *Up Front Albums*. Book 1, I–II; Book 2, I–III. For Eb Bass. Solos by Derek Bourgeois; Arthur Butterworth; Ian Carr; Gordon Crosse; Edward Gregson; Joseph Horovitz; Raymond Premru; Daryl Runswick; Stan Tracey; Guy Woolfenden. Treble and bass clef versions available.

Buchtel, Forrest Lawrence. *The Young Artist's First Book of Solos for BBb Tuba*. M. M. Cole Publishing Co. 1938. Out of print. I–III. Also published for trombone/baritone, cornet/baritone, French horn, Eb mellophone, alto or bari. sax, oboe, flute. Piano accompaniment book available separately. Contains: *The Archer*; *The Ballerina*; *The Cavalier*; *The Courier*; *The Grenadier*; *How Can I Leave Thee?*; *The Hussar*; *The Juggler*; *The Mannequin*; *The Mariner*; *The Ranger*; *Song of the Viking*; *The Spartan*; *The Troubadour*; *The Volunteer*; *The Voyageur*.

Conley, Lloyd, arr. *Christmas Cameos*. Kendor Music, Inc. 1985. $9.00. II–III. Contains: *The First Noel*; *Joy to the World*; *O Come, All Ye Faithful*; *O Little Town of Bethlehem*; *Silent Night*.

CPP/Belwin, Inc. *Tuba Solos, Level One*. CPP/Belwin, Inc. 1984. Tuba $4.50, piano $6.50. I–II. Contains: Barnes, James, *Marching Right Along*; and *Whistlin' Tune*; Bell, William J., *Melodious Etude*; and *The Tubaman*; Billings, William, *Old American Patriotic Song (Chester)*; Gruber, Franz, *Silent Night*; Ostling, Acton, *Aurora*; *Deep Cavern*; and *King Neptune*; Ostling, Acton, arr. *Blow the Man Down*; *Three Famous Melodies*; and *When the Saints Go Marching In*; Popper, David, *Gavotte*; Sousa, John Philip, *Stars and Stripes Forever*.

CPP/Belwin, Inc. *Tuba Solos, Level Two*. CPP/Belwin, Inc. Tuba $4.50, piano $6.50. II–III. Contains: Bach, Johann Sebastian, *Gavotte*; Barnes, James, *In a Modal Mood* and *Work Song, A "Blues Song" for the Young Tubist*; Barnes, James, arr., *Sometimes I Feel Like a*

Motherless Child; Bell, William J., *Chief John*; *Jolly Jumbo*; and *The Spartan*; Gounod, Charles, *Valentine's Song from "Faust"*; Handel, George Frederick, *Bourrée*; Haydn, Franz Joseph, *Haydn Medley (from Symphony No. 94)*; Ostling, Acton, arr., *Gallant Captain*; Schubert, Franz, *Moment Musical*; Swanson, Ken, arr., *Blue Bells of Scotland*.

Daellenbach, Charles, arr. *Book of Beginning Tuba Solos*. Hal Leonard Publishing Corp. 1992. $14.95. I. Contains: Beethoven, Ludwig van, *Ode to Joy*; Benedict, Julius, *Carnival of Venice*; Bourgeois, Louis, and Ken, Thomas, *Doxology*; Boyd, Bill, *Canadian Brass Blues*; Boyd, Bill, arr., *The Cruel War Is Raging*; *The Riddle Song*; *Song of the Volga Boatmen*; *Streets Of Laredo*; and *Yankee Doodle*; Carey, Henry, and Smith, Samuel, *America*; Cohan, George M., *Give My Regards to Broadway*; Foley, Red, *Just a Closer Walk*; Newton, John (lyrics), *Amazing Grace*; Offenbach, Jacques, *Marine's Hymn*; Sibelius, Jean, *Finlandia*; Tilzer, Albert von and Norworth, Jack, *Take Me Out to the Ball Game*; Waldteufel, Emil, *The Skaters*. Comes with practice/performance cassette. Charles Daellenbach, tuba, and Bill Casey, piano on A side; piano accompaniments only on B side.

Daellenbach, Charles, arr. *Book of Easy Tuba Solos*. Hal Leonard Publishing Corp. 1992. $14.95. I–II. Contains: Boyd, Bill, arr. *Come, Thou Fount Of Every Blessing*; *The Erie Canal*; *Hey, Ho! Nobody Home*; *Loch Lomond*; and *The Wayfaring Stranger*; Giordani, Giuseppe, *Love Song (Caro mio ben)*; Grieg, Edvard, *The Last Saturday Evening*; Handel, George Frederick, *Lento*; and *Repentance*; Lully, Jean-Baptiste, *The Lonely Forest*; Schwartz, Jean, and Jerome, William, *Chinatown, My Chinatown*; Sullivan, Arthur, and Gilbert, W. S., *Miya Sama* from *The Mikado*. Comes with practice/performance cassette. Charles Daellenbach, tuba, and Patrick Hansen, piano, on A side; piano accompaniments only on B side.

Daniel-Lesur, and Werner, Jean-Jacques. *Collection Panorama*. Gérard Billaudot. 1990. $16.00. II–III. Db-e'. For French tuba. Contains: Autran, Alphonse, *Quadrille en Forme de Ronds d'Eau*; Clais, Tristan, *Tub' 88*; Guinot, Georges-Léonce, *Simplex pour tuba et piano*; Huuck, Reinhard, *Ariette*; Renaud, Manuel, *Ton Coeur (Tuba)*.

de Ville, Paul, arr. *Pleasant Hours. A Collection of 20 Standard Melodies*. Carl Fischer Inc. 1906. Out of print. Written for Eb Bass. Also published for cornet, baritone (bass and treble clefs), trombone (bass and treble clefs), Eb alto saxophone, soprano saxophone, tenor saxophone, alto saxophone and piano. Contains: Abt, Franz, *Dear Old Songs of Home*; and *Oh, My Home*; Bellini, Vincenzo, *Come Brave the Sea*; Dibdin, *Tom Bowling*; Diehl, Louis, *The Water Mill*; Fischer, Ludwig, *Down Deep within the Cellar*; Gatty, A. S., *Lights Far Out at Sea*; Glover, S., *Faith*; Glover, S., *The Melodies of Many Lands*; Handel, George Frederick, *The Harmonious Blacksmith*; and

See, The Conquering Hero Comes; Marzials, *The Fairy Jane*; Mendelssohn, Felix, *On Wings of Song*; Nelson, S., *The Hour of Prayer*, and *Pilot*; Nicolai, W. F. G., *Minstrel's Song*; Roeckel, J., *Unforgotten Days*; Rubinstein, A., *Romance*; Schubert, Franz, *By the Sea*; Sponholtz, *Peace of Mind*.

Edmunds, John, arr. *Popular Solos for the Young Bandsman*. Columbia Pictures Publications. 1976. II–III. Written for a variety of instruments, contains 29 popular TV, movie, and rock songs. Some contain tricky syncopations.

Eerola, Lasse. *N-sarja*. Finnish Music Information Centre. 1991. III. F-a. Contains: *Nukkahörtsö* (Bassia hirsuta); *Nurmivihvilä* (Juncus tenuis); *Nittynätkelmä* (Lathyrus pratensis); *Närvänä* (Sibbaldia procumbens); *Nuckkurusokki* (Bidens cernua); *Nukkakärsämö* (Achillea tomentoso); *Nurmitädyke* (Veronica chamaedrys); *Nyylähaarikko* (Sagina nodosa). Folk-song quality. Some mixed meters. Conservative range; no major technical problems.

Eerola, Lasse. *Rohtokokoelma*. Finnish Music Information Centre. 1991. II–III. F-a. Contains: *Rohtokuirimo* (Cochlearia officinalis); *Rohtopunaluppu* (Sanguisorba officinalis); *Rohtonenätti* (Nasturtium officinale); *Rohtotädyke* (Veronica officinalis); *Rohtopähkämö* (Stachys officinalis); *Rohtoimikkä* (Pulmonaria officinalis). Very tonal tunes with no major technical problems. One movement has mixed meters.

Feldstein, Sandy, arr. *First Solo Songbook*. CPP/Belwin, Inc. 1990. Book: $3.95. Book and Cassette: $9.95. I. Bb1-G. "Contains 30 songs using only the first six notes taught in all beginning methods." Bayly, T. H., *Long, Long Ago*; Beethoven, Ludwig von, *Ode To Joy*; Feldstein, Sandy, *Rainy Day Rock*; *A-Tisket, A-Tasket*; *Aura Lee*; *Baa, Baa Black Sheep*; Feldstein, Sandy, arr., *Beautiful Brown Eyes*; *Caisson Song*; *Erie Canal*; *For He's a Jolly Good Fellow*; *French Folk Song*; *Frère Jacques*; *Good King Wenceslas*; *Hot Cross Buns*; *Jolly Old St. Nicholas*; *London Bridge*; *Love Somebody*; *Lovely Evening*; *Old McDonald*; *There's a Hole in the Bucket*; *This Old Man*; *Tom Dooley*; *Twinkle, Twinkle Little Star*; *The Victors' March*; and *When the Saints Go Marching In*; Foster, Stephen, *Camptown Races*; Hanby, B. R., *Up on the Housetop*; Hart, Lorenz, and Rodgers, Richard, *Blue Moon*; Martin, Hugh and Blaine, Ralph, *The Trolley Song*; Pierpont, J., *Jingle Bells*. Optional accompaniment/performance cassette available.

Fletcher, John, arr. and ed. *Tuba Solos (Tuba in C) Volume One*. Chester Music. 1982. $9.95. II–III. Contains: Berlioz, Hector, *Sanctus*; Martin, Easthope, *Hey-Ho, Come to the Fair*; Schubert, Franz, *Der Lindenbaum*; Sullivan, Arthur, *Oh, Is There Not One Maiden Breast?*; *The Policeman's Song*; and *When Britain Really Ruled the Waves*.

Fletcher, John, arr. and ed. *Tuba Solos (BBb Bass) Volume One* and *Tuba Solos (Eb Bass) Volume One*.

Chester Music. 1982. Each $9.95. See above listing.

Gershenfeld, Mitchell, ed. *Medici Masterworks Solos Volume 1*. Medici Music Press. 1985. $10.00. II–III. Contains: Buononcini, Giovanni, *Pupille Nere*; Dargomijsky, Aleksander S., *Nur Lieben!*; Dvořák, Antonin, *Gypsy Melody*; Humperdinck, Engelbert, *Children's Prayer*; Rubinstein, Anton, *Be Not Shy, My Pretty One*; Tchaikovsky, Peter I., *At the Dance*.

Graham, James, arr. *Concert Music for Tuba*. TUBA Press. 1967. $12.00. II–IV. Originally published by DePauw University Bands in 1967. Contains: Brahms, Johannes, *Waltz*; Corelli, Arcangelo, *Sonata No. 10, Opus 5*; and *Sonata No. 9*, Op. 5; Gliere, Reinhold, *Intermezzo*; and *Nocturne*; Handel, George Frederick, *Chorus from Judas Maccabaeus*; Mozart, Wolfgang Amadeus, *Concert Rondo*; *Concerto in D (K. 412)*; *Concerto in E flat (K.417)*; *Concerto in E flat (K.447)*; and *Concerto in E flat (K.495)*; Saint-Saëns, Camille, *Romance*; Schumann, Robert, *Adagio and Allegro*; Scriabine, Alexander, *Romance*; Strauss, Richard, *Concerto, Op. 11*; and *Second Horn Concerto*.

Gregson, Edward, and Ridgeon, John. *Nine Miniatures*. Brass Wind Publications. I–II. For E♭ bass/E♭ tuba. Solos with easy piano accompaniments. Treble and bass clef versions available.

Guzii, V., comp. *Pieces for Tuba and Piano*. Moscow: Muzyka. 1976. Contains: Castérède, Jacques, *Fantaisie Concertante*; Ruff, D., *Concert Piece*; Tomasi, Henri, *Etre ou ne pas être*.

Guzii, V., comp. *Pieces for Tuba and Piano*. Moscow: Muzyka. 1978. Contains: Bitsch, M., *Ritcherkar*; Hartley, V., *Concertino*; Kikta, V., *Concert for Tuba and Orchestra*; Kling, G., and Neuling, G., *Grand Cadence*.

Howe, Marvin C., arr. *Three Tuba Solos*. Plymouth Music Co. 1965. $4.00. 6:08. III. G₁–g (a). Contains: Bach, Johann Sebastian, *Rondo from Suite in B Minor for Flute*; Pergolesi, Giovanni Battista, *Spiritoso*; Purcell, Henry, *Next, Winter Comes Slowly*.

Hoza, Václav. *Schule für Tuba in F und in B*. Edio Supraphon Praha. 1983. II-V. See listing under "Methods and Studies." Contains: Blodek, Vilém, *Arie Janeks aus der Oper "Im Brunnen"*; Gregor, Frantisek, *Konzertetüde*; Hoza, Václav, *Ländler für Tuba und Klavier*; Hoza, Václav, and Hála, Jan, *Mosaik*; Hrdina, Eman, *Slow-Fox-Medium*; *Walzer*; and *Westernstil*; Kubes, Ladislav, *Alte Bekannte*.

Hudadoff, Igor, ed., and Wescott, William, piano. acc. *Fifteen Intermediate Tuba Solos*. Pro Art Publications. 1965. Out of print. II–IV. Published for a variety of instruments with piano. Includes: Chopin, Frederick, *Nocturne*; Cohan, George M., *George M. Cohan Medley*; Cui, César, *Orientale*; Debussy, Claude, *Reverie*; Gounod, Charles, *Funeral March of a Marionette*; Granados, E., *Playera*; Haydn, Franz Joseph, *Allegro and Minuet*; Klohr, *Billboard*;

Meyerbeer, Giacomo, *Coronation March*; Moussorgsky, M., *Gopak*; Rimsky-Korsakov, N., *Song of India*; Strauss, Johann, *Artist's Life*; Tchaikovsky, Peter I., *Andante Cantabile*; and *Waltz from Serenade for Strings*; Waldteufel, *Spanish Waltzes*.

Hume, James Ord, arr. *Boosey's Bombardon Solo Album*. Boosey and Co. 1906. Solo E♭ bombardon part written in treble clef. Contains: Handel, George Frederick, *Love That's True Will Live Forever (Si, Tra I Ceppi, from "Berenice")*; Hatton, J. L., *Simon the Cellarer*; Knight, J. P., *Rocked in the Cradle of the Deep*; Meyerbeer, Giacomo, *On Heaven's Just Cause Relying* and *Rataplan Chorus (from "Les Huguenots")*; and *Piff, Paff (from "Les Huguenots")*; Wagner, Richard, *Heav'n, in Pray'r, Thine Aid I Seek* and *Good Subjects of Brabant, 'tis well! (from Lohengrin)*.

Jacobs, Wesley, arr. *Solos from the Classics*. Encore Music Publishers. 1991. $16.50. I–II. Twenty-four classical and folk tunes. Contains: Beethoven, Ludwig van, *Hymn to Joy*; Brahms, J., *Lullaby*; *Sandman*; and *Waltz*; Haydn, J., *Hymn*; and *The Spacious Firmament*; Jacobs, Wesley, arr. *Coventry Carole*; *Dona Nobis Pacem*; *German Waltz*; *Go Down, Moses*; *Greensleeves*; *Harvest Dance*; *In Olden Times*; *In Springtime*; *Little Maiden*; *A Mighty Fortress*; *Nightingale*; *Steal Away*; *The Steeple*, *Thanksgiving*; and *Village Dance*; Mendelssohn, F., *Nocturne*; Sibelius, Jean, *Finlandia*; Ward, S. A., *America the Beautiful*.

Kinyon, John, arr. *Breeze-Easy Recital Pieces for Tuba*. M. Witmark and Sons. 1958. I–II. Thirty recognizable tunes for tuba and piano. Contains: Barnby, Sir Joseph, *Sweet and Low*; Bayley, Thomas Haynes, *Faith Of Our Fathers*; and *Long, Long Ago*; Benedict, Julius, *Carnival of Venice*; Brahms, Johannes, *Cradle Song*; Haydn, Franz Joseph, *Papa Haydn's Tune*; Kinyon, John, arr., *All Through The Night*; *Ash Grove, The*; *Auld Lang Syne*; *Bendemeer's Stream*; *The Blue Bells of Scotland*; *Cockles and Mussels*; *Crusaders' Hymn*; *Drink to Me Only with Thine Eyes*; *The Erie Canal*; *German Waltz*; *Home on the Range*; *John Peel*; *Loch Lomond*; *Londonderry Air*; *Minstrel Boy*; *Red River Valley*; *Steal Away*; *Sweet Betsy from Pike*; *When Love Is Kind*; and *Ye Banks and Braes of Bonny Doon*; Monk, W. H., *Abide with Me*; Spillman, James E., *Flow Gently, Sweet Afton*; Strauss, Johann, *Roses from the South*; Thompson, H. S., *Annie Lisle*.

Kinyon, John, arr. *Instant Band Ensembles (Tuba)*. Alfred Music. 1969. Solo book for any solo instrument and band or piano accompaniment. Sixteen popular songs, Christmas songs, etc.

Lamb, Jack, ed. *Classic Festival Solos*. CPP/Belwin, Inc. Tuba part: $4.50, piano part, $6:50. I–III. Contains: Barnes, James, *Work Song, a "Blues Song" for the Young Tubist*; Bartók, Belá, *Dance of the Slovaks*; Bordogni, Marco, *Bordogni Medley*; Eccles, John, *Minuet*; Handel, George Frederick, *Bourrée*; *Larghetto and Allegro*; and *Where'er You Walk (from Semele)*; Barnes, James, arr., *Sometimes I Feel Like a Motherless Child*; Ostling, Acton, *Aurora*; Ostling, Acton, arr., *Gallant Captain*; Saint-Saëns, Camille, *Allegro*; Stoutamire, Albert L., *Legend; Little*, Donald, C., arr., *Military March*; Weber, Fred, and Garrett, Dorothy, *The Elephant Dance.*

Lamb, Jack, ed. *Solo Sounds for Tuba, Level 1–3*, Vol. 1. CPP/Belwin, Inc. 1987. Tuba $4.50, piano $6.50. I–III. Contains: Arne, Thomas A., *Air from "Comus"*; Belden, George R., *Black Holes in Space*; Bell, William J., arr., *Russian Medley*; Bordogni, Marco, *Bordogni Medley*; Bowles, Richard W., *Deep Rock* and *Venetian Carnival*; Dacre, Harry, *Bicycle Built for Two;* Handel, George Frederick, *Where'er You Walk (from Semele)*; Little, Donald C., *Lazy Lullaby*; Little, Donald C., arr. *Military March*; Peter, C., *The Jolly Coppersmith;* Schumann, Robert, *Sailors' Song*; Weber, Fred, and Garrett, Dorothy, *The Elephant Dance.*

Lamb, Jack, ed. *Solo Sounds for Tuba, Level 3–5*, Vol. 1. CPP/Belwin, Inc. 1987. Tuba $4.50, piano $6.50. II–III. Contains: Bizet, Georges, *Carmen Excerpts*; Bowles, Richard W., *Changing Scene*; Dowling, Robert, *His Majesty the Tuba;* Gretchaninoff, A., *Slumber Song*; Grieg, Edvard, *In the Hall of the Mountain King*; Handel, George Frederick, *Honor and Arms*; Haydn, Franz Joseph, *Sonata No. 7, first movement*; Marcello, Benedetto, *Largo and Presto*; Mozart, Wolfgang Amadeus, *Menuetto*; Vivaldi, Antonio, *Allegro (from Sonata No. 3).*

Larin, J., ed. *Pieces for Tuba and Piano.* Moscow: Muzyka. 1979. Contains: Bernstein, Leonard, *Waltz for Mippy*; Bozza, Eugène, *Allegro and Finale*, and *Prelude and Allegro*; Désenclos, A., *Air;* LeClerc, E., *Concertino*; Moreau, J., *Piece from Suite "Colours in Movement"*; Tchebotarev, S., *Rondo.*

Lawrance, Peter. *Six Modern Pieces.* Brass Wind Publications. II. For E♭ bass/E♭ tuba. Solos with easy accompaniments. Treble and bass clef versions available.

Lebedev, A., ed. *Collection of Pieces for Tuba "Es" and Piano.* Military Band Masters Faculty of Moscow Conservatiore. 1971. Contains: Arutiunian, Alexandre, *Expromt*; Bartók, Belá, *Dance Of The Bear*; Fesh, D., *Prelude*; Gudmen, S., *Dance*; Handel, George Frederick, *Air*; and *Variations; Jurovsky, V., March*; Kaneda, B., *Long, Long Ago*; Karaev, V., *Dance from the Ballet "Seven Beauties"*; Kazadezins, R., *Spanish Dance*; Khatchaturian, A., *Dance from Ballet "Spartak"*; Kotshetov, V., *Adagio from the ballet "Till Eulenspiegel"*; Lebedev, A., arr., *Adagio*; Ledov, A., *Prelude*; Mozart, Wolfgang Amadeus, *Allegro*; Orthel, L., *Prelude*; Pergolesi, Giovanni Battista, *Air*; Prokofiev, Sergei, *Recitative and Kutuzov's Air from the Opera "War and Peace"*; Rachmaninoff, Sergei, *Russian Song*; Rakov, N., *Romance*; Ravel, Maurice, *Pavane*; Rubinstein, A., *A Persian Song*;

Schubert, Franz, *Ave Maria*; Scriabine, Alexander, *Etude*; Shostakovitch, Dimitri, *Romance*; Stepovoi, J., *Cantabile*; Stravinsky, Igor, *Russian Song*; Vasilyev, V., *Melody.*

Lebedev, A., ed. *Tuba Tutor Vol. 1.* Moscow Muzyka. 1984. II–III. "School of Playing on Tuba." Contains: Bartók, Belá, *Adagio, Dance; Hungarian Folk Song*, and *A Song*; Britten, Benjamin, *The Sentimental Sarabande from the "Simple Symphony" for String Orchestra*; Frid, G., *A Little Birch Tree*; Gluck, K. [sic], *Gavotte*; Goedicke, A., *Dance*; Handel, George Frederick, *Bourée*; Lebedev, A., arr., *Estonian Folk Dance; On the Steep High Mountain*; and *A Ring*; Miaskovskii, N., *Song of the Field*; Monushko, S., *A Fairy Tail*; Pozzoli, E., *The Sad Minute*; Samonov, A., *Good Night*; and *Grandfather Is Dancing*; Tchaikovsky, Peter I., *Tomsky's Song from the Opera "Queen Of Spades"*; Zverev, V., *Song.* Also see listing under "Methods and Studies."

Lebedev, A., ed. *Tuba Tutor Vol. 2.* Moscow: Muzyka. 1986. II–IV. "School Of Playing on Tuba." Contains: Bak, M., *A Joke*; Barber, S., *Adagio and Scherzo from Sonata in C minor*; Brahms, S. [sic], *Waltz*; Corelli, A., *Sarabanda*; Duntriev, G., *Ballada*; Greig, E., *In Spring Time*; Kikta, V., *Epic Tale and Procession of the People in Costumes (Festival)*; Lebedev, A., *A Cradle Song*; and Gavotte; Link, I., *Sonatina Movement IV*; Rakov, N., *Sonatina*; Schedrin, R., *Variations from the Ballet Konick-Gorbunoch*; Smirnova, T., *A Joke*; Sviridov, G., *Iago's Song about King Stephen from the Tragedy Othello*; Taktakishvili, O., *Aria from the Opera "Three Lives"*; Tomasi, G. [sic], *Hamlet's Monologue*; Volkov, K., *A Piece.*

Little, Donald C., arr. *Solo-Pak for Tuba, Part One.* CPP/Belwin, Inc. 1989. $5.00. I. Follows the levels of the Medalist Band Method. Contains: Haydn, Franz Joseph, *The Spacious Firmament on High*; Little, Donald, arr., *Flow Gently, Sweet Afton*; Quate, Amy, and Little, Donald, *Texas Horizons.*

Little, Donald C., arr. *Solo-Pak for Tuba, Part Two.* CPP/Belwin, Inc. 1991. $5.00. I–II. Follows the levels of the Medalist Band Method. Contains: Brahms, Johannes, *Sunday (Sonntag, Op. 47, 1868)*; Caccini, Giulio, *Amarilli, Mia Bella*; Quate, Amy, *Los Cocos Locos (Crazy Coconuts).*

Little, Donald C., arr. *Solo-Pak for Tuba, Part Three.* CPP/Belwin, Inc. 1992. $5.00. II–III. Follows the levels of the Medalist Band Method. Contains: Mozart, Wolfgang Amadeus, *Aria from La Clemenza di Tito*; Purcell, Henry, *Song from Timon of Athens*; Quate, Amy, *The Feel Good Blues.*

McLin, Edward, arr. *With Melody for All.* Pro Art Publications. 1963. Out of print. "20 all-time favorite melodies for band, orchestra, ensemble, unison or solo performance."

Melnikov, S., ed. *Pieces for Tuba and Piano.* Moscow: Military Band Masters Institute. 1957. Contains: Assafyev, B., *Scherzo*; Bach, Johann Sebastian, *Bou-*

rée; and *Second Part from Capriccio*; Blazhevich, Vladislav, *Concerto No. 2, Part 3,* and *Miniature No. 7;* Chopin, Frederick, *Prelude No. 6*; Dvarionas, B., *Theme and Variations*; Ekkls, H., *Sonata*; Glinka, M., *Romance*; Handel, George Frederick, *Bourée*; Kalinikov, V., *The Sad Song*; Leonov, I., *Etude de concert;* Marcello, Benedetto, *Largo and Allegro*; Masne, D., *Elegia*; Moniushko, S., *An Air from the Opera "Halka"*; Mozart, Wolfgang Amadeus, *Concert No. 2 Part One*; *Concert No. 4 Part One;* and *Rondo de Concerto*; Rachmaninoff, Sergei, *Elegia*; Rimsky-Korsakov, N., *Song from the Opera "Snow Maiden"*; Rubinstein, A., *Romance*; and *Song from the Cycle "Persian Songs"*; Saint-Saëns, Camille, *Concert Piece*; Tchaikovsky, Peter I., *The Sad Song*; Vivaldi, Antonio, *Sonata*; Weber, K. M. [*sic*], *Adagio.*

Meschke, Dieter, ed. *Zum Uben und Vorspielen/B-Tuba.* arr. Philipp, Gerd, and Schwotzer, Stephan. Hofmeister. 1993. I–III. Contains: Concone, Giuseppe, *Allegretto animato*; Daquin, Louis-Claude, *Rigaudon*; Dragonetti, Domenico, *Kleiner Walzer*; Franck, Melchior, *Allemande*; and *Galliarde;* Fux, Johann Joseph, *Allegro*; Giordani, Giuseppe, *Arietta*; Krebs, Johann Ludwig, *Bourrée*; Mozart, Leopold, *Bourrée*; Pachelbel, Johann, *Gavotte*; Pergolesi, Giovanni Battista, *Arie*, and *Lied*; Pezel, Johann, *Intrade*; Radolt, Wenzel Ludwig Freiherr von, *Menuett im Kanon*; Saint-Saëns, Camille, *L'Éléphant (Der Elefant)*; Schumann, Robert, *Fröhlicher Landmann*; Schwotzer, Stephan, arr. *Altdeutscher Tanz (Narrentanz)*; Stanley, John, *Allegretto grazioso*; Witthauer, Johann Georg, *Allegretto und Gavotte.*

Meschke, Dieter, ed. *Zum Uben und Vorspielen/F-Tuba.* arr. Philipp, Gerd and Schwotzer, Stephan. Hofmeister. 1993. See above listing.

Mitegin, V., ed. *Pieces for Tuba and Piano.* Moscow: Muzyka. 1969. Contains: Arensky, A., *Ballade*; Dubrovsky, I., *A Song and a Dance*; Moussorgsky, M., *"Bydlo" from Suite "Pictures at an Exhibition"*; Rakov, N., *Air*; Tchaikovsky, Peter I., *Arioso from the Opera "Jolanta."*

Mitjagina, V., ed. *Pieces For Tuba and Piano.* Moscow: Muzyka. 1969. II–IV. Contains: Goedicke, A., *Improvisation*; Moussorgsky, M., *Bydlo from Pictures at an Exhibition*; Mozart, V. [*sic*], *Leporello's Aria from Don Juan (Don Giovanni)*; Saint-Saëns, Camille, *Cavatina*; Zverev, V., *Hungarian Melody*, and *Russian Dance.*

Mozart, Wolfgang Amadeus. *Suite No. 1 from The Magic Flute.* arr. Frackenpohl, Arthur, ed. Daellenbach, Charles. Hal Leonard Publishing Corp. 1989. $14.95. 6:01. III–IV. Contains: *How Strong Your Tone with Magic Spell; O Isis and Osiris; All the World is Full of Lovers.* Includes practice/performance cassette by Charles Daellenbach, tuba, and Monica Gaylord, piano. See review in *T.U.B.A. Journal*, Vol. 18, no. 2, p. 19.

Mozart, Wolfgang Amadeus. *Suite No. 2 from The Magic Flute.* arr. Frackenpohl, Arthur, ed. Daellenbach, Charles. Hal Leonard Publishing Corp. 1989. $14.95. 4:49. III–IV. Contains: *I'd Give My Finest Feather; Within These Holy Portals; Ha! Just in the Nick of Time!* Includes practice/performance cassette by Charles Daellenbach, tuba, and Monica Gaylord, piano. See review in *T.U.B.A. Journal*, Vol. 18, no. 2, p. 20.

Niverd, Lucien. *Six Petites Pièces de Style.* Gérard Billaudot. 1939. $6.25. II–III. "Pour Saxhorn-basse en Si♭ ou Trombone en Si♭." (Also written for horn.) *Hymne*; *Romance Sentimentale*; *Complainte*; *Historiette Dramatique*; *Chant Mélancolique*; *Scherzetto.*

Ostling, Acton, and Weber, Fred, arr. *Tuba (Bass) Soloist, Book 1.* CPP/Belwin, Inc. 1969. Tuba part $4.50, piano part: $6.50. I. Contains: *Song*; Herbert, Victor, *Victor Herbert Medley*; Knight, J. P., *Rocked in the Cradle of the Deep*; Lehar, Franz, *Merry Widow Waltz*; Lincke, *Glow Worm, The*; Lincke and Waldteufel, Emil, *Waltz Themes*; Lincoln, *College March;* Mendelssohn, Felix, *On Wings of Song*; Olcott, *My Wild Irish Rose*; Ostling, Acton, arr., *All through the Night*; *Blow the Man Down*; *Folk Song Melodies*; *French Song*; Ostling, *Military Marches Melodies*; *Three Famous Melodies*; and *When the Saints Go Marching In*; Poulton, *Andantino*; and *Aura Lee*; Sousa, John Philip, *Stars and Stripes Forever*; Waldteufel, Emil, *Skater's Waltz*; Weber, *Campus Queen.*

Ostrander, Allen, ed. *Concert Album for Tuba.* Editions Musicus. 1954. $13.00. II–IV. Contains: Bach, Johann Sebastian, *Siciliano*; Beethoven, Ludwig van, *Menuet*, and *Nature's Adoration*; Bizet, Georges, *Adagietto from L'Arlésienne*; Concone, G., *Etude* (Op. 10, no. 11); Corelli, Arcangelo, *Gigue*; Gluck, Chr., *Air*, Handel, George Frederick, *Andante*; and *Bourée*; *Maganini, Quinto, An Ancient Greek Melody*; Martini, Padre [*sic*], *Plaisir d'amour*; Meyerbeer, Giacomo, *Veni Creator*; Rameau, J. Ph., *Rigaudon*; Rimsky-Korsakov, N., *Song of the East*; Stravinsky, Igor, *Berceuse.*

Perantoni, Daniel, ed. *Master Solos Intermediate Level.* Hal Leonard Publishing Corp. 1976. $5.95. Contains: Bach, Johann Sebastian, *Siciliano and Chorale*; Brahms, Johannes, *Two Lieder*; Dowland, John, *Come Again, Sweet Love Doth Now Invite*; *Dear If You Change*; and *Now, O Now I Needs Must Part*; Haydn, Franz Joseph, *Two Classical Themes*; Lawrence, Lucinda, *Piece for Tuba and Piano*; Powell, Morgan, *Introduction and Blues*; Schumann, Robert, *Romance No. 3.* Includes a performance/ practice cassette performed by Daniel Perantoni, tuba, and Eric Dalheim, piano. See review in *T.U.B.A. Journal*, Vol. 8, no. 1, p. 35.

Prendiville, Harry, arr. Six *Popular Solos.* A. Squire. 1888. Out of print. II–III. "E♭ Bass; or, Tuba with Piano or Organ Accompaniment (ad lib)." Contains: Hatton, J. L. , *Simon the Cellarer*; Knight, J.

P., *Rock'd in the Cradle of the Deep*; Nelson, S., *The Pilot;* Prendiville, Harry, arr., *Down Among the Dead Men;* Russell, H., *The Old Sexton;* Shield, *The Friar of Orders Gray.*

Pro Art (publisher). *Fifty Standard Solos.* Pro Art Publications. 1964. Out of print. I–IV. Published for a variety of instruments. The pieces in this series of solo books range from easy waltzes and marches to more difficult excerpts from traditional and classical works.

Roikjer, Kjell. *Tonal Miniature Pieces,* Op. 75. Edition Edtved. 1983. $8.80. 25:00. IV-V. F$_1$-e'. Dedicated to Michael Lind. Fourteen pieces, each in a different major key and its relative minor.

Rubank. *Soloist Folio for Bass (E♭ or BB♭).* Rubank, Inc. 1939. $6.95. II–III. May have been compiled by Voxman, Himie. Contains: Bizet, Georges, *Toreador's Song;* Brahmstedt, N. K., *Stupendo;* DeLamater, E., *Rocked in the Cradle of the Deep;* Grieg, Edvard, *In the Hall of the Mountain King;* Lohr, Frederic N., *Out on the Deep;* Macbeth, Allan, *Forget Me Not;* Phillips, L. Z., *The Marines' Hymn;* Pinsuti, Ciro, *Bedouin Love Song;* Schumann, Robert, *The Jolly Peasant;* Vander Cook, H. A., *Bombastoso.*

Salvation Army Press. *Instrumental Albums Number 14: Solos and Duets for Soprano E♭, Horn E♭, and Bass E♭ with Pianoforte Accompaniment.* Salvation Army Press. 1929. *Nearer My Home* (duet); *O Lovely Peace* (duet); *Swiss Melodies; Whosoever; Sing Glory, Hallelujah; Isle of Beaty; In the Army, Rocked in the Cradle; Shepherd of Israel; Battling for the Lord.*

Schubert, Franz. *Songs from Die Schöne Müllerin.* tr. Feldman, Enrique C. Arizona University Music Press. 1987. 10:33. III–IV. B-e'. Dedicated to James Andrews. Contains: *Die böse Farbe, Die liebe Farbe; Mein!,* and *Wohin?* Best on F tuba or euphonium.

Smith, David E., arr. *Young Tuba Soloist.* David E. Smith Publications. All selections available separately. Contains: *Abide with Me; Away in a Manger; Dare to be a Daniel; Hallelujah What a Survivor!; My Jesus I Love Thee; Praise Him little Children; Tis So Sweet to Trust in Jesus; We Gather Together.*

Voronov, G., ed. *Works for Tuba and Piano by Russian Composers.* Moscow Muzyka. 1984. Contains: Berlin, A., *Ballade;* Burshtin, M., *Legend;* Kolodub, L., *Humorous Dance;* Rakov, N., *Sonatina;* Smironova, T., *Sonata;* and *A Tale;* Strukov, V., *Lento Elegiaco;* Zverev, V., *Concertino;* and for tuba solo: Burshtin, M., *Suite;* Ekimovsky, V., *Romance and Capriccio.*

Voxman, Himie, comp. and ed. *Concert and Contest Collection.* Rubank, Inc. 1972. $10.45. II–IV. "For E♭ or BB♭ Bass (Tuba-Sousaphone)." Piano accompaniment available separately. Contains: Alary, G., *Morceau de Concours;* Berlioz, G. P., *Air Gai;* Clérisse, Robert, *Andante and Allegro;* Corelli,

Arcangelo, *Sarabanda and Gavotta;* Gaucet, Charles, *Adagio and Finale from Concertino;* Handel, George Frederick, *Adagio and Allegro from Sonata No. 7;* and *Two Short Pieces;* Kabalevsky, D., *Waltz and Galop from Petite Suite;* Koepke, Paul, *Persiflage;* Maniet, René, *Premier Solo de Concours;* Marcello, Benedetto, *Largo and Allegro;* Mozart, Wolfgang Amadeus, *First Movement from Concerto for Horn;* Ostransky, Leroy, *Serenade and Scherzo;* Rimsky-Korsakov, N., *Andante Cantabile from Concerto.*

Wastall, Peter, ed. *Learn As You Play Tuba.* Boosey and Hawkes, Inc. 1985. Tuba part $6.75, piano part $7.50. I–III. Contains: Bogár, István, *Quick Dance;* Cole, Keith Ramon, *Romance, Homage to Peter Ilyich;* Cole, Keith Ramon, *Solstice;* Debussy, Claude, *Jimbo's Lullaby from Children's Corner;* Grétry, André, *Air from Richard Coeur de Lion;* Gurlitt, Cornelius, *Andante from First Steps,* Op. 82; Hyde, Derek, *Promenade;* and *Tuba-Talk;* Mozart, Wolfgang Amadeus, *Aria "O Isis and Osiris";* Norton, Christopher, *Make Mine a Tuba;* Schumann, Robert, *The Merry Peasant from Album for the Young.*

Weber, Carl, arr. *First Solo Album (Bass Clef).* Theodore Presser Company. $1.00. I–II. Easy beginning solos—55 recognizable tunes.

Weber, Carl, arr. *Nineteen Solos for E♭ Bass with Piano Accompaniment.* J. W. Pepper and Son. 1914. Out of print. Contains: Arban, Jean Baptiste, *Arban's Fantaisie Brillante;* Ascher, *Alice, Where Art Thou?;* Bell, J. H., *Sans Pareil;* Bottesini, Giovanni, *Bombardon Polka;* Giovanini, J., *Challenge Concert Polka;* Innes, F. N., *La Coquette Concert Polka;* Jennings, *Pomposo Polka;* Lange, *Heather Rose Caprice;* Legendre, *Souvenir du Poitou;* Mercadante, Giuseppe, *Solitude Caprice;* Owen, J. A., *Serenade;* Prendiville, Harry, *The Approach of the Lion;* Pryor, Arthur, *Exposition Echoes Polka;* Rollinson, T. H., *Hear Our Prayer—Paraphrase;* Rose, Phil. S., *Chromatic Concert Polka;* Verdi, Giuseppe, *Aria from Falstaff;* Wallace, *Let Me Like a Soldier Fall from "Maritana";* Weber, Carl, arr., *The Old Sexton;* and *Pretty as a Butterfly.*

Wekselblatt, Herbert, arr., and Kagan, Susan, piano realizations. *First Solos for the Tuba Player.* G. Schirmer Inc. 1972. $9.95. II–IV. Contains: *Hornpipe* (American folk dance); Arban, J. B., *The Carnival of Venice (Variations);* Bach, Johann Sebastian, *Musette;* Beethoven, Ludwig van, *Country Dance;* Fischer, Ludwig, *Down in the Deep Deep Cellar;* Gounod, Charles, *March of a Marionette;* Grieg, Edvard, *In the Hall of the Mountain King (from Peer Gynt);* Kagan, Susan, *Oxford Gavotte;* Lully, Jean-Baptiste, *Gavotte;* Mozart, Wolfgang Amadeus, *Marche (from Les Petits Riens);* Nicolai, Otto, *Falstaff's Drinking Song (from The Merry Wives of Windsor);* Petrie, H. W., *Asleep in the Deep;* Rameau, Jean Philippe,

La Villageoise; Schumann, Robert, *The Happy Farmer (Variations from "Album for the Young")*; and *The Wild Horseman (from Album for the Young)*; various composers, *Seven Duets*; Wekselblatt, Herbert, arr., *Civil War Medley*; Wekselblatt, Herbert , arr. *Military Suite*. See review in *T.U.B.A. Journal*, Vol. 12, no. 2, p. 16.

Wekselblatt, Herbert, ed. *Solos for the Tuba Player*. G. Schirmer Inc. 1972. $13.95. II-V. Contains: Bernstein, Leonard, *Waltz for Mippy III*; Mozart, Wolfgang Amadeus, *O Isis and Osiris (from The Magic Flute)*; and *Romanze and Rondo (from Horn Concerto No. 3)*; Shostakovitch, Dimitri, *Polka from The Age of Gold*; Stamitz, Karl, *Rondo Alla Scherzo (from Clarinet Concerto in E♭)*; Tchaikovsky, Peter I., *None But the Lonely Heart, Op. 6*; *Die Meistersinger von Nürnberg (from the Prelude, Act One)*; *Die Walküre (from Act III)*; and *Siegfried (from Act II, Prelude and First Scene)*. See review in *T.U.B.A. Journal*, Vol. 12, No. 2, Page 16.

Yasumoto, Hiroyuki, arr. *Tuba Volume #1*. Toa Music International Co. 1986. II–IV. Contains: Bizet, Georges, *Habanera from Carmen*; Bland, J., *Carry Me Back to Old Virginny*; Boccherini, L., *Menuette*; Couperin, F., *Concertpièce*; Eccles, H., *First and Second Movements from Violin Sonata*; Foster, Stephen C., *Foster Medley*; Giordani, Giuseppe, *Caro mio ben*; Martini, J. P. A., *Plaisir d'amour*; Saint-Saëns, Camille, *Elephant from Carnival of the Animals*; Wagner, Richard, *Die Meistersinger von Nürnberg*; Wagner, Richard, *O du mein holder Abendstern, from "Tannhäuser"*; Yasumoto, Hiroyuki, arr. *Barcarolle for Tuba*; *Londonderry Air*; *Nobody Knows the Trouble I've Seen*.

Yasumoto, Hiroyuki, arr. *Tuba Volume #2*. Toa Music International Co. 1989. III–IV. Contains: Tanimunei, Kocho, *Fantasy for Tuba and Piano*; Handel, G. F., *Concerto No. 3 for Tuba and String Orchestra*; Kopprasch, C., *No. 15, Etüden für Tuba*; Kopprasch, C., *No. 19, Etüden für Tuba*; Kreisler, F., *Leibesfreud*; Lennon, John, and McCartney, Paul, *Yesterday*; Marcello, B., *Sonata I, from 6 Solos for a Violoncello*; McHugh, Jim, and Fields, Dorothy, *On the Sunny Side of the Street*; Reiche, E., *Adagio from Concerto No. 2*; Schumann, Robert, *Träumerei*.

Yasumoto, Hiroyuki, arr. *Tuba Volume #3*. Toa Music International Co. 1989. III–IV. Contains: Bach, J. S., *Sarabande (from BWV 1013)*; Bordogni, G. M., *No. 10 from 24 Easy Vocalises*; Bordogni, G. M., *No. 4 from 24 Easy Vocalises*; Bordogni, G. M., *No. 9 from 24 Easy Vocalises*; Bozza, Eugène, *Prélude et Allegro*; Censhu, Jiro, *Verdurous Aubade for Tuba and Piano*; Konagaya, Soichi, *Celebration for Tuba and Piano*; Kreisler, Fritz, *Schön Rosmarin;* Lennon, John, and McCartney, Paul, *Hey Jude!*; Livingston, J., and Evans, R., *To Each His Own;* Schubert, Franz, *Ständchen*.

Tuba and Keyboard Other than Piano

The following list is offered for players interested in creating recitals for tuba and organ, harpsichord, synthesizer, or celeste. Most of the pieces can also be performed with piano, but in some cases (e.g., Barney Child's *Mary's Idea*) the composers have expressly requested that they not be presented with piano. Refer to the section "Works Listed by Composer" for specific information.

Tuba and Organ

Bach, Johann Sebastian. *O Mensch, bewein' dein' Sünde gross*. arr. Hilgers, Walter. Editions Marc Reift.

Bach, Johann Sebastian. *Sonata II*. arr. Hilgers, Walter. Editions Marc Reift.

Callahan, Charles. *In the Beginning, Biblical Poem for Tuba (Cello) and Organ*. Morning Star Music Publishers.

Ehmann, Heinrich. *Drei Stücke für Tuba und Orgel*.

Hatton, J. L. *Simon the Cellarer*. arr. Prendiville, Harry. A. Squire.

Knight, J. P. *Rock'd in the Cradle of the Deep*. arr. Prendiville, Harry. A. Squire.

Koetsier, Jan. *Choralfantasie über "Es ist ein Schnitter, Der Heisst Tod."*

Kulesha, Gary Alan. *Sonata for Tuba & Organ*. Canadian Music Centre.

Mueller, J. I. *Praeludium, Chorale, Variations and Fugue*. arr. Ostrander, Allen. Editions Musicus.

Nelson, S. *Pilot, The*. arr. Prendiville, Harry. A. Squire.

Prendiville, Harry, arr. *Down among the Dead Men*. A. Squire.

Prendiville, Harry, arr. *Six Popular Solos*. A. Squire.

Russell, H. *The Old Sexton*. arr. Prendiville, Harry. A. Squire.

Schmutz, Albert D. *Chorale Prelude*. Available from the composer.

Shield. *The Friar of Orders Gray*. arr. Prendiville, Harry. A. Squire.

Tuba and Harpsichord

Butterfield, Don. *Journal of Days*. D. B. Publishing Co.

Childs, Barney. *Mary's Idea*. Seesaw Music Corporation.

Enciña, Juan Del. *Triste España Sin Ventura*. tr. Buttery, Gary A. Whaling Music Publishers.

Forez, Henri. *Opus Open*.

Loelliet, Jean-Baptiste. *Vivace, from Sonata in E minor*. arr. Buttery, Gary. Whaling Music Publishers.

Marcello, Benedetto. *Adagio from Sonata C-Dur*. arr. Buttery, Gary A. Whaling Music Publishers.

Marcello, Benedetto. *Sonata No. 1 in F Major.* arr. Little, Donald C., and Nelson, Richard B. Southern Music Company.

Marcello, Benedetto. *Sonata No. 5 in C Major.* arr. Little, Donald C., and Nelson, Richard B. Southern Music Company.

Purcell, Henry. *Gavotte.* arr. Vedeski, Anton. Medici Music Press.

Stratton, Don. *In F.* Trombone Association Publishing.

Tuba and Synthesizer

Fritze, Gregory. *Basso Concertino.* Manuscript.

Tuba and Celeste

Louvier, Alain. *Cromagnon.*

3. Music for Tuba and Band
Skip Gray

The tuba's beginnings as a solo instrument can be traced to the last decades of the nineteenth century, when the growth of professional and town bands was at its zenith. Among the earliest original solo works for the tuba are *The Thunderer* (1891) by J. S. Cox, *Tuba Polka* (1886) by J. J. Davis, *The Beauty Polka* (1887) by D. L. Ferrazzi, and *Dream of Peace* (1888) by W. C. Ripley. George Southwell is credited with at least five works for solo tuba with band between the years 1881 and 1902. Most of these early solo pieces are formal relatives of cornet solos, such as those by Herbert L. Clarke, which are well known and are still played often. The standard structure of these works consists of an introduction, a brief cadenza, a polka, and a trio. Although most of the early pieces for solo tuba and band are out of print or lost, several publishing companies are beginning to make some available again, and as they reappear, it becomes evident that these works offered significant technical and musical challenges to tubists of more than one hundred years ago.

In the early to middle twentieth century, the public school music education movement created a need and a new market for music of wide ability levels. There were more concerts and new contests not only for bands but also for ensembles and soloists on many instruments. Beginners through advanced students needed solo material fit to their level of proficiency, and band directors wanted to spotlight their young artists in front of the group in concerts. Publishers brought out series of graded solo literature for a variety of instruments, and the tubists received a great deal of literature from composers such as H. A. Vandercook, Forrest Buchtel, and Fred Weber.

In the 1960s and 70s there was a conscious movement to make the tuba the equal of other instruments, to gain respect for it as a musical instrument in its own right, and to create opportunities for its performers. The great players of this period, paired with the uninhibited experimental spirit of composers, led to a large body of works in a wide variety of styles. In this time period, many colleges and universities added tuba professors to faculty rosters, and many works for

solo tuba and band were commissioned to help promote these new artists in residence as well as to attract students for them to teach. In addition to college bands and professional military bands seeking new works featuring tuba soloists, professional tubists needed works to play with high school groups and at the ever-growing number of music conventions and conferences.

Compositions featuring the solo tubist with band have evolved beyond the "polka and trio" into the complete spectrum of styles, from modern, experimental works with avant-garde techniques required of both soloist and band members, to works which could function as soundtracks for the latest Hollywood cinema productions.

A scholarly study which has been most helpful in preparing this listing of compositions for solo tuba and band, especially for the very early works, is L. Richmond Sparks, *An Annotated Bibliography of Tuba Solos with Band Accompaniment* (Ann Arbor: University Microfilms, 1990), referred to below in abbreviated form. Special thanks also to Bert Wiley at Bernel Music for his assistance with works for tuba and brass band.

Akiyoshi, Toshiko. *I Ain't Gonna Ask No More.* Kendor Music, Inc. Solo tuba (or bass trombone) and jazz ensemble. 1974. 5:30. III. F_1–f. Single movement. A good bluesy solo with great back-up licks. Also contains an open ad lib solo with simple changes. Recorded by Toshiko Akiyoshi and Lew Tabackin Big Band.

Albian, Franco. *Alla Siciliana (Aria and Variations).* Available from the composer. Solo tuba and band. 1993. 6:30. III. F_1–bb. Theme and five variations, with two solo cadenzas. Musically, this piece is very conservative; it is typical of solo works written in the late nineteenth century, centering on Bb major and closely related keys. A strong Italian flavor permeates this piece, which is fun for both the player and the audience.

Allmend, Robert. *Doppelten Dings.* Molenaar, N.V. Solo tuba (or two baritones) and band. 1989. III–IV. Updated polka-type solo featuring the tuba.

Anderson, Eugene D. *Concert Piece for Tuba and Band.* Anderson's Arizona Originals. Solo tuba and concert band. $30.00. 6:00. III–IV. F_1–f'. Single movement in four sections. Dedicated to the Mesa City Band. Tuba solo part is primarily diatonic with several broken-chord passages. The work is centered in B♭ major with departures to the parallel minor and a Largo section in C major. Band accompaniment is playable by most high school and community bands. See: Bird, Gary, ed., *Program Notes for the Solo Tuba*.

Andrieu, Fernand. *L'Angelus du soir—Melodie*. Editions Musicales. Solo tuba (or saxophone, baritone, horn, trombone) and band. 3:30. III. G–c'. See: Sparks, L. Richmond, *An Annotated Bibliography*.

Angst, Adolf. *Die swingende Tuba—Solo for Tuba in E♭ or B♭*. Eigentum u. Verlag. Solo tuba and band. 4:30. III–IV. F_1–d♭'. A German march written in swing style. See: Sparks, L. Richmond, *An Annotated Bibliography*.

Arban, Jean Baptiste. *Variations on the Carnival of Venice*. Arranged by William Schmidt. Western International Music, Inc. Solo tuba (in F) and symphonic wind ensemble. 1993. Score and parts are rental. 8:00. V. C–b♭'. For Ron Davis. This version in the key of B♭ major sits well for the F tuba; the accompanimental sections are scored for good balance with the soloist.

Arban, Jean Baptiste. *Variations on the Carnival of Venice*. Arranged by Frank Berry. Carl Fischer, Inc. Solo tuba (in F) and band (also for tuba and orchestra). 1988. Score and parts are rental from the publisher. 8:00. V. C–b♭'. For Roger Bobo. This version in the key of B♭ major sits well for the F tuba; the accompanimental sections are scored for good balance with the soloist. Recorded by Roger Bobo.

Arend, A. Den. *Concerto—Voor Tuba, Basse Solo, Baryton or Tenorhorn—Harmonie Fanfare*. Molenaar N.V. Solo tuba and band. 1963. 9:30. IV. F_1–a. Continuous movement with an introduction, theme, and variations. See: Sparks, L. Richmond, *An Annotated Bibliography*.

Bach, Johann Sebastian. *Air and Bourée*. Arranged by William Bell and Jerry Lackey. Carl Fischer, Inc. Solo tuba and band. Rental. 5 minutes. III. An easy-moderate band arrangement of the William Bell classic arrangement for tuba and piano.

Barat, J. Edouard. *Introduction and Dance*. Arranged by Daniel Phillips. T.U.B.A. Press. Solo tuba and band (piano accompaniment available). $30.00. 4:00. IV. C–g♭'. An easy band arrangement of the standard tuba solo. See listing under "Music for Tuba and Keyboard."

Baratto, Paolo. *Jumbo-Baby*. Available from the composer. Solo tuba (or bass trombone, bassoon) with wind band or brass band (piano reduction available). CF 60 with wind band, CF 30 with brass band. 2:30. II. C–g. A simple, cute little work with an easy accompaniment.

Barnhouse, Charles L. *Barbarossa—Air Varié*. C. L. Barnhouse. Out of print. Piano accompaniment available. Solo tuba and band. 1897. 5:30. III. $E♭_1$–e♭'. A true classic in the turn-of-the-century repertoire.

Barry, Darrol. *Impromptu for Tuba*. Studio Music. Solo tuba and brass band. 1981. 5:22. III–IV. $B♭_1(F_1)$–f'. Written for Ian Duckworth. A tuneful work with most material for the soloist diatonic and a nice cadenza. Recorded by Kenneth Ferguson and the Desford Colliery Caterpillar Band.

Bartles, Alfred. *Scherzo for Tuba and Wind Ensemble*. Sam Fox Publishing. Piano reduction out of print. 1970. Rental through Theodore Presser Co. 4:30. III–IV. F_1–d♯'. Single movement. To Harvey Phillips. An enjoyable, tuneful piece with jazz influences in both tuba solo part and accompaniment.

Beasley, Rule. *Concerto for Tuba and Band*. Available from the composer. Piano reduction available. 1969. 13:30. III–IV. F_1–f'. Three movements: Allegro moderato; Adagio; Allegro. Commissioned by David Kuehn. The music sounds modern yet conventional. See: Bird, Gary, ed., *Program Notes for the Solo Tuba*.

Bell, J. H. *Sans Pareil*. J. W. Pepper and Son. Out of print. Solo tuba and band. 1901. 3:45. III–IV. $A♭_1$–f'. See: Sparks, L. Richmond, *An Annotated Bibliography*.

Bell, William J. *The Tubaman*. Arranged by Fred Weber. Belwin Mills Publishing Corporation. Out of print. Solo tuba and band (piano accompaniment available). 1962. 2:00. I. $B♭_1$–c. A very easy solo and band accompaniment from Fred Weber's *First Division Band Course*.

Bencriscutto, Frank. *Concertino for Tuba and Band*. Shawnee Press. Piano reduction available. 1969. $50.00. 10:00. III. $E♭_1$–c'. Single movement work. For Stanford Freese. A diatonic work centered in the tuba's middle register with two extensive solo cadenzas. Band accompaniment is easy. Recorded by Stanford Freese.

Bennet, David. *Basses Berserk*. Carl Fischer, Inc. Tuba section (or tuba solo) and band. Out of print. 1953. 2:30. II. B♭–f. A simple, entertaining work performable by high school or good junior high players.

Benson, Warren. *Helix*. Carl Fischer. Solo tuba and concert band (piano reduction available). 1967. $6.00 (score), parts on rental. 14:00. III–IV. F_1–e'. Two movements: Dancing—rollicking; Singing—pensive. Commissioned by and dedicated to Harvey Phillips. Tuba part not extremely demanding. Band accompaniment difficult and requires extensive percussion. Recorded by Harvey Phillips; Jack Robinson; and John Turk.

Berg, Thomas. *Bass—Solo—Polka*. Adlerverlag. Solo tuba and band. 1974. 2:50. III. C–b♭. See: Sparks, L. Richmond, *An Annotated Bibliography*.

Bilik, Jerry. *Introduction and Dance*. RBC Publications. Solo tuba and band. 1969. $50.00. 4:30. II–III. G_1–b. Continuous work in three sections: Andante; Allegro ma non troppo; Allegro ma non troppo. A musically simple yet solid composition. This music could be handled by a good junior high school level soloist and band.

Blank, Allan. *Divertimento for Tuba and Band*. American Composers Alliance. 1979. 28:00.

Blank, Hans. *Variationen über ein Volkslied (Ein Männlein steht im Walde)*. Musikverlag Siegfried Rundel. Solo tuba (or baritone, bassoon) and band. 4:00. III. E♭₁–e♭. See: Sparks, L. Richmond, *An Annotated Bibliography*.

Blemant, L. *Le Triomphe—Fantasie pour Tuba*. Editions Robert Martin. Solo tuba (or trombone, baritone) and band. 7:00. III–IV. D–c'. Continuous work in four sections with solo cadenza. See: Sparks, L. Richmond, *An Annotated Bibliography*.

Bourgeois, Derek. *Rondo Grottesco*. William Allen Music, Inc. Solo tuba and band. $70.00.

Bowles, Richard. *Venetian Carnival*. Belwin Mills Publishing Inc. Solo tuba and band. 1973. 2:30. II. B♭–e♭. An easy solo with brief cadenza based on the melody "The Carnival of Venice."

Brahmstedt, N. K. *Stupendo—Concert Polka*. Rubank, Inc. Solo tuba and band (piano accompaniment available). 1937. 3:30. II–III. A₁–a♭. An easy, mostly diatonic work.

Brand, Michael. *Tuba Tapestry*. R. Smith & Co. Ltd. Solo tuba with brass band. 1978. $34.00. 4:45. IV. D–g'. Single movement. Written for John Fletcher and the Fodens' Band. A pretty, tuneful piece with a fairly extensive cadenza for the solo tubist. Recorded by Hans Anderson; John Fletcher; and Sibley Graham.

Briccetti, Thomas. *Ecologue No. 4 for Solo Tuba and Concert Band*. Available from the composer. 1962. 9:00. III. E₁–b♭. Two movements: Lento; Allegro. Composed for the Pinellas County (Florida) School System under a grant from the Contemporary Music Project, funded by the Ford Foundation and administered by Music Educators National Conference. A good solo tuba—symphonic band work with melodic, rhythmic, and coloristic interest. The solo part contains little technically difficult material. Meter changes in the second movement will be challenging to high school groups.

Briegel, George F. *Basso Profundo*. Available from the composer. Solo tuba and band (piano accompaniment available). 1952. 3:30. B♭–f. An easy polka for solo tuba.

Broughton, Bruce. *Concerto for Tuba Solo and Wind Ensemble*. Edwin F. Kalmus & Co. Piano arrangement available as *Sonata for Tuba and Piano*. 1976 (1985). $60.00. 7:30. IV. C₁–e'. Three movements: Allegro moderato; Aria; Allegro Leggero. For Tommy Johnson. The composer's arrangement of his *Sonata for Tuba and Piano* works very well; the very coloristic scoring includes harp. See: Bird, Gary, ed., *Program Notes for the Solo Tuba*.

Brubaker, Jerry. *Song and Dance*. Horizon Press. Tuba (or euphonium) solo and band. $85.00.

Bruniau, A. *Sur la montagne*. Editions Billaudot. Tuba and band (also tuba and brass band).

Camphouse, Mark. *Poème for Solo Tuba and Symphonic Band*. Manuscript available from the composer.

1986. 12:00. IV–V. E–a'. Single movement. For Jeffrey Arwood and the United States Army Band. A slow, brooding work with many wide leaps in the solo tuba part. There are long sections in which the soloist does not play, as well as interludes in which the tubist plays alone or with just one other instrument. The emotional work is difficult but is not perceived as virtuosic. Recorded by Jeffrey Arwood.

Cardillo, S. *Catari, Catari*. Molenaar Music N.V. Solo tuba (or euphonium) and band. 1912. 2:30. IV. C–g'. See: Sparks, L. Richmond, *An Annotated Bibliography*.

Catelinet, Philip. *Three Sketches for Tuba*. Solo tuba and brass band. Available from Bernel Music Ltd. $53.00.

Catozzi, A. *Beelzebub*. Arranged by Julius S. Seredy. Carl Fischer, Inc. Tuba and band (piano reduction available). 1932. $30.00. 5:30. III. A₁–c'(e♭'). Theme and four variations. Dedicated to G. Marquardt, tuba soloist. A classic air-and-variation solo portraying several characters. A good technical showpiece with short cadenza. See listing under "Music for Tuba and Keyboard."

Childs, Barney. *Concert Piece for Tuba and Band*. Manuscript available from the composer. 1973. Out of print. 9:00. III–IV. D₁–d' (f' or B♭'). Six connected sections: Introduction; Lively; Dialogue; Surprises,...; ...Cadenza...; ...and Coda. Commissioned by and dedicated to Rex Conner, Ivan Hammond, David Kuehn, R. Winston Morris, Dan Perantoni, Harvey Phillips, Jack C. Robinson, and James Self. An interesting, modern work with moderately easy band accompaniment. Tuba solo is not difficult except for hemiolas and five-against-four passages. This work could serve as a good introduction to modern sounds for a younger group.

Clark, Maurice. *Tyrolean Tubas*. Molenaar Music N.V. Solo tuba(s) and brass band. 1963. $22.00. 3:30. III–IV. G₁–f'. See: Sparks, L. Richmond, *An Annotated Bibliography*. Recorded by Mary Stern.

Condon, Leslie. *Celestial Morn*. Salvationist Publishing and Supplies, Ltd. Solo tuba and brass band. 1962. 9:00. IV. E♭₁–e♭'. Beautiful, neo-romantic. Recorded by Albert Hornsberger.

Condon, Leslie. *Radiant Pathway*. Salvationist Publishing and Supplies, Ltd. Tuba duet (or euphonium-tuba duet, solo tuba) and brass band. 1975. 7:00. IV. Tuba I: B♭₁ (E♭₁)–f' (b♭'); Tuba II: E♭₁(G♭₁)–d♭'. Continuous work in three sections: Allegro moderato; Largo con espressivo; Allegro ritmico. A nicely written work intended as a duet for E♭ and B♭ tubas with brass band. A devotional showpiece with lots of finger technique required. Recorded by Graham Patterson; David Stokes.

Cox, J.S. *The Thunderer—Solo for Bombardon*. Jean White. Out of print. Solo tuba and band. 1891. 2:45. III. B♭–e♭'. See: Sparks, L. Richmond, *An Annotated Bibliography*.

Curnow, Jim. *Concertino for Tuba and Band*.

T.U.B.A. Press. 1980. $27.00. 6:30. III–IV. F₁ (A♭₂)–e♭'. Single movement in three sections. For Barton Cummings. A tuneful piece with traditional harmonic orientation. Heavy scoring creates balance problems with large accompanying ensembles. Recorded by Charles McAdams, Daniel Perantoni.

Curnow, Jim. *Fantasia for Tuba and Band.* T.U.B.A. Press. 1987. $50.00. 8:00. IV. D₁–f '. Continuous movement with six sections. Commissioned by the Roanoke Rapids (NC) Band Boosters. Dedicated to the Roanoke Rapids High School Band. David L. Hanks, Director. A dramatic work with much quartal and diatonic writing in the solo tuba part typical of Curnow's style. Band accompaniment is easily playable by most high school bands and does not overpower the tuba soloist.

Daniels, George F. *Orpheus.* J. G. Richards & Co. Out of print. Solo tuba and band. 1891. 2:30. II–III. D♭–f. See: Sparks, L. Richmond, *An Annotated Bibliography.*

Davis, J. J. *Tuba Polka—The Eureka.* Publisher not listed. Out of print. Solo tuba and band. 1886. 3:00. III. B♭1–a♭. Original copy in United States Library of Congress. See: Sparks, L. Richmond, *An Annotated Bibliography.*

Davis, William. *Variations on a Theme of Robert Schumann—"The Happy Farmer."* Southern Music Company. Solo tuba (or bass other instruments in the band) and band (Piano accompaniment available). 1983. $40.00. 4:15. IV. B♭₁–c'. A great deal of technique and flexibility required of the soloist throughout the four variations and in the cadenza.

DeCosta, Harry, and the Original Dixieland Band. *Tuba Tiger Rag.* Arranged by Luther Henderson, adapted for band by David Marshall. Hal Leonard Publishing Corporation. Solo tuba and band. 1991. $55.00. 5:00. III. F₁ (B♭₂)–b♭ (c'). A fun tuba solo featuring the old Dixieland favorite. Band accompaniment is fairly easy. Recorded by the Canadian Brass.

Dedrick, Art. *A Touch of Tuba.* Kendor Music Inc. Tuba and concert band (piano reduction available). 1959. $32.00. 4:00. II. F₁–b♭ (e♭'). One movement with two sections: Moderato; Fast. Dedicated to Harold L. Walters. A good solo work for a young high school or junior high school student. A cadenza links the two large sections of the piece. Recorded by Peter Popiel. Recorded accompaniment available: *Vivace: A Complete Practice System.* See listing under "Discography, Recorded Accompaniments."

DeLamater, E. *Auld Lang Syne.* Rubank, Inc. Solo tuba and band (piano accompaniment available). 1948. 4:00. II. C–f. A traditional solo in format of introduction, theme, and two variations. The material is mostly diatonic with the closing variation in triplets being the most technically difficult. Recorded accompaniment available.

DeLamater, E. *Rocked in the Cradle of the Deep.* Rubank, Inc. Solo tuba and band (piano accompaniment available). 1937. 3:00. II. B♭₁–f. Theme with two variations. Active yet mostly diatonic writing for the soloist lying mostly within the staff. The second variation is in triplets.

DeLamater, E. *Tramp! Tramp! Tramp!.* Rubank, Inc. Solo tuba and band (piano accompaniment available). 1948. 3:30. II. B♭₁–e♭. Theme with two variations. Mostly diatonic writing with greatest technical demand in the second variation, consisting of running triplets. Contains several short cadenzas.

Delbecq, Alfred. *Air Varie.* Molenaar Music N.V. Solo tuba and band. 1968. 4:00. III–IV. E♭–e♭'. See: Sparks, L. Richmond, *An Annotated Bibliography.*

Dersen. *Im Winzerkeller.* Huhn/Nobile Verlag. Arranged by Kothera. Tuba and band. Piano accompaniment available.

DeWitt, L. O. *Pride of America—Polka.* Carl Fischer, Inc. Out of print. Solo tuba and band. 1895. 5:00. III–IV. B♭–e♭'. Dedicated to Eldon Baker. See: Sparks, L. Richmond, *An Annotated Bibliography.*

Dumitru, Ionel. *Romanian Dance.* In preparation by Editions Bim. Solo tuba and band. 1993.

Eklund, Hans. *Concerto for Tuba and Wind Orchestra.* Swedish Music Information Center. Sola Tuba and wind ensemble. 1982.

Eklund, Hans. *Concerto per Tuba e Orchestra a Fiati.* Manuscript available from the Tuba Center. Solo tuba and band. 1982. 8:00. IV. F♯₁–f '. See: Sparks, L. Richmond, *An Annotated Bibliography.*

Engelhardt, Ernst. *Tuba—Sepp'l.* Musikverlag Wilhelm Halter GmbH. Solo tuba and band (piano accompaniment available). 2:30. III. F₁–b♭. A concert polka featuring the solo tuba. See: Sparks, L. Richmond, *An Annotated Bibliography.*

Ferrazzi, D. L. *"The Beauty" Polka.* Originally published by Carl Fischer, republished and available from Piston, Reed, Stick, and Bow. Solo tuba and band. 1887. $15.00. 3:15. III. B♭–b♭. A typical turn-of-the-century solo in Introduction (Cadenza)—Polka–Trio form.

Fillmore, Henry. *Deep Bass.* Carl Fischer, Inc. Solo tuba and band (piano accompaniment available). 1927. 1:00. I–II. F₁–e. A very easy solo with a short cadenza.

Flowers, Herbie. *Tuba Smarties.* Arranged by Denzil Stephens. Sarnia Music. Solo tuba and brassband (wind band arrangement also available). 1982. 2:20. III. B♭₁–b♭. A clever novelty solo for the tuba. Recorded by Herbie Flowers.

Follas, Ronald W. *Concertpiece for Tuba and Band.* T.U.B.A. Press. Tuba and concert band (piano reduction available). 1982. $45.00. 11:30. IV. F♯₂–f♯'. One continuous movement. The very easy band parts and "Hollywood" sound make this an appealing work. The solo part is both tuneful and flashy. An extensive cadenza toward the end of the piece explores the tuba's expansive range.

Foster, Stephen. *Gentle Tuba (Old Black Joe).* Arranged by Conley and Lloyd. Studio PR Publications. Solo tuba and band. 1980. $36.00. 3:00. II. E♭–e♭. An easy arrangement with updated harmonies.

Frackenpohl, Arthur. *Song and Dance for Euphonium, Tuba, and Band.* Horizon Press. 1991. Commissioned by the Lake Braddock Secondary School Band, Roy C. Holder, director, Burke, Virginia. Recorded by David Porter.

Frackenpohl, Arthur. *Variations on "The Cobbler's Bench."* Shawnee Press, Inc. Tuba and concert band (piano reduction available). 1973. $25.00. 5:30. III–IV. G₁–c¹(e♭¹). Theme and four variations with cadenza. For Peter Popiel. A nicely scored work which allows the soloist to be heard easily. Recorded by Ronald Davis, Peter Popiel. Recorded accompaniment available: *Vivace: A Complete Practice System.* See listing under "Discography, Recorded Accompaniments."

Fucik, Julius. *Der Alte Brummbär (Basse Solo).* Arranged by John Maston. Musikverlag Wilhelm Halter GmbH. Solo tuba (or bassoon, saxophone, baritone) and band (piano accompaniment available). 1964. 3:45. III. C–b. Traditional concert polka with the solo part staying in the upper tessitura. See: Sparks, L. Richmond, *An Annotated Bibliography.*

George, Thom Ritter. *Concertino for Tuba and Wind Ensemble.* Manuscript available from the composer. Also for solo tuba with string orchestra and solo tuba and piano. 1984. 7:30. IV. B♭–e♭¹. Three movements: Allegro ma non troppo; Cantabile e simplice; Vivace. Traditional melodic writing with modern harmonies. See: Bird, Gary, ed., *Program Notes for the Solo Tuba.*

Giovanini, J. *Challenge Concert Polka.* J. W. Pepper. Out of print. Solo tuba and band. 1901. 4:00. II–III. D♭–a♭. See: Sparks, L. Richmond, *An Annotated Bibliography.*

Giroux, George. *Solo Blues.* Southern Music Company. Solo tuba (or clarinet, saxophone, trumpet, trombone, baritone). 1974. $20.00. 1:30. I. C–d♭. A very easy work with a pop-music sound.

Graetsch, Hans. *Chiemgauer—Bass—Sololander.* Arranged by Karl Jugel-Janson. Wilhelm Halter GmbH. Solo tuba and band (piano accompaniment available). 4:00. II. A♭₁–e♭. A waltz in three sections. See: Sparks, L. Richmond, *An Annotated Bibliography.*

Graetsch, Hans. *Tuba Kapriolen.* Regina. Tuba and band (piano accompaniment available).

Gregson, Edward. *Tuba Concerto.* Novello & Co., Ltd. Solo tuba and concert band (solo tuba and brass band, solo tuba and concert band, solo tuba and orchestra, and piano reduction available). 1976. $75.00. 15:00. IV. D₁–e¹. Three movements: Allegro deciso; Lento e mesto; Allegro giocoso. Commissioned by the Besses O' Th'

Barn Band with funds from the Arts Council of Great Britain. For John Fletcher. An excellent accompaniment lets the soloist shine in this finely crafted work. Nice melodies and cadenzas provide a perfect solo vehicle for the tubist. See: Bird, Gary, ed., *Program Notes for the Solo Tuba.* Recorded with wind band by Josef Maierhofer; Lennart Nord. Recorded with brass band by John Fletcher; James Gourlay; Michael Lind; Michael Wagner.

Grieg, Edvard. *In the Hall of the Mountain King.* Arranged by G. E. Holmes. Rubank, Inc. Solo tuba and band (piano accompaniment available). 1939. 2:00. II. C–e. A popular melody from the classics which works well for the young tubist. Mostly diatonic writing; some chromatic alterations and accidentals carrying through the bar will demand the attention of a novice player.

Grundman, Claire. *Tuba Rhapsody.* Boosey & Hawkes. Tuba and concert band (piano reduction available). 1976. $65.00. 9:30. III. G₁–b♭. One continuous movement. To Martin D. Erickson, tuba soloist, and the U.S. Navy Band. Simple tunes and light scoring in solo passages allow the tubist to be heard. Band parts are moderately difficult, playable by most high school groups. Recorded by Lesley Varner.

Haddad, Don. *Suite for Tuba.* Arranged by Robert E. Clemons. Shawnee Press. Tuba and concert band (piano accompaniment available). 1978. $50.00. 9:00. III. B♭₁–c¹. Three movements: Allegro Maestoso; Andante Espressivo; Allegro con Brio. Nice melodies and sensible scoring make this an effective work for tuba soloists, whether they be accomplished students or professionals. The band parts are playable by a good high school band. Tuba and piano version recorded by Rex Conner, Ronald Davis. Recorded accompaniment available: *Vivace: A Complete Practice System.* See listing under "Discography, Recorded Accompaniments."

Harris, John H. *Tempesta Polka.* Carl Fischer, Inc. Out of print. Solo tuba and band (piano accompaniment available). 1896. 5:00. III–IV. B♭–e♭¹. See: Sparks, L. Richmond, *An Annotated Bibliography.*

Hartley, Walter. *Concertino for Tuba and Wind Ensemble.* Theodore Presser Co. Piano reduction available. 1968–69. $21.00. 9:00. IV. F₁–e♭¹. Two movements: Lento; Allegro non troppo. For Rex Conner. Requires sensitive playing by the soloist as well as the ability to execute a triple *forte* which takes place at the work's main climax, just before the cadenza in the second movement. Recorded by John Turk.

Hartzell, Doug. *Ballad for Young Cats.* Shawnee Press. Solo tuba and band. $18.00. II.

Hartzell, Doug. *The Egotistical Elephant,.* Shawnee Press. Tuba and concert band (piano reduction available). 1967. $18.00. 3:30. II. C–d♭. Single movement. A simple, melodic work appropriate for a first- or second-year student. Band accompaniment is very easy.

Hastings, Ross. *Prelude and Faràndola for Tuba and Band*. T.U.B.A. Press. Piano reduction available. 1987. $30.00. 6:30. III–IV. F₁–e♭'. The *Prelude* is melodic and quite expressive. The *Faràndola* is a driving dance with some changing meters and several tricky rhythmic passages. Tuba solo contains very few wide intervallic leaps. Other than the occasionally changing meters, the band parts are not difficult.

Hayes, Al. *Solo Pomposo*. Carl Fischer Inc. Tuba and band (piano reduction available). 1911. $35.00. 4:00. II–III. B♭₁–b♭. An old, traditional tuba solo in the Introduction—Cadenza—Polka—Trio format. The solo part is mostly diatonic in the key of B♭ and E♭ and in the lower half of the bass staff.

Heinl, Otto. *Bärentanz*. Musikverlag Wilhelm Halter GmbH. Solo tuba and band (piano accompaniment available). 3:00. III. B♭–f'. See: Sparks, L. Richmond, *An Annotated Bibliography*.

Heinl, Otto. *Der verliebte Teddybär*. Musikverlag Wilhelm Halter GmbH. Solo tuba and band. 3:00. III. A₁(C₁)–f'. Simple diatonic and chordal melodies in this cute, novelty solo. The tuba solo part is mostly in the upper tessitura and, although technically simple, might be best suited for the F or E♭ tuba.

Holmes, G. E. *Emmett's Lullaby*. Rubank, Inc. Solo tuba and band (piano accompaniment available). 1933. 5:30. III. F₁–f. An old favorite theme-and-variations solo. See listing under "Music for Tuba and Keyboard."

Hopkinson, Michael E. *Concerto for Tuba*. Solo tuba and brass band. Kirklees Music. $18.90.

Hopkinson, Michael E. *In Lively Spirits*. Solo tuba and brass band (piano accompaniment available). Kirklees Music. 1992. $9.50. 4:30. III–IV. G₁–e♭'. A quasi-jazz style arrangement of *Andante and Allegro Spiritoso* by J. B. Senaillé. The main challenge to the soloist is playing with a swing feeling; there are no substantial technical demands.

Horovitz, Joseph. *Tuba Concerto*. Manuscript available from the composer. Solo tuba and brass band (concert band accompaniment in preparation, piano reduction available). 1989. 21:00. IV–V. F₁–f#'. Three movements: Allegro; Andante; Con moto. Commissioned by the Besses O' Th' Barn Band, for James Gourlay, with funds from the Musicians' Union. A substantial concerto consisting of modern harmonies and traditional style. A good deal of interplay between soloist and accompanying ensemble creates a texture that allows the tubist to be heard. An extensive cadenza follows the dramatic climax toward the end of the third movement. Recorded by James Gourlay.

Hubert, Roger. *Elegie*. Editions Robert Martin. Solo tuba (or saxophone, horn, trombone, baritone) and band. 1961. 2:30. I–II. F–b. A very simple work, probably intended primarily for horn solo.

See: Sparks, L. Richmond, *An Annotated Bibliography*.

Huffine, G. *Them Basses*. Carl Fischer Inc. Tuba/low-brass soli with band. $30.00. III. A traditional march in 6/8 featuring the low brass section.

Hupfield, Herman. *When Yuba Plays the Rumba on the Tuba*. Arranged by Bob Foster. Warner Bros. Publications Inc. Solo tuba (or tubas) with marching band. 1982. 2:00. II. B♭₁–f. Single movement. A fun and easy arrangement of the popular classic tuba solo. Recorded by William Bell; Harvey Phillips; Joe Tarto; Joe "Country" Washburn.

Jacobsen, Julius. *Tuba buffo (Concerto for Tuba and Wind Orchestra)*. Swedish Music Information Center. Solo tuba and wind ensemble. 1977. 9:30. IV–V. A truly humorous and tuneful work. Recorded by Michael Lind.

Jager, Robert. *Concerto for Bass Tuba and Concert Band*. Belwin-Mills, Inc. Arrangement for tuba and orchestra and piano reduction available. 1978. Score and parts available on rental from Theodore Presser. 13:20. IV–V. D₁–a♭'. One continuous movement with five sections. Commissioned by the University of Illinois Band for Daniel Perantoni. A beautiful concerto in the romantic style reminiscent of Rachmaninoff or Brahms. See: Bird, Gary, ed., *Program Notes for the Solo Tuba*. Recorded by R. Winston Morris; Daniel Perantoni.

Jansson, Leif A. *Lassie*. Lema Musikförlag, Sweden. Solo tuba and band. 1990. 7:00. IV.

Jude, W. H. *The Mighty Deep*. Arranged by Paul de Ville. Originally published by Carl Fisher, Inc.; republished and available from Piston Reed Stick and Bow. Solo tuba and band. 1898. $15.00. 3:30. II–III. B♭₁–a. An easy tuneful solo.

Kabec, Vlad. *Der Knurrhahn*. Musikverlag Wilhelm Halter GmbH. Solo tuba and band. 1987. 2:45. II. Primarily diatonic, easy work.

Kabec, Vlad. *Der Wurzelseppl'—Polka for Tuba*. Musikverlag Wilhelm Halter GmbH. Solo tuba and band. 1986. 2:45. II. B♭–f. Published in tandem with a solo horn piece entitled *Harlem—Lullaby* by Jean Treves.

Kessler, James. *Solo Overture for Tuba and Band*. Available from the composer. 1977. 11:00. III–IV. F₁–d#'. Written for Jeff Arwood. A work characterized as dark and brooding with a great deal of shifting meters and repetitive melodic fragments.

King, Karl L. *The Devil and the Deep Blue Sea—Humoreske*. Originally published by C. L. Barnhouse; republished and available from Piston Reed Stick and Bow. Solo tuba and band. $15.00. 3:30. II–III. C–g. A novelty solo from the early twentieth century.

Kleinsinger, George. *Tubby the Tuba*. Arranged by George Roach. G. Schirmer. Tuba and band (also available for tuba and orchestra). 1945. $75.00. 12:00. III. E♭₁–e♭'. Single movement. The classic work featuring the tuba in a story setting with narrator and ensemble. The beautiful tuba melody and nice story make this a good pops or children's concert piece. Numerous recordings and videos are available.

Kolditz, Hans. *Die Kellerasseln*. Musikverlag Wilhelm Halter GmbH. Tuba and band.

Kolditz, Hans. *Rondo for Tuba and Large Wind Orchestra*. Musikverlag Wilhelm Halter GmbH. 1988. 3:45. II–III. B♭$_1$–e♭. Continuous work in three sections: Allegro; Andante cantabile; Allegro. An easy, tuneful work in A-B-A form. Band parts not difficult.

Kothera, Georg. *Mit Lust und Liebe*. Georg Bauer Musikverlag. Solo tuba and band. 1977. 3:20. II. B♭$_1$–g. See: Sparks, L. Richmond, *An Annotated Bibliography*.

Kottaun, Celian. *Billy Blowhard—Concert Polka*. Carl Fischer, Inc. Solo tuba and band (piano accompaniment available). 1909. 4:00. II–III. B♭$_1$–b♭. An old standard in the tuba solo with band repertoire.

Koumans, R. *Concerto for Basstuba and Band*. Molenaar Music N.V. In preparation.

Kroepsch, F. *Down in the Deep Cellar—Grand Fantasia*. Arranged by L. P. Laurendeau. Carl Fischer, Inc. Out of print. Solo tuba (or clarinet, cornet, trombone, baritone) and band (solo tuba with brass quintet and solo tuba and piano also available). 1908. 6:45. IV. E♭$_1$–g'. A traditional yet technically demanding work for the solo tubist.

Kulesha, Gary. *Concerto for Tuba*. Canadian Music Centre. Solo tuba and band (orchestra accompaniment and piano accompaniment, four hands also available). 1979. Rental from the publisher. 18:00. IV. C$_1$–d'. Three movements: Prelude and Fugue; Scherzo; Finale. Commissioned by the Scarborough Concert Band of Ontario, Canada.

Kumstedt, Paul. *Humoreske for Tuba and Wind Orchestra*. Georg Bauer Musikverlag. 1985. 3:30. III. F$_1$–d'. A well scored piece with pop music influences. See: Sparks, L. Richmond, *An Annotated Bibliography*.

Lackey, Jerry. *Concertpiece for Three Tubas and Band*. Available from the composer. Three solo tubas (one small, two large) and band (piano reduction available). 1963. Score and parts rental (tubas and piano $25.00). 8 minutes. IV. Part I: A$_1$–f♯'; Part II: G♭$_1$–d'; Part III: E$_1$(D$_1$)–d'. One movement with multiple sections.

Lackey, Jerry. *Jazz Concerto for Tuba and Band*. Available from the composer. Solo tuba and band, drum set, piano, and electric bass (also versions for tuba and orchestra, tuba and piano). 1984. Rental from composer. 12 minutes. IV. G$_2$–b♭'. Three movements: Fast Swing, Rock, Simple Waltz, Fast Swing; Slow, Tranquillo; Fast, with Energy. Originally for solo tuba and orchestra; this arrangement by the composer is a great solo tuba showpiece, especially for pops concerts.

Lackey, Jerry. *Short Stuff*. Available from the composer. Solo tuba and band. 1964. Tuba and band rental from composer (piano reduction $15.00). 1:00. IV. G$_1$–c'. Written for William Bell. A quick, humorous encore piece.

Lange, Willy. *Launische Tuba—Heitere Polka für Tuba*. Musikverlag Wilhelm Halter GmbH. Solo tuba and band. 2:30. II. A♭$_1$–f. See: Sparks, L. Richmond, *An Annotated Bibliography*.

Lange, Willy. *Tubistenfreud, Op. 176*. Musikverlag Wilhelm Halter GmbH. Solo tuba and band (piano accompaniment available). 3:00. II–III. E♭$_1$–e♭. See: Sparks, L. Richmond, *An Annotated Bibliography*.

Lange, Willy. *Tubistenlaune*. Musikverlag Wilhelm Halter GmbH. Solo tuba and band. 1:30. II–III. F–a (b♭). An easy polka with no substantial technical demands.

Lange, Willy. *Ein Tubistenscherz*. Musikverlag Wilhelm Halter GmbH. Solo tuba and band. 1:45. III. F$_1$–f'. A technical polka-style solo which lies mostly in and above the bass staff. Several arpeggios demand dexterity, rapid passages require double tonguing, and a cadenza requires some triple tonguing.

Lange, Willy. *Tubistenschreck, Op. 77*. Musikverlag Wilhelm Halter GmbH. Solo tuba and band. 1983. 3:30. IV. C$_1$ (F$_1$)–a' (a). See: Sparks, L. Richmond, *An Annotated Bibliography*.

Lange, Willy. *Tubistentraum, Op. 216*. Musikverlag Wilhelm Halter GmbH. Solo tuba and band. 1983. 2:00. III–IV. F (F$_1$)–b♭' (b♭). See: Sparks, L. Richmond, *An Annotated Bibliography*.

Laurendeau, L. P. *Elephantine Polka*. Originally published by Carl Fischer, Inc., republished and available from Piston Reed Stick and Bow. Solo tuba and band. 1903. $15.00. 1:30. III. D♭–d♭'. A good solo in polka-and-trio form with two short cadenzas.

Legrady, Thomas. *Tubantella*. Molenaar Music N.V. Solo tuba and band. 1987. 2:40. II. F$_1$–b♭. A simple tarantella with no substantial technical demands of the soloist.

Loder, E. J. *The Diver—Tuba Solo*. Arranged by Paul de Ville. Carl Fischer, Inc. Out of print. Solo tuba and band. 1893. 3:30. II. A$_1$–g. See: Sparks, L. Richmond, *An Annotated Bibliography*.

Loeffler. *Der Herr Tubist*. Arranged by Cosmar. Musikverlag Rundel GmbH. Tuba and band (piano accompaniment available).

Losch, Margot. *Auf Freierstuber—Polka*. Arranged by H. Ruckauer. Margot Losch Musikverlag. Solo tuba and band. 1978. 2:30. II. G$_1$–f. A concert polka featuring the soloist in the bread-and-butter register.

Madsen, Trygve. *Introduction and Allegro*. Norwegian Music Information Center. Tuba and band. 10:00. IV–V. For Michael Lind.

Manas, Franz. *Lustiger Bassist Konzertpolka*. Johann Kliment. Solo tuba and band. 1970. 2:30. II. A$_1$–f. See: Sparks, L. Richmond, *An Annotated Bibliography*.

Marais, Marin. *Le Basque*. Transcribed by Dan Phillips. Thompson Edition. Tuba and band. 1987. $35.00. 1:00. IV. C–c'. Single movement. A short, light, flashy work which serves as a nice encore. Easy band accompaniment.

Martin, W., arr. *Rocked in the Cradle*. Wright & Round, Ltd. Solo tuba with brass band. 1985. $23.00. 1:30. II. A♭–E♭. A very simple arrangement in a paired edition, which also contains a solo tenor horn version of *Annie Laurie Variations*.

Masso, George. *Suite for Louise*. Arranged by Robert Rÿker. Kendor Music, Inc. Solo tuba and concert band (piano accompaniment available). 1966. 5:40. II. A₁–f. Three movements: Bourée; Pavane; Gigue. Three simple movements of contrasting character make this a nice solo for a young tubist. Band accompaniment is easy.

Matteson, Rich. *Be-Bop Minor*. Available from the composer. Solo tuba and jazz ensemble. 1978. 3–5 minutes. V. B₁–g'. Commissioned by and composed for Michael Lind. A hot and difficult chart with several openings for ad lib solos. Several written solos are provided with the arrangement.

Matteson, Rich. *Just the Two of Us*. Available from the composer. Solo tuba and jazz ensemble. 1978. 4:00. IV–V. C–a'. Commissioned by and composed for Michael Lind. A pretty ballad with completely notated solo part, which stays in the upper tessitura.

McBeth, Francis. *Daniel in the Lion's Den*. Southern Music Company. Solo tuba and concert band. 1992. Rental from the publisher. 3:10. V. G₁–b'. Composed for and dedicated to Daniel Perantoni. A technical tour de force nearly always lying at the top of or above the bass staff; intended as an encore piece for tuba soloist with band. Very high tessitura and some difficult sixteenth-note passages. Premiered by Dan Perantoni with the United States Air Force Band at the 1992 International Tuba-Euphonium Conference in Lexington, Kentucky.

McKimm, Barry. *Tuba Concerto*. Yarra Yarra Music Services. Tuba and concert band (piano reduction available). 1983. 18:00. III. G–c♯'. Three movements: Andante sostenuto—Allegro; Adagio; Allegro vigoroso. Commissioned by Peter Sykes. An introspective, lyrical work intended for the contrabass tuba. The original version of this concerto, for tuba and piano, has been shortened considerably. The concert band parts are somewhat difficult, probably requiring college-level players. An edition for solo tuba with brass band is in preparation by the composer.

Medberg, Gunnar. *Divertimento*. Swedish Music Information Center. Solo tuba and wind ensemble. 1988. Four movements: Allegro con brio; Andante; Allegretto; Allegro vivace.

Meier, Jost. *Eclipse finale?* Editions Bim. Solo tuba with brass band (also available for tuba and chamber orchestra, tuba and piano). 1991. Rental from the publisher. 19:30. V. D₁–a♭'. Commissioned for the 1991 Geneva Competition by the Christiane and Jean Henneberger-Mercier Foundation. Variations on the German folksong "Der Mond ist aufgegangen" (The Moon Has Risen). The tuba solo plays a dramatic role, portraying humanity's increasing concern at the destruction of nature and the environment. A dramatic and difficult modern work with wide, irregular intervals, complex rhythms and ensemble cuings, and other avant-garde effects. Recorded by Øystein Baadsvik and the Bienne Brass Band.

Merle, John. *Mummers—Danse Grotesque*. Carl Fischer, Inc. Out of print. Solo tuba and band (piano accompaniment available). 1938. 2:00. I–II. G₁–c. An easy little solo in 6/8 time. Recorded by William Bell.

Methehen, E. *Ramses*. Tuba Center. Tuba and band.

Mozart, W. A. *Concert Rondo*. Arranged by Andy Clark. C. L. Barnhouse Co. Solo tuba (baritone or horn) and band. $55.00.

Mozart, W. A. *Horn Concerto No. 1*. Transcribed by Otto Zurmuhle. Molenaar Music N.V. Solo tuba (or tenorhorn, baritone) and band. 1959. 9:00. III. F–g♭. A good band arrangement of this classic.

Mueller, Frederick. *Variations on a Theme of Samuel Barber*. Manuscript available from the composer. Solo tuba and band (also solo tuba and strings, solo tuba and piano). See listing under "Music for Tuba and Orchestra."

Muscroft, Fred. *Carnival for Bass*. Studio Music Co. Solo tuba with brass band (piano accompaniment available). 1981. $22.75. 5:00. III–IV. B♭₁–e♭'. A theme-and-variation solo based on "Carnival of Venice" complete with opening cadenza, theme, and three variation sections. Recorded by Fred Baker.

Nelhybel, Vaclav. *Concert Piece*. E. C. Kerby, Ltd. Tuba (or alto saxophone, tenor saxophone, baritone saxophone, trumpet, trombone, or baritone) and band (piano accompaniment available). 1973. $27.00. 4:00. III. C–f. Three continuous sections: Allegro marcato; Più vivo; Molto vivo. A dramatic dialogue between the solo tuba and band.

Nelhybel, Vaclav. *Concerto Grosso for Tubas and Band*. Hope Publishing Co. 1980. $28.00. 10:00. III. G₁–d♭. Three movements: Con brio; Sostenuto; Allegro. Commissioned by the Dauphin County Music Educators Association, Harrisburg, Pennsylvania. Music typical of the composer's well-known style and sound. For good balance, it is recommended that at least four tubists perform this work with a typical symphonic band.

Nelhybel, Vaclav. *Concerto for Tuba (or Horn)*. Great Works Publishing, Inc. Solo tuba (or horn), two flutes, oboe, English horn, two clarinets, bassoon, harp, double bass, two trumpets, trombone, three percussion (vibraphone, bells, xylophone). 1993.

14:00. IV. Three movements: Allegro; Adagio; Moderato—Allegro. An effectively written work. Although it employs many of the composer's familiar idioms, it sounds especially fresh because of the orchestration.

Nelson, S. *Bonnie Mary of Argyle.* Arranged by A. Kriek. Molenaar Music N.V. Solo tuba and band. 1960. 2:30. II. C–g. An easy folk-song arrangement.

Newsome, Roy. *The Bass in the Ballroom.* Studio Music Company. Solo tuba and brass band (piano accompaniment available). 1971. $14.00. 4:45. III–IV. A_1–e♭'. A good pops concert arrangement which takes the solo tuba through two dance styles: tango and waltz. Recorded by Stephen Sykes.

Newsome, Roy. *Swiss Air.* Studio Music Company. Solo tuba and brass band (piano accompaniment available). $14.00. Recorded by Shaun Crowther.

Newton, Rodney. *Capriccio.* Rosehill Music Publishing Company. Solo tuba and brass band (piano accompaniment available). 1991. 35.50. 8:30. IV. E_1–e'. Single movement. For James Gourlay. An interesting work which presents two contrasting themes, the first dancelike, the second lyrical and romantic. A very nice display piece for the solo tubist which includes one short and two fairly extensive cadenzas. Recorded by James Gourlay; Stephen Sykes.

Novello, Ivor. *Shine through My Dreams.* Molenaar Music N.V. Solo tuba (or tenorhorn, trombone, baritone, euphonium) and band. 1935. 2:30. I–II. D♭–f. See: Sparks, L. Richmond, *An Annotated Bibliography.*

Payer. *Tuba Capriolen.* Arranged by Gottlöber. Simton Musikproduktion und Verlag. Solo tuba and band.

Petrie, H. W. *Asleep in the Deep.* Arranged by Harold L. Walters. Rubank, Inc. Solo tuba and band (piano accompaniment available). 1954. 3:00. II. C(F_1)–d. A popular old theme-and-variations solo. Recorded by William Bell; Barney Mallon.

Pettee, W. E. M. *Tuba Solo—Osceola.* J. G. Richards & Co. Out of print. Solo tuba and band. 1889. 3:30. I–II. B♭–a♭. See: Sparks, L. Richmond, *An Annotated Bibliography.*

Plog, Anthony. *Three Miniatures.* Editions Bim. Tuba and wind ensemble (originally for tuba and piano, also available from the publisher). 1992. CHF 35 (score), parts rental. 5:30. V. D–e'. Three movements: Allegro; Freely—Slowly; Allegro vivace. For Daniel Perantoni. See listing under "Music for Tuba and Keyboard." Version for solo tuba and wind ensemble premiered by Dan Perantoni with the United States Air Force Band at the 1992 International Tuba-Euphonium Conference in Lexington, Kentucky. Recorded in tuba and piano edition by Roger Bobo.

Ployhar, James D. *Tubas on the Run.* CPP/Belwin Inc. Tuba and/or baritone section soli with band. 1992.

$32.00. 2:00. II.

Precker, Jean. *Air et Divertissement.* Molenaar Music N.V. Solo tuba and band. 1971. $45.00. 5:40. III. D♭$_1$–a♭. Two movements. A tuneful work with no substantial technical difficulties.

Presser, William. *Capriccio for Tuba and Band.* Tenuto Publications. Piano reduction available. 1969. $22.00. 5:26. III–IV. E_1–c'. One continuous movement. For Rex Conner. A quick showpiece with few technical difficulties. Two extended cadenzas allow the soloist to also display some expressive quality. Band scoring does not cover the soloist. See: Bird, Gary, ed., *Program Notes for the Solo Tuba.* Recorded by Michael Astwood.

Putnam, C. S. *The Elephant's Dance (A Jungle Episode).* Fillmore Bros. Co. Out of print. Solo tuba and band. 1940. 6:00. III. F_1–c'. A melodic work written in the traditional form of band solo works in the early twentieth century. This time, an elephant dances a polka.

Raich, Heribert. *Bassistengruss.* Adler Musikverlag. Solo tuba and band (piano accompaniment available).

Ramsdell, E. C. *Polka di Basso—Tuba Solo.* E. C. Ramsdell. Out of print. Solo tuba and band. 1896. 3:00. III. B♭$_1$–a♭. See: Sparks, L. Richmond, *An Annotated Bibliography.*

Read, L. C. *"Thunderer" Polka.* W. H. Cundy Publishers. Out of print. Solo tuba and band. 1881. 3:30. III–IV. A♭$_1$–e♭'. See: Sparks, L. Richmond, *An Annotated Bibliography.*

Rehfeld, Kurt. *Elefanten-Ballet.* Georg Bauer Musikverlag. Solo tuba and band. 1978. 3:15. II. G_1–g. A very easy, tuneful work for the young tubist and band. See: Sparks, L. Richmond, *An Annotated Bibliography.*

Rehfeld, Kurt. *Launische Tuba.* Georg Bauer Musikverlag. Solo tuba and band. 1978. 3:30. III–IV. F_1–f'. A technically demanding work for the soloist reminiscent of can-can. See: Sparks, L. Richmond, *An Annotated Bibliography.*

Reinhart, Wolfgang. *Bombardon—Polka für Bass-Solo.* Georg Bauer Musikverlag. Solo tuba and band. 1985. 3:15. III. F–c'. See: Sparks, L. Richmond, *An Annotated Bibliography.*

Relton, William. *"The Trouble with the Tuba is..."* Kirklees Music. Solo tuba and brass band. 1991. $27.00. 4:30. III. B♭–b. Single movement in four sections: Maestoso, Allegro, Andante, Allegro. For Colin Aspinall. A humorous work with few technical demands.

Rimmer, William. *Variations on Jenny Jones.* Arranged by Thomas Wyss. Kirklees Music. Solo tuba and brass band. 1989. $25.50. 5:00. IV. A_1–f'. Continuous work with introduction, cadenza, theme, and three variations. A nice arrangement of the traditional British song providing ample display of the solo tubist's technique.

Rimsky-Korsakov, Nikolai. *Flight of the Bumble Bee.* Arranged by Thomas Wyss. Kirklees Music. Solo

tuba and brass band. 1989. $21.00. 1:30. IV. A₁–
e'. The traditional virtuoso display piece arranged
nicely for solo tuba and brass band.

Ringleben, J. *The Storm King—Grand Fantasia*. Originally published by Carl Fischer, Inc., republished
and available from Piston Reed Stick and Bow. Solo
tuba and band (piano accompaniment available).
1896. $15.00. 6:00. III–IV. B♭₁–c'(f '). A chal-
lenging traditional theme-and-variations solo.

Ripley, W. C. *The Close of Day*. George Southwell
Publishers. Out of print. Solo tuba and band. 1891.
3:30. II. B♭₁–e♭. See: Sparks, L. Richmond, *An
Annotated Bibliography*.

Ripley, W. C. *Dream of Peace*. J. G. Richards & Co.
Out of print. Solo tuba and band. 1888. 3:00. II–
III. B♭₁–g♭. See: Sparks, L. Richmond, *An Anno-
tated Bibliography*.

Ripley, W. C. *Tuba Obligato—Majenta*. J. C. Richards
& Co. Out of print. Tuba section soli with band.
1885. 3:30. II–III. B♭₁–e♭. See: Sparks, L. Richmond, *An Annotated Bibliography*.

Robertson, Dave. *Tuba-riff-ic*. Laissez-Faire Music.
Out of print. Solo tuba (or tuba section) and band.
1981. 2:00. II. F₁–g. A cute, pop-oriented piece
usable as a solo or featuring the entire tuba section.

Rollinson, T. H. *Bombastes Polka*. W. H. Cundy Publishers. Out of print. Solo tuba and band. 1886.
3:30. III. B♭₁–c'. This work would have been considered a virtuoso tuba solo in the late nineteenth
century, with high tessitura and a fair amount of
technique required. See: Sparks, L. Richmond, *An
Annotated Bibliography*.

Rooy, J. de. *Watching the Wheat*. Molenaar Music N.V.
Solo tuba (or baritone) and band. 1961. 2:40. II.
E♭–a. A nice arrangement of the Dutch folk song.

Rooy, Jan de. *The Twelve Rovers (Les douze Brigands)*.
Molenaar Music N.V. Solo tuba (or euphonium)
and band. 1961. 2:00. I–II. C–c. See: Sparks, L.
Richmond, *An Annotated Bibliography*.

Ross, Walter. *Tuba Concerto*. Boosey & Hawkes. Tuba
and band (piano reduction available). 1973.
$36.00. 11:30. IV. F#₁–e♭'. Three movements:
Overture; Berceuse; Toccata. For R. Winston
Morris. A well-scored work for full symphonic
band craftily written so that the soloist is not
obscured. An interesting accompaniment easily
playable by a good high school band. Very good
use of solo tuba with percussion. See: Bird, Gary,
ed., *Program Notes for the Solo Tuba*. Recorded by
Harvey Phillips.

Rossini, Gioacchino. *Largo al Factotum*. Arranged by
Stephen Roberts. Obrasso Verlag AG. Solo tuba
and brass band. 1992. $72.50. 4:30. III. B♭₁–e♭'. A
good arrangement of the famous operatic solo.
Recorded by Shaun Crowther; James Gourlay.

Round, H. *The Men of Harlech—Air Varié*. Arranged
by Red Fences. Molenaar Music N.V. Solo tuba (or
trombone, euphonium) and band. 1966. 6:45. II–
III. E♭–g. Theme and five interesting contrasted
variations.

Rückauer, H. *Der fidele Bassist*. Musikverlag Rundel
GmbH. Solo tuba and band (piano accompaniment available).

Saint-Saëns, Camille. *Chumbo the Elephant from "Carnival of the Animals."* Arranged by D. W. Stauffer.
Stauffer Press. Solo tuba and concert band. $10.00.
1:20. II. A♭₁–e.

Sauter, Eddie. *Conjectures*. Mentor Music, Inc. Solo
tuba and band (piano accompaniment with optional percussion available). 1968. Band accompaniment rental from the publisher. 9:00. IV–V. F#₁–
e'. Two connected movements. Written for and
first performed by Harvey Phillips, the work contains a great deal of rubato and expression as one
might infer from the title. Frequent tempo changes,
unstable tonality, dramatic scoring, and extensive
use of percussion make this a difficult yet interesting work. Recorded by Harvey Phillips.

Schmidt, William. *Tuba Mirum—Variations on a
Gregorian Chant*. Western International Music,
Inc. Solo tuba, winds, and percussion, with harp
and piano. 1984. $80.00. 18:22. IV. A₁–f '. One
continuous movement. For Michael Lind. This
interesting and significant work in the wind ensemble literature could be the focal point of a
group's program. It contains imaginative variations
and colorful orchestration that is sensitive to the
soloist. See: Bird, Gary, ed., *Program Notes for the
Solo Tuba*.

Schmidt, William. *Tunes*. Western International Music, Inc. Solo tuba, winds, and percussion. 1990.
12:22. V. F₁–b'. Three movements: A Little Off; A
Little Under; A Little Out. Commissioned by the
Sapporo International Music Festival '90 and dedicated to Tubists Universal Brotherhood Association. A demanding work for soloist and accompanying ensemble. In the first movement, which has
a Latin feel, the tubist is required to use alternate
fingerings for intonation shadings. A cup mute is
specified for the second movement, which is blues
oriented. The third movement contrasts "straight"
and jazz musical styles. See: Bird, Gary, ed., *Program Notes for the Solo Tuba*.

Schneebiegl, Rolf. *Der Kellermeister—Konzertpolka*.
Bosworth & Co. Solo tuba and band. 1979. 2:40.
III. F₁–b♭. A cute, novelty solo containing few
technical difficulties except for some melodic leaps.

Senaillé, J. B. *In Lively Spirits*. See: Hopkinson,
Michael E., above.

Shahin, Ray. *Mr. Bass*. Southern Music Company. Solo
tuba (or baritone) and band. 1962. $25.00. 2:30.
II. B♭–e♭. A very easy work for both solo tuba and
band.

Siebert, Edrich. *The Bombastic Bombardon*. Molenaar
Music N.V. Solo tuba and band. 1952. 4:15. II–
III. A₁–f. A traditional concerto polka featuring the
tuba.

Siebert, Edrich. *Dear to My Heart—Air Varié*. Studio
Music Company. Solo tuba and brass band (piano
accompaniment available). 1972. $21.00. 3:45. II–

III. D (A♭₁)–b♭ (e♭'). A traditional waltzlike theme with three variations, a brief cadenza, and a coda.

Smith, Claude T. *Ballade and Presto Dance.* Arranged by Gary Lewis. To be published by Wingert-Jones. Solo tuba and band (piano accompaniment available). 1988. 7:30. IV. F–a'. Written for Steve Seward. See listing under "Music for Tuba and Keyboard." Recorded by Robert Daniel.

Sorbon, Kurt. *"Die Poltergeist—Polka."* Musikverlag Wilhelm Halter GmbH. Solo tuba and concert band. 1990. 1:40. A–c'. A traditional German polka in basic arrangement for solo tuba.

Southwell, George. *Monte Cristo.* George Southwell Publisher. Out of print. Solo tuba and band. 1895. 4:00. III–IV. D–f ' (a♭). A late nineteenth-century virtuoso work. See: Sparks, L. Richmond, *An Annotated Bibliography.*

Southwell, George. *My Tuba Solo.* Volkwein Bros., Inc. Out of print. Solo tuba and band (piano accompaniment available). 1954; originally published in 1887. 4:30. III. C–a♭ (c'). A typical concert polka for solo tuba.

Southwell, George. *Natoma.* George Southwell Publications. Out of print. Solo tuba and band. 1902. 2:15. II. C–f. A very easy concert polka. See: Sparks, L. Richmond, *An Annotated Bibliography.*

Southwell, George. *Quickstep (Fun for the Basses).* Southwell & Streeter Publishers. Out of print. Tuba section soli and band. 1881. 1:50. II–III. C–a♭. An easy novelty march with mostly diatonic writing for the tubas. See: Sparks, L. Richmond, *An Annotated Bibliography.*

Southwell, George. *Sounds from the Tuba.* George Southwell Publisher. Out of print. Solo tuba and band. 1886. 3:45. III. B♭₁–a♭. See: Sparks, L. Richmond, *An Annotated Bibliography.*

Sparke, Philip. *Concertino for Tuba and Brass Band.* Studio Music. 1988. 13:00. IV–V. C₁–g'. Two large connected sections: Lento; Vivo. An extensive, technically difficult solo work for tuba. The opening Lento is highly melismatic with the tuba playing many notes per beat, similar to the middle section of the Romanza from the Vaughan Williams *Concerto;* and it has two moderate solo cadenzas. The Vivo contains nonstop tonal pyrotechnics for the solo tuba and an extensive written and ad lib cadenza. This work is a major virtuoso showpiece for tuba and brass band.

Steadman-Allen, Ray. *Dashing Away with the Smoothing Iron.* Rosehill Music Publishing Company. Solo tuba and brass band. 1991. $27.50. 3:00. III–IV. A♭–e♭'. Continuous movement in three sections: Allegro giocoso, Andante, Allegro vivace. A good arrangement of the traditional British tune with some humorous moments.

Stephens, Denzil S. *Albertie.* Wright & Round, Ltd. Solo tuba and brass band. 1984. $23.00. 3:30. III. A₁–c' (d'). A novelty solo with no significant technical or musical demands.

Stephens, Denzil. *The Dancing Tuba.* Sarnia Music.

Solo tuba and band. 1985. 3:30. III–IV. C–e♭'. A waltz featuring the solo tuba.

Stephens, Denzil S. *The Imp.* Wright & Round, Ltd. Solo tuba and brass band. $23.00. 3:00. III. B♭₁ (G₁)–d'. A little rondo with cute tunes and nice contrasting sections.

Stewart, Joseph. *Tuba.* Kendor Music, Inc. Tuba and band with optional SATB choral parts (piano accompaniment available). 1977. $42.00. 3:00. III. B♭₁–b♭. Two connected sections: Presto, Jazz Waltz. Dedicated to Andy Peruzzini and the Maryvale High School Chorale. Some stylistic and technical challenges for the soloist. Band accompaniment is fairly easy.

Storm, Charles W. *Bouquet for Basses.* Volkwein Bros., Inc. Out of print. Solo tuba and brass band (piano accompaniment available). 1954. 5:00. II. B♭₁–e♭. A traditional polka for tuba solo.

Strauss, Richard. *Concerto No. 1 for Horn and Symphonic Band.* Band transcription by John Boyd. Tuba solo transcribed by John Anderson. Thompson Edition, Inc. Tuba and band. 1987. Purchase price $120.00; also available from the publisher on rental. 18:00. IV. G₁–e♭'. Three connected movements: Allegro; Andante; Allegro. Band arrangement "For Louis Stout." This arrangement of the great romantic horn concerto works very well for tuba.

Sullivan, Arthur. *The Lost Chord.* Arranged by A. C. van Leeuwen. Molenaar Music N.V. Solo tuba (or trombone) and band. 1950. 3:30. I. C–c. A very easy melodic solo for tuba and band.

Sutton, E. *The Cavalier.* Molenaar N.V. Solo tuba (or tenorhorn, baritone) and band. 4:15. II–III. G₁–a♭. An old-style theme and polka. See: Sparks, L. Richmond, *An Annotated Bibliography.*

Thingnæs, Frode. *Song for Michael—To Be or Not Tuba.* Frost Music A/S. Solo tuba (or baritone) and concert band. $60.00. 4:00. IV. A♭–g'. For Michael Lind. A pretty, lyrical work displaying the tuba's upper register.

Tuthill, Burnett. *Fantasia for Tuba, Op. 57.* Lyceum Press. Solo tuba (or bass trombone) and band (piano accompaniment available). 1968. 8:00. III–IV. G₁–g'(e'). For Rex Conner. Brief Andante introduction followed by an Allegro. Relatively traditional tonal writing with some larger, irregular intervals for the soloist on and above the staff.

Vadala, Chris. *Lonely Road.* Whaling Music. Solo tuba (or euphonium) and jazz band (or concert band and rhythm section). 1978. $30.00. 5:00. III–IV. D–d'. A slow jazz ballad. Contains choice of written-out or improvised solos.

Vaughan, Rodger. *Elegy.* Available from the composer. Solo tuba and wind ensemble (piano accompaniment also available). 1986–87. 3:45. III–IV. A₁–c'. Single movement. For Roger Bobo. A slow, gentle, expressive work. Band accompaniment is very easy.

Vaughan Williams, Ralph. *Concerto for Bass Tuba.* Arranged by Robert Hare. Oxford University Press.

Tuba and band (also tuba and orchestra, tuba and piano). 1976. Score and parts rental from the publisher. Arranged for Daniel Perantoni. This arrangement is as difficult and heavily scored as the original orchestral version, and it takes a great deal of preparation and care to ensure a successful performance. See listings under "Music for Tuba and Orchestra" and "Music for Tuba and Keyboard." See: Bird, Gary, ed., *Program Notes for the Solo Tuba*. Recorded by Jeffrey Arwood; Daniel Perantoni. Recorded accompaniment available: *Vivace: A Complete Practice System*. See listing under "Discography, Recorded Accompaniments."

Vivaldi, Antonio. *Concerto in A Minor* (first movement). Arranged by Richard R. Trevarthen. Bernel Music LTD. Solo tuba and brass band. 1993. $35.00. 3:45. III. A_1–d#'. A good arrangement of this standard tuba solo; see Vivaldi, arr. Ostrander under "Music for Tuba and Keyboard." Fairly wide intervallic leaps and rapid scale passages, mostly in the middle register.

Wagner, Richard. *Lied Aan de Avondster*. Arranged by F. Diepenbeek. Molenaar Music N.V. Solo tuba (or baritone) and band. 1949. 2:45. III. B–e♭'. An arrangement of an aria from the third act of "Tannhäuser."

Walters, Harold L. *Concertante*. Rubank, Inc. Solo tuba and band (piano accompaniment available). 1960. $19.50. 4:45. III–IV. E♭$_1$–d'. Continuous work in three sections.

Walters, Harold L. *Forty Fathoms*. Rubank, Inc. Solo tuba and band (piano accompaniment available). 1952. 3:00. III. A♭$_1$–e♭. An easy work with a nautical flavor.

Walters, Harold L. *Scherzo Pomposo*. Rubank, Inc. Solo tuba and band (piano accompaniment available). 1958. 4:00. II–III. B♭$_1$–f (b♭ or e♭'). This melodic work contains trills, hemiola, and optional quintuplets and triplet scale passages, which can be added to increase the difficulty of the piece. Several descending chromatic sequences will challenge the younger player.

Walters, Harold L. *Tarantelle*. Ludwig. Tuba and band (piano accompaniment available). 1946. $42.50. 3:30. II. B$_1$–f. Continuous work in two sections: Andante; Allegro. Opening Andante section is majestic and primarily diatonic. Allegro is a rollicking 6/8 in F minor.

Wantier, Firmin. *Air et Variations*. Editions Musicales Brogneaux. Out of print. Solo tuba (or saxophone, trombone, baritone) and band. 1957. 6:30. IV. A♭$_1$–g'. A substantial and characteristically French work with a theme and three variations. See: Sparks, L. Richmond, *An Annotated Bibliography*.

Ward, Norman. *The Happy Hippo*. Kendor Music, Inc. Out of print. Solo tuba and band (piano accompaniment available). 1967. 3:00. II. B♭$_1$–f. A very easy work for the soloist; band parts are slightly more difficult.

Watz, Franz. *Concertino in drei Saetzen*. Musikverlag Rundel GmbH. Solo tuba and band (piano accompaniment available).

Watz, Franz. *Der Fröliche Tubist*. Ewoton Musikverlag. Solo tuba and band. (piano accompaniment available).

Weber, Fred. *Big Boy*. Arranged by Howard Kilbert. Belwin Mill Corporation. Solo tuba and band (piano accompaniment available). Out of print. 1953. 1:30. I. E♭–d♭. A very easy arrangement for solo tuba and band.

Werle, Floyd E. *Concertino for Three Brass and Band*. Bourne Co. Solo trumpet, trombone, tuba, and band (piano reduction available). 1970. $30.00. 6:30. III. B$_1$–c'. Three movements: Vintage Foxtrot; Lullaby; Greek Dance. A well-scored work with a pop feel showcasing three solo brass. The first movement is in a fast two; the second is a slow interplay between the three solo instruments; and the final, "Greek Dance," is a driving movement in 7/8. Recorded by Fred Angerstein.

Wiegand, George. *The Leviathan—Fantasia*. Harry Coleman Publisher. Out of print. Solo tuba and band (piano accompaniment available). 1894. 6:45. III–IV. B♭$_1$–e♭'. A substantial and demanding work for the solo tubist. See: Sparks, L. Richmond, *An Annotated Bibliography*.

Wilder, Alec. *Concerto for Tuba and Concert Band*. Margun Music, Inc. Piano reduction available. 1965. Score and parts rental from the publisher. 12:00. IV. F#$_1$–g'. Four movements: Lively; Andante; Jauntily; Allegro. For Harvey Phillips. A work containing typical lyrical and technical demands of most of Wilder's tuba music. Some wide, irregular intervals.

Wilhelm, Rolf. *Concertino for Tuba*. Tuba Center. Solo tuba and band (piano reduction available). Strube Verlag GmbH. 1983. 11:45. IV–V. F$_1$–f'. Three movements: Moderato, deciso; Andante lirico; Allegro comodo. Written for Robert Tucci. A delightful work which excellently displays the soloist's virtuosity and musicianship. See: Bird, Gary, ed., *Program Notes for the Solo Tuba*. Recorded by Michael Bunn, Jens Bjorn-Larsen.

Williams, Ernest. *Concerto No. 2*. Charles Colin. Solo tuba (or trumpet) and band (piano accompaniment available). 1937. 17:00. III–IV. E♭$_1$–b♭. Three movements: Allegro Moderato; Adagio; Allegro. See listing under "Music for Tuba and Keyboard."

Woods, J. H. *Carter's March*. Thompson & Odell Publishers. Out of print. Solo tuba and band. 1887. 3:30. II. B♭$_1$–e♭. Dedicated to T. M. Carter, Esquire. See: Sparks, L. Richmond, *An Annotated Bibliography*.

Woods, J. H. *A Castle in Spain*. Op. 48. Thompson & Odell Publishers. Out of print. Solo tuba and band. 1887. 4:20. II–III. F$_1$–e♭. See: Sparks, L. Richmond, *An Annotated Bibliography*.

Woods, J. H. *Helicon Schottische, Op.46*. Thompson &

Odell Publishers. Out of print. Solo tuba and band. 1887. 2:30. III. B♭₁–c'. See: Sparks, L. Richmond, *An Annotated Bibliography.*

Wuorinen, Charles. *Chamber Concerto for Tuba with Twelve Winds and Twelve Drums.* C. F. Peters Corporation. Solo tuba, four flutes (doubling piccolo and alto flute), two oboes (doubling English horn), two bassoons (doubling contrabassoon), four horns, percussion (single player requiring twelve equidistant drums). 1970. Available on rental from the publisher. 17:00. IV–V. C₁–f♯'. A very demanding contemporary work with difficult parts for all players. Recorded by David Brainard; Don Butterfield.

Yarrow, Peter, and Lipton, Leonard. *Puff (The Magic Dragon).* Arranged by Richard Maltby. Warner Bros. Out of print. Solo tuba (or tuba section) and band (piano accompaniment available). 1967. 3:00. II–III. A♭₁–a'. A nice arrangement in variations of the Sixties pop tune.

Youmans, Vincent. *The Carioca.* Arranged by Lon Norman. Manuscript. Out of print. Solo tuba and band. 1972. 3:15. IV. E♭₁–e♭'. Arranged for Harvey Phillips and the U.S. Army Band. A classic rumba which works as a great popular feature for the solo

tuba. Recorded by Jeffrey Arwood; Harvey Phillips; Sam Pilafian.

Zaninelli, Luigi. *Peg Leg Pete.* Boosey & Hawkes. Out of print. Solo tuba (or bass clarinet) and band (piano accompaniment available). 1963. 2:30. II. B♭₁(A♭₁)–f. A tuneful novelty solo with a cadenza and the added demand on the soloist to produce several half-valve glissandos.

Zinke, Gerhard. *Der Basskarle—Polka.* Wilhelm Halter GmbH. Solo tuba and band. 2:30. II–III. C–a. See: Sparks, L. Richmond, *An Annotated Bibliography.*

Zinke, Gerhard. *Der Klettermaxe Polka.* Musikverlag Wilhelm Halter GmbH. Solo tuba (or tenorhorn, baritone, trombone, or bassoon) and concert band. 3:00. III. G₁–d♭. A good novelty solo to play with the "town band."

Zonn, Paul Martin. *Exchanges.* Available from the composer. Solo tuba and symphonic wind ensemble. 1980. 8:00. IV–V. E₁–g'. For the De Paul University Wind Ensemble and Don DeRoche, Conductor. To the memory of Thomas Harris. A difficult, contemporary work with gestural writing, including wide, irregular intervallic leaps and difficult polyrhythms. Interesting ensemble colors.

4. Music for Tuba and Orchestra
Skip Gray

Not many years ago tubists had very little choice of solo works with orchestral accompaniment. The venerable Ralph Vaughan Williams's *Concerto for Bass Tuba* was the usual selection, not necessarily because it was a great piece of music, but more often than not, because it was the only piece by a major composer available to the instrument. The first comprehensive guide to tuba repertoire, *Encyclopedia of Literature for the Tuba* by William J. Bell and R. Winston Morris, published in 1967, identified only six original works for solo tuba and orchestra. By 1973 and the publication of Morris's *Tuba Music Guide*, twenty-six works in this genre are listed. Today, there are well over one hundred works featuring the solo tuba with orchestra. They range from pops to experimental, from works in traditional forms to those which are almost completely improvisatory.

For a composer, the creation of a major work for solo tuba and orchestra is a true labor of love. Some pieces have been commissioned with a fairly substantial fee or grant, but many of these compositions were written by a composer for a tubist friend, a musician whom the composer honestly respected, even admired. This is evidenced in Joachim Grunner's *Concerto for Tuba and Orchestra*, written for Dietrich Unkrodt, as well as John Williams's *Tuba Concerto*, dedicated to Chester Schmitz. There are also compositions of significant duration, some as long and intricate as symphonies. These works show great care and devotion to the instrument, as the composers must have realized, down-deep, that their great investment of thought, time, and creative turmoil would probably not be rewarded in a similar manner for a composition for a more traditional musical medium. Tuba concerti are not performed as regularly (or regarded as critically) as symphonies, tone poems, or even solo works for the more popular orchestral instruments. Yet composers are writing works of sizable duration, complexity, and intellect for tuba and orchestra, for example, Derek Bourgeois's *Tuba Concerto, Op.38* (duration 43 minutes), Eugene Anderson's *Tuba Concerto No. 1 in B Minor* (36 minutes), and Frank Proto's *Sinfonia Concertante for Solo Tuba, Percussion, Flutes, and Strings* (33 minutes).

In addition to formal concerti for tuba and orchestra, there are now works putting the solo tubist in new solo roles with the orchestra. William Kraft's *Concerto for Tuba with Three Chamber Groups and Orchestra* actually has the soloist moving to different locations on stage during various sections of the work. A new work by Canadian composer Elizabeth Raum, entitled *The Legend of Heimdall for Solo Tuba and Orchestra*, is a sort of music drama with the solo tuba cast in the leading role. In the more popular vein, the solo tubist has works like Jerry Lackey's *Jazz Concerto for Tuba and Orchestra*.

The works briefly highlighted here illustrate the diversity of fine literature available for solo tuba and orchestra. Today, tubists can choose from a wide range of music featuring them with orchestra and can select particular roles in which they wish to be cast. This variety of literature should not only make it possible for more tubists to be heard and appreciated but also offer greater opportunities for tuba players to receive critical respect and acclaim.

Albam, Manny. *Concertino for Tuba and Chamber Orchestra*. Manuscript available from the composer. Solo tuba, strings, and harp. Three movements. For Michael Lind.

Almila, Atso. *Concerto for Tuba and String Orchestra*. Finnish Music Information Center. 1986. Rental from the publisher. 16:00. IV. F_1–d'. Three movements: Moderato; Tranquillo; Presto. To Michael Lind. Good, colorful string scoring with many opportunities for expressive interpretation by the soloist, whose part is fairly straightforward. There is an extensive cadenza in the first movement, and a mute is required in the second.

Anderson, Eugene D. *Tuba Concerto No. 1 in B Minor*. Anderson's Arizona Originals. Solo tuba and symphony orchestra (piano reduction available). 1970. Score and parts $90.00 (also available on rental). Original version 35:50. Revised version 27:00. IV. C_1–g#'. Three movements: Legato expressivo—Allegro; Largo; Allegro. To Arnold Jacobs. With its lush harmonies and melodic lines, this concerto could be considered neo-romantic. Although the main body of the solo tuba part is on or below the staff, the very long duration of the work, with little rest, makes it physically demanding. The orchestral scoring is sometimes very heavy, and attention needs to be directed to maintaining correct balance for the soloist. Reviewed in *T.U.B.A. Journal,* Winter 1991. See: Bird, Gary, ed., *Program Notes for the Solo Tuba.*

Andriessen, Jurriaan. *Concertino.* Donemus Publishing House. Solo tuba and orchestra (part indicates "solo sousaphone in e-flat"). 1967. $32.50. 12:00. IV. C–c''. A work mostly in the very upper tessitura.

Arban, Jean Baptiste *Variations on the "Carnival of Venice."* Arranged by Jerry Lackey. Carl Fischer. Solo tuba and orchestra. Rental. 8 minutes. VI. G_1– a. This arrangement is in the key of F, so it will lie well for the C tuba.

Arban, Jean Baptiste. *Variations on the "Carnival of Venice."* Arranged by Richard Domek. Available from Richard Domek. Solo tuba and orchestra (also available for tuba and piano, tuba and woodwind quintet, tuba and brass band, tuba and symphonic band). 1983. Rental. 8:00. VI. C–d' (B♭). For Skip Gray. This arrangement, in the key of B♭, is well suited to the F tuba. Contains interesting new material in the accompanying episodes between solo sections.

Arban, Jean Baptiste. *Variations on the "Carnival of Venice."* Arranged by Frank Berry. Carl Fischer, Inc. Solo tuba and orchestra. Rental. 8 minutes. VI. G_1–a. For Roger Bobo. In the key of B♭, so it will lie well for the F tuba. Recorded by Roger Bobo.

Arutiunian, Alexandre. *Concerto for Tuba and Orchestra.* In preparation by Editions Bim. Piano reduction 1995. Rental from the publisher.

Bentzon, Niels Viggo. *Capriccio, Op. 396.* Edition Wilhelm Hansen. Solo tuba, trumpet, percussion, piano, strings. 1977. Rental from the publisher. 7:00.

Bentzon, Niels Viggo. *Concerto for Tuba, Op. 373.* Edition Wilhelm Hansen. Solo tuba and orchestra. 1975. Rental from the publisher. 20:00.

Blank, Alan. *Divertimento for Tuba and String Orchestra.* American Composers Alliance. 1979. 28:00.

Blanquer, Amando. *L'os hispánic.* Sociedad General de Autores de España. Solo tuba with orchestra (piano reduction available). 1976. 6:00. Four movements: De gaubança; La Passió; L'espera; La tombearella. Original contrabass version dedicated to Jaime Antonio Robles. A work originally for contrabass and piano arranged by the composer for tuba, later for tuba and orchestra.

Borg, Kim. *Finnish Rhapsody, Op. 32B.* Finnish Music Information Centre. Solo tuba, flute, oboe, clarinet, bassoon, horn, trumpet, and strings (piano accompaniment available). 1985. 6:30. III–IV. A_1–d'. Three movements: On the Road; Summer Night; Wedding. A light, tuneful work nicely scored so that the solo tubist will be easily heard.

Bottje, Will Gay. *Concerto for Tuba and Orchestra.* American Composers Alliance. Solo tuba and or-

chestra (piano accompaniment available). 1973. 16:00. III–IV. E_1–c'. Three movements: Very Quietly; Dance Variations; Dramatic. A work with few range or intervallic demands. The second movement has continually shifting polymeters.

Bourgeois, Derek. *Tuba Concerto, Op. 38.* R. Smith & Company. Solo tuba and orchestra (piano reduction available). 1972. Rental from the publisher. 43:00. IV–V. $F_1(G\sharp_2$ in cadenza)–f '. Four movements: Allegro moderato; Rondo (Grave); Scherzo (Allegro Scherzando); Finale (Maestoso—Allegro vivace). For John Fletcher. A major extended work, blending jazz and popular elements into a classical setting. Rhythmic writing in some places quite difficult. Scored for large orchestra. Recorded by John Fletcher.

Boutry, Roger. *Tubaroque.* Alphonse Leduc. Solo tuba with orchestra (piano accompaniment available). 1955. Rental from the publisher. 4:30. IV. A_1– g'(a♭'). For Paul Bernard. See listing under "Music for Tuba and Keyboard." Also see: Thompson/ Lemke, *French Music for Low Brass Instruments.*

Bozza, Eugene. *Concertino for Tuba and Orchestra.* Alphonse Leduc. Piano reduction available. 1967. Rental from the publisher. 13:00. V. $F\sharp_1$–ab'. Three movements: Allegro vivo; Andante ma non troppo; Allegro vivo. A true technical and musical showpiece with important cadenzas in each movement. Although the work was originally intended for the small French tuba, it is regularly performed on the bass and sometimes the contrabass tuba. The work is full of interesting, tuneful melodies, rapid chromatic passages, and wide leaps. Orchestral scoring is light and presents no balance problems for the soloist. See: Thompson/Lemke, *French Music for Low Brass Instruments.* Tuba and piano version recorded by Steven Seward.

Brehm, Alvin. *Concerto for Tuba.* G. Schirmer. Solo tuba and orchestra. 1982. Rental from the publisher. 22:00.

Broadstock, Brenton. *Tuba Concerto.* G. Schirmer (Australia). Tuba and orchestra. 1985. Score and parts rental from the publisher. 17:00. V. $F\sharp_1$–b' (also a notation to "very high note"). Two movements: Pensoso sempre sostenuto; Drammatico. A lyrical work in a modern style with tone clusters, string harmonics, mutings, stopped effects, and quarter-tone trills. A major work of great difficulty for both the soloist and the accompanying ensemble. Four extensive solo cadenzas contain support/interaction from the orchestra. This work is actually Broadstock's second major concerto for the tuba. The first is much more conservative in musical nature and difficulty; at this time, it is not available for performance.

Brown, Jonathan Bruce. *Lyric Variations for Tuba and String Orchestra.* Seesaw Music Corporation. 1975. $13.50 (score). 5:15. III–IV. Ab_1–eb'. A work of mainly diatonic, melodic nature for the soloist with a theme and seven variations.

Bull, Edvard Hagerup. *Giocoso Bucolico: La Muse Legère: Concertino for Tuba and Chamber Orchestra*. Norwegian Music Information Center. Solo tuba, flute, oboe, horn, piano, strings. 1992. 12:00. IV–V. C$\sharp_1$–c''. Three movements: Allegretto; Adagio; Allegro Energico. In memoriam Darius Milhaud. The score specifies "Tuba (à 6 Pistons en Ut)" signifying the French Tuba. The solo part lies in an extremely high tessitura (35 c'''s, and many b' and b♭'s) throughout; this is truly the primary difficulty in this overall nice, conservative, French-influenced work.

Cioffari, Richard J. *Rhapsody for Tuba and Orchestra*. Trombone Association Publishing. Piano reduction available. 1975. $75.00. 7:30. III–IV. G$_1$–b. For Ivan Hammond. The soloist plays continuously with few rests. The part lies mostly on the staff; the main difficulty, other than endurance, being a few wide intervallic leaps.

Dennison, Sam. *Lyric Piece and Rondo for Tuba and Strings*. Kalmus. 1982. $32.00. *Lyric Piece* 5:00. *Rondo* 3:20. IV. F$_1$–g'. A tuneful work which presents no major difficulties and goes together very easily with the accompanying string ensemble.

Domazlicky, František. *Concerto, Op. 53*. Artia Foreign Trade Corporation of Czechoslovakia. Solo tuba and string orchestra. 1983. IV.

Dupriez, Christian. *Piccolo Capriccio*. Available from the composer. Tuba and orchestra (piano accompaniment also available). 2:30. IV. A$_1$–g'. Dedicated to Edward R. Goldstein. A melodic little work in four sections.

Eerola, Lasse. *Music for Tuba and Orchestra*. Finnish Music Information Center. Solo tuba, two flutes, two clarinets, bassoon, two horns in F, piano, two percussion, strings (piano reduction available). 1991. 11:00. IV–V. F$_1$–ab'. Two movements: Adagio; Scherzo. Extensive solo cadenzas precede each movement (and actually link the two together) and foreshadow material to come. A difficult work for both soloist and orchestra.

Fleming, Robert. *Concerto for Tuba*. Canadian Music Centre. Solo tuba and orchestra (two flutes, oboe, two clarinets, bassoon, two horns, timpani, strings). Piano reduction available. 1966. Orchestral part rental. 13:00. III–IV. E♭$_1$–f♯'. Three movements: Allegro con Moto; Andantino e Grazioso; Allegro Vivace. Dedicated to Robert Ryker. A good, conservatively written work.

Frackenpohl, Arthur. *Concertino for Tuba and String Orchestra*. Robert King Music. Piano reduction available. 1962. $17.25. 8:45. III. G$_1$–c'. Three movements: Moderato; Lento; Allegro. Written for Abe Torchinsky. A tuneful, approachable work easily put together.

Gagneux, Renaud. *Concerto*. Editions Durand et Cie. Solo tuba and orchestra. 1984. Rental from the publisher.

Gagneux, Renaud. *La Chasse des carillons crie dans les gorges pour tuba, cor, et orchestre*. Editions Durand et

Cie. Tuba, horn, and orchestra. 1991. Rental from the publisher. Premiered by Hervé Brisse.

George, Thom Ritter. *Concertino for Tuba and String Orchestra*. Available from the composer. Also versions for solo tuba and wind ensemble, solo tuba and piano. 1984. Three movements: Allegro ma non troppo; Cantabile e simplice; Vivace. See: Bird, Gary, ed., *Program Notes for the Solo Tuba*.

Gregson, Edward. *Concerto for Tuba*. Novello and Co., Ltd. Solo tuba and orchestra (solo tuba and concert band, solo tuba and brass band, and piano reduction available). 1976. Rental from the publisher. See listing under "Music for Tuba and Band." See: Bird, Gary, ed., *Program Notes for the Solo Tuba*.

Gruner, Joachim. *Double Concerto for Contrabass Clarinet and Tuba*. Available from the composer. Solo contrabass clarinet, solo tuba, and orchestra. 1991. 22:00. Four movements: Parallel; Trionfante; "Etude"; Passacaglia.

Gruner, Joachim. *Konzert für Tuba und Orchester*. Verlag Neue Musik Berlin. 1977. Score $29.95. Parts rental from the publisher. 22:00. VI. E$_1$–a'. Three movements: Recitative; Aria; Scenes. For Dietrich Unkrodt. A dramatic, energetic work requiring a great deal of control of the instrument by the soloist, who in addition to playing notated pitches, must sing and play during three poignant sections of the "Aria," ad lib, and make some very quick mute changes. Recorded by Dietrich Unkrodt.

Gruner, Joachim. *Triple Concerto for Trumpet, Trombone, Tuba and Large Orchestra*. Verlag Neue Musik Berlin. 1983–84. Rental from the publisher. 21:00. Four movements.

Hahn, Gunnar. *Per Svinagerde: Ballad*. Swedish Music Information Center. Solo tuba and string orchestra. 1982.

Hartley, Walter S. *Fantasia for Tuba and Chamber Orchestra*. Wingert-Jones Music, Inc. Solo tuba, two flutes, oboe, bassoon, two clarinets, two trumpets, two horns, two trombones, and strings (piano reduction available). 1991. $35.00. 8:30. IV–V. E♭$_1$–a'. Continuous work in four sections: Andante; Allegro molto; Adagio; Presto. Commissioned by Scott Watson with a General Research Grant from the University of Kansas. A solid musical work, conservative in compositional style yet approachable by a wide body of listeners.

Heiden, Bernard. *Concerto for Tuba and Orchestra*. Southern Music Publishing Company (dist. by Theodore Presser). Piano reduction available. 1976. Rental from the publisher. 17:00. IV. D$_1$–f♯'. Three movements: Allegro risoluto; Andante; Vivace. Composed under a grant from the National Endowment for the Arts. For Harvey Phillips. The opening, dancing solo phrase in the waltzlike first movement quickly takes the tubist through nearly the entire range required in the composition. The Andante has the tuba playing lyrical variations mostly over a fifteen-note ground. The Vivace combines a diatonic, marchlike melody with a chromatically varied sixteenth-note line played in varied forms later by the soloist. A traditionally written work with few excessive demands on the soloist. See: Bird, Gary, ed., *Program Notes for the Solo Tuba.*

Hollomon, Samuel. *Concerto for Tuba and Orchestra.* Manuscript from the composer. Band accompaniment and piano reduction by the composer available. 1990. Rental from the composer. 23:00. IV. C_1–a'. Three movements: Allegro moderato; Andante (Theme); Variations. For James Edward Shearer. A neo-romantic work with some nice lines for the soloist. Extensive solo cadenza in the first movement. The movements end somewhat abruptly, and there are few climaxes featuring the soloist.

Holmboe, Vagn. *Concerto for Tuba, Op. 127.* G. Schirmer, Inc. Solo tuba and orchestra. 17:00. V.

Holmboe, Vagn. *Intermezzo Concertante.* G. Schirmer, Inc. Solo tuba and orchestra. 8:00.

Jager, Robert. *Concerto for Bass Tuba and Symphony Orchestra.* Belwin-Mills Music Corporation. Also tuba and band, tuba and piano. 1981. Rental from the publisher. 13:00. See listing under "Music for Tuba and Band." See: Bird, Gary, ed., *Program Notes for the Solo Tuba.*

Jevtic, Ivan. *Concerto for Tuba and Symphony Orchestra.* Editions BIM. Piano reduction available. 1992. Rental from the Publisher. 22:00. IV–V. F_1–ab'. Four movements: Maestoso; Scherzo diabolico; Adagio; Allegro giusto. A powerful, major work. Melodically oriented writing with no avant-garde techniques required.

Karkoff, Maurice. *Concertino for Tuba and String Orchestra.* Swedish Music Information Center. 1991. 12:00. Three movements: Moderato; Adagio; Finale.

Kayser, Leif. *Concerto for Tuba and String Orchestra.* Leif Kayser. 1979.

Kellaway, Roger. *Songs of Ascent (Concerto).* In preparation by Editions Bim. Tuba and orchestra (piano reduction in preparation). 1988/89. Rental from the publisher. V. Extremely high tessitura for the soloist throughout. See: Bird, Gary, ed., *Program Notes for the Solo Tuba.*

Kleinsinger, George. *The Further Adventures of Tubby the Tuba.* Music Theatre International. Solo tuba and orchestra. Rental from the publisher. Contains the most involved playing for the tubist of the "Tubby" pieces, including much lyrical playing and extensive technical material toward the end of the work. Recorded by Tommy Johnson.

Kleinsinger, George. *Tubby Joins the Circus.* Music Theatre International. Solo tuba and orchestra. Rental from the publisher. Less playing for the tubist than in the other "Tubby" works. Recorded by Tommy Johnson.

Kleinsinger, George. *Tubby Meets the Jazz Band.* Music Theatre International. Solo tuba, clarinet, trumpet, trombone, drums, piano, and orchestra. Rental from the publisher. Recorded by Tommy Johnson.

Kleinsinger, George. *Tubby the Tuba.* Music Theatre International. Solo tuba and orchestra (tuba and band arrangement available). 1945. Rental from the publisher. 12:00. III. Eb_1–eb'. Narration by Paul Tripp. The classic story of the tuba wanting to play a melody. Beautiful tunes and a nice story. Many recordings available.

Koch, Erland von. *Concerto for Tuba.* AB Carl Gehrmans Musikforlag. Tuba and strings (piano reduction available). 1978. $19.50 (score), parts rental from the publisher. 14:00. IV–V. E_1 ($F\sharp_1$)–g'(ab'). Three movements: Allegro moderato; Siciliano; Presto. Dedicated to Michael Lind. A conservative melodic work somewhat romantic in character.

Koetsier, Jan. *Concertino for Tuba and String Orchestra, Op. 77.* Editions Bim. Piano reduction available. 1978, revised 1982. Parts rental from the publisher. 15:00. V. F_1–gb'. Three movements: Allegro con brio; Romanza e Scherzino; Rondo Bavarèse. Dedicated to Manfred Hoppert. A tonal, melodic work with virtuosic and humorous moments. Tessitura and agility required would suggest appropriateness of an F or Eb tuba in the performance of this work. Recorded by Manfred Hoppert.

Köper, Karl-Heinz. *Tuba-Tabu.* Musikverlag K. H. Köper. Tuba and orchestra (tuba and piano version also published). 10:00. IV. F_1–f'. One continuous movement with four large sections. A pleasant, tuneful work with few outstanding technical demands. Recorded by Michael Lind.

Kosteck, Gregory. *The Enchanted Island: Symphonic Poem for Tuba and Orchestra.* Manuscript previously available from the composer, out of print. Piano reduction available. 1981. 11:00. IV. C_1–e'. Continuous work in four large sections plus a coda (Tranquillo; Scherzando; Arioso; Finale; Adagio). Commissioned by, composed for, and dedicated to Sande and Paula MacMorran. An extensive, coloristic, modern tone poem for orchestra with a great deal of soloistic tuba writing. Although not a virtuoso work, the tuba solo serves as a principal melodic component. Because of the tessitura of the part and the weight of orchestration, a contrabass tuba would probably work best in performance of this piece.

Kraft, William. *Tuba Concerto.* New Music West. Solo tuba with three chamber groups and orchestra. 1979. Rental from the publisher. 18:00. V. $F\sharp_2$–a$\sharp$'. Commissioned by Zubin Mehta for Roger Bobo and the Los Angeles Philharmonic with partial assistance of a grant from the National Endowment for the Arts. An extensive contemporary work, revised and rescored by the composer from his 1977 work *Andirivieni.* The work contains material very reminiscent of the composer's *Encounters II for Solo Tuba*, including rapid, nontonal passages, very wide intervallic leaps, the complete spectrum of dynamics, and various avant-garde effects, including singing into the instrument, double stops, glissandos. A demanding piece for both the performers and the audience. See: Bird, Gary, ed., *Program Notes for the Solo Tuba*.

Krol, Bernhard. *Falstaff Concerto, Op. 119*. Editions Bim. Solo tuba and string orchestra (piano reduction available). 1990. Rental from the publisher. 15:00. IV–V. G$_1$–f♯'. Three movements. Commissioned by Editions Bim. A neoclassical work in both melodic style and form. The second movement contains some beautiful, lyrical writing, while the greatest technical demands for the tubist are in the driving and humorous third movement, entitled "Homage to Giuseppe Verdi."

Krzywicki, Jan. *Fantasy for Tuba and Strings*. Available from the composer. 1964. 8:00. III. E$_1$–b. Two movements: Andante; Allegro. For Abe Torchinsky. A melodic work with the tuba part written within and below the bass staff.

Kulesha, Gary. *Concerto for Tuba and Orchestra*. Canadian Music Centre. Band accompaniment and piano accompaniment, four hands, also available. 1979. Rental from the publisher. 18:00. IV. C$_1$–d'. Three movements: Prelude and Fugue; Scherzo; Finale. Commissioned by the Scarborough Concert Band of Ontario, Canada. Written for Scott Irvine. See listing under "Music for Tuba and Band."

Kupferman, Meyer. *Concerto for Tuba*. Soundspells Productions. V.

Lachenmann, Helmut. *Harmonica—Music for Full Orchestra with Tuba-Solo*. Breitkopf & Härtel. 1981–83. 31:00. V. A$_2$–c" (highest note possible). For Richard Nahatzki. A difficult and complex work for both the tubist and the orchestra. Extensive range and leaps, very challenging rhythms and polymeters, and other avant-garde effects throughout. Recorded by Richard Nahatzki.

Lackey, Jerry. *Jazz Concerto for Tuba and Orchestra*. Available from the composer. Solo tuba and orchestra, drum set, piano, and electric bass (also versions for tuba and band, tuba and piano). 1984. Rental from composer. 12:00. V. G$_2$–b♭'. Three movements: Fast Swing, Rock, Simple Waltz, Fast Swing; Slow, Tranquillo; Fast, with Energy. A very good, challenging pops-style feature work for tuba and orchestra.

Larsson, Mats. *Homage to the Neon Sign of las Palaz Bingo: Concerto for Tuba and String Orchestra*. Swedish Music Information Center. 1991. 14:00–15:00. For Gene Pokorny.

Leichtling, Alan. *Concerto for Tuba, Strings, and Two Harps, Op. 83*. Seesaw Music Corporation. 1980–81. 21:00. IV–V. F$_1$–g'. Two movements: Aria with fantasy variations; Finale: allegro con brio. Dedi-

cated to Robert Starer. Primarily diatonic writing in the solo part with some difficult polymeters and rhythmic interaction between solo part and ensemble. An extensive cadenza precedes the brief transition between the last variation in the first movement and the Finale.

Levy, Frank. *Dialogue*. Seesaw Music Corporation. Tuba, harp, timpani, and strings. 1962. $13.00 (score). 10:00. IV. F$_1$–f'. The work is in two connected large sections: Adagio e molto mesto; Allegro marcato. Open scoring and effective use of dissonance make this work interesting although by no means virtuosic. "Contrabass" tuba is specified in the score, but an F or E♭ tuba would also be effective within the instrumentation, especially in sections juxtaposing the tuba with harp.

Linkola, Jukka. *Concerto for Tuba and Orchestra*. Finnish Music Information Center. 1992. 24:00. V. F$_1$–b♭'. Three movements: Introduction; Choral; Shades of Rhythm. Commissioned by NOMUS. Dedicated to Michael Lind. An extensive, virtuosic work employing less-exploratory melodic and harmonic styles yet still possessing interesting, coloristic writing in both the solo and the accompanying ensemble.

Lorge, John S. *Fantasia for Tuba and Orchestra*. Available from the composer. 1992. 15:00. IV. E$_1$–g'. Four movements: Andante, Allegro non Troppo molto pesante; Andante; Senza Misura, Poco Allegretto, Senza Misura Ancora; Allegro. For Matthew Garbutt. A substantial modern work in which the soloist is often playing dialogues with various orchestral combinations. Wide, irregular intervallic leaps throughout. There are no avant-garde effects except some improvised half-valve passages in the third movement.

Lovelock, William. *Concerto for Tuba and Orchestra*. Allans Publishing Pty. Ltd. Out of print. Piano reduction by the composer. c. 1965. 11:30. IV–V. F$_1$–f'. Continuous work in three large sections: Allegro; Adagio; Tempo primo. For John Woods. A tonal, neo-romantic work written in Australia with some very demanding technical passages. Works best on the F or E♭ tuba.

Lundquist, Torbjorn Iwan. *Landskap for Tuba and Orchestra*. Swedish Music Information Center. Tuba and strings. 1978. 16:00. IV–V. F$_1$–a♭'. Continuous work in three large sections. For Michael Lind. A beautiful work with nice melodies and quartal and chromatic melodic and harmonic influences. The opening section with allegro moderato feeling moves into an expressive Largamente; the following substantial cadenza provides a transition to the final Presto. Recorded by Michael Lind.

Madsen, Trige. *Concerto for Tuba and Orchestra, Op. 35*. Musikk-Huset Forlag, Norway. Piano reduction available. 1986. IV.

Markl, Max. *Concertino for Tuba and Orchestra*. Tuba Center. Tuba and orchestra.

Martin, Vernon. *Concerto for Tuba and Strings.* Composers Autograph Publications. Out of print. Piano reduction available. 1956. 14:00. III–IV. G₁–e♭'. Three movements. Conservative writing for the tuba and orchestra.

Meier, Jost. *Eclipse finale?* Editions Bim. Solo tuba and chamber orchestra (also available for tuba and brass band, tuba and piano). 1991. Rental from the publisher. 19:30. V. See listing under "Music for Tuba and Band."

Mortimer, John Glenesk. *Tuba Concerto.* Editions Marc Reift. Tuba and string orchestra (piano accompaniment available). 1983. For David LeClair.

Mueller, Florian. *Concert Music for Tuba.* University Publications. Out of print. Tuba and orchestra (two flutes doubling piccolo, two oboes, two clarinets, two bassoons, two horns, strings). Piano reduction available. 1961. 5:00. III–IV. E₁–e'. For Arnold Jacobs. See listing under "Music for Tuba and Keyboard." Tuba and piano version recorded by Rex Conner.

Mueller, Frederick. *Variations on a Theme of Samuel Barber.* Manuscript available from the composer. Solo tuba and strings (also solo tuba and band, solo tuba and piano). 1972. 9:00. III–IV. C♯–d'(g'). Commissioned by and dedicated to Robert Tucci. A mostly lyrical work in seven variations and cadenza.

Muradian, Vazgen. *Concerto for Tuba and Orchestra, Op. 85.* Rental from the composer. Solo tuba and string orchestra (piano reduction available). 1984. 15:30. IV. C₁–g'. Three movements: Allegro grazioso; Romanza; Presto. A melodic, neo-romantic work which takes the soloist through much of the range in a mostly diatonic fashion. The music contains passion reminiscent of the composer's Armenian homeland. Vazgen Muradian has written a very large body of music, including concerti for every orchestral instrument. His *Concerto for Contrabassoon and String Orchestra* also works quite well for the tuba and is in the same style.

Premru, Raymond. *Concerto for Tuba and Orchestra.* T.U.B.A Press. Piano accompaniment available. 1992. 15:00. IV. F₁–f'. Three movements: Adagio—Allegro ma non troppo; Molto Allegro; Adagio. Commissioned by Tubists Universal Brotherhood Association and premiered at the 1992 International Tuba-Euphonium Conference in Lexington, Kentucky. Dedicated to the memory of John Fletcher. A highly melodic work in which the composer depicts the personality and memories of his friend and colleague John Fletcher. The hauntingly beautiful third movement, a soliloquy for solo tuba with strings, is about seven minutes long and can very effectively stand by itself in performance.

Presser, William. *Concerto for Tuba and Strings.* Theodore Presser Company. Solo tuba and string orchestra (piano reduction available). 1970. Rental from the publisher. 16:30. IV. C₁–e'. Three move-

ments. See: Bird, Gary, ed., *Program Notes for the Solo Tuba.*

Proto, Frank. *The Four Seasons.* Liben Music Publishers. Tuba, percussion, strings, and tape. 1980. Score and parts rental from the publisher. 30:00. IV–V. A₂–a'. Five movements: Introduction; Spring; Summer; Autumn; Winter. Commissioned by the Cincinnati Symphony Orchestra. A fulfilling work from both the performers' and the audience's perspective; combines popular and modern musical idioms. A duo concertante for tuba and percussion with orchestra and tape. Recorded by Michael Thornton.

Proto, Frank. *The New Seasons—Sinfonia Concertante for Tuba, Percussion, Flutes and Strings.* Liben Music Publishers. Solo tuba, two solo percussion, four flutes (with piccolos and alto flutes), two tutti percussion, and strings. 1991. Rental from the publisher. 32:30. IV–V. E♭₁–g♭'. Three movements. An extensive modern work with a demanding tuba part and very demanding percussion parts. Although probably not a work that would fit on a pops concert, there are jazz and popular influences in the composition. Both solo percussion parts require improvisation within a jazz style.

Raum, Elizabeth. *The Legend of Heimdall for Solo Tuba and Orchestra.* Canadian Music Centre. 1991. 19:00. IV–V. G₁–g'. Three movements: Heimdall's Gjallarhorn; The Song of the Bard; The Battle of Asgard. Commissioned by the Canadian Broadcasting Corporation and dedicated to John Griffiths. Lyrical program music in a neo-romantic style based on themes from Norse myths. The composer specifies CC tuba for the outer movements and F for the middle movement.

Ridout, Alan. *Concertino for Tuba and Strings.* Emerson Edition. Solo tuba and strings or string quartet (piano reduction available). 1985. 4:45. IV. F₁–e'. Three movements: Allegro; Lento; Vivace. Tuneful, conservative music. Meter in third movement shifts irregularly between three and two beats per bar.

Roikjer, Kjell. *Capriccio for Tuba and Orchestra, Op. 66.* Musikforlaget IMUDICO. Piano reduction available. 1974. 7:30. IV–V. F₁–g'. Continuous work in three large sections. For Michael Lind. A flashy work for the solo tuba with mostly diatonic and chordal writing.

Roikjer, Kjell. *Concerto for Tuba and Orchestra.* Musikforlaget IMUDICO. Piano reduction available.

Rottler, Werner. *Concerto for Tuba and Orchestra.* Available from the composer. Piano accompaniment available. 1980. IV. Three movements: Allegro moderato; Adagio quieto e religioso; Allegretto vivace. For Robert Tucci.

Sagvik, Stellan. *Svensk Concertino, Op. 114j.* Swedish Music Information Center. Solo tuba and string orchestra. 1983. 10:00. IV.

Schilling, Hans Ludwig. *Tuba & Co.—Concerto für Basstuba und Streichorchester.* Available from the composer. Solo tuba and string orchestra.

Schmidt, Ole. *Concerto for Tuba and Orchestra.* Edition Wilhelm Hansen. Piano reduction available. 1976. 14:20. V. Three movements: Allegro moderato; Lento; Allegro giusto. See: Bird, Gary, ed., *Program Notes for the Solo Tuba.* Recorded by Michael Lind.

Schmidt, William. *Concerto for Tuba and Chamber Orchestra.* Available from the composer. Solo tuba and chamber orchestra (flute, oboe, clarinet, bassoon, trumpet, two horns, bass trombone, percussion, and strings). 1993. Rental. 15:30. IV. A_1–$g\sharp'$. Three movements: 1; 2; 3. A great deal of interplay between soloist and accompanying ensemble and some very coloristic instrumental doublings make this an interesting yet not overly difficult work. The third movement contains a great deal of shifting meters.

Schuller, Gunther. *Capriccio for Tuba and Orchestra.* Mentor Music, Inc. Solo tuba and small orchestra (piano reduction available). 1969. Rental from the publisher. 10:00. IV. Eb_1–e'. For Harvey Phillips. Substantial technical demands made of the soloist, including extensive lip trills. See: Bird, Gary, ed., *Program Notes for the Solo Tuba.* Recorded by Harvey Phillips.

Segerstam, Leif. *Orchestral Diary Sheet No. 11i.* Finnish Music Information Center. Solo tuba (or trombone) in the orchestra. 1981. V. An unmetered orchestral sound-piece with solo obbligato instrumental solo, originally cello; later rewritten by the composer for various solo instruments.

Shaughnessy, Robert. *Concertino for Tuba and String Orchestra.* Peer International Corp. Piano reduction available. 1969. Score and parts on rental from the publisher. 12:00. III–IV. A_1–b. Three movements: I; II. Lento; III. Allegro non troppo. A work without significant difficulty, unusual in that all three movements are in a compound meter—the first movement in 6/4, the second in 9/8, and the third in 12/8.

Sorensen, Erling Ingemann. *Sensonner, Op. 10.* Danish Music Information Center. Solo tuba and string orchestra. 1981. 10:00. IV.

Steptoe, Roger. *Concerto for Tuba and Strings.* Stainer & Bell. Piano reduction available. 1983. Rental from the publisher. 15:00. V. F_1–g'. Three movements: Con poco moto—Allegro; Giocoso; Molto calmo. For James Gourlay. The opening of the first movement and the third movement are quite melodic. Very difficult technical material which, depending on the tempo, will require double tonguing.

Stevens, Thomas. *Variations in Olden Style (after Bach).* Editions Bim. Solo tuba, strings, continuo (piano accompaniment available). 1989. Parts on rental from the publisher. 4:45. IV. F–f '. Theme and five variations. For Roger Bobo. Good, traditional theme and variations based on the Sarabande from J.S. Bach's Sixth Cello Suite. The tuba part is within or slightly above the staff and lies very well for the F tuba. Recorded in tuba-piano version by Roger Bobo.

Stokes, Eric. *A Center Harbor Holiday.* Manuscript. Out of print. Tuba and orchestra. 1963; revised 1972. 14:00. IV. E_1–g'. For Roger Bobo. A concerto in one movement with patriotic American flavor.

Strukow, Valerie. *Concerto for Tuba and Orchestra.* Editions Bim. Piano reduction available. 1980. Rental from the publisher. 13:45. V. C_1–a' (with suggested "ossia" sections down an octave). Three movements: Allegro moderato; Lento elegiaco; Vivo scherzando. A technically demanding modern work in a style interesting and accessible to broad audiences. In the first movement, many hybrid scale passages quickly take the player through much of the tuba's range; the movement ends with an extensive solo cadenza. The second movement is lyrical and expressive. The finale resembles a wild tarantella. Recorded by Jens Bjørn-Larsen.

Tischhauser, Franz. *Eve's Meditation on Love.* Margun Music, Inc. Soprano, solo tuba, and orchestra. 1971. Work in preparation for publication.

Tomasi, Henri. *Danse Sacrée: No. 3 from "Cinc danses profanes et sacrées."* Alphonse Leduc. Solo tuba and chamber orchestra (piano reduction available). 1960. 5:00. III. G_1–ab'. See: Thompson/Lemke, *French Music for Low Brass Instruments.*

Vaughan Williams, Ralph. *Concerto for Bass Tuba.* Oxford University Press. Solo tuba and orchestra (solo tuba and band, piano reduction also available). 1954. Rental from the publisher. 13:00. IV. Eb_1–$f'(ab')$. Three movements: Prelude (Allegro moderato); Romanza; Finale—Rondo alla Tedesca. Dedicated to the London Symphony Orchestra. Although written in 1954, this is a truly conservative work, firmly within the bounds of traditional harmony, tonality, and notation. Despite the fact that there are now over one hundred works for solo tuba and orchestra, this concerto is still regarded by many musicians and conductors as the primary work in the tubist's solo repertoire, and it is a required selection for many auditions and competitions. The first movement takes the soloist through much of the instrument's range, from low eb to optional high ab in the cadenza. The Romanza is a beautifully expressive, melodic scene providing the soloist with a very nice vehicle in which to express emotion and exhibit musicality. The Finale contains some opportunity for pyrotechnic display, although it winds to a halt with the final cadenza and ends with a unsatisfying fizzle. See: Bird, Gary, ed., *Program Notes for the Solo Tuba.* Recorded by Philip Catelinet; Eugene Dowling; John Fletcher; Patrick Harrild; Manfred Hoppert; Arnold Jacobs;

Ian King; Michael Lind; Richard Nahatzki; Harvey Phillips; Donald Strand; Floyd Cooley. Recorded accompaniment available: *Vivace: A Complete Practice System*. See listing under "Discography, Recorded Accompaniments."

Villette, Pierre. *Fantaisie concertante*. Alphonse Leduc. Solo tuba and chamber orchestra (piano reduction available). 1962. Rental from the publisher. IV–V. G_1–a♭'. See: Thompson/Lemke, *French Music for Low Brass Instruments*.

Wilder, Alec. *Elegy for the Whale*. Margun Music Inc. Solo tuba and orchestra (piano accompaniment also available). Rental from the publisher. 1981. 3:20. IV. F_1–g'. Written for Harvey Phillips. A somber, brooding piece. The tuba part is mostly in the upper register and contains many intricate, irregular tonal shifts. Although melodic in nature, this work lacks the "popular feel" inherent in much of Wilder's music. It is truly a difficult piece for performer and audience alike.

Wilder, Alec. *Sonata for Tuba and Orchestra*. Wilder Music Inc. (Out of print). Tuba and piano available. An arrangement for orchestral accompaniment of the composer's *Sonata for Tuba and Piano*.

Wilder, Alec. *Suite No. 1 for Tuba and Orchestra, "Effie."* Margun Music Inc. Rental from the publisher. The popular solo tuba work arranged nicely with orchestral accompaniment. See listings under "Music for Tuba and Keyboard" and "Music for Tuba in Mixed Ensemble."

Williams, John. *Concerto for Tuba*. Rodgers & Hammerstein Concert Library. Solo tuba and orchestra (piano reduction available). 1985. 16:30. V. F_1–g'. Three movements: Allegro moderato; Andante; Allegro molto. To Chester Schmitz. An incredible, virtuosic work with John Williams's familiar melodic and harmonic style. Some of the technical demands in the solo part arise because of the stringlike nature of the writing: rapid, smooth arpeggiations and double-tongue sections perhaps more idiomatic to bowed instruments. See: Bird, Gary, ed., *Program Notes for the Solo Tuba*.

Winteregg, Steven. *Concerto for Tuba*. Available from the composer. Tuba and orchestra (flute, clarinet, bassoon, horn, trumpet, trombone, two percussion, strings). 1992. Rental from the composer. 16:30. IV. G_1–e'. Three movements: I; II; III. Written with the CC tuba in mind, although the piece would certainly work very well on one of the smaller tubas. A modern, dramatic work very well scored so that the soloist is easily heard.

Woolf, Gregory. *Per Tuba Ad Astram (A Concertino for Tuba in Stilo Antico)*. Previously available from the composer. Out of print. Solo tuba and orchestra (piano reduction by the composer). 12:00. IV. F_1–g'. Three movements: Allegro; Adagio; Molto Allegro. For Daniel Perantoni. An expressive work filled with haunting, quirky melodies which truly demonstrate the tubists' ability to "sing" with their instrument.

Zur, Menachem. *Tuba Concerto*. Israel Music Center. Solo tuba and orchestra (piano reduction available). 16:00. IV–V. 1992. Three connected sections: Fast; Slow; Fast. For Adi Hershko. A modern, neo-romantic work with serial influences. In many places, this piece resembles the *Violin Concerto* of Alban Berg.

5. Music for Tuba in Mixed Ensemble

Skip Gray

Over the past twenty-five years, there has been tremendous growth in the number of works for tuba in various chamber ensemble settings. Both composers and performers like to experiment and discover new sounds and innovative media for expression. Works for tuba in mixed ensemble often exemplify this creative spirit. Another motivation for seeking works with different instrumental combinations is to reach audiences who might not have been exposed to the tuba's capabilities or those who reject the pairing of tuba with piano. Certainly, if a string quartet performs a work that includes the tuba, the tubist will undoubtedly be cast in front of a new group of listeners. Performing with say, a fine vocalist, or flutist, creates an opportunity to draw an expanded audience, persons who might not be interested in attending a tuba recital.

Several chamber works have become standard tuba solo repertoire: Armand Russell's *Suite Concertante for Tuba and Woodwind Quintet* and Alec Wilder's *Suite No. 1 for French Horn, Tuba, and Piano* come immediately to mind. But as can be seen in the following pages, works for many diverse combinations feature or at least employ the tuba as an equal partner. Compositions for tuba with such established ensembles as string quartet, horn quartet, rhythm section, and percussion ensemble, as well as experimental combinations often appear on programs and recitals.

This chapter lists pieces which feature the tuba in chamber settings as well as those in which the tuba is an equal partner in the ensemble. The established brass quintet repertoire has been omitted here, with the exception of works specifically emphasizing the tuba.

Adomavicis, T. *Ballade Aria.* Valentin Avvakoumov. Trombone and tuba. 1985. 2:30. III. Trombone: c♯–a♭'; Tuba: A_1–a♭. A nicely written little rondo in conventional tonality featuring the trombone as the melodic voice.

Albam, Manny. *Quintet for Tuba and Strings.* Manuscript available from the composer. Solo tuba and string quartet. For Harvey Phillips.

Albam, Manny. *Sextet for Tuba and Winds.* Manuscript available from the composer. Solo tuba and woodwind quintet. For Harvey Phillips.

Alexander, Josef. *Three Miniatures from Two Extremes.* Margun Music. Piccolo and tuba (F). 1987. $20.00. 10:45. IV–V. F♯$_1$–f'. Three movements: Downstream; Midstream; Upstream. Mixed meters and wide, nonmelodic intervallic leaps add difficulty to this unusual yet interesting work.

Amato, Bruno. *Two Together.* Seesaw Music Corporation. Soprano and tuba. 1971. $20.00. 8:00. V. F♯$_1$–e'. In six sections. To Les Varner. Text by Walt Whitman. A very demanding "new music" work for both soprano and tubist, with difficult rhythms and wide melodic leaps. Tubist has extensive sing and play sections as well as passages of simultaneously playing and tapping the tuba. Recorded by John Turk.

Amellér, André. *Epigraphe.* Alphonse Leduc. Three trombones and tuba. $16.00.

Amis, Kenneth. *Suite for Bass Tuba.* Seesaw Music Corporation. Tuba, violin, viola, violoncello, three flutes, piano, three percussion. 1987. $26.00. 7:00. IV. B♭$_2$–f'. Five movements: Pastorale (tuba and piano); Anima (tuba and percussion); Agitato (tuba and flutes); Impromptu (tuba and strings); Allegro (tuba and full ensemble). The tuba is accompanied in traditional tonal idioms. Except for the wide range of the brief cadenza at the end of the fifth movement, the tuba part lies very comfortably below and within the staff and is mostly diatonic.

Anderson, Eugene. *Fugue for Low Brass Trio.* Anderson's Arizona Originals. Horn, trombone, tuba. 1988. $6.00. 4:30. III. G_1–b♭'. Lack of rests could present endurance problems for less-developed players. A good opportunity for three players to work on matching style.

Anderson, Eugene. *Quintuple Overlays.* Anderson's Arizona Originals. Two trumpets, two euphoniums, two tubas, three percussion (snare drum, cymbals, timpani). 1988. $9.00. 2:30. III–IV. Tuba I: D♯–c♯'; Tuba II: D_1–g. An interesting instrumental combination, literally an extended tuba-euphonium ensemble with percussion. Tonal and melodic aspects are very conventional. Tuba II part requires good technique below the staff going down to pedal D.

Applebaum, Allyson Brown. *Premises.* MMB Music, Inc. Solo tuba, two trumpets, two horns, two trombones, narrator or pre-recorded narration . 1984. Rental from the publisher. 10:00. IV–V. D_1–g'. Three movements: Emergence; Point of Departure; Elements. A well-written modern piece, melodic in overall character. Although unlike a renaissance canzona, the first movement has a contrapuntal flavor. The second movement is a tuba cadenza accompanying the reading of a poem (by live or pre-recorded speaker). The final movement consists of melodic fragments and gestures. Several avant-garde techniques are required of the tubist, including limited double stops and "pitch boxes," in which notes are to be played with varied rhythms and articulations.

Arban, Jean Baptiste. *Variations on the "Carnival of Venice."* Arranged by Richard Domek. Available from Richard Domek. Solo tuba and woodwind quintet (also available for solo tuba and piano, chamber orchestra, brass band, and symphonic band). 1982. 8:00. VI. C–d'(Bb). For Skip Gray. This arrangement is in the key of Bb and is well suited to the F tuba. Contains interesting new material in the accompanying episodes between solo sections. Well scored for the accompanying woodwind quintet.

Arensky, Anton. *Serenade No. 3 for Three Trombones and Tuba, Op. 39.* Edited by Keith Brown. International Music Company. $5.50.

Arrigo, G. *Petit Requiem.* Aldo Bruzzichelli. Horn, trombone, tuba, violin, cello, bass, piano, percussion. Score $10.00.

Bach, J.S. *Bach Duets for B-flat and Bass Clef Instruments.* Arranged by Branch. Accentuate Music. Trumpet and tuba (or trombone). $4.95.

Bach, J.S. *Bandinerie.* Arranged by Jan Koetsier. Donemus. Tuba, two trumpets, horn, trombone. IV.

Bach, J.S. *Contrapunctus I from "Art of Fugue."* Arranged by Lewis Waldeck. Cor Publishing Company. trumpet, horn, trombone, tuba. $4.00.

Bach, J.S. *Goldberg Suite from "Aria with Thirty Variations."* Arranged by Arthur Frackenpohl. T.U.B.A. Press. Horn and tuba. 1989. $7.00. 8:50. III–IV. F$_1$–eb'. Four movements: Overture; Canon; Gigue; Finale. For Phil Myers and Warren Deck. Good music which works well for the combination of horn and tuba. A musical challenge for both seasoned professionals as well as students.

Bach, J.S. *Motet, BWV 118.* Nichols Music Company. Two trumpets, two horns, trombone, tuba, and voices. $10.00.

Bach, J.S. *Two Choruses from the Motet "Jesu, meine Freude."* Arranged by Lowell E. Shaw. The Hornists' Nest. Four horns and tuba (or five horns). 1970. $4.00. 4:45. III. B$_1$–a. Two movements: Andante; Allegro non tanto—Andante. An effective arrangement for five horns (the tuba is a substitute for Horn 4).

Bach, Jan. *Quintet for Solo Tuba and Strings.* T.U.B.A. Press. Solo tuba and string quartet. 1978. $30.00. 23:00. IV–V. E$_1$–b'. Four movements: Introit; Scherzo in moto perpetuo; Chaconne; Ripresa e fandango. To Harvey Phillips. A "notey" work with little gratification for the soloist. Interesting string writing adds great coloristic effect. A demanding work for all members of the quintet. See: Bird, Gary, ed., *Program Notes for the Solo Tuba.*

Bach, P.D.Q. (Peter Schickele). *"Dutch" Suite in G Major.* Theodore Presser Company. Bassoon and tuba. 1980. $5.50. 10:00. III–IV. C$_1$–e'. Four movements: Mr. Minuit's Minuet; Panther Dance; Dance of the Grand Dams; The Lowland Fling. For Ellen Brinkman and Jon Jackson. A work laden with Schickele's typical compositional humor. A challenge for the tubist to balance artistically with the bassoon. Recorded by Ronald Bishop.

Bach, P.D.Q. (Peter Schickele). *Trio Sonata.* Theodore Presser Company. Two flutes, tambourine, and tuba. $7.95.

Baer, Howard J., arr. *Amazing Grace.* Sonante Publications. Two trumpets, trombone, tuba. 1989. $5.50. 2:45. II–III. Bb–a. An easy, conventional brass quartet arrangement with two tasteful variation sections.

Baker, David. *Sonata for Tuba and String Quartet.* MMB Music, Inc. 1982. $24.95. 18:30. IV. C$_1$–f#'. Four movements: Slow—Moderato; Easy swing "blues"; Very slow; Fast. To Harvey Phillips. An extensive solo work for the tubist. Although individual string parts are not extremely difficult, extended harmonies and shifting meters make adequate rehearsal time a requisite. See: Bird, Gary, ed., *Program Notes for the Solo Tuba.* Recorded by Harvey Phillips.

Bakke, Ruth. *Rock Bottom.* Norwegian Music Information Center. Tuba and timpani. 1988. 12:00. IV–V. Absence of bar lines makes this a very free piece in terms of rhythm.

Baldwin, David. *Divertimento for Flute and Tuba.* Cleveland Chamber Music Publishers. 1973. 9:00. IV. A$_2$–e'. Three movements: Largo—mysterioso, Allegro; Andante espressivo; Quasi pomposo, Allegro vivo. For Kenneth and Elizabeth Singleton. Modern music for flute and tuba with wide irregular leaps and rhythms, non-metered aleatory passages, and avant-garde effects, including long rips, screaming through the tuba, pitch bends, flutter tonguing, and feet stomps.

Baldwin, David. *The Last Days.* Philharmusica Corporation. Horn and tuba. 1974. $10.00. 8:00. IV. C$_1$–bb'. A modern, interactive dialogue with some difficult cross-rhythms between the parts and a limited number of effects, including glissandi, flutter tonguing, pitch bending, and kicking over music stands.

Banco, Gerhart. *Trio in Four Styles.* Edition Helbling. Trumpet, tenor horn (or trombone), and tuba. $18.00. Four movements: À la invention; Adagio espressivo; Sehr lebhaft; Mässig rasch, musikantisch. Each movement is written in the style of a specific composer: J.S. Bach (two movements), Beethoven, and Bruckner.

Barber, Clarence. *Theme and Variations for Tuba and Percussion.* Music for Percussion, Inc. Single player requiring four timpani, three glass bowls, ice bell, bongo, small tamtam, bucket of water, wind gong. 1987. $4.00. 6:20. IV. G$_1$–f'. Theme and four variations (Lightly; Freely; Serenely; Barbaric, driving). To Mark Carson and Gilbert Corella. A well-written work which uses the instruments idiomatically. A limited amount of polyrhythms. The tubist is required to perform several avant-garde effects, including some easy double stops and flutter tonguing. Requires a mute.

Barber, Clarence. *Uriel: A Flourish of Joy.* Great Works Publishing, Inc. Euphonium, tuba, and percussion (vibraphone, snare drum, four tom-toms, bass drum). 1993. 5:30. III–IV. Euphonium: F–c''; Tuba: F#$_1$–g. The high tessitura and constantly shifting meters of the euphonium part make this nicely written, tuneful piece deceivingly difficult. The percussion part is playable by a single performer.

Barboteu, Georges. *Divertissement for Tuba and Brass Quartet.* Editions Choudens. Solo tuba, two trumpets, horn, and trombone. 1973. 27.75. 2:30. V. Dedicated to E. Raynaud. Recorded by Walter Hilgers.

Bartles, Alfred. *Beersheba Neo-Baroque Suite.* Brass Press. Tuba and cello (or euphonium, trombone). 1975. $5.00. 7:30. III–IV. D$_1$–e'. Four movements: Prelude; Gavotte; Sarabande; Gigue—Postlude. To R. Winston Morris. A well-written duet in Baroque style idiomatically suited for any of the instrumental combinations. See listing under "Music for Multiple Tubas."

Bassett, Leslie. *Nonet.* C.F. Peters Corporation. Flute, oboe, clarinet, bassoon, trumpet, horn, trombone, tuba, and piano. $17.05.

Baxley, W.S. *Chorale in E Major.* Clark-Baxley Publications. Horn, trombone, euphonium, and tuba. $7.25.

Beach, Bennie. *Dance Suite for Tuba and Triangle.* Neil A. Kjos Music Co. 1978. $5.00. 6:00. III–IV. A$_1$–d'. Three movements: Cracovienne; Roundance; Jazz. Dedicated to Barton Cummings. Wide intervallic leaps and shifting tonal centers produce primary difficulties. Three contrasting movements. Recorded by Barton Cummings.

Becker, Günther. *Un poco giocoso—Konzertante Szenen für Basstuba und Kammerensemble.* Breitkopf & Härtel. Solo tuba and chamber ensemble (flute, oboe, clarinet, bassoon, horn, trumpet, trombone, percussion, harp, piano, violin, viola, cello, bass). 1983. Rental from the publisher. 20:00. V. B♭$_2$–f'. Continuous multisection work. Dedicated to Dr. Wilfried Brennecke. Premiered by Melvyn Poore and the Düsseldorf Chamber Ensemble. A difficult and powerful work for both tubist and ensemble members. In addition to standard notation of music, the soloist is asked to ad lib, flutter tongue, produce wide glissandos, sing and play, mutter vocal sounds, and play the tuba with a saxophone mouthpiece and a bassoon reed.

Beethoven, Ludwig van. *Excerpt from the "Appassionata Sonata."* Arranged by J. Strautman. Valen-

tin Avvakoumov. Solo tuba and four trombones. 1986. 0:45. II–III. G$_1$(E♭$_1$)–c. A nice little arrangement featuring the tuba in the "bread and butter" register.

Beethoven, Ludwig van. *Joyful, Joyful.* Arranged by Howard J. Baer. Sonante Publications. Two trumpets, trombone, tuba (or bass trombone). 1982. $5.50. 2:00. II. F$_1$–g. An easy arrangement of the "Ode to Joy" from Beethoven's Ninth Symphony.

Belden, George. *They All Have Flown Away.* Manuscript available from the composer. Tuba, horn, and percussion (single player requiring marimba, four tom-toms, suspeneded cymbals, maracas, triangle, and tambourine). 1978. 8:10. III–IV. F$_1$–d'. Commissioned by and dedicated to Sue Hudson and Mark Wolfe. This work in three large connected sections is traditionally notated and contains idiomatically written parts for all three players. A good chamber work.

Benson, Warren. *Canon.* Carl Fischer. Tuba and hand drum. 1971. $10.00. 3:15. IV. Approximate pitch notation used, with all notes being on or slightly above the staff. Single movement. Commissioned by Harvey Phillips in memory of William Bell. The tubist creates only percussive effects, including half-valve pitches, sung pitches into the horn, fingernail on the bell, horn slaps, etc., in this canonic duet with hand drum.

Bergsma, W. *Suite.* Carl Fischer. Two trumpets, trombone, and tuba. $6.50.

Bernstein, Leonard. *Fanfare for Bima.* Boosey & Hawkes. Trumpet, horn, trombone, and tuba. $8.50. 1:00. III–IV.

Blahnik, J. *Die Weihnacht—Christmas.* GIA Publications, Inc. Two trumpets, trombone, and tuba. $7.00.

Blank, Allan. *American Medley.* Associated Music Publishers. Flute, two trumpets, horn, trombone, tuba, and percussion. $22.50.

Bliss, P. P. *Wonderful Words.* Arranged by Howard J. Baer. Sonante Publications. Two trumpets, trombone, tuba. 1989. $5.50. 1:45. II. E♭ (E♭$_1$)–g. A good, simple church arrangement.

Blum, Thomas. *Confutatis.* Swedish Music Information Center. Soprano, tuba, and piano. 1992. 5:00. For Kerstin Pettersson, Mattias Johansson, and Mattias Gummesson.

Blumenfeld, A. *Trio Sonata.* T.A.P. Music Sales. Flute, tuba, and piano. $22.00.

Bogar, I. *Three Movements.* Editio Musica Budapest. Two trumpets, trombone, and tuba. $12.50.

Börtz, Daniel. *Winter Pieces 1.* Swedish Music Information Center. Tuba, piano, and percussion. 1981-82. 8:00.

Bradbury, William B. *Just as I Am.* Arranged by Gordon A. Adnams. Sonante Publications. Cornet, flugelhorn, euphonium, and tuba. 1982. $5.50. 1:20. I–II. B♭ (E♭$_1$)–e♭. A very easy, devotional piece arranged for all conical instruments but playable by alternate instrumentation (trumpets, trombone).

Brahms, Johannes. *Three Songs from Opus 62.* Arranged by Howland. Touch of Brass Publications. Trumpet, horn, trombone, and tuba. $9.00.

Brandon, Sy. *Serenade for Oboe and Tuba.* Co-op Press. Oboe and tuba. 1979. $4.00. 3:00. III–IV. F_1–e♭'. One continuous movement with three sections. To Harry and Betty Hewitt. Some interesting music; very poor quality of manuscript produces greatest performance difficulty.

Brandon, Sy. *Summer Suite for Oboe and Tuba.* Co-op Press. 1987. $6.00. 8:45. IV. F_1–f'. Four movements: Rain Dance; Garden Serenade; Harvest Dance; Celebration Dance. For Anita. "An exploration of the use of the twelve tones around a changing tonal center."

Brandon, Sy. *Three Amusement Park Pieces.* Co-op Press. Tuba and percussionist. 1988. $4.00. 4:15. III–IV. G_1–e'. Three movements: Shooting Gallery; Carousel; Rollercoaster. Three light, contrasting pieces. Several wide intervallic leaps for the tubist, but mostly diatonic writing in dialogue with the percussionist.

Breit, Stan, and Ward, Norman. *The Boy Who Wanted a Tuba—A Christmas Story.* Byron-Douglas Publications. Flute, clarinet, trumpet, tuba, and narrator. 1971. 3:00. I–II. F–D'. A simple yet cute story with small ensemble geared toward young children.

Briegel, George F., arr. *Im Tiefen Keller.* George F. Briegel. Out of print. Solo tuba (or trombone) and three trumpets. 1937. 3:00. III. F–f'. A traditional tuba solo with trumpet accompaniment. Trumpet parts are not difficult and contain nice fanfare introduction and interlude.

Broege, Timothy. *Benedictus.* Allaire Music Publications. Mezzo-soprano or contralto voice, tuba, and piano. 1971. 4:30. IV–V. D_1–f'. One continuous movement. Composed for Gary and Barbara Shulze. "In memory of my Father." Except for three very difficult measures, consisting of wide intervallic leaps, the tuba part is not extremely difficult. Sensitive playing is a requisite so that the voice and transparent piano are not overshadowed.

Brott, A. *World Sophisticate.* Berandol Music. Two trumpets, horn, trombone, tuba, soprano, and percussion. $12.50.

Broughton, Bruce. *Bipartition for Tuba and Cello.* Magnolia Manor Press. Tuba and amplified cello. 7:00. V. Two movements. For Keith and Tommy Johnson.

Brown, Jonathan Bruce. *Strata: Five Pieces for Percussion Quintet and Tuba.* Seesaw Music Corporation. Five percussionists (playing five timpani, vibraphone, orchestra chimes, suspended cymbals, mixing bowls, claves, wood blocks, bongoes, piccolo snare drum, bass drum, marimba) and tuba. 1974. $19.00. 10:45. III–IV. E♭–d'. Five movements: Andante; Moderately Slow, Reflective; Allegro con fuoco; Lento Espressivo; Allegro Moderato, Maestoso. An extensive percussion ensemble work with

a tuba obbligato, which serves as an effective coloristic addition. Tuba part is not technically demanding.

Brown, Newell Kay. *Dialogue and Dance.* Seesaw Music Corporation. Trombone and tuba. $11.00.

Brown, Newel Kay. *Silhouettes.* Seesaw Music Corporation. Trumpet and tuba. 1978. 6:30. IV. A_1–f♯'. To Robert Levy and Robert Yeats. Continuous work in seven contrasting sections, from the chant-like opening to non-specific, chance music dialogues.

Brown, Newell Kay. *Windart 1.* Seesaw. Tuba, soprano, piano. 1978. $17.00. 9:00. IV–V. E♭–a♭'. Continuous work in seven sections. For Cherry Beauregard. Text based on the poem "Leben," by G. Meurer. Difficult yet expressive chamber music in a nontonal setting.

Brown, Raynor. *Six Fugues.* Western International Music. Horn, trombone, and tuba. 1969. $9.00. 13:00. III–IV. E_1–d'. Few technical problems. No tempo markings and very few expression indications. The trombone has the most difficult part, with a range of B♭$_1$–c''. Endurance could also be a problem, as there are very few rests.

Brown, Raynor. *Variations.* Western International Music. Two trumpets, horn, trombone, tuba, and piano. 1973. $15.00. 18:40. III–IV. G_1–b. Theme and ten variations. For Sharon Davis. The piano part, while not very difficult, is the most demanding writing of this interesting, modern chamber work.

Brün, Herbert. *twice upon three times...* Smith Publications. Bass clarinet and tuba. 1988. 4:30. V. B_2–a'. Three movements: I; II; III. Interesting timbral effects resulting from orchestration and harmonic intervals between bass clarinet and tuba parts. Difficulties for the tubist include wide, nontonal leaps and balancing with the volume level of the bass clarinet to attain the composer's desired sonorities.

Bury, Peter, arr. *Deep Down in the Cellar—Demonstration Piece for Tuba.* Camara Music Publishers. Solo tuba in brass quintet. 1966. $7.50. 3:00. III. B♭$_2$–g. A good, light arrangement of the traditional tuba solo. Accompanying parts are not difficult and do not cause balance problems for the soloist.

Buss, H.J. *Sonic Fables.* Brixton Publications. Two trumpets, horn, trombone, tuba, and percussion. $27.50.

Buss, H.J. *Trigon.* Brixton Publications. Trumpet, trombone, and tuba. $17.00.

Capuzzi, Antonio. *Concerto for Double Bass.* Arranged by Jim Self. Basset Hound Music. Solo tuba, two trumpets, horn, tenor trombone, bass trombone (or euphonium). 1993. 14:45. IV. F_1–g'. Three movements: Allegro moderato; Andante cantabile; Rondo Allegro. The complete concerto is not regularly performed, as only the second and third movements are arranged for solo tuba with brass quintet. The key is changed from the standard version to B♭, which because of the higher tessitura, lies much better on the F or E♭ tuba. Third movement re-corded by Jim Self.

Carion, M. *Toccata Sax.* J. Maurer Editions Musicales. Saxophone and tuba. $7.95.

Carpenter, Bud. *Basso Bossa.* Swing Lane Publications. Tuba (or bass trombone, bassoon), guitar, bass, piano (vibes, accordion, and/or electric guitar), drums. 1963. 2:15. II–III. C–g. A good little piece for tuba and rhythm section.

Castérède, Jacques. *Prelude et Danse.* Alphonse Leduc. Three trombones, tuba, piano, percussion. $37.00.

Chamberlin, Robert. *Daysong.* Available from the composer. Tuba, marimba, and tape. 1985. 9:30. IV. D♭₁–g'. One movement. For Scott and Mary Watson. Most of this work, which can be described as a "sound piece," is in non-metered, time-delineated sections. In addition to normal pitch material, the tuba is required to perform several effects, including producing wind sounds, singing, and playing double stops and sub-tones. This piece could serve as a good introduction to contemporary performance styles for a younger student, as there are no great technical difficulties except for a few isolated high-note entrances. See: Bird, Gary, ed., *Program Notes for the Solo Tuba.*

Chihara, P. *Willow, Willow.* C.F. Peters Corporation. Tuba, amplified bass flute, three percussion. 1968. $14.50. 8:00. IV. C–f'. Four movements. To Sheridan Stokes. The amplified bass flute is featured in this sound piece. The largest demand is putting the tuba part together within the ensemble.

Childs, Barney. *A Question of Summer for Tuba and Harp.* Composers Facsimile Edition. 1976. 9:20. IV–V. C₁–b'. One continuous movement. Commissioned by Ivan Hammond. Although both parts are precisely notated, there is great deal of truly independent activity taking place between the tuba and harp. This is chamber music in which the performers do not have to listen to each other much of the time. Contains jazz influences and some avant-garde effects. See: Bird, Gary, ed., *Program Notes for the Solo Tuba.* Recorded by Ivan Hammond.

Christensen, James. *Ballad for Tuba.* Whaling Music. Solo tuba and brass ensemble. $12.00. 2:30. IV.

Coles, G. *Chorale Variations on Oh Sacred Head Sore and Wounded.* Berandol Music. Two trumpets, trombone, and tuba. $12.50.

Couperin, F. *Les Ondes.* Arranged by Krzywicki. Theodore Presser Company. Trombone (or baritone) and tuba. $7.50.

Cummings, Barton, arr. *Song of the Trouvères.* Tuba and self-played percussion. See listing under "Music for Unaccompanied Tuba."

Curnow, Jim. *Variations on an Aboriginal Melody.* T.U.B.A. Press. Tuba and woodwind quintet. 1982. $20.00. 10:00. IV–V. E₁–g'. Four movements: Allegro con Spirito; Andante moderato con

espressivo; Allegro Giocoso; Allegro con Energetico. For Skip Gray. A melodic *tour de force* for solo tuba within the accompanying woodwind quintet.

Danielsson, Christer. *Capriccio da Camera.* Nordiska Musikförlag. Solo tuba, two trumpets, horn, two trombones. 1976. 6:45. IV. A₁–f'. One continuous movement in three sections. Dedicated to Michael Lind and the Stockholm Philharmonic Brass ensemble. A tuneful, brief showpiece for the solo tuba. Recorded by Michael Lind and Walter Hilgers.

Danielsson, Christer. *Little Suite for Four Brass.* Throre Ehrling Musik AB. trombone, trombone (or horn), trombone (or baritone), and tuba (or bass trombone). 1972. $22.50. 8:00. III–IV. Part I: d–c''; Part II: d♭–a'; Part III: A♭–d'; Part IV: A₁–e♭. Three movements: Moderato; Lento; Scherzo. Tuneful work with a great deal of pop-jazz influences. Because of the general high tessitura of all parts, this piece also works well for a tuba-euphonium ensemble.

Danielsson, Christer. *Suite Concertante.* Gehrmans Musikförlag. Tuba and four horns (alternate parts for other brass instrument combinations). 1977. 12:30. IV. F♯₁–e'. Four movements: Largo—Allegro Vivo; Moderato misterioso; Andante con Sentimento; Alla Marcia. Composed for Michael Lind and the First Swedish Tuba Workshop. Nice, melodic music scored very effectively showcasing both the solo tubist and the horns. Recorded by Michael Lind.

Davidson, John. *Sonata.* T.A.P. Music Sales. Trombone, tuba, and piano. $18.00.

Deason, David. *Sy-Anita Suite for Tuba and Oboe.* T.U.B.A. Press. $5.00. 4:00. B₁–e♭'. Three movements: Andante; Lento; Allegretto. Contains shifting meters and some wide intervallic leaps.

DeCosta, Harry, and the Original Dixieland Band. *Tuba Tiger Rag.* Arranged by Luther Henderson. Brassworks Music (G. Schirmer). Tuba in brass quintet. $34.00. 5:00. III. F₁(B♭₂)–b♭ (c'). Recorded by Canadian Brass.

Diemente, E. *Forms of Flight.* Smith Publications. Two trumpets, horn, trombone, tuba, soprano. $35.50.

Diercks, John. *Figures on China.* Theodore Presser Company. Horn, trombone, and tuba. $4.00.

Doane, William H. *To God Be the Glory.* Arranged by Howard J. Baer. Sonante Publications. Two trumpets, trombone, tuba (or bass trombone). 1978. $5.50. 2:15. II–III. A₁–b♭.

Dorsey, A. *Brass Music II.* MS Publications. Two trumpets, trombone, and tuba. $6.00.

Druckman, Jacob. *Dark Upon the Harp.* Theodore Presser. Two trumpets, horn, trombone, tuba, soprano, and percussion. Rental from the publisher (score $4.00). V. A difficult nontonal work. The soprano must have perfect pitch.

Dubenski, Arcady. *Concerto Grosso.* Ricordi. Three trombones, tuba, orchestra. 1950. Orchestral accompaniment rental from the publisher. 6:30. III–IV. A_1–c#'. Three movements (if played without orchestral accompaniment): Prelude; Toccata; Fugue. Five movements (if played with orchestral accompaniment): Introduction (tacet for solo instruments); Prelude; Toccata; Interlude (tacet for solo instruments); Fugue. A good neoclassical work which may be performed with or without the orchestral accompaniment. Written in truly orchestral keys of A and E major.

Dubois, Rob. *Espaces à Remplir.* Donemus. Two clarinets, saxophone, trumpet, trombone, tuba, bass, piano, vibraphone, percussion. $30.00.

Dubois, Rob. *Trio Agitato.* Donemus. Horn, trombone, and tuba. 1969. $29.75. Indeterminate length. IV. G_1–f#'. For Kees Blokker. A nonmetered work with only pitch group successions given. Contemporary techniques required also include approximate pitch notation and flutter tonguing. There are many wide leaps, and a mute is required.

Dutton, Brent. *Brass Trio.* Seesaw Music Corporation. Trumpet, trombone, tuba. 1968-71. $13.50. 4:30. IV. Eb_1–c'. Three movements: 7th. Yellow Song; Squelch; March for an Invalid. Conventional writing in the first and third movements. The second movement contains modern effects including flutter tonguing, gestures played "as fast as possible," wide glissandos over the harmonic series, and simultaneous singing and playing.

Dutton, Brent. *Evidently, Occasional Music.* Seesaw Music. Cello, double bass, tuba. 1973. $16.00. 8:45. IV. C–d'. Three movements: Muzerwug's Skither; Folktune; Ending. Written for Mark Jamison and Guy Fouquet. The tubist's challenges include rapidly shifting meters, balancing with the cellist and double bassist, and a brief improvisatory passage.

Dutton, Brent. *Tuba Concerto No. 1.* Seesaw Music Corporation. Tuba, three trumpets, three trombones, percussion (single player on timpani and vibes), Piano. 1968. $50.00. 9:00. IV–V. C_1–g'. Three movements: Andante—Allegro; Andante; Allegro. A very challenging work which lies outside the bounds of common tonality. The tuba soloist encounters wide, irregular intervallic leaps as well as many changes in tempo and meter.

Dutton, Brent. *Tuesday Overture.* Seesaw Music Corporation. Tuba and percussion. 1975. $15.00. 4:00. IV. D_1–d'. An interactive piece for percussionist and tuba with extensive avant-garde techniques for the tubist, including hissing sounds, simultaneous singing and playing, and improvised sections. Very little conventional pitch notation other than eight bars in D major and several other brief passages.

Elvey, George J. *Crown Him with Many Crowns.* Arranged by Howard J. Baer. Sonante Publications. Two trumpets, trombone, tuba or bass trombone. 1982. $5.50. 1:45. III. Gb_1–eb'.

Erb, Donald. *Three Pieces.* Merion Music, Inc. Two trumpets, horn, trombone, tuba, and piano. 1973. 6:15. III–IV. B_1–a. Three movements: I; II; III. A contemporary work requiring tapping on bell, muttering, hissing into instrument, kissing sounds, etc.

Fauré, Gabriel. *Lydia.* Nichols Music Company. Two trumpets, horn, and tuba. $4.00.

Feldman, Enrique Cañez. *Sueños Negros.* Available from the composer. Tuba, piano, percussion (four tom-toms and suspended cymbal). 1991. 6:30. IV. B_2–gb'. A dramatic, generally melodic work which, as the composer states in his preface, "is a musical depiction of the human mind during its dream state." Its high tessitura makes performance on the F tuba advisable.

Feldman, Morton. *Durations III for Violin, Tuba, and Piano.* C.F. Peters Corporation. 1961. $15.00. 10:00. IV. F#–g'. An example of "chance music." Tuba is muted throughout. Pitches are notated but rhythms are free. Recorded by Don Butterfield.

Fernandez, C. *Musical Confrontations.* Margun Music. Woodwind quintet and brass quintet. $40.00.

Filippi, Amedeo di. *Divertimento for Brass Duo.* Robert King Music Company. Baritone (or horn) and tuba. 1968. $5.85. 9:00. III. G_1–c'. Five movements: March; Intermezzo I; Tempo de Valse; Intermezzo II; Rondino. A straight-ahead little suite of tonal music.

Finko, David. *The Klezmers (One Act Opera).* Dako Publishers. Bass-baritone, mezzo-soprano, two violins, double bass, clarinet, cornet, tuba, percussion. 1989. 20:00. IV. F_1–d'. Dedicated to Dr. Lawrence Bernstein. An interesting little opera with glimpses of Jewish culture. As a member of the klezmer band, the tubist actually performs onstage. The part contains some difficult passages, especially those interplaying with the cornet.

Fote, R. *Twelve Christmas Carols.* Kendor Publications, Inc. Trumpet, horn (or trombone), and tuba (or trombone). $19.50.

Frackenpohl, Arthur. *Brass Duo.* Robert King Music Company. Horn (or baritone) and tuba. 1972. $5.55. 6:45. III. F_1–bb. Four movements: Prelude; Ballad; Scherzo; Variations. Traditional writing with few difficulties except an occasional irregular rhythm and shifting meters.

Frackenpohl, Arthur. *Pop Suite No. 2.* Horizon Press. Trombone (or euphonium) and tuba. 1991.

Frackenpohl, Arthur. *Sonata for Trumpet, Tuba and Piano.* PP Music. 1977. For Ivan Hammond.

Frackenpohl, Arthur. *Song and Dance.* Horizon Publications. Tuba, euphonium, and piano. $10.00. See listing under "Music for Tuba and Band."

Frackenpohl, Arthur. *Three Dances for Horn and Tuba.* Tenuto Publications. 1989. $7.00. 8:00. IV. G_1–c'. Three movements: Rag; Waltz; Bossa. For Phil Myers and Warren Deck. Light music with enough difficulty to make interesting recital material.

Françaix, Jean. *Petite Valse Européenne.* B. Schott's Söhne. Tuba and double wind quintet (piano reduction available). 1979. Parts are rental from the publisher. 8:00. IV–V. G_1–a♭'. One continuous movement. "For my little son Eric." High tessitura and wide leaps permeate this brief, entertaining work. Certainly intended for the F tuba.

Franck, César. *Arioso from "L'Organist, Vol. 1."* Transcribed by Howard J. Baer. Sonante Publications. Two trumpets, trombone, tuba (or bass trombone). 1982. $5.50. 1:45. II. E–e.

Frederickson, Thomas. *Tubalied.* Available from the composer. Solo tuba and chamber ensemble (piano reduction also available). V. D_1–f♯'. For Daniel Perantoni. A "new music" piece, both original scoring and piano reduction are very difficult. Recorded by Dan Perantoni.

Friedman, Stanley. *Parodie III.* Seesaw Music Corporation. $40.00. Solo tuba, solo trumpet, and brass quintet. V.

Friedman, Stanley. *Parodie VI.* Seesaw Music Corporation. $85.00. Solo tuba, two horns, two trumpets, two trombones, percussion. V.

Fritze, Gregory. *Basso Concertino.* Available from the composer. Solo tuba (or bass trombone), two trumpets, horn, trombone (version for solo tuba and synthesizer available). 1984. 7:00. IV–V. C_1–a' A serial work which serves as a very nice, lyrical display for the solo tuba in the traditional brass quintet instrumentation. Recorded by Gregory Fritze and the Cambridge Symphonic Brass Ensemble.

Gaathaug, Morten. *Sonata Concertante for Tuba and Brass Quintet, Op.41.* Norwegian Music Information Centre. Solo tuba two trumpets, horn, trombone, and tuba. 1991-92. 18:00. IV–V. E_1–a♭'(c''). Three connected movements: Allegro; Andante molto moderato; Molto allegro. To Øystein Baadsvik. A tuneful, pyrotechnic display piece for the tubist. The very high tessitura would make performance on the F tuba a wise choice. Fun music for performers and listeners alike. Recorded by Øystein Baadsvik.

Gabrieli, Andrea. *Three Ricercare.* Arranged by Lewis Waldeck. Cor Publishing Company. Two trumpets, trombone, tuba. $5.00.

Gates, Crawford. *Suite for Tuba with Percussion, Celesta, Harp, and Piano, Op. 53.* Pacific Publications. 1978. 14:30. IV–V. D_1–g'. Six movements: Intrada; Allemande; Courante; Sarabande; Gavotte; Gigue. Commissioned by Cherry Beauregard. Unique, well-crafted orchestration and good writing for the solo tuba.

Geier, Oskar. *Conzert-Fantasie.* Musikverlag Barbara Evans. Trumpet, tuba, and piano.

Geminiani, F. *Concerto Grosso.* Shawnee Press, Inc. Two trombones (or euphoniums) and tuba. $12.50. See listing under "Music for Multiple Tubas."

Gerhard, R. *Hymnody.* Oxford University Press. Flute, oboe, clarinet, trumpet, horn, trombone, tuba, two pianos, percussion. Rental from the publisher (score $7.35).

Ghiselin, Johannes. *La Alfonsina.* Edited by the Empire Brass Quintet. G. Schirmer. Horn, trombone, and tuba (or baritone). 1979. $3.95. 1:20. III–IV. G–d'. A Renaissance contrapuntal work which works well for low brass trio.

Gillis, L. *Ten Duets.* Virgo Music Publishers. Bass trombone and tuba. $7.95.

Gillis, L. *Ten More Duets.* Virgo Music Publishers. Bass trombone and tuba (or two bass trombones). $9.00.

Glandien, Lutz. *"4:1" for Four Trombones and Tuba.* Verlag Neue Musik Berlin. 1985. 9:00. IV. D_1–f' Four movements: I; II; III; IV. Good modern chamber music.

Goedicke, Alexander. *Concert Suite.* Philharmusica Corporation. Trombone (or euphonium) and tuba. $5.95.

Gottschalk, Arthur. *Fanfare.* Seesaw Music Corporation. Trumpet, horn, trombone, and tuba. $9.00.

Gould, Morton. *Tuba Suite.* G. Schirmer. Solo tuba and three horns. 1971. $12.00. 9:30. IV. F_1–E♭'. Five movements: Prelude; Chorale; Waltz; Elegy; Quickstep. For Bill Bell in memoriam. The solo tuba part is substantially more difficult than the horn accompaniment parts. See: Bird, Gary, ed., *Program Notes for the Solo Tuba.* Recorded by Harvey Phillips.

Grape, John T. *Jesus Paid It All.* Arranged by Howard J. Baer. Sonante Publications. Cornet/flugelhorn, flugelhorn, trombone, tuba. 1989. $5.50. 3:15. III. F_1–a.

Gryc, Stephen. *Music for Tuba and Timpani.* Robert King Music Company. 1990. $6.75. 7:15. III. G_1–a♭. Three movements: Deciso; Lirico; Energico. Commissioned by Rosemary Small. Dedicated to Alexander Lepak. Very few difficulties for the tubist other than staying together with the timpanist, whose part is more demanding than the tubist's.

Guy, Noa. *The Forbidden Fruit.* Available from the composer. Tuba and female choir. 1992. 20:00. IV. $G♯_1$–g'. Three movements: The Garden of Eden; The Seduction; The Realization. Dedicated to Roger Bobo. An extensive, modern tuba solo work which interacts in dialogues with the female choir. The choir performs standard vocalization, sprechstimme, clapping, finger snapping, and hand rubbing sounds. Text by the composer.

Hackbarth, Glenn. *Duo.* Smith Publications. Tuba and percussion (single player: xylophone, vibraphone, four tom-toms, three cymbals). 1976. $13.00. 4:45. V. D_1–a'. Single movement. For Dan Perantoni. A typical experimental work from the seventies with gestures passed between tubist and percussionist, polyrhythms, "free" sections, and other effects.

Hallnäs, Eyvind. *Myggan och elefanten.* Swedish Music Information Center. Piccolo and tuba. 1983. 3:30.

Handel, G.F. *The Trumpet Shall Sound.* Editions Musicus. Trombone and tuba (with optional piano accompaniment). $4.50.

Hartley, Walter. *Concerto for Tuba and Percussion Orchestra*. Accura Music, Inc. Tuba and six percussionists. 1974. $60.00. 15:00. IV–V. B$_2$–g$^\#$'. Four movements: Adagio—Allegro; Molto vivace; Largo; Allegro molto. Dedicated to C. Rudolph Emilson (tubist) and Theodore C. Frazeur (percussionist). A work full of interesting colors and worth the work of preparation for performance.

Hartley, Walter. *Double Concerto for Saxophone, Tuba, and Wind Octet*. Theodore Presser. Saxophone, tuba, flute, oboe, bassoon, two trumpets, horn, and trombone. 1969. $18.00. 5:00. III–IV. F$_1$–c$^\flat$'. Three movements: Allegro con brio; Andante; Presto. An interesting instrumental combination and a good chamber work overall. Recorded by Martin Erickson.

Hartley, Walter. *Duet for Flute and Tuba*. Theodore Presser. 1963. $6.00. 3:00. III. G$_1$–b. Three movements: Allegretto; Andante; Vivace. Pleasant music which goes together easily. Recorded by Harvey Phillips.

Harvey, Paul. *Six for Six in Six Inns*. Manuscript available from the composer. Tuba and woodwind quintet. 1981. 12:00. IV. F$_1$–d'. Six movements: The Royal Oak; The Golden Ball; The Lord Nelson; Pope's Grotto; The Lemon Tree; The Coach and Horses. To Skip Gray. Delightful chamber music picturing six pubs in London frequented by musicians.

Heiden, Bernhard. *Variations for Solo Tuba and Nine Horns*. Associated Music Publishers. 1974. $12.00. 12:00. IV–V. D$_1$–f'. Single movement with nine sections. Written for Harvey Phillips and dedicated to the memory of John Barrows. See: Bird, Gary, ed., *Program Notes for the Solo Tuba*. Recorded by Harvey Phillips.

Heilmann, Harald. *Trauerode für vier Wagner-Tuben und Kontrabasstuba*. Heinrichshofen Verlag (C.F. Peters Corporation).

Heinichen, Johannes David. *Sonata in C minor*. Transcribed by Skip Gray. Available from Skip Gray. Horn and tuba. $4.00. 6:00. III–IV. G$_1$–B$\flat$. Four movements: Grave; Allegro; Larghetto e cantabile; Allegro. A Baroque duo originally for oboe and bassoon.

Heiss, J. *Inventions, Contours, and Colors*. Boosey & Hawkes. Flute, clarinet, bassoon, tuba, violin, viola, cello, bass. Rental from the publisher (score $7.50).

Helperin, Salomon. *Capris 41*. Swedish Music Information Center. Tuba, clarinet, and electro-accoustic instruments. 1986.

Heussenstamm, George. *Dialogue*. Dorn Publications Inc. Tuba and saxophone. $15.00.

Hewitt, Harry. *Discourse for Tuba and Guitar (Op. 452, No. 3)*. Harry Hewitt. 1983. 3:30. IV. F$^\#_1$–g$^\flat$'. Single movement.

Hewitt, Harry. *Leaf in the Stream (Op. 456, No. 2)*. Harry Hewitt. Oboe and tuba. 1979. 4:00. III–IV. D$\flat$–f'. Single movement. Consists of a series of

rubato gestures with rather free interplay between oboe and tuba parts.

Hewitt, Harry. *Six Preludes for Flute and Tuba (Op. 452, No. 1)*. T.U.B.A. Press. 1977. $5.00. 12:15. IV. E$\flat_1$–a'. Six movements.

Hidas, Frigyes. *Quartettino*. Editio Musica Budapest. Two trumpets, trombone, and tuba. $11.75.

Hidas, Frigyes. *Trio for Horn, Trombone, and Tuba*. Editio Musica Budapest. 1981. $12.00. 4:15. III–IV. A$_1$–d$\flat$'. Single movement with four sections. Some engaging harmonies and shifting meters.

Hoag, Charles. *TUBAPLAY*. Manuscript available from the composer. Solo tuba and self-played percussion. 1985. 6:00. IV. D$_1$–a'. Eight movements: Prelude; Gong with the Wind; Interlude; Tango; Interlude; Soft-Shoe Dance; Interlude; Final Bounce. Commissioned by Scott Watson, Skip Gray, and Jerry Young. The performer is required to play the tuba and, simultaneously in various movements, gong, pedal bass drum, and suspended cymbal. An effective work for both its music and its theatrical appeal. See listing under "Music for Unaccompanied Tuba."

Hogg, Merle E. *Seven for Four*. Music Graphics Press. Trumpet, horn, trombone, and tuba. $105.75.

Hollingworth, W. *Dear Is My Little Vale*. Molenaar Music N.V. Two trumpets, horn, and tuba. $8.00.

Horovitz, Joseph. *Brass Polka*. Chester Music. Trumpet, horn, trombone, and tuba. $14.95.

Horwood, M.S. *Residue*. Theodore Presser. Tuba and vibraphone. 1981. $4.00. V.

Hovhaness, Alan. *Tower Music*. Broude Brothers. Woodwind quintet and brass quintet. Rental from the publisher.

Hoyt, George M. *Introduction and Allegro for Brass Trio*. Hoyt Editions. Horn in F, trombone, and tuba. 1983. $12/00. 5:30. III–IV. B$_1$–e$\flat$'. Single continuous movement. For Bill and Jack.

Hoyt, George M. *Suite for Horn and Tuba*. Hoyt Editions. $14.00. 12:00. III–IV. F$_1$–d'. Five movements: Chorale; Canonic Invention; Poem; Elegy; Dance.

Iannacone, Anthony. *Sonatina for Trumpet and Tuba*. Theodore Presser. 1976. $4.50. 10:15. III–IV. F$_1$–d'. For Carter Eggers and J.R. Smith. A modern work with hybrid scales, shifting meters, and irregular rhythms. A very playable work for college students. Endurance may be a problem because there are few periods of rest for either part. Recorded by J.R. Smith.

Irish Traditional. *Be Thou My Vision*. Arranged by Howard J. Baer. Sonante Publications. Two trumpets, trombone, tuba. 1989. $5.50. 3:15. II–III. A$\flat_1$–a$\flat$. A nice arrangement whose main difficulty is the 5/4 middle section, which goes into the key of E major. A good piece for church services.

Isaac, Heinrich. *Four Pieces*. Transcribed by Kenneth Singleton. Peer International Corporation. Horn, trombone (or baritone), tuba (or bass trombone). 1976. $8.00. 3:45. II–III. F–g. Four Renaissance contrapuntal pieces with little technical difficulty other than occasional imitative entrances on "odd" parts of the beat.

Jacobsen, Julius. *Tuba Ballet.* Swedish Music Information Center. Tuba and woodwind quintet. 1978. 7:45. IV. F_1–e'. Four movements: Arabesque—Battement; Pas de Deux; Gr. Battement; Polka—Can Can. Commissioned by Rikskonserter for Michael Lind. Delightful music inspired by the ballet. Recorded by Michael Lind.

Jager, Robert. *Fantasy Variations.* T.U.B.A. Press. Flute (doubling piccolo), tuba, and piano. 1982. $10.00. 7:30. IV. A_1–eb'. Continuous work with theme and five variations. Interesting yet conservative chamber music for an unusual instrumental combination. Recorded by Robert N. Daniel.

Josquin Des Prez. *De Tous Biens Playne.* Southern Music Company. Trumpet, horn, trombone, and tuba. $3.00.

Josquin Des Prez. *Se je perdu mon ami.* Arranged by George M. Hoyt. Hoyt Editions. Horn, trombone, and tuba. $10.00.

Kapr, J. *Omaggio alla Tromba.* Artia Foreign Trade Corporation. Two trumpets, three horns, trombone, tuba, piccolo, flute, clarinet, bass clarinet, contrabassoon, piano, and timpani. $8.00.

Kayser, Leif. *In dulci jubilo.* Leif Kayser. Trumpet, horn, trombone, and tuba. 1955.

Kayser, Leif. *Notturno saccro.* Leif Kayser. Trumpet, horn, trombone, and tuba. 1958.

Kayser, Leif. *Variationer over Lovet være du Jesu Christ.* Leif Kayser. Trumpet, horn, trombone, and tuba. 1957.

Kellaway, Roger. *Dance of the Ocean Breeze.* Edition BIM. Horn, tuba, and piano. 1979. 3:45. III–IV. F_1–c'. Single movement. For Froydis Vekre and Roger Bobo. A delightful light piece. Recorded by Roger Bobo.

Kellaway, Roger. *Sonoro.* Edition BIM. Tuba, horn, and piano. 1979. 10:00. IV. C_1–d'. Single, multi-section movement. For Froydis Vekre and Roger Bobo. Very lyrical writing with a tricky bridge section in 5/16. Recorded by Roger Bobo.

Knox, Charles. *Solo for Tuba with Brass Trio.* Tenuto Publications. Solo tuba, trumpet, horn, and trombone. 1968. $4.50. 8:45. III–IV. F_1–c'. Three movements: I; II; III. A good work with modern harmonies, easily put together.

Kodály, Zoltán. *Lament.* Arranged by Skip Gray. Shawnee Press, Inc. Trombone (or euphonium) and two tubas. $5.00. See listing under "Music for Multiple Tubas."

Kont, P. *Quartet #2.* Ludwig Doblinger. Trumpet, horn, trombone, and tuba. $20.50.

Kraft, William. *Double Trio for Piano, Prepared Piano, and Small Ensemble.* New Music West. Trio I: Piano, tuba, percussion; Trio II: prepared piano, electric guitar, percussion. 1966. Rental from the publisher. 24:13. V. A_2 (or lowest possible note)–g'

(highest note possible). Five movements: Prelude: Presto Energico; Tempo Rubato e Andante; Presto Delicato; Cadenze: Adagio; Allegro Molto. Difficult and complex contemporary chamber music with avant-garde effects. Recorded with Roger Bobo (Cambria CD 1071).

Kraft, William. *Nonet for Brass and Percussion.* New Music West. Two trumpets, horn, trombone, tuba, four percussion. 1958. $25.00. 25:00. III–IV. E_1–bb. Six movements: Presto; Andante; Interlude 1—Scherzo a Tre; Allegretto; Interlude 2: Scherzo a Quatro; Maestoso e Rubato. Extensive percussion parts.

Krol, Bernard. *Cathedrale in Three Naves, Op. 85.* Bote & Bock K.G. Horn (or alto trombone), trombone, and tuba (or bass trombone). 1982. $15.50. 7:45. III. G_1–ab. Three movements: Natus est nobis hodie; Victimae paschali laudes; Veni, Creator Spiritus. Music influenced by chant and ecclesiastical modes. Parts are melodically inspired and sound like medieval music in new clothing. Very little of technical difficulty.

Kröpsch, Fritz. *Im tiefen Keller (Down in the Deep Cellar)—Grosse Fantasie.* Arranged by Mark Evans. Musikverlag Barbara Evans. Solo tuba in brass quintet (piano accompaniment also available). 1989. 6:45. IV. Eb_1–g'. A good transcription for brass quartet accompaniment of the classical "Grand Fantasia" for solo tuba published in 1908.

Krush, Jay. *Two Madrigals.* Plymouth Music Company. Horn, trombone (or euphonium), and tuba. $5.95.

Kulesha, Gary. *Three Complacencies.* Sonante Publications. Bass clarinet and tuba. 1978. $4.00. 3:00. III–IV. G_1–d'. Three movements: I; II; III. Humorous little contrasting pieces written in conventional tonality. A few difficult leaps in the tuba part.

Langer, K. *Cortege for Tuba.* Encore Music Publishers. Tuba and three percussion (marimba and gong, two timpanists). 1986. $13.00. 4:00. III. F_1–g#. Continuous work in cantabile style. Some effective writing, especially in section requiring glissandi by the tubist in counterpoint with timpani.

Langley, James W. *Suite.* Hinrichsen Editions Ltd. Three trombones and tuba (or four trombones). 1961. 7:00. III. Part I: c–bb'; Part II: A–g'; Part III: Gb–eb'; Tuba Part: D–d'. Five movements: Intrada; Chorale; Scherzetto; Canon; Moto Perpetuo. Two upper parts in tenor clef. A nice demonstration piece for the orchestral trombone section or contest piece for high school students. Also usable by tuba-euphonium quartet or ensemble.

Lanza, A. *Eidesis II.* Boosey & Hawkes. Two horns, two trombones, tuba, three cellos, two basses, three percussion. $3.00.

Lassus, Orlandus. *Two Pieces.* Transcribed by Randall Block. Philharmusica Corporation. Flute (or oboe) and tuba. 1975. $4.50. 3:00. II–III. F–bb. Two movements. The tuba part stays within the staff throughout and moves at moderate pace in mostly diatonic motion. There is no rest, so endurance could be a problem for a younger player.

Lendvay, Kamilló. *Five Movements in Quotation-Marks*. Editio Musica Budapest. Horn, trombone, and tuba. 1980. $13.00. 7:15. IV. $G\flat_1$–e'. Five movements: Hommage à Stravinsky; Hommage à Count Basie; Hommage à Johann Strauss; Hommage à Robert Stolz; Hommage à Moi... For Horst Küblböck and his ensemble.

Leontyev, A. *Folk Song for Three Trombones and Tuba*. Edited by Keith Brown. International Music Company. $5.50.

Levinas, M. *Clov et Hamm*. Éditions Salabert. Trombone, tuba, percussion, and tape. 1974. 8:00. III. $D\flat_1$–b. For Marcel Galiegue and Fernand Lelong. Relies almost completely on the tape. Tuba and trombone parts not difficult. Some nonmetered sections.

Lindberg, Nils. *Movements for Tuba and Wind Quintet*. Swedish Music Information Center. Tuba, alto flute, English horn, bass clarinet, horn, and bassoon. 1979.

Locke, Matthew. *One Dozen Duets*. MS Publications. Trombone and tuba (or two trombones). $5.00.

Locke, Matthew. *Suite No. 2*. Arranged by Lewis Waldeck. Cor Publishing Company. Trumpet, horn, trombone, tuba. $4.00.

Loeb, D. *Aubade and Villanelle*. Accentuate Music. Tuba, violin, and percussion. $20.00 (score).

Loeb, D. *Three Invocations*. Accentuate Music. Horn and uba. $4.50.

Lovreglio, E. *Évocation*. Editions Musicales Transatlantiques. Three trombones, tuba, timpani. 1972. $26.00. 10:00. IV. $F\sharp_1$–$f\sharp'$. An episodic work with many tempo changes. Good post-Romantic chamber music in which all instrumental parts are fairly equal.

Luedeke, Raymond. *Krishna*. Seesaw Music Corporation. Tuba, seven percussion, and piano. 1975. $52.00. 8:30. V. C_1–$e\flat'$. Single movement with five sections. For Don Harry. A dramatic work incorporating the tuba into the percussion ensemble. No avant-garde effects other than singing and playing.

Luedeke, Raymond. *New Hampshire—His Majesty the Tuba*. Seesaw Music Corporation. Tuba, tenor, and piano. 1968. 2:50. III–IV. E_1–$f\sharp'$. Two brief whimsical songs. Some wide leaps in the tuba part, which serves as a true equal to the tenor.

Lund, Erik. *Music for Tuba and Mallet Instruments*. T.U.B.A. Press. Tuba and percussion (single performer playing crotale, vibraphone, marimba with low a). 1983. $12.00. 8:00. V. $D\sharp_1$–c'' (continuing as high as possible). A difficult work for both tubist and percussionist consisting mainly of dialogues and gestures passed between the two performers.

Lunde, Ivar, Jr. *Embellishments, Op. 60, No. 1*. Norsk Musikforlag. Piccolo trumpet and tuba. 1976. 2:30. IV. G_1–d'. Single movement in two sections:

Moderately Fast, Majestic; Very Fast & Light. To Gary Albrecht and Steve Allen. Difficult rhythms and mixed meters throughout.

Macero, Teo. *One-Three Quarters*. C.F. Peters Corporation. Two pianos, piccolo/flute, violin, cello, trombone, and tuba. 1970. $7.50. 8:00. A colorful exploratory piece with dramatic gestures. One piano is tuned down a quarter tone, and there are quarter-tone pitch variances in other parts.

Madsen, Trygve. *Divertimento, Op. 43*. Musikk-Huset Forlag, Norway. Horn and tuba. 8:00. V.

Maganini, Quinto. *The Boa-constrictor and the Bobolink (Humorous Sketch)*. Editions Musicus. Piccolo and tuba. $2.50. 1:30. III. C–$b\flat$. Single movement in waltz tempo.

Maneri, J. *Ephphatha*. Margun Music. Clarinet, trombone, tuba, and piano. $35.00.

Mantia, Simone. *Believe Me If All Those Endearing Young Charms*. Arranged by David R. Werden. Whaling Music Publishers. Tuba solo in brass quintet. 1983. $9.50. 6:00. V. F_1–$g'(a')$. The great barn-burner solo nicely arranged with brass quartet accompaniment.

Marcello, Benedetto. *Adagio from Sonata in C Major*. Arranged by Gary Buttery. Whaling Music. Tuba, harp, cello, bassoon. $3.50.

Marks, Günther. *Hymnus für vier Wagner-Tuben und Kontrabass-Tuba*. Edition Kunzelmann. Published 1985. 4:40. II. G_1–$a\flat$. Single movement in three parts. A work inspired by the Adagio from Bruckner's Seventh Symphony.

Maros, Miklós. *Concertino for Tuba (or Contrabass) and Winds*. Swedish Music Information Center. Solo tuba (or bass), flute, clarinet, baritone saxophone, trumpet, horn, percussion. 1971. 9:00.

Martinson, Rolf. *Monogram, Op. 30 for basstuba och blaskvintett*. Swedish Music Information Center. Tuba and woodwind quintet. 1991.

Matthus, Siegfried. *Sonate for Brass, Piano and Timpani*. VEB Deutscher Verlag für Musik. Trumpet in $B\flat$, horn, trombone, tuba, piano, and timpani. 1983. Rental from publisher. 4:30. III–IV. $F\sharp_1$–f. Continuous work in seven sections. A "sound" piece with few technical demands other than some difficult rhythmic interplay and two sections in which all the parts are in completely different meters.

Mendelssohn, Felix. *Scherzo*. Arranged by A.E. Goldstein. Cor Publishing Company. Trumpet, horn, trombone, and tuba. $5.00.

Miller Ragne, Philip. *Interlacements*. Swedish Music Information Center. Flute, oboe, clarinet, trumpet, horn, and tuba. 1989.

Mitchell, W. Roy. *Jazz Suite for Tuba and Jazz Trio*. T.U.B.A. Press. Solo tuba, piano, bass, and drums. 1988. $16.00. 19:00. IV–V. $B\flat_2$–$b\flat'$. Three movements: Samba; Ballad; Fusion-Rock. Written especially for Gary Bird. Although F tuba is specified for Samba and Fusion-Rock, and CC tuba for Ballad, the *Suite* is completely playable on either instrument. Fusion-Rock requires a great deal of agility and contains optional open ad lib solo sections.

Molineux, Allen. *Dichotomic Diversion for Tuba and Percussionists*. T.U.B.A. Press. Tuba and three percussionists (playing multi set-ups). $15.00. 8:00. IV. E_1–c'. Nice percussion writing and muted tuba passages create timbral variety. No significant ensemble problems.

Mozart, W.A. *Fugue, K. 401*. Robert King Music Sales. Flexible brass quartet with tuba. $3.40.

Mozart, W.A. *O Isis and Osiris from "The Magic Flute."* Transcribed by Arthur Frackenpohl. Brassworks Music. Solo tuba in brass quintet (trumpets playing flugelhorns). 1985. $15.00. 2:30. III. F_1–c'. A good version of the standard tuba solo transcription, mostly within the staff. A nice opportunity for the tubist to be featured playing a beautiful melody.

Mozart, W.A. *Two Themes*. Robert King Music Sales. Flexible brass quartet with tuba. $3.40.

Murray, Greg. *"...a whale for the killing."* Music for Percussion, Inc. Tuba and two percussionists. 1983. 8:30. V. Db_1–gb'. Single movement with eleven episodes. Written for Daniel Perantoni and the Rosewood Percussion Duo. An effective, introspective work demanding various nontraditional techniques (wind sounds, singing/playing, rips, etc.) from the tubist.

Nagel, Robert. *Suite*. Mentor Music. Trumpet, horn, trombone, tuba, and piano. $6.50.

Nash, Richard. *Trio Number 1 for Tuba, Horn, and Piano*. T.U.B.A. Press. 1992. $8.00. 7:30. IV. Bb_2–e'. Three movements: Marche; Adagio; Allegro. Looks like Alec Wilder's music but lacks its melodic character.

Nash, Richard T. *Variations for Tuba*. Available from the composer. Solo tuba in brass quintet. 6:30. IV. A_2–e'. Three movements. Dedicated to Tommy Johnson. Three contrasting movements with a strong post-Romantic flavor. The tuba part is lyrical with few technical difficulties; solo cadenza in the third movement.

Naulais, Jerôme. *Choral*. Alphonse Leduc & Cie. Three trombones and tuba. 1986. $9.50. 2:45. II–III. Bb_1–f♯.

Nelhybel, Vaclav. *Concerto for Tuba (or Horn)*. Great Works Publishing, Inc. Solo tuba (or horn), two flutes, oboe, English horn, two clarinets, bassoon, harp, double bass, two trumpets, trombone, three percussion (vibraphone, bells, xylophone). See listing under "Music for Tuba and Band."

Nelhybel, Vaclav. *Octet*. Jerona Music Corporation. Tuba, bass guitar, strings, percussion. $44.00.

Newman, Ron. *Duo for Bass Trombone and Tuba*. Available from he composer. 1991. 10:45. IV–V. Bass Trombone: Gb_1–gb'; Tuba: E_1–f '. Three movements: That Old Refrain; Jobim; Ritual Fire Fugue. Written for Curtis Olson and Philip Sinder. Con-

stantly shifting polymeters in the first movement (14/16, 2/4, 12/16, and 13/16 in the first four measures!) require diligent preparation. In the second movement, the tuba spins out a liquid melody high above the bossa nova rhythms in the bass trombone. The last movement is a study of metric modulation with a modern jazz feel. This duet cannot be quickly "thrown together," but it can be rewarding for players who take the time to realize a fine performance of this good piece of music.

Nielsen, Erik. *Spiritual Alloys (Musings IV)*. For F tuba and vibraphone. Available from the composer. For Mark Nelson. 12:00. IV–V. 1993. A moderately difficult modern work with shifting meters and melodically wide, nontonal writing for the tuba. Requires simultaneous singing and playing by the tubist.

Nilsson, Bo. *Bass*. Edition Reimers. Tuba, percussion (six buckelgongs, tamtam) and electric sound reinforcement. 1977. $6.75. 10:30. IV–V. E_1–g♯'. Continuous work in nine sections. For Michael Lind. A new-music electro-acoustical composition requiring amplification and filtered sound processing of the tuba and percussion. Although the part is notated in strict meters, the music consists of gestures and melodic passages. Recorded by Michael Lind.

Nono, Luigi. *Guai ai gelidi Mostri*. Ricordi. Two altos, flute, clarinet, tuba, viola, cello, bass, live electronics. 1987.

Nono, Luigi. *Hommage to Gyorgy Kurtag*. Ricordi. Alto, flute, clarinet, tuba. 1986.

Nono, Luigi. *Risonanze Erranti*. Ricordi. Alto, flute, tuba, percussion, live electronics. 1987.

Nordhagen, Stig. *Equilibrium for Tuba and Two Percussionists*. Norwegian Music Information Centre. Tuba, two percussion (each playing mutliple set-ups). 1991. 12:10. IV–V. G_1–g♯'. Continuous work in three sections. Written for Sten Cranner, Tomas Nilsson, and Rolf Lennart Stenso. A modern work with a great deal of difficult rhythmic interaction between the tubist and percussionists.

Orowan, T. *Trio No. 1*. Editions Musicus. Trombone, euphonium, and tuba. 1965. $6.00. 10:00. IV. Eb_1–eb. A technical work with the tuba part mostly in the low register.

Pachelbel, Johann. *Fugue on "Ein Feste Burg."* Transcribed by J. Kent Mason. Sonante Publications. Two trumpets, trombone, tuba (or bass trombone). 1978. $5.50. 1:30. II–III. D–a.

Pachelbel, Johann. *Two Magnificats*. Robert King Music Sales. Flexible brass quartet with tuba. $3.40.

Palestrina, G.P. *Adoramus*. Arranged by Lewis Waldeck. Cor Publishing Company. Trumpet, horn, trombone, tuba. $3.00.

Palestrina, G.P. *Ricercare del Primo Tono*. Robert King Music Sales. Flexible brass quartet with tuba. $4.20.

Palestrina, G.P. *Three Hymns*. Robert King Music Sales. Flexible brass quartet with tuba. $3.40.

Parker, J. *Music for Two—Six Duets*. Patterson's Publications. Trombone and tuba (or euphonium). $8.95.

Payne, Frank Lynn. *Canzona de Sonare*. Manuscript available from the composer. Tuba and woodwind quintet. 1982. 10:00. IV. E_1–f'. Single movement with three sections. To Skip Gray. An energetic chamber work exploring Renaissance counterpoint ideas within modern tonal and harmonic practice. See: Bird, Gary, ed., *Program Notes for the Solo Tuba*.

Pearsall, Ed. *Duet for Tuba and Piccolo*. T.U.B.A. Press. 1991. $10.00. 12:00. III. F_1–c'. Two movements: Lightly; Slowly. Simple, characteristic writing.

Peaslee, Richard. *The Devil's Herald*. Margun Music. Tuba, four horns, percussion. 1975. $15.00. 8:45. V. $E\flat_1$–a$\flat$'. One continuous movement. For Harvey Phillips. An interesting and powerful work with varied colors resulting from both the orchestration and special effects, including wind sounds and flutter-tongue sections. See: Bird, Gary, ed., *Program Notes for the Solo Tuba*.

Penn, William. *Capriccio for Tuba and Marimba*. Keyboard Percussion Publications. 1992. 9:10. III–IV. F_1–e' (glissando from nondescript low note to highest note possible). Continuous work in rondo form. Written for John Turk and Rosemary Small. A tuneful, entertaining work reminiscent of movie sound tracks. Both parts well written. See listing under "Music for Tuba and Tape."

Persichetti, Vincent. *Serenade No. 1 for Ten Wind Instruments, Op.1*. Elkan-Vogel Inc. Flute, oboe, clarinet, bassoon, two trumpets, two horns, trombone, tuba. 1929. $20.00. 6:30. III. $F\#_1$–g$\flat$. Five movements: Prelude; Episode; Song; Interlude; Dance. Pleasant chamber music foreshadowing *Serenade No. 12* for solo tuba, which is much more demanding. Recorded by the United States Coast Guard Band.

Peterson, T. *Allegro*. Arranged by J. Strautman. Valentin Avvakoumov. Four trombones and tuba. 1978. 1:30. III–IV. G_1–b$\flat$. A energetic, melodic work employing Romantic harmonies. A good opener or encore piece for a concert.

Petit, Philip. *Les quatre Vents*. Alphonse Leduc. Trumpet, two horns, and tuba. $42.00.

Pluister, S. *Divertimento*. Donemus. Two flutes, oboe, clarinet, bassoon, trumpet, horn, tuba, bass, percussion. $15.50.

Polin, Claire. *The Death of Procris (Studies after a Painting by Piero de Cosimo)*. Seesaw Music Corporation. Flute and tuba. 1972-73. $11.00. 5:30. IV–V. D_1–e'. Two movements: Background; Foreground. Commissioned by Kenneth and Elizabeth Singleton. A difficult "modern" work requiring much rhythmically free interplay between flute and tuba. Nontraditional performance requirements include humming, slap-clicks, and extensive multiphonics in the flute part.

Powell, Morgan. *Transitions for Solo Tuba and Chamber Ensemble*. T.U.B.A. Press. Solo tuba, flute, clarinet, oboe, tenor saxophone, trumpet, trombone, violin, bass, two percussion, piano. 1991. $30.00. 10:20. V. $E\flat_1$–b$\flat$' (also "highest note possible" indicated). For Daniel Perantoni and Edwin London. A very difficult work featuring the solo tuba. Performers required to play strict rhythms in some sections and make free gestures in others. Recorded live by Daniel Perantoni following a performance of Morgan Powell's unaccompanied tuba solo *Midnight Realities*.

Presser, William. *Five Duets for Trombone and Tuba*. Theodore Presser Company. $7.00.

Presser, William. *Five Duets for Trumpet and Tuba*. Theodore Presser Company. 1985. $6.00. 6:19. III–IV. G_1–a (trumpet part goes to high c). Five movements: Adagio; Allegretto; Allegretto; Allegro; Adagio. The work could serve as a good change of pace on a recital. There is little rest, so endurance could be a problem for the trumpeter, whose part lies mainly at the top and above the staff.

Presser, William. *Five Duets for Tuba and Timpani*. Theodore Presser Company. 1981. $4.00. 6:30. III. G_1–c'. Five movements: Adagio; Andante; Tempo de valse; Andante; Finale. A simple work with lots of interplay between the tuba and timpani.

Presser, William. *Quintet for Horns and Tuba*. Tenuto Publications. Four horns and tuba. 1988. $12.00. 5:15. III. F_1–b$\flat$. Four movements: Allegretto; Adagio; Poco allegro; Allegro moderato. Tuba part is somewhat simple yet soloistic.

Presser, William. *Seven Duets for Horn and Tuba*. Seesaw Music Corporation. 1972. $9.00. 7:00. III–IV. $E_1(D_1)$–d'. Seven movements: Andante; Allegro; Allegro; Allegro molto; Adagio—Allegro; Vivace; Allegro. These duets, reminiscent of Bach's two-part inventions, employ more modern tonal boundaries. They can be used for casual playing or in recital.

Presser, William. *Seven Duets for Tuba and Violin*. Theodore Presser. $4.50.

Pryor, Arthur. *The Whistler and His Dog—A Caprice*. Arranged by John Hoesly. Piston Reed Stick and Bow Publisher. Solo tuba in brass quintet. 1985. $11.00. 2:45. II–III. $B\flat_1$–g. An easy arrangement of an old classic tune.

Purcell, Henry. *Allegro and Air from "King Arthur."* Robert King Music Sales. Flexible brass quartet with tuba. $3.40.

Purcell, Henry. *Canon on a Ground Bass*. Arranged by Skip Gray. Shawnee Press, Inc. Trombone (or euphonium) and two tubas. $4.00. See listing under "Music for Multiple Tubas."

Purcell, Henry. *Fantasia #1*. Arranged by Irving Rosenthal. Western International Music. Horn, trombone, and tuba. 1968. $5.00. 2:00. III–IV. G_1–d$\flat$'. A good arrangement for low brass trio. The tuba part is mostly in the upper tessitura.

Purcell, Henry. *Music for Queen Mary II*. Robert King Music Sales. Flexible brass quartet with tuba. $3.40.

Purcell, Henry. *Two Trumpet Tunes and Air*. Robert King Music Sales. Flexible brass quartet with tuba. $5.55.

Rasmussen, Mary, arr. *Christmas Music (40 Carols)*. Robert King Music Sales. Flexible brass quartet with tuba. $26.45.

Read, Thomas. *Brillenbass*. ACA Music Publishers. Solo tuba and celeste (also playing two suspended cymbals). 1993. $18.00. 11:00. IV. C_1–f'. Single movement with contrasting sections. For Mark Nelson. A powerful work with melodic material reminiscent of chant or folk songs. Controlled soft playing in the pedal register and long *forte* sections above the staff.

Reed, Alfred. *Double Wind Quintet*. Marks Music Corporation. Flute, oboe, clarinet, bassoon, two trumpets, two horns, trombone, tuba. 1973. $25.00. 16:00. IV. G_1–b♭. Three movements: Intrada (Fanfares, Entrances and Marches); Pavane (Elegy); Toccata (Rock). Enjoyable chamber music of a popular nature. Although the tuba part is not soloistic, the player has plenty of material with which to keep and be noticed!

Reiche, Gottfried. *Sonatas No. 1, 15, 18, 19, 24, 7, 21, and 22*. Robert King Music Sales. Flexible brass quartet with tuba. $3.40 each.

Revueltas, Sylvestre. *Tres Sonetos*. Southern Music Publishing Company (dist. Theodore Presser). Two clarinets, bass clarinet, bassoon, two trumpets, horn, tuba, piano, percussion. $12.00.

Reynolds, R. *Blind Men*. C. F. Peters Corporation. Three trumpets, three trombones, tuba, percussion, and piano. $10.00.

Reynolds, R. *Wedge*. C. F. Peters Corporation. Two trumpets, two trombones, tuba, two flutes, bass, piano, percussion, and celeste. Rental from the publisher.

Reynolds, Verne. *Signals for Trumpet, Tuba, and Brass Ensemble*. Available from the composer. 1976. 10:50. IV–V. D_1–a♭'. Continuous work in three large sections. Commissioned by Thomas Stevens and Roger Bobo. In several sections the soloists are required to play somewhat freely over ostinato figures in the brass ensemble. Many wide, irregular leaps, and interactive dovetailing between solo parts. Recorded by Roger Bobo.

Reynolds, Verne. *Trio for Horn, Trombone, and Tuba*. Margun Music. 1978. $16.00.

Rice, Thomas. *Bass Quartet*. Seesaw Music Corporation. Tuba, string bass, contrabassoon, timpani. $18.00.

Rice, Thomas. *Music for Brass Duo, Op. 53F*. Seesaw Music Corporation. Trumpet and tuba. $9.00.

Rice, Thomas. *Music for Brass Quartet, Op. 53A*. Seesaw Music Corporation. Trumpet, horn, trombone, and tuba. $30.00.

Rice, Thomas. *Thing for Tuba and Timpani, Op. 52*. Seesaw Music Corporation. 1982. $15.00 6:10. III. G_1–b♭. Single movement with four sections. No substantial demands. Neither instrument is used particularly melodically but most often pass timpani-like figures to each another.

Riddle, Peter. *Concertino*. Seesaw Music Corporation. Tuba, flute, six percussion. V.

Ridout, Alan. *Concertino for Tuba and Strings*. Emerson Edition Ltd. Solo tuba and strings or string quartet (piano reduction available). See listing under "Music for Tuba and Orchestra."

Rimsky-Korsakov, Nicolai. *Flight of the Tuba Bee*. Arranged by Howard Cable. Canadian Brass Publications (G. Schirmer). Solo tuba, two trumpets, horn, trombone. 1979. $16.00. 1:30. V. E_1–e'. The classic virtuoso encore arranged excellently for solo tuba in brass quintet. Recorded by Canadian Brass.

Roikjer, Kjell. *Variations and Fugue*. Wilhelm Hansen Musikforlag. Two trumpets, trombone, and tuba. $9.25.

Rollin, Robert. *Chamber Concerto*. Seesaw Music Corporation. Solo tuba, piccolo, oboe, clarinet, saxophone, trumpet, trombone, and percussion. 1993.

Rollin, Robert. *Concertino No. 2*. Seesaw Music Corporation. Flute, tuba, percussion ensemble. $30.00.

Rollin, Robert. *The Raven and the First Men*. Seesaw Music Corporation. Horn, tuba, piano, tape. $40.00.

Rollin, Robert. *Trio for Trumpet, Trombone, and Tuba*. Seesaw Music Corporation. 1993.

Rubenstein, Arthur B. *Bruegel-Dance Visions*. In preparation by Editions BIM. Solo tuba, viola, cello, bass, harp, percussion, and synthesizer. 1991. 14:45. IV. $F\sharp_1$–g♭'. Four movements: Aubade (The Misanthrope); Estampie (Children's Games); Pavanne (Land of Cockaigne); Rondeau (Struggle between Carnival and Lent). Commissioned by Jim Self. Four movements based on paintings by the sixteenth-century Flemish painter Pieter Bruegel. Some difficult rhythmic writing. Recorded by Jim Self.

Russell, Armand. *Suite Concertante*. Accura Music. Tuba and woodwind quintet (piano reduction available). 1961. $36.00. 11:15. IV. G_1–f♯'. Four movements: Capriccio; Ballade; Scherzo; Burlesca. Good chamber music employing traditional musical idioms. See: Bird, Gary, ed.: *Program Notes for the Solo Tuba*. Recorded by Floyd Cooley.

Rybrant, Stig. *Deep Brass Joke: Scherzo*. H. Busch. (Swedish Music Information Center). Four trombones and tuba. 1954. 3:30.

Sabatini, G. *Ecstasy*. Camara Music Publishers. Solo tuba, two trumpets, horn, trombone, violin, and harp. $9.00.

Saglietti, Corrado Maria. *Concerto for Tuba and Four Horns*. Edition BIM. Piano accompaniment also available. 1985. 8:45. III–IV. G♭₁–e'. Three movements: Allegro; Adagio; Allegro con Spirito. Very approachable melodic work with difficult horn parts.

Saint-Saëns, Camille. *Adagio from the "Third Symphony."* Arranged by J. Strautman. Valentin Avvakoumov. Four trombones and tuba. 1978. 4:00. III. A♭₁–g. A nice low brass arrangement of the famous chorale from the "Organ Symphony."

Saint-Saëns, Camille, and Mussorgsky, Modest. *Two Tuba Solos: The Elephant and Bydlo.* Arranged by David Camesi. Western International Music, Inc. Solo tuba in brass quintet. 1974. $7.00. 2:00. III. E₁–e'. Two pieces which can be played individually. A good arrangement, mostly in the bread-and-butter range of two works often assimilated with the tuba. "Bydlo" is a major third lower than in the Ravel orchestration key and is thus much easier to play.

Sandström, Sven-David. *Ratio.* Swedish Music Information Center. Tuba and bass drum. 1974. 6:00.

Schelle, Michael. *Blue Plate Special.* American Composers Edition, Inc. Solo tuba and percussion. 1983. $6.35. 18:00.

Schickele, Peter. *Little Suite for Winter.* Theodore Presser Company. Clarinet and tuba. 1981. $18.00. 11:00. III–IV. E♭₁–c♯'. Five movements: Fantasia; Blues Bounce; Lullaby; Rondo; Traveling Music. Commissioned by Rodger Vaughan for the occasion of his 50th birthday tuba recital. Nice, effervescent chamber music.

Schilling, Hans Ludwig. *Meeting.* Hans Ludwig Schilling. Tuba and contrabassoon.

Schilling, Hans Ludwig. *Sonate en Trio.* J.P. Tonger Verlag, Köln. Trumpet, tuba, and piano.

Schmidt, F. *Tullnerbacher Blasmusik.* Ludwig Doblinger K.G. Two trumpets, three horns, tuba, and two oboes. $15.15.

Schmidt, William. *Concertino.* Western International Music, Inc. Piano, two trumpets, horn, trombone, and tuba (or bass trombone). 1969. IV. Three movements: Allegro con brio; Largo; Allegro con spirito. A true mini-concerto with extended albeit conservative harmonies and influences of American musical idioms.

Schmidt, William. *Concertino for Tuba (or Bass Trombone) and Woodwind Quintet.* Western International Music, Inc. 1980. $15.00. 12:00. III. A♭₁–c♯'. Three movements. For Terry Cravens. Good chamber music featuring the tuba which goes together without difficulty. Tuba mute is required in the second movement. See: Bird, Gary, ed., *Program Notes for the Solo Tuba.*

Schmidt, William. *Latin Rhythms.* Western International Music, Inc. Tuba and percussion. 1989. $18.00. 9:00. IV. E₁–g'. Four movements: Introduction; Tangoletto; Bossalina Nova; Chat Chat Chat. To Gary Brittin. Fairly complex rhythms. Much of the time, the tuba is scored like an exten-

sion of the percussion instruments. A true chamber duet. Tuba bucket and cup mutes required.

Schmidt, William. *Music for Scrimshaws.* Western International Music, Inc. Two trumpets, horn, trombone, tuba, and harp. $15.00.

Schmidt, William. *Sonatina.* Western International Music, Inc. Horn, trombone, and tuba. $7.00.

Schmidt, William. *Tony and The Elephant or Jim and The Road Runner.* Western International Music Inc. Trumpet and tuba. 1984. $8.00. 8:30. IV–V. G₁–e'. Five movements: Stomp'n'; Waltz'n'; Blues'n'; Swing'n'; Trip'n'. For Tony Plog and Jim Self. Cup, bucket, and straight mutes requested. Contrasting movements present a stylistic challenge. See: Bird, Gary, ed., *Program Notes for the Solo Tuba.*

Schmitt, F. *Quatuor.* Editions Billaudot. Three trombones and tuba. $29.00.

Schmitt, M. *Trio.* Bote & Bock K.G. Trumpet, trombone, and tuba. $26.40.

Schooley, John H. *Partita for Brass Quartet.* Kendor Music, Inc. Two trumpets, trombone, tuba. 1969. 6:20. II–III. F₁–a. Six movements: Chorale; Invention for Two Trumpets; Pastorale; Invention for Trombone and Tuba; Fugato; Finale. A good contest or recital work for a high school group.

Schuback, Peter. *Lignes parallèles.* Swedish Music Information Center. Flute, alto, and tuba. 1975.

Schuller, Gunther. *Little Brass Music.* Mentor Music. Trumpet, horn, trombone, and tuba. 1963. $5.00. 4:00. IV–V. F₁–d♭'. A difficult modern chamber work.

Schuller, Gunther. *Perpetuum Mobile.* Margun Music Inc. Four horns and tuba (or bassoon). $10.00. Horns are muted throughout. A light work reminiscent of twentieth-century French chamber music.

Schust, Alfred. *Duo for Tuba and Flute.* Musikverlag Barbara Evans. 1989. 7:45. IV. G₁–g'. Four movements: I; II. Presto agitato; III. Adagio; IV. Presto. Good post-Romantic chamber music. The tubist is required to change registers and roles (from accompanying to lead) quite rapidly. Some difficult, irregular chromatic alterations in some passages, especially in the fourth movement.

Schust, Alfred. *Trio for Flute (Doubling Piccolo), Alto Sax, and Tuba.* Musikverlag Barbara Evans. 1984. 7:15. III–IV. E♯₁(D₁)–e'. Three movements. Nice neo-Romantic chamber music in three well-balanced, contrasting movements—an opening allegro moderato, Waltz "à la mode," and a concluding marchlike movement. Although the flute is truly the lead voice, the saxophone and tuba parts are challenging and rewarding to play

Sear, Walter. *Quartet.* Cor Publishing. Two trumpets, trombone, and tuba. $14.00.

Self, Jim. *Courante.* Jim Self. Tuba, trombone, alto saxophone. 1991. 6:30. IV–V. Tuba: D₁–a' (trombone: A₁–e♭"!). The work is based on the French Baroque dance form, in triple meter with rhythmic variations. Includes an improvistory section for the tubist. The trombone part is more difficult than the tuba part, with its high tessitura, wide intervallic leaps, and lack of rests, which could present an endurance challenge. Recorded by Jim Self.

Sigurbjörsson, Thorkell. *Donkey Dance*. Iceland Music Information Centre. Tuba, double bass, and piano. 4:00. V. E$_1$–f♯'. A work which attempts to imitate the polymetric freedom of ethnic folk music.

Silverman, Faye-Ellen. *Dialogue*. Seesaw Music Corporation. Horn and tuba. 1975-76. $10.00. 4:30. III. F$_1$–d'. Continuous work in two sections. The opening section consists of steady eighth notes and long, sustained trill passages exchanged between horn and tuba. The second section is contrapuntal, featuring frequent dissonance, several half-valve glissandos, and one short phrase requiring simultaneous singing and playing by the tubist.

Singleton, Ken, trans. and ed. *Ars Nova Duets*. PP Music. F horn and tuba. 1984. $9.00. 22 pages. III. b♭–d'. Fifteen individual works. Very little music from the fourteenth century has been transcribed for tubists, and this collection is a good introduction. These duets, lying within to slightly above the staff, will extend a younger player's range and security in the upper register.

Smit, Leo, arr. *Taps*. Theodore Presser Company. Five trombones and tuba. 1980. $6.00. 0:35. II. E$_1$ (optional octave higher)–G$_1$. Composed for the 1980 Brevard Music Center Trombone Choir. A simple harmonization of the old standard bugle call featuring the first trombone on the melody.

Smith, Glenn. *Beyond the Dream and to the Sun*. Seesaw Music Corporation. Solo tuba, flute, oboe, bass clarinet, bassoon, piano. $26.50.

Smith, Glenn. *Forowen*. Seesaw Music Corporation. Alto flute and tuba. 1972. $7.00. 3:45. IV. B♭$_2$–highest note possible (highest notated pitch is e'). Dedicated to John and Sally Turk. Interestingly orchestrated music requiring both players to sing and play simultaneously in several sections. The three *Forowen* pieces work very well when performed as a set on a recital program.

Smith, Glenn. *Forowen 2*. Seesaw Music Corporation. Flute and tuba. 1979. $7.00. 3:00. IV. C$_1$–g'. A brief reflective work with a haunting melody and unresolved dissonance, which can leave the conservative listener unnerved. The composer uses a wide range in both parts to attain coloristic variety. A brief section with some difficult sixteenth-note interplay with wide intervallic leaps.

Smith, Glenn. *Forowen 3*. Seesaw Music Corporation. Piccolo and tuba. 1979. $7.00. 2:30. IV. F$_1$–g'. For John and Laurie Turk. An interesting two-part invention with some difficult nontonal sixteenth-note passages and simultaneous sing-and-play sections. *Forowen 3* contains fewer traditional dissonances than its two predecessors, but it is much

more energetic and technically demanding. Recorded by John Turk.

Smith, Glenn. *Music for Horns, Tuba, and Violas*. Seesaw Music Corporation. Two horns, tuba, two violas. $28.00.

Stepanyan, A. *Nocturne for Three Trombones and Tuba*. Edited by Keith Brown. International Music Company. $5.50.

Stephens, Denzil. *Rondo Rotundo*. Sarnia Music. Solo tuba with brass ensemble or brass band. 1989. $23.00. 3:00. IV. G$_1$–f'. A brisk tuba showpiece with contrasting technical and lyrical sections.

Stevens, John. *City Suite*. Available from the composer. Tuba, flute, flugelhorn, trombone, vibes, guitar, piano, bass, and drums. 1978. 20:00. IV. B♭$_1$–f'. Three movements: Home Again; Central Park Down; Crush Hour. Composed for Toby Hanks. A jazz work requiring improvisation.

Stevens, John. *Country Suite*. Available from the composer. Tuba, flute, flugelhorn, vibes, guitar, piano, bass, and drums. 1977. 20:00. IV. C–d'. Three movements: Amazing Place "How Sweet the Sound"; Lazy Day Song; Saturday Night Stompin'. Composed for Toby Hanks. A companion to *City Suite*. Improvisation by the tubist is required.

Stevens, John. *Dialogues for Horn and Tuba*. Manuscript from the composer. 1987. 12:00. IV–V. C$_1$–e'. Five movements: Prologue and Dance; March; Scherzo; Lament; Dance and Epilogue. The styles of the movements are contrasted with pop and jazz influences throughout. The tuba part is rhythmically demanding.

Stevens, John. *Dialogues for Trombone and Tuba*. Southern Music Publishing Company (dist. Theodore Presser). 1987. $8.50. 10:00. IV–V. E♭$_1$–f♯'. Four movements: Fanfare; Aria; Scherzo; Finale. Much melodic and rhythmic interaction between the two instruments. The "fast" tempos are extremely quick, and the tuba part is rhythmically demanding.

Stevens, John. *Dialogues for Trumpet and Tuba*. Manuscript available from the composer. 1988. 10:00. IV–V. E♭$_1$–g'. Four movements: Fanfare; Scherzo; Chant; Finale. More exploratory music than is typical of Stevens's work, with greater use of dissonance, free sections, and multiphonics. Mute required of the tubist.

Stevens, John. *Triangles*. Gordon V. Thompson Music. Horn, trombone, and tuba. 1978. $18.00. 11:00. IV–V. G$_1$–f'. A one-movement work with four sections connected by solo cadenzas. Good chamber music employing jazz rhythms and style. Recorded by John Stevens.

Stewart, Joseph. *TUBA*. Kendor Music, Inc. Solo tuba, SATB chorus, string bass (version for solo tuba and band, solo tuba and piano available). 1973. 3:00 III. B♭–b♭. Two connected sections: Presto; Jazz Waltz. Dedicated to Andy Peruzzini and the Maryvale High School Chorale. Some stylistic and technical challenges for the soloist. The choral accompaniment is more difficult than the band accompaniment and may require that the piano accompaniment be played also.

Stewart, Robert. *Heart Attack*. American Composers Alliance. Tuba and two percussionists (I: xylophone, vibes, orchestra bells; II: conga, timbales, brake drum, triangle, maracas). 1973. 9:00. D♭₁–a♭'. For Barton Cummings. A difficult contemporary work with wide-interval, disjunct-note groupings and several effects, including glissandi and slapping the instrument.

Strautman, J. *Ragtime*. Valentin Avvakoumov. Four trombones and tuba. 1991. 5:30. III. B♭₁–a. A well-crafted little rag with a tricky six-bar tuba solo in the middle.

Strautman, J. *Serenade*. Valentin Avvakoumov. Four trombones and tuba. 1990. 3:00. III–IV. G–b♭. An expressive, melodic work which features the tuba.

Strautman, J. *Waltz in "5 x 5."* Valentin Avvakoumov. Four trombones and tuba. 1992. 4:00. III–IV. A♭₁–d♭'. A traditional waltz-style work in quintuple meter. Although the tuba does not have the principal part throughout, it is featured.

Tackett, Fred. *Yellow Bird*. Hoceanna Music. Solo tuba, guitar, piano, bass, drums. 1971-72. 15:45. V. C–b♭'. Three sections: Fast; Not So Fast; Real Fast. Commissioned by and written for Roger Bobo. One of the first pop-jazz works featuring the tuba. Contains ad lib solo section. Recorded by Roger Bobo. See: Bird, Gary, ed., *Program Notes for the Solo Tuba*.

Tartini, Giusseppe. *Andante Cantabile*. Arranged by A. Reisman. Camara Music Publishers. Solo tuba, two trumpets, horn, trombone, violin. $6.00.

Tautenhahn, G. *Trio No. 2*. Seesaw Music Corporation. Tuba, English horn, glockenspiel. $16.00.

Telemann, G.P. *Three Chorale Preludes*. Arranged by Arthur Frackenpohl. Horizon Press. Trombone (or euphonium) and tuba. 1991.

Telemann, G.P. *Three Dances in A Minor*. Arranged by Walter Hartley. Ensemble Publications, Inc. Flute and tuba. 1972. $4.00. 5:00. III–IV. A₁–c'. Three movements: Moderato; Allegro; Vivace. Chamber music which works very well for flute and tuba.

Tenney, J. *3 Indigenous Songs*. Smith Publications. Tuba or bassoon, two piccolos, alto flute, two percussion. $75.00.

Teuber, Fred W. *Duet Set for Horn and Tuba*. Broad River Press, Inc. 1975. $4.00. 6:15. IV. A♭₁–c#'. Five movements: Starter; Song-Like; Near March; Rock-a-bye; Bog-Hunt Chase. Fun music to play when getting together with a hornist friend.

Thomas, T. Donley. *Bicinia*. Medici Music. Trombone (or euphonium) and tuba. $10.00. See listing under "Music for Multiple Tubas."

Tomasi, Henri. *Être ou ne pas être*. Alphonse Leduc. Solo tuba (or bass trombone) and three trombones (piano accompaniment also available). 1963.

$12.20. 6:10. IV. B♭₁–d'. Single movement. For the Trombone Quartet of the National Orchestra of the French Radio Theater. A dramatic musical setting of the famous monologue from Shakespeare's *Hamlet*. Recorded by Arnold Jacobs and Toby Hanks.

Tómasson, Jónas. *Sonata XVII*. Iceland Music Information Centre. Horn, tuba, and piano. 1986. 12:00. III–IV. F₁–f'. Six movements: Preludia; Intermezzo I; Danza; Canto; Intermezzo II; Finale. Interesting chamber music with some difficult rhythmic interplay in the Danza and Finale movements.

Traditional. *Nobody Knows*. Arranged by Gordon A. Adnams. Sonante Publications. Two trumpets, trombone, tuba (or bass trombone). 1982. $5.50. 1:45. II. C–c. An easy arrangement in slow swing of the old favorite.

Tull, Fisher. *Concerto da Camera*. Southern Music Company. Alto saxophone, two trumpets, horn, trombone, and tuba. $29.95.

Tull, Fisher. *Lament, Op. 32*. Manuscript available from the composer. Four horns and tuba. 5:30. III. B₁–a. Single movement. Good chamber music featuring the first horn.

Uber, David. *Caricatura, Op. 89*. Available from the composer. Solo tuba and brass ensemble. 1970. 5:20. III. B♭₁–c'. Single movement. Commissioned by Harvey Phillips. A tuneful piece with mostly diatonic writing for the soloist. The brass ensemble parts are not difficult, and this is an easy work to put together.

Uber, David. *Double Portraits—The City—Concert Sketches for Trombone and Tuba*. Brodt Music Company. 1967. $4.00. 7:30. III–IV. A♭₁–b♭'. Three movements: Times Square; Twilight; The City Awakens. Light music with "pop" sound. Recorded by Michael Lind.

Uber, David. *The Giraffe and the Bear: A Concert Duo for Flute and Tuba*. Medici Music. 1981. $13.00. 6:40. IV. A♭₁–e♭' (f '). Three movements: Allegro vivo; Andante tranquillo; Allegro con fuoco. A tonal piece with much dialogue between the two parts. Third movement has a great deal of shifting polymeters (5/8, 4/8, 7/8, etc.).

Uber, David. *Rhythmic Contours (Op. 135)*. Available from the composer. Solo tuba and percussion (four players). Piano reduction available from the composer. $15.00. 10:30. IV–V. A₁–b♭'. One continuous work in five sections. Composed for Barton Cummings. A driving work with little rest for the tubist. Good, active percussion writing keeps the composition moving forward.

Uber, David. *Skylines (Op. 296)*. Hidalgo Music. Solo tuba (bass trombone) and brass ensemble. 1992. $30.00. 7:15. IV–V. G₁–a'. Three movements: Manhattan; Chicago; Boston. Composed for and dedicated to Douglas Yeo. Movements have highly individual characters. High tessitura of the solo part makes performance on an E♭ or F tuba logical.

Uber, David. *Sonatuba for Solo Tuba, Brass and Percussion (Op. 291)*. T.U.B.A. Press. Piano reduction available. 1991. $30.00. 8:00. IV. A♭₁–f¹ (a♭¹). Three movements: Allegro moderato; Valse, poco lento; Allegro. For Harvey Phillips. A tuneful work nicely scored so that the tuba is not over-balanced.

Uber, David. *Three Cameos*. In preparation by the composer. Solo tuba and saxophone quartet. 1992. For Harvey Phillips.

Van der Velden, Renier. *Concertino*. Centre Belge de Documentation. Two pianos, two trumpets, horn, trombone, and tuba. 1965. 12:00.

Van Vactor, David. *Song and Dance (Economy Band No. 2 for Horn, Tuba, and Percussion)*. Roger Rhodes Music, Ltd. Out of print. Single percussionist plays bells, chimes, marimba, bass drum, snare drum, timpani, cymbal. 1969. 7:00. III–IV. E₁–c¹. Two connected sections: Lento—(Meno mosso, con licenza)—Allegretto. A good, conventional work. Few rests in the horn part could present endurance problems.

Vasconi, Eugene. *Images*. Southern Music Company, Inc. Two trumpets, trombone, tuba. $10.00.

Vasconi, Eugene. *Promenade*. Southern Music Company, Inc. Two trumpets, trombone (or euphonium), tuba. $5.00. See listing under "Music for Multiple Tubas."

Vaughan, Rodger. *Quattro Bicinie for Clarinet and Tuba*. Philharmusica Corporation. Tuba and B♭ clarinet. 1967. $7.95. 5:00. III–IV. F₁–d¹. Four movements: Intrada; Gavotte; Sarabande; Gigue. To Donal Michalsky. Light music requiring tasteful playing by the tubist.

Vaughan, Rodger. *Quinte Bicinie for Viola and Tuba*. Rodger Vaughan. 1972. 8:00. III–IV. G₁–c¹. Five movements: Preludio; Basse Danse; Pavane; Passamezzo; Saltarello. Commissioned by Pamela Goldsmith. Effective chamber music with some nice lines and colors, including a small amount of sing-and-play sections in the tuba part.

Vaughan, Rodger. *Three Miniatures*. T.U.B.A. Press. Tuba and cello. 1982. $4.00. 5:20. III. C–b♭. Three movements: Allegretto; Canon at the inversion; Greeley Jazz. For Mattie Robinson on her twelfth birthday. Simple yet interesting works for a change of pace on a recital or a brief fling with a cellist.

Vaughan, Rodger. *Three Songs for Soprano and Tuba—Poems by John Updike*. Trigram Music. 1968. $7.95. 5:15. IV. E♭₁–e♭¹. Three movements: The Clan; Lament for Cocoa; Headline in the Times. For Marjorie Tall.

Vazzana, Anthony. *Cambi for Tuba and Percussion*. Available from the composer. Tuba (in F) and percussionist. 1976. 9:00. V. D₁–b♭¹. Three movements: Toccata; Canzona; Giga. For James Self. A difficult work in both technical and ensemble aspects. Some very interesting colors and musical interplay between tubist and percussionist. Piece

uses micro tones, singing through instrument, and multiphonics. See: Bird, Gary, ed., *Program Notes for the Solo Tuba*.

Vitali. T. *Ciaccona*. Arranged by G. Sabatini. Camara Music Publishers. Solo tuba, two Trumpets, horn, trombone, violin. $22.00.

Vizzutti, Allen. *Fantasia for Solo Tuba, Brass and Percussion*. Allen Vizzutti. Piano reduction available. 1990. 8:00. V. C–g¹ (c¹¹). Single movement with three sections. Commissioned by and written for Skip Gray. A showpiece for solo tuba with rapid as well as lyrical expressive sections.

Wallach, Joelle. *Cantares de los Peredis*. American Composers Alliance. Mezzo soprano, baritone, tenor or soprano, tuba, timpani, crotales. 1987. 11:00.

Warren, Frank E. *Music for Tuba with Violoncello and Vibraharp*. Frank E. Warren Music Service. 1989. 10:30. IV. F₁–f¹. Single movement. For Richard Armandi. Requires tuba mute.

Warren, Frank E. *Seven Duets for Tuba and Bassoon*. Frank E. Warren Music Service. 1983. $5.00. 11:00. IV. C–f¹. Commissioned by Gary and Judy Buttery. Dedicated to Gary and Judy Buttery. A good, interactive composition for bassoon and tuba. The movements are in contrasting styles. Balance between the instruments is not a major problem.

Washburn, Robert. *Concertino for Wind and Brass Quintets*. Oxford University Press. Flute, oboe, clarinet, bassoon, two trumpets, two horns, trombone, tuba. 1971. $15.00. 8:00. III–IV. G₁–a. Two movements: Adagio—Allegro vivo; Theme and Variants. Allegro vivo section of first movement contains many meter changes with three through nine eighth notes to the bar. Tuba part in Theme and Variants contains a rapid sixteenth-note passage.

Wilder, Alec. *Effie Joins the Carnival, from "Suite No. 1."* Arranged by Ronald Bishop. Margun Music. Tuba in brass quintet. $7.00. III.

Wilder, Alec. *Elegy*. Margun Music Inc. Solo tuba and brass ensemble (three trumpets, three horns, three trombones). 1971. 4:00. III–IV. A₁–f♯¹. Written in tribute to and memory of William Bell. A beautiful, lyrical work. Accompanying brass ensemble parts are very easy.

Wilder, Alec. *Movement III. Tuba Showpiece from "Brass Quintet No. 1."* Margun Music, Inc. Tuba in brass quintet. 1959. $12.00 (complete work). 2:45. IV. F₁–b♭¹. Written for the New York Brass Quintet. This single movement featuring the tuba is part of a six-movement work which showcases each member of the brass quintet. The movements may be performed as a suite or separately. Recorded by Harvey Phillips.

Wilder, Alec. *Nonet for Brass*. Margun Music. Eight horns, tuba. $28.00. IV. Four movements. Jazz style throughout.

Wilder, Alec. *Suite for Brass Quintet and Strings.* Margun Music Inc. Two trumpets, horn, trombone, tuba, strings, percussion (one player). 1979. 11:45. III–IV. G_1–eb'. Four movements. Music typical of Alec Wilder with no substantial difficulties in any part. The fourth movement is in a jazz style and is the only movement in which the percussionist plays, simply providing time.

Wilder, Alec. *Suite for Trumpet and Tuba.* Margun Music, Inc. Published 1980. $15.00. 7:00. IV. G_1–f'. Six movements. Nicely written music which sounds good for the difficult combination of trumpet and tuba.

Wilder, Alec. *Suite No. 1 "Effie" for Tuba and Woodwind Quintet.* Arranged by William Stanton. Margun Music, Inc. 1991. $20.00. 11:15. III–IV. F_1–e'. Six movements: Effie Chases a Monkey; Effie Falls in Love; Effie Takes a Dancing Lesson; Effie Joins the Carnival; Effie Goes Folk Dancing; Effie Sings a Lullabye.

Wilder, Alec. *Suite No. 1 for Horn, Tuba, and Piano.* Margun Music, Inc. 1971. $15.00. 14:00. IV–V. Ab_1–g'. Five movements: Maestoso; Pesante; In a Jazz Manner; Berceuse (for Carol); Alla cacia. For John Barrows and Harvey Phillips. Challenging chamber music. See: Bird, Gary, ed., *Program Notes for the Solo Tuba.* Recorded by Harvey Phillips.

Wilder, Alec. *Suite No. 2 for Horn, Tuba, and Piano.* Margun Music. 1971. 10:00. IV–V. F_1–f'. Five movements. Written for John Barrows and Harvey Phillips. Recorded by Harvey Phillips.

Wilder, Alec. *Suite No. 1 for Tuba, Double Bass, and Piano.* Margun Music. 1962. $12.00. 10:00. IV. F_1–g'. Written for bassist Gary Karr and tubist Harvey Phillips.

Wilder, Alec. *Suite No. 1 for Tuba, "Effie the Elephant."* Arranged by Walter Hilgers. Available from the arranger. Solo tuba and brass quintet. 1988. 12:30. See listing under "Music for Tuba and Keyboard." Recorded by Walter Hilgers.

Wilder, Alec. *Twelve Duets for Horn and Tuba.* Margun Music, Inc. In preparation 1992. 1968.

Wright, Rayburn. *Undercurrents.* Seesaw Music Corporation. Flute, seven tubas, two percussion. See listing under "Music for Multiple Tubas."

Wyatt, Scott. *Lifepoints.* Available from the composer. Solo tuba, percussion, electronic tape. 1990. See listing under "Music for Tuba and Tape."

Wyre, John. *Maruba for Tuba and Marimba.* Malarkey Music. Tuba and marimba (with low A). 1987. 12:30. III. C–d'. Single movement with three sections. Commissioned by Ex Tenebris with assistance of the Ontario Arts Council. Written and dedicated to Beverly Johnson and J. Scott Irvine. A work containing interesting colors and somewhat "New Age" in character.

Xenakis, Iannis. *Linaia-Agon.* Éditions Salabert. Horn, trombone, and tuba. 1972. At least 13:30. V. G_1–a'. Dedicated to Lina Lalandi. This atonal work is a true musical game or play depicting a fight between the Classical gods Linos and Apollo, each player assuming the role of one of the adversaries. The prelude, entr'acte music, and closing music are conventionally notated. The four internal episodes, which represent combat between the gods, is chance music chosen by the players in interactive response to what other players have chosen to play and determined with a scoring matrix.

Yen, Lu. *Quartet.* Seesaw Music Corporation. Clarinet, tuba, two percussionists (playing multiple setups). 1970. $14.00. 6:30. IV–V. Bb_2–f'. Continuous work in four sections: Adagio; Allegro; Andante; Adagio. Many interactive, free gestures with notated pitches, air sound, and simultaneous singing and playing. Music duration is notated in approximate time spans rather than meters.

Zaninelli, Luigi. *Berlin Suite.* Shawnee Press. Trumpet, trombone, and tuba. $10.00.

Ziffrin, Marilyn. *Trio.* Available from the composer. Xylophone, soprano, and tuba. 8:30. IV. D_1–g'. Continuous work. For Barton Cummings. Atonal, nonmetered. All three parts are quite active. The soprano is required to produce nineteen different vocal sounds, all notated on specific pitches. Recorded by Barton Cummings.

Zonn, Paul Martin. *Divertimento #1.* Available from the composer. Tuba, double bass, two percussion (I: marimba and xylophone; II: vibraphone and xylophone). 1965. 10:00. IV–V. Bb_2–f'. Three movements: Moderato; Poco Lento; Allegro. For Robert Whaley. A contemporary, virtuoso piece for all members of the ensemble, written in traditional notation. The tuba part contains some half-valve glissandos, flutter tongue, and muted passages. Wide, irregular intervals throughout. Recorded by Daniel Perantoni.

Zonn, Paul Martin. *Varia V.* Available from the composer. Clarinet, trumpet, trombone, tuba, and piano. 1979. 5:00. IV–V. C_1–g'. Interesting contemporary chamber music with wide intervallic leaps and difficult rhythms. The work's five sections could be construed as four variations and a concluding theme (*Livery Stable Blues* in Dixieland style).

Zonn, Paul Martin. *Winter Paths.* Paul Zonn. Tuba and woodwind quintet. 1982. 10:30. V. A_1–g#'. Single movement. For Skip Gray. An interesting and demanding chamber work containing traditional, unmetered, and aleatory notation. There are wide, irregular intervallic leaps and difficult rhythmic relationships.

6. Music for Unaccompanied Tuba

Jeffrey L. Funderburk

Music for unaccompanied tuba encompasses a great diversity of musical styles and experiences. The unique limitations and inherent freedom of this medium have encouraged composers to experiment. Because of the limited number of sounds produced by an unaccompanied instrument, many new techniques have evolved and are often incorporated into the texture of a work. This is not to say, however, that all of this literature relies on extended technique. While many works exhibit a high degree of experimentation and exploration of the instrument's possibilities, others represent very traditional musical experiences.

Besides the presentation of new and nontraditional performance techniques, there are other important reasons to examine this literature. The performer benefits from the unaccompanied solo by becoming aware of all aspects of playing. Without accompaniment to help furnish melodic, rhythmic, and dynamic contrasts, the tubist has total control of the interpretation. This is a valuable expansion of a performer's musical experience, one that keyboard musicians have long been faced with. With unaccompanied music, the tubist can also have the experience of total control of the music and, it is hoped, will grow musically from the increased responsibilities.

With proper selection, the unaccompanied literature need not be reserved for advanced students and professionals, but may be used by all tuba players. Experiences gained from etudes can be significantly enhanced by study of unaccompanied works requiring similar techniques.

Because of the great diversity of compositional and notational styles within the unaccompanied medium, in the following annotations three categories of composition were identified:

Traditional: These works rely on traditional technique and range. The musical language is based on traditional harmony and is represented in standard notation.

Contemporary: These works often represent a more modern use of the instrument in terms of technical demands. The range is generally expanded, and some extended techniques may be used. The basic material lies within the realm of traditional performance practice but represents a limited departure from the norm for performer and audience. Notation is primarily standard though some use of newer techniques may appear.

Avant-garde: These works make extensive use of expanded range and extended techniques. Nontraditional notation and theatrical techniques may be in evidence. These works are the most challenging for the general audience and the least familiar to the average performer.

The notational systems were identified as belonging to one of four categories: *traditional*, the notation used in the "common practice" period of music history; *proportional notation*, in which durational values are given proportionally, often by extending the ligatures of the notes; *frame notation*, which employs a frame or enclosure that contains the events to be performed in a specified amount of time; and *graphic notation*, which employs pictures or drawings to be interpreted by the performer.

Because of the nature of this medium, many sketches of works and brief manuscripts exist which are, for all practical purposes, generally unavailable. For this reason, some works which were identified have not been included.

Special thanks are extended to W. Ryan Thomas for his hours of assistance in helping to make this project possible.

Adler, Samuel. *Canto VII*. Boosey & Hawkes, Inc. 1974. $6.50. 9:00. IV–V. D_1–f¹. Four movements: Quite Fast; Light, fluffy and quick; Slowly and with great expression; Fast and triumphant. For Harvey Phillips. This piece, composed in 1972, is interesting and very approachable. The general range requirements are moderate, with most playing in the middle register while utilizing the entire range of the instrument. The general compositional style is contemporary with traditional notation, sometimes modified to represent the non-pitched sounds. The most interesting movement is the second, which combines percussive effects with played sounds sometimes altered with flutter tonguing. This movement effectively converts the tuba to a percussion instrument. The other three movements rely on traditional performance techniques. Wide intervals are the greatest technical demand. Brief explanations of the symbols are provided. Extended techniques include: breath sounds, fingernails on the bell, valve clicks, flutter tonguing, glissandi, white noise. See: Bird, Gary, ed., *Program Notes for the Solo Tuba*. Recorded by Cherry Beauregard.

Albert, Thomas. *Latticework*. 1973. 4:00. IV. E♭–d'. One movement. For Daniel Perantoni. This is an avant-garde work which relies entirely on proportional and frame notation. A good explanation of the notation is included. Multiphonics and general interpretation are the primary challenges.

Anderson, Eugene. *Lyri-Tech I*. Anderson's Arizona Originals. 1991. 6:00. III–IV. D₁–e'. One movement. Commissioned by and dedicated to David Aubuchon. This work is rhythmically simple and theatrically based. There are no particular technical challenges, but the piece requires attention in order to achieve an interesting musical presentation.

Anonymous. *Hijazker Longa*. Gary Buttery. Whaling Music Publishers. 1978. $2.50. 5:00. III. C–e♭'. One movement. An interesting and entertaining transcription of a traditional Syrian Oud concert piece. This dancelike work is tuneful and within the normal technical demands of the instrument.

Antonij, Giovanni Battista degl'. *Ricercata Quarta*. arr. Gordon J. Kinney. Queen City Brass Publications. 1981. $6.50. 4:00. IV. B♭₁–g'. Originally a work for cello, this is an interesting study in Baroque style. Technical requirements are limited to range and extended rapid passages. It is well edited and should prove an interesting work for study and performance.

Antoniou, Theodor. *Six Likes for Solo Tuba*. Bärenreiter-Verlag, Kassel. 1968. $18.00. 12:00. V. A♭₂–b♭'. Six movements: Like a Duet; Like a Study; Like a March; Like a Cackling; Like a Song; Like a Murmuring. Composed in 1967, this avant-garde composition relies on both traditional and proportional notation. The general tessitura is quite high with considerable demands made on the upper middle and extreme high register. Perhaps its most effective utilization is as a study piece in extended techniques. Each movement is a depiction of its title. It is a very difficult work with great demands on multiphonics and coordination of finger taps in "Like a March." Very wide interval glissandi are required in the "Like a cackling." A clear explanation of symbols is included. Extended techniques used include: bends, breath sounds, valve clicks, finger taps, flutter tonguing, glissandi, indefinite rhythm, multiphonics, quarter-tone bends, trills, vocal sounds (singing). See: Bird, Gary, ed., *Program Notes for the Solo Tuba*.

Arnold, Malcolm. *Fantasy for Tuba*. Faber Music Inc. 1969. $6.95. 5:00. III–IV. F₁–c'. One movement. The range requirements of this work are modest, with most playing in the middle and lower middle register. The compositional style and notational systems are traditional. The work is a traditional fantasy with a recurring melodic theme contrasted by various sections, in almost like a rondo. With the

exception of a few measures in the Allegro section at letter C, it is a very easy work for the performer. The rapid arpeggiated passages at that point are difficult. This is a light work with few demands on performer or audience. Recorded by John Fletcher; Rodney Newman.

Bach, Johann Sebastian. *Allemande from Partita II in D Minor*. Arr. Paul Hartin. 3:30. III–IV. G♯–d'. One movement. A well-conceived transcription. The primary difficulty is to phrase and breathe without disrupting the musical flow.

Bach, Johann Sebastian. *Dance Movements*. Arr. Abe Torchinsky. G. Schirmer. 1974. $2.50. IV. D–G'. Selected dances from the unaccompanied cello suite. Similar to other collections.

Bach, Johann Sebastian. *Six Short Solo Suites*. Arr. Robert King. Robert King Music Company 1990. $4.80. III. E₁–a. 22 movements from J.S. Bach's six suites for unaccompanied cello. Well suited to the tuba and not technically demanding. These selections are good study and recital material, and should prove musically satisfying to the performer.

Bach, Johann Sebastian. *Suite #1 (cello)*. Cazes Cuivres.

Baker, Claude. *Canzonet*. Southern Music Company. 1973. $1.00. IV. F₁–e'. One movement. For Alan Estes. This work is rhythmically complex and has an improvisational character. It relies entirely on traditional technique and notation. Rhythmic interpretation and wide intervals are the primary technical challenges.

Ballif, Claude. *Solfeggietto VII*.

Bamert, Matthias. *Icon-sequenza*. G. Schirmer Inc. 1973. $1.50. 4:30. V. E₁–f♯'. One movement. To Ronald Bishop. An avant-garde composition which relies heavily on proportional and graphic notation and on extended technique and extramusical sounds, including singing in the horn, playing tam-tam and tambourine, and popping the mouthpiece.

Bashmakov, Leonid. *Cassazione*. Edition Fazer, Helsinki. 1976. $5.50. 5:00. IV–V. E₁–d'. One movement. Commissioned by 1976 Brass Congress. The general range requirements are moderate with an emphasis on performance below and just within the staff. This work is particularly idiomatic for the large tuba. It exploits the instrument without resorting to extreme registers or nontraditional techniques. The compositional style and notational system are traditional. A multisection work with numerous tempo and style changes. A brief introduction presents much of the basic material of the composition. A motive involving slurred harmonics from the second to the tenth recurs three times during the composition and serves as a unifying element. Technically, many extended passages of rapid notes, both slurred and articulated, are the primary challenge. Tremolos are the only extended technique used.

Bates, Jeremiah. *Variations on a Theme of Villa-Lobos.* Musical Evergreen. 1977. $6.50. 2:30. III–IV. F_1–a♭'. One movement. The general tessitura of this work is moderate to somewhat high, with most of the requirements within the staff. The range is much less an issue on the smaller tuba. Traditional compositional style and notational system employed. Frequent tempo shifts. The variations are separated by fermatas. Technical demands beyond range requirements are quite modest, though some instances of wide interval work are demanding. Trills are the only extended technique employed.

Baxley, Wayne S. *Tuba McDifficult Unaccompanied Multi-phonic Solo.* Clark-Baxley Publications. 1989. $5.50. 1:30. IV. G_1–e'. One movement. The general range requirements are moderate, with most of the playing within the staff. Generally, the work should provide no particular problems provided the performer is capable of multiphonics. The general compositional style and notational system are traditional. The work is loosely organized in an ABA' form. A short melody in eighth notes marked by wide intervals serves as the primary musical theme. As the subtitle suggests, multiphonics are a dominant idea in the work and basically serve as the purpose of the work.

Baxton, Anthony. *Golden Gate Scenes.*

Beach, Bennie. *Divertissement for Tuba.* Tenuto Publications. 1975. $2.00. 6:00. IV. $B♭_1$–d♭'. Three movements: Statement; Waltz; Chant. For Kent Campbell. This composition relies on solid control of the middle register and should present no special endurance concerns. This simple piece is most interesting for the younger or less-advanced performer. It should be a successful recital piece. The general style is traditional, tending toward the contemporary, and the notation is traditional. There are no great technical demands. The first movement is organized around a rhythmic/thematic motive of two sixteenths and an eighth. The second movement is a fast waltz in one. The final movement is based on an opening chantlike motive. Following the initial slow tempo, the work moves to a quicker middle section which uses many compound/complex meters with much of the same thematic material as before. It then returns to the opening style and tempo. See: Bird, Gary, ed., *Program Notes for the Solo Tuba.*

Bernaud. *Humoresque.* Associated Music Publishers.

Beveridge, Thomas. *Etude in piano e forte.* T.U.B.A. Gem, Vol. XII, no. 1. 1981. 3:00. III–IV. D♭–f'. One movement.

Blank, Allan. *Three for Barton.* Associated Music Publishers. 1974. $3.50. 6:00. IV–V. D_1–g♭'. Three movements: A Short Fantasy; Burlesque; Scene. For Barton Cummings. The general tessitura of this work is moderate, with a well-dispersed use of the middle register. There is significant use of the upper middle register throughout, but it is always

balanced with lower playing. Written in 1973, the compositional style would best be described as contemporary. Most of the notation is traditional, though it is often unmetered, and there are also instances of proportional notation. The first movement consists of contrasting sections, one dominated by repeated notes while the other is slower, more legato, and marked by multiphonics. The second movement is roughly in the form ABA'B'(C)A''. The third movement utilizes a single prominent theme set off by short episodes. Repeated-note figures hark back to the first movement. The work is technically challenging, but not unattainable for most strong players. Most technical demands lie in the areas of range, wide intervals, and control of extended techniques, which include breath sounds, foot stamps, high/low sounds/noises, flutter tonguing, glissandi, indefinite pitch, multiphonics, quarter-tone bends, one half air/one half tone.

Blatter, Alfred. *Cameos.* Media Press.

Bliss, Marilyn. *Aria.* 1:00. IV. $D♯_1$–e'. One movement. This brief work written in 1982 explores the lyric qualities of the tuba. The range and the wide intervals, often slurred, are the primary technical challenges. The work is interesting for study and very useful for performance because of its brevity.

Bliss, Marilyn. *Evocations.* New York Women Composers, Inc. 5:30. IV–V. $E♭_1$–f'. Four movements: Praeludium; Burlesque; Arioso; Largo—Finale. To Albert Plugasch. Written in 1982, this work seeks, in the composer's words, to "explore the broad range of sound, timbre, register, and emotion obtainable" with the tuba. This mildly contemporary piece relies entirely on traditional notation. The primary challenges are range, extended rapid passages, and heavy reliance on multiphonics in the final movement. An interesting work worthy of study and performance.

Borkowski, M. *Vox per uno strumento at ottone.* Polskie Wydawnictwo Muzyczne. 5:40.

Borwick, Doug. *Tuba Sonata.* Three movements: Recitative and Aria; Theme and Variations; Rondo. See: Bird, Gary, ed., *Program Notes for the Solo Tuba.*

Braun, Yehezkel. *Tubae Cantus Ante Lucem.* Israeli Music Institute. 1975. 3:30. III–IV. G–f'. Four movements: I; II; III; IV. A melodic work with interesting rhythmic diversity. Often dancelike, it is entertaining for performer and audience.

Brings, Allen. *Scherzetto.* Seesaw Music Corp. 1975. $3.00. 1:20. IV. F_1–f'. One movement. This composition places moderate demands on range but utilizes the complete range. The compositional style is contemporary, with nontonal organization. It relies entirely on traditional notation. It is a very melodic work in general format. The material is based on elements of serial technique. Without fully utilizing a single row, there are extended passages of nonrepeated pitches. This short work is rich in study material, particularly from a compositional standpoint. Extended rapid passages of a nonscale nature, wide intervallic work, and a very wide range make this a rather difficult work.

Brizzi, Aldo. *De La Tramutazione Dei Metalli II.*

Brown, Anthony. *Interim Structures.* Seesaw Music Corp. 1977. $10.00. 9:00. IV. C–bb. One movement. Range requirements in the traditional sense are not applicable here. The limited traditional playing is in a very modest register. Slides were not provided with the score and must be sought from another source. Avant-garde composition. The primary notational system is graphic, with some unmetered traditional notation. The soloist enters, lights candles, and begins with the slides. Three musical/sound events are set off between four slide sections. The primary challenge is interpreting the symbols. There is a helpful explanation of all symbols used. Very little of the piece requires actual playing, and only one of these short played passages is at all difficult. Extended techniques employed include breath sounds, fingernails on bell, half-valve, indefinite pitch, mouthpiece buzzing (with sung pitch), theatrics, vocal sounds (mumbling through horn), white noise.

Brown, Francis James. *Small Suite for Tuba Solo.* American Composers Edition. $6.98. 6:00.

Bujanovsky, Vitali. *Improvisation.* 4:00. IV. F_1–c'. One movement. The compositional style and notational systems are traditional. Many brief sections of contrasting styles and tempi are connected by a recurring thematic motive. No technical demands other than occasional wide intervals. The work should prove interesting for study and performance.

Bujanovsky, Vitali. *Monodie.* 2:00. III. F_1–db'. One movement. This brief work in a traditional style is essentially a short monologue for tuba. Few technical demands. The melodic basis of the work should be particularly interesting for younger players.

Buss, Howard J. *A Day in the City: 7 Vignettes for Unaccompanied Tuba or Bass Trombone.* Brixton Publications. 1986. $4.75. 9:30. III. Gb_1–a. Seven movements: Another Sunrise; Off to a Busy Day; Lost Key Episode; The Waitin' in Line Blues; Romantic Interlude; Sudden Storm; Out on the Town. Range requirements are quite modest with demands limited to middle-register playing. The compositional style and notation are traditional. The work is mildly programmatic, as each vignette has a descriptive title. Traditional tonal techniques are the primary harmonic language. Movements are in varying styles and show some jazz influences. The second movement has an awkward rhythmic, repeated-note passage and several rapid passages. The fourth movement is marked by a series of wide intervals which consistently return to a constant lower pitch. No great technical demands.

Buttery, Gary. *Suite for Unaccompanied Broque* [sic] *Tuba (and Tubaist* [sic]*).* Whaling Music Publishers. 1975. $3.00. 4:00. III. F_1–f'. Three movements: Allemande; Sarabande; Gigue. Tends to linger in the upper middle register and above. Written in 1973, this is an excellent work for studying the Baroque dance forms, but it is also very entertaining for performer and audience and a very effective recital piece. The compositional style and notation of this work are traditional. Though this is contemporary music, the form remains true to the Baroque suite in style and selection of dance movements. The general tessitura and extended passages of rapid sixteenths are the primary technical challenges.

Campbell, D.E. *Sonata for Unaccompanied Tuba.* TUBA Gem Vol. XII, no. 2.

Chamberlain, Robert. *Elegy.* MMB Music Inc. $2.95. 5:00. IV. One movement. For Jerry Young. This work is contemporary in style and uses some nontraditional notation. It is intended to be played into the lid of a grand piano with the damper pedal held down. The work was written in 1981 in response to the assassination of Anwar Sadat and the resulting strong feelings experienced by the composer. Extended techniques utilized include multiphonics, glissandi, speaking into the instrument, half-valve notes, and the use of a mute. Very effective work in performance. See: Bird, Gary, ed., *Program Notes for the Solo Tuba.*

Christiansen, Henning. *Kirkeby and Munch.*

Christiansen, Henning. *Kredslobsforstyrrelse.*

Cionek, Edmund. *Lamentations for Manfred (Tuba and Narrator).* Tuba-Euphonium Music Pub.

Clark, William. *Jeremy.* RBC Publications. 1989. $3.50. 2:00. I. C–eb. One movement. An excellent introduction to the unaccompanied literature and a fine teaching piece. The extended middle section is intended for bell tree and triangle, which may be performed by a nonskilled percussionist. None of the rhythms are more complicated than the dotted-eighth-and-sixteenth-note pattern.

Clark, William. *Timothy.* RBC Publications. 1989. $3.50. 2:30. II. Eb–g. One movement. This simple work is interesting study material for the young tubist. The middle section, which is written for brake drum and 20 penny nails, is a nice break. The only technical concern may be the reliance on performance within the staff.

Clark, William. *The Water Valley Flash.* RBC Publications. 1989. $3.50. 1:30. I. Bb–d. One movement. For Jim Shearer. For the beginner player. The jazz style should be entertaining. A middle section for suspended cymbal gives a break and musical contrast. None of the rhythms are more complicated than the dotted-eighth and sixteenth-note patterns.

Colding-Jørgensen, Henrik. *Boast.* Dansk Musik. 1984. 3:00. V. D_1–g'. One movement. For Michael

Lind. Composed in 1980. Relies heavily on the extreme high register. As its name suggests, perhaps the greatest value of this work is to boast of one's technical prowess. Nevertheless, if performed convincingly, it can be an audience thriller. The general compositional style is traditional, as is the notational system, though it is unmetered. The work derives from the tradition of the fantasia and is in many regards an extended, stand-alone cadenza. The single movement is marked in sections by many tempo and style changes. The work relies heavily on advanced traditional technique, particularly in its use of extended rapid passages often in the extreme high register. Many very wide intervallic leaps and phrases of extreme range. Glissandi are the only extended technique.

Constantinides, Dinos. *Piece for Solo Tuba.* T.A.P. 1979. $2.00. 4:00. IV–V. F#$_1$–f '. One movement. In a contemporary style, rhythmically complex. There is significant use of proportional notation. Technical challenges include rapid arpeggiated slurs and wide leaps.

Cooper, Steve. *7 Modal Tunes for Tuba.* T.U.B.A. GEM Vol. XI, no. 2. 1978. 3:00. III. A–b♭'. Seven movements: Dorian; Aeolian; Lydian; Phrygian; Ionian; Locrian; Mixolydian. Extended passages of rapid notes and occasional wide leaps dominate these short studies.

Cope, David. *BTRB.* Brass Music Ltd. 1974. $7.00. IV. One movement. For Tom Everett. This work is theatrical in nature and relies almost entirely on extramusical sounds. Various special effects are achieved by using bassoon reeds, foot stomps, and the like. The work was originally written for Bass Trombone but it may be adapted for any brass instrument.

Cresswell, Lyell. *Drones IV.* ALM. 1977. 6:00. IV–V. G$_1$–f#'. One movement. For Melvyn Poore. This avant-garde composition is primarily a sound painting. It calls for a high-pitched drone. Notation is entirely proportional and graphic. Events are measured in seconds. There is considerable use of vocalization.

Creuze, Roland. *Eria.* Editions Gérard Billaudot. 1985. $6.50. 6:30. V. G♭$_1$–a'. One movement. For Fernand Lelong. Written in 1980. Relies on high-register playing. An explanation of the symbols would be helpful, as there are several nontraditional symbols. The general compositional style is contemporary, mostly unmetered traditional notation with some instances of proportional notation. There is considerable use of flutter-tongued passages and repeated-note patterns in proportional notation which accelerate or slow. Extended flutter-tongued passages of rapidly changing pitches are difficult. Changes between normal tonguing and flutter tonguing occur regularly within a line. Awkward intervals and a rather disjunct style are additional difficulties. Extended techniques include

bends and flutter tonguing. Recorded by Fernand LeLong. See Thompson/Lemke, *French Literature for Low Brass Instruments.*

Croley, Randel. *Variazioni.* Avant Music. 1968. $4.95. 7:00. III–IV. E$_1$–b. One movement. The range of this work is moderate but requires control throughout the middle register. The majority of the writing is within the staff. The single greatest challenge is to make the composition musically interesting as it has a tendency to ramble. The general compositional style is contemporary; the traditional notation is unmetered but uses bar lines. The single movement is highly sectionalized with many tempo and style changes. Two primary sections serve as thematic material for the variation. No special technical demands, though control of the middle register and accurate rhythmic interpretation are essential.

Cummings, Barton. *Brief Moments.* PRB Productions. 1989. $6.00. 4:30. III. F$_1$–e'. Five movements: Sprightly Dance; Melancholia; Crisply Clean; Waltzing; Marching. The simple melodic character and reliance on basic technique make this an excellent first unaccompanied work. Technical demands are limited to sixteenth-note passages, which are not extensive except in the third movement.

Cummings, Barton. *Musings.* Kiwi Music Press. 1985. $1.50. 2:00. IV. E$_1$–e'. Three movements: Reflections; Currents; Reflections Two. The general range is moderate with a tendency to emphasize the upper middle and high registers, with most writing within the staff. The compositional style is contemporary and the notation system is primarily traditional though often unmetered, and it uses a single incident of proportional notation. The outer movements are generally lyric and, though unmetered, are dominated by a quarter-note pulse. The second movement begins with a brief quasi-cadenza, moves to a rapid section of frequently shifting meter emphasizing the compound subdivisions, returns to the quasi-cadenza style, and finally finishes with a brief Allegro. Technical demands are quite modest, with wide slurred intervals and control of range the major concerns.

Cummings, Barton. *Three Moods.* Musical Evergreen. 1976. $3.95. 3:00. III. C$_1$–f '. Three movements: Lightly; Lento—Rubato; Lightly—Staccato. The general range requirements of this work are moderate. The compositional style and notation system used are traditional. Very wide dynamic shifts occur throughout the work. Technical demands are moderate. Low-register passages in the second movement and rapid rearticulated pitches in the third movement are the primary technical requirements.

Cummings, Barton, arr. *Song of the Trouvères.* Edition Musicus. 1980. $2.50. 5:00. II–III. E–a. Seven movements: En ma dame; Ja nuns hon pris; C'est la fin; Douce dame; E, dame jolie; Vos n'aler; Pour mon cuer. Simple tunes from the Renaissance and

Middle Ages with suggested (optional) percussion parts. The works provide no particular technical challenges but may prove an interesting experience in an often neglected musical style.

Dalbavie, Marc. *Petite Interlude*. Editions Gérard Billaudot. 1992. $4.95. 4:00. V. C–f#'. One movement. For Fernand Lelong. See: Thompson/Lemke, *French Literature for Low Brass Instruments*.

Danburg, Russell. *Five Extemporizations*. Kendor Music Company Inc. 1985. $5.00. 9:00. IV. F₁–d'. Five movements: Lento e doloroso; Andante maestoso (tempo di polacca) with fervor but not fast; Adagio con espressivo; Allegretto (tempo di valse); Andantino giocoso (tempo di boogie) in a rollicking style, but not fast. For Harvey Phillips. This work relies on middle and upper middle register playing, making the general range demands moderate with most requirements within the staff. Very approachable for most good performers and all audiences. The general compositional style and notation are traditional. The four movements are in a slow, fast, slow, fast arrangement, with slow movements being songlike and fast movements dancelike. Solid control of lyric playing, particularly in the wide intervals, is required throughout. Technical demands are modest, though control of sixteenth-triplets in the second movement and accurate dotted eighths and sixteens in contrast to eighth triplets in the fifth movement are essential.

Danburg, Russell. *Sonatina*. Wing. $4.00.

Dobrowolski, Andrzej. *Muzyka na tubę*. Polskie Wydawnictwo Muzyczne. 12:05. V–VI. Three movements. Written in 1973, this avant-garde work is unusual for its use of prepared tuba in the second movement. Besides great demands on traditional technique, a great portion of the work relies on extended techniques. Primarily this is an exploration of the sound possibilities of the tuba.

Dragonetti, D. *Concert Etude*. arr. Randall Block. Musical Evergreen. $3.95. 2:30. III–IV. E–g'. One movement. The primary technical demands of this work are extended passages of sixteenths and the somewhat high tessitura. It is an entertaining work that works particularly well on the F tuba.

Dubrovay, László. *Solo No. 3*. Editio Musica Budapest. 1986. 8:40. V. B♭₂–d♭". Three movements: I; II; III. Relies almost entirely on graphic notation, which is fully explained, though in German. Musically it is an exploration of sounds and colors with considerable latitude for performer interpretation.

Dutton, Brent. *Four Expansions*. Seesaw Music Corp. 1976. $5.00. 3:00. V. B♭₂–b♭'. Four movements: Moderato; Slow; Dance; Moderato. For Ron Bishop. While this work generally lies in the middle register, there are frequent occurrences of both extremes. It demands complete control of the instrument's entire range. The general compositional style is contemporary and the notation traditional.

An additional challenge is the cluttered appearance of the manuscript. Glissandi are the only extended technique.

Dutton, Brent. *Polis for Unaided Tuba*. Seesaw Music Corp. 1977. $6.00. 3:00. V. B♭₂–e♭". One movement. The general range requirements of this work are quite extensive and relatively evenly divided between the extreme high and low registers. This avant-garde composition, written in 1970, utilizes proportional, frame, and traditional notation. A glissando effect simulating a motorcycle serves as a unifying element; it occurs at the beginning and end as well as once more in the body of the work. Another, more-traditional line occurs twice and serves as a second unifying motive. Many contrasts are exploited in this work, such as the juxtaposition of great range extremes, muted versus natural sounds, and breath sounds versus played pitches. Once the technical demands of range and coordination of mute insertion and withdrawal while performing are surmounted, there remains the great challenge to make musical sense of the work. The extensive notes are helpful in interpretation, but their occasional inclusion between lines adds to the untidy appearance of the score. Extended techniques used include breath sounds, glissandi, and multiphonics, and a mute is required.

Dutton, Brent. *Thème Varié*. Seesaw Music Corp. 1980. $4.00. 5:30. V. B₂–a'. One movement. Though most of the work is in the middle register, extended passages during the opening place great demands on the high register. The general compositional style is contemporary; the notation is primarily traditional with significant use of proportional notation. The work is a very free set of variations. A fermata marks the end of most sections, and often there is a tempo change for the new section. The work culminates in a three-to-five second section of "totally chaotic playing," which is entirely without notation except to give the final pitch. Technical demands inclue extensive use of multiphonics with independence of each line, random pitch selection, and lengthy passages of rapid arpeggiation which are sometimes played and sometimes sung in a multiphonic.

Emmerson, Simon. *Variations for Tuba*. Arts Lab Music Publishing. 1977. $7.00. 3:00. V. E♭₂–e♭". One movement. Range requirements are extensive in both directions, with equal emphasis on high and low registers. Composed in 1976, this piece is in contemporary style and utilizes proportional notation almost entirely, except for some instances of graphic notation depicting the general contour of glissando lines. This work has an improvisatory character. The opening is dominated by sustained pitches with increased activity between each occurrence as the pace increases. The body of the work is dominated by a series of pitches performed as fast as possible. The wide range and long passages of rapid pitches with irregular accents are the primary technical difficulties. Extended techniques include bends, glissandi, indefinite pitch, microtonal pitch (in sung parts only), multiphonics, mouthpiece buzzing, timbre trills, trills.

Feiler, Christian. *Fünf Schritte.* E_1–$c\sharp^1$. Five movements: I; II; III; IV; V. See below, Unkrodt, *Reige Vortragsliteratur.*

Fennelly, Brian. *Tesserae V.* American Composers Edition. 1980. 7:00. V. C_1–$g\sharp^1$. Three movements: Introduction—Pilafony I—Sombre Sounds (A); Pilafony II—Sombre Sounds (B)—Solemn Song; Coda: Toccata. A rhythmically and technically complex work. Absolute control is required to achieve an effective musical performance. Extended techniques include multiphonics, tonguing noises, and theatrical instructions.

Fodi, John. *Four Bagatelles.* Canadian Music Centre. 1979. 4:00. IV. E_1–$f\sharp^1$. Four movements: ♩ = 72; ♩ = 64; ♩ = 84; ♩ = 72. Rhythmic complexities with a great deal of syncopation and wide intervals are the challenging technical aspects of this work. Without careful interpretation, these movements take on a rambling character.

Frackenpohl, Arthur. *Sonata for Solo Tuba.* TUBA Press. 1993. 8:35. IV. C_1–d^1. Four movements: Slowly; Very Fast; Freely; Fast. With the exception of the third movement, which is unmetered and has proportional notation, this work is essentially traditional in style. It requires absolute technical control of the instrument and has many extended passages of rapid notes and disjunct intervals.

Frackenpohl, Arthur. *Studies on Christmas Carols.* Kendor Music Company Inc. 1981. $6.50. II–III. G_1–$b\flat$. Twelve songs: O Come, All ye Faithful; We Wish You a Merry Christmas; Away in a Manger; Go, Tell It on the Mountain; Angels We Have Heard on High; The Friendly Beasts; Jolly Old St. Nicholas; Hark! The Herald Angels Sing; What Child Is This?; Jingle Bells; Fum! Fum! Fum!; Deck the Halls. Each of these traditional carols is dealt with in a simple theme-and-variation form. They are interesting for younger players and very functional for seasonal performances by any tubist.

Frackenpohl, Arthur. *Tubatunes.* Almitra Music/Kendor Music. 1981. $6.00. 15:00 (10:30 with cuts). III. C_1–$e\flat^1$(F_1–$c\sharp^1$). Four movements: Rag; Waltz Ballad; Latin Jazz; Blues. For Daniel Perantoni. Range requirements are moderate, with all demands within the middle register. The compositional style and notational system are traditional. A very light work with considerable jazz influence. The movements are very simple, with optional cuts and ossia parts provided to make this work accessible to the younger player, who would most enjoy it. There are optional improvisation sections in the third and fourth movements with chord symbols provided. The most difficult aspect is coordinating playing and percussive effects within a single inte-

grated line. Otherwise, technical demands are quite modest and confined to rapid articulations in sixteenths and smooth, lyric performance within the staff. Extended techniques include bends, foot stamps, glissandi, and timbre trill (articulation with valves).

Frank, Marcel G. *Andante and Allegro.* 3:00. III. $B\flat_1$–$e\flat^1$. Two movements: Moderately Slow; Lively. Written in 1973, this work is traditional in notation and style. No unusual technical demands.

Frank, Marcel G. *Sonata.* 7:30. III–IV. $D\flat_1$–e^1. Five movements: Brightly; Moderately; Slowly; Gaily; Moderately Fast. To Winston Morris. Traditional notation and style. The music is thematically and melodically based. No particular technical challenges.

Freedman, Harry. *Caper.* Canadian Music Centre. 1978. 5:00. IV. A_1–f^1. One movement. Commissioned by Dennis Miller with the assistance of the Canada Council. An interesting work of a mildly theatrical mature. Foot stomps, valve clicks, multiphonics, and vocalization permeate the work. There is a great element of humor in this very successful and entertaining work.

Friedman, Stan. *Ossia.* Seesaw Music Corp. 1984. $6.00. 8:00. IV–V. $C\sharp_1$–$f\sharp^1$. One movement. North Carolina State Music Teachers Association. Moderate range requirements, with generally well-balanced use of the entire middle register with some emphasis on the upper middle and upper register. Composed in 1980 (revised 1983) in contemporary style and entirely in proportional notation. Tempo is estimated by the statement that each system is approximately ten seconds in duration. Interpreting all symbols and presenting all accents and nuances are critical to the success of this work. There are very few explanations, but the work is generally easy to interpret. Control of wide slurs, often into the high register, rapid slurred passages, and multiphonics are the primary challenges. Extended techniques include glissandi, multiphonics, trills.

Fritze, Gregory. *Yevrah Yad Thrib Bypah.* $5.00. 7:00. IV. C_1–f^1. Four movements: Slow and Dramatic; Lento Rubato; Dancelike; Allegro non troppo. To Harvey Phillips. The notation is primarily traditional, though there are instances of approximate pitch notation. The compositional style is essentially traditional with the addition of extended techniques including multiphonics, mouthpiece pops, and taps to extend the sound palette. Wide intervals are the primary technical challenge. See: Bird, Gary, ed., *Program Notes for the Solo Tuba.*

Fulkerson, James. *Patterns III.* Media Press. 1969. 4:00. IV. $B\flat_2$–g^1. One movement. This work relies heavily on extended techniques. It uses the full range of the instrument, including extremes in both directions during traditional performance sections. This difficult avant-garde composition utilizes frame and graphic notation as well as traditional notation. An explanation of symbols is included. The work is an exploration of sound possibilities. Some sections are pointillistic as isolated notes occur in varied registers. The work may be best described as a "sound scape," a painting with sounds. Besides the great range requirements, there are intricate alternations between singing, playing, and vocal clicks/clucks within a continuous line. It also calls for removing the mute while maintaining a multiphonic. Extended techniques include breath sounds, Doppler effect, mouthpiece pops, flutter tonguing, multiphonics, timbre trill, trills, vocal sounds, whistle tone, white noise, mute.

Gabrieli, Domenico. *Ricercar.* arr. by R. Winston Morris . Shawnee Press Inc. 1974. $1.75. 3:30. III–IV. G_1–c^1. One movement. Originally for unaccompanied cello. An excellent study or recital piece in the Baroque style. Technical demands are limited to extended passages of sixteenth notes. Recorded by Ronald Davis; Edward R. McKee.

Gallagher, Jack. *Sonata Breve.* The Brass Press. 1983. $4.00. 4:30. III. G_1–c^1 (G_1–$e^{\flat1}$). Four movements: With conviction; Introspectively; Swaggeringly; With energy. For Tucker Jolly. This work relies heavily on the middle register, thereby making limited demands on endurance or general range. It is interesting for its use of a traditional Classical structure in an unaccompanied work and is therefore a good study and teaching piece. The first movement is in sonata allegro form. The second movement is songlike. The third movement is a dance in compound time, and the fourth is a short rondo-like movement.

Galloway, Scott. *Essay for Tuba.*

Geissler, Siegfried. *Studie V für Tuba.* 3:30. F_1–g^1. One movement. See below, Unkrodt, *Reige Vortragsliteratur.*

Ghezzo, Dinu. *Sound Shapes II.* Seesaw Music Corp.

Glaser, Verner Wolf. *Two Tuba Tunes.* Swedish Music Information Center.

Globokar, Vinko. *Echanges für einen Blechbläser.* Henry Litolff's Verlag/C.F.Peters. 1975. $44.35. 8:00. IV. One movement. Written in 1973, in avant-garde compositional style and entirely graphic notation. Intended for any brass instrument. A tone row is given which may be used in interpreting the symbols. A microphone is placed near specific slide/valve openings and loudspeakers are placed behind the audience. The work is basically an exploration of sounds and sound possibilities. The primary difficulty is in interpreting the symbols, for which an explanation is given in German. A great deal of time and effort are required to prepare this work. Extended techniques include bends, flutter tonguing, glissandi, trills, mute, varied mouthpieces, and reeds.

Globokar, Vinko. *Introspection d'un Tubist.*

Globokar, Vinko. *Res/As/Ex/Ins-pirer.*

Golightly, D.F. *Serenade for Solo Tuba, Op. 4.* Modrana. 1979. $2.45. 4:30. IV. D_1–$a^{\sharp1}$. Three movements: March; Elegy; Galop. For James Anderson. Range requirements are quite significant, with frequent use of extreme registers in both directions requiring complete control of the instrument. The compositional style and notation system are traditional. The title of each movement is an accurate portrayal of the material which follows. The primary technical demands are the very wide range, and the use of wide intervals, extended passages of articulated sixteenth notes in March, and complicated rhythmic subdivisions of the beat in Galop.

Golob, Jani. *TubaBlues.*

Grant, James. *Three Furies.* Grantwood Music Press. 1993. $9.50 (+ $1.50 shipping). 10:15. V. $C^{\flat}_1$–g^1. Three movements: Fury I; Fury II; Fury III. For Mark Nelson. This work in a contemporary style relies entirely on traditional notation. Rhythmically, the work is very complex. Extended rapid passages, very wide leaps, and passages encompassing extremes of range make this a tremendously difficult work. The only extended technique involves half-valve effects. Motivically based, this is a very interesting work.

Gregson, Edward. *Alarum.* Recorded by James Gourlay.

Gruner, Joachim. *Solo für Tuba.* 5:00. C_1–a^1. One movement. See below, Unkrodt, *Reige Vortragsliteratur.*

Ha, Jae Eun. *Three Abstracts for Tuba.* Neil A. Kjos Music Company. 1978. $6.00. 8:00. IV–V. C_1–ab^1 (Eb_1–ab^1). Three movements: With much freedom in improvisational style; Molto tranquillo; Freely and fantastically. To Barton Cummings. Range requirements are quite demanding, from extreme low to extreme high. Complete flexibility within and between registers is required. A very difficult work which is very effective in performance. This avant-garde composition utilizes proportional, frame, and graphic notation as well as unmetered traditional notation. Generally, motives tend to grow from a basic germ of an idea to a larger form by extension. This work involves extreme range, very rapid passages, and very wide intervallic work. Extended techniques include breath sounds, flutter tonguing, glissandi, key clicks, quarter-tone bends, tremolos, and use of a mute. Recorded by Barton Cummings.

Haddad, Don. *Short Suite.* Seesaw Music Corp. 1975. $5.50. 4:00. III. G_1–$e^{\flat1}$. Four movements: Freely; ♩. = c.60; Freely; ♩ = c.138. The range demands of this work are moderate with an emphasis on work within the staff. A good introductory work for those unfamiliar with the unaccompanied genre. The compositional style and notation are traditional. Each movement is short, simple, and tuneful, more in the style of well-crafted etudes. Technical demands are modest in every regard. There is passage work in sixteenth notes with many accidentals, but most lines are scalewise with all notes true to a given key.

Hahn, Gunnar. *4 Winds.*

Hanks, Paul. *Solo No.1; Three Short Pieces.* Tomorrow Brass Series. 4:00. IV. C$\sharp_1$–f'. Three movements: $\downarrow$ = 90; $\downarrow$ = 50; $\downarrow$ = 90. For Tom Hancock. This work in a contemporary style is like a series of monologues. Two of the three movements are unmetered, and there are many instances of proportional notation. Requires a great deal of flutter tonguing and the use of a mute. Rhythmically, the work is complex.

Hanson, Ronald D. *Escapement.* To Mark Nelson. 7:00. V. F$_1$–eb'. One movement. This work relies entirely on traditional notation and displays a very complex rhythmic palette. Because of the constant rhythmic flow, it is tremendously difficult.

Harmon, R. C. *Suite for Solo Tuba.* 8:30. IV. G$_1$–f'. Six movements: Praeludium; Marcia; Sarabande; Bourrée; Minuetto; Finale. This work is traditional in notation and style and is primarily based on thematic and motivic development. Wide leaps and passages which span a very wide range are the primary technical challenges.

Harris, Roger. *Suite for Solo Tuba.* Seesaw Music Corp. 1976. $7.50. 4:45. III. F$_1$–c'. Four movements: Fanfare; Badinage; Loure; March. Modest range requirements, with emphasis on the middle register and an avoidance of extreme registers. Composed in 1970. Traditional compositional style and notational system. This work is dominated by melodic/thematic material.

Hartley, Walter S. *Music for Tuba Solo.* Philharmusica Corp. 1974. $7.50. 5:00. IV. Eb$_1$–g'. Four movements: I. Andante; II. Allegro; III. Largo; IV. Presto. For Harvey Phillips. Moderate range requirements with a well-distributed use of the middle register. Contemporary compositional style in traditional notation. The first movement is dominated by wide intervals usually in the context of long phrases. The second movement is in 5/8 time with shifting subdivision of the bar. The third movement has very wide intervals reached by glissando, rapid passages in 32nd notes, and very wide intervals within sixteenth-note passages. It is technically the most demanding movement. The fourth movement is in cut time, utilizing a repeated-note motive in eighth notes, contrasted with passages of moving eighth notes. Extended techniques include flutter tonguing, glissandi, trills.

Hartley, Walter S. *Suite for Unaccompanied Tuba.* Elkan-Vogel. 1964. $2.00. 5:00. IV. G$_1$–b. Four movements: Intrada; Valse; Air; Galop. Moderate range with emphasis on upper middle-register playing. Written in 1962, this work is widely used as an introductory piece to the unaccompanied literature for tuba. Its compositional style is mildly contemporary, and it utilizes traditional notation. This loose interpretation of the dance suite does not rely

on actual dance forms, but its movements are dancelike. The primary difficulty lies in the disjunct nature of the melodic/harmonic contour, which makes use of many awkward intervals. Pitch accuracy and interpretive skills are the major challenges technically and musically for the performer. See: Bird, Gary, ed., *Program Notes for the Solo Tuba.* Recorded by Peter Popiel; John Fletcher; and Rex Conner.

Hartzell, Eugene. *Monologue 17: Toying for Tuba.* Ludwig Doblinger KG. 1987. $11.10. 6:00. IV. C$_1$–c'. One movement. Written in 1983. Moderate range requirements with an emphasis on the lower middle register. A solid composition worthy of attention. In contemporary style using traditional notation. Considerable rhythmic diversity utilizes duple subdivisions as small as the 32nd note, as well as triplets, sextuplets, and septuplets. Excellent melodic use of the extreme low register. Tempo shifts mark sections of the work. The only extended techniques required are trills and the use of a mute.

Hermanson, Christer. *Waves.* MIC.

Hewitt, Harry. *Twelve Preludes, Op. 376A.* 1973. 17:00. IV. D$_1$–ab'. Can be performed with or without tape accompaniment prepared by the tubist or as a duet for two tubas. In any event, the work seems inadequate without the second part. Range is the only technical problem.

Hilprecht, Uwe. *Vier Haltungen zu einem alten Thema.* Ab$_2$–ab''. Five movements: Thema; Der Melancholiker; Der Sanguiniker; Der Phlegmatiker; Der Choleriker. See below, Unkrodt, *Reige Vortragsliteratur.*

Hoag, Charles. *Tubaplay.* 6:00. V–VI. Bb$_2$–a'. Eight movements: Prelude; Gung with the Wind; Interlude; Tango; Interlude; Soft-shoe Dance; Interlude; Final Bounce. Commissioned by Scott Watson, Skip Gray, and Jerry Young. The tubist is also required to play gong, bass drum, and suspended cymbal. Probably the greatest challenge is the coordination between the percussion and tuba playing, as the parts are thoroughly integrated. The piece is very effective in performances, but requires extensive preparation.

Israel, Brian. *Suite for Unaccompanied Tuba.* Tritone Press. 1982. $2.50. 5:30. III–IV. F$_1$–d'. Four movements: Allemande; Courante; Gavotte; Gigue. For Randal Foil. Written in 1980. Moderate range requirements with some significant upper middle-register passages. Every effort should be made to understand and portray the traditional dance form of each movement in order to allow the contrast of the more modern extended tonality to work. Essentially traditional compositional style and notation. The work applies the broad architecture of the Baroque dance suite to a more modern tonal palette. The tonal twists of the melodies make the work challenging in initial stages of study. Extended passages of rapid notes, both scalewise and arpeggiated, often with numerous accidentals, are the primary technical demand.

Jager, Robert. *Diverse Moments #1*. Wingert-Jones Music Inc. 1978. $4.00. 5:30. III. B_1–c'. Five movements: March; Elegy; Waltz; Ballad; Scherzo. For R. Winston Morris. This work relies primarily on middle- and lower middle-register playing. The compositional style and notational system are traditional. Technical and musical demands are kept to a minimum, although the moving eighth-note passages in the Waltz (in one) and the alternation between cut time and 3/4 meter in the Scherzo are challenging.

Johnson, Tom. *Monologue for Tuba*. Two-Eighteen Press. 1976. A theatrical work for tuba, talking and playing. A fun piece for performer and audience alike.

Jones, Roger. *Design No. 1*. Laissez-Faire Music/TUBA Press. 1983. 4:00. IV. E_1–e'. Two movements: ♩ = c.60; ♩ = c.72. For Constance Weldon. Moderate range requirements with a well-balanced use of the entire middle register and some emphasis on the upper register. The compositional style and notation are traditional. The general style of the work is simple. The numerous technical demands include wide intervals and rather complicated rhythmic activity. Perhaps the greatest challenge is to arrive at an interesting interpretation of the music.

Joubert, Claude-Henry. *Petite Suite*. Editions M. Combre. 1982. $6.00. 6:30. III. A_1–e'. Four movements: Prélude et Fugue; Sarabande; Menuet; Gigue. For Jean-Pierre Besançon. Moderate range requirements with an emphasis on the upper middle register. An excellent study and recital piece, entertaining for audience and performer alike. This reinterpretation of the unaccompanied suite is light in style and particularly useful for the study of traditional dance forms. It is designated as an elementary piece on the score, and with some minor octave transposition would work well as an elementary piece for euphonium. A very lyric work that makes solid demands on general technique. Wide intervals are not uncommon, and the general style concerns of each dance are important to proper interpretation.

Kagel, Mauricio. *Mirum*. Universal Edition A.G. 1974. $4.00. IV. D♭₁–g'. One movement. The general tessitura of this work is quite high. Composed in 1965, it is particularly worthy of performance and study because of the international stature of the composer and the unique quality of the work. An avant-garde composition which relies heavily on theatrics. The pitch/rhythmic notation is traditional, but short staves are used without meter to notate individual events, each set off from the next by text. The work is a series of events often using words or other theatrical elements between performed passages. Several isolated passages are

technically difficult and require special attention. In general, individual passages are relatively less difficult than the pacing and continuity considerations of the work as a whole. Extended techniques include flutter tonguing and glissandi.

Kasai, Kiyoshiro. *Music for Tuba*. 1985. 4:00. IV–V. G_2–c". One movement. For Takashi Abo. This work is very free in style and contemporary in its musical language. There are passages of graphic notation as well as note stems without pitch designation. The extreme range is the greatest challenge.

Katzenbeier, Hubert. *Drei Spielstücke für Tuba Solo*. 7:25. D_1–f'. Three movements: Spielstücke I; Spielstücke II; Spielstücke III. See below, Unkrodt, *Reige Vortragsliteratur*.

Kavanaugh, Patrick. *Debussy Variations: No. 14 for Solo Tuba*. Pembroke Music Co. 1977. $5.00. 5:00. IV–V. One movement. For Lynn Robinson. The score is cluttered and difficult to interpret. Coordination of slide removal and the like is at least as much of a challenge as performance technique. The compositional style is avant-garde and there is considerable proportional and graphic notation. This is an extensive exploration of nontraditional sounds on the tuba. Valve slides must be almost constantly manipulated, often removed quickly to produce a "pop." Several staves are intended to be interpreted simultaneously. Even though extensive explanations are given, some notation is not completely clear. In general, the work relies on gestures and rapid flourishes to create a sound environment. Extended techniques include breath sounds, mouthpiece pops, flutter tonguing, half-valve, lip trills, lip buzzing, multiphonics, quick removal of slides, finger-stopping slides, vocal sounds.

Kayser, Leif. *Monolog for Solo Tuba*.

Kessler, Jim. *Etude*. 0:30. III. D_1–c'. One movement. This very short work is a useful study in 7/8 meter. No unusual technical challenges.

Khoudoyan, Adam. *Elégie*. Editions BIM. $10.50.

Kibbe, Michael. *Three Lyric Pieces*. Seesaw Music Corp. 1975. $5.50. 2:30. III. F_1–c'. Three movements: Andante; Allegro; Moderato. Composed in 1968. Modest range. This work is useful as study material for younger students. The compositional style and notational system are traditional, and the harmonic language is tonal. The three very short movements are more like etudes than concert material. They make minimal demands on technique and provide sight-reading material for good players. The primary demand is control of legato playing.

Kinney, Gordon J. *Improvisation for Solo Tuba*. T.U.B.A. Gem. 1976. 1:30. III–IV. A♭–f'. One movement. For Rex Conner. This work is traditional in style and notation. There are no particular technical challenges other than a somewhat high tessitura and a couple of rapid passages.

Kinney, Gordon J. *Little Suite for Tuba*. Studio P/R. 1973. $2.50. 7:00. III. G_1–e♭'. Four movements:

Prelude; Caprice; Air tendre; Bourrée. For Rex Conner. Moderate range requirements with an emphasis on the upper middle register. The compositional style and notational system are traditional. This collection of dances and dancelike movements is simple and tuneful. It requires solid control of the middle and upper-middle register. Wide interval slurs are the single most demanding technical aspect.

Kinney, Gordon J. *Ricercar for Tuba*. Studio P/R. 1973. $2.00. 2:00. III. B_1–d'. One movement. Moderate range requirements with no extreme demands in either direction. The bulk of the composition lies within the staff. The compositional style and notation are traditional. A short, very simple work in ABA' form with each section labeled in the score. No significant technical demands other than control of lyric playing in the upper middle register.

Kjär, Vildfred. *3 Plays the Tuba*.

Klauss, Kenneth. *Sonata for Solo Tuba*. Composers Autograph Pub. 1969.

Klucevsek, Guy. *Elegy for Solo Tuba*. 2:30. III–IV. $G\sharp$–$g\sharp'$. One movement. In memory of Dr. Martin Luther King, Jr. Written in 1970, this improvisatory work relies on traditional notation. The often high tessitura is its primary technical challenge. An interesting and evocative work.

Knudsen, Per Egil. *Tre Miniatyrer*.

Koch, Erland von. *Monolog nr 9*. Carl Gehrmans Musikförlag. 1977. $8.00. 5:00. III–IV. F_1–bb' (F_1–e'). Two movements: Andante; Allegro vivace. Range requirements are moderate if the lower ossia parts are performed. Most of the work is within the staff with extended use of upper middle-register playing. Without ossia parts, there are significant high-register demands. Composed in 1975, this entertaining work is equally pleasurable for performer and audience. The compositional style and notation are traditional. Each movement begins with the statement of a theme which forms the basis for the movement. The work is very melodic, simple in form, musically light, and very pleasing. The primary technical demand is range, which in most cases is simplified in an ossia part. See: Bird, Gary, ed., *Program Notes for the Solo Tuba*. Recorded by Michael Lind.

Kochan, Günter. *Monolog*. Gb–g'. One movement. See below, Unkrodt, *Reige Vortragsliteratur*.

Kohlenberg, Oliver. *Le torre di Bologna* (*The Towers of Bologna*). Jasemusiikki. 1991. IV. Eb_1–f'. Seven movements and coda: A. Maestoso e lugubre; B. Poco agitato; C. Più agitato; D. Cantabile; E. Lugubre e sombre; F. Poco scherzando; G. Lamentoso, con dolore; Coda. The composer suggests that the piece should always begin with movement (section) A and end with section G and Coda, but the other sections may be played in any order or omitted. Each section is marked with a repeat, which is also optional. The composer also suggests

that pauses of any length may occur between sections and that other works may be performed during pauses. The work uses traditional notation throughout but utilizes syncopations to break the normal feel of the meter. Melodic lines are angular and contemporary in style.

Kraft, William. *Encounters II*. MCA Music / Editions BIM. 1970 / 1991. 6:00. V. C_2–bb'. One movement. For Roger Bobo. This work exploits the complete range of the tuba, with particular emphasis on the upper middle and high registers. Composed in 1966, this is one of the most performed works in the tuba's repertoire. It is in contemporary style and relies on traditional notation. According to the composer, it is a set of variations, but that is not obvious. Each section is marked by a double bar and a change of tempo and/or style. The extended multiphonic section demands pitch accuracy for effective performance, and the technical demands of the final page are very substantial. The overall technical demands are enormous, but the greater challenge is to surmount them and move toward a purely musical interpretation and performance. Extended techniques include glissandi, multiphonics, timbre trills, trills. See: Bird, Gary, ed., *Program Notes for the Solo Tuba*. Recorded by Roger Bobo; Oystein Baadsvik.

Krush, Jay. *I Will Speak Briefly On....* 9:00. IV. C_1–c'. One movement. This theatre piece consists of a very long text with brief musical interludes involving passages of proportional notation and passages of vocalizations through the instrument. This work was written in 1973 and is unique within the medium.

Krzanowski, Andrzej. *Sonata*. Polskie Wydawnictwo Muzyczne. 1985. 14:00. IV. $C\sharp_1$–ab'. One movement. For Zdzislawowi Piernikowi. Modest range requirements with a few extended passages in the high register. Written in 1978, this is an important piece in the genre because of its minimalist tendencies. It is not appropriate for every audience and will not prove fulfilling for many performers, but it is unique within the literature and worthy of study. The general style is contemporary and, though there is some use of proportional notation, the notations is primarily traditional without meter. This work relies on a motivic idea repeated endlessly with only slight variation. Distinct sections are marked by tempo changes and fermatas. As an element of contrast, there are slow, lyric passages at much lower dynamic levels, but the original cell always dominates. If the range is within grasp, the only technical difficulty is endurance. The only extended technique employed is indefinite pitch. Recorded by Zdzislaw Piernik.

Kuehn, Mikel. *Jigsaw*. Available from the composer. 9:15. V–VI. B_1–g'. Three movements: I; II; III. Written for Mark Cox, dedicated to David Kuehn. As the composer states, "each movement possesses a separate structural design and emphasizes a different model of time—movement I is non-linear, movement II linear, and movement III combines both non-linear and linear elements." Very advanced traditional notation, with nontraditional notation clearly explained in performance notes. Wide intervals and very complex rhythmic patterns are the primary technical demands. Extended techniques include flutter tonguing, multiphonics, glissandi, tone alteration, and circular breathing.

Kuhn, Charles. *Improvisation for Unaccompanied Tuba*. Tomorrow Brass Series. 1972. 3:00. IV. D–e♭'. One movement. This work is traditional in general style and relies on traditional notation. Other than a few wide leaps and rapid passages, it presents no special challenges.

Kühnl, Claus. *Hommage à Schubert*. Breitkopf & Härtel. 1986. 5:00. F₁–e". One movement. For Malte Burba and Klaus Burger. This work is intended for alphorn or any brass instrument. It is a theatrical piece and relies heavily on the performer's acting ability in the portrayal of frame characters. Extended techniques include breath sounds, multiphonics, and knocking on the instrument. There are extensive explanatory notes covering notation and performance suggestions.

Kurylewicz, A. *Tubesque for Solo Tuba*. TUBA Press. $7.00. 9:00. V. C₁–a'. Four movements: Allegro; Canzona; Tango—Grotesque; Presto. This work employs graphic and frame notation as well as traditional notation. All movements are without meter. A very difficult work involving wide intervals, often with glissando, extreme range, and extended rapid passages. No explanation of the notation is included, and some notes are missing in the manuscript. Movements are based on motives, which should make the work more easily understood by performer and audience.

Laiosa, Mark. *Traun*. 2:00. III–IV. A₁–f'. One movement. This short lyric piece presents no special problems. It is in traditional style and traditional notation and is melodic in nature.

Lang, David. *Are You Experienced?* Based on a Jimi Hendrix song of the same name. Recorded by Jay Rozen.

Láng, István. *Aria di Coloratura*. Editio Musica Budapest. 1984. $7.00. 5:00. V. C₁–g'. One movement. For László Ujfalusi. This work uses a wide and well-distributed range. Most work is within the middle register, but there is definite emphasis on both extremes. In contemporary style, with unmetered traditional notation as well as some proportional notation. The single movement is divided into sections by tempo changes. The lengthy opening in a slow tempo with many fermatas gradually reveals an eleven-note row through a process of gradual addition of notes. Throughout, the work maintains an improvisatory character. Technically, the most demanding aspects are rapid-note passages often

encompassing a very wide range, sometimes as much as two and a half octaves. Extended techniques include flutter tonguing, multiphonics, trills, tremolos with tongue, tongue clicking, vocal sounds.

Langgård, Rued. *Dies Irae*. RDB.

Lawes, William. *Five Pieces*. arr. Gordon J. Kinney. Queen City Brass Publications. 1981. $6.50. 3:00. III. G₁–d'. For Rex Conner. These simple Baroque dance tunes are entertaining. They are excellent for study material with limited technical demands.

Lebedev, I. *Three Pieces*. Musical Evergreen. 1975. $5.50. 4:00. III–IV. E₁–g. Three movements: Allegro moderato; Moderato; Grave. Modest range requirements with most writing below the staff. The compositional style and notation are traditional, and the material is melodic. Technical demands are very modest, with the main challenges being some rather low articulated eighth-note passages in the second movement and octave leaps in the middle register in the third movement.

Leichtling, Alan. *Fantasy Piece VII*. Seesaw Music Corp. 1983. $6.00. 8:00. IV. F₁–f♯'. One movement. For Barton Cummings. Composed in 1982, this work uses a well-distributed wide range with some emphasis on the upper middle and high register. Its general compositional style is contemporary, and it uses complex traditional notation. This work is rhythmically very complex, utilizing many meter changes, a great variety of subdivisions of the individual beat, and multiple beats. Most of the work is marked at an eighth-note pulse, which makes the rhythm more manageable.

Leitermeyer, F. *Tubissimo*. 1990. $7.95. 5:00. IV. C₁–g'. This work is traditional in its use of thematic material and unmetered traditional notation. The primary technical challenge is its use of very wide intervals, often slurred and exceeding two octaves. Sections of contrasting styles combine to make a very interesting work.

Lennon, John, and McCartney, Paul. *Blackbird*. arr. Lars Holmgaard. 3:00. IV. B♭₁–e♭'. One movement. The primary technical challenge of this work is the extensive use of multiphonics. Besides solid technical control, an accurate stylistic approach is essential for effective performance.

Lerstad, Terje. *Two Pieces for Solo Tuba*.

Lewis, Robert Hall. *Monophony IX*. Ludwig Doblinger KG. 1977. $5.00. 9:00. IV–V. F♯₁–f'. Five movements: Liveramente; Adagio; Moderato; Quasi Cadenza; Moderato. For Harvey Phillips. This composition relies on upper middle-register playing, which is taxing. Though CC tuba would clearly work, the F tuba allows for greater comfort and control in prolonged playing through this high work. In contemporary style and traditional notation. The work has a tendency to ramble, much in the style of a literary monologue. Extended techniques include breath sounds, flutter tonguing, glissandi, multiphonics, trills, tremolos, and use of a mute.

Lipp, Charles. *Tuba Magritte.* TUBA Press. 1991. $5.00. 4:30. IV. G_1–f#'. Three movements: The Fair Captive; Threatening Weather; Ladder of Fire. Wide intervals and accurate rhythmic execution are the primary technical challenges of this work. The second movement employs a mute throughout and requires flutter tonguing and multiphonics. Overall, this is a challenging and musically satisfying work.

List, Garret. *Le Maire de Courbevoie.*

Little, David. *Stonehenge Study 9.* Donemus Publishing House. 1990. 5:00. V–VI. G_1–g'. One movement. Relies primarily on traditional notation though there are sections of proportional notation. Extended techniques include slap tonguing, hissing in the mouthpiece, and a brief optional passage of multiphonics. Technically demanding; the extensive use of high range and rapid passages across a wide range are the primary difficulties.

Lubet, Alex. *Lament.* Alex Lubet. 1979. $5.00. 1:30. IV. E_1–eb'. One movement. Moderate range, well distributed throughout the middle register. In contemporary style with traditional notation. Rhythmic complexity is the primary technical challenge of this very short etude-like work. It is interesting for its use of a tone row. The only extended technique employed is eighth-tone bends.

Lys, Marc. *Tubastone.* Editions Robert Martin. 1988. $7.50. 3:00. IV–V. F_1–ab'. One movement. Theme and ten variations. Though there are instances of extremely high register, they are well balanced with passages in the lower middle register, and ossia parts mediate some of the endurance problems. In contemporary style with traditional notation. The many technical demands include very complex rhythms and extended rapid passages, sometimes with very wide intervals.

Macauley, Janice. *Tuba Contra Mundum.* TUBA Press. 1991. $4.00. 3:00. IV. G_2–c". One movement. Phrases alternate moods with instructions such as "jokingly" and "wistful." A very effective and interesting work for study and performance, with no unusual demands other than range.

MacBride, David. *Tuba Mirum.* American Composer's Edition. $2.98. 6:00.

Macy, Carleton. *Music for Tuba Alone.* 7:00. IV. A_1–b". Five movements: I Allegro Moderato; Prelude; II Andante Sostenuto; Prelude; III Fugue. For Carla Rutschman. This contemporary composition relies on a combination of traditional, proportional, and graphic notation. Extended rapid passages and wide leaps are the primary technical challenges.

Mannino, Franco. *Tre Impressioni Serial.* Edizioni Curci. 1990. 11:00. IV. C#$_1$–gb'. Three movements: L'infinito; Marcetta; Canto d'amore. The first and third movements are unmetered, but otherwise these works are traditionally notated. Each one is based on a theme or motive. Range is the primary technical challenge.

Maros, Miklós. *Etudes for Tuba (Etyder för Tuba).* Nordiska Musikforlag. 1976. 6:30. IV. Indications for highest and lowest possible pitch. Five movements: Dolce; II; Cantabile; Umoristico; Espr Legato. Relies entirely on proportional and graphic notation. Extended techniques include multiphonics, glissandi, and blowing air through the horn. Interpretation should prove the primary challenge.

Martinsson, Rolf. *Monodi, Op. 31.* Swedish Music Information Center. 9:00. For Sven-Olof Juvas.

Mattern, Daniell. *Five Sequential Studies for Solo Tuba.* 8:00. IV. E_1–bb. Five movements: Fast; Slow; Fast; Slow; Rubato. Written in 1969, this work is traditional in style and notation. Movements are based on motivic development. No particular technical challenges. Useful as a study piece because it requires no high-register work.

McCarty, Frank. *Color-Etudes.* Media Press. 1970. 6:50. III. Eb$_1$–e'. Three movements: Black; Green; Red. For Rodger Vaughan. Well distributed through the general range with limited use of either extreme. This is a very playable and entertaining work to study and perform. Its compositional style is contemporary but it uses traditional notation. Repeated notes are important in all movements. The first movement is marked by a swell motive, so-called for its repeated crescendo and decrescendo on a sustained pitch. In the second movement, the triple repetition of a pitch at the beginning of a line is particularly important. The third movement utilizes a constant motion in eighth notes with few interruptions, and the repeated note continues to be an important device. The third movement will take work for the rapid execution and the constant motion, but other requirements are minimal.

McIntosh, Ian. *Inner Voices.*

Menoche, Charles. *Perceptions for Solo Tuba.*

Mitsuoka, I. *Whales.* Musical Evergreen. 1976. $5.50. 5:00. IV. Indeterminant range. One movement. An avant-garde composition which relies entirely on graphic notation. Pitch is approximated by horizontal lines and lines of different shapes on a staff. Time is denoted by numbers over the staff which represent seconds. The length of individual occurrences and the total length of the work are flexible, according to the performer's interpretation, but the score advises proceeding slowly. The work is presumed to mimic whale song. Pitch level and direction of musical line are represented by straight, jagged, and curved lines. There are no explanatory notes, but the score is easily interpreted. The technical challenge is to produce an effective glissando sound which can work throughout the registers of the tuba and to control it in order to bring out marked accents within the line, as well as accurately represent the contour of each line.

Morecki, Krzysztof. *Quasars*. Musical Evergreen. 1976. $3.89. 2:00. IV. G₁–b'. One movement. The majority of the pitches in this work are in the extreme high register. This avant-garde composition makes use of a varied form of proportional notation. On a time line drawn above the staff, 2 cm. is approximately equal to a metronome marking of 52 beats per minute. There are no explanatory notes or performance suggestions other than the indication regarding the time line. Pitches are placed on the staff with no indication of rhythm. Density of the occurrences varies, being determined by the approximate placement of the pitches on the staff in relation to the time line. The work is essentially pointillistic, with individual pitches treated as occurrences. With the exception of two flourishes, the texture is quite sparse. Extreme intervals are often juxtaposed. The primary technical demands other than the generally high tessitura are the wide intervals and accuracy of pitch, as high pitches frequently follow extended rests.

Morgenstern, Tobias. *1-2-3 für Tuba*. C–e'. Three Movements: Mässig Schreitend; II; Schnelle Viertel. See below, Unkrodt, *Reige Vortragsliteratur*.

Moylan, William. *Solo and Duo*. See listing under "Music for Tuba and Keyboard."

Mozart, [Wolfgang Amadeus]. *Alleluja, Exultate*. arr. Matthews. WING. $5.00.

Muczynski, Robert. *Impromptus*. G. Schirmer. 1973. $2.00. 4:30. III. D₁–eb'. Five movements: Allegro con moto; Andante; Allegro Moderato; Moderato; Allegro giocoso. This composition relies on middle-register playing with few demands in either extreme, making very modest demands on endurance. It is entertaining for performer and audience alike. It should be easily playable by anyone who can manage the range requirements. The compositional style and notation system are traditional. Syncopations and accents are important elements of the first, third, and fifth movements, which are dancelike. The second movement is lyric; it uses the upper middle register and demands control of legato style in a soft dynamic setting. The fourth movement is also songlike, but in 5/8 meter and a lower tessitura than the second. Another technical concern may be the fifth movement's alternations between 6/8 and 3/4 meter.

Müller, Achim. *Vier Kapitel für Tuba Solo*. arr. Weinberg. 10:30. E₁–f'. Four movements: Evolution; Stagnation; Depression; Revolution. See below, Unkrodt, *Reige Vortragsliteratur*.

Nelson, Gary. *Verdigris*. TUBA Press. 1991. $4.00. 5:30. IV. E₁–eb'. Rhythmically, this work is simple, though it uses no metric marking. Careful interpretation of the many dynamic markings is essential for accurate interpretation. A poem is spoken in fragments throughout the piece, adding an interesting wrinkle to the composition.

Nielsen, John. *Landlig Suite for Solo Tuba*.

Olson, C. G. Sparre. *Canto II*. Norsk Musikforlag. 1981. 1:30. II–III. G₁–f♯. One movement. A lively work in an ABA form with a short lyric section as the B section. The outer sections have a folk-dance character dominated by simple eighth-note rhythmic patterns. A fun work for younger tubists.

Osmon, L. *Concert Etudes*. Southern Music Company. $3.50.

Paganini, Niccolo. *4 Caprices*. arr. by David Werden. Whaling Music Publishers. $12.50.

Para, D. J. *Variations*. T.U.B.A. GEM. 1975. 1:30. IV. F–b'. One movement. This very short avant-garde composition is based on a series of pitches derived from the name of tubist Robert Whaley. The notation is a mixture of traditional, frame, and proportional notation.

Parker, Charlie. *Charlie Parker Omnibook*. Atlantic Music Supply Corporation. 1978. $11.95. IV. Eb–ab'. This collection of 60 solos transcribed from recordings of Charlie Parker is intended for use by any bass clef instrument. Also included is a scale syllabus which explains chord symbols, lists scales which can be used with each symbol and spells various types of scales. Each solo provides the head and solo as well as the appropriate chord changes. Technique is quite demanding at the marked tempi and considering the range. These are excellent and entertaining study material. Many may be used down an octave.

Pearsall, Ed. *Two Motets*. TUBA Press. $5.00. 4:30. IV–V. A₁–g'. Two movements: Intrada; Aire. An interesting but very difficult work. Absolute control of multiphonics is required, as a majority of the composition relies on this technique. An added twist is the use of finger taps in the first movement. The work is interesting and challenging for the performer and works well as a recital piece.

Pellay, Paul. *Capriccio for Tuba, Op. 41a*. 1989. 5:30. IV–V. Eb₁–f'. One movement. This work is improvisatory in style and relies entirely on traditional technique.

Penderecki, Krzysztof. *Capriccio*. B. Schott's Söhne Mainz. 1987. $8.95. 5:00. V. Eb₁–g'. One movement. The general tessitura tends to be moderately high with an emphasis on performance within and above the staff. Composed in 1980, this is an excellent work deserving the attention of every serious tubist. Its general compositional style is contemporary, and it uses unmetered traditional notation with three exceptions: special notation depicts the highest and lowest possible pitch, note flags represent rhythm without note heads, and a curved line denotes the general musical contour. The majority of the work is in a quick tempo; a brief middle section in a waltz style and slightly slower. The opening theme supplies most of the motivic material for the work and returns following the waltz section. The primary technical demands beyond those of range are wide intervals and extended passages of rapid sixteenths. The notation and sparse markings leave a great deal of freedom for interpretation, requiring special attention on the part of the performer to arrive at a satisfactory musical solution. Extended techniques include flutter tonguing, glissandi, indefinite pitch, trills. Recorded by Roger Bobo; James Gourlay; Rodney Neuman; Zdzislaw Piernik.

Penn, William. *Three Essays*. Seesaw Music Corp. 1975. $9.00. 10:55. V. A_2–c^1. Three movements: Prelude; Interlude; Postlude. For Gene Pokorny, dedicated to Barney Childs. The primary demands on traditional techniques are in the upper middle register, with extremes in both directions. Composed in 1973, this is a very interesting work, particularly for study and certainly worthy of performance. This avant-garde composition utilizes proportional and frame notation as well as traditional notation. A very good explanation of the symbols used greatly aids in the interpretation of the score. The first movement emphasizes repeated patterns. The second movement uses an indefinite time notation with notes and effects spaced on the staff to reflect relative time. The third movement is lyric and uses many very wide slurs in succession. The opening two-thirds of the movement are traditionally notated and performed, then the third slide is withdrawn, and the final section is a mixture of natural and altered sounds produced by playing and singing through the unsealed third valve. Extended techniques include glissandi, indefinite pitch, tremolos (with voice), vocal sounds, removal of slides.

Persichetti, Vincent. *Parable XXII*. Elkan-Vogel. 1983. $4.00. 13:30. V. D_1–g^1. One movement. For Harvey Phillips. This work requires a very wide range with full use of both extremes. Control of both upper and lower registers is required, and because of the length, endurance is a concern. A significant commitment of time is required to give an effective rendering of this work. Though limited in its use of extended techniques, it requires complete control of all traditional techniques at a professional performance level. The compositional style is contemporary, but the work relies entirely on traditional notation. Though it is a single continuous movement, there are sections marked by tempo changes. Very rapid tongued passages coupled with wide, sometimes awkward intervals are particularly demanding. Musically the work demands considerable attention in order to arrive at an adequate interpretation. Extended techniques include glissandi, trills. See: Bird, Gary, ed., *Program Notes for the Solo Tuba*. Recorded by Mark Nelson.

Persichetti, Vincent. *Serenade No. 12*. Elkan-Vogel. 1963. $3.00. 7:00. IV. D_1–e^1. Six movements: Intrada; Arietta; Mascherata; Capriccio; Intermezzo; Marcia. For Harvey Phillips. The range is generally moderate to high with extremes utilized in both directions. Though this work is normally performed on CC, it does work well on F tuba. This set of dancelike movements is a mainstay of the genre and deserves attention and study by every serious tubist. The compositional style and notation are traditional. Though no extended techniques are required, the work relies on a very advanced level of traditional technique. The first and sixth movements require control of wide interval slurs and sudden dynamic changes, which must not be allowed to interfere with the flow of the melody. The second and fifth movements explore the lyric qualities of the instrument in long phrases. The third movement is the most awkward musically and generally requires the greatest interpretive efforts. The fourth movement is difficult because of its speed and the awkward slurs within the triplet line. See: Bird, Gary, ed., *Program Notes for the Solo Tuba*. Recorded by Harvey Phillips.

Pinkham, Daniel. *Tucket IV*. E. C. Schirmer Company Inc. 1981. 1:30. IV. G_1–eb^1. One movement. A very short work in a contemporary style, chromatic in nature. Wide intervals and changing meter are the primary technical challenges. An exciting short piece, excellent as an encore piece.

Poore, Melvyn. *Variations*.

Poore, Melvyn. *Vox Superius*. Arts Lab Music Publishing. 1977. $8.00. 8:00. IV–V. Bb_1–f^1. One movement. Composed in 1976. The general tessitura is moderate, with most playing within the staff. This work is perhaps a bit long. The compositional style is best described as contemporary bordering on the avant-garde. The dominant notational system is proportional with some use of advanced traditional notation of rhythm. The symbols are explained, and the score is very clean and clear. This piece is a study in timbres and effects possible on the tuba and an exploration of the instrument's other potentials. An interesting effect is the use in a multiphonic section of pronounced syllables and even words with the sung line. Some patterns do emerge, such as a motive of wide repeated intervals alternating rather rapidly. Wide leaps, frequent use of multiphonics, and rapid passages containing extreme dynamic shifts are among the more demanding technical aspects of this work. Extended techniques include flutter tonguing, multiphonics, trills (valve trill while singing), tremolos, vocal sounds, and use of a mute.

Powell, Morgan. *Midnight Realities*. Brass Music, Lt. 1974. $3.50. 5:00. V. C_1–a^1. One movement. For Daniel Perantoni. Composed in 1972, this is a tremendously difficult work. It is an avant-garde composition which uses proportional and frame notation as well as traditional notation. Durations of events are sometimes given in seconds. The work is a sound painting more than a traditional form. The music is based on timbres sometimes produced by multiphonics and percussive sounds, which create a descriptive atmosphere. Though most of the piece relies on nontraditional technique and sounds, that which is traditional tends to be quite high. Many difficulties are encountered, including a multiphonic section in which each part is fully independent and passages of very rapid articulated notes which encompass a very wide range. Extended techniques include breath sounds, valve clicks, glissandi, indefinite pitch, multiphonics, and use of a mute. See: Bird, Gary, ed., *Program Notes for the Solo Tuba*. Recorded by Daniel Perantoni.

Presser, William. *Suite*. Ensemble Publications / Lyceum Music Press. 1967. $4.00. 8:10. III–IV. E_1–eb'. Three movements: Allegretto; Adagio; Adagio. For Rex Conner. Range demands are very modest, with most playing below the staff or just within it. One of the few unaccopanied pieces which relies on lower middle register playing almost exclusively, so that range should not be a problem for any performer. The general compositional style and notation system are traditional. There are no great technical demands. The second and third movements each have a short opening in a slow tempo before moving to the moderately rapid pace of the entire composition.

Ptaszynska, Marta. *Two Poems*. Polskie Wydawnictwo Muzyczne (Marks Music). 1979. $5.00. 8:00. V. $F\#_1$–$f\#'$. Two movements: Cantabile, con espressione; Scherzando, con bravura. The range of the tuba is thoroughly exploited, with special emphasis on the high register. Endurance is an important consideration. Composed in 1975. The compositional style is contemporary tending toward the avant-garde. There is proportional notation, though most of the notation is traditional or modified so that it includes bar lines. When there is a change in the pulse from the previous measure, a number indicating how many quarters or eighths will occur within the measure appears over the bar line. A brief explanation of the symbols is provided. The first movement is slow and expressive with a rearticulated pitch motive serving as a unifying element. Multiphonics occur throughout, often with both parts moving in rhythmic unison as intervals continuously change. Another difficulty of the multiphonics section involves sung pitches below the played line. The second movement involves some very rapid runs sometimes coupled with very wide intervallic leaps. There is interesting use of vocal syllables to alter the timbre of the played sound. Very rapid triple tonguing is also required. Extended techniques include flutter tonguing, glissandi, multiphonics, quarter-tone bends, vocal sounds.

Reck, David. *Five Studies*. Edition Peters. 1968. $9.25. 10:00. V. B_2–f'. Five movements: Tempo Rubato; As fast as possible, with clarity; Like a Song; Make like a Wallenda, man!; Blues. The total range of the tuba is fully exploited in this work, but demands are well paced for endurance considerations. This work is an excellent study piece, particularly for alternative notational systems. The explanations and symbols are clear enough for use as a first study piece in this genre provided the player is technically very strong. This avant-garde work explores a wide range of styles and employs proportional and frame notation as well as unmetered traditional notation. Notation is perhaps its most interesting feature, as it makes extensive use of frame notation for both sound and silence. Technically, the work is quite difficult, requiring control of rapidly articulated, non-scale passages, wide leaps in rapid succession with changing accent patterns, multiphonics, and a very wide range. Extended techniques include breath sounds, flutter tonguing, glissandi, multiphonics, lip trills. See: Bird, Gary, ed., *Program Notes for the Solo Tuba*. Recorded by Toby Hanks.

Reed, Marlyce P. *Two Autumn Moods*.

Reményi, Attila. *Solo for Tuba*. Editio Musica Budapest.

Roikjer, Kjell. *Five Unaccompanied Pieces*.

Roikjer, Kjell. *Study for Tuba Solo*. 1:30. IV. C–f'. One movement. This short work written in 1979, is traditional in style and notation. The improvisatory character and flowing lines are very entertaining. Rapid slurred passages across a wide range are the primary technical challenge.

Ross, Walter. *Escher's Sketches*. Mark Tezak. 1986. 8:00. IV. Gb_1–f'. Five movements: Comodo; Estravagante; Agitato; Ballo Lento; Fantastico. This contemporary work uses very traditional musical language. All movements are without meter, however rhythm and pulse are simple throughout. Each movement is based on a lithograph by M.C. Escher and uses musical devices to depict that picture. It is an interesting work, worthy of study, and a solid recital piece. Recorded by Mark Nelson.

Rozen, Jay. *In the 90% (Sturgeon's Law) for Solo Tuba*. TUBA Press.

Russell, Gilmour. *Mud*. American Music Center.

Sacco, Peter. *Tuba Mirum*. Western International Music. 1969. $2.00. 10:00. IV. Eb_1–eb'. Five movements (named for sections of the Catholic liturgy): Tuba Mirum; Lacrymosa; Libera Me; Sanctus Benedictus; Allegro con Brio. Moderate range with most playing well distributed in the middle register. The performance of this work can be very effective if a narrator reads the text before each movement. The general compositional style is traditional, though it is unique in this medium for its coupling of a religious text with music. The movements reflect the sentiments of the text; for example, the mention of the trumpet call in the text of the first movement is depicted in the double-dotted rhythm reminiscent of trumpet fanfares. The second movement is marked by a sob motive. Notation is traditional throughout. Though five movements are labeled, there is no pause between the fourth and fifth movements, and the da capo returns to the beginning of the fourth movement, so in practical terms, there are only four movements. Technically the work presents no unusual demands.

Samkopf. *Solo Piece for Tuba*.

Sandgren, Joachim. *Rave*. Swedish Music Information Center.

Sandgren, Joachim. *Resonance*. Swedish Music Information Center.

Sarcich, Paul. *Chaconne*. American Music Center. 6:00.

Saul, Walter. *De Profundis*. TUBA Press.

Sauter, Ed. *Eight Random Thoughts*. 11:00. IV. F_1–a♭'. Eight movements: ♩ = 88; ♩ = 112; ♩ = 104; ♩ = 48; ♩ = 66; ♩ = 48; ♩ = 60; ♩ = 66. To Kurt Vonnegut, Jr. This interesting work takes traditional technique to the limits. Wide intervals of as much as two octaves are common, and a smooth legato style is required throughout.

Scelsi, Giac. *Maknongan*. Salabert. 1956.

Schilling, Hans Ludwig. *Tuba Prima*. Möseler Verlag. 1981. 6:00. V. B♭₁–b♭". Two movements: Recitando; Valse musette. An extremely difficult work in a contemporary style. The notation is entirely traditional, but the rhythmic notation is quite complex in the first movement. Considerable use of multiphonics, very rapid passages covering a wide range, and a non-stop rapid rhythmic flow in the waltz are the primary technical challenges.

Schlünz, Annette. *Ach, es... Musik für Tuba Solo*. Bote & Bock. 1993. 7:00. V. C_1–e♭'. One movement. For Michael Vogt. Written in 1991, this is a tremendously difficult work in a contemporary style. The notation is a mix of traditional and proportional notation, with many markings signifying extended techniques. All symbols are clearly explained. The rhythmic notation is complex. Musically, the work is a collage of sounds, colors and flourishes. A short poem by the composer and a quote from René Char suggest the general emotional character of the work. Though very demanding, this work has great potential in performance.

Schneider, John. *TBA (To Be Arranged)*. Arts Lab Music. 1978. May be performed by any bass wind or brass instrument.

Schudel, Thomas. *Line Drawings*. Canadian Music Centre. 1985. 3:30. IV. G_1–g♭'. Two movements: Adagio; Allegro con brio. For Michael Moran. This work is melodic and generally traditional. The primary technical demand is range, with all other aspects well within normal technical demands. A solid composition of value both as a study piece and as a recital work.

Sear, Walter E. *Sonata*. Western International Music. 1966. $3.00. 8:00. III. F_1–d'. Four movements: Andante; Presto; Andantino; Giocoso. Range requirements are moderate with much of the work in the lower middle register. This composition should work well as study material to supplement basic etudes. The compositional style and notation are traditional. No special technical demands. The work is melodic in character. The first movement is smooth with extended slurred passages across intervals, which are generally a perfect fifth or less. The second movement is marked by a double-dotted eighth note and 32nd-note figure in a very fast tempo. The third movement is similar in tempo and style to the first movement.

Selmer-Collery, Jules. *Tuba Nova*. Associated Music Publishers.

Sera, Carlo. *Lyric Suite*. Musical Evergreen. 1977. $3.89. 3:30. III–IV. E_1–f♯'. Four movements: Allegro molto; Adagio; Allegretto; Allegro. Range requirements generally moderate with most playing within the staff. Composed in 1976. This work provides excellent study material to supplement basic etudes, and it is a worthy recital piece though it is rather short. The compositional style and notation system are traditional. The first movement is dominated by very wide leaps and a very sparse texture with a sporadic, rhythmic flow. The second movement is more lyric, again dominated by wide intervals often slurred. The third movement returns to a thin texture reminiscent of the first one, though in 3/8 meter and in a somewhat higher tessitura. The final movement is marked by frequent meter changes, wide intervals, and a sometimes sporadic rhythmic flow, here created by a reliance on syncopations and irregularly placed accents. Technical demands are moderate. Pitch accuracy is critical particularly in the first movement, as high notes frequently occur after rests.

Silverman, Faye-Ellen. *Zigzags*. Seesaw Music Corp. 1988. $7.00. 8:30. IV–V. C♯₁–b♭'. One movement. This work tends to emphasize the high register. Few if any breaks make it very taxing. A very difficult work that will require a significant time commitment. The general compositional style is contemporary, but the notation is traditional. Seven different tempi recur throughout and mark changes in style and section. Each successive tempo marking is referenced to a previous one, for instance, Tempo VI is three times the speed of Tempo I. Although they seem complicated at first, these references aid in matching style with previous sections and assist in understanding the relationship between sections. Wide leaps and rapid passages across a very wide range abound. These difficulties, the endurance factor, and the extended techniques make this a very demanding composition. Extended techniques include flutter tonguing, glissandi, multiphonics.

Smith, Glenn. *Magniloquentia*. 4:00. V. C–d'. Two movements: I; II. Extended passages of rapid notes and complex rhythmic figures dominate this work. The second movement makes extensive use of multiphonics. While notationally the work is traditional, the general musical effect is that of a contemporary work and a technical exploration of the instrument.

Smith, Glenn. *The Survival.* 7:00. V. E♭₂–c″. Two movements: Future Schock; Discorporation. For John Turk. Written in 1972, this contemporary composition uses passages of proportional and graphic notation as well as traditional notation. Multiphonics and extended passages of multiple tonguing and vocalizations are used. A very difficult and long work.

Smith, Jason. *Episodes.* 3:00. III–IV. C₁–e♭'. One movement. Traditional notation with numerous meter changes. This work is essentially an extended etude.

Songer, Lewis. *Tuballet.* KoKo Enterprises. 1983. $3.50. 5:00. III–IV. G₁–e♭'. Four movements: Stately—mysterious; Moderato, dolce e simplice; Easy 1; Spirited. Modest range with most playing well distributed in the middle register. An excellent study piece for the advancing student and good sightreading material for the more advanced. The compositional style and notation are traditional. Each movement is dominated by a basic theme or motive. Technical demands are modest. The first movement has rapid passages of sixteenth notes as well as eighth and sixteenth triplets and presents the most diverse rhythmic palette.

Spillman, Robert A. *Four Greek Preludes.* Editions Musicus. 1969. $3.75. 13:00. IV. E₁–f'. Four movements: Lento, molto liberamente; Andante moderato e cantabile; Recitativo: largamente; Allegro giocoso. For Rex Conner. This work relies on middle-register playing and makes moderate demands on endurance, though extremes of range are used. These preludes are very approachable and enjoyable for the advanced player. They are worthy of programming, but should probably not be performed as a full set because of the overall length and similarity of the movements. The compositional style and notation are traditional, with the first and third movements unmetered. The work maintains a unique modal character. The first three movements are highly melodic, with very singable themes. The third movement is dominated by a fanfare motive that remains somewhat tentative in its progress, never developing into a full theme. This work is moderately challenging, with rapid scale passages the dominant technical feature. The greatest musical challenge is to maintain the character of each movement despite the technical demands.

Stanley, Helen. *Excursions for Solo Tuba.* TUBA Press. 1986. $4.00. 4:00. III. F₁–d'. Three movements: Allegro dramatico; Andantino romantico; Allegretto burlando. This interesting work is a useful introduction to the unaccompanied medium. All movements are thematically based. Occasional wide intervals are the only technical challenge; the musical content should maintain the interest of performer and audience.

Steadman, Robert. *Sonata in One Movement.* MGP. 1983. $1.00. 8.25. IV–V. A₂–f'. One movement. This work is dominated by changing meters with sections marked by tempo changes. The drive of the work is primarily rhythmic with some motivic use.

Stein, Leon. *Solo Sonata for Tuba.* Composers Facsimile Edition. 10:00. IV. F♯₁–c'. Two movements: Variations; Recitative. This very long work is traditional in style and notation. There are many style and time changes through each movement. Extended passages of rapidly articulated notes are the primary technical challenge.

Stein, Leon. *Two Pieces.* Dorn Publications Inc. 1981. 6:30. III–IV. F♯₁–c'. Two movements: Transformations (Twelve mini-etudes in variation form); Duplex. The general range demands of this work are moderate with most playing in the staff. Composed in 1969, the compositional style and notation are traditional. The first movement is a set of variations which place great demands on the performers facility through numerous rapid passages which are primarily scalar. The second movement utilizes two themes which serve as the basic thematic material in a sectionalized movement. The primary technical demands are extended passages of sixteenth notes which seem to proceed endlessly.

Stephens. *Slow Melody Solos.*

Stevens, John. *Suite #1.* Philharmusica Corp. 1977. 6:00. IV–V. E1–f'. Five movements: Slow and Rubato; Ponderous; Slow and Freely; March; Slow and Sombre. This work is primarily melodic in nature and makes traditional demands on technique. With its limited use of the high register, it is a valuable piece for study and performance. See: Bird, Gary, ed., *Program Notes for the Solo Tuba.* Recorded by John Stevens.

Stevens, John. *Triumph of the Demon Gods.* Queen City Brass Publications. 1981. $5.00. 3:30. IV. E♭₁–e'. One movement. The range requirements are well balanced, with somewhat more emphasis on the middle and low register. The compositional style is essentially traditional though not particularly tonal, and the notational system is traditional. The music depicts a struggle between the forces of good and evil. Sections contrast a relatively low tessitura line with a marked style utilizing accents and short/long rhythm versus a higher, more legato melodic section. There are frequent tempo shifts and meter shifts, but always in a quarter-note pulse. Technical requirements are moderate, with rapid sixteenth-note passages and regular style shifts the primary demands. See: Bird, Gary, ed., *Program Notes for the Solo Tuba.* Recorded by John Stevens.

Stevens, Thomas. *Encore: Boz.* Wimbledon Music Inc. 1977. $4.00. 3:00. IV. C–c″. One movement. For Roger Bobo. This work uses the performer's complete range. Though much of the playing is in the upper and upper middle register, the short duration should prevent endurance problems. Composed in 1976, this work is contemporary in style and relies primarily on traditional notation with some examples of proportional notation. It is a "mirror piece" in that after the material is presented it is played in retrograde, making the end and the beginning identical. At the center of the composition, between the presentation and the retrograde, a "Little Concert" is to be improvised. The instructions for it call for a gradual crescendo from pianissimo to fortissimo and a return to pianissimo to maintain the mirror idea. It is also suggested in the score that in place of the improvised section, the opening and closing of the work may be used as a general entrance and exit for another work or group of works, and, in fact, the work is recorded in this fashion. The greatest technical demands are the very wide intervals. Thematically the piece is a decreasing interval beginning from the highest possible to the lowest possible pitch and arriving at a unison. Also challenging is the flutter tonguing on individual notes within a rapid line. Extended techniques include foot stamps, flutter tonguing, indefinite pitch. Recorded by Roger Bobo.

Stöckigt, Michael. *Monogramm.* F_1–f'. One movement. See below, Unkrodt, *Reige Vortragsliteratur.*

Stratton, Don. *Won't He Get Lonely?* PP Music. 1986. $5.00. 3:30. III. F_1–d'. One movement. For George Shaffer. This work uses a well-distributed range primarily in the middle register. A work of modest difficulty, it is good study material for a younger tubist. The compositional style and notation are traditional. Though it has only one movement, there are many sections marked by tempo and style changes. The many instances of arpeggiation and arpeggiated sequences are the most demanding technical elements. Numerous meter changes and extensive use of compound meters give a rhythmic vitality to the composition.

Stroud, Richard. *A Variation of East African Calls.* One movement. For R. Winston Morris. See: Bird, Gary, ed., *Program Notes for the Solo Tuba.*

Szalonek, W. *Piernikiana.* 1978. 12:03. V. Indeterminate range. One movement. Relies entirely on graphic and proportional notations. Numerous extended techniques, including use of tenor saxophone mouthpiece, air sounds, glissandi, other brass instrument bells in slide openings, and many others. The primary challenge of this work is assembling the needed equipment and interpreting the score. Extensive notes in Polish and German explain the notation.

Szeto, Caroline. *Study No. 1.*

Szeto, Caroline. *Study No. 2.*

Takahashi, Tohru. *Canzon.* 4:00. IV–V. D_1–f'. One movement. To Tsutomu Morimoto. Written in 1982, this avant-garde composition utilizes proportional, graphic, and traditional notation. There

are extended passages of indefinite pitch and much use of vocalization.

Terzakis, D. *Stixis III for Tuba Solo.* Breitkopf & Härtel. 1974. 3:00. III. A_1–d'. One movement. The primary challenge of this work is its musical interpretation. The notation includes some nontraditional markings which are not explained and may not be familiar to everyone. The work relies on short patterns which are repeated, generally with an increase in speed before beginning the next pattern.

Thommesen, Olav Anton. *Two Pieces.*

Thow, John. *Living Room Music.* 2:30. III–IV. A_1–eb'. One movement. To Michael A. McClain. Written in 1967, this work is traditional in style and notation. Regular meter changes and tempo changes mark several sections. This work is probably best used as a study piece.

Tisné, Antoine. *Monodie III.* Editions Billaudot. 1990. $7.00. 9:30. V. B_2–f'. One movement. For Fernand Lelong. This very difficult work relies almost entirely on proportional notation. Those sections in traditional notation use complex time signatures. Rapid articulated passages, which are rhythmically complex, and very wide intervals make a technically challenging work.

Toulon, Jacques. *Trois Caricatures.* Editions Robert Martin. 1989. $4.00. 2:10. III. G_1–bb'. Three movements: Dinosaurus; Valse; Presto. The general tessitura is high and is generally more appropriate to the euphonium. This very pleasant work is appropriate for a lower-level euphonium student but is of limited value to the tubist. The general compositional style and notation are traditional. Musically, the three movements are organized around traditional melodic and thematic ideas. The work is listed as elementary, but its range is not appropriate for the tuba; musically, however, this is a very accurate characterization. The general high tessitura and the passages of extended sixteenth notes in the third movement are the only technical challenges.

Tuominen, Seppo. *Tubaniana.* FMI Finnish Music Information Centre. 3:00. III. D_1–db'. One movement. This work is simple in concept and should present no problems other than range for the average high school student. There are few extended passages of sixteenth runs.

Tuthill, Burnet. *Ten Tiny Tunes for Tuba.* Tenuto Publications. 1974. $2.00. 10:33. IV. F_1–f' (D_1–eb). Ten movements: Slow; Allegro; Andante; Vivace; Allegretto; Moderato, cantabile; Snappy; Allegro; Slowly; Fast. For R. Winston Morris. All movements are characterized by moderate middle-register demands, well within the general range of the instrument. Endurance should be no problem, particularly with the many chances to pause between movements. As study pieces, these are effective because of their brevity—half are a minute or less in length— and the option to choose appropriate movements. In performance, all or a selection may be used. The general compositional style is traditional with reliance on traditional notation. Technical demands are minimal for the most part; though the last three movements contain rapid passages, sometimes in arpeggiation and sometimes as florid embellishment to the line.

Unkrodt, Dietrich. *Reige Vortragsliteratur, Tuba 1 und Tuba 2*. Verlag Neue Musik, Berlin. 1989. V. This two-volume collection contains eleven works for solo tuba. They represent a wide variety of styles tending toward the contemporary and avant-garde. Most rely to some extent on extended techniques. The general tessitura tends to be high.

Vadala, C. *Lonely Road*. Whaling Music Publishers. $5.00.

Van Nostrand, Burr. *Tuba-Tuba*. American Composers Edition. $2.45. 5:00.

Vaughan, Rodger. *Suite for Tuba*. Joseph Boonin. 1976. 7:00. III–IV. F_1–c'. Four movements: ♩ = 112; ♩ = 112–116; ♩ = 72–76; ♩ = 96. For Benton Minor. The general tessitura is moderate with no extended high-register demands. Composed in 1971. Both the compositional style and the notation are traditional. This work is very approachable technically and musically by any good player. Placement of accents in the first movement, accurate handling of the meter in the second movement, and accurate rendering of triplets versus dotted eighths and sixteenths in the third movement are the major technical demands.

Waagemans, Peter-Jan. *Nuage Gris*.

Warren, Frank E. *Leeann*. Seesaw Music Corp. 1975. $5.00. 5:00. V. G_2–e^b'. One movement. For Rob Weller and Leeann. The range is well distributed throughout the middle register, with considerable low-register demands as well. Composed in 1974. The general compositional style is contemporary, and the notation is traditional. There is a brief key to the notation for extended techniques. The dominant tempo is slow, and the general character is lyric. Control of multiphonics is necessary for an effective performance, as there are somewhat extended passages of melodic work in the voice part. Also problematic is the half-valve melodic section. Extended techniques include glissandi, half-valve, multiphonics, trills.

Warren, Frank E. *Tuba Music, Op. 13*. Frank E. Warren Music Service. 1980. $4.50. 5:00. IV–V. F_2–e'. One movement. The general range is moderate and well distributed, primarily in the middle register. The compositional style and notation are traditional. Several tempo changes mark sections within the movement. The prevalent tempo is quick with many rapid-note passages. Many of the more extended rapid passages have simpler ossia parts. Some extreme low passages may be problematic. One interesting section involves bringing out a two-part counterpoint within the context of a constantly moving sixteenth-note line.

Watz, Franz. *Fantasie*.

Wefelmeyer, Bernd. *Sieben durch Acht*. C–f♯. One movement. See above, Unkrodt, *Reige Vortragsliteratur*.

Werner, Sven Erik. *Tale for Tuba*.

Wilder, Alec. *Convalescence Suite*. Margun Music Inc. 1982. $9.50. 20:00. IV. E^b_1–g'. Eighteen movements (in three parts): Dolce; ♩ = 120; ♩. = 50; Gently & otherwise; Forcefully; ♩ = 144; Expressive e rubato; Muscularly; Giocoso; Dolce; As fast as 16ths will permit; Gently and romantically; Fast; ♪ = 160; Andante; Flowingly Rubato; Up tempo jazz style; Epilogue. For Harvey Phillips. The range tends to favor the upper and upper-middle registers. This exceptionally long work is not appropriate for performance as a single unit. It is an excellent source of study material with many possible combinations of movements for performance. Endurance considerations will depend on the selection of movements for performance. The compositional style and notational system are traditional. Much of this work displays definite jazz influence. A primary technical demand is control of smooth, lyric playing, sometimes in rapid tempos. Melodic lines tend to cover a wide range in the course of a phrase, with the direction of motion changing often. Though the harmony is traditional, many resolutions require careful attention to establish them firmly in the ear. Performance demands are traditional, but tax all aspects of technique to the fullest extent. Extended techniques include flutter tonguing, glissandi, trills.

Wiley, Frank. *Caverns*. Ludwig Music. 1988. $4.95. 8:00. V. B^b_1–g'. One movement. To Ronald Bishop. Written in 1982. Three distinct sections marked by pauses. Primarily based on traditional notation, with passages of proportional notation. An interesting feature is the use of timbral changes produced by altering the mouth formation while playing. In addition, there is significant use of multiphonics and passages of flutter tonguing without playing.

Winteregg, Steven. *A Time for...*. Pasticcio Music. 1991. $5.00. 3:30. IV. A_1–e^b'. Two movements: Searching; Living. To Robert LeBlanc. The compositional style of this work is contemporary with a reliance on traditional notation and technique. Rhythmic complexity is the primary technical challenge. The driving second movement is exciting and enjoyable.

Wolff, Christian. *Tuba Song*. C.F. Peters Corp. 1992.

Yost, Michael. *Variations on a Theme for Tuba*. 3:00. III–IV. G_1–d'. One movement. This contemporary work notates pitch but no rhythm. Its success depends on the performer's interpretive abilities.

Zerbe, Hannes. *Gamma*. G_1–e'. One movement. See above, Unkrodt, *Reige Vortragsliteratur*.

Ziffrin, Marilyn J. *Four Pieces for Tuba*. Music Graphics Press. 1982. $4.95. 10:00. IV. E_2–g' (Bb_2–g'). Four movements: ♩ = 68; ♩ = 100; Largo; Fast, but very rhythmical. For Barton Cummings. This work utilizes the complete range of the instrument, including both extremes, with a general tendency to be somewhat high. The general compositional style is contemporary and the work uses traditional notation. The first movement is characterized by its opening fanfare motive, which recurs near the end of the movement in inversion. The second movement is based on a rapidly repeated note pattern. The third movement is slow and melodic with repeated note passages harkening back to the previ-ous movement. The fourth movement is quick and rhythmically challenging. Extended techniques employed include flutter tonguing and glissandi. Recorded by Barton Cummings.

Zindars, Earl. *Trigon*. For Floyd Cooley. Recorded by Floyd Cooley.

Zonn, Paul. *Red Wiggler*. T.U.B.A. GEM. 1:30. IV. F_1–f'. One movement. This short work utilizes proportional and graphic as well as traditional notation. Wide intervals and multiphonics are the primary technical demands. This work is a brief exploration of the tuba's extramusical possibilities in a contemporary musical setting.

7. Music for Tuba and Tape
Jeffrey L. Funderburk

The medium described as tuba and tape is actually expanding to include tuba and electronic media of greater variety. With the increased capabilities of the current generation of synthesizers and advances in electronic music, it is expected that there will be a significant increase in composition in this medium in coming years. This development is welcomed by many tubists who have never been completely satisfied with the acoustic combination of tuba and piano. This medium combines the independence of the unaccompanied medium with the much broader tonal palette provided by the tape or electronic accompaniment.

Unfortunately, these works have not been as successful in securing publication as works in other media. For this reason, most of them are available from very small publishers or directly from the composers. It is hoped that with greater attention by performers and an increase in composition, these works will become more available. This medium offers a truly unlimited potential for the tubist and can be one of the most interesting and exciting areas of performance and programming available to the soloist.

I would like to thank Barton Cummings for identifying works in this area and providing information on several of the pieces listed here.

Ayers, Jesse. *The Dancing King*. TUBA Press. 1991. $15.00. 6:00. IV–V. F_1–g'. One movement. For Frank Banton. This work utilizes a tape-recorded synthesized accompaniment, but there is no score showing the tape part. A rhythmically driving work in an almost popular style. The tape provided has several versions, including an accompaniment track for performance, a performance track with a synthesized tuba sound producing the solo part, and a slow practice track. Substantial technical challenges, complex meters, and a scarcity of rests make this a difficult work.

Bark, Jan. *Malumna (Music-Theatre for Tuba and Tape)*. Swedish Music Information Center.

Báthory-Kitsz, Dennis. *Llama Butter*. Westleaf Editions. 1993. 23:00. IV–V. Db_1–cb'. One movement. Commissioned by Mark Nelson. In addition to the tuba and tape, this piece has two recommended stage settings and suggests using dancers as well. Careful instructions are provided for staging and costuming. The tape primarily provides environmental sounds—a combination of breathing sounds, viols, vocalizations, and animal sounds. The tuba part is synchronized by timings, and the tuba score does not attempt to give a graphic rendering of the tape. Most of the tuba part is traditionally notated, though there are passages of graphic notation, and the entire work is without meter. There are also extended multiphonic sections with both parts moving in unison rhythm.

Berling, David. *Colloquy*. 6:00. IV. Eb–f'. One movement. Written in 1992. This work is unusual in that it calls for the tape to be turned on and off at various points, allowing for very free passages of solo tuba. The score offers no graphic representation of the tape, but does provide timings.

Biggs, John. *Invention for Tuba and Tape*. Consort Press.

Bottje, Will Gay. *Triangles*. Composers Facsimile Edition. 1972. 7:00. One movement. Written for tuba, trumpet, and tape. An aleatory work in which each performer has three different parts, consisting of five sections. In performance, each player selects five sections from the three available sets.

Byers, David. *St. Columbus and the Crane*.

Cisternino, Nic. *Morgana...il segreto del quarto tempo*.

Cope, David. *Spirals*. Seesaw. 6:30. IV. E_1–g#'. One movement. For Barton Cummings. This work utilizes a tape prepared by the performer. The tape part is traditionally notated and involves four tracks of music. Full instructions are included.

Corwell, Neal. *New England Reveries*. Nicolai Music. $21.00 (+ $2.00 shipping). 8:45. IV. D_1–b'. One movement. For Mark Nelson. Despite the medium, this is an essentially traditional work, very melodic and with definite pop-music influences. The score is very clear and easily followed, as it is entirely in traditional notation. The tape is a synthesized voicing of the accompaniment. The work is very pleasant and entertaining. Other than extended passages of sextuplets, the tuba part presents no special technical problems.

Cresswell, Lyell. *Drones IV*. See listing under "Music for Unaccompanied Tuba."

Dunn, David. *Interjacence*. 20:00. Written for Barton Cummings. Written in 1977, the final realization has no live performers. The work includes nontraditional notation utilizing frame notation of indeterminate length. A pre-recorded tape part is used with live tuba, clarinet, and tam-tam to make a final tape, which is presented in the final performance.

Dutton, Brent. *Subterrestrial Sounds*. Seesaw Music. 1978. $34.00. 7:00. IV. C_1–f'. Four movements: Prologue; II; III; Epilogue. This work is intended for use with a tape made by the performer. The score includes five staves, four of which should be recorded. Alternate performance is possible with five tubists. The compositional style is contemporary. Occasional nontraditional notation is used, but performance notes make these markings clear. Range and general timing of the solo with the tape are the primary concerns. It is suggested that a technician run the tape in performance to assist with timings, as the tape needs to be stopped and restarted several times. The work is based on sections dominated by color while other sections are canonic.

Ernst, David. *Coludes for Tuba and Tape.* 10:00. V. One movement. Written for Barton Cummings. A very colorful work using musique-concrète for the tape. An extremely difficult work that will require significant rehearsal time with tape and a stopwatch.

Escobar, Aylton. *Poética IV.* Editora Novas Metas. 1980. V. This very interesting work requires the performer to prepare a rather elaborate tape, which will require a studio to produce. Two scores are provided, one for performance and one for preparation of the tape. The tape is primarily tuba performance on multiple tracks with various electronic manipulations. The performer personalizes the tape at the end by including his or her name in the final text. This work requires a significant commitment of time, but should result in a very effective performance.

Felciano. *"and from the abyss" for tuba and tape.* Recorded by Floyd Cooley.

Furukawa, Kiyoshi. *Music for Tuba and Tonband.*

Giuliano, Giuseppe. *Aleph Infinito.*

Hanson, Stan. *Play Power 6.* Medi.

Hatzis, Christos. *Pavilliones en l'air.*

Hewitt, Harry. *Twelve Preludes for Solo Tuba.* See listing under "Music for Unaccompanied Tuba."

Hiller, Lejaren. *Malta.* Theodore Presser Co. 1971. $15.00. 20:16. IV–V. B_1–b#". Four movements: Geographical; Historical; Carnival; Personal. To Barton Cummings. A very difficult work with extensive range and length. The tape is a mixture of sounds on two separate channels, primarily acoustic sounds ranging from a narrator to church bells to a village band. The score graphically represents events on the tape and gives clock timings to simplify synchronization. The tuba part is often in treble clef and is dominated by very wide intervals, extremely high register, and extended passages of rapid notes. Recorded by Barton Cummings.

Jacobs, Kenneth. *Children of the Hermit and Their Mountain Handiwork.* Seesaw. 1987. $42.00. 15:00. IV–V. Bb_1–gb'. This composition relies on traditional performance technique from the tubist and uses unmetered traditional notation. The score provides a rather sketchy depiction of the tape events.

Kulesha, Gary. *Demons.*

Larson, Forrest. *Syncronic for Tuba and Tape.* 8:00. IV. G_1–d#'. One movement. For Phil Vanouse. Composed in 1993. Performance requires use of a stopwatch, as the score offers no graphic representation of the tape. A brief work with minimal endurance requirements, as the tuba plays only about half the time.

Lazarof, Henri. *Cadence VI.* Bote & Bock. 1974. $12.25. 6:25. V. G_2–ab'. One movement. Commissioned by and dedicated to Roger Bobo. Utilizes a tape prepared by the performer. The score presents both parts. Except for three clusters of four notes near the end, this is essentially a duet. Compositionally, the piece is a set of variations based on a six-note tone row. It utilizes proportional notation and a little graphic notation, in addition to unmetered traditional notation. Multiphonics and use of a mute expand the sound palette. Recorded by Roger Bobo.

McLean, Priscilla. *Beneath the Horizon III.* MLC. 1978. 12:30. IV–V. C_1–a'. One movement. This very interesting work combines a tape of recorded whale sounds (sometimes electronically manipulated) with live tuba performance dominated by extended techniques resulting in nontraditional sounds. The score uses graphic representations of events on the tape as well as a time line, which gives placement in number of minutes and seconds for large events on the tape. The composer suggests using a stopwatch in the learning process to aid in synchronization. Many extended techniques are required, including fingernail tapping, glissandi, whistling with the mouthpiece, flutter tonguing, and vocalizations. Thorough explanatory notes are included. Recorded by Melvyn Poore.

Montague, Stephen. *Paramell IV.*

Nono, Luigi. *Post-prae-ludium per Donau.* Ricordi. 1987. To Giancarlo Schiaffini.

Ostrander, Linda. *Time Out for Tuba and Tape Recorder.* V. For Barton Cummings. Written in 1979, this work calls for a tape made by the performer which will require multi-track recording equipment, a stopwatch and a lot of patience.

Ott, Joseph. *Bart's Piece.* Claude Benny Press. $9.00. 9:30. III–IV. A_1–a. One movement. For Barton Cummings. The score graphically represents the tape and gives event timings in seconds for the tuba part. There is only loose synchronization in the piece, and there are sections of improvisation. Notation and performance techniques are primarily traditional, though there are notations for the highest and the lowest possible notes. Recorded by Barton Cummings.

Ott, Joseph. *Concerto with Tape.* Claude Benny Press. 1974. $14.00. 18:00. IV. D_1–db'. One movement. Performance requires a technician, as the tape must be stopped and restarted several times on cue. The score gives a reasonably clear representation of the tape. The tuba part makes no unusual demands. Notation of the tuba part is primarily traditional, though the part is sometimes unmetered and there are a few instances of proportional notation.

Ott, Joseph. *Music for Tuba and Two Channel Tape.* Benny Press. 1972. 8:00–10:00. IV. C_1–c♯'. One movement. Composed at the request of Barton Cummings. This work calls for the performer to make the tape. The score for the tape part consists of eight staves, four per channel, and a tape overlay at certain points. The tape part is composed primarily of clusters and sequenced statements and will require considerable time to arrive at an adequate realization. The tuba part uses several extended techniques, including double tonguing, glissandi, and key clicks. There are instances of proportional notation and sections of free improvisation. The overall effect is that of a very large tuba ensemble.

Penn, William. *Capriccio.* See listing under "Music for Tuba in Mixed Ensemble."

Poore, Melvyn. *And Finally... for Tuba and Live Electronics.*

Poore, Melvyn. *One, Two, Three for Tuba and Delay System.*

Poore, Melvyn. *Playback I for Tuba and Recording/ Playback System.*

Poore, Melvyn. *Tubassoon for Tuba and 4-Channel Amplification System.*

Price, Joseph. *The Search for the Missing Marble.* V–VI. C_1–a♭'. One movement. Written in 1993. Also available for tuba and piano. There is no representation of the tape in the tuba score. The work is written in traditional meters with numerous metric and tempo changes. There are few rests for the tubist.

Riley, James. *Tubagogic.* This work requires significant studio taping and is very difficult.

Rollin, R. *The Raven and the First Men.* Seesaw. For tuba, horn, piano, and tape.

Ross, Walter. *Midnight Variations.* Dorn. 1971. 7:00. IV. F♯$_1$–c'. One movement. For Barton Cummings. An effective if somewhat dated composition for tuba and tape. The score very clearly depicts events on the tape with graphic notation. The tape is primarily electronically produced sounds. Most of the tuba part relies on extended techniques, including vocalizations, half-valve performance, and glissandi. See: Bird, Gary, ed., *Program Notes for the Solo Tuba.* Recorded by Bart Cummings.

Ross, Walter. *Piltdown Fragments.* Walter Ross. 1975. 9:15. IV–V. F$_1$–e'. One movement. For Barton Cummings. A very interesting work of many colors. The tape is primarily electronically generated, with some vocalization added. The texture tends to be thin throughout. The score uses a very clear graphic depiction of events on the tape and provides a time line with slashes representing a pulse to help place events. The tuba part is notated in a traditional fashion, though it occasionally uses vocalizations

and half-valve effects, which are depicted graphically. An excellent work worthy of attention. Recorded by Barton Cummings.

Ruggiero, Charles. *Fractured Mambos.* $45.00. 10:00. V. E♭$_1$–e'. One movement. For Philip Sinder. The tape combines recorded acoustic sounds as well as synthesized sounds in a dance/jazz setting. The rehearsal tape that is provided has an excellent tuba performance, which is very helpful in learning the work. It is more an ensemble feature than a technical display and should prove very popular in performance. See: Bird, Gary, ed., *Program Notes for the Solo Tuba.*

Schiaffini, Giancarlo. *Canzon "La volupiense."* Edipan. 1986.

Souster, Tim. *Heavy Reductions.*

Stevens, John D. *Soliloquy—Peace in Our Time with Tape.* 9:00. One movement. This composition relies entirely on improvisation. The tape is a prerecorded improvisation by the composer playing the piano. There is no written music for the tuba. See: Bird, Gary, ed., *Program Notes for the Solo Tuba.*

Stockhausen, Karlheinz. *Solo for Tuba and Tape.* Universal Edition. V. Written for tuba and tape prepared by the performer.

Winsor, Phillip. *Asleep in the Deep.* Pembroke Music. 1975. IV. One movement. The tape is made by the performer by overdubbing four other tuba parts. There is significant use of improvisation. The work may be performed as an ensemble. See listing under "Music for Multiple Tubas."

Witkin, Beatrice. *Breath and Sounds.* Belwin-Mills. 1975. $15.00. 9:00. IV. C_1–g♯'. Four movements: I; II; III; IV. The tape comes with both a performance track and a recorded performance of the work by Toby Hanks. The depiction of the tape in the score is sketchy but adequate. In addition to the graphic portrayal of the tape, every second on the work is marked by a dotted line and the number of seconds, thus setting a pulse. Much of the tuba part is freely interpreted. The third movement involves only vocalizations and nontraditional sounds.

Wraggett, Wes. *Cetecea.*

Wyatt, Scott A. *Lifepoints for Tuba with Percussion and Tape.* Scott Wyatt. 1990. 9:00. V. A♭$_1$–a'. Three movements: I; II; III. Commisioned for and dedicated to Skip Gray. This work is tremendously difficult from an ensemble standpoint. A high degree of proficiency is required of both musicians. The tape is a combination of electronically generated sounds and recorded acoustic sounds. The score combines both performers' parts and the tape part on three staves in traditional notation. The tuba part is extremely demanding technically. A contemporary work with minimalist influence.

Wyatt, Scott A. *Three for One.* TUBA Press. $18.00. 10:30. IV–V. C_1–a'. Three movements: I; II; III. A very entertaining and challenging work. Though it is in three movements, the tape runs continuously. The score clearly depicts events on the tape in a modified traditional notation. The tape consists of electronically generated sounds and recorded acoustic sounds. Of particular interest is the second movement's use of pre-recorded tuba sounds which combine with the live performance to create echo effects. A tremendously effective work, worthy of study and performance. Recorded by Dan Perantoni.

8. Music for Multiple Tubas
Charles A. McAdams

The published repertoire for multiple tubas has grown enormously in the last twenty years, not only in arrangements and transcriptions but also in original compositions. The more than 1,100 compositions listed in this chapter indicate this recent growth. As a matter of fact, the number of two-part listings in *The Tuba Source Book* exceeds the total of multiple tuba entries in *Tuba Music Guide* (Morris, 1973). Fortunately, as the quantity of literature has increased, so has the quality. Composers continue to discover the potential for expression with an ensemble consisting of tubas or euphoniums and tubas.

Although many of these compositions for multiple tubas are available from established publishers (i.e., Kendor, Shawnee Press, Theodore Presser, etc.), the bulk of this literature is being produced by smaller publishers, who often devote more than half of their catalogs to publications for the tuba.

"Multiple tubas" is defined as two or more tubas or any combination of euphoniums and tubas. However, for a composition to be listed here at least one of the parts has to be marked "tuba." Compositions for four euphoniums are not included, but compositions for three euphoniums and one tuba are. While there are many compositions for multiple trombones, bassoons, cellos, or string basses that are easily adapted for tuba and euphonium ensembles, the present listing is limited to those works composed or published for tubas.

Publishers and composers, in addition to our international consultants, provided materials and information to examine for this project. If part of an entry for a composition is missing (e.g., price, copyright date, range), it is because that information was not provided or could not be verified. Compositions whose entries are incomplete may also be more difficult to obtain.

The duration and grade level listed for each piece are meant to be guides, not absolutes. A composition for four tubas may be extremely challenging because of the range and technical demands of the first and second parts. However, with euphoniums playing the first or second part, the composition may be as much as a grade level easier and more approachable.

The annotations indicate whether a euphonium may be substituted for a tuba part or vice versa. There are, of course, tuba duets, trios, quartets, etc., where the composer had in mind only tubas, not tubas and euphoniums. The instrumentation given in the listing is exactly what appears on the printed score or part. Tubists have been transcribing music for years. Certainly Scott Joplin did not envision ragtime melodies played by euphonium and tubas, yet there are 21 arrangements of his "rags" published for two euphoniums and two tubas. Generally, performers should feel free to use whatever instrumentation best fits their needs.

Purchasing music from publishers encourages them to continue issuing music for multiple tubas. Many works are listed as out of print and no longer available; supporting the publishers of this music can prevent further loss of literature.

The research for this chapter was an enormous undertaking, and I would like to thank those who helped with this task: the publishers and composers who provided examination copies; Michael Bersin, Central Missouri State University, for his assistance in developing a database program to store and manage the information on all the compositions; Wesley True, Central Missouri State University, for his help with translations of international publications; and Kazuhisa Nishida, Osaka University of Arts, for obtaining and translating numerous Japanese publications. Others who provided invaluable information and materials include Jim Self, free-lance artist, Los Angeles; David Miles, editor of TUBA Press; Jan Bodeux and the Microsoft Corporation; and the staff at Wingert-Jones Music, Kansas City, Missouri. I would also like to thank my fellow assistant editors, Co-editor Edward Goldstein, and especially Senior Editor Winston Morris for his encouragement and support. And finally to my wife, Carol, and my children, James and Kathryn, I would like to express my gratitude for their support and patience.

Two Parts

Albam, Manny. *The Odd Couple*. Manncy Music. Two tubas.

Albert, Thomas. *Five for Two Tubas*. Brass Music Limited (The Brass Press). 1971. $3.50. 5:00. IV. Part I: A$_1$–a, Part II: F$_1$–a. Five movements: Prelude; Rondo; Meditation; Scherzo; Postlude. Dedicated to Daniel Perantoni. This piece uses very contemporary harmonies and rhythms. The first two movements are in mixed meter, the third movement requires a mute for both parts. Some sections are technically challenging.

Anderson, Eugene. *Baroque'n Brass*. Anderson's Arizona Originals. Trumpet or euphonium and tuba. 1991. $6.00. 5:00. IV. Part I: G#–d", Part II: D$_1$–d'. Commissioned by and dedicated to David L. Aubuchon, U.S. Army Band, Ft. Dix, New Jersey. A moderate tempo fugue. Technically challenging for both players. The tessitura of the first part is high.

Anderson, Eugene. *Teuphm'isms I*. Anderson's Arizona Originals. Euphonium and tuba. 1990. $5.00. 5:00. IV. Part I: G–c", Part II: F$_1$–f'. Dedicated to Brian Bowman and Harvey Phillips. Technically challenging for both parts. The tessitura of the first part is high. There are many syncopated rhythms in both parts.

Anderson, Eugene. *Teuphm'isms II*. Anderson's Arizona Originals. Euphonium and tuba. 1992. $5.00. 5:00. IV. Part I: G–c#", Part II: E$_1$–f'. Dedication: Dedicated to Brian Bowman and Harvey Phillips. Fanfare-like in character. Switches back and forth from 6/8 to 2/4. Both parts are challenging technically and have large range demands.

Anderson, Eugene. *Three Contrasts for Two Tubas*. Anderson's Arizona Originals. 1988. $5.00. 4:30. IV. Part I: G$_1$–d', Part II: E$_1$–b♭. Three movements: Allegretto; Rubato Espressivo; Forcefully. The first movement is in a canon-like style. The last movement has a few meter changes with many syncopated rhythms.

Bach, J.S. *Bach for Two Tubas*. arr. Scott MacMorran. Tuba/Euphonium Music Publications. Out of print. III–IV. Part I: D–d, Part II: G$_1$–f#. A collection of twelve minuets, marches, and one bourrée. Each lasts approximately two minutes. Selected movements may be combined into a suite for concert use.

Bach, J.S. *Duets and Trios*. arr. Daniel S. Augustine. Southern Music Company. Two or three tubas. 1972. $7.95. 17 pp. III–IV. Part I: F–f', Part II: F$_1$–b♭, Part III: F$_1$–f. A collection of short minuets, marches, and other dances, including thirteen duets and three trios. Ten of the sixteen arrangements are from the *Clavier Book of Anna Magdalena Bach,* the composer's second wife. The first part works equally well on euphonium. Individual movements may be played alone or combined into a suite.

Bach, J.S. *Tuba Duo Nine*. arr. James Self. Basset Hound Music. Two tubas. 1988. $5.00. 4:00. IV–V. Part I: G$_1$–d', Part II: G$_1$–d'. This transcription is

from the second movement (Largo) of Bach's Concerto for Two Violins. A beautiful melody that is lyrical and technically challenging. Works very well.

Bach, J.S. *Twelve Duets*. arr. Ronald Dishinger. Medici Music Press. Two tubas. 1993. $9.50.

Bach, J.S. *Twelve Two-Part Inventions*. Miller. David McNaughton. Two tubas.

Bach, J.S. *Two-Part Inventions*. arr. Allen Ostrander. Kendor Music, Incorporated. Two tubas. 1976. $6.50. 5:20. IV–V. Part I: C–e♭', Part II: (F$_1$)G$_1$–d'. Four movements. Dedicated to Bill Bell. Bach wrote fifteen two-part inventions and fifteen three-part inventions for the clavier. These arrangements of Nos. 1, 3, 12, and 15 of the Two-Part Inventions are transposed down a major sixth for the tuba. They may be played individually or in any combination. The Inventions contrast in meter and tempo and are very challenging to play at the tempos marked.

Bach, J.S. *Vivace from Concerto No. 3 in D minor*. arr. James Self. Wimbledon Music Incorporated. Two tubas. 1979. $7.00. 5:00. IV. Part I: A$_1$–d', Part II: G$_1$–d'. This concerto was originally written for two violins. Written in a fugal style, this composition requires good technique and a strong sense of rhythm. Effective as a finale in a recital.

Bach, W.F. *Tuba Duo Five*. arr. James Self. Basset Hound Music. Two tubas. 1984. $5.00. 4:45. IV. Part I: B♭$_1$–e♭', Part II: E♭$_1$–e♭'. The texture is very polyphonic. There are many large skips. Requires light and agile playing. Many technically challenging sections.

Bach, W.F. *Tuba Duo Six*. arr. James Self. Basset Hound Music. Two tubas. 1985. $5.00. 4:00. IV. Part I: C–d', Part II: A$_1$–d'. Both parts are technically challenging. The texture is very polyphonic and the parts are quite interesting. Requires strong players.

Badarak, Mary Lynn. *Bass Lied and Valse to Bass*. T.U.B.A. Journal. Euphonium and tuba. 1976. $7.50. 2:30. IV. Part I: A–d', Part II: F$_1$–a. Two movements: Bass Lied; Valse to Bass. The first movement is slow and lyrical with contemporary harmonies. The second is multimetric, switching between 5/8, 4/8, and 6/8. Written as part of the T.U.B.A. GEM series and published in the *T.U.B.A. Journal,* Vol. 3, no. 3.

Bartles, Alfred H. *Beersheba Neo-Baroque Suite*. Brass Music Limited (The Brass Press). 1975. $5.00. 5:30. IV. Part I: G–g, Part II: F$_1$–e'. Four movements: Prelude; Gavotte; Sarabande; Gigue—Postlude. For Winston Morris. The first part may be played on cello, euphonium, or trombone. See listing under "Music for Tuba in Mixed Ensemble."

Bartles, Alfred H. *T.U.B.A. Canon*. T.U.B.A. Journal. Two tubas. 1975. $7.50. 2:30. IV. Part I: D$_1$–c#', Part II: D$_1$–c#'. For Winston Morris. The first section is a canon two measures apart. The second section is a canon one measure apart with a 6/4 time signature. Written as part of the T.U.B.A. GEM Series and published in the *T.U.B.A. Journal*, Vol. 2, no. 3.

Beasley, R. *Four Miniatures for Trombone and Tuba*. Trombone and tuba.

Belden, George R. *Ginnungigap*. T.U.B.A. Journal. Euphonium and tuba. 1977. $7.50. 2:30. IV. Part I: F♯–b♭', Part II: F♯$_1$–f '. A programmatic description of the creation of the world as told in Scandinavian mythology. Both parts are difficult and have extreme range demands. Very contemporary harmonies. Written as part of the T.U.B.A. GEM series and published in the *T.U.B.A. Journal*, Vol. 5, no. 1.

Belden, George R. *Ragnarok*. Tenuto Publications. Euphonium and tuba. 1983. $3.50. 2:20. IV. Part I: c–b♭', Part II: E$_1$–b♭. Originally written in 1978. A programmatic description of the final destruction of the world, a companion piece to *Ginnungigap*. Contains many syncopated rhythms.

Bell, William, arr. *Artistic Solos and Duets*. Charles Colin. Euphonium and tuba. 1975. $5.95. 15 pp. IV. Part I: B–a', Part II: F–f '. A collection of thirteen duets arranged for two low brass instruments taken from the *Complete Tuba Method* by William Bell. Not technically difficult, but the tessitura of the second part is high. Several of the passages may be played down an octave. See also "Methods and Studies."

Benson, Warren. *Serpentine Shadows*. T.U.B.A. Journal. Two tubas. 1973. $7.50. 4:15. III–IV. Part I: C$_1$–e♭', Part II: C$_1$–e♭'. Four movements: Song; Dance; Hymn; Riff. Written as part of the T.U.B.A. GEM Series and published in the *T.U.B.A. Journal*, Vol.1, no. 2.

Blazhevich, Vladislav. *Two Concert Duets*. arr. Herbert Wekselblatt. G. Schirmer Incorporated. Two tubas. 1964. $13.95. 2:30. III–IV. Part I: G$_1$–c', Part II: F$_1$–g. Two movements: Andante; Allegro Vivo. The first movement is very slow and lyrical. The second is in a bright 6/8 meter in a polyphonic style. This is one of two duets published in a collection of tuba solos. See Wekselblatt, H., *Solos for the Tuba Player* in "Music for Tuba and Keyboard."

Boccherini, Luigi. *Tuba Duo Eleven, Op. 5*. arr. James Self. Basset Hound Music. Two tubas. 1990. $5.00. 5:30. IV–V. Part I: B♭$_1$–e♭', Part II: G$_1$–e♭'. A nice melody that is technically challenging and frequently passed between the two parts. There are many large skips in the second part. Works very well. Will require strong players.

Bourgeois, Derek. *March and Fugue for Two Tubas, Op. 40 and 55*. Vanderbeek and Imirie Limited. Two tubas. 1985. 5:30. IV. Part I: B♭$_1$–e', Part II: E♭$_1$–g. Two movements: March; Fugue. The top part is written for an E♭ or F tuba. Most of the work is in the first part. There are some meter changes

and the harmonies in the first movement are dissonant. The last two measures of the first movement require multiphonics in both parts. Originally published by Tuba/Euphonium Ensemble Publications, a project of the local chapter of T.U.B.A. at Ball State University.

Brandon, Sy. *Recital Duets for Two Tubas*. TUBA Press. 1981. $7.00. 9:00. III–IV. Part I: A$_1$–a, Part II: G♭$_1$–a. Seven movements: Fanfare; Waltz; Chorale; March; Bel Canto; Canons; Gigue. Utilizes traditional harmonies. The fifth movement contains several recitatives and rubato sections. Players will need to listen and count carefully. Playable by good high school players.

Brown, Newel Kay. *Dialogue and Dance*. Seesaw Music Corporation Publishers. Trombone (euphonium) and tuba. 1978. $12.00. 6:00. IV–V. Part I: G$_1$–b♭', Part II: A♭$_1$–e'. Two movements: Resolutely; Gay. Dedicated to David Kuehn and G. B. Lane. Very contemporary harmonies. Both parts are technically challenging. Sections of the first part are printed in tenor clef. Both players read from a single score. Requires strong players.

Butterfield, Don. *Seven Duets for Tubas*. DB Publishing Company. 1960. 15:00. III–IV. Part I: C–c, Part II: E♭$_1$–g. Seven movements: To The Spartans; Archaic Portrait; Swingsville; Toccata; Abstraction; Sound Imagery; Construction in Keys. Dedicated to William J. Bell. A collection of duets in varying styles. Technical difficulty ranges from moderate to very difficult. The first part may also be played on euphonium. The duets may be performed individually or arranged into a suite.

Buttery, Gary. *Wallowed Out*. Whaling Music Publishers. Two tubas. 1975. $5.00. 4:30. IV. Part I: F♯–g', Part II: G$_1$–b. Three movements: June 17, 1972; Periodicity of Infinity; 'Pardon Me' March. The first movement alternates between 3/4 and 4/4 with the 3/4 section played in one. The third movement is marked "very rapid" in 6/8. Buttery wrote this for a composition recital; it was premiered on June 18, 1975. The composition is programmatic and is a satire of the Watergate affair. The first part may be played on euphonium.

Carnardy, J. *Thirty Progressive Duos*. Two tubas.

Catelinet, Philip. *The Alpha Suite*. Philip Catelinet. Out of print. Euphonium and tuba. 7:30. IV. Part I: B♭–a♯', Part II: A$_1$–a♭. Three movements: Aerimony; Amiability; Affinity. All three movements are very polyphonic. No significant technical problems, but players will need to count carefully. Fairly traditional harmonic structure.

Catelinet, Philip. *Suite in Miniature*. Hinrichsen Edition Limited (C.F. Peters). Two tubas. 1952. $4.20. 5:30. III–IV. Part I: E♭–d', Part II: C–a. Three movements: Minuet; Invocata; Ecossaise. Three movements in contrasting styles published for trombones, euphoniums, or tubas. The first part may be performed on either euphonium or tuba. First and third movements are recorded by Karl Megules, Recorded Publications Company, Z434471.

Chedeville, Philippe. *Three Rococo Dances.* arr. Randall Block. The Musical Evergreen. Two tubas. 1975. $3.50. 4:30. III–IV. Part I: F–c', Part II: F–b♭. Three movements: Rondeau; Contredance; Gigue. The dances are very polyphonic and typical of the style invoked by the title.

Conley, Lloyd, arr. *Christmas for Two.* Kendor Music, Incorporated. Euphonium and tuba. 1981. $9.50. 21 pp. III. Part I: A–f ', Part II: A♭₁–f. Easy arrangements of ten familiar Christmas carols: O Come All Ye Faithful; We Three Kings; Deck the Halls; O Little Town;The First Noel; Hark, the Herald; It Came Upon A Midnight Clear; Jingle Bells; Silent Night; and Joy to the World. Traditional harmonies often used in a contrapuntal style. Arrangements are very appropriate for high school concerts or church. The last three are more technically challenging.

Constantinides, Dinos. *Dedications for Baritone and Tuba.* Dinos Constantinides. Euphonium and tuba. 1989. $5.00. 6:20. IV–V. Part I: G–a', Part II: G₁–f '. Three movements: Pandiatonic; Polytonal; Quartal. Good technique is required of both players at the tempo marked. Harmonies are representative of the names of the movements. The third movement is multimetric, and the second has some tenor clef lines in the first part. Originally written in 1970.

Corelli, Arcangelo. *Sonata da Chiesa.* arr. R. Winston Morris. Ludwig Music Publishing Company. Two tubas and piano. 1970. $7.00. 8:00. IV. Part I: D–d', Part II: C–d'. Five movements: Grave; Allegro Moderato; Allegretto; Adagio; Allegro Vivace. Very nice Baroque melodies. The music is polyphonic, but not overly demanding technically. A harpsichord could be substituted for the piano. Fun to play.

Danburg, Russell. *Prelude and Tarantella.* Wingert-Jones Music, Incorporated. Two tubas. 1982. $5.00. 4:00. IV. Part I: F₁–c', Part II: A♭₁–c'. Two movements: Prelude; Tarantella. The first movement is slow and lyrical and provides some very interesting harmonies as it weaves in and out of major and minor modes. The second movement is a frolicking dance. Both parts have similar range demands and responsibilities.

De Filippi, Amedeo. *Divertimento.* Robert King Music Sales, Incorporated. Euphonium and tuba. 1968. $5.55. 9:00. III. Part I: c–g', Part II: G₁–b♭. Five movements: March; Intermezzo I; Tempo Di Valse; Intermezzo II; Rondino. Ranges and level of technical difficulty make this very appropriate for high school use.

De Jong, Conrad. *Music for Two Tubas.* Elkan-Vogel. Two tubas or euphonium and tuba. 1964. $1.95. 5:00. III. Part I: D–c', Part II: G₁–e♭. Three move-

ments: Fanfare; Canon; Finale. Dedicated to Dick and Don. Three contrasting movements. The canon is in a lyrical style. These three contrasting movements work particularly well for high school students. The first part may be played by a euphonium.

Defaye, Jean-Michel. *Six Etudes.* Alphonse Leduc Editions. Two tubas.

Devienne, Francois. *Duet in F.* arr. Kenneth Singleton. Peer International Corporation. Out of print. Two tubas. 1976. $3.50. 8:00. IV. Part I: E–e', Part II: E–e'. Two movements: Allegro; Grazioso con Variatione. Originally part of *Six Duets, Op. 18*, for flutes. In the second movement, the final variation is quite technical, with the melody constantly switching between the two parts.

Devienne, Francois. *Four Duets, Op. 82.* arr. Mitchell Gershenfeld. Medici Music Press. Two tubas. 1984. $9.50. 9:00. III–IV. Part I: C–b♭, Part II: G₁–g. Four movements: I; II; III; IV. The movements contrast in key and meter, but they all begin with a section in moderate tempo, followed by a Rondo/Trio. No significant technical problems. Works well.

Dutton, Brent. *One Slow, One Fast.* Seesaw Music Corporation Publishers. Two tubas. 1978. $12.00. 5:30. IV. Part I: F₁–f ', Part II: F₁–e♭'. Two movements: I; II Rondo. For Stevie. The first movement is slow and fairly conservative. The second movement is multimetric and more challenging technically. Some dissonant harmonies.

Dutton, Brent. *Pretty Forms.* Seesaw Music Corporation Publishers. Two tubas. 1977. $12.00. 4:00. V. Part I: A₁–e', Part II: B♭₂–g'. Four movements: Liturgical Circles; Spots; Fugue; A Very Peasant Dance. Extreme technical and range demands required of both parts. The second movement contains mostly multiphonics. Very contemporary in character.

Dutton, Brent. *Some Loose Canons.* Seesaw Music Corporation Publishers. Two tubas. 1977. $12.00. 6:00. IV–V. Part I: D♭₁–e', Part II: B♭2–e'. Six movements: I; II; III; IV; V; VI. Dedicated to Ronald Bishop. A few mixed meters with many triplets, quintuplets, and septuplets. Numerous octave, eleventh, and thirteenth skips in the melody. Originally written in 1971. Very challenging to play.

Dutton, Brent. *Then and Now.* Seesaw Music Corporation Publishers. Euphonium and tuba. 1978. $12.00. 5:00. IV–V. Part I: G♭–b♭', Part II: G♭₁–d'. Two movements: Then; Now. Written for Ken Henning and Mark Edwards. The second movement contains many twentieth-century techniques, including singing and yelling through the horn, slapping the bell, and foot stomps. The first movement is in a more traditional style. Very difficult.

Ferstl, Herbert, arr. *Sechs und Zwanzig Tuba Duette.* Georg Bauer Musikverlag. Two tubas. 1987.

$12.00. 24 pp. III. Part I: E–b♭, Part II: F₁–f. A collection of 26 melodies by German and French composers. No significant range or technical problems. The duets are short and excellent for study. They may be grouped together as a suite for performance.

Frackenpohl, Arthur. *Brass Duo*. Robert King Music Sales, Incorporated. Horn (euphonium) and tuba. 1972. $5.55. 7:00. IV. Part I: B♭–b'(c"), Part II: F₁–b♭. Four movements: Prelude; Ballad; Scherzo; Variations. Fine traditional writing. May be performed with F horn and tuba or euphonium and tuba. The tessitura of the first part is high. See listing under "Tuba in Mixed Ensemble."

Frackenpohl, Arthur. *Pop Suite No. 2*. Horizon Press. Euphonium and tuba. 1991. $5.00. 9:30. IV. Part I: c–c", Part II: F₁–b♭. Three movements: Tango; Waltz; March. The tango and march are very syncopated and will require very careful counting. All three movements are tuneful, and fun to play, but challenging.

Frackenpohl, Arthur. *Song and Dance*. Horizon Press. Euphonium, tuba, and piano. 1991. $10.00. 8:00. IV–V. Part I: B♭–c', Part II: G₁–c♭'. Two movements: Slowly; Moderately. A challenging piece for both parts. Each one has an opportunity to play the melody. Ossia sections provide alternatives to some of the rhythmic and range demands.

Frackenpohl, Arthur, arr. *Five Bach Duos for Euphonium and Tuba*. Williams Music Publishing Company. Euphonium and tuba. 1993. $10.00. 8:45. IV. Part I: B♭–c", Part II: F₁–b♭. Five movements: Two-part Invention No. 4; Sarabande; Aria; Minuett; Chorale Prelude. Traditional arrangement of these famous Bach melodies. The first part is written in tenor clef.

Fritze, Gregory. *Fifteen Spectrum Duets for Tubas*. Gregory Fritze. 1990. $10.00. 30 pp. IV–V. Part I: C₁–f', Part II: C₁–c'. Fifteen movements: Serenade; Gallop; Waltz; Dance; untitled; Rock and Jazz Dance; Pastoral; Song; untitled; Invention; Light Swing; Double/Half Tempo; Song; Gallop; Fanfare. Contrasting movements in a traditional style, except for one that is very contemporary in design. Both parts have melodic responsibility and have many technical challenges. The duets may be played individually or in small groups as a suite.

Fux, Johann Joseph. *Sonata Pastorale (K. 397)*. arr. Paul F. Hartin. Cellar Press. Two tubas and piano. 1974. 3:00. III–IV. Part I: D–d', Part II: E–a. Two movements: Adagio; Un poco allegro. Two contrasting movements in Classical style. Not technically difficult, playable by high school students.

Garrett, James A. *Duet for Tubas*. The Brass Press. Out of print. 1974. 5:00. III–IV. Part I: A♭₁–c', Part II: G♭₁–c'. A one-movement work in 3/8 with both marcato and lyrical sections. Not rhythmically difficult. Large skips in the melody.

Garrett, James A. *Fantasia for Tuba Duo*. The Brass Press. 1974. $3.50. 5:00. IV. Part I: A₁–e♭', Part II: A♭₁–c'. Three movements: Adagio Sonoro; Agitato; Andante Sonoro. Very interesting writing contrasting sections. Numerous meter and style changes. The two parts are of equal difficulty.

Gearhart, Livingston, arr. *Bass Clef Sessions*. Shawnee Press, Incorporated. 1954. $7.50. 50 pp. III–IV. Part I: c–b♭', Part II: F–g'. A collection of 62 two-, three-, and four-part arrangements for euphonium and tuba. Styles range from Renaissance to jazz. See listing below under "Four Parts."

Geer, Karen. *Suite for Two Tubas*. Ludwig Music Publishing Company. Two tubas. 1984. $4.50. 5:00. III–IV. Part I: C–e♭', Part II: E₁–c'. Three movements: March; Canon; Waltz. The march contains many major sevenths and ninths. The last movement is very tonal and harmonically simple. The texture of the outer two movements is homophonic.

Geib, Fred. *A Joyous Dialogue, Op. 11*. Mills Music. Out of print. 1941. 3:00. III. Part I: C–g, Part II: E–b♭. For tuba and piano with an optional second tuba part, making a tuba duet possible. Contains a traditional theme, cadenza, and variation section.

Gibbons, Orlando. *Fantasia*. The Musical Evergreen. Two tubas. 1971. $2.50. 2:00. IV. Part I: D♭–c', Part II: D♭–c'. Typical Renaissance polyphonic fantasia. A lot of syncopation and rhythmic challenges associated with this type of close canon-like writing.

Gillam, Russell C. *Tuba Duet No. 1*. Two tubas and piano. 1967. 3:00. III. Part I: C–f, Part II: G₁–e. Very usable by high school players, as the piano accompaniment strongly supports the melody. No real technical problems.

Gillis, Lew. *Ten Duets*. Virgo Music Publishers. Trombone (euphonium) and tuba. 1986. $7.95. 13 pp. IV. Part I: D♭₁–f', Part II: G–a'. Movements vary in difficulty, depending on range, and in style, key, and tempo. Several combinations of movements will work on a program.

Gillis, Lew. *Ten More Duets, Book 2*. Virgo Music Publishers.

Goedicke, Alexander. *Concert Suite*. Philharmusica Corporation. Euphonium and tuba. 1974. $6.00. 7:30. IV. Part I: B♭–ab', Part II: B♭₁–e♭'. Six movements: I; II; III; IV; V; VI. Very polyphonic, but not technically difficult. The tessitura of both parts is high.

Goldman, Richard Franko. *Duo for Tubas*. Mercury Music Corporation. Out of print. 1950. 3:00. IV. Part I: G₁–c', Part II: F₁–b. Three movements: Allegro commodo; Andante pessimistico; Vigoroso. For Frederick W. Prausnitz. Written in twelve-tone technique. The second movement is based on an inversion of the theme, the third movement is based on the retrograde. Not rhythmically challenging.

Handel, G.F. *Nine Duets.* arr. Ronald Dishinger. Medici Music Press. Two tubas. 1993. $10.50.

Hartin, Paul F. *Two Medieval Carols.* Cellar Press. Two tubas. 1974. IV. Part I: c–d', Part II: C–f. Two movements: Parit Virgo Filium; Cantilena: Princeps Serenissine. Typical Renaissance syncopated rhythms. Euphonium may be used on the first part.

Hartley, Walter. *Bivalve Suite.* Autograph Editions. Euphonium and tuba. 1971. $8.50. 3:00. IV. Part I: F–a', Part II: E♭₁–d♭'. Three movements: Allegro moderato; Lento; Presto. For Edward Bahr and C. Rudolph Emilson. Fun to play but there are several challenging ensemble problems. Recorded by Robert LeBlanc and Paul Droste, *Euphonium Favorites for Recital and Contest,* Coronet, LPS 3203.

Hartzell, Doug. *Ten Jazz Duos and Solos.* Shawnee Press, Incorporated. Euphonium and tuba. 1974. $6.00. 7:30. IV–V. Part I: B♭–a♭', Part II: F–a♭'. Six movements: Funky Monkeys; Split-Level; Swingin' in Seven; Tri-Level; Rock Pile; Short Ballad for Short Chicks. From a collection of ten jazz melodies: four solos, five duets, and one trio. Written for any two bass-clef instruments but would work best with one euphonium and one tuba. Technically challenging for both parts. Chord symbols are included so piano, bass, and drums may be easily added for concert use.

Haugland, A. Oscar. *Suite No. 16 for Two Tubas.* HOA Music Publishers. 1993. $4.00. 4:20. IV. Part I: F♯–c', Part II: F♯–d♭. Four movements: Allegro con brio; Allegretto; Tempo giusto; Andantino. Traditional harmonic structure. No significant technical demands except in the third movement, which is multimetric. This suite works pretty well.

Haugland, A. Oscar. *Suite No. 17 for Two Tubas.* HOA Music Publishers. 1993. $4.00. 4:20. IV. Part I: G–b, Part II: E₁–c. Four movements: Allegro; Moderato; Lento; Allegretto. The technical demands and harmonies are more complex than in *Suite No. 16.* No range problems. Good reading material.

Haugland, A. Oscar. *Suite No. 18 for Two Tubas.* HOA Music Publishers. 1993. $5.00. 6:00. IV. Part I: E–b, Part II: E₁–e. Five movements: Allegro non troppo; Lento; Allegretto amabile; Allegretto; Scherzo. More complicated than the previous Suites with regard to key and technique. The movements contrast in style, meter, and key. Interesting writing.

Haugland, A. Oscar. *Suite No. 19 for Two Tubas.* HOA Music Publishers. 1993. $5.00. 4:30. IV. Part I: A–c♯', Part II: A₁–g♯. Five movements: Andantino; Andante; Andante; Adagio; Risoluto. Parts have equal responsibility for the melody. Melodies are frequently passed back and forth between parts. Movements contrast in key and style.

Haugland, A. Oscar. *Suite No. 20 for Two Tubas.* HOA Music Publishers. 1993. $5.00. 6:00. IV. Part I: G–e', Part II: G₁–d. Five movements: Allegro giocoso;

Allegro moderato; Allegro; Moderato; Allegro non troppo. More challenging technically than the other suites by Haugland. Rhythms are more complex and syncopated, the third movement is multimetric and complicated. Requires strong players.

Hawkins, Alan, arr. *Twenty Duets from Symphonic Masterworks.* Shawnee Press, Incorporated. Euphonium and tuba. 1985. $4.95. 32 pp. IV. Part I: G–c", Part II: B♭₁–f. Twenty famous melodies from symphonies by Haydn, Mozart, Beethoven, Schubert, Brahms, etc. The first part is responsible for the melody most of the time. Because of their familiarity, these melodies are enjoyable to play.

Haydn, F.J. *Tuba Duo Ten, Op. 99.* arr. James Self. Basset Hound Music. 1989. $5.00. 4:45. IV–V. Part I: A₁–e♭', Part II: A₁–d'. A very nice melody. Technically challenging, several skips of one to two octaves. Parts are of equal difficulty. Fun to play.

Heidler, Manfred, arr. *Drie Duette für Tuba, Band I.* Carpe-Diem Music Verlag Claudia Wölpper. Two tubas. 1993. $18.00

Heidler, Manfred, arr. *Drie Duette für Tuba, Band II.* Carpe-Diem Music Verlag Claudia Wölpper. Two tubas. 1993. $18.00

Hewitt, Harry. *Six Preludes for Euphonium and Tuba, Op. 246C.* TUBA Press. Out of print. Euphonium and tuba. 1991. 14:00. IV. Part I: A♭–g♭', Part II: B♭₁–f♭'. Six movements; 1; 2; 3; 4; 5; 6. Challenging pieces in a contemporary harmonic setting. Technical and rhythmic challenges especially in the fourth movement. Several movements have ad lib. sections requiring players to watch the score and listen carefully. Requires strong players. Originally written in 1983 and titled *Six Preludes for Baritone and Tuba.*

Hewitt, Harry. *Suite for Harp and Two Tubas.* Harry Hewitt. 1977. 8:00. IV. Part I: E–f♯', Part II: F₁–f♯. Four movements: I; II; III; IV. The harp part may be played by celeste or vibes. Tuba parts are not very interesting or challenging except for the range demands of the first part. The tubas primarily provide accompaniment for the harp.

Hewitt, Harry. *Suite for Tuba Duo, Op. 376.* Harry Hewitt. 1972. 9:30. IV. Part I: A♭₁–e'(a♭'), Part II: F₁–e♭. Five movements. Contemporary tonal style with each movement differing in key and tempo. In some movements the first part may be played by a euphonium.

Hoesly, John, arr. *Christmas Collection—Duets For Brass.* Piston Reed Stick and Bow Publisher. Two tubas. 1990. $17.00. 19 pp. III–IV. Part I: B♭₁–b♭, Part II: G₁–g. Fourteen movements: Jingle Bells; Good King Wenceslas; We Three Kings; Deck the Halls; God Rest Ye Merry Gentlemen; Angels We Have Heard on High; O Come All Ye Faithful; O, Christmas Tree; It Came Upon a Midnight Clear; Joy to the World; We Wish You a Merry Christmas; Hark, The Herald Angels Sing; The First Noel;

Silent Night. Both parts have only moderate technical challenges and no range problems. Ideal for good high school players or anyone looking for fun arrangements of Christmas music. There is another version available for euphonium and tuba. The parts and score are all sold separately.

Hudadoff, Igor, arr. *Concert and Ensemble Folio (Bandsembles).* Pro Art Publications (see CPP Belwin Incorporated). Out of print. Two tubas. 1961. 24 pp. II–III. A collection of 22 popular tunes usable as easy duets for junior high or high school.

Israel, Brian. *Sonata No. One.* Tritone Press. Two tubas. 1979. $4.00. 6:05. IV. Part I: F₁–d♭, Part II: F₁–c'. Three movements: 1; 2; 3. To Rick and Al Balestra. Moderate technical challenges. The two parts have equal responsibility for the melody. Interesting two-part writing.

Israel, Brian. *Sonata No. Two.* Tritone Press. Two tubas. 1977. $3.00. 4:30. III–IV. Part I: B♭₁–c♯', Part II: A₁–b. Three movements: Allegro non troppo; Andante; Vivace. Question-and-answer style in the first movement. Part one may be played by a euphonium in the first two movements.

Jacobsen, Julius. *Ten Duets for Two Tubas.* Swedish Music Information Center—STIM. 1983. 15:00. IV–V. Part I: B♭₁–e', Part II: F₁–e♭'. Technically challenging for both parts. The movements vary in meter, key, and style. Fun to play, but challenging. Movements may be performed individually or grouped together in small suites.

Jones, Roger. *21 Distinctive Duets for Tuba.* University of Miami Press. Out of print. 1973. 32 pp. III–IV. Part I: G₁–d', Part II: F₁–a. Each duet is in a different style and tempo. Many will work well for good high school players. They may be played individually or arranged in small suites. Some of the movements are quite tuneful. Duet No. 12 recorded by the University of Miami Tuba Ensemble, Miami United Tuba Society, 14568.

Jones, Roger. *Two Tuba Suites, Book 1.* Roger Jones. Two tubas. 1981. $10.00. 24 pp. IV. Part I: G₁–g, Part II: F₁–f. Six suites: 1; 2; 3; 4; 5; 6. Suites 1, 2, 3, and 5 contain three movements, suites 4 and 6 have four movements. Both parts are interesting and share melodic responsibilities. The movements in each suite contrast in meter and key. These work well.

Jones, Roger. *Two Tuba Suites, Book 2.* Roger Jones. Two tubas. 1988. $15.00. 42 pp. IV. Part I: F₁–c', Part II: F₁–g. Four suites: 7; 8; 9; 10. Each suite contains four movements that contrast in meter and tempo. The melodies are often syncopated and at times are technically challenging.

Joplin, Scott. *Easy Winners.* Arr. David LeClair. ITC Editions Marc Reift. Euphonium, tuba, and piano. 1979. 2:45. IV. Part I: B♭–d♭", Part II: A♭₁–d♭'. Recorded by David LeClair, Contraband, *Swingin' Low*, Marcophon CD 940-2.

Joubert, Claude-Henry. *Ten Duos Concertants.*

Kelly, Michael S. *Sonata.* Euphonium and tuba. 1979.

Krush, Jay. *Largo and Allegro.* The Brass Press. Two tubas. 1974. $3.50. 3:00. III–IV. Part I: G–a, Part II: C₁–a. One-movement work that alternates in tempo between Largo and Allegro. Works well with high school students but also interesting for university level.

Lasso, Orlando di. *Fantasias.* arr. Richard E. Powell. Southern Music Company. Out of print. Euphonium and tuba. 1970. 4:00. IV.

Leavitt, Daniel Joe. *Sub-Voce Entropy.* West Wind Music Company. Two tubas. 1986. 3:00. 3:30. IV. Part I: E–e♭', Part II: E–e♭'. This is an aleatory composition. The players read from a chart consisting of 40 measures. They start anywhere and play the measures in any order as long as every measure is played only once by each player. Technical demands depend on the speed of the performance. Good introduction to aleatory music.

LeClair, David. *Growing Up Together.* ITC Editions Marc Reift. Euphonium and tuba. 1993. 4:25. IV–IV. Part I: G–b', Part II: A♭₁–f'. Recorded by David LeClair, Contraband, *Swingin' Low*, Marcophon CD 940-2.

Luedeke, Raymond. *Eight Bagatelles.* Tenuto Publications. Two tubas. 1970. $7.00. 9:00. IV. Part I: E₁–e♭', Part II: B♭₂–c'. For Lee Richardson. May be performed completely, or selections may be chosen for a suite. The second part has several occurrences of B₂ and C♯₂. Several technically challenging sections, two-octave leaps, etc. The sixth and seventh movements are in mixed meter.

Luedeke, Raymond. *Wonderland Duets.* Tenuto Publications. Two tubas and narrator. 1971. $6.00. 5:00. IV. Part I: D₁–d♭', Part II: D₁–d♭'. Based on Lewis Carroll's *Alice in Wonderland.* The tuba parts are very challenging. The narrator should be able to read the text in rhythm. Good recital material, a real audience pleaser.

Mason, J. Kent, arr. *Serpent Duets.* Sonante Publications. Two tubas. 1990. $5.00. 6:00. Part I: G₁–c', Part II: G₁–g. Five movements. Dedication: To commemorate the 400th anniversary of the Serpent. These duets were originally published in the *Method de Serpent* by the Conservatoire de Paris in 1812. The second movement is challenging rhythmically, but all movements are very approachable and quite enjoyable to play.

McCurdy, Gary L. *Chorale and Gigue.* TMC Publications. Out of print. Euphonium and tuba.

McCurdy, Gary L. *The Coloring Book.* TMC Publications. Out of print. Two tubas. 1975. 4:00. II–III. Part I: C–d, Part II: B♭₁–c. Four movements. Range and technical demands make this suitable for young tubists.

McCurdy, Gary L. *Prelude and Fugue.* TMC Publications. Out of print. Two tubas. 1971. 3:00. III. Part I: C–c', Part II: A₁–g. Fugue is in typical

Baroque style, very polyphonic. Technical demands, however, allow this to be performed by high school players.

McCurdy, Gary L. *Twelve Duets for Tubas.* TMC Publications. (Out of print). 1971. 9 pp. III–IV. Part I: Bb_1–c', Part II: F_1–e. Twelve short duets, each twelve measures in length, in twelve different keys. The challenge of these movements are the different keys and some slight technical demands.

McCurdy, Gary L. *Two Impressions.* TMC Publications. Out of print. Two tubas. 1971. 2:00. III. Part I: Bb–f, Part II: E_1–db.

McCurdy, Gary L. *Waltz of the Walrus.* TMC Publications. Out of print. Two tubas. 1972. 2:00. III–IV Part I: F–f, Part II: Bb_1–eb. May be performed by two tubas, or by tuba with piano or band accompaniment.

Morley, Thomas. *Tuba Duets.* arr. Leigh Anne Hunsaker. Harold Gore Publishing Company. 1991. $10.00. 41 pp. III. Part I: G_1–g, Part II: F_1–g. Transcription of 21 songs by Thomas Morley. There are very few technical demands, and the ranges are well within the capabilities of a high school player.

Mozart, W.A. *Duets for Tuba.* arr. Wesley Jacobs. Encore Music Publishers. 1989. $16.00. 23 pp. IV. Part I: D–d', Part II: F#$_1$–ab. Twelve movements, varying in technical and range demands, key, meter, and style. Several of the movements are very tuneful and enjoyable to play.

Mozart, W.A. *Eleven Mozart Duets for Bass Clef Instruments.* arr. Richard E. Powell. Shawnee Press, Incorporated. 1972. $7.00. 15 pp. IV. Part I: d–c", Part II: c_1–f'. Duets of varying style and tempo originally written for two horns. The first part should be played on euphonium, the second on tuba. Younger tubists may wish to play some of the passages an octave lower.

Mozart, W.A. *Five Duets.* arr. Paul F. Hartin. Cellar Press. Two tubas. 1974. 6:00. IV. Part I: F–f ', Part II: F_1–gb. Five movements: Allegro; Menuetto; Polonaise; Larghetto; Allegro. Five contrasting movements of familiar Mozart melodies. First part is very playable by a euphonium. Arrangements work very well.

Mozart, W.A. *Seven Menuets K. 65A.* arr. Ronald C. Dishinger. Medici Music Press. Two tubas. 1990. $7.50. 8 pp. III–IV. Part I: C_1–c', Part II: F_1–f. In standard minuet, trio, minuet form. Originally written by Mozart when he was thirteen years old. The first piece is in the key of Ab; the rest are in the key of Bb. Movements may be performed individually or grouped together in any number. A couple of these work really well.

Mozart, W.A. *Sonata for Two Tubas, K. 292.* arr. Rex Conner. PP Music. 1993. $6.50. 13:00. IV. Part I: C–d', Part II: Bb_1–c'. Three movements: Moderato; Andante; Rondo—Allegro. Originally written for bassoon and cello, now transposed down a fifth.

Both parts are tuneful and technically challenging. Would also work well for euphonium and tuba. Requires strong players.

Mozart, W.A. *Tuba Duo Eight.* arr. James Self. Basset Hound Music. Two tubas. 1987. $5.00. 4:45. IV–V. Part I: G_1–f ', Part II: F_1–d'. A very lyrical but challenging melody. Both parts have the opportunity to play the melody. Good writing.

Mozart, W.A. *Tuba Duo Four, K. 380.* arr. James Self. Basset Hound Music. Two tubas. 1983. $5.00. 5:30. IV–V. Part I: G_1–f ', Part II: F_1–d'. A transcription of the first movement of the *Sonata for Klavier and Violin in Eb*, 1781. Parts have equal responsibility for the melody and are very demanding in range and technique. Interesting writing.

Mozart, W.A. *Tuba Duo One, K. 378.* arr. James Self. Basset Hound Music. Two tubas. 1976. $5.00. 7:30. IV–V. Part I: G_1–d', Part II: F_1–d'. From the first movement of a sonata for klavier and violin, 1779. A very melodic but challenging duet. Parts are of equal difficulty, and each has the opportunity to play the melody. This duet works very well.

Mozart, W.A. *Tuba Duo Seven, K. 380.* arr. James Self. Basset Hound Music. Two tubas. 1986. $5.00. 6:00. IV–V. Part I: F_1–f ', Part II: E_1–c'. Third movement, Rondo, of *Sonata for Klavier and Violin*, 1781. In a moderate 6/8 meter. Parts are very challenging but also quite interesting. A lot of work, but well worth the effort.

Mozart, W.A. *Tuba Duo Three, K. 454.* arr. James Self. Basset Hound Music. Two tubas. 1981. $5.00. 5:00. IV–V. Part I: G_1–e', Part II: (C_1) E_1–e'. First movement of *Sonata for Klavier and Violin*, 1784. The melody is very lyrical and is played by both parts. There are many range and technical challenges for both parts. Works well.

Mozart, W.A. *Tuba Duo Two (Rondo alla Tubas) K. 564.* arr. James Self. Basset Hound Music. Two tubas. 1979. $5.00. 5:00. IV–V. Part I: F_1–f ', Part II: F_1–d'. Rondo from *Trio for Klavier, Violin, and Cello*, 1788. Both parts are interesting and technically very challenging. Excellent writing.

Mozart, W.A. *Twelve Duets, K. 487.* arr. Ronald Dishinger. Medici Music Press. Two tubas. 1993. $9.50. 12 pp. III–IV. Part I: C–d', Part II: F_1–f. Each duet varies in style, tempo, and meter. Most are very tuneful and not technically difficult. A couple of these could be played by good high school students.

Mozart, W.A. *Twelve Duos for Two Tubas.* arr. Rex A. Conner. Queen City Brass Publications. 1981. $8.00. 15 pp. IV. Part I: Eb–eb', Part II: Eb_1–gb. A collection of minuets, andantes, and polonaises. The first part may easily be played on euphonium or F tuba. Movements may be used individually, or a small number may serve as a suite for concert use.

Mozart, W.A. *Twelve Easy Duets for Winds.* arr. Henry Charles Smith. G. Schirmer Incorporate. Out of print. Euphonium and tuba. 1972.

Mozart, W.A. *Two Wind Duets (K. 487).* arr. Randall Block. The Musical Evergreen. Euphonium and tuba. 1975. $3.50. 3:00. III–IV. Part I: B♭–c', Part II: B♭₁–g. Two movements: Allegro; Andante. Two contrasting movements in Classical style. Parts are of equal difficulty.

Mueller, Frederick A. *Duet.* Frederick Mueller. Euphonium and tuba. $6.00.

Nakagawa, Ryohei, arr. *My Melody Book.* Sohgaku-Sha. Two tubas. 1990. $42.00. 160 pp. III–IV. Part I: B♭₁–b♭, Part II: F₁–f. Dedicated to K. Yamashita. A collection of 109 familiar melodies. European folk songs, American folk songs, popular songs, Christmas songs, jazz, and a few Japanese folk songs. The technical challenges range from moderate to moderately difficult. Many of these pieces work quite well and would be appropriate for study, for concert use, or just for fun.

Nelhybel, Vaclav. *Counterpoint No. 6.* Barta Music Company. Two tubas. 1979. $6.50. 9 pp. IV. Part I: A♭₁–g, Part II: G₁–a♭. Eight movements. A collection of original polyphonic duets. Movements are of varying difficulty depending on their rhythmic complexity. Ranges are not a problem. The first three movements are very playable by high school students.

Nelhybel, Vaclav. *Eleven Duets for Tuba.* General Music Publishing Company. Two tubas. 1966. $4.95. 8 pp. II–IV. Part I: A₁–e, Part II: A₁–e. Rhythmically quite interesting. Selected movements may serve as suites for concerts. Rhythms are moderately challenging. Tempos may be varied for high school players.

Nicolai, Otto. *Duet No. 1 in E♭ Major.* arr. Rex Connor. PP Music. Two tubas. 1993. $7.00. 11:30. IV. Part I: E♭–d', Part II: E♭₁–b♭. Three movements: Allegro; Adagio; Allegretto. Originally written for two horns. May also be played by one euphonium and one tuba. Some very nice melodies. Technically challenging at times for both parts.

Pachelbel, Johann. *Canon in D.* arr. Frank H. Siekmann. Brelmat Music. Euphonium, tuba, and piano. 1994. $5.00. 4:30. III. Part I: A–f♯', Part II: C♯–a. A very nice arrangement of this famous canon. No significant range or technical problems. The piano part is necessary for performance. Works well.

Patterson, Merlin E. *Two-Part Inventions.* Euphonium and tuba. 1974. 5:50. IV. Part I: A♭–b♭', Part II: G♯₁–c'. Four movements: Fughetta; Ostinato; Gigue; Allemande. Euphonium part is printed in tenor clef. Movements are in mixed meter and rhythmically very challenging.

Pederson, Tommy. *Ten Duets for Bass Trombone.* Kendor Music, Incorporated. Two bass trombones (tubas). 1976. $9.50. 20 pp. IV. Part I: G₁–d', Part II: F₁–e♭'. Ten movements: Empty Boxes; The Whether Man; Hippo in the Cabbage Patch; Rumble on 6th Street; Riot of the Red Ants; Fibulee, Tibula; Mel-

issa; The Walrus Ordered Waffles; Tigger Talk; Adrift on a Waterbed. Very tuneful and humorous duets. Movements vary in technical and range demands, but all require strong players. Fun to play.

Porret, Julien. *Twelve Divertissements en Duos, Op. 670.* Editions Robert Martin. Two tubas. 1980. $16.00. 23 pp. IV. Part I: B–e', Part II: G–e'. Twelve original duets that may be performed individually or in any order. Parts are of equal technical difficulty. Predominantly polyphonic in character, but not technically challenging. The tessitura is a little high for both parts. The first part could be played by a euphonium.

Powell, Morgan. *Short Piece for Tuba and Euphonium.* T.U.B.A. Journal. 1974. $7.50. 1:30. IV. Part I: B♭–b♭", Part II: G–d'. Short duet with mixed meters and numerous tempo changes. Challenging rhythmically to put together. Uses some flutter tonguing, and the last note is muted. This was written as part of the T.U.B.A. GEM series and is published in the *T.U.B.A. Journal*, Vol. 1, no. 3.

Presser, William. *Five Hag Pieces.* Theodore Presser Company. Euphonium and tuba. 1987. $5.50. 4:20. IV. Part I: E–b♭', Part II: E₁–b♭. Five movements: Gee, Dad Gaffed a Faded Hag; H.H.A. Beach Egged a Caged Hag; Abe Bach Bagged a Bead-Headed Hag; Each Fagged Hag Had a Bad Headache; A Chafed Hag Fed a Chef Chaff. Using German spellings (B = B♭ and H = B), the themes spell out the titles of each movement. The two parts have equal responsibility for the melody. Some technical challenges in both parts. Interesting writing and fun to play. This composition is a sequel to *Two Hag Pieces*, published by the *T.U.B.A. Journal*, Winter 1984.

Presser, William. *Seven Tuba Duets.* Tenuto Publications. 1970. $6.00. 9:00. IV. Part I: F₁–b♭, Part II: E₁–b♭. Seven movements: Prologue; Invention I; Passacaglia; Invention II; Fugue; Invention III; Epilogue. The movements contrast in style, meter, and key. They are short and may be performed alone, or in a variety of combinations. Some movements are technically challenging, especially at the tempos indicated.

Presser, William. *Two Hag Pieces for Euphonium and Tuba.* T.U.B.A. Journal. 1984. $7.50. 2:50. IV. Part I: G–b♭', Part II: G₁–a. Two movements: A Deaf, Aged, Bad Hag; A Gagged Hag Abed, Dead, Hee–Hee, Ha–Ha. Using German spellings (B = B♭ and H = B), the themes spell the titles of the movement. The first movement begins like a canon and remains polyphonic throughout. The second movement is in 6/8 and has traditional harmonies. Written as part of the T.U.B.A. GEM series and published in the *T.U.B.A. Journal*, Vol. 11, no. 3.

Purcell, Henry. *Chaconne.* arr. R. Winston Morris. Shawnee Press, Incorporated. Two tubas with optional piano or harpsichord. 1982. $7.00. 2:20. III–IV. Part I: G–d', Part II: G–d'. The famous

Purcell *Chaconne* arranged in canonic form. The addition of the harpsichord can add a Baroque flavor and a tone color not often heard with two tubas. The arrangement works very well.

Purvis, Stanley H. *Appalachian Echos.* Kendor Music, Incorporated. Two tubas. 1991. $5.00. 2:50. III–IV. Part I: E♭–b♭(c'), Part II: E♭₁–f. The melody is like a folk song that is presented in a question-and-answer format. There are several tempo changes within the basic ABA (slow fast slow) form. Very tuneful and enjoyable to play.

Rener, Hermann. *Spielheft 1.* Philipp Grosch Musikverlag. Euphonium and tuba. $10.00. 10:00. IV. Part I: c–f', Part II: F–d'. Ten movements. Written for two trombones or any two bass-clef instruments; works well with euphonium and tuba. Parts have equal responsibility for the melody. A lot of imitation. Not technically difficult.

Roikjer, Kjell. *Ten Inventions for Two Tubas, Op. 55.* Wilhelm Hansen Musikforlag. 1969. $16.00. 17 pp. IV. Part I: B₁–e', Part II: F₁–a. Excellent study material. Quite challenging rhythmically and in terms of key.

Ryker, Robert. *Petite Marche.* Euphonium, tuba, and piano. 1983. 4:00. IV. Part I: C♭–b♭', Part II: C–d♭'. A lot of imitation between the piano accompaniment and the wind instruments. Parts are of equal difficulty.

Ryker, Robert. *Sonata for Two Bass Tubas.* Robert King Music Sales, Incorporated. Out of print. 1959. 4:00. IV. Part I: D₁–d', Part II: D₁–d'. Parts are of equal difficulty. Texture is mostly homophonic. Three sections have varying tempo. First performed March 23, 1959. A good recital piece.

Sainte-Jacome. *Duet.* arr. Herbert Wekselblatt. G. Schirmer Incorporated. Two tubas. 1964. $13.95. 3:20. III–IV. Part I: F₁–g, Part II: F₁–g. Very polyphonic and technically challenging in a few sections. Players need to count carefully. Originally written for two trumpets. One of two duets published in a collection of tuba solos. See Wekselblatt, H., *Solos for the Tuba Player* under "Music for Tuba and Keyboard."

Scarmolin, A. Louis. *Duet Time.* arr. Michael Boo. Ludwig Music Publishing Company. Euphonium and tuba. 1982. $5.50. 15 pp. IV. Part I: F–f', Part II: F–e♭'. Twelve movements: Dialogue; Rondolette; Jumpin' Bean; Andantino; Fiesta; Drawing Room; Here and There; Swans; Spring Dance; Bambolina; Follow Me; Fughetta. The melodies are very traditional in style and harmonic structure. The parts are of equal difficulty. There are no significant technical problems. May be performed individually or in a small group, as a suite. Fun to play. Originally copyrighted 1966.

Scherzer, Edward. *Twenty-Four Duettes, Op. 73.* Two tubas.

Schmidt, William. *Variations on a Theme of Prokofieff.* Western International Music. Euphonium and tu-

ba. 1990. $5.00. 5:00. IV. Part I: B–g', Part II: D♯–e'. Scored for either two euphoniums or euphonium and tuba. The range demands on the second part are not great, but the tessitura is high. Technically challenging in only a couple of spots, but the harmonies are quite dissonant and very contemporary.

Sear, Walter. *Advanced Duets for Tuba, Vol. I.* Cor Publishing Company. 1969. $6.00. 24 pp. III–IV. Part I: F₁–d', Part II: F₁–d'. A collection of 21 original duets in contrasting tempo and style. Difficulty ranges from moderate to difficult. Many of these duets are very tuneful and enjoyable to play and listen to. They may be performed individually or in small groups as a suite.

Sear, Walter. *Advanced Duets for Tuba, Vol. II.* Cor Publishing Company. 1974. $6.00. 24 pp. IV. Part I: F♯₁–d', Part II: E₁–c'. Ten different movements mostly in the style of strict canons and inventions. They vary in range and technical demands but are generally more difficult and less tuneful than the duets in Vol. I. These may also be played individually or in small groups as a suite.

Singleton, Kenneth, arr. *Three Renaissance Duets.* Peer International Corporation. Two tubas. 1976. $8.00. 5:00. IV. Part I: D–d', Part II: D–c'. Three movements: Fantasia; Canon; Duo. These duets represent the imitative polyphony typical of the fifteenth and sixteenth centuries. Fantasia was originally written for two bass viols. Canon is originally by Obrecht and served as a Credo for the *Missa Salve Dive Parens.* Technically not very difficult, but counting correctly can be a challenge.

Singleton, Kenneth, arr. *Twenty-Five Baroque and Classical Duets, Book I.* Peer International Corporation. Two tubas. 1981. $8.00. 24 pp. IV. Part I: B♭₁–d', Part II: B♭₁–c'. Contains the first thirteen melodies. Originally composed for two flutes or recorders. Most of the pieces are individual movements from larger compositions, but a few are entire suites. They vary in technical and range demands. Most are very tuneful and work exceptionally well for two tubas.

Singleton, Kenneth, arr. *Twenty-Five Baroque and Classical Duets, Book II.* Peer International Corporation. Two tubas. 1981. $8.00. 24 pp. IV. Part I: D–d', Part II: C–d'. The last twelve movements (of the set of 25) from a different movement from larger compositions, originally written for two flutes. Each movement presents different range and technical demands. They are fun to play and work quite well for two tubas.

Sparke, Philip, arr. *Sweet 'n' Low, Book 1.* Studio Music Company. Euphonium and tuba. 1989. $8.00. 8 pp. III. Part I: d–f', Part II: B♭₁–e♭. Eight movements: Barbara Allen; Loch Lomond; Silver Threads among the Gold; The Ash Grove; Drink to Me Only; When the Saints; Swing Low, Sweet Chariot; Early One Morning. All five books of duets arranged by Sparke follow the same format. Each duet appears twice, once in bass clef, once in treble clef. The same duets are also available for treble-clef instruments in *Mix'n' Match* by the same arranger and publisher. Consequently the tuba may be combined with any other bass or treble instrument to play these same melodies. These are not technically challenging and are very appropriate for high school students.

Sparke, Philip, arr. *Sweet 'n' Low, Book 2.* Studio Music Company. Euphonium and tuba. 1989. $8.00. 8 pp. III. Part I: Eb–f '. Part II: Bb–eb. Eight movements: The Blue Bells of Scotland; Marching through Georgia; All through the Night; Cockles and Mussels; Santa Lucia; Müss Ich Denn?; Ye Banks and Braes; The Camptown Races. May be played individually or grouped together as a suite. No technical problems.

Sparke, Philip, arr. *Sweet 'n' Low, Book 3: A First Christmas Selection.* Studio Music Company. Euphonium and tuba. 1989. $8.00. 8 pp. III. Part I: d–f. Part II: Bb–eb. Eight movements: Away in a Manger; Ding Dong, Merrily on High; The First Noel; God Rest Ye Merry, Gentlemen; Good King Wenceslas; Hark, The Herald Angels Sing; The Holly and the Ivy; Jingle Bells. Both parts have the opportunity to play the melody. Not technically difficult. Each movement lasts approximately one minute.

Sparke, Philip, arr. *Sweet 'n' Low, Book 4: A Second Christmas Selection.* Studio Music Company. Euphonium and tuba. 1989. $8.00. 8 pp. II–III. Part I: c–f '. Part II: Bb$_1$–eb. Eight movements: Infant Holy; O Come, All Ye Faithful; Silent Night; O Little Town of Bethlehem; One in Royal David's City; We Three Kings of Orient Are; While Shepherds Watched; We Wish You a Merry Christmas. Both parts are of equal difficulty. The movements are short and are fun for young players.

Sparke, Philip, arr. *Sweet 'n' Low, Book 5: Caribbean Cocktail.* Studio Music Company. Euphonium and tuba. 1989. $8.00. 8 pp. III. Part I: d–f '. Part II: Bb$_1$–eb. Eight movements: Banana Boat Song; Mary Ann; The Mocking Bird; Mango Walk; Sloop John B; Sly Mongoose; Matilda; Jamaican Farewell. Both parts have opportunities to play the melody. No significant technical problems. These melodies are fun to play and are appropriate for young players.

Stamitz, Karl. *Duet for Tubas.* arr. Newell H. Long. The Brass Press. Out of print. 1974. 2:00. III. Part I: G–c'. Part II: Bb$_1$–eb. Work very well for high school students. The first part may be played on euphonium. Treble- and bass-clef parts are provided for the first part.

Stevens, John. *Splinters.* T.U.B.A. Journal. Two tubas or euphonium and tuba. 1982. $7.50. 1:00. IV. Part I: (Bb$_1$)F–f '. Part II: F$_1$–f. A short rock duet with challenging rhythmic figures. The first part

needs a strong player because of the range. Rhythmically and dynamically fun but challenging to play. Written as part of the T.U.B.A. GEM Series and published in the *T.U.B.A. Journal*, Vol. 9, no. 4. Recorded by John Stevens, *Power Classical*, Mark Records, MRS 20699.

Stevens, John. *Suite for Two.* Brassworks Music, Gordon V. Thompson Limited. Two tubas. 1985. $20.00. 6:00. IV. Part I: A$_1$–d'. Part II: F$_1$–c'. Four movements: Prelude; Scherzo; Song; Coda. The Scherzo and Coda are in a jazz style. Parts have equal responsibility for the melody. Good writing for two tubas. Recorded by John Stevens, *Power Classical*, Mark Records, MRS 20699.

Stoker, Richard. *Four Dialogues.* Hinrichsen Edition Limited. Out of print. Two tubas or euphonium and tuba. 1966. 5:00. IV. Part I: A–d'. Part II: C–g. Four movements: Interview; Debate; Interrogation; Argument. The third movement is in 5/8 but is not very difficult.

Stouffer, Paul, arr. *Easy Classics for Two.* Kendor Music, Incorporated. Two tubas. 1993. $5.50. 5:30. II. Part I: G$_1$–d, Part II: G$_1$–d. Six movements: Andante (Mozart); Bourrée (Telemann); Dance (Haydn); Andantino (Schubert); Minuet (Purcell); Imitation (Baton). No technical or range problems. Both parts have an opportunity to play the melody. Ideal for young players.

Stoutamire, Albert, and Henderson, Kenneth, arr. *Duets for All.* CPP Belwin, Incorporated. Two tubas. 1973. $5.00. 24 pp. III–IV. Part I: D–c'. Part II: Ab$_1$–c'. A collection of eighteen different melodies from famous composers, ranging from Baroque to contemporary styles. These same duets are arranged for a variety of instruments (e.g. two flutes, two trumpets), so a tuba can play the first part and a trumpet or clarinet the second. Excellent material to challenge or reward intermediate to advanced high school players. The higher parts are all written with 8va for younger players.

Stroud, Richard. *Tubantiphon.* Seesaw Music Corporation Publishers. Two tubas. 1976. $12.00. 5:30. IV. Part I: G$_1$–bb'. Part II: G$_1$–bb. Very complex rhythmically. There are multimetric sections, several sixteenth-note runs, syncopations, and trills. Requires strong players.

Sweelinck, Jan P. *Io mi son giovanetta.* arr. Paul F. Hartin. Cellar Press. Two tubas. 1974. 3:30. III–IV. Part I: G–c'. Part II: C–f. The first part is easily performed on euphonium, making this very playable by high school students. Not rhythmically complex.

Sweelinck, Jan P. *Polyphonic Rhyme No. 4.* arr. Randall Block. The Musical Evergreen. Two tubas. 1974. $2.50. 2:30. III. Part I: F–ab. Part II: Bb$_1$–c. Duet is marked "Alla Breve" but there are no bar lines. Not technically difficult, but varying the tempo can make this playable by high school students or more challenging for college students.

Sweelinck, Jan P. *Voci du gai printemps*. arr. Paul F. Hartin. Cellar Press. Two tubas. 1974. 2:30. III–IV. Part I: Bb–c', Part II: Bb₁–f. Two movements: Allegro; March–like. A lively duet featuring contrasting lyrical and technical sections. The first part may be performed on euphonium.

Telemann, George Phillip. *Canonic Sonata*. arr. Paul F. Hartin. Cellar Press. Two tubas. 1974. 5:00. IV. Part I: D–d', Part II: D–d'. Three movements: Spirituoso; Larghetto; Allegro assai. Each movement is a pure canon. The first player begins and the second player, reading from the same music, starts at the beginning when the first player reaches the second measure. There is a fermata at the end of each movement for the two players to catch up to each other. Rhythmically very challenging.

Telemann, George Phillip. *Sonata, Op. 5, No. 4*. arr. Brent Dutton. Brent Dutton. Two tubas. 1973. $5.00. 6:00. IV. Part I: F–f ', Part II: F–f '. Three movements: Vivace; Piacevole; Presto. Typical Baroque style, each part is technically difficult in some section. The tessitura of both parts is high. Other instrumentation possibilities include euphonium and tuba, or two F tubas.

Telemann, George Phillip. *Three Chorale Preludes*. arr. Arthur Frackenpohl. Horizon Press. Euphonium and tuba. 1991. $5.00. 6:30. IV. Part I: G–bb', Part II: G₁–a'. Three movements: Allein gott in der Hoh Sei Ehr (All Glory Be to God on High); Vater Unser im Himmelreich (Our Father in Heaven); Christ Lag In Todesbanden (Christ Lay in Death's Bonds). The two parts take turns playing the slow chorale theme and the faster accompaniment. No significant technical problems. Works well.

Thomas, T. Donley. *Bicinia, Op. 5*. Medici Music Press. Trombone or euphonium and tuba. 1986. $11.00. 10:00. IV. Part I: Gb–b', Part II: A₁–a. Five movements: Pomposo, Quasi Marcia; Allegro con Fuoco; Andante Cantabile; Scherzo; Maestoso. Both parts are interesting and challenging. The movements are multimetric and rhythmically very interesting. The third movement is a theme and variations.

Thornton, Michael. *Two English Madrigals*. PP Music. Two tubas.

Torchinsky, Abe, arr. *Ten Duets*. Encore Music Publishers. Two tubas. 1988. $16.00. 29 pp. IV–V. Part I: D–f ', Part II: A₁–g'. Transcriptions of duets for ophicleides by Hartmann and by F. Vobaron. Moderate to very difficult because of the varying technical and range demands.

Uber, David. *Double Portraits*. Brodt Music Company. Euphonium and tuba. 1967. $4.00. 7:30. III–IV. Part I: Bb–g', Part II: Ab₁–b'. Four movements: The City; Times Square; Twilight; The City Awakes. A programmatic description of life in a big city. Originally written for trombone and tuba, it is often performed on euphonium and tuba. Excellent recital piece. See listing under "Music for Tuba

in Mixed Ensemble." Recorded by Michael Lind , tuba and Christer Torgé, trombone, BIS LP 95.

Uber, David. *Duo Concertante for Two Tubas, Op. 97*. Almitra Music Company/Kendor Music, Incorporated. 1978. $6.00. 5:40. III–IV. Part I: Cb–c, Part II: G₁–g. Three movements: Poco Allegretto; Andante, poco Agitato; Allegro Moderato. Works well for good high school or college players. First movement is very rhythmic, the second lyrical, and the third is a bouncy 6/8. Moderate technical demands on both players. Other instrumentation possibilities include euphonium and tuba, and bass trombone and tuba.

Uber, David. *Silent Streets for Euphonium and Tuba*. REBU Music Publications. Euphonium and tuba. 1993. $5.00. 2:20.

Vaughan, Rodger. *Ronda's First Suite*. Rodger Vaughan. Two tubas. 1992. $5.00. 5:45. II–III. Part I: Bb–bb, Part II: A₁–Bb. Four movements: March; Song; Minuet; Galop. For Ronda Ellis. The first part requires a good high school player, but the second part may be played by a younger student. Most of the melody is in the top part. Harmonies are fairly traditional.

Vaughan, Rodger. *Sonatina for Two Tubas*. Rodger Vaughan. Two tubas. 1975. $5.00. 7:30. IV. Part I: G₁–g', Part II: D₁–bb. Three movements. For James Self. The first part would work well on F tuba because of the range. Very interesting writing and dynamic contrasts, especially in the last movement. A few meter changes in the last movement.

Wadowick, James L. *Two for the Tuba*. Concert Music Publishing Company. Two tubas and piano. 1969. 4:00. III. Part I: Db–bb, Part II: Ab₁–eb. A very usable duet for high school players with piano accompaniment. In a traditional tonal style.

Warren, Christopher. *Four Etudes for Two Tubas*, in *Twenty Etudes*. TUBA Press. 1992. $10.00. 6:30. IV. Part I: E₁–d', Part II: Eb₁–c'. Four movements: Bouncy; Moderate; Mysterious; Marcia. Very contemporary style. Both parts are technically challenging in some sections.

White, William. *Fantasia*. arr. David Baldwin. The Musical Evergreen. Two tubas. 1975. $2.50. 2:00. III–IV. Part I: C₁–a, Part II: A₁–a. Polyphonic texture with some syncopation. Playable by high school students at a slightly slower tempo. There are a few 32nd note patterns in the first part.

White, William. *Fantasia*. arr. Paul F. Hartin. Cellar Press. Two tubas. 1975. 2:00. Part I: F–d', Part II: D–d'. Transposed from the original in C to the key of F. Playable by high school or college students.

Wilder, Alec. *Suite for Two Tubas*. Margun Music, Incorporated. 1971. $8.00. 14:00. IV. Part I: D₁–f♯, Part II: F₁–eb'. Written at the request of Harvey Phillips. Ten original duets with classic Wilder melodic and harmonic writing. Can be organized into small suites for performance. Large interval skips make this a challenging work.

Wilhelm, Rolf. *Ragtime*. T.U.B.A. Journal. Two tubas. 1986. $7.50. 1:45. IV. Part I: A–f ', Part II: A♭₁–a♭. A nice rag that features the two parts equally. The first part has a high tessitura and may be played on an F tuba. Written as part of the T.U.B.A. GEM Series and published in the *T.U.B.A. Journal*, Vol. 13, no. 3.

Wilson, David. *Duet for Two Tubas and Understanding Audience*. Cleveland Chamber Music Publishers (Philharmusica Corporation). 1973. 2:30. IV. Part I: F–d', Part II: F₁–a. Four movements: Arrive; Volta; Song; Humoresque. Not difficult except for the second movement. Could be used by high school students with a euphonium on the first part. Traditional harmonies.

Wolfe, Gordon. *Canon in the Lydian Mode*. T.U.B.A. Journal. Euphonium and tuba. 1983. $7.50. 1:30. III–IV. Part I: F♯–e♭', Part II: B₁–a♭. The canon is written in treble clef. The tuba plays it as an E♭ instrument (reading the notation as if it were in the bass clef and adding three flats) while the euphonium plays the canon as a B♭ transposing instrument. Not technically difficult. Written as part of the T.U.B.A. GEM series and published in the *T.U.B.A. Journal*, Vol. 10, no. 4.

Zemp, Daniel. *Twenty Petite Duos*. Gérard Billaudot (Theodore Presser). Euphonium and tuba or two F tubas. 1985. $14.50. 6:00. IV. Part I: A–f ', Part II: D–e'. The tessitura of the second part is high. Not technically demanding until the last movement. The movements can be grouped together in any number or order. Parts have equal responsibility for the melody.

Zettler, Richard. *Alt und Neu für Zwei (Old and New for Two)*. Elisabeth Thomi-Berg. Euphonium and tuba. $8.50. 12:30. IV. Part I: (E♭)A–a', Part II: F–f '. Six movements: I—Andante; Menuett; Allegretto Commodo; II—Tango Sentimental; Valse Viennoise; Tarantella. Parts have equal responsibility for the melody. No significant technical problems. The tessitura of the second part is high, but there are some ossia sections.

Zychowicz, James L. *Six Baroque Pieces for Two Tubas*. Shawnee Press, Incorporated. Out of print. 1981. 8:00. III–IV. Part I: F–b♭, Part II: E₁–G. A transcription of six Baroque songs by six different composers. Range is not demanding, and a few of the movements are playable by high school students. A couple of the movements are quite tuneful and work very well. They may be performed individually or grouped together in small suites.

Three Parts

Anderson, Eugene. *Sea Chanty for Three*. Anderson's Arizona Originals. Three tubas. 1990. $5.00. 2:20. III–IV. Part I: D–g, Part II: B♭₁–e♭, Part III: G₁–B♭. Most of the melody is in the top part. There are

moderate technical demands and traditional harmonies. Parts may be doubled for a large ensemble.

Anderson, Mogens. *Ebbe Skammelson*. Royal Danish Brass Publications. Three tubas. 1976. IV. Part I: G–d', Part II: A₁–b, Part III: G₁–e. Four movements. To the Danish Tuba-Klub. No significant range or technical problems. The second movement features an "ad lib" solo for each part. A euphonium may be used on the first part. Fun to play.

Bach, J.S. *Come, Sweet Death*. arr. Eddie Sauter. T.U.B.A. Journal. Euphonium and two tubas. 1973. 1:30. III–IV. Part I: c–g', Part II: G–c' Part III: G₁–c'. To the memory of William J. Bell. Arranged May 26, 1973, at the conclusion of the first International Tuba Symposium Workshop. Some of the third part may be played down an octave to make it playable by high school students. Works well for large ensembles. A traditional closer for many Octubafest concerts and T.U.B.A. Conferences. Published in the first organizational Newsletter, Fall 1973. There is a misprint in the original score: the third line, third measure, second beat of the first tuba part should be d♭, not d♮. Given to T.U.B.A. by Eddie Sauter and may be freely duplicated by tubists everywhere and performed in the memory of William J. Bell. Recorded by the Tennessee Technological University Tuba Ensemble, Golden Crest Records, CRS 4139; Garden State Tuba Ensemble, *Karl Megules,* Recorded Publications Company, Z434471; and *Harvey Phillips/TubaChristmas,* Harvey Phillips Foundation, HPF NR1111.

Bach, J.S. *Fugue in C Minor for Low Brass.* arr. R. Winston Morris. Ludwig Music Publishing Company. Euphonium and two tubas. 1992. 1:40. III–IV. Part I: d–b♭', Part II: C–c', Part III: G₁–d. Arranged for the Tennessee Technological University Tuba Ensemble. A transcription of a well-known Bach fugue. The style is meant to be smooth and lyrical. The first part is written in both bass and treble-clef. The tessitura of the first part is high. Parts may be doubled for a large ensemble.

Bach, J.S. *Fugue in F Major.* arr. Paul Schmidt. Heavy Metal Music. Two euphoniums and one tuba. 1991. $7.00. 2:20. IV. Part I: G–f ', Part II: D–f ', Part III: (F₁) C–f. Requires very clean playing in the low register of all parts. Works well for this instrumentation. Parts may be doubled for a large ensemble.

Bergenfeld, Nathan. *Chaconne*. Tempo Music Publications. Out of print. Two euphoniums and one tuba. 1975. 4:00. III. Part I: f–f ', Part II: d–d♭', Part III: G–a♭. A fairly easy composition with simple rhythms. Very appropriate for high school concerts or contests.

Bewley, Norlan. *Pinata*. Bewley Music Incorporated. Two euphoniums and one tuba or one euphonium and two tubas 1991. $10.00. 1:20. III–IV. Part I:

d–f ', Part II: A–b♭, Part III: G₁–d. A lot of syncopation, but not technically difficult. All three parts have an opportunity to play the melody. Parts may be doubled for a large ensemble.

Blair, Dean. *The Serious Suite for Three Tubas*. T.A.P. Music. 1986. $6.00. 4:20. IV. Part I: c–d", Part II: E₁–a, Part III: F₁–c'. Four movements: Moderato; March; Chant; Finale. Technically not very demanding, but the tessitura of the first part is high. The third part is higher and more challenging than the second part. No score available. Originally written and copyrighted by Blair in 1970.

Bruckner, Anton. *Aequale*. arr. Paul Schmidt. Heavy Metal Music. Euphonium and two tubas. $3.00. 1:20. III. Part I: f♯–f ', Part II: G–c', Part III: G₁–g. A very slow chorale. The second part may be played by a euphonium or tuba. Players read from a score. Parts may be doubled for a large ensemble.

Butterfield, Don, arr. *Them Baces*. DB Publishing Company. Euphonium and two tubas. 1973. 4:00. IV. Part I: F–f ', Part II: F₁–b♭, Part III: F₁–g. Dedicated to the memory of William J. Bell. A cute arrangement that paraphrases *Them Basses, Under the Double Eagle, Bombasto, When Yuba Plays the Rhumba...*, and *Tubby the Tuba*. Written to be performed at the first Annual New York Brass Conference for Scholarships held February 3–4 1973.

Byrd, William. *In Crystal Towers, from Psalms, Songs, and Sonnets*. arr. Paul F. Hartin. Cellar Press. Three tubas. 1974. 3:00. III. Part I: G–c', Part II: A–c', Part III: G₁–d. Will work best for high school ensembles with a euphonium on the first part. Rhythms are not difficult, and harmonic structure is consistent with Baroque writings. Parts may be doubled for a large ensemble.

Carmody, Bill. *Disco Tuba*. T.U.B.A. Journal. Euphonium and two tubas. 1978. $7.50. 3:00. IV. Part I: B–a', Part II: C₁–d', Part III: A₁–e. Bass line is in a funky style. A few challenging rhythmic figures for all parts. There is a four-measure section that may be repeated for improvisation. Parts may be doubled for a large ensemble. Much fun to play. Written as part of the T.U.B.A. GEM Series and published in *T.U.B.A. Journal*, Vol. 6, no. 1.

Censhu, Jiro. *Doguu Sansai* (Three Clay Puppets). Jiro Censhu. Three tubas. 1986. $10.00. 4:00. IV. Part I: d–f ', Part II: G–e', Part III: F₁–a. Three movements: Con moto; Con grazia; Con spirito. For R. Winston Morris. The first and second parts could easily be played on euphonium. The last movement is very lively and interesting to play. Revised in 1988.

Corelli, Arcangelo. *Sonata da Chiesa a Tre*. arr. Brent Dutton. Brent Dutton. Three tubas. 1970. $5.00. 5:30. IV. Part I: D–d', Part II: D–d', Part III: D–f. Four movements: Grave; Presto; Adagio; Allegro. The top two parts are the solo parts and the third part is the continuo. Requires light playing, works well.

Corelli, Arcangelo. *Sonata da Chiesa in E Minor, Op. 3, No. 7*. arr. Larry Pitts. The Brass Press. Out of print. Three tubas. 1974. 5:30. III–IV. Part I: E–d', Part II: E–d', Part III: E₁–e. Four movements: Grave; Allegro; Adagio; Allegro. In the style of a typical Baroque sonata. Excellent for teaching Baroque style. Very playable by high school players, especially if the second movement is taken at a moderate tempo.

Corelli, Arcangelo. *Trio Sonata, Op. 1, No. 5*. arr. Paul Schmidt. Heavy Metal Music. Two euphoniums and one tuba. 1990. $7.00. 6:30. IV. Part I: c–g', Part II: A–g', Part III: C–g (c'). Four movements: Grave; Allegro; Adagio; Allegro. Parts one and two are the melody, and part three is primarily the continuo part. The third movement alternates every few measures between 3/2 and 4/4 and a slow and fast tempo. No score available.

Corelli, Arcangelo. *Trio Sonata, Op. 1, No. 10*. arr. Paul Schmidt. Heavy Metal Music. Two euphoniums and tuba. 1990. $7.00. 6:45. IV. Part I: E–a', Part II: A–f ', Part III: A–a. Four movements: Grave; Allegro; Adagio; Allegro. The top two parts are more challenging than in the other Corelli sonatas arranged by Schmidt. The third part (continuo) is also more challenging, but very interesting to play. No score available.

Corelli, Arcangelo. *Trio Sonata, Op. 3, No. 2*. arr. Paul Schmidt. Heavy Metal Music. Two euphoniums and one tuba. 1990. $7.00. 7:00. IV. Part I: F–f ', Part II: G–d', Part III: F₁–g. Four movements: Grave; Allegro; Adagio; Allegro. The first two parts present the melody polyphonically. Moderate technical demands of all parts. No score available.

Corelli, Arcangelo. *Trio Sonata, Op. 3, No. 7*. arr. Paul Schmidt. Heavy Metal Music. Two euphoniums and one tuba. 1990. $7.00. 6:30. IV. Part I: B♭–f ', Part II: G–f ', Part III: G₁–g. Four movements: Grave; Allegro; Adagio; Allegro. The top two parts are polyphonic and very syncopated, but not technically challenging. The third part plays the continuo. These arrangements work well for this instrumentation. No score available.

Couperin, Francois. *Les Ondes Rondeau*. arr. Jan Krzywicki. Theodore Presser Company. Two euphoniums and one tuba. 1984. $7.50. 2:30. IV. Part I: A–e', Part II: F–f ', Part III: F₁–f. For Paul, Pete and Hal. Originally written for harpsichord in 1713. A slow, flowing, lyrical melody in 6/8. No significant technical or range problems. Can also be performed by three tubas or one euphonium and two tubas.

Danburg, Russell. *Nocturne and Dance for Three Tubas*. Wingert-Jones Music, Incorporated. 1983. $6.00. 3:20. IV. Part I: G–c', Part II: C₁–b♭, Part III: F₁–b♭. Two movements: Nocturne; Dance. All three parts have equal responsibility for the melody. The Dance is especially rhythmic and exciting and has a brief cadenza for the first part. Range of the parts is not high but the technical challenges require three strong players.

Daughtry, Russ. *The Plains of Esdraelon*. Tuba/Euphonium Music Publications. Out of print. Euphonium and two tubas. 3:30. IV. Part I: B–d', Part II: G₁–ab, Part III: G₁–d. Each part is featured as a soloist at different times during this mixed meter trio. Technically challenging, especially for the first and second parts.

Dutton, Brent. *Choral and Folksong*. Brent Dutton. Two trombones (euphoniums), one tuba, and piano. 1968. $10.00. 6:00. IV–V. Part I: E–b', Part II: F–g♯', Part III: Bb₂–gb'. Two movements: Choral; Folksong. Very contemporary in harmony and notation. Most of the second movement uses spatial notation for all parts. The piano part is very difficult. Extreme range demands for the third part.

Dutton, Brent. *Troisième Suite*. Seesaw Music Corporation Publishers. Three tubas. 1977. $17.00. 4:00. IV. Part I: A₁–e', Part II: F₁–d', Part III: Db₁–f'. The third part has the largest range of the three, although all three are equal in technical difficulty. Special techniques required of all players include multiphonics, improvisation, and mutes. Challenging to play.

Garbáge, Pierre. *Chaser #1*. James Garrett. Two euphoniums and one tuba, or one euphonium and two tubas. 1972. $10.00. 1:20. IV. Part I: a–f', Part II: d–d', Part III: B₁–c(b). Written for R. Winston Morris and the Tennessee Technological University Tuba Ensemble. A highly syncopated melody at a "hoedown" tempo. Fun to play. Pierre Garbáge says of this composition, "Heavy in every way but one." Parts may be doubled for a large ensemble.

Garrett, James A., arr. *Clementine*. James Garrett. Euphonium and two tubas. 1971. $5.00. 1:00. II–III. Part I: Bb–c', Part II: F–eb, Part III: Bb₁–Bb. A very usable arrangement for junior high school students. The second part could be played on euphonium or tuba. Parts may be doubled for a large ensemble.

Garrett, James A., arr. *Im Wald und auf der Heide*. James Garrett. Two euphoniums and one tuba, or one euphonium and two tubas. 1974. $5.00. 1:00. III. Part I: d–f', Part II: Bb–d, Part III: Bb₁–f. Very traditional harmonies. Easily playable by young students. Parts may be doubled for a large ensemble.

Garrett, James A., arr. *I've Been Working on the Railroad*. James Garrett. Euphonium and two tubas. 1971. $5.00. 1:00. II–III. Part I: Bb–ab, Part II: G–g, Part III: Bb₁–Bb. Could also be played with two euphoniums and one tuba or by three tubas. No technical or range problems. Parts may be doubled for a large ensemble.

Garrett, James, arr. *Red River Valley*. James Garrett. Euphonium and two tubas. 1971. $5.00. 1:00. I–

II. Part I: Bb–c', Part II: G–eb, Part III: Bb₁–c. A simple arrangement of this American folk song. The third part has the melody for half of the song. No technical or range problems. Ideal for very young players. Parts may be doubled for a large ensemble.

Geminiani, Francesco. *Concerto Grosso*. arr. R. Winston Morris. Shawnee Press, Incorporated. Two euphoniums and one tuba. 1974. $12.50. 6:30. III–IV. Part I: c–a', Part II: A–a', Part III: G₁–e (g). Three movements: Moderato; Adagio; Allegro. Written for the Tennessee Technological University Tuba Ensemble. Both euphonium parts are printed in bass and treble clef. Easily playable by high school students if the euphonium players have a good high a (a'). The arrangement is not muddy at all, works very well. Parts may be doubled for a large ensemble.

Gershenfeld, Mitchell, arr. *Two English Madrigals*. Medici Music Press. 1983. $5.00. 4:30. III–IV. Part I: F♯–a, Part II: E–a, Part III: G₁–c. Two movements: Weep, Oh Mine Eyes; In the Merry Month of May. Two short madrigals originally by John Wilbye and Henry Youll respectively. The texture is very polyphonic, but the pieces are not technically challenging. Works well. Parts may be doubled for a large ensemble.

Gessner, John M. *Two Pieces for Three Tubas*. 1969. 5:00. IV. Part I: F♯–f♯, Part II: E–b, Part III: F♯₁–f♯. Two movements: Slowly, Very fast. First part has a high tessitura and may require an F tuba. Many complex rhythms. Requires three strong players.

Gillam, Russell C. *Innocuous Incident*. Three tubas. 1971. 4:00. III. Part I: G–d', Part II: C–bb, Part III: G₁–a. If the first part is performed by a euphonium the piece is easily performed by high school ensembles.

Hancock, Thomas M., arr. *Tuba Carols*. Ludwig Music Publishing Company. Euphonium and two tubas. 1987. $5.00. 14 pp. III–IV. Part I: Bb–c', Part II: F–b, Part III: F₁–c. A collection of twelve familiar Christmas Carols. Score, but no separate parts. Because of the ranges other possible instrumentations are three tubas or two euphoniums and tuba. The first and second parts are printed in treble clef at the end of the book. Some of these work really well. Parts may be doubled for a large ensemble.

Handel, G.F. *Sonata No. 4*. arr. George R. Belden and Donald C. Little. Great Works Publishing, Incorporated. Two euphoniums and one tuba. 1992. $8.00. 6:00. IV. Part I: c–bb', Part II: c–c", Part III: F₁–c'. Four movements: Adagio; Allegro; Largo; Allegro. In a trio sonata format with the top two parts playing the solo parts and the tuba playing the continuo. The tessitura of both euphonium parts is high. Technically challenging for all parts.

Hartin, Paul F., arr. *A Suite of Elizabethan Madrigals*. Cellar Press. Three tubas. 1974. 4:30. III. Part I: Bb–c', Part II: Bb–c', Part III: A₁–c. Four movements: O

Sleep, Fond Fancy; Ha Ha, This World Doth Pass; Come Sirrah Jack, Ho!; The Nightingale. The first and second parts can be played on euphoniums to make this suite playable by a high school ensemble. Parts may be doubled for a large ensemble.

Hastings, Ross. *Little Madrigal for Big Horns*. Southern Music Company. Out of print. Euphonium and two tubas. 1972. 2:30. III–IV. Part I: c–g', Part II: G–c', Part III: F_1–d♭. Nice melodic madrigal, not very polyphonic. Frequent meter changes but the quarter note remains constant. Very tuneful, a lot of music in this short composition. Parts may be doubled for a large ensemble. Recorded by the University of Miami Tuba Ensemble, Miami United Tuba Ensemble Society, 14568.

Heger, Owe, arr. *Leichte Ragtime-Trios* (Easy Ragtime Trios). Noetzel Edition (C.F. Peters). Two euphoniums and one tuba. 1988. $15.95. 18:00. IV. Part I: F–g', Part II: F–g', Part III: F–d'. Five movements: The Easy Winners; The Entertainer; Dickie's Rag; The Strenuous Life; The Sycamore. Dedicated to Wilhelm Ebeling. A collection of one original and four Joplin rags. A lot of syncopation, some technical challenges in all three parts. The movements are complete rags and may be played separately or in small groups. Fun to play.

Heger, Owe, arr. *Leichte Volkslieder-Trios 6* (Easy Folksong Trios). Noetzel Edition (C.F. Peters). Three tubas. 1988. $14.50. 8:30. IV. Part I: F–d', Part II: F–d', Part III: F–d'. Six movements: Guten Abend, Gute Nacht; Bruder Jakob; Weisst du, wieviel Sternlein stehen; Guter Mond, du Stehst so stille; Dat du min Leevsten büst; Es warren zwei Königskinder. Dedicated to Volker Kähler and Gerke Swyter. Arranged for any three bass-clef instruments. The movements are short and not technically challenging. The same melodies are arranged for three trumpets and three horns, thus allowing combinations of any three brass instruments.

Henderson, Kenneth, and Stoutamire, Albert, arr. *Trios for All*. CPP Belwin, Incorporated. Two euphoniums and one tuba. 1974. $5.00. 21 pp. II–III. Part I: B♭–g', Part II: A–e♭', Part III: F_1–e. Seventeen compositions by Purcell, Mozart, Shostakovich, Grieg, and thirteen other notable composers. Some work very well for junior high as well as high school players. Parts may be doubled for a large ensemble.

Hewitt, Harry. *Three Preludes for Three Tubas, Op. 376C*. Harry Hewitt. 1968. $4.00. 7:00. IV. Part I: F_1–d', Part II: D_1–b, Part III: F_1–d. Three movements. Technical challenges are primarily in the first and second parts. Very dissonant harmonies at times. Performers play from a score.

Isbell, Thomas, arr. *Dona Nobis Pacem*. The Brass Press. Euphonium and two tubas, or three tubas. 1969. $3.50. 3:00. II–III. Part I: c–d', Part II: C–d, Part III: C–d. Written for R. Winston Morris and

the Tennessee Technological University Tuba Ensemble. The second and third parts are relatively easy, with no technical or range problems. Excellent piece for young students, or any players wishing to work on lyrical playing. Parts may be doubled for a large ensemble.

Israel, Brian. *Tower Music*. Tritone Press. Two euphoniums and one tuba. 1983. $3.50. 4:17. III–IV. Part I: G–d', Part II: F♯–b, Part III: G_1–g♭. Three movements: Praeludium; Fugua, Carol. To Jack Gallagher. The second part is not high and could be performed on tuba. The Fugua and Carol are lively and playable by good high school players. Parts may be doubled for a large ensemble.

Jacobsen, Julius. *Ten Trios for Three Tubas*. Swedish Music Information Center—STIM. 14:00. IV–V. Part I: A_1–f', Part II: C–e♭', Part III: A_1–b♭. Ten movements, which vary in key, meter, and style. Many technical challenges for all three parts. The tessitura of the first part is high. An F tuba is recommended, though a euphonium may also be used.

Jacobson, I.D. *Three Temperaments for Tubas*. Israel Composers League. Out of print. Three tubas. 1963. 3:30. III–IV. Part I: G–f', Part II: G_1–a. Part III: C–d'. Three movements: I; II; III. The top part has a high tessitura and may be played on euphonium or F tuba. No technical demands, very traditional harmonies. Parts may be doubled for a large ensemble.

Jager, Robert. *Variations on a Motive by Wagner*. Elkan-Vogel. Euphonium and two tubas. 1976. $15.00. 5:00. IV. Part I: G–b♭', Part II: D♯–d', Part III: $D♯_1$–f. Composed for Harvey Phillips, Earle Louder, and R. Winston Morris. A single movement with contrasting sections. The last section is particularly challenging technically, but worth the effort.

Jones, Roger. *Suite for Three Tubas*. Roger Jones. Three tubas. 1992. $15.00. 5.00. IV. Part I: F♯–d', Part II: B♭$_1$–g, Part III: F_1–e. Three movements: Moderately Fast and with a Stealy Pulse; Very Slow; Fast. All three parts are challenging and have responsibility for the melody. The melodies are often syncopated but are tuneful and work very well.

Jones, Roger. *Switched-Down Bach*. Roger Jones. Euphonium and two tubas, or three tubas. 1992. $5.00. 2:00. IV. Part I: A♭–f, Part II: A♭$_1$–a, Part III: A♭$_1$–d♭. Written in a jazz style. All parts play the melody at different times. The melody is syncopated and requires a good jazz feel of all players. Parts may be doubled for a large ensemble.

Jones, Roger. *Three Tubas Two*. Roger Jones. 1971. $6.00. 3:30. III–IV. Part I: C–f(c'), Part II: A♭$_1$–f, Part III: A♭$_1$–c. The melody is primarily in the first and second parts. The melody has some syncopations but contains very traditional harmonies. The top part may be played on euphonium, making this very playable by high school students.

Jones, Roger. *Toe Tapping Tuba Tune*. Roger Jones. Three tubas. 1993. $5.00. 2:30. IV. Part I: A♭₁–a♭, Part II: B♭₁–f, Part III: F₁–d. The melody is very syncopated and multimetric. No significant technical problems. Parts may be doubled for a large ensemble.

Jones, Roger. *Trio for Tubas*. Roger Jones. Euphonium and two tubas. 1970. $10.00. 4:20. IV. Part I: G–a', Part II: F–d', Part III: C–c'. Two movements: Slow But Moving; Lively. The second movement is multimetric and rhythmically challenging. All three parts are interesting to play.

Kerll, J.C. *Canzone*. arr. Newell H. Long. The Brass Press. Euphonium and two tubas. 1974. $3.50. 2:00. III. Part I: A–e', Part II: A₁–f, Part III: A₁–f. Imitative counterpoint that works very well. No technical problems, but players need to count carefully. Parts may be doubled.

Kinyon, John, arr. *Fun for Band*. Alfred Publishing Company Incorporated. Out of print. 1972. 16 pp. I–II. Part I: A♭–f, Part II: A♭–f, Part III: A♭–f. A collection of easy duets and trios. Works very well for tubists who have been playing only one or two years.

Kodály, Zoltán. *Lament*. arr. Skip Gray. Shawnee Press, Incorporated. Euphonium and two tubas. 1980. $6.95. 2:30. III–IV. Part I: c♭–c″, Part II: C–f, Part III: F₁–B♭. The first part is written in tenor clef in the score, although the part is in bass clef. Parts are technically easy, but the range of the first part is difficult for the euphonium. This arrangement works very well. Parts may be doubled for a large ensemble.

Kresin, Willibald, arr. *Swing Low, Sweet Chariot*. ITC Editions Marc Reift. Two euphoniums and two tubas. 3:40. IV. Part I: B♭–d♭″, Part II: E–b♭', Part III: F₁–d♭, Part IV: F₁–b. Recorded by David LeClair, Contraband, *Swingin' Low*, Marcophon CD 940-2.

Larrick, Geary. *Trio for Tubas*. Geary Larrick. Three tubas. 1992. $12.00. 4:00. III. Part I: C–f♯, Part II: C–e, Part III: B♭₁–f♯. Three movements: Recitative; Song; March. No range or technical problems. The texture is very thin—it is rare for even two parts to play at the same time.

Lindenfeld, Harris. *Inflation*. Tritone Press. Three tubas. 1975. $6.00. 8:30. IV. Part I: A₁–d', Part II: A♭₁–c♯', Part III: G₁–g. Three movements: Moderately and smoothly; Very slowly; Fast and light. The technical demands are moderate but there are many ensemble challenges, especially in the multimetric third movement. The piece is atonal and thus quite dissonant.

Lupo, Thomas. *Fantasia*. arr. David Baldwin. The Musical Evergreen. Three tubas. 1974. $3.50. 2:00. IV. Part I: C–a, Part II: B–b, Part III: A₁–a. Very contrapuntal and syncopated. While range is not a problem for high school players, the piece is rhythmically and technically challenging.

Lupo, Thomas. *Fantasia*. arr. Paul F. Hartin. Cellar Press. Three tubas. 1975. 2:00. IV. Part I: F–d',

Part II: E–e', Part III: D₁–d. Same as the Baldwin arrangement above, but transposed up a fourth to the key of C.

Marcellus, John, arr. *Trios for Brass, Volume I, Easy–Intermediate*. CPP Belwin, Incorporated. Two euphoniums and one tuba. 1986. $6.50. 15 pp. II–III. Part I: B♭–g', Part II: B♭–f', Part III: G₁–f. Collection of eight melodies from the Renaissance, Baroque, and Classical periods. Very appropriate for young players. A treble-clef book is available, so any combination of brass instruments is possible. Parts may be doubled for a large ensemble.

Marcellus, John, arr. *Trios for Brass, Volume I, Intermediate*. CPP Belwin, Incorporated. Two euphoniums and one tuba. 1986. $6.50. 15 pp. III. Part I: F–a', Part II: F–e', Part III: A₁–f. Collection of eight melodies from the Baroque and Classical periods. The melodies are more polyphonic and slightly more challenging than the Easy–Intermediate arrangements. Parts may be doubled for a large ensemble.

Marcellus, John, arr. *Trios for Brass, Volume I, Advanced*. CPP Belwin, Incorporated. Two euphoniums and one tuba. 1986. $6.50. 15 pp. III–IV. Part I: F–b♭', Part II: A–g', Part III: A♭₁–f. Five melodies from the Baroque and Classical style periods. As with the other books in this series, a treble-clef book is available, allowing any combination of brass instruments to play these trios. The tessitura of the top part is much higher than that of the previous books in this series, and there are more technical challenges. Parts may be doubled for a large ensemble.

McAdams, Charles A., arr. *Swing Low, Sweet Chariot*. Encore Music Publishers. Euphonium and two tubas. 1991. $8.50. 3:00. III–IV. Part I: f–g', Part II: B♭–b♭', Part III: B♭₁–c. The tubas begin this familiar melody in a slow lyrical fashion. The middle section is an up-tempo swing treatment of the melody; the slow lyrical section returns at the end. Drum set may be added. Works well and is a good introduction to teaching swing style. Parts may be doubled for a large ensemble.

McCurdy, Gary. *Chorale*. TMC Publications. Out of print. Two euphoniums and one tuba. 1973. 2:00. III. Part I: B♭–d', Part II: A–c', Part III: C–d. The top part could be played by a tuba. The chorale is in a very traditional style with the melody primarily in the top part. Parts may be doubled for a large ensemble.

McCurdy, Gary. *Demon Dance*. TMC Publications. Out of print. Three tubas. 1971. 2:00. III. Part I: B♭–d', Part II: D–a, Part III: F₁–A.

McCurdy, Gary. *Five Hundred Pound Polka*. TMC Publications. Out of print. Three tubas and piano. 1971. 2:00. II–III. Part I: A–g, Part II: E–d, Part III: C–d.

McCurdy, Gary. *Three Dances for Three Tubas*. TMC Publications. Out of print. 1971. 4:00. IV. Part I:

G♭–d', Part II: E–b♭, Part III: F₁–d. Three movements: Minuet; Two–Step; Tango.

Morita, Kazuhiro, arr. *Euphonium and Tuba: Ensemble Works for the First Time.* Yamaha Kyohan Company Limited. Two euphoniums and one tuba. 1983. $8.00. 20 pp. III–IV. Part I: B♭–g', Part II: A–f ', Part III: G₁–d. Seven duets (for two euphoniums) and seven trios (two euphoniums and one tuba). Three of the duets have an optional third part for tuba so they are notated in three parts. Compositions are by Western composers, including Grieg, Mussorgsky, Brahms, Bach, and Beethoven and one non-Western composer. The arrangements are short and are of moderate technical difficulty.

Mozart, W.A. *Allegro,* from *Divertimento No. 1, K. 229.* arr. Paul Schmidt. Heavy Metal Music. Two euphoniums and one tuba. 1992. $5.00. 4:30. IV. Part I: c–f ', Part II: F–e', Part III: B♭₁–f. A workout for all three parts, but fun to play. No score available.

Mueller, Frederick A. *Tuba Trio.* Frederick A. Mueller. Euphonium and two tubas. 1973. $12.00. 8:30. IV. Part I: E–a♭', Part II: A₁–e♭', Part III: E₁–d♭'. Five movements: Adagio; Presto-staccato; Lament; Cadenza; Perpetuum mobile. To Earle, David, and Winston, in memory of William J. Bell. Very interesting trio. Parts are challenging to put together. A few twentieth-century techniques, very modern harmonies.

Murzin, V. *Impromptu.* The Musical Evergreen. Two trombones (or euphoniums) and one tuba. 1975. $7.50. 1:20. III–IV. Part I: g–a', Part II: f–e, Part III: A–f. The top two parts are written in tenor clef. The melody is primarily in the third part.

Nelhybel, Vaclav. *Ludus for Three Tubas.* E.C. Kerby Limited (Hal Leonard Publishing Corporation). Three tubas. 1975. $10.00. 9:00. V. Part I: G₁–g', Part II: G₁–g', Part III: F♯₁–g'. Three movements Commissioned by Rudolf Meinl Tubas and dedicated to the First International Tuba Symposium, 1973. First Performed by Daniel Perantoni, Robert Tucci, and J. Lesley Varner. Extensive technical and range demands on all parts. There are frequent and extreme dynamic contrasts, complex rhythms, large skips, and a contemporary harmonic structure. A very demanding but an exciting piece of music.

Olsen, Ole. *Fanitul.* arr. L.A. Rauchut. KIWI Music Press. Out of print. Two euphoniums and one tuba. 2:00. IV. Part I: c–a', Part II: G♯–e', Part III: A₁–c'. The technical demands are greatest on the two euphonium parts. Brief high sections of the tuba part may be played an octave lower if necessary.

O'Reilly, J., and Kinyon, J., arr. *Yamaha Band Ensembles, Tuba/Book 1.* Alfred Publishing Company Incorporated. Three tubas and optional piano. 1990. $4.50. 23 pp. I–II. Part I: B♭₁–c, Part II: A₁–A♭, Part III: A₁–A♭. Seventeen different American folk and Christmas songs that correlate with the

Yamaha Band Student Method Book series. These same melodies are arranged for several different groups of instruments and may be purchased separately. The top line is always the melody, the second line the harmony, and the third line an accompaniment. Very appropriate for beginning and young players.

O'Reilly, J., and Kinyon, J., arr. *Yamaha Band Ensembles, Tuba/Book 2.* Alfred Publishing Company Incorporated. Three tubas and optional piano. 1990. $4.50. 23 pp. II. Part I: B♭₁–e♭, Part II: A♭₁–B♭, Part III: G₁–c. Fourteen different melodies. Correlates with Book 2 of the *Yamaha Band Student Method Book.* No range or technical problems.

O'Reilly, J., and Kinyon, J., arr. *Yamaha Band Ensembles, Tuba/Book 3.* Alfred Publishing Company Incorporated. Three tubas and optional piano. 1990. $4.50. 23 pp. II–III. Part I: A₁–e♭, Part II: A₁–c, Part III: A₁–c. Thirteen melodies that correlate with the *Yamaha Band Student Method Book.* Though they can get muddy at times, they give young tuba players a fine chance to play melodies and harmonies.

Pappas, Joseph. *Pastorale and March.* JPM Publications. 1993. $8.00. 3.00. III. Part I: B♭₁–d♭, Part II: B♭₁–c, Part III: B♭–c. Two movements: Pastorale; March. No significant range or technical problems. The melody is mostly in the first part. Well suited for young players.

Potter, David. *Aria and Rondo.* Southern Music Company. Two euphoniums and one tuba. 1983. $5.95. 4:30. IV. Part I: c♯–b', Part II: c♯–g', Part III: G₁–e♭'. Two movements: Aria; Rondo. For Susan Smith, Dan Satterwhite, and a friend. The Rondo is in mixed meter with alternating technical and lyrical sections. Brief sections of the tuba part may be played an octave lower if necessary as the tessitura is a bit high.

Presser, William. *Suite for Three Tubas.* Tenuto Publications. 1968. $6.00. 8:00. III–IV. Part I: A₁–a. Part II: A₁–a♭, Part III: E₁–d. Three movements: Allegretto; Andante; Allegro. Although individual parts are not difficult, there are some complicated rhythmic figures in the first movement that can cause ensemble problems. Good program material.

Purcell, Henry. *Canon on a Ground Bass.* arr. Skip Gray. Shawnee Press, Incorporated. Euphonium and two tubas. 1980. $7.50. 2:20. III–IV. Part I: e–a', Part II: E–b, Part III: A₁–e. From an instrumental interlude in Purcell's opera *Dioclesian.* The third part plays the ground bass, while the two top parts play the melody in canon. Very tuneful and enjoyable to play and listen to. Good for high school ensemble although the second part may get a little high for some high school players. Parts may be doubled for a large ensemble.

Purcell, Henry. *Chaconne.* arr. Paul F. Hartin. Cellar Press. Three tubas. 1975. 2:30. III. Part I: G₁–a♭',

Part II: G$_1$–e♭', Part III: G$_1$–b♭. Arrangement of the Purcell *Canon* above. First part should be played on the euphonium or F tuba. Parts may be doubled for a large ensemble.

Racussen, David. *Canonic Etudes.* Shawnee Press, Incorporated. Out of print. Three tubas. 1971. 37 pp. III–IV. A collection of canons for one to four players. The books were printed for all wind instruments.

Rodgers, Thomas. *Three Pieces for Low Brass Trio.* The Brass Press. Out of print. Two euphoniums and one tuba. 1974. 7:00. IV. Part I: c♭–g', Part II: G–f, Part III: G$_1$–b♭. Three movements: Fanfare; Contrapunctus; Scherzo. Written for R. Winston Morris and the Tennessee Technological University Tuba Ensemble. While range is not a problem for any of the parts, there are several sections that challenge the ensemble. A good concert piece.

Roikjer, Kjell. *Ten Inventions for Three Tubas.* Engström and Sodring Musikverlag. Three tubas. 1990. 8 pp. IV–V. Part I: c–e', Part II: c♯–e', Part III: A$_1$–c. Ten contrasting movements. Excellent writing for this genre. Movements are musically and technically challenging for the advanced player. They may be performed individually or in small groups as a suite.

Ross, Walter. *Fancy Dances.* Dorn Publications, Incorporated. Three tubas. 1972. 6:00. IV. Part I: B$_1$–e♭', Part II: A♭$_1$–c', Part III: F♯$_1$–f. Three movements: Galop; Saraband; Saltarello. Parts are of equal difficulty. The third movement is especially rhythmically challenging. Recorded by the New York Tuba Quartet, *Tubby's Revenge,* Crystal Records, S221.

Scheidt, Samuel. *Selections from Symphonien auf Conzerten-Manier.* arr. Paul F. Hartin. Cellar Press. Three tubas. 1974. 5:00. IV. Part I: c♯–b', Part II: A–f ', Part III: F♯$_1$–e. Four movements: I; II; III; IV. The first part should be played on euphonium, and the second part may require an F tuba. The third movement is very challenging technically, but the others do not present much of a problem.

Schmidt, Paul, arr. *Five Trios of King Henry VIII.* Heavy Metal Music. Two euphoniums and one tuba. 1992. $5.00. 5:00. III–IV. Part I: F–f ', Part II: F–e♭', Part III: B♭$_1$–f. Five movements: Pastime with Good Company; If Love Now Reigned; O My Hart; Fantasy; With Owt Dyscorde. Nice arrangement of these famous English melodies. Younger players will need a conductor because of the many fermatas and tempo changes. No score available. Parts may be doubled for a large ensemble.

Schubert, Franz. *Four Choruses.* arr. Kenneth Singleton. Peer International Corporation. Three tubas. 1977. $8.50. 5:00. IV. Part I: F–d', Part II: F–d', Part III: D–f '. Four movements: Dessen Fahne Donnesturme wallte (The Colors Churn within the Thunderstorm); Die zwei Tugendwege (The Two Ways of Virtue); Totengraberlied (Grave Digger's

Song); Tronend auf Erhabnem Sitz (In Majesty upon the Sublime Throne). Parts are of equal difficulty and have the same range. The first part has a higher tessitura and would be appropriate on euphonium or F tuba. The movements are tuneful and are in a traditional harmonic setting.

Schumann, Robert. *Two Canons.* arr. Kenneth Singleton. Peer International Corporation. Out of print. Three tubas. 1977. 1:45. IV. Part I: F–e♭', Part II: F–d', Part III: F–d'. Two movements: Gibt mir zu Trinken! (Let Me Drink!); Lässt Lautenspiel und Becherklang nicht Rasten (Let the Lute Playing and the Clinking of Goblets not Cease). Two contrasting canons, the first very aggressive and fast, the second a little slower paced. Range and technical demands of all parts are equal. F tubas or euphoniums could easily be used on any of the parts.

Singleton, Kenneth, arr. *Two English Madrigals.* Peer International Corporation Out of print. Three tubas. 1977. 2:30. IV. Part I: E♭–d', Part II: D–d', Part III: D–d'. Two movements: Come, Merry Lads, Let us Away; Lady Those Eyes. Parts are of equal difficulty regarding range. The first movement is polyphonic; the second is in a canon-like style. Requires three strong players.

Stewart, Frank G. *Heavyweights.* Seesaw Music Corporation Publishers. Three tubas. 1974. $18.00. 5:00. IV. Part I: D–e', Part II: D–b♭, Part III: F♯$_1$–a. Several contrasting sections within one movement. There are mixed meters (3/8, 6/8, 7/8, etc.) in the fast section. The first part may be played on euphonium.

Telemann, G.P. *Three Chorale Preludes.* arr. William Schmidt. Western International Music. Euphonium and two tubas. 1985. $7.00. 5:30. IV. Part I: d–f ', Part II: D–c', Part III: G$_1$–f. Three movements: Komm, heiliger Geist, Herr Gott; Vater unser im Himmelreich; Herr Jesu Christ, Dich zu uns Wend. The chorale melodies are in the top part. Interesting writing in the second and third parts. There are no articulation markings, so players will need to exercise sensitivity in phrasing. Parts may be doubled for a large ensemble.

Thornton, Michael, arr. *Three Diverse Drinking Songs.* Queen City Brass Publications. Three tubas. 1991. $8.00. 2:00. IV. Part I: C–e♭', Part II: C–c', Part III: C–b♭. Three movements: Would you have a young Virgin?; He that will an Alehouse keepe; Trinklied im Winter. A lively collection. A euphonium may be used for the first part. Parts may be doubled for a large ensemble. Originally copyrighted in 1980.

Thornton, Michael, arr. *Three Pieces from King Henry VIII.* Queen City Brass Publications. Three tubas. 1980. $5.00. 2:30. IV. Part I: F–e', Part II: F–e♭', Part III: G$_1$–d'. Three movements: O My Hart; Blow Thy Horne Hunter; With Owt Dyscorde. Transcriptions of three Renaissance songs. Not technically difficult, but the range requirements make this more suited for college players.

Uber, David. *Signals for Tuba Trio*. TUBA Press. 1992. $10.00. 3:00. IV. Part I: F–b♭, Part II: B♭–g, Part III: G₁–e♭. Three movements: I; II; III. Technically challenging, but no range problems. Parts have equal melodic and technical responsibilities. Requires three strong players. Interesting writing and fun to play.

Warren, Frank E. *Suite for Three Tubas, Op. 3*. Frank E. Warren Music Service. Three tubas. 1976. 6:00. IV. Part I: C₁–e', Part II: E₁–f ', Part III: C₁–d♭'. Extreme range and technical demands of all three parts. Several tempo changes and mixed meters throughout. A companion piece (Op. 3a) is exactly the same composition scored for one euphonium and two tubas.

Weelkes, Thomas. *Three Madrigals*. arr. Paul Schmidt. Heavy Metal Music. Two euphoniums and one tuba. 1990. $7.00. 4:00. IV. Part I: e♭–f ', Part II: B♭–e♭', Part III: E♭–f. Three movements: Come, Sirrah Jack, Ho!; Since Robin Hood; Strike It Up, Tabor. Three very spirited madrigals. The third is the most polyphonic, though none of the movements are difficult technically. No score available; parts may be doubled.

Wilder, Alec. *Ten Trios for Tubas*. Margun Music, Incorporated. 1980. $8.00. 7 pp. IV. Part I: G₁–g', Part II: G₁–g♭', Part III: F₁–d'. Ten movements in contrasting styles, including jazz. The first part may be played on euphonium or F tuba because of the high tessitura. The technical and range demands require advanced players.

Wilder, Alec. *Tuba Trio Number 1*. Margun Music, Incorporated. 1983. $4.50. 1:45. IV. Part I: G♭–f ', Part II: D–f ', Part III: C–d'. Very polyphonic, canon-like in the middle section. Harmonies are rich and typical of Wilder's music—consequently angular melodies and skips are common.

Willaert, Adrian. *Ricercar a Tre Voci*. arr. Paul F. Hartin. Cellar Press. 1974. 2:00. III–IV. Part I: A–d', Part II: E–g, Part III: G₁–B♭. Has a limited range for all parts. Very usable with a high school ensemble with a euphonium on the first part. Parts may be doubled for a large ensemble.

Zindars, Earl. *Tuba Trio*. T.U.B.A. Journal. Three tubas. 1981. $7.50. 1:00. III–IV. Part I: d–e', Part II: A–d', Part III: G₁–a. Top two parts are much more suited for euphoniums or F tubas. No real technical difficulties, may be performed by high schools players if euphoniums are playing the first two parts. Parts may be doubled for a large ensemble. Written as part of the T.U.B.A. GEM Series and published in *T.U.B.A. Journal* Vol. 9, no. 2.

Four Parts

Abt, Franz. *Postlude on "Willingham."* arr. Gregory Bright. Tuba/Euphonium Music Publications. Out of Print. Two euphoniums and two tubas. 4:00. III.

Adson, John. *Two Airs*. arr. John Stevens. Encore Music Publishers. Two euphoniums and two tubas. 1988. $12.50. 2:20. III–IV. Part I: d–g', Part II: d–e', Part III: A–a, Part IV: A₁–d. Two movements: Allegro; Allegretto. Most of the melody is in the first euphonium part. The second movement has primarily tutti rhythms in a very traditional harmonic setting. A very playable arrangement by high school or college ensembles. Parts may be doubled for a large ensemble.

Ahrendt, Karl. *Three Movements for Four Tubas*. T.A.P. Music. Four tubas. 1989. Parts, $15.00., score $4.00. 12:00. IV. Part I: B♭–b♭', Part II: F–f ', Part III: C–d', Part IV: C₁–g. Three movements: Intrada; Aria; Canzona. The top two parts indicate a tuba in F, though a euphonium could also be used. Some sections are technically difficult; strong players are required to put this together.

Albeniz, I.M.F. *Tango Espana*. arr. Paul Schmidt. Heavy Metal Music. Two euphoniums and two tubas. 1991. $7.00. 1:30. IV. Part I: G–f ', Part II: G–b♭, Part III: G–d♭'(e♭'), Part IV: G₁–a♭. Rhythmically complex for the top three parts. Several large skips in the first part. Fun to play. No score available. Parts may be doubled for a large ensemble.

Albert, Thomas. *TubaCanon*. T.U.B.A. Journal. Four tubas. 1975. $7.50. Indeterminate. IV–V. Part I: G–g, Part II: G–g, Part III: G–g, Part IV: G–g. Based on a larger indeterminate (aleatory) work entitled *A Maze with Grace*. All players read from the score. Players begin one at a time at the upper left-hand corner and proceed to the other notes in any order they choose. The length and structure players will use should be decided prior to the performance. Written as part of the T.U.B.A. GEM series and published in the *T.U.B.A. Journal*, Vol. 2, no. 2.

Albinoni, Tomaso. *Adagio*. arr. Hirokazu Hiraishi. Sonic Arts, Incorporated. Four euphoniums. 1992. $11.00. 6:00. III–IV. Part I: G–a', Part II: F–e', Part III: F–d♭', Part IV: C–c'. May also be played with two euphoniums and two tubas, or three euphoniums and one tuba. A slow lyrical melody with most of the melodic responsibility in the top two parts. No significant technical problems. Parts may be doubled for a large ensemble.

Alexander, Joseph. *Dyad for Four Tubas*. Margun Music, Incorporated. Four tubas. 1989. $30.00. 8:30. IV–V. Part I: C♯–g', Part II: D–f ', Part III: A₁–g', Part IV: F♯₁–f '. Two movements. Extensive range demands for all parts. Could be performed by two euphoniums and two tubas. Technically very challenging, both movements are multimetric. Harmonies are contemporary and very dissonant.

Alexander, Lois, arr. *Swing Low, Sweet Chariot*. Southern Music Company. Two euphoniums and two tubas. 1990. $5.00. 3:00. IV. Part I: c–c", Part II:

A–b♭', Part III: B♭₁–b♭, Part IV: E♭₁–f. Tessitura of the first two parts is quite high. The middle section is pointillistic. Parts may be doubled for a large ensemble.

Alford, Kenneth. *Colonel Bogey March* (Bridge Over the River Kwai). arr. Paul Schmidt. Heavy Metal Music. Two euphoniums and two tubas. 1991. $7.00. 3:20. IV. Part I: A–a', Part II: F–c', Part III: F–c', Part IV: F₁–c. Good arrangement of the march used in the motion picture *Bridge Over The River Kwai*. Most of the melody is in the first part. No score available. Parts may be doubled for a large ensemble.

Alpert, Herb. *El Solo Toro-Marriachi*. arr. James Self. James Self. Out of print. Two euphoniums and two tubas. 2:30. III. Part I: c–f ', Part II: G–b♭, Part III: (F₁)B♭₁–f, Part IV: F₁–c. No technical problems. A Mexican flavor designed for young players.

Amellér, André. *Adagio, Choral et Scherzetto*. André Amellér. Four tubas. 1981.

Amellér, André. *Concertstück*. André Amellér. Four tubas. 1982.

Amellér, André. *Lento Espressivo*. T.U.B.A. Journal,. Four tubas. 1980. $7.50. 2:00. IV. Part I: g–g♭', Part II: C–c', Part III: F–d♭', Part IV: F₁–d. The tessitura of the first part is high and may require an F tuba. A very lyrical chorale. Written as part of the T.U.B.A. GEM Series and published in *T.U.B.A. Journal*, Vol. 8, no. 1.

Anderson, Eugene. *Celebration*. Anderson's Arizona Originals. Three euphoniums and tuba. 1988. $5.00. 1:45. III–IV. Part I: g–a', Part II: g–e♭', Part III: G–b, Part IV: (C₁)G₁–e♭. A fanfare with all parts having equal melodic responsibility and technical demands. Good for a concert opener. Parts may be doubled for a large ensemble.

Anderson, Eugene. *Chorale Quartet*. Anderson's Arizona Originals. Two euphoniums and two tubas. 1989. $5.00. 2:30. III. Part I: A–a', Part II: E–c♯', Part III: F–c♯, Part IV: (D₁)E–d. A very lyrical chorale. No technical problems, very appropriate for younger players. Parts may be doubled for a large ensemble.

Anderson, Eugene. *Fanfare for Tubafour*. Anderson's Arizona Originals. Two euphoniums and two tubas. 1988. $5.00. 1:45. IV. Part I: d–b♭', Part II: d–e', Part III: G–b, Part IV: G♭₁–d. Slow and mysterious in character. The melody is based on dotted-eighth note and triplet figures. Parts may be doubled for a large ensemble.

Anderson, Eugene. *Great Chromatic Fugue in G*. Anderson's Arizona Originals. Three euphoniums and one tuba. 1988. $6.00. 3:00. IV. Part I: d–c″, Part II: G–g', Part III: D–a, Part IV: G₁–b♭. The technical challenges are moderate. The tessitura of the first part is high. Players need to count carefully.

Anderson, Eugene. *Heavy Metal*. Anderson's Arizona Originals. Two euphoniums, two tubas, and drum set. 1989. $5.00. 2:30. IV. Part I: B♭–b♭', Part II:

A–f ', Part III: f–d', Part IV: A♭₁–d♭. A rock-style melody with most of the melody in the first part. The tubas have an interesting bass line. The drum set helps establish a rock feel. The tessitura of the first part is high. Parts may be doubled for a large ensemble.

Anderson, Eugene. *Outback Brass*. Anderson's Arizona Originals. Two euphoniums and two tubas. 1989. $5.00. 1:30 IV. Part I: e–b♭', Part II: F–d', Part III: E–b♭, Part IV: G₁–f. Based on an aboriginal melody dating from 1788. There are many driving rhythmic figures and large skips. Interesting writing. Parts may be doubled for a large ensemble.

Anderson, Eugene. *Theme and Six Derivations*. Anderson's Arizona Originals. Two euphoniums and two tubas. 1988. $8.00. 11:00. IV. Part I: G–c″, Part II: G–a♭', Part III: B♭₁–f ', Part IV: D₁–g. A single movement with seven different sections. The derivations contrast in key, tempo, and style. Only moderate technical demands, but the tessitura for the first part is high. Mutes are required.

Anderson, Eugene, arr. *Beautiful Savior*. Anderson's Arizona Originals. Two euphoniums and two tubas. 1988. $5.00. 2:20. IV. Part I: f♯–g', Part II: d–d', Part III: G–d', Part IV: G₁–a. Arrangement in a lyrical and chorale style of the hymn "Fairest Lord Jesus." No significant technical problems. Parts may be doubled for a large ensemble.

Anderson, Eugene, arr. *Beer Barrel Polka*. Anderson's Arizona Originals. Two euphoniums and two tubas. 1990. $5.00. 1:45. IV. Part I: B♭–b♭', Part II: F–f ', Part III: F–f ', Part IV: F₁–f. The first part has primary melodic responsibility throughout the piece. The tessitura of the first and third parts is high. Perfect for those Octubafest parties! Parts may be doubled for a large ensemble.

Anderson, Eugene, arr. *The Caroling Quartet*, Anderson's Arizona Originals. Two euphoniums and two tubas. 1988. $5.00. 2:00. IV. Part I: e♭–b♭', Part II: B♭–a', Part III: A–d', Part IV: F₁–b♭. A Christmas medley featuring brief excerpts of: "Do You Hear What I Hear?," "Santa Claus Comes Tonight," "Jingle Bells," and "Rudolph the Red-Nosed Reindeer." Most of the melody is in the first part, and its tessitura is high. Parts may be doubled for a large ensemble.

Anderson, Eugene, arr. *Chiapanecas* (Advanced). Anderson's Arizona Originals. Three euphoniums and one tuba. 1988. $5.00. 2:30. IV–V. Part I: g–b♭', Part II: F–g', Part III: F–g♭', Part IV: F₁–e♭'. A fun arrangement of the "Mexican Hat Dance." The tessitura of the first and fourth parts is high. A few technical challenges. Parts may be doubled for a large ensemble.

Anderson, Eugene, arr. *Chiapanecas* (Easy). Anderson's Arizona Originals. Two euphoniums and two tubas. 1988. $5.00. 2:30. III–IV. Part I: b♭', Part II: d–g', Part III: B♭–c(d'), Part IV: F₁–c. An easier arrangement of the same Mexican melody.

The tessitura of the top part is still a little high, but the fourth part is much more suited for younger players. Parts may be doubled for a large ensemble.

Anderson, Eugene, arr. *Christmas Bells A-Plenty*. Anderson's Arizona Originals. Two euphoniums and two tubas. 1988. $5.00. 3:00. IV. Part I: d–bb', Part II: E–f ', Part III: D–eb', Part IV: Eb₁–c'. An arrangement of three Christmas melodies with the word "Bell" in the title: "Ring Christmas Bells;" "I Heard the Bells on Christmas Day;" and "Children's Bell Choir." The melody is primarily in the first part. Parts may be doubled for a large ensemble.

Anderson, Eugene, arr. *Deutschland über Alles*. Anderson's Arizona Originals. Two euphoniums and two tubas. 1988. $5.00. 2:00. III–IV. Part I: c–g', Part II: A–e', Part III: A–c', Part IV: G₁–g. A chorale-like arrangement of the German national anthem. Most of the melodic responsibility is in the first part. Parts may be doubled for a large ensemble.

Anderson, Eugene, arr. *The Echo Carol*. Anderson's Arizona Originals. Two euphoniums and two tubas. 1990. $5.00. 2:30. IV. Part I: c#–a', Part II: A–f ', Part III: F–c', Part IV: F₁–f '. Good arrangement of this traditional melody. No significant technical demands. Parts may be doubled for a large ensemble.

Anderson, Eugene, arr. *Kimiga-Yo*. Anderson's Arizona Originals. Two euphoniums and two tubas. 1989. $5.00. 2:00. III–IV. Part I: c–a', Part II: b–e', Part III: D–a, Part IV: D₁–d. A traditional setting of this Japanese melody. The melody is primarily in the first part. Parts may be doubled for a large ensemble.

Anderson, Eugene, arr. *Minuet*. Anderson's Arizona Originals. Two euphoniums and two tubas. 1988. $5.00. 2:00. IV. Part I: A–g', Part II: f–e', Part III: F–f ', Part IV: F₁–f. The third part has a high tessitura and may be played by a euphonium. Uses very traditional harmonies and works very well. Parts may be doubled for a large ensemble.

Anderson, Eugene, arr. *Sixteen Tons*. Anderson's Arizona Originals. Solo tuba and three euphoniums. 1988. $5.00. 1:45. III–IV. Part I: Ab₁,–bb, Part II: Ab–b, Part III: A–f, Part IV: (Bb₁)E–d'. A light jazzy arrangement of the Tennessee Ernie Ford classic. Features a tuba solo with three euphoniums accompanying. Swing feel is necessary. Could be used to highlight a high school tuba player with trombones or euphoniums playing the other parts. An optional part is included that is a combination of parts II and III for use as a trio. Parts may be doubled for a large ensemble.

Anderson, Leroy. *Sleigh Ride*. arr. Peter Rauch. Ohio Valley Tuba Quartet Press. Two euphoniums and two tubas. $13.00. 3:45. IV. Part I: d–a', Part II: c–g', Part III: C–b, Part IV: C₁–A. A fun arrangement of this Anderson classic. The melody is primarily in the first and third parts. The tessitura of the first part

is high. Sleigh bells and slap stick may be added for effect. Parts may be doubled for a large ensemble.

Anonymous. *Lute Dances for Four-Part Tuba Ensemble*. arr. John Baker. The Brass Press. Two euphoniums and two tubas. 1975. $4.00. 1:40. II–III. Part I: e–c', Part II: d–d', Part III: B–f#, Part IV: (A₁)B₁–A. Two movements: Der Prinzentanz; Proportz. Written for R. Winston Morris and the Tennessee Technological University Tuba Ensemble. The limited range and simple rhythms allow this to work well for high school or college ensembles. The difficulty of the performance is determined by the tempo at which the second movement is taken. The Proportz is written in 3/4 but should be felt in one. The first and second parts are printed in both treble and bass clefs. Parts may be doubled for a large ensemble. Recorded by the British Tuba Quartet, *In at the Deep End*, Heavyweight Records Limited, HR008/D.

Aoshima, Hiroshi. *Gnome*. Tokyo Bari-Tuba Ensemble. Two euphoniums and two tubas.

Arcadelt, Jacob. *Ave Maria*. arr. James Self. Wimbledon Music Incorporated. Four tubas. 1979. $7.00. 2:30. III–IV. Part I: db–db', Part II: c–bb, Part III: Ab–f, Part IV: Db–d. While the published title suggests four tubas, the first two parts are designated "tenor tuba" in the music. Can be played by four tubas, but it is very playable by high school students with euphoniums on the first and second parts. A very nice setting of this slow chorale. Recorded by the Melton Tuba Quartet, *Premiere*, Diavolo Records, DR-D-93-C-001.

Ayers, Jesse. *Into the Magical Rain Forest for Tuba/Euphonium Ensemble and Tape*. TUBA Press. Two euphoniums, two tubas, and tape. 1993. $15.00. 5:30. IV. Part I: f–g', Part II: A–f ', Part III: E–ab, Part IV: E₁–d. Commissioned by R. Winston Morris and the Tennessee Technological University Tuba Ensemble. The tape has many melodic and percussive sounds and is often the focal point of the composition. The composition is tonal but with some very interesting harmonies. No significant technical problems. Enjoyable for both performers and audience. Parts may be doubled for a large ensemble.

Bach, C.P.E. *Solfeggietto*. arr. F. Chester Roberts. Southern Music Company. Two euphoniums and two tubas. 1986. $3.00. 1:30. IV. Part I: G–a', Part II: Eb–c', Part III: Ab–ab, Part IV: G₁–g. Dedicated to the U.S. Coast Guard Tuba-Euphonium Quartet. A very usable arrangement of C.P.E. Bach's most famous keyboard composition. Constant sixteenth-note runs traded between the parts, technically very challenging. Players must count carefully to make the phrases seamless as the technical melody is passed from one part to the next.

Bach, C.P.E. *Solfegietto*. arr. Michael Howard. BTQ Publications. Two euphoniums and two tubas. 1993. $8.00.

Bach, J.S. *Air from Suite No. 3 in D.* arr. David Werden. Whaling Music Publishers. Two euphoniums and two tubas. 1978. $5.00. 3:10. IV. Part I: c–b♭', Part II: B♭–a', Part III: A–f ', Part IV: G$_1$–d'. The third part has a high tessitura and may be played on an F tuba or euphonium. The first part is printed only in treble clef. This arrangement is in the key of C, transposed up from the original in G. This beautiful simple melody requires a great deal of finesse to play as an ensemble. Parts may be doubled for a large ensemble. Recorded by the Atlantic Tuba Quartet, Golden Crest Records, CRS 4173; the British Tuba Quartet, *Euphonic Sounds,* Polyphonic Reproductions Limited, QPRZ 009D.

Bach, J.S. *Anna Magdalena Suite.* arr. John Stevens. John Stevens. Two euphoniums and two tubas. 1981. 7:00. III–IV. Part I: G–ab', Part II: F–A', Part III: B♭$_1$–c', Part IV: F$_1$–e♭. Four movements: Menuet; Musette; Bist du bei Mir; Marche. A straightforward transcription of this group of well-known keyboard compositions.

Bach, J.S. *Bist du bei Mir.* arr. David Werden. Whaling Music Publishers. Two euphoniums and two tubas. 1978. $5.00. 2:30. III–IV. Part I: d–ab', Part II: B♭–e♭, Part III: F–f ', Part IV: G$_1$–d. An excellent arrangement of one of Bach's most famous secular songs, written as a love song for his second wife Anna Magdalena. The two euphonium parts are in tenor clef in the score, and the first euphonium part is printed in treble clef only. Not difficult rhythmically—the challenge here is playing together as an ensemble. The first tuba part may be too high for high school tuba players, and a euphonium may be substituted. Recorded by the Atlantic Tuba Quartet, Golden Crest Records, CRS 4173; the Melton Tuba Quartet, *Premiere,* Diavolo Records, DR-D-93-C-001; U.S. Armed Forces Tuba/Euphonium Ensemble and Massed Ensemble, U.S. Army Records.

Bach, J.S. *Come Sweet Death.* arr. Eugene Anderson. Anderson's Arizona Originals. Two euphoniums and two tubas. 1988. $5.00. 1:30. III–IV. Part I: c–g', Part II: G–c', Part III: C–b♭, Part IV: (C$_1$)F$_1$–c. A four-part version and slightly easier arrangement of the Bach melody that Sauter arranged for one euphonium and two tubas. The euphonium parts are not high, and the first tuba part is not overly challenging. Parts may be doubled for a large ensemble.

Bach, J.S. *Contrapunctus III from Art of Fugue.* arr. Mark Nelson. Whaling Music Publishers. Two euphoniums and two tubas. 1991. $15.00. 3:20. IV. Part I: c♯–b♭', Part II: G–f ', Part III: B♭$_1$–g, Part IV: (D$_1$)F$_1$–d. Very polyphonic and technically challenging at times. Players need to count carefully. No significant range demands.

Bach, J.S. *Contrapunctus IX.* arr. Larry Pitts. The Brass Press. Out of print. Two euphoniums and two tubas. 4:45. IV. Part I: c–a', Part II: G♯–e', Part III: D–c', Part IV: G♯$_1$–d. Written for R. Winston Morris and the Tennessee Technological University Tuba Ensemble. Good arrangement of this very contrapuntal composition in a key which does not pose great range demands on any of the parts. All parts are technically demanding and need to be played very lightly and cleanly. Parts may be carefully doubled for a large ensemble.

Bach, J.S. *Contrapunctus IX.* arr. Peter Rauch. Ohio Valley Tuba Quartet Press. Two euphoniums and two tubas. 1988. $10.00. 4:45. IV–V. Part I: d–c", Part II: G♯–b♭', Part III: C–a, Part IV: D$_1$–d. Very challenging for all four parts. The tessitura of the first part is high, but there are some ossia sections an octave lower. Written in four, this fugue should be felt in two when performed. Requires four strong players.

Bach, J.S. *Contrapunctus IX.* arr. Paul Schmidt. Heavy Metal Music. Two euphoniums and two tubas. 1991. $7.00. 4:45. IV. Part I: G–d', Part II: F–d', Part III: C♯–a, Part IV: F$_1$–g. All parts have the opportunity to play the theme. Technically challenging at times; all players need to count carefully. No score available. Parts may be doubled for a large ensemble.

Bach, J.S. *Fantasia in C.* arr. David Sabourin. Touch of Brass Music Corporation. Two euphoniums and two tubas. 1981. 1:20. IV. Part I: c–c", Part II: c♯–a', Part III: F–a, Part IV: A$_1$–f '. Technically not extremely difficult, but putting the parts together can be challenging because of the polyphony. The tessitura of the top two parts is quite high. The score indicates a copyright date of 1981, the parts show a date of 1982.

Bach, J.S. *Four Bach Chorales.* arr. Keith Mehlan. Horizon Press. Two euphoniums and two tubas. 1991. $12.00. 6:30. IV. Part I: d–b♭', Part II: A–ab', Part III: B♭–f ', Part IV: D$_1$–e♭. Four widely contrasting movements: Haupt voll Blunt und Wunden; Ein Feste Burg ist unser Gott; Christ Lag in Todesbanden; In Dulci Jubilo. All parts have an opportunity to play the melody. The tessitura of the top three parts is high. This arrangement could also work well with three euphoniums and one tuba.

Bach, J.S. *Fuga VII from WTC I.* arr. James Self. James Self. Out of print. Two euphoniums and two tubas. 1972. 2:00. IV. Part I: e♭–c", Part II: B♭–g', Part III: D–b♭, Part IV: F♭$_1$–e♭. Very polyphonic; players must count carefully.

Bach, J.S. *Fugue No. 16 for Four Low Brass Instruments.* arr. Ray Grim. Prima Musica. Two euphoniums and two tubas. 1988. 2:00. IV. Part I: c♯–b♭', Part II: E–f ', Part III: C–f, Part IV: D$_1$–d. This has been transcribed from the *Well-Tempered Clavier,* Book One. Technically not very demanding, but the first part requires a strong player because of the range. The fourth part will need very clean articulation in the low register.

Bach, J.S. *Fugue in G Minor (Little)*. arr. Skip Gray. Shawnee Press, Incorporated. Two euphoniums and two tubas. 1984. $9.00. 3:15. IV. Part I: A–c', Part II: F–a♭', Part III: B♭₁–b♭, Part IV: G₁–d. While the greatest technical demands are on the two euphonium parts, all four parts have the subject and countersubject in exposed places. The first euphonium part is printed in tenor clef. Requires very light and clean playing by all parts. A first-rate arrangement of Bach's best-known fugue. Parts may be doubled for a large ensemble. Recorded by the British Tuba Quartet, *In at the Deep End*, Heavyweight Records, Limited, HR008/D.

Bach, J.S. *Fugue in G Minor (Little)*. arr. Albert Peoples. Southern Music Company. Two euphoniums and two tubas. 1990. $8.00. 4:00. IV. Part I: A–c", Part II: F–a♭', Part III: F♯₁–b♭, Part IV: D₁–c. The tessitura of the first part is high. Technically demanding, especially of the first and third parts. Requires strong players. Parts may be carefully doubled for a large ensemble.

Bach, J.S. *Jesu, Joy of Man's Desiring*. arr. H. Hiraishi. Sonic Arts, Incorporated. Two euphoniums and two tubas. 1986. $11.00. 2:10. III–IV. Part I: E–f', Part II: E–c', Part III: D–g, Part IV: G₁–e. The tessitura of the top two parts is low. The melody is in the euphonium parts exclusively. No technical difficulties. Parts may be doubled for a large ensemble.

Bach, J.S. *Jesu, Joy of Man's Desiring*. arr. David Werden. Whaling Music Publishers. Two euphoniums and two tubas. 1978. $5.00. 2:10. IV. Part I: c–g', Part II: B♭–f', Part III: E–b♭, Part IV: F₁–B♭. Nice arrangement of this famous melody. No real technical problems. A lyrical triplet feel must be maintained throughout. The top part is printed in tenor clef, and parts I and II are in tenor clef in the score. Parts may be doubled for a large ensemble. Recorded by the British Tuba Quartet, *In at the Deep End*, Heavyweight Records Limited, HR008/D.

Bach, J.S. *Minuet*. arr. Paul Schmidt. Heavy Metal Music. Two euphoniums and two tubas. 1991. $3.00. 1:20. III. Part I: d–d', Part II: c♯–g', Part III: F–g, Part IV: C♯–d. An interesting minuet with a highly polyphonic middle section. The second part has a higher tessitura and is more challenging than the first part. No score available. Parts may be doubled for a large ensemble.

Bach, J.S. *Prelude and Fugue No. 16*, from *Well-Tempered Clavier*, Book One. arr. Paul Schmidt. Heavy Metal Music. Two euphoniums and two tubas. 1992. $5.00. 3:30. IV. Part I: G♯–g', Part II: A–f', Part III: B♭₁–c', Part IV: G₁–a'. Two movements: Prelude; Fugue. Challenging for all four parts. No score available. Parts may be doubled for a large ensemble.

Bach, J.S. *Prelude and Fugue in C Minor*, from *Well-Tempered Clavier*, Book One. arr. Skip Gray.

Shawnee Press, Incorporated. Two euphoniums and two tubas. 1984. $9.00. 3:00. IV. Part I: A♭–b♭', Part II: A♭–f', Part III: E♭₁–a, Part IV: D₁–f. Typical of the *WTC* keyboard style, there is a flowing sixteenth-note melodic line passed between parts I and III and parts II and IV. Most of the first euphonium part is notated in tenor clef. Parts may be doubled for a large ensemble, but the two measures of cadenza-like material should be played as a solo.

Bach, J.S. *Prelude and Fugue in G Minor*. arr. David Sabourin. Touch of Brass Music Corporation. Two euphoniums and two tubas.

Bach, J.S. *Prelude and Fugue in G*. arr. David Sabourin. Touch of Brass Music Corporation. Two euphoniums and two tubas. $10.00. 3:00. IV. Part I: B♭–a', Part II: B♭–a', Part III: D–c', Part IV: F₁–d. No significant technical challenges, but the fugue section should not be played too quickly. Parts may be carefully doubled for a large ensemble.

Bach, J.S. *Sarabande*. arr. Michael Howard. BTQ Publications. Two euphoniums and two tubas. 1993. $9.00.

Bach, J.S. *Sarabande and Bourrée*. arr. Akira Yodo. TUBA Press. Two euphoniums and two tubas. 1991. $6.00. 7:00. IV. Part I: A♭–b♭', Part II: G–g', Part III: F–b♭, Part IV: G₁–f. Two movements: Sarabande; Bourrée. No real range or technical difficulties. The Bourrée is more polyphonic and consequently more difficult to play together. Though in a different key, this is the same violin partita that Bill Bell transcribed for tuba and piano in *Air and Bourrée*. Parts may be doubled for a large ensemble.

Bach, J.S. *Sonate en Trio Vivace*. arr. Alain Cazes. Cazes-Cuivres. Four tubas. 1986. 2:00. IV. Part I: G–c", Part II: B♭–b♭', Part III: C–c, Part IV: D₁–e♭. The tessitura of the top two parts is quite high, and both of these parts are printed in tenor clef. Technical demands are greatest on the first part.

Bach, J.S. *Wachet Auf,* from *Cantata No. 104*. arr. Gary A. Buttery. Whaling Music Publishers. Two euphoniums and two tubas. 1978. $9.00. 3:20. IV. Part I: G–a♭', Part II: G–a', Part III: G₁–e♭', Part IV: F₁–c'. Nice arrangement. This beautiful melody is passed around through all four parts. Very lyrical in style at a moderate tempo. Both tuba parts have a high tessitura. Parts may be doubled for a large ensemble.

Bale, Maurice, arr. *Three Early Dances*. Godiva Music. Two euphoniums and two tubas. 1994. $8.50. 4:00. III–IV. Part I: c–f', Part II: B♭–c', Part III: C–g, Part IV: F₁–c. Three movements: Almande; The Choice; Almande.

Ball, Eric. *Friendly Giants*. R. Smith and Company Limited. Four tubas. 1961. $5.00. 5:45. IV. Part I: B♭₁–e♭', Part II: B♭₁–b♭, Part III: A–e♭', Part IV: E–d. Two movements: I; II. All four parts are printed in treble clef. Parts I and II are for E♭ tubas, and parts III and IV are for B♭ tubas. Very traditional harmonies. The second movement is technically challenging and contains exposed sections for all parts.

Ball, Eric. *Quartet for Tubas.* R. Smith and Company Limited. Two E♭ tubas and two BB♭ tubas. 1950. $10.00. 5:30. IV. Part I: A–d', Part II: B♭–b♭, Part III: A–d', Part IV: F–d'. Two movements: Moderato; Largo. Very traditional style. No real technical challenges. The score and parts are both printed in treble clef and must be transposed.

Bartles, Alfred H. *When Tubas Waltz.* Kendor Music, Incorporated. Two euphoniums and two tubas. 1976. $11.00. 4:20. IV. Part I: d–b♭', Part II: B♭–g', Part III: B♭₁–b, Part IV: B♭₁–b♭. Dedicated to R. Winston Morris and the Tennessee Technological University Tuba Ensemble. A classic early composition for tuba/euphonium ensemble. A jazz waltz in a scherzo—trio—scherzo form. Players must have a good jazz feel. Not easy to play, but works very well. Trap set with brushes can be used to support the feel of a jazz waltz. Parts may be doubled for a large ensemble. Recorded by the Tennessee Technological University Tuba Ensemble, Golden Crest Records, CRS 4139; the Tubadours, *Ya Ve Iss Da Mighty Tubadours,* Crystal Records, S421; David Le Clair, *Swingin' Low,* Marcophon.

Beadell, Robert. *Three Sketches.* Brass Music Limited/ The Brass Press. Out of print. Two euphoniums and two tubas. 1974. 6:00. IV. Part I: A♭–c♭"(d♭"), Part II: G♯–g', Part III: B♭₁–c', Part IV: B♭₁–c'. Three movements: I; II; III. Commissioned by R. Winston Morris and the Tennessee Technological University Tuba Ensemble. There are many syncopated and jazz-influenced rhythms. The texture can get very thick at times. The third movement is especially challenging technically. Originally published in 1970 by Manuscripts for Tuba.

Beethoven, L.V. *Sonata "Pathétique."* arr. David R. Werden. Whaling Music Publishers. Two euphoniums and two tubas. 1993. $9.00. IV. Part I: c–d", Part II: c–b♭', Part III: C–f♭', Part IV: E♭₁–d♭'. Second movement of the *Sonata in C minor, Op. 13* (1798) for piano. Slow and very melodic, but challenging to play. The tessitura of the first part is high. The first part is printed in bass and treble clef. Parts may be doubled for a large ensemble.

Berlin, Irving. *Alexander's Ragtime Band.* arr. John Hoesly. Piston Reed Stick and Bow Publisher. Two euphoniums and two tubas. 1991. $7.00. 2:20. IV. Part I: d–b♭', Part II: F♯–f ', Part III: C–c♭', Part IV: F₁–g. A good jazz style is required for this swinging arrangement. Some technical challenges in all parts. Drums may be added for stylistic effect. No score available; parts may be doubled for a large ensemble.

Berlin, Irving. *Alexander's Ragtime Band.* arr. Paul Schmidt. Heavy Metal Music. Two euphoniums and two tubas. 1990. $5.00. 1:45. III–IV. Part I: B♭–f ', Part II: A–e♭', Part III: E♭–e♭, Part IV: F₁–A♭. Good arrangement of this famous melody. Most of the melody is in the first part. No score available; parts may be doubled for a large ensemble.

Berlioz, Hector. *Hungarian March from The Damnation of Faust.* arr. David R. Werden. Whaling Music Publishers. Two euphoniums and two tubas. 1979. $9.00. 2:30. IV. Part I: G–c", Part II: c–a', Part III: G–e', Part IV: G₁–a. Technically challenging for the first and second parts. The tessitura of the first and third parts is high. Requires mature players. The first part is printed in treble and tenor clef.

Bewley, Norlan. *Cinnamon Downs.* Bewley Music Incorporated. Two euphoniums, two tubas, and three harps. 1992. $25.00. 5:00. IV. Part I: c–a', Part II: c–a', Part III: G₁–c', Part IV: G₁–d. With the exception of a few solo sections, the primary role of the euphoniums and tubas is to accompany the three harps. All parts are very syncopated and rhythmic. Requires precise rhythmic execution between the harps and tubas. Harp parts are demanding.

Bewley, Norlan. *The Octubafest Song.* Bewley Music Incorporated. Two euphoniums, two tubas, and vocal solo. 1992. $20.00. 2:30. IV. Part I: B♭–ab', Part II: B♭–ab', Part III: E♭–e♭', Part IV: E♭₁–g. The text and vocal melody are fairly simple. However, the middle instrumental interlude is challenging, especially for the euphoniums. The tessitura of the third part is high. Parts may be doubled for a large ensemble.

Bewley, Norlan. *Runabout.* Bewley Music Incorporated. Two euphoniums and two tubas. 1993. $15.00. 4:30. IV. Part I: f–b♭', Part II: c–f ', Part III: F–f ', Part IV: F–g. A good jazz feel is necessary for the syncopation and swing eighth-notes. All parts have the opportunity to play the melody. Drums may be added for effect. Parts may be doubled for a large ensemble.

Bewley, Norlan. *Santa Wants a Tuba for Christmas.* Bewley Music Incorporated. Two euphoniums, two tubas, optional vocal and rhythm. 1992. $20.00. 4:00. IV. Part I: B♭–a', Part II: B♭–e♭', Part III: B♭₁–f ', Part IV: F₁–c. An exceptionally cute tune, especially when used with the vocal solo and rhythm. The first tuba part has two challenging sections, but otherwise the parts are not difficult. A good swing feel is necessary for all players. The second part has extended divisi sections. Fun to play and delightful for audiences. Parts may be doubled for a large ensemble. Recorded by Harvey Phillips and his TubaSantas, *Merry Tuba Christmas,* HPF #1000-1.

Billings, William. *Canon.* arr. Paul Schmidt. Heavy Metal Music. Two euphoniums and two tubas. 1991. $5.00. 2:30. III. Part I: c–f ', Part II: A–d', Part III: C–a, Part IV: F₁–c. The melody and technical demands are most appropriate for high school students. All parts have the opportunity to play the melody. No score available. Parts may be doubled for a large ensemble.

Bizet, Georges. *Overture from Carmen*. arr. Bruno Seitz. Musikverlag Martin Scherbacher. Two euphoniums and two tubas. 1993. $15.00. 5.00. IV. Part I: B♭–b♭', Part II: F–g', Part III: C–b♭, Part IV: F₁–g. Fun arrangement of this famous overture. Technically challenging for the top three parts. The top part is printed in bass and treble clef. Parts may be doubled for a large ensemble.

Blahnik, F., and Gratz, E. *The Last Polka*. arr. Paul Schmidt. Heavy Metal Music. Two euphoniums and two tubas. 1992. $7.00. 3:00. IV. Part I: G♭–e♭', Part II: G♭–f', Part III: A♭₁–b♭, Part IV: G₁–d♭(e♭). While the melody is primarily in the first part, the second part is technically more challenging. A good arrangement for Octubafests and other social events. No score available. Parts may be doubled for a large ensemble.

Blank, Allan. *Music for Tubas*. T.A.P. Music. Four tubas. 1977. $12.00. 9:30. IV–V. Part I: C–b', Part II: C–b', Part III: A₁–a', Part IV: E₁–c'. Three movements. There are extreme range and technical demands of all parts. Euphoniums could be used on any of the first three parts. Requires four strong players. Score not available.

Blatter, Alfred. *Images for Tuba Quartet*. Alfred Blatter. Four tubas. 1974. 5:20. IV–V. Part I: B♭–f', Part II: D♭–f♯, Part III: C–f♯, Part IV: E♭₁–e♭. Dedicated to the great musicians in T.U.B.A. An early avant-garde work for tuba quartet. Uses mutes and several twentieth-century techniques, including flutter tonguing, multiphonics, and some improvisation. Each measure lasts approximately five seconds. Requires four strong players.

Bock, Jerry. *Sunrise, Sunset*. arr. Eugene Anderson. Anderson's Arizona Originals. Three euphoniums and one tuba. 1988. $5.00. 2:10. III–IV. Part I: A–g', Part II: A–g', Part III: G–g', Part IV: G₁–g. Probably the most famous selection from *Fiddler on the Roof*. No real technical challenges. The melody is primarily in the top two parts. Parts may be doubled for a large ensemble.

Bottje, Will Gay. *Incognitos*. The Brass Press. Out of print. Two euphoniums and two tubas. 1974. 7:00. IV. Part I: G–b', Part II: F♯–g', Part III: G–e♭', Part IV: F♯₁–c'. Two movements: I; II. Commissioned by R. Winston Morris and the Tennessee Technological University Tuba Ensemble. Very contemporary sounding harmonies with many dissonances. The second movement is multimetric and more challenging to play. Requires four strong players.

Boyce, William. *Alleluia*. arr. F.H. Laws. Ohio Valley Tuba Quartet Press. Two euphoniums and two tubas. 1988. $9.00. 1:45. III–IV. Part I: c–f', Part II: c–e', Part III: C–d, Part IV: G₁–d. An eight-measure theme repeated by each part. The texture is very polyphonic but fits together quite well. Parts may be doubled for a large ensemble.

Brahms, Johannes. *Hungarian Dance No. 5*. arr. Bruno Seitz. Musikverlag Martin Scherbacher. Four tubas. 1993. $15.00. 3:30. IV. Part I: c–a♭', Part II: B♭–d', Part III: F–f, Part IV: F₁–c. The tessitura of the first part is high. Euphoniums may be used on the top two parts to make this playable by most college and some high school students. The melody is primarily in the top part. Parts may be doubled for a large ensemble.

Brahms, Johannes. *Hungarian Dance No. 5*. arr. David Woodcock. Green Bay Music. Two euphoniums and two tubas. 1992. $22.00. 2:20. IV. Part I: d–b♭', Part II: c♯–f', Part III: F♯–b♭, Part IV: C–f. The euphonium parts are the most challenging as they have the primary melodic responsibility. There are several tempo changes. Requires a light, clean style. All four parts are printed in both bass and treble clef.

Brahms, Johannes. *Hungarian Dance No. 6*. arr. David Woodcock. Green Bay Music. Two euphoniums and two tubas. 1993. $22.00. 4:00. IV. Similar in character to *Hungarian Dance No. 5* by the same arranger, but more technically challenging.

Brahms, Johannes. *Marienlieder, Op. 22*. arr. John Stevens. John Stevens. Two euphoniums and two tubas. 1987. 8:30. IV. Part I: f–b♭', Part II: d♭–g', Part III: B♭–d', Part IV: B♭₁–g♭. Seven movements: Con Moto; Andante con Moto; Con Moto; Allegro; Poco Adagio—Legato; Poco Lento; Allegro. Transcriptions of characteristic Brahms songs.

Brahms, Johannes. *Waldesnacht, du Wunder Kühle* (Wondrous Cool, Thou Woodland Quiet). arr. Mark Nelson. Whaling Music Publishers. Two euphoniums and two tubas. 1988. $5.50. 1:45. III–IV. Part I: f♯–a', Part II: d–e', Part III: G–a, Part IV: G₁–d. Nice chorale-like arrangement of this tranquil melody. No significant technical or range problems. Parts may be doubled for a large ensemble.

Brandon, Sy. *Quartet for Tubas*. Co-op Press. Two euphoniums and two tubas. 1988. 4:20. IV. Part I: f–c", Part II: c–g', Part III: F–b♭, Part IV: F₁–c. No real technical problems, but there are several high b♭s in the first part. Some interesting melodic passages and tasteful contemporary harmonies. Good writing. Parts may be doubled for a large ensemble.

Britain, Radie. *The World Does Not Wish for Beauty*. T.A.P. Music. Four tubas. 1980. $5.00. 4:20. IV. Part I: E♭–f', Part II: C–c', Part III: B₁–g♭, Part IV: E₁–b♭. The tessitura of the first part is high. No significant technical problems. Parts may be doubled for a large ensemble. Score not available.

Bruckner, Anton. *Ave Maria*. arr. David Sabourin. Touch of Brass Music Corporation. Two euphoniums and two tubas. $6.50.

Bruckner, Anton. *Locus Iste*. arr. David Sabourin. Touch of Brass Music Corporation. Two euphoniums and two tubas. $6.50.

Bruckner, Anton. *Three Motets*. arr. John Stevens. John Stevens. Two euphoniums and two tubas. 1986.

6:00. IV. Part I: d–b♭', Part II: B♭–d', Part III: E♭–c', Part IV: G₁–f. Three movements: Vexilla Regis; Locus Iste; Pange Lingua. Three very sonorous vocal motets. Very polyphonic.

Bruckner, Anton. *Virga Jesse Floruit.* arr. Mark Nelson. TUBA Press. Two euphoniums and two tubas. 1994. $8.00. 2:00. IV. Part I: d♯–a', Part II: G♯–e♭', Part III: C♯–b, Part IV: E₁–c♯. For the Hokkaido Euphonium/Tuba Camp. Nice arrangement of this chorale. The tessitura of the fourth part is low. Works especially well with parts doubled.

Bull, John. *The King's Hunt.* arr. Michael Howard. BTQ Publications. Two euphoniums and two tubas. 1993. $9.00. 2:30. Recorded by the British Tuba Quartet, *Elite Syncopations,* Polyphonic Reproductions Limited, QPRZ 012D.

Bulla, Stephen. *Celestial Suite.* Rosehill Music Publishing Company, Limited. Two euphoniums and two tubas. 1989. $14.95. 8:00. IV. Part I: c–c", Part II: F–g♭', Part III: C–c', Part IV: E₁–f. Three movements: Eclipse; Canzone Lunaire; Solar Plexus. A very tuneful virtuosic work for tuba/euphonium quartet. The tessitura of the first part is high. All four parts are technically challenging . The third part has a brief improvised cadenza, and the player has to blow into the instrument to imitate the sound of wind. All four parts are printed in treble and bass clef. Recorded by the British Tuba Quartet, *Euphonic Sounds,* Polyphonic Reproductions Limited, QPRZ 009D.

Bulla, Stephen. *Quartet for Low Brass.* Kendor Music, Incorporated Out of print. Two euphoniums and two tubas. 1978. 4:00. IV. Part I: A–e', Part II: G–c', Part III: C–f, Part IV: G₁–d. A single-movement work in three sections; a bright fanfare, a lyrical middle section, and a march-like finale. Range is not demanding but there are a couple of technical sections that can be tricky. The piece generally fits together quite nicely. The composition works very well and is a good audience pleaser. Parts may be doubled for a large ensemble. Recorded by the British Tuba Quartet, *In at the Deep End,* Heavyweight Records, HR008/D; U.S. Navy Tuba Quartet, U.S. Navy Band Recordings.

Bulla, Stephen, arr. *Quartets for Low Brass, Volume I: Traditional Favorites.* TUBA Press. Two euphoniums and two tubas. 1992. $25.00. 16 pp. III–IV. Part I: A♭–c", Part II: G–g', Part III: A♭₁–a♭, Part IV: F₁–e♭. Ten movements: The Blue Bells of Scotland; Blow the Man Down; Auld Lang Syne; Polly Wolly Doodle; Listen to the Mockingbird; Sourwood Mountain; Oh, Susanna; The Last Rose of Summer; He's a Jolly Good Fellow; Good Night Ladies. The range demands vary greatly from one movement to another. Since there are very few technical challenges, many of these are very playable by high school ensembles. The arrangements are very short and are more appropriate for recreational use than for a formal concert. The settings of the move-ments are very traditional. The top two parts are printed in bass and treble clef. Parts may be doubled for a large ensemble.

Bulla, Stephen, arr. *Quartets for Low Brass, Volume II: Spirituals.* TUBA Press. Two euphoniums and two tubas. 1992. $25.00. 11 pp. IV. Part I: F–c"(d"), Part II: F–g', Part III: C–b♭, Part IV: F₁–e. Ten movements: Little David Play; Down by the Riverside; Go Down Moses; Deep River; Swing Low, Sweet Chariot; Every Time I Feel the Spirit; Amazing Grace; Joshua; Precious Lord Take My Hand; Hand Me Down My Silver Tuba. These arrangements are of moderate technical difficulty, but the tessitura of the first part is high. Movements are relatively short, just one verse of each song. Designed for school or recreational use, not for a formal concert. The top two parts are printed in both treble and bass clef. Parts may be doubled for a large ensemble.

Bulla, Stephen, arr. *Quartets for Low Brass, Volume III: Fanfares and Anthems.* TUBA Press. Two euphoniums and two tubas. 1992. $25.00. 13 pp. III–IV. Part I: B♭–b♭', Part II: B♭–e♭, Part III: B♭₁–b♭, Part IV: F₁–d. Twelve movements: Hail to the Chief; Star-Spangled Banner; America the Beautiful; God Save the Queen (My Country 'Tis of Thee); O Canada; Rule Britannia; La Marseillaise; Fanfare of Tribute; Fanfare D'Sousa; Canonic Fanfare; Quatre Fanfares Générique; Choral Anthem (Now the Day Is Over). Short traditional arrangements of familiar fanfares and national anthems. No significant technical problems. Designed as study material or for use on specific occasions. Parts may be doubled for a large ensemble.

Bullet, William. *Greensleeves.* arr. Gary A. Buttery. Whaling Music Publishers. Two euphoniums and two tubas. 1978. $5.00. 2:00. III–IV. Part I: B♭–f ', Part II: A–e', Part III: D–a, Part IV: D₁–B♭. A very lush arrangement of this traditional melody. The melody is all in the euphonium parts, but the tessitura is not high. The first tuba part has several measures of flowing sixteenth-notes. Parts may be doubled for a large ensemble. Recorded by the Atlantic Tuba Quartet, *Euphonic Sounds,* Golden Crest Records, CRS 4173; the British Tuba Quartet, *Euphonic Sounds,* Polyphonic Records, QPRZ009D.

Buttery, Gary. *An English Folk Christmas.* Whaling Music Publishers. Four tubas. 1978. $7.50. 3:30. IV–V. Part I: B♭–b♭', Part II: G–g', Part III: E♭–e, Part IV: F♯₁–e. A nice medley in a single movement of five English folk/Christmas songs: Glouchestershire Wassail, God Rest Ye Merry Gentlemen, All You That Are to Mirth Inclined, King Herod and the Cock, and Here We Come A-Wassailing. Each part has the opportunity to play one of the melodies. The tessitura of the first part is high. Euphoniums may be used for the first and second parts. Parts may be doubled for a large ensemble. Recorded by the U.S. Coast Guard Tuba/Euphonium Quartet, U.S. Coast Guard Recordings.

Buttery, Gary. *Musica De Lupus: Scenarios for the Continued Existence of a Misunderstood Friend— The Wolf.* Whaling Music Publishers. Four tubas. 1978. $12.00. 12:30. IV–V. Part I: F–g♯', Part II: D–f', Part III: (D₁)E₁–f', Part IV: B₂–d♯. A very contemporary programmatic work. The single movement contains four sections: Vocalise for the Survivors, The Hunted, Orphans of the Wind, and A Right to Life. The music portrays the struggle faced by the wolf in the never-ending encroachment upon its wilderness home. The work is technically very challenging and places great range demands on all four parts. Twentieth-century techniques required include glissandos, blowing wind through the tuba, half-valve notes, quarter tones, and a free rhythmic section. Requires mutes for all four parts. Won Honorable Mention in the 1978 Mirafone Tuba Quartet Composition Competition.

Buttery, Gary, arr. *Sponger Money.* Whaling Music Publishers. Two euphoniums, two tubas, and percussion. 1983. $7.50. 2:50. IV. Part I: A–d", Part II: A–c", Part III: C–f', Part IV: F₁–f. Good arrangement of this familiar Latin melody with a calypso beat. The percussion parts are written into the euphonium and tuba parts and are to be played by the brass musicians. In a section with only chord symbols the tubists improvise a solo. The top part requires a mute, and the bottom three parts are asked to sing. The tessitura is high for the top three parts. Fun for performers and audience.

Butts, Carol M. *March and Chorale.* Pro Art Publications. Out of print. Two trombones (euphoniums) and two tubas. 1971. 3:00. III–IV. Part I: e♭–g♭', Part II: B♭–f', Part III: B♭₁–f, Part IV: B♭₁–e♭. Published for originally for trombones and tubas but works just as well with euphoniums on the first and second parts. Very basic rhythms in the 6/8 section, the chorale section is in cut time. Traditional harmonies. Parts may be doubled for a large ensemble.

Byrd, William. *Ave Verum Corpus.* arr. Michael Howard. BTQ Publications. Two euphoniums and two tubas. 1993. $8.00.

Byrd, William. *Ave Verum Corpus.* arr. Paul Schmidt. Heavy Metal Music. Two euphoniums and two tubas. 1991. $5.00. 4:00. III. Part I: e–e', Part II: G–a, Part III: G–g, Part IV: A₁–c. All parts have a chance to play the theme. Very polyphonic, but fits together very nicely. No score available. Parts may be doubled for a large ensemble.

Byrd, William. *Jhon Come Kisse Me Now.* arr. Denis Winter. Whaling Music Publisher. Two euphonium and two tubas. 1978. $7.00. 2:00. IV. Part I: F–g', Part II: F–g', Part III: C–e', Part IV: F₁–c'. A nice lyrical melody. The high tessitura of the third

and fourth parts requires mature players. Requires rhythmic accuracy. The first and second parts are printed in treble clef. Recorded by the Atlantic Tuba Quartet, *Euphonic Sounds,* Golden Crest Records, CRS 4173; the British Tuba Quartet, *Euphonic Sounds,* Polyphonic Reproductions Limited, QPRZ009D.

Byrd, William. *Stately Procession.* arr. Gregory Bright. Tuba/Euphonium Music Publications. Out of print. Two euphoniums and two tubas. 4:00. III. Permanently out of print.

Camphouse, Mark. *Ceremonial Sketch.* Mark Camphouse. Two euphoniums and two tubas. 1988. $6.00. 4:30. IV–V. Part I: G–d♭", Part II: G♭–c", Part III: G₁–f', Part IV: D♯₁–c'. Written for R. Winston Morris and the Tennessee Technological University Tuba Ensemble. A major work. Many sections are divisi, making it necessary to double the players on each part. Range demands are extreme and require four strong players. Recorded by the Tennessee Technological University Tuba Ensemble, Mark Custom Recording Service, MENC88-1-4; the U.S. Armed Forces Tuba/Euphonium Ensemble and Massed Ensemble, U.S. Army Band.

Cannon, Hughie. *Rev Bill Bailey.* arr. Rodger Vaughan. Rodger Vaughan. Two euphoniums and two tubas. 1986. $5.00. 1:20. IV. Part I: f–b♭', Part II: e♭–f', Part III: F♯–b♭, Part IV: C–d. For Bert Harclerode's birthday. A medium-tempo version of "Bill Bailey." No significant technical problems. The melody is primarily in the first part. Drums may be added for stylistic effect. No score available. Parts may be doubled for a large ensemble.

Canter, James A. *Appalachian Carol* (Quartet No. 2). TUBA Press. Two euphoniums and two tubas. 1992. $10.00. 5:20. IV. Part I: A–a♭', Part II: A–d', Part III: B♭₁–e♭, Part IV: A₁–d. Written for R. Winston Morris and the Tennessee Technological University Tuba Ensemble. A unique and tuneful composition based on the hymn "What Wondrous Love Is This?" The composition is in a slow—fast— slow—fast form. Some brief technical challenges. Fun to play and enjoyable for audiences. Parts may be doubled for a large ensemble. Originally copyrighted in 1980 and published by Kendor Music, Incorporated. Recorded by the U.S. Armed Forces Tuba/Euphonium Ensemble and Massed Ensemble, U.S. Army Band Records.

Canter, James A. *Paraklesis.* TUBA Press. Two euphoniums, two tubas, and tambourine. 1993. $15.00. 5:00. V. Part I: A₁–g', Part II: A₁–e', Part III: G₁–a, Part IV: F₁–c♯. Commissioned by and written for R. Winston Morris and the Tennessee Technological University Tuba Ensemble. A very contemporary and complex composition. Numerous twentieth-century techniques, including blowing through the instrument, bending pitches, quarter tones, playing pitches and rhythms in a random order, and frequent odd meter changes. Requires very strong players. Originally written and first performed in 1981. Parts may be doubled for a large ensemble.

Canter, James A. *Siamang Suite*. TUBA Press. Two euphoniums and two tubas. 1992. $10.00. 6:00. IV. Part I: c–d♭", Part II: c–a', Part III: B♭₁–c', Part IV: G₁–a. Three movements: Introduction; Song; Dance. To the Tennessee Technological University Tuba Ensemble, R. Winston Morris, Director. A classic work for tuba/euphonium ensemble. All four parts require mutes in the eerie second movement. The third movement is a fast-paced, vibrant, multimetric dance. Technically the composition is moderately demanding, but it is a challenge to put together without a conductor. Parts may be doubled for a large ensemble. Originally published by Kendor Music, Incorporated and copyrighted in 1978.

Canter, James A., arr. *Twelve Days of Housetops!*. Kendor Music, Incorporated. Two euphoniums and two tubas. 1985. $9.50. 3:15. III–IV. Part I: B♭–g', Part II: A–e♭', Part III: A♭₁–g♭, Part IV: F₁–B. Commissioned by the Franklin (TN) Junior H.S. Tuba Ensemble, Bill Marley and Bob Horne, directors. A cute arrangement combining *The Twelve Days of Christmas* and *Up on the Housetop*. Players are asked to speak through their instruments, and some parts are required to play half-valve glissandos. Many tempo and style changes. Very entertaining for both performers and audience. Parts may be doubled for a large ensemble.

Carmody, Bill. *Fifteen Easy Pieces for Bass Clef Instruments*. Whaling Music Publishers. Two euphoniums and two tubas. $15.00. 18 pp. III–IV. Part I: (B♭)c–e♭', Part II: B♭–c', Part III: E♭–c', Part IV: A♭₁–d. Short compositions contrasting in key, style, and tempo. Consists of two duets, two trios, a euphonium solo with trio accompaniment, and ten quartets. Most are not technically demanding and are suitable for a good high school ensemble. Parts I and II are in one booklet, and parts III and IV in another. Parts may be doubled for a large ensemble. Fun to play.

Carmody, Bill, and Francis, Mike. *Hard Way*. Whaling Music Publishers. Four tubas. $5.00. 4:00. IV. Part I: d–c", Part II: F–f ', Part III: F₁–f ', Part IV: F₁–e♭. A hard rock bass line passed between the third and fourth parts becomes the foundation of this piece. There is a section with chord symbols in all four parts for improvised solos and bass lines. The first two parts have a high tessitura and may be played by euphonium. Drums may be added for stylistic effect. Parts may be doubled for a large ensemble.

Censhu, Jiro. *No No Hate Yori* (From Beyond the Field). Jiro Censhu. Two euphoniums and two tubas. 1992. $10.00. 9:30. IV. Part I: e♭–c", Part II: B♭–a', Part III: G₁–f ', Part IV: G₁–g. Commissioned by and dedicated to the Sendai Tuba/Eu-

phonium Ensemble. A slow introduction in 3/4 followed by a very fast animated section in 4/4. The melody is primarily in the euphoniums, but all parts are interesting. The tessitura of the first part is very high. There is a challenging cadenza for the third part. Works well. Parts may be doubled for a large ensemble.

Censhu, Jiro. *Sai Kai* (The Reunion). Jiro Censhu. Two euphoniums and two tubas. 1992. $10.00. 5:00. IV. Part I: c–a', Part II: F–f ', Part III: E♭–b♭, Part IV: A₁–b♭. Commissioned by and dedicated to the Sendai Tuba/Euphonium Ensemble. The melody is in a moderate 6/8 tempo with very traditional harmonies. No significant range or technical problems. Parts may be doubled for a large ensemble.

Censhu, Jiro. *Shinju* (May Tree). Jiro Censhu. Two euphoniums and two tubas. 1991. $10.00. 8:30. IV. Part I: c–b♭', Part II: G–b♭', Part III: C–c', Part IV: F₁–b♭. Two movements: I; II. Commissioned by and dedicated to the Sendai Tuba/Euphonium Ensemble. The first movement is in a slow 4/4, and the second movement in a spirited 6/8. All four parts are interesting and challenging. The tessitura of the first part is high. Parts may be doubled for a large ensemble.

Cheetham, John. *Consortium for Euphoniums and Tubas*. Shawnee Press, Incorporated. Two euphoniums and two tubas. 1980. $18.00. 5:30. IV. Part I: F–b♭', Part II: F♯–g', Part III: C–c', Part IV: F₁–g. Commissioned by R. Winston Morris for the Tennessee Technological University Tuba Ensemble. The numerous divisi sections make it necessary to have four euphonium and four tuba players. The first section contains a lyrical melody, and the second section is a technically aggressive treatment of the same melody. A first-rate work appropriate for any program. Requires tuba players who can articulate cleanly in the low register. Euphonium parts are also printed in treble clef. Designed to be performed by a large ensemble. Recorded by the Tennessee Technological University Tuba Ensemble, KM Records, KM 4631 and the U.S. Armed Forces Tuba/Euphonium Ensemble, Mark Records, MW89MCD-8; the British Tuba Quartet, *In at the Deep End*, Heavyweight Records Limited, HR008/D.

Cheyette, Irving, and Roberts, Charles, arr. *Fourtone Folio, Volume I*. Carl Fischer Incorporated. Out of print. Three euphoniums and one tuba. 1931. 16 pp. I–II. Part I: c–g', Part II: d–g', Part III: B♭–e', Part IV: B♭₁–a. Arrangements of thirteen Classical and folk tunes. Actually published for any four bass-clef instruments but works best with euphoniums on the first three parts. Good for junior high school students. The melody is always in the top part. Parts may be doubled for a large ensemble.

Cheyette, Irving, and Roberts, Charles, arr. *Fourtone Folio, Volume II (More 4-Tones)*. Carl Fischer Incorporated. Out of print. Three euphoniums and one tuba. 1933. 15 pp. II. Part I: c–a', Part II: c–f ', Part III: B♭–e♭', Part IV: A♭₁–e♭. Eleven short arrangements of popular Baroque, Classical, and Romantic melodies. The top part always has the melody. These are slightly more challenging than Volume I, but still very playable by young students.

Childs, Barney. *Quartet Fantasy.* Barney Childs. Four tubas. 1978. 15:00. IV–V. Part I: B♭₂–f '(a♭'), Part II: D₁–c♯', Part III: E₁–d', Part IV: E₁–c♯'. Two movements: 1; 2. To Gene Pokorny, Ivan Hammond, Daniel Perantoni, and Bart Cummings. All parts are technically challenging and have many exposed places. The harmonies are contemporary and the meter is constantly changing. A couple of twentieth-century techniques are required, but most of the work involves traditional performance techniques. Requires four strong players.

Chopin, Frederic. *Four Preludes Op. 28, Nos. 4, 7, 22, 28.* arr. Peter Rauch. Ohio Valley Tuba Quartet Press. Two euphoniums and two tubas. 1988. $12.00. 4:00. IV. Part I: B–c", Part II: G–a♯', Part III: E♭–c', Part IV: E₁–c. Four movements. Four well-known piano preludes transcribed for tuba/euphonium quartet. Careful dynamic control is necessary to maintain proper balance.

Chopin, Frederic. *Minute Waltz.* arr. Steven Mead. BTQ Publications. Two euphoniums and two tubas. 1993. 1:45. Recorded by the British Tuba Quartet, *Elite Syncopations,* Polyphonic Reproductions Limited, QPRZ 012D.

Chopin, Frederic. *Minute Waltz.* arr. David R. Werden. Whaling Music Publishers. Two euphoniums and two tubas. 1979. $5.50. 1:20. IV–V. Part I: A–d", Part II: B♭–b♭', Part III: c–f ', Part IV: B♭₁–f. Solo euphonium accompanied by one euphonium and two tubas. The solo part is virtuosic in its technical demands, and its tessitura is very high. The accompanying parts are not difficult.

Chopin, Frederic. *Prelude No. 4 for Tuba Quartet.* arr. Chris Hendricks. Hidalgo Music. Four tubas. 1992. $4.00. 2:00. IV. Part I: F–f ', Part II: (A₁)D♯–a, Part III: e–b, Part IV: E–f. Nice arrangement. Other than a single high note in the first part (f ') the parts are all playable by high school students. Parts may be doubled for a large ensemble.

Chopin, Frederic. *Tuba Quartet—Chopin Mazurka, Op. 68, No. 48.* arr. Eugene Anderson. Anderson's Arizona Originals. Four tubas. 1988. $5.00. 2:30. III–IV. Part I: F–c', Part II: B♭₁–a♭, Part III: B♭₁–f, Part IV: F₁–c'. Dedicated to Professor Raymond F. Dvorak. The melody is primarily in the first part, which may be played by a euphonium. The fourth part requires a c', so a stronger player is needed for it than for the second or third parts. Includes an additional part that is a combination of parts II and III allowing this to be played as a trio. Parts may be doubled for a large ensemble.

Clarke, Jeremiah. *Trumpet Voluntary.* arr. Maurice Bale. Godiva Music. Two euphoniums and two tubas. 1994. $8.50. 3:00. III-IV. Part I: e♭–f ', Part II: c–c', Part III: A♭–a♭, Part IV: (E♭₁) A♭₁–c.

Collins, Judy. *Since You've Asked.* arr. Gary Buttery. Whaling Music Publishers. Two euphoniums and two tubas. 1967. $7.50. 2:20. IV. Part I: F–g', Part II: f–g', Part III: D–c', Part IV: C–a. A very lyrical flowing melody, primarily in the first two parts. Parts may be doubled for a large ensemble. Recorded by the Atlantic Tuba Quartet, *Euphonic Sounds,* Golden Crest, CRS 4173.

Confrey, Zez. *Charleston Chuckles.* arr. Rodger Vaughan. Rodger Vaughan. Two euphoniums and two tubas. 1988. $5.00. 1:20. IV. Part I: f–b♭', Part II: f–e♭', Part III: B♭–a, Part IV: B♭₁–d♭. A toe-tapping syncopated melody. The melody is primarily in the top two parts. Drums may be added for stylistic enhancement. Parts may be doubled for a large ensemble.

Confrey, Zez. *Dizzy Fingers.* arr. Rodger Vaughan. Rodger Vaughan. Two euphoniums and two tubas. 1989. $5.00. 3:30. IV. Part I: d–b♭', Part II: B♭–e', Part III: B♭–b♭, Part IV: B♭₁–f. Arranged for the TUBADOURS. An up-tempo arrangement of this jazz-like melody. Technically challenging for the top two parts. Fun to play and for audiences.

Confrey, Zez. *High Hattin' from African Suite.* arr. Rodger Vaughan. Rodger Vaughan. Two euphoniums and two tubas. 1988. $5.00. 2:10. IV. Part I: c♯–b♭', Part II: f–e♭', Part III: B♭–a♭, Part IV: B♭₁–d. For the TUBADOURS. A jazz melody from the 1920s. Most of the melody is in the first part. Drums may be added to enhance the jazz style. Fun to play. Parts may be doubled for a large ensemble.

Constantinides, Dinos. *Eight Miniatures for Four Tubas.* T.A.P. Music. 1978. $10.00. 12:00. IV–V. Part I: E♭–a', Part II: C–f♯', Part III: F₁–d♯', Part IV: D₁–b♭. A virtuosic-level quartet. Extreme range and technical demands of all parts. Could also be performed with one euphonium and three tubas. Odd meters, complicated rhythms, and many contemporary harmonies. Winner of Honorable Mention in the Tuba Quartet Composition Contest sponsored by the Mirafone Corporation and the Los Angeles Tuba Quartet.

Constantinides, Dinos. *I Never Saw a Moor for Four Tubas.* T.A.P. Music. 1980. $4.00. 3:00. III–IV. Part I: B–e', Part II: G♯–e', Part III: D–g, Part IV: (F₁) G₁–e. For Lennax. The tessitura of the top two parts is high. No real technical demands, top parts could be played on euphonium. No parts available, players must read off score. Parts may be doubled for a large ensemble.

Cook, Kenneth. *Introduction and Rondino.* Hinrichsen Edition Limited Out of print. Four tubas. 1951. 4:45. IV. Part I: D–c', Part II: F♭–b♭, Part III: A♭₁–e♭, Part IV: F♭₁–B♭. In the British brass band tradition and one of the first tuba quartets ever published. All four parts are in treble clef. The first and second parts are in Eb and the third and fourth are for Bb tubas. Slow chorale-like section followed by a more aggressive and lively second half.

Coucounaras, S. *Elegy for Four Tubas*. ITC Editions Marc Reift. $20.00.

Cummings, Barton. *From Darkness...Emerging*. TUBA Press. Two euphoniums and two tubas. 1992. $10.00. 6:30. IV. Part I: E–c", Part II: A–bb', Part III: E₁–bb, Part IV: E₁–bb. Three movements. Technically challenging, and the tessitura of the first part is high. Dissonant harmonies reflect the title of the composition. The first and third parts have cadenzas in the last movement.

Cummings, Barton. *In Darkness...Dreaming*. Heavy Metal Music. Two euphoniums and two tubas. 1991. $10.00. 6:50. IV–V. Part I: F–bb', Part II: Eb–a', Part III: F₁–f ', Part IV: D₁–f '. Three movements: The Last Dying Rays; Flight; To Wake. Dedicated to the Colonial Tuba Quartet. A programmatic work whose dissonant harmonies and technical challenges reflect the titles of the movements. There are extreme range demands of all parts. Very interesting writing. The first, third, and fourth parts have cadenzas in the last movement.

Cummings, Barton, arr. *Three Renaissance Quartets*. Editions Musicus. Two euphoniums and two tubas. 1980. $5.00. 8:00. IV. Part I: c–g', Part II: E–d', Part III: D–a, Part IV: F₁–c. Three movements: Canzona; Canzona; Song. The first movement was composed by Florentio Maschera, the second and third by Heinrich Isaac. Range is not demanding, but the highly polyphonic canzonas can be challenging to put together. The top two parts could be played by F tubas for use as a tuba quartet. Parts may be doubled for a large ensemble.

Cunningham, Michael G. *Chaconne, Op. 148*. Seesaw Music Corporation Publishers. Two euphoniums and two tubas. 1991. $12.00. 4:00. IV. Part I: Db–bb', Part II: A–f ', Part III: d–eb', Part IV: G₁–g. Technically challenging, especially for the euphoniums. Very contemporary harmonies. All players read from a five-page score.

Danburg, Russell. *Chorale and Gigue for a Quartet of Tubas*. Wingert-Jones Music, Incorporated. 1990. $7.00. 4:20. IV. Part I: A–c', Part II: F–c', Part III: A₁–ab, Part IV: G₁–c#. Dedicated to my grandson, Jarrid. The Chorale is quite lyrical and traditional in its harmony. The Gigue is more rhythmically complex but contains mostly tutti rhythms. The top two parts are often pitted melodically against the bottom two. Parts may be doubled for a large ensemble.

Davison, Peter. *Tuba Quartet*. Peter Davison. Four tubas. 1977. V. Part I: c–c", Part II: A–c", Part III: D–g#', Part IV: E#₁–f#'. A very challenging work. The tessitura is extremely high for all four parts (many occurrences of c"). Skips of an octave or greater are frequent.

Day, Joel, arr. *International Tuba Day Music Books, Numbers 1 and 2*. Joel Day. Two euphoniums and two tubas. $5.00.

De Filippi, Amedeo. *Cassation for Four Tubas*. General Music Publications Company. 1975. $8.50. 8:00. IV. Part I: eb–ab', Part II: Gb–f ', Part III: Gb₁–eb', Part IV: F#₁–d#'. Three movements: Cortège; Nocturne; Rondo alla Caccia. Fun to play but very challenging. The top two parts may be played by euphoniums or F tubas, otherwise the range is very demanding. The third movement is marked Allegro Giocoso and is in 6/8. All four players use mutes in the second movement. Parts may be doubled for a large ensemble.

De Jong, Conrad. *Grab Bag*. Brass Music Limited (The Brass Press). Four tubas. 1974. $6.00. 3:30. IV. Part I: a–a', Part II: Ab–db', Part III: A–g, Part IV: F#₁–Gb. Three movements: Warm-Up; Sear and Yellow Leaf (MacBeth); Fanfare Variations. Commissioned by R. Winston Morris and the Tennessee Technological University Tuba Ensemble. The first tuba part should be played on euphonium or F tuba. The first movement contains fragments from nineteen different tuba solos, ensembles, and orchestral literature. Players perform at least eight to ten of the fragments in random order. Fragments may be segmented, or repeated in any fashion as one would in a practice session. The third movement contains sections where only the rhythms are notated and the players are free to choose their own pitches. It is based on the first movement of De Jong's *Music for Two Tubas* ; see listing above, under "Two Parts."

De Vento, Ivo. *Die Brinlein die da fliessen*. arr. Paul Schmidt. Heavy Metal Music. Two euphoniums and two tubas. 1990. $5.00. 1:00. III–IV. Part I: c–c', Part II: f–g', Part III: D–d, Part IV: F₁–Bb. The second part has a much higher tessitura than the first part. No significant technical problems. No score available; parts may be doubled for a large ensemble.

Deak, Csaba. *Quartet for Tubas*. Swedish Music Information Center. One euphonium and three tubas. 1990. $11.00. 10:00. IV–V. Part I: Db–c", Part II: F#₁–f ', Part III: F₁–eb', Part IV: Eb₁–b. A demanding work regarding both technique and range. The composition has very contemporary harmonies, uses pitch bending, flutter tonguing, blowing air through the instrument, and mutes.

Debussy, Claude. *Golliwogg's Cakewalk*. arr. Paul Schmidt. Heavy Metal Music. Two euphoniums and two tubas. 1991. $7.00. 2:10. IV. Part I: (Bb₁) Gb–g', Part II: F–g', Part III: Bb–d' (eb'), Part IV: Eb₁–ab. All parts have an opportunity to play the melody. No significant technical problems, but light and lyrical playing is required. No score available. Parts may be doubled for a large ensemble.

Debussy, Claude. *The Little Negro*. arr. Hirokazu Hiraishi. Sonic Arts, Incorporated. Two euphoniums and two tubas. 1986. $11.00. 2:00. IV. Part I: E–g', Part II: G–d', Part III: C–f, Part IV: E$_1$–c♯. The melody begins syncopated and ends very lyrical. All parts have an opportunity to play the melody. Parts may be doubled for a large ensemble.

Debussy, Claude. *The Little Negro*. arr. Harold Sandmann. Carpe-Diem Musikverlag Claudia Wölpper. Two euphoniums and two tubas. 1993. $21.00. 1:00. III–IV. Part I: A–g', Part II: G–f ', Part III: D–c', Part IV: C$_1$–f. This arrangement is based on a movement from a piano suite.

Dempsey, Raymond. *Now Hear This*. Horizon Press. Two euphoniums and two tubas.

Dempsey, Raymond. *Quatre Chansons pour Tuba Quatuor* (French Suite for Tuba Quartet). Horizon Press. Two euphoniums and two tubas. 1991. $16.00. 9:00. IV. Part I: A–b', Part II: g–e', Part III: E–e', Part IV: E$_1$–e'. Four movements: Ma Normandie; V'là l'bon Vent; Le Temps des Cerises; Auprès de ma blonde. The second movement is very challenging, all four parts have an extended cadenza. The French text and English translation are provided for each Chanson. Parts may be doubled for a large ensemble. The first, third, and fourth movements are recorded by the British Tuba Quartet, *Elite Syncopations*, Polyphonic Reproductions Ltd., QPRZ012D; and the Monarch Tuba/Euphonium Quartet.

Diero, Pietro. *March: Il Ritorno*. arr. Ken Ferguson. Studio Music Company. Two euphoniums and two tubas. 2:50. Recorded by the British Tuba Quartet, *Euphonic Sounds*, Polyphonic Reproductions Limited, QPRZ 009D.

DiGiovanni, Rocco. *Tubas at Play*. Rocco DiGiovanni. Four tubas. 1978. $18.00. 3:30. IV–V. Part I: C–f ', Part II: A$_1$–d♯', Part III: G$_1$–a, Part IV: F$_1$–g. The tessitura of the first part is high. Very melodically driven, with most of the melody in the top two parts. Very rich harmonies, nice lyrical writing. Formerly called *Shining Star*. Euphoniums may be used for the first and second parts. Parts may be doubled for a large ensemble.

Dowland, John. *Two Madrigals*. arr. Mark Nelson. Whaling Music Publishers. Two euphoniums and two tubas. 1988. $5.50. 3:30. III. Part I: d–e', Part II: G–b♭, Part III: F♯–g, Part IV: F♯$_1$–G. Two movements: What If I Never Speed?; Now, O Now I Needs Must Part. Good arrangement of two simple madrigals. Very appropriate for high school students. The texture is homophonic much of the time. Parts may be doubled for a large ensemble.

Dutton, Brent. *Resonances*. Seesaw Music Corporation Publishers. Two euphoniums and two tubas. 1991. $17.00. 4:45. IV. Part I: e♭–b♭', Part II: B♭–g', Part III: F$_1$–a, Part IV: E♭$_1$–f. Not difficult technically. A very approachable and playable dissonant, contemporary quartet. Parts may be doubled for a large ensemble.

Dutton, Brent. *Song and Dance No. 3*. Seesaw Music Corporation Publishers. Four tubas. 1979. $17.00. 3:30. IV–V. Part I: G♭$_1$–f ', Part II: E♭$_1$–c', Part III: E♭$_1$–e♭', Part IV: D♭$_1$–e♭'. A fast-paced work with very contemporary harmonies, changing meters, and large range requirements for all parts. Technically challenging for all four parts. Mutes needed for third and fourth parts.

Dvořák, Anton. *Humoresk, Op. 101, No. 7*. arr. Paul Schmidt. Heavy Metal Music. Two euphoniums and two tubas. 1992. $7.00. 2:20. IV. Part I: B♭–a', Part II: G–g♭', Part III: A♭$_1$–c', Part IV: F$_1$–g♭. A cute arrangement of this famous melody, in which the tubas frequently have the melody. No score available. Parts may be doubled for a large ensemble.

Ellington, Duke. *Mean Thing Swing*. arr. Rodger Vaughan. Rodger Vaughan. Two euphoniums and two tubas. 1990. $5.00. 2:20. IV–V. Part I: g♭–g', Part II: c–f ', Part III: F–b♭, Part IV: G$_1$–f. For the TUBADOURS. A fun arrangement of the jazz classic "It Don't Mean a Thing if it Ain't Got That Swing." Technically challenging for all parts at the tempo indicated. Performers need a good jazz feel.

Ellington, Duke. *Mood Indigo*. arr. Rodger Vaughan. Rodger Vaughan. Two euphoniums and two tubas. 1976. $5.00. 3:00. III–IV. Part I: g♯–f ', Part II: c–d', Part III: B–b♭, Part IV: F$_1$–e. Nice arrangement of this classic jazz ballad. Drums may be added to support the jazz style. Most of the melody is in the first part. Parts may be doubled for a large ensemble. Recorded by the TUBADOURS, *Ve Iss Da Mighty TUBADOURS Ya?*, Crystal Records, S421.

Ellington, Duke. *Satin Doll*. arr. Rodger Vaughan. Rodger Vaughan. Two euphoniums and two tubas. 1978. $5.00. 1:30. IV. Part I: f–g', Part II: g–e', Part III: c–b♭, Part IV: F$_1$–f. A famous moderate swing melody. Good arrangement for this instrumentation. Drums may be added for effect. No score available. Parts may be doubled for a large ensemble. Recorded by the TUBADOURS, *Ve Iss Da Mighty TUBADOURS Ya?*, Crystal Records, S421.

Ellmenreich, Albert. *Spinning Song*. arr. Peter Rauch. Ohio Valley Tuba Quartet Press. Two euphoniums and two tubas. 1990. $9.00. 1:20. IV. Part I: g–a', Part II: A–f ', Part III: F–f, Part IV: F$_1$–d. A fairly aggressive syncopated melody. Most of the melodic responsibility is in the top two parts. Some interesting harmonies in the accompaniment. Parts may be doubled for a large ensemble.

Emberson, Steven, arr. *Five Foot Two—Eyes of Blue*. Steven Emberson. Two euphoniums and two tubas.

Emberson, Steven, arr. *From a Distance*. Steven Emberson. Two euphoniums and two tubas.

Emberson, Steven, arr. *Happy Birthday with Fanfare*. Steven Emberson. Two euphoniums and two tubas.

Emberson, Steven, arr. *Longer.* Steven Emberson. Two euphoniums and two tubas. 3:00. IV. Part I: Ab–ab', Part II: Ab–g', Part III: Ab₁–ab, Part IV: Ab₁–gb. An arrangement of the folk/rock melody made famous by Dan Fogelberg. The melody is primarily in the top two parts. No significant technical problems. Parts may be doubled for a large ensemble.

Emberson, Steven, arr. *New York, New York.* Steven Emberson. Two euphoniums and two tubas.

Emberson, Steven, arr. *You Light Up My Life.* Steven Emberson. Two euphoniums and two tubas.

Evans, G. *In the Good Old Summertime.* arr. Arthur Frackenpohl. T.A.P. Music. Two euphoniums and two tubas. 1990. $16.00. 1:30. IV. Part I: Bb–bb', Part II: A–f ', Part III: A₁–bb, Part IV: G₁–bb. For Harvey Phillips and Friends. Fun arrangement of this familiar melody. Technical challenges depend on the performance tempo. Parts may be doubled for a large ensemble.

Ewazen, Eric. *Devil Septet.* Seesaw Music Corporation Publishers. Four tubas, piano, and percussion. 1976. $33.00. 7:00. IV–V. Part I: F#₁–f ', Part II: A₁–f ', Part III: Ab₁–e', Part IV: F₁–e'. Very contemporary and dissonant. Techniques include singing, talking, hissing, and roaring through the mouthpiece. There are two improvisation sections for all four parts and a spot for the house and stage lights to dim. A very effective piece requiring four strong players.

Fentress, Stephen S. *Song of Memory.* T.U.B.A. Journal. Three euphoniums and one tuba. 1980. $7.50. 1:00. III–IV. Part I: g–eb", Part II: d–gb', Part III: G–db', Part IV: Bb₁–ab. A slow lyrical song in a minor key. Meter constantly shifts between 2/4, 3/4, and 4/4. The first part is written in treble clef though in concert pitch, unlike the normal transposition. Players read from the score. Parts may be doubled for a large ensemble. Written as part of the T.U.B.A. GEM Series and distributed in the *T.U.B.A. Journal,* Vol. 8, no. 4.

Ferguson, Edmund. *Total Tubosity.* Heavy Metal Music. Two euphoniums and two tubas. 1991. $5.00. 2:45. IV. Part I: c–ab', Part II: c–g', Part III: F–bb, Part IV: Ab₁–g. For the Heavy Metal Society Tuba Quartet. The second tuba part plays a rock bass line with a euphonium melody above. A tutti rhythmic shout chorus is in the middle. Fun to play, drums may be added for style enhancement. No score available. Parts may be doubled for a large ensemble.

Ferguson, Ken, arr. *Fascinatin' Gershwin.* BTQ Publications. Two euphoniums and two tubas. 1993. $15.00. 8:45. A medley of "Swanee," "Fascinatin' Rhythm," "It Ain't Necessarily So," "A Foggy Day," and "Strike Up the Band." Recorded by the British Tuba Quartet, *Elite Syncopations,* Polyphonic Reproductions Limited, QPRZ 012D.

Fischer, Fred. *Come Josephine (In My Flying Machine).* arr. Paul Schmidt. Heavy Metal Music. Two eu-

phoniums and two tubas. 1990. $3.00. 2:00. III. Part I: e–e', Part II: G–c', Part III: E–f, Part IV: G₁–B. A moderate waltz with the melody in the first part. Very playable by high school students. No score available. Parts may be doubled for a large ensemble.

Forte, Aldo. *Adagio and Rondo.* TUBA Press. Two euphoniums and two tubas. 1992. $10.00. 4:00. IV. Part I: C–c", Part II: B–a', Part III: E–d', Part IV: G#₁–a. Written for R. Winston Morris and the Tennessee Technological University Tuba Ensemble. The tessitura of the first part is high. The rondo section is challenging technically, very fast-paced, and multimetric. Contains some contemporary sounding harmonies, a very exciting composition. Parts may be doubled for a large ensemble. Originally copyrighted by the composer in 1973.

Frackenpohl, Arthur. *A Little Four Tuba Music.* T.A.P. Music. Four tubas. 1990. $10.00. 12:30. IV. Part I: Eb₁–d', Part II: Eb₁–db', Part III: Eb₁–db', Part IV: Eb₁–bb. Five movements: Prelude; Waltz; Air; Dance; Intro; March. All four parts require good range and technical facility. Some of the movements are tuneful and have fairly traditional harmonies. A conductor may be helpful in the fourth and fifth movements because of the complicated meter changes.

Frackenpohl, Arthur. *Pop Suite.* Kendor Music, Incorporated. Two euphoniums and two tubas. 1974. $10.50. 7:00. IV. Part I: Bb–bb', Part II: Bb–g' Part III: Bb₁–ab, Part IV: G₁–ab. Three movements: Rock; Refrain; Rag. Written for R. Winston Morris and the Tennessee Technological University Tuba Ensemble. This is exactly like the brass quintet with the same name. The first movement is slightly stilted for rock enthusiasts, but the Refrain is a beautiful melody, and the Rag works quite well. All parts have written-out solos to play. While the range is not demanding, rhythmically there are enough challenges to make this primarily a college-level piece. Parts may be doubled for a large ensemble. Recorded by the University of Miami Tuba Ensemble, Miami United Tuba Society, 14568; Karl Megules, *Garden State Tuba Ensemble,* Recorded Publications, Company, Z43471; the British Tuba Quartet, *In at the Deep End,* Heavyweight Records Limited, HR008/D.

Frackenpohl, Arthur. *Suite for Tuba Quartet.* Horizon Press. Two euphoniums and two tubas. 1991. $16.00. 6:50. IV. Part I: B–bb', Part II: B–ab', Part III: Bb₁–c', Part IV: Ab₁–eb. Three movements: Fanfare; Air; March. Commissioned by the Colonial Tuba Quartet. Nice quartet writing. The last movement is multimetric and more technically challenging, but is also very aggressive and exciting. The top two parts are printed in treble clef. Parts may be doubled for a large ensemble.

Friederich, G.W.E. *Lilly Bell Quick Step.* arr. Paul Schmidt. Heavy Metal Music. Two euphoniums and two tubas. 1991. $7.00. 2:00. IV. Part I: e♭–a♭', Part II: A♭–d♭', Part III: A♭₁–a♭, Part IV: A♭₁–A♭. A lively march with the melody shared by the top three parts. There are some technical challenges depending on performance tempos. No score available. Parts may be doubled for a large ensemble.

Friederich, G.W.E. *Ocean Tide March with Hail Columbia.* arr. Paul Schmidt. Heavy Metal Music. Two euphoniums and two tubas. 1990. $7.00. 3:30. IV. Part I: B♭–g', Part II: F–f ', Part III: D–e♭', Part IV: F₁–f. "Hail Columbia" serves as a 29-measure introduction to this march. The melody is passed among the three upper parts. There are some range and technical demands of the three top parts. No score available. Parts may be doubled for a large ensemble.

Friederich, G.W.E. *Prima Donna Waltz.* arr. Paul Schmidt. Heavy Metal Music. Two euphoniums and two tubas. 1991. $7.00. 2:20. III–IV. Part I: c–g', Part II: G–a', Part III: A♭₁–f, Part IV: (E♭₁)F₁–g. All parts have an opportunity to play the melody in this waltz. No significant technical problems. No score available. Parts may be doubled for a large ensemble.

Fritze, Gregory. *Pacman Gets Caught.* Gregory Fritze. Two euphoniums and two tubas. 1982. $10.00. 4:00. IV. Part I: B♭–b♭', Part II: B♭–g♭', Part III: B♭₁–c', Part IV: A♭₁–g♭. For the Boston Tuba-Four. One melody is "chased" by the rest of the parts and is finally caught programmatic of the popular late 1970s video game. All parts are interesting and challenging. Parts may be doubled for a large ensemble.

Fritze, Gregory. *Prelude and Dance.* TUBA Press. Two euphoniums and two tubas. 1990. $18.00. 9:00. IV. Part I: G–b♭', Part II: F–b♭', Part III: B♭–f♭', Part IV: F♯₁–a♭. Commissioned by and composed for the Colonial Tuba Quartet. The Prelude is very lyrical, the Dance is in a rock style. The tessitura is a little high for the first tuba part. Good writing for mature players. The first performance of this piece was at the International T.U.B.A. Conference in Sapporo, Japan, August 1990.

Fucik, Julius. *Entry of the Gladiators.* arr. Bruno Seitz. Musikverlag Martin Scherbacher. Two euphoniums and two tubas. 1993. $15.00. 4:00. IV. Part I: e♭–b♭', Part II: A♭–e♭', Part III: E♭–d', Part IV: G₁–d♭. Good arrangement of this famous fanfare. All four parts are interesting and challenging. Parts may be doubled for a large ensemble.

Fucik, Julius. *Thunder and Blazes.* arr. Skip Gray. Dedicated to the Tokyo Bari-Tuba Ensemble.

Gabrieli, A. *Canzona.* arr. J. Lesley Varner. Tuba/Euphonium Music Publications. Out of print. Two euphoniums and two tubas.

Gabrieli, Andrea. *Ricercar del Duodecimo Tuono.* arr. Richard Barth. Music Arts Company. Two euphoniums and two tubas. 1979. $10.00. 3:20. III–IV. Part I: B♭–g', Part II: A–c', Part III: E♭–g, Part IV:

B♭₁–c. An instrumental canzona, very polyphonic, but not technically demanding. Two top parts are printed in bass and treble clef. Fun to play, works very well. Parts may be doubled for a large ensemble.

Gabrieli, Andrea. *Ricercar del Duodecimo Tuono.* arr. Paul Schmidt. Heavy Metal Music. Two euphoniums and two tubas. 1990. $7.00. 2:30. III. Part I: A♭–e♭', Part II: G–a♭, Part III: D♭–f, Part IV: A♭₁–B♭. A typical late Renaissance instrumental canzona with the middle section in triple meter. Very polyphonic, but not technically difficult. Ideal for high school students. No score available. Parts may be doubled for a large ensemble.

Gabrieli, Giovanni. *Canzona, "La Spiritata."* arr. Peter Rauch. Ohio Valley Tuba Quartet Press. Two euphoniums and two tubas. 1988. $9.00. 1988. III–IV. Part I: d–a', Part II: B♭–d', Part III: B♭₁–b♭, Part IV: G₁–e♭. Typical polyphonic instrumental canzona. All parts have the opportunity to play the theme. Players must count carefully and play cleanly. Recorded by the British Tuba Quartet, *Elite Syncopations,* Polyphonic Reproductions Limited.

Gabrieli, Giovanni. *Canzona per Sonare II.* arr. Paul Schmidt. Heavy Metal Music. Two euphoniums and two tubas. 1992. $7.00. 3:00. IV. Part I: e♭–g', Part II: A–c', Part III: E–g, Part IV: F₁–c. An instrumental canzona well-known in the brass quintet repertoire. All parts have an opportunity to play the melody. Technical difficulty depends on performance tempo. No score available.

Gabrieli, Giovanni. *Sonata.* arr. Paul Schmidt. Heavy Metal Music. Two euphoniums and two tubas. 1991. $7.00. 4:00. IV. Part I: B♭–e♭', Part II: F–e♭', Part III: F–c', Part IV: B♭₁–a♭. A polyphonic instrumental work that shifts back and forth from duple to triple meter. Not technically difficult. No score available. Parts may be doubled for a large ensemble.

Garbáge, Pierre. *Chaser No. 3.* James Garrett. Two euphoniums and two tubas. 1974. $10.00. 2:00. IV. Part I: (B♭₁) d–f '(c"), Part II: (B♭₁) B♭–d', Part III: (C₁) G₁–b, Part IV: (C₁) G₁–d. Written for R. Winston Morris and the Tennessee Technological University Tuba Ensemble. The melody is primarily in the fourth part. Written in cut time but should be performed in a moderate four. This work has lyrics for group sing-along activities and is also known as *I'm Walkin' the Dog.* A very catchy melody. Parts may be doubled for a large ensemble. As the composer says, "Real heavy, nearly."

Garbáge, Pierre. *Songs in the Fight against Rum (Songs of Might to Cheer the Fight against the Blight of Liquordom).* James Garrett. Two euphoniums, two tubas, tenor solo, barbershop quartet, mixed chorus, female speaker, male speaker, country band, chimes, collection takers, and three clarinets. 1975. $75.00. 25:00. IV–V. Part I: E–b♭', Part II: G–e♭', Part III: F♯₁–c', Part

IV: B♭$_2$–f♯. A monumental work requiring strong performers on all parts. This opera-like production has vocal solos, chorus selections, instrumental interludes, and speaking parts. The tongue-in-cheek melodies and text must be performed genuinely yet in the spirit of pure fun. Very enjoyable for performers and audience. All parts require mutes. Parts may be doubled for a large ensemble. The composer says, "A burning plea for Bromo-Seltzer."

Garrett, James A. *Miniature Jazz Suite*. James Garrett. Two euphoniums and two tubas, piano, bass, and drums. 1977. $35.00. 6:50. IV. Part I: a♭–b', Part II: D–b', Part III: C–c♯', Part IV: G$_1$–c♭. Written for R. Winston Morris and the Tennessee Technological University Tuba Ensemble. This single-movement suite contains sections in moderate swing, slow swing, and rock. There are written-out solos and sections for improvised solos. Many tutti lines in the accompaniment. Technically challenging in some spots. Parts may be doubled for a large ensemble. Recorded by the Tennessee Technological University Tuba Ensemble, *Heavy Metal*, Mark Records, MES-20759.

Garrett, James A. *Mystical Music*. The Brass Press. Out of print. Two euphoniums and two tubas. 1974. 7:30. IV. Part I: e♭–b♭', Part II: G♯–a', Part III: G♯$_1$–c♭', Part IV: F$_1$–g♯. A single-movement with several contrasting sections. The tessitura of the first part is high. Technically challenging at times for the first two parts. Most effective with all four parts doubled.

Garrett, James A., arr. *Bill Bailey*. James Garrett. Two euphoniums and two tubas with optional keyboard and drums. 1984. $15.00. 4:00. IV. Part I: B♭–f♯', Part II: B♭–e♭', Part III: B♭$_1$–a♭, Part IV: B♭$_1$–e♭. Commissioned by and dedicated to Allen Jaffe. A fun but technically difficult arrangement of this popular tune. The melody and accompaniment is very syncopated. There is a 32-measure section that may be repeated for improvised solos. Requires strong players. Parts may be doubled for a large ensemble. Recorded by the Tennessee Technological University Tuba Ensemble, *All That Jazz*, Mark Records, MES-20608.

Garrett, James A., arr. *Chimes Blues*. James Garrett. Two euphoniums and two tubas with optional keyboard and drums. 1984. $10.00. 4:50. IV. Part I: f–f', Part II: B♭–b♭, Part III: B♭–g, Part IV: G$_1$–f. Commissioned by and dedicated to Allan Jaffe. Nice arrangement of this Dixieland standard. Twelve-bar blues in B♭. No significant range or technical challenges. Tubas have major responsibility for the melody. Parts I and II are available in both treble and bass clef. The top two parts have divisi sections. Parts may be doubled for a large ensemble. Recorded by the Tennessee Technological University Tuba Ensemble, *All That Jazz*, Mark Records, MES-20608.

Garrett, James A., arr. *Down on the Farm*. James Garrett. Two euphoniums and two tubas. 1984. $10.00. 2:30. IV. Part I: B–f', Part II: B–f', Part III: B♭$_1$–a♭, Part IV: B♭$_1$–f. Good Dixieland style arrangement. A section of sixteen measures in B♭ in the middle for improvised solos is followed by a unison shout chorus. Some technical challenges, but fun to play. Parts may be doubled for a large ensemble.

Garrett, James A., arr. *Joe Avery*. James Garrett. Two euphoniums and two tubas. 1984. $10.00. 2:00. IV. Part I: B♭–f', Part II: B♭–d', Part III: B♭$_1$–a♭, Part IV: B♭$_1$–e♭. Twelve-bar blues in B♭. The middle section may be repeated for improvised solos. The addition of drums is suggested. Parts may be doubled for a large ensemble.

Garrett, James A., arr. *Just a Closer Walk with Thee*. James Garrett. Two euphoniums and two tubas with optional keyboard and drums. 1984. $10.00. 3:00. IV. Part I: e–e', Part II: c–c', Part III: C–g, Part IV: C–c. Commissioned by and dedicated to Allan Jaffe. This arrangement begins slowly and solemnly and ends with a fast swing feel. A lot of syncopated, jazz rhythms. Works very well. Parts may be doubled for a large ensemble. Recorded by the Tennessee Technological University Tuba Ensemble, *All That Jazz*, Mark Records, MES-20608.

Garrett, James A., arr. *Rip'em Up, Joe*. James Garrett. Two euphoniums and two tubas with optional keyboard and drums. 1984. $10.00. 2:20. IV. Part I: f–g', Part II: e–f', Part III: G♯–g, Part IV: A$_1$–d. Commissioned by and dedicated to Allan Jaffe. Sixteen-bar blues in F at a moderate tempo. Sections may be repeated with chord symbols for improvised solos. Parts may be doubled for a large ensemble.

Garrett, James A., arr. *Wabash Cannon Ball for Tuba-Euphonium Ensemble*. Ludwig Music Publishing Company. Two euphoniums and two tubas. 1987. $15.50. 1:45 III–IV. Part I: A♭–g', Part II: A♭–f', Part III: B♭$_1$–g, Part IV: A♭$_1$–f. Written for R. Winston Morris and the Tennessee Technological University Tuba Ensemble. Excellent arrangement of this classic country/folk song. The melody is in both euphonium and tuba parts. The work can be a challenge to keep together at fast tempos. It could be played by a tuba quartet with F tubas on the first two parts. The top two parts are printed in both bass and treble clef. Parts may be doubled for a large ensemble. Recorded by the British Tuba Quartet, *In at the Deep End*, Heavyweight Records Limited, HR008/D.

Garrett, James A., arr. *When the Saints Come Marchin' In*. James Garrett. Two euphoniums and two tubas. 1984. $10.00. 2:00. IV. Part I: B–f', Part II: B–f', Part III: B$_1$–a, Part IV: B$_1$–f. A fast-paced arrangement that includes a repeated section for improvised solos. There is a 16-measure shout chorus that follows the improvised solos. Technically challenging, especially at the tempos indicated. Parts may be doubled for a large ensemble.

Gates, Crawford. *Tuba Quartet, Op. 59*. Intrada Music Group. Two euphoniums and two tubas. 1991. $15.00. 14:05. IV–V. Part I: B–c", Part II: E–ab', Part III: G₁–f ', Part IV: G₂–eb'. Three movements: Preludium; Chorale; Finale. Commissioned by Mitch Gershenfeld. The second part is marked Eb tuba or second euphonium, although a euphonium is typically used, as the tessitura is high. A wonderful work for tuba/euphonium ensemble, but there are great range and technical demands on all parts. The second movement is very lyrical with lush harmonies. The two outer movements are very technical and full of energy. Requires four very strong players. Parts may be doubled for a large ensemble. Recorded by the Tennessee Technological University Tuba Ensemble, Mark Records, MES-20759.

Gautier, Leonard. *Le Secret*. arr. David R. Werden. Whaling Music Publishers. Three euphoniums and one tuba. 1979. $6.00. 2:10. IV. Part I: Bb–g', Part II: G–bb', Part III: Bb–g', Part IV: Eb₁–bb. Arrangement for solo euphonium accompanied by two euphoniums and one tuba. Excellent for showing off a strong euphonium player. The other three parts are not technically demanding. Parts may be doubled for a large ensemble.

Gearhart, Livingston; Cassel, Don; and Hornibrook, Wallace. *Bass Clef Sessions*. Shawnee Press, Incorporated. Two euphoniums and two tubas. 1954. $7.50. 50 pp. III–IV. Part I: c–bb', Part II: F–g', Part III: G–d', Part IV: F₁–g. A collection of 62 two-, three-, and four-part arrangements for euphonium and tuba ranging in style from Palestrina to jazz. Technical challenges vary from easy to moderately difficult. Parts may be doubled for a large ensemble.

George, Thom Ritter. *TUBASONATINA*. Thom Ritter George. Two euphoniums and two tubas. 1977. $13.00. 8:20. IV. Part I: Bb–bb', Part II: G–bb', Part III: B₁–d', Part IV: F₁–b. Three movements: Sea Chanty; Meditation; Dance. Commissioned by and dedicated to R. Winston Morris and the Tennessee Technological University Tuba Ensemble. A real classic in the tuba ensemble repertoire. A very tuneful composition in which all four parts have an opportunity to play a melodic role. The second movement requires mutes for all parts. The last movement is fast-paced and challenging to play, with all its mixed meters. Enjoyable to perform and for audiences. Parts may be doubled for a large ensemble. Recorded by the Tennessee Technological University Tuba Ensemble, KM Records, KM 6431.

Gershenfeld, Mitchell, arr. *Three Chorales*. Medici Music Press. Four tubas. 1983. $5.00. 3:00. III–IV. Part I: c–d', Part II: G–a, Part III: D–eb, Part IV: F₁–B. Three movements: Christ lag in To-

desbanden; Wer nur den lieben Gott lässt walten; Lobt Gott, unsern Herren in seinem Heiligtum. A very nice setting of chorales by J.S. Bach, G. Neumark, and M. Praetorius respectively. No real technical difficulties. Easily playable by high school students if euphoniums are used for the two top parts. Parts may be doubled for a large ensemble.

Gervaise, Claude. *Dance Suite*. arr. David R. Werden. Whaling Music Publishers. Two euphoniums and two tubas. 1979. $8.50. 5:00. III–IV. Part I: c–bb', Part II: d–f ', Part III: Bb–ab, Part IV: Ab₁–eb. Three movements: Bransle de Bourgone; Bransle Gai; Allemande. Three French Renaissance dances. Technically very playable by high school ensembles. The first part is printed in treble clef. Parts may be doubled for a large ensemble.

Gesualdo, [Don Carlo]. *Moro Lasso*. Two euphoniums and two tubas.

Gibbons, Orlando. *Prelude and Voluntary for Four Tubas*. arr. James Self. Wimbledon Music Incorporated. 1979. $7.00. 2:50. IV. Part I: e–a', Part II: G–d', Part III: D–bb, Part IV: C₁–f. Two movements: Prelude; Voluntary. The tessitura of the first part is high and requires a very strong player on F tuba or euphonium. Rhythms in the Voluntary are not difficult but players must count carefully because of the close counterpoint. There is a divisi in the last measure of the top three parts. Parts may be doubled for a large ensemble.

Gillis, Lew. *Four Kuehn ("Keen") Guys*. Virgo Music Publishers. Four tubas. 1986. $8.95. 3:00. IV. Part I: C₁–f ', Part II: Ab–f ', Part III: G–d', Part IV: Bb₁–f '. Range demands require four strong players, in fact, the fourth part is higher than the third part. Sections of the music alternate between 6/8, 9/8, and 4/4. Written for David Kuehn when he was Dean of the School of Music at the University of North Texas.

Glinka, Michael. *Overture from Russlan and Ludmila*. arr. Ken Ferguson. BTQ Publications. Two euphoniums and two tubas. 1993. $12.00. 5:20. Recorded by the British Tuba Quartet, *Elite Syncopations,* Polyphonic Reproductions Limited, QPRZ 012D.

Glover, Jim, arr. *Amazing Grace*. Jim Glover. Two euphoniums and two tubas. 1982. $12.00.

Glover, Jim, arr. *Frosty the Snowman*. Jim Glover. Two euphoniums and two tubas. 1992. $8.00.

Glover, Jim, arr. *God Save the Queen*. Jim Glover. Two euphoniums and two tubas. 1991. $3.50.

Glover, Jim, arr. *In Heaven There Is No Beer*. Jim Glover. Two euphoniums and two tubas. 1992. $12.00.

Glover, Jim, arr. *Moon River*. Jim Glover. Two euphoniums and two tubas. 1992. $12.00.

Glover, Jim, arr. *O Canada*. Jim Glover. Two euphoniums and two tubas. 1991. $3.50.

Glover, Jim, arr. *Old Comrades (Alte Kamaraden).* Jim Glover. Two euphoniums and two tubas. 1992. $12.00.

Glover, Jim, arr. *Paloma Blanca.* Jim Glover. Two euphoniums and two tubas. 1991. $10.00.

Glover, Jim, arr. *Sleigh Ride.* Jim Glover. Two euphoniums and two tubas. 1993. $10.00.

Glover, Jim, arr. *Star-Spangled Banner.* Jim Glover. Two euphoniums and two tubas. 1991. $3.50.

Glover, Jim, arr. *Those Lazy, Hazy, Crazy Days of Summer.* Jim Glover. Two euphoniums and two tubas. 1991. $12.00. 2:00. III–IV. Part I: d–g', Part II: c–g', Part III: C–g, Part IV: C–e. Moderately difficult, could be played by high school ensembles depending on the performance tempo. All four parts have the opportunity to play the melody. Parts may be doubled for a large ensemble.

Glover, Jim, arr. *Too Fat Polka.* Jim Glover. Two euphoniums and two tubas. 1991. $12.00.

Goble, Joseph D. *Leviathans.* TUBA Press. Two euphoniums and two tubas. 1993. $5.00. 1:20. IV. Part I: B♭–ab', Part II: B♭–eb', Part III: B₁–ab, Part IV: G₁–g. For the T.O.P. Quartet; Andy, Phil, Kary, and Matt. Fanfare-like in a brisk 6/8 meter. All parts are interesting and moderately challenging. Parts may be doubled for a large ensemble.

Gottschalk, Arthur. *Tubas at Christmas.* Arthur Gottschalk. One euphonium and three tubas. 1974. 2:45. IV. Part I: c–g', Part II: C–c', Part III: C–a, Part IV: C₁–c. Three movements: Deck the Halls; Silent Night; Jolly Old St. Nicholas. Traditional arrangements. All parts have an opportunity to play the melody. No significant technical problems. Parts may be doubled for a large ensemble.

Gounod, Charles François. *Funeral March of a Marionette.* arr. Arthur Frackenpohl. Almitra Music Company (Kendor Music, Incorporated). Two euphoniums and two tubas. 1992. $11.00. 4:00. IV. Part I: A–g', Part II: G–g', Part III: G₁–c', Part IV: G₁–ab. A fun arrangement of the theme song of the Alfred Hitchcock television series. Technically not a problem once the 6/8 feel is established. Parts may be doubled for a large ensemble.

Gounod, Charles François. *Funeral March of a Marionette.* arr. Paul Schmidt. Heavy Metal Music. Two euphoniums and two tubas. 1990. $7.00. 4:20. III–IV. Part I: c–f', Part II: F–d', Part III: D–d', Part IV: C–d. The range and technical demands of the euphoniums are well within the abilities of good high school students. The first tuba part is high in some sections but does have ossia parts written an octave lower. No score available. Parts may be doubled for a large ensemble.

Grieg, Edward. *Arietta and Waltz.* arr. Hirokazu Hiraishi. Sonic Arts, Incorporated. Two euphoniums and two tubas. 1987. $11.00. 2:45. IV. Part I: d–g', Part II: F–cb', Part III: Eb–g, Part IV: Ab₁–d. Two movements: Arietta; Waltz. A fairly simple melody in a very traditional setting. No significant

technical problems. Parts may be doubled for a large ensemble.

Grieg, Edward. *Four Pieces.* arr. Peter Rauch. Ohio Valley Tuba Quartet Press. Two euphoniums and two tubas. 1988. $12.00. 5:00. IV. Part I: c–ab', Part II: G♯–ab', Part III: c–bb, Part IV: C₁–d. Four movements: National Song; At Home; Sailors Song; Waltz. Most of the melody is in the top two parts. Contains mostly tutti rhythms and traditional harmonies in the accompaniment. Parts may be doubled for a large ensemble.

Grieg, Edward. *In the Hall of the Mountain King.* arr. David R. Werden. Whaling Music Publishers. Two euphoniums and two tubas. 1992. $9.00. 3:00. IV. Part I: F–bb', Part II: E–bb', Part III: Bb₁–db', Part IV: Bb₁–ab. A fun melody played by William Bell on his solo tuba album. All parts have the opportunity to play the melody. The tessitura of the first part is high. Parts may be doubled for a large ensemble.

Grieg, Edward. *Wachterlied (Watchman's Song), Op. 12.* arr. Paul Schmidt. Heavy Metal Music. Two euphoniums and two tubas. 1991. $5.00. 2:00. III Part I: c–gb', Part II: A–d', Part III: A₁–bb, Part IV: F₁–d. Nice arrangement of this familiar song. Very appropriate for high school students. No score available. Parts may be doubled for a large ensemble.

Gussago, Cesario. *La Nicolina.* arr. Paul Schmidt. Heavy Metal Music. Two euphoniums and two tubas. 1992. $7.00. 3:40. III–IV. Part I: d–g', Part II: Ab–bb, Part III: Eb–ab, Part IV: Ab₁–d. A canon with no real technical problems. Players need to count carefully. No score available. Parts may be doubled for a large ensemble.

Haddad, Don. *Quartet for Tubas.* Don Haddad. 1974. 3:00. IV. Part I: F–f', Part II: Bb–c', Part III: Eb–f, Part IV: Bb₁–c. The first part has primary responsibility for the melody and is the most challenging technically. The other three parts are not very difficult. The first part has a high tessitura and may be played by a euphonium.

Handel, G.F. *Allegro, from Water Music.* arr. Peter Rauch. Ohio Valley Tuba Quartet Press. Two euphoniums and two tubas. 1988. $11.00. 3:00. IV. Part I: d–bb', Part II: A–a', Part III: F–bb, Part IV: D₁–d. Nice arrangement. Most challenging for the top two parts. Parts must be played cleanly and lightly.

Handel, G.F. *The Hallelujah Chorus.* arr. David Sabourin. Touch of Brass Music Corporation. Two euphoniums and two tubas. 1981. $10.00. 3:00. IV. Part I: Bb–bb', Part II: A–bb', Part III: F–a, Part IV: F₁–f. A good arrangement of this classic Baroque choral work. Requires euphonium players with a strong bb' and light, clean articulation in the low tuba register. Parts may be doubled for a large ensemble.

Handel, G.F. *Hallelujah Chorus.* arr. John Stevens. John Stevens. Two euphoniums and two tubas.

1986. 2:00. III–IV. Part I: c–g', Part II: F–E', Part III: C–g, Part IV: F_1–c.

Handel, G.F. *Hallelujah! from "Messiah."* arr. Daniel Heiman. Heavy Metal Music. Two euphoniums and two tubas. 1991. $7.00. 8:00. III–IV. Part I: c–a♭', Part II: F–d', Part III: C–g, Part IV: F_1–d. Three movements (fast—slow—fast): Hallelujah Chorus; Pifa; And with His Stripes We Are Healed. Most of the melodic responsibility is in the top two parts. No score available. Parts may be doubled for a large ensemble.

Handel, G.F. *Sarabande and Variations.* arr. Richard Barth. Music Arts Company. Two euphoniums and two tubas. 1978. $10.00. 5:00. III. Part I: B–e♭', Part II: A–c', Part III: B_1–g, Part IV: $(C_1)G_1$–c. Very moderate technical demands. Good for young players. The top two parts are printed in both bass and treble clef. Parts may be doubled for a large ensemble.

Handel, G.F. *Two Baroque Dances.* arr. Grady Greene. Music Arts Company. Two euphoniums and two tubas. 1987. $15.00. 2:30. III–IV. Part I: e–a♭', Part II: B♭–f ', Part III: A–g, Part IV: A♭–d♭. Two movements: Gavotte; Gigue. Works well for high school or college ensembles as there are no significant technical problems. The top two parts are printed in both bass and treble clef. Parts may be doubled for a large ensemble.

Handel, G.F. *Water and Fireworks Music.* arr. Daniel Heiman. Heavy Metal Music. Two euphoniums and two tubas. 1991. $5.00. 3:20. IV. Part I: G–g', Part II: G–e♭', Part III: A_1–a, Part IV: F_1–g. Three movements: Hornpipe; Coro; Bourrée. The melody is primarily in the first part. Performers should play lightly and cleanly to avoid making the melody muddy in the low register of the euphonium. No score available. Parts may be doubled for a large ensemble.

Handy, W.C. *St. Louis Blues.* arr. Bill Holcombe. Musicians Publications. Two euphoniums and two tubas. 1992. $12.00. 5:00. IV. Part I: d♯–g', Part II: G–e', Part III: D–b, Part IV: G_1–e. Fun arrangement of this classic blues melody. All four parts have interesting lines and the harmonization is typical of this style. Drums may be added for effect. Parts may be doubled for a large ensemble. Recorded by the Melton Tuba Quartet, *Premiere,* Diavolo Records, DR-D-93-C 001.

Hardt, Victor H. *Lullaby and Dance.* Tempo Music Publications, Incorporated. Out of print. Two euphoniums and two tubas. 1968. 2:30. III–IV. Part I: e–f♯', Part II: d♭–f ', Part III: A♭–d', Part IV: F–d'. Two movements: Lullaby; Dance. Not very difficult but there are some very musical sections in both movements. The Dance has some rhythmic challenges, so high school ensembles may need to perform it at a more conservative tempo. There are two measures that high school tuba players may wish to play down an octave, all other range re-

quirements are appropriate. Parts may be doubled for a large ensemble.

Harrison, Wayne. *Beneath the Surface.* Laissez-Faire Music Publishing Company. Out of print. Two euphoniums, two tubas, piano, guitar, bass, and drums. 1981. 4:30. IV. Part I: d–b♭, Part II: d–f ', Part III: B♭₁–d', Part IV: F_1–f. Dedicated to R. Winston Morris and the Tennessee Technological University Tuba Ensemble. Starts in a swing style, then has sections in a bossa-nova and funk. Not too difficult rhythmically but challenging stylistically. The first euphonium has a high tessitura and requires a strong player. All players need a good jazz feel. Parts may be doubled for a large ensemble. Recorded by the Tennessee Technological University Tuba Ensemble, *All That Jazz,* Mark Records, MES-20608.

Harrold, Robert. *The Night (It Has a Thousand Faces).* TUBA Press. Two euphoniums and two tubas. 1991. $10.00. 4:00. IV. Part I: c–b♭', Part II: c–f, Part III: F_1–b♭, Part IV: F_1–b♭. For Laura. The first section features a slow lyrical melody accompanied by sustained block chords. The second section begins with a rhythmic bass line passed between the third and fourth parts underneath a syncopated melody. No great technical demands, but a strong sense of rhythm and a good upper register for the euphoniums are required. Top two parts are printed in both bass and treble clef. Parts may be doubled for a large ensemble.

Harrold, Robert. *Three Traveling Shorts.* TUBA Press. Two euphoniums and two tubas. 1991. $10.00. 6:00. IV. Part I: A–c'(a"), Part II: G–g'(a'), Part III: C_1–g, Part IV: F_1–e♭. Three movements. The first movement is fast and multimetric, constantly repeating 3/8, 2/8, and 4/4. The second movement is slower-paced and uses traditional harmonies in a chorale-like style. The third movement is very fast and more technically demanding for the first euphonium player. The last twelve measures of the third movement get significantly slower, perhaps signifying the end of the "trip," thus the composition. The top two parts are printed in both treble and bass clef. Parts may be doubled for a large ensemble.

Hartin, Paul F. , arr. *An Old German Folk Song.* Cellar Press. Two euphoniums and two tubas. 1975. 2:00. II–III. Part I: g–e', Part II: e♭–c', Part III: c–a♭, Part IV: A♭₁–f. A nice chorale setting of the German folk song *Ich Schwing mein Horn in Jammersthal.* The melodic characteristics, range, and technical demands make this excellent for high school students. Parts may be doubled for a large ensemble.

Hartley, Walter. *Miniatures for Four Valve Instruments.* Galaxy Music Corporation. Two euphoniums and two tubas. 1984. $11.25. 5:20. IV. Part I: F–b♭', Part II: F–g♭', Part III: B–e♭', Part IV: E♭₁–c'. Four movements: Marche Manquée; Shizo; Pavane; Four Valve Rag. The first movement is a short multimetric march, the last movement is the most challenging of the piece. The euphoniums have greater technical and range demands than do the tubas. Written in 1976, published in 1984. Recorded by the Atlantic Tuba Quartet, Golden Crest Records, CRS 4173.

Hassler, Hans Leo. *Two Motets.* arr. Paul Schmidt. Heavy Metal Music. Two euphoniums and two tubas. 1991. $5.00. 3:00. III–IV. Part I: d–e', Part II: A–bb, Part III: A–a, Part IV: C–e. The first movement is homophonic with mostly tutti rhythms. The second movement is polyphonic. No significant technical problems. No score available. Parts may be doubled for a large ensemble.

Hawker, John. *Romance for Bass Tuba.* T.U.B.A. Journal. Two tubas and two euphoniums. 1977. $7.50. 3:30. IV. Part I: e–g', Part II: B$_1$–c', Part III: F$_1$–b, Solo/Part IV: Eb_1–e'. Challenging tuba solo with an accompaniment of two euphoniums and one tuba. Contrasting sections of a fast 3/8, slow 3/4, and fast 2/4. Written as part of the T.U.B.A. GEM Series and published in the *T.U.B.A. Journal,* Vol. 5, no. 2.

Hawkins, Erskine. *Tuxedo Junction.* arr. Paul Schmidt. Heavy Metal Music. Two euphoniums and two tubas. 1991. $7.00. 4:30. IV. Part I: F–g', Part II: Bb–bb', Part III: D–bb, Part IV: A$_1$–db. Fun arrangement of this big-band classic. The top three parts require mutes with a closed and open effect (players are instructed to use the lid of a plastic bucket). Opportunities exist for improvisation. Drums may be added to enhance swing style. No score available. Parts may be doubled for a large ensemble.

Haydn, Franz J. *Menuett, from Quartet Op. 76, no. 13* [*sic*]. arr. Karl Humble. T.A.P. Music. Two euphoniums and two tubas. 1989. $5.00. 4:00. IV. Part I: F#–bb', Part II: G–f ', Part III: D–bb, Part IV: E$_1$–e. A nice transcription of the third movement of the work often referred to as the "Kaiser Quartet." No extreme range or technical demands. Parts may be carefully doubled for a large ensemble. There is a misprint on the parts, this quartet is Op. 76, no. 3, not no. 13.

Heidler, Manfred, arr. *Concert für 4.* Carpe-Diem Musikverlag Claudia Wölpper. Two euphoniums and two tubas. 1994. $21.00.

Heidler, Manfred, arr. *Struktur in Blech—The Brummi Brass Band.* Carpe-Diem Musikverlag Claudia Wölpper. Four tubas. 1993. $18.00 IV. Four movements: Ruhig-Cantable; March; Waltz; Ragtime—The Entertainer. Parts are available in bass or treble clef.

Heiman, Daniel. *La Guercia.* Heavy Metal Music. Two euphoniums and two tubas. 1991. $5.00. 1:45. III–IV. Part I: d–f ', Part II: (C) G–bb, Part III: Eb–c', Part IV: Bb–f. All parts are syncopated, and the texture is polyphonic. No significant tech-

nical demands. No score available. Parts may be doubled for a large ensemble.

Heiman, Daniel, arr. *Three Barbershop Songs.* Heavy Metal Music. Two euphoniums and two tubas. 1991. $7.00. 4:00. III. Part I: gb–f ', Part II: B–c', Part III: G–a, Part IV: Db–f. Three movements: I Had a Dream Dear; My Old Kentucky Home; Aura Lee. Very traditional arrangements. Most of the melody is in the top two parts. Not difficult, but fun to play. No score available. Parts may be doubled for a large ensemble.

Heiman, Daniel, arr. *Three Motets.* Heavy Metal Music. Two euphoniums and two tubas. 1991. $7.00. 4:00. IV. Part I: d–f ', Part II: c–c', Part III: C#–bb, Part IV: (D$_1$)F$_1$–eb. Three movements: Sanctus; Motet for Four Voices; Cantate Domino. Three very polyphonic motets by Byrd, Crose, and Hassler respectively. Many meter changes; not technically difficult. No score available. Parts may be doubled for a large ensemble.

Henderson, Ray. *Five Foot Two, Eyes of Blue (Has Anybody Seen My Kim?).* arr. Steve Emberson. Steve Emberson. Two euphoniums and two tubas. 2:00. IV. Part I: bb–bb', Part II: a–g', Part III: Bb–d', Part IV: F$_1$–g. Cute arrangement of this peppy classic melody. It is written in four but should be played in cut time. Technical difficulty is determined by the speed of performance. Parts may be doubled for a large ensemble.

Heussenstamm, George. *Tuba Quartet, Op. 65, No. 3.* George Heussenstamm. Four F tubas. 1977. $22.00. 9:00. IV. Part I: F$_1$–f#', Part II: D$_1$–ab', Part III: D#$_1$–e', Part IV: E$_1$–d. A contemporary composition with many complicated rhythms and mixed meters. Some spoken parts and mouthpiece buzzing. The score indicates a specific certain staging for the performance.

Heussenstamm, George. *Tubacussion, Op. 62.* Seesaw Music Corporation Publishers. Four tubas and percussion. 1977. $31.00. 10:00. IV–V. Part I: c–eb', Part II: A#$_1$–b, Part III: E$_1$–eb', Part IV: Eb$_1$–ab. An avant-garde work with many twentieth-century techniques, including tapping the instrument, floor stomps, humming, rattling of keys, indeterminate sections, and random selection of pitches. A very difficult work.

Heussenstamm, George. *TubaFour, Op. 30.* Seesaw Music Corporation Publishers. Euphonium and three tubas. 1976. $24.00. 8:30. IV. Part I: Db$_1$–b', Part II: B$_1$–d', Part III: G$_1$–b, Part IV: D$_1$–b. In a contemporary style. The pitches in some sections are determined by the position of dots on the page. Very challenging technical demands and complex harmonic structure. The composer indicates a conductor is necessary. Recorded by the New York Tuba Quartet, *Tubby's Revenge,* Crystal Records, S221.

Hewitt, Harry. *Bird in the Forest, Op. 376F.* Harry Hewitt. Four tubas with a high solo instrument (flute or clarinet) and optional echo part. 1972. $15.00. 3:00. IV. Part I: D♭–f♯', Part II: D♭–b, Part III: D♭–b, Part IV: D♭–b. To R. Winston Morris and the Tennessee Technological University Tuba Ensemble. A second optional high part echoes the solo part. The solo and echo parts often play in a manner that is totally unrelated to the tuba ensemble. Numerous dynamic contrasts and tempo changes. With a few adjustments, the top part could be played by a euphonium.

Hewitt, Harry. *Four Preludes for Four Tubas*. Harry Hewitt. 1973. $9.00. 13:00. IV. Part I: B♭–f ', Part II: B♭₁–c', Part III: G♭₁–c', Part IV: E₁–c'. Four movements contrasting in tempo and character. Contemporary harmonies. Very interesting interplay between the parts. No extreme technical demands, but the parts are still challenging. Originally composed and copyrighted in 1971.

Hewitt, Harry. *In the Shadows, Op. 376B*. Harry Hewitt. Four tubas and celeste. 1971. $8.00 4:00 IV. Part I: A♭–f ', Part II: B♭₁–c', Part III: F₁–c, Part IV: E₁–A. The fourth part (optional) only plays for 22 measures. The first part is high and may be played on an F tuba or euphonium. Technically only moderately challenging but with many tempo and meter changes. A conductor is necessary.

Hill, William H. *Fantasia on "Dies Irae" for Tuba Ensemble*. Neil A. Kjos Music Company. Two euphoniums and two tubas. 1980. $7.00. 5:00. IV. Part I: G–b', Part II: F–b', Part III: G₁–c', Part IV: F₁–b. Commissioned by the Tubists Universal Brotherhood Association for the Second National Tuba/Euphonium Workshop, 1980. Based on the Gregorian Chant *Dies Irae*. Plainsong line introduction is followed by a very dissonant contrasting Allegro molto section. The first and second tuba parts have divisi sections; all parts use mutes. Good writing for tuba/euphonium ensemble. Parts may be doubled for a large ensemble.

Hoesly, John. *Quadrant*. Piston Reed Stick and Bow Publisher. Two euphoniums and two tubas. 1992. Parts $15.00, score $4.00. 20:00. IV–V. Part I: F–b', Part II: A♭–a', Part III: A♭₁–c', Part IV: F₁–b♭. Four movements: Amorphous; Bemorphous; Seamorphous; Fourmorphous. A contemporary tonal composition. There are numerous meter changes, a multiphonic section, glissandos, and players are asked to blow air through their instruments at different pitch levels. All four parts are technically challenging. Very interesting writing.

Hoesly, John, arr. *Ballin' the Jack*. Piston Reed Stick and Bow Publisher. Two euphoniums and two tubas. 1990. Parts $7.00, score $2.00. 2:00. IV. Part I: c–a♭', Part II: F♯–e', Part III: C–g♭, Part IV: (D₁) G₁–e. Begins with a slow introduction followed by a moderate jazz section. The first and second parts are the most technically challenging. Parts may be doubled for a large ensemble.

Hoesly, John, arr. *Just a Closer Walk with Thee*. Piston Reed Stick and Bow Publisher. Two euphoniums and two tubas. 1990. Parts $7.00, score $2.00. 3:00. IV. Part I: B♭–b♭', Part II: A–e♭', Part III: B♭₁–a♭, Part IV: B♭₁–d(b♭). Begins with a slow chorale, then moves to swing, then Dixieland, and ends slowly. Most challenging for the top two parts. Drums may be added for stylistic support. Parts may be doubled for a large ensemble.

Hoesly, John, arr. *St. Louis Blues*. Piston Reed Stick and Bow Publisher. Two euphoniums and two tubas. 1990. Parts $7.00, score $2.00. 4:30. IV. Part I: e–g', Part II: B♭–f ', Part III: B♭₁–f, Part IV: G₁–e♭. Good arrangement of this famous blues melody. Most of the melodic responsibility is in the first part. Many syncopated rhythms in the melody and accompaniment. Fun to play.

Hoesly, John, arr. *That's A Plenty*. Piston Reed Stick and Bow Publisher. Two euphoniums and two tubas. 1990. Parts $7.00, score $2.00. 3:00. IV. Part I: B♭–g', Part II: B♭–f ', Part III: D–a, Part IV: A₁–f. The melody is primarily in the first and second parts. A middle section with chord symbols may be repeated for improvised solos. A rhythm section is recommended for stylistic effect. Parts may be doubled for a large ensemble.

Holborne, Anthony. *Ten Pieces for Tuba Ensemble*. arr. John Stevens. TUBA Press. Two euphoniums and two tubas. 1992. $10.00. 14:00. IV. Part I: d–g', Part II: G–g', Part III: F–c', Part IV: F₁–d. Ten movements: Muy Linda; Honie-Suckle; Pavan; The Marie-Golde; The Choice; Patiencia; The New Yeres Gift; Night Watch; Last Will and Testament; Galliard. A conglomeration of Renaissance style songs in a variety of keys, meters, and styles. Technically not difficult but there are many polyphonic sections. Some movements could be played by high school ensembles. Parts may be doubled for a large ensemble. No score available.

Holmes, Paul. *Quartet for Tubas*. TRN Music Publishers. Two euphoniums and two tubas. 1980. $20.00. 10:00. IV. Part I: B–g', Part II: B–e', Part III: D–b, Part IV: G₁–a. Four movements: Adagio; Andante and Allegro; Lento; Allegro Moderato in a Jazz Style. Commissioned by R. Winston Morris and the Tennessee Technological University Tuba Ensemble. Very melodic and rhythmically interesting. Second and fourth movements have a lot of syncopated rhythms and hemiolas. Fun to play and satisfying for audiences. Parts may be doubled for a large ensemble. Recorded by the University of Michigan Tuba and Euphonium Ensemble, University of Michigan Records, SM0011; the British Tuba Quartet, *In at the Deep End*, Heavyweight Records Limited, HR008/D.

Hook, James. *Rondo*. arr. James A. Garrett. James Garrett. Two euphoniums and two tubas. 1973. $15.00. 2:00. IV. Part I: f–g', Part II: c–d', Part III: F–b♭, Part IV: A₁–f. Written for R. Winston Morris and the Tennessee Technological University Tuba Ensemble. A very energetic melody equally demanding of all instruments. This transcription works very well for tubas and euphoniums. The top two parts are available in bass and treble clef. Parts may be doubled for a large ensemble. Recorded by the British Tuba Quartet, *In at the Deep End,* Heavyweight Records Limited, HR008/D.

Howard, Ronald. *Chorale.* Ronald Howard. Two euphoniums and two tubas. 1979. 1:10. III–IV. Part I: db–e', Part II: F–f, Part III: F–a, Part IV: B₁–d. A very slow chorale, alternating between 3/4, 5/4, and 6/4. Uses contemporary harmonies. Players read from a score. No significant technical problems. Parts may be doubled for a large ensemble.

Hughey, J., and Jernigan, P., arr. *Gay 90's Medley.* University of Tennessee Series. Out of print. Two euphoniums and two tubas. 1971. 4:00. IV. Part I: d–db', Part II: F–ab, Part III: F–f, Part IV: Bb₁–d.

Humperdink, Engelbert. *Gebet aus Hänsel und Gretel.* arr. Bruno Seitz. Musikverlag Martin Scherbacher. Two euphoniums and two tubas. 1991. $13.50. 3:30. IV. Part I: Bb–bb', Part II: A–g, Part III: Bb₁–d', Part IV: E₁–g. A slow and very lyrical melody, primarily in the first part. No significant technical problems. Parts may be doubled for a large ensemble.

Hurt, Eddie. *Melissma.* Queen City Brass Publications. Four tubas. 1981. $6.50. 2:00. IV. Part I: Bb–bb', Part II: Ab–c', Part III: C–f, Part IV: Bb₁–eb. For Rex Conner. The major demand of this piece is range, not technique. It would be considered a Level V if tubas were to play all four parts. If performed with two euphoniums and two tubas it is playable by a good high school ensemble. Parts may be doubled for a large ensemble.

Hutchinson, Terry. *Tuba Juba Duba.* The Brass Press. Two euphoniums and two tubas. 1974. $5.00. 3:10. III. Part I: c♯–g'(b'), Part II: c♯–c', Part III: D–e, Part IV: B–d. The simple catchy melody makes this a thoroughly fun piece to perform and to listen to. Simple mixed meters; slow, lyrical middle section. Includes finger snaps or a woodblock part and a foot stomp at the end. Very entertaining. Parts may be doubled for a large ensemble. Recorded by the Tennessee Technological University Tuba Ensemble, Golden Crest Records, CRS 4139; the Melton Tuba Quartett, *Premiere,* Diavolo Records, DR-D-93-C-001.

Iannaccone, Anthony. *Hades.* Seesaw Music Corporation Publishers. Two euphoniums and two tubas. 1975. $12.00. 5:30. IV–V. Part I: c–bb', Part II: A–a', Part III: D–d', Part IV: D₁–b. Very contemporary in harmony and style. Special techniques include blowing through the instrument while clicking valves, quarter-tones, glissandos, and multiphonics. All four parts require mutes. Many difficult rhythmic figures. Requires four strong players. Recorded by the University of Michigan Tuba/Euphonium Ensemble, Golden Crest Records, CRS-4145.

Iannaccone, Anthony. *Three Mythical Sketches.* Tenuto Publications. Two euphoniums and two tubas. 1973. $4.00 6:30. IV. Part I: A–a', Part II: A–gb', Part III: C♯–eb', Part IV: G₁–c♯'. Three movements: Pluto; Persephone; Poseidon. All parts are technically and rhythmically challenging. Harmonically very dissonant at times. All parts need mutes. Requires four strong players. Recorded by the University of Michigan Tuba/Euphonium Ensemble, Golden Crest Records, CRS–4145.

Israel, Brian. *Canzona and Hornpipe.* Tritone Press. Four tubas. 1982. $5.00. 5:20. IV. Part I: A₁–d', Part II: A₁–d', Part III: A₁–d', Part IV: E₁–d'. The Canzona is very contrapuntal; the Hornpipe is also very imitative and rhythmically more challenging than the Canzona. All parts are similar in their range demands (all four tubas have a d'). Requires four strong players.

Ivanovici, J. *Waves of the Danube.* arr. Soichi Konagaya. Sonic Arts, Incorporated. Two euphoniums and two tubas. 1986. $12.00. 3:45. IV. Part I: c–ab', Part II: Bb–ab', Part III: D–ab, Part IV: (Eb₁) F₁–d. A medley of three different moderate waltzes. Brief cadenza for the first part near the beginning of the piece. All parts play portions of the melody. Parts may be doubled for a large ensemble.

Jacob, Gordon. *Four Pieces for Tuba Quartet.* Whaling Music Publishers. Two euphoniums and two tubas. 1981. $15.00. 6:00. IV. Part I: d–c", Part II: G–bb', Part III: Eb–d', Part IV: Eb₁–bb. Dedicated to the Denis Winter Quartet. The movements are in a variety of meters. The melody is often written in a folk style. While only the first euphonium part is printed in treble clef, both parts are notated in treble clef in the score. Requires strong euphonium players for the high tessitura. Parts may be doubled for a large ensemble.

Jacobsen, Julius. *Ten Quartets.* Swedish Music Information Center—STIM. Four tubas. 1983. 15:00. IV–V. Part I: C♯–f', Part II: A₁–e', Part III: F₁–e', Part IV: E₁–c. Ten movements. All parts are musically and technically challenging. Many sections with mixed meters and complex harmonies. Very interesting writing; requires four strong players. Parts may be doubled for a large ensemble.

Jager, Robert. *Mixtures and Mutations.* TUBA Press. Two euphoniums and two tubas. 1992. $10.00. 6:30. IV. Part I: c–c", Part II: Gb–gb', Part III: G₁–b, Part IV: E₁–gb. Four movements: Slowly; Aggressively; Moderately; Boldly. To R. Winston Morris and the Tennessee Technological University Tuba Ensemble. Contemporary harmonies and and intricate rhythms in some of the movements. The fourth movement is multimetric and the tessitura of the first part is high. Mutes are required of all parts. Originally published and copyrighted in 1981 by Laissez-Faire Music Publishing Company.

Johnson, Charles Leslie. *Dill Pickles Rag: A Ragtime Two-Step*. arr. Mark Nelson. TUBA Press. Two euphoniums and two tubas. 1994. $8.00. 2:30. IV. Part I: B–a' (c"), Part II: d–f ', Part III: D–a, Part IV: (C$_1$) G$_1$–d. For the Hokkaido Euphonium/ Tuba Camp. Most of the technical challenges are in the first part. Fun to play. Parts may be doubled for a large ensemble.

Jones, Roger. *Allegro for Tuba Quartet*. Roger Jones. 1969. $12.00. 5:00. IV. Part I: G–e', Part II: B♭$_1$– b♭, Part III: G$_1$–g, Part IV: F$_1$–d. The melody and accompaniment are very syncopated. The first and third parts are the most technically challenging. Works well.

Jones, Roger. *Canticles*. Roger Jones. Four tubas. 1978. $50.00. 15:00. IV. Part I: A–a', Part II: C– e', Part III: E$_1$–d', Part IV: D$_1$–g. Three movements. A major work for tuba/euphonium quartet. The music is multimetric and harmonically complex, and there are cadenzas in many of the parts. All parts require mutes and are technically challenging.

Jones, Roger. *Cantilena*. Roger Jones. Two euphoniums and two tubas. 1975. $5.00. 1:45. III–IV. Part I: c–f ', Part II: c–c', Part III: C–a♭, Part IV: F$_1$–e. A nice lyrical melody in a slow 3/4. No technical problems. Very appropriate for high school students. Parts may be doubled for a large ensemble.

Jones, Roger. *Chant and Fantasie*. Roger Jones. Four tubas. 1969. $20.00. 5:00. IV. Part I: C–e♭', Part II: C–b♭, Part III: G$_1$–f, Part IV: F$_1$–d. The Chant is slow and somber. The Fantasie shifts frequently between 2/4 and 3/4. All parts play portions of the melody. No significant technical difficulties, but players need to count carefully.

Jones, Roger. *Quartet for Tubas*. Roger Jones. 1972. $10.00. 4:50. IV. Part I: C–e', Part II: C–b♭, Part III: C–g, Part IV: F$_1$–c. Three movements: Intrada; Air; Ballabile. Very good writing for tuba quartet. The third movement is rhythmically more interesting and challenging. All parts require mutes.

Jones, Roger. *TUBAFUGALFANFARE*. Roger Jones. Four tubas. 1992. $6.00. 1:20. IV. Part I: F–a, Part II: G♭$_1$–d, Part III: F–f, Part IV: F$_1$–d. A short but dramatic fanfare based on one main fugal subject. All parts have equal responsibility for the melody. Works very well. Parts may be doubled for a large ensemble.

Joplin, Scott. *The Easy Winners*. arr. Hirokazu Hiraishi. Sonic Arts, Incorporated. Two euphoniums and two tubas. 1986. $12.00. 2:45. IV. Part I: G–a', Part II: F–a', Part III: F–c', Part IV: F$_1$–e♭. All parts have the opportunity to play this syncopated melody. Technically challenging in several sections. Fun to play.

Joplin, Scott. *The Easy Winners*. arr. Paul Schmidt. Heavy Metal Music. Two euphoniums and two tubas. 1991. $7.00. 2:45. IV. Part I: f–a♭', Part II: E♭–g', Part III: B♭$_1$–c', Part IV: E♭$_1$–a. Highly syn-

copated melody. Technically challenging for all parts, but fun to play. No score available.

Joplin, Scott. *The Easy Winners*. arr. David R. Werden. Whaling Music Publishers. Two euphoniums and two tubas. 1980. $6.00. 2:45. IV. Part I: G–b♭', Part II: G–a', Part III: G–d', Part IV: F$_1$–a. The tessitura is high for the top two parts of this Joplin rag. A few tricky rhythms. Requires strong players. The first euphonium part is printed in treble clef. Parts may be doubled for a large ensemble.

Joplin, Scott. *Elite Syncopations*. arr. William Picher. PP Music. Two euphoniums and two tubas. 1986. $8.00. 3:30. IV. Part I: B♭–c', Part II: B♭–g', Part III: D–d', Part IV: A♭$_1$–g. Not many technical difficulties, but counting, which can be tricky, is the primary challenge of most of these Joplin rags. The tubas get a brief opportunity to play the melody, but most of the work is in the euphoniums. The first part is printed in treble clef in the score and the part. Parts may be doubled for a large ensemble. Recorded by the British Tuba Quartet, *Elite Syncopations*, Polyphonic Reproductions Ltd., QPRZ012D.

Joplin, Scott. *The Entertainer*. arr. Maurice Bale. Godiva Music. Two euphoniums and two tubas. 1994. $9.00. 3:00. IV. Part I: B♭–f ', Part II: A–d', Part III: E♭–a♭, Part IV: (E♭$_1$) F$_1$–f.

Joplin, Scott. *The Entertainer*. arr. Hirokazu Hiraishi. Sonic Arts, Incorporated. Three euphoniums and one tuba. 1987. $12.00. 3:30. IV. Part I: d–a', Part II: A–g', Part III: G–e', Part IV: F$_1$–d. The third part could be played by a tuba, as the tessitura is not high. The melody is primarily in the top three parts. Fun to play. Parts may be doubled for a large ensemble.

Joplin, Scott. *Euphonic Sounds*. arr. Hirokazu Hiraishi. Sonic Arts, Incorporated. Two euphoniums and two tubas. 1986. $12.00. 2:50. IV. Part I: G–b♭', Part II: F♯–e♭', Part III: D♭–f, Part IV: G♭$_1$–d. A very syncopated melody shared by all parts. Requires light and clean playing. Technically challenging in some sections. Parts may be doubled for a large ensemble.

Joplin, Scott. *Euphonic Sounds*. arr. David R. Werden. Whaling Music Publishers. Two euphoniums and two tubas. 1978. $8.00. 2:50. IV. Part I: c–d", Part II: c–a', Part III: c♯–c', Part IV: F$_1$–f. A medium tempo rag with a very syncopated melody and accompaniment. Most of the melodic work is in the first and second parts, both of which are printed in treble clef. These Joplin arrangements are challenging to play, and when played correctly are enjoyable for both performers and audience. Recorded by the Atlantic Tuba Quartet, *Euphonic Sounds*, Golden Crest, CRS 4173; the British Tuba Quartet, *Euphonic Sounds*, Polyphonic Reproductions Limited, QPRZ009D.

Joplin, Scott. *The Favorite Rag*. arr. David Sabourin. Touch of Brass Music Corporation. Two euphoniums and two tubas. 1981. $10.00. 2:20. IV. Part I: c–g', Part II: c–d', Part III: G–b, Part IV: A₁–e. Technically quite challenging for the euphoniums. Tuba parts are primarily accompaniment. Parts may be doubled for a large ensemble.

Joplin, Scott. *The Great Crush Collision*. arr. Paul Schmidt. Heavy Metal Music. Two euphoniums and two tubas. 1991. $7.00. 2:30. IV. Part I: A–f ', Part II: E–f ', Part III: G♯₁–b♭, Part IV: F₁–c. Originally written by Joplin to describe a staged steam locomotive crash in 1896. The parts are challenging, but fun to play. No score available.

Joplin, Scott. *Maple Leaf Rag*. arr. Karl Humble. T.A.P. Music. Two euphoniums and two tubas. 1989. $6.00. 3:20. IV. Part I: c–c", Part II: A♭–c", Part III: D♭–b♭, Part IV: E♭₁–f♭. Technically challenging for the top three parts. The tessitura of the first part is high. Players need to count carefully. Fun to play.

Joplin, Scott. *Peacherine Rag*. arr. Hirokazu Hiraishi. Sonic Arts, Incorporated. Two euphoniums and two tubas. 1992. $11.00. 4:00. III–IV. Part I: d–a♭, Part II: G–e♭, Part III: F–c', Part IV: F₁–d. A moderate tempo rag. No significant technical problems, but many of the rhythmic patterns are very syncopated. Parts may be doubled for a large ensemble.

Joplin, Scott. *Pineapple Rag*. arr. Hirokazu Hiraishi. Sonic Arts, Incorporated. Two euphoniums and two tubas. 1986. $12.00. 4:00. IV. Part I: B♭–g', Part II: F–e♭', Part III: E–g, Part IV: G₁–c. A moderate tempo rag. The melody is primarily in the top two parts. A lot of syncopation requiring accurate counting and playing. Parts may be doubled for a large ensemble.

Joplin, Scott. *Pleasant Moments Rag*. arr. Paul Schmidt. Heavy Metal Music. Two euphoniums and two tubas. 1990. $7.00. 2:30. IV. Part I: F–f ', Part II: F–d', Part III: F₁–b♭, Part IV: F₁–f. A rag in 3/4 time. A lot of syncopation in the top three parts. Challenging, but fun to play. No score available.

Joplin, Scott. *Rag-Time Dance*. arr. David R. Werden. Whaling Music Publishers. Two euphoniums and two tubas. 1979. $7.00. 2:45. IV–V. Part I: A♭–b♭'(d"), Part II: A♭–b♭', Part III: A♭₁–e♭', Part IV: A♭₁–e♭'. Medium tempo rag. While most of the work is in the first part, both tuba parts have opportunities to play the melody. Technically challenging. The tessitura of all four parts is high. Recorded by the U.S. Navy Tuba Quartet, U.S. Navy Band recordings.

Joplin, Scott. *Rag-Time Dance*. arr. Paul Schmidt. Heavy Metal Music. Two euphoniums and two tubas. 1991. $7.00. 3:30. IV. Part I: F–g', Part II: C–f ', Part III: E–b, Part IV: F₁–c. The top two parts have the most technical demands. A very interesting rag. No score available.

Joplin, Scott. *The Strenuous Life*. arr. Hirokazu Hiraishi. Sonic Arts, Incorporated. Two euphoniums and two tubas. 1986. $12.00. 4:00. IV. Part I: A–g', Part II: A–e', Part III: C–g, Part IV: G₁–d. All parts have the opportunity to play this syncopated melody. No range problems. Parts may be doubled for a large ensemble.

Joplin, Scott. *The Strenuous Life: A Ragtime Two-Step*. arr. Walter Lex. PP Music. Two euphoniums and two tubas. 1986. $8.00. 4:00. IV–V. Part I: d–c", Part II: F–b♭', Part III: C–d', Part IV: E♭₁–f. To Roger Behrend. A challenging Joplin rag. The tessitura of both euphonium parts is quite high. Requires strong players to produce a flowing ragtime feel. All four parts have responsibility for the melody.

Joplin, Scott. *Swipesy*. arr. David R. Werden. Whaling Music Publishers. Two euphoniums and two tubas. 1981. $7.00. 3:00. IV. Part I: c–c♭", Part II: d♭–b♭', Part III: A♭–d♭', Part IV: A♭₁–f. Rhythmically challenging, and the euphoniums have a high tessitura. The first euphonium part is printed in treble clef. This arrangement works very well. Parts may be doubled for a large ensemble.

Joplin, Scott. *Two Rags, Volume 1*. arr. David Sabourin. Touch of Brass Music Corporation. Two euphoniums and two tubas. $10.00. Two movements: The Cascades; The Favorite Rag. The Cascades is recorded by the British Tuba Quartet, *In at the Deep End*, Heavyweight Records, Limited, HR008/D.

Joplin, Scott. *Two Rags, Volume 2*. arr. David Sabourin. Touch of Brass Music Corporation. Two euphoniums and two tubas. $10.00. Two movements: Pleasant Moments; Heliotrope Bouquet.

Kern, Jerome. *They Didn't Believe Me*. arr. Bill Holcombe. Musicians Publications. Two euphoniums and two tubas. 1991. $12.00. 2:45. IV. Part I: e♭–e', Part II: c–d', Part III: B♭–g, Part IV: F₁–e. A nice lyrical melody with lush jazz harmonies. The second section is in a faster swing style. This arrangement works quite well. Drums may be added for effect. Parts may be doubled for a large ensemble. Recorded by the British Tuba Quartet, *Euphonic Sounds*, Polyphonic Reproductions Limited, QPRZ 009D.

Key, Francis Scott. *The Star-Spangled Banner*. arr. Eugene Anderson. Anderson's Arizona Originals. Three euphoniums and one tuba. 1988. $5.00. 1:10. IV. Part I: B♭–b♭', Part II: B♭–d', Part III: G–f ', Part IV: F₁–f. Technically not very difficult, but requires a strong player on the first part because the five high b♭' occurs five times. Parts may be doubled for a large ensemble.

Khachaturian, Aram. *Sabeltanz*. arr. Bruno Seitz. Musikverlag Martin Scherbacher. Two euphoniums and two tubas. 1991. $13.50. 2:00. IV. Part I: B–g', Part II: F–d', Part III: F–b♭, Part IV: F₁–f. Khachaturian's well-known, fast-paced melody, often played as a solo. While most of the melodic work is in the first part, there are numerous tutti figures that make this technically challenging for all parts. Performers need to play cleanly and lightly. The first part is printed in treble clef. Parts may be doubled for a large ensemble.

King, Karl. *The Melody Shop.* arr. David R. Werden. Whaling Music Publishers. Two euphoniums and two tubas. 1987. $8.00. 2:30. IV–V. Part I: B♭–c", Part II: B♭–a♭', Part III: B♭–e♭', Part IV: A♭₁–e♭. Good arrangement of this famous march. Technically most demanding of the top two parts. The tessitura of the first part is especially high. The top two parts are printed in bass and treble clef. Challenging, but worth the effort. Recorded by the U.S. Armed Forces Tuba/Euphonium Ensemble, Mark Records, MW89MCD-8.

Kochan, Gunter. *Sieben Miniaturen für Vier Tuben* (Seven Miniatures for Four Tubas). Verlag Neue Musik Berlin. 1978. $11.00. 13:00. V. Part I: G♭₁–a♭', Part II: F₁–g♭', Part III: G₁–f♯', Part IV: F₁–e♭'. Seven movements: Moderato; Lento; Allegretto; Largo—Agitato; Allegro Molto; Adagio; Prestissimo. For Dietrich Unkrodt. A virtuosic piece. Extremely challenging rhythmically and in terms of range. All four parts were written with an F tuba in mind. Has some elements of "third-stream music" and contains many twentieth-century techniques, including multiphonics, flutter tonguing, and glissandos. Winner of first prize in the 1978 tuba quartet composition contest sponsored by The Los Angeles Tuba Quartet and the Mirafone Corporation. Recorded by Jim Self, *Changing Colors,* Summit Records, DCD 132.

Koltz, Michael. *Tuba Quartet: Study in Motion, Hymn, and Finale.* TUBA Press. Two euphoniums and two tubas. 1992. $12.00. 3:20. IV. Part I: F♯–e", Part II: D–f♯', Part III: d–f♯', Part IV: F₁–c'. Three movements: Motion; Hymn; Finale. The first movement is fast, multimetric, and technically challenging. The tessitura of the first part is high. Portions of the first part are printed in tenor clef. Very interesting writing.

Kosteck, Gregory. *Serene Voices: Music for Tuba Quartet.* Rochester Music Company, Incorporated. Four tubas. 1978. 5:15. V. Part I: D–f', Part II: A♯₁–e', Part III: G₁–d♭', Part IV: C₁–d'. Three movements: Motivic Theme; Fantasie; Canons. Composed especially for and dedicated to Sande MacMorran. Extreme ranges and technical demands required of all four parts. Very interesting writing. Requires four superb players.

Krebs, Johann Ludwig. *Fugue on B.A.C.H.* arr. Rayner Brown. Western International Music. Two euphoniums and two tubas. 1986. $7.00. 4:30. IV. Part I: D–g', Part II: c–e♭', Part III: E♭–d', Part IV: G₁–b♭. Nice arrangement of this fugue. At times the brief low tessitura of the first part can make this arrangement sound a bit muddy. Parts may be doubled with care.

Kreisler, Fritz. *Liebesleid.* arr. David Woodcock. Green Bay Music. Two euphoniums and two tubas. 1992. $22.00. 3:20. IV. Part I: c–b♭', Part II: d–g', Part III: G–b♭, Part IV: G₁–d. A moderate tempo waltz with the melody in the first and second parts. No significant technical problems. Parts may be doubled for a large ensemble.

Kresin, Willibald. *Chin Up!* ITC Editions Marc Reift. Two euphoniums and two tubas. 3:10. IV. Part I: d–b♭', Part II: B♭–a', Part III: E♭–d', Part IV: E♭1–a. Recorded by David LeClair, Contraband, *Swingin' Low,* Marcophon CD 940-2.

Kupferman, Meyer. *Kierkegaard for Four Tubas.* General Music Publishing. 1982. $8.00. 3:20. IV–V. Part I: C♯–e', Part II: E–e♭', Part III: C–d', Part IV: E♭₁–g♭. For Roger Bobo. A slow but very rhythmically challenging composition. Scoring is very thick. The first two parts could be played on euphonium. A conductor might be helpful for some quartets.

Lasso, Orlando di. *Mon Coeur se Recommende à Vous: Madrigal for Tuba Quartet.* arr. Jack Robinson. Whaling Music Publishers. 1979. $5.00. 2:00. III. Part I: e–f', Part II: c–b♭, Part III: F–f, Part IV: F₁–b♭. Playable by high school students if the first two parts are played by euphoniums. The madrigal has both chorale and imitative sections. Very easy, with some beautiful melodic sections. A very nice short concert piece. Parts may be doubled for a large ensemble. Recorded by the British Tuba Quartet, *Euphonic Sounds,* Polyphonic Reproductions Limited, QPRZ009D.

LeClair, David, arr. *Carnival of Venice.* ITC Editions Marc Reift. Two euphoniums and two tubas. 1990. 7:44. V. Part I: B♭–b♭', Part II: B♭–b♭', Part III: E♭₁–f', Part IV: E♭₁–b♭. Five movements: Introduction; Theme and Variation I; Rumba; Swing; Perpetuo Mobile. Written for the Contraband Tuba Quartet. According to the arranger, "This is a tour de force meant to display the varied technical and stylistic capabilities of a tuba quartet." A virtuosic piece, extremely challenging for all four parts. Recorded by the Monarch Tuba-Euphonium Quartet, *Metamorphosis,* IMPS Music; Contraband, *Swingin' Low,* Marcophon, CD 940-2.

Le Jeune, Claude. *Quand la Terre au Printemps.* Claude Le Jeune. Four tubas. 1974. 1:30. III–IV. Part I: F–b♭, Part II: E♭–g, Part III: E♭–e♭, Part IV: B♭–c.

Lemeland, Aubert. *Partita, Op. 109.* Four tubas.

Lennon, John, and McCartney, Paul. *Michelle.* arr. Rodger Vaughan. Rodger Vaughan. Two euphoniums and two tubas. 1990! $5.00. 2:10. III–IV. Part I: e–f', Part II: c–d♭', Part III: A–a, Part IV: A₁–f. For the TUBADOURS. A lyrical chorale-like arrangement of this Beatles' ballad. Most of the melody is in the top part. Playable by good high school players. Parts may be doubled for a large ensemble.

Lennon, John, and McCartney, Paul. *Yesterday.* arr. Akira Miyagawa. Yamaha Music Foundation. Two euphoniums and two tubas. 1990. $21.00. 3:00. IV. Part I: d–a', Part II: c♯–f', Part III: A–a', Part IV: A₁–f. A very interesting arrangement of this famous Beatles' melody. The first part has primary responsibility for the melody. Works quite well. Parts may be doubled for a large ensemble.

Leontovich, M. *Ukrainian Carol* (Ring Christmas Bells). arr. Peter Rauch. Ohio Valley Tuba Quartet Press. Two euphoniums and two tubas. 1990. $6.00. 1:10. IV. Part I: f–b♭', Part II: f–d', Part III: B♭–b♭, Part IV: B♭₁–B♭. Also known as *Carol of the Bells*. The melody, which is primarily in the first part, seems natural for a tuba/euphonium ensemble. Enjoyable to play. Parts may be doubled for a large ensemble.

Liszt, Franz. *Hungarian Rhapsodie No. 2*. arr. Bruno Seitz. Musikverlag Martin Scherbacher. Two euphoniums and two tubas. 1990. $13.50. 2:30. IV. Part I: B–b♭', Part II: F–f', Part III: B₁–d', Part IV: F₁–f. A fun arrangement of this famous Hungarian melody. No significant technical problems. Parts may be doubled for a large ensemble.

Livingston, Jay, and Evans, Ray. *Buttons and Bows*. arr. Paul Schmidt. Heavy Metal Music. Two euphoniums and two tubas. 1990. $7.00. 1:30. IV. Part I: F–g', Part II: G–e♭', Part III: A♭–e♭', Part IV: B♭₁–d. Most of this familiar melody is in the first part. Some range challenges for the third part. Fun to play. No score available. Parts may be doubled for a large ensemble.

London, Edwin. *Love in the Afternoon: A Tone Poem*. Henmar Press Incorporated. Four tubas. 1979. $17.50. 4:00. IV–V. Part I: C₁–d', Part II: C₁–e', Part III: D₁–e', Part IV: B₂–e♭'. A programmatic work depicting the physical act of love. The tessitura of all four parts is quite low. Many twentieth-century techniques, including flutter-tonguing, double/triple tonguing, extra wide vibrato, and a free nonmetered section. This humorous piece requires four strong players.

Lully, Jean-Baptiste. *Air from Amadis*. arr. Paul E. Hartin. Cellar Press. Four tubas. 1975. 2:00. III. Part I: d–f, Part II: A–c', Part III: F–a, Part IV: C–e. Works especially well for high schools if euphoniums are used on the first two parts; a college quartet should use four tubas. Good writing in this genre. Parts may be doubled for a large ensemble.

Lundquist, Torbjorn. *Triplet for Four Tubas*. Swedish Music Information Center. 1977. $12.00. 5:00. IV. Part I: d–a♭', Part II: G♯–d', Part III: E♭–c♯, Part IV: E₁–e♭. Three movements. The tessitura of the first part is high and may require an F tuba or euphonium. The first and third movements are slow, with contemporary harmonies. The second movement is fast, more rhythmically challenging, and multimetric.

Lupo, Thomas. *Fantasia for Basses*. arr. Paul Schmidt. Heavy Metal Music. Two euphoniums and two tubas. 1992. $5.00. 4:00. IV. Part I: A♭–g', Part II: A♭–g', Part III: F–c', Part IV: F₁–f. A slow tempo, but very polyphonic. Players need to count carefully. Parts are included to allow this to be played as a trio with just three euphoniums. No score available. Parts may be doubled for a large ensemble.

Lyon, Max J. *Suite for Four Bass Instruments*. Shawnee Press, Incorporated. Two euphoniums and two tubas, or one euphonium and three tubas. 1975. $10.00. 5:00. IV. Part I: c♯–a', Part II: B♭–e♭', Part III: C♯–b, Part IV: A♭₁–g♯. Three movements: Chorale; Rhyme; Motion. The second movement is in a moderate 3/8 and the last one alternates between 3/8, 5/8, and 7/8 in a lively tempo. The piece fits together well. Parts may be doubled for a large ensemble. Recorded by the Atlantic Tuba Quartet, Golden Crest Records, CRS 4173.

MacDowell, Edward. *To a Wild Rose*. arr. Peter Rauch. Ohio Valley Tuba Quartet Press. Two euphoniums and two tubas. 1990. $8.00. 1:45. IV. Part I: d–b♭', Part II: D–b♭', Part III: B♭₁–b♭, Part IV: F₁–b♭. All parts have the opportunity to play this very lyrical melody. Very traditional harmonies. Parts may be doubled for a large ensemble.

Mack, Cecil. *Charleston*. arr. Clifford Bevan and Paul Schmidt. Heavy Metal Music. Two euphoniums and two tubas. 1991. $7.00. 2:00. IV. Part I: B–f', Part II: F–e♭', Part III: B♭₁–b♭, Part IV: F₁–g♭. A fun arrangement of this melody associated with the Roaring 20s. Most of the melody is in the first part. Very syncopated, but no significant technical problems. No score available. Parts may be doubled for a large ensemble.

Mancini, Henry. *Baby Elephant Walk*. arr. Eugene Anderson. Anderson's Arizona Originals. Two euphoniums and two tubas. 1988. $5.00. 2:45. IV. Part I: G♯–a', Part II: F–a', Part III: F–d', Part IV: F₁–a. Fun arrangement of this familiar Mancini melody. The melody is primarily in the fourth part, alternating some with the first part. The first and second parts need a secure a'. Parts may be doubled for a large ensemble.

Mancini, Henry. *The Pink Panther*. arr. Jay Krush. Northride Music, Incorporated/Kendor Music, Incorporated. Two euphoniums and two tubas. 1982. $8.50. 3:45. III–IV. Part I: d–b♭', Part II: G–d♯', Part III: C–b♭, Part IV: E₁–e. A cute jazzy arrangement of this familiar tune. While not very fast, it is rhythmically challenging in a couple of sections. Fun to play and to listen to. Parts may be doubled for a large ensemble. Recorded by the British Tuba Quartet, *Euphonic Sounds*, Polyphonic Reproductions Limited, QPRZ009D; the Melton Tuba-Quartet, *Premiere*, Diavolo Records, DR-D-93-C-001; and the Northern Tuba Lights.

Marcellus, John, arr. *Quartets for Brass, Volume I: Easy-Intermediate*. CPP Belwin, Incorporated. Three euphoniums and one tuba. 1986. $6.50. 15 pp. II–III. Part I: d–a', Part II: B♭–f', Part III: A–

d', Part IV: B♭₁–f♯. Nine melodies from the Baroque and Classical periods. The parts are technically very easy. The third part may be played by an advanced tuba player, but is designed for a euphonium. The quartets start out very easy but get increasingly difficult. Treble-clef books are available, allowing these quartets to be played by almost any combination of brass instruments. Parts may be doubled for a large ensemble.

Marcellus, John, arr. *Quartets for Brass, Volume I: Intermediate.* CPP Belwin, Incorporated. Three euphoniums and one tuba. 1986. $6.50. 15 pp. III. Part I: e♭–b♭', Part II: c–g♭', Part III: A–f ', Part IV: F–e♭. Eight melodies from the Baroque, Classical, and Romantic periods. The tessitura of the first part is high, and that part also has most of the technical challenges. Treble-clef books are available, allowing these arrangements to be played by almost any combination of brass instruments. Parts may be doubled for a large ensemble.

Marcellus, John, arr. *Quartets for Brass, Volume I: Advanced.* CPP Belwin, Incorporated. Three euphoniums and one tuba. 1986. $6.50. 15 pp. III–IV. Part I: c–c", Part II: c–f ', Part III: F–d', Part IV: A₁–e. Seven melodies from the Baroque, Classical, and Romantic periods. The first part in two of the arrangements is printed in tenor clef. Treble-clef books are available, allowing these to be performed by any combination of brass instruments. Parts may be doubled for a large ensemble.

Marks, Johnny. *Rudolph the Red-Nosed Reindeer.* arr. Keith Mehlan. PP Music. Two euphoniums and two tubas. 1987. $10.00. 2:20. IV. Part I: c'–c", Part II: c–g', Part III: c–c', Part IV: B♭₁–d. Technically fairly easy, but the tessitura of the first part is quite high. The melody is featured in both euphonium and tuba parts. Parts may be doubled for a large ensemble.

Martino, Ralph. *Fantasy for Tuba/Euphonium Quartet.* PP Music. Two euphoniums and two tubas. 1992. $11.00. 5:00. IV. Part I: c♯–b', Part II: c♯–b♭', Part III: B₁–c♭', Part IV: F₁–a. Written for the U.S. Navy Band Tuba/Euphonium Quartet. A very driving and exciting composition. It is technically challenging and is often multimetric as it progresses through different styles. Works very well. Recorded by the British Tuba Quartet, *Elite Syncopations,* Polyphonic Reproductions Limited, QPRZ 012D; and the Monarch Tuba/Euphonium Quartet.

Massenet, J.E.F. *Aragonaise from "Le Cid"* (1885). arr. M.S. Erickson. PP Music. Two euphoniums and two tubas. 1986. $6.00. 1:45. IV. Part I: e♭–c", Part II: c–f ', Part III: E♭–a♭, Part IV: A♭₁–d♭. This marchlike composition is in 6/8 and is technically challenging for all four parts. Good writing. Recorded by the U.S. Navy Tuba Quartet, U.S. Navy Band Records; and the Monarch Tuba/Euphonium Quartet.

Masuda, Kouzou. *Suite for Four Tubas.* Tokyo Bari-Tuba Ensemble.

Matchett, Steve. *Sounding for Tuba/Euphonium Quartet.* RBC Publications. Two euphoniums and two tubas. 1991. $8.00. 7:20. IV. Part I: B♭–a♭', Part II: G–g♭', Part III: B♭₁–c♭', Part IV: F₁–f. Two movements: I; II. Dedicated to Joe Gannon, Robert Muñoz, Glenn Pistoll, and Larry Porter. The first movement is chorale-like. The second is very aggressive rhythmically, with several meter changes. All parts play portions of the melody and are technically challenging at times. The first and second parts are printed in treble and bass clef. Parts may be doubled for a large ensemble.

McAdams, Charles A., arr. *The Saints.* Encore Music Publishers. Two euphoniums and two tubas. 1991. $8.50. 1:30. III–IV. Part I: b♭–b♭', Part II: f–d', Part III: B♭–b♭, Part IV: B♭₁–e♭. A swing arrangement of this traditional Dixieland tune. A slower middle section features the first tuba part. Ranges are easy except for the b', the last note of the first part. Parts may be doubled for a large ensemble.

McCurdy, Gary, arr. *Saints.* TMC Publications Out of print. Four tubas. 1979. 1:30. II–III. Part I: B♭–f ', Part II: B♭–c', Part III: B♭–g, Part IV: B♭₁–e♭. Easily playable by high school students if the first two parts are played by euphoniums. Not technically difficult. Melody stays in the top two parts, and the moving bass line is doubled in the third and fourth parts. Parts may be doubled for a large ensemble.

McCurdy, Gary, arr. *Two Patriotic Songs.* TMC Publications. Out of print. Four tubas. 1976. 1:45. II–III. Part I: A–e♭', Part II: A–e♭', Part III: A₁–d, Part IV: A₁–B♭. Two movements: My Country 'Tis of Thee; Yankee Doodle. Very playable by junior or senior high school students if the first and second parts are played by euphoniums. No real technical difficulties. Fun for students to play. Parts may be doubled for a large ensemble.

McCurdy, Gary. *Bentonsport 1895.* TMC Publications. Out of print. Four tubas. 1981. 1:45. III–IV. Part I: B♭–f ', Part II: B♭–d, Part III: B♭–f, Part IV: B♭₁–b♭. A fast, old-fashioned sounding waltz. Can work well for high school ensembles if the first and second parts are played on euphonium. Not difficult rhythmically. Parts may be doubled for a large ensemble.

McCurdy, Gary. *Blues for Bill.* TMC Publications. Out of print. Four tubas. 1980. 2:45. III–IV. Part I: B♭–e♭', Part II: B♭–d', Part III: B♭₁–d, Part IV: A♭₁–d♭. Dedicated to the late William J. Bell. Basic twelve-bar blues in B♭. The middle sections may be used for improvised solos. A rhythm section may be added, though it is not called for in the score. Top two parts should be taken by euphoniums when played by high school students. Parts may be doubled for a large ensemble.

McCurdy, Gary. *Recitative for Four Tubas and Cantor.* TMC Publications. Out of print. Four tubas and male vocalist. 1971. 2:00. III. Part I: c–f, Part II: E–A, Part III: F#₁–E, Part IV: C₁–C. A short humorous piece.

McCurdy, Gary. *Things Are Tough All Over, Tubby.* TMC Publications Out of print. Four tubas and male vocalist. 1971. 2:00. III–IV. Part I: A–g, Part II: G–d, Part III: E–A, Part IV: C–E. A humorous piece.

McCurdy, Gary. *Two Folk Songs.* TMC Publications. Out of print. Two euphoniums and two tubas. 1973. 2:00. III. Part I: c–g', Part II: B♭–e♭', Part III: B♭₁–f, Part IV: A₁–c. Melody and harmony in a very traditional style. No technical problems. Parts may be doubled for a large ensemble.

Meacham, F.W. *American Tuba Patrol.* arr. Soichi Konagaya. Sonic Arts, Incorporated. Two euphoniums and two tubas. 1986. $12.00. 3:20. III–IV. Part I: B♭–g', Part II: F–e♭', Part III: B♭–g, Part IV: (E♭₁)F₁–e♭. An arrangement of the march "American Patrol." The melody is in both the tuba and the euphonium parts. No real technical or range problems. Fun to play. Parts may be doubled for a large ensemble.

Medek, Ivo. *Reflections.* T.A.P. Music. Four tubas, or with two euphoniums and two tubas. 1985. $6.00. 8:00. IV–V. Part I: A–a', Part II: E♭–a', Part III: F–d', Part IV: F₁–a. Three movements: I; II; III. Extreme technical and range demands of all four parts. Some contemporary harmonies.

Mehlan, Keith. *Bottoms Up Rag.* Horizon Press. Two euphoniums and two tubas. 1991. $8.00. 2:45. IV. Part I: e–c", Part II: e♭–a', Part III: f–b♭, Part IV: F₁–f. Each part has the opportunity to play this ragtime melody. The top two parts always have the melody together. Works very well. Parts may be doubled for a large ensemble. Recorded by the Monarch Tuba/Euphonium Quartet.

Mehlan, Keith. *Tubalation Rag.* PP Music. Two euphoniums and two tubas. 1987. $8.00. 3:00. IV. Part I: d–a', Part II: c–f ', Part III: B♭₁–b♭, Part IV: A₁–g. An original composition in the ragtime style of Scott Joplin. All four parts have an opportunity to play the solo. Fun to play. Parts may be doubled for a large ensemble.

Mehlan, Keith, arr. *Londonderry Air.* Horizon Press. Two euphoniums and two tubas. 1991. $7.00. 2:20. IV. Part I: c#–a', Part II: d–f ', Part III: G–d', Part IV: F₁–d. Begins with a euphonium solo, then the melody is traded among all four parts. The phrases are clearly marked and should be followed exactly. Works well for this genre. Parts may be doubled for a large ensemble. Recorded by the Monarch Tuba/Euphonium Quartet.

Mendelssohn, Felix. *Tarantella from Songs Without Words, Op. 182, No. 3.* arr. Norihisa Yamamoto. KIWI Music Press. Two euphoniums and two tubas. 1987. $3.95. 1:20. IV. Part I: e♭–b♭', Part II: B♭–d', Part III: F#–g, Part IV: A♭₁–e♭. Most of the melodic work is in the top three parts, with numerous rapid triplets. The first part is printed in tenor clef and requires a mute. Parts may be doubled for a large ensemble.

Minerd, Doug, arr. *Sea Tubas.* Whaling Music Publishers. Two euphoniums and two tubas. 1982. $12.50. 5:10. IV. Part I: F–g', Part II: F–e', Part III: A₁–c', Part IV: F₁–g'. A very cute medley of "What Do You Do with a Drunken Sailor," "Blow The Man Down," "Asleep in the Deep," "Barnacle Bill the Sailor," and "Shenandoah." Technically challenging for all parts, some potential for ensemble problems. Well received by audiences. The first part is printed in treble clef. Parts may be doubled for a large ensemble. Recorded by the Northern Tuba Lights.

Monaco, Keith. *You Made Me Love You.* arr. Bill Holcombe. Musicians Publications. Two euphoniums and two tubas. 1991. $12.00. 3:20. IV. Part I: d–a', Part II: B–e', Part III: D–c', Part IV: F#₁–d♭. Good arrangement of this old popular song. It begins in a slow ballad style then ends with an uptempo swing section. A good swing feel is necessary for all players. Drums may be added for effect. Recorded by the British Tuba Quartet, *Euphonic Sounds,* Polyphonic Reproductions, Limited, QPRZ 009D.

Monteverdi, Claudio. *Toccata for L'Orfeo.* arr. Donald C. Little. KIWI Music Press. Two euphoniums and two tubas. 1987. $2.75. 1:30. III. Part I: b♭–g', Part II: B♭–b♭, Part III: F–d, Part IV: B♭₁–B♭₁(e'). The fourth part has the same pitch for the entire piece, but it has optional divisi chords for up to four different pitches. Other possible instrumentations are one euphonium and three tubas, or four tubas. No real technical problems. All players read from a single score. Parts may be doubled for a large ensemble.

Morel, Jean-Marie. *Sept Péchés Capitau* (Seven Major Sins). Editions Robert Martin. Four tubas. 1989. $35.00. 9:45. IV–V. Part I: B♭–b♭', Part II: G–a♭', Part III: G#₁–g♭', Part IV: D₁–g♭'. Seven movements: L'Orgueil est une estime exagérée de soi-même (Pride is an inordinate self-esteem); L'Avarice nous fait user de nos richesses avec une excessive parcimonie (Avarice makes us dispose of our wealth with parsimony); La Luxure est un abandon immodéré aux plaisirs de la chair (Lust means unrestrained addition to the pleasures of the flesh); L'Envie consiste à s'attrister du bien et à se réjouir du mal qui arrive au prochain (Envy makes us sad about the good fortune of others and delights us about their misfortune); La Gourmandise est l'amour déréglé du manger et du boire (Greediness means an immoderate love for food and drink); La Colère est un mouvement déréglé de l'âme, qui fait que l'on s'emporte contre ce qui déplait (Anger is a disordered state of mind which makes us lose our temper when something displeases us); La Paresse est un amour excessif du repos (Laziness means an immoderate love for rest). A programmatic work describing in detail the seven major sins. The tessitura of all four parts is quite high. The top two parts will require F tubas or euphoniums. There are a few technical problems; players need to count carefully. The composer asks that the players "loudly give notice of the subtitles before each number."

Morley, Thomas. *April Is in My Mistress' Face.* arr. Michael Howard. BTQ Publications. Two euphoniums and two tubas. 1993. $8.00.

Morley, Thomas. *April Is in My Mistress' Face.* arr. Mark Nelson. Whaling Music Publishers. Two euphoniums and two tubas. 1991. $8.00. 1:30. III–IV. Part I: g–f ', Part II: d–c', Part III: G–f, Part IV: G_1–B♭. Good arrangement of this famous Renaissance madrigal. Easily playable by good high school students. Parts may be doubled for a large ensemble.

Mortaro, Antonia. *L'Albergona.* arr. Daniel Heiman. Heavy Metal Music. Two euphoniums and two tubas. 1991. $5.00. 1:45. IV. Part I: d–f ', Part II: F–c', Part III: E♭–g, Part IV: $A♭_1$–c. Not technically difficult, but very polyphonic. Players need to count carefully. No score available. Parts may be doubled for a large ensemble.

Mouret, Jean Joseph. *Fanfare and Rondeau from "Premiere Suite."* arr. Paul Schmidt. Heavy Metal Music. Two euphoniums and two tubas. 1991. $7.00. 2:45. IV. Part I: G–f ', Part II: G–f ', Part III: E–f ', Part IV: G_1–g. Two movements: Fanfare; Rondeau. The tessitura of the third part is high and may be played on euphonium. Movements work well together. No score available. Parts may be doubled for a large ensemble.

Mouret, Jean Joseph. *Rondeau.* arr. John Stevens. Encore Music Publishers. Two euphoniums and two tubas. 1988. $13.00. 1:30. IV. Part I: c–b♭', Part II: c–g', Part III: E–c', Part IV: G_1–e♭. A very playable arrangement of the famous *Masterpiece Theatre* theme. No significant technical or range problems. Parts may be doubled but care should be taken to keep the character light and the articulations clean.

Mozart, W.A. *Adoramus Te, Christe.* arr. Mark Nelson. Whaling Music Publishers. Two euphoniums and two tubas. 1991. $8.00. 1:30. III. Part I: d–f ', Part II: A–b♭, Part III: G–g, Part IV: G_1–B♭. Nice slow chorale. Very playable by high school students, but enough musical material for mature ensembles. Parts may be doubled for a large ensemble.

Mozart, W.A. *Allegro from Eine Kleine Nachtmusik, K. 525.* arr. Albert Peoples. Southern Music Company. Two euphoniums and two tubas. 1990. $12.50. 5:00. IV. Part I: D–e', Part II: B–e', Part III: A_1–d', Part IV: G_1–e. Good arrangement of this familiar melody. Most of the melodic work is in the first part. Parts may be doubled for a large ensemble.

Mozart, W.A. *Ave Verum.* arr. David Sabourin. Touch of Brass Music Corporation. Two euphoniums and two tubas. $6.50.

Mozart, W.A. *Ave Verum Corpus.* arr. Bruno Seitz. Musikverlag Martin Scherbacher. Two euphoniums and two tubas. 1993. $13.00. 2:30. III–IV. Part I: f–g', Part II: d–c', Part III: B♭–g, Part IV: B–d. Nice chorale with traditional harmonies. Ranges lie well for high school players. The euphonium parts are printed in bass and treble clef. Parts may be doubled for a large ensemble.

Mozart, W.A. *Das Butterbrot.* arr. Hans Dorner. Four tubas.

Mozart, W.A. *Eine Kleine Nachtmusik, K. 525.* arr. Grady Greene. Music Arts Company. Two euphoniums and two tubas. 1987. $15.00. 5:00. IV. Part I: c–g', Part II: G–d', Part III: B–g, Part IV: G_1–d. Moderate technical challenges and no real range problems. This arrangement works well for less-experienced performers. The top two parts are printed in bass and treble clef. Parts may be doubled for a large ensemble.

Mozart, W.A. *Eine Kleine Nachtmusik K. 525.* arr. Paul Schmidt. Heavy Metal Music. Two euphoniums and two tubas. 1991. $20.00. 22:30. IV–V. Part I: ($B♭_1$)E–g', Part II: C–f ', Part III: $B♭_1$–d', Part IV: $E♭_1$–g. Four movements: Allegro; Romance; Menuetto; Rondo (The complete Serenade). The melody is primarily in the euphoniums and most challenging for them. This arrangements works well for this genre. No score available. Parts may be doubled for a large ensemble.

Mozart, W.A. *Eine Kleine Nachtmusik.* arr. Bruno Seitz. Musikverlag Martin Scherbacher. Two euphoniums and two tubas. 1989. $15.00. 5:00. IV. Part I: B♭–g', Part II: F–d', Part III: B♭–g, Part IV: E_1–f. Arranged in the key of B♭, the tessitura of the first part is approachable by many high school students. The melody remains primarily in the euphoniums. Parts may be doubled for a large ensemble.

Mozart, W.A. *Eine Kleine Nachtmusik for Tuba Quartet.* arr. James Self. Basset Hound Music. 1976. $10.00. 5:00. IV. Part I: B♭–a', Part II: G–g', Part III: G_1–a, Part IV: F_1–a. The top two parts have a high tessitura and could be played by euphoniums. Technically challenging in some sections depending on the performance tempo. This transcription is in the key of C and works very well for two euphoniums and two tubas. Parts may be doubled for a large ensemble. Recorded by the TUBADOURS, *Ve Iss da Mighty TUBADOURS, Ya?,* Crystal Records, S421.

Mozart, W.A. *Fugue K. 401.* arr. Paul Schmidt. Heavy Metal Music. Two euphoniums and two tubas. 1990. $7.00. 4:00. IV. Part I: d–g', Part II: A–c', Part III: C♯–b, Part IV: G_1–d. All parts are challenging. Players need to count carefully and play cleanly and lightly. No score available.

Mozart, W.A. *March of the Priests from "The Magic Flute."* arr. Donald Sherman. Horizon Press. Two euphoniums and two tubas. 1991. $6.00. 3:00. III. Part I: c–f', Part II: A–d', Part III: A–f, Part IV: B♭₁–d. The melody is primarily in the top two parts. Not technically challenging, very appropriate for high school students. Parts may be doubled for a large ensemble.

Mozart, W.A. *Overture from the Marriage of Figaro.* arr. Ken Ferguson. BTQ Publications. Two euphoniums and two tubas. $15.00. Recorded by the British Tuba Quartet, *In At the Deep End,* Heavyweight Records Limited, HR008/D.

Mozart, W.A. *Overture to The Magic Flute.* arr. Jay Rozen. KIWI Music Press. Two euphoniums and two tubas. 1987. $10.00. 6:30. IV. Part I: B♭–b♭', Part II: B♭–g', Part III: B♭–f', Part IV: G–d♭'. Dedicated to the Little Big Horns. An arrangement for four male voices (TTBB) transcribed by an anonymous arranger in the 1830s. There are only moderate technical demands, but the tessitura of the third and fourth parts is high. However, the higher sections have optional section at the lower octave for younger players.

Mozart, W.A. *Serenade Eine Kleine Tuba Musik for Four Tubas, K. 525.* arr. John Fletcher. Emerson Edition Limited. 1984. $21.50. 5:00. IV. Part I: G–a, Part II: E–e', Part III: A₁–g, Part IV: G₁–e. Fine arrangement of this classic composition. The tessitura of the top two parts is high. According to the score, "the top part can be played on a euphonium, but a bass (F) tuba is preferable." There are several turns and trills in the top two parts. Parts may be doubled for a large ensemble. Recorded by the Melton Tuba Quartet, *Premiere,* Diavolo Records, DR-D-93-C-001; John Fletcher and the Philip Jones Brass Ensemble, Argo Records, ZRG895.

Mozart, W.A. *Turkish March K. 331.* arr. Keith Mehlan. PP Music. Two euphoniums and two tubas. 1986. $8.00. 3:30. IV. Part I: B♭–c", Part II: B♭₁–a', Part III: B♭₁–d', Part IV: B♭₁–b♭. Nice arrangement of this march. Tessitura is high for all four parts. Technically challenging if played at the tempo indicated. Recorded by the Monarch Tuba/Euphonium Quartet.

Mozart, W.A. *Two Waltzes, K. 600, Nos.1 and 4.* arr. Paul Schmidt. Heavy Metal Music. Two euphoniums and two tubas. 1990. $5.00. 2:50. III–IV. Part I: B♭–f', Part II: F–e♭', Part III: B♭₁–b♭, Part IV: A₁–e♭. All parts have an opportunity to play the melody. Technically not difficult, but the tessitura of the second part is low. No score available. Parts may be doubled for a large ensemble.

Muller, Francisco J. *The Death of Beowulf.* Francisco Muller. Four tubas. 1969. 5:50. IV. Part I: f–f', Part II: G♯–d♭, Part III: E–b, Part IV: E₁–d. Can also be performed with one euphonium and three tubas. While the tempo is slow, there are many meter changes and challenging rhythmic figures.

Nash, Richard. *Tublue.* Whaling Music Publishers. Four tubas, piano, bass and drums. 1979. $14.00. 5:30. IV. Part I: d–c"(d"), Part II: E–f' (g'), Part III: B–c' (d'), Part IV: (C₁) E₁–c'. Written for the Los Angeles Tuba Quartet: Roger Bobo, Tommy Johnson, Jim Self, and Don Waldrop. An original composition for tuba quartet in a jazz idiom. All players need good jazz phrasing and style. The tessitura of the first two parts is high. Other possible instrumentations are one euphonium and three tubas, or two euphoniums and two tubas. The first part is printed in treble clef.

Necke, Hermann. *Csikos Post.* arr. Soichi Konagaya. Sonic Arts, Incorporated. Two euphoniums and two tubas. 1986. $12.00. 2:20. IV. Part I: B–b', Part II: B–b, Part III: C–a, Part IV: E₁–f♯. Fun melody that is passed back and forth between the euphoniums and the tubas. A lot of sudden dynamic changes. No significant technical problems. Parts may be doubled for a large ensemble.

Necke, Hermann. *Csikos Post.* arr. Paul Schmidt. Heavy Metal Music. Two euphoniums and two tubas. 1990. $5.00. 1:45. IV. Part I: G–a♭, Part II: F♯–g', Part III: E♭–e♭', Part IV: F₁–e♭. Cute arrangement of the "Daffy Duck Song," associated with Disney cartoons. Fast-paced and technically challenging in some spots. No score available. Parts may be doubled for a large ensemble.

Newsome. *Dead Man's Cove.* Two euphoniums and two tubas.

Niehaus, Lennie. *All Too Soon.* Kendor Music, Incorporated. Two euphoniums and two tubas. 1986. $9.00. 2:45. IV. Part I: c♭–g', Part II: B–e♭', Part III: E♭–f, Part IV: A₁–d. A moderate jazz waltz with traditional eight-measure phrases. Melodies are tossed between all four parts. Ranges of the Niehaus arrangements are generally not a problem. Drums may be added for additional jazz feel. Parts may be doubled for a large ensemble.

Niehaus, Lennie. *Brass Tacks.* Kendor Music, Incorporated. Two euphoniums and two tubas. 1983. $9.00. 2:40. IV. Part I: e♭–a', Part II: c–f', Part III: F–g, Part IV: A₁–f. Swing style composition at a moderate tempo. While the euphoniums carry much of the responsibility, the two tuba parts have some written solos. Drum set may be added to enhance the swing feel. This arrangement works very well. Parts may be doubled for a large ensemble. Recorded by the Northern Tuba Lights.

Niehaus, Lennie. *Grand Slam.* Kendor Music, Incorporated. Two euphoniums and two tubas. 1986. $9.50. 3:00. IV. Part I: d–g', Part II: c–c', Part III: C–f, Part IV: A₁–c. An original bright swing composition. Range is not demanding on the first euphonium, and there are many tutti jazz rhythms between parts. All four parts share melodic responsibility. Parts may be doubled for a large ensemble. Recorded by the British Tuba Quartet, *Elite Syncopations,* Polyphonic Reproductions Limited, QPRZ012D.

Niehaus, Lennie. *Keystone Chops*. Kendor Music, Incorporated. Two euphoniums and two tubas. 1986. $9.00. 3:10. IV. Part I: Bb–f', Part II: Bb–c', Part III: C–gb, Part IV: G₁–c. A swing tune that works at a moderate or bright tempo, depending on the abilities of the ensemble. Range is not demanding, but players must be able to swing to make the composition work. One of the better examples of this genre. Parts may be doubled for a large ensemble.

Niehaus, Lennie. *Miniature Jazz Suite No. 1*. Kendor Music, Incorporated. Two euphoniums and two tubas. 1987. $12.00. 9:45. IV. Part I: Bb–g', Part II: Bb–c', Part III: Bb–f#, Part IV: (F₁) Ab₁–eb. Four movements: Tubalues; Bebop and Ballad; Change of Heart; Barimetricks. Each movement represents a contrast in jazz styles: swing, ballad, jazz waltz, and swing. The fourth movement has a section where players may improvise. Technically more challenging than the other Niehaus compositions. A good swing feel is necessary for an appropriate performance of this piece. Parts may be doubled for a large ensemble. Recorded by the Melton Tuba Quartet, *Premiere*, Diavolo Records, DR-D-93-C-001.

Niehaus, Lennie. *Pachyderms in Paradise*. Kendor Music, Incorporated. Two euphoniums and two tubas. 1989. $9.50. 3:00. IV. Part I: c–f', Part II: Bb–d', Part III: Bb₁–f, Part IV: A#₁–eb. Range and technical demands make this possible for a good high school quartet. A good swing feel is necessary. All parts have written solos as well as tutti rhythmic accompaniments. The first third of the piece changes meter frequently, but the quarter note remains constant. There is an eight-measure section with chord symbols in the third part for an improvised solo, or the player may play what is written in the part. Parts may be doubled for a large ensemble.

Niehaus, Lennie. *Sleeping Giants*. Kendor Music, Incorporated. Two euphoniums and two tubas. 1986. $9.50. 3:15. IV. Part I: c#–f', Part II: c–d', Part III: Eb–gb, Part IV: G₁–eb. An original swing tune, no real range demands, but players must have a good swing feel to make the piece work. Drum set may be added to help with tempo and style. Many tutti swing rhythms. Parts may be doubled for a large ensemble. Recorded by David LeClair, *Swingin' Low*, Marcophon.

Niehaus, Lennie. *Stephen Foster Jazz Suite*. Kendor Music, Incorporated. Two euphoniums and two tubas. 1989. $11.00. 8:30. IV. Part I: B–g', Part II: c–c', Part III: E–g, Part IV: (F₁)Ab₁–c. Four movements: Beautiful Dreamer; My Old Kentucky Home; Oh! Susanna; Camptown Races. The first and last movements are in a fast swing style. The second movement is a ballad, and the third is a jazz waltz. Range is not hard, but a good swing feel is necessary. The fourth movement contains a section with chord symbols in the first part for an improvised solo, or the player may elect to play the solo

written in the part. Any of the movements can stand alone in a concert. Parts may be doubled for a large ensemble.

Niehaus, Lennie. *Tuba Turf*. Cojarro Music, Incorporated (Kendor Music, Incorporated). Two euphoniums and two tubas. 1992. $10.00. 2:50. III–IV. Part I: e–f', Part II: c–c', Part III: D–f, Part IV: (F₁) Bb₁–d. A jazz waltz at a moderate tempo. Many tutti passages and sections where two parts pass the melody back and forth. The addition of a drum set would be beneficial. Parts may be doubled for a large ensemble.

Niehaus, Lennie. *Tubalation*. Kendor Music, Incorporated. Two euphoniums and two tubas. 1987. $9.50. 3:35. IV. Part I: f–g', Part II: d–d', Part III: Eb–f, Part IV: Bb₁–c. A moderate swing style composition. The melody is often passed back and forth between the euphoniums and the tubas. Each part has the opportunity to play the melody as a brief solo. No great technical or range demands.

Niehaus, Lennie. *Tubarometer*. Kendor Music, Incorporated. Two euphoniums and two tubas. 1991. $9.50. 2:55. IV. Part I: Bb–f', Part II: Bb–c', Part III: Bb₁–f, Part IV: Bb₁–db. As the "barometer" rises, so does the key. This moderate swing tune modulates from Bb to B then finally to the key of C. There are a few meter changes, but no real technical challenges. A good swing feel is essential. Parts may be doubled for a large ensemble.

Niehaus, Lennie. *A Whale's Tale*. Kendor Music, Incorporated. Two euphoniums and two tubas. 1984. $9.00. 2:20. IV. Part I: f–g', Part II: d–c', Part III: F–a, Part IV: A₁–eb. A jazz waltz at a moderate tempo. Individual parts are more exposed than in other Niehaus compositions, as the melody shifts from part to part. Not difficult technically, but challenging to count in three. Parts may be doubled for a large ensemble.

Niehaus, Lennie, arr. *A Christmas Jazz Medley*. Kendor Music, Incorporated. Two euphoniums and two tubas. 1984. $9.00. 3:30. IV. Part I: f–g', Part II: c–eb, Part III: F–g, Part IV: Bb₁–eb. A fun and lightly medley of "It Came Upon a Midnight Clear," "Hark the Herald Angels Sing," and "Jingle Bells." All Niehaus's compositions have very playable ranges for all the parts. Not technically difficult, but challenging to play cleanly and stylistically correct at the tempos indicated; moderate swing, ballad, and bright swing. Fun for both performers and audience. Parts may be doubled for a large ensemble.

Niehaus, Lennie, arr. *Spiritual Jazz Suite*. Kendor Music, Incorporated. Two euphoniums and two tubas. 1990. $17.00. 8:50. IV. Part I: F–g', Part II: F–d', Part III: C–f, Part IV: F₁–d. Four movements: Joshua Fought the Battle of Jericho; Deep River; Nobody Knows the Trouble I've Seen; Swing Low, Sweet Chariot. These well-known spirituals are set in contrasting styles: swing, ballad, jazz waltz, and swing. Range is not a problem, but a good swing feel is necessary. This arrangement works very well. Parts may be doubled for a large ensemble. Recorded by the British Tuba Quartet, *Euphonic Sounds,* Polyphonic Reproductions Limited, QPRA009D.

Niehaus, Lennie, arr. *Yuletide Jazz Suite No. 1.* Kendor Music, Incorporated. Two euphoniums and two tubas. 1990. $11.00. 7:30. IV. Part I: d–g', Part II: c–d', Part III: F–f, Part IV: (F$_1$)Ab$_1$–f. Four movements: Joy to the World; Angels We Have Heard on High; We Three Kings; O Little Town of Bethlehem. The first movement has a medium swing feel, the second is a ballad, the third is a jazz waltz, and the last is a bright swing. Good swing feel required to make this work. The movements can be performed separately. Parts may be doubled for a large ensemble.

Niehaus, Lennie, arr. *Yuletide Jazz Suite No. 2.* Kendor Music, Incorporated. Two euphoniums and two tubas. 1993. $16.00. 7:45. IV. Part I: c#–g', Part II: c–eb', Part III: D–f, Part IV: G$_1$–d. Three movements: Deck the Halls; What Child Is This?; The Wassail Song. In a moderate swing, jazz waltz, and bright swing respectively. A good swing feel is necessary from all players. Drums may be added for effect. All parts have the opportunity to play the melody. Parts may be doubled for a large ensemble.

Nilovic, Janko. *Variations aux Quatre Vents.* Symphony Land. Four tubas. 1980. 6:30. III–IV. Part I: c–a', Part II: G#–f#', Part III: F#–c#', Part IV: F#$_1$–g. The first two parts could be played on the euphonium for use by high school students. There are no technical demands; the harmony is very dissonant.

Orzechowski, H. *Grey Horse Polka.* arr. Paul Schmidt. Heavy Metal Music. Two euphoniums and two tubas. 1990. $7.00. 1:30. IV. Part I: Bb–eb', Part II: Bb–eb', Part III: Db–ab, Part IV: G$_1$–e'. A medium difficult polka. The tessitura of part II is higher than that of part I. No score available. Parts may be doubled for a large ensemble.

Ott, Joseph. *7 22 73 forTuba Quartet.* Claude Benny Press. Two euphoniums, two tubas, and tape. 1973. $10.00. 9:30. IV. Part I: d–a', Part II: B–g', Part III: A–b', Part IV: F$_1$–g. Three movements: I; II; III. Commissioned by R. Winston Morris. Title reflects the date the composition was completed. A taped accompaniment is used in movements I and III. Very contemporary (half-valve notes, hissing through the instrument, etc.) and very dissonant. More appropriate for a large ensemble than for a quartet.

Owen, Blythe. *Saraband and Gigue for Tuba Quartet Op. 43.* Hall-Orion Music Press. 1973. $6.00. 4:00. III–IV. Part I: c–f ', Part II: Eb–eb', Part III: B$_1$–a, Part IV: E$_1$–c. The first and second part may be played on euphonium for high school students, F tuba for college students. The tessitura of the

fourth part remains quite low and will require very cleanly playing. A nice light work for tuba quartet. Parts may be doubled for a large ensemble.

Palestrina, Giovanni Pierluigi. *Motet "Christe, Lux Vera."* arr. Randall Block. The Musical Evergreen (Philharmusica). Four tubas. 1976. $8.50. 1:45. III. Part I: Ab–ab, Part II: Eb–c, Part III: Bb$_1$–eb, Part IV: Bb$_1$–Ab. A polyphonic work, but not difficult. Ranges are limited, and the piece is very appropriate for high school students. Players must count carefully. Parts may be doubled for a large ensemble.

Palestrina, Giovanni Pierluigi. *Ricercar del Primo Tuono.* arr. Paul Schmidt. Heavy Metal Music. Two euphoniums and two tubas. 1992. $5.00. 2:00. III–IV. Part I: f–f ', Part II: G–c', Part III: F–a, Part IV: G$_1$–d. Very polyphonic. All parts are of equal difficulty. A limited range, very appropriate for high school ensembles. No score available. Parts may be doubled for a large ensemble.

Payne, Frank Lynn. *Quartet for Tubas.* Shawnee Press, Incorporated. Four tubas. 1971. $18.00. 11:00. IV. Part I: G–e', Part II: F–d', Part III: B$_1$–d', Part IV: D$_1$–a. Three movements: Allegro; Andante; Vivo. The first part has a high tessitura. No real technical problems, but requires four strong players. Good challenging writing for tuba quartet. Awarded first place in the 1969 International Tuba Ensemble Composition Contest sponsored by the University of Miami School of Music. Recorded by the University of Michigan Tuba and Euphonium Ensemble, University of Michigan Records, SM0011; the University of Miami Tuba Ensemble, Miami United Tuba Ensemble Society, 14568; and the Melton Tuba Quartet, *Premiere,* Diavolo Records, DR–D–93–C–001.

Payne, Frank Lynn. *Tubaphonic Suite.* T.A.P. Music. Four tubas. 1989. Parts $7.00, score $4.00. 15:00. IV. Part I: D–f ', Part II: A–f ', Part III: E$_1$–d', Part IV: D$_1$–a. Six movements: Concept; Divergence; Exploration; Postulate; Retreat Canon; Synthesis. A massive work. The first and last movements change meter frequently and are very contemporary. Texture is very thick at times. Range and technical demands will require four strong players.

Payne, Roger. *Suite in Blue.* Fortune Music Publications. Four tubas. 1976. $10.00. 7:30. IV. Part I: C–bb, Part II: D–f#, Part III: F$_1$–f, Part IV: G$_1$–d. Three movements: March Two-step; Meander; Danse Triste. Commissioned by the William Davis Construction Group Band. Dedicated to Charlie Longridge and Phil Porter. The score and parts are printed in treble clef, as the first two parts are for Eb tubas and the third and fourth are for Bb tubas. Some technical problems, especially in the third movement. Fairly traditional harmonies. Players must count carefully.

Petrie, H. W. *Asleep in the Deep.* arr. Paul Schmidt. Heavy Metal Music. Two euphoniums and two tubas. 1990. $5.00. 1:20. III–IV. Part I: (F₁)F–d', Part II: G–c', Part III: G–bb, Part IV: F₁–f. Written for euphonium or ophicleide solo with accompaniment. No significant technical problems; very playable by high school students. No score available. Parts may be doubled for a large ensemble.

Pezel, John. *Sonata No. 2.* arr. John Stevens. Encore Music Publishers. Two euphoniums and two tubas. 1988. $10.00. 2:00. III–IV. Part I: e–f ', Part II: G–c', Part III: C–g, Part IV: F₁–g. A single movement typical of Renaissance instrumental music. The first section is in 4/4, then proceeds to 3/2. Very playable by high school or university ensembles. Parts may be doubled for a large ensemble.

Pierpont, James. *Jingle Bells.* arr. James A. Garrett. James Garrett. Two euphoniums and tubas. 1990. $10.00. 1:00. III–IV. Part I: Bb–bb', Part II: Bb–eb', Part III: Bb₁–bb, Part IV: Bb₁–g. A fun arrangement of this popular Christmas song. No significant technical challenges. Other than a couple of bbs, range is not a problem.

Pierpont, James. *Jingle Bells.* arr. Rodger Vaughan. Rodger Vaughan. Two euphoniums and two tubas. 1990. $5.00. 1:10. III–IV. Part I: a–bb', Part II: f–f ', Part III: F–bb, Part IV: Bb₁–g. For the TUBADOURS. The melody is divided between the first and fourth parts. The arrangement works quite well. No score available. Parts may be doubled for a large ensemble.

Pitoni, Giuseppe. *Cantate Domini and What Child Is This?* arr. Paul Schmidt. Heavy Metal Music. Two euphoniums and two tubas. 1991. $3.00. 1:45. III. Part I: c–eb', Part II: Bb–c', Part III: F–f, Part IV: G₁–d. Two famous Christmas melodies. Very appropriate for high school students. No score available. Parts may be doubled for a large ensemble.

Powell, Baden. *Bocoxe.* arr. Gary Buttery. Whaling Music Publishers. Two euphoniums and two tubas. 1978. $5.00. 1:45. IV. Part I: c–g'(c"), Part II: A–eb', Part III: F–c', Part IV: F₁–f. A lively melody that switches from 6/8 to 2/4 to 3/4. All parts have the opportunity to play the melody. Parts may be doubled for a large ensemble. Recorded by the Atlantic Tuba Quartet, *Euphonic Sounds,* Golden Crest, CRS 4173; and the British Tuba Quartet, *Euphonic Sounds,* Polyphonic Reproductions Limited, QPRZ009D.

Praetorius, Michael. *Three Bourées from "Terpsichore."* arr. Paul F. Hartin. Cellar Press. Four tubas. 1975. 4:00. IV. Part I: d–e', Part II: B–a, Part III: F#–f, Part IV: G₁–G. Three pieces in the same style. Harmony is very traditional. A little muddy at times.

Presser, William. *Serenade for Four Tubas.* Tenuto Publications. 1972. $6.00. 6:00. IV. Part I: E–c', Part II: Bb₁–bb, Part III: F₁–f, Part IV: d₁–eb. Three movements: Allegretto; Adagio (Canon); Allegro. No outstanding range or technical problems, how-

ever the fourth part gets quite low (D₁). Good writing for tuba quartet. Received third place in the 1969 University of Miami International Tuba Ensemble Composition Contest. The Allegro was recorded by the University of Michigan Tuba and Euphonium Ensemble, Golden Crest Records, CRS-4145.

Proctor, Simon. *Light Metal.* Heavy Metal Music. Two euphoniums and two tubas. 1992. $10.00. 11:30. IV. Part I: c–g', Part II: A–f ', Part III: C–b, Part IV: F–f. Four movements: Talatasco; Schmaltz Waltz; Chorale; Jazz Fugue. For the Heavy Metal Society Tuba Quartet and published in the memory of our friend Christopher Monk. A challenging composition encompassing a wide variety of styles. A good jazz style is necessary for all players. All parts have solos. Parts may be doubled for a large ensemble.

Puccini, Giocomo. *Turandot: Two Choruses.* arr. Donald Sherman. Horizon Press. Two euphoniums and two tubas. 1991. $7.00. 2:00. III. Part I: c–g', Part II: Ab–c', Part III: Db–f, Part IV: F₁–f. A single movement containing two Puccini melodies. All parts have the opportunity to play the melody. No significant technical problems. Parts may be doubled for a large ensemble.

Pullig, Ken. *Dances; Four Tubas: A Short Piece for Tuba Quartet.* TUBA Press. Two euphoniums and two tubas. 1993. $15.00. 5:30. IV. Part I: d–bb", Part II: F–a', Part III: F–c', Part IV: (G₁) Bb₁–eb. Good writing for tuba/euphonium quartet. Several tempo and meter changes and some technical challenges. All four parts are interesting. Tessitura of the first part is high. Parts may be doubled for a large ensemble.

Purcell, Henry. *Two Trumpet Tunes and Ayre.* arr. Karl Humble. T.A.P. Music. Two euphoniums and two tubas. 1989. $5.00. 3:20. III–IV. Part I: Bb–g', Part II: A–eb', Part III: Bb₁–f, Part IV: A₁–eb. Three movements: Tune I; Ayre; Tune II. The first tune is the famous "Trumpet Voluntary," which was actually written by Jeremiah Clarke (?–1707). No significant technical or range problems. The movements may be played in any order or individually. Parts may be doubled for a large ensemble.

Purcell, H., and Clarke, J. *Two Trumpet Tunes and Trumpet Voluntary.* arr. Peter Rauch. Ohio Valley Tuba Quartet Press. Two euphoniums and two tubas. 1988. $12.00. 6:20. IV. Part I: A–b', Part II: Bb–b', Part III: Bb₁–a (d'), Part IV: (C₁) G₁–A. Three movements: Trumpet Tune A; Trumpet Tune B; Trumpet Voluntary. Very usable arrangement of these three familiar Baroque trumpet melodies. Most of the melodic responsibility is in the first two parts. Precision in the dotted-eighth-and-sixteenth-note figures and execution of trills is vital. Parts may be carefully doubled for a large ensemble.

Pygott, Richard. *Quid Petis O Fili.* arr. Michael Thornton. Queen City Brass Publications. Four tubas. 1980. $6.50. 3:10. III–IV. Part I: f–d', Part II: A–c', Part III: D–f, Part IV: B♭–d. The first and second parts could be played by euphonium in high school ensembles. A lot of imitation typical of Renaissance instrumental music. Parts may be doubled for a large ensemble.

Ramsoe, Wilhelm. *Quartet for Brass.* arr. Gary Buttery. Whaling Music Publishers. Two euphoniums and two tubas. 1978. $12.00. 9:00. IV–V. Part I: A–a', Part II: G–g', Part III: E–g', Part IV: G₁–e♭'. Three movements: Scherzo; Andante quasi Allegretto; Allegro Molto. Three contrasting movements based on the works of the French composer Ramsoe. Tessitura of all four parts is high. All parts are rhythmically and musically challenging, especially at the suggested tempos. Recorded by the Atlantic Tuba Quartet, *Euphonic Sounds,* Golden Crest, CRS 4173; the British Tuba Quartet, *Euphonic Sounds,* Polyphonic Reproductions Limited, ♯QPRZ009D; the Melton Tuba Quartet, *Premiere,* Diavolo Records, DR-D-93-C-01; U.S. Coast Guard Tuba/Euphonium Quartet, *Soloists and Chamber Players,* U.S.C.G., 122678-A; U.S. Navy Tuba/Euphonium Quartet, U.S. Navy Band Records.

Randalls, Jeremy. *Tuba Quartet.* Scottish Music Information Centre. Four tubas. 1986. $8.00. 7:15. IV. Part I: E♭–f ', Part II: C♯–e', Part III: G₁–e', Part IV: D₁–d♭'. To Willie Young. Allegro section is multimetric and can be challenging. All parts have an opportunity to play the melody. The top two parts have a high tessitura and would be most appropriate on F tubas or perhaps euphoniums.

Raposa, Joe. *Sesame Street.* arr. Rodger Vaughan. Rodger Vaughan. Two euphoniums and two tubas. 1988. $5.00. 2:30. IV. Part I: f–a♭', Part II: B♭–e', Part III: B♭–c', Part IV: F₁–f. The theme from the popular children's television show. The syncopated melody is bounced between the first and third parts. Fun to play. No score available. Parts may be doubled for a large ensemble.

Rauch, Peter. *Folksong Medley.* Ohio Valley Tuba Quartet Press. Two euphoniums and two tubas. 1991. $12.00. 4:00. IV. Part I: B♭–b♭', Part II: B♭–a', Part III: C–b♭, Part IV: E♭₁–f. A medley of "Camptown Races," "Oh Suzanna," "My Old Kentucky Home," "Shennandoah," and "Dixie." All parts have an opportunity to play the melody. Some mixed meters. Parts may be doubled for a large ensemble.

Rauch, Peter, arr. *Greensleeves.* Ohio Valley Tuba Quartet Press. Two euphoniums and two tubas. 1990. $10.00. 2:00. IV. Part I: B–c", Part II: B–b♭', Part III: E–g, Part IV: D₁–f. All four parts have an opportunity to play the melody. Not technically difficult, but the tessitura of the first and second parts is high. Parts may be doubled for a large ensemble.

Rauch, Peter, arr. *With a Little Bit of Flash.* Ohio Valley Tuba Quartet Press. Two euphoniums and two tubas. 1992. $12.00. 3:45. IV–V. Part I: c–b♭', Part II: B♭–b♭', Part III: F₁–a♭, Part IV: E₁–a. A fanfare with many driving eighth- and sixteenth-note patterns. The accompaniment is very syncopated, and the meter changes frequently. Most demanding technically of the first part. An exciting piece; requires four strong players.

Read, Thomas. *Meet These People.* American Composers Alliance. Two euphoniums and two tubas. 1987. $20.00. 7:00. V. Part I: B♭₁–a♭', Part II: F♯₁–f♯', Part III: c–g', Part IV: C₁–g'. Written for the University of Vermont Tuba/Euphonium Ensemble. A very technically challenging piece with extensive range demands of all parts. Very contemporary harmonies. Players are directed to sit very far apart on the stage to surround the audience with sound.

Reicha, Anton. *Four Quartets.* arr. David R. Werden. Whaling Music Publishers. Two euphoniums and two tubas. 1983. $9.50. 8:20. IV. Part I: B♭–b♭', Part II: F–b♭', Part III: F–g♭', Part IV: B♭₁–g. Four movements: Theme and Variations; Minuetto; Andante; Allegro. All parts are technically challenging, though most of the melodic responsibility is in the first part. The last movement features a driving syncopated melody. The first part is printed in treble clef. Parts may be doubled for a large ensemble.

Reiche, Gottfried. *Sonata No.15.* arr. Paul Schmidt. Heavy Metal Music. Two euphoniums and two tubas. 1991. $5.00. 3:10. III. Part I: d–f ', Part II: A–g, Part III: B♭₁–d, Part IV: F₁–d♭. Two movements: Tenuto; Allegro. The first movement is in a chorale style. The second movement is very polyphonic, but not technically challenging. No score available. Parts may be doubled for a large ensemble.

Reiche, Gottfried. *Sonata No. 18.* arr. Paul Schmidt. Heavy Metal Music. Two euphoniums and two tubas. 1991. $5.00. 3:30. III–IV. Part I: B♭₁–g', Part II: F–a, Part III: B♭₁–f, Part IV: F₁–d. The texture is much less polyphonic than what is typical for this style period. Not technically difficult, very appropriate for high school ensembles. No score available. Parts may be doubled for a large ensemble.

Reinhardt, Django. *Nuages.* John Wessner. Two euphoniums and two tubas. 1993. $5.00. 2:00. IV. Part I: d–e♭", Part II: B–c", Part III: G₁–d'(a'), Part IV: G₁–b. The tessitura of the top two parts is high. The fourth part contains a section for an improvised jazz solo. Rhythm parts are included.

Richardson, Sharon. *Three Statements for Four Tubas.* Southern Music Company. Out of print. 1971. 5:00. IV. Part I: A–f ', Part II: C–e', Part III: C–d', Part IV: F₁–g. Could also be performed with euphonium on the first or first and second parts. The second movement requires the second and third players to sing the syllable "doo" through their instrument. The last movement is the most challenging technically.

Rimmer, Frederick. *The Mery Men*. Two euphoniums and two tubas.

Rimsky-Korsakov, Nicholai. *Procession of the Nobles*. arr. David Butler. TUBA Press. Two euphoniums and two tubas. 1993. $15.00. 3:30. IV. Part I: G–bb', Part II: Ab–eb', Part III: Ab–c', Part IV: Ab₁–ab. Written for R. Winston Morris and the Tennessee Technological University Tuba Ensemble. Fine arrangement of this familiar melody. Technically challenging for all parts. Requires eight players (two on a part), as all parts have numerous divisi sections.

Rimsky-Korsakov, Nikolas. *Dance of the Tumbler*. arr. Frank H. Seikman. Brelmat Music. Three euphoniums and tuba. 1986. 1986. $9.00. 3:30. IV. Part I: Bb–bb', Part II: F–bb', Part III: F–g', Part IV: (F₁) Bb₁–bb. A fun melody in a lively polyphonic texture. All four parts have some technical challenges. Parts may be doubled for a large ensemble.

Roark, Larry. *Intonation I*. T.U.B.A. Journal. Two euphoniums and two tubas. 1978. $7.50. 1:45. III. Part I: bb–g', Part II: eb–c', Part III: G–f, Part IV: C–d. Very playable by high school ensembles. Very pleasant quartal harmonies. Not technically demanding. Parts may be doubled for a large ensemble. Written as part of the T.U.B.A. GEM Series and published in the *T.U.B.A. Journal*, Vol. 7, no. 1.

Roark, Larry. *Intonation II*. Larry Roark. Two euphoniums and two tubas. 1:00. IV. Part I: f–bb', Part II: c–eb', Part III: F#–ab', Part IV: Gb₁–db. A nice chorale-like composition. Similar in style to *Intonation I*, but the range is slightlyly more demanding. Parts may be doubled for a large ensemble.

Robertson, Donna N. *Lullaby*. TMC Publications. Out of print. Four tubas. 2:00. III–IV. Part I: d–f ', Part II: c–a, Part III: D–f, Part IV: A₁–d. Based on a thirteenth-century Noel. Easily playable by high school students if the first or first and second parts were played on euphonium. Very simple rhythmically. Parts may be doubled for a large ensemble.

Rodgers, Thomas. *Air for Tuba Ensemble*. TUBA Press. Two euphoniums and two tubas. 1993. $6.00. 4:00. IV. Part I: d–bb', Part II: d–f ', Part III: D–c', Part IV: G₁–g. Written for R. Winston Morris and the Tennessee Technological University Tuba Ensemble. No real technical problems, challenges are with range and playing lyrically. Musically very rewarding for both performers and audience. Written for and works best with a large ensemble. Originally copyrighted in 1981 and published by Laissez-Faire Music Publishing Company.

Rodgers, Thomas. *Preludio*. Two euphoniums and two tubas. 2:00. III–IV. Part I: db–e ', Part II: Bb–bb,

Part III: G–a, Part IV: F₁–d. Written for R. Winston Morris and the Tennessee Technological University Tuba Ensemble. Chorale-like with at least one part moving by itself on each beat of the measure. Many dynamic contrasts. Appropriate for high school students, especially to teach intonation and phrasing. Parts may be doubled for a large ensemble.

Rodgers, Thomas. *Thematic Permutations*. TUBA Press. Two euphoniums and two tubas. 1993. $10.00. 6:40. IV. Part I: Ab–bb', Part II: F–gb', Part III: A₁–c', Part IV: F₁–a. Written for R. Winston Morris and the Tennessee Technological University Tuba Ensemble. A single movement with contrasting sections based on one main theme with several polyphonic sections. Several sections of the first part are notated in tenor clef. Good writing for tuba quartet. Originally published by Laissez-Faire Music Publishing Company and copyrighted in 1981. Parts may be doubled for a large ensemble.

Roikjer, Kjell. *Divertimento, Op. 70*. Kjell Roikjer. Four tubas. 1977. 9:00. IV. Part I: G–f ', Part II: D–c', Part III: C–bb, Part IV: Eb₁–gb. Five movements: Intrada; Intermezzo; Canzonetta; Carillon; Finale. A very interesting and technically challenging composition. The second movement is multimetric but not overly difficult. Requires four strong players.

Roikjer, Kjell. *Polka*. Kjell Roikjer. Four tubas and piano. 1975. IV. Part I: Bb–c', Part II: G–a, Part III: Bb₁–f, Part IV: G₁–b. A fun arrangement available with piano or concert band accompaniment. All four parts have brief technical solo sections.

Roikjer, Kjell. *Ten Inventions for Four Tubas, Op. 64*. Engström and Södring Musikverlag. 1990. 9 pp. IV. Part I: B–gb', Part II: E–db', Part III: C–c', Part IV: E₁–d'. The first part should be played on an F tuba or perhaps a euphonium. The movements contrast in tempo, meter, and key. They may be selected to form a suite or performed individually. Requires skilled performances by all four players.

Rollin, Robert. *Quodlibitus Bibendum (The Drinking Quodlibet) for Tuba Quartet*. Seesaw Music Corporation Publishers. Four tubas. 1983. $24.00. 3:00. IV. Part I: Bb–g#', Part II: F#–b, Part III: Bb₁–f#', Part IV: G₁–b. For John Turk, Ronald Bishop, Tucker Jolly, and Sumner Erickson. A euphonium may be used on the first part. The piece contains small quotations of Irish, French, English, German, and Scottish drinking songs. Not difficult technically, but the tessitura of the first part is high. Parts may be doubled for a large ensemble.

Rollin, Robert. *The Raven and the First Man*. Two euphoniums and two tubas.

Rosenberger, W. *The Lyric Tuba Waltz*. Musikverlag Martin Scherbacher. Two euphoniums and two tubas. 1993. $15.00. 2:20. IV. Part I: A–bb', Part II: A–g', Part III: D#–b, Part IV: B₂–g. All parts have an opportunity to play portions of the melody.

No significant technical problems. The top part is printed in bass and treble clef. Parts may be doubled for a large ensemble.

Ross, Walter. *Shapes in Bronze.* TUBA Press. Two euphoniums and two tubas. 1992. $15.00. 11:00. IV. Part I: B♭–g', Part II: F–f ', Part III: G₁–b♭, Part IV: F₁–g. For R. Winston Morris and the Tennessee Technological University Tuba Ensemble. Four contrasting movements, with the last one the most technically demanding. The tubas frequently have the melody. Works very well, especially with the parts doubled.

Rossini, Gioacchino. *Allegro from William Tell Overture.* arr. Peter Rauch. Ohio Valley Tuba Quartet Press. Two euphoniums and two tubas. 1992. $10.00. 7:30. IV. Part I: A–b♭', Part II: G–e♭', Part III: B♭₁–c', Part IV: E♭₁–e♭. Most of the melodic responsibility is in the top two parts, but the technical challenges are greatest on the top part. All players need accurate multiple tonguing skills. Requires four strong players.

Rossini, Gioacchino. *Overture to Wilhelm Tell.* arr. Bruno Seitz. Musikverlag Martin Scherbacher. Two euphoniums and two tubas. 1990. $13.50. 1:45. IV. Part I: B♭–c", Part II: A–e♭', Part III: D–c', Part IV: E♭₁–e♭. The first part is the most challenging technically and has a high tessitura. All parts need to be played lightly and cleanly. Parts may be doubled for a large ensemble.

Rossini, Gioacchino. *Petit Caprice: In the Style of Offenbach.* arr. Ron Davis. TUBA Press. Two euphoniums and two tubas. 1993. $5.00. 3:20. IV. Part I: B♭–c", Part II: E♭–g', Part III: B♭₁–c', Part IV: E♭₁–f♯. A very lively piece, challenging for all parts. The tessitura of the first part is high, and the fourth part is quite low. Works well. Parts may be doubled for a large ensemble.

Rossini, Gioacchino. *William Tell Overture (abridged).* arr. Paul Schmidt. Heavy Metal Music. Two euphoniums and two tubas. 1991. $7.00. 1:30. IV. Part I: F–g', Part II: F–f ', Part III: F–c♯', Part IV: F₁–f. A shortened version of this famous overture. The melody is passed between the first, second, and third parts. Works very well for this genre and is fun to play. No score available. Parts may be doubled for a large ensemble.

Russell, Armand. *Transforming Realms.* Armand Russell. Two euphoniums and two tubas. 1983. $15.00. 9:00. IV. Part I: F–b♭', Part II: F♯–g', Part III: G₁–c', Part IV: F♯₁–a♭. Technically challenging with several meter changes. Very contemporary harmonies, many polychords and dissonant intervals.

Saint-Saëns, Camille. *Adagio from Symphony No. 3.* arr. Steve Hanson. KIWI Music Press. Two euphoniums and two tubas. $5.00. 3:00. III–IV. Part I: d–g', Part II: c–f ', Part III: C–d', Part IV: B♭₁–d♭. Nice arrangement of this familiar melody. No real technical or range problems. Parts may be doubled for a large ensemble.

Saint-Saëns, Camille. *Chumbo the Elephant.* arr. Donald W. Stauffer. Stauffer Press. Two euphoniums and two tubas. 1992. $10.00. 1:10. IV. Part I: B♭–a', Part II: B♭–e', Part III: B♭₁–a♭, Part IV: (E₁) A♭₁–e. A transcription of the elephant feature from *Carnival of the Animals* . There are no significant technical problems, but the melody is in the bottom part and the tessitura is low. This arrangment is also available for tuba and band.

Saint-Saëns, Camille. *Three Pieces from "Carnival of the Animals."* arr. Maurice Bale. Godiva Music. Four tubas. 1994. $9.00. 6:00. IV. Part I: F–e♭', Part II: F–b♭, Part III: C–e♭, Part IV: (D₁) F₁–c. Three movements: The Elephant; Tortoises; The Swan.

Sample, Steve, arr. *Cole Porter Medley.* T.A.P. Music. Two euphoniums, two tubas, piano/guitar, bass, and drums. 1978. $22.00. 3:45. IV–V. Part I: f–c", Part II: G–a♭', Part III: E♭–f ', Part IV: C–a. Written for R. Winston Morris and the Tennessee Technological University Tuba Ensemble. An excellent arrangement of "Easy to Love," "So in Love," and "You'd Be So Nice to Come Home To." The arrangement features both swing and bossa nova styles. All parts have interesting soli sections. Players need a good swing feel. The top three parts have several divisi sections, so seven players are needed to play all the parts. Requires strong players because of the high tessitura of the top three parts. Very enjoyable for performers and audience. Parts may be further doubled for a large ensemble. Recorded by the Tennessee Technological University Tuba Ensemble, KM Records, KM 4631.

Sample, Steve, arr. *Ellington Medley.* SOS Music Services. Out of print. Two euphoniums, two tubas, piano/guitar, bass, and drums. 1974. 12:00. IV. Part I: d–c", Part II: B♭–f♯', Part III: B♭₁–c', Part IV: A₁–a. Written for R. Winston Morris and the Tennessee Technological University Tuba Ensemble. One of the first jazz medleys for multiple tubas. This arrangement includes the selections "Satin Doll," "Mood Indigo," " Don't Get Around Much Anymore," " Sophisticated Lady," and "Take the A Train." Several tempo and key changes. The tessitura of the top part is quite high and requires a strong player. All parts have some divisi, so each part requires two players. Recorded by the Tennessee Technological University Tuba Ensemble, Golden Crest Records, CRS 4139.

Sample, Steve, arr. *Gershwin Medley.* T.A.P. Music. Two euphoniums, two tubas, piano/guitar, bass, and drums. 1979. $15.00. 3:20. IV–V. Part I: f–c", Part II: e–a', Part III: G–e♭', Part IV: A₁–b♭. Written for R. Winston Morris and the Tennessee Technological University Tuba Ensemble. A swing medley of "They Can't Take That Away from Me," "Soon," and "A Foggy Day." Both euphonium parts have a high tessitura and require a good swing feel to work stylistically. Both tuba parts are featured melodically in different sections. This arrangement works quite well and is a real audience pleaser. All parts (except the fourth) require two players because of the extensive divisi sections. Parts may be further doubled for a large ensemble. Recorded by the Tennessee Technological University Tuba Ensemble, *LIVE!*, KM Records, KM 5661; and the U.S. Armed Forces Tuba/Euphonium Ensemble, Mark Records, MW89MCD-8.

Sample, Steve, arr. *Harold Arlen Medley*. SOS Music Services. Two euphoniums, two tubas, piano/guitar, bass, and drums. 1982. $50.00. 5:20. IV. Part I: f–c″, Part II: B♭–g′, Part III: C–d♭′, Part IV: B♭₁–a. Written for R. Winston Morris and the Tennessee Technological University Tuba Ensemble. A medley of "Somewhere over the Rainbow," "My Shining Hour," "That Old Black Magic," and "Out of This World." Players need a good jazz feel. The tessitura of the first part is high. The top three parts have numerous divisi sections, requiring a minimum of seven players for this arrangement. Parts may be further doubled for a large ensemble.

Sample, Steve, arr. *Nostalgia Medley*. SOS Music Services. Out of print. Two euphoniums, two tubas, piano/guitar, bass, and drums. 1975. IV. Written for R. Winston Morris and the Tennessee Technological University Tuba Ensemble.

Sample, Steve, arr. *Stella by Starlight* SOS Music Services. Two euphoniums, two tubas, piano/guitar, bass, and drums. 1986. $50.00. 4:30. IV. Part I: g–c″, Part II: e–g′, Part III: C–c′, Part IV: A₁–g. The top two parts require a minimum of two players each. Contains an open section for improvised solos. Chord changes occur in all parts. The tessitura of the first part is high. A swing feel is necessary from all players. Parts may be further doubled for a large ensemble.

Sample, Steve, arr. *Tennessee Waltz*. SOS Music Services. Out of print. Two euphoniums, two tubas, piano/guitar, bass, and drums. 1986. 4:30. IV. Part I: e♭–b♭′, Part II: c–f′, Part III: G–b♭, Part IV: B♭₁–g. Written for R. Winston Morris and the Tennessee Technological University Tuba Ensemble. Has sections in 3/4, 2/4, 2/2, 4/4, and 5/4, and one with chord symbols in all parts for improvised solos. Rhythm parts are essential to the performance. Parts may be doubled for a large ensemble.

Sample, Steve, arr. *Two Tunes by Nacio Herb Brown*. SOS Music Services. Two euphoniums, two tubas, piano/guitar, bass, and drums. 1983. $50.00. 5:00. IV–V. Part I: g–d″, Part II: c–f′, Part III: G–d′, Part IV: G₁–g. Written for R. Winston Morris and the Tennessee Technological University Tuba Ensemble. A medley of "You Stepped Out of A Dream" and "Temptation." The tessitura of the first part is very high. The first section is in a mambo style, and bongos, tambourines, and other rhythm instruments should be used. The second section is

a fast swing. Requires a good rhythmic feel by all players. Parts I, II, and IV require a minimum of two players each. Parts may be further doubled for a large ensemble. Recorded by the Tennessee Technological University Tuba Ensemble, *All That Jazz*, Mark Records, MES-20608.

Sample, Steve, arr. *Waltzing with Irving*. SOS Music Services. Two euphoniums, two tubas, piano/guitar, bass, and drums. 1984. $50.00. 3:30. IV. Part I: f–b♭′, Part II: d–a′, Part III: F–d′, Part IV: B♭₁–b♭. Written for R. Winston Morris and the Tennessee Technological University Tuba Ensemble. A medley of "What'll I Do?" "Always," and "Remember." The tessitura of the top part is high. The top three parts have many divisi sections and will require two players each. Rhythm parts are essential to maintain a good jazz waltz feel. Works well. Parts may be further doubled for a large ensemble.

Satie, Erik. *First Gymnopedie*. arr. Peter Rauch. Ohio Valley Tuba Quartet Press. Two euphoniums and two tubas. 1988. $8.00. 2:10. IV. Part I: e–a′, Part II: d–a′, Part III: A₁–b, Part IV: (D₁)A₁–a. A very lyrical melody passed primarily between the top three parts. No significant technical problems. Parts may be doubled for a large ensemble.

Satie, Erik. *Le Piccadilly*. arr. Hirokazu Hiraishi. Sonic Arts, Incorporated. Two euphoniums and two tubas. 1986. $11.00. 2:00. IV. Part I: F–a′, Part II: F–d′, Part III: C–f, Part IV: F₁–d. A cute syncopated melody passed around to each part. No significant technical problems. Parts may be doubled for a large ensemble.

Schein, Johann H. *Pavan a 4*. arr. Paul Schmidt. Heavy Metal Music. Two euphoniums and two tubas. 1991. $5.00. 1:45. IV. Part I: d–d′, Part II: B–g, Part III: G–g, Part IV: B♭₁–B♭. Very polyphonic; the first part is the most technically challenging. No score available. Parts may be doubled for a large ensemble.

Schmelzer, J.H. *Three Pieces for Horseballet*. arr. Paul Schmidt. Heavy Metal Music. Two euphoniums and two tubas. 1990. $3.00. 2:45. III. Part I: e♭–f′, Part II: c–f′, Part III: E♭–a♭, Part IV: A♭₁–E♭. Three movements: Courante for His Majesty the King and All His Calvary; Follia to Begin More of the Jumping and Other Horse Exercises; Sarabande for Concluding the Ballet. A traditional homophonic texture with the melody primarily in the first part. No significant technical problems. No score available. Parts may be doubled for a large ensemble.

Schmidt, Dankwart, arr. *Tuba Muckl*. Dankwart Schmidt. Two euphoniums and two tubas. 1:20. IV. Recorded by David LeClair, Contraband, *Swingin' Low*, Marcophon CD 940-2.

Schmidt, Paul, arr. *Christmas Bell Songs*. Heavy Metal Music. Two euphoniums and two tubas. 1991. $5.00. 2:30. III–IV. Part I: c–f′, Part II: B♭–a♭, Part III: F–e♭, Part IV: F₁–B♭. Two movements: Carol of the Bells; Jingle Bells. Very playable arrangement of these two familiar melodies. The melody is in the first part. No score available. Parts may be doubled for a large ensemble.

Schmidt, Paul, arr. *The Cuckoo*. Heavy Metal Music. Two euphoniums, two tubas, with optional flute, recorder, or whistle. 1990. $5.00. 1:20. IV. Part I: B♭–g', Part II: c–f ', Part III: F–b♭, Part IV: C–e♭. Cute arrangement of this humorous traditional Swiss melody. The Cuckoo notes are written in the fourth part. No score available. Parts may be doubled for a large ensemble.

Schmidt, Paul, arr. *Emilia Polka*. Heavy Metal Music. Two euphoniums and two tubas. 1991. $7.00. 3:30. IV. Part I: B♭–e♭', Part II: A♭–d', Part III: C–c', Part IV: G₁–d♭. A traditional polka with most of the melody in the top part. No range problems. No score available. Parts may be doubled for a large ensemble.

Schmidt, Paul, arr. *Evergreen Polka*. Heavy Metal Music. Two euphoniums and two tubas. 1990. $7.00. 3:30. IV. Part I: c–f ', Part II: A–g', Part III: C–b♭, Part IV: F₁–B♭. Most of the melodic responsibility lies in the top two parts. Drums can be added for stylistic enhancement. Very traditional harmonies. No score available. Parts may be doubled for a large ensemble.

Schmidt, Paul, arr. *Helena Polka*. Heavy Metal Music. Two euphoniums and two tubas. 1991. $7.00. 3:30. IV. Part I: e♭–f ', Part II: c–a♭', Part III: E♭–e♭', Part IV: F₁–e♭. Good arrangement of this traditional polka. Most of the melody is in the top part. No significant technical challenges. No score available. Parts may be doubled for a large ensemble.

Schmidt, Paul, arr. *Three Christmas Carols*. Heavy Metal Music. Two euphoniums and two tubas. 1991. $5.00. 2:45. III. Part I: c–f ', Part II: G–c', Part III: D–g, Part IV: F₁–A. Three movements: O Holy Night; O How Joyfully; O Come, Little Children. A fairly easy arrangement of these three familiar melodies. The melody is primarily in the top part. No score available. Parts may be doubled for a large ensemble.

Schmidt, Paul, arr. *Three Christmas Carols I*. Heavy Metal Music. Two euphoniums and two tubas. 1991. $5.00. 2:30. III–IV. Part I: d–g', Part II: B♭–e♭', Part III: D–g, Part IV: F₁–c. Three movements: Vom Himmel Hoch; In the Bleak Midwinter; O Tannenbaum. Three short and contrasting Christmas melodies in a traditional setting. Very appropriate for high school students. No score available. Parts may be doubled for a large ensemble.

Schmidt, Paul, arr. *Three Christmas Carols II*. Heavy Metal Music. Two euphoniums and two tubas. 1991. $7.00. 3:00. III. Part I: B♭–f ', Part II: A–d♭', Part III: F–a♭, Part IV: G₁–f. Three movements: Macht auf die Tor; Make We Joy; Übers Gebirg Maria Geht. A very traditional arrangement of three familiar Christmas melodies. The third movement has a polyphonic texture but is not difficult techni-

cally. Very appropriate for high school players. No score available. Parts may be doubled for a large ensemble.

Schmidt, Paul, arr. *Three German Songs*. Heavy Metal Music. Two euphoniums and two tubas. 1990. $7.00. 4:30. III–IV. Part I: B–f ', Part II: G–e♭', Part III: B♭₁–e♭', Part IV: F₁–a(b♭). Three movements: Deutschland über Alles; Tomorrow Belongs to Me; Edelweiss. Nice arrangement of these traditional German and Austrian melodies. With just a couple of exceptions, the melody is in the first part. Good programming for fall German festivals. No score available. Parts may be doubled for a large ensemble.

Schmidt, Paul, arr. *Tinker Polka*. Heavy Metal Music. Two euphoniums two tubas. 1990. $7.00. 3:30. III–IV. Part I: d–g', Part II: G–b♭, Part III: F–b♭, Part IV: B♭₁–f. Not technically difficult. The melody is primarily in the top part. No score available. Parts may be doubled for a large ensemble.

Schmidt, Paul, arr. *Two Christmas Carols*. Heavy Metal Music. Two euphoniums and two tubas. 1991. $5.00. 2:00. III–IV. Part I: B♭–g♭', Part II: A–f ', Part III: B♭₁–b♭, Part IV: F₁–e♭. Two movements: Masters in This Hall; Once in Royal David's City. Each part has an opportunity to play the melody. No significant technical problems. No score available. Parts may be doubled for a large ensemble.

Schmidt, Paul, arr. *Two Madrigals*. Heavy Metal Music. Two euphoniums and two tubas. 1990. $7.00. 3:00. III–IV. Part I: d–e', Part II: A–d', Part III: E–f, Part IV: F₁–c. Two movements: Weep, O Mine Eyes; Fair Phyllis I Saw. The first movement is slow and somber, the second is fast and has a humorous character. Both movements are very polyphonic, though not technically difficult. No score available. Parts may be doubled for a large ensemble.

Schmidt, Paul, arr. *Two Old Songs*. Heavy Metal Music. Two euphoniums and two tubas. 1990. $5.00. 2:10. IV. Part I: B–g', Part II: F–f ', Part III: A♭₁–g, Part IV: G₁–d. Two movements: K-K-K-Katy; Toot, Toot Tootsie Goodbye. Fun arrangement of two melodies from the 1920s. No significant technical problems. Drums may be added for effect. No score available. Parts may be doubled for a large ensemble.

Schmidt, Paul, arr. *Two Sackbut Quartets*. Heavy Metal Music. Two euphoniums and two tubas. 1992. $7.00. 3:00. IV. Part I: c–g', Part II: B♭–b♭, Part III: B♭₁–b♭, Part IV: F₁–f. Two movements: In Te Domini, Speravi; In Nomine. For Ascanio Sforza. These two works by Josquin des Prez and Orlando Gibbons respectively are very polyphonic, with primary melodic responsibility in the top three parts. No score available. Parts may be doubled for a large ensemble.

Schooley, John. *Cherokee for Tuba Quartet*. Heilman Music. Two euphoniums and two tubas. 1984.

$15.00. 5:00. IV. Part I: G–a', Part II: G–e', Part III: D–b♭, Part IV: D₁–g. Dedicated to Melodie. Schooley refers to this as a tone poem for tuba ensemble. The piece progresses through various styles, tempos, and tonalities. One section shifts frequently between 3/4, 5/8, and 7/8. The two euphonium parts are printed in both bass and treble clef. Offers a change of pace in a recital program. Parts may be doubled for a large ensemble. Recorded by Northern Tuba Lights.

Schooley, John. *Toccata for Euphonium/Tuba Quartet.* Heilman Music. Two euphoniums and two tubas. 1984. $15.00. 5:00. IV. Part I: B–bb', Part II: F–ab', Part III: C–b♭, Part IV: (C₁)Eb₁–f. Dedicated to Jonathan. A tuneful original composition, very contrapuntal in style. Technically not too difficult. Most of the melodic activity is in the top two euphonium parts, and both parts are printed in bass and treble clef. Parts may be doubled for a large ensemble.

Schubert, Franz. *Heidentüblein.* arr. David LeClair. ITC Editions Marc Reift. Two euphoniums and two tubas. 1992. 1:50. IV. Part I: c♭–bb', Part II: B♭–f ', Part III: A–c', Part IV: F₁–f. Recorded by David LeClair, Contraband, *Swingin' Low,* Marcophon CD 940-2.

Schubert, Franz. *Military March.* arr. David LeClair. ITC Editions Marc Reift. Two euphoniums and two tubas. 1992. 4:20. IV. Part I: A–b', Part II: G–g', Part III: C₁–d', Part IV: G₂–g. Recorded by David LeClair, Contraband, *Swingin' Low,* Marcophon CD 940-2.

Schubert, Franz. *Staendchen.* arr. David LeClair. ITC Editions Marc Reift.Two euphoniums and two tubas. 1992. Part I: d–c", Part II: c–g', Part III: c–eb', Part IV: D₁–a. Recorded by David LeClair, Contraband, *Swingin' Low,* Marcophon CD 940-2.

Schuller, Gunther. *Five Moods for Tuba Quartet.* Associated Music Publishers. Out of print. 1976. 6:45. V. Part I: F♯₁–b', Part II: E₁–f♯', Part III: E₁–d', Part IV: Eb₁–d'. Five movements: Lament; Allegro moderato; Adagio misterioso; Molto lento, Broodingly; Allegro Volando. Commissioned by Harvey Phillips. Dedicated to the memory of William Bell. According to the composer, this composition "tries to capture in vignette portraits the different characteristic traits of this remarkable man." Extreme ranges, technical demands, and wide skips make this a most complex and challenging work. An F tuba would be needed on the first and probably the second parts. Many contemporary techniques, including multiphonics and tapping the mouthpiece and horn. Mutes are required of all four parts. Written for the First International Tuba Symposium-Workshop. Recorded by the New York Tuba Quartet, *Tubby's Revenge,* Crystal Records, S221.

Schumann, Robert. *Classics for Low Brass Quartet, Set No. 1.* arr. David Schanke. Music Arts Company.

Two euphoniums and two tubas. 1991. $12.50. 2:00. III. Part I: B♭–eb', Part II: B♭–c', Part III: A–f, Part IV: Ab₁–eb. Two movements: The Merry Farmer, Op. 68, no. 10; Soldier's March, Op. 68, no. 2. Easy arrangements of two piano pieces by Schumann. Excellent for young players. The top two parts are printed in bass and treble clef. Parts may be doubled for a large ensemble.

Schumann, Robert. *Classics for Low Brass Quartet, Set No. 2.* arr. David Schanke. Music Arts Company. Two euphoniums and two tubas. 1991. $12.50. 2:20. III–IV. Part I: B♭–eb', Part II: B♭–c', Part III: Ab–g, Part IV: Ab₁–db. Two movements: Andante con Expresione, Op. 68, no. 26; The Wild Horseman, Op. 68, no. 8. Two piano pieces that contrast in style and meter. No significant range or technical problems. The top two parts are printed in both bass and treble clef. Parts may be doubled for a large ensemble.

Schumann, Robert. *Piece in Folk Style.* arr. David R. Werden. Whaling Music Publishers. Three euphoniums and one tubas. 1981. $5.00. 2:20. IV. Part I: F–bb', Part II: B♭–ab', Part III: G♭–eb', Part IV: G♭₁–ab. An arrangement of the second movement from *Five Pieces in a Folk Style,* which Paul Droste transcribed for euphonium and piano. No real technical difficulties. The first euphonium part is printed in treble clef. Parts may be doubled for a large ensemble.

Schumann, Robert. *Suite from Album for the Young.* arr. Stephen Shoop. Southern Music Company. Two euphoniums and two tubas. 1993. $7.95. 4:45. III–IV. Part I: B♭–eb', Part II: A–d', Part III: Ab₁–f, Part IV: F₁–eb. Five movements: Chorale; The Happy Farmer; Melody; The Wild Rider; Soldier's March. All four parts have an opportunity to play the melody. No significant range or technical problems. Very appropriate for good high school players. Parts may be doubled for a large ensemble.

Schumann, Robert. *Suite from Album for the Young.* arr. David R. Werden. Whaling Music Publishers. Two euphoniums and two tubas. 1980. $9.50. 5:00. IV. Part I: B–c", Part II: G–g', Part III: G₁–f ', Part IV: G₁–g. Four movements: Wilder Reiter (Wild Rider); Armes Waisenkind (Poor Orphan); Fröhlicher Landmann (Happy Farmer); Kriegslied (War Song). Good arrangement of four contrasting Schumann piano pieces. The tessitura of the first part is high. The top two parts are printed in treble clef. No significant technical challenges. Parts may be doubled for a large ensemble.

Schumann, Robert. *Träumerei.* arr. Bruno Seitz. Musikverlag Martin Scherbacher. Two euphoniums and two tubas, or one euphonium and three tubas. 1991. $13.50. 2:50. III–IV. Part I: Ab–gb', Part II: G♭–c', Part III: D♭–f, Part IV: F₁–B♭. Very lyrical, with the melody predominantly in the first part. The first part is printed in bass and treble clef. Parts may be doubled for a large ensemble. Recorded by the Melton Tuba Quartet, *Premiere,* Diavolo Records, DR-D-93-C001.

Schütz, Heinrich. *Chorale (Psalm 97).* arr. Daniel Heiman. Heavy Metal Music. Two euphoniums and two tubas. 1992. $5.00. 1:00. III–IV. Part I: d–f', Part II: A–a, Part III: D–f, Part IV: G$_1$–A. A slow lyrical chorale. The meter is constantly shifting. No range problems. Players read from a single score. Parts may be doubled for a large ensemble.

Schütz, Heinrich. *Ego Sum Tui Plaga Doloris.* arr. Mark Nelson. Whaling Music Publishers. Two euphoniums and two tubas. 1991. $10.00. 2:20. III–IV. Part I: f–g', Part II: B♭–c', Part III: E♭–g, Part IV: B♭$_1$–e♭. Very playable by high school students. The texture is polyphonic but the piece is not difficult technically. Parts may be doubled for a large ensemble.

Seitz, Bruno. *Tuba Muckl Polka.* Musikverlag Martin Scherbacher. Two euphoniums and two tubas. 1988. $13.50. 2:20. IV. Part I: G–f', Part II: E♭–d', Part III: E♭–b♭, Part IV: F$_1$–d. Could also be played with one euphonium and three tubas, or four tubas. A short, fun polka with most of the melody and technical challenges in the first part. The parts may be doubled for a large ensemble.

Seitz, Bruno. *Vier Tuben im 3/4 Takt-Volksweise.* Musikverlag Martin Scherbacher. Four tubas. 1988. $13.50. 1:45. III–IV. Part I: B♭–e♭', Part II: G–d', Part III: G–g, Part IV: G$_1$–d. A nice lyrical melody with no technical problems. Easily playable by high school students if a euphonium is used on the first and second parts. The parts may be doubled for a large ensemble.

Self, James. *Poker Chips.* Basset Hound Music. Four tubas and vibraphone. 1993. IV–V. A multimovement work with the name of each movement representing a different term in poker and a musical aspect (i.e., five-card stud will be in 5/4). Interesting timbres with the vibraphone. A fun piece for audiences. Work in progress.

Self, James, arr. *Carolina.* James Self. Out of print. Two euphoniums and two tubas. 1969. 1:30. III–IV. Part I: c–c' (a'), Part II: A–a♭ (f'), Part III: F–g (c'), Part IV: C–f. Barbershop style harmonies of this familiar folk song. No significant technical problems.

Shostakovich, Dimitri. *Four Preludes, Op. 34, nos. 4, 7, 14, 16.* arr. Peter Rauch. Ohio Valley Tuba Quartet Press. Two euphoniums and two tubas. 1992. $12.00. 7:30. IV. Part I: B–c", Part II: A–a♭', Part III: B–a♭, Part IV: C$_1$–d. Movements contrast in key, meter, and style. The tessitura of the first part is high, but there are no significant technical problems. Parts may be doubled for a large ensemble.

Silcher, Fr. Von. *Die Lorelei.* arr. Bruno Seitz. Musikverlag Martin Scherbacher. Four tubas. 1993. $15.00. 3:00. IV. Part I: e♭–g', Part II: B♭–c', Part III: E♭–e♭, Part IV: F$_1$–B♭. A standard arrangement

of this famous German waltz. The top part has a high tessitura and may be played on euphonium. No technical problems. Playable by high school students if euphoniums are used on the top two parts. Parts may be doubled for a large ensemble.

Singleton, Kenneth, arr. *Three Sixteenth-Century Flemish Pieces.* Queen City Brass Publications. Two euphoniums and two tubas. 1984. $7.50. 3:00. III. Part I: f–g', Part II: c–d', Part III: B♭–b♭, Part IV: B♭$_1$–e♭. Three movements: Holla hoi per lanerta hoi; Sauff aus ünd machsnit lang; Hilf glüch mit freuden. Fairly easy arrangements of melodies typical of the Renaissance polyphonic style. Measure 15 in the first part of the first movement is missing a half rest. Parts may be doubled for a large ensemble. Recorded by the Monarch Tuba/Euphonium Quartet.

Sloan, Gerald, arr. *Tuba Sunday for Tuba Choir.* Gerald Sloan. Two euphoniums and two tubas. 1983. $5.00. 2:10. III. Part I: d–f', Part II: d♭–e', Part III: F–g, Part IV: B♭$_1$–d. Two movements: How Firm a Foundation; Amazing Grace. For Dr. Jerry Young and his students at Interlochen. Nice arrangement of two traditional Protestant hymns. All parts have an opportunity to play the melody. Very playable by high school students. Parts may be doubled for a large ensemble.

Smaller, Victor, and Adler, Richard. *That Lovin' Rag.* arr. Rodger Vaughan. Rodger Vaughan. Two euphoniums and two tubas. 1988. $5.00. 2:00. IV. Part I: f–a', Part II: e–e', Part III: F–a', Part IV: F$_1$–d. An up-tempo very syncopated rag. Technical challenges depend on the performance tempo.

Snow, David. *Elephants Exotiques.* David Snow. Four tubas. 1978. 9:30. IV–V. Part I: E–b♭', Part II: E–e♭', Part III: E–e♭', Part IV: E♭$_1$–e♭'. Four movements: Preludio Pachydermus; Looking for Peanuts (in the Jungle); Elephant Love Song; Mating Season. The piece is fun to listen to but because of the very contemporary harmonies, it is difficult to play. At the end of the third movement the fourth tuba player stands and recites two paragraphs of text printed in French. The fourth movement is multimetric and involves glissandos and slapping the hand against the mouthpiece. The top two parts have a very high tessitura and may be played by euphoniums. All players read from a score. Winner of second place in the Los Angeles Tuba Quartet/Mirafone composition contest.

Sousa, John Philip. *Belle of Chicago March.* arr. Skip Gray. Shawnee Press, Incorporated. Two euphoniums and two tubas. 1984. $8.00. 2:20. III–IV. Part I: d♭–f', Part II: B♭–e♭', Part III: E♭–g, Part IV: A♭$_1$–c. This arrangement poses the fewest technical demands of any of the Sousa marches published for tuba/euphonium quartet. Range requirements also make this a good high school or college recital piece. The melody is primarily in the euphoniums. Parts may be doubled for a large ensemble.

Sousa, John Philip. *El Capitan.* arr. R. Winston Morris. The Brass Press. Two euphoniums and two tubas. 1974. $5.00. 2:20. III–IV. Part I: B♭–g', Part II: c–f ', Part III: G–a♭, Part IV: A₁–e♭. Written for the Tennessee Technological University Tuba Ensemble. This transcription is in the same key as the original, with most of the melody in the top two parts. It works well and is effective at concerts. Parts may be doubled for a large ensemble. Recorded by the British Tuba Quartet, *In at the Deep End,* Heavyweight Records Limited, HR008/D; and the Monarch Tuba/Euphonium Quartet.

Sousa, John Philip. *Hands across the Sea.* arr. David R. Werden. Whaling Music Publishers. Two euphoniums and two tubas. 1983. $8.00. 3:30. IV. Part I: d–d", Part II: c–b♭', Part III: C–e♭', Part IV: F₁–f. Dedicated to the Tokyo Bari-Tuba Ensemble. Tessitura of both euphoniums parts is high. The first euphonium part is printed in treble clef. The arrangement works well. Parts may be doubled for a large ensemble. Recorded by the Northern Tuba Lights.

Sousa, John Philip. *Semper Fidelis.* arr. R. Winston Morris. Ludwig Music Publishing Company. Two euphoniums and two tubas. 1988. $15.50. 2:30. III–IV. Part I: B–g', Part II: B♭–f ', Part III: C–g, Part IV: G₁–f. Written for the Tennessee Technological University Tuba Ensemble. Excellent arrangement of this traditional Sousa march. Technically not overly challenging, but the moving lines must be played cleanly by all parts. Both euphonium parts are printed in bass and treble clef. Arrangement works very well. Parts may be doubled for a large ensemble. Recorded by the British Tuba Quartet, *In at the Deep End,* Heavyweight Records, HR008/D.

Sousa, John Philip. *Semper Fidelis.* arr. David Sabourin. Touch of Brass Music Corporation. Two euphoniums and two tubas. 1982. $7.50. 2:30. IV. Part I: G–b♭', Part II: G–e♭', Part III: B♭₁–b♭, Part IV: A♭₁–e♭. Good arrangement of this classic march. Tessitura of the first part is high. Most of the work is in the top two parts. Transposed up a fourth from the original key. Parts may be doubled for a large ensemble.

Sousa, John Philip. *The Stars and Stripes Forever.* arr. Paul Schmidt. Heavy Metal Music. Two euphoniums and two tubas. 1990. $7.00. 2:00. III–IV. Part I: B♭–f ', Part II: B♭–f ', Part III: C♭–g(e♭'), Part IV: F₁–e♭. The range and technical demands are very appropriate for good high school players. Drums may be added for effect. No score available. Parts may be added for a large ensemble.

Sousa, John Philip. *The Stars and Stripes Forever.* arr. David R. Werden. Whaling Music Publishers. Two euphoniums and two tubas. 1992. $8.00. 2:00. IV. Part I: B♭–b♭', Part II: A–b♭', Part III: F–f ', Part IV: A₁–c'. Tessitura of the first three parts is high, an F tuba or a euphonium may be used on the third part.

The first and second parts are printed in treble clef and the third and fourth in both treble and bass clef for E♭ tubas. Good arrangement. Originally copyrighted in 1979. Parts may be doubled for a large ensemble. Recorded by the Atlantic Tuba Quartet, Golden Crest Records, CRS 4173; the Northern Tuba Lights.

Sousa, John Philip. *The Thunderer.* arr. David R. Werden. Whaling Music Publishers. Two euphoniums and two tubas. 1989. $8.00. 2:30. IV. Part I: c–b♭', Part II: c–a', Part III: C–c', Part IV: F₁–c'. Most of the melody is in the first part, while the other three parts have a tutti rhythmic accompaniment. Parts may be doubled for a large ensemble.

Sousa, John Philip. *Washington Post.* arr. David Sabourin. Touch of Brass Music Corporation. Two euphoniums and two tubas. 1981. $8.50. 2:30. IV. Part I: B♭–f ', Part II: F–e♭', Part III: F–b♭, Part IV: F₁–c. Excellent arrangement of this traditional march. No real range or technical difficulties for this level. Parts may be doubled for a large ensemble. Recorded by the British Tuba Quartet, *In at the Deep End,* Heavyweight Records, HR008/D; the Melton Tuba Quartet, *Premiere,* Diavolo Records, DR-D-93-C-001.

Sousa, John Philip. *Washington Post.* arr. David R. Werden. Whaling Music Publishers. Two euphoniums and two tubas. 1983. $8.50. 2:30. IV. Part I: F–b♭', Part II: A–g', Part III: F–f ', Part IV: B♭₁–e♭'. Nice arrangement of this famous Sousa march. The tessitura of the third part is high; an F tuba is recommended. The first part is printed in tenor clef. Parts may be doubled for a large ensemble. Recorded by David LeClair, *Swingin' Low,* Marcophon.

Spears, Jared. *Divertimento.* Jared Spears. Two euphoniums and two tubas. 1980. $50.00. 10:45. IV–V. Part I: B♭–c", Part II: F–g', Part III: F–e', Part IV: F♯₁–b. Five movements: Invention; Melodrama; Dance; Chorale; Toccata. Written for R. Winston Morris and the Tennessee Technological University Tuba Ensemble. There are considerable range and technical demands on all parts. All four parts have numerous divisi sections and will require at least two players each. The first, third, and fifth movements are high-spirited and full of energy. Mutes are required for the top three parts. An exceptional piece for an advanced ensemble. Parts may be doubled for a large ensemble. Recorded by the Tennessee Technological University Tuba Ensemble, *Composer Festival,* KM Records, KM 6549.

Speer, Daniel. *Sonata.* arr. Paul Schmidt. Heavy Metal Music. Two euphoniums and two tubas. 1991. $5.00. 3:00. III–IV. Part I: e–e♭, Part II: B♭–c', Part III: A–b♭, Part IV: B♭₁–f. All parts have the same rhythmical technical demands. No range problems. Texture is polyphonic in some sections. No score available. Parts may be doubled for a large ensemble.

Stauffer, Donald W. *Sebastian, the St. Bernard.* Stauffer Press. Two euphoniums and two tubas. 1994. $10.00. 1:30. IV. Part 1: f–ab', Part II: c♯–f', Part III: D₁–c', Part IV: Bb₂–f. One of a collection of compositions called "Canine Capers." The tessitura of the third and fourth parts is very low. No significant technical problems. Also available for tuba and band.

Steffe, W. *Battle Hymn.* arr. Thomas Isbell. The Brass Press. Two euphoniums and two tubas. 1974. $4.00. 2:00. III. Part I: D–f', Part II: Bb–f', Part III: Eb–f, Part IV: G₁–bb. Written for R. Winston Morris and the Tennessee Technological University Tuba Ensemble. The first part has an extended solo in the first section in a free expressive style. The second section is a march-like version of this traditional patriotic melody. Very usable with high school students. Parts may be doubled for a large ensemble.

Steinke, Greg. *Suspended in Frozen Velocity: Image Music IX from "Songs of the Fire Circles."* TUBA Press. Two euphoniums and two tubas. 1992. $12.00. 6:00. IV–V. Ranges for all parts are the lowest note possible to the highest note possible. Dedicated to those dying for freedom as this is played. In a series of pieces of "Image Music" which explore Native American culture based on the "Songs of the Fire Circles." Numerous twentieth-century techniques called for include various "free" pitch and meter sections, randomly chosen rhythms, and glissandos. There are extreme technical and range challenges for all four parts. All parts require mutes.

Stevens, John. *Ballade.* John Stevens. Two euphoniums and two tubas. 1990. 2:00. III. Part I: F–eb'. Part II: d–a, Part III: D–f, Part IV: Bb₁–d. A short jazz ballad. Very sonorous and legato in style throughout. Written especially for high school players.

Stevens, John. *Dances.* Peer International Corporation. Solo tuba and three tubas. 1978. $12.00. 7:30. IV–V. Part I: c–f', Part II: C–c', Part III: Bb₁–g, Part IV: Bb₁–c. One movement is in three sections: moderate 2/2, slow 3/4, and fast 6/8. Rhythmically challenging for the soloist as well as the other three parts. A solo cadenza separates each section. The solo part may be played on euphonium. A very exciting aggressive sounding composition. See: Bird, Gary, ed., *Program Notes for the Solo Tuba.* Recorded by Toby Hanks, *Sampler,* Crystal Records, S395; the Melton Tuba Quartet, *Premiere,* Diavolo Records, DR-D-93-C-001; and the Northern Tuba Lights.

Stevens, John. *Diversions.* Editions Bim. Four tubas. 1978. 14:00. IV. Part I: C–ab', Part II: E–Ab', Part III: C–d', Part IV: G₁–bb. Five movements: Prologue; Latin Feel; Free—Very Down Home; Fast; Epilogue. A jazz composition requiring improvisation by the second and third parts. The Prologue

and Epilogue are short and in a jazz ballad style. The second movement is a funk/rock tune featuring the fourth part in an intricate bass line, and the third movement is a fast jazz waltz. The top two parts may be played on euphonium.

Stevens, John. *Jammin'.* John Stevens. Two euphoniums and two tubas. 1990. 2:30. III. Part I: c–eb', Part II: c–eb', Part III: C–Gb, Part IV: Ab₁–db. A short piece in a rock style. Rock rhythms, syncopations, and unison ensemble figures are stressed.

Stevens, John. *Manhattan Suite.* Southern Music Publishing Company Incorporated. Four tubas. 1979. $12.00. 15:20. IV. Part I: Bb–bb', Part II: Bb₁–g', Part III: F₁–eb, Part IV: Eb₁–f. Four movements: Rock; Slow Swing; Jazz Waltz; Slow and Free. While the score indicates four tubas, the parts suggest that the first part may be played by a euphonium and the second by a euphonium or F tuba. The top three parts have a section for improvised solos. As an alternative to improvisation, players may use solos written by the composer. This is a very lively piece with four contrasting movements. A few ensemble challenges; requires four strong players. Recorded by the University of Michigan Tuba and Euphonium Ensemble, University of Michigan Records, SM0011.

Stevens, John. *Moondance.* Editions Bim. Four tubas. 1991. 7:00. V. Part I: C–gb', Part II: C–eb', Part III: Eb₁–db', Part IV: Eb₁–eb'. Commissioned by and dedicated to the Summit Tuba Quartet. A slow, legato opening section is followed by a solo cadenza that leads to a very rapid, rhythmically energetic section. The opening material returns at the end. The piece is tonal and has a jazz flavor. Very challenging. Recorded by the Summit Tuba Quartet, *Summit Brass-American Tribute,* Summit Records, DCD 127; and the United States Air Force Tuba Section.

Stevens, John. *Music 4 Tubas.* Peer International Corporation. Four tubas. 1978. $12.00. 8:00. IV. Part I: C–f', Part II: Bb₁–g', Part III: G₁–db', Part IV: G₁–d'. Three movements: Lively; Largo; Rock. A very interesting work. The tessitura is rather high for the first two parts, even the fourth part goes up to a d'. A challenge to play but worth the effort. Recorded by the New York Tuba Quartet, *Tubby's Revenge,* Crystal Records, S221.

Stevens, John. *Power for Four Tubas.* Peer International Corporation. Four tubas, or two euphoniums and two tubas. 1978. $12.00. 2:10. IV. Part I: G–eb', Part II: c–eb', Part III: C–f, Part IV: G₁–c. A driving, jazz-like composition which alternates between 2/2 and 7/4. Very challenging, especially at the tempo marked. This exciting piece makes a terrific opener. Recorded by John Stevens, *Power,* Mark Records, MRS-20699; the Northern Tuba Lights.

Stevens, John, arr. *Twenty-Four Christmas Carols.* John Stevens. Two euphoniums and two tubas. 1982. 24

pp. IV. Part I: F–bb', Part II: F–g', Part III: G_1–c', Part IV: F_1–ab. Traditional carols arranged in a variety of traditional classical styles. Use of modulations, trills, ornaments, and countermelodies predominate.

Stolc, C. *Forge in the Forest Polka*. arr. Paul Schmidt. Heavy Metal Music. Two euphoniums and two tubas. 1990. $7.00. 3:00. IV. Part I: A–eb', Part II: F–eb', Part III: Eb–bb, Part IV: F_1–f. There are many technical challenges for the top two parts, especially if the piece is played at a fast tempo. Perfect for Octubafest concerts. No score available. Parts may be doubled for a large ensemble.

Stoutamire, Albert, and Henderson, Kenneth. *Quartets for All*. CPP Belwin, Incorporated. Three euphoniums and one tuba. 1975. $5.00. 23 pp. III. Part I: Bb–g', Part II: Bb–f ', Part III: Ab–f ', Part IV: Bb_1–f. A collection of twelve songs from a variety of composers and styles. No significant technical problems. The melody is almost exclusively in the first part. Works very well for junior high and high school students. Parts may be doubled for a large ensemble.

Strauss, Johann. *An der Schönen Blauen Donau* (Blue Danube Waltz). arr. Bruno Seitz. Musikverlag Martin Scherbacher. Two euphoniums and two tubas. 1989. $15.00. 4:30. IV. Part I: Ab–c", Part II: Gb–eb', Part III: C–db', Part IV: Eb_1–eb. Good arrangement of this famous waltz. The first part has the melody the majority of the time and is the most difficult technically. Fun to play, but also challenging. Parts may be doubled for a large ensemble.

Strauss, Johann. *Tritsch-Tratsch Polka*. arr. Bruno Seitz. Musikverlag Martin Scherbacher. Two euphoniums and two tubas. 1988. $13.50. 2:20. IV. Part I: c–bb', Part II: G–f ', Part III: Db–ab, Part IV: F_1–Ab. A high-spirited polka, technically challenging for the top three parts. Many subito dynamic contrasts for stylistic effect. Fun to play. Parts may be doubled for a large ensemble.

Strauss, Johann. *Valse from Die Fledermaus*. arr. David Schanke. Music Arts Company. Two euphoniums and two tubas. 1992. $10.00. 1:45. III–IV. Part I: eb–g', Part II: F#–c', Part III: Eb–ab, Part IV: G_1–eb. A fun arrangement of this classic waltz. Most of the work is in the first euphonium part, though all four parts get a chance to play the melody occasionally. The top two parts are printed in both bass and treble clef. Parts may be doubled for a large ensemble.

Stroud, Richard. *Night Train for Tubas*. Richard Stroud. Two euphoniums and two tubas. $12.00. 2:30. IV. Part I: db–ab', Part II: c–g', Part III: Bb–c', Part IV: Bb_1–f. Twelve-bar blues in Bb. There is a written-out walking bass line in the fourth part. The melody is primarily in the first and second part. There is a section that may be repeated for improvised solos. Parts may be doubled for a large ensemble. See: Bird, Gary, ed., *Program Notes for the Solo Tuba*.

Stroud, Richard. *Treatments for Tuba*. Seesaw Music Corporation Publishers. Two euphoniums and two tubas. 1976. $33.00. 8:00. IV–V. Part I: Ab–a', Part II: Ab–d', Part III: G_1–bb, Part IV: G_1–ab. Three movements. Rhythmically complex and very dissonant. There is a brief aleatoric section in the second movement. Very interesting writing, and challenging to play.

Stroud, Richard, arr. *Silver Bells*. Richard Stroud. Two euphoniums and two tubas. $10.00. 1:20. IV. Part I: d–g', Part II: d–eb', Part III: Bb_1–g, Part IV: D–d. This arrangement is of "Carol of the Bells," not the popular secular Christmas song, "Silver Bells." Much of the melodic work is in the top two parts, though there are some tutti rhythmic passages in all four parts. No real range or technical demands. The tempo really determines the difficulty of this composition. Parts may be doubled for a large ensemble.

Strukow, Valery. *Tuba Quartet*. Editions Bim. Four tubas. 1992. $22.50.

Stuart, Hugh M. *Soft Shoo for Two Euphoniums and Two Tubas*. Shawnee Press, Incorporated. 1987. $11.00. 2:00. IV. Part I: e–bb', Part II: e–a', Part III: Bb_1–a, Part IV: Bb_1–g. A single soft-shoe style melody is passed around to each part. Technically this is fairly easy, but the range of the first part requires an advanced player.

Sullivan, Arthur. *Two Pieces by Sir Arthur Sullivan*. arr. Maurice Bale. Godiva Music. Two euphoniums and two tubas. 1994. $9.00. 4:00. IV. Part I: d–f ', Part II: Ab–d', Part III: D–ab, Part IV: (Bb) F_1–eb (f). Two movements: The Long Day Closes; Madrigal from "Mikado."

Susato, Tielman. *Ronde and Saltarelle*. arr. Denis Winter. Whaling Music Publishers. Two euphoniums and two tubas. 1978. $7.00. 2:00. IV. Part I: d–ab', Part II: d–ab', Part III: Bb–g, Part IV: Bb_1–d. A nice melody in a fast—slow—fast form. No significant technical problems. The top two parts are written in tenor clef. Parts may be doubled for a large ensemble. Recorded by the Atlantic Tuba Quartet, *Euphonic Sounds*, Golden Crest, CRS 4173.

Sydeman, William. *Music for Low Brass*. Seesaw Music Corporation. Two trombones (euphoniums) and two tubas. 1967. $19.00. 6:30. IV. Part I: E–bb', Part II: Bb_1–a, Part III: C–f ', Part IV: E_1–bb. Two movements. Originally written for three trombones and one tuba, but euphoniums could be used on the top two or three parts. Only moderately difficult, but the harmonies are quite dissonant. Some of the top two parts in tenor clef. The top three parts require mutes.

Tamura, Toru. *Quartet for Tubas*. Tokyo Bari-Tuba Ensemble.

Tautenhahn, Gunther. *Alte Kameraden*. Two euphoniums and two tubas.

Tautenhahn, Gunther. *In—Phase—Out*. Seesaw Music Corporation Publishers. Four tubas. 1978.

$19.00. 9:00. IV–V. Part I: C–e', Part II: A₁–e', Part III: G₁–e', Part IV: G♭₁–e♭'. Designed to alternate phases of sound with silence. There are very contemporary harmonies, and all four parts have large range demands. There are several contrasting sections within this single movement.

Taylor, Jeff. *Fanfare No. 1.* Horizon Press. Two euphoniums and two tubas. 1991. $6.00. 2:30. IV. Part I: c–c♯", Part II: c–g', Part III: A♭₁–g, Part IV: F₁–f. A technically challenging and exciting fanfare for all four parts. The tessitura of the first part is high.

Tchaikovsky, Peter. *Arabian Dance.* arr. David Woodcock. Green Bay Music. Two euphoniums and two tubas. 1993. $22.00. 2:00. III–IV.

Tchaikovsky, Peter. *Chinese Dance.* arr. David Woodcock. Green Bay Music. Two euphoniums and two tubas. 1993. $22.00. 3:00. IV. A well-known excerpt from the ballet *Nutcracker.* Most challenging for the first euphonium.

Tchaikovsky, Peter. *Dance of the Mirlitons.* arr. David Woodcock. Green Bay Music. Two euphoniums and two tubas. 1993. $22.00. 3:00. IV.

Tchaikovsky, Peter. *Russian Dance.* arr. David Woodcock. Green Bay Music. Two euphoniums and two tubas. 1993. $22.00. 2:00. IV. A spirited dance containing long technical passages for the euphoniums. Challenging, but fun to play.

Tchaikovsky, Peter. *March of the Toy Soldiers from the "Nutcracker."* arr. David Woodcock. Green Bay Music. Two euphoniums and two tubas. 1993. $22.00. 1:45. IV. Part I: c–b♭', Part II: B♭–b♭', Part III: D–b, Part IV: G₁–g. Technically challenging for the first and second parts. All parts need to be played lightly and cleanly. Parts may be doubled for a large ensemble.

Tchaikovsky, Peter. *Sleeping Tuba Waltz.* arr. John Fletcher. Emerson Edition. Four tubas. 1983. $24.50. 3:20. IV–V. Part I: B♭₁–b♭', Part II: B♭₁–f ', Part III: B♭₂–b♭, Part IV: B♭₂–d. From the ballet *Sleeping Beauty,* also used in the cartoon version made by Walt Disney. Parts I and II are quite high and were originally conceived for an F or E♭ tuba, but may be played on euphonium. Fun to play but challenging to perform at the tempo marked. Recorded by John Fletcher and The Philip Jones Brass Ensemble, *Brass Splendour,* London 411 9552, and on *Divertimento,* Argo, ARG 851.

Teike, Carl. *Alte Kameraden March.* arr. Paul Schmidt. Heavy Metal Music. Two euphoniums and two tubas. 1992. $7.00. 2:20. IV. Part I: A–g', Part II: A♭–d', Part III: A–f, Part IV: G₁–f. With just a couple of exceptions, the first euphonium has primary responsibility for the melody. No significant technical challenges. No score available. Parts may be doubled for a large ensemble.

Thielmans, Jean ("Boots"). *Bluesette.* arr. Rodger Vaughan. Rodger Vaughan. Two euphoniums and two tubas. 1991. $5.00. 3:30. IV. Part I: c–a', Part

II: d♭–d', Part III: G–a, Part IV: B♭₁–f. For the TUBADOURS. A jazz waltz. The melody is primarily in the top three parts. Drums may be added to enhance the jazz feel. Parts may be doubled for a large ensemble.

Thingnäs, Frode. *Faeroe Island Suite.* Frost Noter. Two euphoniums, two tubas, rhythm section, and orchestra. 12:00. V. Part I: B♭–b', Part II: B♭–a♭', Part III: C–f ', Part IV: A♭₁–e♭'. Three movements: The Nordic House; Perlan; Brandur. A jazz suite with the movements in swing, ballad, and samba styles. All parts are challenging and have sections for improvised solos. Also available with concert band accompaniment. A very effective piece.

Thompson, Bruce G. *Three Miniatures for Tuba Quartet.* Bruce Thompson. Four tubas. 5:00. III–IV. Part I: F–c'(d'), Part II: F♯₁–c', Part III: G₁–a, Part IV: F₁–g. Three movements: Prelude; Song; Introduction and March. A euphonium could be used on the first part to make this playable by high school students. No significant technical problems. Parts may be doubled for a large ensemble.

Thornton, Michael, arr. *Two English Madrigals.* PP Music. Four tubas. 1992. $6.50. 2:10. IV. Part I: E–d', Part II: A₁–d', Part III: G₁–f ', Part IV: B♭₁–f '. Two movements: Tosse Not My Soule; Thus Saith My Cloris Bright. An arrangement of two madrigals by John Dowland and John Wilbye respectively. Range demands are greater on the third and fourth parts than on the first and second. Requires four strong players. Originally published by Queen City Brass Publications and copyrighted in 1980.

Toda, Akira. *Euphonium Tuba Quartet.* Yamaha Kyohan Company Limited. Two euphoniums and two tubas. 1989. $17.50. 30 pp. III–IV. Part I: B♭–g', Part II: A–d', Part III: C–g, Part IV: A–e♭. A collection of 29 American folk songs and Christmas songs. No significant technical or range challenges. Short arrangements that are very playable by high school students, yet interesting enough for university students. Parts may be doubled for a large ensemble.

Tomkins, Thomas. *Oyez! Has Any Found a Lad?* arr. Paul Schmidt. Heavy Metal Music. Two euphoniums and two tubas. 1991. $7.00. 2:00. IV. Part I: d–g', Part II: c–d', Part III: A₁–g, Part IV: A₁–f. An aggressive melody primarily in the upper three parts in a traditional harmonic style. No significant technical problems, but players need to count carefully. No score available. Parts may be doubled for a large ensemble.

Torme, Mel. *The Christmas Song.* arr. Rodger Vaughan. Rodger Vaughan. Two euphoniums and two tubas. 1987. $5.00. 2:00. IV. Part I: F–g', Part II: e–e', Part III: D–b, Part IV: G₁–g. For the TUBADOURS. Probably the most popular secular Christmas song written in the twentieth century. The top three parts take turns playing the melody.

Works very well. No score available. Parts may be doubled for a large ensemble.

Uber, David. *Divertimento*. TUBA Press. Two euphoniums and two tubas. 1992. $12.00. 6:00. IV. Part I: d–d♭", Part II: c–f ', Part III: D–b, Part IV: G₁–g. Three movements: Scherzo; Legend; Marchette. The first movement is very fast and should be felt in one, not three. The second movement is very lyrical, and the third is a slow march. The tessitura of the first part is high. There are no range demands placed on the tubas. The third movement has a fuguelike section and is the most technically challenging of the piece. Originally published by Almitra Music Company, Incorporated (Kendor Music, Incorporated) and copyrighted in 1981. Parts may be doubled for a large ensemble.

Uber, David. *Divertimento No. 2, Op. 130*. Encore Music Publishers. Two euphoniums and two tubas. 1990. $24.50. 9:00. IV–V. Part I: d♭–c", Part II: B♭–g', Part III: B♭₁–b♭, Part IV: F₁–g. Five movements: Prologue; Dance; Diversion; Fete; Celebration. A very interesting and complex work for tuba/euphonium quartet. The tessitura and technical demands are greatest on the first part. Several sections are multimetric. Requires four strong players.

Uber, David. *Music for the Stage, Op. 283*. Rebu Music Publications. Two euphoniums and two tubas. 1993. $12.00. 7:50. IV. Part I: d–b♭', Part II: c–e', Part III: D♭–a, Part IV: G₁–f. Three movements: I Opening Curtain—Act I; II Entr'Acte; III Finale—Act II, Closing Curtain. Designed as a show piece, each part has numerous solo sections. All four parts are challenging but interesting. Close adherence to written dynamics is essential. Parts may be doubled for a large ensemble.

Uber, David. *Suite for Four Bass Tubas, Op. 67*. Almitra Music Company (Kendor Music, Incorporated). 1976. $11.00. 5:30. III–IV. Part I: F₁–b♭, Part II: A♭₁–a♭, Part III: B♭₁–g, Part IV: F₁–e♭. Four movements: Allegretto Misterioso; Allegro; Andante; Scherzo Allegro Molto. A classic work for tuba quartet. Technically it is not very challenging, but players must count carefully. Works well for good high school players or college students. Fun to play and for audiences.

Uber, David. *Three Bagatelles for Euphonium/Tuba Quartet, Op. 286*. Hidalgo Music. Two euphoniums and two tubas. 1992. $9.50. 5:15. IV. Part I: d♭–a♭', Part II: c–f ', Part III: C–b♭, Part IV: G₁–e. Three movements. Three short, fairly easy movements that contrast in key, meter, and style. The final movement is a bit more challenging than the first two. Parts may be doubled for a large ensemble.

Uber, David. *Vaudeville*. Touch of Brass Music Corporation. Two euphoniums and two tubas. 1982. $12.00. 8:00. IV. Part I: c–c", Part II: c–b♭, Part III: B♭₁–b♭, Part IV: F₁–b♭. Four movements:

Moderato; Very Rhythmic; Tempo di Blues; Allegro. Four contrasting movements in styles representative of their titles. The top two parts have a high tessitura, and all four parts are challenging technically. Fun to play.

Van Vactor, David. *Quartetto for Four Tubas*. Southern Music Company. Out of print. Two euphoniums and two tubas. 1974. 13:00. IV. Part I: G–b♭' (c"), Part II: G–f ', Part III: C–c', Part IV: (B♭₂) F₁–f♯. Four movements: Chorales; Allegro Scherzando; Intermezzo; Allegretto Giusto. The movements contrast greatly in style, meter, and key. The second and fourth movements are technically challenging at times. Good writing, fun to play.

Vasconi, Eugene. *Promenade*. Southern Music Company. Two euphoniums and two tubas. 1989. $5.00. 2:30. IV. Part I: d–f ', Part II: G–d', Part III: G–a, Part IV: B♭₁–f. Technically not very challenging. The melody and harmonies are very traditional. The melody resembles a fugue subject. Works quite well for large ensembles. Parts may be doubled for a large ensemble.

Vaughan, Rodger. *Fanfares*. Rodger Vaughan. Two euphoniums and two tubas. 1988. $5.00. 2:00. IV. Part I: d–b♭', Part II: c–f ', Part III: c–b♭, Part IV: A₁–f. Commissioned by Skip Gray and written for the University of Kentucky Tuba Ensemble. A moderate tempo fanfare with the first and second parts often echoing the third and fourth parts. Some divisi sections in the top three parts. Very effective. Parts may be doubled for a large ensemble.

Vaughan, Rodger. *Marce's Blues*. Rodger Vaughan. Two euphoniums and two tubas. 1993. $5.00. 2:45. IV. Part I: f–a', Part II: e–a', Part III: F–a, Part IV: F₁–e♭. For the nineteenth birthday of Cecilia Nocum. A traditonal blues progression and format. Most of the melody is in the top two parts. Drums may be added. Parts may be doubled for a large ensemble.

Vaughan, Rodger. *Petite and Powerful: A Rag for Tuba/Euphonium Quartet*. Rodger Vaughan. Two euphoniums and two tubas. 1991. $5.00. 2:45. IV. Part I: c–b♭', Part II: c–e♭', Part III: C–c♭, Part IV: D♭₁–g. Composed for the 21st birthday of Roxane Requio. A medium tempo rag. The melody is very syncopated, especially in the top two parts. Parts may be doubled for a large ensemble.

Vaughan, Rodger. *Riverwest Rag*. Rodger Vaughan. Two euphoniums and two tubas. 1989. $5.00. 2:30. IV. Part I: b♭–g', Part II: B♭–e♭', Part III: B♭–b♭, Part IV: E♭₁–e♭. Composed for the 21st birthday of Minako Kawanishi. An up-tempo rag. The lively melody is primarily in the top two parts. Fun for both performers and audiences. No score available. Parts may be doubled for a large ensemble.

Vaughan, Rodger. *Wiggleworm Squirm: The Neighbor Note Nocturne, The Semitone Serenade, A Rag*. Rodger Vaughan. Two euphoniums and two tubas.

1989. $5.00. 6:00. IV. Part I: g–bb', Part II: Bb–d', Part III: Eb–ab, Part IV: D$_1$–e. Written for the TUBADOURS and dedicated to Minako Kawanishi. A very fun rag to play. No significant technical difficulties, though the melody is quite syncopated. Drums may be added for effect. No score available. Parts may be doubled for a large ensemble.

Vaughan, Rodger, arr. *Amazing Grace*. Rodger Vaughan. Two euphoniums, two tubas, and garden hose. $5.00.

Vaughan, Rodger, arr. *American Favorites: Tuba Euphonium Quartets*. TUBA Press. Two euphoniums and two tubas. 1992. $15.00. 14 pp. III–IV. Part I: Bb–ab', Part II: Bb–f ', Part III: Bb$_1$–bb, Part IV: Eb$_1$–f. A delightful set of light arrangements of traditional American folk melodies. All parts are featured with the melody at one time or another. No significant technical problems. The euphonium parts are printed in bass and treble clef. Originally published in 1977 by the Mirafone Corporation. Parts may be doubled for a large ensemble.

Vaughan, Rodger, arr. *Away in a Manger*. Rodger Vaughan. Two euphoniums and two tubas. 1984. $5.00.

Vaughan, Rodger, arr. *Down by the Old Mill Stream*. Rodger Vaughan. Two euphoniums and two tubas. 1990. $5.00. 1:30. III–IV. Part I: c–f ', Part II: c–d', Part III: c–a, Part IV: C–e. For the TUBADOURS. Cute arrangement of this familiar melody. Very appropriate for high school or college students. No score available. Parts may be doubled for a large ensemble. Recorded by the TUBADOURS, *Ve Iss Da Mighty TUBADOURS Ya?*, Crystal Records, S421.

Vaughan, Rodger, arr. *Dream*. Rodger Vaughan. Two euphoniums and two tubas. 1988. $5.00. 1:30. IV. Part I: eb–g', Part II: eb–eb', Part III: Eb–ab, Part IV: Eb$_1$–eb. For Abe Torchinsky and the Aspentubas. Nice arrangement of this classic "Big Band" era ballad. The lyrical melody is primarily in the euphoniums. No score available. Parts may be doubled for a large ensemble.

Vaughan, Rodger, arr. *Eight Days of Christmas*. Rodger Vaughan. Two euphoniums and two tubas. 1982. $5.00.

Vaughan, Rodger, arr. *God Rest Ye, Merry Gentlemen*. Rodger Vaughan. Two euphoniums and two tubas. $5.00. 2:00. IV. Part I: f–bb', Part II: d–eb', Part III: G–bb, Part IV: Bb$_1$–g. For the TUBADOURS. Good arrangement of this traditional Christmas carol. No significant technical problems. Parts may be doubled for a large ensemble. Recorded by the TUBADOURS, *Merry Christmas Album*, Crystal Records, S422.

Vaughan, Rodger, arr. *Good Christian Men Rejoice*. Rodger Vaughan. Two euphoniums and two tubas. 1984. $5.00.

Vaughan, Rodger, arr. *Greensleeves*. Rodger Vaughan. Two euphoniums and two tubas. 1976. $5.00.

Vaughan, Rodger, arr. *Infant Holy*. Rodger Vaughan. Two euphoniums and two tubas. 1982. $5.00.

Vaughan, Rodger, arr. *Java*. Rodger Vaughan. Two euphoniums and two tubas. 1990. $5.00. 3:00. IV. Part I: db–ab', Part II: db–ab', Part III: Ab–c', Part IV: Ab$_1$–f. For the TUBADOURS. Interesting arrangement of this jazz standard. The melody is primarily in the first and second euphonium parts. Several meter changes in the middle section. No score available. Parts may be doubled for a large ensemble.

Vaughan, Rodger, arr. *Jingle Bells Waltz*. Rodger Vaughan. Two euphoniums and two tubas. $5.00. 2:00. IV. Part I: eb–bb', Part II: Ab–f ', Part III: Ab–db', Part IV: Db–gb. For the TUBADOURS. A very interesting and fast-paced waltz version of "Jingle Bells." The meter repeats the pattern 3+3+3+2. Drums may be added for effect. Fun to play. No score available. Parts may be doubled for a large ensemble.

Vaughan, Rodger, arr. *Lo How a Rose*. Rodger Vaughan. Two euphoniums and two tubas. 1984. $5.00.

Vaughan, Rodger, arr. *Mack, The Knight*. Rodger Vaughan. Two euphoniums and two tubas. 1988. $5.00. 2:00. IV. Part I: g–g', Part II: f–d', Part III: A–bb, Part IV: Bb$_1$–g. For the TUBADOURS. A humorous combination of "Mack, The Knife" and the music from a McDonald's restaurant commercial featuring "Mac Tonight." Most of the melody is in the upper two parts and the fourth part. Fun to play. Parts may be doubled for a large ensemble. No score available. Premiered at the Octubafest at the University of Kansas, 1988.

Vaughan, Rodger, arr. *March of the Toys*. Rodger Vaughan. Two euphoniums and two tubas. 1975. $5.00.

Vaughan, Rodger, arr. *Moonglow*. Rodger Vaughan. Two euphoniums and two tubas. 1991. $5.00. 2:10. III–IV. Part I: g#–g', Part II: d–d', Part III: F–bb, Part IV: Bb$_1$–f. For the TUBADOURS. A nice slow swing melody with most of the work in the euphonium. Not difficult technically. No score available. Parts may be doubled for a large ensemble.

Vaughan, Rodger, arr. *Santa Claus Is Coming to Town*. Rodger Vaughan. Two euphoniums and two tubas. 1984. $5.00. 1:30. IV. Part I: f–a', Part II: d–f ', Part III: F–bb, Part IV: F$_1$–e. For the TUBADOURS. Cute arrangement of this fun Christmas melody. Many tempo and style changes. Parts may be doubled for a large ensemble. Recorded by the TUBADOURS, *Merry Christmas Album*, Crystal Records, S422.

Vaughan, Rodger, arr. *Sentimental Journey*. Rodger Vaughan. Two euphoniums and two tubas. 1977. $5.00. 1:45. IV. Part I: g#–f ', Part II: d–d', Part III: Gb–bb, Part IV: Bb$_1$–c. For the TUBADOURS. A moderate swing tune with most of the melody primarily in the top two parts. No significant technical problems. Drums may be added. Parts may be doubled for a large ensemble.

Vaughan, Rodger, arr. *Silent Night*. Rodger Vaughan. Two euphoniums and two tubas. 1984. $5.00.

Vaughan, Rodger, arr. *Speak Low*. Rodger Vaughan. Two euphoniums and two tubas. 1990. $5.00.

Vaughan, Rodger, arr. *Take Me Out to the Ballgame*. Rodger Vaughan. Two euphoniums and two tubas. 1988. $5.00.

Vaughan, Rodger, arr. *Undecided*. Rodger Vaughan. Two euphoniums and two tubas. 1988. $5.00. 3:20. IV. Part I: f–ab', Part II: f–eb', Part III: F–g, Part IV: F_1–d. For the TUBADOURS. A famous dance melody from the "Big Band" era. Contains an extended tuba solo. Drums may be added for style enhancement. No score available. Parts may be doubled for a large ensemble.

Vaughan, Rodger, arr. *Veni Emmanuel*. Rodger Vaughan. Two euphoniums and two tubas. 1983. $5.00. 3:00. IV. Part I: f–f ', Part II: c–g', Part III: G–a, Part IV: G_1–e. A very lyrical and traditional arrangement. Works well. Parts may be doubled for a large ensemble.

Vazzana, Anthony. *Montaggi for Four Tubas*. TUBA Press. 1993. $40.00. 12:00. V. Part I: A_1–a', Part II: A_1–g', Part III: A_1–e', Part IV: C#$_1$–c'. A contemporary work that is very technically demanding of all four parts. Twentieth-century techniques include multiphonics, quartertones, hand clapping, shouting, singing, and chanting into the instrument. Each player reads from the score. All parts require mutes, and players are asked in one section players are asked to play from their lowest possible note to their highest possible note. A very dissonant and complex work. Originally written in 1978. Winner of Honorable Mention in the Tuba Quartet Composition Contest sponsored by the Los Angeles Tuba Quartet and the Mirafone Corporation.

Verdi, Guiseppe. *Ave Maria*. arr. Mark Nelson. TUBA Press. Two euphoniums and two tubas. 1994. $6.00. III–IV. Part I: c–f#', Part II: G–d', Part III: F–f#, Part IV: G_1–d. For the Hokkaido Euphonium/Tuba Camp. No technical problems, though players must display sensitivity to the melodic line. Parts may be doubled for a large ensemble.

Verdi, Guiseppe. *Choro di Schiavi Ebrei (Chor der Gefangenen aus der Opera "Nabucco")*. arr. Mark Evans. Musikverlag Barbara Evans. Two euphoniums and two tubas. 1992. $15.00. 3:30. IV. Part I: F–g', Part II: B–f ', Part III: F_1–d', Part IV: F_1–f. All parts have an opportunity to play the lyrical melody. Numerous repeating patterns of triplets and sextuplets accompany the melody. The tempo is quite slow, and the rhythm patterns can be a challenge to fit together. Parts may be doubled for a large ensemble.

Victoria, Thomas Luis de. *O Regem Coeli for Tuba Quartet*. arr. Joseph Schwartz. The Unicorn Music Company, Incorporated. 1990. 4:30. IV. Part I: c–f ', Part II: eb–eb', Part III: Eb–bb', Part IV: Eb–bb'. Two movements. A very nice arrangement of this Renaissance madrigal. The tessitura of the first part is high. Playable by high school students if the first and second parts are played on euphonium. Part II is faster and more polyphonic than Part I. No real technical challenges. Parts may be doubled for a large ensemble.

Victoria, Thomas Luis de. *O Vos Omnes (Motet)*. arr. James Self. Wimbledon Music Incorporated. Four tubas. 1979. $7.00. 2:30. II–III. Part I: f–eb', Part II: d–eb', Part III: Ab–gb, Part IV: (Eb$_1$)Ab$_1$–eb. This motet is marked Lento, with the main theme primarily in the first two parts. The arranger suggests the ideal instrumentation would be euphoniums on the first and second parts and tubas on the third and fourth. Not rhythmically challenging, and with euphoniums playing the top two parts, this is easily playable by high school students. Parts may be doubled for a large ensemble.

Vivaldi, Antonio. *Concerto*. arr. Karl Humble. T.A.P. Music. Two euphoniums and two tubas. 1990. $10.00. 6:00. IV–V. Part I: f–c", Part II: c–bb', Part III: Bb–d', Part IV: F_1–bb. Three movements: Allegro; Largo; Allegro. Originally written for two trumpets and orchestra in the key of C. The tessitura of the first two parts is quite high. Technically challenging in some spots, depending on the tempos used. Parts may be doubled for a large ensemble. No score available.

Wagner, J. F. *Under the Double Eagle*. arr. Paul Schmidt. Heavy Metal Music. Two euphoniums and two tubas. 1990. $7.00. 2:45. IV. Part I: Bb–g', Part II: G–g', Part III: D–c', Part IV: F_1–e(a). All four parts have an opportunity to play the melody. No significant technical challenges. No score available. Parts may be doubled for a large ensemble.

Wagner, Richard. *Bridal Chorus from Lohengrin*. arr. Dan Oliver. Ohio Valley Tuba Quartet Press. Two euphoniums and two tubas. 1988. $9.00. 2:30. III–IV. Part I: d–g', Part II: d–d', Part III: G–a, Part IV: Bb$_1$–Bb. Very usable arrangement of this famous wedding introit. The melody is primarily in the first part, but is not demanding of any of the players. Parts may be doubled for a large ensemble.

Wagner, Richard. *Pilgerchor aus Tannhäuser*. arr. Bruno Seitz. Musikverlag Martin Scherbacher. Four tubas. 1988. $15.00. 3:00. IV. Part I: Ab$_1$–f ', Part II: Ab$_1$–c', Part III: F–a#, Part IV: F_1–eb. No significant technical problems. The first and second parts are written for tubas in F. A euphonium could be used on the first part. Good arrangement; works quite well. Parts may be doubled for a large ensemble.

Wagner, Richard. *Pilgrim's Chorus from Tannhäuser*. arr. Paul Schmidt. Heavy Metal Music. Two euphoniums and two tubas. 1991. $7.00. 3:20. IV. Part I: A♭–f ', Part II: A♭–d', Part III: F–c', Part IV: G♭₁–g♭. Nice arrangement. No technical or range problems. A conductor will help the ensemble performance. Parts may be doubled for a large ensemble.

Waldteufel, E. *The Skaters' Waltzes.* arr. Soichi Konagaya. Sonic Arts, Incorporated. Two euphoniums and two tubas. 1986. $12.00. 5:30. IV. Part I: e♭–a♭', Part II: B♭–e♭', Part III: C–a♭, Part IV: G₁–e♭. A medley of three popular waltzes. The melody is primarily in the first part. No range or technical problems. Parts may be doubled for a large ensemble.

Warren, Harry. *Selections from 42nd Street.* arr. Doug Minerd. PP Music. Two euphoniums and two tubas. 1989. $20.00. 6:00. IV. Part I: B–a', Part II: B–a', Part III: G₁–e', Part IV: G₁–f '. The medley includes "We're in the Money," "Lullaby of Broadway," "Forty-Second Street," and "Shuffle Off to Buffalo." The range of all four parts is quite high. A good swing feel is necessary. The addition of a drum set would benefit the ensemble. Works very well. Parts may be doubled for a large ensemble. Recorded by the British Tuba Quartet, *Elite Syncopations,* Polyphonic Reproductions Limited, QPRZ 012D; and the Monarch Tuba/Euphonium Quartet.

Watts, Charles. *Suite in D♭ for Tubas and Euphoniums.* Charles Watts. Two euphoniums and two tubas. 1992. $5.00. 6:30. IV. Part I: c–b♭', Part II: c–g♭', Part III: A♭₁–b♭, Part IV: A♭₁–a♭. Three movements: Alla Marcia; Moderato; Chaconne. Rhythmically not very difficult, and the melody and harmonies are very traditional. The three movements contrast in key, meter, and style. Parts may be doubled for a large ensemble.

Weber, Carl Maria von. *Hunter's Chorus from "Der Freischütz."* arr. F.H. Laws. Ohio Valley Tuba Quartet Press. Two euphoniums and two tubas. 1988. $9.00. 1:20. III–IV. Part I: f–a', Part II: d–d', Part III: c–b♭, Part IV: E♭–f. Very traditional in its harmonic and rhythmic treatment of this melody. No significant technical problems. Parts may be doubled for a large ensemble.

Weber, Carl Maria von. *Hunter's Chorus from "Der Freischütz."* arr. Paul Schmidt. Heavy Metal Music. Two euphoniums and two tubas. 1991. $7.00. 1:20. III–IV. Part I: c–e', Part II: A–a, Part III: G–f, Part IV: B♭₁–f. The melody is primarily in the top two parts. No significant technical problems. No score available. Parts may be doubled for a large ensemble.

Wedner, Henry Lewis. *O Little Town of Bethlehem.* arr. Rodger Vaughan. Rodger Vaughan. Two euphoniums and two tubas. 1984. $5.00. 2:25. III–IV. Part I: d–a', Part II: d–d', Part III: D–a, Part IV: F₁–d. For the TUBADOURS. A very traditional arrangement. The melody is primarily in the top two parts.

Works well. Parts may be doubled for a large ensemble. Recorded by the TUBADOURS, *Merry Christmas Album,* Crystal Records, S422.

Weelkes, Thomas. *Lo, Country Sports.* arr. Paul F. Hartin. Cellar Press. Four tubas. 1974. 2:00. III–IV. Part I: B♭–c', Part II: B♭–c, Part III: B♭₁–f, Part IV: A₁–c. Playable by high school students if the first and second parts are played on euphonium. A typical contrapuntal madrigal. Not difficult technically. Parts may be doubled for a large ensemble.

Welcher, Dan. *Hauntings for Tuba Ensemble.* Dan Welcher. Two euphoniums and two tubas. 1986. $25.00. 7:30. IV. Part I: G–c", Part II: A♯₁–b', Part III: F♯₁–d♯', Part IV: D₁–c♯'. Four movements: In the Twilight; Kaspar; Poltergeist; Il Commendatore (without pause). Commissioned by Tubists Universal Brotherhood Association. Contemporary tonal harmonies, along with basic twentieth-century techniques. The tessitura of the first two parts is high and requires strong players. All parts require mutes. Parts may be doubled for a large ensemble. First performed by the College All-Star Tuba/Euphonium Ensemble at the 1986 International Tuba-Euphonium Conference.

Werden, David R., arr. *Songs of the British Isles.* Whaling Music Publishers. Two euphoniums and two tubas. 1986. $9.50. 6:30. III–IV. Part I: B♭₁–g', Part II: G–f ' (g'), Part III: (C) E♭–c', Part IV: (E♭₁) B♭₁–g. Four movements: The Minstrel Boy; Molly Malone; Danny Boy; English Country Garden. Four short familiar English folk songs. Technically not challenging and consequently very appropriate for good high school ensembles. The first part is printed in treble clef. Parts may be doubled for a large ensemble.

Wilder, Alec, arr. *Carols for a MERRY TUBA-CHRISTMAS.* Harvey Phillips Foundation. Two euphoniums and two tubas. 1977. $5.00. 20 pp. III–IV. Part I: e–a♭', Part II: A–e, Part III: C–c', Part IV: E♭₁–d. Commissioned by Harvey Phillips. Dedicated to William J. Bell. The book of Christmas carols used in the annual TubaChristmas concerts all over the world. Nineteen familiar carols plus Eddie Sauter's arrangement of *Come, Sweet Death* (three parts). While the technical and range demands are not great, these carols should not be considered easy. They require four moderately strong players, as the melody shifts between all four parts. With Wilder, even the accompaniment parts are interesting, but challenging to play. Designed for and actually work much better with multiple players on a part. A treble clef book is available for the first and second parts. Available from the Harvey Phillips Foundation or at any TubaChristmas concert. Recorded by Harvey Phillips/TubaChristmas, Harvey Phillips Foundation, HPF NR-1111; and Harvey Phillips and his TUBASANTAS, Harvey Phillips Foundation, HPF 1000-1.

Wilder, Alec, and Bewley, Norlan, arr. *Carols for a MERRY TUBACHRISTMAS, Volume II*. Harvey Phillips Foundation. Two euphoniums and two tubas. 1992. $6.00. 66 pp. III–IV. Part I: e–ab', Part II: A–e, Part III: C–c', Part IV: Eb₁–d. Commissioned by Harvey Phillips. Dedicated to William J. Bell and Alec Wilder. Contains all the carols from Volume I plus thirteen new carols arranged by Norlan Bewley for a total of 32 Christmas carols. All but three arrangements are in score form. Technical demands are moderate. A treble clef book is also available. These are designed for a quartet or mass ensemble. Recorded by Harvey Phillips and his TUBASANTAS, Harvey Phillips Foundation, HPF 1000-1.

Williams, William N. *Little Suite for Tuba Quartet*. T.A.P. Music. 1990. $12.00. 10:00. IV. Part I: C–ab', Part II: Bb₁–g', Part III: C–g', Part IV: G₁–eb'. Three movements: Barcarole; Scherzo; March. Range is very demanding for all four parts. Other possible instrumentations include two euphoniums and two tubas, or three euphoniums and one tuba. The third player is asked to tap rhythmically on the rim of the bell with a metal mallet. Parts may be doubled for a large ensemble.

Wilson, Kenyon. *Dance No. 1*. TUBA Press. Two euphoniums and two tubas. 1993. $5.00. 2:00. IV. Part I: f–c", Part II: Bb–f ', Part III: F–bb, Part IV: F₁–Bb. A very lively melody that is multimetric and primarily in the euphoniums. All parts are interesting and have some technical challenges, depending on the performance tempo. Works well for a concert opener. Parts may be doubled for a large ensemble.

Winteregg, Steven L. *Time Structures*. Steven Winteregg. Four tubas. 1979. 11:00. IV–V. Part I: Bb–g', Part II: G–eb', Part III: C–a, Part IV: C₁–g. Four movements: Gothic Cathedral; Brunelleschi's Dome; Bayreuth Festspielhaus; Art Deco Skyscraper. The four contrasting movements vary in tempo and style. All are multimetric and are complex rhythmically. The top two parts could be played by euphonium but are intended to be performed by tubas. A very interesting work, though complex. Requires four strong players.

Wolking, Henry. *Tuba Blues Medley*. Touch of Brass Music Corporation. Two euphoniums, two tubas, and drums. 1984. $10.00. 5:30. IV. Part I: c–b', Part II: Bb₁–g', Part III: G₁–a , Part IV: E₁–c#'. A cute basic twelve-bar blues in the key of C. Features written-out solos for the first tuba part in the slow blues section, then a section opened up for anyone to improvise in the faster swing section. The feel switches back and forth between half time and double time. Drums really help to make the tempo and style changes work. Parts may be doubled for a large ensemble. Recorded by the British Tuba Quartet, *Elite Syncopations*, Polyphonic Reproductions Limited, QPRZ012D; and the Northern Tuba Lights.

Woodcock, David, arr. *How Much Is That Doggy in the Window?* Green Bay Music. Two euphoniums and two tubas. 1993. $22.00. 1:30. IV. Part I: A–bb', Part II: c–g', Part III: C–b, Part IV: F₁–eb. Cute arrangement of this classic children's melody. The tubas have much of the melodic responsibility. No range or technical problems. Parts may be doubled for a large ensemble.

Woodcock, David. *Tiny Tuba Tunes*. Green Bay Music. Two euphoniums and two tubas. 1993. $22.00. 3:34. III. Part I: c–c', Part II: G–a, Part III: D–e, Part IV: A₁–c. Five movements: Austrian Folk Song; Oh, Susanna; Old MacDonald Had a Farm; When the Saints Go Marching In; Greensleeves. Very easy and playable melodies. The melody is passed around to all parts. Ideal for younger players. All four parts are printed in bass and treble clef. Parts may be doubled for a large ensemble.

Five Parts

Anderson, Eugene, arr. *Take Me Out to the Ballgame*. Anderson's Arizona Originals. Three euphoniums and two tubas. 1988. $5.00. 1:10. III–IV. Part I: g–a', Part II: c–f', Part III: G–c', Part IV: A–d', Part V: G₁–d. Fairly easy arrangement of this familiar melody. The first tuba part is too high for most high school players, a euphonium may be used for this part or the tuba player may take some of the passages down an octave. An extra part combines the second and third parts so the arrangement can be played as a quartet. Parts may be doubled for a large ensemble.

Anderson, Eugene. *Hawaiian Quintet '88*. Anderson's Arizona Originals. Three euphoniums and two tubas. 1988. $5.00. 2:00. IV. Part I: f–g', Part II: c–d', Part III: d–ab', Part IV: Bb–db', Part V: F₁–bb. A fanfare-like melody in 6/8. Some syncopation; tubas have an interesting bass line. Two of the euphoniums parts were originally written for two conch shells.

Bach, J.S. *Contrapunctus I*. arr. R. Winston Morris. The Brass Press. Two euphoniums and three tubas. 1974. $5.00. 4:00. IV. Part I: G–ab', Part II: G–g', Part III: F–ab, Part IV: A₁–f, Part V: (C₁)F₁–d. Good arrangement of this traditional Bach Fugue. No real technical or range demands; the challenge is to count correctly to avoid incorrect entrances. Other possible instrumentations include three euphoniums and two tubas; or two euphoniums, one F tuba, and two CC tubas. Parts may be doubled with care. Recorded by Tennessee Technological University, *The Golden Sound of Euphoniums*, Mirafone Corporation promotional recording.

Bach, J.S. *Passacaglia and Fugue in C Minor*. arr. James A. Garrett. James Garrett. Two euphoniums and three tubas. 1987. $50.00. 14:00. IV–V. Part I: c–c", Part II: A–c", Part III: C₁–eb', Part IV: C₁–

c', Part V: C_1–a♭. The tessitura of the first two parts is high. Technical demands are extensive on all five parts. Fine writing. Requires five strong players.

Baskin, Bernard. *Four Excursions for Five Tubas.* Bernard Baskin. 1971. 8:00. IV. Part I: F_1–f, Part II: F_1–f, Part III: F_1–g, Part IV: F_1–a, Part V: F_1–a. Four movements. Technically not very difficult. The harmonies are quite dissonant with numerous seconds, ninths, and augmented fourths. There are many meter changes, but all with the quarter note remaining constant. A conductor is strongly recommended.

Bathory-Kitsz, Dennis. *Quintet for Tubas.* Westleaf Edition. Five tubas. 1974. $50.00. 12:00. V. Part I: $A♭_1$–d", Part II: E♭–b♭', Part III: C–g', Part IV: E♭–d', Part V: C♭$_1$–e♭'. Three movements. Extreme range and technical demands for all parts. The tessitura of the first two parts is very high. Numerous complex meter changes, including 5.5/4, 14/4, 11.25/4, 4.25/4. The composition is tonal, but requires five very strong players.

Colding-Jørgensen, Henrik. *Puer Natus.* Henrik Coling-Jørgensen. Five Tubas. 1976. 7:00. IV. Part I: E♭–e', Part II: E–c, Part III: E–c, Part IV: F_1–a, Part V: F_1–c♭. Seven movements. All parts are interesting and at times technically challenging. Frequently alternates between a chorale and a highly rhythmic style.

Debussy, Claude. *Golliwog's Cake Walk.* arr. Norihisa Yamamoto. KIWI Music Press. Two Euphoniums and three tubas. 1988. $4.95. 2:10. IV. Part I: d–b♭', Part II: B♭–a♭', Part III: E♭–f ', Part IV: E♭$_1$–c', Part V: E♭$_1$–a♭. Good arrangement of this famous melody. No significant technical problems. Fun to play. The first part is printed in tenor clef. No score available. Parts may be doubled for a large ensemble.

Dutton, Brent. *Sub-Terrestrial Sounds.* Seesaw Music Corporation Publishers. Five tubas. 1978. $36.00. IV–V. Solo tuba: C_1–f ', Part II: G♭$_1$–a♭, Part III: G♭$_1$–a♭, Part IV: E_1–d♭', Part V: C_1–a'. For solo tuba with four tubas accompanying or solo tuba and tape. Very contemporary, with enormous range demands, multiphonics, and improvisation. See listing under "Music for Tuba and Tape."

Fiegel, Todd, arr. *Medley of the Third Kind.* UNITUBA Press. Out of Print. Three euphoniums and two tubas. 1978. 7:00. IV. Part I: G–a', Part II: B♭–b', Part III: F–f ', Part IV: E♭$_1$–b♭, Part V: A♭$_1$–f. To The Unitubas. A humorous medley of the themes from *Close Encounters, William Tell Overture,* and *Star Wars.* Parts may be doubled for a large ensemble.

Forte, Aldo. *Tubas Latinas (Overture for Tuba Ensemble).* TUBA Press. Two euphoniums, three tubas, and two optional percussion. 1992. $10.00. 7:00. IV–V. Part I: c–b♭', Part II: c–a', Part III: F–e♭', Part IV: G_1–b, Part V: F_1–b. Commissioned by Ernie Walls for the Tennessee Technological University Tuba Ensemble, R. Winston Morris, Director. Consists of four sections in a slow—fast—slow—fast format with styles of Spanish, Latin American, and jazz rhythms. The tessitura of the first part is very high, and all parts are technically demanding. The second and third parts have several divisi sections. Requires strong players. Parts may be doubled for a large ensemble. The composition was premiered at the 1992 National MENC Convention in New Orleans.

Frank, Marcel G. *Ballad for Five Tubas.* Marcel Frank. Two euphoniums and three tubas. 1972. 4:30. IV. Part I: f–b♭', Part II: c♯–f♯', Part III: F♯–b♭, Part IV: E–f, Part V: A_1–d. A very slow lyrical composition. Responsibility for the melody lies primarily in the first part. The tessitura of the first part is high, but the other parts are not very challenging. Requires players with mature sounds.

Frank, Marcel G. *Lyric Poem for Five Tubas.* University of Miami Press. Out of Press. Two euphoniums and three tubas, or one F tuba and two CC tubas. 1971. $6.00. 4:30. IV. Part I: e♭–b♭', Part II: F♯–g', Part III: F♯–b♭, Part IV: E–f, Part V: A_1–d. To Connie Weldon. A melodically rich composition with most of the difficulty in the first part. The first part has a very high tessitura, but the two tuba parts are not demanding. Parts may be doubled for a large ensemble. Recorded by the University of Miami Tuba Ensemble, Miami United Tuba Society, 14568; U.S. Armed Forces Tuba/Euphonium Ensemble and Massed Ensemble, U.S. Army Band Recordings.

Frederick, Donald R., arr. *Fourteen Familiar Hymns, Carols, and Spirituals.* Accura Music. Three euphoniums and two tubas. 1991. 8 pp. III–IV. Part I: e♭–a', Part II: c–f ', Part III: A–c', Part IV: C–a♭, F_1–A♭. As the fifth part doubles the fourth part at the octave, these selection scould be played as quartets. Very useful for occasions when sacred music is appropriate. Parts may be doubled for a large ensemble.

Fritze, Gregory, arr. *Simple Gifts.* Gregory Fritze. Solo tuba, two euphoniums, and two tubas. 1990. $10.00. 4:00. IV. Solo tuba: C–c', Part II: d–g', Part III: A–e', Part IV: F–g, Part V: F_1–c. This famous folk melody is played by a solo tuba with a simple and very lyrical accompaniment. Also available for solo tuba and three-part accompaniment. Parts may be doubled for a large ensemble.

Fritze, Gregory. *Octubafest Polka for Tuba Ensemble.* Gregory Fritze. Two euphoniums and three tubas. 1976. $10.00. 4:00. IV. Part I: A♭–a♭', Part II: A♭–f ', Part III: E♭–d♭', Part IV: A♭$_1$–f, Part V: A♭$_1$–c. Commissioned by Harvey Phillips in celebration of the annual OCTUBAFEST. A very cute melody with the beginning and end utilizing a brief excerpt from the "Ride of the Valkyries." Not difficult and fun to play. Parts may be doubled for a large ensemble.

Fritze, Gregory. *Salutation Fanfare.* Gregory Fritze. Three euphoniums and two tubas. 1985. $10.00. 2:00. III–IV. Part I: B♭–a♭', Part II: B♭–f♯', Part III: B♭–e', Part IV: B♭₁–b♭, Part V: A₁–f. Commissioned by and written for the 1985 New York Brass Conference. A very syncopated fanfare melody and accompaniment. The melody is not technically challenging, and most moving lines are played by two or more parts at once. Parts may be doubled for a large ensemble.

Garrett, James A., arr. *Londonderry Air.* Ludwig Music Publishing Company. Three euphoniums and two tubas. 1987. $15.50. 2:20. III–IV. Part I: G–a', Part II: d–g', Part III: c–e', Part IV: F–c', Part V: F₁–d. Solo euphonium and four-part tuba/euphonium accompaniment. The arrangement is very lyrical and contains some very lush harmonies. Both euphonium parts are available in treble and bass clef. An excellent selection to feature a guest soloist or outstanding student euphoniumist. Parts may be doubled for a large ensemble. Recorded by the U.S. Armed Forces Tuba/Euphonium Ensemble, Mark Records, MW89MCD-8.

Gates, Crawford. *Psalm.* Intrada Music Group. Three trombones, one euphonium, and one tuba. 1984. $7.50. 3:00. IV. Part I: e–c", Part II: B–g', Part III: G–e', Part IV: G–f ', Part V: E–b. Commissioned by M. Dee Stewart and first performed at the 1984 International Brass Congress. First three parts may be played on euphonium. Nice chorale writing, very melodic. The tessitura of the first part is quite high and requires a very mature player. Mutes are required of all players. Parts may be doubled for a large ensemble. See listing under "Music for Tuba in Mixed Ensemble."

Gesualdo, Carlo. *Moro Lasso.* arr. Eugene Anderson. Anderson's Arizona Originals. Three euphoniums and two tubas. 1988. $5.00. 3:00. III–IV. Part I: f–g', Part II: B♭–e', Part III: B–c', Part IV: E–g, Part V: A₁–c. A highly polyphonic madrigal. All parts have the opportunity to play the theme. No significant technical problems. Parts may be doubled for a large ensemble.

Gesualdo, P. *Madrigale.* arr. John McClernan. Tuba/ Euphonium Music Publications. Out of print. Two euphoniums and three tubas. 1971. 5:00. III–IV.

Henderson, Ray. *Five Foot Two, Eyes of Blue (has anybody seen my girl?).* arr. Mark Nelson. Whaling Music Publishers. Two euphoniums and three tubas. 1988. $7.50. 2:00. IV. Part I: b♭–b♭', Part II: a–g', Part III: F–d', Part IV: C–a, Part V: B♭₂–A. Can also be played by three euphoniums and two tubas. A lot of syncopation. The top part has most of the melodic responsibility. Parts may be doubled for a large ensemble.

Holborne, Anthony. *Pavan: The Funerals.* arr. Paul F. Hartin. Cellar Press. Five tubas. 1975. 2:30. III–IV. Part I: f–f ', Part II: B♭–c', Part III: F–a♭, Part

IV: F–b♭, Part V: F₁–d. The first part has a high tessitura and may be played on an F tuba or euphonium. Not very difficult technically. Parts may be doubled for a large ensemble.

Howard, Bart. *Fly Me to the Moon.* arr. Robert Hughes. Hampshire House Publishing Corporation (Mark Tezak). Four trombones (euphoniums) and one tuba. 1986. 4:00. IV. Part I: g–c♯", Part II: f–a", Part III: e–d", Part IV: A–g', Part V: F₁–d'. Originally written for four trombones and tuba. The top four parts may be played by euphoniums. A popular jazz tune arranged in a bossa nova then swing style then back to bossa nova. Drums may be added for style enhancement.

Jones, Roger. *Yankee Tunes for Tubas.* Roger Jones. Two euphoniums and three tubas. 1993. $12.00. 4:00. IV. Part I: B♭–g', Part II: B♭–f ', Part III: C–d', Part IV: A♭–a', Part V: F₁–c. A medley of "Chester," "Yankee Men of War," and "Drunken Sailor." Very tuneful with traditional harmonies. No significant technical problems. Parts may be doubled for a large ensemble.

Joplin, Scott. *Great Crush Collision March.* arr. L.A. Rauchut. KIWI Music Press. Three euphoniums and two tubas. 1985. $7.95. 2:10. IV. Part I: d–b♭', Part II: (c♯)e–f ', Part III: A–c', Part IV: C–c', Part V: F₁–g. While the euphoniums have primary responsibility for the melody, the tubas have the melody for 32 measures. The fifth part has sixteen measures of divisi, but they can be covered in the other parts. Parts may be doubled for a large ensemble.

Konagaya, Soichi. *Illusion.* TUBA Press. Out of print. Two euphoniums, three tubas, and percussion. 1979. 9:00. IV/V. Part I: e♭–b♭', Part II: A–g♭', Part III: A–c', Part IV: F–c', Part V: F₁–e♭. Dedicated to R. Winston Morris and the Tennessee Technological University Tuba Ensemble. Percussion parts include suspended cymbals, timpani, gong, vibraphone, and chimes, but all can be played by one player. While tonal, this piece contains some contemporary harmonies, oriental sounds, and many unique timbral effects not always associated with a tuba/euphonium ensemble. Effects include blowing air through the instrument without the mouthpiece and playing a roll on a suspended cymbal that is upside down on the timpani. The most interesting sound is the "Bala-euphonium." Recorded by the Tennessee Technological University Tuba Ensemble, *LIVE!,* KM Records, KM 5661.

Krive, Rick. *Lil Short'nin Funk.* T.U.B.A. Journal. Five tubas. 1976. $7.50. 1:30. IV. Part I: b♭–g♭', Part II: B♭₁–d♭', Part III: B♭₁–a♭, Part IV: B♭₁–e, Part V: G₁–c. A jazz-rock feel that is rhythmically exciting and challenging to play. There is a brief multimetric section and one measure where all five players are asked to sing through their instruments. Requires five strong players. Written as part of the T.U.B.A. GEM series and published in the *T.U.B.A. Journal,* Vol. 4, no. 1.

Krol, Bernhard. *Feiertagsmusik* (Festive Music). Editions Bim. Three euphoniums and two tubas. 1989. $22.50. 7:30. IV–V. Part I: c–a', Part II: G–f ', Part III: A–d♭', Part IV: E–a, Part V: D♭₁–e. Commissioned by R. Winston Morris for the Tennessee Technological University Tuba Ensemble April 2, 1990 performance at Weil Recital Hall, Carnegie Hall, New York City. Excellent writing, though not technically challenging. Tessitura of the first part is high. The work is slow, lyrical, and musically challenging. Parts may be doubled for a large ensemble.

Martin, Glenn. *Bluesin' Tubas.* TUBA Press. Three euphoniums, two tubas, piano, bass, drums, and guitar. 1984. $10.00. 4:10. IV. Part I: B–c", Part II: d–a', Part III: c–e', Part IV: B♭–c', Part V: B♭–e♭. Dedicated to R. Winston Morris and the Tennessee Technological University Tuba Ensemble. An original jazz tune with a medium swing feel. Sections can be opened up for improvised solos. Originally published by Laissez-Faire Music Publishing Company. Recorded by the Tennessee Technological University Tuba Ensemble, *Heavy Metal,* Mark Records, MES 20759.

Martin, Glenn. *Chops!* TUBA Press. Three euphoniums, two tubas, and rhythm. 1984. $10.00. 2:40. IV. Part I: d–c", Part II: d–e', Part III: d–e', Part IV: C–a, Part V: A–e♭'. Dedicated to R. Winston Morris and the Tennessee Technological University Tuba Ensemble. Fast swing style with sections for improvised solos. As the title implies, strong players are needed as there are range and technical demands in addition to the need for a good swing style by all players. Parts may be doubled for a large ensemble. Originally published by Laissez-Faire Music Publishing Company. Recorded by the Tennessee Technological University Tuba Ensemble, *All That Jazz,* Mark Records, MES 20608.

Maurer, Ludwig. *Four Pieces.* arr. John Stevens. John Stevens. Two euphoniums and three tubas. 1983. 8:00. III. Part I: c–a', Part II: c–f ', Part III: F–c', Part IV: C–g, Part V: G₁–g. Four movements: Maestoso alla Marcia; Andante con moto; Scherzo; Allegro Grazioso. A traditional arrangement of these Romantic compositions. The style is very light and best performed with one on a part.

Monteverdi, Claudio. *Ecco Mormorar L'onde.* arr. Gary Lee Nelson. TUBA Press. Two euphoniums and three tubas. 1991. $8.00. 3:00. IV. Part I: f–b♭', Part II: f–g', Part III: B♭–b♭, Part IV: F–b♭, Part V: B♭₁–e♭. Very polyphonic, though there are no significant technical problems. Players need to count carefully. Parts may be doubled for a large ensemble.

Monteverdi, Claudio. *Two Pieces from "Orfeo."* arr. Daniel Heiman. Heavy Metal Music. Three euphoniums and two tubas. 1991. $5.00. 1:30. IV. Part I: f–g', Part II: d–d', Part III: B♭–a, Part IV: E♭–g, Part

V: F₁–c. Two movements: Sinfonia; Ballo. The first movement is in a chorale style. The second movement is polyphonic and more challenging. The third part may be played by euphonium or tuba. No score available. Parts may be doubled for a large ensemble.

Moulu, Pierre. *A Lament for Anne of Brittany.* arr. Richard Jacoby. Ludwig Music Publishing Company. Three euphoniums and two tubas. 1986. $9.95. 4:00. III–IV. Part I: g–f ', Part II: d–d', Part III: G₁–c', Part IV: F–f, Part V: A₁–c. Based on a cantus firmus Josquin Des Près used in his lament on the death of Ockeghem. No significant technical or range problems. A translation of the text and performance suggestions are included. Parts may be doubled for a large ensemble.

Mozart, W.A. *Overture to the "Marriage of Figaro."* arr. Arthur Gottschalk. Shawnee Press, Incorporated. Three euphoniums and two tubas. 1981. $14.00. 3:45. IV–V. Part I: A–d", Part II: A–a', Part III: G–f♯', Part IV: D–e', Part V: D–c'. Technically challenging for all parts, but fun to play. The tessitura of the tuba parts is high. The three euphonium parts are printed in tenor clef. Requires strong players. Parts may be doubled for a large ensemble. Recorded by the University of Michigan Tuba Ensemble; U.S. Armed Forces Tuba/Euphonium Massed Ensemble, U.S. Army Records.

Nave, John. *Sjaj Suncece Suncano* (Shine Bright Sun). TUBA Press. Three tubas and two tubas. 1994. $8.00. 2:00. IV. Part I: a♭–b♭', Part II: e♭–g', Part III: c–e♭', Part IV: A♭–f♭, Part V: A♭₁–f♭. This traditional Serbian folk song was transcribed from a recording for four voices. The text reads: "Shine bright sun, I am behind the Turkish frontier. The Turkish cart rattles along and the people gather."

Pezel, Johann. *Three German Dances.* arr. Daniel Heiman. Heavy Metal Music. Two euphoniums and three tubas. 1991. $7.00. 3:30. IV. Part I: f–b♭', Part II: c–a', Part III: F–g, Part IV: C–d, Part V: F₁–G. Three movements: Intrade 10; Intrade 16; Allemande 17. Very close polyphony in the upper four parts. Players need to count very carefully. No score available.

Presser, William. *Divertimento.* Tenuto Publications. Two euphoniums and three tubas. 1976. $7.00. 6:30. IV. Part I: G–b♭', Part II: F–g', Part III: C–f♯', Part IV: G₁–a, Part V: E♭₁–f♯. Three movements: I; II; III. A challenging piece in terms of both technique and range. Technical demands are greatest in the third movement. Good solid writing. Parts may be doubled for a large ensemble.

Rossini, Giochino. *La Corona D'Italia.* arr. Manfred Heidler. Carpe-Diem Musikverlag Claudia Wölpper. Three euphoniums and two tubas. 1993. $21.00.

Scheidt, Samuel. *Canzona XXX.* arr. Skip Gray. Shawnee Press, Incorporated. Two euphoniums and three tubas. 1980. $14.00. 5:30. IV. Part I: c–a',

Part II: B–e', Part III: F–a. Part IV: C–g, Part V: (C₁) G₁–d. Nice arrangement of this canzona, which has been a staple of brass quintet literature for years. Lightness and clarity of the moving lines are a necessity, as it is very polyphonic and technically demanding of all parts. The two euphonium parts are printed in tenor clef in the score, but the parts are printed in bass clef. The arrangement remains true to the original metric form of duple—triple—duple. Parts may be cautiously doubled for a large ensemble.

Schelokov, V. *Movement for Five Tubas*. The Musical Evergreen. Five tubas. 1976. $11.50. 2:20. IV. Part I: G♭–b♭, Part II: E♭–g, Part III: D♭–e♭, Part IV: D♭–d, Part V: B♭₁–B♭. Not very demanding technically for any of the parts, although the first and fourth parts have challenging triplet figures in the fast middle section. Some dissonances in the harmonies. Can sound muddy at times if players are not careful.

Shiner, Marty. *Mexican Carnival*. Kendor Music, Incorporated. Four trombones (euphoniums) and one tuba, or three euphoniums and two tubas. 1972. $8.00. 2:00. IV. Part I: e♭–d", Part II: e♭–g', Part III: A♭–e♭', Part IV: A♭–d', Part V: A♭₁–e♭. A fun piece with a Mexican flavor. It is not difficult technically, but the tessitura of the first part is quite high. Parts may be doubled for a large ensemble.

Smith, Jason. *Five Pieces for Tuba Quintet*. Jason Smith. Three euphoniums and two tubas. 1992. $8.00. 10:00. IV. Part I: B♭–a', Part II: G♭–g', Part III: G–g', Part IV: E₁–d, Part V: A♭₁–b♭. Five contrasting movements with contemporary harmonies: Intreppa; Steps; Marcato; Walsa; Gallop. Several meter changes in the second movement. An F tuba may be used instead of a euphonium on the third part.

Sousa, John Philip. *The Liberty Bell March*. arr. L.A. Rauchut. KIWI Music Press. Three euphoniums and two tubas. $6.95. 3:30. IV. Part I: c–b♭', Part II: c–f ', Part III: B♭–f ', Part IV: E–d♭', Part V: F♯₁–f. Good arrangement. Most of the melody is in the first euphonium part. Several divisi section in the fourth part. Parts may be doubled for a large ensemble.

Sousa, John Philip. *Washington Post*. arr. James Self. Basset Hound Music. Two euphoniums and three tubas. 1993. $7.00. 3:00. IV. Part I: A–g', Part II: A–f ', Part III: A₁–b♭, Part IV: A₁–f, Part V: F₁–f. A good arrangement with some humorous sections. Fun to play. Parts may be doubled for a large ensemble.

Stevens, John, arr. *Suite of English Madrigals*. Encore Music Publishers. Two euphoniums and three tubas. 1988. $19.00. 6:00. IV. Part I: f–b♭', Part II: c–a', Part III: B♭–d', Part IV: F–b♭, Part V: B♭₁–g. Four movements: Down the Hills; Cruel, Wilt Thou Per Server; To the Shady Woods; Now Is the Month of Maying. No significant technical prob-

lems. Good arrangement. Parts may be doubled for a large ensemble.

Stevens, John. *Fanfare for a Friend*. TUBA Press. Five tubas. 1991. $5.00. 1:30. IV. Part I: B–g', Part II: B–f ', Part III: B₁–b♭, Part IV: G₁–g, Part V: G₁–d. For Dietrich Unkrodt and the Berlin Tubists. A very driving and energetic fanfare. The rhythms are complex and syncopated, but most of the time two to five parts are playing the same rhythm. The first part has a very high tessitura and may be played by a euphonium.

Telemann, George Phillip. *Alleluia*. arr. Daniel Heiman. Heavy Metal Music. Two euphoniums and three tubas. 1991. $5.00. 1:20. III–IV. Part I: f–g', Part II: d–e♭', Part III: G–b♭, Part IV: B♭–f, Part V: F₁–d. Based on the last movement of a Cantata by Telemann. The only text is the word "alleluia," repeated over and over. No significant range or technical problems. Parts may be doubled for a large ensemble.

Uber, David. *Exhibitions, Op. 98*. Kendor Music, Incorporated. Out of Print. Four euphoniums and one tuba. 1977. 3:30. IV. Part I: e♭–b', Part II: f–g', Part III: e♭–e♭', Part IV: B♭–e♭', Part V: (B♭₁) F–b. Can be performed by five euphoniums or as many as three tubas, depending on the strengths of the players. The solo euphonium has a high tessitura and is difficult technically. All parts are challenging, as the piece moves through several different styles. Very enjoyable for performers and audience.

Uber, David. *Explorations for Tuba Quintet, Op. 85*. TUBA Press. Five tubas. 1992. $12.00. 8:00. IV. Part I: D–c', Part II: G₁–g, Part III: F₁–g, Part IV: F₁–f, Part V: F₁–e♭. All parts have equal technical demands and are interesting to play. No range problems. Needs a conductor, as there are many challenging rhythmic figures and entrances.

Vaughan, Rodger. *Offering: A Sketch for Euphonium Solo and Tuba/Euphonium Quartet*. Rodger Vaughan. Three euphoniums and two tubas. 1992. $5.00. 1:20. III–IV. Solo euphonium: f–g♭', Part II: e–e', Part III: c–c♯', Part IV: E♭–f♯, Part V: A♭₁–d. A very lyrical and tranquil euphonium solo with a fairly simple accompaniment. None of the parts are technically demanding. Parts may be doubled for a large ensemble.

Von Suppe, Franz. *Poet and Peasant Overture*. arr. Gregory Bright. Tuba/Euphonium Music Publications. Out of print. Two euphoniums and three tubas. 8:00. IV.

Wagner, Richard. *Rienzi Overture*. arr. Gregory Bright. Tuba/Euphonium Music Publications. Out of print. Two euphoniums and three tubas.

Wagner, Richard. *Siegfried's Funeral March*. arr. Gregory Bright. Tuba/Euphonium Music Publications. Out of print. Two euphoniums and three tubas. 6:00. IV.

White, Ian. *Quintet*. John D. Elliott. Three euphoniums and two tubas. 8:00. IV–V. Part I: c–b", Part

II: B–bb', Part III: G–d', Part IV: c#–a, Part V: D#₁–g. Three movements. An exciting and challenging work. The tessitura of the first part is high. The movements are all multimetric and technically challenging. Parts may be doubled for a large ensemble.

Wilson, Ted. *Wot Shigona Dew?* TUBA Press. Three euphoniums, two tubas, and rhythm. 1983. $10.00. 4:00. IV. Part I: eb–c″, Part II: c–bb', Part III: c–ab', Part IV: Bb₁–bb, Part V: Bb₁. A very catchy blues tune with some very nice harmonies. One section with just chord symbols is open for any instrumentalist to play an improvised solo. Technically not very difficult, but a good swing feel is crucial. Works well at a variety of tempos. Originally published by Laissez-Faire Music Publishing Company. Parts may be doubled for a large ensemble. Recorded by the Tennessee Technological University Tuba Ensemble, *Heavy Metal,* Mark Records, MES 20759.

Winsor, Phil. *Asleep in the Deep.* Pembroke Music Company, Incorporated. Five tubas. 1975. 6:00. Can be performed with five tubas or solo tuba and tape. The tape must be made by the performer. This avant-garde composition utilizes contemporary notation and performance techniques, including half-valved notes, improvisation, and singing through the instrument. A very unusual piece.

Six Parts

Arlen, Harold. *Somewhere over the Rainbow.* arr. Rich Matteson. TUBA Press. Three euphoniums, three tubas, and rhythm. 1993. Written for the Matteson-Phillips Tubajazz Consort.

Bewley, Norlan. *Rich Tradition: A Tribute to Rich Matteson.* Bewley Music Incorporated. Three euphoniums, three tubas, and rhythm. 1992. $30.00. 5:45. IV–V. Solo euphonium: db–bb' (f ″), Part II: f–bb', Part III: Bb–f ', Part IV: C–c#', Part V: C–c#', Part VI: Bb₂–eb. Three movements: Chorale; The Call; Jubilee. The first part is for solo euphonium, and the fourth part is for solo tuba. The second movement is for the solo euphonium a cappella. The last movement alternates between Dixieland and swing style. While the two solo parts are the most demanding, there are many tutti sections requiring a good swing feel from all players. A very exciting work.

Boone, Dan. *Three Moods.* The Brass Press. Four euphoniums and two tubas. 1971. $5.00. 4:00. III. Part I: c–g', Part II: eb–ab, Part III: c–f ', Part IV: G–f ', Part V: C–f, Part VI: F₁–f. Three movements: Allegro; Larghetto; Allegro. Written for R. Winston Morris and the Tennessee Technological University Tuba Ensemble. A delightful work playable by high school ensembles. The three contrasting movements provide wide musical variety. The second movement is very lyrical; the third is multi-

metric and fits together very well. The first four parts are printed in both treble and bass clefs. Very enjoyable to play. Parts may be doubled for a large ensemble. Recorded by the University of Miami Tuba Ensemble, Miami United Tuba Society, 14568.

Brahms, Johannes. *Es ist eine Rose Entsprungen.* arr. by Fumio Gotoh. TUBA Press. Three euphoniums and three tubas. 1992. $6.00. 1:20. III–IV. Part I: c–g', Part II: c–d', Part III: eb–ab', Part IV: F–bb, Part V: Eb–ab, Part VI: G₁–db. Parts I and II are marked "euphonium." Part III is marked "tenor tuba" and has a higher range and tessitura than the first two parts. A very nice arrangement of this beautiful melody. No technical problems. Meant for a large ensemble—almost all the parts have some divisi sections, so parts should be doubled.

Carmichael, Hoagy. *Georgia on My Mind.* arr. by Rich Matteson. TUBA Press. Three euphoniums, three tubas, and rhythm. 1993. 4:40. Written for the Matteson-Phillips Tubajazz Consort. Recorded by the Matteson-Phillips Tubajazz Consort, *Super Horn,* Mark Records, MJS 57591.

Childs, Barney. *Music for Tubas ... Six of 'em.* Facsimile Editions (Carl Fischer). 1969. $18.00. 10:00. IV. Part I: Bb₁–f#, Part II: G–d, Part III: A#₁–db', Part IV: A#₁–e#', Part V: G₁–c#', Part VI: F₁–eb'. Four movements: I; II; III; IV. For Barton Cummings. This piece has many complicated rhythms and is challenging to put together. Twentieth-century techniques include flutter tonguing, lip trills, and glissandos. Multiple tonguing and mutes are required of all players. May need a conductor to help keep the ensemble together.

Cummings, Barton. *Fanfare and Chant.* Kendor Music, Incorporated. Out of print. Four euphoniums and two tubas. 1978. 2:30. IV. Part I: e–c″, Part II: e–c″, Part III: A–f#', Part IV: A–f#, Part V: E–b, Part VI: A₁–c. Two movements: Fanfare; Chant. The tessitura of the first part is very high. There are many tutti rhythms in the chant. Parts may be doubled for a large ensemble.

Delius, Frederick. *Serenade from "Hassan."* arr. Maurice Bale. Godiva Music. Two euphoniums and four tubas. 1994. $9.00. 2:30. IV. Part I: e–g', Part II: c–', Part III: Ab–g, Part IV: E–e, Part V: B–c, Part VI: F₁–G.

DiGiovanni, Rocco. *Tuba Magic for Tuba Ensemble.* Shawnee Press, Incorporated. Two euphoniums and four tubas. 1981. $25.00. 6:30. IV–V. Part I: F#–bb', Part II: G–a', Part III: Bb₁–e', Part IV: Bb₁–eb', Part V: F₁–db', Part VI: F₁–a. Written for R. Winston Morris and the Tennessee Technological University Tuba Ensemble. A majestic sounding piece with very lush harmonies that explores the lyrical qualities of the euphonium and the tuba. The first euphonium has a cadenza in the middle section. The lyrical qualities of the euphonium and tuba are explored. The range of all parts is high, and strong players are needed on all parts. The top two parts are printed in both bass and treble clef. Very enjoyable for performers and audience. Parts may be doubled for a large ensemble. Recorded by the Tennessee Technological University Tuba Ensemble, *LIVE!* KM Records, KM 5661; and the U.S. Armed Forces Tuba/Euphonium Ensemble and Massed Ensemble, U.S. Army Band Records.

DiGiovanni, Rocco. *Tubarhumba*. Rocco DiGiovanni. Two euphoniums, four tubas, guitar, bass, drums, claves, and maracas. 1984. $20.00. 4:00. IV. Part I: e–bb', Part II: e–bb', Part III: D–f', Part IV: D–f', Part V: Ab₁–eb', Part VI: F₁–c'. Written for R. Winston Morris and the Tennessee Technological University Tuba Ensemble. A fun melody in a bright rumba and swing style; a good feel for these two styles is necessary. The first euphonium part is very demanding, and the tessitura of the first tuba part is high. The rhythm section is a key ingredient to this piece. Parts may be doubled for a large ensemble.

Dutton, Brent. *Warring*. Seesaw Music Corporation Publishers. Three euphoniums and three tubas. 1980. $17.00. 7:30. IV. Part I: B–bb', Part II: G–bb', Part III: F–bb', Part IV: G₁–b, Part V: Eb₁–f, Part VI: Eb₁–f. Dedicated to the Central Michigan University Tuba Ensemble. Designed for a large ensemble with each part doubled, ideally 12 to 24 players. The euphoniums and tubas should be placed as far from each other as possible (i.e., one group on the stage and the other in a balcony). Technically challenging at times: players sing through their instruments, ad lib. sections for each part, and contemporary harmonies.

Ellington, Duke. *In a Mello Tone*. arr. Rich Matteson. TUBA Press. Three euphoniums, three tubas, and rhythm. 1990. Written for the Matteson-Phillips Tubajazz Consort.

Ellington, Mercer. *Thing's Ain't What They Used to Be*. arr. Rich Matteson. TUBA Press. Three euphoniums, three tubas, and rhythm. 1993. 7:30. Written for the Matteson-Phillips Tubajazz Consort. Recorded by the Matteson-Phillips Tubajazz Consort, *Super Horn*, Mark Records, MJS 57591

Endo, M. *Meiso No Inga*. Tokyo Bari-Tuba Ensemble. Five euphoniums and one tuba.

Fiegel, E. Todd. *Celluloid Tubas: A Score for Barney Oldfield's Race for a Life (1913)*. E. Todd Fiegel. Three euphoniums, three tubas, motion picture equipment. 1992. Rental. 15:00. IV–V. Part I: G–db', Part II: Bb–a', Part III: G–f#', Part IV: Bb₁–a, Part V: Bb₂–a, Part VI: A₂–d. For Fritz Kaenzig with profound admiration. Designed to accompany a select portion of the film *Barney Oldfield's Race for a Life*. Challenging for all parts because of tempo and meter changes and the need to stay with the film. A low tessitura is required for the fifth and sixth parts. Very enjoyable for performers and audi-

ence. Contact the composer for exact rental and performance information.

Frescobaldi, Girolamo. *Toccata*. arr. Joseph Skillen. TUBA Press. Three euphoniums and three tubas. 1992. $10.00. 2:20. IV. Part I: c–c'', Part II: G–a', Part III: G–f', Part IV: E–c', Part V: G₁–a, Part VI: (C₁) E₁–g. Written for R. Winston Morris and the Tennessee Technological University Tuba Ensemble. Most of the melody and technical challenges are in the top three parts. The tessitura of the first part is high. Works well. Parts may be doubled for a large ensemble.

Fritze, Gregory. *Kilimanjaro*. Gregory Fritze. Three trombones (euphoniums), one euphonium, and two tubas. 1991. $10.00. 9:00. V. Part I: F–db'', Part II: Ab–db'', Part III: F₁–f#', Part IV: E₁–db'', Part V: E₁–ab', Part VI: E₁–ab'. Composed for Gary Bird and the Indiana University of Pennsylvania Low Brass Faculty. The top three parts may be played on trombones or euphoniums. A very challenging work with extensive range demands, several smears and glissandos for all parts, and numerous meter changes. Requires very strong players.

Fritze, Gregory. *Tubafest Shuffle*. Gregory Fritze. Three euphoniums, three tubas, and rhythm. 1988. $10.00. 3:30. IV. Part I: f–g', Part II: d–eb', Part III: F–eb', Part IV: F–f, Part V: A₁–eb, Part VI: G₁–eb. Composed for the Berklee Heavy Metal. A driving funk-rock style composition. A basic funk rhythm is repeated throughout the piece. A twelve-measure section can be repeated for improvised solos. Some technical challenges. Another version is available that includes two French horns. Parts may be doubled for a large ensemble.

Fritze, Gregory. *Tu-Bop*. Gregory Fritze. Three euphoniums, three tubas, and rhythm. 1981. $10.00. 10:00. IV. Part I: f–d'', Part II: c–bb', Part III: Bb–f#', Part IV: A₁–e', Part V: B₁–c', Part VI: F₁–a. Composed for the Berklee Heavy Metal. An uptempo swing composition with improvised solos for the first, second, and fourth parts. Very syncopated, a good swing feel is necessary from all players. Parts may be doubled for a large ensemble.

Garbáge, Pierre. *Sousa Surrenders*. James Garrett. Three euphoniums, three tubas and optional timpani. 1974. $35.00. 10:30. IV–V. Part I: cb–bb', Part II: Ab–gb', Part III: Eb–f', Part IV: D–c', Part V: Bb₁–c', Part VI: D₁–c'. Written for R. Winston Morris and the Tennessee Technological University Tuba Ensemble. A humorous arrangement of several Sousa marches. The third part could be played by a euphonium or a tuba. Technically challenging for all parts. All parts require mutes. Expect the unexpected from this arrangement. A lot of fun for performers and audience. Garbáge writes, "Sousa Surrenders and Pierre graciously accepts his sword." Recorded by the U.S. Armed Forces Tuba/Euphonium Ensemble and Massed Ensemble, U.S. Army Band Records.

Garrett, James A. *Expose for Tubas.* James Garrett. Four euphoniums and two tubas. 1976. $20.00. 2:20. IV. Part I: g–c", Part II: g–g', Part III: c–e', Part IV: E♭–d♭', Part V: A♭₁–f, Part VI: C₁–c. Written for R. Winston Morris and the Tennessee Technological University Tuba Ensemble. A single movement that progresses through several different moods in a short period of time. The tessitura of the first part is high. Most of the technical work is for the top two parts. Very dissonant harmonies at times. The top two euphonium parts require mutes. Several divisi sections in all parts. Parts may be doubled for a large ensemble.

Garrett, James A. *Fanfare.* The Brass Press. Three euphoniums and three tubas. 1966. $3.50. 1:00. III–IV. Part I: g–a♭', Part II: c–f ', Part III: d–d', Part IV: c–b♭, Part V: F–f, Part VI: G₁–f. Designed as a fun opener to a concert. Not technically difficult. Parts may be doubled for a large ensemble.

Garrett, James A., arr. *Espana Cami.* James Garrett. Three euphoniums and three tubas. 1970. $20.00. 3:00. IV. Part I: f–b♭', Part II: d♭–f ', Part III: B♭–f ', Part IV: G–f ', Part V: G–b♭, Part VI: B♭₁–b♭. A fun arrangement of this classic Mexican melody. Several syncopated and triplet rhythms, though most rhythm patterns are played by two or more parts. Drums and other percussion instruments may be added for stylistic enhancement. Parts may be doubled for a large ensemble.

Glover, Jim, arr. *Florentiner March.* Jim Glover. Three euphoniums and three tubas. 1992. $15.00.

Glover, Jim, arr. *Here Comes Santa Claus.* Jim Glover. Four euphoniums and two tubas. 1992. $8.00.

Glover, Jim, arr. *Jingle Bell Rock.* Jim Glover. Four euphoniums and two tubas. 1992. $8.00.

Glover, Jim, arr. *Let It Snow.* Jim Glover. Four euphoniums and two tubas. 1992. $8.00.

Glover, Jim, arr. *Santa Claus Is Comin' to Town.* Jim Glover. Four euphoniums and two tubas. 1992. $8.00.

Glover, Jim, arr. *Silver Bells.* Jim Glover. Four euphoniums and two tubas. 1992. $8.00.

Goodman, Benny; Webb, Chick; and Sampson, Edgar. *Stompin' at the Savoy.* arr. Rich Matteson. TUBA Press. Three euphoniums, three tubas, and rhythm. 1976. 6:50. Written for the Matteson-Phillips Tubajazz Consort. Recorded by the Matteson-Phillips Tubajazz Consort, *Super Horn,* Mark Records, MJS 57591.

Handel, G.F. *Allegro from "Water Music."* arr. James Self. Basset Hound Music. Two euphoniums and four tubas. 1972. $10.00. 3:00. IV. Part I: B♭–b♭', Part II: B♭–b♭', Part III: B♭₁–b♭, Part IV: F₁–b♭, Part V: F₁–b♭, Part VI: F₁–b♭. Good arrangement of this Baroque melody. Some technical challenges, especially in the top four parts. Requires good lyrical and detached playing. Some syncopated rhythms.

Hayakawa, M. *Divertimento.* Tokyo Bari-Tuba Ensemble. Three euphoniums and three tubas.

Hill, William H. *Fantasia on "Dies Irae."* Neil A. Kjos Music Company. Two euphoniums and four tubas. 1988. $7.00. 5:30. IV. Part I: G–b♭', Part II: G–b♭', Part III: F₁–b, Part IV: F₁–b, Part V: F₁–b, Part VI: F₁–b. Commissioned by T.U.B.A. The two euphonium parts call for two players each, requiring a minimum of eight players for this piece. Two contrasting sections: a slow chantlike introduction followed by a dissonant Allegro section. All parts are interesting and have sections that are technically challenging.

Holst, Gustav. *Mars, the Bringer of War, from "The Planets."* arr. David Butler. TUBA Press. Three euphoniums and three tubas. 1993. $15.00. 7:00. IV. Part I: B–c", Part II: B–g', Part III: B–g', Part IV: C–d♭', Part V: c–b♭, Part VI: F₁–d'. Written for R. Winston Morris and the Tennessee Technological University Tuba Ensemble. A solid arrangement—the piece almost seems best suited for euphoniums and tubas. Technically challenging for all parts. Players need to count carefully and play cleanly. Several divisi sections, intended for a large ensemble. Fun to play.

Jarrett, Keith. *Lucky Southern.* arr. Rich Matteson. TUBA Press. Three euphoniums, three tubas, and rhythm. 1976. 4:30. Written for the Matteson-Phillips Tubajazz Consort. Recorded by the Matteson-Phillips Tubajazz Consort, Mark Records, MJS 57587.

Knight, Morris. *Colossi.* Woodsum Music, Limited. Six Tubas. 1990. $25.00. 14:00. IV. Part I: D♯–e', Part II: A₁–b, Part III: F₁–c♯', Part IV: A₁–b, Part V: A₁–b, Part VI: F₁–d♭. Seven movements: Elephants; Hippopotamus; Moose; Giraffe; Rhinoceros; Ostrich; Whales. Dedicated to Harvey and Toby and Les and J.S. and John and Sande and Phil and so many other colossal tubists I've always looked "down" to for great performances. The movements contrast in style, meter, and key. Some technical challenges, especially in the bottom two parts. The score and parts are very difficult to read because the ledger lines are printed in an awkward manner.

Lamb, Marvin. *Heavy Metal.* Carl Fischer, Incorporated. Two euphoniums and four tubas. 1985. Rental. 5:12. IV–V. Part I: B♭–b♭', Part II: A♭–b♭', Part III: C–e', Part IV: (F₁) G₁–b, Part V: E₁–d', Part VI: F♯₁–b♭. Written for R. Winston Morris and the Tennessee Technological University Tuba Ensemble and dedicated to the memory of John Dunstable and the Pointer Sisters. This piece stretches the timbres normally associated with the tuba/euphonium ensemble. Following a muted eerie-sounding introduction, a funk feel evolves into a swing section. Performers are asked to sing swing nonsense syllables and perform hand jives (clapping the legs, chest, and hands to a written rhythm). Several sixteenth-note and triplet runs make this technically challenging and exciting to play. Parts may be doubled for a large ensemble. Recorded by the

Tennessee Technological University Tuba Ensemble, *Heavy Metal,* Mark Records, MES 20759.

Lawn, Rick. *Hippochondriac.* UNITUBA Press. Out of print. Four euphoniums and two tubas, or three euphoniums and three tubas. 4:00. IV. Part I: a–c", Part II: d–b♭', Part III: g–f ', Part IV: E–c', Part V: E–c', Part VI: C–a. A good jazz feel is necessary to perform this work. No significant technical demands, but the tessitura of the top two parts is high. The use of a drum set is strongly recommended. Parts may be doubled for a large ensemble.

Matteson, Rich. *Little Ole Softy.* TUBA Press. Three euphoniums, three tubas, and rhythm. 1980. 5:30. Written for the Matteson-Phillips Tubajazz Consort. Recorded by the Matteson-Phillips Tubajazz Consort, *Super Horn,* Mark Records, MJS 57591.

Matteson, Rich. *Spoofy.* TUBA Press. Three euphoniums, three tubas, and rhythm. 1976. 11:45. Written for the Matteson-Phillips Tubajazz Consort. Recorded by the Matteson-Phillips Tubajazz Consort, Mark Records, MJS 57587.

Morris, Mike. *Tubology.* Laissez-Faire Music Publishing Company. Out of print. Three euphoniums, three tubas, and rhythm.

Ott, Joseph. *Suite for Six Tubas.* Claude Benny Press. 1968. $9.00. 7:00. IV. Part I: G_1–b, Part II: Bb_1–a, Part III: G_1–a, Part IV: G_1–g, Part V: Bb_1–b, Part VI: G_1–g. Three movements. No major technical problems, but putting the ensemble together can be challenging. Some close harmonies and tone clusters. Very dissonant at times—can get muddy if players are not careful. Interesting writing.

Presser, William. *Suite for Six Tubas.* Tenuto Publications. 1967. $6.00. 7:00. IV. Part I: B_1–e♭', Part II: Bb_1–b, Part III: Gb_1–b♭, Part IV: Ab_1–d', Part V: Ab_1–b, Part VI: Eb_1–b. Three movements: March; Echo; Song and Scherzo. For Rex Conner. All parts are of equal difficulty. Several melodic and rhythmic tutti sections. The melody frequently alternates between the top three and bottom three parts.

Rollins, Sonny. *Oleo.* arr. Rich Matteson. TUBA Press. Three euphoniums, three tubas, and rhythm. 1993. 4:30. Written for the Matteson-Phillips Tubajazz Consort. Recorded by the Matteson-Phillips Tubajazz Consort, Mark Records, MJS 57587.

Sandstrom, Sven-David. *Fanfare for Six Tubas.* Swedish Music Information Center. 1979. 6:30.

Schmidt, Dankwart. *Bayerische Polka.* Dankwart Schmidt. Two euphoniums and four tubas. 2:35. Recorded by Gerhard Meinl's Tuba Sextet, *A Six-Tuba Musical Romp,* Angel, 54729; and David LeClair, *Swingin' Low,* Marcophon.

Schmidt, Dankwart. *Bayerische Zell.* Dankwart Schmidt. Two euphoniums and four tubas. 2:50. Recorded by Gerhard Meinl's Tuba Sextet, *A Six-Tuba Musical Romp,* Angel, 54729.

Self, James, arr. *Basic Psych-Rock.* James Self. Out of print. Two euphoniums and four tubas. 5:00. IV. Part I: c–b♭', Part II: e♭–f ', Part III: e–b♭, Part IV:

E–g, Part V: G_1–f, Part VI: G_1–f. A hard rock style with rhythm section. Parts may be doubled for a large ensemble.

Shinihara, Keisuke. *Japanese Songs.* Tokyo Bari-Tuba Ensemble. Four euphoniums and two tubas.

Sibelius, Jean. *Finlandia.* arr. James Self. Basset Hound Music. Two euphoniums and four tubas. 1993. $12.00. 8:00. IV. Part I: c–a', Part II: A–e♭', Part III: C–b♭, Part IV: C–g, Part V: F_1–f, Part VI: F_1–d. A very good chorale-like arrangement of this nice melody. Parts may be doubled for a large ensemble.

Silver, Horace. *Gregory Is Here.* arr. Rich Matteson. TUBA Press. Three euphoniums, three tubas, and rhythm. 1993. 7:50. Written for the Matteson-Phillips Tubajazz Consort. Recorded by the Matteson-Phillips Tubajazz Consort, Mark Records, MJS 57587.

Strauss, Richard. *Allerseelen* (All Soul's Day). arr. Fumio Gotoh. TUBA Press. Three euphoniums and three tubas. 1991. $6.00. 2:45. IV. Part I: c–a♭', Part II: A♭–a♭', Part III: G–b♭', Part IV: F–e♭', Part V: G_1–a♭, Part VI: Eb_1–d. Part III is marked "tenor tuba" and has a higher range and tessitura than the first and second parts. No real technical demands other than range. All parts have divisi sections, so twelve players are required to perform the arrangement as written (though the bottom two parts have only two or three notes marked divisi). The bottom tuba part requires several precise Eb_1s.

Sullivan, Arthur. *The Lost Chord.* arr. Barton Cummings. TUBA Press. Three euphoniums and three tubas. 1991. $5.00. 3:30. IV. Part I: c–c", Part II: c–g', Part III: B♭–c', Part IV: C–g, Part V: C–d, Part VI: F_1–A. Other than a single c" in the first part, the arrangement is not difficult. Attention should be paid to the lyricism and dynamics. Parts may be doubled for a large ensemble.

Svarda, William E. *Piece for Six Tubas.* William Svarda. 1969. 6:00. III–IV. Part I: D–c', Part II: Bb_1–b, Part III: D♭–g, Part IV: Ab_1–g, Part V: E_1–c, Part VI: F_1–d♭. Four movements: Moderato; Moderato; Andante; Presto. Traditional harmonies and rhythms. Frequent unison and octave playing, no significant technical or range problems. Parts may be doubled for a large ensemble.

Toyama, Yuzo. *Essay.* Yuzo Toyama. Three euphoniums and three tubas. 1993. $15.00. 4:00. V. Part I: B–c', Part II: A–b♭', Part III: G–b♭', Part IV: G_1–d', Part V: G♭–c', Part VI: F_1–c'. Commissioned by T.U.B.A. Very complex rhythmically and technically challenging to play. The tessitura of the first two parts is high. This piece was premiered by the International All-Star College Ensemble, R. Winston Morris, Director, August 12, 1990, at the International Tuba/Euphonium Conference Sapporo, Japan.

Uber, David. *Intrada, Romanze, and Scherzo.* T.A.P. Music. Four euphoniums and two tubas. 1989.

$20.00. 8:00. IV. Part I: d–c", Part II: d–g', Part III: d♭–f ', Part IV: F–g', Part V: A♭₁–g, Part VI: F₁–g. Three movements: Intrada; Romanze; Scherzo. The tessitura of the top two parts is high. Some technical challenges in all parts. Good writing.

Vaughan, Rodger. *Five Canons for Tuba/Euphonium Sextet*. Rodger Vaughan. 1977. $8.00.

Vaughan, Rodger, arr. *Tubagirls I*. Rodger Vaughan. Two euphoniums and four tubas. 1977. $5.00. 6:30. IV. Part I: f–b♭', Part II: c–a♭', Part III: E♭–c', Part IV: G₁–b, Part V: F₁–c', Part VI: E♭₁–c. This is a medley of "Sweet Sue," "Laura," "Sweet Georgia Brown," "Nancy," and "Liza." All parts except the first have numerous divisi sections requiring two on a part.

Vaughan, Rodger, arr. *Tubagirls II*. Rodger Vaughan. Two euphoniums and four tubas. 1978. $5.00. 6:00. IV. Part I: B♭–c", Part II: B♭–g', Part III: E♭–d', Part IV: F₁–c', Part V: G₁–b♭, Part VI: E♭₁–b♭. A medley of "Sioux City Sue," "Georgia on My Mind," "Jean," "Amy," and "Tootsie." All parts have an opportunity to play the melody. The tessitura of the first part is high. Drums may be added for effect. No score available, parts may be doubled for a large ensemble.

Weisling, Raymond. *Tuba Club*. Raymond Weisling. Out of Print. Six tubas. 1969. 7:00. IV. Parts I–VI: from the lowest possible note to the highest possible note. This composition is intended as an exploration into the "total sound resources" of six tubas. Contemporary notation, flutter tonguing, glissandos, lip trills, and whistling. The piece is very challenging. A conductor is necessary.

Werle, Floyd E. *Variations on an Old Hymn Tune*. Floyd Werle. Two euphoniums and four tubas. 1988. 5:50. IV. Part I: g–a', Part II: e–f ', Part III: A♯–c', Part IV: C–g, Part V: G₁–g♭, Part VI: F₁–A. For R. Winston Morris, Ernie Walls, and the Tennessee Technological University Tuba Ensemble. After the statement of the hymn tune, there are five variations, all in different tempos. The sections in the fast tempos are more technically challenging. No significant range demands. Good six-part writing. Parts may be doubled for a large ensemble. Recorded by the Tennessee Technological University Tuba Ensemble, Mark Custom Recording Service, MENC88-1-4; and the U.S. Armed Forces Tuba/Euphonium Massed Ensemble, U.S. Army Records.

Seven or More Parts

Bach, J.S. *Jesu, Joy of Man's Desiring*. arr. N. Yamamoto. TUBA Press. Six euphoniums and two tubas. 1985. $6.00. 2:00. IV. Part I: B♭–b♭", Part II: B♭–f ', Part III: A–f ', Part IV: F₁–b♭, Part V: f–e♭', Part VI: e–c', Part VII: F–g, Part VIII: F₁–a. Dedicated to Peggy Heinkel and to the Tokyo Bari-Tuba Ensemble. Beautiful arrangement of this fa-mous Bach melody. Technically it is not very difficult, but rhythmic accuracy is necessary to keep the texture from sounding muddy. A tuba may be used on at least one of the euphonium parts. Four of the euphonium parts are printed in tenor clef. Parts may be doubled for a large ensemble.

Bale, Maurice. *Three Fanfares for Tubas*. Godiva Music. Three euphoniums and six tubas. 1994. $11.00. 1:30. IV. Part I: a–b♭' (d"), Part II: e♭–f ', Part III: d–d', Part IV: B♭₁–b♭, Part V: B♭₁–f, Part VI: B♭–f, Part VII: F–d, Part VIII: G₁–B♭, Part IX: (B♭₂) G₁–G. Three movements. Written for the first British Tuba and Euphonium Conference, Birmingham Conservatoire, February 1994. All parts available in treble or bass clef.

Beale, David. *Reflections on a Park Bench*. David Beale. Out of print. Six euphoniums and six tubas. 1973. 24:00. IV–V. Part I: E–c", Part II: E–c", Part III: E–c", Part IV: E–b♭', Part V: E–b♭', Part VI: E–b♭', Part VII: E₁–a, Part VIII: E₁–a, Part IX: E₁–b♭, Part X: E₁–c', Part XI: E₁–c', Part XII: E₁–c'. Written for R. Winston Morris and the Tennessee Technological University Tuba Ensemble. A mammoth work written for three tuba/euphonium quartets. A very complex, challenging, and programmatic work based on an inscription found on the back of a park bench, "To those who shall sit here rejoicing, to those who shall sit here mourning, sympathy and greeting: So have we done in our time," 1892 A.D.W.-H.M.W. This work is extremely difficult and requires twelve strong players. Recorded by the Tennessee Technological University Tuba Ensemble, *Carnegie Hall*, Golden Crest Records, CRSQ-4152.

Brahms, Johannes. *Ballade in D Minor, Op. 10, no. 1*. arr. Frank H. Siekmann. Brelmat Music. Five euphoniums and two tubas. 1994. $30.00. 4:00. IV. Part I: A–c", Part II: A–g', Part III: E–g', Part IV: E–f♯', Part V: E–f♯', Part VI: A₁–d', Part VII: G₁–f♯. Very lyrical writing. There is some doubling in the third part, otherwise the parts are independent. No significant technical problems. Parts may be doubled for a large ensemble.

Berlioz, Hector. *March to the Scaffold from Symphonie Fantastique*. arr. William Granger. Shawnee Press, Incorporated. Four euphoniums and six tubas. 1986. $30.00. 4:30. IV. Part I: G–d", Part II: G–b', Part III: E♭–b♭', Part IV: E♭–b♭', Part V: G₁–c♭', Part VI: B♭₁–e♭', Part VII: G₁–b♭, Part VIII: G₁–a♭, Part IX: G₁–g, Part X: G₁–g. Dedicated to the University of Georgia Tuba-Euphonium Ensemble. Good arrangement of this famous orchestral excerpt. Requires four strong euphonium players because of the high tessituras. Technically not very difficult but challenging to fit all the parts together cleanly. Parts may be doubled for a large ensemble.

Bruckner, Anton. *Os Justi*. arr. David Sabourin. Touch of Brass Music Corporation. Four euphoniums and four tubas. $8.50.

Canter, James A. *Circle VIII: Bowge IV.* TUBA Press. Four euphoniums and four tubas. 1993. $15.00. 8:30. IV. Part I: A♭–g', Part II: A♭–g', Part III: A♭–f♯', Part IV: A♭–f♯', Part V: B♭₁–a♭, Part VI: A♭₁–e♭, Part VII: A₁–e, Part VIII: G₁–A♭. Written for R. Winston Morris and the Tennessee Technological University Tuba Ensemble. A very contemporary piece, with numerous half- and whole-step intervals in the tuba parts. Some basic twentieth–century techniques required. Tubas are muted. No significant range or technical demands on any part.

Censhu, Jiro. *Chi Ni Hikari Arite* (Lux in Terra). Jiro Censhu. Four euphoniums and four tubas. 1987. $15.00. 10:00. IV. Part I: F–b♭', Part II: F–b♭', Part III: G–b♭', Part IV: F–a', Part V: D–e', Part VI: F₁–c', Part VII: F₁–e♭', Part VIII: F₁–a. Three movements: I; II; III. Commissioned by the Osaka Bari-Tuba Ensemble. Players are arranged into two tuba/euphonium quartets. The third movement features a brief cadenza for the first part in each quartet. The tessitura of the euphonium parts is high. Technically challenging in some spots. Good writing.

Clinard, Fred L. *Diversion for Seven Bass Clef Instruments.* Shawnee Press, Incorporated. Four euphoniums and three tubas. 1979. $16.00. 5:00. IV. Part I: e–c", Part II: e–c", Part III: c♯–g', Part IV: c♯–g', Part V: C–a, Part VI: C–a, Part VII: D₁–e. Written for R. Winston Morris and the Tennessee Technological University Tuba Ensemble. A one-movement work in a fast—slow—fast form. The fast section contains a driving multimetric section. The slow section features a hauntingly beautiful melody for a solo euphonium with ensemble accompaniment. The tessitura of the first two parts is very high and requires strong players. Very enjoyable for audiences and performers. Parts may be doubled for a large ensemble.

DiGiovanni, Rocco. *Tuba Musicale.* Encore Music Publishers. Four euphoniums and six tubas. 1993. $30.00. 10:00. IV–V. Part I: d–a', Part II: d–a', Part III: G–f ', Part IV: G–f ', Part V: D–c', Part VI: D–c', Part VII: F₁–d', Part VIII: F₁–d', Part IX: E♭₁–b♭, Part X: E♭₁–f. Dedicated to my two best tuba friends, R. Winston Morris and Charles A. McAdams. A beautiful melody with a slow 3/4 feel. All parts have an opportunity to play the melody, but most of the melodic responsibility is in the top four parts. Requires strong players.

Dutton, Brent. *Suite for Seven Tubas.* Seesaw Music Corporation Publishers. 1978. $26.00. 10:00. IV–V. Part I: B♭₁–f ', Part II: G₁–a, Part III: E♭₁–e♭', Part IV: G₁–c', Part V: D₁–b♭, Part VI: C₁–g, Part VII: B♭₂–B♭. Seven movements: I; II; III; IV; V; VI; VII. Each movement is written for the same number of players as the number of the movement. So the first movement is for one tuba, the second movement for two, etc. The last movement is very challenging. The tessitura of the bottom three parts is very low.

Fiegel, E. Todd. *Pachydermus Pinkus Lowus-Blowus; Adapted from the Score for Dumbo (1941).* E. Todd Fiegel. Four euphoniums, four tubas, auxiliary percussion, and film equipment. 1992. Rental. 8:00. V. Part I: f–d", Part II: F–d", Part III: c–d", Part IV: F–a', Part V: B♭₁–e♭', Part VI: D–e♭', Part VII: E₁–c', Part VIII: E₁–d. For "Mr. Tuba" and the University of Michigan Euphonium/Tuba Ensemble. A tuba ensemble adaptation of a segment of the sound track from the Disney cartoon classic *Dumbo.* Technically challenging at times. Range demands are extensive for the top euphoniums and the bottom parts. All parts require mutes. Fun to play and very entertaining for audiences.

Florinza, Lino. *Typic Rhythm.* Florent Lemirre. Four euphoniums and four tubas. 1987. $55.00. 7:20. IV. Part I: B♭–a', Part II: B♭–a♭', Part III: G–a♭', Part IV: F–e♭', Part V: E♭–g', Part VI: E♭–e♭', Part VII: B♭₁–a♭, Part VIII: E♭₁–g. Four movements: Mambo Calypso; Bolero; Bossa Nova; Samba. Dedicated to Hervé Brisse in total friendship. Each movement rhythmically represents its title. Some technical challenges of all parts. The use of drums is strongly recommended. Lino Florenzo is a pseudonym for the French composer Florent Lemirre.

Frackenpohl, Arthur. *Eine Kleine Octubamusic.* T.A.P. Music. Eight tubas. 1990. $25.00. 10:00. IV. Part I: F♯₁–c', Part II: F♯₁–b♭, Part III: F♯₁–b♭, Part IV: E₁–b♭, Part V: E₁–b, Part VI: F♯₁–b♭, Part VII: F₁–b♭, Part VIII: E₁–b♭. Five movements: Unison Prelude; Round Dance; Sad Waltz; Pair Dance; Intro and March. Each part has an opportunity to play the melody. Often a single part has a portion of the melody without any accompaniment. Pair Dance features two parts at a time, passing the melody back and forth.

Fredrickson, Thomas. *Antiphonies.* Thomas Fredrickson. Four euphoniums and four tubas. 1983. $15.00. 6:00. IV. Part I: F♯–b', Part II: F♯–a♭', Part III: F♯₁–d', Part IV: F♯₁–b♭, Part V: F♯–a', Part VI: F♯–g', Part VII: F♯₁–c', Part VIII: E₁–c'. Commissioned by Tubists Universal Brotherhood Association for the 1983 International Tuba/Euphonium Conference. A very contemporary piece written for two tuba/euphonium quartets. Technically and metrically very complex. A very interesting contemporary composition.

Gabrieli, Giovanni. *Antiphony No. 2 for Double Tuba/Euphonium Choir.* arr. Art Conner. Tuba/Euphonium Music Publications. Out of print. Four euphoniums and four tubas. 4:00. III–IV.

Gabrieli, Giovanni. *Sonata No. 13 for Double Tuba/Euphonium Choir.* arr. J. Lesley Varner. Tuba/Euphonium Music Publications. Out of print. Four euphoniums and four tubas. 4:30. IV.

George, Thom Ritter. *Two Interplays.* Thom Ritter George. Three tenor trombones, one bass trombone, two euphoniums, and tuba tubas. 1985. $7.50. 7:30. IV. Part I: e–b', Part II: A♭–g', Part

III: E–a', Part IV: E–g♭, Part V: E–a', Part VI: E–e♭', Part VII: E₁–f♯, Part VIII: E♭₁–c. Two movements: Andante Sempre; Vivo. Commissioned by the Morehead State University Chapters of the I.T.A. and T.U.B.A. Can be performed by five euphoniums and three tubas. The composition focuses on the interplay between two quartets. Some technical challenges in the second movement. Solid writing. See listing under "Music for Tuba in Mixed Ensemble."

Gottschalk, Arthur. *Substructures I*. Seesaw Music Corporation Publishers. Two euphoniums and eight tubas. 1975. $31.00. 6:00. IV–V. Part I: D–e', Part II: F♯₁–d♭', Part III: F♯₁–a, Part IV: F♯₁–a, Part V: e–b♭', Part VI: e–b♭', Part VII: B–c, Part VIII: G₁–b♭, Part IX: E₁–b, Part X: E₁–c. Parts V and VI are for euphoniums. The players are divided into three groups on the stage. Not very difficult technically, but a challenge to put together. The tessitura of the bottom two parts is very low. Harmonically very dissonant. Recorded by the University of Michigan Tuba/Euphonium Ensemble, Golden Crest Records, CRS 4145.

Haddad, Don. *Knoxville, 1974*. Seesaw Music Corporation Publishers. Two euphoniums and six tubas. 1975. $12.00. 5:20. IV. Part I: g–d", Part II: c♯–a', Part III: G–d', Part IV: C–d', Part V: g–d", Part VI: A–g', Part VII: C–e♭', Part VIII: F₁–c♯. Written for two choirs of one euphonium and three tubas each. The tessitura of the first and second parts of each choir is very high. The second part of each choir may be played by a euphonium. No significant technical problems. No score available.

Hartley, Walter. *Sinfonia No. 10 for Tuba-Euphonium Ensemble*. Walter Hartley. Four euphoniums and four tubas. 1994. 7:45. IV–V. Four movements: Andante/Allegro; Allegro Scherzando; Adagio; Presto. Harmonically and rhythmically conservative. Utilizes the full range of the instruments in the ensemble. Parts may be doubled for a large ensemble.

Hoshina, Hiroshi. *Dialogue*. Tokyo Bari-Tuba Ensemble. Four euphoniums and six tubas.

Ishii, Maki. *Yama No Hibiki*. Tokyo Bari-Tuba Ensemble. Six euphoniums and six tubas.

Ito, Yasuhide. *Cadenzas for 8 Players*. Tokyo Bari-Tuba Ensemble. Four euphoniums and four tubas.

Knox, Charles. *Scherzando for Tubular Octet*. Charles Knox. Four euphoniums and four tubas. 1979. $25.00. 5:45. IV. Part I: B–c", Part II: B♭–a', Part III: B♭–a', Part IV: A–a', Part V: A₁–c', Part VI: A₁–c', Part VII: A₁–a, Part VIII: F♯₁–a. Dedicated to R. Winston Morris and the Tennessee Technological University Tuba Ensemble. Excellent writing for eight-part tuba ensemble. Technically not difficult, but challenging to fit together and requires a conductor. Recorded by the Tennessee Technological University Tuba Ensemble, *LIVE!* KM Records, KM 5661.

Konagaya, Soichi. *Celebration*. Tokyo Bari-Tuba Ensemble. Solo tuba, three euphoniums, and three tubas. Written for Harvey Phillips.

Konagaya, Soichi. *Prophecy*. Tokyo Bari-Tuba Ensemble. Solo euphonium, four euphoniums, and four tubas.

Lasso, Orlando di. *Echo Fantasy for Double Tuba/Euphonium Ensemble*. arr. James Derby. Tuba/Euphonium Music Publications. Out of print. Four euphoniums and six tubas. 3:00. IV.

Lemirre, Florent. *Circus Life*. Florent Lemirre. Four euphoniums and four tubas. 1987. $55.00. 7:30. IV–V. Part I: d–b♭', Part II: A–g', Part III: A♭–e♭', Part IV: G–e♭', Part V: F–f ', Part VI: E♭–e♭', Part VII: D♭–e♭', Part VIII: E♭₁–a♭. Four movements: La Parade (the Parade); Clown et Funambules (Clowns and Tightrope Walkers); Trapèze Volant (Flying Trapeze); Fauves et Dompteur (Beasts and Animal Tamers). Dedicated to Hervé Brisse in total friendship. Four programmatic character pieces. Technical and range demands are great on all parts. The most harmonically complex of Lemirre's compositions. Requires eight strong players.

Lemirre, Florent. *Esquisse Villageoise* (Country Sketches). Florent Lemirre. Four euphoniums and four tubas. 1987. $55.00. 5:50. IV. Part I: d–a♭', Part II: G–a♭', Part III: A♭–g', Part IV: B♭₁–f ', Part V: E♭–f ', Part VI: E♭–d', Part VII: B♭₁–c', Part VIII: A♭₁–a♭. Four movements: Cloche dans le Matin (Morning Bells); Calme et Serein (Calm and Serene); Ronde Enfantine (Children's Round Dance); Farandole de Fête (Festival Farandole). Dedicated to Hervé Brisse in total friendship. Tessitura of the first two tuba parts is high. The harmonies are very traditional, but there are several technically demanding sections.

Lemirre, Florent. *Tuba Séduction (Ballade)*. Florent Lemirre. Four euphoniums and four tubas, or six euphoniums and two tubas. 1987. $30.00. 4:30. IV. Part I: f–a♭', Part II: d–f ', Part III: c–f ', Part IV: G–f ', Part V: B♭–a', Part VI: F–e', Part VII: B♭₁–c', Part VIII: G₁–f. Dedicated to Hervé Brisse in total friendship. The tessitura of the first tuba part is quite high, higher than the first euphonium part. The melody is primarily in the top two parts. No significant technical problems. The composer's last name is spelled with only one *r* on some parts and some compositions.

McCarthy, Daniel. *Two Pieces for Tuba/Euphonium Ensemble*. TUBA Press. Six euphoniums and two tubas. 1993. $20.00. 7:30. IV. Part I: c♯–b♭', Part II: B♭–g', Part III: G–f♯', Part IV: B₁–a, Part V: C–b♭', Part VI: B♭–f♯', Part VII: G–f ', Part VIII: E₁–a. Two movements: Dark Towers; Wind and Wuthering. Dedicated to Elliot Chasanov. Written for two tuba/euphonium quartets. All parts are challenging because of the constantly changing meters and dissonant harmonies. The composition is very programmatic, depicting the names of the movements. Winner of the 1992 Connie Weldon Tuba/Euphonium Ensemble Contest, sponsored by T.U.B.A. and the University of Miami.

McKimm, Barry. *Serenade for Tubas.* Barry McKimm. Four euphoniums and four tubas. 1982. 7:30. IV. Part I: B♭–d♭", Part II: B♭–c♭", Part III: G♭–b♭', Part IV: G♭–g', Part V: B♭$_1$–c', Part VI: B♭$_1$–c', Part VII: G♭$_1$–d♭, Part VIII: (E♭$_1$) G♭$_1$–A. A large single-movement work with several different sections. The tessitura of the top part is high. Some syncopated and complex rhythms in a traditional harmonic style.

McKimm, Barry, arr. *Irish Tune from County Derry.* Barry McKimm. Four euphoniums and four tubas. 1983. 2:20. IV. Part I: A–c", Part II: A–a', Part III: A–a', Part IV: A–b♭', Part V: E♭–d', Part VI: D–d', Part VII: A♭$_1$–e♭, Part VIII: E♭$_1$–d♭. Arranged for the Solitaire Tuba/Euphonium Ensemble. The tessitura of the first part is high. Scoring is a little thick at times. The style is very lyrical.

Mobberley, James C. *On Thin Ice.* Cautious Music. Four euphoniums and five tubas. 1990. $50.00. 5:15. V. Part I: G–d♭", Part II: F♯–b♭', Part III: F–b♭', Part IV: B♭$_1$–a', Part V: E$_1$–e♭', Part VI: F♯$_1$–d♯', Part VII: F$_1$–d♭', Part VIII: E$_1$–c', Part IX: E♭$_1$–g♭. Commissioned by Ernie Walls and dedicated to R. Winston Morris and the Tennessee Technological University Tuba Ensemble. A very well-written and difficult composition. Range demands are extensive for the euphoniums. Several odd meter changes, and some isolated sixteenth-notes in the parts can be difficult to place. Performance techniques include glissandos, flutter tonguing, and mutes. Parts may be doubled, but should begin with doubling the lowest parts first. Originally titled *Bull in a China Shop.* International premiere at the International Tuba/Euphonium Conference by the All-Star University Tuba/Euphonium Ensemble, in August 1990, Sapporo, Japan.

Nelhybel, Vaclav. *Canzona for Four Baritones and Four Tubas.* Great Works Publishing Incorporated. 1993. $25.00. 3:30. IV. Part I: c♯–b♭', Part II: c♯–f ', Part III: c♯–d', Part IV: A$_1$–d', Part V: c–a, Part VI: C♯–e, Part VII: A$_1$–c♯, Part VIII: E$_1$–B♭. Composed for and dedicated to the St. Olaf Tuba/Euphonium Ensemble. Very polyphonic, syncopated, and rhythmically oriented. Several tutti rhythmic figures with very close harmonies. Players need to play in a light style to keep from sounding muddy.

Paganini, N. *Perpetual Motion.* arr. Gary Buttery. Whaling Music Publishers. Two to seven tubas and piano. 1978. $10.00. 4:20. V. All Parts: C$_1$–d'(e'). Eighty percent of the composition is in unison. Technically very challenging. Players must have excellent technique and a good sense of rhythm.

Pegram, Wayne. *Howdy!* Ludwig Music Publishing Company. Three euphoniums, four tubas, and drums. 1992. $17.50. 2:40. IV. Part I: c–a', Part II:

c–f ', Part III: B♭–b♭, Part IV: G$_1$–d', Part V: G$_1$–b♭, Part VI: G$_1$–b♭, Part VII: G$_1$–b♭. Written for R. Winston Morris and the Tennessee Technological University Tuba Ensemble. A high-energy, fast-paced opening fanfare. A few technical challenges, though many of the parts are often doubled. A fun fanfare that is exciting for both performers and audience. Parts may be doubled for a large ensemble. Recorded by the Tennessee Technological University Tuba Ensemble, *Heavy Metal,* Mark Records, MES 20759, and the U.S. Armed Forces Tuba/Euphonium Ensemble, Mark Records, MW89MCD-8.

Piltzecker, Ted. *Cacology.* TUBA Press. Three euphoniums and five tubas. 1992. $10.00. 2:20. IV. Part I: B♭–b♭', Part II: d–g♭', Part III: B–d♭', Part IV: C–c', Part V: D–b♭', Part VI: F$_1$–b♭', Part VII: B♭$_1$–b♭, Part VIII: F$_1$–g♭. Commissioned by John Stevens and the University of Wisconsin Tuba/Euphonium Ensemble. A challenging work for all eight parts. Very interesting writing, very appropriate for recital material. Premiered by the College All-Star Ensemble at the 1992 International Tuba/Euphonium Conference.

Rimsky-Korsakov, Nicolas. *Flight of the Bumblebones.* arr. Wally Gladwin. T.A.P. Music. Six euphoniums and two tubas. 1986. $15.00. 3:45. IV–V. Part I: B$_1$–a', Part II: B$_1$–g', Part III: B♭$_1$–f ', Part IV: B♭$_1$–d♭', Part V: A$_1$–f ', Part VI: A$_1$–f ', Part VII: A$_1$–a', Part VIII: A$_1$–e'. The ranges are extreme, and the tessitura of all parts is very high. Can be performed with a variety of instrumentations especially if some sections are played an octave lower. Technically challenging in several sections.

Ross, Walter. *Concerto Basso.* Dorn Publications, Incorporated. Four euphoniums and four tubas. 1974. 11:00. IV. Part I: c–g♯', Part II: B♭–g', Part III: B♭–f, Part IV: F♯$_1$–B♭, Part V: d♭–g', Part VI: B–g', Part VII: F–f, Part VIII: F♯$_1$–e. Three movements. Written for two euphonium/tuba quartets. Parts I–IV represent one quartet, Parts V–VIII the second quartet. The third movement is multimetric and is more technically challenging. The top four parts require mutes. Recorded by the Tennessee Technological University Tuba Ensemble, Golden Crest Records, QCRS 4139.

Schudel, Thomas. *Richter 7.8 for 12 Low Brass Instruments.* T.A.P. Music. Three euphoniums and nine tubas. 1981. $25.00. 6:00. IV. Part I: c–g', Part II: c♯–g', Part III: c–f♯', Part IV: G♯–d', Part V: G–d♭', Part VI: G♯–c♯', Part VII: C–b♭, Part VIII: C♯–a, Part IX: C–b♭, Part X: G$_1$–e, Part XI: F♯$_1$–f, Part XII: F$_1$–e. Dedicated to John Griffiths. The ensemble is divided into three groups, with one euphonium and three tubas in each group. The texture is very thick and the harmonies very dissonant. It is what one would expect with a title named after a device used to measure the force of earthquakes. A very interesting piece.

Schütz, Heinrich. *Antiphony No. 1 for Double Tuba/ Euphonium Choir.* arr. Tom Hancock. Tuba/Euphonium Music Publications. Out of print. Four euphoniums and six tubas. 4:00. III–IV.

Stevens, John. *Adagio.* Editions Bim. Four euphoniums and four tubas. 1991. 9:00. IV. Part I: g–bb', Part II: g–a', Part III: d–d', Part IV: c–d', Part V: E–c', Part VI: C–c', Part VII: G$_1$–f, Part VIII: F$_1$–e. Commissioned by the Tubists Universal Brotherhood Association for the 1992 International Tuba/ Euphonium Conference, Lexington, KY. A slow, single-movement work in a Romantic style. Lush harmonies and sonorous qualities of the instruments are emphasized.

Stevens, John. *Higashi-Nishi* (East-West). Editions Bim. Four euphoniums and four tubas. 1984. 12:00. V. Part I: F–c", Part II: Db–c", Part III: Db–gb', Part IV: Db–gb', Part V: F$_1$–c', Part VI: F$_1$–c', Part VII: F$_1$–g, Part VIII: Db$_1$–f. Written for the Tokyo Bari-Tuba Ensemble. One movement work in four distinct sections: Slow, Fast, Slow, Fast. The harmonies and melodies show a distinct Asian influence combined with more "American" rhythms.

Stevens, John. *The Liberation of Sisyphus.* Editions Bim. Solo tuba, four euphoniums, and four tubas. 1990. $43.50. 6:00. IV–V. Solo tuba: A$_1$–c", Part II: G–bb', Part III: F–ab', Part IV: G–f ', Part V: F–d', Part VI: F$_1$–c', Part VII: F$_1$–b, Part VIII: F$_1$–f, Part IX: F$_1$–f. For Roger Bobo. The solo part is virtuosic, spanning a huge range and very demanding technically. The ensemble parts are also very challenging. A very exciting and demanding composition. See: Bird, Gary, ed., *Program Notes for the Solo Tuba.* Recorded by Roger Bobo, *The Liberation of Sisyphus,* Crystal Records.

Susato, Tylman. *Five Dances.* arr. John Stevens. Encore Music Publishers. Four euphoniums and four tubas. 1988. $23.00. 8:30. IV. Part I: f–a', Part II: d–g', Part III: c–f ', Part IV: F–c', Part V: G–c', Part VI: D–c', Part VII: C–ab, Part VIII: C$_1$–c. Five movements contrasting in style, meter, and key: La Mourisque; Bransle Quatre Bransles; Ronde; Ronde Mon Amy; Pavane Battaille. No significant technical problems. Works well for a large ensemble. No score available.

Torre, Javier De La. *Preludio and Fuga a 8 for Tuba and Euphonium Octet.* Javier De La Torre. Four euphoniums and four tubas. 1987. 10:00. V. Part I: E–a#', Part II: F–gb', Part III: E–g', Part IV E–g#', Part V: F$_1$–d', Part VI: F$_1$–d#', Part VII: F$_1$–e', Part VIII: F$_1$–f '. Very contemporary piece with many twentieth-century compositional techniques, including flutter tonguing, circular breathing, glissandos, murmuring in the instrument, complex notation, and complex meters. The bottom two tuba parts have higher range requirements than the first two tuba parts. Requires very strong players on each part.

Tull, Fisher. *Tubular Octad.* Boosey & Hawkes, Incorporated. Four euphoniums and four tubas. 1980. $19.00. 8:00. IV–V. Part I: F–c", Part II: G–bb', Part III: F–a', Part IV: F–a', Part V: G$_1$–db', Part VI: G$_1$–bb, Part VII: G$_1$–bb, Part VIII: G$_1$–ab. Commissioned by the Tubists Universal Brotherhood Association. Single movement with several distinct sections, including a canonic passage and a scherzo within an overall arch form. Two double cadenzas featuring one euphonium and one tuba. Range and technical demands require eight very strong players. Premiered May 22, 1980 by the National Collegiate All-Star Tuba-Euphonium Ensemble at the Second National Tuba/Euphonium Symposium/Workshop.

Vaughan, Rodger. *Winds: Five Descriptive Pieces for Tuba/Euphonium Octet.* TUBA Press. Four euphoniums and four tubas. 1992. $20.00. 10:30. IV. Part I: Bb–cb', Part II: Bb–ab', Part III: Bb–f#', Part IV: Bb–f ', Part V: C–bb, Part VI: C–a, Part VII: C$_1$–a, Part VIII: C$_1$–f. Five movements: Khamsin; Zephyrs; Bora; Doldrums; Sirocco. For Jerry Young and his low-down musicians at the University of Wisconsin, Eau Claire. Not technically difficult but a challenge because of the numerous meter changes. The character is descriptive of each movement. Rhythmically very interesting and exciting at times. Enjoyable to play.

Wright, Rayburn. *Undercurrents.* Seesaw Music Corporation Publishers. One flute, seven tubas, and two percussion. 1980. $99.00. 18:00. IV–V. Part I: Eb–eb', Part II: Eb–eb', Part III: Bb$_1$–bb, Part IV: Gb$_1$–c#', Part V: Gb$_1$–a, Part VI: Gb$_1$–c#', Part VII: F#$_1$–g. A large and complex work with numerous tempo and meter changes. Technically challenging. Contains very dissonant harmonies. All parts require mutes. Requires strong players and a conductor. See listing under "Music for Tuba in Mixed Ensemble."

Yoshizawa, Kentaro. *Tuba Chan Chaka Chan.* Tokyo Bari-Tuba Ensemble. Four euphoniums and four tubas.

Ensemble Master List by Title

Adagio. Albinoni/Hiraishi. Four euphoniums.

Adagio. Stevens. Four euphoniums and four tubas.

Adagio, Choral et Scherzetto. Ameller. Four tubas.

Adagio and Rondo. Forte. Two euphoniums and two tubas.

Adagio from Symphony No. 3. Saint-Saëns/Hanson. Two euphoniums and two tubas.

Adoramus Te, Christe. Mozart/Nelson. Two euphoniums and two tubas.

Advanced Duets for Tuba, Volume I. Sear. Two tubas.

Advanced Duets for Tuba, Volume II. Sear. Two tubas.

Aequale. Bruckner/Schmidt. One euphonium and two tubas.

Air for Tuba Ensemble. Rodgers. Two euphoniums and two tubas.

Air from Amadis. Lully/Hartin. Four tubas.

Air from Suite No. 3 in D. Bach/Werden. Two euphoniums and two tubas.

Albergona, L'. Mortaro/Heiman. Two euphoniums and two tubas.

Alexander's Ragtime Band. Berlin/Hoesly. Two euphoniums and two tubas.

Alexander's Ragtime Band. Berlin/Schmidt. Two euphoniums and two tubas.

All Too Soon. Niehaus. Two euphoniums and two tubas.

Allegro for Tuba Quartet. Jones. Four tubas.

Allegro, from Divertimento No. 1, K. 229. Mozart/Schmidt. Two euphoniums and one tuba.

Allegro from Eine Kleine Nachtmusik. Mozart/Peoples. Two euphoniums and two tubas.

Allegro from Water Music. Handel/Rauch. Two euphoniums and two tubas.

Allegro from "Water Music." Handel/Self. Two euphoniums and four tubas.

Allegro from William Tell Overture. Rossini/Rauch. Two euphoniums and two tubas.

Alleluia. Boyce/Laws. Two euphoniums and two tubas.

Alleluia. Telemann/Heiman. Two euphoniums and three tubas.

Allerseelen. Strauss/Gotoh. Three euphoniums and three tubas.

Alpha Suite, The. Catelinet. One euphonium and one tuba.

Alt und Neu für Zwei. Zettler. One euphonium and one tuba.

Alte Kameraden. Tautenhahn. Two euphoniums and two tubas.

Alte Kameraden March. Teike/Schmidt. Two euphoniums and two tubas.

Amazing Grace. Glover. Two euphoniums and two tubas.

Amazing Grace. Vaughan. Two euphoniums, two tubas, and garden hose.

American Favorites: Tuba Euphonium Quartets. Vaughan. Two euphoniums and two tubas.

American Tuba Patrol. Meacham/Konagaya. Two euphoniums and two tubas.

An der Schönen Blauen Donau. Strauss/Seitz. Two euphoniums and two tubas.

Anna Magdalena Suite. Bach/Stevens. Two euphoniums and two tubas.

Antiphonies. Fredrickson. Four euphoniums and four tubas.

Antiphony No. 1 for Double T/E Choir. Schütz/Hancock. Four euphoniums and six tubas.

Antiphony No. 2 for Double T/E Choir. Gabrieli/Conner. Four euphoniums and four tubas.

Appalachian Carol (Quartet No. 2). Canter. Two euphoniums and two tubas.

Appalachian Echos. Purvis. Two tubas.

April Is in My Mistress' Face. Morley/Howard. Two euphoniums and two tubas.

April Is in My Mistress' Face. Morley/Nelson. Two euphoniums and two tubas.

Arabian Dance. Tchaikovsky/Woodcock. Two euphoniums and two tubas.

Aragonaise from "Le Cid." Massenet/Erickson. Two euphoniums and two tubas.

Aria and Rondo. Potter. Two euphoniums and one tuba.

Arietta and Waltz. Grieg/Hiraishi. Two euphoniums and two tubas.

Artistic Solos and Duets. Bell. One euphonium and one tuba.

Asleep in the Deep. Petrie/Schmidt. Two euphoniums and two tubas.

Asleep in the Deep. Winsor. Five tubas

Ave Maria. Arcadelt/Self. Four tubas.

Ave Maria. Bruckner/Sabourin. Two euphoniums and two tubas.

Ave Maria. Verdi/Nelson. Two euphoniums and two tubas.

Ave Verum. Mozart/Sabourin. Two euphoniums and two tubas.

Ave Verum Corpus. Byrd/Howard. Two euphoniums and two tubas.

Ave Verum Corpus. Byrd/Schmidt. Two euphoniums and two tubas.

Ave Verum Corpus. Mozart/Seitz. Two euphoniums and two tubas.

Away in a Manger. Vaughan. Two euphoniums and two tubas.

Baby Elephant Walk. Mancini/Anderson. Two euphoniums and two tubas.

Bach for Two Tubas. Bach/MacMorran. Two tubas.

Ballad for Five Tubas. Frank. Two euphoniums and three tubas.

Ballade. Stevens. Two euphoniums and two tubas.

Ballade in D Minor, Op. 10, no. 1. Brahms/Siekmann. Five euphoniums and two tubas.

Ballin' the Jack. Hoesly. Two euphoniums and two tubas.

Baroque'n Brass. Anderson. One trumpet or euphonium and one tuba.

Basic Psych-Rock. Self. Two euphoniums and four tubas.

Bass Clef Sessions. Gearhart. Two euphoniums and two tubas.

Bass Lied and Valse to Bass. Badarak. One euphonium and one tuba.

Battle Hymn. Steffe/Isbell. Two euphoniums and two tubas.

Bayerische Polka. Schmidt. Two euphoniums and four tubas.

Bayerische Zell. Schmidt. Two euphoniums and four tubas.

Beautiful Savior. Anderson. Two euphoniums and two tubas.

Beer Barrel Polka. Anderson. Two euphoniums and two tubas.

Beersheba Neo-Baroque Suite. Bartles. Tuba and cello (or euphonium).

Belle of Chicago March. Sousa/Ray. Two euphoniums and two tubas.

Beneath the Surface. Harrison. Two euphoniums, two tubas, piano, guitar, bass, and drums.

Bentonsport 1895. McCurdy. Four tubas.

Bicinia, Op. 5. Thomas. One trombone (euphonium) and one tuba.

Bill Bailey. Garrett. Two euphoniums and two tubas with optional keyboard and drums.

Bird in the Forest, Op. 376F. Hewitt. Four tubas with a high solo and optional echo part.

Bist du bei Mir. Bach/Werden. Two euphoniums and two tubas.

Bivalve Suite. Hartley. One euphonium and one tuba.

Blues for Bill. McCurdy. Four tubas.

Bluesette. Thielmans/Vaughan. Two euphoniums and two tubas.

Bluesin' Tubas. Martin. Three euphoniums, two tubas, piano, bass, drums, and guitar.

Bocoxe. Powell/Buttery. Two euphoniums and two tubas.

Bottoms Up Rag. Mehlan. Two euphoniums and two tubas.

Brass Duo. Frackenpohl. One horn (euphonium) and one tuba.

Brass Tacks. Niehaus. Two euphoniums and two tubas.

Bridal Chorus from Lohengrin. Wagner/Oliver. Two euphoniums and two tubas.

Brinklien, die da fliesen, Die. De Vento/Schmidt. Two euphoniums and two tubas.

Butterbrot, Das. Mozart/Dorner. Four tubas.

Buttons and Bows. Livingston and Evans/Schmidt. Two euphoniums and two tubas.

Cacology. Piltzecker. Three euphoniums and five tubas.

Cadenzas for Eight Players. Ito. Four euphoniums and four tubas.

Canon. Billings/Schmidt. Two euphoniums and two tubas.

Canon in D. Pachelbel/Siekmann. One euphonium, one tuba, and piano.

Canon in the Lydian Mode. Wolfe. One euphonium and one tuba.

Canon on a Ground Bass. Purcell/Gray. One euphonium and two tubas.

Canonic Etudes. Racussen. Three tubas.

Canonic Sonata. Telemann/Hartin. Two tubas.

Cantate Domini and What Child Is This? Pitoni/Schmidt. Two euphoniums and two tubas.

Canticles. Jones. Four tubas.

Cantilena. Jones. Two euphoniums and two tubas.

Canzona. Gabrieli/Varner. Two euphoniums and two tubas.

Canzona "La Spiritata." Gabrieli/Rauch. Two euphoniums and two tubas.

Canzona and Hornpipe. Israel. Four tubas.

Canzona for Four Baritones and Four Tubas. Nelhybel. Four euphoniums and four tubas.

Canzona per Sonare II. Gabrieli/Schmidt. Two euphoniums and two tubas.

Canzona XXX. Scheidt/Gray. Two euphoniums and three tubas.

Canzone. Kerll/Long. One euphonium and two tubas.

Carnival of Venice. Le Clair. Two euphoniums and two tubas.

Carolina. Self. Two euphoniums and two tubas.

Caroling Quartet, The. Anderson. Two euphoniums and two tubas.

Carols for a Merry Tubachristmas. Wilder. Two euphoniums and two tubas.

Carols for a Merry Tubachristmas, Vol. II. Wilder and Bewley. Two euphoniums and two tubas.

Cassation for Four Tubas. De Filippi. Four tubas.

Celebration. Anderson. Three euphoniums and one tuba.

Celebration. Konagaya. Solo tuba, three euphoniums, and three tubas.

Celestial Suite. Bulla. Two euphoniums and two tubas.

Celluloid Tubas: A Score for Barney Oldfield's Race for a Life (1913). Fiegel. Three euphoniums, three tubas, and motion picture equipment.

Ceremonial Sketch. Camphouse. Two euphoniums and two tubas.

Chaconne. Bergenfeld. Two euphoniums and one tuba.

Chaconne. Purcell/Hartin. Three tubas.

Chaconne. Purcell/Morris. Two tubas with optional piano or harpsichord.

Chaconne, Op. 148. Cunningham. Two euphoniums and two tubas.

Chant and Fantasie. Jones. Four tubas.

Charleston. Mack/Bevan and Schmidt. Two euphoniums and two tubas.

Charleston Chuckles. Confrey/Vaughan. Two euphoniums and two tubas.

Chaser No. 1. Garbáge. Two euphoniums and one tuba.

Chaser No. 3. Garbáge. Two euphoniums and two tubas.

Cherokee for Tuba Quartet. Schooley. Two euphoniums and two tubas.

Chi Ni Hikari Arite. Censhu. Four euphoniums and four tubas.

Chiapanecas (Advanced). Anderson. Three euphoniums and one tuba.

Chiapanecas (Easy). Anderson. Two euphoniums and two tubas.

Chin Up! Kresin. Two euphoniums and two tubas.

Chinese Dance. Tchaikovsky/Woodcock. Two euphoniums and two tubas.

Chimes Blues. Garrett. Two euphoniums and two tubas with optional keyboard and drums.

Chops! Martin. Three euphoniums, two tubas, and rhythm.

Choral and Folksong. Dutton. Two trombones (euphoniums), one tuba, and piano.

Chorale. Howard. Two euphoniums and two tubas.

Chorale. McCurdy. Two euphoniums and one tuba.

Chorale and Gigue. McCurdy. One euphonium and one tuba.

Chorale and Gigue for a Quartet of Tubas. Danburg. Four tubas.

Chorale (Psalm 97). Schütz/Heiman. Two euphoniums and two tubas.

Chorale Quartet. Anderson. Two euphoniums and two tubas.

Choro di Schiavi Ebrei (from "Nabucco"). Verdi/Evans. Two euphoniums and two tubas.

Christmas Bell Songs. Schmidt. Two euphoniums and two tubas.

Christmas Bells A-Plenty. Anderson. Two euphoniums and two tubas.

Christmas Collection—Duets for Brass. Hoesly. Two tubas.

Christmas Jazz Medley, A. Niehaus. Two euphoniums and two tubas.

Christmas Song, The. Torme/Vaughan. Two euphoniums and two tubas.

Christmas for Two. Conley. One euphonium and one tuba.

Chumbo the Elephant. Saint-Saëns/Stauffer. Two euphoniums and two tubas.

Cinnamon Downs. Bewley. Two euphoniums, two tubas, and three harps.

Circle VIII: Bowge IV. Canter. Four euphoniums and four tubas.

Circus Life. Lemirre. Four euphoniums and four tubas.

Classics for Low Brass Quartet, Set No. 1. Schumann/Schanke. Two euphoniums and two tubas.

Classics for Low Brass Quartet, Set No. 2. Schumann/Schanke. Two euphoniums and two tubas.

Clementine. Garrett. One euphonium and two tubas.

Cole Porter Medley. Sample. Two euphoniums, two tubas, piano/guitar, bass, and drums.

Colonel Bogey March. Alford/Schmidt. Two euphoniums and two tubas.

Coloring Book, The. McCurdy. Two tubas.

Colossi. Knight. Six Tubas.

Come Josephine (In My Flying Machine). Fischer/Schmidt. Two euphoniums and two tubas.

Come Sweet Death. Bach/Anderson. Two euphoniums and two tubas.

Come Sweet Death. Bach/Sauter. One euphonium and two tubas.

Concert and Ensemble Folio (Bandsembles). Hudadoff. Two tubas.

Concert für 4. Heidler. Two euphoniums and two tubas.

Concert Suite. Goedicke. One euphonium and one tuba.

Concerto. Vivaldi/Humble. Two euphoniums and two tubas.

Concerto Basso. Ross. Four euphoniums and four tubas.

Concerto Grosso. Geminiani/Morris. Two euphoniums and one tuba.

Concertstück. Amellér. Four tubas.

Consortium for Euphoniums and Tubas. Cheetham. Two euphoniums and two tubas.

Contrapunctus I. Bach/Morris. Two euphoniums and three tubas.

Contrapunctus III from Art of Fugue. Bach/Nelson. Two euphoniums and two tubas.

Contrapunctus IX. Bach/Pitts. Two euphoniums and two tubas.

Contrapunctus IX. Bach/Rauch. Two euphoniums and two tubas.

Contrapunctus IX. Bach/Schmidt. Two euphoniums and two tubas.

Corona D' Italia, La. Rossini/Heidler. Three euphoniums and two tubas.

Counterpoint No. 6. Nelhybel. Two tubas.

Csikos Post. Necke/Konagaya. Two euphoniums and two tubas.

Csikos Post. Necke/Schmidt. Two euphoniums and two tubas.

Cuckoo, The. Schmidt. Two euphoniums, two tubas, with optional flute, recorder, or whistle.

Dance No. 1. Wilson. Two euphoniums and two tubas.

Dance of the Mirlitons. Tchaikovsky/Woodcock. Two euphoniums and two tubas.

Dance of the Tumblers. Rimsky-Korsakov/Siekmann. Two euphoniums and two tubas.

Dance Suite. Gervaise/Werden. Two euphoniums and two tubas.

Dances. Stevens. Solo tuba and three tubas.

Dances; Four Tubas: A Short Piece for Tuba Quartet. Pullig. Two euphoniums and two tubas.

Dead Man's Cove. Newsome. Two euphoniums and two tubas.

Death of Beowulf, The. Muller. Four tubas.

Dedications for Baritone and Tuba. Constantinides. One euphonium and one tuba.

Demon Dance. McCurdy. Three tubas.

Deutschland über Alles. Anderson. Two euphoniums and two tubas.

Devil Septet. Ewazen. Four tubas, piano, and percussion.

Dialog for Tubas. Atherton. Four tubas.

Dialogue. Hoshina. Four euphoniums and six tubas.

Dialogue and Dance. Brown. One trombone (euphonium) and one tuba.

Dill Pickles Rag: A Ragtime Two-Step. Johnson/Nelson. Two euphoniums and two tubas.

Disco Tuba. Carmody. One euphonium and two tubas.

Diversion for Seven Bass Clef Instruments. Clinard. Four euphoniums and three tubas.

Diversions. Stevens. Four tubas.

Divertimento. De Filippi. One euphonium and one tuba.

Divertimento. Hayakawa. Three euphoniums and three tubas.

Divertimento. Presser. Two euphoniums and three tubas.

Divertimento. Spears. Two euphoniums and two tubas.

Divertimento. Uber. Two euphoniums and two tubas.

Divertimento No. 1, K. 229. Mozart/Schmidt. Two euphoniums and one tuba.

Divertimento No. 2, Op. 130. Uber. Two euphoniums and two tubas.

Divertimento, Op. 70. Roikjer. Two tubas.

Dizzy Fingers. Confrey/Vaughan. Two euphoniums and two tubas.

Doguu Sansai. Censhu. Three tubas.

Dona Nobis Pacem. Isbell. One euphonium and two tubas.

Double Portraits. Uber. One euphonium and one tuba.

Down by the Old Mill Stream. Vaughan. Two euphoniums and two tubas.

Down on the Farm. Garrett. Two euphoniums and two tubas.

Dream. Vaughan. Two euphoniums and two tubas.

Drei Duette für Tuba, Band I. Heidler. Two tubas.

Drei Duette für Tuba, Band II. Heidler. Two tubas.

Duet. Mueller. One euphonium and one tuba.

Duet. Sainte-Jacome/Wekselblatt. Two tubas.

Duet for Tubas. Garrett. Two tubas.

Duet for Tubas. Stamitz/Long. Two tubas.

Duet for Two Tubas and Understanding Audience. Wilson. Two tubas.

Duet in F. Devienne/Singleton. Two tubas.

Duet No. 1 in Eb Major. Nicolai/Conner. Two tubas.

Duet Time. Scarmolin/Boo. One euphonium and one tuba.

Duets and Trios. Bach/Augustine. Two or three tubas.

Duets for All. Stoutamire and Albert. Two tubas.

Duets for Tuba. Mozart/Jacobs. Two Tubas.

Duo Concertante for Two Tubas, Op. 97. Uber. Two tubas.

Duo for Tubas. Goldman. Two tubas.

Dyad for Four Tubas. Alexander. Four tubas.

Easy Classics for Two. Stouffer. Two tubas.

Easy Winners, The. Joplin/Hiraishi. Two euphoniums and two tubas.

Easy Winners, The. Joplin/Le Clair. One euphonium, one tuba, and piano.

Easy Winners, The. Joplin/Schmidt. Two euphoniums and two tubas.

Easy Winners, The. Joplin/Werden. Two euphoniums and two tubas.

Ebbe Skammelsen. Anderson. Three tubas.

Ecco Mormorar L'onde. Monteverdi/Nelson. Two euphoniums and three tubas.

Echo Carol, The. Anderson. Two euphoniums and two tubas.

Echo Fantasy for Double T/E Ensemble. Lasso/Derby. Four euphoniums and six tubas.

Ego Sum Tui Plaga Doloris. Schutz/Nelson. Two euphoniums and two tubas.

Eight Bagatelles. Luedeke. Two tubas.

Eight Days of Christmas. Vaughan. Two euphoniums and two tubas.

Eight Miniatures for Four Tubas. Constantinides. Four tubas.

Eine Kleine Nachtmusik. K. 525. Mozart/Greene. Two euphoniums and two tubas.

Eine Kleine Nachtmusik K. 525. Mozart/Schmidt. Two euphoniums and two tubas.

Eine Kleine Nachtmusik. Mozart/Seitz. Two euphoniums and two tubas.

Eine Kleine Nachtmusik for Tuba Quartet. Mozart/Self. Four tubas.

Eine Kleine Octubamusic. Frackenpohl. Eight tubas.

El Capitan. Sousa/Morris. Two euphoniums and two tuba.

El Solo Toro-Marriachi. Alpert/Self. Two euphoniums and two tubas.

Elegy for Four Tubas. Coucounaras. Four tubas.

Elephants Exotiques. Snow. Four tubas.

Eleven Duets for Tuba. Nelhybel. Two tubas.

Eleven Mozart Duets for Bass Clef Instruments. Mozart/Powell. Two bass-clef instruments.

Elite Syncopations. Joplin/Picher. Two euphoniums and two tubas.

Ellington Medley. Sample. Two euphoniums, two tubas, piano/guitar, bass, and drums.

Emilia Polka. Schmidt. Two euphoniums and two tubas.

English Folk Christmas, An. Buttery. Four tubas.

Entertainer, The. Joplin/Bale. Two euphoniums and two tubas.

Entertainer, The. Joplin/Hiraishi. Three euphoniums and one tuba.

Entry of the Gladiators. Fucik/Seitz. Two euphoniums and two tubas.

Es ist eine Rose Entsprungen. Brahms/Gotoh. Three euphoniums and three tubas.

Espana Cami. Garrett. Three euphoniums and three tubas.

Esquisse Villageoise (Country Sketches). Lemirre. Four euphoniums and four tubas.

Essay. Toyama. Three euphoniums and three tubas.

Euphonic Sounds. Joplin/Hiraishi. Two euphoniums and two tubas.

Euphonic Sounds. Joplin/Werden. Two euphoniums and two tubas.

Euphonium and Tuba: Ensemble Works for the First Time. Morita. Two euphoniums and one tuba.

Euphonium Tuba Quartet. Toda. Two euphoniums and two tubas.

Evergreen Polka. Schmidt. Two euphoniums and two tubas.

Exhibitions, Op. 98. Uber. Four euphoniums and one tuba.

Explorations for Tuba Quintet, Op. 85. Uber. Five tubas.

Expose for Tubas. Garrett. Four euphoniums and two tubas.

Faeroe Island Suite. Thingnäs. Two euphoniums, two tubas, rhythm section, and orchestra.

Fancy Dances. Ross. Three tubas.

Fanfare. Garrett. Three euphoniums and three tubas.

Fanfare and Chant. Cummings. Four euphoniums and two tubas.

Fanfare and Rondeau. Mouret/Schmidt. Two euphoniums and two tubas.

Fanfare for a Friend. Stevens. Five tubas.

Fanfare for Six Tubas. Sandstrom. Six Tubas.

Fanfare for Tubafour. Anderson. Two euphoniums and two tubas.

Fanfare No. 1. Taylor. Two euphoniums and two tubas.

Fanfares. Vaughan. Two euphoniums and two tubas.

Fanitul. Olsen/Rauchut. Two euphoniums and one tuba.

Fantasia. Gibbons. Two tubas.

Fantasia. Lupo/Baldwin. Three tubas.

Fantasia. Lupo/Hartin. Three tubas.

Fantasia. White/Baldwin. Two tubas.

Fantasia. White/Hartin. Two tubas.

Fantasia for Basses. Lupo/Schmidt. Two euphoniums and two tubas.

Fantasia for Tuba Duo. Garrett. Two tubas.

Fantasia in C. Bach/Sabourin. Two euphoniums and two tubas.

Fantasia on "Dies Irae." Hill. Two euphoniums and four tubas.

Fantasias. Lasso/Powell. One euphonium and one tuba.

Fantasy for Tuba/Euphonium Quartet. Martino. Two euphoniums and two tubas.

Fascinatin' Gershwin. Ferguson. Two euphoniums and two tubas.

Favorite Rag, The. Joplin/Sabourin. Two euphoniums and two tubas.

Feiertagsmusik. Krol. Three euphoniums and two tubas.

Fifteen Easy Pieces for Bass Clef Instruments. Carmody. Two euphoniums and two tubas.

Fifteen Spectrum Duets for Tubas. Fritze. Two tubas.

Finlandia. Sibelius/Self. Two euphoniums and four tubas.

First Gymnopedie. Satie/Rauch. Two euphoniums and two tubas.

Five Bach Duos for Euphonium and Tuba. Frackenpohl. One euphonium and one tuba.

Five Canons for Tuba/Euphonium Sextet. Vaughan.

Five Dances. Susato/Stevens. Four euphoniums and four tubas.

Five Duets. Mozart/Hartin. Two tubas.

Five Foot Two—Eyes of Blue. Emberson. Two euphoniums and two tubas.

Five Foot Two, Eyes of Blue. Henderson/Emberson. Two euphoniums and two tubas.

Five Foot Two, Eyes of Blue. Henderson/Nelson. Two euphoniums and three tubas.

Five for Two Tubas. Albert. Two tubas.

Five Hag Pieces. Presser. One euphonium and one tuba.

Five Hundred Pound Polka. McCurdy. Three tubas with piano.

Five Moods for Tuba Quartet. Schuller. Four tubas.

Five Pieces for Tuba Quintet. Smith. Three euphoniums and two tubas.

Five Trios of King Henry VIII. Schmidt. Two euphoniums and one tuba.

Flight of the Bumblebones. Rimsky-Korsakov/Gladwin. Six euphoniums and two tubas.

Florentiner March. Glover. Three euphoniums and three tubas.

Fly Me to the Moon. Howard/Hughes. Four trombones (euphoniums) and one tuba.

Folksong Medley. Rauch. Two euphoniums and two tubas.

Forge in the Forest Polka. Stolc/Schmidt. Two euphoniums and two tubas.

Four Bach Chorales. Bach/Mehlan. Two euphoniums and two tubas.

Four Choruses. Schubert/Singleton. Three tubas.

Four Dialogues. Stoker. One euphonium and one tuba.

Four Duets, Op. 82. Devienne/Gershenfeld. Two tubas.

Four Etudes for Two Tubas. Warren. Two tubas.

Four Excursions for Five Tubas. Baskin. Five tubas.

Four Kuehn ("Keen") Guys. Gillis. Four tubas.

Four Miniatures for Trombone and Tuba. Beasley. One trombone and one tuba.

Four Pieces. Grieg/Rauch. Two euphoniums and two tubas.

Four Pieces. Maurer/Stevens. Two euphoniums and three tubas.

Four Pieces for Tuba Quartet. Jacob. Two euphoniums and two tubas.

Four Preludes for Four Tubas. Hewitt. Four tubas.

Four Preludes, Op. 28. Nos. 4, 7, 22, 28, Chopin/Rauch. Two euphoniums and two tubas.

Four Preludes, Op. 34. Shostakovich/Rauch. Two euphoniums and two tubas.

Four Quartets. Dressler. Two euphoniums and two tubas.

Four Quartets. Reicha/Werden. Two euphoniums and two tubas.

Fourteen Familiar Hymns, Carols, and Spirituals. Frederick. Three euphoniums and two tubas.

Fourtone Folio, Volume I. Cheyette and Roberts. Three euphoniums and one tuba.

Fourtone Folio, Volume II. Cheyette and Roberts. Three euphoniums and one tuba.

Friendly Giants. Ball. Four tubas.

From Darkness...Emerging. Cummings. Two euphoniums and two tubas.

From a Distance. Emberson. Two euphoniums and two tubas.

Frosty the Snowman. Glover. Two euphoniums and two tubas.

Fuga VII from WTC. Bach/Self. Two euphoniums and two tubas.

Fugue in C Minor for Low Brass. Bach/Morris. One euphonium and two tubas.

Fugue in F Major. Bach/Schmidt. Two euphoniums and one tuba.

Fugue in G Minor (Little). Bach/Gray. Two euphoniums and two tubas.

Fugue in G Minor (Little). Bach/Peoples. Two euphoniums and two tubas.

Fugue K. 401. Mozart/Schmidt. Two euphoniums and two tubas.

Fugue No. 16 for Four Low Brass Instruments. Bach/Grim. Two euphoniums and two tubas.

Fugue on B.A.C.H. Krebs/Brown. Two euphoniums and two tubas.

Fun for Band. Kinyon.

Funeral March of a Marionette. Gounod/Frackenpohl. Two euphoniums and two tubas.

Funeral March of a Marionette. Gounod/Schmidt. Two euphoniums and two tubas.

Gay 90's Medley. Hughey and Jernigan. Two euphoniums and two tubas.

Gebet aus "Hansel und Gretel." Humperdink/Seitz. Two euphoniums and two tubas.

Georgia on My Mind. Carmichael/Matteson. Three euphoniums, three tubas, and rhythm.

Gershwin Medley. Sample. Two euphoniums, two tubas, piano/guitar, bass, and drums.

Ginnungigap. Belden. One euphonium and one tuba.

Gnome. Aoshima. Two euphoniums and two tubas.

God Rest Ye, Merry Gentlemen. Vaughan. Two euphoniums and two tubas.

God Save the Queen. Glover. Two euphoniums and two tubas.

Golliwog's Cake Walk. Debussy/Yamamoto. Two Euphoniums and three tubas.

Golliwogg's Cakewalk. Debussy/Schmidt. Two euphoniums and two tubas.

Good Christian Men Rejoice. Vaughan. Two euphoniums and two tubas.

Grab Bag. De Jong. Four tubas.

Grand Slam. Niehaus. Two euphoniums and two tubas.

Great Chromatic Fugue in G. Anderson. Three euphoniums and one tuba.

Great Crush Collision, The. Joplin/Schmidt. Two euphoniums and two tubas.

Great Crush Collision March. Joplin/Rauchut. Three euphoniums and two tubas.

Greensleeves. Bullet/Buttery. Two euphoniums and two tubas.

Greensleeves. Rauch. Two euphoniums and two tubas.

Greensleeves. Vaughan. Two euphoniums and two tubas.

Gregory Is Here. Silver/Matteson. Three euphoniums, three tubas, and rhythm.

Grey Horse Polka. Orzechowski/Schmidt. Two euphoniums and two tubas.

Growing Up Together. Le Clair. One euphonium and one tuba.

Guercia, La. Heiman. Two euphoniums and two tubas.

Hades. Iannaccone. Two euphoniums and two tubas.

Hallelujah Chorus, The. Handel/Sabourin. Two euphoniums and two tubas.

Hallelujah Chorus, The. Handel/Stevens. Two euphoniums and two tubas.

Hallelujah! from "Messiah." Handel/Heiman. Two euphoniums and two tubas.

Hands across the Sea. Sousa/Werden. Two euphoniums and two tubas.

Happy Birthday with Fanfare. Emberson. Two euphoniums and two tubas.

Hard Way. Carmody. Four tubas.

Harold Arlen Medley. Sample. Two euphoniums, two tubas, piano/guitar, bass, and drums.

Hauntings for Tuba Ensemble. Welcher. Two euphoniums and two tubas.

Hawaiian Quintet '88. Anderson. Three euphoniums and two tubas.

Heavy Metal. Anderson. Two euphoniums, two tubas, and drum set.

Heavy Metal. Lamb. Two euphoniums and four tubas.

Heavyweights. Stewart. Three tubas.

Heidentüblein. Schubert/Le Clair. Two euphoniums and two tubas.

Helena Polka. Schmidt. Two euphoniums and two tubas.

Here Comes Santa Claus. Glover. Four euphoniums and two tubas.

Higashi-Nishi. Stevens. Four euphoniums and four tubas.

High Hattin' from "African Suite." Confrey/Vaughan. Two euphoniums and two tubas.

Hippochondriac. Lawn. Four euphoniums and two tubas.

Hoffnung Festival. Hoffnung. Two euphoniums and two tubas.

How Much Is That Doggy in the Window? Woodcock. Two euphoniums and two tubas.

Howdy! Pegram. Three euphoniums, four tubas, and drums.

Humoresk, Op. 101, No. 7. Dvorak/Schmidt. Two euphoniums and two tubas.

Hungarian Dance No. 5. Brahms/Seitz. Four tubas.

Hungarian Dance No. 5. Brahms/Woodcock. Two euphoniums and two tubas.

Hungarian Dance No. 6. Brahms/Woodcock. Two euphoniums and two tubas.

Hungarian March from "Faust." Berlioz/Werden. Two euphoniums and two tubas.

Hungarian Rhapsodie No. 2. Liszt/Seitz. Two euphoniums and two tubas.

Hunter's Chorus from "Der Freischütz." Weber/Laws. Two euphoniums and two tubas.

Hunter's Chorus from "Der Freischütz." Weber/ Schmidt. Two euphoniums and two tubas.

I Never Saw a Moor for Four Tubas. Constantinides. Four tubas.

IIlusion. Konagaya. Two euphoniums, three tubas, and percussion.

Im Wald und auf der Heide. Garrett. Two euphoniums and one tuba.

Images for Tuba Quartet. Blatter. Four tubas.

Impromptu. Murzin. Two trombones (euphoniums) and one tuba.

In a Mello Tone. Ellington/Matteson. Three euphoniums, three tubas, and rhythm.

In Crystal Towers, from Psalms, Songs, and Sonnets. Byrd/Hartin. Three tubas.

In Darkness...Dreaming. Cummings. Two euphoniums and two tubas.

In Heaven There Is No Beer. Glover. Two euphoniums and two tubas.

In the Good Old Summertime. Evans/Frackenpohl. Two euphoniums and two tubas.

In the Hall of the Mountain King. Grieg/Werden. Two euphoniums and two tubas.

In the Shadows, Op. 376B. Hewitt. Four tubas and celeste.

In—Phase—Out. Tautenhahn. Four tubas.

Incognitos. Bottje. Two euphoniums and two tubas.

Infant Holy. Vaughan. Two euphoniums and two tubas.

Inflation. Lindenfeld. Three tubas.

Innocuous Incident. Gillam. Three tubas.

International Tuba Day Music Books, Numbers 1 and 2. Day. Two euphoniums and two tubas.

Into the Magical Rain Forest for T/E Ens. and Tape. Ayers. Two euphoniums, two tubas, and tape.

Intonation I. Roark. Two euphoniums and two tubas.

Intonation II. Roark. Two euphoniums and two tubas.

Intrada. Romanze. and Scherzo. Uber. Four euphoniums and two tubas.

Introduction and Rondino. Cook. Four tubas.

Io mi son giovanetta. Sweelinck/Hartin. Two tubas.

Irish Tune from County Derry. McKimm. Four euphoniums and four tubas.

I've Been Working on the Railroad. Garrett. One euphonium and two tubas.

Jammin'. Stevens. Two euphoniums and two tubas.

Japanese Songs. Shinihara. Four euphoniums and two tubas.

Java. Vaughan. Two euphoniums and two tubas.

Jesu, Joy of Man's Desiring. Bach/Hiraishi. Two euphoniums and two tubas.

Jesu, Joy of Man's Desiring. Bach/Werden. Two euphoniums and two tubas.

Jesu, Joy of Man's Desiring. Bach/Yamamoto. Six euphoniums and two tubas.

Jhon Come Kisse Me Now. Byrd/Winter. Two euphonium and two tubas.

Jingle Bell Rock. Glover. Four euphoniums and two tubas.

Jingle Bells. Pierpont/Garrett. Two euphoniums and two tubas.

Jingle Bells. Pierpont/Vaughan. Two euphoniums and two tubas.

Jingle Bells Waltz. Vaughan. Two euphoniums and two tubas.

Joe Avery. Garrett. Two euphoniums and two tubas.

Joyous Dialogue, A. Op. 11. Geib. Two tubas.

Just a Closer Walk with Thee. Garrett. Two euphoniums and two tubas with optional keyboard and drums.

Just a Closer Walk with Thee. Hoesly. Two euphoniums and two tubas.

Keystone Chops. Niehaus. Two euphoniums and two tubas.

Kierkegaard for Four Tubas. Kupferman. Four tubas.

Kilimanjaro. Fritze. Three trombones (euphoniums), one euphonium, and two tubas.

Kimiga-Yo. Anderson. Two euphoniums and two tubas.

King's Hunt, The. Bull/Howard. Two euphoniums and two tubas.

Knoxville, 1974. Haddad. Two euphoniums and six tubas.

Lament. Kodaly/Gray. One euphonium and two tubas.

Lament for Anne of Brittany, A. Moulu/Jacoby. Three euphoniums and two tubas.

Largo and Allegro. Krush. Two tubas.

Last Polka, The. Blahnik and Schmidt. Two euphoniums and two tubas.

Leichte Ragtime-Trios . Heger. Two euphoniums and one tuba.

Leichte Volkslieder-Trios 6 . Heger. Three tubas.

Lento Espressivo. Amellér. Four tubas.

Let It Snow. Glover. Four euphoniums and two tubas.

Leviathans. Goble. Two euphoniums and two tubas.

Liberation of Sisyphus, The. Stevens. Solo tuba, four euphoniums, and four tubas.

Liberty Bell March, The. Sousa/Rauchut. Three euphoniums and two tubas.

Liebesleid. Kreisler. Woodcock. Two euphoniums and two tubas.

Light Metal. Proctor. Two euphoniums and two tubas.

Lil Short'nin Funk. Krive. Five tubas.

Lilly Bell Quick Step. Friederich/Schmidt. Two euphoniums and two tubas.

Little Four Tuba Music, A. Frackenpohl. Four tubas.

Little Madrigal for Big Horns. Hastings. One euphonium and two tubas.

Little Negro, The. Debussy/Hiraishi. Two euphoniums and two tubas.

Little Ole Softy. Matteson. Three euphoniums, three tubas, and rhythm.

Little Suite for Tuba Quartet. Williams. Four tubas.

Lo, Country Sports. Weelkes/Hartin. Four tubas.

Lo How a Rose. Vaughan. Two euphoniums and two tubas.

Locus Iste. Bruckner/Sabourin. Two euphoniums and two tubas.

Londonderry Air. Garrett. Three euphoniums and two tubas.

Londonderry Air. Mehlan. Two euphoniums and two tubas.

Longer. Emberson. Two euphoniums and two tubas.

Lorelei, Die. Silcher/Seitz. Four tubas.

Lost Chord, The. Sullivan/Cummings. Three euphoniums and three tubas.

Love in the Afternoon: A Tone Poem. London. Four tubas.

Lucky Southern. Jarrett/Matteson. Three euphoniums, three tubas, and rhythm.

Ludus for Three Tubas. Nelhybel. Three tubas.

Lullaby. Robertson. Four tubas.

Lullaby and Dance. Hardt. Two euphoniums and two tubas.

Lute Dances. Anonymous/Baker. Two euphoniums and two tubas.

Lyric Poem for Five Tubas. Frank. Two euphoniums and three tubas.

Lyric Tuba Waltz, The. Rosenberger. Two euphoniums and two tubas.

Mack, the Knight. Vaughan. Two euphoniums and two tubas.

Madrigale. Gesualdo/McClernan. Two euphoniums and three tubas.

Manhattan Suite. Stevens. Four tubas.

Maple Leaf Rag. Joplin/Humble. Two euphoniums and two tubas.

Marce's Blues. Vaughan. Two euphoniums and two tubas.

March: Il Ritorno. Diero/Ferguson. Two euphoniums and two tubas.

March and Chorale. Butts. Two trombones (euphoniums) and two tubas.

March and Fugue for Two Tubas, Op. 40 and 55. Bourgeois. Two Tubas.

March of the Priests from "The Magic Flute." Mozart/Sherman. Two euphoniums and two tubas.

March of the Toy Soldiers from the "Nutcracker." Tchaikovsky/Woodcock. Two euphoniums and two tubas.

March of the Toys. Vaughan. Two euphoniums and two tubas.

March to the Scaffold from Symphonie Fantastique. Berlioz/Granger. Four euphoniums and six tubas.

Marienlieder, Op. 22. Brahms/Stevens. Two euphoniums and two tubas.

Mars, the Bringer of War, from "The Planets." Holst/Butler. Three euphoniums and three tubas.

Mean Thing Swing. Ellington/Vaughan. Two euphoniums and two tubas.

Medley of the Third Kind. Fiegel. Three euphoniums and two tubas.

Meet These People. Read. Two euphoniums and two tubas.

Meiso No Inga. Endo. Five euphoniums and one tuba.

Melissma. Hurt. Four tubas.

Melody Shop, The. King/Werden. Two euphoniums and two tubas.

Menuett, from Quartet Op. 76, No. 3. Haydn/Humble. Two euphoniums and two tubas.

Mery Men, The. Rimmer. Two euphoniums and two tubas.

Mexican Carnival. Shiner. Four trombones (euphoniums) and one tuba.

Michelle. Lennon and McCartney/Vaughan. Two euphoniums and two tubas.

Military March. Schubert/Le Clair. Two euphoniums and two tubas.

Miniature Jazz Suite. Garrett. Two euphoniums and two tubas, piano, bass, and drums.

Miniature Jazz Suite No. 1. Niehaus. Two euphoniums and two tubas.

Miniatures for Four Valve Instruments. Hartley. Two euphoniums and two tubas.

Minuet. Anderson. Two euphoniums and two tubas.

Minuet. Bach/Schmidt. Two euphoniums and two tubas.

Minute Waltz. Chopin/Mead. Two euphoniums and two tubas.

Minute Waltz. Chopin/Werden. Two euphoniums and two tubas.

Mixtures and Mutations. Jager. Two euphoniums and two tubas.

Mon Coeur se Recommende à Vous: Madrigal. Lasso/Robinson. Four tubas.

Montaggi for Four Tubas. Vazzana. Four tubas.

Mood Indigo. Ellington/Vaughan. Two euphoniums and two tubas.

Moon River. Glover. Two euphoniums and two tubas.

Moondance. Stevens. Four tubas.

Moonglow. Vaughan. Two euphoniums and two tubas.

Moro Lasso. Gesualdo. Two euphoniums and two tubas.

Moro Lasso. Gesualdo/Anderson. Three euphoniums and two tubas.

Motet "Christe, Lux Vera." Palestrina/Block. Four tubas.

Movement for Five Tubas. Schelokov. Five tubas.

Music for Low Brass. Sydeman. Two trombones (euphoniums) and two tubas.

Music for the Stage, Op. 283. Uber. Two euphoniums and two tubas.

Music for Tubas. Blank. Four tubas.

Music 4 Tubas. Stevens. Four tubas.

Music for Tubas ... Six of 'em. Childs. Six tubas.

Music for Two Tubas. De Jong. Two tubas.

Musica De Lupus: Scenarios for the Continued Existence of a Misunderstood Friend—The Wolf. Buttery. Four tubas.

My Melody Book. Nakagawa. Two tubas.

Mystical Music. Garrett. Two euphoniums and two tubas.

New York, New York. Emberson. Two euphoniums and two tubas.

Nicolina, La. Gussago/Schmidt. Two euphoniums and two tubas.

Night, The (It Has a Thousand Faces). Harrold. Two euphoniums and two tubas.

Night Train for Tubas. Stroud. Two euphoniums and two tubas.

Nine Duets. Handel/Dishinger. Two tubas.

No No Hate Yori . Censhu. Two euphoniums and two tubas.

Nocturne and Dance for Three Tubas. Danburg. Three tubas.

Nostalgia Medley. Sample. Two euphoniums, two tubas, piano/guitar, bass, and drums.

Now Hear This. Dempsey. Two euphoniums and two tubas.

Nuages. Reinhardt. Two euphoniums and two tubas.

O Canada. Glover. Two euphoniums and two tubas.

O Little Town of Bethlehem. Wedner/Vaughan. Two euphoniums and two tubas.

O Regem Coeli for Tuba Quartet. Victoria/Schwartz. Four tubas.

O Vos Omnes (Motet). Victoria/Self. Four tubas.

Ocean Tide March with Hail Columbia. Friederich/Schmidt. Two euphoniums and two tubas.

Octubafest Polka for Tuba Ensemble. Fritze. Two euphoniums and three tubas.

Octubafest Song, The. Bewley. Two euphoniums, two tubas, and vocal solo.

Odd Couple, The. Albam. Two tubas.

Offering: A Sketch for Euphonium Solo and Tuba/ Euphonium Quartet. Vaughan. Three euphoniums and two tubas.

Old Comrades. Glover. Two euphoniums and two tubas.

Old German Folk Song, An. Hartin. Two euphoniums and two tubas.

Oleo. Rollins/Matteson. Three euphoniums, three tubas, and rhythm.

On Thin Ice. Mobberley. Four euphoniums and five tubas.

Ondes Rondeau., Les. Couperin/Krzywicki. Two euphoniums and one tuba.

One Slow, One Fast. Dutton. Two tubas.

Os Justi. Bruckner/Sabourin. Four euphoniums and four tubas.

Outback Brass. Anderson. Two euphoniums and two tubas.

Overture from Carmen. Bizet/Seitz. Two euphoniums and two tubas.

Overture from Russlan and Ludmila. Glinka/Ferguson. Two euphoniums and two tubas.

Overture from the Marriage of Figaro. Mozart/Ferguson. Two euphoniums and two tubas.

Overture to "The Magic Flute." Mozart/Rozen. Two euphoniums and two tubas.

Overture to the "Marriage of Figaro." Mozart/Gottschalk. Three euphoniums and two tubas.

Overture to Wilhelm Tell. Rossini/Seitz. Two euphoniums and two tubas.

Oyez! Has Any Found a Lad? Tomkins/Schmidt. Two euphoniums and two tubas.

Pachyderms in Paradise. Niehaus. Two euphoniums and two tubas.

Pachydermus Pinkus Lowus-Blowus; Adapted from the Score for Dumbo (1941). Fiegel. Four euphoniums, four tubas, auxiliary percussion, and film equipment.

Pacman Gets Caught. Fritze. Two euphoniums and two tubas.

Pains of Esdraelon, The. Daughtry. One euphonium and two tubas.

Paloma Blanca. Glover. Two euphoniums and two tubas.

Paraklesis. Canter. Two euphoniums, two tubas, and tambourine.

Partita, Op. 109. Lemeland. Four tubas.

Passacaglia and Fugue in C Minor. Bach/Garrett. Two euphoniums and three tubas.

Pastorella and March. Pappas. Three tubas.

Pavan a 4. Schein/Schmidt. Two euphoniums and two tubas.

Pavan: The Funerals. Holborne/Hartin. Five tubas.

Peacherine Rag. Joplin/Hiraishi. Two euphoniums and two tubas.

Perpetual Motion. Paganini/Buttery. Two to seven players with piano.

Petit Caprice: In the Style of Offenbach. Rossini/Davis. Two euphoniums and two tubas.

Petite and Powerful: A Rag for T/E Quartet. Vaughan. Two euphoniums and two tubas.

Petite Marche. Ryker. One euphonium, one tuba, and piano.

Piccadilly, Le. Satie/Hiraishi. Two euphoniums and two tubas.

Piece for Six Tubas. Svarda. Six tubas.

Piece in Folk Style. Schumann/Werden. Three euphoniums and one tubas.

Pilgerchor aus Tannhäuser. Wagner/Seitz. Four tubas.

Pilgrim's Chorus from Tannhäuser. Wagner/Schmidt. Two euphoniums and two tubas.

Pinata. Bewley. Two euphoniums and one tuba.

Pineapple Rag. Joplin/Hiraishi. Two euphoniums and two tubas.

Pink Panther, The. Mancini/Krush. Two euphoniums and two tubas.

Pleasant Moments Rag. Joplin/Schmidt. Two euphoniums and two tubas.

Poet and Peasant Overture. Von Suppe/Bright. Two euphoniums and three tubas.

Poker Chips. Self. Four tubas and vibraphone.

Polka. Roikjer. Four tubas and piano.

Polyphonic Rhyme No. 4. Sweelinck/Block. Two tubas.

Pop Suite. Frackenpohl. Two euphoniums and two tubas.

Pop Suite No. 2. Frackenpohl. One euphonium and one tuba.

Postlude on "Willingham." Abt/Bright. Two euphoniums and two tubas.

Power for Four Tubas. Stevens. Four tubas.

Prelude and Dance. Fritze. Two euphoniums and two tubas.

Prelude and Fugue. McCurdy. Two tubas.

Prelude and Fugue in C Minor. Bach/Gray. Two euphoniums and two tubas.

Prelude and Fugue in G. Bach/Sabourin. Two euphoniums and two tubas.

Prelude and Fugue in G Minor. Bach/Sabourin. Two euphoniums and two tubas.

Prelude and Fugue No. 16. Bach/Schmidt. Two euphoniums and two tubas.

Prelude and Tarantella. Danburg. Two tubas.

Prelude and Voluntary for Four Tubas. Gibbons/Self. Four tubas.

Prelude No. 4 for Tuba Quartet. Chopin/Hendricks. Four tubas.

Preludio. Rodgers. Two euphoniums and two tubas.

Preludio and Fuga a 8 for T/E Octet. Torre. Four euphoniums and four tubas.

Pretty Forms. Dutton. Two tubas.

Prima Donna Waltz. Friederich/Schmidt. Two euphoniums and two tubas.

Procession of the Nobles. Rimsky-Korsakov/Butler. Two euphoniums and two tubas.

Promenade. Vasconi. Two euphoniums and two tubas.

Prophecy. Konagaya. Solo euphonium, four euphoniums, and four tubas.

Psalm. Gates. Three trombones, one euphonium, and one tuba.

Puer Natus. Colding-Jørgensen. Five tubas.

Quadrant. Hoesly. Two euphoniums and two tubas.

Quand la Terre au Printemps. Le Jeune. Four tubas.

Quartet Fantasy. Childs. Four tubas.

Quartet for Brass. Ramsoe/Buttery. Two euphoniums and two tubas.

Quartet for Low Brass. Bulla. Two euphoniums and two tubas.

Quartet for Tubas. Ball. Two E♭ tubas and two BB♭ tubas.

Quartet for Tubas. Brandon. Two euphoniums and two tubas.

Quartet for Tubas. Deak. One euphonium and three tubas.

Quartet for Tubas. Haddad. Four tubas.

Quartet for Tubas. Holmes. Two euphoniums and two tubas.

Quartet for Tubas. Jones. Four tubas.

Quartet for Tubas. Payne. Four tubas.

Quartet for Tubas. Tamura. Four tubas.

Quartets for All. Stoutamire and Henderson. Three euphoniums and one tuba.

Quartets for Brass, Volume I: Easy-Intermediate. Marcellus. Three euphoniums and one tuba.

Quartets for Brass, Volume I: Intermediate. Marcellus. Three euphoniums and one tuba.

Quartets for Brass, Volume I: Advanced. Marcellus. Three euphoniums and one tuba.

Quartets for Low Brass, Volume I: Traditional Favorites. Bulla. Two euphoniums and two tubas.

Quartets for Low Brass, Volume II: Spirituals. Bulla. Two euphoniums and two tubas.

Quartets for Low Brass, Volume III: Fanfares and Anthems. Bulla. Two euphoniums and two tubas.

Quartetto for Four Tubas. Van Vactor. Two euphoniums and two tubas.

Quartour pour Tubas. Fasce. Four tubas.

Quatre Chansons pour Tuba Quatuor. Dempsey. Two euphoniums and two tubas.

Quid Petis O Fili. Pygott/Thornton. Four tubas.

Quintet. White. Three euphoniums and two tubas.

Quintet for Tubas. Bathory-Kitsz. Five tubas.

Quodlibitus Bibendum for Tuba Quartet. Rollin. Four tubas.

Ragnarok. Belden. One euphonium and one tuba.

Ragtime. Wilhelm. Two tubas.

Rag-time Dance. Joplin/Schmidt. Two euphoniums and two tubas.

Rag-Time Dance. Joplin/Werden. Two euphoniums and two tubas.

Raven and the First Man, The. Rollin. Two euphoniums and two tubas.

Recital Duets for Two Tubas. Brandon. Two tubas.

Recitative for Four Tubas and Cantor. McCurdy. Four tubas and male vocalist.

Red River Valley. Garrett. One euphonium and two tubas.

Reflections. Medek. Four tubas.

Reflections on a Park Bench. Beale. Six euphoniums and six tubas.

Resonances. Dutton. Two euphoniums and two tubas.

Rev Bill Bailey. Cannon/Vaughan. Two euphoniums and two tubas.

Ricercar a Tre Voci. Willaert/Hartin. Three tubas.

Ricercar del Duodecimo Tuono. Gabrieli/Barth. Two euphoniums and two tubas.

Ricercar del Duodecimo Tuono. Gabrieli/Schmidt. Two euphoniums and two tubas.

Ricercar del Primo Tuono. Palestrina/Schmidt. Two euphoniums and two tubas.

Rich Tradition: A Tribute to Rich Matteson. Bewley. Three euphoniums, three tubas, and rhythm.

Richter 7.8 for 12 Low Brass Instruments. Schudel. Three euphoniums and nine tubas.

Rienzi Overture. Wagner/Bright. Two euphoniums and three tubas.

Rip'em Up. Joe. Garrett. Two euphoniums and two tubas with optional keyboard and drums.

Riverwest Rag. Vaughan. Two euphoniums and two tubas.

Romance for Bass Tuba. Hawker. Solo tuba, two euphoniums, and one tuba.

Ronda's First Suite. Vaughan. Two tubas.

Ronde and Saltarelle. Susato/Winter. Two euphoniums and two tubas.

Rondeau. Mouret/Stevens. Two euphoniums and two tubas.

Rondo. Hook/Garrett. Two euphoniums and two tubas.

Rudolph the Red-Nosed Reindeer. Marks/Mehlan. Two euphoniums and two tubas.

Runabout. Bewley. Two euphoniums and two tubas.

Russian Dances. Tchaikovsky/Woodcock. Two euphoniums and two tubas.

Sabeltanz. Khachaturian/Seitz. Two euphoniums and two tubas.

Sai Kai. Censhu. Two euphoniums and two tubas.

Saints, The. McAdams. Two euphoniums and two tubas.

Saints. McCurdy. Four tubas.

Salutation Fanfare. Fritze. Three euphoniums and two tubas.

Santa Claus Is Comin' to Town. Glover. Four euphoniums and two tubas.

Santa Claus Is Coming to Town. Vaughan. Two euphoniums and two tubas.

Santa Wants a Tuba for Christmas. Bewley. Two euphoniums, two tubas, optional vocal and rhythm.

Saraband and Gigue for Tuba Quartet Op. 43. Owen. Four tubas.

Sarabande. Bach/Howard. Two euphoniums and two tubas.

Sarabande and Bourrée. Bach/Yodo. Two euphoniums and two tubas.

Sarabande and Variations. Handel/Barth. Two euphoniums and two tubas.

Satin Doll. Ellington/Vaughan. Two euphoniums and two tubas.

Scherzando for Tubular Octet. Knox. Four euphoniums and four tubas.

Scherziapriori II. Dressler. Two euphoniums and two tubas.

Sea Chanty for Three. Anderson. Three tubas.

Sea Tubas. Minerd. Two euphoniums and two tubas.

Sebastian the St. Bernard. Stauffer. Two euphoniums and two tubas.

Sechs und Zwanzig Tuba Duette. Ferstl. Two tubas.

Secret, Le. Gautier. Werden. Three euphoniums and one tuba.

Selections from 42nd Street. Warren/Minerd. Two euphoniums and two tubas.

Selections from Symphonien auf Conzerten-Manier. Scheidt/Hartin. Three tubas.

Semper Fidelis. Sousa/Morris. Two euphoniums and two tubas.

Semper Fidelis. Sousa/Sabourin. Two euphoniums and two tubas.

Sentimental Journey. Vaughan. Two euphoniums and two tubas.

Sept Péchés Capitaux. Morel. Four tubas.

Serenade Eine Kleine Tuba Musik for Four Tubas, K. 525. Mozart/Fletcher. Four tubas.

Serenade for Four Tubas. Presser. Four tubas.

Serenade for Tubas. McKimm. Four euphoniums and four tubas.

Serenade from "Hassan." Delius/Bale. Two euphoniums and four tubas.

Serene Voices: Music for Tuba Quartet. Kosteck. Four tubas.

Serious Suite for Three Tubas, The. Blair. Three tubas.

Serpent Duets. Mason. Two tubas.

Serpentine Shadows. Benson. Two tubas.

Sesame Street. Raposa/Vaughan. Two euphoniums and two tubas.

Seven Duets for Tubas. Butterfield. Two tubas.

Seven Menuets KV65A. Mozart/Dishinger. Two tubas.

Seven Tuba Duets. Presser. Two tubas.

7 22 73 for Tuba Quartet. Ott. Two euphoniums, two tubas, and tape.

Shapes in Bronze. Ross. Two euphoniums and two tubas.

Shinju. Censhu. Two euphoniums and two tubas.

Short Piece for Tuba and Euphonium. Powell. One euphonium and one tuba.

Siamang Suite. Canter. Two euphoniums and two tubas.

Sieben Miniaturen für Vier Tuben. Kochan. Four tubas.

Siegfried's Funeral March. Wagner/Bright. Two euphoniums and three tubas.

Signals for Tuba Trio. Uber. Three tubas.

Silent Night. Vaughan. Two euphoniums and two tubas.

Silent Streets for Euphonium and Tuba. Uber. One euphonium and one tuba.

Silver Bells. Glover. Four euphoniums and two tubas.

Silver Bells. Stroud. Two euphoniums and two tubas.

Simple Gifts. Fritze. Solo tuba, two euphoniums, and two tubas.

Since You've Asked. Collins/Buttery. Two euphoniums and two tubas.

Sinfonia No. 10 for Tuba-Euphonium Ensemble. Hartley. Four euphoniums and four tubas.

Six Baroque Pieces for Two Tubas. Zychowicz. Two tubas.

Six Etudes. Defaye. Two tubas.

Six Preludes for Euphonium and Tuba, Op. 246C. Hewitt. One euphonium and one tuba.

Sixteen Tons. Anderson. Solo tuba and three euphoniums.

Sjaj Suncece Suncano. Nave. Three tubas and two tubas.

Skaters' Waltzes, The. Waldteufel/Konagaya. Two euphoniums and two tubas.

Sleeping Giants. Niehaus. Two euphoniums and two tubas.

Sleeping Tuba Waltz. Tchaikovsky/Fletcher. Four tubas.

Sleigh Ride. Anderson/Glover. Two euphoniums and two tubas.

Sleigh Ride. Anderson/Rauch. Two euphoniums and two tubas.

Soft Shoo for Two Euphoniums and Two Tubas. Stuart. Two euphoniums and two tubas.

Solfeggietto. Bach, C.P.E./Roberts. Two euphoniums and two tubas.

Solfegietto. Bach, C.P.E./Howard. Two euphoniums and two tubas.

Some Loose Canons. Dutton. Two tubas.

Somewhere over the Rainbow. Arlen/Matteson. Three euphoniums, three tubas, and rhythm.

Sonata. Gabrieli/Schmidt. Two euphoniums and two tubas.

Sonata. Kelly. One euphonium and one tuba.

Sonata. Speer/Schmidt. Two euphoniums and two tubas.

Sonata, Op. 5, no. 4. Telemann/Dutton. Two tubas.

Sonata da Chiesa. Corelli/Morris. Two tubas and piano.

Sonata da Chiesa a Tre. Corelli/Dutton. Three tubas.

Sonata da Chiesa in E Minor, Op. 3, No. 7. Corelli/Pitts. Three tubas.

Sonata for Two Bass Tubas. Ryker. Two tubas.

Sonata for Two Tubas. K.V. 292. Mozart/Conner. Two tubas.

Sonata No. One. Israel. Two tubas.

Sonata No. Two. Israel. Two tubas.

Sonata No. 2. Pezel/Stevens. Two euphoniums and two tubas.

Sonata No. 4. Handel/Little. Two euphoniums and one tuba.

Sonata No. 13 for Double T/E Choir. Gabrieli/Varner. Four euphoniums and four tubas.

Sonata No. 15. Reiche/Schmidt. Two euphoniums and two tubas.

Sonata No. 18. Reiche/Schmidt. Two euphoniums and two tubas.

Sonata Pastorale (K. 397). Fux/Hartin. Two tubas and piano.

Sonata "Pathétique." Beethoven/Werden. Two euphoniums and two tubas.

Sonate en Trio Vivace. Bach/Cazes. Four tubas.

Sonatina for Two Tubas. Vaughan. Two tubas.

Song and Dance. Frackenpohl. One euphonium, one tuba, and piano.

Song and Dance No. 3. Dutton. Four tubas.

Song of Memory. Fentress. Three euphoniums and one tuba.

Songs in the Fight against Rum (Songs of Might to Cheer the Fight in the Blight of Liquordom). Garbáge. Two euphoniums, two tubas, tenor solo, barbershop quartet, and mixed chorus.

Songs of the British Isles. Werden. Two euphoniums and two tubas.

Sounding for Tuba/Euphonium Quartet. Matchett. Two euphoniums and two tubas.

Sousa Surrenders. Garbáge. Three euphoniums, three tubas, and optional timpani.

Speak Low. Vaughan. Two euphoniums and two tubas.

Spielheft 1. Rener. One euphonium and one tuba.

Spinning Song. Ellmenreich/Rauch. Two euphoniums and two tubas.

Spiritual Jazz Suite. Niehaus. Two euphoniums and two tubas.

Splinters. Stevens. Two tubas.

Sponger Money. Buttery. Two euphoniums, two tubas, and percussion.

Spoofy. Matteson. Three euphoniums, three tubas, and rhythm.

St. Louis Blues. Handy/Holcombe. Two euphoniums and two tubas.

St. Louis Blues. Hoesly. Two euphoniums and two tubas.

Staendchen. Schubert/Le Clair. Two euphoniums and two tubas.

Star-Spangled Banner. Glover. Two euphoniums and two tubas.

Star-Spangled Banner, The. Key/Anderson. Three euphoniums and one tuba.

Stars and Stripes Forever, The. Sousa/Schmidt. Two euphoniums and two tubas.

Stars and Stripes Forever, The. Sousa/Werden. Two euphoniums and two tubas.

Stately Procession. Byrd/Bright. Two euphoniums and two tubas.

Stella by Starlight. Sample. Two euphoniums, two tubas, piano/guitar, bass, and drums.

Stephen Foster Jazz Suite. Niehaus. Two euphoniums and two tubas.

Stompin' at the Savoy. Goodman, Webb, and Sampson/Matteson. Three euphoniums, three tubas, and rhythm.

Strenuous Life, The. Joplin/Hiraishi. Two euphoniums and two tubas.

Strenuous Life, The: A Ragtime Two-Step. Joplin/Lex. Two euphoniums and two tubas.

Struktur in Blech. Heidler. Four tubas.

Substructures I. Gottschalk. Two euphoniums and eight tubas.

Sub-Terrestrial Sounds. Dutton. Five tubas.

Sub-Voce Entropy. Leavitt. Two tubas.

Suite for Four Bass Instruments. Lyon. Two euphoniums and two tubas.

Suite for Four Bass Tubas, Op. 67. Uber. Four tubas.

Suite for Four Tubas. Masuda. Four tubas.

Suite for Harp and Two Tubas. Hewitt. Two tubas and harp.

Suite for Seven Tubas. Dutton. Seven tubas.

Suite for Six Tubas. Ott. Six tubas.

Suite for Six Tubas. Presser. Six tubas.

Suite for Three Tubas. Jones. Three tubas.

Suite for Three Tubas. Presser. Three tubas.

Suite for Three Tubas., Op. 3. Warren. Three tubas.

Suite for Tuba Duo, Op. 376. Hewitt. Two tubas.

Suite for Tuba Quartet. Frackenpohl. Two euphoniums and two tubas.

Suite for Two. Stevens. Two tubas.

Suite for Two Tubas. Geer. Two tubas.

Suite for Two Tubas. Wilder. Two tubas.

Suite from Album for the Young. Schumann/Shoop. Two euphoniums and two tubas.

Suite from Album for the Young. Schumann/Werden. Two euphoniums and two tubas.

Suite in Blue. Payne. Four tubas.

Suite in D♭ for Tubas and Euphoniums. Watts. Two euphoniums and two tubas.

Suite in Miniature. Catelinet. Two tubas.

Suite No. 16 for Two Tubas. Haugland. Two tubas.

Suite No. 17 for Two Tubas. Haugland. Two tubas.

Suite No. 18 for Two Tubas. Haugland. Two tubas.

Suite No. 19 for Two Tubas. Haugland. Two tubas.

Suite No. 20 for Two Tubas. Haugland. Two tubas.

Suite of Elizabethan Madrigals, A. Hartin. Three tubas.

Suite of English Madrigals. Stevens. Two euphoniums and three tubas.

Sunrise, Sunset. Bock/Anderson. Three euphoniums and one tuba.

Suspended in Frozen Velocity: Image Music IX from "Songs of the Fire Circles." Steinke. Two euphoniums and two tubas.

Sweet 'n' Low, Book 1. Sparke. One euphonium and one tuba.

Sweet 'n' Low, Book 2. Sparke. One euphonium and one tuba.

Sweet 'n' Low, Book 3: A First Christmas Selection. Sparke. One euphonium and one tuba.

Sweet 'n' Low, Book 4: A Second Christmas Selection. Sparke. One euphonium and one tuba.

Sweet 'n' Low, Book 5: Caribbean Cocktail. Sparke. One euphonium and one tuba.

Swing Low, Sweet Chariot. Alexander. Two euphoniums and two tubas.

Swing Low, Sweet Chariot. Kresin. Two euphoniums and two tubas.

Swing Low, Sweet Chariot. McAdams. One euphonium and two tubas.

Swipesy. Joplin/Werden. Two euphoniums and two tubas.

Switched-Down Bach. Jones. One euphonium and two tubas.

Take Me Out to the Ballgame. Anderson. Three euphoniums and two tubas.

Take Me Out to the Ballgame. Vaughan. Two euphoniums and two tubas.

Tango Espana. Albeniz/Schmidt. Two euphoniums and two tubas.

Tarantella from Songs Without Words, Op. 182, No. 3. Mendelssohn/Yamamoto. Two euphoniums and two tubas.

Ten Duets. Gillis. One trombone (euphonium) and one tuba.

Ten Duets. Torchinsky. Two tubas.

Ten Duets for Bass Trombone. Pederson. Two bass trombones (tubas).

Ten Duets for Two Tubas. Jacobsen. Two tubas.

Ten Duos Concertants. Joubert.

Ten Inventions for Four Tubas, Op. 64. Roikjer. Four tubas.

Ten Inventions for Three Tubas. Roikjer. Three tubas.

Ten Inventions for Two Tubas, Op. 55. Roikjer. Two tubas.

Ten Jazz Duos and Solos. Hartzell. One euphonium and one tuba.

Ten More Duets. Book 2. Gillis.

Ten Pieces for Tuba Ensemble. Holborne/Stevens. Two euphoniums and two tubas.

Ten Quartets. Jacobsen. Four tubas.

Ten Trios for Three Tubas. Jacobsen. Three tubas.

Ten Trios for Tubas. Wilder. Three tubas.

Tennessee Waltz. Sample. Two euphoniums, two tubas, piano/guitar, bass, and drums.

Teuphm'isms I. Anderson. One euphonium and one tuba.

Teuphm'isms II. Anderson. One euphonium and one tuba.

That Lovin' Rag. Smaller and Adler/Vaughan. Two euphoniums and two tubas.

That's A Plenty. Hoesly. Two euphoniums and two tubas.

Them Baces. Butterfield. One euphonium and two tubas.

Thematic Permutations. Rodgers. Two euphoniums and two tubas.

Theme and Six Derivations. Anderson. Two euphoniums and two tubas.

Then and Now. Dutton. One euphonium and one tuba.

They Didn't Believe Me. Kern/Holcombe. Two euphoniums and two tubas.

Things Ain't What They Used to Be. Ellington/Matteson. Three euphoniums, three tubas, and rhythm.

Things Are Tough All Over, Tubby. McCurdy. Four tubas and male vocalist.

Thirty Progressive Duos. Carnardy. Two tubas.

Those Lazy, Hazy, Crazy Days of Summer. Glover. Two euphoniums and two tubas.

Three Bagatelles for Euphonium/Tuba Quartet. Uber. Two euphoniums and two tubas.

Three Barbershop Songs. Heiman. Two euphoniums and two tubas.

Three Bourrées from "Terpsichore." Praetorius/Hartin. Four tubas.

Three Chorale Preludes. Telemann/Frackenpohl. One euphonium and one tuba.

Three Chorale Preludes. Telemann/Schmidt. One euphoniums and two tubas.

Three Chorales. Gershenfeld. Four tubas.

Three Christmas Carols. Schmidt. Two euphoniums and two tubas.

Three Christmas Carols I. Schmidt. Two euphoniums and two tubas.

Three Christmas Carols II. Schmidt. Two euphoniums and two tubas.

Three Contrasts for Two Tubas. Anderson. Two tubas.

Three Dances for Three Tubas. McCurdy. Three tubas.

Three Diverse Drinking Songs. Thornton. Three tubas.

Three Early Pieces. Bale. Two euphoniums and two tubas.

Three Fanfares for Tubas. Bale. Three euphoniums and six tubas.

Three German Dances. Pezel/Heiman. Two euphoniums and three tubas.

Three German Songs. Schmidt. Two euphoniums and two tubas.

Three Madrigals. Weelkes/Schmidt. Two euphoniums and one tuba.

Three Miniatures for Tuba Quartet. Thompson. Four tubas.

Three Moods. Boone. Four euphoniums and two tubas.

Three Motets. Bruckner/Stevens. Two euphoniums and two tubas.

Three Motets. Heiman. Two euphoniums and two tubas.

Three Movements for Four Tubas. Ahrendt. Four tubas.

Three Mythical Sketches. Iannaccone. Two euphoniums and two tubas.

Three Pieces for Horseballet. Schmelzer/Schmidt. Two euphoniums and two tubas.

Three Pieces for Low Brass Trio. Rodgers. Two euphoniums and one tuba.

Three Pieces from "Carnival of the Animals." Saint-Saëns/Bale. Four tubas.

Three Pieces from King Henry VIII. Thornton. Three tubas.

Three Preludes for Three Tubas, Op. 376C. Hewitt. Three tubas.

Three Renaissance Duets. Singleton. Two tubas.

Three Renaissance Quartets. Cummings. Two euphoniums and two tubas.

Three Rococo Dances. Chedeville/Block. Two tubas.

Three Sixteenth-Century Flemish Pieces. Singleton. Two euphoniums and two tubas.

Three Sketches. Beadell. Two euphoniums and two tubas.

Three Statements for Four Tubas. Richardson. Four tubas.

Three Temperaments for Tubas. Jacobson. Three tubas.

Three Traveling Shorts. Harrold. Two euphoniums and two tubas.

Three Tubas Two. Jones. Three tubas.

Thunder and Blazes. Fucik/Gray.

Thunderer, The. Sousa/Werden. Two euphoniums and two tubas.

Time Structures. Winteregg. Four tubas.

Tinker Polka. Schmidt. Two euphoniums two tubas.

Tiny Tuba Tunes. Woodcock. Two euphoniums and two tubas.

To a Wild Rose. MacDowell/Rauch. Two euphoniums and two tubas.

Toccata. Frescobaldi/Skillen. Three euphoniums and three tubas.

Toccata for Euphonium/Tuba Quartet. Schooley. Two euphoniums and two tubas.

Toccata for L'Orfeo. Monteverdi/Little. Two euphoniums and two tubas.

Toe Tapping Tuba Tune. Jones. Three tubas.

Too Fat Polka. Glover. Two euphoniums and two tubas.

Total Tubosity. Ferguson. Two euphoniums and two tubas.

Tower Music. Israel. Two euphoniums and one tuba.

Transforming Realms. Russell. Two euphoniums and two tubas.

Träumerei. Schumann/Seitz. Two euphoniums and two tubas.

Treatments for Tuba. Stroud. Two euphoniums and two tubas.

Trio for Three Tubas. Keays. Three tubas.

Trio for Tubas. Jones. One euphonium and two tubas.

Trio for Tubas. Larrick. Three Tubas.

Trio Sonata, Op. 1, No. 5. Corelli/Schmidt. Two euphoniums and one tuba.

Trio Sonata, Op. 1, No. 10. Corelli/Schmidt. Two euphoniums and one tuba.

Trio Sonata, Op. 3, No. 2. Corelli/Schmidt. Two euphoniums and one tuba.

Trio Sonata, Op. 3, No. 7. Corelli/Schmidt. Two euphoniums and one tuba.

Trios for All. Henderson. Two euphoniums and one tuba.

Trios for Brass, Volume I, Advanced. Marcellus. Two euphoniums and one tuba.

Trios for Brass, Volume I, Easy-Intermediate. Marcellus. Two euphoniums and one tuba.

Trios for Brass, Volume I, Intermediate. Marcellus. Two euphoniums and one tuba.

Triplet for Four Tubas. Lundquist. Four tubas.

Tritsch-Tratsch Polka. Strauss/Seitz. Two euphoniums and two tubas.

Troisième Suite. Dutton. Three tubas.

Trumpet Voluntary. Clarke/Bale. Two euphoniums and two tubas.

Tuba Blues Medley. Wolking. Two euphoniums, two tubas, and drums.

T.U.B.A. Canon. Bartles. Two tubas.

Tuba Carols. Hancock. One euphonium and two tubas.

Tuba Chan Chaka Chan. Yoshizawa. Four euphoniums and four tubas.

Tuba Club. Weisling. Six tubas.

Tuba Duet No. 1. Gillam. Two tubas and piano.

Tuba Duets. Morley/Hunsaker. Two tubas.

Tuba Duo Eight. Mozart/Self. Two tubas.

Tuba Duo Eleven, Op. 5. Boccherini/Self. Two tubas.

Tuba Duo Five. Bach/Self. Two tubas.

Tuba Duo Four, K. 380. Mozart/Self. Two tubas.

Tuba Duo Nine. Bach/Self. Two tubas.

Tuba Duo One, K. 378. Mozart/Self. Two tubas.

Tuba Duo Seven, K. 380. Mozart/Self. Two tubas.

Tuba Duo Six. Bach/Self. Two tubas.

Tuba Duo Ten, Op. 99. Haydn/Self. Two tubas.

Tuba Duo Three, K. 454. Mozart/Self. Two tubas.

Tuba Duo Two (Rondo alla Tubas) K. 564. Mozart/Self. Two tubas.

Tuba Juba Duba. Hutchinson. Two euphoniums and two tubas.

Tuba Magic for Tuba Ensemble. DiGiovanni. Two euphoniums and four tubas.

Tuba Muckl. Schmidt. Two euphoniums and two tubas.

Tuba Muckl Polka. Seitz. Two euphoniums and two tubas.

Tuba Musicale. DiGiovanni. Four euphoniums and four tubas.

Tuba Quartet. Davison. Four tubas.

Tuba Quartet. Randalls. Four tubas.

Tuba Quartet. Strukow. Four tubas.

Tuba Quartet, Op. 59. Gates. Two euphoniums and two tubas.

Tuba Quartet, Op. 65, No. 3. Heussenstamm. Four tubas.

Tuba Quartet—Chopin Mazurka, Op. 68, No. 48. Chopin/Anderson. Four tubas.

Tuba Quartet: Study in Motion, Hymn, and Finale. Koltz. Two euphoniums and two tubas.

Tuba Seduction (Ballade). Lemirre. Four euphoniums and four tubas.

Tuba Sunday for Tuba Choir. Sloan. Two euphoniums and two tubas.

Tuba Trio. Mueller. One euphonium and two tubas.

Tuba Trio. Zindars. Three tubas.

Tuba Trio Number 1. Wilder. Three tubas.

Tuba Turf. Niehaus. Two euphoniums and two tubas.

TubaCanon. Albert. Four tubas.

TubaFour, Op. 30. Heussenstamm. One euphonium and three tubas.

Tubacussion, Op. 62. Heussenstamm. Four tubas and percussion.

Tubafest Shuffle. Fritze. Three euphoniums, three tubas, and rhythm.

Tubafugalfanfare. Jones. Four tubas.

Tubagirls I. Vaughan. Two euphoniums and four tubas.

Tubagirls II. Vaughan. Two euphoniums and four tubas.

Tubalation. Niehaus. Two euphoniums and two tubas.

Tubalation Rag. Mehlan. Two euphoniums and two tubas.

Tubantiphon. Stroud. Two tubas.

Tubaphonic Suite. Payne. Four tubas.

Tubarhumba. DiGiovanni. Two euphoniums, four tubas, and rhythm.

Tubarometer. Niehaus. Two euphoniums and two tubas.

Tubas at Christmas. Gottschalk. One euphonium and three tubas.

Tubas at Play. DiGiovanni. Four tubas.

Tubas Latinas (Overture for Tuba Ensemble). Forte. Two euphoniums, three tubas, and two optional percussion.

Tubasonatina. George. Two euphoniums and two tubas.

Tublue. Nash. Four tubas, piano, bass, and drums.

Tubology. Morris. Three euphoniums, three tubas, and rhythm.

Tu-Bop. Fritze. Three euphoniums, three tubas, and rhythm.

Tubular Octad. Tull. Four euphoniums and four tubas.

Turandot: Two Choruses. Puccini/Sherman. Two euphoniums and two tubas.

Turkish March K. 331. Mozart/Mehlan. Two euphoniums and two tubas.

Tuxedo Junction. Hawkins/Schmidt. Two euphoniums and two tubas.

12 Days of Housetops! Canter. Two euphoniums and two tubas.

Twelve Divertissements en Duos, Op. 670. Porret. Two tubas.

Twelve Duets. Bach/Dishinger. Two tubas.

Twelve Duets, K. 487. Mozart/Dishinger. Two tubas.

Twelve Duets for Tubas. McCurdy. Two tubas.

Twelve Duos for Two Tubas. Mozart/Conner. Two tubas.

Twelve Easy Duets for Winds. Mozart/Smith. One euphonium and one tuba.

Twelve Two-Part Inventions. Bach/Miller. Two tubas.

Twenty Duets from Symphonic Masterworks. Hawkins. One euphonium and one tuba.

Twenty-Five Baroque and Classical Duets, Book I. Singleton. Two tubas.

Twenty-Five Baroque and Classical Duets, Book II. Singleton. Two tubas.

Twenty-Four Christmas Carols. Stevens. Two euphoniums and two tubas.

Twenty-Four Duettes, Op. 73. Scherzer. Two tubas.

21 Distinctive Duets for Tuba. Jones. Two tubas.

Twenty Petite Duos. Zemp. One euphonium and one tuba.

Two Airs. Adson/Stevens. Two euphoniums and two tubas.

Two Baroque Dances. Handel/Greene. Two euphoniums and two tubas.

Two Canons. Schumann/Singleton. Three tubas.

Two Christmas Carols. Schmidt. Two euphoniums and two tubas.

Two Concert Duets. Blazhevich/Wekselblatt. Two tubas.

Two English Madrigals. Gershenfeld. Three tubas.

Two English Madrigals. Singleton. Three tubas.

Two English Madrigals. Thornton. Four tubas.

Two English Madrigals. Thornton. Two tubas.

Two Folk Songs. McCurdy. Two euphoniums and two tubas.

Two for the Tuba. Wadowick. Two tubas and piano.

Two Hag Pieces for Euphonium and Tuba. Presser. One euphonium and one tuba.

Two Impressions. McCurdy. Two tubas.

Two Interplays. George. Three tenor trombones, one bass trombone, two euphoniums, and tuba.

Two Madrigals. Dowland/Nelson. Two euphoniums and two tubas.

Two Madrigals. Schmidt. Two euphoniums and two tubas.

Two Medieval Carols. Hartin. Two tubas.

Two Motets. Hassler/Schmidt. Two euphoniums and two tubas.

Two Old Songs. Schmidt. Two euphoniums and two tubas.

Two-Part Inventions. Bach/Ostrander. Two tubas.

Two-Part Inventions. Patterson. One euphonium and one tuba.

Two Patriotic Songs. McCurdy. Four tubas.

Two Pieces by Sir Arthur Sullivan. Sullivan/Bale. Two euphoniums and two tubas.

Two Pieces for Three Tubas. Gessner. Three tubas.

Two Pieces for Tuba/Euphonium Ensemble. McCarthy. Six euphoniums and two tubas.

Two Pieces from "Orfeo." Monteverdi/Heiman. Three euphoniums and two tubas.

Two Rags, Volume 1. Joplin/Sabourin. Two euphoniums and two tubas.

Two Rags, Volume 2. Joplin/Sabourin. Two euphoniums and two tubas.

Two Sackbut Quartets. Schmidt. Two euphoniums and two tubas.

Two Trumpet Tunes and Ayre. Purcell/Humble. Two euphoniums and two tubas.

Two Trumpet Tunes and Trumpet Voluntary. Purcell and Clarke/Rauch. Two euphoniums and two tubas.

Two Tuba Suites, Book 1. Jones. Two tubas.

Two Tuba Suites, Book 2. Jones. Two tubas.

Two Tunes by Herb Brown. Sample. Two euphoniums, two tubas, piano/guitar, bass, and drums.

Two Waltzes. K. 600, Nos. 1 and 4. Mozart/Schmidt. Two euphoniums and two tubas.

Two Wind Duets (K.487). Mozart/Block. One euphonium and one tuba.

Typic Rhythm. Florinza. Four euphoniums and four tubas.

Ukrainian Carol (Ring Christmas Bells). Leontovich/Rauch. Two euphoniums and two tubas.

Undecided. Vaughan. Two euphoniums and two tubas.

Under the Double Eagle. Wagner/Schmidt. Two euphoniums and two tubas.

Undercurrents. Wright. One flute, seven tubas, and two percussion.

Valse from Die Fledermaus. Strauss/Schanke. Two euphoniums and two tubas.

Variations aux Quatre Vents. Nilovic. Four tubas.

Variations on a Motive by Wagner. Jager. One euphonium and two tubas.

Variations on a Theme of Prokofieff. Schmidt. One euphonium and one tuba.

Variations on an Old Hymn Tune. Werle. Two euphoniums and four tubas.

Vaudeville. Uber. Two euphoniums and two tubas.

Veni Emmanuel. Vaughan. Two euphoniums and two tubas.

Vier Tuben im 3/4 Takt-Volksweise. Seitz. Four tubas.

Virga Jesse Floruit. Bruckner/Nelson. Two euphoniums and two tubas.

Vivace from Concerto No. 3 in D minor. Bach/Self. Two tubas.

Voci du gai Printemps. Sweelinck/Hartin. Two tubas.

Wabash Cannon Ball for Tuba-Euphonium Ensemble. Garrett. Two euphoniums and two tubas.

Wachet Auf. Bach/Buttery. Two euphoniums and two tubas.

Wachterlied, Op. 12. Grieg/Schmidt. Two euphoniums and two tubas.

Waldesnacht, du Wunder Kuhle. Brahms/Nelson. Two euphoniums and two tubas.

Wallowed Out. Buttery. Two tubas.

Waltz of the Walrus. McCurdy. Two tubas.

Waltzing with Irving. Sample. Two euphoniums, two tubas, piano/guitar. bass, and drums.

Warring. Dutton. Three euphoniums and three tubas.

Washington Post. Sousa/Sabourin. Two euphoniums and two tubas.

Washington Post. Sousa/Self. Two euphoniums and three tubas.

Washington Post. Sousa/Werden. Two euphoniums and two tubas.

Water and Fireworks Music. Handel/Heiman. Two euphoniums and two tubas.

Waves of the Danube. Ivanovici/Konagaya. Two euphoniums and two tubas.

We Run Them In. Offenbach. Three tubas.

Wedding March. Mendelssohn/Emberson. Two euphoniums and two tubas.

Whale's Tale, A. Niehaus. Two euphoniums and two tubas.

When the Saints Come Marchin' In. Garrett. Two euphoniums and two tubas.

When Tubas Waltz. Bartles. Two euphoniums and two tubas.

Wiggleworm Squirm. Vaughan. Two euphoniums and two tubas.

William Tell Overture (abridged). Rossini/Schmidt. Two euphoniums and two tubas.

Winds: Five Descriptive Pieces for T/E Octet. Vaughan. Four euphoniums and four tubas.

With a Little Bit of Flash. Rauch. Two euphoniums and two tubas.

Wonderland Duets. Luedeke. Two tubas and narrator.

World Does Not Wish for Beauty, The. Britain. Four tubas.

Wot Shigona Dew? Wilson. Three euphoniums, two tubas, and rhythm.

Yama No Hibiki. Ishii. Six euphoniums and six tubas.

Yamaha Band Ensembles, Tuba/Book 1. O'Reilly. Three tubas with optional piano.

Yamaha Band Ensembles, Tuba/Book 2. O'Reilly. Three tubas with optional piano.

Yamaha Band Ensembles, Tuba/Book 3. O'Reilly. Three tubas with optional piano.

Yankee Tunes for Tubas. Jones. Two euphoniums and three tubas.

Yesterday. Lennon and McCartney/Miyagawa. Two euphoniums and two tubas.

You Light Up My Life. Emberson. Two euphoniums and two tubas.

You Made Me Love You. Monaco/Holcombe. Two euphoniums and two tubas.

Yuletide Jazz Suite No. 1. Niehaus. Two euphoniums and two tubas.

Yuletide Jazz Suite No. 2. Niehaus. Two euphoniums and two tubas.

9. Methods and Studies

Jerry A. Young and David D. Graves, editorial assistant

Pedagogical literature for the tuba dates from the nineteenth century. Early tubists probably borrowed study materials from methods for other brass instruments—trumpet, horn, and trombone, serpent and ophicleide—and studies from the vocal literature. Material specific to the tuba emerged in the last half of the nineteenth century. In the present survey of these materials, it is apparent that pedagogical practice has changed drastically over the years, with common practice becoming slightly more standardized since 1980.

Catalogs from music publishers, computer databases, and numerous other sources provided information for this chapter. Almost all currently available materials and a very large portion of materials that have been in print in the past are included here. Thanks are extended to those in the music publishing industry who furnished review copies of pedagogical materials, and to the music retailers who allowed access to their inventory, particularly Groth Music of Minneapolis, Minnesota, and Alan Hager of that firm. The many International Consultants furnished copies of works available in their countries, and low brass colleagues across the United States provided materials from their libraries. Finally, special thanks go to the University of Wisconsin—Eau Claire School of Graduate Study and Research, Dr. Ronald Satz, Dean; and the Department of Music, Dr. David Baker, Chair. Through their generous support, David Graves (tubist, scholar, teacher, and master's degree candidate) was able to assist with the research for and preparation of this chapter.

Our goal was to determine the availability of published methods and studies for the tuba. If it was determined that a work is out of print, this fact is indicated in the bibliographic information. However, the lack of an out-of-print notation does not guarantee that the item is indeed available. The prices given are the most recent ones. In the case of out-of-print material or where no other source was available, the cover price is listed. Since some publishers did not furnish current catalogs with up-to-date price information, some prices may not be accurate. Entries that appear in the following listing without annotation and/or with incomplete bibliographic in-

formation were not made available to the editor for examination. The editorial staff of *The Tuba Source Book* felt that it was important that all items be documented in this project, regardless of availability. Some items were not furnished for review by the publisher, while others (appearing in old catalogs or bibliographies) are presumably out of print and lost.

Adler, Samuel. *Tubetudes*. Southern Music Company. 1978. $3.50. 7 pp. II–III. These etudes range from very playable by an intermediate student to challenging for a good high school student. All sixteen etudes were written as musical studies, as well as to challenge some technical aspect of musicianship, and are appropriate for recital presentation. A particularly good choice for the pedagogical library of the junior and senior high school teacher.

Amis, K. *Pre-Audition Warm-up for Tuba*. Seesaw Music Corporation. $29.00.

Anderson, Eugene, and Harvey Phillips. *Musically Mastering the Low Range of the Tuba and Euphonium: A College Method Book*. Anderson's Arizona Originals. 1992. 75 pp. III–IV. Although designed for the college-level student, these etudes work well for the very advanced high school student. The etudes are organized in sets of three with each set working one half step lower than the previous one. Each set includes etudes in Baroque, Romantic, and contemporary style, and a variety of performance techniques are employed. Also includes pedagogical hints and fingering charts.

Appelghem and Zemp. *Methode pour Tuba I et II*. Lille. 1982.

Arban, J. B. *Arban Scales*. ed. Wesley Jacobs. Encore Music Publishers. $20.00. 98 pp. II–V. Arban scale patterns are presented in all keys, complete with articulation and rhythmic variations. A good resource for developing thorough acquaintance with scales from the intermediate years forward.

Arban, J. B. *Arban-Bell Interpretations*. ed. William Bell. Charles Colin. 1975. $25.00. 126 pp. III–V. This volume presents significant portions of the original Arban *Complete Method for Trumpet* in bass clef for the tubist or euphoniumist (all exercises are presented in octaves). Includes sections on dotted eighths and sixteenths, lip slurs, the simple grace note, the triple tongue, the double tongue. All sections are accompanied by instructive comments from the legendary William Bell.

Arban, J. B. *Exercises in Double Crotchets*. tr./ed. Wesley Jacobs. Encore Music Publishers. 1988.

$20.00. 99 pp. IV–V. The original Arban double crochet studies transposed into all keys, complete with listing of all Arban articulation variations plus additional articulation variations from the editor. A fine route to better time and articulation while improving reading in all keys.

Arban, Joseph Jean Baptiste Laurent. *The Arban-Bell Tuba Method.* ed. William J. Bell. Charles Colin. Out of print. 1968. 196 pp. III–IV. Although this volume is out of print, it is included in Bell's *Complete Method for Tuba* from the same publisher.

Arban/Prescott. *Arban-Prescott First and Second Year.* Carl Fischer, Incorporated. 1937. $8.50. 51 pp. I–III. An abbreviated version of the complete Arban method designed especially for use in heterogeneous brass instrument class settings. Emphasizes the most fundamental aspects of proper brass playing.

Associated Board (United Kingdom). *Studies for Tuba, Grades III–VIII.* Associated Board of the Royal Schools of Music.

Atkinson, M. *National Self-Teacher for Tuba or E♭ Bass.* M. Atkinson. Out of print. 1904. $.25. I–III. Contains exercises, popular songs, easy duets, and presents only flat scales in study of rudiments. The cover describes the text as: "An easy system by which, after slight practice, anyone can play at sight all the popular airs and any music adapted for the instrument. No tedious study of notes or scales is required as the only necessary rudiments are given in condensed form."

Augustine, Daniel S. *Seventeen Etudes for Tuba.* Daniel Augustine. 1975. 12 pp. IV–V. Only the most advanced student or professional player will benefit from these etudes. These very challenging studies contain very wide leaps to both extreme registers combined with difficult and odd technical and rhythmic figures. Excellent material for the athletic tubist who needs to "stretch."

Bach, J. S. *Bach for the Tuba, Volume I.* arr. Douglas Bixby; tr. Roger Bobo. Western International Music. 1971. $8.00. 34 pp. IV–V. Study of the music of Bach with emphasis on phrasing, low register, style, and ornamentation. Preparatory exercises for volume II (see following entry). Some selections are appropriate for solo performance.

Bach, J.S. *Bach for the Tuba, Volume II.* arr. Douglas Bixby; tr. Roger Bobo. Western International Music. 1972. $8.00. 36 pp. IV–V. Continued study of the music of Bach with emphasis on phrasing, low register, style, and ornamentation. This volume consists largely of arrangements of works suitable for recital use.

Balent, Andrew. *Sounds Spectacular Band Course (Tuba), Books I and II.* Carl Fischer, Incorporated. 1991. $4.95 each. 32 pp. each. I–II. A band method with attractive covers which includes instruction in theory (with an emphasis on terminology) and ensemble playing, theory puzzles, and full band arrangements.

Balent, Andrew, and Quincy Hilliard. *Sounds Spectacular Skill Builders: Warmups and Technical Studies for the Developing Performer (Tuba), Book I.* Carl Fischer, Incorporated. 1992. $3.95. 16 pp. I–II. Intended as a supplement to the *Sounds Spectacular Band Course,* this work is divided into separate units, with exercises specifically designed for the proper development of embouchure, breathing, counting, articulation, and ensemble balance.

Bauer, G. *Elementarschule für Bläser in B, Es, C im violin-/Bassschlüssel.* Georg Bauer Musikverlag. 1980.

Bauer, G. *Technisch-rhythmische Studien für Bläser (Bassschlüssel).* Georg Bauer Musikverlag. 1965.

Bayley, W. R. *Scales for E♭ Bombardone (E♭ Bass).* W. R. Bayley Philadelphia. Out of print. 1860. 1 p. II. A simple introduction to fingerings for the E♭ tuba, the chromatic scale, the overtone series for each valve, and flat scales.

Becker, G. *Method for the B♭ Tuba* in three volumes. Remick.

Beeler, Walter. *Method for BB flat Tuba—Book I.* Warner Brothers Music. 1946. $7.95. 72 pp. I–II. A "first book" for private instruction. It includes many familiar tunes and logically introduces new notes, keys, and concepts. An outstanding feature is the inclusion of duets for teacher and student.

Beeler, Walter. *Method for BB flat Tuba—Book II.* Remick. 1962. $7.95. 48 pp. II–III. Intended for the advanced intermediate to advanced high school student, this book continues with familiar traditional and classical melodies and concludes with a good set of characteristic etudes. Includes fine material for use in high school level auditions.

Beeler, Walter. *Play Away! for BB♭ and E♭ Tubas (Sousaphone).* G. Schirmer, Incorporated. 1960. $1.00. 32 pp. I. Typical of the fine pedagogical thought of Walter Beeler, this book provides a decelerated approach for the very young beginner. It proceeds at a very slow pace and provides plenty of review as new ideas and concepts are introduced.

Behm. *Sharps and Flats (Tuba).* Belwin-Mills.

Bell, William J. *Blazhevich Tuba Interpretations.* Charles Colin. 1975. $7.95. 79 pp. III–IV. These studies, edited by William Bell, are presented with very instructive comments. They include a variety of unusual meters as well as etudes in all keys. Whether used for concentrated study or as a resource for challenging sight reading material, this is an excellent text. (Also included in Bell's *Complete Method for Tuba.*)

Bell, William J. *Complete Method for Tuba.* Charles Colin. 1975. $45. 260 pp. I–IV. A comprehensive text for tuba study. Included is an abridged and edited version of the Arban *Complete Method for Trumpet* (including some of the *Art of Phrasing* and duets from that text), as well as Bell's *Bla-zhevich Tuba Interpretations* (also available from the publisher in separate editions). "Artistic Solos and Duets" include classics such as *The Carnival of Venice*.

Bell, William J. *Daily Routine and Blazhevich Interpretations, Volumes 1 and 2.* ed. Charles Colin. New Sounds in Modern Music. Out of print. 1954. $1.95. 31 pp. III–IV. Includes a brief introduction to Bell's pedagogical approach plus the solo parts to two solos: "Tuba Man" and "Gus the Hippo." One of the most historically significant methods in the repertoire.

Bell, William J. *Foundation to Tuba and Sousaphone Playing.* Carl Fischer, Incorporated. 1931. $12.00. 106 pp. I–III Covers fundamentals of tuba playing with pedagogical comments directed to the teacher. Includes a variety of progressive etudes and some simple solos.

Bell, William J. *Tuba Warm-Ups and Daily Routine.* Charles Colin. Out of print. 1975. $3.50. 39 pp. III–IV. This text includes William Bell's prescribed warm-up procedure covering long tones, flexibilities, tonguing, scales and arpeggios, interval studies, etc. (This material is included in its entirety in Bell's *Complete Method for Tuba* from the same publisher.)

Bell, William. *William Bell Daily Routine for Tuba.* ed. Abe Torchinsky. Encore Music Publishers. 1989. $17.50. 28 pp. III–IV. The daily routine recommended by William Bell, edited and explained by his student Abe Torchinsky. Exercises in breathing, flexibility, tonguing, etc., with specific directions on the way Bell intended them to be played.

Bencriscutto, Frank, and Hal Freese. *Total Musicianship (Tuba).* Neil A. Kjos Music Company. 1983. $4.50. 48 pp. III–IV. Designed for the intermediate to advanced musician, this method is appropriate for individual or group study. Its primary objectives are establishing a solid warm-up routine, developing technique, and learning to improvise in the jazz idiom. Especially helpful are the simplicity of the improvisation section and the scope of the fingering chart (for BB♭, CC, E♭, and F tubas).

Bergeim, Joseph. *Instrumental Course for E flat and BB flat Tubas.* Joseph E. Skornicka. Boosey & Hawkes, Incorporated. 1946. 48 pp. I.

Bernard, Paul. *Douze Pièces Mélodiques.* Alphonse Leduc Editions Musicales. 1947. $14.25. 16 pp. III–IV. See Thompson/Lemke; *French Music for Low Brass Instruments.*

Bernard, Paul. *Etudes et Exercises pour Tuba et Saxhorn Basse.* ed. J. Forestier. Alphonse Leduc Editions Musicales. 1948. $14.20. 17 pp. III–IV. Good studies in a variety of keys. They work best on F tuba or even tenor tuba, although they present reasonable range challenges for the contrabass tubist. For the most advanced high school students and second year (or higher) college students. See:

Thompson/Lemke, *French Music for Low Brass Instruments.*

Bernard, Paul. *Méthode Complète pour Trombone Basse, Tuba, Saxhorns Basses et Contrebasse.* Alphonse Leduc Editions Musicales. 1960. $36.50. 136 pp. I–IV. Although directed toward the broader low brass family, this method is best suited to the tenor tuba. Because of the high tessitura of the exercises, it is probably intended for the French C tuba, an instrument that is actually smaller than the euphonium. See: Thompson/Lemke, *French Music for Low Brass Instruments.*

Bernard, Paul. *Quarante Etudes d'Après Forestier.* Alphonse Leduc Editions Musicales. 1948. $14.20. 17 pp. III–IV. See: Thompson/Lemke; *French Music for Low Brass Instruments.*

Berninger, H. *Bläserübungen, Tonleitern und tägliche Studien für Bass-Tuba oder Helikon.* Friedrich Hofmeister.

Bianchini. *Popular Method.* Editions Salabert.

Bimboni, Cav. Giovacchino. *Metodo Graduato e Progressivo per Elicon Si B.* Adolpho Lapini. Out of print. 1928. 44 pp.

Bing, W. *The Bing Book.* Whipple Music. $21.00.

Bitsch, M. *Quatorze Etudes de Rythme (Greiner).* Alphonse Leduc Editions Musicales. 1988. 29 pp. IV–V. See: Thompson/Lemke; *French Music for Low Brass Instruments.*

Blazewitsch, Vladislav. *Advanced Daily Drills for Trombone and Tuba.* ed. Alan Ostrander. Editions Musicus. 1961. $5.60. 18 pp. III–IV. These studies can be used either as warm-up or study material. Focus is on development of tone, articulation, and flexibility through intensive scale study. The author's pedagogical approach is presented briefly in English translation at the beginning of the text.

Blazhevich, V. *26 Melodic Studies in Sequences.* ed. Joel Zimmerman. Shawnee Press. 1988. $10.00. 53 pp. IV. Challenging etudes that cover a variety of rhythmic and phrasing problems. A broad range of meters and keys are represented. Excellent studies for the advanced college student who needs to refine reading skills and improve general musicality.

Blazhevich, V. M. *Textbook for Tuba in B♭.* Encore Music Publishers. 1939/1990. $32. 62 pp. II–V. The first Russian etude book specifically for tuba. These etudes are totally different from those transcribed from the trombone etudes in the King and Knaub Blazhevich editions. This is a complete method for tuba in the spirit of Arban.

Blazhevich, Vladislav. *70 Studies for BB flat Tuba, Vols. I and II.* Robert King Music Company. 1965. $3.40 each. 52 pp. each. III–IV. Excellent studies in all keys for low range, odd meters. These studies (transcribed from the original trombone etudes) have become a standard of tuba pedagogical repertoire. See also: Knaub, D., *Progressive Techniques for Tuba.*

Blazhewitsch, V. *Schule für Bass-Tuba in B* (Hochschule der Künste Berlin). SSV. 1925.

Bleger, M. *Méthode Complète de Saxhorn-Basse*. ed. M. Job. Alphonse Leduc Editions Musicales. 1932. 83 pp. IV.

Bleger, M. *Méthode Elementaire*.

Bleger, M. *Nouvelle Méthode Complète*. Alphonse Leduc Editions Musicales. 1932.

Bleger, M. *10 Caprices*. Alphonse Leduc Editions Musicales.

Bleger, M. *31 Etudes Brillantes*. Alphonse Leduc Editions Musicales.

Blume, O. *36 Übungen, Band 1-3*. ed. Emil Teuchert. C. F. Schmidt. 1972.

Bobo, Roger. *Mastering the Tuba*. 3 Vols. Editions BIM. 1993–1995. The first volume will cover fundamental exercises and warm-ups; the second (anticipated release 1994) will include special etudes by contemporary composers, with special instructional material for each etude; and the third (anticipated release 1995) will be on "how to be your own teacher."

Bordogni, Marco. *43 Bel Canto Studies for Tuba*. ed. Chester Roberts. Robert King Music Company. 1972. 52 pp. III–IV. These studies, transcribed from Bordogni vocalises, focus on phrasing and lyricism. Roberts has transposed many of the etudes from their original keys. A standard college/university text in the United States.

Bordogni, Marco. *Legato Etudes for Tuba, Volume I*. trans. Wesley Jacobs. Encore Music Publishers. 1990. $10.00. 16 pp. III–V. Fifteen etudes from the vocalises of Bordogni emphasizing lyric style and phrasing. This edition has recorded accompaniments available from the publisher.

Bordogni, Marco. *Low Legato Etudes for Tuba, Volume I*. tr. Wesley Jacobs. Encore Music Publishers. 1990. $11.00. 17 pp. IV–V. Five etudes from the vocalises of Bordogni. Each is presented an octave lower than in other editions and in three different (progressively lower) keys (for an actual total of fifteen etudes). An excellent approach to low register study.

Bower, and [Charles] Colin. *Advanced Rhythms*.

Bower, and [Charles] Colin. *Rhythms, Volumes I and II*.

Brightmore, Victor. *Forty-Three Easy Melodic Studies for Beginners on Brass Instruments (Bass Clef Edition)*. Chappell & Company, Limited. II.

Brightmore, Victor. *Twenty-five Melodic Studies for Brass (Bass Clef Version)*. Chappell & Company, Limited. 1964. 12 pp. III–IV.

Brothers, H. P. *Squire's Melodic School for the Bb Bass*. A. Squire Cincinnati. Out of print. 1883. 58 pp. I–III. Although published in the same year as the next entry by the same author and publisher and with virtually the same title, this is a quite different work in format and content. It introduces the bass clef (instead of the G clef) and has a much abbreviated

pedagogical section (only 24 pages), but that section is in a similar format (concept introduction followed by musical material) to that of the next entry. A large number of contemporary popular melodies and duets are included.

Brothers, H. P. *Squire's Melodic School for the Bb Bass, G Clef*. A. Squire Cincinnati. Out of print. 1883. 43 pp. I–III. A self-instruction book that includes basic rudiments. Unlike most late nineteeth-century tutors, this method uses a truly progressive approach, with unusual clarity, incorporating each new concept into an exercise or melody with some degree of musical value before moving on to a new concept.

Brothers, H. P. *Squire's Melodic School for the Eb Bass*. A. Squire Cincinnati. Out of print. 1883. I–III. This method for Eb tuba was designed to fulfill the same purpose as the two previous entries, but contains different comments and studies. All exercises are in bass clef.

Bruggen, P. van. *Etudes*.

Buck, Lawrence. *Elementary Method for Tuba (Eb or BBb)*. Neil A. Kjos Music Company. Out of print. 1954. $1.25. 40 pp. I. Although this text is described as a method for similar-instrument or private instruction, it is most suitable for the private setting. A new idea or concept is introduced every one to two pages, and considerable individual attention/explanation from the teacher would be desirable, as there is no explanatory text in the body of the book.

Buehlman, Barbara, and Ken Whitcomb. *Sessions in Sound, Books I and II (Tuba/Sousaphone)*. Heritage Music Press. 1976. $4.50 each. 32 pp. each. I–II. A beginning band method which introduces new ideas at the top of each page. Contains a brief glossary.

Burden, James H. *Head Start Band Method, Book 1 (Tuba)*. Columbia Lady Music. 1977. $5.50. 24 pp. I–II. A beginning band method which highlights new ideas and concepts with textual coloration and cartoons.

Burke, E. *A–B–C Instructor for the Bb Bass, G Clef*. A. Squire Cincinnati. Out of print. 1885. I–III. Probably designed for the aspiring, self-taught tubist, this method contains rudiments of music theory, simple etudes, and 70 contemporary popular melodies.

Butterfield, Don. *Advanced Solo-Studies for Bass Clef Instruments*. D. B. Publishing Company.

Carbone, E. *Methodo teorico-practico: Posaune, Tuba, Bombardon*. Carisch Edizioni Musicali.

Cardoni, A. *Introduzione Allo Studio Del Flicorno Contrabbasso in Si Bemolle*. G. Ricordi e C. 1927. 22 pp.

Carnaud, Jeune. *Vingt-cinq Etudes pour Tuba*.

Carnaud, Jeune. *Vingt-cinq Exercises pour Saxhorn basse*.

Carnaud, Jeune. *Complete Method, Volumes I and II*.

Caruso, Carmine; Hal Graham; and Shelton Booth. *Caruso Band Method (Tuba)—Book I*. Samuel French. 1969. $2.00. 30 pp. I. A beginning method for group instruction, this approach is based in the pedagogical ideas of prominent brass teacher Carmine Caruso. The tuba book has very good pedagogical comments, but little material of melodic interest for the young student.

Catelinet, Philip. *The Essential Tubaist*. Cinque Port Music Publishers. 1985. 30 pp. III–IV. A guide to daily practice covering tone flexibility, precision and pitch, scales, and arpeggios. The format that takes the student from Monday through Saturday (resting on Sunday). All keys are covered. Pedagogical suggestions are offered at the beginning of the book.

Caton. *Progressive Eb Tuba Instruction for Public School Classes*. Volkwein.

Charlier, Théo. *Trente-deux études de perfectionnement pour trombone in si bénik á 4 pistons ou tuba*. Henri Lemoine and Cie. 1946. 55 pp. III–IV. See: Thompson/Lemke; *French Music for Low Brass Instruments*.

Childs, Robert and Nicholas. *Warm-ups and Studies*. Obrasso-Verlag AG. 1988. 11 pp. II–IV. Comprising six warm-up studies and two etudes, this book is intended for all brass instruments. Long tones, flexibilities, articulation, and technique are represented. As the work is aimed principally at a brass band audience, notation is presented in treble-clef only. Text in English and German.

Christensen, Kerstein. *Tuba Skole*. Wilhelm Hansen Musikforlag. 1949. $4.00. 67 pp. I–III. Aimed principally at the beginning tubist who is using the F tuba, this small book is not dissimilar to the abbreviated versions of the Arban Method, covering all basic fundamentals of performance. At the end of the book are a few good, intermediate—early advanced etudes. Text in Scandinavian dialects.

Cimera, Jaroslav. *73 Advanced Tuba Studies*. Belwin-Mills. 1955. $5.50. 31 pp. IV. These etudes emphasize technique and rhythmic development. A variety of keys and meters are represented. The style of the etudes compares favorably with the Tyrell and Kopprasch studies.

Clark, Andy. *Five Minutes a Day (Tuba)*. C. L. Barnhouse Company. 1992. $3.95. 12 pp. II–III. This method for band contains twelve individual lessons, including chorales, technical studies, and tuning exercises.

Clarke, Harry F. *Elementary Method for Tuba*. Belwin-Mills. I.

Clodomir. *Méthode Complète pour tous les Saxhorns*. Alphonse Leduc Editions Musicales. 1948. 112 pp. IV.

Clodomir. *Méthodes Elementaires pour tous les Saxhorns*. Alphonse Leduc Editions Musicales.

Colin, C. *100 Original Warm-Ups*.

Concone, G. *Advanced Concone Studies*. ed. Reinhardt. Theodore Presser Company. $5.50.

Concone and Marchesi. *60 Musical Studies for Tuba (Book I)*. tr. David L. Kuehn. Southern Music Company. 1969. $7.50. 21 pp. II–III. Studies in legato style from the vocalises of Concone and Marchesi, with special attention to phrasing and reading problems. On the whole, these studies are less challenging than traditional Rochut-style studies, but are very worthwhile for the late intermediate/early advanced student.

Culbertson, Melvin. *Muscle Up, Volumes I and II*.

Cummings, Barton. *Seventeen Virtuoso Studies after Maxime-Alphonse for Tuba, Bass Trombone, Bass and Contrebass Saxhorn*. Alphonse Leduc Editions Musicales. $16.25. See: Thompson/Lemke; *French Music for Low Brass Instruments*.

Cummings, Barton. *Thirty Studies for Tuba, Bass Trombone, Bass and Contrabass Saxhorn after Maxime-Alphonse*. Alphonse Leduc Editions Musicales. 1978. $11.40. 12 pp. III–IV. These etudes are especially fine for work on articulation and technique. They would work especially well for the advanced high school or beginning college student. Per Cummings's reputation as a fine composer as well as gifted tuba artist, the etudes are very musical in character. See: Thompson/Lemke; *French Music for Low Brass Instruments*.

D'Erasmo. *Method (Tuba)*. Editions Salabert.

de Ville, Paul. *The Eclipse Self Instructor for BBb Bass*. Carl Fischer, Incorporated. Out of print. 1905. 64 pp. II–III. Although the title indication is for contrabass tuba, the tessitura of all exercises appears to be principally for euphonium or trombone. A thorough introduction to rudiments of music is included, together with a few early exercises and "seventy-three standard national and sacred melodies." Comments of interest to the scholar of pedagogical history appear at the beginning of the method.

Defaye. *Six Etudes Tuba*. Alphonse Leduc Editions Musicales. $11.40. See: Thompson/Lemke; *French Music for Low Brass Instruments*.

Defaye. *Six Etudes —Two Tubas*. Alphonse Leduc Editions Musicales. $25.30.

Delgiudice, Michel. *Douze Etudes Rythmiques et Mélodiques*. Eschig. 1954. 25 pp. IV. See: Thompson/Lemke; *French Music for Low Brass Instruments*.

Delgiudice, Michel. *10 Kleine Text*.

Dijoux, Marc. *Déchiffrage du debutant*.

Dodson, Thomas. *Music Creativity (Tuba)*. Neil A. Kjos Music Company. 1991. $4.95. 32 pp. I. This method is unique in its emphasis on developing the creative process. Typical etudes are presented in alternation with incomplete etudes. The student is given guidelines within which to complete the incomplete etude, after which it is to be performed.

Dondeyne, D. *Cinq Etudes*.

Dondeyne, D. *Douze Déchiffrages.* See: Thompson/ Lemke; *French Music for Low Brass Instruments.*

Dondeyne, D. *Neuf Déchiffrages.*

Dondeyne, D. *Treize Déchiffrages.*

Douglas, Wayne, and Fred Weber. *Belwin Band Builder for Bass (Tuba) in 3 Volumes.* Belwin-Mills. 1953/57. $5.50 each. 27 pp. each. I–II. This classic band method quickly introduces the tuba as both a soloistic and accompaniment instrument. This is accomplished through the early presentation of several harmonized tunes, each of which includes both the melody and a bass part. Volumes II and III give additional attention to the development of technique through progressive scale studies.

Downey and Meehan. *Ensemble Techniques in two volumes (Tuba).* Hal Leonard Publishing Corporation. $2.95 each.

Dubois, Pierre Max. *Douze Soli en form d'Etudes.* Alphonse Leduc Editions Musicales. 1961. $14.25. 16 pp. IV. See: Thompson/Lemke; *French Music for Low Brass Instruments.*

Dufresne, Gaston. *Sight Reading Studies for Bass Trombone/Tuba.* ed. Don Schaeffer. Charles Colin. 1964. 25 pp. IV.

Eby, Walter M. *Eby's Scientific Method for BB flat Bass, Sousaphone, E flat Tuba and CC Bass Part 1.* Walter Jacobs (Big Three). Out of print. 1930. 60 pp. I–II. One of the early methods emphasizing the contrabass tuba, this method was intended for private instruction. It covers all fundamental areas of performance and provides detailed explanation of pedagogical practice.

Eby, Walter M. *Eby's Scientific Method for BB flat Bass, Sousaphone, E flat Tuba and CC Bass Part 2.* Walter Jacobs (Big Three). Out of print. 1930. 175 pp. III. A continuation of Eby *Method*, Part I. This section of the work is aimed toward the more advanced player, developing and building on ideas presented in Part 1.

Eerola, Lasse. *Thirty Etydia Tuuballe.* Finnish Music Information Centre. 1992. 30 pp. II. A particularly fine book of etudes for the serious young student. Virtually all basic rhythm problems are addressed, and the etudes focus on developing the mid-register of the instrument, an important focus for any young student. Various studies focus on intervals, flexibility, articulation, etc.

Eidson, Alonzo B. *Belwin Brass Bass Method, Books I and II.* ed. Nilo W. Hovey. Belwin-Mills. 1947. $1.25 each. 32 pp. each. I–II. This basic beginning method includes several piano accompaniments for exercises within the book and a fingering chart which extends up to f '.

Elledge, Robert, and Haddad, Donald. *Band Technique—Step by Step (Tuba).* Neil A. Kjos Music Company. 1992. $4.95. 36 pp. II. An intermediate level method which progresses through most major and minor keys. Features enrichment through "Advanced Rhythms" pages and through an extensive fingering chart, which both extends to BBB♭ and includes fingerings for F, E♭, CC, and BB♭ tubas.

Endresen, R. M. *BB♭ Tuba Method* (two books). M. M. Cole Publishing Company. Out of print. 1937. $1.00. 63 pp. I–II. Intended for private instruction, this classic method introduces basic music fundamentals at an accelerated pace. In addition to etudes emphasizing all aspects of development, a number of recognizable melodies and duets for student and teacher are included.

Endresen, R. M. *E♭ Tuba Method* (two books). M. M. Cole Publishing Company. Out of print. 1937. $1.00. 63 pp. I–II. This text is essentially identical to the previously described Endresen *BB♭ Tuba Method.* A few photographs and the Foreword are different, but, all instructional material is the same.

Endressen, R. M. *Supplementary Studies for E♭ or BB♭ Bass.* Rubank, Incorporated. 1936. $3.95. 24 pp. II–III. Contains progressively arranged, brief etudes in various styles emphasizing various aspects of melodic and technical playing. A good review/ sight-reading book for junior/senior high.

Erickson, Frank. *Belwin Comprehensive Band Method (BB♭ Tuba), Volumes I, II, and III.* Belwin-Mills. 1988/88/89. $5.00 each. 40 pp. each. I–II. Each volume is divided into two sections: one for individual instruction and the other for group study. Features of each section include harmonized etudes, progressively introduced rhythmic patterns, and (Volume III only) alternating etudes/program works.

Erickson, Frank. *Technique through Melody for Band (Tuba).* Belwin-Mills. 1983. $5.50. 24 pp. II–III. With an emphasis on lyrical playing, this method includes both modal and tonal etudes, some of which are designed for aural development through the repetition of specific intervallic relationships.

Erickson, Frank; Eric Osterling; and James D. Ployhar. *Band Today, Part I.* Belwin-Mills. 1977. $5.50. 32 pp. I. A traditional band method designed for group or individual instruction. Covers fundamentals of music reading and playing.

Feldstein, Sandy. *Alfred's New Band Method, Book I.* Alfred Music Company. $4.95. I.

Feldstein, Sandy, and John O'Reilly. *Alfred's Basic Band Method, I, II, III (Tuba).* Alfred Music Company. 1977. $5.50 each. 32 pp. each. I–II. Each section/chapter begins with the new material for that section and continues with reinforcing etudes, occasionally including a duet for two tubas.

Feldstein, Sandy, and John O'Reilly. *Yamaha Band Student, Books I and II (Tuba).* Alfred Music Company. 1988. $5.50. 31 pp. I. Contains a variety of repertoire. A colorful and widely used band method. Newly introduced fundamentals are presented in highlighted areas.

Feldstein, Sandy, and Joseph Scianni. *The Sound of Rock (Tuba).* Alfred Music Company. 1971. $1.95.

32 pp. II–III. Designed to introduce elements of rock/jazz to the student through group instruction. Emphasis is on rhythm patterns and articulation styles typically found in rock music. The tuba part emphasizes bass-like playing, but with opportunities to play solos.

Fink, Reginald H., ed. and comp. *Studies in Legato.* Carl Fischer, Incorporated. 1967. $9.00. 43 pp. III–IV. Legato studies for tuba or bass trombone "Based on the works of Concone, Marchesi and Panofka." Includes suggestions for efficient study of each etude. Well suited to the advanced high school or beginning college student.

Fischer, Carl. *Carl Fischer's New and Revised Edition of Celebrated Tutors: BB♭ Bass.* Carl Fischer, Incorporated. Out of print. 1908. 77 pp. II–III. Virtually identical to the later method attributed to O. H. Langey and published by Carl Fischer, apparently printed from the same plates. See below *Langey— Carl Fischer Tutors for BB♭ Bass.*

Fitchhorn, E. *Practical Procedures for Sight Reading for Band (Tuba).* ed. O. W. Margrave. Henri Elkan Music Publisher.

Fitz-Gerald, John. *Practical Tutor for the B♭ and BB♭ Basses (in the Treble Clef).* Hawkes & Son New York. Out of print. 107 pp. I–III. Contains rudiments of music, melodies, duets, and etudes in addition to a short section of excerpts from contemporary popular marches and solos.

Fontbonne, L. *Méthode Complète.* Costallat & Cie. Out of print. 1908. 45 pp.

Frank, Steven. *The Good Book: Supplementary Exercises for Winds—Tuba, Volume I.* Frankenbush Publishing. 1987. 42 pp. I–II. Designed to provide supplemental material for any beginning text, this text contains a wealth of material for reinforcing concepts and developing sightreading skills. The table of contents is particularly useful in that it refers to the performance problem treated on each page in music notation. Although the target audience is young players, this material would be valuable to any teacher at any level in reviewing any basic aspects of music performance. Uses the keys of F, B♭, and E♭ major.

Frank, Steven. *The Good Book: Supplementary Exercises for Winds—Tuba, Volume II.* Frankenbush Publishing. 1987. 42 pp. I–II. This text covers more complex rhythms than the first volume, compound meters, and the keys of C, G, D, and A major.

Franz, A. *Schule für Tuba oder Helikon in F mit 4 Ventilen* (Hochschule der Künste, Berlin). Bellmann & Thymer O.J.

Freese, Hal. *Advanced Band Method (Tuba).* Belwin-Mills. 1972. $5.50. 39 pp. II.

Freese, Hal. *Elementary Band Method (Tuba).* Belwin-Mills. 1967. $5.50. 33 pp. I.

Freese, Hal. *Intermediate Band Method (Tuba).* Belwin-Mills. 1968. $5.50. 40 pp. I–II.

Fritze, Gregory. *Twenty Characteristic Etudes for Tuba.* T.U.B.A. Press. 1991. $12.00. 40 pp. III–IV. Winner of the 1992 T.U.B.A. Etude Contest. Directed toward the preparation of orchestral, chamber, and solo literature and principally toward the advanced collegiate or professional performer. The composer notes that there are several direct quotations from the repertoire to help direct learning. All keys are represented, and the etudes are intended for tubas in all keys.

Froseth, James. *Listen, Move, Sing and Play for Band (Tuba), Book 1.* Gia Publications, Incorporated. 1984. $3.50. 33 pp. I. This highly comprehensive band method emphasizes the firm establishment of fundamental performance skills through a variety of exercises and etudes, including rounds, duets, and rhythmic drills.

Froseth, James. *Listen, Move, Sing and Play for Band (Tuba), Book II.* Gia Publications, Incorporated. 1984. $3.95. 31 pp. I–II.

Froseth, James O. *The Comprehensive Music Instructor for Band, Books I, II, III (Tuba).* Gia Publications, Incorporated. $4.95 each.

Froseth, James O. *The Individualized Instructor, Preliminary Book (Tuba).* Gia Publications, Incorporated. $5.95.

Froseth, James O. *The Individualized Instructor, Books I, II, III (Tuba).* Gia Publications, Incorporated. 1970/72/73. $4.95 each. 31 pp. each. I–III. Designed as a self-guided, individual course. Includes rhythm exercises, technical studies, and ensembles.

Gallay, J. F. *Thirty Etudes for Tuba, Op.13.* ed. Robert King. Robert King Music Company. 1978. $3.95. 31 pp. IV. Originally for valveless horn, these difficult etudes present exceptional challenges in flexibility and overall technique for either the advanced college student or the professional player seeking to "stretch."

Gallay, Jacques. *Fifteen Style Studies.* ed. Gerard Billaudot. Editions Billaudot. 1974. $9.25. 14 pp. IV–V. Played in the written octave, this method provides excellent melodic material for the F tuba. The longer studies may be used as performance works.

Gallay, Jacques. *Twelve Etudes.* ed. Estevan Dax. Editions Billaudot. $9.50. 15 pp. IV.

Geib, Fred. *The Geib Method for Tuba.* Carl Fischer, Incorporated. 1941. $12.00. 117 pp. I–III. Written by one of the early great figures in tuba pedagogy, this text is similar to the Arban method for trumpet, but at a simpler level. The work does not have melodies, but does incorporate a few orchestral excerpts at its conclusion. See listing under "Orchestral Excerpts."

Getchell, Robert W. *Practical Studies (Books I and II).* ed. Nilo Hovey. Belwin-Mills. 1955. $6.50. 32 pp. II–III. An introduction to the study of technique and, particularly, rhythm. Basic rhythmic figures receive concentrated treatment in brief, interesting etudes.

Giovannoli, S. *Method for E♭ and B♭ Bass for Beginners, Part I: Rudiments and Easy Exercises.* New York: Middle Village. 1959. $1.50. 31 pp. I–II. A beginning method for private instruction. This simple text introduces basic rudiments of playing together with very easy exercises for the beginning and early intermediate student. There are no pedagogical comments in the book, however, the simple etudes work well for supplementary material for the young person.

Giuffre, Jimmy. *Jazz Phrasing and Interpretation (Bass Instruments).* Associated Music Publishers. 1969. 61 pp. III–IV.

Gland, H., and A. Franz. *Schule für Tuba oder Helikon in B mit 4 Ventilen* (Hochschule der Künste, Berlin). Bellman & Thymer, O. J.

Goldman, Edwin Franko. *Daily Embouchure Studies.* Carl Fischer, Incorporated. Out of print. 1909. 9 pp. III–IV.

Gornston, David. *Fun with Scales in Bass Clef.* MCA.

Gornston, David. *The Very First BB♭ or E♭ Bass method.* Edward Schuberth & Co. 1953. $.60. 32 pp. I.

Gornston, David, and W. Musser. *Tuba Dailies.* Neil A. Kjos Music Company. 1960. $1.00. 17 pp. I–V. A book (principally) of lip slurs, with various rhythms and articulations. It is intended as a guide to establishing a daily routine, drilling fundamentals of good playing.

Goudenhooft, André. *Quinze Etudes complementaires.* Editions Billadout. See: Thompson/Lemke; *French Music for Low Brass Instruments.*

Goudenhooft, André. *Vingt-quatre Etudes pour le Trombone Basse et le Tuba Basse.* ed. Gerard Billaudot. Editions Billaudot. 1985. $19.50. 30 pp. V. Use of wide range, various keys, contrasting articulations and tenor-clef make this a challenging method for the most advanced performers. See: Thompson/Lemke; *French Music for Low Brass Instruments.*

Gouse, Charles F. *Learn to Play the Tuba! (Books I and II).* Alfred Music Company. 1970. 48 pp. I. Part of a method series intended for group brass instruction or as a private tutor. It covers basics of music reading and playing fundamentals.

Gower, William, and Himie Voxman. *Rubank Advanced Method for E flat or BB flat Bass, Vol. I.* Rubank, Incorporated. 1951. $6.95. 72 pp. III. Provides excellent challenges for the serious young high school student. Short etudes cover scales, arpeggios, flexibility and other aspects of development of good, fundamental playing skills.

Gower, William, and Himie Voxman. *Rubank Advanced Method for E flat or BB flat Bass, Vol. II.* Rubank, Incorporated. 1959. $6.95. 95 pp. III–IV. These etudes emphasize articulation, flexibility, ornamentation, and scales. Includes several full-length solos.

Green, Barry, and Timothy Gallwey. *The Inner Game of Music: Workbook for Band (Tuba/String Bass).* Gia Publications, Incorporated. 1991. $4.50. 21 pp. II–III. Designed as a supplement to *The Inner Game of Music,* this method reinforces positive performance concepts with musical examples from the Classical music repertoire.

Gregson, E. *New Horizons for the Young Brass Player (Tuba).*

Gregson, E. *Twenty Supplementary Tunes.*

Grigoriev, Boris. *Fifty Etudes for Tuba, Volume 1.* ed. Keating Johnson. Encore Music Publishers. 1986. $15.00. 27 pp. III–IV. Etudes in all keys with particular emphasis on low register. They are best suited for students who have established good fundamentals, as well as for professional players.

Grigoriev, Boris. *Fifty Etudes for Tuba, Volume 2.* ed. Keating Johnson. Encore Music Publishers. 1986. $15.00. 29 pp. III–V.

Grigoriev, Boris. *Seventy-eight Studies for Tuba.* Robert King Music Company. 1983. $5.20. 72 pp. III–IV. These etudes cover all keys (major and relative minor), moving through sharps and flats progressively. Although some technical problems are presented, the emphasis is on lyric playing and low register, very comparable in some ways to the Blazhevich studies published by Robert King.

Grunow, Richard F., and Edwin E. Gordon. *Jump Right In! Book I (Tuba).* Gia Publications, Incorporated. $4.95.

Guthrie, James. *Twenty-Nine Etudes for Tuba.* T.U.B.A. Press. 1992. $12.00. 35 pp. IV–V. Not for the faint of heart, these etudes are recommended for the very advanced, serious student or professional. Very good, challenging rhythmic problems are presented, both in terms of meters and basic time, and range and technical demands really push the performer to the limit. An excellent choice for the performer who needs to be totally prepared in any reading situation.

Haddad, Don. *Twenty Short Etudes.* Southern Music Company. 1990. $7.95. 15 pp. II–III. Very nice etudes for the intermediate to early advanced player. Melodic and rhythmic problems are presented in a musically attractive way. These etudes appropriately test the range of the young player to middle C.

Haines, Harry, and J. R. McEntyre. *Division of Beat (Tuba/Bass), Books Ia, Ib, and II.* Southern Music Company. 1981/81/89. $4.50 each. I–II. This band method places emphasis on the development of correct rhythmic skills through the use of a breath impulse. It is recommended that the method be used in conjunction with matching rhythm slides, also available from Southern Music Company.

Hawkes & Sons. *Simplicity Tutor.*

Hawkes & Sons' Instruction Books: The BB♭ Bass (in the Treble Clef). Hawkes & Sons London. Out of print. 1904. 31 pp. Contains technical and melodic studies together with exerpts from popular marches and songs of the time.

Hejda. *Etudes for BB flat Tuba*. Artia, Foreign Trade Corporation. 1958. Hejda. Studies.

Herfurth, C. Paul, and Vernon R. Miller. *A Tune a Day for Tuba or Sousaphone*. Boston Music Company. 1954. $6.95. 48 pp. I. Includes a review of musical and playing fundamentals, but the main content focuses on essentially American folk and hymn tunes presented in a simple format.

Herfurth, C. Paul, and Hugh M. Stuart. *Our Band Class Book for Basses (Levels I and II for BB flat and E flat Tubas)*. Carl Fischer, Incorporated. 1967. $3.95 each. 34 pp. I.

Herfurth, C. Paul, and Hugh M. Stuart. *Sounds of the Winds (Tuba), Book I and II*. Carl Fischer, Incorporated.

Hilgers, Walter. *Tägliche Übungen für Tuba*. Editions Marc Reift.

Hindsley, Mark H. *Carl Fischer Basic Method for BBb Tuba*. Carl Fischer, Incorporated. Out of print. 1938. $1.00. 48 pp. I–II. A rapidly moving yet well-organized method covering various rhythms, keys, and interpretive skills.

Hofmeister, Friedrich, ed. *Tonleitern und tägliche Studien: Bass-Tuba und Helikon*. Friedrich Hofmeister. 1933/53.

Hoppert, Manfred. *B-Tuba/Kontrabasstuba Grifftabellen*. Wilhelm Zimmerman.

Hornung, A. and O. Heinl. *Schule für Blasorchester: Tuba*. Halter O. J. 1968.

Hovey, Howard. *Universal's Fundamental Method for the Tuba and Sousaphone*. Universal Music Publishers. Out of print. 1942. $1.75. 48 pp. I–II. An elementary method for private instruction that includes an introduction to basic musical skills and a variety of short solos and familiar tunes.

Hovey, Nilo W. *Advanced Techniques for Eb and BBb Basses*. M. M. Cole Publishing Company.

Hovey, Nilo W. *Basic Technique for Eb or BBb Bass*. M. M. Cole Publishing Company.

Hovey, Nilo W. *Rubank Elementary Method—E flat or BB flat Bass*. Rubank, Incorporated. 1934. $4.95 48 pp. I–II. This book rapidly introduces basic musical concepts and most major keys. It works particularly well as an initial text for private study.

Hovey, Nilo W. *Supplementary Drill Book for Eb and BBb Basses*. M. M. Cole Publishing Company.

Hovey, Nilo W. *T-I-P-P-S for Bands (Bass/Tuba)*. Belwin-Mills. 1959. $4.50. 23 pp. II–III. With studies in most "band keys," this ensemble method emphasizes fundamentals such as tone, intonation, phrasing, precision, and style through the use scalar, arpeggiated, and chorale-type studies.

Hoza, Vaclav, ed. *One Hundred Etudes for Tuba*. Editio Supraphon veb Deutscher Verlag für Musik Leipzig.

Hoza, Vaclav. *Schule für Tuba in F und in B*. Editio Supraphon veb Deutscher Verlag für Musik Leipzig. 1983. 135 pp. I–IV. Vaclav Hoza is a legendary performer and teacher in Czechoslova-kia. This comprehensive method includes a history of the tuba and a complete introduction to musical skills and brass playing skills. Similar in format to the Arban Method, it presents one of the most sensible progressive approaches to playing in existence for tuba players. Text is printed in Czech and German.

Hubbell, Fred. *Rounds Plus*. Heritage Music Press. 1991. $3.95. 24 pp. I–II. Scales and short melodies which may be played as rounds and are organized by key.

Hudadoff, Igor. *A Rhythm a Day*. Pro Art Publications. 1963. 24 pp. II–III.

Hudadoff, Igor, and Norman Ward. *Sight Reader for Young Bands (Tuba)—Book I*. Shawnee Press. 1968. 16 pp. I.

Hudadoff, Igor, and Norman Ward. *Sight Reader for Young Bands (Tuba)—Book II*. Shawnee Press. 1969. 16 pp. I–II

Jacobs, Wesley. *Daily Routine and Warm Up Studies for Tuba*. Encore Music Publishers. 1990. $12.00. 16 pp. I–V. A complete warm-up routine covering flexibility, articulation, intervals, scales, and tone production. Each section is preceded by practice suggestions.

Jacobs, Wesley. *Flexibility Studies for Tuba*. Encore Music Publishers. 1989. $11.00. 23 pp. III–V. Flexibility etudes are each presented in all keys and cover a variety of interval problems. The book opens with detailed practice hints and suggestions.

Jacobs, Wesley. *Low Register Studies for Tuba*. Encore Music Publishers. $22.00. 121 pp. II–V. A progressive book for study of low register that includes fingering charts and a guide to practice. Each chapter has exercises followed by musical etudes.

Jacobs, Wesley. *Technical Studies for Tuba*. Encore Music Publishers. 1990. $15.00. 40 pp. IV–V. A series of etudes (in all keys) that present a variety of pattern and interval studies together with a variety of suggested rhythm and articulation patterns. Excellent study repertoire for the serious student or the professional who wants material to maintain or sharpen skills.

Jacobs, Wesley, ed. *Restructured Etudes for Tuba, Volume I*. Encore Music Publishers. 1989. $12.00. 22 pp. IV–V. The five etudes in this volume are each presented in three different keys provide interesting technical and musical challenges. The editor makes suggestions for effective study and recommends these etudes for tubas in all keys.

Jacobs, Wesley, ed. *Restructured Etudes for Tuba, Volume II*. Encore Music Publishers. 1986. $15.00. 45 pp. IV–V. Each etude in this volume is presented in three different keys, and one of the occurrences is in a different meter. As in Volume I, the etudes are musically interesting and present challenges in all areas of technique. The editor recommends these etudes for tubas in all keys.

Jacobs, Wesley, ed. *Restructured Etudes for Tuba, Volume III.* Encore Music Publishers. 1986. $13.50 37 pp. IV–V. As in the previous two volumes, each etude is presented in three different keys, and, as in Volume II, one of the occurrences is in a different meter. The editor recommends these etudes for tubas in all keys.

Jacobs, Wesley, ed. *Restructured Etudes for Tuba, Volume IV.* Encore Music Publishers. 1986. $12.00. 33 pp. IV–V. The format for this volume is identical to that of the previous volumes in the same series.

Jacobs, Wesley, ed. *Restructured Etudes for Tuba, Volume V.* Encore Music Publishers. 1991. $17.00. 27 pp. IV–V. The format for this volume is identical to that of the previous volumes in the same series.

Jenson, Art. *Learning Unlimited—Audio Visual/Cassette Series (BB♭ Bass), Levels I and II.* Hal Leonard Publishing Corporation. 1971. $9.95 each. 48 pp. each. I–II. Designed primarily for individual instruction, this combination book/cassette method is usable by groups of like instruments and as supplementary material for any band method. The material is progressively organized according to complexity of each concept, beginning (in Level I) with buzzing the mouthpiece and concluding (in Level II) with playing in compound meter.

Jenson, Art. *Learning Unlimited—Class Series (BB♭ Bass), Level I.* Hal Leonard Publishing Corporation. 1973. $4.95. 64 pp. I. A beginning band method whose primary features include reference charts (listing each exercise by primary concept emphasized and as unison, duet, or full band), illustrations, and textual coloration.

Jenson, Art. *Learning Unlimited—Class Series (BB♭ Bass), Level II.* Hal Leonard Publishing Corporation. 1974. $4.95. 48 pp. II. Continues the expansion of harmonic, formal, and expressive skills, begun in the Level I book above.

Job, M., ed. *Ecole de Chant et de Style—Trente Airs Classiques.* Alphonse Leduc Editions Musicales. 1949. 11 pp. IV. See: Thompson/Lemke; *French Music for Low Brass Instruments.*

Johnson, Harold M. *Aeolian Method for E♭ or BB♭ Bass.* H. T. Fitzsimmons. Out of print. 1945. $1.00. 48 pp. I–II. Although billed as a method for group or private instruction, this method is definitely best suited to the individual lesson format, as little supplemental or explanatory material is included, and the pace is brisk. The selection of melodies included is excellent, and the brief etudes are well written.

Johnson, Keith. *Progressive Studies for the High Register.* Harold Gore Publishing. 1991. $10.00. 35 pp. III–V. These progressive studies in range development are intended for use as part of the player's daily routine. A good guide to study is provided at the beginning of the book.

Johnson, Stuart. *New Horizons Tuneful Tuba.*

Johnson, Tommy; Mark McDunn; and Harold Rusch. *The Tommy Johnson Tuba Methods, Book 1.* Neil A. Kjos Music Company. 1975. $1.75. 32 pp. I. Tommy Johnson is best known in the tuba world as a studio musician. For many years he has also been a successful teacher of young students. Here are his ideas for teaching the young tubist set for private instruction. The method includes familiar melodies and good preliminary comments on playing fundamentals.

Kietzer, Robert. *School for Self-instruction on the Tuba or Helicon, Op. 84* (in two parts). Verlag von Jul. Heinr. Zimmerman. Out of print. 1891.

Kietzer, Robert. *Schule für Tuba in B♭ oder C, Helikon, bombardon, Sousaphon, Op. 85.* (complete or in two parts). Wilhelm Zimmerman. Out of print. 112 pp. II–III. An early German tuba tutor that begins with a review of basic fundamentals of music reading and instrument address. The volume consists principally of short etudes in all keys suitable for the intermediate to advanced high school student. All fundamental areas of brass study are covered thoroughly. Text in German, English, and Russian.

Kietzer, Robert. *Schule für Tuba in F und E♭ oder Helikon, Op. 84.* Wilhelm Zimmerman. $13.25. 87 pp. I–IV.

Kinyon, John. *Basic Training Course for Tuba, Book 1.* Alfred Music Company. 1970. $5.50. 32 pp. I. A progressively organized method containing many short melodies. Although it is intended for private instruction, like-instrument classes, mixed ensembles, or beginning bands, its most appropriate use is as part of a beginning band course.

Kinyon, John. *Basic Training Course for Tuba, Book 2.* Alfred Music Company. 1971. $5.50. 32 pp. I–II.

Kinyon, John. *Breeze-Easy Method for BB flat Tuba, Book I.* Witmark. 1954. $5.95. 32 pp. I. A true classic, this text is designed for use individually or with other brass instruments. It introduces principles of musicianship and basic musical skills, as well as performance fundamentals in a thorough, logical manner.

Kinyon, John. *Breeze-Easy Method for BB flat Tuba, Book II.* Witmark. 1960. $5.95. 32 pp. I–II.

Kinyon, John. *Daily Half Dozens for Young Bands (Tuba).* Alfred Music Company. 1968. $1.00. 15 pp. I–II. Intended for group instruction, this book includes seven six exercise pre-rehearsal routines for full band. Each set includes a warm-up, scale study, rhythm exercise, round, contrapunctal study, and technique drill. Contains good suggestions for home practice.

Kinyon, John. *The MPH John Kinyon Band Method (Tuba).* Warner Brothers Music.

Kinyon, John. *Stepping Stones to Band Performance (Tuba).* Alfred Music Company. 1970. $1.00. 17 pp. I–II. This simple book for group instruction moves the ensemble from playing unison melodies to playing independent lines in a full band composition. Except for two full-length compositions at the end of the book, exercises are two to three lines long.

Kitchner, O. *Schule für Tuba.* (Stadt Bibliotheken, Munich). Domkowsky O. J. ca. 1910.

Kliment, Hans. *Anfänger-Schule für B-Tuba.*

Kliment, Hans. *Anfänger-Schule für F-Tuba oder Bass Posaune.*

Kliment. *B-Bass-Schule für Fortgeschrittene (Mittelstufe).* Musikverlag Johann Kliment, Vienna and Leipzig. Out of print..

Kliment. *Grifftabelle und Anfangsbrunde.*

Kling, H. *Leicht fassliche praktische Schule.* Louis Oertle. Out of print. 1898.

Kling, Henri. *32 Technical and Musical Studies for Tuba or Bass Trombone.* tr. Peter Popiel. Accura Music. $15.95. III–IV.

Klose and Vanasek. *270 Tone and Technique Exercises.*

Knaub, Donald. *Progressive Techniques for Tuba.* Hal Leonard Publishing Corporation. 1970. $14.95. 128 pp. III–IV. This method contains the 70 studies by Blazhevich with the addition of warm-up studies, scale studies, and editorial comments. The warm-up routine, based on the famous Emory Remington warm-up studies, together with Knaub's pedagogical comments make this a particularly valuable work for the tubist's library.

Kopprasch, C. *Sechzig usgewahlte Etuden* (60 Etudes). Two volumes. ed. Franz Seyffarth (Hofmeister). Freidrich Hofmeister. 27 pp. each. III–IV. This book (originally from the horn repertoire) represents one of the basic resources for study of brass technique. It has a wealth of interval and articulation studies and should be in every player's library. Also published for trumpet and trombone. Now also available from Hofmeister in a single volume.

Kopprasch, C. *Sixty Studies for Tuba.* Robert King Music Company. $4.80. 52 pp. III–IV. (See previous entry.)

Krzystek, W. *Studia na puzon i tube.* Polish Music Edition (P. W. M.), Krakow.

Kuhn, John M., and Jaroslav Cimera. *Kuhn-Cimera Method for Tuba (BB flat and E flat).* Belwin-Mills. 1941. $5.50. 48 pp. I–II. Intended as an introductory method for private study. Written by two of the "giants" of low brass pedagogy early in the twentieth century. Covers basic fundamentals, and includes familiar tunes from Classical and folk repertoire.

Laas, Bill, and Fred Weber. *Advanced Fun with Fundamentals (Tuba).* Belwin-Mills. $5.50. II–III.

Laas, Bill, and Fred Weber. *Fun with Fundamentals (Tuba).* Belwin-Mills. 1963. $5.50. 28 pp. I–II. A supplemental method which emphasizes technical development through elementary scales, etudes, and duets.

Laas, Bill, and Fred Weber. *Studies and Melodious Etudes for Tuba (Bass), Level I.* Belwin-Mills. 1969. $5.50. 32 pp. I–II. The first in a series of three books (for Books II and III, see Swanson, Vincent, and Ployhar, below) designed as a supplementary

technique book to be used with the Tuba (Bass) Student Instrumental Course. It addresses the development of musicianship through scales and technical/melodic etudes.

Labole, P. *Méthode Complète I et II.* See: Thompson/ Lemke; *French Music for Low Brass Instruments.*

Lachmann, Hans. *25 Etuden nach Josef Hrabe.* Friedrich Hofmeister. 1956. IV–V.

Lachmann, Hans. *26 Etudes für Tuba.* Friedrich Hofmeister. 1956. 15 pp. III. These fine etudes for the average high school student or good intermediate student also present good fundamental review possibilities for the beginning college student. They are principally studies in technique, time, and articulation, similar to the Robert Getchell studies.

Lange, W. *Etüden und Vortragstücke: Tuba I (F–Es).* Schulz. 1980.

Lange, W. *Etüden und Vortragstücke: Tuba II (C).* Schulz. 1980.

Langey, O.K. *The Bass.*

Langey, O.K. *Langey–Carl Fischer Tutors for BBb Bass.* Carl Fischer, Incorporated. Out of print. 1944. $1.50 80 pp. II–III. Although an introduction to the rudiments of music starts this text, it is probably not intended for a beginner, as it moves at an accelerated pace through all fundamental aspects of playing. Studies are arranged according to key. This method is similar to the Arban and Rubank methods in its approach to the introduction of new material and exercises.

Langey, O. K. *Practical Tutor for Bb Bass.* Boosey & Hawkes, Incorporated.

Langey, O. K. *Practical Tutor for Eb Bass.* Boosey & Hawkes, Incorporated.

Lebedjev, A. *Tuba Tutor, Vol. 1.* Moscow Muzyka. 1984. 70 pp. II–III. The text of this method by the most famous Russian tuba pedagogues is in Russian only. It includes warm-up etudes in various keys, progressive technical and melodic etudes, and solos well suited to the average high school student. Piano accompaniment is included for most etudes and solos.

Lee, William F., and James Progris. *I Wanna Play the Tuba.* Charles Hanson II Music and Books of California, Inc. 1979. $2.95. 33 pp. I. A basic beginning method for private instruction. It introduces music reading and fundamentals using simple but (generally) well-known melodies.

Lehman, Cliff, and Susan Taylor. *Sound Method for Band in Four Volumes (Tuba).* Belwin-Mills. $5.50 each.

Leidig, Vernon. *Visual Band Method, Books I and II (Tuba—Eb and BBb).* ed. Lennie Niehaus. Highland Music Company. 1965. $1.00. each 35 pp. I–II. A method for full beginning band instruction. It is typical of such methods with regard to presentation of basic material and very short etudes and melodies. Fingerings for new notes are supplemented with photographs of fingers depressing appropriate valves.

Leidig, Vernon, and Lennie Niehaus. *Visual Intermediate Band Method (Tuba—E♭ and BB♭)*. Highland Music Company. 1968. $1.25. 27 pp. II. A continuation of the method above. Contains eight lessons covering eight major and two minor keys, with scales, thirds and varied articulations, rhythms, and meters. Several parts for works for full band are included at the end of the book.

Lelong, F. *Special Exercises for Flexibility and Scales for B♭ Euphonium and Tenor and Bass Tuba in Two Books*. Alphonse Leduc Editions Musicales. 1981. $15.00. each. 20 pp. each. I–IV. Written by Paris Conservatoire Professor Lelong. The first book deals with flexibility exercises, the second with development of technique through scales. The exercises can be adapted to virtually any level of student and provide good material for daily routine.

Lelong, F. *Tuba Method, Books I, II, III*. Editions Billaudot. $13.25.

Lesaffre, C., and Lelong, F. *Petite Chanson pour Marion*. Editions Billaudot. $5.75.

Linderman. *Melodious Fundamentals*.

Lindkvist, Janne. *Tore Tuba's Første Spelbok; Nybørjarskola Før Tuba*. Mo Brass Musikförlag, Sweden. 1988. 46 pp. I. Intended for private instruction at the beginning level, this volume is filled with entertaining caricatures and simple songs (with Scandinavian text), duets, and tunes with piano harmonization. Intended primarily for beginning E♭ tubists, but also suitable for the BB♭ tuba.

Linke, E., ed. *Tonstudien und Orchesterauszüge berühmter Meister für F und Es-Tuba* (Hochschule der Künste, Berlin). Verlag Militärmusik-Zeitung.

Little, Donald C., with James D. Ployhar *Practical Hints on Playing the Tuba*. Belwin-Mills. 1984. $5.50. 41 pp. II–III. A concise method-text with several explanatory pages devoted to proper instrument/mouthpiece selection, playing position, tone production, instrument maintenance, and other aspects of playing. Includes photos.

Little, Lowell. *Embouchure Builder for BB♭ Bass (Tuba)*. Pro Art Publications. 1954. $4.50. 16 pp. II–III. A supplementary method which stresses long tone and flexibility practice. Intended for use during the warm-up period.

Maddy, J. E. and Thadeus P. Giddings. *Universal Teacher for Orchestra and Band (E♭ and BB♭ tuba)*. Willis Music Company. Out of print. 1923. $3.00. 34 pp. II–III. A historic first method for group band instruction. (Maddy and Giddings were also the founders of the Interlochen National Music Camp.) A rapidly moving, progressive method. Includes developmental etudes, and band parts to works arranged by Maddy.

Maenz, Otto. *Zwölf Spezialastudien für Tuba*. Friedrich Hofmeister. $12.25. 16 pp. IV.

Magnell, Elmer P. *68 Pares Studies for E♭ or BB♭ Tuba*. Belwin-Mills. 1957. II–III.

Magnell, Elmer P. *29 Schantl Studies for Tuba*. Belwin-Mills. 1959. III.

Makela, Steven. *Thirteen Etudes for Tuba*. T.U.B.A. Press. 1992. $8.00. 25 pp. III–V. Intended primarily for the college or professional player, although a few of the etudes are useful for the serious high school student. While the studies are very musical, the technical emphasis is on development of even tone across the full range of the tuba, most covering a three-octave range.

Marchesi, Mathilde, and Heinrich Panofka. *28 Advanced Studies for Tuba*. tr. David L. Kuehn. Southern Music Company. 1972. $15.00. 55 pp. IV–V. These advanced etudes in legato style and technique are suitable for the advanced, serious high school student, but are also interesting practice material for the college or professional player. A variety of keys and meters are covered.

Mariani, A. *Popular Method for Tuba*. Editions Salabert.

Mariani, Giuseppe. *Metodo Popolare per Flicorno Contrabasso Si♭*. G. Ricordi & Company. 1957.

Maros, M. *Etydes for Tuba*. AB Nordiska Musikforlaget. 1943.

Maxwell, Roger. *Fourteen Weeks to a Better Band (Tuba)*, *Vol. I*. C. L. Barnhouse Company. $4.00. I–II. For grades 7-9. A group method designed to improve sight reading through the study of basic rhythmic figures and their use across musical styles.

Maxwell, Roger. *Fourteen Weeks to a Better Band (Tuba)*, *Vol. II*. C. L. Barnhouse Company. $4.50. II–III. For grades 9-12. An advanced version of Vol. I. The rhythmic figures are virtually the same, but more challenging exercises are presented for the high school student.

Maxwell, Roger. *Fourteen Weeks to an Improved Band (Tuba)*. Roger Maxwell Publications. 1985. $3.50. 31 pp. I–II. For grade 5-7 students. A rapidly progressive method which quickly addresses dotted-eighth–sixteenth-note rhythms, syncopation, and other intermediate skills.

McLeod, James, and Norman Staska. *Rhythm Etudes (Tuba)*. Belwin-Mills. 1966. $5.00. 31 pp. II. A progressively organized method with emphasis on a variety of keys and meters.

McLeod, James, and Norman Staska. *Scale Etudes (Tuba, String Bass)*. Belwin-Mills. 1963. $5.50. 33 pp. I–II. Contains scale-based etudes, each written in octaves.

Meschke, D. *Tuba Fibel*.

Meschke, Dieter. *60 Etüden für Kontrabasstuba*. Friedrich Hofmeister.

Mestdagh, P. *Methoden voor Trombone, Tuba*. Metropolis.

Michalek, J. *Method*.

Michel, J. Fr. *Blattlese-Schule*. Editions Marc Reift.

Michel, J. Fr. *Schule für B und Es Bass*. Editions Marc Reift.

Mityagin. *37 Selected Etudes for Tuba*. MCA.

Moeck, Walter. *Tuba Warm-Ups*. C. L. Barnhouse Company. 1976. $1.50. 5 pp. II–III. A warm-up routine with lip slurs in various meters and up to c¹. A good "taking off place" in establishing a solid daily routine.

Moore, E. C. *Elements of Band Technic (Tuba)*. Summy-Birchard Publishing Company. 1958. 16 pp. III.

Moore, E. C. *The Moore Band Course (BB♭ Bass)*. Carl Fischer, Incorporated. Out of print. 1930. 39 pp. I–II. Intended for group instruction, this early band method includes rudiments of musicianship and numerous exercises in solo and duet form based on familiar tunes. Pedagogical comments given on the facing page describe each exercise's intent and suggestions for its accomplishment.

Moore, E. C. *The Moore Band Course (E♭ Bass)*. Carl Fischer, Incorporated. Out of print. 1930. 39 pp. I–II. Identical to the above entry with appropriate adjustments for range, etc., applicable to the E♭ tuba.

Moore, E. C., and A. O. Sieg. *Preparatory Instructor for Basses (BB♭ and E♭)*. Carl Fischer, Incorporated. 1937/67. $.75. 32 pp. I–II. An elementary tutor for private instruction, this book gives a rudimentary introduction to addressing the instrument, breath, and articulation. Although the exercises are somewhat pedantic, they are pedagogically well thought out and, supplemented with melodic material, they are quite useful.

Mühlbacher, F. *Schule für Bass-Tuba in B oder C, F und Es-Tuba/Helikon*. Solistenverlag.

Müller. *Technische Studien für Bassposaune und Tuba*.

Murphy, Bower. *Advanced Tuba Etudes*. ed. Constance Weldon. Charles Colin. 1969. 63 pp. III–IV. Written by a noted American brass pedagogue. These etudes are in all major and minor keys and cover both lyric and technical styles. Very good for use with serious high school students, and excellent, challenging reading material for the college student.

Muzzi, Pietro. *Raccolta di pezzi di autori classici per Flicorni Bassi Gravi e Contrabassi (Tube)*. Musicali Ortipe.

O'Reilly, John, and John Kinyon. *Yamaha Band Student, Book III (Tuba)*. Alfred Music Company. 1989. $5.50. 31 pp. II. A continuation of the first two volumes (see above, Feldstein and O'Reilly), this book is directed more toward skill improvement for intermediate players. Compound meters and more major and minor keys are explored.

Osmon, Leroy. *Concert Etudes for Solo Tuba*. Southern Music Company. 1991. $3.50. 7 pp. IV–V. Intended for concert performance, these etudes are somewhat programmatic and definitely challenging for the most serious performer. High range, technique, and flexibility are all thoroughly tested.

Ostling, Acton, and Fred Weber. *Tunes for Tuba (Bass) Technic, Levels I and II*. Belwin-Mills. 1969/70. $5.50 each. 32 pp. each. I–II. Like the *Studies and Melodious Etudes for Tuba (Bass)* series (see above, Laas and Weber), this series is a member of the Belwin Student Instrumental Course and is designed as a supplement to the primary series, *The Tuba (Bass) Student*. Whereas the *Studies and Melodious Etudes* series is primarily of a technical nature, the *Tunes for Tuba* series is purely melodic and thus emphasizes the development of musicality.

Ostling, Acton, and Nilo W. Hovey. *Section Studies for Low Range Basses*. Belwin-Mills.

Ostrander, Allen. *Low Tone Studies*. Charles Colin. $4.95.

Ostrander, Allen. *Shifting Meter Studies for Bass Trombone or Tuba*. Robert King Music Company. 1965. $2.00. 20 pp. III–IV. Primarily intended for the double-valved bass trombone, these studies provide excellent material for improving a student's sense of time and sight reading. They do not present undue technical challenges, thus allowing the student to focus on the principal objective of the etudes.

Ostrander, Allen. *Twenty-Minute Warmup*. Charles Colin.

Pares, G. *Daily Exercises and Scales for BB♭ Bass*. rev. E. Claus. Carl Fischer, Incorporated. 1912. $6.00. 32 pp. II–III. A classic text for scale study for band students. Emphasis is on flat major and minor keys with short sections on chromatic scales and arpeggios. Scales are presented in a variety of rhythmic and articulation patterns.

Pares, G. *Gammes et Exercices Journaliers pour Basse*. Henry Lemoine et Co. Out of print. 1896. 31 pp.

Pares, G. *Gammes et Exercices Journaliers pour Contre-Basse ou Saxhorn Contre-Basse*. Henry Lemoine et Co. Out of print. 1896. 31 pp.

Pares, G. *Méthode de Contrebasse (ou Saxhorn-Contrebasse)*. Chez Henry Lemoine. 47 pp.

Pares, G. *Méthode Elémentaire de Tuba*.

Pares, G. *Pares Scales for BB♭ Bass*. rev. and ed. by Harvey S. Whistler. Rubank, Incorporated. 1946. $4.95. 48 pp. II–III. Contains all the major and minor scales in a variety of rhythmic patterns. An excellent review or introductory text for scale study.

Pares, G. *Pares Scales for E flat Tuba*. rev. and ed. by Harvey S. Whistler. Rubank, Incorporated. 1946. $4.95. 48 pp. II–III. Identical to the book listed above with appropriate adjustments made for the E♭ instrument.

Paudert, Ernst. *Etudes for Tuba*. Encore Music Publishers. $9.00. 12 pp. IV–V. The emphasis is on technique for the advanced player. These studies are well suited to the F tuba and the euphonium, and cover all the major keys.

Paulson, Joseph. *Get in Rhythm (Basses and String Bass)*. Pro Art Publications. 1948. 31 pp. I–II.

Paulson, Joseph. *Play Right Away*. Pro Art Publications. Out of print. 1953. 36 pp. I. This is a march-size publication for beginning instruction.

Pearson, Bruce. *Best in Class, Books I and II (Tuba).* ed. Gerald Anderson and Charles Forque. Neil A. Kjos Music Company. 1982/83. $4.95 each. 32 pp. each. I. A standard band method which is correlated with a series of compositions for full band and is published for both E♭ and BB♭ tubas, in both treble and bass clefs.

Pearson, Bruce. *Encore (Tuba)!* ed. Gerald Anderson and Charles Forque. Neil A. Kjos Music Company. 1985. $3.95. 32 pp. I. Intended as a supplement to the *Best in Class* series. Provides solos, duets, trios, rounds, and full band arrangements (tuba part) as a reinforcement of basic performance skills.

Pearson, Bruce, and Chuck Elledge. *A Best in Class Christmas (Tuba).* Neil A. Kjos Music Company. 1988. $3.45. 24 pp. I. A supplement to the *Best in Class* series of method books. Contains several familiar carols, all of which include the melody, the bass part, and a harmony part.

Pearson, Bruce, and Chuck Elledge. *A Best in Class Showcase (Tuba).* Neil A. Kjos Music Company. 1989. $3.95. 24 pp. I. Presents popular march, folk, or Classical melodies.

Pease, Donald J. *Pro Art E♭ or BB♭ Bass (Tuba and Sousaphone) Method.* Pro Art Publications. 1964. $5.00. 48 pp. I–II. A rapidly progressive method with special emphasis on exposure to a variety of keys.

Pease, Donald J. *Starting the Band—Basses.* Pro Art Publications. 1951. 36 pp. I. A march-size publication for beginning instruction.

Pepper, J. W. *J. W. Pepper's New and Popular Self Instructor for the B♭ Bass.* J. W. Pepper. Out of print. 1886. 64 pp. I–III. This very early American method for the tuba or euphonium includes rudiments of musicianship and a wealth of melodies from contemporary European and American composers, many of which remain important today. Includes beginning etudes introducing various concepts essential for the development of basic skills.

Pepper, J. W. *J. W. Pepper's Self Instructor for B♭ Bass.* J. W. Pepper. Out of print. 1879. $.50. I–III. Contains etudes in all major and minor keys and 50 classic, popular, and operatic melodies.

Pepper, J. W. *J. W. Pepper's Self Instructor for E♭ Bass.* J. W. Pepper. Out of print. 1879. $.50. I–III. Contains etudes in all major and minor keys and 50 classic, popular, and operatic melodies.

Peters, Charles, and Matt Betton. *Take One (Basses).* Neil A. Kjos Music Company. 1972. $1.95. 32 pp. I. A beginning method which is traditional in its introduction of fundamental theory and basic playing skills and nontraditional in its inclusion of several contest-length solos (including piano accompaniment), band-related photographs, and jazz pedagogy.

Peters, Charles S. *Master Method for Band, Book I (Basses).* ed. Paul Yoder. Neil A. Kjos Music Company. 1958. $3.45. 32 pp. I. Progresses rapidly

through the first year of instrumental instruction with an emphasis on rhythmic, harmonic, and pedagogical development through "count-time" exercises, duets, and instructional ideas within each lesson.

Peters, Charles S. *Master Method for Band, Book II (Basses).* ed. Paul Yoder. Neil A. Kjos Music Company. 1959. $3.45. 32 pp. I–II. A continuation of Book I, with the addition of "artist variation" exercises—exercises which are technically oriented variations of previously introduced etudes.

Peters, Charles S. *Master Method for Band, Book III (Basses).* ed. Paul Yoder. Neil A. Kjos Music Company. 1964. $3.45. 31 pp. II–III. Emphasizes the development of articulation, phrasing, and ensemble skills. Continues the "artist variation" concept of Book II, with the addition of concert-length, full band accompaniments to the variations.

Peters, Charles S. *Total Range (Tuba).* Neil A. Kjos Music Company. 1976. $2.45. 36 pp. II–V. Presents a progressive, cumulative approach to range development from low to high. Lessons are presented in a format of weekly goals and exercises, always building on and including material studied previously.

Peters, Charles S., and Paul Yoder. *Master Drills: Scales and Skills (Basses).* Neil A. Kjos Music Company. 1962. 17 pp. I–II.

Pethel, Stan. *Twenty Etudes for Tuba.* T.U.B.A. Press. 1992. $10.00. 41 pp. IV. These advanced etudes cover a broad range of styles (song, waltz, blues, etc.) and keys. Most focus on the mid-range of the instrument and avoid the extreme outside ranges. Recommended for the serious college student.

Phillips, Harry I. *Silver Burdett Instrumental Series (E♭ and BB♭ Tubas), Volumes I and II.* Hal Leonard Publishing Corporation. 1969. $3.95 each. 74 pp. each. I–III. Simple yet thorough method by one of the most respected music textbook publishers. Includes duets and trios in addition to technical and lyrical studies.

Phillips, Harvey G., and William Winkle. *The Art of Tuba and Euphonium.* Summy-Birchard Publishing Company. 1992. $14.95. 98 pp. I–V. Covers all aspects of tuba performance and pedagogy. The chapter on developing and maintaining performance skills includes a suggested warm-up routine and short exercises emphasizing aspects of proper fundamental development.

Pilant, F. *Bass Tuba School.*

Pilant, F. *Pro Art Method.*

Ployhar, James, and George Zepp. *3-D Band Book (Bass/Tuba).* Belwin-Mills. 1983. $5.50. 40 pp. II–III. A supplemental method for full band which emphasizes the development of tuning, counting, and scale skills.

Ployhar, James D. *Band Today, Part I and II (Tuba).* Belwin-Mills. 1977. $5.50 each. 32 pp. each. I–II. A standard band method for individual or group instruction.

Ployhar, James D. *Band Today, Part III*. Belwin-Mills. 1978. $5.50. 32 pp. II. Contains a small amount of work in Gb major and a section which teaches rudimental ornamentation.

Ployhar, James D. *I Recommend*. Belwin-Mills. 1972. $5.50. 32 pp. II–III. A supplemental warm-up book, this volume covers scales and arpeggios, as well as articulation, intervals, dynamics, and rhythm. A review of musical rudiments concludes the book.

Ployhar, James D. *Medalist Band Method (Tuba) in Three Volumes*. Belwin-Mills. $5.00 each. I–II.

Ployhar, James D. *Technic Today (Tuba) in Three Volumes*. Belwin-Mills. 1977/78/79. $5.50 each. 24 pp. each. I–III. A supplemental series organized according to key.

Ployhar, James D., and George Zepp. *Tone and Technic through Chorales and Etudes (Tuba)*. Belwin-Mills. $5.50 each. II. Includes exercises in four-part harmony for full band, duets, and technical studies for individual instruments, all intended to be used in the ensemble setting, although the technical studies may be used in individual practice as well.

Pniak, Jan. *Mala Szdola na Tube*. Polish Music Edition (P. W. M.), Krakow. 1986.

Pniak, Jan. *Szkola na tube BB, CC, Es, F*. Polish Music Edition (P. W. M.), Krakow. In progress.

Popiel, Peter. *Thirty Vocalises for Tuba*. Accura Music. 1992. 64 pp. IV. These etudes from works of composers of the Baroque, Classic, and Romantic periods emphasize low-register legato style. They progress from least to most difficult. Each etude is well thought-out and presents an excellent challenge for the college student.

Porret, J. *Mécanisme (A)*.

Porret, J. *Méthode Progressive*.

Porret, J. *Vingt-quatre Etudes Mélodiques*.

Poullot, François. *Préambule* (Preamble), *Book 1. Saxhorn Basse/Contrebasse Sib., Tuba en ut (six valves)*. Alphonse Leduc Editions Musicales. 1982. $37.95. 55 pp. I–II. An elementary text for the tuba, introducing basic aspects of playing (tone production, rhythm reading, scales, etc.). Includes a history of the tuba and euphonium. The mode of presentation is not far removed from that of the classic Arban method.

Poullot, François. *Préambule* (Preamble), *Book 2. Saxhorn Basse/Contrebasse Sib., Tuba en ut (six valves)*. Alphonse Leduc Editions Musicales. 1982. $37.95. 58 pp. III–IV. Systematically organized according to meter, this book includes scalar, intervallic, and arpeggiated exercises in the keys of C major, A minor, F major, D minor, G major, and E minor. A book for the very serious intermediate to early advanced player. Considerable upper-register demands. Pedagogical comments included.

Poullot, François. *Préambule* (Preamble), *Book 3. Saxhorn Basse/Contrebasse Sib., Tuba en ut (six valves)*. Alphonse Leduc Editions Musicales. 1986. $44.35.

74 pp. III–IV. Continuation of the series with a more involved study of range and meter.

Poullot, François. *Traité des Gammes d'Après Balay. Volume 1, Tuba/Saxhorns Basses*. Alphonse Leduc Editions Musicales. $25.30.

Poullot, François. *Traité des Gammes d'Après Balay. Volume 2, Tuba/Saxhorns Basses*. Alphonse Leduc Editions Musicales. $25.30.

Prescott, Gerald R. *The Prescott Technic System, Parts I and II*. Carl Fischer, Incorporated. 1935/63. $1.40. 10 pp. A set of lesson plans designed as a guide to teaching the *Complete Arban Method*. Part I includes the first and second sets of preparatory exercises and plans for the first through fourth years of studies. Part II includes fifth- through twelfth-year lesson plans.

Prevet, H. *Méthode pour Saxhorn Basse*.

Pucci, Salvatore. *Studi per Bassi Gravi e Contrabassi Sib*. Musicali Florio.

Ranieri, V. *30 Instruktive und Melodisce Übungsstücke für Tuba oder Fagott* (in three volumes). Louis Oertel & Co. Out of print. 11 pp. each. III–IV. Each volume of this set contains 10 tonal etudes in progressively more difficult keys.

Rascusen, David. *Canonic Etudes*. See same work under "Music for Multiple Tubas: Three Part."

Reger, Wayne M. *The Talking Tuba*. Charles Colin. 1967. $4.95. 24 pp. I–III. A basic method designed to supplement other texts and emphasize very basic fundamentals. This work features cartoon illustrations with a humorous flavor.

Reift, Marc. *Einspielübung* . Editions Marc Reift.

Reift, Marc. *Rhythmus-Schule*. Editions Marc Reift.

Rhodes, Tom, and Donald Bierschenk. *Symphonic Band Technique (Tuba)*. Southern Music Company. 1986. $4.50. 32 pp. III–IV. Supplemental warm-up method for the high school/college-level band. Emphasizes the development of tone and phrasing as well as the development of technique through major and minor scale study in various meters, with various articulations.

Rhodes, Tom C.; Donald Bierschenk; and Tim Lautzenheiser. *Essential Elements: A Comprehensive Band Method:Tuba* (in two volumes). Hal Leonard Publishing Corporation. 1991. 32 pp. each. $5.50 each. I–II. A beginning method that includes much supplementary material. Extra attention has been given to using a broad range of tunes, ranging from Classical repertoire to melodies from around the world, together with the history of the melody and/or information about the melody's ethnic origin. An introduction to conducting is one of the more unusual inclusions.

Rhodes, Tom C.; Donald Bierschenk; and Tim Lautzenheiser. *Essential Technique: Intermediate to Advanced Studies Essential Elements Band Method: Tuba*. Hal Leonard Publishing Corporation. 1993. 48 pp. $5.95. II.

Rhodes, Tom C.; Donald Bierschenk; and Tim Lautzenheiser. *Instant Success: Tuba*. Hal Leonard Publishing Corporation. 1993. 16 pp. $3.50. I. This book is useful for the first two to three weeks of beginning instruction, introducing the most basic fundamentals of tone production and music reading. It is designed to complement any beginning method.

Ridgeon, John. *Brass for Beginners: Studies for Brass Instruments in Bass Clef.* Boosey & Hawkes, Incorporated.

Ridgeon, John. *Eight Graded Lip Flexibility Studies.* Belwin-Mills. 1981. I. Boosey & Hawkes, Incorporated.

Rieunier, Françoise. *Twenty-two Rhythmic Instrumental Sightreading Exercises (for All Instruments).* Alphonse Leduc Editions Musicales. 1972. 15 pp. IV–V. These challenging and interesting etudes provide the ultimate in sight-reading practice for the advanced student or professional. None of the etudes have clefs or keys, so those factors may be adjusted for each instrument appropriately. In addition to standard meters, beat groupings of 5/2, 3/2, etc., are found. See: Thompson/Lemke; *French Music for Low Brass Instruments.*

Rinderspacher, Karl. *Neue Schule für Tuba in F oder Es.*

Rinderspacher, Karl. *Schule für Tuba in B oder C.*

Robinson, Jack. *Advanced Conditioning Studies.* Whaling Music Publishers. $12.50. 72 pp. III–V. A comprehensive text on warm-up and daily routine as related to building strength and endurance. Includes extensive text explaining the author's position and pedagogical philosophy and exercises for implementation. The author was influenced in his writing by experts in Nautilus training and by tuba pedagogues William Bell and Don Harry.

Robinson, Jack. *Musical Tuba Playing.* Encore Music Publishers. 1992. $42.00. 116 pp. III–V. A complete text with detailed instruction and etudes that cover traditional areas (tuning, breath, articulation, etc.) for BBb, CC, and F tubas, as well as some less commonly discussed topics. An interesting addition to every teacher's and student's library.

Rollinson, T. H. *Rollinson's Modern School for the Eb and Double Bb Bass.* Oliver Ditson Company Boston. Out of print. 1905. 96 pp. I–III. A typical tutor that introduces all rudiments of music and contains technical studies, etudes, scales, and contemporary popular melodies. This method is unusual in that it contains twenty military band excerpts/preparatory studies.

Ronka, Ilmari. *Modern Daily Warm-ups and Drills.* Carl Fischer, Incorporated.

Rossari and Muzzi. *Studi di Perfezionamento per Tuba (Flicorno Basso Grave e Contrabasso).* 2 Volumes. Musicali Ortipe.

Rusch, Harold W. *Eighteen Barrett and Jancourt Studies for Tuba.* Belwin-Mills.

Rusch, Harold W. *Hal Leonard Elementary Band Method (Tuba).* Hal Leonard Publishing Corporation. $3.50.

Rusch, Harold W. *Hal Leonard Intermediate Band Method (Tuba).* Hal Leonard Publishing Corporation. 1961. $3.50. 44 pp. I–II. Emphasizes rhythmic development through the use of rhythm charts.

Rusch, Harold W. *Hal Leonard Advanced Band Method for Basses.* Hal Leonard Publishing Corporation. 1963. 64. III–IV. Includes nineteen pages of exercises/etudes composed and/or compiled by Arnold Jacobs, with brief commentary by this legendary master teacher. The remainder of the book is a class method for band.

Rusch, Harold W. *Twenty-five Lazarus-Concone Studies for Tuba.* Belwin-Mills. 1956. $5.50. 28 pp. II–III. A follow-up text to the *Arban-Klose-Concone Studies* but with emphasis on articulation, phrasing, and dynamics rather than rhythm. Each etude has a direct and obvious emphasis on correct performance of a particular fundamental area.

Rusch, Harold W. *Twenty-four Arban-Klose-Concone Studies.* Belwin-Mills. 1956. $5.50. 29 pp. II–III. For private lesson or class/full band instruction. Specific etudes have been chosen from the more complete methods listed in the title to provide focus for specific performance problems, generally based in rhythm. Each study consists of a unison etude and an accompaniment part to be played by other class members when used in a band setting.

Rusch, Harold W., and Alfred F. Barto. *Breath Control and Tuning and Intonation Studies for Wind Instrument Players.* Fillmore Music House. Out of print. 1949. $1.25. 32 pp. III. Detailed suggestions for breath control and tuning that apply to all instruments are followed by specific intonation correction solutions for each of the traditional bass-clef band instruments. Sixteen lessons follow, each with specific objectives and pedagogical comments regarding improvement of breath and intonation. Although much information is out-dated, much remains valuable.

Rys, Gilbert. *Cinquante [50] Etudes de Perfectionnement pour Tuba Contrebasse Ut, Tuba B, Tenor Ut.* Alphonse Leduc Editions Musicales. $16.40. See: Thompson/Lemke; *French Music for Low Brass Instruments.*

Rys, Gilbert. *Cinquante [50] Etudes Faciles pour Tuba Contrebasse Ut, Tuba Basse Fa, Tuba Tenor Ut.* Alphonse Leduc Editions Musicales. $22.40. See: Thompson/Lemke; *French Music for Low Brass Instruments.*

Rys, Gilbert. *Cinquante [50] Etudes Progressives.* Robert Martin Editions Musicales. $12.50. See: Thompson/Lemke; *French Music for Low Brass Instruments.*

Salvo, Victor. *Fun Workbook for Tuba.* Pro Art Publications. 1973. $1.50. 37 pp. I–II. A book of theory worksheets at the beginning level applied to the tuba range. Includes fingering charts. A possible supplement to any method book.

Salvo, Victor V. *241 Double and Triple Tonguing Exercises for Trombone-Baritone-Tuba.* Belwin-Mills.

1973. $5.50. 36 pp. III–IV. A progressive method for the study of multiple tonguing. Includes suggestions for practice procedures, measuring progress, and additional sources of material.

Sargent, W. A. Barrington. *Lip Builders or Daily Stimulants.* Cundy-Bettoney. Out of print. 1911. $.75. 8 pp. I–III. Very simple warm-up and flexibility studies designed to improve tone quality, endurance, and articulation. Pedagogical suggestions occur at the beginning of the book as well as between the four series of studies.

Sawhill, Clarence, and Frank Erickson. *Bourne Guide to the Band (Tuba), Book I.* Bourne Company. 1955. 31 pp. I. Intended only for group instruction. Integrates unison melodies and exercises with short pieces in parts, requiring independence on the part of each section.

Sawhill, Clarence, and Frank Erickson. *Bourne Guide to the Band (Tuba), Book II.* Bourne Company. 1956. 28 pp. I–II.

Sear, Walter. *Etudes for Tuba.* Cor Publishing Company. 1969. $6.00. 32 pp. IV. Forty-five challenging etudes for the advanced tubist that present balanced study of upper and lower registers. Contains arrangements of excerpts from three of the Bach cello suites.

Sebesky, Gerald. *Fundamentals for Beginning Bands (Tuba).* C. L. Barnhouse Company. $2.25. I. Supplementary material for group methods. An activity book to enhance study of music fundamentals for young students.

Senon, G., *Préludes Faciles pour Tuba Tenor (Vol. 1).* Robert Martin Editions Musicales. 1983. $12.75. 32 pp. III–IV. Though the first several pages of this method are playable by an advanced junior high student, it is generally suited to the high school and college levels. The overall tessitura is high and there are many studies in changing meters.

Senon, G., and Ferdinand Lelong. *Kaleidoscope (in Three Volumes).* Editions Billaudot. 1983. $13.50 each. 23 pp.each. III–IV. Although designated as elementary, these etudes would be challenging melodically and rhythmically for the advanced intermediate student and in range for the advanced student. A very good choice for the developing F or E♭ tuba player. See: Thompson/Lemke, *French Music for Low Brass Instruments.*

Shoemaker, John. *Legato Etudes for Tuba Based on the Vocalises of Giuseppe Concone.* Carl Fischer, Incorporated. 1969. $8.00. 30 pp. III–IV. Similar to the Concone etudes edited by David Kuehn. Very good pedagogical comments on legato style and how to perform it properly are included in the Foreword.

Sieber, Ferdinand. *Sixty Musical Studies for Tuba (Book II).* tr. David L. Kuehn. Southern Music Company. 1969. $7.50. 21 pp. III–IV. Studies in legato style from the vocalises of Concone and Marchesi, with special attention to phrasing and reading problems. Very nice studies for the high school student or a

good beginning lyrical study book for the college student.

Singer, Larry. *Etudes for Tuba, Volume I.* ed. Wesley Jacobs. Encore Music Publishers. 1986. $15.00. 43 pp. III–V. Very appropriate for bass or contrabass tubas. Some of the etudes are built on familiar melodies. Some excellent challenges in the areas of interval study and unusual rhythmic figures. Each etude is presented in three different keys.

Singer, Larry. *Etudes for Tuba, Volume II.* ed. Wesley Jacobs. Encore Music Publishers. 1986. $15.00. 45 pp. III–V.

Skornicka, J. E., and E. G. Boltz. *Rubank Intermediate Method for E♭ and BB♭ Bass.* Rubank, Incorporated. 1934. $4.95. 48 pp. II–III. A continuation of the Hovey *Rubank Elementary Method,* this work progresses through various keys and uses pleasing, familiar melodies. A perennial good choice for the interested, young student who needs listenable tunes to help solve fundamental problems.

Skornicka, J. E. and Joseph Bergheim. *The Boosey and Hawkes Band Method (Tuba).* Boosey & Hawkes, Incorporated. Out of print. 1947. $.75. 32 pp. I–II. A method for group band study, this text introduces basic rudiments of musicianship using familiar tunes. Pedagogical comments given at the beginning of the book are spare.

Slama, Anton. *66 Etudes in All Major and Minor Keys for Trombone, Tuba, Bassoon, String Bass.* Carl Fischer, Incorporated. 1922. $7.00. 45 pp. III–V. These etudes provide the advanced student with fine material for all aspects of articulation and technique. The material is particularly well suited to the F tuba; however, it is very beneficial to the contrabass tubist who needs to improve upper-register facility, or it could be read down one octave for solid work on technique and articulation.

Slokar, B. *Tägliche Übungen* . Editions Marc Reift.

Slokar, B. *Tonleitern/Gammes/Scales, Vol. I und II.* ed. Marc Reift. Editions Marc Reift.

Smith, Claude; Paul Yoder; and Harold Bachman. *Smith-Yoder-Bachman Ensemble Band Method (Basses).* Neil A. Kjos Music Company. 1939. $1.00. 32 pp. I. A group method with emphasis on developing player independence through use of two-, three-, and four-part exercises, as well as full band arrangements. A series of theory lessons as well as familiar melodies.

Smith, Claude B. *All-State Band Method.* Pro Art Publications. 1961. 24 pp. I.

Smith, Claude T. *Symphonic Rhythms and Scales (Tuba).* Hal Leonard Publishing Corporation. 1984. $3.95. 24 pp. II–III. A supplementary method with emphasis on rhythmic development through the use of syncopation, ties, and accentuation.

Smith, Claude T. *Symphonic Techniques for Band (Tuba).* Hal Leonard Publishing Corporation. 1987. $3.95. 32 pp. III–IV. Consists primarily of technical studies and chorales for full band.

Smith, Claude T. *Symphonic Warm-Ups for Band (Tuba)*. Hal Leonard Publishing Corporation. 1982. $4.95. 24 pp. II–IV. This supplementary method emphasizes the development of tone, technique, and style through scales, etudes, and chorales.

Smith, Leonard B. *A Treasury of Scales for Band and Orchestra (Tuba)*. Belwin-Mills. 1952. $4.00. 8 pp. I–II. A collection of all the major and minor scales.

Snedecor, Phil. *Low Etudes for Tuba*. PAS Music. 1991. $8.95. 34 pp. III–V. Contains etudes in various keys and styles for the development of the tuba's low register. Designed with both the professional and the advanced student in mind. Contains mostly original material, plus two excerpt-based etudes at the end of the book.

Sparke, Philip. *Scales and Arpeggios, Grades 1-8 in Grade Order*.

Steckeler. *Tuba-Schule für Anfänger (für Tuba in B, F, Es aus: Neue Trossinger Instrumentalmethoden)*.

Stegmann. *Elementarschule*. Richard Stegmann. $15.60.

Street, A. *Scales and Arpeggios for the Tuba*. Boosey & Hawkes, Incorporated. 1977. $6.00. 16 pp. III–IV. Designed for the student preparing for the Royal Schools of Music board exams. Presents a detailed practice regimen for preparation of scales and arpeggios for all the major and minor scales, as well as chromatic and whole-tone scales. The student's attention is directed to variance of phrasing and articulation patterns and the need to practice intonation as well as technique.

Stuart, and C. Paul Herfurth. *Sounds of the Winds*.

Sueta, Ed. *Band Method, Volumes I, II, III (Tuba)*. Macie Publishing Co. 1974. $5.50 each. 40 pp. each. I–II. An unusual band method which emphasizes rhythmic reading and perception through use of familiar repertoire. Pedagogical comments peculiar to the tuba are included in Vol III.

Swan. *Practice Routine*. Trombacor Music. $10.00.

Swanson, Kenneth, and James Ployhar. *Tunes for Tuba (Bass) Technic, Level III*. Belwin-Mills. 1971. $5.50. 32 pp. II–III. The third in a series of three books/levels (see above, Ostling for Levels I and II). Emphasizes the development of musicality through the presentation of advanced-intermediate level melodies.

Swanson, Kenneth; Herman Vincent; and James Ployhar. *Studies and Melodious Etudes for Tuba (Bass), Levels II and III*. Belwin-Mills. 1970/71. $5.50 each. 32 pp. each. II–III. The second and third books in a series of three (see Laas and Weber, above). Adds coverage of advanced meters and keys.

Swanson, Kenneth; Herman Vincent; and James Ployhar. *Tuba (Bass) Student, Level III*. Belwin-Mills. 1971. $5.50 each. 40 pp. each. II–III. The third in a series of three books/levels (see Weber, below, for Books I and II). Includes technical etudes in a variety of meters and keys.

Swearingen, James. *Go for Technique (Tuba), Books I, II, and III*. Belwin-Mills. 1990. $5.00 each. 24 pp. each. I–II. Each book of this method is divided into individual units, and each unit contains "technique builders," rhythmic studies, scale studies, and melodious etudes.

Swearingen, James. *Unison Plus (Tuba)*. Heritage Music Press. 1988. $2.50. 15 pp. I. Contains eight popular folk tunes, each including both the basic melody and the tuba part to a full band arrangement.

Swearingen, James, and Barbara Buehlman. *Band Encounters, Book 1 (Tuba)*. Heritage Music Press. 1984. $4.50. 32 pp. I. This band method uses a combined theoretical and cartoon approach to introduce the fundamentals of first-year performance.

Swearingen, James, and Barbara Buehlman. *Band Encounters, Book 2 (Tuba)*. Heritage Music Press. 1984. $4.50. 32 pp. I–II. Introduces sixteenth notes, expressive terminology, and other basic concepts of musical performance.

Swearingen, James, and Barbara Buehlman. *Band Plus, Book 1 (Tuba)*. Heritage Music Press. 1989. $4.95. 48 pp. I. Contains the *Band Encounters* series plus a number of theory puzzles (find-a-word, word scramble, matching, etc.).

Swearingen, James, and Barbara Buehlman. *Band Plus, Book 2 (Tuba)*. Heritage Music Press. 1989. $4.95. 48 pp. I–II. Introduces sixteenth-notes, expressive terminology, and other basic concepts of musical performance.

Swearingen, James, and Barbara Buehlman. *Technique Encounters, Books 1 and 2 (Tuba)*. Heritage Music Press. 1984. $1.95 each. 15 pp. each. I–II. Ideal as a supplement to any beginning method book, Book 1 places emphasis on rhythmic development at the beginning level, while Book 2 introduces more complex rhythms in a progressive manner.

Tarto, Joe. *Basic Rhythms and the Art of Jazz Improvisation*. Charles Colin. 1976. $7.50. 102 pp. III–V. Written by one of the original tuba artist/teacher virtuosi, this book serves as a thorough introduction to jazz playing for the bass line player. It includes pattern drills and a good representation of standard tunes from the early to middle years of the development of the jazz art form. The blues, boogie-woogie, and Latin styles are among those introduced along with such basic techniques as "walking bass."

Tarto, Joe. *Bass Noodles: Modulation Breaks and Hot Choruses for Tuba, Trombone, Mellophone, String Bass, and Bari Sax.* Alfred and Company. Out of print. 1929. $1.00. 33 pp. III–IV. Includes a variety of examples of modulation breaks in a variety of keys, in addition to several solos and choruses as performed by Tarto himself. A valuable work for the aspiring young bass player, regardless of the particular bass instrument chosen.

Tarto, Joe. *Joe Tarto's Modern Method for Improvising for Tuba and Double Bass for the Dance Orchestra.* Robbins-Engel, Inc. New York. Out of print. 1926. $.75. 16 pp. II–III. One of the earliest tutors for jazz improvisation by one of the legendary tubists of the twentieth century. It contains simple, direct instruction in various contemporary jazz styles and notated examples to represent proper musical results. A short biographical sketch of Tarto of interest to historical scholars is included.

Taube, L. H. *Leichte Übungen für Bläser—Heft I: Baritone/Tuba.* ed. Otto Ebner. Pro Musica Verlag.

Taylor, Maurice D. *Band Fundamentals in Easy Steps (Basses)—Books One, Two, Three.* Belwin-Mills. 1960/ 63/ 66. 32 pp. each I–II. Principally intended for group band instruction. Includes a good introduction to basic musicianship fundamentals and one- to two-line exercises and melodies, as well as band-type parts.

Taylor, Maurice D. *Easy Steps to Band (Basses).* Belwin-Mills. 1967. 32 pp. I.

Taylor, Maurice. *Easy Steps to the Band (Tuba).* Belwin-Mills. 1939. $3.95. 32 pp. I–II. A rapidly progressive method divided into twenty-five individual lessons, including scale studies, duets, and full band arrangements (tuba part).

Taylor, Maurice D. *Intermediate Steps to Band (Basses).* Belwin-Mills. 1947. 32 pp. II. Intended primarily for class use with early intermediate students. Includes thirty lessons, each with a clearly stated objective dealing with a specific area such as rhythm, phrasing, articulation, etc. Exercises are typically only one or two lines in length.

Teuchert, Emil. *Grosse Praktische Tubaschule.* Carl Fischer, Incorporated.

Teuchert, Emil. *Lehrgang.*

Teuchert, Emil. *Schule für B oder C-Tuba, Teil I.* Friedrich Hofmeister.

Teuchert, Emil. *Schule für die Basstuba in F oder Eb und für Kontrabass-tuba in CC oder BBb.* ed. Franz Seyffarth. Friedrich Hofmeister. 63 pp. II–III. Offers a good approach to private instruction for the late intermediate student. Scale and interval studies are presented together with short, interesting etudes in virtually all keys. A review of music fundamentals is presented in the introductory section. All text is in German.

Teuchert, Emil. *Tägliche Übungen für Tuba mit einem Anhang der Schwierigsten Orchesterstellen und Soli aus Blas und Streichmusik.* Seeling/Erdmann. 1936/64.

Teuchert, Emil, and Uetz, Bruno. *26 Studien in allen Dur- und moll-Tonarten und (Uetz) Technische Studien.* Friedrich Hofmeister.

Todorov, G. *School.*

Tortoriello, V. T. See Tarto, Joe.

Tutor for the Eb Bombardon, A. W. H. Paling & Co., Ltd., Sydney. Out of print. 1918. I–III. Part of a series called "Paling's Victor Series," this is a self-instructor with information on rudiments of music, instructions for use and care of the instrument, scales and exercises.

Tyrrell, H. W. *Advanced Studies for BBb Bass.* Boosey & Hawkes, Incorporated. 1948. $9.00. 40 pp. III–IV. A standard method for the serious high school student with particular focus on rhythmic and melodic patterns. An excellent resource for private study and for audition material for honors bands, etc.

Tyrrell, H.W. *Advanced Studies for Eb Bass.* Boosey & Hawkes, Incorporated. 1948. 40 pp. III–IV. These etudes are identical to those in the BBb book, but with appropriate editings for range, etc., to facilitate development of skills appropriate to the Eb tuba.

Uber, David. *Concert Etudes for Tuba (or Bass Trombone).* Robert King Music Company. 1985. $3.50. 32 pp. IV. These etudes will challenge the advanced performer both musically and technically. The composer explores a variety of keys and both extremes of range for the tuba, as well as interesting rhythmic challenges. These studies offer more musical satisfaction than usually found in worthwhile etudes.

Uber, David. *David Uber Warm-Up Procedure for Tuba.* Charles Colin. 1980. $5.95. 20 pp. II–IV. A well thought-out routine which may be used as a whole or in parts. All basic, fundamental aspects of performance are covered, including long tones, scales, flexibilities, etc. Pedagogically sound instructions occur at the beginning of the text as well as with each emphasis area.

Uber, David. *Fifteen Progressive Etudes for Tuba (or Bass Trombone).* Touch of Brass. $7.95.

Uber, David. *First Studies for BBb Tuba.* Kendor Music Company. 1988. $9.00. 25 pp. II–III. These etudes work well for the intermediate/early advanced player. The composer has made special effort to accommodate the problems encountered by the young student with orthodontic braces.

Uber, David. *Thirty Studies for the Bass Tuba.* Southern Music Company. 1977. $3.75. 28 pp. III–IV. Excellent musical etudes for the advanced student. Contains challenges for all areas of musical skills. Only the most advanced high school students should tackle these studies, as they are most appropriate for college students.

Uber, David. *Thirty-five Conservatory Etudes.* Touch of Brass. $9.95.

Uber, David. *Tuba Method (in Three Books).* Peer-Southern Organization.

Uber, David. *Twenty-five Early Studies for Tuba.* Southern Music Company. 1980. $7.50. 28 pp. II–III. Appropriate etudes for the second- or third-year tuba student. Fine musical studies that emphasize tonguing, legato, rhythm, breath control, and phrasing. Tonally, principally flat keys are represented.

Uetz, Bruno. *Elementarschule für Tuba in B*.

Uetz, Bruno. *Technische Studien mit Toneleiterstudein nach Arban (I und II)*.

Ujfalusi, Laszlo; Andras Pehl; and Jozsef Perlaki. *Tuba-iskola (Tubaschule)*. Editio Musica Budapest. 1962. 133 pp. I–IV. Includes parallel Hungarian and German text. A comprehensive method for the study of the F tuba. Includes rudimentary studies, exercises in all keys, and several solos with piano accompaniment.

U.S. Department of the Army. *Soldier's Manual: Tuba Player, Levels I, II, and III*. Washington: Department of Defense, Department of the Army. 1978. 109 pp.

Uth, Lothar. *Schule für Tuba*. Uth O. J.

Van Beekum, Jan. *Fondamento*.

Van Uffelen, P. C. *Voordrachtstukken en Etudes*. Molenaar N.V. 1963. 18 pp. IV.

Vander Cook, H. A. *Vander Cook Etudes for E flat or BB flat Bass (Tuba)*. Rubank, Incorporated. 1941. $3.50. 26 pp. II–III. From one of the great legends of instrumental pedagogy, here are principally short etudes in a variety of styles and covering the broad range of fundamental areas from legato tonguing to technical development. The volume concludes with two of Vander Cook's classic solos, *Bombastoso* and *Colossus*.

Vasiliev, S. *Twenty-four Melodious Etudes for Tuba*. Robert King Music Company. $3.40. 39 pp. III–IV. Good studies for phrasing, interpretation, and flexibility in mostly lyric settings. A nice alternative to Bordogni and, in some instances, more challenging in terms of range and technique.

Vaughan, Rodger. *Randolph Etudes for Tuba and Bass Trombone, Book 1 (Introductory)*. 1991. 24 pp. II. At press time these etudes had been submitted for publication. Contact the composer for publication information at California State University—Fullerton. Designed with the very young player in mind, these are mainly interesting half note/quarter note studies in which modal, as well as major and minor, keys are explored. All studies are lyrical in nature.

Vaughan, Rodger. *Randolph Etudes for Tuba and Bass Trombone, Book 2 (Intermediate)*. 1991. 25 pp. II–III. At press time these etudes had been submitted for publication. Contact the composer for publication information at California State University—Fullerton. These studies, exploring modal and major/minor keys, are suitable for the advanced junior high/early senior high student. More rhythmic challenges are presented than in Book I.

Vaughan, Rodger. *Randolph Etudes for Tuba and Bass Trombone, Book 3 (Advanced)*. 1991. 26 pp. III. At press time these etudes had been submitted for publication. Contact the composer for publication information at California State University—Fullerton. This set presents excellent challenges for the high school tubist and tunes the ear to work well in keys outside the standard major and minor fare.

Victor. *Victor Method (Tuba)*. Belwin-Mills.

Vieulou, E. *Études Caractéristiques*. Editions Gras. $44.75. See: Thompson/Lemke; *French Music for Low Brass Instruments*.

Vieulou, E. *Études Caractéristiques. Saxhorn Basse, 4/5/6 Pistons*. Alphonse Leduc Editions Musicales. $22.40.

Ward, N. *Elementary School Beginner for E♭ Tuba*. Consolidated. 1956.

Warren, Christopher. *Twenty Etudes for Tuba*. T.U.B.A. Press. 1992. $10.00. 48 pp. III–IV. A very helpful text that includes a comprehensive section on scales, a warm-up routine, and etudes in a variety of styles. Pedagogical suggestions help guide the student who might not have a professional tuba teacher. A very good book for the library of a serious high school student or early college student. Concludes with four nice duets for tuba.

Wastall, Peter. *Learn as You Play Tuba*. Boosey & Hawkes, Incorporated. $11.50.

Wastall, Peter. *Scales and Arpeggios for Tuba*. Boosey & Hawkes, Incorporated. 1990. $6.50. 19 pp. II–III. Includes the scale and arpeggio exercises required for the five levels of the Associated Board of the Royal Schools of Music in England for E♭ and BB♭ tubas. All scales and arpeggios for each grade are included in order, and a practice planner/comment from the teacher precedes each section. A good resource for the student who needs extra work on scales.

Watelle, Jules. *Grande Méthode de Basse et Tuba*. Editions Salabert. Out of print. 1912. 196 pp. III–V. This French method is aimed particularly at the French tuba in C, although much of the material is useful in the development of upper-register facility on the F tuba. The etudes are, for the most part, very advanced and cover every aspect of technical development. A few melodic studies and solos are included.

Weast. *Valuable Repetitions*. McGinnis & Marx Music Publications. $10.00.

Weber, Carl. *The Premier Method for E♭ Bass or Tuba*. J. W. Pepper. Out of print. 1887. 104 pp. I–III. Rudiments of music theory, musicianship, and other basic aspects of performance are covered in the first 40 pages of this work. The remainder of the text holds 119 solos and duets drawn from the contemporary popular and Classic repertoire.

Weber, Fred. *Belwin Elementary Band Method for Bass (Tuba)*. ed. Nilo W. Hovey. Belwin-Mills. 1945. $1.00. 39 pp. I. A beginning method for full band instruction. Includes some unisonal melodies as well as ensemble works for the full band. As the book progresses, less emphasis is placed on the melodic aspect of the tuba, and more emphasis on the tuba as an accompaniment/background instrument.

Weber, Fred. *Belwin Intermediate Band Method for Bass (Tuba)*. ed. Nilo W. Hovey. Belwin-Mills.

1947. $5.50. 31 pp. II. Places more emphasis on the development of individual technique.

Weber, Fred. *Belwin Progressive Band Studies for Bass (Tuba).* Belwin-Mills. 1949. II–III.

Weber, Fred. *First Division Band Method for Tuba, Parts I, II, III, and IV.* Belwin-Mills. 1962/63/64/65. $5.50 each. I–III. A classic progressive group method for band that still enjoys immense popularity in the United States. Presentation of fundamentals is combined with singable melodies and brief ensemble works.

Weber, Fred. *Rehearsal Fundamentals for Bass (Tuba).* Belwin-Mills. 1956. II–III.

Weber, Fred. *Tuba Note Speller.* Belwin-Mills. 1951. $5.50. 32 pp. I. A workbook to assist the young student with note reading, fingerings, and rhythmic reading.

Weber, Fred, and Kenneth Swanson. *Tuba (Bass) Student, Levels I and II.* Belwin-Mills. 1969/70. $5.50 each. 40 pp. each. I–II. This three-volume method (for Level III, see Swanson, Vincent, and Ployhar, above) is designed for use in private instruction from the elementary through the advanced-intermediate levels. It includes the introduction and review of fundamentals throughout.

White, William C., comp. and ed. *Unisonal Scales, Chords & Rhythmic Studies for Bands—Tuba.* Carl Fischer, Incorporated. Out of print. 1921. 30 pp. II–III.

Wltschek. *Lippenbindungen für Tuba in F und B.*

Woodruff, Frank. *Twenty-four Artistic Studies for Tuba.* Southern Music Company. 1986. $7.50. 32 pp. III. A collection of studies from the etudes of Bordogni, Blazhevich, Vasiliev, and Kopprasch freely edited by Woodruff, who reworked the etudes to make them better suited for competition or other uses. Stylistic, tempo, and other expressive indications have been added to give the performer more ideas for musical interpretation of the etudes.

Wouda. *Voordrachstukken Etudes Ten Behoeve van de Muziekexamens.* Uitgave Molenaar, N. V.

Wright, D., and H. Round. *Complete Method.* Wright.

Yaus, Grover C. *Forty Rhythmical Studies for Basses (E♭ & BB♭).* Belwin-Mills. 1958. $2.95. 23 pp. II–III. These studies are designed for unison band, however, they will work very well for private instruction, particularly for intermediate or early advanced students who need help with rhythm. Rhythms presented are common figures, not "tricks" presented for difficulty's sake.

Yaus, Grover C. *Forty-seven Foundation Studies for E♭ or BB♭ Tuba.* Belwin-Mills. II.

Yaus, Grover C. *Harmonized Rest Patterns (Tuba).* Belwin-Mills.

Yaus, Grover C. *101 Rhythmic Rest Patterns (for Basses).* Belwin-Mills. 1953. $5.50. 21 pp. I–II. This method, published for unison band, focuses on the development of rhythmic reading skills.

Yaus, Grover C. *127 Original Exercises for Bass Clef Instruments.* Belwin-Mills. 1956. III.

Yaus, Grover C. *32 All in One Studies for Basses.* Belwin-Mills.

Yaus, Grover C. *20 Rhythmical Studies for Basses (E♭ or BB♭).* Belwin-Mills. 1952. $3.95. 21 pp. II–III. Emphasizes rhythmic development through the inclusion of various meters and the strategic placement of accentuation.

Yaus, Grover C., comp. and ed. *Division of Measure for E♭ and BB♭.* Belwin-Mills. II–III.

Yaus, Grover C., and Roy C. Miller. *150 Original Exercises for Bass Clef Instruments.* Belwin-Mills. 1944.

Zepp, George. *Notes for Today (Bass), Parts I and II.* Belwin-Mills. 1977/78. $5.00 each. 24 pp. each. I–II. A book of word games intended as a supplement to any band method for the reinforcement of basic music theory skills.

10. Orchestral Excerpts

Jerry A. Young and David D. Graves, editorial assistant

The study of orchestral repertoire consumes a considerable portion of the serious tubist's practice time. In addition to the *Albums of Orchestra Parts* published by Kalmus, there are many collections created by other publishers that furnish either entire parts or important passages for the tubist. Many contain specific pedagogical and interpretational information and suggestions. Although the bulk of the literature for tuba in this area has been produced since the late 1940s, such materials for tuba have existed since the latter part of the nineteenth century.

Special thanks are extended to Eugene Pokorny of the Chicago Symphony Orchestra, Ronald Bishop of the Cleveland Orchestra, and Douglas Yeo of the Boston Symphony Orchestra for their assistance in obtaining some of the more difficult-to-locate orchestral study texts. Several International Consultants provided information about publications from their respective parts of the world. In addition, special thanks go to the University of Wisconsin—Eau Claire School of Graduate Study and Research, Dr. Ronald Satz, Dean; and the Department of Music, Dr. David Baker, Chair. Because of their generous support, David Graves was able to assist with the research for and preparation of this chapter.

Our goal was to determine the availability of published orchestral excerpts for the tuba. If it was determined that a given work is out of print, this fact is indicated in the bibliographic information. However, the lack of an out-of-print notation does not guarantee that the item is indeed available. The prices given are the most recent ones. In the case of out-of-print material or where no other source was available, the cover price is listed. Since some publishers did not furnish current catalogs with up-to-date price information, some prices may not be accurate. Entries that appear in the following listing without annotation and/or with incomplete bibliographic information were not made available to the editor for examination. The editorial staff of *The Tuba Source Book* felt that it was important that all items be documented in this project, regardless of current availability. Some items were not furnished for review by the publisher while others (appearing in old catalogs or bibliographies) are presumably out of print and lost.

For works published for both trombone and tuba, the full contents are listed, but every work listed does not necessarily include a tuba part. Spelling of composers' names and titles of works are given here just as they appear in the tables of contents of the listed publications. No attempt has been made to make spellings consistent.

Bartók, Béla. *Albums of Orchestra Parts, # 8610.* Edwin F. Kalmus. $9.00. A set of complete parts to *Two Portraits*, Op. 5; *Two Pictures*, Op. 10; *First Suite.*

Belwin Mills. *Tuba Excerpts from Standard Orchestral Repertoire, Book One.* Belwin-Mills. $6.50. 57 pp. Contains excerpts from D'Albert: *Der Rubin, Gernot;* Bantock: *Der Zeitgeist, Helena;* Berger: *Symphonie B dur;* Berlioz: *Symphony Fantastique, Romeo and Juliet, Trojan Marsch, Requiem, Damnation of Faust, Benvenuto Cellini;* Chabrier: *Gwendoline,* Donizetti: *Lucia di Lammermoor;* Dräseke: *Herat;* Glazounow: *Symphony;* Halévy: *Die Jüdin;* Kretzschmer: *Die Folkunger;* Liszt: *Ce qu'on entend sur la montagne (Symphonische Dichtung Nr. 1), Tasso (Symphonische Dichtung Nr. 2), Die Ideale (Symphonische Dichtung Nr. 12);* Mascagni: *Cavalleria Rusticana;* Mendelssohn: *Midsummer Night's Dream;* Nicodé: *Das Meer;* Novak: *Von ewiger Sehnsucht (Tondichtung);* Saint-Saëns: *Samson and Delilah;* Sibelius: *Symphony Nr. 1, Symphony Nr. 2;* Strauss: *Til Eulenspiegel, Also sprach Zarathustra;* Thomas: *Hamlet;* Tinel: *Franziskus, Drei Symphonische Tongemälde,* Overture to *Godoleva;* Tchaikowsky: *Symphony Nr. 4;* Verdi: *Rigoletto;* Volbach: *Es waren zwei Königskinder;* Wagner: *Lohengrin, Tristan und Isolde, Eine Faust Overture;* Weingartner: *Symphony Nr. 2;* Zoellner: *Der Überfall, Die versunkene Glocke.*

Belwin Mills. *Tuba Excerpts from Standard Orchestral Repertoire, Book Two.* Belwin-Mills. $4.00. 25 pp. Contains excerpts from Wagner: *Rienzi, Der Fliegende Holländer, Tannhäuser, Lohengrin, Tristan und Isolde.*

Belwin Mills. *Tuba Excerpts from Standard Orchestral Repertoire, Book Three.* Belwin-Mills. $4.00. 25 pp. Contains excerpts from Wagner's *Die Meistersinger, Das Rheingold, Die Walküre, Siegfried, Götterdämmerung, Parsifal, Eine Faust-Ouvertüre, Huldigungs-Marsch.*

Berlioz, Hector. *Albums of Orchestra Parts, #8616.* Edwin F. Kalmus. $9.00. Complete parts to the overtures to *King Lear, Judges of the Secret Court, Der Corsair, Benvenuto Cellini.*

Berlioz, Hector. *Albums of Orchestra Parts, #8617.* Edwin F. Kalmus. $9.00. Complete parts to *Romeo and Juliet, Fantastic Symphony, Harold in Italy.*

Bernard, Paul. *Traits Difficiles: Tuba.* Alphonse Leduc Editions Musicales. 4 pp. Contains excerpts for tuba from Delvincourt: *Radio Serenade;* Wagner: *La Walkyrie, Eine Faust Overture;* Roussel: *Fourth Symphony;* Stravinsky: *Petrouchka;* Tchaikowsky: *Fourth Symphony;* Liszt: *Les Ideals de Schiller;* Halévy: *La Juive;* Berlioz: *Requiem;* Saint-Saëns: *Le Deluge;* Thomas: *Hamlet.*

Berthold, Otto. *Orchesterstudien: Strauss (Symphonic Werken).*

Beversdorf, Thomas. *Orchestral Literature for Trombone and Tuba.* $15.00.

Borodin, Alexander, and Reinhold Gliere. *Albums of Orchestra Parts, #8608.* Edwin F. Kalmus. $9.00. Complete parts to Borodin: *Symphony No. 2, Prince Igor Overture, Polovetsian Dances;* Gliere: *Russian Sailors' Dance.*

Brahms, Johannes. *Orchestral Literature für Trombone und Tuba: Die 4 Sinfonien + 2 Ouvertüren.*

Brahms, Johannes, and Max Bruch. *Albums of Orchestra Parts, # 8609.* Edwin F. Kalmus. $9.00. Complete parts to Brahms: *Academic Festival Overture, Tragic Overture, Symphony No. 2;* Bruch: *Scottish Fantasie Op. 46.*

Brown, Keith, ed. *Orchestral Excerpts from the Symphonic Repertoire for Trombone, Vol. I.* International Music Company. 1964. $9.00. 63 pp. Includes trombone and tuba (when applicable) excerpts from Berlioz: "Hungarian March" from *The Damnation of Faust, Overture to the Roman Carnival;* Borodin: *Symphony No. 2;* Brahms: *Symphony No. 2, Tragic Overture;* Dvořák: *Symphony Nos. 8 and 9;* Elgar: *Enigma Variations;* Hindemith: *Konzertmusik for Strings and Brass;* d'Indy: *Symphony on a French Mountain Air;* Liszt: *Les Preludes;* Prokofiev: *Symphony No. 5;* Rimsky-Korsakow: *Russian Easter Overture;* Rossini: *Overture to la Gaza Ladra;* Schumann: *Symphony No. 4;* Sibelius: *Symphony No. 2;* Stravinsky: *Firebird Suite;* Tchaikovsky: *Symphony No. 4, 1812 Overture;* Vaughan Williams: *A London Symphony;* Verdi: *Othello;* Weber: *Overture to Der Freischutz.*

Brown, Keith, ed. *Orchestral Excerpts from the Symphonic Repertoire for Trombone, Vol. II.* International Music Company. 1965. $9.00. 62 pp. Contains trombone and tuba (when applicable) excerpts from Berlioz: *Symphony Fantastique;* Brahms: *Academic Festival Overture;* Chausson: *Symphony in Bb;* Delibes: *Coppelia;* Prokofiev: *Lt. Kije;* Rachmaninoff: *Isle of the Dead;* Saint-Saëns: *Symphony No.3 in C;* Schumann: *Symphonies Nos. 2 and 3;* Shostakovich: *Symphony No. 1;* Sibelius: *Finlandia;* Smetana: *Overture to The Bartered Bride;* Strauss: *Ein Heldenleben, Don Juan, Salome's Dance, Till Eulenspiegel;* Stravinsky: *Fireworks, Petrouchka;* Tchaikovsky: *Francesca da Rimini;* Verdi: *Aida.*

Brown, Keith, ed. *Orchestral Excerpts from the Symphonic Repertoire for Trombone, Vol. III.* International Music Company. 1965. $9.00. 62 pp. Contains trombone and tuba (where applicable) excerpts from Berlioz: *Overture to Beatrice and Benedict;* Bizet: *L'Arlesienne Suite No. 2;* Borodin: *Polovetsian Dances;* Brahms: *Requiem, Symphonies Nos. 1 and 2;* Bruckner: *Symphony No. 4;* Debussy: *Nocturnes;* Dukas: *The Sorcerer's Apprentice;* Franck: *Symphony in D Minor;* Humperdinck: *Hansel and Gretel;* d'Indy: *Istar;* Kabalevsky: *Overture to Colas Breugnon;* Lalo: *Overture to Le Roi d'Ys;* Mahler: *Symphony No. 1;* Mussorgsky: *Night on the Bare Mountain;* Rimsky-Korsakov: *Symphony No. 2, Suite Coq d'Or;* Shostakovich: *Symphony No.5;* Stravinsky: *L'Histoire du Soldat, Le Sacre du Printemps;* Tchaikowsky: *Symphony No. 6;* Verdi: *Overture to la Forza del Destino, Requiem;* Weber: *Overture to Euryanthe.*

Brown, Keith, ed. *Orchestral Excerpts from the Symphonic Repertoire for Trombone, Vol. IV.* International Music Company. 1965. $9.00. 62 pp. Contains trombone and tuba (where applicable) excerpts from Berlioz: *Harold in Italy, Overture to Judges of the Secret Court;* Brahms: *Symphony No. 4;* Chabrier: *España;* Dvořák: *Cello Concerto;* Hindemith: *Symphonic Metamorphosis;* Liszt: *Piano Concerto No. 2;* Milhaud: *The Creation of the World;* Orff: *Carmina Burana;* Prokofiev: *Romeo and Juliet Suites 1 and 2, Scythia Suite;* Rachmaninoff: *Symphony No. 2;* Ravel: *Alborada del Gracioso;* Sibelius: *Symphony No. 1;* Strauss: *Don Quixote;* Stravinsky: *Song of the Nightingale;* Tchaikowsky: *Suite No. 3.*

Brown, Keith, ed. *Orchestral Excerpts from the Symphonic Repertoire for Trombone, Vol. V.* International Music Company. 1966. $9.00. 62 pp. Contains trombone and tuba (where applicable) excerpts from Berg: *Violin Concerto;* Berlioz: "Funeral Oration" from *Symphonie Funèbre et Triomphale;* Bruckner: *Symphony No. 5;* Chabrier: *Overture to Gwendoline;* Hindemith: *Sinfonietta;* Kodály: *Hary Janos Suite;* Mahler: *Symphony No. 5;* Mendelssohn: *Symphony No. 5, Wedding March;* Prokofiev: *Symphony No. 6;* Sibelius: *Symphony No. 5;* Strauss: *Also Sprach Zarathustra;* Stravinsky: *Symphony in C;* Tchaikovsky: *Symphony No. 5.*

Brown, Keith, ed. *Orchestral Excerpts from the Symphonic Repertoire for Trombone, Vol. VI.* International Music Company. 1967. $9.00. 62 pp. Contains trombone and tuba (where applicable) excerpts from Berg: *Kammerkonzert;* Bruckner: *Symphony No. 7;* Dvořak: *Scherzo Cappricioso;* Gliere: *Symphony No. 3;* Hindemith: *Harmonie der Welt;* Mahler: *Symphony No. 7;* Poulenc: *Suite Française;* Ravel: *L'Heure Espagnole, Piano Concerto for the Left Hand, L'Enfant et les Sortilèges;* Rimsky-Korsakow: *Scheherazade;* Schoenberg: *Variations;* Tchaikovsky: *Nutcracker Suite;* Verdi: *Don Carlo.*

Brown, Keith, ed. *Orchestral Excerpts from the Symphonic Repertoire for Trombone, Vol. VII.* International Music Company. 1967. $9.00. 62 pp. Contains trombone and tuba (where applicable) excerpts from Berg: *Wozzeck*; Berlioz: *Romeo and Juliet*; Bruckner: *Symphony No. 6*; Glazunov: *Symphony No. 4*; Hindemith: *Nobilissima Vissione*; Mahler: *Symphonies Nos. 5 and 8*; Shostakovich: *Symphony No. 9*; Tchaikowsky: *Swan Lake*; Webern: *Six Pieces*.

Brown, Keith, ed. *Orchestral Excerpts from the Symphonic Repertoire for Trombone, Vol. VIII.* International Music Company. 1968. $9.00. 62 pp. Contains trombone and tuba (where applicable) excerpts from Berlioz: *Requiem*; Blacher: *Variations on a Theme by Paganini*; Bruckner: *Symphony No. 1*; Debussy: *Le Martyre de St. Sebastian*; Dukas: *Fanfare La Peri*; Hindemith: *Mathis der Maler*; Ibert: *Divertissement*; Janaček: *Sinfonietta*; Mahler: *Symphony No. 3*; Poulenc: *Suite Française*; Ravel: *Daphnis et Chloe Suites I and II, La Valse*; Roussel: *Symphony No. 4*; Sibelius: *Symphony No. 3*; Strauss: *Le Bourgeois Gentilhomme, Tod und Verklärung*; Stravinsky: *Symphony in Three Movements*; Tchaikowsky: *Manfred Symphony, The Sleeping Beauty*; Verdi: *Nabucco*.

Brown, Keith, ed. *Orchestral Excerpts from the Symphonic Repertoire for Trombone, Vol. IX.* International Music Company. 1969. $9.00. 62 pp. This collection of orchestral studies contains trombone and tuba (where applicable) excerpts from the following works: Berg: *Lulu*; Berlioz: *The Damnation of Faust*; Bruckner: *Symphony No.8*; Hindemith: *Cello Concerto*; Liszt: *Hungarian Rhapsody No.2*; Mahler: *Symphonies Nos. 6 and 9*; Ravel: *Bolero*; Sibelius: *Symphony No.7*; Smetana: *From Bohemia's Fields and Meadows*; Strauss: *Salome*; Tchaikowsky: *Symphony No.2*.

Brown, Keith, ed. *Orchestral Excerpts from the Symphonic Repertoire for Trombone, Vol. X.* International Music Company. 1970. $9.00. 62 pp. Contains trombone and tuba (where applicable) excerpts from Berlioz: *The Royal Hunt and Storm*; Bruckner: *Symphonies Nos. 3 and 9*; Debussy: *Iberia*; Dvořák: *Symphony No. 7*; Franck: *Le Chasseur Maudit*; Ibert: *Escales*; Mussorgsky: *Boris Godunov*; Puccini: *La Boheme, Tosca*; Ravel: *Rhapsodie Espagnole*; Rimsky-Korsakow: *Capriccio Espagnole*; Rossini: *Overture to William Tell*; Roussel: *Symphony No. 3*; Strauss: *Macbeth*; Stravinsky: *Jeu de Cartes*, Tchaikowsky: *Hamlet Overture-Fantasy, Romeo and Juliet*; Vaughan Williams: *Symphony No. 4*; Verdi: *Falstaff, La Forza del Destino, Rigoletto*.

Brown, Keith, ed. *Orchestral Excerpts from the Symphonic Repertoire for Trombone—Strauss.* International Music Company. 1969. $9.00. 28 pp. Contains trombone and tuba (where applicable) excerpts from *Don Juan, Til Eulenspiegel, Tod und Verklärung, Salome's Dance, Also Sprach Zarathu-*

stra, *Le Bourgeois Gentilhomme, Ein Heldenleben, Don Quixote, Symphonica Domestica*.

Brown, T. Conway. *Tuba Passages (Bass Clef), Band Edition.* Boosey & Hawkes, Incorporated. Out of print. 1940. $1.00. 48 pp. Contains excerpts from the following band works/transcriptions: Bach: *Air* (from Suite No. 3), *Fugue à la Gigue*; Beethoven: *Symphony No. 5*; Borodin: *In the Steppes of Central Asia*; Coleridge-Taylor: *The Bamboula* (Rhapsodic Dance), *Petite Suite de Concert, Christmas Overture*; Curzon: *La Gitana* (Czardas), *Robin Hood* (Suite), *Zingaresca* (Gipsy Caprice); Debussy: *The Children's Corner* (Suite); Dukas: *L'Apprenti Sorcier* (Scherzo); Dvořák: *Largo and Scherzo* (from "New World" Symphony); Enesco: *Roumanian Rhapsody No. 1*; Friedemann: *Slavonic Rhapsody No. 1, Slavonic Rhapsody No. 2*; Glinka: *Russlan and Ludmilla* (Overture); Liszt: *Hungarian Rhapsody No. 2*; Mancini, S.: *Symphonic March*; Mozart: *The Marriage of Figaro* (Overture); Nicolai: *Merry Wives of Windsor* (Overture); Rachmaninoff: *Prelude in G Minor* (Op. 23, No. 5), *Prelude*; Rimsky-Korsakov: *Scheherazade, Capriccio Espagnol, Dance of the Tumblers* (from *The Snow Maiden*), *The Flight of the Bumble Bee, Polonaise* (from *Christmas Night*); Saint-Saëns: *Marche Heroïque*; Sibelius: *Valse Lyrique, Valse Triste, Finlandia*; Tschaikowsky: *Two Movements from the Fifth Symphony, Valse des Fleurs* (from *The Nutcracker*), *Two Excerpts from the Pathéique Symphony*; Wagner: *Lohengrin* (Introduction to Act III and "Bridal Chorus"); Wallace: *Maritana* (Overture); Woodforde-Finden: *Four Indian Love Lyrics*; Wood: *Frescoes* (Suite).

Bruckner, Anton. *Albums of Orchestra Parts, #8611.* Edwin F. Kalmus. $9.00. Complete parts to Symphonies Nos. 4, 7, 8, 9.

Bruckner-Seyffarth. *Orchesterstudien, Volume One.*

Bruckner-Seyffarth. *Orchesterstudien, Volume Two.*

Chabrier, Emmanuel, and Ernest Chausson. *Albums of Orchestra Parts, #8612.* Edwin F. Kalmus. $9.00. Complete parts to Chabrier: *Marche Joyeuse, España*; Chausson: *Symphony in Bb*.

de Ville, Paul. *The Tuba Player's Studio.* Carl Fischer, Incorporated. Out of print. Includes excerpts for tuba from Tchaikowsky: *1812 Overture, Capriccio Italien*; Moses-Tobani: *Auld Lang Syne, Unfinished Symphony* (Schubert, arr.), *Fantasia from Fidelio* (Beethoven, arr.), *Grand War March and Battle Hymn from Rienzi* (Wagner, arr.), *Souvenir de Meyerbeer, Andante from Fifth Symphony* (Beethoven, arr.), *Selections from Martha* (Flotow, arr.), *Souvenir de Meyerbeer* (Fantasia), *Fantasia from Götterdamerung* (Wagner, arr.), *Attila* (selection from Verdi's opera), *The Bohemian Girl* (selection from Balfe's opera) *Creme de la Creme, A Trip to Coney Island, Grand Fantasia from Siegfried* (Wagner, arr.), *Vorspiel to Der Meistersinger von Nurnburg* (Wagner, arr.); Johnson: *The Death of Custer* (from the *Battle of Little Big Horn*); Suppe: *Isabella Overture*, *Pique Dame* (Overture); Laurendeau: *Selections from Samson and Delilah* (Saint-Saëns, arr.); Godfrey: *Reminiscences of Scotland* (Grand Selection of Scotch Melodies), *Reminiscences of Verdi* (Grand Selection); Kucken: *The Warriors Return* (Descriptive Fantasia); Mendelssohn-Bartholdy: *Ruy Blas Overture*; Moszkowski: *From Foreign Lands*; Lassen: *Fest Overture* (Festival); Thomas: *Mignon Overture*; Luscombe: *A Trip to the Country* (Descriptive Fantasia); Baetens: *Albion* (Grand Fantasia on Scotch, Irish and English Airs); Ackermann: *Arie Concertante*; Rossini: *Semiramide Overture*; Wagner: *Tannhäuser* (March), *Rienzi Overture*; Auber: *Zanetta Overture*, *Le Lac des Fees*; Bishop: *Guy Mannering Overture*; Mercadante: *Overture from Stabat Mater* (Rossini, arr.); Flotow: *Martha Overture*; Suppe: *Poet and Peasant Overture*; Litolff: *Maximillian Robespierre Overture*; Beethoven: *Overture Leonore* (*Fidelio*); Herman: *Columbus* (Grand Descriptive Fantasia); Meyrelles: "Andante" from *Surprise Symphony* (Haydn, arr.), *Selection from Tannhäuser* (Wagner, arr.), *Bouquet of Melodies* (potpourri); Luigini: *Ballet Egyptien*; Massenet: *Scènes Pittoresques*; Langey: *Sounds from England*; Gomez: *Il Guarany*; Bizet: *L'Arlesienne* (Suite de Concert); Keler-Bela: *Roumanian Festival Overture*.

Debussy, Claude, and Leo Delibes. *Albums of Orchestra Parts, # 8613*. Edwin F. Kalmus. $9.00. Complete parts to Debussy: *La Mer, Nocturnes*; Delibes: *Prelude and Mazurka, Ballade and Theme, Entr' Acte and Waltz from Coppelia Ballet*.

Dreyer, Franz. *Orchestral Studies from Operas for the Trombone, Volume 1*. C. F. Schmidt. This entire series of excerpts contains portions of the tuba parts (when applicable) to works listed. Volume 1 contains excerpts from Wagner: *Rienzi, Fliegende Holländer, Tannhäuser*; Weber: *Freischütz*; Verdi: *Rigoletto*; Tschaikowsky: *Iolanthe*; Spohr: *Jessonda*; Smetana: *Der Kuss*; Oberleithner: *Aphrodite*; Mozart: *Don Juan, Zauberflöte*; Mascagni: *Rantzau*; Lortzing: *Undine*; Donizetti: *Don Pasquale*; Flotow: *Martha*.

Dreyer, Franz. *Orchestral Studies from Operas for the Trombone, Volume 2*. C. F. Schmidt. $4.00. 61 pp. (See annotation for Volume 1.) Volume 2 contains excerpts from Wagner: *Parsifal, Tristan und Isolde, Lohengrin*; Waltershausen: *Oberst Chabert*; Verdi: *Othello*; Tschaikowsky: *Eugen Onegin*; Smareglia: *Der Vasall von Szigeth*; Schillings: *Moloch*; Meyerbeer: *Nordstern*.

Dreyer, Franz. *Orchestral Studies from Operas for the Trombone, Volume 3*. C. F. Schmidt. (See annotation for Volume 1.) Volume 3 contains excerpts from Wagner: *Rheingold, Walküre, Meistersinger*; Weber: *Euryanthe*; Verdi: *Falstaff*; Saint-Saëns: *Samson and Dalila*; Rossini: *Diebische Elster*; Puccini: *Manon Lescaut*; Mascagni: *Freund Fritz*; Gou-

nod: *Faust* (*Margarethe*); Kienzl: *Evangelimann*; Herold and Halévy: *Ludovic*; Wallace: *Maritana*; Thomas: *Hamlet*.

Dreyer, Franz. *Orchestral Studies from Operas for the Trombone, Volume 4*. C. F. Schmidt. (See annotation for Volume 1.) Volume 4 contains excerpts from Wagner: *Siegfried, Götterdämmerung*; Nicolai: *Die lustigen Weiber*; Verdi: *Troubadour, Maskenball*; Puccini: *Boheme*; Meyerbeer: *Robert der Teufel*; Goldmark: *Heimchen am Herd, Gotz von Berlichingen*; Schumann: *Genoveva*.

Dreyer, Franz. *Orchestral Studies from Operas for the Trombone, Volume 5*. C. F. Schmidt. (See annotation for Volume 1.) Volume 5 contains excerpts from Auber: *Stumme von Portici*; d'Albert: *Tiefland*; Berlioz: *Benvenuto Cellini*; Bittner: *Der Musikant*; Cornelius: *Barbier von Bagdad*; Donizetti: *Regimentstochter*; Goldmark: *Königin von Saba*; Lortzing: *Der Wildschütz*; Halévy: *Der Blitz*; Istel: *Tribunals Gebot*; Gorter: *Das süsse Gift*.

Dreyer, Franz. *Orchestral Studies from Operas for the Trombone, Volume 6*. C. F. Schmidt. (See annotation for Volume 1.) Volume 6 contains excerpts from Meyerbeer: *Hugenotten*; Bizet: *Djamileh*; Bittner: *Der Bergsee*; Cornelius: *Gunlod*; Goldmark: *Merlin*; Lortzing: *Zar und Zimmermann*; Nessler: *Trompeter von Sackingen*; Herold: *Zampa*; Offenbach: *Hoffmann's Erzahlungen*.

Dreyer, Franz. *Orchestral Studies from Operas for the Trombone, Volume 7*. C. F. Schmidt. (See annotation for Volume 1.) Volume 7 contains excerpts from Meyerbeer: *Der Prophet*; Massenet: *Werther*; Mendelssohn: *Loreley*; Smetana: *Dalibor, Die verkaufte Braut*; Thomas: *Mignon*; Rossini: *Wilhelm Tell*; Gluck: *Orpheus*; Boito: *Mephistofeles*; and Dohnányi: *Der Schleier der Pierrette*.

Dreyer, Franz. *Orchestral Studies from Operas for the Trombone, Volume 8*. C. F. Schmidt. (See annotation for Volume 1.) Volume 8 contains excerpts from Auber: *Fra Diavolo*; d'Albert: *Kain*; Berlioz: *Die Trojaner*; Beethoven: *Fidelio, Leonoren Ouverture Nr. 2*; Bizet: *Carmen*; Delibes: *Lakme*; Flotow: *Stradella*; Kaskel: *Der Gefangene der Zarin*; Kreutzer: *Nachtlager*; Marschner: *Vampyr*; Massenet: *Der Gaukler unserer l. Frau*; Cherubini: *Wasserträger*; Brull: *Prince Gringoire*.

Dreyer, Franz. *Orchestral Studies from Operas for the Trombone, Volume 9*. C. F. Schmidt. (See annotation for Volume 1.) Volume 9 contains excerpts from Verdi: *Aida*; Puccini: *Tosca*; Meyerbeer: *Afrikanerin*; Marschner: *Hans Heiling*; Marenco: *Excelsior*; Goldmark: *Die Kriegsgefangene*; Gluck: *Iphigenie auf Tauris, Alceste*; Giordano: *Fedora*; Mascagni: *Cavalleria Rusticana*; Bittner: *Die rote Gred*.

Dreyer, Franz. *Orchestral Studies from Operas for the Trombone, Volume 10*. C. F. Schmidt. (See annotation for Volume 1.) Volume 10 contains excerpts from Verdi: *Ernani*; Tschaikowsky: *Pique Dame*;

Reznicek: *Donna Diana*; Puccini: *Madame Butter-fly*; Nougues: *Quo vadis?*; Marschner: *Templer und Judin*; Maillart: *Glöckchen des Eremiten*; Goldmark: *Wintermärchen*; Goldberger: *Mondweibchen*.

Dvořák, Antonin. *Albums of Orchestra Parts, #8614*. Edwin F. Kalmus. $9.00. Complete set of parts to *Carnival Overture, Scherzo Capriccioso Op. 66, Cello Concerto*.

Dvořák, Antonin. *Albums of Orchestra Parts, #8615*. Edwin F. Kalmus. $9.00. Complete set of parts to Symphonies Nos. 1, 4, 5.

Elgar, Edward. *Albums of Orchestra Parts, #8618*. Edwin F. Kalmus. $9.00. Complete set of parts to *Enigma Variations, Cockaigne Overture, Pomp and Circumstance No. 1*.

Ferrari, Bruno. *Passi Difficili e "A Solo" per trombone e basso tuba, Vol. I*. G. Ricordi & Company. 1970. $18.00. 43 pp. Contains trombone and tuba (where applicable) excerpts from the following Italian operatic works: Rossini: *La Gazza Ladra*; Verdi: *Nabucco, Macbeth, Aida*; Catalani: *Loreley*; Puccini: *Manon Lescaut, La Boheme*; Mascagni: *Iris*.

Ferrari, Bruno. *Passi Difficili e "A Solo" per trombone e basso tuba, Vol. II*. G. Ricordi & Company. 1970. $10.50. 39 pp. Collection contains trombone and tuba (where applicable) excerpts from the following Italian operatic works: Rossini: *Guglielmo Tell*; Verdi: *Ernani, La Forza del Destino, Falstaff*; Catalani: *La Wally*; Puccini: *Madama Butterfly*; Mascagni: *Cavalleria Rusticana*; Giordano: *Fedora*.

Ferrari, Bruno. *Passi Difficili e "A Solo" per Trombone e Basso Tuba, Vol. III*. G. Ricordi & Company. 1970. $10.50. 39 pp. Contains trombone and tuba (where applicable) excerpts from the following Italian operatic works: Donizetti: *Lucia di Lammermoor*; Verdi: *Il trovatore, Messa di Requiem, Simon Boccanegra, Don Carlo*; Leoncavallo: *I Pagliacci*; Puccini: *Tosca, La Fanciulla del West*.

Ferrari, Bruno. *Passi Difficili e "A Solo" per Trombone e Basso Tuba, Vol. IV*. G. Ricordi & Company. 1970. $10.50. 49 pp. Contains trombone and tuba (where applicable) excerpts from the following Italian operatic works: Donizetti: *La Favorita*; Verdi: *La Battaglia di Legnano, Rigoletto, I Vespri Siciliani, Otello*; Boito: *Mefistofele*; Puccini: *Turandot*; Mascagni: *L'amico Fritz*.

Franck, César, and Leo Delibes. *Albums of Orchestra Parts, #8619*. Edwin F. Kalmus. $9.00. Complete parts to Franck: *Symphony in D Minor, Le Chasseur Maudit*; Delibes: *Sylvia Ballet Suite*.

Geib, Fred. *The Geib Method for Tuba*. Carl Fischer, Incorporated. 1941. $12.00. 117 pp. Basically an etude/method book, this work contains excerpts from Meyerbeer: *Fackeltanz*; Gounod: *Queen of Sheba*; Strauss: *Death and Transfiguration, Till Eulenspiegel*; Mascagni: *Cavalleria Rusticana*; Franck: *Symphony in D Minor*; Berlioz: *Symphony Fantastique*; Delibes: *Sylvia*; Bach: *Fugue à la Gigue*; Berlioz: *Benvenuto Cellini*.

Grieg, Edvard. *Albums of Orchestra Parts, #8620*. Edwin F. Kalmus. $9.00. Set of complete parts to *Peer Gynt Suites Nos. 1 and 2, Norwegian Dance Op. 35, Lyric Suite,Symphonic Dances*.

Heber, P., and H. Müller. *Orchesterstudien für Tuba Symphonien von Bruckner und Bach*. Friedrich Hofmeister. 1974.

Hoppert, Manfred. *Orchester Studien für Tuba: Wagner: Der Ring des Nibelungen*. Zimmermann-Frankfurt. 47 pp. Contains tuba excerpts from the *Ring* operas including *Das Rheingold, Die Walküre, Siegfried*, and *Götterdämmerung*.

Hoppert, Manfred. *Orchester Studien für Tuba: Wagner I*. Zimmermann-Frankfurt. 51 pp. Contains tuba excerpts from Wagner's *The Flying Dutchman, Tannhäuser, Lohengrin, Tristan und Isolde, Die Meistersinger von Nürnberg, Parsifal, Eine Faust Ouverture*.

Kabalevsky, Dmitri, and Aram Khachaturian. *Albums of Orchestra Parts, #8621*. Edwin F. Kalmus. $9.00. A set of complete parts to Kabalevsky: *Colas Breugnon Overture, The Comedians*; Khachaturian: *Masquerade Suite*.

Kalmus, Edwin. *Tuba Excerpts from Standard Orchestral Repertoire, Book One*. Edwin F. Kalmus.

Kalmus, Edwin. *Tuba Excerpts from Standard Orchestral Repertoire, Book Two*. Edwin F. Kalmus.

Kalmus, Edwin. *Tuba Excerpts from Standard Orchestral Repertoire, Book Three*. Edwin F. Kalmus.

Kalmus, Edwin. *Tuba Excerpts from Standard Orchestral Repertoire, Book Four*. Edwin F. Kalmus. $5.50. 24 pp. Contains excerpts from Auber: *Die Stumme von Portici*; Bendel: *Rotkäppchen*; Reger: *Variationen und Fugue*; Wallace: *Maritana*; Büttner-Tartier: *Die Heilblume*; Hartmann: *Eine nordische Heerfahrt*; Lortzing: *Undine*; Smetana: *Richard III*; Verdi: *La Traviata*; Volbach: *Sinfonie H-moll*; Leoncavallo: *Der Bajazzo*; Scheinpfug: *Frühling*; Verdi: *Falstaff*.

Kalmus, Edwin. *Tuba Excerpts from Standard Orchestral Repertoire, Book Five*. Edwin F. Kalmus. $5.50. 22 pp. Contains excerpts from: Hausmann: *Fortuna*; Huber: *Sinfonie No. 3*; Kalafati: *Ouverture-Fantasie*; Pierson: *Musik zu Faust*; Berlioz: *Marsch für die Überreichung der Fahnen* (from *Te Deum*); Schmidt: *Sinfonie in E-dur*; Smetana: *Aus Böhmens Hain und Flur*; Verdi: *Aida*; Wolf: *Penthesilea*; Berlioz: *Trauermarsch* (from *Hamlet*), *Heroide funèbre, Die Vehmrichter*; Dohnányi: *Der Schleier der Pierrette*; Lange: *Komisches Sextett*.

Kalmus, Edwin. *Tuba Excerpts from Standard Orchestral Repertoire, Book Six*. Edwin F. Kalmus. $4.00. 36 pp. Contains excerpts from Berlioz: *Damnation of Faust, Symphonie Fantastique, Corsair Overture, Harold in Italy, King Lear Overture*; Mendelssohn: *Elijah, St. Paul, Midsummer Night's Dream*; Meyerbeer: *The African, The Huguenots, The Prophet, Roberto Diavolo, Fackeltanz No. 1*.

Laurendeau, L.P. *The Tuba Player's Vade Mecum: Tonal Studies, Solos and Extracts from Well Known Works of Celebrated Masters.* Carl Fischer. Out of print. 66 pp. A very few exercises and solos begin this text, and it ends with five solos that are obviously so placed for advertisement purposes. The body of the book is orchestral repertoire. Contains excerpts from Auber: *Crown Diamonds Overture*; Balfe: *Bohemian Girl Overture in F Minor, Bohemian Girl Overture in A Minor*; Boieldieu: *Jean de Paris, La Dame Blanche Overture*; Brüll: *The Golden Cross Overture*; Cherubini: *Anacreon Overture, Medea Overture*; *Lodoiska Overture*; Conradi: *Die Weiber von Weinsberg Overture*; Donizetti: *La Fille du Regiment Overture, Lucia di Lammermoor Overture*; Gluck: *Armide Overture*; Grieg: *Norwegian Dance No. 1*; Gounod: *La Reine de Saba; Faust Fantasia*; Kontski: *Reveil du Lion*; Kreutzer: *A Night in Granada Overture*; Lortzing: *Wildschütz Overture*; Löschhorn: *La Belle Amazone*; Mendelssohn: *Hebriden Overture, Ruy Blas Overture, Athalia Overture*; Mercadante: *Giuramento Fantasia*; Meyerbeer: *Festmarch zur Schillerfeier, Coronation March, The Huguenots, Fantasia, Ein Feldlager in Schlesien, Struensee, Fackeltanz in Bb major, L'Africaine, Robert le Diable*; Mozart: *The Magic Flute Overture, Adagio, Largo, and Larghetto—Andante from the Magic Flute, Titus Overture, Arie der Vitellia, Figaro's Wedding Overture*; Nicolai: *Merry Wives of Windsor Overture, The Templar Finale*; Prinz Friedrich Wilhelm: *Fackeltanz*; Redern: *Fackeltanz*; Rossini: *Tell Overture, Belagerung von Corinth, Tancred Overture, Stabat Mater Air, Italian in Algeria Overture, La Gazza Ladra Overture*; Rubinstein: *Maccabäer Fantasia*; Schneider: *Overture über den Dessauer Marsch*; Schubert: *Rosamunde Overture, Erlkoenig Overture*; Shulz: *Ein Faust Overture*; Suppe: *Banditenstreiche Overture in Db major, Banditenstreiche Overture in Bb major*; Verdi: *La Traviata*; Wagner: *Walküre, Liebes Duett (Walküre), Rheingold, Lohengrin*; Wallace: *Maritana*; Weber: *Oberon Overture, Euryanthe Overture, Jubel Overture, Freischütz Overture, Freischütz Air, Preziosa Overture.*

Liszt, Franz. *Albums of Orchestra Parts,* #8622. Edwin F. Kalmus. $9.00. Complete parts to *Faust Symphony, Tasso, Totentanz, Mephisto Waltz, Mazeppa.*

Mahler, Gustav. *Albums of Orchestra Parts,* #8623. Edwin F. Kalmus. $9.00. Set of complete parts to *Symphonies Nos. 1, 2, 5.*

Mahler, Gustav. *Sinfonie Nr. 1–6 (für Posaune und Tuba).* ed. Göss.

Mahler, Gustav. *Sinfonie Nr. 7–10 und Das Lied von der Erde (für Posaune und Tuba).* ed. Göss.

Massenet, Jules, and Giacomo Meyerbeer. *Albums of Orchestra Parts,* #8624. Edwin F. Kalmus. $9.00. Set of complete parts to Massenet: *Phèdre Overture, Le Cid Ballet*; Meyerbeer: "Coronation March" from *The Prophet.*

Meschke, Dieter, ed. *Orchestral Studies: Tuba.* VEB Deutscher Verlag für Musik Leipzig. 1989. 127 pp. Contains excerpts from Meyerbeer: *Fackeltanz* (Torch Dance); Lortzing: *Undine*; Adam: *Giselle*; Berlioz: *Symphonie Fantastique, The Corsair, Benvenuto Cellini, The Damnation of Faust*; Mendelssohn: *Calm Sea and Prosperous Voyage, A Midsummer Night's Dream, St. Paul, Elijah*; Liszt: *Les Preludes*; Wallace: *Maritana;* von Flotow: *Martha*; Wagner: *Eine Faust Overture, Rienzi, The Flying Dutchman, Tannhäuser, Lohengrin, Das Rheingold, Die Walküre, Siegfried, Götterdämmerung, Tristan und Isolde, Die Meistersinger, Parsifal*; Verdi: *Nabucco, Macbeth, Luisa Miller, Rigoletto, Il Trovatore, La Traviata, Simone Boccanegra, La forza del destino, Don Carlos, Aida, Othello, Falstaff, Requiem*; Moniuszko: *Halka*; Franck: *Symphony in D Minor, Psyche*; Smetana: *Richard III, Wallenstein's Camp, Hakon Jarl, Ma Vlast, Vysehrad, Die Moldau, Sarka, From the Fields and Groves of Bohemia, Tabor, Blanik*; Bruckner: *Symphonies Nos. 4–9, Te Deum*; Brahms: *Symphony No. 2, Academic Festival Overture, Overture in C Minor, Ein Deutsches Requiem*; Borodin: *Symphony No. 2, Prince Igor.*

Morris, R. Winston. *An Introduction to Orchestral Excerpts for Tuba.* Shawnee Press. 1974. $8.00. 39 pp. Excellent for the introduction of orchestral playing, this anthology includes excerpts from Prokofiev: "Kije's Wedding" (from *Lieutenant Kije*); Moussorgsky: *Night on Bald Mountain*; Rimsky-Korsakoff: *Russian Easter Overture*; Mahler: *Symphony No. 1* (mvt. 3); Saint-Saëns: *Symphony No. 3* (mvt. 2); Shostakovich: "Polka and Dance" (from *The Age of Gold*), *Symphony No. 5* (mvts. 1 and 4), *Symphony No. 9* (Finale), *Festival Overture*; Liszt: *Les Preludes*; Sibelius: *Finlandia*; Brahms: *Academic Festival Overture*; Tchaikowsky: *Symphony No. 6* (mvts. 1, 2, 3), *Romeo et Juliette, Symphony No. 4* (mvt. 4), *Overture 1812*; Franck: *Symphony in D Minor* (mvts. 1 and 3); Wagner: *Ride of the Valkyries, Die Meistersinger* (Prelude to Act I), *Lohengrin* (Prelude to Act III); Berlioz: *The Damnation of Faust* ("Hungarian March"), *Symphonie Fantastique* (mvts. 4 and 5).

Müller, Heinz. *Intonation Studies for Trombone.* VEB Friedrich Hofmeister—Leipzig. 56 pp. Though written for trombone, this book includes portions of the tuba parts to Bruckner: *Symphony No. 4* (mvt. 4), *Symphony No. 5* (mvt. 4), *Symphony No. 6* (mvts. 2 and 4), *Symphony No. 9* (mvts. 1 and 3); Brahms: *Symphony No. 2* (mvts. 1 and 2); Tschaikowski: *Symphony No. 4* (mvt. 1), *Symphony No. 6* (mvts. 1 and 4), *Schwanensee*; Dvořák: *Symphony No. 9* ("New World," mvt. 2); Verdi: *Don Carlos, Nabucco, Othello*; Wagner: *The Flying Dutchman, Tannhäuser, Lohengrin.*

Müller, Robert, and Teuchert, E. *Orchester Studien für alle Instrumente für Tuba, Heft I.* Verlag Friedrich Hofmeister, Leipzig. Out of print. One of the few clues to Teuchert's background in his etude and study works is found on the title page of this text: "Emile Teuchert: kammervirtuos und Tubaist der Sächs. Staatskapelle Dresden." Contents include Richard Strauss: *Don Quixote, Don Juan, Macbeth, Tod und Verklärung, Till Eulenspiegel, Also sprach Zarathustra, Symphony Domestica.*

Müller, Robert, and Teuchert, E. *Orchester Studien für alle Instrumente für Tuba, Heft II.* Verlag Friedrich Hofmeister, Leipzig. Out of print. This volume is very similar in content to the 1911 work attributed only to Teuchert (below). Contains excerpts from Auber: *Die Stumme von Portici;* Bendel: *Rothkäppchen;* Reger: *Variationen und Fuge;* Wallace: *Maritana Overture;* Büttner-Tartier: *Die Heilblume;* Hartmann: *Eine Nordische Heerfahrt;* Lortzing: *Undine;* Smetana: *Richard III;* Verdi: *La Traviata, Falstaff;* Volbach: *Sinfonie H moll;* Leoncavallo: *Der Bajazzo;* Scheinpflug: *Frühling: Ein Kampf und Lebensbild.*

Müller, Robert, and Teuchert, E. *Orchester Studien für alle Instrumente für Tuba, Heft III.* Verlag Friedrich Hofmeister, Leipzig. Out of print. Contains excerpts from Hausmann: *Fortuna;* Huber: *Sinfonie No. 3 (heroische) in C dur;* Kalafati: *Ouverture-Fantasie, Op. 8;* Pierson: *Musik zu "Faust,"* Berlioz: *Marsch für die Überreichung der Fahnen, Trauermarsch, Heroide Funèbre, Die Vehmrichter;* Schmidt: *Sinfonie in E dur;* Smetana: *Aus Böhmens Hein und Flur;* Verdi: *Aida;* Wolf: *Penthesilia;* Dohnányi: *Der Schlier der Pierre;* Lange: *Komisches Sextett.*

Nielsen, Carl. *Orchestral Studies for Trombone and Tuba, Volume One.* Edition Wilhelm Hansen. 1984. 29 pp. Includes excerpts from Nielsen: *Symphony No. 1 in G Minor,* "Aladdin" (No. 6 from *Dance of the Prisoners*), *Symphony No. 2* ("The Four Temperaments"), *Concerto for Flute and Orchestra, Rhapsodic Overture, Masquerade* ("Overture" and "Cock's Dance").

Nielsen, Carl. *Orchestral Studies for Trombone and Tuba, Volume Two.* Edition Wilhelm Hansen. 1984. 35 pp. Contains excerpts from Nielsen: *Symphony No. 3* ("Sinfonia Expansive"), *Symphony No. 4* ("The Inextinguishable").

Nielsen, Carl. *Orchestral Studies for Trombone and Tuba, Volume Three.* Edition Wilhelm Hansen. 1984. 19 pp. Contains excerpts from Nielsen: *Symphony No. 5, Concerto for Violin and Orchestra, Symphony No. 6* ("Sinfonia Semplice"), *Saul and David* (Prelude to Act II).

Pniak, Jan. *Studia orkiestrowe na tube.* In preparation.

Prokofieff, Serge. *Albums of Orchestra Parts, #8625.* Edwin F. Kalmus. $9.00. Complete parts to *Symphonies* Nos. 5, 6, 7.

Prokofieff, Serge. *Albums of Orchestra Parts, #8626.* Edwin F. Kalmus. $9.00. This is a set of complete parts to "Suite" from the *Love for Three Oranges* Op. 33, *Lt. Kije Suite* Op. 60, *Cinderella Suite No. 3.*

Prokofieff, Serge. *Albums of Orchestra Parts, #8627.* Edwin F. Kalmus. $9.00. Complete parts to *Romeo and Juliet Suites* Nos. 1, 2, 3.

Prokofieff, Serge. *Albums of Orchestra Parts, #8628.* Edwin F. Kalmus. $9. Complete parts to *Piano Concertos Nos. 1 and 5, Violin Concerto No. 1.*

Rachmaninoff, Serge. *Albums of Orchestra Parts, #8629.* Edwin F. Kalmus. $9.00. Complete parts to *Piano Concertos Nos. 2 and 3, Isle of the Dead.*

Rimsky-Korsakoff, Nicholas. *Albums of Orchestra Parts, #8630.* Edwin F. Kalmus. $9.00. Complete parts to *Capriccio Espagnol, Sheherazade, Russian Easter Overture.*

Rimsky-Korsakoff, Nicholas. *Albums of Orchestra Parts, #8631.* Edwin F. Kalmus. $9.00. Complete parts to *Le Coq d'Or Introduction, Le Coq d'Or Suite, Mlada Suite,* "Polonaise" from *Christmas Eve.*

Saint-Saëns, Camille. *Albums of Orchestra Parts, #8632.* Edwin F. Kalmus. $9.00. Complete parts to "Bacchanale" from *Samson, Symphony No. 3* Op. 78, *Suite Algerienne* Op. 60.

Sear, Walter, and Lewis Waldeck. *Tuba Excerpts, Volume I.* Cor Publishing Company. 1966. $6.00. 32 pp. Contains excerpts from Berlioz: *Damnation of Faust, Symphonie Fantastique, Corsaire Overture, Harold in Italy, Benvenuto Cellini, Romeo and Juliet, Trojan March, Requiem, King Lear,* "Funeral March" from *Hamlet, Heroide Funèbre;* Brahms: *Academic Festival Overture, Symphony No. 2, Tragic Overture;* Bach: *Passacaglia and Fugue in C Minor;* Borodin: *Symphony No. 2;* Bruckner: *Symphony No. 4, Symphony No. 5, Symphony No. 6, Symphony No. 7, Symphony No. 8, Symphony No. 9, Te Deum;* Donizetti: *Lucia di Lammermoor;* Debussy: *Iberia, La Mer;* Delibes: *Coppelia;* Elgar: *Cockaigne Overture.*

Sear, Walter, and Lewis Waldeck. *Tuba Excerpts, Volume II.* Cor Publishing Company. 1966. $6.00. 32 pp. Contains excerpts from Elgar: *Enigma Variations;* Franck: *Symphony in D Minor;* Ibert: *Escales;* Leoncavallo: *I Pagliacci;* Liszt: *Les Preludes;* Mahler: *Das Lied von der Erde, Symphonies 1, 2, 9, 10;* Mascagni: *Cavalleria Rusticana;* Mendelssohn: *Midsummer Night's Dream;* Meyerbeer: *Fackeltanz;* Mussorgsky: *Night on Bald Mountain;* Prokofiev: *Lt. Kije, Piano Concerto No.1, Symphony No.5, Romeo and Juliet No. 2, Scythian Suite;* Respighi: *Pines of Rome, Feste Romane, Fountains of Rome;* Shostakovich: *Symphony No. 1, Symphony No. 5, Symphony No. 6, Symphony No. 7, Symphony No. 9, Golden Age;* Sibelius: *Finlandia, Symphonies 1, 2;* Smetana: *Die Moldau, From Bohemia's Fields and Forest;* Strauss: *Don Quixote, Ein Heldenleben, Death and Transfiguration, Don Juan, Macbeth, Also Sprach Zarathustra, Til Eulenspiegel's Lustige Streiche;* Tchaikowsky: *Symphonies 4, 5, 6, Sleeping Beauty, Romeo and Juliet, 1812 Overture;* Rossini: *Thieving Magpie;* Rimsky-Korsakov: *Capriccio Es-*

pagnol, Russian Easter Overture, Coq D'or, Sheherazade.

Sear, Walter, and Lewis Waldeck. *Tuba Excerpts, Volume III.* Cor Publishing Company. 1969. $6.00. 32 pp. Contains excerpts from Wagner's *Der Fliegende Holländer, Tannhäuser, Lohengrin, Die Meistersinger, Das Rheingold, Die Walküre, Siegfried, Eine Faust Overture, Götterdämmerung, Parsifal.*

Seyffarth, F. *Orchesterstudien (Complete), Volume One.*

Seyffarth, F. *Orchesterstudien (Complete), Volume Two.*

Shifrin, Ken, and Danny Longstaff. *British Orchestral Excerpts for Trombone and Tuba, Volume I.* Virgo Music Publishers. 1986. 58 pp. Contains trombone and tuba (where applicable) excerpts from Arnold: *Tam O'Shanter Overture*; Britten: *Peter Grimes—Four Sea Interludes from the Opera, War Requiem, The Young Person's Guide to the Orchestra*; Elgar: *The Dream of Gerontius*; Holst: *The Perfect Fool Ballet*; Walton: *Concerto for Viola and Orchestra.*

Shifrin, Ken, and Danny Longstaff. *British Orchestral Excerpts for Trombone and Tuba, Volume II.* Virgo Music Publishers (in preparation). Contains trombone and tuba (where applicable) excerpts from Britten: *Sinfonia da Requiem*; Elgar: *Symphony No. 2*; Holst: *The Planets*; Tippett: *Child of Our Time*; Vaughan Williams: *Sea Symphony*; Walton: *Symphony No. 1.*

Shifrin, Ken, and Danny Longstaff. *British Orchestral Excerpts for Trombone and Tuba, Volume III.* Virgo Music Publishers (in preparation). Contains trombone and tuba (where applicable) excerpts from Britten: *Spring Symphony*; Delius: *Brigg Fair*; Elgar: *Symphony No. 1*; Vaughan Williams: *Symphony No. 5*; Walton: *Belshazzar's Feast*; Wood: *Sea Songs.*

Shifrin, Ken, and Danny Longstaff. *British Orchestral Excerpts for Trombone and Tuba, Volume IV.* Virgo Music Publishers (in preparation). Contains trombone and tuba (where applicable) excerpts from Bax: *Tentagel*; Britten: "Passacaglia" from *Peter Grimes*; Elgar: *Cockaigne Overture, Music Makers, Pomp and Circumstance No. 1*; Tippett: *Symphony No. 4*; Vaughan Williams: *Symphony No. 6*; Walton: *Henry V, Portsmouth Point.*

Shostakovich, Dmitri. *Albums of Orchestra Parts, #8633.* Edwin F. Kalmus. $9.00. Complete parts to Symphonies Nos. 5, 9, 10.

Shostakovich, Dmitri. *Albums of Orchestra Parts, #8634.* Edwin F. Kalmus. $9.00. Complete parts to *Hamlet, Festive Overture, Golden Age Ballet Suite.*

Sibelius, Jean. *Albums of Orchestra Parts, #8635.* Edwin F. Kalmus. $9.00. Complete parts to Symphonies *Nos. 1 and 2, Finlandia, Karelia Suite.*

Smetana, Frederick. *Albums of Orchestra Parts, #8636.* Edwin F. Kalmus. $9.00. Complete parts to *Moldau, Sarka, Blanik, From Bohemia's Meadows and Forests.*

Stoneberg, Alfred. *Moderne Orchesterstudien für Posaune und Basstuba, Volume 1.* Musikverlage Hans Gerig Koln. 1953. $17.50. 35 pp. This series of orchestral studies includes trombone and tuba (when applicable) excerpts from "the most technically difficult passages in operatic and concert music." Volume 1 contains excerpts from Mozart: *Tuba mirum aus dem Requiem*; Berlioz: *Faust's Verdammung Op. 24*; Schumann: *Symphonie Nr. 2 in C-Dur, Symphonie Nr. 3 in Es-Dur*; Rimsky-Korsakow: *Scheherazade*; D'Albert: *Tiefland*; Brahms: *Symphonie Nr. 1 in C-Moll Op. 68, Symphonie Nr. 2 in D-Dur Op. 73*; Ravel: *Bolero*; Strawinsky: *Pulcinella, Petruschka, Psalmen Symphonie*; Hindemith: *Sinfonische Metamorphosen*; Barber: *Medea.*

Stoneberg, Alfred. *Moderne Orchesterstudien für Posaune und Basstuba, Volume 2.* Musikverlage Hans Gerig Koln. 1953. $17.50. 34 pp. (See annotation for Volume 1.) Volume 2 contains excerpts from Berlioz: *Roman Carnival Ouverture*; Tschaikowsky: *Klavier-Konzert Nr. 1, Francesca da Rimini, 1812 Ouverture Solenelle*; Borodine: *Die Polewetzer Tanze a.d. Oper "Furst Igor"*; Reger: *Requiem*; Wolf-Ferrari: *Der Schmuck der Madonna*; Ravel: *La Valse, Daphnis et Chloe*; Strawinsky: *Der Feuervogel, Symphonie en Ut*; Hindemith: *Konzertmusik fur Streicher und Blechbläser.*

Stoneberg, Alfred. *Moderne Orchesterstudien für Posaune und Basstuba, Volume 3.* Musikverlage Hans Gerig Koln. 1953. $17.50. 39 pp. (See annotation for Volume 1.) Volume 3 contains excerpts from Schumann: *Symphonie Nr. 4 in D-moll*; Verdi: *Die Macht des Schicksals* (Ouverture); Cornelius: *Der Barbier von Bagdad*; Bruckner: *Symphonie Nr. 3 in D-moll* (second version, 1878), *Symphonie Nr. 4 in Es-Dur* (original version), *Symphonie Nr. 5 in B-Dur* (original version); Mussorgsky: *Tableaux d'une exposition (Bilder einer Ausstellung)*; Bartók: *Konzert für Orchester, Violin-Konzert*; Weinberger: *Schwanda der Dudelsackpfeifer*; Prokofieff: *Peter and the Wolf* (Op. 67).

Stoneberg, Alfred. *Moderne Orchesterstudien für Posaune und Basstuba, Volume 4.* Musikverlage Hans Gerig Koln. 1953. $17.50. 49 pp. (See annotation for Volume 1.) Volume 4 contains excerpts from Bruckner: *Symphonie Nr. 7 in E-Dur* (original version), *Symphonie Nr. 8 in C-Moll* (Original version); Brahms: *Tragische Ouverture*; Dvořák: *Symphonie Nr. 5 (Aus der neuen Welt)*; Rimsky-Korsakoff: *Russiche Ostern* (Ouverture); Martin: *Konzert fur sieben Bläser und Orchester*; Bartók: *Tanz-Suite*; Blacher: *Orchestervariationen über ein Thema von Paganini*; Tschaikowsky: *Symphonie Nr. 4 in F-Moll, Symphonie Nr. 6 in H-Moll* (Pathétique); Berg: *Violin-Konzert*; Mahler: *Symphonie Nr. 3*; Liszt: *Les Preludes, Zweite Ungarische Rhapsodie.*

Stoneberg, Alfred. *Moderne Orchesterstudien für Posaune und Basstuba, Volume 5.* Musikverlage Hans

Gerig Koln. 1953. $17.50. 47 pp. (See annotation for Volume 1.) Volume 5 contains excerpts from Bach: *Christ lag in Todesbanden* (Kantate am Osterfeste); Rietz: *Ouverture in A-Dur*; Smetana: *Die verkaufte Braut* (Ouverture); Strauss: *Eine Alpensinfonie, Der Bürger als Edelmann*; Pfitzner: *Palestrina, Von Deutscher Seele*; Mohaupt: *Die Gaunerstreiche der Courasche.*

Stoneberg, Alfred. *Moderne Orchesterstudien für Posaune und Basstuba, Volume 6.* Musikverlage Hans Gerig Koln. 1953. $17.50. 44 pp. (See annotation for Volume 1.) Volume 6 contains excerpts from Beethoven: *Symphonie Nr. 5* Op. 67, *Fidelio* Op. 72, *Missa Solemnis* Op. 123, *Symphonie Nr. 9* Op. 125; Maillart: *Das Glöckchen des Eremiten*; Berlioz: *Phantastische Symphonie*; Pfitzner: *Konzert für Violine in H-moll*; Orff: *Carmina Burana.*

Stoneberg, Alfred. *Moderne Orchesterstudien für Posaune und Basstuba, Volume 7.* Musikverlage Hans Gerig Koln. 1953. $17.50. 42 pp. (See annotation for Volume 1.) Volume 7 contains excerpts from Bruckner: *Symphonie Nr. 1 in C-moll* (Linz version), *Symphonie Nr. 2 in C-moll* (original version), *Symphonie Nr. 4 in A-dur* (original version), *Symphonie Nr. 9 in D-moll* (original version); Hindemith: *Mathis der Maler* (Oper in sieben Bildern).

Stoneberg, Alfred. *Moderne Orchesterstudien für Posaune und Basstuba, Volume 8.* Musikverlage Hans Gerig Koln. 1953. $17.50. 46 pp. (See annotation for Volume 1.) Volume 8 contains excerpts from Mozart: *Die Zauberflöte, Don Juan* (*Don Giovanni*); Humperdinck: *Hänsel und Gretel*; Berg: *Wozzeck.*

Stöneberg, Alfred. *Verdi Orchesterstudien, Vol. I.* Musikverlage Hans Gerig Koln. $19.50. Contains trombone and tuba (where applicable) excerpts from the Verdi operas *Troubadour*, and *Macbeth.*

Stöneberg, Alfred. *Verdi Orchesterstudien, Vol. II.* Musikverlage Hans Gerig Koln. $13.50. Contains trombone and tuba (where applicable) excerpts from the Verdi operas *Aida*, and *Sizilianische Vesper.*

Stöneberg, Alfred. *Verdi Orchesterstudien, Vol. III.* Musikverlage Hans Gerig Koln. $13.50. Contains trombone and tuba (where applicable) excerpts from the Verdi operas: *Othello*, and *Nabucco.*

Stöneberg, Alfred. *Verdi Orchesterstudien, Vol. IV.* Musikverlage Hans Gerig Koln. $13.50. Contains trombone and tuba (where applicable) excerpts from the following Verdi operas *Don Carlos*, and *Rigoletto.*

Stöneberg, Alfred. *Verdi Orchesterstudien, Vol. V.* Musikverlage Hans Gerig Koln. $13.50. Contains trombone and tuba (where applicable) excerpts from the Verdi operas *Macht des Schicksals, Simone Boccanegra, La Traviata.*

Stöneberg, Alfred. *Verdi Orchesterstudien, Vol. VI.* Musikverlage Hans Gerig Koln. $13.50. Contains trombone and tuba (where applicable) excerpts from the Verdi operas *Maskenball*, and *Falstaff.*

Strauss, Johann. *Albums of Orchestra Parts, #8641.* Edwin F. Kalmus. $9.00. A set of complete parts to *Tales from the Vienna Woods, Blue Danube Waltz, Artists Life, Thunder and Lightning.*

Strauss, Richard. *Albums of Orchestra Parts, #8639.* Edwin F. Kalmus. $9.00. A set of complete parts to *Death and Transfiguration, Till Eulenspiegel, Don Juan.*

Strauss, Richard. *Albums of Orchestra Parts, #8640.* Edwin F. Kalmus. $9.00. A set of complete parts to *Also Sprach Zarathustra, Don Quixote, Ein Heldenleben.*

Strauss-Berthold. *Orchestra Studies.*

Stravinsky, Igor. *Albums of Orchestra Parts, #8637.* Edwin F. Kalmus. $9.00. A set of complete parts to *Petroushka, Firebird* (1919), *Fireworks.*

Stravinsky, Igor. *Albums of Orchestra Parts, #8638.* Edwin F. Kalmus. $9.00. A set of complete parts to *The Rite of Spring*, and *Symphony No. 1.*

Tchaikovsky. See Tschaikowsky.

Teuchert, E.T. *Orchesterstudien für Basstuba.* Breitkopf & Haertel, Leipzig. 57 pp. Contains tuba excerpts from: d'Albert: *Der Rubin, Gernot*; Bantock: *Der Zeitgeist, Helena*; Berger: *Symphonie in B dur*; Berlioz: *Phantastische Symphonie, Trojanischer Marsch, Requiem, Fausts Verdämmung, Benvenuto Cellini*; Chabrier: *Gwendoline*; Donizetti: *Lucia di Lammermoor*; Dräske: *Herrat*; Glazounow: *Symphonie*; Halévy: *Die Jüdin*; Kretzschmer: *Die Folkunger*; Liszt: *Ce qu'on entend sur la montage, Tasso, Die Ideale*; Mascagni: *Cavalleria Rusticana*; Mendelssohn: *Musik zu Shakespeares Sommernachtstraum*; Nicodé: *Das Meer*; Novak: *Von ewiger Sehnsucht*; Saint-Saëns: *Samson und Dalila*; Sibelius: *Symphonie Nrs. 1 and 2*; Strauss: *Till Eulenspiegels lustige Streiche, Also sprach Zarathustra*; Thomas: *Hamlet*; Tinel: *Franziskus, Drei symphonische Tongemälde, Godoleva*; Tschaikowsky: *Symphonie Nr. 4*; Verdi: *Rigoletto*; Volbach: *Es waren zwei Königskinder*; Wagner: *Lohengrin, Tristan und Isolde, Eine Faust-Ouvertüre*; Weingartner: *Symphonie Nr. 2*; Zoellner: *Der Überfall, Die versunkene Glocke.*

Teuchert, Emil. *Orchesterstudien für Basstuba (Serpent-Ophikleide) aus Oratorien, Opern, Sinfonien und anderen Orchesterwerken, Heft I.* Verlag Friedrich Hofmeister, Leipzig. Out of print. 1911. Contains excerpts from Auber: *Die Stumme von Portici*; Bendel: *Rothkäppchen*; Berlioz: *Harold en Italien*; Büttner-Tartier: *Die Heilblume*; Hartmann: *Eine Nordische Heerfahrt*; Lortzing: *Undine*; Mendelssohn: *Elias*; Meyerbeer: *Der Prohet, Struensee*; Pierson: *Musik zu Faust*; Reger: *Variationen und Fuge*; Smetana: *Richard III*; Verdi: *La Traviata*, Volbach: *Sinfonie H moll*; Wallace: *Maritana Overture.*

Teuchert, Emil. *Tägliche Übungen für Tuba, mit Anhang der Schwierigsten Orchesterstellen.* Seeling/Erdmann. 1936/64.

Torchinsky, Abe. *The Tuba Player's Orchestral Repertoire, Volume One.* European American Music Corporation. Out of print. 1975. $14.95. 68 pp. Contains complete parts from Mendelssohn: *A Midsummer Night's Dream, Elijah*; Berlioz: *King Lear, Waverly, The Judges of the Secret Court* (tubas I and II), *Grand Death-Mass* (orchestras I and II), *Fantastic Symphony* (tubas I and II), *Harold in Italy, Romeo and Juliet, The Corsair, Te Deum* (tubas I and II), *Benvenuto Cellini, The Damnation of Faust, Trojan March, Symphonie Descriptive: Chasse et Orange, Lelio, Funeral and Triumphal Symphony* (tubas I and II).

Torchinsky, Abe. *The Tuba Player's Orchestral Repertoire, Volume Two*. European American Music Corporation. Out of print. 1976. $10.00. 26 pp. Contains complete parts from Wagner: *A Faust Overture; Overture to Rienzi; Overture to The Flying Dutchman; Tannhäuser* (Overture, Overture and Scene One [Venusberg], and Chorus ["Arrival of the Guests at Wartburg"]); Lohengrin (Prelude to the opera and Introduction to Act III); *The Mastersingers of Nuremberg* (Prelude to the opera, Prelude to Act III, "Dance of the Apprentices," "Procession of the Mastersingers," and "Greeting to Hans Sachs"); Prelude and "Isolde's Love Death" from *Tristan and Isolde*; "Entrance of the Gods into Valhalla" from *The Rhinegold; The Valkyrie* ("The Ride of the Valkyries," "Wotan's Farewell," and "Magic Fire Music"); *The Twilight of the Gods* ("Siegfried's Rhine Journey" and "Siegfried's Narrative/Death with Funeral March"); *Parsifal* (end of Act III and "Good Friday Spell").

Torchinsky, Abe. *The Tuba Player's Orchestral Repertoire, Volume Three*. Encore Music Publishers. 1989. $24.00. 58 pp. Previously published by Joseph Boonin, Incorporated. Contains complete parts from Brahms: *A German Requiem, Symphony No. 2, Academic Festival Overture, Tragic Overture, Song of the Fates*; Dvořák: *Symphony in E♭ Major (No. 3), Symphony in D Major* (No. 6, old No. 3), *Scherzo Capriccioso, Husitska, Symphony in G Major* (No. 8, old No. 4), *Requiem Mass, Carnival, In Nature's Realm, Othello, Symphony in E Minor* (No. 9, old No. 5), *Suite in A Major, Concerto for Violoncello and Orchestra, The Noon Witch, The Golden Spinning Wheel*.

Torchinsky, Abe. *The Tuba Player's Orchestral Repertoire, Volume Four*. Encore Music Publishers. $27. 63 pp. Previously published by Joseph Boonin, Incorporated. Contains complete parts from Strauss: *Serenade in E♭ Major, Don Juan, Macbeth, Tod und Verklärung, Till Eulenspiegels Lustige Streiche, Also Sprach Zarathustra* (tubas I and II), *Don Quixote* (tenor tuba in B♭, tenor tuba in C, and bass tuba parts), *Ein Heldenleben* (tenor tuba in B♭, tenor tuba in C, and bass tuba parts), *Symphonia Domestica, Eine Alpensinfonie* (tubas I and II), and *Salome's Tanz*.

Torchinsky, Abe. *The Tuba Player's Orchestral Repertoire, Volume Five*. Jerona Music Corporation.

1980. $11.95. 35 pp. Contains complete parts from Tchaikovsky: *Symphony No. 1, Symphony No. 2, Symphony No. 3, Symphony No. 4, Symphony No. 5, Symphony No. 6*.

Torchinsky, Abe. *The Tuba Player's Orchestral Repertoire, Volume Six*. Jerona Music Corporation. 1980. $10.95. 35 pp. Contains complete parts from Tchaikovsky: *The Tempest, Swan Lake Suite, Marche Slave, Francesca da Rimini, Capriccio Italien, 1812 Overture, Suite No. 2, Suite No. 3*.

Torchinsky, Abe. *The Tuba Player's Orchestral Repertoire, Volume Seven*. Jerona Music Corporation. 1980. $7.95. 28 pp. Contains complete parts from Tchaikovsky: *Manfred Symphony, Sleeping Beauty Suite, Hamlet, The Nutcracker Suite, Concerto No. 3 for Piano and Orchestra, Overture to L'Orage, Fatum, Le Voyvode, Marche Solennelle*, and *Romeo and Juliet*.

Torchinsky, Abe. *The Tuba Player's Orchestral Repertoire, Volume Eight*. Jerona Music Corporation. 1981. $14.95. 78 pp. Contains complete parts from Prokofiev: *Symphony No. 2, Symphony No. 3, Symphony No. 4, Symphony No. 5, Symphony No. 6, Symphony No. 7*.

Torchinsky, Abe. *The Tuba Player's Orchestral Repertoire, Volume Nine*. Jerona Music Corporation. 1981. $16.95. 87 pp. Contains complete parts from Prokofiev: *Piano Concerto No. 1, Piano Concerto No. 2, Violin Concerto No. 1*, Symphonic Suite from *The Love of Three Oranges, Piano Concerto No. 5, Lieutenant Kije Suite, Romeo and Juliet* (Suites Nos. 1, 2, and 3), *Alexander Nevsky, Cinderella* (Suites Nos. 1 and 3), *Summer Night Suite*.

Torchinsky, Abe. *The Tuba Player's Orchestral Repertoire, Volume Ten*. Jerona Music Corporation. 1982. $11.95. 50 pp. Contains complete parts from Stravinsky: *The Rite of Spring* (tubas I and II), *Firebird Suite* (1919 edition), *Petrouchka*.

Torchinsky, Abe. *The Tuba Player's Orchestral Repertoire, Volume Eleven*. Jerona Music Corporation. 1983. $13.95. 53 pp. Contains complete parts from Mahler: *Symphony No. 1, Symphony No. 2, Symphony No. 3, Symphony No. 5, Symphony No. 6*.

Torchinsky, Abe. *The Tuba Player's Orchestral Repertoire, Volume Twelve*. Jerona Music Corporation. 1985. $7.95. 23 pp. Contains complete parts from Franck: *Symphony in D Minor*; Saint-Saëns: *Third Symphony*; Chausson: *Symphony in B♭ Major*; Debussy: *Nocturnes, La Mer*.

Torchinsky, Abe. *The Tuba Player's Orchestral Repertoire, Volume Thirteen*. Jerona Music Corporation. 1985. $17.95. 56 pp. Contains complete parts from Bruckner (Nowak edition): *Symphony No. 4, Symphony No. 5, Symphony No. 6, Symphony No. 7, Symphony No. 8, Symphony No. 9*.

Torchinsky, Abe. *Twentieth Century Orchestra Studies for Tuba*. G. Schirmer, Incorporated. 1969. $13.75.

79 pp. Contains excerpts from Barber: *Medea's Meditation, Second Essay*; Bernstein: *On the Waterfront*; Bloch: *Schelomo*; Carter: *Variations*; Creston: *Invocation and Dance*; Diamond: *Fourth Symphony*; Einem: *Concerto for Orchestra*; Harris: *Third Symphony*; Hartmann: *Sixth Symphony*; Hindemith: *Konzertmusik, Mathis der Maler, Nobilissima Visione, Symphonic Metamorphosis*; Holst: *The Planets*; Mahler: *Tenth Symphony*; Orff: *Carmina Burana*; Piston: *The Incredible Flutist*; Prokofiev: *Cinderella Suite No.1, Lieutenant Kije Suite, Romeo and Juliet No. 1, Romeo and Juliet No. 2, Scythian Suite, Fifth Symphony, Sixth Symphony, Seventh Symphony, Violin Concerto No. 1*; Revueltas: *Sensemaya*; Riegger: *Third Symphony*; Schoenberg: *Theme and Variations*; Schuman: *Circus Overture, Third Symphony, Sixth Symphony*; Sessions: *Second Symphony*; Shostakovitch: *The Golden Age*; *First Symphony, Fifth Symphony, Seventh Symphony, Ninth Symphony*; Stravinsky: *Circus Polka, Scenes de Ballet, Symphony in Three Movements*; Thomson: *Louisiana Story, The Seine at Night, A Solemn Music*; Villa-Lobos: *Choros No. 8*; Weinberger: *Fugue from Shvanda*.

Tschaikowsky, Peter Ilich. *Albums of Orchestra Parts, #8643*. Edwin F. Kalmus. $9.00. Complete parts to Symphonies Nos. 1, 2, 3.

Tschaikowsky, Peter Ilich. *Albums of Orchestra Parts, #8644*. Edwin F. Kalmus. $9.00. Complete parts for Symphonies Nos. 4, 5, 6.

Tschaikowsky, Peter Ilich. *Albums of Orchestra Parts, #8645*. Edwin F. Kalmus. $9.00. Complete parts for *Marche Slave, Fransesca da Rimini, 1812 Overture, Romeo and Juliet Overture*.

Tschaikowsky, Peter Ilich. *Albums of Orchestra Parts, #8646*. Edwin F. Kalmus. $9.00. Complete parts for *Swan Lake Suite, Sleeping Beauty Suite, Nutcracker Suite No. 1*.

Tschaikowsky, Peter Ilich. *Albums of Orchestra Parts, #8647*. Edwin F. Kalmus. $9.00. Complete parts for *Suite No. 3, Nutcracker Suite No. 2, Capriccio Italien*.

Verdi, Giuseppe. *Albums of Orchestra Parts, #8642*. Edwin F. Kalmus. $9.00. Complete parts for *I Vespri Siciliani Overture, Forza del Destino Overture, Nabucco Overture*.

Wagner, Richard. *Albums of Orchestra Parts, #8648*. Edwin F. Kalmus. $9.00. Complete parts for the overtures to *Flying Dutchman, Tannhäuser, Meistersinger, Rienzi*, and "Prelude and Love Death" from *Tristan*.

Wagner, Richard. *Albums of Orchestra Parts, #8649*. Edwin F. Kalmus. $9.00. Complete parts for *The Ride of the Valkyries, Entry of the Gods into Valhalla, Siegfried's Rhine Journey, Wotan's Farewell, Magic Fire Music*.

Wagner, Richard. *Albums of Orchestra Parts, #8650*. Edwin F. Kalmus. $9.00. Complete parts for *Siegfried's Death and Funeral Music, Arrival of the Guests at Wartburg, Faust Overture, Venusberg Music*.

Wagner, Richard. *Wagner Orchester-Studien*. ed. F. Seyffarth. DV.

Wagner, Richard. *Werke Orchesterstudien aus seinen Bühnen und Konzertwerken: Tuba*. ed. Emil Teuchert. Breitkopf & Haertel. ca. 1910.

Watelle, Jules. *Choix de Passages Importants ou Difficiles d'Ouvrages Classiques ou Modernes pour le Tuba d'Orchestre*. Éditions Musicales E. Gaudet. Out of print. 1926. 26 pp.

Wekselblatt, Herbert. *Solos for the Tuba Player*. G. Schirmer, Incorporated. 1964. $13.95. 38 pp. Principally a collection of solos, but also contains several orchestral studies including Berlioz: *Hungarian March, Symphonie Fantastique*; Verdi: *Rigoletto, Ernani, Otello, Falstaff*; Wagner: *Lohengrin, Eine Faust Overture, Siegfried, Das Rheingold*; Strauss: *Salome, Also Sprach Zarathustra*.

Yeo, Douglas. *Orchestral Excerpts for Trombone and Tuba, Vol. I: Shostakovich*. Virgo Music Publishers. 1989. $12.50. 24 pp. Contains excerpts from Shostakovich's Third and Fourth Symphonies. Contains comments in the excerpted portions of the score describing texture and other information critical to proper performance, historical notes about each work, and a discography.

11. Recommended Basic Repertoire

For the High School Student

William Troiano

This writer's experience in teaching high school tubists, playing the literature, working on the New York State School Music Association contest manual for tuba, and chairing Long Island's annual Octubafests has provided valuable insight into the capabilities and limitations of high school tubists. With the assistance of a committee of *TSB* international consultants, the following lists of solos and method books were compiled. They reflect the best and most readily available literature for high school tuba students. However, these lists were conceived primarily for performance on BB♭ and CC tubas. Although most of this literature is playable on all keyed tubas, some selections might be inappropriate on F or E♭ tubas, largely because of the range. Teachers of students playing F or E♭ tubas should take this into consideration when assigning this literature for study.

The most challenging aspect of teaching high school tuba players is developing their musical skill to equal that of players of the higher-pitched instruments of the concert band. This effort can be very difficult if their abilities have not been encouraged from the start. It is interesting to observe their lack of progress between the time they began playing the tuba in elementary school (at nine or ten years of age, if they started as early as the school music program permitted) until they reach high school. Of course, there are exceptions, but, for the most part, high school tuba players are not prepared as complete musicians on their instruments.

Most students progress at a rate dictated by the musical requirements of the ensembles in which they perform, which, for wind players, is usually the concert band. Such factors as the amount of time they practice and their natural musical talent can affect their progress, but for the most part, they all start out as musical equals when they begin lessons at an early age. In most school music programs, the flute player, the trumpet player, and the tuba player all begin lessons the same week, with the same teacher, using the same method book. Their first lessons present the basics necessary for reading music, assembling the instrument, holding it, and producing a sound. As the weeks pass, they learn more notes and some complicated rhythms. The big moment arrives when they are accepted to play in the band. It is at this time that they begin to progress at different rates. Playing tuba parts in a band does not carry the same rewards as playing melody instruments, which are generally higher in pitch. After a few years, although the tuba player is a great asset to the band, the youngster is not ready to perform solo material at the same level as the flute or trumpet player. By high school, the tuba player has not encountered the range, complex rhythms, and musical phrases that players of higher-pitched instruments have.

Even if musical aptitude and time spent practicing are equal, it is more difficult for the tuba player to be a complete musician than it is for the trumpet or flute player. Students acquire much of their musical skill through band practice, and for the tubists that is not sufficient. It is, therefore, very important for young tubists to be carefully guided through the proper course of study so that they might also become self-fulfilled and complete instrumentalists, capable of playing various kinds of music at various levels of difficulty.

Several instrumental lesson books and band methods are suitable for beginning and intermediate tubists and should be used along with a minimum of long-tone, lip slur, and scale work. At an early age, it is more important to "feed" them songs! The method books, for the most part, tend to satisfy this deficiency. The songs can be supplemented with easy solos, most of which are available through the same publishers that supply the materials on the following basic repertoire lists.

Through solo work young tubists learn about melodic playing, and in the band they get experience in serving as the foundation of an ensemble. After about a year of study, it is also important to start playing duets, trios, and quartets with other euphonium and tuba players. If those instruments are lacking in the school program, young tubists should be encouraged to play small ensemble music with any available instruments. Band method books are perfect for this activity. As soon as possible, students should get involved in local Octubafests and TubaChristmases. These events, conceived and developed by Harvey Phillips of Indiana University, give tubists the marvellous experience of performing various voices of a four-part ensemble. As they perform and hear each other, perhaps along with a guest soloist, they become tremendously motivated.

The recommended basic repertoire for the high school student is intended for the serious player who is interested in becoming a more complete tubist. Most of the solo selections are written for tuba and piano; a few, as indicated, are unaccompanied. The lists of solos and method books do not pretend to include all the literature that exists for this level. New and obscure music has not been included, as these selections have not endured the test of time. All the recommended music is widely used among tubists, is of good quality, is published, and is readily available.

Although many solos and method books written for other instruments can be adapted or transposed for the tuba, the music listed here is written or arranged specifically for the tuba. It was decided not to include advanced multimovement solo works in which only individual movements are appropriate for high school tubists. The solos on the basic repertoire list should be studied as complete works so that the student can obtain the maximum benefits each piece has to offer. High school tubists may study more-advanced works that are not on the list and music written for other instruments at the discretion of their teachers.

The materials in the method books emphasize scales, arpeggios, articulation studies, legato studies, and other basic routines that are necessary to advancement as a tubist. The list also contains etude books, which are good for musical development, much as solos are, and the two are equally important to the high school tubist's development. The numbers in parentheses following the titles refer to the levels the method covers: I, freshman (14–15 years of age); II, sophomore (15–16 years of age); III, junior (16–17 years of age); and IV, senior (17–18 years of age). Level four material overlaps college-level methods.

The list of solos is also divided into four grade levels, and the technical challenges gradually increase. One encounters more complicated rhythms; greater range, especially in the higher register of the instrument; and longer pieces, including multimovement works.

A high school tubist would not have to play all the material on the lists to accomplish the goal of becoming a complete, self-fulfilled, and fine tubist. With careful guidance from a good teacher, opportunities to play in ensembles other than a concert band, and a good amount of time devoted to practice, the high school tubist who utilizes some of the material from each grade level will be well on the way to becoming a complete musician and and will be well prepared for study at the college level.

Appreciation and thanks are extended to the consultants who participated in compiling the recommended basic repertoire for the high school student: William D. Porter II, United States Air Force Concert Band; Jørgen Vøigt Arnsted, Symphonyorch of Odense, Denmark; Nicholas Zervopoulos, Philippos Naxas Conservatory, Greece; Steven Wassell, teacher, London, England; Bill Thiessen, Oak Ridge (Tennessee) Wind Ensemble; James Allen Garrett, Tennessee; Jerry Young, University of Wisconsin-Eau Claire; C. Rudolph Emilson, Fredonia State Universiy College, New York; and Michael Eastep, Calgary Philharmonic, Canada.

Method Books

Adler, S.	*Tubetudes* (II–IV)	Southern Music
Bell, W.	*Foundation to Tuba Playing* (I–II)	Carl Fischer
Beeler, W.	*Method for BB♭ Tuba, Book 1* (I)	Warner Bros.
Beeler, W.	*Method for BB♭ Tuba, Book 2* (II–IV)	Warner Bros.
Blazhevich, V.	*70 Studies—Vol. 1* (II–IV)	Robert King
Blazhevich, V.	*70 Studies—Vol. 2* (III–IV)	Robert King
Blazhevich, V./ Ostrander, A.	*Advanced Daily Drills* (III–IV)	Edition Musicus

Endresen, R.M.	*Supplementary Studies for Eb or BBb Bass* (I–IV)	Rubank, Inc.
Fink, R.H.	*Studies in Legato* (III–IV)	Carl Fischer
Geib, F.	*Method for Tuba* (I–IV)	Carl Fischer
Getchell, R.W./ Hovey, N.W.	*First Book of Practical Studies* (I)	Belwin Mills
Getchell, R.W./ Hovey, N.W.	*Second Book of Practical Studies* (I)	Belwin Mills
Gower, W./ Voxman, H.	*Advanced Method, Vol. 1* (I–IV)	Rubank, Inc.
Gower, W./ Voxman, H.	*Advanced Method, Vol. 2* (II–IV)	Rubank, Inc.
Kopprasch, C.	*60 Selected Studies* (III–IV)	Robert King
Kuehn, D.L.	*60 Musical Studies for Tuba, Book 1* (I–II)	Southern Music
Kuehn, D.L.	*60 Musical Studies for Tuba, Book 2* (II–IV)	Southern Music
Little, L.	*Embouchure Builder* (I–IV)	Pro Art
Pares, G.	*Daily Exercises and Scales* (I–IV)	Carl Fischer
Pares, G./ Whistler, H.S.	*Pares Scales for BBb Tuba* (I–IV)	Rubank, Inc.
Reger, W.M.	*The Talking Tuba* (I–III)	Charles Colin
Rusch, H.W.	*Hal Leonard Intermediate Band Method* (I–II)	Hal Leonard
Rusch, H.W.	*Hal Leonard Advanced Method* (II–IV)	Hal Leonard
Sear, W.	*Etudes for Tuba* (IV)	Cor Publishing Company
Skornicka, J.E./ Boltz, E.G.	*Rubank Intermediate Method for Eb or BBb Bass* (I)	Rubank, Inc.
Street, A.	*Scales and Arpeggios* (IV)	Boosey and Hawkes
Tyrell, H.W.	*40 Advanced Studies* (IV)	Boosey and Hawkes
Uber, D.	*First Studies for BBb Tuba* (I–II)	Kendor Music
Uber, D.	*25 Early Studies* (II–IV)	Southern Music
Uber, D.	*Warm-Up Procedure* (II–IV)	Charles Colin
Vandercook, H.A.	*Vandercook Etudes* (I–III)	Rubank, Inc.
Woodruff, F.	*24 Artistic Studies* (III–IV)	Southern Music

Solo Repertoire

LEVEL I. FRESHMAN (14–15 YEARS OF AGE)

Bach, J.S./ Weskelblatt, H.	*Two Bourées (Solos for the Tuba Player)*	G. Schirmer, Inc.
Dedrick, A.	*A Touch of Tuba*	Kendor Music
Handel, G.F./ Little, D.C.	*Larghetto and Allegro*	Belwin Mills
Handel, G.F./ Morris, R.W.	*Thrice Happy the Monarch*	Ludwig Music
Handel, G.F./ Voxman, H.	*Adagio and Allegro (Concert and Contest Collection)*	Rubank, Inc.
Haydn, F.J./ Bowles, R.W.	*Sonato No. 7 (First Movement) (Solo Sounds, levels 3–5, Vol. 1)*	Belwin Mills
Koepke, P./ Voxman, H.	*Persiflage (Concert and Contest Collection)*	Rubank, Inc.
Marcello, B./ Little, D.C.	*Largo and Presto (Solo Sounds, levels III–V, Vol. 1)*	Belwin Mills
Purcell, H./ Ostrander, A.	*Arise Ye Subterranean Winds*	Edition Musicus
Sear, W.	*Sonata*	Cor Publishing Company

| Vivaldi, A./ Maganini, Q. | *Praeludium in C Minor* | Edition Musicus |
| Vivaldi, A./ Swanson, K. | *Allegro from Sonato No. 3 (Solo Sounds, levels 3–5, Vol. 1)* | Belwin Mills |

LEVEL II. SOPHOMORE (15–16 YEARS OF AGE)

Alary, G. / Voxman, H.	*Morceau de Concours (Concert and Contest Collection)*	Rubank, Inc.
Denmark, M.	*Scène de Concert*	Ludwig Music
Dowling, R.	*His Majesty the Tuba (Solo Sounds, levels 3–5, Vol. 1)*	Belwin Mills
Holmes, G.E.	*Emmett's Lullaby*	Rubank, Inc.
Jaffe, G.	*Centone Buffo Concertante*	Southern Music
Marcello, B. / Little, D.C. / Nelson, R.B.	*Sonata No. 5 in C Major*	Southern Music
Mozart, W.A. / Voxman, H.	*First Movement (Concert and Contest Collection)*	Rubank, Inc.
Muller, J.I. / Ostrander, A.	*Praeludium, Chorale, Variations, and Fugue*	Edition Musicus
Ostransky, L. / Voxman, H.	*Serenade and Scherzo (Concert and Contest Collection)*	Rubank, Inc.
Painparé, H. / Voxman, H.	*Concertpiece*	Rubank, Inc.
Troje-Miller, N.	*Sonatina Classica*	Belwin Mills
Uber, D.	*Romance*	Kendor Music
Walters, H.	*Concertante*	Rubank, Inc.

LEVEL III. JUNIOR (16–17 YEARS OF AGE)

Bach, J.S. / Bell, W.	*Air and Bourrée*	Carl Fischer
Beethoven, L.van / Bell, W.	*Variations on the Theme of Judas Maccabeas*	Carl Fischer
Beversdorf, T.	*Sonata*	Southern Music
Catozzi, A. / Seredy, J.	*Beelzebub*	Carl Fischer
Frackenpohl, A.	*Concertino*	Robert King
Grundman, C.	*Tuba Rhapsody*	Boosey & Hawkes
Haddad, D.	*Suite*	Shawnee Press
Hartley, W.	*Aria*	Theodore Presser
Hartley, W.	*Sonatina*	Theodore Presser
Hartley, W.	*Suite for Unaccompanied Tuba*	Theodore Presser
Hogg, M.E.	*Sonatina*	Ensemble Publ.
Holmes, P.	*Lento*	Shawnee Press
Marcello, B. / Little, D.C. /Nelson, R.B.	*Sonata No.1 in F Major*	Southern Music
Nelhybel, V.	*Suite*	General Music
Presser, W.	*Rondo*	C.L. Barnhouse
Presser, W.	*Second Sonatina*	Theodore Presser
Ross, W.	*Tuba Concerto*	Boosey and Hawkes
Schooley, J.	*Serenata*	Glouchester Press
Telemann, G.P. / Friedman, N.F.	*Adagio and Allegro*	Southern Music
Uber, D.	*Evensong*	Kendor Music
Uber, D.	*Sonatina*	Southern Music
Uber, D.	*Summer Nocturne*	Southern Music
Vaughan, R.	*Concertpiece No.1*	Fema Music

LEVEL IV. SENIOR (17–18 YEARS OF AGE)

| Barat, J. Ed. | *Introduction and Dance* | Southern Music |
| Bencriscutto, F. | *Concertino* | Shawnee Press |

Frackenpohl, A.	*Sonata*	Kendor Music
Gabrieli, D. / Morris, R.W.	*Ricercar* (unaccompanied)	Shawnee Press
Handel, G.F. / Morris, R.W.	*Sonata No. 6*	Shawnee Press
Hartley, W.	*Concertino*	Theodore Presser
Hartley, W.	*Sonata*	Theodore Presser
Lebedev, A.	*Concerto in One Movement*	Edition Musicus
Mozart, W.A. / Morris, R.W.	*Serenade*	Shawnee Press
Mozart, W.A. / Wekselblatt, H.	*Romance and Rondo (Solos for the Tuba Player)*	G. Schirmer, Inc.
Persichetti, V.	*Serenade No.12 for Solo Tuba* (unaccompanied)	Theodore Presser
Presser, W.	*Capriccio*	Theodore Presser
Presser, W.	*Suite*	Ensemble Publ.
Sibbing, R.	*Sonata*	Theodore Presser
Stamitz, K.	*Rondo alla Scherzo (Solos for the Tuba Player)*	G. Schirmer, Inc.
Uber, D.	*Legend of the Sleeping Bear*	Kendor Music
Uber, D.	*Sonata*	Edition Musicus
Vivaldi, A. / Morris, R.W.	*Sonata No.3*	Shawnee Press
Vivaldi, A. / Ostrander, A.	*Concerto in A Minor*	Edition Musicus
Williams, E.S.	*Second Concerto*	Charles Colin

For the University Student

Daniel T. Perantoni and Michael Dunn, editorial assistant

The materials in this section encompass five levels of ability, from the freshman level in a college or university through the professional level. Players develop at varying rates, and a tubist may be weak in one area and quite strong in others. Therefore, one should be flexible when choosing literature from the various levels. Even if a student is able to perform a Level IV solo, there may be techniques that do not occur there that the player needs to work on in a Level III book. Since the term "cross-training" caught on a few years back, professionals from all walks of life have tried to incorporate that concept into their work. Everyone benefits from working on materials from various levels. It makes sense to continue to incorporate tone building and technical exercises into practice routines to maintain the basics.

This following list of method books, etudes, and solo literature is not intended to be comprehensive; rather it is quite subjective. Neither is it supposed to replace a private teacher, for only an experienced teacher can inspire and guide a student.

Only those materials currently in print were considered for this list, which contains 45 entries, ranging from elementary to very difficult and encompasses all styles of musical challenges. The materials are graded as follows: Level I, Pre-College; Level II, College Sophomore; Level III, College Junior; Level IV, College Senior–Graduate; Level V, D.M.A.–Professional.

The following individuals have submitted materials for consideration in this chapter: Jørgen V. Arnsted, Symphony Orchestra Odense; Cherry Beauregard, Eastman School of Music; Phillip C. Black, Wichita State University; Robert Brewer, Colorado State University; Gary Buttery, U.S. Coast Guard Band; Larry Campbell, Louisiana State University; Alain Cazes, Montreal Symphony; Barton Cummings, Walnut Creek Concert Band; Brent Dutton, San Diego State University; Dan Ellis, Furman University; Thomas R. Ervin, University of Arizona; Michael Formeck, Grove City College; Edward Goldstein, Towson State University; Skip Gray, University of Kentucky; Karl Hovey, Stephen F. Austin University; Jeff Jarvis, East Carolina University; Tommy Johnson, University of Southern California; Chitate Kagawa, Sapporo Symphony; Tony Kniffen, University of Hawaii; Steve Layman, University of Virginia; Don Little, University of North

Texas; Sande MacMorran, University of Tennessee; Rex Martin, Northwestern University; Charles McAdams, Central Missouri State University; William Mickelsen, University of South Florida; Mickey Moore, University of Illinois; R. Winston Morris, Tennessee Technological University; Douglas A. Nelson, Keene State College; Mark Nelson, Millikin University; Harvey Phillips, Indiana University; Eugene Pokorny, Chicago Symphony; Richard Powell, West Virginia University; David Randolph, University of Georgia; Steve Rossé, Sydney Symphony Orchestra; Jim Self, L.A. Studio Musician/Recording; Kevin Stees, James Madison University; Abe Torchinsky, University of Michigan and Robert Tucci, Bavarian State Opera Orchestra

Etudes and Studies

Adler, Samuel. *Tubetudes.* Southern Music Co., 1978. Level I–II. Sixteen very short etudes that progress quickly from junior high level to college freshman level. Contains many accidentals instead of key signatures. The last few exercises are technical in nature.

Arban, J. *Complete Conservatory Method for Trombone and Euphonium.* Randall and Simone Mantia. Carl Fischer. Level I–V. In bass clef. Part I: elementary studies, syncopation studies, dotted rhythms, slurs, and scales. Part II: ornamentation, intervals, sixteenth notes, triplets, arpeggio studies, multiple tonguing, characteristic studies, fanfares, and arias. Can be played an octave lower as well as in the register written. A must for all tubists to develop excellent technique.

Baker, David. *Bebop Jazz Solos.* Correlated with Volumes 10 and 13 of Jamey Aebersold's Play-A-Long Book and Record Series. Bass Clef edition, 1981.

Baker, David. *How to Play Bebop.* Vol. 1., The Bebop Scale and Other Scales in Common Use. Vol. 2., Learning the Bebop Language: Patterns, Formulae, and Other Linking Materials. Vol. 3., Techniques for Learning and Utilizing Bebop Tunes. Alfred Publishing Co., 1985. I–V.

Baker, David. *Improvisational Patterns: The Blues.* Bass-clef edition. New York: Charles Colin, 1980. I–V.

Baker, David. *Jazz Improvisation: A Comprehensive Method of Study for All Players.* Revised edition, 1983. Alfred Publishing Co. Level I–V.

Baker, David. *Jazz Solos.* Correlated with Volumes 5 and 6 of Jamey Aebersold's *Play-A-Long Book and Record Series.* Bass clef edition, 1979.

Baker, David. *A New Approach to Ear Training for the Jazz Musician.* Columbia Pictures Publications/ Belwin Mills, 1976.

Bell, William. *Foundation to Tuba and Sousaphone Playing.* Carl Fischer, 1931. I. Intended for the

serious high school tuba player. Contains excellent treatments of articulation and lip slurs. Useful band excerpts and musical examples balance the technical emphasis.

Bernard, Paul. *Quarante Etudes d'Après J. Forestier.* Alphonse-Leduc, 1948. I–III. A most useful French etude book. Very effective for the mastery of all the embellishments students tend to neglect.

Bernard, Paul. *Quarante Etudes pour Tuba.* Alphonse-Leduc, 1940. I–II. French method containing trills, mordents, turns, and other embellishments. Contains technical studies in a variety of keys.

Blazevich, V. *Seventy Studies for BBb Tuba,* Vols. I & II. Robert King. I–V. A highly recommended series for the serious tubist. Excellent studies in the "bread-and-butter" register. Contains melodious etudes, mixed meters, twentieth-century intervals, intricate rhythms, and technical studies in a variety of keys.

Blume, O. *Thirty-six Studies for Trombone with F Attachment.* ed. Reginald Fink. Carl Fischer, 1962. II–IV. Although originally written for trombone, this book contains a wealth of good etudes usable for the tuba.

Bobo, R. *Bach for the Tuba.* Western International Music. III–V. Transcriptions of the J. S. Bach cello suites have been carefully edited and phrased by one of the premier tuba soloists of our time. Excellent studies in phrasing and musicality.

Bordogni, M. *Melodious Etudes for Trombone,* Vols. I, II, and III. Trans. and progressively arr. by Johannes Rochut. Carl Fischer, 1928. I–V. Can be played an octave higher, where written, or one or two octaves lower. Highly recommended for developing smooth legato style and dark sound. Phrases are especially long for the tubist and sub-phrasing is recommended. Player should add dynamic contrasts. These books are standards and present musically rewarding exercises.

Bordogni, M./Roberts, C. *Forty-three Bel Canto Studies for Tuba.* Robert King, 1972. I–III. Contains some of the Rochut studies (Bordogni melodies) for trombone written an octave lower. Valuable introductory remarks. Very useful melodious studies. Sub-phrasing the longer phrases will be necessary to avoid tensions caused by air depletion.

Charlier, T. *Trente-Six Etudes Trancendentes.* Alphonse Leduc, 1946. III–V. Lyrical and technical etudes. Double and triple tonguing necessary. Many articulations, meters, and keys explored. Difficult.

Cimera, J. *Seventy-three Advanced Tuba Studies.* Belwin, 1955. I–II. Especially useful studies written in a variety of rhythms and keys. Stresses major as well as harmonic and melodic minor modes. Highly recommended.

Clark, Herbert. *Technical Studies.* Carl Fischer. III–IV. Bass clef and cornet edition. Read an octave lower accordingly. Good technical exercises, mostly scale oriented.

Concone, G. *Vocalises (Legato Etudes for Trombone)*. Carl Fischer. II–IV. Fine etude book offering lyrical solutions to the problems of phrasing and line shaping.

Delgiudice, Michel. *Dix Petite Textes*. Eschig, 1954. IV–V. Melodious and technical studies with piano accompaniment that are especially useful for the Eb and F tubas. Dwells in the high register and can be played by advanced players on the CC and BBb tubas. Wide range and difficult keys.

Dubois, Pierre Max. *Douze Soli en form d'Etudes*. Alphonse-Leduc, 1964. III–V. Lyrical and technical etudes for maintaining musicality and flexibility. No unusual rhythms or keys.

Fink, Reginald. *Studies in Legato for Bass Trombone and Tuba*. Carl Fischer, 1969. I–III. Although originally conceived for bass trombone, this book is useful for the tubist. Well-edited studies based on the works of Concone, Marchesi, and Panafka.

Fritze, Gregory. *Twenty Characteristic Etudes for Tuba*. TUBA Press. III–V. Good for intervallic study and basic musicianship. This book should be a part of every tubist's library.

Gallay, Jacques. *Thirty Etudes, Op. 13*. Robert King. I–III. These fine etudes are transcribed from the excellent original French horn method. Highly recommended.

Getchell, Robert. *Practical Studies*, Books 1 and 2. Belwin, 1955. I. Excellent books which systematically cover basic rhythms. Mostly in flat keys. Provides good fundamental material in the middle register.

Grigoriev, Boris. *Fifty Etudes*. King. II–IV. Reminiscent of the second volume of the Blazevich studies. Focuses on work in various meters and all keys. An often overlooked etude book.

Grigoriev, Boris. *Twenty-four Studies for Bass Trombone*. International. II–III. Very fine studies emphasizing various meters and intervallic work. Quite rangy but manageable even for the young student.

Hickman, David. *Music Speed Reading*. Wimbledon, 1979. I–III. An ingenious approach to sight reading. Uses an eye training method that has proven successful. Highly recommended.

Jacobs, Wesley. *Technical Series—Low Register Development for Tuba*. Encore. II–IV. One aspect of tuba playing which is often ignored by most methods and etude books is the low-register work. This book and the Snedecor book (below) go a long way toward answering this need. Lyrical melodies aid in keeping the air flow and musicality uppermost in the player's mind.

Knaub, Donald. *Progressive Techniques for Tuba*. M.C.A., 1970. I–IV. Preface contains a daily routine plus the harmonic series for the F, Eb, BBb, and CC tubas. Also contains fingering charts, including charts for the Eb and BBb compensating instruments. Includes the 70 etudes by Blazevich with instructions before each exercise to aid the student with interpretation and performance.

Kopprasch, C. *Sixty Selected Studies*. Robert King. I–IV. Covers a wide range of technical material in a variety of keys and meters. Highly recommended.

Kuehn, David. *Sixty Musical Studies for Tuba*. Southern Music Co., 1969. I–III. Book 1, excellent legato material in the middle to low range from the vocalises of Concone and Marchesi. Sub-phrasing the longer vocal phrases is necessary. Highly recommended. Book 2, excellent middle- and low-register playing from the vocalises of Ferdinand Sieber. Sub-phrasing is recommended. Encompasses a greater variety of keys than Book 1.

Kuehn, David. *Twenty-eight Advanced Studies*. Southern Music Co., 1972. I–IV. Advanced legato studies offering a wide range of musical challenges. Transcribed from the vocalises of Marchesi and Panofka. Keys go through five sharps and seven flats. Extremely long phrases demand sub-phrasing for best results.

Lachmann, Hans. *Funf-und-zwanzig Etuden für Bass Tuba* (25 Etudes). Hofmeister, 1956. IV–V. Can be used by tubas in any key for developing and controlling the upper register (fine F-tuba book). Excellent method utilizing all keys.

Lachmann, Hans. *Sechs-und-zwanzig Tuba Etuden* (26 Etudes). Hofmeister. IV–V. Very challenging etudes for F-tuba. Dwells on the upper register and contains very musical studies in a variety of keys.

Maenz, Otto. *Zwölf Spezialstudien für Tuba* (12 Special Studies). Hofmeister. IV–V. Some very challenging technical works containing mixed meters and contemporary intervals. Extreme range. Highly recommended for the advanced player.

Mueller, R. *Technical Studies*. Carl Fischer. III–V. An excellent set of studies for refining technical problems. Good compound meter work with an emphasis on various harmonies.

Ostrander, Allen. *Shifting Meter Studies*. Robert King, 1965. I–III. Contains unusual meters and rhythms in a contemporary setting. Good sight-reading material.

Pares, B. *Pares Scales*. ed. H. Whistler. Rubank, 1956. I. Contains essential technical exercises on scales with various articulations and keys. Highly recommended for the intermediate to advanced high school player.

Paudert, Ernst. *Eighteen Etudes*. Encore. III–IV. A fabulous book of etudes designed to refine one's musicianship and song style.

Paudert, Ernst. *Virtuoso Studies*. Encore. IV–V. These studies are not for the faint-hearted. Excellent technical challenges for the upper-level student and professional.

Pietzsch, H. *Twenty-two Virtuosity Studies*. rev. Georges Mager. Alphonse Leduc. IV–V. Originally for trumpet. Legato and technical studies using different styles of articulation. Double and triple tonguing. Medium difficulty.

Pottag, Max. *335 Selected Melodious, Progressive and Technical Studies,* Vols. 1 and 2. Southern Music Co. I–V. Comprehensive method book containing miscellaneous standard etudes and solos. Originally written for horn by some of the finer teachers and virtuosos of that instrument. These volumes start with relatively simple intervallic work and progress to extremely difficult exercises. Several short solos follow the method.

Reynolds, Verne. *Forty-eight Etudes for French Horn.* G. Schirmer, Inc., 1961. IV–V. Very difficult etudes encompassing a wide range of styles, articulations, and meters. Suitable as unaccompanied recital pieces. Highly recommended.

Rusch, Harold. *Hal Leonard Advanced Band Method for Basses (Tuba).* Hal Leonard, 1963. I–III. One of the best method books. Contains fifteen studies by Arnold Jacobs that should be in every tuba player's library.

Schlossberg, Max. *Daily Drills and Technical Studies for Trumpet.* M. Baron Co., 1941. III–V. Contains long-note drills, octave drills, lip drills, chord drills, scale drills, chromatic scale drills, and etudes.

Shoemaker, John. *Legato Studies for Tuba.* Carl Fischer, 2nd ed., 1973. I–II. Based on the vocalises of Concone. Thoughtful phrase markings. Mostly in the middle range with a good variety of keys.

Smith, W. *Top Tones for the Trumpeter, Thirty Modern Etudes.* Charles Colin. V. Very difficult book featuring innovative and effective method for increasing and maintaining range. Recommended for stu-

dents having problems comprehending the subtleties of upper-register playing.

Snedecor, Phil. *Low Etudes.* Robert King. II–V. Excellent book that focuses on a much-neglected element of tuba playing: the low register. These etudes are melodic, challenging, and, as much as possible, make low-register practice enjoyable. Highly recommended.

Torchinsky, Abe. *The Tuba Player's Orchestral Repertoire,* 12 vols. European-American Music. I–V. These books should be in every tuba player's library. They cover every major composer who wrote orchestral repertoire for tuba. Each book contains complete, uncut parts taken directly from the published parts, allowing the player to practice exactly what will be encountered in rehearsal. Each book has an invaluable preface, which describes difficulties, sensitive passages, and potential pitfalls in each excerpt. A must.

Tyrell, H.W. *Advanced Studies for BBb Bass (Tuba).* Boosey & Hawkes, 1948. I–III. Forty etudes, primarily in flat keys, that are especially beneficial for band musicians. Good rhythmical and technical studies. Highly recommended for the advanced high school and college student.

Vasiliev, S. *Twenty-four Melodious Etudes for Tuba.* Robert King. I–II. Very melodious "Russian" studies covering difficult intervals in a variety of keys.

Vernon, Charles. *Singing Approach to the Trombone and Other Brass.* Atlanta Brass Society Press. III–V. Novel approach to teaching and playing brass instruments. If you can play your way through this book, you can play anything.

Solo Repertoire

The following list of solos is selective and includes the most essential literature. Unaccompanied pieces are labeled (U), transcriptions (T), and taped accompaniments (T&t).

LEVEL I

Bach/Bell	*Air and Bourée* (T)	Carl Fischer
Bencriscutto	*Concertino*	Shawnee Press
Beversdorf	*Sonato*	Southern
Boda, John	*Sonatina*	Robert King
Frackenpohl, A.	*Concertino*	Robert King
Gabrieli/Morris	*Ricercar* (U/T)	Shawnee Press
Handel/Morris	*Sonata No. 6* (T)	Ludwig Music
Haddad	*Suite*	Shawnee Press
Hartley	*Aria*	Elkan-Vogel
Hartley	*Sonatina*	Fema Music
Hartley	*Unaccompanied Suite* (U)	Interlochen Press
Holmes	*Lento*	Shawnee Press
Lebedev	*Concerto*	Editions Musicus
Marcello	*Sonata No. 1* (T)	International Edition
Marcello	*Sonata No. 5* (T)	International Edition
Nelhybel	*Suite*	General Music

Perantoni, D.	*Master Solos*	Hal Leonard
Scott, Kathleen	*Andante and Allegro*	Queen City Brass Publications
Telemann/Chidster	*Adagio and Allegro* (T)	Southern Music
Uber	*Sonata*	Editions Musicus
Vaughan	*Concertpiece No. 1*	Fema Music

LEVEL II

Arnold	*Fantasy* (U)	Faber Music
Galliard	*Sonata No. 6* (T)	International Edition
Grundman, C.	*Tuba Rhapsody*	Boosey & Hawkes
Hartley	*Sonata*	Tenuto Publications
Jacob	*Tuba Suite*	Boosey & Hawkes
Marcello/Little	*Sonata No. 1*	Southern Music
Marcello/Little	*Sonata No. 5*	Southern Music
McFarland	*Sketches*	Theodore Presser
Schmidt, Wm.	*Serenade*	Avant Publications
Sibbing	*Sonata*	Theodore Presser
Stabile, James	*Sonata*	Wimbledon
Vaughan Williams	*Six Studies in English Folk Song* (T)	Galaxy Music
Vivaldi	*Concerto in A minor* (T)	Editions Musicus

LEVEL III

Benker, H.	*Miniaturen-Suite*	Zinneberg Musikverlag
Benson, Warren	*Helix*	Carl Fischer
Bernstein, L.	*Waltz for Mippy III*	Jaini Publications
Capuzzi	*Andante and Rondo* (T)	Hinrichsen
Crockett, E.	*Mystique* (T&t)	T.U.B.A. Press
Curnow, J.	*Fantasia for Tuba and Concert Band*	T.U.B.A. Press
Downey, John	*Tabu for Tuba*	Mentor Music
Glass, Jennifer	*Sonatina*	Emerson Edition
Heiden, Bernard	*Concerto for Tuba and Orchestra*	Southern Music
Hindemith	*Sonate*	Schott Söhne
Koetsier	*Sonatina*	Donemus
Ross, Walter	*Tuba Concerto*	Boosey & Hawkes
Sibbing, R.	*Sonata*	Tenuto Publications
Stevens, Halsey	*Sonatina*	Peer International
Stevens, John	*Triumph of the Demon Gods* (U)	Queen City Brass Publications
Swann	*Two Moods*	Chamber Music Library
Takacs, Jeno	*Sonato Capricciosa, Op. 81*	Verlag Doblinger
Wilder	*Suite No. 1 (Effie)*	Sam Fox
Wilder	*Sonata*	Margun Music

LEVEL IV

Barat	*Introduction and Dance*	Alphonse Leduc
Broughton	*Sonata*	MMP
George, Thom Ritter	*Sonata*	Thom Ritter George
Gregson	*Concerto*	Novello Publications
Hummel, Bertold	*Sonatine*	Hoffmeister
Jager, R.	*Concerto*	Piedmont Music
Kellaway	*The Morning Song*	Editions BIM
Koch, Erland von	*Monologue No. 9* (U)	Carl Gehrmans
Koetsier	*Concerto Op. 77*	Editions BIM
Kroll, Bernard	*Concerto*	Editions BIM
Lazarof, H.	*Cadence VI* (T&t)	Bote and Bock
Madsen, T.	*Conzert Op. 35*	Musikk-Huset A/S Norway
Madsen, T.	*Sonata Op. 34*	Musikk-Huset A/S Norway
Mahler/Perantoni	*Songs of a Wayfarer* (T)	Encore Music

Payne, Frank	Sonata	Shawnee Press
Persichetti	Serenade No. 12 (U)	Theodore Presser
Reck, D.	Five Studies	C.F. Peters
Reed	Fantasia a Due	Belwin-Mills
Reynolds	Sonata	Carl Fischer
Roikjer, K.	Andante	Imudico
Roikjer, K.	Sonate	Imudico
Ross	Concerto	Boosey & Hawkes
Russel	Suite Concertante	Accura Music
Schmidt, W.	Sonata	Western International Music
Strauss, R.	Horn Concerto No. 1 (T)	G. Schirmer, Inc.
Vaughan Williams	Concerto	Oxford University Press
White, D.H.	Sonata	Ludwig Music
Wilhelm, Rolf	Concertino	Strubverlaag GmbH

LEVEL V

Adler, Samuel	Canto VII (U)	Boosey & Hawkes
Bozza	Concertino	Alphonse Leduc
Jacobsen, J.	Tuba Buffo	STIM
Koch, Erland von	Tubania	STIM
Koeck, L.	Promenade	Dehaske Muziekuitgave BV
Kraft	Encounters II (U)	Editions BIM
Lundquist, T.	Landskap for Solo Tuba	STIM
Murguir, Jacques	Concertstück	Edition Musicales
Pauer, Jari	Tubonetta	Editions BIM
Penderecki	Capriccio for Tuba Solo (U)	Schott Söhne
Plog, A.	Three Miniatures	Editions BIM
Roikjer, K.	Capriccio	Imudico
Schmidt, O.	Concerto	Wilhelm Hansen Edition
Williams, John	Concerto	Warner Bros.
Wyatt, S.	Three for One (T&t)	Media Press

Recommended Four-Year Undergraduate Program

Three items are essential in the pursuit of the art of musicianship: a metronome, a tuner, and a good tape recorder. Without these helpful tools, one's development is unquestionably hindered.

FRESHMAN TUBA MAJOR

Etudes: Rochut, *Melodious Etudes;* Tyrell, *Advanced Studies;* Arban, *Complete Method;* Blazhevich, *70 Studies;* Bell, *Studies, Hal Leonard Advanced Band Method;* Kuehn, *28 Advanced Studies,* Kopprasch, *60 Selected Studies,* Vasiliev, *24 Melodious Etudes.*
Solos: Holmes, *Lento;* Bach, *Air and Bourée;* Haddad, *Suite;* Frackenpohl, *Concertino;* Hartley, *Suite for Unaccompanied Tuba;* Gabrieli, *Ricercar;* Telemann, *Adagio and Allegro;* Perantoni, *Master Solos—Intermediate Level;* Hartley, *Concertino.*
Orchestral Excerpts: Wagner, *Meistersinger;* Prokofiev, *Symphony No. 5;* Shostakovich, *Symphony No. 5;* Mahler, *Symphony No. 1;* Wagner, *Eine Faust Overture;* Gershwin, *An American in Paris;* Tchaikowsky, *1812 Overture, Symphony No. 4, Capriccio Italien.*

SOPHOMORE TUBA MAJOR

Etudes: Blume, *36 Studies;* Cimera, *73 Advanced Tuba Studies;* continue with Rochut, Blazhevich, Arban, and Kopprasch.
Solos: Galliard, *Sonatas Nos. 5 and 6;* Beversdorf, *Sonata;* Sibbing, *Sonata;* Schmidt, *Serenade;* Persichetti, *Serenade No. 12;* Vaughan Williams, *Six Studies in English Folk Song;* Vaughn, *Suite;* Ross, *Tuba Concerto.*
Orchestral Excerpts: Wagner, *Walküre;* Franck, *Symphony in D minor;* Berlioz, *Hungarian March;* Tchaikowsky, *Symphonies No. 5 and 6;* Brahms, *Symphony No. 2;* Berlioz, *Symphonie Fantastique;* Holst, *Planets.*
Duets: Jones, *21 Distinctive Duets;* Sear, *Advanced Duets;* Singleton ed., *25 Baroque and Classical Duets;* Hartley, *Bivalve Suite.*
F-Tuba: Marcello, *Sonata in F.*

JUNIOR TUBA MAJOR

Etudes: Rochut, *Melodious Etudes Book II;* Pottag, *Selected Melodious, Progressive and Technical Studies for Horn;* Kuehn, *60 Musical Studies;* continue with Kopprasch, Blume, and Arbans.

Solos: Benker, *Miniaturen-Suite;* Hindemith, *Sonate;* Wilder, *Effie Suite;* Crockett, *Mystique;* Capuzzi, *Andante and Rondo;* Downey, *Tabu for Tuba;* Stevens, *Triumph of the Demon Gods;* Koetsier, *Sonatina.*
Orchestral Excerpts: Mussorgsky/Ravel, *Pictures at an Exhibition;* Mahler, *Symphony No. 5;* Stravinsky, *Petrouchka;* Strauss, *Ein Heldenleben, Also Sprach Zarathustra;* Bruckner, *Symphony No. 4.*
F-Tuba: Swann, *Two Moods;* Kellaway, *The Morning Song.*

Senior Tuba Major

Etudes: Bobo, *Bach for the Tuba;* Charlier, *Transcendental Etudes;* Clarke, *Technical Studies;* Schlossberg, *Daily Drills and Technical Studies for the Trumpet;* Snedecor, *Low Etudes;* Vernon, *Singing Approach to the Trombone and Other Brass,* continue with Rochut and Arban.
Solos: Bach, *Sonata in Eb Major;* Broughton, *Sonata;* Gregson, *Concerto;* Mahler, *Songs of the Wayfarer;* Russell, *Suite Concertante;* Vaughan Williams, *Concerto;* Wilhelm, *Concertino.*
Orchestral Excerpts: Berlioz, *Romeo and Juliet, Benvenuto Cellini, Corsair;* Bruckner, *Symphonies No. 7 and 8;* Mahler, *Symphonies No. 2 and 6;* Revueltas, *Sensamaya;* Stravinsky, *Rite of Spring;* Wagner, *Prelude to Act III of Lohengrin.*
F-Tuba: Barat, *Introduction and Dance;* Kraft, *Encounters II;* Penderecki, *Capriccio for Tuba Solo.*

For Multiple Tubas

Charles A. McAdams

Perhaps the most important decision teachers and performers make is the selection of literature to study and perform. Literature for tuba/euphonium ensembles has experienced a tremendous increase in the last twenty years. For the following selected list compositions had to meet three criteria: They had to be scored for two or more tubas, in print and readily available internationally, and of exceptional quality. The list was compiled from responses received from high school and university teachers who have had experience with tuba/euphonium ensembles. They were asked to name published compositions of significant musical value. All the compositions listed were selected by a majority of respondents. The grade level given (I = Beginner; II = Intermediate; III = High School; IV = University; V = Professional) corresponds to the grade level assigned to the composition in the chapter "Music for Multiple Tubas." For full information on each composition, refer to its complete entry in that chapter.

The final judgment of the appropriateness of any piece of music must be left to the teacher or the player. It is hoped that this recommended repertoire list and the complete listing of compositions and arrangements for multiple tubas will aid in exploring the vastness and exceptional quality of multiple tuba literature. An expression of deep gratitude goes to teachers who participated in this survey: Steve Bryant, University of Texas; Gary Buttery, U.S. Coast Guard Band; Ron Davis, University of South Carolina; Martin Erickson, U.S. Navy Band; Skip Gray, University of Kentucky; Fritz Kaenzig, University of Michigan; Chitate Kagawa, Sapporo Symphony; David LeClair, Basler Conservatory; Donald Little, University of North Texas; R. Winston Morris, Tennessee Technological University; Daniel Perantoni, Arizona State University; Jim Self, free-lance artist, Los Angeles, California; Stephen Shoop, High School Band Director, Garland, Texas; John Stevens, University of Wisconsin; Scott Watson, University of Kansas; David Werden, U.S. Coast Guard Band; Denis Winter, University of Central Arkansas; and Jerry Young, University of Wisconsin-Eau Claire.

High School Level: Grades I, II, III, and III–IV

Two Parts

Bach, J.S./Augustine	*Duets and Trios* (III–IV)	Southern Music
De Jong, C.	*Music for Two Tubas* (III–IV)	Theodore Presser
Nelhybel, V.	*Eleven Duets for Tubas* (II–IV)	General Music
Purcell, H./Morris	*Chaconne* (III–IV)	Shawnee Press
Sear, W.	*Advanced Duets,* Book 1 (III–IV)	Cor Publishing Company
Sparke, P.	*Sweet 'n' Low,* Books 1–5 (III)	Studio Music
Stamitz, K./Long	*Duet for Tubas* (III)	Brass Press
Stoutamire, A.	*Duets for All* (III–IV)	CPP Belwin

THREE PARTS

Bach, J.S./Sauter	*Come, Sweet Death* (III–IV)	Harvey Phillips Foundation
Bach, J.S./Morris	*Fugue in C minor for Low Brass Trio* (III–IV)	Ludwig Music
Geminiani, F./Morris	*Concerto Grosso* (III–IV)	Shawnee Press
Isbell, T.	*Dona Nobis Pacem* (III)	Brass Press
Marcellus, J.	*Trios for Brass, Books* 1, 2, 3 (II–III)	CPP Belwin
McAdams, C.	*Swing Low, Sweet Chariot* (III–IV)	Encore Music
O'Reilly, J.	*Yamaha Band Ensembles* Books I and II (I–II)	Alfred Publishing
Presser, W.	*Suite for Three Tubas* (III–IV)	Tenuto Publications
Purcell, H./Gray	*Canon on a Ground Bass* (III)	Shawnee Press

FOUR PARTS

Anonymous/Baker	*Lute Dances* (II–III)	Brass Press
Bach, J.S./Werden	*Bist Du bei Mir* (III–IV)	Whaling Music
Hutchinson, T.	*Tuba Juba Duba* (III)	Brass Press
Lasso, O./Robinson	*Madrigal for Tuba Quartet* (III)	Whaling Music
Mancini, H./Krush	*The Pink Panther* (III–IV)	Kendor Music
Marcellus, J.	*Quartets for Brass,* Books 1, 2, 3 (II–III)	CPP Belwin Incorporated
McAdams, C.	*The Saints* (III–IV)	Encore Music
Saint-Saëns, C./ Hanson	*Adagio from Symphony No. 3* (III–IV)	KIWI Music Press
Sousa, J./Gray	*Belle of Chicago March* (III–IV)	Shawnee Press
Sousa, J./Morris	*El Capitan* (III–IV)	Brass Press
Sousa, J./Morris	*Semper Fidelis* (III–IV)	Ludwig Music
Steffe, W./Isbell	*Battle Hymn* (III)	Brass Press
Uber, D.	*Suite for Four Bass Tubas* (III–IV)	Kendor Music
Wilder, A.	*Carols For A Merry TubaChristmas* (III–IV)	Harvey Phillips Foundation

FIVE PARTS

| Garrett, J. | *Londonderry Air* (III–IV) | Ludwig Music |

SIX PARTS

| Boone, D. | *Three Moods* (III) | Brass Press |

University and Professional Level: Grades III–IV, IV, and V

TWO PARTS

Bach, J.S./Augustine	*Duets and Trios* (III–IV)	Southern Music
Bach, J.S./Self	*Vivace from Concerto No. 3 in D minor* (IV)	Wimbledon Music
Bartles, A.	*Beersheba Neo-Baroque Suite* (IV)	Brass Press
Corelli, A./Morris	*Sonata da Chiesa* (IV)	Ludwig Music
De Jong, C.	*Music for Two Tubas* (III–IV)	Elkan-Vogel Company
Devienne, F./Singleton	*Duet in F* (IV)	Peer International
Hartley, W.	*Bivalve Suite* (IV)	Autograph Editions
Luedeke, R.	*Eight Bagatelles* (IV)	Tenuto Publications
Luedeke, R.	*Wonderland Duets* (IV)	Tenuto Publications
Mozart, W.A./Conner	*Twelve Duos for Two Tubas* (IV)	Queen City Brass Publications
Nelhybel, V.	*Eleven Duets for Tuba* (II–IV)	General Music
Purcell, H./Morris	*Chaconne* (III–IV)	Shawnee Press
Roikjer, K.	*Ten Inventions for Two Tubas* (IV)	Wilhelm Hansen Edition
Sear, W.	*Advanced Duets, Book 1* (III–IV)	Cor Publishing Company
Singleton, K.	*Twenty-five Baroque and Classical Duets,* Book 1 (IV)	Peer International

Singleton, K.	*Twenty-five Baroque and Classical Duets*, Book 2 (IV)	Peer International
Wilder, A.	*Suite for Two Tubas* (IV)	Margun Music Incorporated

THREE PARTS

Bach, J.S./Sauter	*Come, Sweet Death* (III–IV)	Harvey Phillips Foundation
Bach, J.S./Morris	*Fugue in C Minor for Low Brass Trio* (III–IV)	Ludwig Music
Geminiani, F./Morris	*Concerto Grosso* (III–IV)	Shawnee Press
Jager, R.	*Variations on a Motive by Wagner* (IV)	Elkan-Vogel
McAdams, C.	*Swing Low, Sweet Chariot* (III–IV)	Encore Music
Presser, W.	*Suite for Three Tubas* (III–IV)	Tenuto Publications
Schubert, F./Singleton	*Four Choruses* (IV)	Peer International
Wilder, A.	*Ten Trios for Tuba Trio* (IV)	Margun Music

FOUR PARTS

Bach, J.S./Werden	*Air from Suite No. 3* (IV)	Whaling Music
Bach, J.S./Werden	*Bist Du bei Mir* (III–IV)	Whaling Music
Bach, J.S./Gray	*Fugue in G Minor* (IV)	Shawnee Press
Bartles, A.	*When Tubas Waltz* (IV)	Kendor Music
Bulla, S.	*Celestial Suite* (IV)	Rosehill Music
Canter, J.	*Appalachian Carol* (IV)	T.U.B.A. Press
Canter, J.	*Siamang Suite* (IV)	T.U.B.A. Press
Cheetham, J.	*Consortium* (IV)	Shawnee Press
Frackenpohl, A.	*Pop Suite* (IV)	Kendor Music
Gates, C.	*Tuba Quartet* (IV–V)	Intrada Music Group
George, T.R.	*Tubasonatina* (IV)	Thom Ritter George
Gibbons, O./Self	*Prelude and Voluntary for Four Tubas* (IV)	Wimbledon Music
Hartley, W.	*Miniatures for Four Valve Instruments* (IV)	Galaxy Music
Holmes, P.	*Quartet for Tubas* (IV)	TRN Music
Joplin, S./Werden	*Easy Winners* (IV)	Whaling Music
Joplin, S./Werden	*Euphonic Sounds* (IV)	Whaling Music
Kern, J./Holcombe	*They Didn't Believe Me* (IV)	Musicians Publications
King, K./Werden	*The Melody Shop* (IV–V)	Whaling Music
Kochan, G.	*Seven Miniatures for Four Tubas* (V)	Verlag Neue Musik Berlin
Lyon, M.	*Suite for Four Bass Instruments* (IV)	Shawnee Press
Mancini, H./Krush	*The Pink Panther* (III–IV)	Kendor Music
McAdams, C.	*The Saints* (III–IV)	Encore Music
Niehaus, L.	*Brass Tacks* (IV)	Kendor Music
Niehaus, L.	*Keystone Chops* (IV)	Kendor Music
Payne, F. L.	*Quartet for Tubas* (IV)	Shawnee Press
Powell, B./Buttery	*Bocoxe* (IV)	Whaling Music
Ramsoe, W./Buttery	*Quartet for Tubas* (IV–V)	Whaling Music
Rodgers, T.	*Air for Tuba Ensemble* (IV)	T.U.B.A. Press
Saint-Saëns, C./Hanson	*Adagio from Symphony No. 3* (III–IV)	KIWI Music
Sample, S.	*Cole Porter Medley* (IV)	T.A.P. Music
Sample, S.	*Gershwin Medley* (IV–V)	T.A.P. Music
Sousa, J./Gray	*Belle of Chicago March* (III–IV)	Shawnee Press
Sousa, J./Morris	*El Capitan* (III–IV)	Brass Press
Sousa, J./Morris	*Semper Fidelis* (III–IV)	Ludwig Music
Sousa, J./Werden	*Stars and Stripes Forever* (IV)	Whaling Music
Sousa, J./Werden	*Washington Post* (IV)	Whaling Music
Stevens, J.	*Dances* (IV–V)	Peer International
Stevens, J.	*Music 4 Tubas* (IV)	Peer International
Stevens, J.	*Power for Four Tubas* (IV)	Peer International
Susato, T./Winter	*Ronde and Saltarelle* (IV)	Whaling Music

Thornton, M.	*Two English Madrigals* (IV–V)	PP Music
Victoria, T./Self	*O Vos Omnes* (Motet) (IV)	Wimbledon Music
Uber, D.	*Suite for Four Bass Tubas* (III–IV)	Kendor Music
Wilder, A.	*Carols for a MerryTubaChristmas* (III–IV)	Harvey Phillips Foundation

FIVE PARTS

Bach, J.S./Morris	*Contrapunctas I* (IV)	Brass Press
Garrett, J.	*Londonderry Air* (III–IV)	Ludwig Music
Krol, B.	*Feiertagsmusik* (Festive Music) (IV–V)	Editions BIM
Martin, G.	*Bluesin' Tubas* (IV)	T.U.B.A. Press
Martin, G.	*Chops!* (IV)	T.U.B.A. Press
Stevens, J.	*Fanfare for a Friend* (IV)	T.U.B.A. Press
Stevens, J.	*Suite of English Madrigals* (IV)	Encore Music
Wilson, T.	*Wot Shigona Dew?* (IV)	T.U.B.A. Press

SIX PARTS

| Brahms, J./Gotch | *Es ist eine Rose entsprungen* (IV) | T.U.B.A. Press |
| DiGiovanni, R. | *Tuba Magic for Tuba Ensemble* (IV) | Shawnee Press |

SEVEN OR MORE PARTS

Clinard, F.	*Diversion for Seven Bass Clef Instruments* (IV)	Shawnee Press
Pegram, W.	*Howdy!* (IV)	Ludwig Music
Stevens, J.	*The Liberation of Sisyphus* (IV–V)	Editions BIM
Tull, F.	*Tubular Octad* (IV–V)	Boosey & Hawkes

For Military Band Auditions

Martin D. Erickson

Playing in a military band can be very rewarding musically and can provide security for young musicians and their families because of the benefits that accompany a career in the armed forces. Auditioning for one of the major service bands (sometimes called the "premiere" bands) requires a broad knowledge not only of the traditional band literature but also of the basic orchestral repertoire. Be prepared to perform band transcriptions in a key other than that of the orchestral versions. Additionally, be aware that the band tuba part is very often a composite and may include excerpts from the cello and bass parts (or any other parts), in addition to the "regular" tuba part. In fact, the original tuba part may be found in the euphonium or trombone band part.

The first step for most military band auditions is the preliminary tape round. Persons auditioning are usually required to send a cassette tape with a prepared solo or excerpts or a recent tape of suitable nature (such as a student recital performance). An exception to this procedure is followed by the "President's Own" United States Marine Band, which has no preliminary round of evaluating audition tapes. A resumé and a recent picture may be required. The reason for the picture is to satisfy the United States armed forces guidelines regarding personal fitness and military appearance. Naturally, all the United States service bands are equal opportunity employers.

If an applicant's tape is accepted, the audition supervisor will provide information regarding the audition schedule, location, and requirements. Most service bands do not pay for transportation and lodging, but ask anyway! A word of caution: Do not expect local recruiters to have all the answers to questions about the service bands. At best, they have only general information about military careers. Get the specifics from the people providing the job!

The recommended basic repertoire that follows could be classified as the military bands' "Most Wanted" list. These are the selections that should be in everyone's repertoire, and being adequately prepared will greatly increase the chance of winning a position in one of the military bands. These selections are the most frequently requested, but the service bands also have music not readily available to auditionees. These works may consist of transcriptions, original compositions, or arrangements specifically for those bands and are very often in manuscript form. Sightreading material could come from this list. In some cases, band audition boards may choose an etude from the standard repertoire before listening to the prepared piece or audition selections. The most frequently requested are selections from the Blazevich and Rochut etudes.

In most cases, finalists are interviewed by the audition board and/or officers of the band to determine the individual's ability to enlist in the service or to obtain a White House security clearance.

Many thanks go to representatives of the various service bands for their assistance in preparing this material: Jeffrey Arwood, United States Army Band "Pershing's Own," Ft. Myer, VA; Gary Buttery, United States Coast Guard Band, New London, CT; Frank Byrne, The "President's Own" United States Marine Band, Washington, DC; Tim Loehr, United States Army Field Band, Fort Meade, MD; Bruce Mosier, United States Air Force Band, Washington, DC; Joseph J. Roccaro, Jr., United States Military Academy Band, West Point, NY; and Scott Tarabour, United States Naval Academy Band, Annapolis, MD.

Alford, Harry: *The Purple Carnival*
Alford, Harry: *Skyliner*
Barnhouse/John Paynter: *The Battle of Shiloh*
Berlioz/L. Smith: *Damnation of Faust* (Hungarian March Rakoczy)
Berlioz/M.L. Lake: *March Hongroise* (Hungarian March)
Berlioz/Erik Leidzen: *March to the Scaffold* (Symphony Fantastique)
Berlioz/V.F. Safranek: *Roman Carnival Overture*
Bernstein/W. Beeler: *Overture to Candide*
Chance, John Barnes: *Blue Lake Overture*
Creston, Paul: *Celebration Overture*
Elgar, E.: *Pomp and Circumstance*
Enesco, George: *Roumanian Rhapsody No. 1*
Fucik, Julius/Laurendeau: *Thunder and Blazes March*
Gliere, R./Leidzen: *Russian Sailors' Dance*
Glinka, M./Winterbottom or Hennig: *Russlan and Ludmilla*
Goldman, E. F.: *Chimes of Liberty*
Gould, Morton: *Symphony for Band* (West Point Symphony)
Grainger, Percy: *Lincolnshire Posey* (No. 3, Rufford Park Poachers)
Hindemith, Paul: *Symphony for Band*

Hindemith, Paul/Wilson: March from *Symphonic Metamorphosis*
Holst, Gustav: *First Military Suite in E♭*
Holst, Gustav: *The Planets* (Mars and Jupiter)
Holst, Gustav: *Second Suite for Military Band*
Holst, Gustav: *Suite in F for Military Band*
Huffine: *Them Basses*
Jacob, Gordon: *Flag of Stars*
King, Karl: *Barnum and Bailey's Favorite*
King, Karl: *The Melody Shop*
Liszt, Franz/T. Conway Brown: *Les Préludes*
Litolff, Henry/M.C. Meyerelles: *Maximilien Robespierre*
Mendelssohn, F.: *Italian Symphony* (Saltarello)
Mendelssohn, F./V.F. Safranek: *Fingal's Cave* (Hebrides)
Moussorgsky, M.: *Pictures at an Exhibition* (Hut, Great Gate)
Mozart, W.A./W.J. Duthoit: *The Marriage of Figaro Overture*
Nicolai, G.: *Merry Wives of Windsor*
Respighi, O./Guy Duker: *The Pines of Rome*
Rimsky-Korsakov, N.: *Scheherazade* (Festival at Bagdad)
Rossini, G./T. Moses-Tobani: *The Italian in Algiers*
Rossini, G./V.F. Safranek: *Semiramide Overture*
Shostakovich, D.: *Polka from the Golden Age*
Smetana, Bedrich: *The Bartered Bride*
Smith, Claude T.: *Dance Folatre*
Smith, Claude T.: *Eternal Father*
Sousa, John P.: *Free Lance March*
Sousa, John P.: *George Washington Bicentennial*
Sousa, John P.: *Semper Fidelis March*
Sousa, John P.: *Stars and Stripes Forever*
Tchaikovsky, Peter I.: *1812 Overture*
Tchaikovsky, Peter I.: *Finale to Symphony No. 4*
Texidor, Jaime: *Amparita Roca*
Vaughan Williams, R.: *Folk Song Suite No.2* (Intermezzo)
Vaughan Williams, R.: *Toccata Marziale*
Verdi, G./Mollenhauer: *Manzoni Requiem*
Verdi, G./M.L. Lake: *La Forza Del Destino*
von Reznicek/Carl D. Meyers: *Donna Diana Overture*
Wagner, Richard: *Lohengrin* (Introduction to Act III)
Wagner, Richard: *Overture to Rienzi*
Walton, William/W.J. Duthoit: *Crown Imperial*
Weber, C.M./Lake: *Oberon Overture*
Weber, C.M./V.F. Safranek: *Euryanthe*
Weber, C.M./T. Moses-Tobani: *Der Freischütz*

For Orchestral Auditions

Gene Pokorny

Symphony, ballet, and opera orchestras usually fill openings in their organizations by holding auditions. In an audition, candidates are judged on their performance of selected orchestral excerpts. This section presents a list of orchestral excerpts for bass tuba. Though there is occasional mention of the tenor tuba, the survey that was conducted to compile this audition list was limited to excerpts for bass tuba.

The orchestral excerpts that have been used for the past fifteen years continue to be useful in judging whether a tubist is up to the task of handling an orchestra job. However, in conducting the research for this section, it seemed wise to add some unfamiliar pieces to the traditional list. Including relatively unknown pieces is a way of keeping up with the changing times. These nontraditional pieces sometimes present different technical challenges, and there is always the possibility that they might appear on an audition. In focusing on this audition repertoire, one should not lose sight of the fact that this is music to be studied, learned, appreciated, and enjoyed as an inspiring project whether one is preparing for an audition or not.

This list of orchestral excerpts for the bass tuba was prepared based on a survey sent to professional symphony, opera, and ballet orchestra tubists around the world. Naturally, some of these pieces appeared on almost all the returned questionnaires, while others were suggested only once. Not surprisingly, Scandinavian tubists listed Carl Nielsen, while their Polish counterparts listed Szymanowski. Few European tubists listed Gershwin's *An American in Paris*. Some of the respondents went to the trouble of making copies of lesser-known pieces to back up their assertions that a particular piece be included.

Special care should be given in preparing excerpts for audition with ballet and opera companies. Although these excerpts occasionally appear on symphony orchestra auditions, ballet and opera musicians are usually responsible for more than the "top ten" (i.e., there is more to play in *Die Walküre* than just the "Ride"). It is clear that one has to know more than just the most familiar excerpt from an opera, ballet, or symphony. American players who audition for European opera orchestras usually have to do a lot of makeup work in order to compete. For example, for the American tubist, most of the Verdi, Wagner, and Leoncavallo pieces on the list below register a "zero" on the recognition scale, except for isolated excerpts. On the other hand, few non-American tubists have even heard of Ferde Grofé, to say nothing of knowing the "Cloudburst" section from *The Grand Canyon Suite*.

A clear change in the marketing of symphony orchestras in America in the last decade of the twentieth century has also affected the audition list. With the decline of music education in the schools and the desperate financial condition of many orchestras today, pops concerts have become more than just once-a-month events. Consequently, it is not unusual for a pops piece to appear on an audition list even if it comes under the heading of sightreading. As ready as trumpet players may be with the second *Brandenburg Concerto*, they may be asked to play *Boogie Woogie Bugle Boy* next. For the tubist, *An American in Paris* may be as "down and dirty" as it gets, but if the Ellington/Dankworth *Satin Doll* appears, the auditionee should be prepared.

The pieces listed all have a prominent tuba part. A Schnittke symphony will take on sudden importance if it is listed just once for some major audition. Therefore, the possibility exists that a piece found in the local music library, virtually ignored even as a curiosity, will cosmetically increase in importance because of the urgency of an upcoming audition. The list is long because of the abundance of challenging music from which to choose. One should examine and study these pieces well before an employment opportunity presents itself. The urgency of learning an unfamiliar piece is, unfortunately, one of the few stimulants that actually motivate people to learn. Learning pieces for an audition is much easier if one has listened to them previously simply to get acquainted with them and enjoy them.

An asterisk (*) indicates a piece that has shown up in many auditions for American symphony orchestras since the mid-1970s, as documented by the American Symphony Orchestra League. The League not only listed the pieces which were frequently requested for all instruments, but also ranked them according to the frequency with which they were requested. The results are reported in the 1980 publication *Facing the Maestro: A Musician's Guide to Orchestra Audition Repertoire*, which may be ordered from American Symphony Orchestra League, 777 Fourteenth Street, N.W., Suite 500, Washington, DC 20005; phone: 202-628-0099 or FAX: 202-783-7228. The 1993 cost is $7.50.

Adams: *The Chairman Dances*
Bartók: *Concerto for Orchestra*
Bartók: *The Miraculous Mandarin*
Berg: *Drei Orchesterstücke*
Berg: *Violin Concerto*

Berg: *Wozzeck* (onstage solo part and orchestra part, especially the beginning of Act III)
Berlioz: *"Overture" from *Le Corsaire*
Berlioz: *"Overture" to *Benevenuto Cellini*
Berlioz: "Overture" to *Les Francs-Juges*
Berlioz: "Overture" to *King Lear*
Berlioz: *"Hungarian March" from *Damnation of Faust*
Berlioz: *Romeo and Juliet*
Berlioz: *Requiem*
Berlioz: * *Symphonie Fantastique*
Berlioz: *Symphonie funèbre et triomphale*
Bernstein: "Symphonic Dances" from *West Side Story*
Brahms: *Academic Festival Overture*
Brahms: *Requiem*
Brahms: * *Symphony No. 2*
Brahms: *Tragic Overture*
Britten: *Cello Concerto*
Britten: *Young Person's Guide to the Orchestra*
Bruckner: * *Symphony No. 4*
Bruckner: * *Symphony No. 7*
Bruckner: *Symphony No. 8*
Bruckner: *Symphony No. 9*
Corgliano: *Symphony No. 1*
Delibes: *Coppélia* (ballet)
Denisov, E.: *Symphonie pour Orchestre*
Elgar: *Cockaigne Overture*
Elgar: *Enigma Variations*
Ellington/Dankworth: *Satin Doll*
Erb: *Concerto for Brass and Orchestra*
Franck: *Le Chasseur Maudit*
Franck: * *Symphony in D minor*
Gershwin: * *An American in Paris*
Ginastera: *Popol Vuh*
Glazunov: *Raymonda* (ballet)
Gliere: *Russian Sailors' Dance*
Goehr: *Concerto for Piano and Orchestra, Op. 33*
Gomes, Carlos: *Overture "Guarany" Protofonio*
Grofé: *Grand Canyon Suite*
Guanieri, Carmargo: *Symphony No. 4*
Guanieri, Carmargo: *Symphony No. 5*
Guanieri, Carmargo: *Three Dances for Orchestra*
Herold: *La Fille mal gardée* (ballet)
Hindemith: *Die Harmonie der Welt*
Hindemith: *Mathis der Maler*
Hindemith: *Sinfonische Metamorphosen*
Holst: *The Planets*
Honegger: *Symphony No. 5*
Kodály: *Háry János*
Koechlin: *Les Bandar-Log*
Lacerda, Osvaldo: *Symphony for Orchestra*
Leoncavallo: *Pagliacci*
Ligeti: *Melodien*
Lutoslawski: *Concerto for Orchestra*
Lutoslawski: *Symphony No. 3*
Mahle, Ernest: *Symphony Nordestino*
Mahler: * *Symphony No. 1*
Mahler: *Symphony No. 2*
Mahler: *Symphony No. 3*

Mahler: * *Symphony No. 5*
Mahler: *Symphony No. 6*
Mahler: *Symphony No. 10* (Cooke version)
Mendelssohn: *"Overture" to *Midsummer Night's Dream*
Mendelssohn: *St. Paul* (oratorio)
Mussorgsky: *Night on Bald Mountain*
Mussorgsky/Ravel: * *Pictures at an Exhibition* (including "Bydlo")
Mussorgsky/Ravel: * *Pictures at an Exhibition* (excluding "Bydlo")
Nielsen: *Symphony No. 4*
Nielsen: *Symphony No. 5*
Nielsen: *Symphony No. 6*
Orff: *Der Mond*
Poulenc: *Histoire de Babar*
Prado, Almeida: *Estaços*
Prado, Almeida: *Estigma*
Prokofiev: *Cinderella* (ballet)
Prokofiev: *Lieutenant Kije*
Prokofiev: *Romeo and Juliet* (Suites 1 and 2)
Prokofiev: * *Symphony No. 5*
Prokofiev: * *Symphony No. 6*
Prokofiev: *Violin Concerto No. 1*
Ravel: *Daphnis and Chloe*, Suite No. 2
Respighi: *Fountains of Rome*
Revueltas: * *Sensemaya*
Revueltas: *Homenaje a Federico Garcia Lorca*
Rimsky-Korsakov: *Scheherezade*
Rimsky-Korsakov: *Happy Holiday* (approximate translation)
Santoro, Claudio: *Symphony No. 6*
Schnittke: *Symphony No. 3*
Schnittke: *Symphony No. 5*
Shostakovich: * *Symphony No. 5*
Shostakovich: *Symphony No. 7*
Shostakovich: *Symphony No. 9*
Shostakovich: *Violin Concerto No. 1*
Sibelius: *Symphony No. 2*
Smetana: *Die Moldau*
Strauss: *Eine Alpensinfonie*
Strauss: * *Also Sprach Zarathustra*
Strauss: * *Don Juan*
Strauss: *Ein Heldenleben*
Strauss: *Elektra* (opera)
Strauss: *Die Frau ohne Schatten* (opera)
Strauss: *Der Rosenkavalier*
Strauss: *Salome* (opera)
Strauss: * *Till Eulenspiegels lustige Streiche*
Strauss: *Tod und Verklärung*
Stravinsky: * *Jeu de Cartes*
Stravinsky: * *Le Sacre du Printemps*
Stravinsky: * *Petrouchka*
Stravinsky: *Suite No. 2 for small orchestra*
Stravinsky: *Violin Concerto*
Szymanowski: *Concert Overture* (approximate translation)
Szymanowski: *Harnasie* (ballet)
Tchaikovsky: *1812 Overture*

Tchaikovsky: *Francesca da Rimini*
Tchaikovsky: *Suite No. 3*
Tchaikovsky: **Symphony No. 4*
Tchaikovsky: *Symphony No. 5*
Tchaikovsky: **Symphony No. 6*
Tippett: *Symphony No. 4*
Tower: *Concerto for Orchestra*
Vaughan Williams: *Sinfonia Antartica*
Vaughan Williams: *Symphony No. 4*
Verdi: *Aida* (especially the ballet in Act II)
Verdi: *Falstaff* (opera)
Verdi: "Overture" to *La Forza del Destino*
Verdi: *Otello*, Act II (opera)
Verdi: *Rigoletto* (opera)
Verdi: *Requiem*
Verdi: *Il Trovatore* (opera)
Verdi: *I Vespri Siciliani* (opera)
Villa-Lobos: *Piano Concerto No. 3*
Villa-Lobos: *Erosao*
Villa-Lobos: *The Amazone*
Wagner: **Eine Faust Overture*
Wagner: "Overture" to *Der Fliegende Holländer*
Wagner: **Götterdämmerung* ("Siegfried's Funeral
    Music," "Rhine Journey", etc.)
Wagner: *Act I and Prelude to Act III of *Lohengrin*
Wagner: *"Overture" to *Die Meistersinger*
Wagner: *Das Rheingold* (Fafner, the dragon, solo)
Wagner: *Siegfried* (introduction to Act II)
Wagner: "Overture" to *Tannhäuser* (including Paris
    version "Venusberg" music)
Wagner: Act I of *Tristan und Isolde*
Wagner: **Die Walküre* (many parts, not just the
    "Ride")
Webern: *Six Pieces, Op. 6*

In many cases, particular passages within pieces are not singled out because orchestras expect a player to play any passage. There is the danger of preparing one section of a piece while another goes unexplored because it seems simple. In the 1980s, at an audition held by the Pittsburgh Symphony, a tubist was asked to play Prokofiev's *Fifth Symphony*. The request was not a surprise. What turned out to be a surprise was that he was asked to perform rehearsal numbers 8–10. At first glance this section is not very interesting and looks easy, but it exposes a player's low register, and many candidates were disqualified by this passage. The point is that anything may be asked. If *Pictures at an Exhibition* is on the audition list, do not assume it means just "Bydlo." One may be asked to perform the low B major promenade or the soft section with harp in "Baba Yaga."

Instruments to Use at Auditions

In deciding the instrument on which to audi-

tion, tradition, in terms of the instrument for which an excerpt was originally intended and the particular country in the audition is held, is a major factor. The tradition for the particular orchestra should also be taken into consideration. Some orchestras have no hard and fast traditions, but others do. Many German orchestras use BB♭ and F tubas for their contrabass tuba and bass tuba parts, and Italian orchestras adhere to cimbasso markings, so it is important to research the field beforehand. Just because one performs well on an F tuba does not mean that that instrument will be right for every job. Some information about traditions is available in Clifford Bevan's *The Tuba Family* and in several articles in the *T.U.B.A. Journal* (listed below).

The instrument one plays at an audition should be one that fits both the performer and the music. Generally speaking (at least in America), the bigger the instrument one can control, the better the chances of getting a job. But too often players will choose the biggest instruments they can find, even to the extent of auditioning on an unfamiliar instrument. However, bigger instruments are harder to control: clarity can be difficult, and tone can easily become a deep, nebulous, shapeless mass. One must play the instrument and not let the instrument play the player. To that end, a person playing a 4/4 size instrument and who exercises great control over it (knowing its quirks, its dynamic limits, its particular intonation idiosyncrasies) will be better off than one who plays a 6/4 size instrument and cannot control it.

In the matter of control, consider using an F, E♭, or smaller instrument to perform excerpts in a higher register. When I performed *Petrouchka* in my college orchestra with a CC tuba, I played all the notes and maybe even made some music out of it. Given the option of playing it on an F tuba, as I have today, I would not play the "Peasant and Bear" section on a CC tuba for three reasons: With an F tuba I can exercise more control over the high notes; with greater control in the technical area, I can pay more attention to expressing myself in the musical area; and—it sounds better!

Certain pieces in the repertoire require both a small and a large instrument. Several of the Strauss tone poems require tenor tuba. Mahler's *Seventh Symphony* requires a tenor horn. The "Bydlo" excerpt from Mussorgsky/Ravel's *Pictures at an Exhibition* was written for a single C French tenor tuba, and this excerpt seems to find itself on audition lists frequently.

"Bydlo" can be a controversial piece for a tuba audition. It is on many excerpt lists because it is one of the most prominent solos in the repertoire. Unfortunately, many orchestra committees and conductors put an inordinate amount of value on the solo. Actually, 99 percent of the tuba player's job is in another register, fulfilling another role, yet, because importance goes up with pitch, otherwise fine contrabass tuba players are eliminated because the high g♯ may get clipped. Nevertheless, as an auditionee, one has no choice other than to play the excerpt if it is requested. Once the audition is won, a player should objectively examine his or her capabilities in light of the high tessitura of the solo and assess whether its musicality is being served. Deciding whether to perform the solo may depend on what toll the tenor tuba preparation may take on the contrabass tuba portion of the piece. Finally, the tubist may wish to consider having a trombonist colleague who doubles on valves perform the piece, which is in the trombone's normal tessitura. Few tuba players actually transcend the difficulty of getting past the notes to make music. "Bydlo" is certainly a *tour de force*, but that does not necessarily mean one is making good music. One question on the survey asked whether "Bydlo" should be requested at an audition. Unfortunately, the responses were not definitive. That is why *Pictures* is listed twice: once with and once without "Bydlo."

Finding the Music

Where does one find the pieces on the list? Except for the obscure pieces, they may be found in several sources listed in Chapter 10, "Orchestral Excerpts." If at all possible, get the actual part. Some publishers will sell a separate part for several dollars or carry an "album" of music (sometimes consisting of three or four pieces) of a particular composer (Kalmus offers such a product). These publications can be expensive, but the parts will be identical to those required at an audition (unless a different edition is used). Thus, it is advantageous to be exposed to the "real" part as much as possible, typographical errors and all (many of the original printing plates are still in use today). Excerpt books which include the authentic parts are good ones to get. To that end, I recommend Abe Torchinsky's *The Tuba Player's Orchestral Repertoire*, not only for the real parts but for the compiler's introductory comments on the pieces. From years of first-hand experience Torchinsky makes practical suggestions that

might not otherwise be noted. *Die Orchesterstudien* (Orchestral Studies), edited by Dieter Meschke of the Gewandhaus Orchestra (published by the Deutscher Verlag für Musik, Leipzig), is an excellent source of study materials. It has been carefully edited and contains suggested metronome markings. In addition to major and minor works of German origin, there is also a good sample of excerpts from Mendelssohn, Franck, Smetana, and Verdi. There are also some specialized publications. *British Orchestral Excerpts for Trombone and Tuba*, edited by Ken Shifrin and Danny Longstaff (published by Virgo Music Publishers), offers an excellent source of material for the entire low brass section. The music is transcribed in reasonably good manuscript form with helpful playing suggestions. The bounteous music of Britten, Vaughan Williams, Malcolm Arnold, and others are well represented here. Much of this music is ignored in other excerpt books. The music of Carl Nielsen can be found in *Orchestral Studies for Trombone and Tuba*, vols. 1–3, edited by Per Gade (published by Edition Wilhelm Hansen, Copenhagen). This music is very easy to read and is a good source of material not found in other excerpt books. Vol. I of Douglas Yeo's *Orchestral Excerpts for Trombones and Tuba* is devoted to the music of Shostakovich. An upcoming publication in Torchinsky's series of orchestral excerpts also will feature the music of Shostakovich.

Unfortunately, there is no legal means of acquiring some of the selections found on many audition lists: Respighi's *Fountains of Rome*, the Mussorgsky/Ravel *Pictures at an Exhibition*, and the latest editions of Stravinsky's ballets, Mahler's *Symphony No. 10*, some work by Hindemith, Holst's *The Planets*, and Gershwin's *An American in Paris*. Letters to the publishers of these and other works, inquiring about their availability, went unanswered. Therefore, it must be assumed that, without specific approval, it is illegal to copy these pieces. Until publishers and copyright owners of music with restricted accessibility realize that, for the most part, present and aspiring orchestral musicians simply want the music to study and practice, the "black market" is going to exist, and they will obtain these parts in other ways. When an orchestra requires these pieces on an audition, it should provide the parts in question. As a matter of fact, the St. Louis Symphony did so for all the excerpts in a recent tuba audition. In the music business, rights to pieces are constantly changing hands and takeovers in the publishing arena are rampant. So when an excerpt book appears, if it is good, buy it, as many publications go out of print very quickly.

Solo Pieces to Play at an Audition

In many orchestra auditions the performer is asked to play a solo. Some recent lists of the required pieces have included the Vaughan Williams *Concerto*, the Hindemith *Sonate*, J. S. Bach's *Sonata in E♭* for flute, and the Strauss *Horn Concerto No. 1*. Playing a solo is one of the few opportunities to show one's musicality. The orchestral excerpts are limited in the freedom they give an individual and only demonstrate the basic role of the orchestral tubist: to produce a good sound with dynamic contrast, to be in tune, and to keep the tempo without missing too many notes. Few excerpts demand expressive playing, and that is why the solo is important. The auditionee who is given free choice of solo should consider several matters: What kind of playing is not being demonstrated in the chosen excerpts? What are the judges looking for? What do they want to hear? What are the outstanding qualities of one's own playing, and what piece would best express that expertise? Is there some special individual talent one has that probably would not be obvious from the audition repertoire alone?

What Is Being Sought at an Audition

The purpose of an audition is to find the best-qualified player for the repertoire, one who has mastered the basic skills of playing his or her instrument. The overall impression a player should try to make onstage is that he or she is in control of the instrument. The first step is to have a world-class sound; technical prowess without the right sound is meaningless. The next most-important qualities are rhythmic homogeneity—the ability to be rhythmically solid and unwavering—and the ability to play softly. All dynamics are important in an audition, but the soft ones are seldom explored as much as audition committees would like. Intonation, higher tessitura, and greater dynamic levels are all important but are not as important as these three factors. Weakness in the low register becomes apparent pretty quickly and is usually accompanied by a lack of solid tone quality in that range. This is the most difficult and least-practiced register on the horn. If a person can do all of the fundamental steps in playing, a position beyond the preliminary round can be virtually guaranteed. Obviously, musical-

ity is also very important and is integral in finding the right player for a position, but the ability to express a musical phrase and stand out as a great interpreter of line is secondary to the more-routine functions of an orchestral tubist. Generally, the conductor, who is usually present just for the finals, is interested more in the player's musicianship than in the technical aspects of the instrument.

Particular pieces demonstrate a player's abilities in certain areas. The following works from the American Symphony Orchestra League list emphasize particular attributes:

Wagner, *Die Meistersinger*: Tone quality, steadiness in tempo, ability to distinguish different types of articulation, some high range, smoothness at higher dynamic levels.

Stravinsky, *Petrouchka*: High range, some articulation, loud and soft playing in the high register.

Berlioz, *Symphonie Fantastique*: High register, some intonation, ability to control the type of articulation desired (especially in the "Dies Irae"), clean and fast playing, steady tempo.

Mendelssohn, *Midsummer Night's Dream:* High, smooth playing.

Berlioz, "Hungarian March" from *Damnation of Faust:* High register, clean articulation, intonation, steady tempo.

Bruckner, *Symphony No. 7*: A little bit of everything at various times.

Franck, *Symphony in D Minor*: High register.

Mahler, *Symphony No. 1*: Medium-to-high-register playing in a soft dynamic level.

Mahler, *Symphony No. 5*: Clean articulation in the lower register, controlled loud playing.

Mussorgsky/Ravel: *Pictures at an Exhibition*: Extreme high register, intonation, tone quality, controlled loud and soft playing.

Prokofiev, *Symphony No. 5:* Low register control.

Shostakovich, *Symphony No. 5*: Quick facility, low register, high dynamic levels.

Strauss, *Till Eulenspiegel*: Medium-to-high soft playing, contrast in dynamics, articulation, low register at high dynamics.

An Audition Overview

An audition is a complicated affair. Among the many things one could explore are audition preparation, study of recordings, psychological factors, accessories, foods, drugs, exercises, the taped audition, the confidence factor, playing in the section, auditioning in a foreign country, negotiating the contract, survival on the job, being a team player, tenure review, getting along with co-workers. The following books are recommended for additional information on the auditioning process:

Julie Lyonn Lieberman, *You Are Your Instrument* (New York: Huiksi Music, 1991).
James Loehr, *Mental Toughness Training for Sports* (Lexington, MA: Greene Press, 1986).
Chris Stevens with Dr. Ken Ravizza, *Head Control* (available from Chris Stevens, 1848 Hackett Ave., Long Beach, CA 90815, n.d.).
Barry Green and W. Timothy Gallwey, *Inner Game of Music* (New York: Doubleday, 1986).
Eloise Ristad, *Soprano on Her Head* (Moab, UT: Real People Press, 1982).
Stuart Edward Dunkel, *The Audition Process* (Stuyvesant, NY: Pendragon Press, 1990).
Stephen R. Covey, *The Seven Habits of Highly Effective People* (New York: Simon and Schuster, 1989).

Generally, these books deal with the psychology of performance under pressure. If one is nervous in performance or at an audition, it is infinitely better to find out why the nervousness exists than to find a solution for the nervousness itself. Exploring the cause rather than its manifestation is a cleansing process for the performer.

The following articles in the *T.U.B.A. Journal* describe several aspects of auditioning, including historical instruments, traditions in different countries, recordings, and the audition procedure itself:

Vol. 1, No. 1: "The Tuba in Europe" (reprinted in Vol. 4, No. 3).
Vol. 4, No. 1: "Tuba Pedagogy in Germany."
Vol. 4, No. 2: "T.U.B.A. Profile: Arnold M. Jacobs."
Vol. 5, No. 3: "The Evolution of the Tuba in France."
Vol. 7, No. 2: "Orchestra Literature including Euphonium or Tenor Tuba."
Vol. 9, No. 1: "The History and Development of the Serpent."
Vol. 9, No. 3: "Ancestors of the Tuba."
Vol. 10, No. 4: "Views of Berlioz on the Use of the Ophicleide and Tuba in His Orchestral Works."
Vol. 11, No. 1: "The Tuba in Norway."
Vol. 11, No. 2: "The Torchinsky Books."
Vol. 11, No. 3: "Mock Symphony Audition."
Vol. 11, No. 3: "Everything You Always Wanted to Know about Symphony Auditions."
Vol. 11, No. 4: "Development of the Tuba in the Romantic Period."
Vol. 12, No. 2: "Tales of the Cultural Revolution."
Vol. 13, No. 3: "The United States Copyright Law."
Vol. 14, No. 1: "Ophicleide."
Vol. 15, No. 2: "Cimbasso—Verdi's Bass."
Vol. 15, No. 2: "Tuba in England."
Vol. 15, No. 4: "Arnold Jacobs on Record: Its Influence on Me."
Vol. 16, No. 3: "Use of the F Tuba in the College Teaching Studio."
Vol. 17, No. 2: "Will the Gentleman in the Back Row Please Stand Up?"
Vol 17, No. 4: "The Tenor Tuba: Richard Strauss' Orchestration and the Revival of an Instrument."
Vol. 18, No. 3: "Audition Strategy."

There are a number of aids that do not yet exist that would be extremely helpful to anyone preparing for auditions. A very valuable addition would be recordings of orchestral excerpts by fine tuba players. Along the same line are books that show how to utilize tuba exercises in perfecting orchestral excerpts. No one book deals specifically with that subject; the closest is Phil Snedecor's *Low Etudes for Tuba*, in which two studies are somewhat related to Stravinsky and Prokofiev. By contrast, trumpet players have several books to choose from: Rob Roy McGregor's multivolume *Audition and Performance Preparation for Trumpet: Orchestral Literature Studies* coordinates specific excerpts with various studies to facilitate learning. A similar publication for the tuba is needed. Another helpful project would be a collection of some of the more obscure excerpts on the audition list. Influenced by everything that has happened for the tuba since the First International Tuba Symposium-Workshop in 1973 and by the many fine tuba recordings available today, composers have been writing more and more demanding tuba parts, not just for soloists but for orchestral tubists as well. A compilation of late twentieth-century tuba parts available in a single book would be a welcome addition.

It is with profound gratitude that I thank those who responded to my questionnaire. In several cases they even had to translate it. Their input made my job much easier, and I learned much from their ideas: D. K. Annema, Conservatory Groningen, The Netherlands; Jørgen Voigt Arnsted, Odense Symphony Orchestra, Denmark; Alan Baer, Los Angeles; Cherry Beauregard, Rochester Philharmonic Orchestra; Ronald T. Bishop, The Cleveland Orchestra; Donald Blakeslee, Royal Concertgebouw Orchestra, The Netherlands; Alain Cazes, Orchestre Métropolitain de Montréal; Floyd Cooley, San Francisco Symphony; Craig Cunningham, Queensland Symphony Orchestra, Australia; Bernard Ebbinghouse, Royal Oman Symphony Orchestra; David T. Fedderly, Baltimore Symphony Orchestra; Craig L. Fuller, Omaha Symphony; Thompson Hanks, New York City Ballet; Adi Hershko, Israel Philharmonic Orchestra; Steven Johns, New York City Opera; Fritz Kaenzig, Grant Park Symphony; Carl Kleinsteuber, The Hague Philharmonic; Anthony R. Kniffen, Honolulu Symphony Orchestra; Alexander Krauter, Russia; Patrick Krysatis, Luxembourg; David LeClair, Radio Sinfonie, Basel, Switzerland; Michael Lind, Stockholm Philharmonic; Rob Roy McGregor, Los Angeles Philharmonic; David J. Murphy, Irish Army Band; David Moen, Orquesta Sinfonico del Principado de Asturias, Spain; Steve Norrell, Metropolitan Opera Orchestra; Sadayuki Ogura, Tokyo Kosei Wind Orchestra; Daniel Perantoni, Arizona State University; Jeffrey Reynolds, Los Angeles Philharmonic; Jan Pniak, A. Rubinstein Philharmonic Orchestra, Poland; Chester Roberts, Boston Conservatory, Gordon College, former member Cleveland Orchestra; Michael Sanders, St. Louis Symphony Orchestra; Donald Smith, São Paulo State Symphony Orchestra, Brazil; Wally Stormont, Orquesta Sinfonica de Madrid; Abe Torchinsky, former member NBC Symphony and Philadelphia Orchestra; Heiko Triebener, Bamberger Symphoniker, Germany; Robert Tucci, Bavarian State Opera Orchestra, Germany; Peter Wahrhaftig, San Francisco Ballet; Steven Winteregg, Dayton Philharmonic Orchestra; Thomas Joseph Walsh, Munich Philharmonic; Herb Wekselblatt, Metropolitan Opera Orchestra; and Nicholas Zervopoulos, Athens State Symphony Orchestra, Greece.

12. Discography
Ronald Davis

In 1978 the *Tuba Music Guide* discography identified 33 record albums. For *The Tuba Source Book* discography, information on more than 400 recordings was received. The main section, "Tuba Recordings by Artist," lists albums that feature the tuba as a prominent solo instrument. Solo tuba, tuba and piano, tuba and orchestra or band, tuba and brass ensembles, tuba/euphonium ensembles, and jazz recordings are all included. Several categories are not included: orchestral recordings with the tuba as a section instrument, brass quintets, and with one or two exceptions, promotional recordings from publishers. All recording formats are included: long playing records, cassette tapes, and compact discs.

The first approach to this research was to consult every issue of *T.U.B.A. Journal* for recording information and enter it into a database. The next step was to survey all available sources and fill in any missing information. A complete entry provides the name of the tuba artist, the album title, other personnel performing, the record label, the year of recording or release, the format (long-playing record "LP," cassette tape "CS," compact disc "CD"), the catalogue number(s), and the selections on the album that feature the tuba listed by composer, arranger, and title. Compositions are generally listed in the order in which they appear on the album. Information on price and availability of each album was not reliable, so these items were dropped.

The main purpose of this discography is to identify recordings that have been produced, and many of the albums listed may no longer be available. Every attempt was made to secure copies of each recording for accurate, first-hand information. Record catalogues, record stores, distributors, and music libraries were consulted, as were other discographies, most notably the Schwann catalogues and the *Trombone/Euphonium Discography* by Edward Bahr.

The listings under "Tuba Recordings by Artist" include all information on each album. In the listings by title and by composer the names following the colon are those of the recording artists. Information on conference recordings was supplied by the directors of each conference, who were asked to specify whether the recordings are available and whether they exist as tapes.

Every effort was made to secure the most recent address for each company, with the Schwann catalogue serving as the major source. Many of the companies have moved, merged, or gone out of business. In such instances the most reliable reference is provided.

Several individuals are sincerely thanked for their assistance with this chapter: Dr. Reginald Bain of the University of South Carolina School of Music for all of his computer expertise; Barton Cummings for his careful reading and encouragement; and Bert Wiley of Bernel Music, for information on British brass bands; and Ted Meyer for an outstanding job of proofreading. And finally, a loving thank-you to my wife, Phyllis, for enduring this entire project.

Tuba Recordings by Artist

Acuff, Bill. See Tennessee Tech Tuba-Euphonium Quintet, *The Golden Sound of Euphoniums*

Amberst, Nigel. See Hoffnung, Gerard, *Hoffnung Music Festival Concert*

Anderson, Hans
  Album Title:
  Personnel:
  Label: Borgen Records LP: 5202-8
  Christiansen, Henning: *Betrayal* for tuba, violin and vibraphone, Op. 144

Anderson, Hans
  Album Title:
  Personnel:
  Label: Rondo Grammofon LP: RLP 8317
  Brand, Michael: *Tuba Tapestry* for tuba and brass band

Anderson, Hans
  Album Title:
  Personnel:
  Label: Borgen Records LP: ISBN 87-418-7146-4
  Christiansen, Henning: Maskemåned for trumpet and tuba, Op. 148

Anderson, Hans
  Album Title: *Kirkeby and Edvard Munch*
  Personnel:
  Label: Borgen Records/Weltmelodie 1983 LP: WM-LP-4718
  Christiansen, Henning: *Kirkeby and Edvard Munch* (in 12 movements)

Angerstein, Fred
    Album Title: *University of Houston Wind
        Ensemble, Vol. VI*
    Personnel: James Matthews, conductor
    Label: Century Records, 1970. LP: Houston
        Music Series Vol. 4
    Werle, Floyd: *Concertino for Three Brass and
        Band*
Anonymous
    Album Title: *Diadem of Gold*
    Personnel: Brighouse and Rastick Band Label:
        Polyphonic CS: CPRL 017
    Brand, Michael: *Tuba Tapestry*
Anonymous
    Album Title: *Masterpieces for Brass*, Vol. 1
    Personnel:
    Label: Rondo Grammofon. CD: RCD 8322
        (Also RLP 8315 and RMC 8315
        under title *Music from the Old Tivoli
        Bandstand*)
    Nielsen, Hans Peter: *The Satyr*
Anonymous
    Album Title: *Mid-West National Band and
        Orchestra Clinic 1981*
    Personnel: Northshore Concert Band; John
        Painter, conductor
    Label: Silver Crest, 1981 LP: MID-81-15C
    Nelhybel, Vaclav: *Concerto Grosso for Tubas and
        Band*
Anonymous
    Album Title: *Tell Me a Story*
    Personnel: MGM Orchestra; Jose Ferrer,
        narrator
    Label: MGM LP: PX 106
    Kleinsinger, George, and Tripp, Paul: *Tubby
        the Tuba*
Anonymous
    Album Title: *Tubby the Tuba*
    Personnel:
    Label: Simon Says LP: 19
    Kleinsinger, George, and Tripp, Paul: *Tubby the
        Tuba*
Anonymous
    Album Title: *Tubby the Tuba*
    Personnel:
    Label: Wonderland LP: 8
    Kleinsinger, George, and Tripp, Paul: *Tubby the
        Tuba*
Anonymous
    Album Title: *Tubby the Tuba*
    Personnel: Peter Pan Players and Orchestra
    Label: Peter Pan Records 45 RPM: PP1020/
        8044
    Kleinsinger, George, and Tripp, Paul: *Tubby
        the Tuba*
Anonymous
    Album Title: *Tubby the Tuba*
    Personnel: Stuttgart Symphony Orchestra; Carl
        Bamberger, conductor; Paul Tripp, narrator

Label: Golden Records LP: GLP 8
    Kleinsinger, George, and Tripp, Paul: *Tubby
        the Tuba*
Anonymous
    Album Title: *Tubby the Tuba* (*Peter and the
        Wolf; The Story of Celeste*)
    Personnel: Not listed
    Label: MGM Children's Series LP: CHS 505
    Kleinsinger, George, and Tripp, Paul: *Tubby
        the Tuba*
Anonymous
    Album Title:
    Personnel:
    Label: Mark Educational Recordings LP: 1244
    Vaughan Williams, Ralph: *Concerto for Bass
        Tuba and Orchestra*
Arnsted, Jørgen Voight
    Album Title: *Masterpieces for Brass*, Vol. 2
    Personnel:
    Label: Rondo Grammofon CD: RCD 8333
Arnsted, Jørgen Voight
    Album Title: *Old Danish Masterpieces for Brass*,
        Vol. 1
    Personnel:
    Label: Rondo Grammofon LP: RLP 8314; CS:
        RMC 8314
    Langgaard, Rued: *Dies Irae* for tuba and piano
Arnsted, Jørgen Voight
    Album Title: *Scandinavian Trombone*
    Personnel:
    Label: Rondo Grammofon LP: RLP 8307; CS:
        RMC 8307
    Holmboe, Vagn: *Notater* for three trombones
        and tuba
Arwood, Jeffrey
    Album Title: *ASBDA Convention*, June 1985,
        Charlotte, NC
    Personnel: The United States Army Band
        (Pershing's Own); Colonel Eugene W. Allen,
        conductor
    Label: New Age Sight and Sound, 1985 CS
    Vaughan Williams, Ralph/Hare: *Concerto for
        Bass Tuba and Band*
Arwood, Jeffrey
    Album Title: *Augustiana College 32nd Annual
        Concert Band Festival*
    Personnel: Augustiana College Concert Band;
        Dr. Bruce T. Amman, conductor
    Label: Westmark Tapes, 1989 CS
    Taylor, Mark: *Latin Fantasy*
    Abreu, Zequinha/A. Smith: *Tico-Tico*
Arwood, Jeffrey
    Album Title: *Pennsylvania Inter-Collegiate
        Band Festival Concert–1989*
    Personnel: Pennsylvania Inter-Collegiate; Dr.
        Stanley F. Michalski, Jr., conductor
    Label: Al Teare Digital Recordings, 1989 CS
    Lebedev, Alexander/A. Cohen: *Concerto in
        One Movement*

Abreu, Zequinha/A. Smith: *Tico-Tico*
Arwood, Jeffrey
    Album Title: *South Dakota State University Symphonic Band–1975*
    Personnel: South Dakota State University Symphonic Band; Dr. Darwin Walker, conductor
    Label: Mark Records, 1975 LP: MC6106
    Youmans, Vincent/ Norman: *Carioca*
    Rogers, Walter: *The Volunteer*
    Brennard, George/Arwood: *The Old Rugged Cross*
Arwood, Jeffrey
    Album Title: *27th Annual South Dakota All-State Band*
    Personnel: South Dakota All-State Band; Major Allen C. Crowell, conductor
    Label: Mark Records, 1977 LP: MC 6107
    Galliard, Johann Ernst/R. Clemons: *Allegro from Sonata No. 3 in F major*
    Van Heusen, Jimmy, and Silvers, Phil/A. Smith: *Nancy with the Laughing Face*
    Abreu, Zequinha/A. Smith: *Tico-Tico*
Arwood, Jeffrey
    Album Title: *The Army Ground Forces Band in Concert—Texas Bandmasters Association*
    Personnel: The Army Ground Forces Band (Atlanta, Georgia); Major Michael Pyatt, conductor, Forces Command, Ft. McPherson
    Label: The Army Ground Forces Band, 1990 CS: Public service, not for sale
    Camphouse, Mark: *Poème*
Arwood, Jeffrey
    Album Title: *The United States Army Band featuring Overture "1812"*
    Personnel: The United States Army Band (Pershing's Own); Colonel Samuel R. Loboda, conductor
    Label: United States Army Band, 1974 LP: S 19741 Public service, not for sale
    Abreu, Zequinha/A. Smith: *Tico-Tico*
Arwood, Jeffrey
    Album Title: *The United States Army Band in Residence—Wilber M. Brucker Hall*
    Personnel: The United States Army Band (Pershing's Own); Colonel Eugene W. Allen, conductor
    Label: United States Army Band, 1979 LP: S 19791 Public service, not for sale
    Taylor, Mark: *Latin Fantasy*
Astwood, Michael
    Album Title: *1974 Mid-West Band and Orchestra Clinic*
    Personnel: Coronado High School Symphonic Band
    Label: Crest, 1974 LP: MID-74-13
    Presser, William: *Capriccio for Tuba and Band*
Atlantic Tuba Quartet
    Album Title: *Euphonic Sounds*

    Personnel: David Werden, Dennis Winter, euphoniums; Gary Buttery, David Chaput, tubas
    Label: Golden Crest, 1978 LP: CRS 4173
    Susato, Tielman/Winter: *Ronde and Saltarelle "Pour Quoy"*
    Bach, Johann Sebastian/Myers: *Allegro from Toccata in D minor for Klavier,* BWV 913
    Bach, Johann Sebastian/Werden: *Bist du bei mir,* BWV 508
    Lyon, Max J.: *Suite for Low Brass*
    Anonymous/Buttery: *Greensleeves*
    Joplin, Scott/Werden: *Euphonic Sounds*
    Sousa, John Philip/Werden: *Stars and Stripes Forever*
    Bach, Johann Sebastian/Werden: *"Air" from Suite No. 3 for Orchestra,* BWV 1068
    Ramsoe, Emilio Wilhelm/Buttery: *Quartet No. 4 (Allegro molto)*
    Byrd, William/Winter: *Jhon Come Kisse Me Now*
    Hartley, Walter: *Miniatures for 4 Four Valve Instruments*
    Collins, Judy/Buttery: *Since You've Asked*
    Powell, Baden/Buttery: *Bocoxe*
    Best, Denzil Decosta/Buttery: *Move*
Augustin, Rudiger
    Album Title: *Hindemith Chamber Works, Vol. II*
    Personnel: Richard Laugs, piano
    Label: Musical Heritage Society Orpheus LP: OR H-290
    Hindemith, Paul: *Sonata for Bass Tuba and Piano*
Baadsvik, Øystein
    Album Title: *International Competition for Musical Performers Geneva 1991*
    Personnel: Bienne Brass Band; Martin Aakerwall, piano; Orchester de la Suisse Romande
    Label: Musica Helvetica, 1992 CD: MH CD 77.2
    Meier, Jost: *Eclipse finale?* for tuba and brass band (Øystein Baadsvik, tuba)
    Baader-Nobs, Heidi: *Bifurcation* for tuba and piano (Jens Bjørn-Larsen, tuba)
    Strukov, Valery: *Concerto for Tuba and Orchestra* (Jens Bjørn-Larsen, tuba)
Baadsvik, Øystein
    Album Title:
    Personnel: Niklas Sivelöv, piano; Swedish Brass Quintet
    Label: SIMAX-PSC, 1993 CD: 1101
    Kraft, William: *Encounters II for Solo Tuba*
    Hindemith, Paul: *Sonata for Bass Tuba and Piano*
    Madsen, Trygve: *Sonata for Tuba and Piano*
    Sivelov, Niklas: *Sonata for Tuba and Piano*
    Gaathaug, Morten: *Sonata Concertante for Solo Tuba and Brass Quintet*

Baker, Fred
  Album Title: *Brass Ablaze*
  Personnel: Hammonds Sause Works Band
  Label: Polyphonic CS: CPRL 005
  Muscroft, Fred: *Carnival for Bass*
Banker, John. *See* United States Coast Guard Tuba-
  Euphonium Quartet, *The Musical Sounds of the
  Seasons*
Barber, John William (Bill)
  Album Title: *Miles Davis, Birth of the Cool*
  Personnel: Miles Davis Groups, 1948–50
  Label: Capital LP: DT1974
  Best, Denzil Decosta: *Move*
  Wallington, George: *Godchild*
  Henry, Cleo: *Boplicity*
Barber, John William (Bill)
  Album Title: *Miles Davis—Porgy and Bess*
  Personnel: Miles Davis
  Label: Columbia, 1958 LP: 8085
  Gershwin, George/Evans: *The Buzzard Song*
Barber, John William (Bill)
  Album Title: *Musica Jazz Presents Miles Davis*
  Personnel: Miles Davis and His Tuba Band
  Label: Musica Jazz, 1986. LP
  S'il vous plait
Barber, John William (Bill)
  Album Title: *Rugolomania*
  Personnel: Pete Rugolo and his Orchestra with
  the Rugolettes
  Label: Philips LP: BBL 7069
  Adamson/B. Lane: *Everything I Have Is Yours*
Bargeron, Dave
  Album Title: *Blood, Sweat and Tears—Live and
  Improvised*
  Personnel: Blood, Sweat and Tears
  Label: Columbia Legacy/Sony Music Enter-
  tainment 2CDs: C2K4618/ 2CS: C2T46918
  Traditional/Hooker, John Lee/Clayton-
  Thomas: *One Room Country Shack*
Bargeron, Dave
  Album Title: *Blood, Sweat and Tears Featuring
  David Clayton-Thomas/New City*
  Personnel: Blood, Sweat and Tears
  Label: Columbia, 1975 LP: 33484
  Traditional/Hooker, John Lee/Clayton-
  Thomas: *One Room Country Shack*
Bargeron, Dave
  Album Title: *B. S. & T. 4*
  Personnel: Blood, Sweat and Tears
  Label: Columbia LP: MK 30590
  Go Down Gamblin'
Bargeron, Dave
  Album Title: *Dance of Passion*
  Personnel: Johnny Griffin Quartet Plus 3
  Label: Antilles/Polygram, 1993 CD:
  314512604-2
  Griffin, Johnny: *Dance of Passion*
  Griffin, Johnny: *You've Never Been There*

Bargeron, Dave
  Album Title: *New Blood*
  Personnel: Blood, Sweat and Tears
  Label: Columbia LP: MK 31780
  Alone
Beauregard, Cherry
  Album Title: *Music of Samuel Adler*
  Personnel:
  Label: Mark Educational Reocrdings LP:
  MM 1117
  Adler, Samuel: *Canto VII for Solo Tuba*
Bell, William
  Album Title: *A Children's Introduction to the
  Orchestra*
  Personnel: The Golden Symphony Orchestra
  and Sandpiper Chorus; Mitch Miller,
  conductor
  Label: Golden Records LP: GLP 1
  Wilder, Alec: *Poobah the Tuba*
Bell, William
  Album Title: *Bill Bell and His Tuba*
  Personnel:
  Label: Golden Crest LP: CR 4027 / CS:
  CRS4211
  Hupfeld, Herman: *When Yuba Plays the
  Rhumba on the Tuba Down in Cuba*
  Petrie, H. W.: *Asleep in the Deep*
  Grieg, Edvard: *In the Hall of the Moun-
  tain King*
  Carr, S./Bell: *Tuba Man*
  Landes, B.: *The Elephant Tango*
  Merle, John: *Mummers (Dance Grotesque)*
  Arban, J. B./Bell: *Carnival of Venice*
  Mozart, Wolfgang Amadeus: *O Isis and Osiris*
  Beethoven, Ludwig/Bell: *Variations on a Theme
  from "Judas Maccabeus"*
  Schumann, Robert/Bell: *The Jolly Farmer Goes
  to Town*
Bell, William
  Album Title: *The Directors Band*
  Personnel: Directors Band, Morehead State
  University; Robert Hawkins, conductor
  Label: Audicom Corporation 7 inch record:
  KM2038 R634 (first released by Morehead
  State University Book Store)
  Landes, B.: *The Elephant's Tango*
  Paganini, Niccolo: *Moto Perpetuo* (with Arnold
  Jacobs and Harvey Phillips)
Bell, William
  Album Title: *The Neighbors Band*
  Personnel: Robert McClellend, trumpet; Joseph
  Songer, horn; Lawrence Alpeter, trombone
  Label: Young People's 78rpm: 726-A
Bell, William
  Album Title: *The Revelli Years*
  Personnel: University of Michigan Sym-
  phonic Band
  Label: Golden Crest, 1981 LP
  Paganini, Niccolo/Bell: *Moto Perpetuo*

Birnie, Stuart. *See* British Tuba Quartet
Bishop, Ronald
    Album Title: *Music for an Awful Lot of Winds*
    and Percussion
    Personnel: David McGill, bassoon
    Label: Telarc CD: CD-80307
    Bach, P. D. Q.: *Dutch Suite for Bassoon*
    and Tuba
Bjørn-Larsen, Jens
    Album Title: *Concert Band Music*
    Personnel: Danish Concert Band
    Label: Rondo Grammofon CD: RCD 8331
    Wilhelm, Rolf: *Concertino* for tuba and
    concert band
Bjørn-Larsen, Jens
    Album Title: *International Competition for*
    Musical Performers Geneva 1991
    Personnel: Bienne Brass Band; Martin Aaker-
    wall, piano; Orchester de la Suisse-Romande
    Label: Musica Helvetica, 1992 CD: MH
    CD 77.2
    Meier, Jost: *Eclipse finale?* for tuba and brass
    band (Øystein Baadsvik, tuba)
    Baader-Nobs, Heidi: *Bifurcation* for tuba and
    piano (Jens Bjørn-Larsen, tuba)
    Strukov, Valery: *Concerto for Tuba and*
    Orchestra (Jens Bjørn-Larsen, tuba)
Bobo, Roger
    Album Title: *Bobissimo! The Best of Roger Bobo*
    Personnel: Ralph Grierson, piano
    Label: Crystal, 1991 CD: CD125
    Galliard, Johann Ernst: *Sonata No. 5 in*
    D Minor
    Barat, Joseph Eduoard: *Introduction*
    and Dance
    Hindemith, Paul: *Sonata for Bass Tuba*
    and Piano
    Wilder, Alec: *Suite No. 1 for Tuba and Piano*
    (Effie)
    Kraft, William: *Encounters II for Solo Tuba*
    Spillman, Robert: *Two Songs*
    Lazarof, Henri: *Cadence VI* for tuba and tape
    Wilder, Alec: *Encore Piece*
Bobo, Roger
    Album Title: *BOTUBA*
    Personnel: Thomas Stevens, trumpet; Ralph
    Grierson, piano
    Label: Crystal, 1978 LP: S392 / CS: C392
    Stevens, Thomas: *Encore Boz*
    Spillman, Robert: *Two Songs*
    Kraft, William: *Encounters II for Solo Tuba*
    Wilder, Alec: *Tuba Encore Piece (A Tubist's*
    Showcase)
    Lazarof, Henri: *Cadence VI* for tuba and tape
    Reynolds, Verne: *Signals* for trumpet, tuba, and
    brass choir
    zoB erocnE :samohT ,snevetS
Bobo, Roger
    Album Title: *Gravity Is Light Today*

Personnel: Roger Kellaway, piano; Fred
    Tackett, guitar; Ralph Grierson, piano;
    Skip Moser, bass; Ray Rich, drums
    Label: Crystal, 1979 LP: S396
    Kellaway, Roger: *The Morning Song*
    Kellaway, Roger: *The Westwood Song*
    Tackett, Fred: *The Yellow Bird*
Bobo, Roger
    Album Title: *Tuba Libera*
    Personnel: Marie Condamin, piano; European
    Tuba Octet
    Label: Crystal, 1994 CD: CD690
    Stevens, Thomas: *Variations in Olden Style*
    Penderecki, Krzysztof: *Capriccio for Solo Tuba*
    Madsen, Trygve: *Sonata for Tuba and Piano*
    Plog, Anthony: *Three Miniatures for Tuba*
    and Piano
    Arban, J. B./Berry: *Fantaisie and Variations on*
    the Carnival of Venice
    Dumitru, Ionel: *Romanian Dance No. 2*
    Shostakovich, Dimitri: *Adagio*
    Stevens, John: *The Liberation of Sisyphus* (solo
    tuba with euphonium/tuba ensemble)
Bobo, Roger
    Album Title: *Music of Henry Lazarof*
    Personnel:
    Label: Avant, 1974 LP: AV 1019
    Lazarof, Henri: *Cadence VI* for tuba and tape
Bobo, Roger
    Album Title: *Prunes*
    Personnel: Froydis Ree Werke, horn; Zita
    Carno, piano; Roger Kellaway, piano
    Label: Crystal, 1980 LP: S126
    Bach, Johann Sebastian: *Air for the G String*
    Sinigaglia, Leone: *Song and Humoreske*
    Schubert, Franz Peter: *Serenade*
    Cui, Cesar: *Perpetual Motion*
    Kellaway, Roger: *Sonoro* for horn, bass horn,
    and piano
    Kellaway, Roger: *Dance of the Ocean Breeze* for
    horn, bass horn, and piano
Bobo, Roger
    Album Title: *Roger Bobo and Tuba*
    Personnel: Ralph Grierson, piano
    Label: Crystal, 1969 LP: S125
    Galliard, Johann Ernst: *Sonata No. 5 in*
    D Minor
    Hindemith, Paul: *Sonata for Bass Tuba*
    and Piano
    Barat, Joseph Eduoard: *Introduction and Dance*
    Kraft, William: *Encounters II*
    Wilder, Alec: *Suite No. 1 for Tuba and Piano*
    (Effie)
Bobo, Roger. *See* Summit Tubas
Bobo, Roger. *See* United States Army Band,
  "Pershing's Own"
Bobo, Roger
    Album Title: *Solo Brass: New Perspectives*
    Personnel: Fred Tackett, guitar; Ralph Grier-

son, piano; Skip Moser, bass; Ray Rich,
  drums
  Label: Avant LP: AV 1009
  Tackett, Fred: *The Yellow Bird*
Bobo, Roger
  Album Title: *Thomas Stevens, trumpet*
  Label: Crystal CD: CD667
  Reynolds, Verne: *Signals* (solo trumpet, tuba
    and brass choir)
Bobo, Roger
  Album Title: *Tuba Nova*
  Personnel: Dan Rothmuller, cello; Ralph
    Grierson, piano
  Label: Crystal,1981 LP: S398
  Kupferman, Meyer: *Saturnalis* (tuba and
    amplified cello)
  Subotnick, Morton: *First Dream of Light* (tuba,
    piano, electronic ghost score)
Boujie, George
  Album Title: *Danny Kaye's Hans Christian
    Andersen*
  Personnel: Danny Kaye, narrator; Victor Young
    Orchestra
  Label: Decca LP: DL 8479
  Kleinsinger, George, and Tripp, Paul: *Tubby the
    Tuba*
  Kleinsinger, George, and Tripp, Paul: *Tubby the
    Tuba at the Circus*
Boujie, George
  Album Title: *Tubby the Tuba*
  Personnel: Danny Kaye, narrator; Victor Young
    Orchestra
  Label: MCA LP: 148
  Kleinsinger, George, and Tripp, Paul: *Tubby
    the Tuba*
Brainard, David
  Album Title: *American Contemporary Series*
  Personnel: Group for Contemporary Music
  Label: Composer's Recordings, Inc.LP: SD491
  Wuorinen, Charles: *Tuba Concerto*
British Tuba Quartet
  Album Title: *Boosey and Hawkes National Brass
    Band Championship of Great Britain 1991*
  Personnel: Steven Mead, Michael Howard,
    euphoniums; Ken Ferguson, Stuart
    Birnie, tubas
  Label: Polyphonic, 1991 CD: QDRL 049D
  Frackenpohl, Arthur: *Pop Suite* (last movement)
British Tuba Quartet
  Album Title: *Elite Syncopations*
  Personnel: Steven Mead, Michael Howard,
    euphoniums; Ken Ferguson, Stuart Birnie,
    tubas
  Label: Polyphonic, 1993 CD: QPRZ 012D
  Glinka, Michael/Smalley: *Overture to Russlan
    and Ludmila*
  Rossini, Gioacchino/Smalley: *La Danza*
  Chopin, Frederic/Mead: *Minute Waltz*

Martino, Ralph: *Fantasy*
Bull, John/Howard: *The King's Hunt*
Gabrieli, Giovanni/Rauch: *Canzona, La
  Spiritata*
Tchaikovsky, Peter Ilyitch/Smalley: *Trepek*
Strauss, Johann, Jr./Smalley: *Chit Chat Polka*
Gershwin, George/Ferguson: *Fascinatin'
  Gershwin*
Sherwin, Manning/Smalley: *A Nightingale
  Sang in Berkley Square*
Dubin and Warren/Minard: *42nd Street
  Selections*
Schoenberg, C. M./Mead: *On My Own from
  "Les Miserables"*
Joplin, Scott/Picher: *Elite Syncopations*
Horovitz, Joseph: *Rumpole of the Bailey*
Berlin, Irving/Gout: *Puttin' on the Ritz*
arr. Dempsey: *Three Movements from "Quatre
  Chansons"*
Niehaus, Lennie: *Grand Slam*
Wolking, Henry: *Tuba Blues*
British Tuba Quartet
  Album Title: *Euphonic Sounds*
  Personnel: Steven Mead, Michael Howard,
    euphoniums; Ken Ferguson, Stuart
    Birnie, tubas
  Label: Polyphonic, 1992 CD: QPRZ 009D
  Bulla, Stephen: *Celestial Suite*
  Diero/Ferguson: *Il Ritorno*
  Kern, Jerome/Holcomb: *They Didn't
    Believe Me*
  Ramsoe, Emilio Wilhelm/Buttery: *Quartet
    for Brass*
  Di Lasso, Orlando/Robinson: *Mon Coeur se
    Recommende a Vous*
  Byrd, William/Winter: *Jhon Come Kisse Me Now*
  Powell, Baden/Buttery: *Bocoxe*
  Joplin, Scott/Powell: *The Favorite Rag*
  arr. Niehaus: *Spiritual Jazz Suite*
  arr. Buttery: *Greensleeves*
  Lerner, Alan Jay/Belsha: *Get Me to the Church
    on Time*
  Bach, Johann Sebastian/Werden: *Air from
    Suite No. 3*
  Mancini, Henry/Krush: *The Pink Panther*
  Joplin, Scott/Werden: *Euphonic Sounds*
  Monaco/Holcombe: *You Made Me Love You*
  Rossini, Gioacchino/Smalley: *William Tell
    Overture*
British Tuba Quartet
  Album Title: *In at the Deep End*
  Personnel: Steven Mead, Michael Howard,
    euphoniums; Ken Ferguson, Stuart
    Birnie, tubas
  Label: Heavyweight Records LTD, 1991 CD:
    HR008/D
  Bulla, Stephen: *Quartet for Low Brass*
  Sousa, John Philip/Morris: *Semper Fidelis*

Frackenpohl, Arthur: *Pop Suite*
Saint-Saëns, Camille/Murley: *Adagio from Symphony No. 3*
Bach, Johann Sebastian/Werden: *Jesu, Joy of Man's Desiring*
Mozart, Wolfgang Amadeus/Ferguson: *Overture to the "Marriage of Figaro"*
Rimsky-Korsakov, Nicholas: *Notturno*
Heusen, Van/Barton: *Here's That Rainy Day*
Bach, Johann Sebastian/Gray: *Fugue in G Minor*
Sousa, John Philip/Morris: *El Capitan*
Cheetham, John: *Consortium*
Joplin, Scott/Sabourin: *The Cascades*
Anonymous/Baker: *Lute Dances*
Holmes, Paul: *Quartet for Tubas*
Hook, J./Garrett: *Rondo*
Bach, Johann Sebastian/Howard: *Rondo*
Traditional/Garrett: *Wabash Cannonball*
Traditional/Trippet/Howard: *Steal Away*
Sousa, John Philip/Sabourin: *Washington Post*
Bruno, Jerry
   Album Title: *Tubby the Tuba*
   Personnel: The Playmates and Orchestra; Maury Laws, conductor
   Label: Cricket Records 45 rpm: C-46A
   Kleinsinger, George, and Tripp, Paul: *Tubby the Tuba*
Bunn, Michael. *See* United States Army Band, "Pershing's Own"
Busch, Sigi
   Album Title: *Age of Miracles*
   Personnel:
   Label: MPS RecordsLP: 2022451-1
   Busch, Sigi: *Tuba or Not Tuba*
Butterfield, Don
   Album Title: *Gil Melle Quintet*
   Personnel: Gil Melle, bassoon
   Label: Blue Note, 1955. LP: PLP 5063
Butterfield, Don
   Album Title: *Gil's Guest*
   Personnel: Gil Melle, bassoon
   Label: Prestige, 1956. LP: PRLP 7063
Butterfield, Don
   Album Title: *Music of Morton Feldman and Earle Brown*
   Personnel: Don Hammond, alto flute; David Tudor, piano; Philip Kraus, vibraphone; Matthew Raimondi, violin; David Soyer, cello
   Label: Time Records LP: 58007
   Feldman, Morton: *Durations*
Butterfield, Don
   Album Title: *Top and Bottom Brass*
   Personnel: Clark Terry
   Label: Riverside, 1959. LP:
Buttery, Gary
   Album Title: *A Different Village*
   Personnel: David Schoenfeld, Deborah Szajnbeng, Premjit Talwar, Bruce Batts,

Tony Morris, Sue Lowenkron Morris
   Label: 1992 CD, CS
   Traditional/Buttery: *Tsiganochka* for solo tuba, guitar, mandocello, accordian, and bazuki
Buttery, Gary. *See* Atlantic Tuba Quartet, *Euphonic Sounds*
Call, R. Steven
   Album Title: *Tubby the Tuba*
   Personnel:
   Label: Macmillan/McGraw Hill Publishing, 1994. General Music Program
   Kleinsinger, George, and Tripp, Paul: *Tubby the Tuba*
Callender, George Sylvester "Red"
   Album Title: *Basin Street Brass*
   Personnel: Al Aarons, trumpet; Grover Mitchell, trombone; Buddy Collette, reeds; Harold Jones, Walter Sage, drums; Al Viola, guitar/banjo; Leroy Vinnegar, bass; Patrick Boyle, tambourine
   Label: Legend Record Company, 1973 LP: 1003
   Williams, Spencer/Mitchell: *Basin Street Blues*
   arr. Boyle: *Primrose Lane*
   arr. Boyle: *When the Saints Go Marchin' In*
   arr. Boyle: *Just a Closer Walk with Thee*
   Ellington, Duke/Callender: *Sophisticated Lady*
   arr. Callender: *Dedicated to the Blues*
   arr. Mitchell: *I Want a Little Girl*
   arr. Mitchell: *Magna*
   arr. Mitchell: *Fat Cat*
   arr. Callender: *Lush Life*
Callender, George Sylvester "Red"
   Album Title: *Moon Mist Blues*
   Personnel:
   Label: Hemisphere Records LP: 1002
   Callender, Red: *Moon Mist Blues*
Callender, George Sylvester "Red"
   Album Title: *Red Callender Speaks Low*
   Personnel: Vince DeRosa, horn; Bob Bain, guitar; Bill Douglas, drums; Buddy Collette, reeds; Irving Rosenthal, horn; Red Mitchell, bass
   Label: Crown Records, 1957 LP: CLP 5012
   Weill, Kurt/Nash: *Speak Low*
   Collette, Buddy: *Nice Day*
   Ellington, Duke: *In a Sentimental Mood*
   Gershwin, George: *Foggy Day*
   Callender, Red: *Cris*
   DeLange/Van Heusen: *Darn That Dream*
   Wrubel/Magidson: *Gone with the Wind*
Carroll, Bill
   Album Title: *Southern Stomps*
   Personnel: Turk Murphy Jazz Band
   Label: Stomp Off, 1985. LP: S. O. S. 1161
Carroll, Bill
   Album Title: *Turk at Carnegie*
   Personnel: Turk Murphy's San Francisco Jazz Band

Label: Stomp Off, 1987. LP: S. O. S. 1155
Catelinet, Philip
   Album Title:
   Personnel: London Symphony Orchestra
   Label: Barbirolli Society, 1955 LP: SJB102
   Vaughan Williams, Ralph: *Concerto for Bass Tuba and Orchestra*
Chaput, David. *See* Atlantic Tuba Quartet, *Euphonic Sounds*
Conger, Al
   Album Title: *Live at Easy Street*
   Personnel: Turk Murphy's San Francisco Jazz Band
   Label: Cadillac Music, 1958. DC 12018
Conner, Rex
   Album Title: *1969 Midwest National Band and Orchestra Clinic*
   Personnel: Waukegan Grade School Band; Bernard Stiner, director
   Label: Golden Crest, 1969 LP: MID 69-6
   Boccalari, E./Akers: *Fantasia di Concerto*
Conner, Rex
   Album Title: *Rex Conner National Contest List Tuba Solos*
   Personnel: Patricia Lasswell, piano
   Label: Coronet LP: LPS 1259
   Handel, George Friderik: *Air and Bourrée*
   Beethoven, Ludwig: *Minuet*
   Schmidt, William: *Serenade for Tuba and Piano*
   Vaughan, Rodger: *Concertpiece No.1*
   Bach, Johann Sebastian/Bell: *Air and Bourrée*
   Beach, Bennie: *Lamento*
   Haddad, Don: *Suite for Tuba*
   Mueller, Florian: *Concert Music for Bass Tuba*
   Holmes, Paul: *Lento*
   Hartley, Walter: *Suite for Unaccompanied Tuba*
The Contraband
   Album Title: *Swingin' Low*
   Personnel: Martin Kym, Martin Meier, euphoniums; Ernest May, David LeClair, tubas; Andy Lüscher, drums; Thomas Thüring, piano
   Label: Marcophon, 1993 CD: CD 940-2
   LeClair, David: *Heidentüblein*
   arr. Willibald Kresin: *Swing Low*
   Schubert, Franz Peter/LeClair: *Ständchen*
   Carmichael, Hoagy/LeClair: *Georgia on My Mind*
   Bartles, Alfred: *When Tubas Waltz*
   Niehaus, Lennie: *Sleeping Giants*
   arr. Dankwart Schmidt: *Tuba Muckl*
   Lohmann, Georg/Schmidt: *Bayerische Polka*
   LeClair, David: *Carnival of Venice*
   Schubert, Franz Peter/LeClair: *Militärmarsch*
   Kresin, Willibald: *Chin Up!*
   Sousa, John Philip/Werden: *Washington Post*
   LeClair, David: *Growing Up Together* (euphonium and tuba duet)
   Joplin, Scott/LeClair: *The Easy Winners*

Clarke, Herbert L./LeClair: *Cousins*
Cooley, Floyd
   Album Title: *The Romantic Tuba*
   Personnel: Naomi Cooley, harpsichord and piano
   Label: Crystal, 1983 LP: S120 (rerelease of Avant Records 1020)
   Bach, Johann Sebastian: *Sonata in E♭ Major*
   Brahms, Johannes: *Vier ernste Gesänge*
   Zindar, Earl: *Trigon*
   Russell, Armand: *Suite Concertante*
Cooley, Floyd
   Album Title: *School Broadcast "Music Makers"— Brass*
   Personnel:
   Label: SoCal, 1975 CS: M-51
   Vaughan Williams, Ralph: *Concerto for Bass Tuba and Orchestra*
   Wagner, Richard: *Siegfried* (excerpts)
   Brahms, Johannes: *Vier ernste Gesänge* (excerpts)
Cooley, Floyd
   Album Title: *A Schumann Fantasy*
   Personnel: Robin Sutherland, piano
   Label: Summit Records, 1993. CD: DCD 156
   Schumann, Robert: *Fantasiestücke*, Op. 73
   Schumann, Robert: *Drei Romanzen*, Op. 94
   Schumann, Robert: *Märchenbilder* (Pictures of Fairyland), Op. 113
   Schumann, Robert: *Adagio and Allegro*, Op. 70
Cooley, Floyd
   Album Title:
   Personnel:
   Label: Crystal LP: S690
   Schumann, Robert: *Scenes from Fairyland*
   Schumann, Robert: *Three Romanzes*
Cooley, Floyd
   Album Title:
   Personnel:
   Label: Op. One LP: 29
   Felciano, Richard: *"and from the abyss"* for tuba and tape
Crowther, Shaun
   Album Title: *Let's Go*
   Personnel: Williams Fairey Engineering
   Label: Abrasso, CD: 832
   Rossini, Gioacchino/Roberts: *Largo al Factotum*
Crowther, Shaun
   Album Title: *Master Brass, Vol. 1*
   Personnel: Williams Fairey Engineering Band; Major Peter Parks, director
   Label: Polyphonic, 1990 CD: QDRL 046D
   Butler/Gay: *The Sun Has Got His Hat On*
Crowther, Shaun
   Album Title:
   Personnel: Williams Fairey Engineering
   Label: Grasmere CD: GRCD 35
   Butler, Gay, Sparke: *The Sun Has Got His Hat On*

Relton, William: *The Trouble with the Tuba Is*
Newsome, Roy: *Swiss Air*
Cummings, Barton
 Album Title: *Barton Cummings, Music for Tuba*
 Personnel: Sharon Dudley, piano; Pat Pfiffner, percussion
 Label: Coronet LP: LPS 3065
 Butts, Carrol: *Suite for Tuba and Piano*
 Ott, Joseph: *Bart's Piece for Tuba and Electronic Tape*
 Rasbach: *Trees*
 Beach, Bennie: *Dance Suite for Tuba and Triangle*
 Williams, Howard: *Concertino for Tuba, Percussion and Piano*
Cummings, Barton
 Album Title: *Hilles*
 Personnel:
 Label: Capra, 1979 LP: 1206
 Hiller, Lejaren: *Malta for Tuba and Tape*
Cummings, Barton
 Album Title: *On Tuba: Barton Cummings*
 Personnel: Mary Jane Moore, piano
 Label: Crystal LP: S391
 Ross, Walter: *Piltdown Fragments* (tuba and tape)
 Ziffrin, Marilyn J.: *Four Pieces for Tuba*
 Zinos, Frederick: *Elegy*
 Jae Eun Ha: *Three Pieces*
Cummings, Barton
 Album Title: *Paths*
 Personnel: Dean Anderson, xylophone; Neva Pilgrim, soprano
 Label: Capra, 1981 LP: CRS 1210
 Ross, Walter: *Midnight Variations* for tuba and tape
 Ziffrin, Marilyn J.: *Trio for Xylophone, Soprano and Tuba*
Daley, Joe
 Album Title: *Crystals*
 Personnel: Sam Rivers
 Label: Impulse LP
Daley, Joe
 Album Title: *Waves*
 Personnel: Sam Rivers
 Label: Tomato Records LP
Daley, Joe. See Johnson, Howard, *Second Childhood*
Daley, Joseph. See Johnson, Howard, *Taj Mahal: The Real Thing*
Daniel, Robert
 Album Title: *Archival Series, Volume 1: Solo Flight*
 Pesonnel: United States Air Force Band
 Label: U. S. Air Force 1990 CS: BOL-8908T
 Public service, not for sale
 Smith, Claude T.: *Ballade and Presto Dance*
Daniel, Robert. *See* United States Army Band, "Pershing's Own"
Daniel, Robert, N. *See* United States Air Force

Concert Band Tuba Section
Davis, Ronald
 Album Title: *The Magic Place*
 Personnel: Robbie Clement, guitar; John Berquist, button accordian
 Label: Tomorrow River Music, 1985 CS: E1232
 Marxsen, Dale: *Waltzing with Bears*
 Wozniak, Doug: *The Fishy Song*
Davis, Ronald
 Album Title: *SoloPro: Contest Music for Tuba*
 Personnel: Theodor Lichtmann, piano
 Label: Summit, 1990 CS: DCD 106
 Haddad, Don: *Suite for Tuba*
 Holmes, Paul: *Lento*
 Gabrieli, Domenico/R. W. Morris: *Ricercar*
 Frackenpohl, Arthur: *Variations on the Cobbler's Bench*
 Vaughan, Rodger: *Concertpiece No. 1*
 Bach, Johann Sebastian/Bell: *Air and Bourrée*
 Sowerby, Leo: *Chaconne*
 Sear, Walter: *Sonatina*
 Martin, Carroll: *Pompola*
 Little, Donald: *Lazy Lullaby*
Deck, Warren. *See* Gerhard Meinl's Tuba Sextet
Dowling, Eugene
 Album Title: *The English Tuba*
 Personnel: London Symphony; Edward Norman, conductor
 Label: Fanfare, 1992 CD: CD D595
 Vaughan Williams, Ralph: *Concerto for Bass Tuba and Orchestra*
 Vaughan Williams, Ralph: *Six Studies in English Folksong*
 Handel, George Friderik: *Air con Variazioni from Suite No. 5 in E major*
 Elgar, Edward: *Romance*
 Jacob, Gordon: *Tuba Suite*
Dowling, Eugene
 Album Title: *Music Featuring the Tuba*
 Personnel: London Symphony Orchestra; Paul Freeman, conductor
 Label: Digitally Encoded Cassette Classics CS: EC-6033
 Vaughan Williams, Ralph: *Concerto for Bass Tuba and Orchestra*
 Vaughan Williams, Ralph: *Six Studies in English Folksong*
 Bach, Johann Sebastian/Dowling/Norman: *Sonata No. 4 in C*
 Ravel, Maurice: *Pièce en forme de habanera*
 Schumann, Robert: *Adagio and Allegro in Ab, Op. 70*
Draper, Ray
 Album Title: *Jackie McLean and Company*
 Personnel: Jackie McLean Sextet; Jackie McLean, alto saxophone; Bill Hardman, trumpet
 Label: Prestige, 1957. LP: PR LP 7087

Draper, Ray
    Album Title: *John Coltrane/Ray Draper Quintet*
    Personnel: John Coltrane, tenor sax; Gil Coggins, piano; Spanky De Brest, bass; Larry Ritchie, drums
    Label: Prestige, 1980 LP: MPP 2507
    Draper, Ray: *Clifford's Kappa*
    Draper, Ray: *Filidia*
    Draper, Ray: *Two Sons*
    Draper, Ray: *Paul's Pal*
    Draper, Ray: *Under Paris Skies*
    Draper, Ray: *I Hadn't Anyone Til You*
Draper, Ray
    Album Title: *Ray Draper*
    Personnel: Webster Young, trumpet; Jackie McLean, alto sax
    Label: Prestige, 1957. LP: PR LP 7096
Draper, Ray
    Album Title: *Ray Draper/Jackie McLean*
    Personnel: Jackie McLean, alto sax; Webster Young, trumpet
    Label: Prestige, 1957. LP: PR LP 7500
Draper, Ray
    Album Title: *Ray Draper Quintet*
    Personnel: John Coltrane, tenor sax
    Label: Prestige, 1957. LP: PR LP 7229
Draper, Ray
    Album Title: *Red Beans and Rice*
    Personnel: Phil Wood, trumpet; Richard Aplan, reeds; David Dahlsten, trombone; Bob Hogans, organ; Tommy Trujillo, guitar; Ron Johnson, bass; Paul Lagos, drums; Rodney Gooden, bass clarinet
    Label: Epic, 1969 LP: BN 26461
    Draper, Ray: *Happiness*
    Draper, Ray: *Empty Streets*
    Wood, Philip D.: *Trilogy*
    Wood, Philip D.: *Gentle Old Sea*
    Draper, Ray, and Aplan, Richard: *Let My People Go*
    Draper, Ray: *Mess Around*
    Wood, Philip D.: *Home*
    Trujillo, Tommy: *If You Ever Wanna*
Draper, Ray
    Album Title: *Sonny's Dream*
    Personnel: Sonny Criss Orchestra
    Label: Prestige, 1968. LP: PR 7576
Draper, Ray
    Album Title: *A Tuba Jazz*
    Personnel: John Coltrane, tenor sax; John Maher, piano; Spanky De Brest, bass; Larry Ritchie, drums
    Label: Fresh Sound Records, 1989 CD: FSR-CD 20
    Draper, Ray: *Essii's Dance*
    Rollins, Sonny: *Doxy*
    Lerner, Alan Jay: *I Talk to the Trees*
    Harbach, Otto, and Kern, Jerome: *Yesterdays*

    Rollins, Sonny: *Oleo*
    Dennis, Matt, and Brent, Earl: *Angel Eyes*
Draper, Ray
    Album Title: *Who Knows What Tomorrow's Gonna Bring*
    Personnel: Brother Jack McDuff
    Label: Blue Note, 1970. LP: BST 84358
Duga, Jan Z *See* United States Air Force Concert Band Tuba Section
Dumitru, Ionel
    Album Title: *Tuba Recital*
    Personnel: Irina Botez, piano
    Label: Electrecord 7 inch, 33 1/3: ECC 839
    Paganini, Niccolo: *Theme and Variations*
    Wieniawski: *Mazurcă*
    Dumitru, Ionel: *Fantezie Pentru Tuba si Pian*
Erickson, Martin
    Album Title: *Dale Underwood, Saxophone Soloist*
    Personnel:
    Label: Golden Crest LP: 4136
    Hartley, Walter: *Double Concerto for Saxophone, Tuba and Winds*
    Whitney: *Introduction and Samba*
Erickson, Martin. *See* Monarch Tuba-Euphonium Quartet
Erickson, Martin. *See* United States Navy Band Tuba-Euphonium Quartet
Ferguson, Ken. *See* British Tuba Quartet
Ferguson, Kenneth
    Album Title: *Desford Live in Canada*
    Personnel: Desford Colliery Catapillar Band
    Label: Hermitage, 1990 CD: HMCD 001 (same recording released as *Making Tracks*, Polyphonic QPRL 045D)
    Barry, Darrol: *Impromptu for Tuba*
Fletcher, John
    Album Title: *Baroque Brass: The Philip Jones Ensemble*
    Personnel: The Philip Jones Brass Ensemble
    Label: Argo LP: ZRG 898
    Bach, Johann Sebastian: *Suite No. 1 in G Major for Solo Cello* (Minuet, Courante)
Fletcher, John
    Album Title: *The Best of Fletch*
    Personnel: Besses O' Th' Barn Band; Roy Newsome, conductor/London Symphony Orchestra; André Previn, conductor
    Label: John Fletcher Trust Fund, 1988 CS
    Mozart, Wolfgang Amadeus/Fletcher: *Tuba Serenade (Eine kleine Nachtmusik)*
    Gregson, Edward: *Tuba Concerto*
    Ramsoe, Wilhelm: *Allegro Vivace from Quartet No. 5, Op. 38*
    Howarth, Elgar: *Carnival of Venice*
    Rimsky-Korsakov, Nicholas/Fletcher: *Flight of the Bumblebee*
    Arnold, Malcom: *Fantasy for Solo Tuba*
    arr. Howarth: *The Cuckoo, Lucerne Song*
    Bach, Johann Sebastian: *Suite No. 1 in G Major*

for Solo Cello (Minuet, Courante)
Vaughan Williams, Ralph: *Concerto for Bass Tuba and Orchestra*
Tchaikovsky, Peter Ilyitch/Fletcher: *Waltz from "Sleeping Beauty"*
Fletcher, John
    Album Title: *Brass Splendour*
    Personnel: The Philip Jones Brass Ensemble
    Label: London, 1984 CD: 411 955-2 LH
    Tchaikovsky, Peter Ilyitch/Fletcher: *Waltz from "Sleeping Beauty"*
Fletcher, John
    Album Title: *Divertimento*
    Personnel: The Philip Jones Brass Ensemble
    Label: Argo LP: ZRG 851
    Tchaikovsky, Peter Ilyitch/Fletcher: *Waltz from "Sleeping Beauty"*
Fletcher, John
    Album Title: *Easy Winners*
    Personnel: The Philip Jones Brass Ensemble
    Label: Argo, 1978 LP: ZRG 895; CS: KZRC 895
    Mozart, Wolfgang Amadeus/Fletcher: *Tuba Serenade (Eine kleine Nachtmusik)*
Fletcher, John
    Album Title: *Oliver Cromwell*
    Personnel: Stanshawe Band (Bristol); Walter Hargreaves, conductor
    Label: Twoten LP: TT 001
    Brand, Michael: *Tuba Tapestry*
    Arnold, Malcom: *Fantasy for Solo Tuba*
Fletcher, John
    Album Title: *Le Tuba Enchantée*
    Personnel: Michael Reeves, piano
    Label: Seven Seas Records 1980 LP: K28C-65
    Tchaikovsky, Peter Ilyitch: *Overture Miniature from "Nutcracker"*
    Elgar, Edward: *Chanson de Matin*
    Wagner, Richard: *O Du Mein Holder Abendstern from "Tannhäuser"*
    Mussorgsky, Modest: *Song of the Flea*
    Mozart, Wolfgang Amadeus: *Non Più Andrai from "Le Nozze di Figaro"*
    Hartley, Walter: *Suite for Unaccompanied Tuba*
    Hindemith, Paul: *Sonata for Bass Tuba and Piano*
    Glass: *Sonatine for Basstuba and Piano*
Fletcher, John
    Album Title: *Twentieth Century Soloists*
    Personnel: Besses O' Th' Barn Band; Roy Newsome, conductor
    Label: Chandos, 1982 LP: BBR 1013
    Gregson, Edward: *Concerto for Tuba and Brass Band*
Fletcher, John
    Album Title: *Vaughan Williams: Pastoral Symphony/Tuba Concerto*
    Personnel: London Symphony Orchestra; André Previn, conductor

Label: RCA Red Seal, 1972 LP: LSC-3281; CD: 60586-2-RG; CS: AGK1-5872
    Vaughan Williams, Ralph: *Concerto for Bass Tuba and Orchestra*
Flowers, Herbie
    Album Title: *Sky 2*
    Personnel:
    Label: Ariola LP: 204510
    Traditional: *Tuba Smarties*
Flowers, Herbie
    Album Title: *Sky 3*
    Personnel:
    Label: Ariola LP: 203413-320
    Traditional: *Dance of the Big Fairies*
Frazier, Philip. *See* New Orleans Jazz Bands, *Down Yonder*
Frazier, Richard
    Album Title: *The Brass and the Band*
    Personnel: Dallas Symphonic Wind Ensemble
    Label: Crystal, 1987 CD: 431
    Clarke, Herbert L.: *Bride of the Waves*
Freese, Stanford
    Album Title: *25th Anniversary Midwest National Band and Orchestra Clinic*
    Personnel: Thomas Jefferson Senior High School Band; Earl Benson, director
    Label: Golden Crest, 1971 LP: MID-71-7
    Bencriscutto, Frank: *Concertino for Tuba and Band*
Frey, Michael
    Album Title: *Interkantonale Blasabfuhr*
    Personnel:
    Label: Kompost Rekords, 1989 CD: AM 08.14
Frey, Michael
    Album Title: *Interkantonale Blasabfuhr II*
    Personnel: Interkantonale Blasabfuhr
    Label: Unit Records, 1991 CD: UTR 4044CD
Fritsch, Philippe. *See* Steckar Elephant Tuba Horde
Fritze, Gregory
    Album Title: *Cambridge Symphonic Brass Ensemble*
    Personnel: Russell De Vuyst, Ken Pullis, trumpets; Richard Hudson, horn; Kevin Henry, trombone
    Label: Crystal, 1986 LP: S552
    Fritze, Gregory: *Basso Continuo*
    Holmes, Brian: *Tales of the Cultural Revolution*
Gannett, Dave
    Album Title: *Christmas Cookies*
    Personnel: Randy Morris, piano and frets; Charles Bertini, trumpet and flugelhorn; Renee Dover, strings; Ed Metz, drums
    Label: Arbor Jazz Records, 1993 CD, CS
Gannett, Dave
    Album Title: *Tubas from Hell*
    Personnel: Tom Hook, keyboards, trombone, frets, percussion; Ed Metz, drums; Renee Dover, strings; Randy Morris, piano, marimba, mandolin; Anthony Dixon, banjo

Label: Summit Records, 1994 CD, CS:
DcD155 (reissue of 1992 CS)
'Deed I Do
Waller, Thomas "Fats": *Keepin' Out of
Mischief Now*
Fields and McHugh: *On the Sunny Side of the
Street*
Tubas in the Moonlight
Mercer, Johnny: *Tangerine*
Young and Meyer: *Sugar*
Williams, Mason: *Samba Beach*
Loesser, Frank: *On a Slow Boat to China*
Carmichael, Hoagy: *Ol' Rockin' Chair's Got
Me*
Burke and Johnston: *Pennies from Heaven*
Joplin, Scott: *Solace*
Yakkety Tuba
Gay, Les
Album Title: *Music of BL Lacerta*
Personnel: Robert Price, winds; Maurice Hood,
viola and violin; David Anderson, flute,
percussion, and electronics
Label: IRIDA, 1981 LP: IR-0009
BL Lacerta: *High Energy*
BL Lacerta: *Starts Same But Beautiful*
BL Lacerta: *Flutes and Tuba*
BL Lacerta: *Powerful*
BL Lacerta: *Estampie*
BL Lacerta: *My Mother Is Here*
BL Lacerta: *Stravinsky*
BL Lacerta: *Third*
BL Lacerta: *Monkey Chant*
Georgie, Gerhard
Album Title:
Personnel: Maria Bergman, piano
Label: Tontraeger LP: 0123506 SWF
Bozza, Eugene: *Allegro et Finale*
Georgie, Gerhard
Album Title:
Personnel: Maria Bergman, piano
Label: Tontraeger LP: 0123505 SWF
Hindemith, Paul: *Sonata for Bass Tuba and
Piano*
Gerhard Meinl's Tuba Sextet
Album Title: *Tuba! A Six-Tuba Musical Romp*
Personnel: Enrique Crespo, Warren Deck,
Walter Hilgers, Samuel Pilafian, Jonathon
Sass, Dankwart Schmidt
Label: Angel, 1992 CD: CDC 7 54729 2
(USA: CDC 54729)
Mozart, Wolfgang Amadeus/Crespo, Hilgers,
Pilafian: *Divertimento No. 2 in B♭*
Bach, Johann Sebastian/D. Schmidt: *Fugue in
G Minor*
Couperin, F./Pilafian: *Les Barricades
Mystérieuses*
Di Lasso, Orlando/Pilafian: *Ola, O che
bon eccho*

Gabrieli, Giovanni/Gray: *Canzona per
Sonare No. 4*
Rosler, J. J./D. Schmidt: *Partita—Polacca*
Hilgers, Walter: *Praeludium*
Crespo, Enrique: *Bruckner Etude*
Crespo, Enrique: *Three Milongas*
Denson, Frank: *Three Folksongs for Four Brass*
Sass, Jonathon: *Meltdown*
Watz, F.: *Melton March*
Traditional/D. Schmidt: *Bayrische Zell*
Lohmann, Georg/D. Schmidt: *Bayrische Polka*
Godard, Michel. *See* Steckar Tubapack
Gourlay, James
Album Title: *CWS Glasgow Band Meet the
Sovereign Soloists*
Personnel:
Label: Doyen, 1991 CD: DOY CD 012; CS:
DOY MC 012
Rossini, Gioacchino/Roberts: *Largo al
Factotum*
Rimsky-Korsakov, Nicholas/Gourlay: *Flight of
the Bumblebee*
Gourlay, James
Album Title:
Personnel:
Label: Doyen, 1994. CD: Released through
Summit Records
Gregson, Edward: *Tuba Concerto*
Horowitz, Joseph: *Tuba Concerto*
Penderecki, Krystof: *Capriccio for Solo Tuba*
Newton, Rodney: *Capriccio*
Arnold, Malcolm: *Fantasy for Tuba*
Gregson, Edward: *Alarum* (Solo Tuba)
Green, Carlton. *See* Johnson, Howard, *Second
Childhood*
Haas, Uli. *See* Melton Tuba-Quartett
Haering, Bernhard
Album Title: *Tuba Virtuoso*
Personnel: Orchester Emmerich Smola
Label: Caprice
Hammond, Ivan
Album Title:
Personnel: Ruth Inglefield, harp
Label: Composer's Recording, Inc. CD: CRI
SD-556
Childs, Barney: *A Question of Summer* for harp
and tuba
Hanks, Thompson (Toby)
Album Title: *Music of Beatrice Witkin*
Personnel:
Label: Op. One LP: 12
Witkin, Beatrice: *Breath and Sounds for Tuba
and Tape*
Hanks, Thompson (Toby)
Album Title: *Sampler*
Personnel: Gary Kirkpatrick, piano; New York
Tuba Quartet; New York City Ballet
Orchestra Trombones
Label: Crystal LP: S395

Telemann, Georg Philipp: *Fantasy in C Minor*
Hindemith, Paul: *Three Easy Pieces*
Stevens, John: *Dances*
Tomasi, Henri: *Etre ou ne pas Etre (monolog d'Hamlet)* for tuba and three trombones
Reck, David: *Five Studies for Tuba Alone*
Clarke, Herbert L.: *From the Shores of the Mighty Pacific*

Hanks, Thompson (Toby). *See* Megules, Karl
Hanks, Thompson (Toby). *See* New York Tuba Quartet
Harclerode, Albert. *See* Tubadours
Harrild, Patrick
Album Title: *Music by British Composers*
Personnel: Kent Youth Wind Orchestra
Label: Euphonia, 1994. CD: EUPCD012
Ellerby, Martin: *Tuba Concerto*

Harrild, Patrick
Album Title: *Vaughan Williams*
Personnel: London Symphony Orchestra; Bryden Thomson, conductor
Label: Chandos, 1989 LP: ABTD 1379; CD: CHAN-8740
Vaughan Williams, Ralph: *Concerto for Bass Tuba and Orchestra*

Havet, Didier. *See* Steckar Elephant Tuba Horde/ Steckar Tubapack
Hershko, Adi. *See* Tubadours
Hershko, Adi
Album Title: *And Two-Ba Too . . . Music for Tuba and Piano*
Personnel: Yaron Shavit, piano
Label: Kibutz Movement League of Composers 1993. CD
Arbel, Chaya: *Roundarounds*
Yoffe, Shlomo: *Andante and Rondo*
Cohen, Michael: *Diversita Continua*
Rufeisen, Arie: *A Short Suspense Story*
Gasner, Moshe: *Science Fiction*
Kilon, Moshe: *Sine Nomine*
Levy, Yehuda: *Mediterranean Rondo*

Hilgers, Walter. *See* Gerhard Meinl's Tuba Sextet
Hilgers, Walter
Album Title: *Tuba Tubissima*
Personnel: The Hamburg Brass Soloists; Herbert Drees, organ
Label: audite, 1993 CD: 368.403
Bach, Johann Sebastian/Hilgers: *Adagio from Toccata, Adagio and Fugue in C Major*
Handel, George Friderik/Hilgers: *Sonata in C Major, Op. 1 No. 7 for Tuba and Organ*
Bach, Johann Sebastian/Hilgers: *"O Mensch bewein' dein Sünde gross" BWV 622*
Danielssohn, Christer: *"Capriccio da Camera" for Tuba and Brass Ensemble*
Wilder, Alec/Hilgers: *Suite No. 1 for Tuba and Brass Quintet (Effie Suite)*
Barboteu, George: *Divertissement for Tuba and Brass Quartet*

Hilgers, Walter
Album Title: *Tubadour*
Personnel:
Label: Macrophon CD: 939-2 CS: 939-2
Bach, Johann Sebastian: *Nun komm der Heiden Heiland*
Bach, Johann Sebastian: *Sonate II*
Wolf, Hugo: *Der Genesene an die Hoffnung*
Crespo, Enrique: *Escenas Latinas*
Monti, V.: *Czardas*
Danielssohn, Christer: *Concertante Suite for Tuba and Four Horns*

Hoffnung, Gerard
Album Title: *Hoffnung Music Festival Concert*
Personnel: Hoffnung Tuba Quartet; Nigel Amberst, Gerard Hoffnung, Jim Powell, John L. Wilson
Label: Angel, 1956 LP: 35500
Chopin, Frederic/Abrams: *Mazurka No. 49*

Hoppert, Manfred
Album Title:
Personnel:
Label: Colosseum Records/Bayrischen Rundfunkes SM 631
Hindemith, Paul: *Sonata for Bass Tuba and Piano*
Koetsier, Jan: *Concertino for Tuba and String Orchestra*
Koetsier, Jan: *Sonatina for Tuba and Piano*
Lebedev, Alexander: *Concerto in One Movement*
Tcherepnin, Alexander: *Andante for Tuba and Piano*
Vaughan Williams, Ralph: *Concerto for Bass Tuba and Orchestra*

Hornsberger, Albert
Album Title:
Personnel: New York Staff Band— Salvation Army
Label:
Condon, Leslie: *Celestial Morn*

Jacobs, Arnold
Album Title:
Personnel: Directors Band, Gunnison Music Camp; Robert Hawkins, conductor
Label: Century Recordings LP: V15357
Strauss, Richard: *Concerto No. 1 for Horn*

Jacobs, Arnold
Album Title: *Concert Works and Orchestral Excerpts from Wagner, Berlioz, Mahler and More!*
Personnel: Chicago Symphony Orchestra trombone and tuba section
Label: Educational Brass Recordings, 1971 LP: Stereo ERB 1000
Berlioz, Hector: *Rakoczy (Hungarian) March from "Damnation of Faust"* (excerpt)
Brahms, Johannes/Fote: *Chorale Prelude, Op. 122 No. 8, "Es ist ein Ros' entsprungen"*

Bruckner, Anton: *Symphony No. 4* (first
movement excerpt); *Symphony No. 8* (fourth
movement excerpt)
Holst, Gustav: *Mars from "The Planets"*
(excerpts with tenor tuba)
Kreines: *Chorale Variations, "Jesu meine Freude"*
Mahler, Gustav: *Symphony No. 2* (fifth move-
ment excerpt); *Symphony No. 3* (first move-
ment excerpts)
Tchaikovsky, Peter Ilyitch: *1812 Overture*
(excerpt); *Symphony No. 6* (fourth movement)
Tomasi, Henri: *Etre ou ne pas Etre (monolog
d'Hamlet)* for tuba and three trombones
Verdi, Giuseppe: *Nabucco Overture* (excerpt)
Wagner, Richard: excerpts from *Valkyrie (Magic
Fire Music, Ride of the Valkyries)*; *Lohengrin*
(Prelude Act III); *Tannhäuser Overture*
Jacobs, Arnold
    Album Title: *Concerto for Tuba*
    Personnel: Chicago Symphony Orchestra
    Label: Deutsche Grammophone LP: 2530 906
    Vaughan Williams, Ralph: *Concerto for Bass
    Tuba and Orchestra*
Jacobs, Arnold. *See* Bell, William, *The Directors Band*
Jenkel, Herbert
    Album Title: *Tubby the Tuba*
    Personnel: All-American Orchestra; Leon
    Barzin, conductor; Victor Jory, narrator
    Label: Columbia Records, 1945 LP: CL 671
    Kleinsinger, George, and Tripp, Paul: *Tubby
    the Tuba*
Jenkins, James. *See* Stevens, John, *Power*
Johns, Steven. *See* New York Tuba Quartet, *Tubby's
Revenge*
Johnson, Howard
    Album Title: *Album, Album*
    Personnel: Jack De Johnette's Special Edition
    Label: ECM LP: 1280 823 467-1 (LC 2516)
    Johnson, Howard: *Album, Album*
Johnson, Howard
    Album Title: *Composers Workshop Ensemble*
    Personnel: Composers Workshop Ensemble
    Label: Strata-East Records, 1972 LP: SES
    1972-3
    Taylor, Coleridge: *Substructure*
    Smith, Warren: *Lament*
    Smith, Warren: *Blues for E. L. C.*
    Monk, Thelonius: *Blues by Monk*
    Smith, Warren: *Hello Julius*
    Smith, Warren: *Introduction to the Blues*
Johnson, Howard
    Album Title:
    Personnel: Dicky Wells
    Label: Prestige LP: PRT 7593
Johnson, Howard
    Album Title: *Mitschnitte vom Jazz Fest
    Berlin 1984*
    Personnel:
    Label: Bayrischen Rundfunk

Johnson, Howard
    Album Title: *Recycling the Blues & Other Stuff*
    Personnel: Taj Mahal
    Label: Columbia, 1972. Stereo 31605
    Cakewalk into Town
Johnson, Howard
    Album Title: *The Rest of Gil Evans Live at Royal
    Festival Hall, London*
    Personnel:
    Label: Mole Records, 1978 LP
    Where Flamingos Fly
Johnson, Howard
    Album Title: *Second Childhood*
    Personnel: Phoebe Snow, Howard Johnson,
    John Stevens, Carleton Green, Joseph Daley
    Label: Columbia, 1976 LP: 33952
    Snow, Phoebe: *Sweet Disposition* (tubas
    arranged by Howard Johnson)
Johnson, Howard
    Album Title: *A Slice of the Top*
    Personnel: Hank Mobley, tenor sax; Lee
    Morgan, trumpet; Kaine Zawadi, euphonium;
    James Spaulding, flute and alto sax
    Label: Blue Note, 1966. LP: BN LT 995
Johnson, Howard
    Album Title: *Taj Mahal: The Real Thing*
    Personnel: Bob Stewart, Howard Johnson,
    Joseph Daley, Earl McIntyre, tubas
    Label: Columbia Records, 1971 LP: CG 30619
    Thomas, Henry/Mahal: *Fishin' Blues*
    Mahal, Taj: *Ain't Gwine to Whistle Dixie (Any
    Mo')*
    Mahal, Taj: *Sweet Mama Janisse*
    Mahal, Taj: *Going Up to the Country and Paint
    My Mailbox Blue*
    Mahal, Taj: *Big Kneed Gal*
    Johnson, Blind Willie/Mahal: *You're Going to
    Need Somebody on Your Bond*
    Mahal, Taj: *Tom and Sally Drake*
    Estes, Sleepy John/Mahal: *Diving Duck Blues*
    Mahal, Taj: *John, Ain't It Hard?*
    Mahal, Taj: *You Ain't No Streetwalker, Mama
    Honey, But I Do Love the Way You Strut
    Your Stuff*
Johnson, Howard
    Album Title:
    Personnel:
    Label: East Coasting LP: JW001311
    Johnson, Howard: *Music Written for Monterey*
Johnson, John Thomas (Tommy)
    Album Title: *Beetlejuice*
    Personnel: Music by Danny Elfman
    Label: Geffin Records, 1988 CD: 24202-2; CS:
    M5G-24202
Johnson, John Thomas (Tommy)
    Album Title: *Brass Tacks*
    Personnel: Sharon Davis, piano
    Label: Western International Music LP:
    WIMR-14

Schmidt, William: *Serenade* for tuba and piano
Johnson, John Thomas (Tommy)
    Album Title: *Capricorn One*
    Personnel: Music by Jerry Goldsmith
    Label: Warner Brothers
Johnson, John Thomas (Tommy)
    Album Title: *Kermit the Frog Presents the Muppet Musicians of Bremen*
    Personnel: Guido Basso, trumpet; Ed Bickert, banjo; Rob McConnell, trombone; Moe Koffman, clarinet; lyrics by Jerry Juhl; music by Jack Elliott
    Label: Children's Records of America, 1972 LP: CTW 22073
Johnson, Tommy
    Album Title: *The Manhattan Transfer Meets Tubby the Tuba*
    Personnel: Manhattan Transfer; Naples (Florida) Philharmonic ; Timothy Russell, conductor
    Label: Summit Records, 1994. CD: DCD 152
    Kleinsinger, George, and Tripp, Paul: *Tubby the Tuba*
    Kleinsinger, George, and Tripp, Paul: *Tubby at the Circus*
    Kleinsinger, George, and Tripp, Paul: *Tubby Meets a Jazz Band*
    Kleinsinger, George, and Tripp, Paul: *The Further Adventures of Tubby the Tuba*
Johnson, John Thomas (Tommy)
    Album Title: *Music from the TV Series—The Mancini Generation*
    Personnel: Henry Mancini and his Orchestra
    Label: RCA Victor, 1972 LP: LSP-4689
    arr. Mancini: *Amazing Grace*
    Mouret, Jean Joseph/Mancini: *The Masterpiece*
Johnson, John Thomas (Tommy)
    Album Title: *Rampal Plays Scott Joplin*
    Personnel: Jean-Pierre Rampal, flute; John Steele Ritter, piano and harpsichord; Shelly Manne, drums
    Label: Columbia Records, 1983 LP: M 37818
Johnson, John Thomas (Tommy)
    Album Title: *Star Trek—The Motion Picture*
    Personnel: Music by Jerry Goldsmith
    Label: Columbia, 1979 CD: CK-3633; /CS: PST-36334
Johnson, John Thomas (Tommy)
    Album Title: *Tubby the Tuba*
    Personnel: Annette Funicello, narrator
    Label: Disneyland 1963 LP: 1287
    Kleinsinger, George and Tripp, Paul: *Tubby the Tuba*
Joseph, Kirk
    Album Title: *Mardi Gras in Montreux*
    Personnel: Dirty Dozen Brass Band
    Label: Rounder Records, 1985 CD: 2052
Joseph, Kirk
    Album Title: *My Feet Can't Fail Me Now*

    Personnel: Dirty Dozen Brass Band
    Label: Concord Jazz, 1984 GW-3005
Joseph, Kirk. *See* New Orleans Jazz Bands, *Down Yonder*
Joseph, Kirk
    Album Title: *Voodoo*
    Personnel: Dirty Dozen Brass Band
    Label: Columbia Records, 1987 FC 45042
Joseph, Kirk
    Album Title: *Whatcha Gonna Do for the Rest of Your Life*
    Personnel: The Dirty Dozen Brass Band
    Label: Columbia, 1991 CD: 47383
Kaenzig, Fritz
    Album Title: *Mixed Doubles*
    Personnel: Michael Tunnell, trumpet; Meme Tunnell, piano
    Label: Coronet LP: LPS 3210
    White, Donald: *Sonata for Tuba and Piano*
    Liptak, David: *Mixed Doubles* for trumpet, tuba, violin, and contrabass
Karella, Clarange
    Album Title: *Tubby the Tuba*
    Personnel: Johnny Andrews, narrator
    Label: Peter Pan LP: S8044
    Kleinsinger, George, and Tripp, Paul: *Tubby the Tuba*
King, Ian
    Album Title:
    Personnel: SWF Orchester
    Label: SWF, 1962 LP: 11652
    Vaughan Williams, Ralph: *Concerto for Bass Tuba and Orchestra*
Koller, Urs. *See* Frey, Michael, *Interkantonale Blasabfuhr*
Krzywicki, Paul
    Album Title: *The Philadelphia Lower Brass Section*
    Personnel: M. Dee Stewart, Glenn Dodson, Joseph Allessi, Charles Vernon
    Label: Excerpt Recording Company LP
Lacen, Anthony. *See* New Orleans Jazz Bands, *Down Yonder*
Landreat, Daniel. *See* Steckar Elephant Tuba Horde/ Steckar Tubapack
Lawhern, Tim
    Album Title: *Mr. Jack Daniel's Original Silver Cornet Band on Tour across America*
    Personnel: Mr. Jack Daniel's Original Silver Cornet Band
    Label: Silver Cornet Productions CD
    Rollinson, T. H.: *Rocked in the Cradle of the Deep*
LeBlanc, Robert
    Album Title: *Euphonium Favorites for Recital and Contest*
    Personnel: Paul Droste, euphonium
    Label: Coronet, 1986 LP: LPS 3203

Hartley, Walter: *Bivalve Suite for Euphonium and Tuba*
LeBlanc, Robert
  Album Title: *Robert LeBlanc Tuba Solos*
  Personnel: Myra Baker, piano
  Label: Coronet LP: 1721
  Holmes, Paul: *Lento*
  Beach, Bennie: *Lamento*
  Hartley, Walter: *Sonata*
  Rachmaninoff, Sergei: *Vocalise*
  Beversdorf, Thomas: *Sonata for Bass Tuba and Piano*
LeClair, David
  Album Title: *Galina Ustvolskaya Nr. 2*
  Personnel: Marianne Schroeder, piano; Felix Renggli, piccolo
  Label: Hat Art, 1993 CD: CD6130
  Ustvolskaya, Galina: *Dona Nobis Pacem* for piccolo, tuba, and piano
LeClair, David. *See* Contraband, The
Lefever, Christian
  Album Title: *Turk at Carnegie*
  Personnel: Hot Antics Jazz Band
  Label: Stomp Off, 1987. S. O. S. 1155
Legris, Philippe. See Steckar Elephant Tuba Horde/ Steckar Tubapack
Lehr, David "Red"
  Album Title: *The Jazz Incredibles . . . an Incredible Trio*
  Personnel: John Becker, banjo; Jean Kitrell, piano
  Label: Red Lehr LP: JI-84; CS: MCRP-85
  Williams, Spencer: *Basin Street*
  Lockhart and Seitz: *The World Is Waiting for the Sunrise/Ragtime Rosie*
  Steele and Melrose: *High Society Original Rags*
  Robin and Shavers: *Undecided Now*
  Fields and McHugh: *I Can't Give You Anything But Love*
  Cumana
  Zing Went the Strings of My Heart
  Pollack, Lew: *That's A-Plenty*
Lehr, David "Red"
  Album Title: *The Old St. Louis Levee Band Live at the Rockville Opry House*
  Personnel: The Old St. Louis Levee Band
  Label: LP: OSLLB-85-104; CS:
  Hanley, James: *Indiana*
  Oh, Daddy
  Henderson, Ray: *Alabamy Bound*
  Ringle and Meinken: *Wabash Blues*
  Traditional: *Wabash Cannonball*
  Morton, F. "Jellyroll": *Wolverine Blues*
  Traditional: *Just a Closer Walk with Thee*
  DeCosta and LaRocca: *Tiger Rag*
  Howe, Julia Ward: *Battle Hymn of the Republic*
Lehr, David "Red"
  Album Title: *The Old St. Louis Levee Band Plays the Blues*

Personnel: The Old St. Louis Levee Band
Label: Red Lehr LP: OSLLB-1091; CS:
Handy, W. C.: *St. Louis Blues*
Williams, Spencer: *Basin Street Blues*
Swanstone, McCarron, and Morgan: *The Blues My Naughty Sweetie Gave to Me*
Trombone Man Blues
Williams, C. and Williams, S.: *Royal Garden Blues*
Handy, W. C.: *Beale Street Blues*
Schoebel, Maras, and Rapollo: *Farewell Blues*
Lewis, George
  Album Title:
  Personnel: George Lewis, sousaphone, and various instruments
  Label: Black Saint, 1978. LP:
  Monads
  Triple Slow Mix
  Cycle
  Shadowgraph 5
  Sextet
Lienard, Bernard. *See* Steckar Elephant Tuba Horde
Lind, Michael
  Album Title: *Christer Torgé, Trombone and Michael Lind, Tuba*
  Personnel: Steven Harlos, piano
  Label: Grammonfirma BIS, 1978 LP: BIS LP 95 (Released on CD in 1993)
  Marcello, Benedetto: *Sonata in F Major for Tuba and Piano*
  Hindemith, Paul: *Sonata for Bass Tuba and Piano*
  Uber, David: *Double Portraits for Trombone and Tuba*
Lind, Michael
  Album Title: *Michael Lind—Tuba*
  Personnel: Swedish Radio Orchestra; Stockholm Philharmonic; Malmo Symphony Orchestra; Bjørn Liljequist, percussion
  Label: Caprice Records, 1979 LP: CAP 1143
  Lundquist, Torbjørn Iwan: *Landscape for Tuba and Strings*
  Vaughan Williams, Ralph: *Concerto for Bass Tuba and Orchestra*
  Jacobsen, Julius: *Tuba Buffo*
  Nilsson, Bo: *Bass* for solo tuba and buckle gongs
Lind, Michael
  Album Title: *Michael Lind Plays Tuba*
  Personnel: Steve Harlos, piano; Stockholm Philharmonic Winds and Brass
  Label: Four Leaf Records, 1980 LP: FLC 5045 / CD: FLC CD 102
  Arban, J. B.: *Fantaisie and Variations on the "Carnival of Venice"*
  Koch, Erland von: *Monolog No. 9 for Unaccompanied Tuba*
  Jacobsen, Julius: *Tuba Ballet* for tuba and woodwind quintet

Wilder, Alec: *Suite No. 1 for Tuba and Piano (Effie)*

Danielssohn, Christer: *Concertante Suite for Tuba and Four Horns*

Gregson, Edward: *Concerto for Tuba and Brass Band* (on CD only)

Lind, Michael
  Album Title: *National Brass Band Festival 1979*
  Personnel: Besses O' Th' Barn Brass Band; Roy Newsome, conductor
  Label: Chandos, 1979 LP: BBR 103
  Arban, J. B.: *Fantaisie and Variations on the Carnival of Venice*

Lind, Michael
  Album Title: *Ole Schmidt Plays Ole Schmidt: Concertos for Brass Instruments*
  Personnel: Aarhus Symphony Orchestra; Ole Schmidt, conductor
  Label: Edition Wilhelm Hansen LP: LPWH 111
  Schmidt, Ole: *Concerto for Tuba and Orchestra*

Lind, Michael. *See* Scandinavian Tuba Jazz

Lind, Michael
  Album Title:
  Personnel: Stockholm Philharmonic Brass Ensemble
  Label: Swedish Society Discofil LP: SLT-33254
  Danielssohn, Christer: *Capriccio da Camera* for solo tuba and brass quintet

Lusher, David. *See* Tubadours

Maierhofer, Josef
  Album Title: *Secunda Volta vom Pannonischen Blasorchester*
  Personnel: Pannonischen Blasorchester; Peter Forcher, conductor
  Label: Sica-Sound-Music, 1992 CD: CD 020145-2; CS: MC 020-145-4
  Gregson, Edward: *Concerto for Tuba and Brass Band*

Mallon, Barney
  Album Title: *Circus Time with the Dukes of Dixieland*
  Personnel: Frank Assunto, trumpet; Fred Assunto, trombone; Jack Mahev, clarinet; Stanley Mendelson, piano; Tommy Rundell, drums
  Label: Audio Fidelity LP: AFLP 1863
  Petrie, H. W./Lamb: *Asleep in the Deep*

Marshall, Oren
  Album Title: *Clowning Around: London Brass Entertains*
  Personnel: London Brass
  Label: Teldec, 1990 CD: 2292-46069-2
  Bach, Johann Sebastian: *Bandinerie*

Mas, Vicente Navarro
  Album Title:
  Personnel: Fermin Ruiz Escovez, flute
  Label: Discophon
  Casas, Bartolomé Perez/Mas: *Concerto for Tuba*

Escovez, Fermin Ruiz: *Dualismo for Tuba and Flute*

Matteson, Rich
  Album Title: *Best of Dixieland*
  Personnel: Bob Scobey's Frisco Jazz Band; Rich Matteson, helicon
  Label: RCA Victor, 1964 LP: LSP-2982(e)
  Barris, Harry, and Cavanaugh, James: *Mississippi Mud*

Matteson, Rich
  Album Title: *18th and 19th on Chestnut Street*
  Personnel: Bob Scobey's Frisco Jazz Band; Rich Matteson, helicon
  Label: RCA Victor, 1959 LP:

Matteson, Rich
  Album Title: *Louie and the Dukes of Dixieland*
  Personnel: Rich Matteson, helicon
  Label: Audio Fidelity, 1960 LP: AFSD 5924 (Reissued as CD: S522; CS: S524 Leisure Audio 1988)
  Charles, Moten, and Hayes: *South*
  Robbins, Allen, and Sheafe: *Washington and Lee Swing*
  Jolson and Rose: *Avalon*
  Bernie, Pinkard, and Casey: *Sweet Georgia Brown*
  Furber and Braham: *Limehouse Blues*

Matteson, Rich
  Album Title: *The Riverboat Five on a Swinging Date*
  Personnel: Rich Matteson, helicon; Rick Nelson, trombone; Baird Jones, piano; Ed Reed, clarinet; Nappy Lamare, banjo; Ray Baudue, drums
  Label: Mercury, 1959 LP: MG 20509
  Palmer and Williams: *I Found a New Baby*
  Bernie, Pinkard, and Casey: *Sweet Georgia Brown*

Matteson, Rich
  Album Title: *Rompin' and Stompin'*
  Personnel: Bob Scobey's Frisco Jazz Band; Rich Matteson, helicon
  Label: RCA Victor, 1958 LP: LSP 2086
  Stitzel, Mel: *The Chant*
  Gershwin, George: *Fidgety Feet*

Matteson, Rich
  Album Title: *Something's Always Happening on the River*
  Personnel: Bob Scobey's Frisco Jazz Band; Rich Matteson, helicon and bass trumpet
  Label: RCA Victor, 1958 LP: LPM-1889
  Barris, Harry and Cavanaugh, James: *Mississippi Mud*
  Riverboat Shuffle
  Foster, Stephen: *Swannee River*

Matteson, Rich
  Album Title: *Sound of the Wasp*
  Personnel: Rich Matteson, tuba; Phil Wilson, trombone; Jack Peterson, guitar; Lyle Mays,

piano; Ed Soph, drums; Kirby Stewart, bass
Label: ASI Records, 1975 LP: 203
Wilson, Phil: *The Sound of the Wasp*
Wilson, Phil: *What's Her Name?*
Matteson-Phillips TubaJazz Consort
  Album Title: *Matteson-Phillips TubaJazz
    Consort*
  Personnel: Rich Matteson, Ashley Alexander,
    Buddy Baker, euphoniums; Harvey Phillips,
    Dan Perantoni, Winston Morris, tubas; Jack
    Petersen, guitar; Tommy Ferguson, Dan
    Haerle, piano; Rufus Reid, bass; Ed Soph,
    drums
  Label: A & R Records, 1976 LP
  Silver, Horace/Matteson: *Gregory Is Here*
  Jarret, Keith/Matteson: *Lucky Southern*
  Gershwin, George/Matteson: *Summertime*
  Rollins, Sonny/Matteson: *Oleo*
  Matteson, Rich: *Spoofy*
Matteson-Phillips TubaJazz Consort
  Album Title: *SUPERHORN*
  Personnel: Rich Matteson, Ashley Alexander,
    Buddy Baker, euphoniums; Harvey Phillips,
    Dan Perantoni, Winston Morris, tubas; Jack
    Petersen, guitar; Tommy Ferguson, piano;
    Kelli Sills, bass; Steve Houghton, drums
  Label: Mark Recordings, 1982 LP: MJS 57591
  Sampson/Recaf/Foodman/Webb: *Stompin' at
    the Savoy*
  Matteson, Rich: *Little Ole Softy*
  Peterson, Oscar/J. Petersen: *Noreen's Nocturn*
  Ellington, Duke/Matteson: *Things Ain't What
    They Used to Be*
  Carmichael, Hoagy/Matteson: *Georgia on
    My Mind*
  arr. Matteson: *Waltzing Matilda*
Matteson-Phillips TubaJazz Consort
  Album Title: *Superhorn*
  Personnel: Rich Matteson, Ashley Alexander,
    Buddy Baker, euphoniums; Harvey Phillips,
    Dan Perantoni, Winston Morris, tubas; Jack
    Petersen, guitar; Tommy Ferguson, Dan
    Haerle, piano; Kelli Sills, Rufus Reid, bass;
    Ed Soph, Steve Houghton, drums
  Label: Mark Recordings CD: MJS 57626CD
  "*Matteson-Phillips TubaJazz Consort*" and
    "*SUPERHORN*" LPs combined on one CD.
May, Ernest. *See* Contraband, The
McAdams, Charles
  Album Title: *The Forty-First Annual Mid-West
    International Band and Orchestra
    Clinic 1987*
  Personnel: North Side Junior High Band,
    Jackson, Tennessee; Janet Warren, conductor
  Label: Mark Records, 1988 CS:
    MW87-MC-13
  Curnow, James: *Concertino* for tuba and band
McIntyre, Earl
  Album Title: *Carla Bley: Dinner Music*

Personnel:
Label: Watt Works, 1976 LP: 6
Social Studies
McIntyre, Earl. *See* Johnson, Howard, *Taj Mahal:
  The Real Thing*
McIntyre, Earl
  Album Title: *Taj Mahal: Happy Just to Be
    Like I Am*
  Personnel:
  Label: Columbia Records LP:
Megules, Karl
  Album Title: *Karl I. Megules, Tuba*
  Personnel: Bernie Leighton, piano; Garden
    State Tuba Ensemble; Toby Hanks,
    guest artist
  Label: Recorded Publications Company, 1976
    LP: Z 434471
  Weeks, Clifford: *Triptych*
  Ferreira and Einhorn/Megules: *Batida
    Diferente*
  Stradella, Alessandro: *Pièta, Signora*
  Bach, Johann Sebastian/Sauter: *Komm
    Süsser Tod*
  Frackenpohl, Arthur: *Pop Suite*
  Sear, Walter: *Sonatina*
  Croft: *Duet for Tenor Tuba and Bass Tuba*
  Tarlow, Lawrence: *Quintet for Tubas*
  Eccles, Henry/Megules: *Adagio*
  Catelinet, Philip: *Suite in Miniature* (first and
    third movements)
  Butts, Carrol: *Ode to Low Brass*
Mehlan, Keith. *See* Monarch Tuba-Euphonium
  Quartet
Mehlan, Keith. *See* United States Navy Band Tuba-
  Euphonium Quartet
Melton Tuba-Quartett
  Album Title: *Melton Tuba-Quartett "Premiere"*
  Personnel: Uli Haas, Heiko Triebener, Henrik
    Tietz, Hartmut Müller
  Label: Diavolo Records, 1993 CD: DR-D-
    93-C-001
  Sousa, John Philip/Sabourin: *Washington
    Post March*
  Frackenpohl, Arthur: *Ragtime*
  Handy, W. C./Holcombe: *Saint Louis Blues*
  Mozart, Wolfgang Amadeus/Fletcher: *Eine
    kleine Nachtmusik*
  Ramsoe, Wilhelm/Buttery: *Andante Quasi
    Allegretto*
  Payne, Frank Lynn: *Quartet for Tubas*
  Arcadelt, Jacob/Self: *Ave Maria*
  Niehaus, Lennie: *Miniature Jazz Suite*
  Mancini, Henry/Luis: *Baby Elephant Walk*
  Stevens, John: *Dances*
  Bach, Johann Sebastian/Werden: *Bist Du
    bei Mir*
  Schumann, Robert/Seitz: *Träumerei*
  Mancini, Henry/Krush: *The Pink Panther*
  Hutchinson, Terry: *Tuba Juba Duba*

Monarch Tuba-Euphonium Quartet
  Album Title: *Metamorphosis*
  Personnel: Roger Behrend, David Miles,
    euphoniums; Martin Erickson, Keith
    Mehlan, tubas
  Label: Campro Productions, 1993. CD:
  Rossini, Gioacchino/Davis: *Petit Caprice in the
    Style of Offenbach*
  Mehlan, Keith: *Bottoms Up Rag*
  Mozart, Wolfgang Amadeus/Fabrizio: *Overture
    to the "Marriage of Figaro"*
  arr. Singleton, Kenneth: *Three Sixteenth
    Century Flemish Pieces*
  Mozart, Wolfgang Amadeus/Mehlan:
    Turkish Rondo
  Martino, Ralph: *Fantasy*
  Sherwin, Manning/Mehlan: *A Nightingale
    Sang in Berkeley Square*
  Sousa, John Philip/Morris: *El Capitan*
  arr. Dempsey: *Quatre Chansons*
  Massenet, Jules/Margaret Erickson: *Argonaise
    from "Le Cid"*
  Dempsey, Raymond: *Now Hear This!*
  LeClair, David: *Carnival of Venice*
  arr. Mehlan: *Londonderry Air*
  Taylor, Jeffery: *Fanfare No. 1*
  Mehlan, Keith: *Eine kleine Schreckens Musik* (A
    Little Fright Music)
Morris, R. Winston
  Album Title: *Music of Robert Jager*
  Personnel: Tokyo Kosei Wind Orchestra;
    Robert Jager, conductor
  Label: Kosei Publishing Company, 1987 LP:
    KOR8104; CD: KOC3504
  Jager, Roger: *Concerto for Bass Tuba and Band*
Morris, R. Winston. *See* Matteson-Phillips TubaJazz
  Consort
Morris, R. Winston. *See* Tennessee Tech Tuba-
  Euphonium Quintet and Tennessee Technological
  University Tuba/Euphonium Ensemble
Moschner, Pinguin
  Album Title: *Hannes Zerbe Blech Band*
  Personnel: Hannes Zerbe Blech Band
  Label: Plaene LP: 88416 (LC 0972)
Moschner, Pinguin
  Album Title: *Pinguin Moschner: A Tuba
    Love Story*
  Personnel:
  Label: sound aspects LP: sas 005 digital
  Moschner, Pinguin: *Love Story (und dann ging's
    heiss hier)*
  Moschner, Pinguin: *Majobiwomo*
  Moschner, Pinguin: *Sax-Machine*
  Moschner, Pinguin: *Bouillabaisse (Thanks,
    Maggie)*
  Moschner, Pinguin: *Deep Throb*
  Moschner, Pinguin: *Antartic Love Song*
  Moschner, Pinguin: *Der Wurst lebt*
  Moschner, Pinguin: *Waterloo*

Müller, Hartmut. *See* Melton Tuba-Quartett
Nahatzki, Richard
  Album Title:
  Personnel: Berlin Radio Orchestra
  Label: Schwann Records, 1994. In preparation
  Vaughan Williams, Ralph: *Concerto for Bass
    Tuba and Orchestra*
Nahatzki, Richard
  Album Title:
  Personnel:
  Label: Rundfunk-Sifonieorchesters Saarbrucken
  Vaughan Williams, Ralph: *Concerto for Bass
    Tuba and Orchestra*
  Lachenmann: *Harmonica—Music for Large
    Orchestra with Solo Tuba*
Nelson, Mark
  Album Title: *New England Reveries*
  Personnel: Sylvia Parker, piano
  Label: Crystal, 1991 CD: CD 691; CS: C691
  Cummings, Barton: *Fantasia Breve*
  Persichetti, Vincent: *Parable for Solo Tuba*,
    Op. 147
  Corwell, Neal: *New England Reveries*
  Ross, Walter: *Escher's Sketches*
  Calabro, Louis: *Sonata-Fantasia*
New Orleans Jazz Bands
  Album Title: *Down Yonder*
  Personnel: Olympia Jazz Band; Chosen Few;
    Rebirth Marching Jazz Band; Dirty Dozen
    Brass Band
  Label: Rounder Records LP: 2062
New York Tuba Quartet
  Album Title: *New York Tuba Quartet: Tubby's
    Revenge*
  Personnel: Toby Hanks, Steven Johns, Sam
    Pilafian, Tony Price
  Label: Crystal, 1976 LP: S221
  Schuller, Gunther: *Five Moods for Tuba Quartet*
  Heussenstamm, George: *Tubafour*
  Purcell, Henry: *Allegro and Air*
  Ross, Walter: *Fancy Dances for Three Bass Tubas*
  Stevens, John: *Music 4 Tubas*
  Parker, Charlie: *Au Privave*
Newberger, Eli
  Album Title: *Don't Monkey with It*
  Personnel: Black Eagle Jazz Band
  Label: Stomp Off Records, 1987 LP: S. O. S.
    1147, Vol. 6
  Monsborough, Abe: *Don't Monkey with It*
  Oliver, Joe: *Chimes Blues*
  Kassel and Stitzel: *Sobbin' Blues*
  Armstrong and Morton: *Wild Man Blues*
  Johnson, Bunk: *Moose Blues*
  Brown, Sandy: *Tree Top Tall Papa*
  Novick, Billy: *When She Cries*
  Stitzel, Mel: *The Chant*
Newberger, Eli
  Album Title: *Shake It Down*
  Personnel: Jimmy Mazzy, banjo

Label: Stomp Off, 1985 LP: 1109
Williams and Urquhart: *Shake It Down*
Rainey and Arant: *Jelly Bean Blues*
Jones and Dickerson: *Tia Juanna Man*
Gershwin, George: *Prelude in C# Minor*
Graham and Williams: *I Ain't Got Nobody*
Europe, Sissle, and Blake: *Goodnight, Angeline*
Smith, Jabbo: *Lina Blues*
MacDonald, Goodwin, and Hanley: *Breeze*
Lockhart and Seitz: *The World Is Waiting for the Sunrise*
Washington and Harline: *When You Wish upon a Star*
Morton, F. "Jelly Roll": *Chicago Breakdown*
Moret, Neil: *Song of the Wanderer*
Brown and Von Tilzer: *Dapper Dan*
Nord, Lennart
  Album Title:
  Personnel: Stockholm Symphonic Wind Orchestra; Martin Turnovsky, conductor
  Label: Caprice LP: 214 14
  Gregson, Edward: *Concerto for Tuba and Band*
Northern Tuba Lights
  Album Title: *The Northern Tuba Lights*
  Personnel: The Northern Tuba Lights
  Label: The Northern Tuba Lights, 1991 CS
  Stevens, John: *Power*
  Traditional/Minerd: *Sea Tubas*
  Sousa, John Philip/Werden: *Stars and Stripes Forever*
  Schooley, John: *Cherokee*
  Niehaus, Lennie: *Brass Tacks*
  Bach, Johann Sebastian/Sabourin: *Preludium*
  Stevens, John: *Dances*
  Sousa, John Philip/Werden: *Hands across the Sea*
  Wolking, Henry: *Tuba Blues*
  Mancini, Henry/Krush: *The Pink Panther*
  Offenbach, Jacques/Fletcher: *Orpheus in the Underworld*
Palmer, Singleton
  Album Title: *Dixie by Gaslight*
  Personnel: Singleton Palmer and His Dixieland Band
  Label: GNP Crescendo LP: DJS 511
  Melrose, Walter: *Tin Roof Blues*
  Steele and Melrose: *High Society*
  Koenig, Williams, and Handy: *Careless Love*
  Bernie, Pinkard, and Casey: *Sweet Georgia Brown*
  Maryland, My Maryland
  Handy, W. C.: *St. Louis Blues*
  Burris and Smith: *Ballin' the Jack*
  Gilbert and Ory: *Muskrat Ramble*
  Traditional: *When the Saints Go Marching In*
Patterson, Graham. See Stokes, David, and Patterson, Graham, Chalk Farm Band—Salvation Army

Pearson, Norman. *See* Tubadours
Perantoni, Daniel
  Album Title: *Curnow at Illinois*
  Personnel: University of Illinois Band
  Label: University of Illinois Band, 1983 LP: 108
  Curnow, James: *Concertino for Tuba and Band*
Perantoni, Daniel
  AlbumTitle: *Daniel in the Lion's Den*
  Personnel: Eckart Selheim, piano; Arizona State University Band; St. Louis Brass Quintet
  Label: Summit Records, 1994. CD: DCD 163
  McBeth, Francis: *Daniel in the Lion's Den*
  Plog, Anthony: *Three Miniatures*
  Mahler, Gustave/Perantoni and Yutzy: *Lieder eines Fahrenden Gesellen*
  Penderecki, Krzystof: *Capriccio for Solo Tuba*
  Arban, Jean Baptist/Domek: *Carnival of Venice*
  Rachmaninoff, Serge/Perantoni: *Vocalise*, Op. 34, No. 14
  Pinkard, Maico/Sellers: *Sweet Georgia Brown*
Perantoni, Daniel
  Album Title: *In Concert with the University of Illinois Symphonic Band*
  Personnel: University of Illinois Symphonic Band; Harry Begian, conductor
  Label: University of Illinois Band LP: 87
  Jager, Robert: *Concerto for Bass Tuba*
Perantoni, Daniel
  Album Title: *In Concert with the University of Illinois Symphonic Band*
  Personnel: University of Illinois Symphonic Band; Harry Begian, conductor
  Label: College Presentation Series LP: 106
  Vaughan Williams, Ralph/Hare: *Concerto for Bass Tuba and Band*
Perantoni, Daniel
  Album Title: *Morgan Powell: Music for Brass*
  Personnel:
  Label: University Brass Recording Series, 1975 LP: EN 203 Stereo
  Powell, Morgan: *Midnight Realities*
Perantoni, Daniel. *See* Matteson-Phillips TubaJazz Consort
Perantoni, Daniel. *See* Summit Tubas
Perantoni, Daniel
  Album Title: *Sterling Brass*
  Personnel: David Hickman, Illinois Chamber Players, Paul Zonn, Edwin London
  Label: Crystal LP: S394
  Hackbarth, Glenn: *Double Concerto*
  Powell, Morgan: *Nocturnes*
Perantoni, Daniel
  Album Title: *Tuba in Recital*
  Personnel: Eric Dalheim, piano
  Label: University Brass Recording Series LP: SN-101
  Stevens, Halsey: *Sonatina for Tuba and Piano*

Hindemith, Paul: *Sonata for Bass Tuba
and Piano*
Sibbing, Robert: *Sonata*
Zonn, Paul: *Divertimento No. 1* (tuba, string
bass, percussion)
Perantoni, Daniel
Album Title: *Tuba N' Spice*
Personnel: Eric Dalheim, piano; Illinois
Contemporary Chamber Players; University
of Illinois Symphonic Band
Label: Mark Educational Recordings, 1983 LP:
MRS 37879
Fredrickson, Thomas: *Tubalied*
Jager, Robert: *Concerto for Bass Tuba*
George, Thom Ritter: *Sonata for Tuba
and Piano*
Wyatt, Scott: *Three for One*
(Note: On many copies of this record the labels
are on the wrong sides.)
Phillips, Harvey
Album Title: *All-Star Concert Band*
Personnel: James Burke, conductor
Label: Golden Crest LP: CRS 4025
Youmans, Vincent/ Norman: *Carioca*
Phillips, Harvey
Album Title: *The Burke-Phillips All Star Concert
Band, Vol. II*
Personnel: James Burke, director
Label: Golden Crest LP: CR 4040
Kling, H.: *The Elephant and the Fly*
Phillips, Harvey
Album Title: *Cabin in the Sky—Curtis Fuller*
Personnel: Manny Albam, conductor
Label: Impulse Records
Phillips, Harvey
Album Title: *Cornell University Wind Ensemble*
Personnel: Cornell University Wind Ensemble;
Maurice Stith, conductor
Label: LP: CUWE 17
Ross, Walter: *Tuba Concerto with Band*
Phillips, Harvey
Album Title: *David Baker's 21st Century
Bebop Band*
Personnel: David Baker, cello; Hunt Butler,
tenor sax; Jim Beard, piano; Kurt Bahn, bass;
Keith Cronin, drums
Label: Laurel, 1983 LP: LR-503
Phillips, Harvey
Album Title: *Extended Voices*
Personnel: Brandeis University Chorus; Alvin
Lucier, director
Label: Odyssey LP: 32160156
Feldman, Morton: *Chorus and Instruments (II)*
Phillips, Harvey
Album Title: *Faculty Concert Band, Volume 1*
Personnel: Armed Forces School of Music Band
Label: Century, 1968 LP: FV 31721
Youman, Vincent/Norman: *Carioca*

Phillips, Harvey
Album Title: *The Further Adventures of Tubby
the Tuba*
Personnel:
Label: Golden Crest, 1960 LP: CR6000
Kleinsinger, George, and Tripp, Paul: *The
Further Adventures of Tubby the Tuba*
Wilder, Alec: *Suite No. 1 (Effie the Elephant)*
Phillips, Harvey
Album Title: *Harvey Phillips in Recital, Vol. III*
Personnel: New York Horn Trio
Label: Golden Crest LP: CRS 4122
Gould, Morton: *Tuba Suite* for tuba and
three horns
Baker, David N.: *Sonata for Tuba and String
Quartet*
Phillips, Harvey
Album Title: *Harvey Phillips, Tuba*
Personnel: Milton Kaye, Bernie Leighton, piano
Label: Golden Crest LP: RE 7006
Wilder, Alec: *Sonata*
Bach, Johann Sebastian/Bell: *Air and Bourrée*
Handel, George Friderik: *Andante*
Corelli, Archangelo: *Gigue*
Mozart, Wolfgang Amadeus: *O Isis and Osiris*
Swann, Donald: *Two Moods for Tuba*
Phillips, Harvey
Album Title: *Harvey Phillips in Recital for
Family and Friends*
Personnel: Arthur Harris, Bernie Leighton,
piano; Andrew J. Lolya, flute; Bradley
Spinney, percussion
Label: Golden Crest LP: RE 7054
Hartley, Walter: *Suite for Flute and Tuba*
Bach, Johann Sebastian: *Invention No. 1* (flute
and tuba)
Handel, George Friderik: *Selected Movements
from Sonatas for Flute*
Wilder, Alec: *Suite No. 1 for Tuba and Piano
(Effie)*
Wilder, Alec: *Suite No. 2 (Jessie)*
Wilder, Alec: *Suite No. 3 (Little Harvey)*
Wilder, Alec: *Suite No. 4 (Thomas)*
Wilder, Alec: *Suite No. 5 (Ethan Ayer)*
Wilder, Alec: *Song for Carol*
Phillips, Harvey
Album Title: *Hello, Louis!: Bobby Hackett Plays
the Music of Louis Armstrong*
Personnel: Bobby Hackett, trumpet
Label: Epic LP: LN 24099
Phillips, Harvey
Album Title: *Interlochen Music Camp*
Personnel: Interlochen High School
Camp Band
Label: Golden Crest LP: S 403
Benson, Warren: *Helix for Solo Tuba and
Concert Band*
Phillips, Harvey
Album Title: *Ithaca High School Band*

Personnel: Frank Battisti, director
Label: Golden Crest, 1967 LP: CR 6001
Benson, Warren: *Helix for Solo Tuba and Concert Band*
Phillips, Harvey
   Album Title: *John Downey Plays John Downey*
   Personnel: John Downey, piano
   Label: Gasparo LP: GS-243
   Downey, John: *Tabu for Tuba*
Phillips, Harvey
   Album Title: *Lavalle in Hi-Fi*
   Personnel: Paul Lavalle—His Woodwinds and His Band
   Label: RCA Victor, 1958 LP: LSP-1516
   Hupfeld, Herman: *When Yuba Plays the Rumba on the Tuba Down in Cuba* (with Joe Tarto)
Phillips, Harvey
   Album Title: *Leasebreakers*
   Personnel:
   Label: United Artists, 1967 LP: LA 3423
Phillips, Harvey
   Album Title: *Music for the Underdogs of the Orchestra*
   Personnel: New England Conservatory Orchestra; Gunther Schuller, director
   Label: GM Recordings, 1984 LP: GM 2004
   Vaughan Williams, Ralph: *Concerto for Bass Tuba and Orchestra*
   Schuller, Gunther: *Capriccio for Tuba and Orchestra*
Phillips, Harvey
   Album Title: *Music for Tuba and French Horn*
   Personnel: Bernie Leighton, Tait Sanford, piano; John Barrows, horn
   Label: Golden Crest, 1963 LP: RE 7018
   Persichetti, Vincent: *Serenade No. 12 for Solo Tuba*
   Wilder, Alec: *Sonata for French Horn, Tuba and Piano*
Phillips, Harvey. *See* Bell, William, *The Directors Band*
Phillips, Harvey. *See* Matteson-Phillips TubaJazz Consort
Phillips, Harvey. *See* Summit Tubas
Phillips, Harvey
   Album Title: *Tribute to a Friend*
   Personnel: Milton Kaye, piano; John Barrows, horn; Valhalla Horn Choir
   Label: Golden CrestLP: CRS 4147
   Heiden, Bernard: *Variationen for Tuba and Nine Horns*
   Wilder, Alec: *Suite No. 2 for French Horn and Tuba*
Phillips, Harvey
   Album Title: *20th Anniversary Mid-west Band and Orchestra Clinic*
   Personnel: Clarence Central Senior High School Band; Norbert Buskey, director
   Label: Century of Chicago, 1966 LP: 25834

Sauter, Eddie: *Conjectures for Tuba and Band*
Phillips, Harvey
   Album Title: *Two Contemporary Composers: Alec Wilder and Don Hammond*
   Personnel: New York Brass Quintet
   Label: Golden Crest LP: CR4017
   Wilder, Alec: *Quintet for Brass (Mvt. III, Tuba Showpiece)*
Phillips, Harvey
   Album Title: *Virtuosity—A Contemporary Look*
   Personnel: Phil Smith, trumpet
   Label: GM Recordings CD: GM3017CD
   Peasley, Richard: *The Devil's Herald*
Phillips, Harvey/TubaChristmas
   Album Title: *Harvey Phillips and His TubaSantas and Merry TubaChristmas*
   Personnel: Harvey Phillips' TubaSantas
   Label: HPF Records and Tapes, 1991 CS: 1000-1
   Bewley: *Santa Wants a Tuba for Christmas* (vocal by Harvey Phillips)
   Martin, Blaine/Bewley: *Have Yourself a Merry Little Christmas*
   Torme and Wells/Bewley: *The Christmas Song*
   arr. Bewley: *TubaChristmas Suite*
   arr. Bewley: *Fum, Fum, Fum*
   arr. Bewley: *Good Christian Men Rejoice*
   arr. Bewley: *Greensleeves*
   arr. Bewley: *Bring a Torch, Jeanette Isabella*
   arr. Bewley: *Pat-A-Pan*
   arr. Bewley: *Carol of the Bells*
   Wilder, Alec: *Carols for a Merry TubaChristmas*
Phillips, Harvey/TubaChristmas
   Album Title: *Merry TubaChristmas*
   Personnel: TubaChristmas Choirs; Bloomington, Chicago, New York, Los Angeles, Dallas
   Label: Harvey Phillips Foundation, 1980 LP: NR-1111-4; CS:
   O Come All Ye Faithful
   Deck the Halls
   The First Noel
   Go Tell It on the Mountain
   O Little Town of Bethlehem
   O Come, Oh Come Immanuel
   We Three Kings
   Joy to the World
   Angels We Have Heard on High
   Good King Wenceslas
   It Came Upon a Midnight Clear
   God Rest Ye Merry Gentlemen
   Komm Süsser Tod
   Silent Night
Piernik, Zdizislaw
   Album Title: *Music from International Festival of Contemporary Music*
   Personnel:
   Label: SX 1847
   Warsaw Autumn

Piernik, Zdizislaw
  Album Title: *Plays Z. Piernik*
  Personnel:
  Label:
  Penderecki, Krystof: *Capriccio for Solo Tuba*
  Borkowski, Marian: *VOX per uno stromento ad ottone*
  Kranowski, A.: *Sonata for Solo Tuba*
  Dobrowski, A.: *Muzyka for Tuba Solo*
  Szalonek, W.: *Piernikiana for Solo Tuba*
Piernik, Zdizislaw
  Album Title: *Tuba Universale*
  Personnel: Maciej Paderewski, piano
  Label: Proviva/Deutsche Austrophon GMBH, 1980 LP: LC 6542
  Piernik, Zdizislaw: *Dialogue für Tuba und Tonband*
  Schäffer, Boguslaw: *Projekt für Tuba und Tonband*
  Zajaczek, Roman: *Tema Cantabile con Piernicazioni per tuba universale e pianoforte*
  Borkowski, Marian;: *VOX per uno stromento ad ottone*
  Sikora, Elzbieta: *Il Viaggio 1 per tuba solo con pianoforte*
Piernik, Zdizislaw
  Album Title: *Virtuoso Tuba: Zdizislaw Piernik in Recital*
  Personnel: Lech Lesniak, piano
  Label: Stolat/Arista Records, 1981 LP: SZM 0115 (reissue of Polskie Nagrania "MUZA" SX 1210)
  Boccherini, Luigi: *Minuet*
  Schubert, Franz Peter: *Serenade*
  Dvořák, Anton: *Humoresque*
  Mussorgsky, Modest: *Bydlo from "Pictures at an Exhibition"*
  Eccles, Henry: *Sonata in G Minor* (I Prelude; II Courant)
  Mozart, Wolfgang Amadeus: *Rondo in E♭ Major*, K. 371
  Paderewski, Ignacy Jan: *Minuet*
  Saint-Saëns, Camille: *Morceau de Concerto* (III, Allegro non troppo)
  Schumann, Robert: *Träumerei*
  Saint-Saëns, Camille: *Carnival of the Animals* (The Elephant; The Swan)
Pilafian, Sam
  Album Title: *Barbara Cook: It's Better with a Band*
  Personnel: Barbara Cook, vocals; Wally Harper, piano; Jimmy Mitchell, banjo
  Label: 1980 LP, CS, CD
  Pinkard, Casey, and Tauber: *Them There Eyes*
Pilafian, Sam
  Album Title: *Boyadjian: Sonata, Epistles, Sareebar*
  Personnel: John Ziarko, percussion
  Label: Op. One, 1984 CD: 109

Boyadjian, Hayg: *Sareebar for Tuba and Percussion*
Pilafian, Sam
  Album Title: *The Last Elephant: The Mandala Octet*
  Personnel: John Medesk, piano; John Leaman, bass; Gene Caldarazzo, drums
  Label: Accurate Recordings, 1993 CS: CD: *The Unknown Soldier*
Pilafian, Sam
  Album Title: *Light Christmas: Travelin' Light*
  Personnel: Frank Vignola, guitar; Ken Peplowski, clarinet; Don Keiling, rhythm guitar; Joe Ascione, drums; Andy Kubiszewski, percussion
  Label: Telarc, 1993 CD: 83330; CS: 83330
Pilafian, Sam
  Album Title: *Makin' Whoopee*
  Personnel: Frank Vignola, guitar; Ken Peplowski, clarinet; Don Keiling, rhythm guitar; Joe Ascione, drums; Andy Kubiszewski, percussion
  Label: Telarc, 1993 CD: CD83324
  Reinhardt, Django: *Micro*
  Reinken, Fred: *Wabash Blues*
  Winfree, Dick: *China Boy*
  Davis, Jimmie: *You Are My Sunshine*
  Cannon, Hughie: *Bill Bailey Won't You Please Come Home*
  Weill, Kurt: *Mack the Knife*
  Berlin, Irving: *Alexander's Ragtime Band*
  Vignola, Frank: *Chasin' the Antelope*
  Carmichael, Hoagy: *New Orleans*
  Carmichael, Hoagy: *Up a Lazy River*
  Parker, Charlie: *Little Suede Shoes*
  Donalson, Walter, and Kahn, Gus: *Makin' Whoopee*
  Henley, James: *Indiana*
  Williams, Hank: *Jumbalaya*
  Carmichael, Hoagy: *Georgia on My Mind*
  Youmans, Vincent: *Carioca*
  Berlin, Irving: *What'll I Do?*
Pilafian, Sam
  Album Title: *Ready and Able: Frank Vignola*
  Personnel: Frank Vignola, guitar; Billy Mitchell, tenor sax; Junior Mance, piano; John Golosky, bass
  Label: Concord Jazz, 1993 CS: CD *Whirly Twirly*
  Ready and Able
Pilafian, Sam. *See* Gerhard Meinl's Tuba Sextet
Pilafian, Sam. *See* New York Tuba Quartet
Pilafian, Sam
  Album Title: *Silks and Rags*
  Personnel: Ken Cooper, piano; Mark Gould, trumpet; Charles Nedich, clarinet
  Label: Angel EMI, 1991 CS, CD: CDC 7541312
  Joplin, Scott: *The Cascades*
  Joplin, Scott: *Peacherine Rag*

Pilafian, Sam
    Album Title: *Travelin' Light*
    Personnel: Frank Vignola, guitar; Jimmy
        George, guitar; Mark Shane, piano
    Label: Telarc, 1991 CD: CD80281
    Bernie, Casey, Pickard: *Sweet Georgia Brown*
    Ellington, Duke: *Don't Get Around Much
        Anymore*
    Arlen and Harburg: *If I Only Had a Brain*
    Rose, Jolson, and DeSylva: *Avalon*
    Kern, Jerome: *Ol' Man River*
    Razof and Johnson: *Louisiana*
    Palmer and Williams: *I Found a New Baby*
    Fisher, Goodwin, and Shay: *When You're
        Smiling*
    Williams, Spencer: *Basin Street Blues*
    DeCosta and La Rocca: *Tiger Rag*
    Waller, Thomas "Fats": *Black and Blue*
    Rheinhart, Django: *Rhythm Futur*
    Barham and Fuber: *Limehouse Blues*
    Gershwin, George: *Someone to Watch over Me*
Pokorny, Gene
    Album Title: *Hindemith, Paul: Complete
        Brass Works*
    Personnel: Theodor Lichtmann, Piano
    Label: Summit, 1991 2CDs: DCD 115-2
    Hindemith, Paul: *Sonata for Bass Tuba
        and Piano*
Pokorny, Eugene
    Album Title: *OrchestraPro: Tuba* (in
        preparation)
    Personnel:
    Label: Summit Records, 1994. CD: DCD 142
Pokorny, Gene. *See* Summit Tubas
Pokorny, Gene
    Album Title: *Star Wars Trilogy*
    Personnel: Utah Symphony Orchestra; Varnjan
        Kojian, conductor
    Label: Varèse-Sarabande, 1983 CD: VCD47201
    Williams, John: *Jabba the Hutt from "Return of
        the Jedi"*
Pokorny, Gene
    Album Title: *Tuba Tracks*
    Personnel: Roberta Garten, piano; Mary Mottl,
        piano; David "Red" Lehr and the Jazz
        Incredibles
    Label: Summit, 1991 CD: DCD129; CS:
        DCD129
    Handel, George Friderik: *Sonata in G Major*
    Bach, Johann Sebastian: *Partita in A Minor for
        Flute Alone*
    Debussy, Claude/Schaefer: *General Lavine—
        Eccentric*
    Rachmaninoff, Sergei: *Three Songs*
    Castérède, Jacques: *Serenade from Sonatine for
        Bass Saxhorn and Piano*
    Ravel, Maurice: *Pavane pour une enfante
        défunte*

Debussy, Claude: *Prélude à l'après midi
    d'un faune*
Vaughan Williams, Ralph: *Six Studies in English
    Folksong*
Pryor, Arthur: *Theme and Variation on the
    "Blue Bells of Scotland"*
Blake, Eubie: *Memories of You*
Poore, Melvyn
    Album Title: *Electric Surrealistic Landscapes:
        The McClean Mix*
    Personnel: Priscilla and Barton McClean
    Label: Op. One CD: 96
    McLean, Priscilla: *Beneath the Horizon for Tuba
        and Taped Whale Songs*
Popiel, Peter
    Album Title: *Music for Young Bands, Vol.II*
    Personnel: State University of New York—
        Fredonia Wind Ensemble
    Label: Century Custom Recording Service LP
    Dedrick, Art: *A Touch of Tuba*
Popiel, Peter
    Album Title: *1974 Mid-west Band and Orchestra
        Clinic*
    Personnel: Indian Trail Junior High School
        Concert Band
    Label: Golden Crest LP: MID-74-12
    Frackenpohl, Arthur: *Variations for Tuba
        and Winds*
Popiel, Peter
    Album Title: *Peter Popiel: Recital Music
        for Tuba*
    Personnel: Henry Fuchs, piano
    Label: Mark Educational Recordings LP: MRS
        28437
    Bach, Johann Sebastian/Bell: *Air and Bourrée*
    Handel, George Friderik/Ostrander: *Bourrée
        from the Sixth Flute Sonata*
    Mendelssohn, Felix: *"It Is Enough" from Elijah*
    Semler-Collery, Jules: *Barcarolle et Chanson
        Bachique*
    Hartley, Walter: *Sonatina*
    Handel, George Friderik/Lafosse: *Concerto in
        G Minor for Oboe and Orchestra*
    Benson, Warren: *Arioso*
    Hartley, Walter: *Suite for Unaccompanied Tuba*
Porter, William D. (David)
    Album Title: *44th Annual Mid-West Interna-
        tional Band and Orchestra Clinic 1990*
    Personnel: Roger Behrend, euphonium; Lake
        Braddock Secondary School Symphonic
        Band; Roy Holder and Jim Stegner,
        conductors
    Label: Mark Recordings, 1990 CS:
        MW-90MC-19
    Frackenpohl, Arthur: *Song and Dance for
        Euphonium, Tuba and Band*
Porter, William David. *See* United States Air Force
    Concert Band Tuba Section

Poulsen, Heick
    Album Title: *Atlantis Transit*
    Personnel:
    Label: Olufsen Records LP: DOC 5068
Powell, Jim. *See* Hoffnung, Gerard, *Hoffnung Music Festival Concert*
Price, Tony
    Album Title: *Together Again—For the First Time: Mel Torme and Buddy Rich*
    Personnel: The Buddy Rich Band
    Label: Jazz Heritage, 1978 CD: 512742L
    Mercer and Arlen: *Blues in the Night*
Price, Tony. *See* New York Tuba Quartet
Price, Tony
    Album Title: *Tree Music by Paul Chihara*
    Personnel:
    Label: Composer's Recordings, Inc. LP: CRI 269
    Chihara, Paul: *Willow, Willow* (bass flute, tuba, percussion)
Randolph, David
    Album Title: *Contrasts in Contemporary Music*
    Personnel: Peggy Randolph, piano; Richard Zimdars, piano
    Label: ACA Digital Recording, 1992 CD: CM20018-18
    George, Thom Ritter: *Sonata for Tuba and Piano*
    Takács, Jenö: *Sonata Capricciosa, Op. 81*
    Stevens, Halsey: *Sonatina for Tuba and Piano*
    Baker, Claude: *Omaggi e Fantasie*
Reilly, Timothy. See Tubadours
Robinson, Jack
    Album Title: *Windsongs*
    Personnel: University of Northern Colorado Symphonic Band; David Wallace, conductorLabel: Soundmark, 1981 LP: R894 KM6748
    Benson, Warren: *Helix for Solo Tuba and Concert Band*
Rozen, Jay
    Album Title: *Music of David Lang*
    Personnel: Jay Rozen, electric tuba
    Label: CRI CD: 625
Sass, Jonathon. See Gerhard Meinl's Tuba Sextet, *Tubas! A Six-Tuba Musical Romp*
Scandinavian Tuba Jazz
    Album Title: *How Deep Is the Ocean*
    Personnel: Michael Lind, Stein-Erik Tafjord, tubas; Torolf Mölgård, Frode Thingnäs, euphoniums; Göran Söderlund, piano; Sture Nordin, bass; Bjarne Rostvold, drums
    Label: Four Leaf Records, 1986 LP: FLC 5093
    Thingnäs, Frode: *Fink Finster*
    McDermot, Ragni, and Rado/Bergman: *Dead End*
    Hermann, Heinz: *Korn Blues*
    Davis, Miles: *All Blues*
    Berlin, Irving/Windfeld: *How Deep Is the Ocean*

    Hermann, Herman: *Υ Luego*
    Thingnäs, Frode: *Samba Loco*
Schiaffini, Giancarlo
    Album Title: *Infernal Dream*
    Personnel:
    Label: Rofo Records, 1986 CPRr 17001
    Schiaffini, Giancarlo: *Infernal Dream*
Schiaffini, Giancarlo
    Album Title: *Space Blossoms—Dino Vander Noot*
    Personnel:
    Label: Innowo, 1989 CD: IN 813
    Betti, Dino: *Space Blossoms*
Schmearer, William. See Stevens, John, *Power*
Schmitz, Chester
    Album Title: *The Boston Pops: Out of This World*
    Personnel: The Boston Pops Orchestra; John Williams, conductor
    Label: Philips, 1983 LP: 411 185-1
    Williams, John: *Jabba the Hutt from "Return of the Jedi"*
Schmitz, Chester
    Album Title: *Tubby the Tuba*
    Personnel: Julia Child, narrator; Boston Pops; Arthur Fiedler, conductor
    Label: Polydor, 1970 LP: RD 5032
    Kleinsinger, George, and Tripp, Paul: *Tubby the Tuba*
Self, James
    Album Title: *An American Tail II—Fieval Goes West*
    Personnel: Music by James Horner
    Label: MCA, 1991 CD: MCAD-10416; CS: MCAC-10416;
Self, James
    Album Title: *Changing Colors*
    Personnel: Terry Trotter, piano; Doug Masek, alto saxophone; Burnette Dillon, Tony Ellis, trumpets; John Reynolds, horn; William Booth, trombone; Robert Sanders, bass trombone; Janet Lakatos, viola; David Speltz, cello; David Young, double bass; Gayle Levant, harp; Thomas Raney, percussion; David Rubenstein, synthesizer
    Label: Summit, 1992 CD: DCD 132
    Debussy, Claude: *Syrinx*
    Stevens, Halsey: *Sonatina for Tuba and Piano*
    Kochan, Gunter: *Sieben Miniaturen für Vier Tuben*
    Self, James: *Courante*
    Schumann, Robert/Self: *Scenes from Childhood, Op. 15*
    Rubinstein, Arthur: *Bruegel—Dance Visions*
    Capuzzi, Antonio/Self: *Rondo Allegro* (tuba with brass quintet)
Self, James
    Album Title: *Close Encounters of the Third Kind*
    Personnel:
    Label: Varèse-Sarabande, 1977 CD: VSD 5275
    Williams, John: *The Conversation*

Self, James
    Album Title: *Don Ellis—Live at Montreux*
    Personnel: Don Ellis Band
    Label: Atlantic
Self, James
    Album Title: *Home Alone*
    Personnel: Music by John Williams
    Label: CBS, 1990 CD: SK 46595; CS: ST
        46595
Self, James
    Album Title: *Home Alone II*
    Personnel: Music by John Williams
    Label: Fox, 1992 CD: 07822-11000-2
Self, James
    Album Title: *Hook*
    Personnel: Music by John Williams
    Label: Epic Soundtrax, 1991 CD: EK-4888;
        CS: ET-4888
Self, James
    Album Title: *In Concert Tokyo*
    Personnel: Mel Torme and Marty Paitch
    Label: Concord
Self, James
    Album Title: *Jim Morris—Brass Plus: Montage*
    Personnel: Jim Morris, bass trombone; Bruce
        Fowler, trombone; Suzette Moriarty, horn;
        Steve Huffsteter, trumpet; Tom Adams,
        piano; Steve Moore, guitar; Jack Le Compte,
        drums; Jim Self, tuba and electric bass
    Label: Mama Foundation, 1992 CD: MF 1005
    Gale, Jack: *Picture of Dorian Blue*
Self, James
    Album Title: *Jim Self and Friends "New Stuff"*
    Personnel: James Self, tuba, bass trombone,
        electric bass, EVI (electronic valve instru-
        ment); Jon Kurnick, guitar; John Magnussen,
        percussion; Harvey Mason, drums; Ernie
        McDaniel, bass
    Label: Trend Records, 1988 CD: TRCD-548
    Harlos, Steve: *Breakthrough*
    Brown, Tom: *New Stuff*
    Morell, John: *Windsong*
    Myers, Stanley: *Cavatina*
    Brown, Tom: *Kilo*
    Kurnick, Jon: *Bosque De Manaus*
    Bach, Johann Sebastian/Self: *Sinfonia III*
    Kalina, Ron: *Children at Play*
    Waller, Thomas "Fats": *Jitterbug Waltz*
    Eldsvoog, John: *Walt's Samba*
    Rowles, Jimmy: *The Peacocks*
    Mingus, Charlie: *Peggy's Blue Skylight*
    McDaniel, Ernie: *Secrets*
Self, James
    Album Title: *Jim Self Quintet: Children at Play*
    Personnel: Ron Kalina, harmonica; Jon Kurnick,
        guitar; Ernie McDaniel, bass; Harold Mason,
        drums; Steve Forman, percussion
    Label: Discovery, 1983 LP: DS-886
    Kalina, Ron: *Children at Play*

Waller, Thomas "Fats": *Jitterbug Waltz*
Eldsvoog, John: *Walt's Samba*
Rowles, Jimmy: *The Peacocks*
Mingus, Charlie: *Peggy's Blue Skylight*
McDaniel, Ernie: *Secrets*
Self, James
    Album Title: *The Linguini Incident*
    Personnel: Music by Thomas Newman
    Label: Varèse-Sarabande, 1992 CD: VSD-5372;
        CS: VSC-5372
Self, James
    Album Title: *Music from Star Wars and Other
        Galaxies*
    Personnel: Don Ellis Band
    Label: Atlantic
Self, James
    Album Title: *Mystic Solar Dance*
    Personnel: Bingo Miki
    Label: Kitty Jazz
Self, James
    Album Title: *Reunion*
    Personnel: Mel Torme, Marty Paitch Decktette
    Label: Concord
Self, James. *See* Johnson, John Thomas (Tommy),
    Capricorn One
Self, James. *See* Johnson, John Thomas (Tommy),
    Beetlejuice
Self, James. *See* Johnson, John Thomas (Tommy),
    Star Trek—The Motion Picture
Self, James
    Album Title: *Tricky Lix*
    Personnel: Gary Foster, woodwinds; Warren
        Luening, trumpet; Bill Booth, trombone; Jon
        Kurnick, guitar; Joel Hamilton, bass; Alan
        Estes, drums
    Label: Concord Records, 1990 CD: CCD-4430
    Aldcroft, Randy: *Tricky Lix*
    Berg, Curt: *Take the Stairs*
    Monk, Williams Hanighen: *'Round Midnight*
    Brown, Tom: *Night Lights*
    Broadbent, Alan: *Another Time*
    Aldcroft, Randy: *Somebody's Samba*
    Lerner, Alan Jay: *Heather on the Hill*
    Porter, Cole: *I Love You*
    Rodgers, Hart: *My Funny Valentine*
    Berg, Curt: *The Farewell Burn*
Seward, Steven
    Album Title: *The Virtuoso Tuba*
    Personnel: Vicki Berneking, piano; Eric
        Anderson, euphonium
    Label: Golden Crest, 1979 LP: RE 7083
    Bach, Johann Sebastian: *Suite in B♭ Minor for
        Flute*
    Handel, George Friderik/Fitzgerald: *Aria con
        Variazioni*
    Bozza, Eugene: *Concertino for Tuba and Piano*
    Telemann, Georg Philipp: *Sonata in F Minor*
    Vivaldi, Antonio: *Concerto in C major for Two
        Trumpets*

Seward, Steven
    Album Title: *The Virtuoso Tuba, Vol. II*
    Personnel: Vicki Berneking, piano
    Label: Golden Crest, 1984 LP: RE-7096
    Strauss, Richard: *Second Horn Concerto*
    Pryor, Arthur: *The Blue Bells of Scotland*
    Picchi, Ermanno/Mantia: *Fantasie Original*
    Bach, Vincent: *Hungarian Melodies*
Short, Bob
    Album Title: *New Orleans Shuffle*
    Personnel: Turk Murphy's San Francisco
      Jazz Band
    Label: Columbia LP: CL 927
Sibley, Graham
    Album Title:
    Personnel: Hendon Band
    Bratton, John W./Roberts: *Teddy Bears' Picnic*
Smith, Edgar. *See* New Orleans Jazz Bands, *Down
Yonder*
Smith, J. R.
    Album Title: *Chamber Music of Anthony
      Iannoccone*
    Personnel: Carter Eggers, trumpet
    Label: Coronet LP: LPS 3038
    Iannocone, Anthony: *Sonatina for Trumpet and
      Tuba*
Steckar, Marc
    Album Title: *Tuba International*
    Personnel:
    Label: Disc BIM LP: O1TU
    Galliano, R.: *French Tuba in Los Angeles*
    Bologneisi, J.: *Quand le Tuba valse a Paris*
    Steckar, Marc/Delaporte: *African Tuba Safari*
    Galliano, R.: *Tubabando*
    Steckar, Marc/Colombo: *Tuba Banjo Dixie*
    Quibel, R.: *Tuba Bouchka*
    Janin, D.: *Swingin' Little Swiss Tuba . . .Cuckoo-
      clock*
    Steckar, Marc/Galliano: *Tubacuba*
    Steckar, Marc: *Tubas on Fujiyama*
    Steckar, Marc/Galliano: *Bayerische Pop Tuba*
    Steckar, Marc/Colombo: *Butacudatuba*
    Coeuriot, M.: *Tuba Space*
Steckar Elephant Tuba Horde
    Album Title: *Steckar Elephant Tuba Horde*
    Personnel: Jean-Jacques Justafre, tuben; Jean-
      Louis Damant, Christian Jous, Michel
      Nicolle, Marc Steckar, tenor tubas; Philippe
      Legris, Philippe Fritsch, Thierry Thibault,
      bass tubas; Bernard Lienard, Daniel Landreat,
      Didier Havet, contrabass tubas
    Label: IDA Records, 1987 LP: IDA 011/
      OMD 520
    Steckar, Franck: *Rouleaux de Printemps*
    Cugny, Laurent: *Molloy*
    Michel, Marc: *Le Jour ou les Tubas*
    Emler, Andy: *Gicael Mibbs*
    Vigneron, Louis: *Sentier de Nuit*
    Steckar, Franck: *Stabillo Steckardello*

Steckar, Marc: *Tubas au Fujiyama*
    Goret, Didier: *Detournement Mineur*
Steckar Tubapack
    Album Title: *Suite à suivre*
    Personnel: Marc Steckar, Christian Jous,
      euphoniums; Michel Godard, Daniel
      Landreat, tubas
    Label: JAM DISC, 1982 LP: 0183/MS 036
    Steckar: *Suite à suivre*
    Monk, Thelonius: *Blue Monk*
    Godard/Steckar: *Et le Klaxon Retentit Derechef
      comme un Lézard hongrois Enrhumé*
    Steckar: *Danse pour un Kangourou*
    Bologneisi, J.: *Maria Alm*
    Solal: *Tuba Only*
Steckar Tubapack
    Album Title: *Tubakoustic*
    Personnel: Marc Steckar, Christian Jous,
      euphoniums; Michel Godard, Daniel
      Landreat, tubas
    Label: IDA Records, 1989 CD:
Stern, Mary
    Album Title: *Celebration*
    Personnel: Staff Band of the Women's Royal
      Army Corps
    Label: Band Leader, 1990 CD: BNA 5036
    Clark, M.: *Tyrolean Tuba*
Stevens, John
    Album Title: *Barnum!*
    Personnel: Original Broadway Cast
    Label: CBS Masterworks, 1980 LP: 36576; CS:
      36576
    Coleman, Cy, and Kay, Hershey: *Come Follow
      the Band*
Stevens, John
    Album Title: *A Horn of a Different Color*
    Personnel: Jerry Peel, horn
    Label: Friendly Bull Recordings, 1982 LP:
    Stevens, John: *Thunder and Lightning*
Stevens, John
    Album Title: *Power*
    Personnel: James Jenkins, tuba; William
      Schmearer, tuba; Ray Stewart, tuba; Jerry
      Peel, horn; Joseph Stierli, trombone
    Label: Mark Records, 1988 CD: MRS 20699
    Stevens, John: *Suite No. 1 for Solo Tuba*
    Stevens, John: *Triumph of the Demon Gods*
    Stevens, John: *Splinters*
    Stevens, John: *Suite for II*
    Stevens, John: *Power for Four Tubas*
Stevens, John. *See* Johnson, Howard, *Second Childhood*
Stewart, Bob
    Album Title: *Blythe Spirit*
    Personnel: Arthur Blythe
    Label: Columbia, 1981 LP: FC 37427
Stewart, Bob
    Album Title: *Bush Baby*
    Personnel: Arthur Blythe
    Label: Adelphi, 1977 LP: 5008

Stewart, Bob
    Album Title: *Charles Mingus Live at Avery
       Fisher Hall*
    Personnel:
    Label: Columbia LP:
    Let My Children Hear Music
Stewart, Bob
    Album Title: *David Murray Big Band Live at
       Sweet Basil*
    Personnel: David Murray Big Band
    Label: Black Saint, 1984 BSR 0085
Stewart, Bob
    Album Title: *Elaborations*
    Personnel: Arthur Blythe
    Label: Columbia LP: 7464-38163-1
Stewart, Bob
    Album Title: *European Tour 1977*
    Personnel: Carla Bley Band
    Label: Watt Works, 1977 LP: 8
Stewart, Bob
    Album Title: *First Line*
    Personnel: First Line Band
    Label: JMT, 1987 LP: 834 414-1; CD:
       834 414-2
    Stewart, Bob: *First Line*
    Stewart, Bob: *CJ*
    Blythe, Arthur: *Metamorphosis*
    Traditional: *Sometimes I Feel Like a Mother-
       less Child*
    Stewart, Bob: *Nonet*
    Traditional: *Hey Mama*
    Blythe, Arthur: *Bush Baby*
    Traditional: *Surinam*
    Stewart, Bob: *Hambone*
Stewart, Bob
    Album Title: *Goin' Home*
    Personnel: First Line Band
    Label: JMT, 1988 LP: 834 427-1; CD: 834
       427-2; CS: 834 427-3
    Bell, Kelvyn: *Suba La Nas Alturas*
    Cherry, Don: *Art Deco*
    Dara, Olu: *Bell and Ponce*
    Stewart, Bob: *Tunk*
    Stewart, Bob: *Sweet Georgia Brown Sweet*
    Harper, Billy: *Priestess*
Stewart, Bob
    Album Title: *The Grip*
    Personnel: Arthur Blythe
    Label: India Navigation, 1977 LP: 1029
Stewart, Bob
    Album Title: *Heavy Life*
    Personnel: Edward Vesala
    Label: Leo Records, 1980 LP: 009
Stewart, Bob
    Album Title: *Illusions*
    Personnel: Arthur Blythe
    Label: Columbia, 1980 LP: JC 36583
Stewart, Bob
    Album Title: *Lenox Avenue Breakdown*

    Personnel: Arthur Blythe
    Label: Columbia, 1979 LP: JC 35638
Stewart, Bob
    Album Title: *Light Blue*
    Personnel: Arthur Blythe, Abdul Wadud,
       Kelvyn Bell, Bobby Battle
    Label: Columbia, 1983. LP: 7464-38661-1
    Monk, Thelonius: *Light Blue*
    Monk, Thelonius: *Off Minor*
    Monk, Thelonius: *Epistrophy*
    Monk, Thelonius: *Coming on the Hudson*
    Monk, Thelonius: *Nutty*
Stewart, Bob
    Album Title: *Live in Germany*
    Label: Circle Records, 1978 RK 101978/13
Stewart, Bob
    Album Title: *Metamorphosis*
    Personnel: Arthur Blythe
    Label: Navigation, 1977 LP: 1038
Stewart, Bob
    Album Title: *Musique Mecanique*
    Personnel: Carla Bley Band
    Label: Watt Works, 1978 LP: 9
Stewart, Bob
    Album Title: *Rambler*
    Personnel: Bill Frisell
    Label: ECM, 1984 LP: 1287
Stewart, Bob
    Album Title: *13th House*
    Personnel: McCoy Tyner
    Label: Milestone, 1980 LP: M-9102
    13th House
    Song of the New World
Stewart, Bob. *See* Daley, Joseph, *Taj Mahal: The
    Real Thing*
Stewart, Bob
    Album Title: *The Village*
    Personnel: Henry Butler, piano; Ron Carter,
       bass; Jack DeJohnette, drums; Alvin Batista,
       clarinet; John Purcell, oboe
    Label: MCA Impulse, 1987. CD:
    What's Up
    Beautiful She Is
    Joanna
    The Village
    Reflections
    Expressions of Quietude
    Swinging at the Palace
    Soft Platonicism
    The Entertainer
Stewart, Ray. *See* Stevens, John, *Power*
Stokes, David, and Patterson, Graham
    Album Title:
    Personnel: Chalk Farm Band—Salvation Army
    Label:
    Condon, Leslie: *Radiant Pathway*
Strand, Donald
    Album Title: *1979 Music Teachers National
      Association Collegiate Artists Winners*

Personnel: Peggy Randolph, piano
Label: Silver Crest, 1979 LP: MTNA-79-2B
Vaughan Williams, Ralph: *Concerto for Bass Tuba and Orchestra*
Stringer, Myron. *See* Tennessee Tech Tuba-Euphonium Quintet, *The Golden Sound of Euphoniums*
Summit Tubas
   Album Title: *American Tribute—Summit Brass*
   Personnel: Roger Bobo, Dan Perantoni, Harvey Phillips, Gene Pokorny
   Label: Summit, 1991 CD: DCD 127
   Stevens, John: *Moondance*
Sykes, Stephen
   Album Title: *Firebird*
   Personnel: Grimethorpe Colliery Band; Ray Farr, conductor
   Label: Polyphonic, 1982 LP: PRL010 / CS:
   Golland, John: *Scherzo*
Sykes, Stephen
   Album Title: *The Land of the Mountain and the Flood*
   Personnel: C. W. S. Band, Glasgow
   Label: Harlequin Recording, 1994. CD: HAR 1123 CD
   Ellerby, Martin: *Tuba Concerto*
Sykes, Stephen
   Album Title: *Sovereign Soloists, Vol. I*
   Personnel: Rochdale Band; Richard Evans, conductor
   Label: Doyen CD: DOY CD 003; CS: DOY MC 003
   arr. Sykes: *Hefje Kati*
   Newsome, Roy: *The Bass in the Ballroom*
Sykes, Steven
   Album Title:
   Personnel:
   Label: KRO Records KKCD 9204
   Newton, Rodney: *Capriccio for E♭ Bass*
   Mendez, Rafael: *Sambe Guitana*
Szabo, Laszlo
   Album Title: *Barcs 1986*
   Personnel: Budapest Brass Quintet
   Label: Hungaroton, 1987 LP: SLPX 12953
   Farkas, Antal: *Tuba Variations*
Tafjord, Stein-Erik
   Album Title: *Brazzy Landscapes*
   Personnel: Jarle Forde and Jan Forde, trumpets; Runar Tafjorf, horn; Helga Forde, trombone; Egil Johansen, drums; Phil Minton, vocals
   Label: Odin, 1987.
   First Landscape
   Bop Goes to Church
   Wind-up Landscape
   I Can Swing a Sousa
   Brubeck, Dave: Blue Rondo alla Turk
   Crusin' the Big Easy
   Sphinx
   Last Landscape

Reincarnation of a Love Bird
Tafjord, Stein-Erik. *See* Scandinavian Tuba Jazz
Tarto, Joe. *See* Phillips, Harvey, *Lavalle in Hi-Fi*
Tarto, Joe
   Album Title: *Titan of the Tuba*
   Personnel: Red Nichols, Cliff Edwards, Joe Venuti, Carson Robison
   Label: Broadway LP: BR 108
   My Best Girl
   Sob Sister Sadie
   Steppin' in Society
   Row Row Rosie
   Marguerite
   Black Horse Stomp
   Bass Ale Blues
   Song of the Wanderer
   When You See That Aunt of Mine
   Hittin' the Ceiling
   I Must Have That Man
   Less Than That
   Onyx Club Review
   Just an Echo in the Valley
   Boy Scout Be Prepared
   Salty Sailor Tunes
   Trumpet Polka
Tennessee Tech Tuba-Euphonium Quintet
   Album Title: *The Golden Sound of Euphoniums*
   Personnel: R. Winston Morris, Bill Acuff, Myron Stringer, tubas; Bill Cherry, Alan Clark, euphoniums
   Label: Mirafone, flexible 33 1/3, promotional
   Bach, Johann Sebastian/Morris: *Contrapunctus I*
   Joplin, Scott/Self: *The Entertainer*
Tennessee Technological University Tuba/Euphonium Ensemble
   Album Title: *All That Jazz*
   Personnel: R. Winston Morris, director
   Label: Mark College Jazz Series LP: MES 20608
   arr. Garrett: *Just a Closer Walk with Thee*
   arr. Garrett: *Won't You Come Home Bill Bailey*
   arr. Garrett: *Chimes Blues*
   Ahbez, Eden/Cherry: *Nature Boy*
   Harrison, Wayne: *Beneath the Surface*
   Green, Freddie/Esleck: *Corner Pocket*
   Morrison, Van/Kile: *Moondance*
   Brown, Nacio Herb/Sample: *Two Tunes (You Stepped Out of a Dream; Temptation)*
   Martin, Glenn: *Chops!*
   Corea, Chick: *Spain*
   Zawinul, Josef/Arnold: *Birdland*
Tennessee Technological University Tuba/Euphonium Ensemble
   Album Title: *Fifty-First Meeting Music Educators National Conference*
   Personnel: R. Winston Morris, director
   Label: Mark Custom Recording Services, 1988 CD: MENC88-1-4

Tchaikovsky, Peter Ilyitch/O'Conner: *Serenade for Tubas*
Camphouse, Mark: *Ceremonial Sketch*
Werle, Floyd: *Variations on an Old Hymn Tune*
O'Hara, Betty: *Euphonics*
Brubeck, Dave/Esleck: *Blue Rondo alla Turk*
Hancock, Herbie/Perry: *Cameleon*
Tennessee Technological University Tuba/Euphonium Ensemble
    Album Title: *Heavy Metal*
    Personnel: R. Winston Morris, director
    Label: Mark Custom Recording Services, 1987 LP: MES 20759
    Pegram, Wayne: *Howdy!*
    Gates, Crawford: *Tuba Quartet*, Op. 59
    Lamb, Marvin: *Heavy Metal*
    Shearing, George/Perry: *Lullaby of Birdland*
    Wilson, Ted: *Wot Shigona Dew*
    Garrett, James: *Miniature Jazz Suite*
    Martin, Glenn: *Bluesin' Tubas*
    Jarreau, Al/Murphy: *Boogie Down*
Tennessee Technological University Tuba/Euphonium Ensemble
    Album Title: *Live!!!*
    Personnel: R. Winston Morris, director
    Label: KM Educational Library, 1980 LP: KM 5661
    Konagaya, Soichi: *Illusion*
    Knox, Charles: *Scherzando for Tubular Octet*
    Ruth, Matthew: *Exigencies*
    DiGiovanni, Rocco: *Tuba Magic*
    Gershwin, George/Sample: *Gershwin Medley* arr. Arnold Corazon
Tennessee Technological University Tuba/Euphonium Ensemble
    Album Title: *Music of Jared Spears*
    Personnel: R. Winston Morris, director
    Label: KM Records, 1981 LP: KM 6549
    Spears, Jared: *Divertimento for Tuba Ensemble*
Tennessee Technological University Tuba/Euphonium Ensemble
    Album Title: *Tennessee Tech Tuba Ensemble, Vol. I*
    Personnel: R. Winston Morris, director
    Label: Golden Crest, 1975 LP: CRS 4139
    Bartles, Alfred: *When Tubas Waltz*
    Barroso, Ary/Morris: *Brazil*
    Hutchinson, Terry: *Tuba Juba Duba*
    Lecuona, Ernesto/Morris: *Malagueña*
    Ellington, Duke/Sample: *Tribute to Duke Ellington*
    Bach, Johann Sebastian/Morris: *Toccata and Fugue in D Minor*
    Ross, Walter: *Concerto Basso*
    Bach, Johann Sebastian/Sauter: *Come, Sweet Death*
Tennessee Technological University Tuba/Euphonium Ensemble

Album Title: *Tennessee Tech Tuba Ensemble Presents Their Carnegie Recital Hall Program*
Personnel: R. Winston Morris, director
Label: Golden Crest, 1976 LP: CRS 4152
Beale, David: *Reflections on a Park Bench*
Bach, Johann Sebastian/Phillips: *"Air" from Suite No. 3 in D Major for Orchestra*, BWV 1068
Stroud, Richard: *Treatments for Tuba*
Sample, Steve: *Nostalgia Medley*
Tennessee Technological University Tuba/Euphonium Ensemble
    Album Title: *The Tennessee Technological University Tuba Ensemble*
    Personnel: R. Winston Morris, director
    Label: KM Educational Library, 1980 LP: 4631
    Cheetham, John: *Consortium*
    George, Thom Ritter: *Tubasonatina*
    Dodson, John: *Out of the Depths*
    Porter, Cole/Sample: *Cole Porter Medley*
    Bernie, Pinkard, and Casey/Garrett: *Sweet Georgia Brown*
    Nyro, Laura/Cherry: *Eli's Coming*
    Garrett, James: *A Tubalee Jubalee*
    Rodgers, Richard/Cherry: *My Favorite Things*
Thibault, Thierry. *See* Steckar Elephant Tuba Horde
Thornton, Donald
    Album Title: *Metropolis: The Klezmorim*
    Personnel: *The Klezmorim*
    Label: Flying Fish Records LP: *Tuba Doina*
Thornton, Michael
    Album Title: *The Sound of a Tuba*
    Personnel: Richard Jensen, percussion; Lise Proto, piano; Barry Green, doublebass; Frank Proto, conductor
    Label: QCA Red Mark/Liben Records, 1982 LP: RML 8202
    Proto, Frank: *The Four Seasons* for tuba, percussion, strings, and stereo tape
    Beethoven, Ludwig/Proto: *Sonata in G Major* for tuba and piano (Horn Sonata in F)
    Elgar, Edward/Thornton: *Chanson de Matin*, Op. 15, No. 2
Thorton, Michael
    Album Title: *Tubby the Tuba*
    Personnel: Carol Channing, narrator
    Label: Caedmon LP: TC 1623
    Kleinsinger, George, and Tripp, Paul: *Tubby the Tuba*
Tietz, Henrik. *See* Melton Tuba-Quartett, *Premiere*
Torchinsky, Abe
    Album Title: *Complete Brass Sonatas of Hindemith*
    Personnel: Glenn Gould, piano
    Label: Columbia Records, 1976 2 LPs: M2-33971 (rereleased on 2 CDs)
    Hindemith, Paul: *Sonata for Bass Tuba and Piano*

Trice, Jerry
  Album Title: *Opus One, Number Four*
  Personnel: Robert Woodbury, tuba
  Label: Op. One LP: 4
  Birchall, Steven: *Reciprocals II for Two Tubas*
Triebener, Heiko. *See* Melton Tuba-Quartett
Tubadours
  Album Title: *The Mighty Tubadours Merry Christmas Album*
  Personnel: Albert Harclerode, Norm Pearson, tubas; Loren Marstellar, Gil Zimmerman, euphoniums
  Label: Crystal, 1984 LP: S422
  Herbert, Victor/Vaughan: *March of the Toy Soldiers*
  Redner/Vaughan: *Oh Little Town of Bethlehem*
  arr. Vaughan: *Hail the Lord's Annointed*
  arr. Harclerode: *March of the Three Kings*
  Mueller/Vaughan: *Away in a Manger*
  Hopkins/Lycan: *We Three Kings*
  Bach, Johann Sebastian/Falconer: *Von Himmel Hoch*
  arr. Harclerode: *Gloustershire Wassail Song*
  arr. Vaughan: *O Come, O Come Emmanuel*
  Tchaikovsky, Peter Ilyitch/Self: *Dance of the Reedpipes*
  Tchaikovsky, Peter Ilyitch/Charlton: *March–Overture from "Nutcracker"*
  arr. Vaughan: *Coventry Carol*
  arr. Harclerode: *O Tannenbaum*
  Kingsbury/Harclerode: *Infant Holy*
  Schop/Vaughan: *Break Forth O Beauteous Light*
  Willis/Harclerode: *It Came Upon a Midnight Clear*
  arr. Charlton: *First Noel*
  Berlin, Irving/Vaughan: *White Christmas*
  arr. Harclerode: *O Sanctissumus*
  Gillespie/Vaughan: *Santa Claus Is Coming to Town*
  arr. Harclerode: *Good King Wenceslas; Il Est Né*
  arr. Vaughan: *God Rest Ye Merry Gentlemen*
  Schulz/Harclerode: *O Come Little Children*
Tubadours
  Album Title: *Ve Iss Da Mighty Tubadours, Ya?*
  Personnel: Frank Berry, Loren Marstellar, Gil Zimmerman euphoniums; Albert Harclerode, Adi Hershko, David Lusher, Norman Pearson, Timothy Reilly, tubas
  Label: Crystal, 1991 CD: CD420 (Combined *Ya, Ve Iss Da Mighty Tubadours* and *Tubadour Merry Christmas* albums)
  Vaughan, Rodger: *Jingle Bell Waltz*
Tubadours
  Album Title: *Ya, Ve Iss Da Mighty Tubadours*
  Personnel: Frank Berry, euphonium; Albert Harclerode, Adi Hershko, David Lusher, Timothy Reilly, tubas
  Label: Crystal, 1978 LP: S42
  Herbert, Victor/Vaughan: *March of Toy Soldiers*

Strauss, Johann Jr./Berry: *Waltz from "Die Fledermaus"*
King, Karl L./Berry: *Barnum and Bailey's Favorite*
Bartles, Alfred: *When Tubas Waltz*
Mouret, Jean Joseph/Self: *Rondo*
Taylor, Tell/Vaughan: *Down by the Old Mill Stream*
Tchaikovsky, Peter Ilyitch/Self: *Dance of the Reedpipes*
Gounod, Charles/Berry: *Funeral March for a Marionette*
Bach, Johann Sebastian/Berry: *Fugue in G Minor*
Anonymous/Lusher: *Come Dearest, the Daylight Is Gone*
Richardson, Arthur/McLean/Whitcomb: *Too Fat Polka*
Kabalevski, Dmitri/Berry: *Comedian's Galop*
Ellington, Duke/Vaughan: *Mood Indigo/ Satin Doll*
Mozart, Wolfgang Amadeus/Self: *Allegro from Eine kleine Nachtmusik*
Turk, John
  Album Title: *Low Blows*
  Personnel: Dora Ohrenstein, soprano; Randall Fusco, piano; Lori Turk, piccolo; William Slocum, horn
  Label: Dana Recording Project, 1991 CD: DRP-4
  Hindemith, Paul: *Sonata for Bass Tuba and Piano*
  Penn, William: *Three Essays for Solo Tuba*
  Smith, Glenn: *Forowen 3* (tuba and piccolo)
  Largent, Edward: *Four Shorts for Tuba and Piano*
  Amato, Bruno: *Two Together* (tuba and soprano)
  Rollin, Robert: *The Raven and the First Men* (tuba, horn, piano, electronics)
Turk, John
  Album Title: *The Music of Warren Benson*
  Personnel: Indiana University Symphonic Band; Fredrick Ebbs, director
  Label: Coronet, 1966 LP: 2736
  Benson, Warren: *Helix for Solo Tuba and Concert Band*
Turk, John
  Album Title: *1974 Mid-West National Band and Orchestra Clinic*
  Personnel: Cambridge High School Symphonic Band
  Label: Silver Crest, 1974 LP: MID-74-9
  Hartley, Walter: *Concertino for Tuba and Wind Ensemble*
United States Air Force Concert Band Tuba Section
  Album Title: *Moon Dance*
  Personnel: Robert N. Daniel, Edward R. McKee, William D. Porter II, Jan Z Duga, tubas; Kathryn Hutchins Daniel, flute; Marek Vastek, piano; Carl Long, conductor

Label: U. S. Air Force, 1994. CS: Public service, not for sale

Stevens, John: *Moondance*

Jager, Robert: *Fantasy-Variations* (for flute, tuba, and piano; Robert N. Daniel, tuba)

Butterfield, Don: *Sonority Study for Three Tubas*

Koetsier, Jan: *Sonatina for Tuba and Piano*, Op. 57 (Jan Z Duga, tuba)

Traditional/Funderburk: *La Tuba* (tubas and percussion)

Reed, Alfred: *Fantasia a due*

Miller, Sy and Jackson, Jill: *Let There Be Peace on Earth* (William D. Porter, tuba)

Chopin, Frederic/Abrams: *Mazurka No. 49 in A minor*, Op. 68, No. 2 (tuba quartet)

Gabrieli, Domenico/R. W. Morris: *Ricercar* (Edward R. McKee, tuba)

Raph, Alan: *Rock* (Edward R. McKee, tuba)

Anonymous/Funderburk: *O Welt, ich muss dich lassen*

United States Armed Forces Tuba-Euphonium Ensemble

Album Title: *Forty-Third Annual Mid-West International Band and Orchestra Clinic*

Personnel: R. Winston Morris, conductor

Label: Mark Custom Recording Services, 1989 CD: MW89MCD-8

Pegram, Wayne: *"Howdy!"*

Mozart, Wolfgang Amadeus/Gottschalk: *Overture to the "Marriage of Figaro"*

Rossini, Gioacchino/Kile: *Overture to the "Barber of Seville"*

Cheetham, John: *Consortium*

arr. Garrett: *The Londonderry Air*

Garret, James: *A Tubalee Jubalee*

Gershwin, George/Sample: *Gershwin Medley*

King, Karl L./Werden: *The Melody Shop*

King, Karl L./Morris: *Barnum and Bailey's Favorite*

United States Armed Forces Tuba-Euphonium Ensemble and Massed Ensemble

Album Title: *The United States Army Band Tuba-Euphonium Conference 1989*

Personnel: R. Winston Morris, conductor

Label: United States Army Band, 1989 CS: Public service, not for sale

Also released by Mark Custom Recording Services, 1989 CD: MW89MCD-8

Bach, Johann Sebastian/Beckman: *St. Anne's Fugue*

Saint-Saëns, Camille/Cohen: *Marche Militaire Francaise*

Werle, Floyd: *Variations on an Old Hymn*

Camphouse, Mark: *Ceremonial Sketch*

Garbáge, Pierre: *Sousa Surrenders*

Bach, Johann Sebastian: *Bist Du bei Mir*

Frank, Marcel: *Lyric Poem*

Canter, James: *Appalachian Carol*

DiGiovanni, Rocco: *Tuba Magic*

Joplin, Scott/Self: *The Entertainer*

Huffine, G. H.: *Them Basses*

(Note: The Mark CD incorrectly lists Sousa: *Stars and Stripes Forever* as being on the album.)

United States Army Band "Pershing's Own"

Album Title: *United States Army Band Tuba-Euphonium Workshop Grand Concert*

Personnel: The United States Army Band "Pershing's Own"; Colonel Eugene W. Allen, conductor

Label: United States Army Band, 1989 CS: Public service, not for sale

Wilhelm, Rolf: *Concertino* for tuba and wind instruments (Michael Bunn, soloist)

Smith, Claude T.: *Ballade and Presto Dance* (Robert Daniel, soloist)

Barat, Joseph Eduoard/Phillips: *Introduction and Dance* (Roger Bobo, soloist)

Dumitru, Ionel: *Romanian Dance* (Roger Bobo, soloist)

Arban, J. B./Berry: *Carnival of Venice* (Roger Bobo, soloist)

United States Coast Guard Tuba-Euphonium Quartet

Album Title: *The Musical Sounds of the Seasons: The United States Coast Guard Band*

Personnel: John Banker, Gary Buttery, tubas; Roger Behrend, David Werden, euphoniums

Label: U. S. Coast Guard, 1984 LP: Public service, not for sale

Buttery, Gary: *An English Folk Christmas*

United States Coast Guard Tuba-Euphonium Quartet

Album Title: *The United States Coast Guard Band, Soloists and Chamber Players*

Personnel: Gary Buttery, David Chaput, tubas; David Werden, Dennis Winter, euphoniums

Label: U. S. Coast Guard, 1978 LP: USCG 122678-A; Public service, not for sale

Persichetti, Vincent: *Serenade for Ten Wind Instruments*

Ramsoe, Emilio Wilhelm/Buttery: *Quartet for Brass*

United States Navy Band Tuba-Euphonium Quartet

Album Title: *The United States Navy Band Presents the Tuba Quartet*

Personnel: Roger Behrend, John Bowman, euphoniums; Keith Mehlan, Martin Erickson, tubas

Label: United States Navy Band, 1986 CS: Public service, not for sale

Bulla, Stephen: *Quartet for Low Brass*

Ramsoe, Emilio Wilhelm/Buttery: *Quartet for Brass* (third movement)

Massenet, Jules/ Margaret Erickson: *Argonaise from "Le Cid"*

Joplin, Scott/Werden: *Ragtime Dance*

University of Illinois Tuba Quintet
  Album Title: *CDCM Computer Music Series, Volume 3*
  Personnel: Bill Chamberlain, Scott Forsythe, Chris Hall, Richard Perry, James Willett, tubas; William Brooks, conductor
  Label: Centaur Records, 1989. CD: CRC 2045
  Tipei, Sever: *Cuniculi for Five Tubas*
University of Miami Tuba Ensemble
  Album Title: *University of Miami Tuba Ensemble Greatest Hits*
  Personnel: Constance Weldon, director
  Label: Miami United Tuba Ensemble Society LP: 14568
  Payne, Frank Lynn: *Quartet for Tubas (The Condor)*
  Frank, Marcel G.: *Lyric Poem for Five Tubas*
  Hastings, Ross: *Little Madrigal for Big Horns*
  Rogers, Thomas: *Music for Tuba Ensemble*
  Boone, Dan: *Three Moods*
  Donaldson, W./Self: *Carolina in the Morning*
  Gould, Morton/Woo: *Pavanne from the "Latin America Suite"*
  Frackenpohl, Arthur: *Pop Suite for Barituba Ensemble*
  Jones, Roger: *Duet No. 12 from "21 Distinctive Duets"*
  Davis, Akst/Woo: *Baby Face*
  Sousa, John Philip/Weldon: *Stars and Stripes Forever*
University of Michigan Tuba and Euphonium Ensemble
  Album Title: *The Brass Menagerie*
  Personnel: Abe Torchinsky, conductor
  Label: School of Music LP Records, 1979 LP: SM0011
  Byrd, William: *Agnus Dei*
  Payne, Frank Lynn: *Quartet for Tubas*
  Holmes, Paul: *Quartet for Tubas*
  Stevens, John: *Manhattan Suite*
  Mozart, Wolfgang Amadeus/Gottschalk: *Overture to the "Marriage of Figaro"*
University of Michigan Tuba Ensemble
  Album Title: *University of Michigan Percussion and Tuba Ensembles*
  Personnel: Abe Torchinsky, director; Uri Mayer, conductor
  Label: Golden Crest, 1975 LP: CRS 4145
  Iannaccone, Anthony: *Hades* for two euphoniums and two tubas
  Presser, William: *Serenade for Four Tubas* (3rd movement, Allegro)
  Iannaccone, Anthony: *Three Mythical Sketches* for four tubas
  Gottschalk, Arthur: *Substructures* for ten tubas
Unkrodt, Dietrich
  Album Title: *Dixieland Allstars Berlin— AMIGA*

Personnel:
  Label: AMIGA Deutsche Schallplatten LP: Stereo 855-350
Unkrodt, Dietrich
  Album Title: *Musik für Blechbläser; Gruner Tubakonzert*
  Personnel: Rundfunk-Sinfonie-Orchester Berlin; Joachim Willert; Berliner Blech-bläserquintett
  Label: NOVA Deutsche Schallplatten, 1982 LP: 885-208
  Gruner, Joachim: *Konzert für Tuba und Orchester*
Unkrodt, Dietrich
  Album Title: *Unkrodt/Zerbe*
  Personnel: Hannes Zerbe, piano and synthesizer
  Label: AMIGA, 1987 Stereo 856-336
  Kanon
  Die haltbare Graugans
  Für H. S.
  Spiralen
  Calvados
Van Lier, Erik
  Album Title: *First Brass*
  Personnel: Allan Botschinsky, Derek Watkins, trumpet and fluegelhorn; Bart Van Lier, trombone and euphonium
  Label: M-A Music, 1986 LP:
  Botschinsky, Allan: *Interlude No. 4*
  Botschinsky, Allan: *October Sunshine*
  Botschinsky, Allan: *Kubismus 502*
  Brahms, Johannes: *Wiegenlied*
  Botschinsky, Allan: *Don't Shoot the Banjo Player ('Cause We've Done It Already)*
  Botschinsky, Allan: *Toot Your Roots*
  Botschinsky, Allan: *The Lady in Blue*
  Botschinsky, Allan: *Alster Promenade*
  Botschinsky, Allan: *Chops a la Salsa*
  Botschinsky, Allan: *Love Waltz*
Varner, Lesley
  Album Title: *1977 Mid-West National Band and Orchestra Clinic*
  Personnel: Victoria High School Band
  Label: Crest Records, 1977 LP:
  Grundman, Clare: *Tuba Rhapsody*
Wagner, Michael
  Album Title: *The United States Army Ceremonial Brass and Percussion*
  Personnel: The United States Army Ceremonial Brass and Percussion
  Label: U. S. Army, 1986 LP: Public service, not for saleGregson, Edward: *Concerto for Tuba*
Wagner, Michael
  Album Title: *Firestorm*
  Personnel: U. S. Army Brass Band
  Label: U. S. Army Brass Band. Public service, not for sale

Rimsky-Korsakov, Nicholas/Wagner: *Flight of the Bumblebee*
Washburn, Joe "Country"
  Album Title:
  Personnel: Spike Jones and His City Slickers
  Label: RCA LP: 10-2118
  Hupfield, Herman: *When Yuba Plays the Rhumba on the Tuba Down in Cuba*
Well, Christoph
  Album Title: *Grüss Gott mein Bayernland*
  Personnel:
  Label: Mood Records LP: 28631
  Well, Christoph: *Wann der Dudelsack kräht u. a.*
Wilhelm, Matthias
  Album Title: *Amiri Baraka and Artra Live at the Amerikahaus Munich*
  Personnel:
  Label: Artra, 1981 LP: 1003
Wilhelm, Matthias
  Album Title: *Artra-Artra*
  Personnel: Loft
  Label: Loft, 1980 LP: L1002
Wilhelm, Matthias
  Album Title: *Band of Man—Carborundum*
  Personnel:
  Label: Artra, 1983 LP: 1001
Wilhelm, Matthias
  Album Title: *Das Liedmobil*
  Personnel:
  Label: Deutsche Grammophon, 1981 LP: 254
Wilson, John L. *See* Hoffnung, Gerard, *Hoffnung Music Festival Concert*
Woodbury, Robert. *See* Trice, Jerry, *Op. One, Number One*
Yasumoto, Hiroyuki
  Album Title: *Solo Album for Wind Instruments: Tuba*
  Personnel: Yuko Kusuyama, piano; Atsuhi Hairu, percussion
  Label: Nippon Columbia Company, LTD, 1990 CD: COCG 6536
  Censhu, Jiro: *Verdurous Aubade for Tuba and Piano*
  Konagaya, Soichi: *Fantasy for Tuba and Piano*
  Toyama, Yuzo: *Trio Sonata for Tuba, Batteries [percussion], and Piano*
  Kreisler, Fritz/Yasumoto: *Liebesfreud*
  Martini, J. P. E./Yodo: *Piacer d'Amor*
  Saint-Saëns, Camille/Yodo: *The Elephant from "Carnival of the Animals"*
  Mori, Yoshiko: *Barcarolle for Tuba*
  Traditional/Yamamoto: *Sakura Sakura*
  Livingston, J., and Evans, R./Inomata: *To Each His Own*
  Lennon, John, and McCartney, Paul/Ito: *Yesterday*
  McHugh, J., and Fields, D./Ito: *On the Sunny Side of the Street*

Tuba Recordings by Title

Titles beginning with an article are alphabetized according to the first substantive word.

Adagio, Eccles, Henry/Megules: Megules, Karl
Adagio, Shostakovich, Dimitri: Bobo, Roger
Adagio and Allegro in Ab, Op. 70, Schumann, Robert: Dowling, Eugene; Cooley, Floyd
Adagio from Symphony No. 3, Saint-Saëns, Camille/Murley: British Tuba Quartet
Adagio from *Toccata, Adagio and Fugue in C major* BWV 564, Bach, Johann Sebastian/Hilgers: Hilgers, Walter
African Tuba Safari, Steckar and Delaporte: Steckar, Marc
Agnus Dei, Byrd, William: University of Michigan Tuba and Euphonium Ensemble
Ain't Gwine to Whistle Dixie (Any Mo'),: Johnson, Howard
Air and Bourrée, Bach, Johann Sebastian/Bell: Conner, Rex; Davis, Ronald; Phillips, Harvey; Popiel, Peter
Air and Bourrée, Handel, George Friderik: Conner, Rex
Air con Variazioni from Suite No. 5 in E Major, Handel, George Friderik: Dowling, Eugene
Air for the G String, Bach, Johann Sebastian: Bobo, Roger
Air from Suite No. 3 for Orchestra, BWV 1068, Bach, Johann Sebastian/Werden: British Tuba Quartet; Atlantic Tuba Quartet
Air from Suite No. 3 in D Major for Orchestra, BWV 1068, Bach, Johann Sebastian/Phillips: Tennessee Technological University Tuba/Euphonium Ensemble
Alabamy Bound, Henderson, Ray: Lehr, David "Red"
Alarum (solo tuba), Gregson, Edward: Gourlay, James
Album Album, Johnson, Howard: Johnson, Howard
Alexander's Ragtime Band, Berlin, Irving: Pilafian, Sam
All Blues, Davis, Miles: Scandinavian Tuba Jazz
Allegro and Air, Purcell, Henry: New York Tuba Quartet
Allegro et Finale, Bozza, Eugene: Georgie, Gerhard
Allegro from *Eine kleine Nachtmusik*, Mozart, Wolfgang Amadeus/Self: Tubadours
Allegro from Sonata No. 3 in F Major, Galliard, Johann Ernst/Clemons, R.: Arwood, Jeffrey
Allegro from Toccata in D Minor for Klavier, BWV 913, Bach, Johann Sebastian/Myers: Atlantic Tuba Quartet
Allegro Vivace from Quartet No. 5, Op. 38, Ramsoe, Emilio Wilhelm: Fletcher, John
Alone: Bargeron, Dave
Alster Promenade, Botschinsky, Allan: Van Lier, Erik
Amazing Grace, Traditional/Mancini: Johnson, John Thomas (Tommy)

"and from the abyss" for tuba and tape, Felciano, Richard: Cooley, Floyd

Andante, Handel, George Friderik: Phillips, Harvey

Andante and Rondo, Yoffe, Shlomo: Hershko, Adi

Andante for tuba and piano, Tcherepnin, Alexander: Hoppert, Manfred

Andante Quasi Allegretto, Ramsoe, Emilio Wilhelm/Buttery: Melton Tuba-Quartett

Angel Eyes, Dennis and Brent: Draper, Ray

Angels We Have Heard on High, Wilder: Phillips, Harvey/TubaChristmas

Another Time, Broadbent, Alan: Self, James

Antartic Love Song, Moschner, Pinguin: Moschner, Pinguin

Appalachian Carol, Canter, James: United States Armed Forces Tuba-Euphonium Ensemble

Aragonaise from "Le Cid," Massenet, Jules/Erickson, Margaret: Monarch Tuba-Euphonium Quartet; United States Navy Band Tuba-Euphonium Quartet

Aria con Variazioni, Handel, George Friderik/Fitzgerald: Seward, Steven

Arioso, Benson, Warren: Popiel, Peter

Art Deco, Cherry, Don: Stewart, Bob

Asleep in the Deep, Petrie, H. W.: Bell, William

Asleep in the Deep, Petrie, H. W./Lamb: Mallon, Barney

Au Privave, Parker, Charlie: New York Tuba Quartet

Avalon, Rose, Jolson, and DeSylva: Matteson, Rich; Pilafian, Sam

Ave Maria, Arcadelt, Jacob/Self: Melton Tuba-Quartett

Away in a Manger, Mueller/Vaughan: Tubadours

Baby Elephant Walk, Mancini, Henry/Luis: Melton Tuba-Quartett

Baby Face, Davis, Akst/Woo: University of Miami Tuba Ensemble

Ballade and Presto Dance, Smith, Claude T.: Daniel, Robert

Ballin' the Jack, Burris and Smith: Palmer, Singleton

Bandinerie, Bach, Johann Sebastian: Marshall, Oren

Barcarolle et Chanson Bachique, Semler-Collery, Jules: Popiel, Peter

Barcarolle for Tuba, Mori, Yoshiko: Yasumoto, Hiroyuki

Barnum and Bailey's Favorite, King, Karl L./Berry: Tubadours

Barnum and Bailey's Favorite, King, Karl L./Morris: United States Armed Forces Tuba-Euphonium Ensemble

Les Barricades Mystérieuses, Couperin, F./Pilafian: Gerhard Meinl's Tuba Sextet

Bart's Piece for Tuba and Electronic Tape, Ott, Joseph: Cummings, Barton

Basin Street Blues, Williams, Spencer: Lehr, David "Red"; Pilafian, Sam

Basin Street Blues, Williams, Spencer/Mitchell: Callender, Red

Bass Ale Blues: Tarto, Joe

Bass for solo tuba and buckle gongs, Nilsson, Bo: Lind, Michael

The Bass in the Ballroom, Newsome, Roy: Sykes, Stephen

Basso Continuo, Fritze, Gregory: Fritze, Gregory

Batida Diferente, Ferreira and Einhorn/Megules: Megules, Karl

Battle Hymn of the Republic, Howe, Julia Ward: Lehr, David "Red"

Bayerische Polka, Lohmann, Georg/D. Schmidt: The Contraband; Gerhard Meinl's Tuba Sextet

Bayerische Pop Tuba, Steckar and Galliano: Steckar, Marc

Bayerische Zell, Traditional/D. Schmidt: Gerhard Meinl's Tuba Sextet

Beale Street Blues, Handy, W. C.: Lehr, David "Red"

Beau Jack, McLean, Jackie: Draper, Ray

Beautiful She Is: Stewart, Bob

Bell and Ponce, Dara, Olu: Stewart, Bob

Beneath the Horizon for Tuba and Taped Whale Songs, McLean, Priscilla: Poore, Melvyn

Beneath the Surface, Harrison, Wayne: Tennessee Technological University Tuba/Euphonium Ensemble

Betrayal for tuba, violin and vibraphone, Op.144, Christiansen, Henning: Anderson, Hans

Bifurcation for tuba and piano, Baader-Nobs, Heidi: Bjørn-Larsen, Jens

Big Kneed Gal, Mahal, Taj: Johnson, Howard

Bill Bailey Won't You Please Come Home, Cannon, Hughie: Pilafian, Sam

Birdland, Zawinul, Josef/Arnold: Tennessee Technological University Tuba/Euphonium Ensemble

Bist du bei Mir, BWV 508, Bach, Johann Sebastian/Werden: Atlantic Tuba Quartet; Melton Tuba-Quartett; United States Armed Forces Tuba-Euphonium Ensemble

Bivalve Suite for Euphonium and Tuba, Hartley, Walter: LeBlanc, Robert

Black and Blue, Waller, Thomas "Fats": Pilafian, Sam

Black Horse Stomp: Tarto, Joe

Blue Monk, Monk, Thelonius: Steckar Tubapack

Blue Rondo alla Turk, Brubeck, Dave: Tafjord, Stein-Erik

Blue Rondo alla Turk, Brubeck, Dave/Esleck: Tennessee Technological University Tuba/Euphonium Ensemble

Blues by Monk, Monk, Thelonius: Johnson, Howard

Blues for E. L. C., Smith, Warren: Johnson, Howard

Blues in the Night, Mercer and Arlen: Price, Tony

The Blues My Naughty Sweetie Gave to Me, Swanstone, McCarron, and Morgan: Lehr, David "Red"

Bluesin' Tubas, Martin, Glenn: Tennessee Technological University Tuba/Euphonium Ensemble

Bocoxe, Powell, Baden/Buttery: Atlantic Tuba Quartet; British Tuba Quartet

Boogie Down, Jarreau, Al/Murphy: Tennessee Technological University Tuba/Euphonium Ensemble

Bop Goes to Church: Tafjord, Stein-Erik

Boplicity, Henry, Cleo: Barber, John William (Bill)

Bosque De Manaus, Kurnick, Jon: Self, James

Bottoms Up Rag, Mehlan, Keith: Monarch Tuba-Euphonium Quartet

Bouillabaisse (Thanks, Maggie), Moschner, Pinguin: Moschner, Pinguin

Bourrée I & II from Suite for Unaccompanied Cello, Bach, Johann Sebastian: Bobo, Roger

Boy Scout Be Prepared: Tarto, Joe

Brass Tacks, Niehaus, Lennie: Northern Tuba Lights

Brazil, Barroso, Ary/Morris: Tennessee Technological University Tuba/Euphonium Ensemble

Break Forth O Beauteous Light, Schop/Vaughan: Tubadours

Breakthrough, Harlos, Steve: Self, James

Breath and Sounds for Tuba and Tape, Witkin, Beatrice: Hanks, Thompson

Breeze, McDonald, Goodwin, and Hanley: Newberger, Eli

Bride of the Waves, Clarke, Herbert L.: Frazier, Richard

Bring a Torch, Jeanette Isabella, Bewley: Phillips, Harvey/TubaChristmas

Bruckner Etude, Crespo, Enrique: Gerhard Meinl's Tuba Sextet

Bruegel—Dance Visions, Rubinstein, Arthur: Self, James

Bush Baby, Blythe, Arthur: Stewart, Bob

Butacudatuba, Steckar and Colombo: Steckar, Marc

The Buzzard Song, Gershwin, George/Evans: Barber, John William (Bill)

Bydlo from "Pictures at an Exhibition," Mussorgsky, Modest: Piernik, Zdizislaw

Cadence VI for Tuba and Tape, Lazarof, Henri: Bobo, Roger

Cakewalk into Town: Johnson, Howard

Calvados: Unkrodt, Dietrich

Cameleon, Hancock, Herbie/Perry: Tennessee Technological University Tuba/Euphonium Ensemble

Canto VII for Solo Tuba, Adler, Samuel: Beauregard, Cherry

Canzona, La Spiritata, Gabrieli, Giovanni/Rauch: British Tuba Quartet

Canzona per Sonare No. 4, Gabrieli, Giovanni/Gray: Gerhard Meinl's Tuba Sextet

Capriccio, Newton, Rodney: Gourlay, James

Capriccio da Camera for solo tuba and brass quintet, Danielssohn, Christer: Hilgers, Walter; Lind, Michael

Capriccio for Eb Bass, Newton, Rodney: Sykes, Steven

Capriccio for Solo Tuba, Penderecki, Krystof: Piernik, Zdizislaw; Bobo, Roger; Gourlay, James; Perantoni, Daniel

Capriccio for Tuba and Band, Presser, William: Astwood, Michael

Capriccio for Tuba and Orchestra, Schuller, Gunther: Phillips, Harvey

Careless Love, Koenig, Williams, and Handy: Palmer, Singleton

Carioca, Youmans, Vincent: Arwood, Jeffrey; Pilafian, Sam

Carioca, Youmans, Vincent/Norman: Phillips, Harvey

Carnival for Bass, Muscroft, Fred: Baker, Fred

Carnival of the Animals ("The Elephant"), Saint-Saëns, Camille/Yodo: Yasumoto, Hiroyuki

Carnival of the Animals ("The Elephant," "The Swan"), Saint-Saëns, Camille: Piernik, Zdizislaw

Carnival of Venice, Arban, J. B./Bell: Bell, William

Carnival of Venice, Arban, J. B./Berry: Bobo, Roger

Carnival of Venice, Arban, J. B./Domek: Perantoni, Daniel

Carnival of Venice, Dutton, Brent: Dutton, Brent

Carnival of Venice, Howarth, Elgar: Fletcher, John

Carnival of Venice, LeClair, David: The Contraband; Monarch Tuba-Euphonium Quartet

Carol of the Bells, Bewley: Phillips, Harvey/TubaChristmas

Carolina in the Morning, Donaldson, W./Self: University of Miami Tuba Ensemble

Carols for a Merry TubaChristmas, Wilder, Alec: Phillips, Harvey/TubaChristmas

The Cascades, Joplin, Scott: Pilafian, Sam

The Cascades, Joplin, Scott/Sabourin: British Tuba Quartet

Cavatina, Myers, Stanley: Self, James

Celestial Morn, Condon, Leslie: Hornsberger, Albert

Celestial Suite, Bulla, Stephen: British Tuba Quartet

Ceremonial Sketch, Camphouse, Mark: Tennessee Technological University Tuba/Euphonium Ensemble; United States Armed Forces Tuba-Euphonium Ensemble

Chaconne, Sowerby, Leo: Davis, Ronald

Chanson de Matin, Elgar, Edward: Fletcher, John

Chanson de Matin, Op. 15, No. 2, Elgar, Edward/Thornton: Thornton, Michael

The Chant, Stitzel, Mel: Newberger, Eli; Matteson, Rich

Chasin' the Antelope, Vignola, Frank: Pilafian, Sam

Cherokee for tuba quartet, Schooley, John: Northern Tuba Lights

Chicago Breakdown, Morton, F. "Jelly Roll": Newberger, Eli

Children at Play, Kalina, Ron: Self, James

Chimes Blues, Garrett: Tennessee Technological University Tuba/Euphonium Ensemble

Chimes Blues, Oliver, Joe: Newberger, Eli

Chin Up! Kresin, Willibald: The Contraband

China Boy, Winfree, Dick: Pilafian, Sam

Chit Chat Polka, Strauss, Johann Jr./Smalley: British Tuba Quartet

Chops! Martin, Glenn: Tennessee Technological University Tuba/Euphonium Ensemble

Chops a la Salsa, Botschinsky, Allan: Van Lier, Erik

Chorale Prelude, Op. 122, No. 8, "Es ist ein Ros' entsprungen,"* Brahms, Johannes/Fote: Jacobs, Arnold

Chorale Variations, "Jesu meine Freude," Kreines: Jacobs, Arnold

Darn That Dream, DeLange and Van Heusen: Callender, Red

Dead End, McDermot: Scandinavian Tuba Jazz

Deck the Halls, Wilder: Phillips, Harvey/Tuba-Christmas

Dedicated to the Blues, Callender: Callender, Red

'Deed I Do: Gannett, Dave

Deep Throb, Moschner, Pinguin: Moschner, Pinguin

Detournement Mineur, Goret, Didier: Steckar Elephant Tuba Horde

The Devil's Herald, Peasley, Richard: Phillips, Harvey

Dialogue für Tuba und Tonband, Piernik, Zdizislaw: Piernik, Zdizislaw

Dies Irae for tuba and piano, Langgaard, Rued: Arnsted, Jørgen Voight

Diversita Continua, Cohen, Michael: Hershko, Adi

Divertimento for Tuba Ensemble, Spears, Jared: Tennessee Technological University Tuba/Euphonium Ensemble

Divertimento No. 1 (tuba, string bass, percussion), Zonn, Paul: Perantoni, Daniel

Divertimento No. 2 in Bb, Mozart, Wolfgang Amadeus/Crespo, Hilgers, and Pilafian: Gerhard Meinl's Tuba Sextet

Divertissement for tuba and brass quartet, Barboteu, George: Hilgers, Walter

Diving Duck Blues, Estes, Sleepy John/Mahal: Johnson, Howard

Dona Nobis Pacem for tuba, piccolo, and piano, Ustvolskaya, Galina: LeClair, David

Don't Get Around Much Anymore, Ellington, Duke: Pilafian, Sam

Don't Monkey with It, Monsborough, Abe: Newberger, Eli

Don't Shoot the Banjo Player ('Cause We've Done It Already), Botschinsky, Allan: Van Lier, Erik

Double Concerto, Hackbarth, Glenn: Perantoni, Daniel

Double Concerto for Saxophone, Tuba and Winds, Hartley, Walter: Erickson, Martin

Double Portraits (The City) for trombone and tuba, Uber, David: Lind, Michael

Down by the Old Mill Stream, Taylor, Tell/Vaughan: Tubadours

Doxy, Rollins, Sonny: Draper, Ray

Drei Romanzen, Op. 94, Schumann, Robert: Cooley, Floyd

Dualismo for tuba and flute, Escovez, Fermin Ruiz: Mas, Vincente Navarro

Duet for Tenor Tuba and Bass Tuba, Croft: Megules, Karl

Duet No. 12 from "21 Distinctive Duets," Jones, Roger: University of Miami Tuba Ensemble

Durations, Feldman, Morton: Butterfield, Don

Dutch Suite for Bassoon and Tuba, Bach, P. D. Q.: Bishop, Ronald

The Easy Winners, Joplin, Scott/LeClair: The Contraband

Eclipse finale? for tuba and brass band, Meier, Jost: Baadsvik, Øystein

1812 Overture (excerpt), Tchaikovsky, Peter Ilyitch: Jacobs, Arnold

Eine kleine Nachtmusik, Mozart, Wolfgang Amadeus/Fletcher: Melton Tuba-Quartett

Eine kleine Schreckens Musik (A Little Fright Music), Mehlan, Keith: Monarch Tuba-Euphonium Quartet

El Capitan, Sousa, John Philip/Morris: British Tuba Quartet; Monarch Tuba-Euphonium Quartet

Elegy, Zinos, Frederick: Cummings, Barton

The Elephant and the Fly, Kling, H.: Phillips, Harvey

The Elephant Tango, Landes, B.: Bell, William

Eli's Coming, Nyro, Laura/Cherry: Tennessee Technological University Tuba/Euphonium Ensemble

Elite Syncopations, Joplin, Scott/Picher: British Tuba Quartet

Empty Streets, Draper, Ray: Draper, Ray

Encore Boz, Stevens, Thomas: Bobo, Roger

Encounters II for Solo Tuba, Kraft, William: Bobo, Roger; Baadsvik, Øystein

An English Folk Christmas, Buttery, Gary: United States Coast Guard Tuba-Euphonium Quartet

The Entertainer, Joplin, Scott/Self: Tennessee Tech Tuba-Euphonium Quintet; United States Armed Forces Tuba-Euphonium Ensemble

The Entertainer: Stewart, Bob

Epistrophy, Monk, Thelonius: Stewart, Bob

Eria, Creuze: LeLong, Fernand

Escenas Latinas, Crespo, Enrique: Hilgers, Walter

Escher's Sketches, Ross, Walter: Nelson, Mark

Essii's Dance, Draper, Ray: Draper, Ray

Estampie: Gay, Les

Et le Klaxon Retentit Derechef comme un Lézard Hongrois Enrhumé, Godard and Steckar: Steckar Tubapack

Etre ou ne pas Etre (monolog d'Hamlet) for tuba and three trombones, Tomasi, Henri: Jacobs, Arnold; Hanks, Toby

Euphonic Sounds, Joplin, Scott/Werden: Atlantic Tuba Quartet; British Tuba Quartet

Euphonics, O'Hara, Betty: Tennessee Technological University Tuba/Euphonium Ensemble

Everything I Have Is Yours, Adamson/B. Lane: Barber, John William (Bill)

Exigencies, Ruth, Matthew: Tennessee Technological University Tuba/Euphonium Ensemble

Expressions of Quietude: Stewart, Bob

Fancy Dances for Three Bass Tubas, Ross, Walter: New York Tuba Quartet

Fanfare No. 1, Taylor, Jeffery: Monarch Tuba-Euphonium Quartet

Fantaisie and Variations on the "Carnival of Venice," Arban, J. B.: Lind, Michael

Fantaisie and Variations on the "Carnival of Venice," Arban, J. B./Bobo: Bobo, Roger

Fantaisie and Variations on the "Carnival of Venice" (with band), Arban, J. B./Berry: Bobo, Roger

Fantasia a due, Reed, Alfred: United States Air Force Concert Band Tuba Section

Fantasia Breve, Cummings, Barton: Nelson, Mark

Fantasia di Concerto, Boccalari, E./Akers: Conner, Rex

Fantasie Original, Picchi, Ermanno/Mantia: Seward, Steven

Fantasiestücke, Op. 73, Schumann, Robert: Cooley, Floyd

Fantasy, Martino, Ralph: British Tuba Quartet; Monarch Tuba-Euphonium Quartet

Fantasy for Solo Tuba, Arnold, Malcom: Fletcher, John; Gourlay, James

Fantasy for Tuba and Piano, Konagaya, Soichi: Yasumoto, Hiroyuki

Fantasy in C Minor, Telemann, Georg Philipp: Hanks, Toby

Fantasy-Variations, Jager, Robert: Daniel, Robert N.

Fantezie Pentru Tuba si Pian, Dumitru, Ionel: Dumitru, Ionel

Farewell Blues, Schoebel, Mares, and Rappolo: Lehr, David "Red"

The Farewell Burn, Berg, Curt: Self, James

Fascinatin' Gershwin, Gershwin, George/Ferguson: British Tuba Quartet

Fat Cat, Mitchell: Callender, Red

The Favorite Rag, Joplin, Scott/Powell: British Tuba Quartet

Fidgety Feet, Gershwin, George: Matteson, Rich

Filidia, Draper, Ray: Draper, Ray

Fink Finster, Thingnäs, Frode: Scandinavian Tuba Jazz

First Dream of Light (tuba, piano, electronic ghost score), Subotnick, Morton: Bobo, Roger

First Landscape: Tafjord, Stein-Erik

First Line, Stewart, Bob: Stewart, Bob

The First Noel, Charlton: Tubadours

The First Noel, Wilder: Phillips, Harvey/TubaChristmas

Fishin' Blues, Thomas, Henry/Mahal: Johnson, Howard

Fishy Song, Wozniak, Doug: Davis, Ronald

Five Moods for Tuba Quartet, Schuller, Gunther: New York Tuba Quartet

Five Studies for Tuba Alone, Reck, David: Hanks, Toby

Flickers, Waldron, Mal: Draper, Ray

Flight of the Bumblebee, Rimsky-Korsakov, Nicholas/Fletcher: Fletcher, John

Flight of the Bumblebee, Rimsky-Korsakov, Nicholas/Gourlay: Gourlay, James

Flight of the Bumblebee, Rimsky-Korsakov, Nicholas/Wagner: Wagner, Michael

Flutes and Tuba: Gay, Les

Foggy Day, Gershwin, George: Callender, Red

Forowen 3 (tuba and piccolo), Smith, Glenn: Turk, John

42nd Street Selections, Dubin and Warren/Minard: British Tuba Quartet

Four Pieces for Tuba, Ziffrin, Marilyn J.: Cummings, Barton

The Four Seasons for tuba, percussion, strings, and stereo tape, Proto, Frank: Thornton, Michael

Four Shorts for Tuba and Piano, Largent, Edward: Turk, John

French Tuba in Los Angeles, Galliano, R.: Steckar, Marc

From the Shores of the Mighty Pacific, Clarke, Herbert L.: Hanks, Toby

Fugue in G Minor, Bach, Johann Sebastian/Berry: Tubadours

Fugue in G Minor, Bach, Johann Sebastian/Gray: British Tuba Quartet

Fugue in G Minor, Bach, Johann Sebastian/D. Schmidt: Gerhard Meinl's Tuba Sextet

Fum, Fum, Fum, Bewley: Phillips, Harvey/TubaChristmas

Funeral March for a Marionette, Gounod, Charles/Berry: Tubadours

Für H. S.: Unkrodt, Dietrich

The Further Adventures of Tubby the Tuba, Kleinsinger and Tripp: Johnson, John Thomas (Tommy); Phillips, Harvey

General Lavine—Eccentric, Debussy, Claude/Schaefer: Pokorny, Gene

Der Genesene an die Hoffnung, Wolf, Hugo: Hilgers, Walter

Gentle Old Sea, Wood, Philip D.: Draper, Ray

Georgia on My Mind, Carmichael, Hoagy: Pilafian, Sam

Georgia on My Mind, Carmichael, Hoagy/LeClair: The Contraband

Georgia on My Mind, Carmichael, Hoagy/Matteson: Matteson-Phillips TubaJazz Consort

Gershwin Medley, Gershwin, George/Sample: Tennessee Technological University Tuba/Euphonium Ensemble; United States Armed Forces Tuba-Euphonium Ensemble

Get Me to the Church on Time, Lerner, Alan Jay/Belsha: British Tuba Quartet

Gicael Mibbs, Emler, Andy: Steckar Elephant Tuba Horde

Gigue, Corelli, Archangelo: Phillips, Harvey

Gloustershire Wassail Song, Harclerode: Tubadours

Go Down Gamblin': Bargeron, Dave

Go Tell It on the Mountain, Wilder: Phillips, Harvey/TubaChristmas

God Rest Ye Merry Gentlemen, Vaughan: Tubadours

God Rest Ye Merry Gentlemen, Wilder: Phillips, Harvey/TubaChristmas

Godchild, Wallington, George: Barber, John William (Bill)

Going Up to the Country and Paint My Mailbox Blue: Johnson, Howard

Gone with the Wind, Wrubel/Magidson: Callender, Red

Good Christian Men Rejoice, Bewley: Phillips, Harvey/TubaChristmas

Good King Wenceslas, Harclerode: Tubadours

Good King Wenceslas, Wilder: Phillips, Harvey/Tuba-Christmas

Goodnight, Angeline, Blake, Eubie: Newberger, Eli

Grand Slam, Niehaus, Lennie: British Tuba Quartet

Greensleeves, Anonymous/Buttery: Atlantic Tuba Quartet; British Tuba Quartet
Greensleeves, Bewley: Phillips, Harvey/TubaChristmas
Gregory Is Here, Silver, Horace/Matteson: Matteson-Phillips TubaJazz Consort
Growing Up Together (euphonium and tuba duet), LeClair, David: The Contraband
G. S., Schiaffini, Giancarlo: Schiaffini, Giancarlo
Hades for two euphoniums and two tubas, Iannaccone, Anthony: University of Michigan Tuba Ensemble
Hail the Lord's Annointed, Vaughan: Tubadours
Die haltbare Graugans: Unkrodt, Dietrich
Hambone, Stewart, Bob: Stewart, Bob
Hands across the Sea, Sousa, John Philip/Werden: Northern Tuba Lights
Happiness, Draper, Ray: Draper, Ray
Harmonica—Music for Large Orchestra with Solo Tuba, Lachenmann: Nahatzki, Richard
Have Yourself a Merry Little Christmas, Martin, Blaine/Bewley: Phillips, Harvey/TubaChristmas
Heather on the Hill, Lerner, Alan Jay: Self, James
Heavy Metal, Lamb, Marvin: Tennessee Technological University Tuba/Euphonium Ensemble
Hefje Kati, Sykes: Sykes, Stephen
Heidentüblein, LeClair, David: The Contraband
Helix for Solo Tuba and Concert Band, Benson, Warren: Phillips, Harvey; Turk, John; Robinson, Jack
Hello Julius, Smith, Warren: Johnson, Howard
Help, Watkins, Doug: Draper, Ray
Here's That Rainy Day, Heusen, Van/Barton: British Tuba Quartet
Hey Mama, Traditional: Stewart, Bob
High Energy: Gay, Les
High Society, Steele and Melrose: Lehr, David "Red"; Palmer, Singleton
Hittin' the Ceiling: Tarto, Joe
Home, Wood, Philip D.: Draper, Ray
How Deep Is the Ocean, Berlin, Irving: Scandinavian Tuba Jazz
Howdy! Pegram, Wayne: Tennessee Technological University Tuba/Euphonium Ensemble; United States Armed Forces Tuba-Euphonium Ensemble
Humoresque, Dvořák, Anton: Piernik, Zdizislaw
Hungarian Melodies, Bach, Vincent: Seward, Steven
I Ain't Got Nobody, Graham and Williams: Newberger, Eli
I Can Swing a Sousa: Tafjord, Stein-Erik
I Can't Give You Anything But Love, Fields and McHugh: Lehr, David "Red"
I Found a New Baby, Palmer and Williams: Matteson, Rich; Pilafian, Sam
I Hadn't Anyone Til You, Draper, Ray: Draper, Ray
I Love You, Porter, Cole: Self, James
I Must Have That Man: Tarto, Joe
I Talk to the Trees, Lerner, Alan Jay: Draper, Ray
I Want a Little Girl, Mitchell: Callender, Red
If I Only Had a Brain, Arlen and Harburg: Pilafian, Sam
If You Ever Wanna, Trujillo, Tommy: Draper, Ray

Il Est Né, Harclerode: Tubadours
Il Ritorno, Diero/Ferguson: British Tuba Quartet
Il Viaggio 1 per tuba solo con pianoforte, Sikora, Elzbieta: Piernik, Zdizislaw
Illusion, Konagaya, Soichi: Tennessee Technological University Tuba/Euphonium Ensemble
Impromptu for Tuba, Barry, Darrol: Ferguson, Ken
In a Sentimental Mood, Ellington, Duke: Callender, Red
In the Hall of the Mountain King, Grieg, Edvard: Bell, William
Indiana, Henley, James: Pilafian, Sam; Lehr, David "Red"
Infant Holy, Kingsbury/Harclerode: Tubadours
Infernal Dream, Schiaffini, Giancarlo: Schiaffini, Giancarlo
Interlude No. 4, Botschinsky, Allan: Van Lier, Erik
Introduction and Dance, Barat, Joseph Eduoard: Bobo, Roger
Introduction and Dance, Barat, Joseph Eduoard/Phillips: Bobo, Roger
Introduction and Samba, Whitney: Erickson, Martin
Introduction to the Blues, Smith, Warren: Johnson, Howard
Invention No. 1 (flute and tuba), Bach, Johann Sebastian: Phillips, Harvey
It Came Upon a Midnight Clear, Willis/Harclerode: Tubadours
It Came Upon a Midnight Clear, Wilder: Phillips, Harvey/TubaChristmas
It Is Enough from "Elijah," Mendelssohn, Felix: Popiel, Peter
Jabba the Hutt from "Return of the Jedi," Williams, John: Pokorny, Gene; Schmitz, Chester
Jelly Bean Blues, Rainey and Arant: Newberger, Eli
Jesu, Joy of Man's Desiring, Bach, Johann Sebastian/Werden: British Tuba Quartet
Jhon, Come Kisse Me Now, Byrd, William/Winter: Atlantic Tuba Quartet; British Tuba Quartet
Jingle Bell Waltz, Vaughan, Rodger: Tubadours
Jitterbug Waltz, Waller, Thomas "Fats": Self, James
Joanna: Stewart, Bob
John, Ain't It Hard? Mahal, Taj: Johnson, Howard
The Jolly Farmer Goes to Town, Schumann, Robert/Bell: Bell, William
Le Jour ou les Tubas, Michel, Marc: Steckar Elephant Tuba Horde
Joy to the World, Handel, George Friderik: Phillips, Harvey/TubaChristmas
Jumbalaya, Williams, Hank: Pilafian, Sam
Just a Closer Walk with Thee, Boyle: Callender, Red
Just a Closer Walk with Thee, Garrett: Tennessee Technological University Tuba/Euphonium Ensemble
Just a Closer Walk with Thee, Traditional: Lehr, David "Red"
Just an Echo in the Valley: Tarto, Joe
Kanon: Unkrodt, Dietrich
Keepin' Out of Mischief Now, Waller, Thomas "Fats": Gannett, Dave
Kilo, Brown, Tom: Self, James

The King's Hunt, Bull, John/Howard: British Tuba Quartet

Kirkeby and Edvard Munch (in 12 movements), Christiansen, Henning: Anderson, Hans

Komm Süsser Tod, Bach, Johann Sebastian/Sauter: Megules, Karl; Phillips, Harvey/TubaChristmas; Tennessee Technological University Tuba/Euphonium Ensemble

Konzert für Tuba und Orchester, Gruner, Joachim: Unkrodt, Dietrich

Korn Blues, Hermann, Heinz: Scandinavian Tuba Jazz

Kubismus 502, Botschinsky, Allan: Van Lier, Erik

The Lady in Blue, Botschinsky, Allan: Van Lier, Erik

Lament, Smith, Warren: Johnson, Howard

Lamento, Beach, Bennie: Conner, Rex; LeBlanc, Robert

Landscape for Tuba and Strings, Lundquist, Torbjørn Iwan: Lind, Michael

Largo al Factotum, Rossini, Gioacchino/Roberts: Crowther, Shaun; Gourlay, James

Last Landscape: Tafjord, Stein-Erik

Latin Fantasy, Taylor, Mark: Arwood, Jeffrey

Lazy Lullaby, Little, Donald: Davis, Ronald

Lento, Holmes, Paul: Conner, Rex; Davis, Ronald; LeBlanc, Robert

Less Than That: Tarto, Joe

Let My Children Hear Music: Stewart, Bob

Let My People Go, Draper and Aplan: Draper, Ray

Let There Be Peace on Earth, Miller, Sy and Jackson, Jill: Porter, William D. (David)

The Liberation of Sisyphus, Stevens, John: Bobo, Roger

Liebesfreud, Kreisler, Fritz/Yasumoto: Yasumoto, Hiroyuki

Lieder eines Fahrenden Gessellen, Mahler, Gustav/Perantoni and Yutzy: Perantoni, Daniel

Light Blue, Monk, Thelonius: Stewart, Bob

Limehouse Blues, Braham and Furber: Matteson, Rich; Pilafian, Sam

Lina Blues, Smith, Jabbo: Newberger, Eli

Little Madrigal for Big Horns, Hastings, Ross: University of Miami Tuba Ensemble

Little Ole Softy, Matteson, Rich: Matteson-Phillips TubaJazz Consort

Little Suede Shoes, Parker, Charlie: Pilafian, Sam

Lohengrin (Prelude Act III, excerpt), Wagner, Richard: Jacobs, Arnold

The Londonderry Air, Garrett: United States Armed Forces Tuba-Euphonium Ensemble

The Londonderry Air, Mehlan: Monarch Tuba-Euphonium Quartet

Louisiana, Razof, Johnson: Pilafian, Sam

Love Story (und dann ging's heiss hier), Moschner, Pinguin: Moschner, Pinguin

Love Waltz, Botschinsky, Allan: Van Lier, Erik

Lucerne Song, Howarth: Fletcher, John

Lucky Southern, Jarrett, Keith/Matteson: Matteson-Phillips TubaJazz Consort

Lullaby of Birdland, Shearing, George/Perry: Tennessee Technological University Tuba/Euphonium Ensemble

Lush Life, Callender: Callender, Red

Lute Dances, Anonymous/Baker: British Tuba Quartet

Lyric Poem, Frank, Marcel G.: United States Armed Forces Tuba-Euphonium Ensemble; University of Miami Tuba Ensemble

Mack the Knife, Weill, Kurt: Pilafian, Sam

Magna, Mitchell: Callender, Red

Majobiwomo, Moschner, Pinguin: Moschner, Pinguin

Makin' Whoopee, Donalson and Kahn: Pilafian, Sam

Malagueña, Lecuona, Ernesto/Morris: Tennessee Technological University Tuba/Euphonium Ensemble

Malta for Tuba and Tape, Hiller, Lejaren: Cummings, Barton

Manhattan Suite, Stevens, John: University of Michigan Tuba and Euphonium Ensemble

March, Watz, F. Melton: Gerhard Meinl's Tuba Sextet

March of the Three Kings, Harclerode: Tubadours

March of the Toy Soldiers, Herbert, Victor/Vaughan: Tubadours

March—Overture from "Nutcracker," Tchaikovsky, Peter Ilyitch/Charlton: Tubadours

Marche Militaire Française, Saint-Saëns, Camille/Cohen: United States Armed Forces Tuba-Euphonium Ensemble

Märchenbilder (Pictures of Fairyland), Op. 113, Schumann, Robert: Cooley, Floyd

Marguerite: Tarto, Joe

Maria Alm, Bologneisi, J.: Steckar Tubapack

Mars from "The Planets," Holst, Gustav: Jacobs, Arnold

Maryland, My Maryland: Palmer, Singleton

Maskemåned for trumpet and tuba, Op.148, Christiansen, Henning: Anderson, Hans

The Masterpiece, Mouret, Jean Joseph/Mancini: Johnson, John Thomas (Tommy)

Mazurcă, Wieniawski: Dumitru, Ionel

Mazurka No. 49 in A Minor, Op. 68, No. 2 Chopin, Frederic/Abrams: Hoffnung, Gerard; United States Air Force Concert Tuba Section

Mediterranean Rondo, Levy, Yehuda: Hershko, Adi

The Melody Shop, King, Karl L./Werden: United States Armed Forces Tuba-Euphonium Ensemble

Meltdown, Sass, Jonathon: Gerhard Meinl's Tuba Sextet

Memories of You, Blake, Eubie: Pokorny, Gene

Mess Around, Draper, Ray: Draper, Ray

Metamorphosis, Blythe, Arthur: Stewart, Bob

Micro, Reinhardt, Django: Pilafian, Sam

Midnight Realities, Powell, Morgan: Perantoni, Daniel

Midnight Variations for tuba and tape, Ross, Walter: Cummings, Barton

Militärmarsch, Schubert, Franz Peter/LeClair: The Contraband

Miniature Jazz Suite, Garrett, James: Tennessee Technological University Tuba/Euphonium Ensemble

Miniature Jazz Suite, Niehaus, Lennie: Melton Tuba-Quartett

Miniatures for 4 Four Valve Instruments, Hartley, Walter: Atlantic Tuba Quartet

Minor Dream, Draper, Ray: Draper, Ray

Minuet, Beethoven, Ludwig: Conner, Rex

Minuet, Boccherini, Luigi: Piernik, Zdzislaw

Minuet, Paderewski, Ignacy Jan: Piernik, Zdzislaw

Minute Waltz, Chopin, Frederic/Mead: British Tuba Quartet

Mirage, Waldron, Mal: Draper, Ray

Mississippi Mud, Barris and Cavanaugh: Matteson, Rich

Mixed Doubles for trumpet, tuba, violin, and contrabass, Liptak, David: Kaenzig, Fritz

Molloy, Cugny, Laurent: Steckar Elephant Tuba Horde

Mon Coeur se Recommende à Vous, Di Lasso, Orlando/Robinson: British Tuba Quartet

Monads: Lewis, George

Monkey Chant: Gay, Les

Monolog No. 9 for Unaccompanied Tuba, Koch, Erland von: Lind, Michael

Mood Indigo—Satin Doll, Ellington, Duke/Vaughan: Tubadours

Moon Mist Blues, Callender, Red: Callender, Red

Moondance, Morrison, Van/Kile: Tennessee Technological University Tuba/Euphonium Ensemble

Moondance, Stevens, John: United States Air Force Concert Tuba Section

Moose Blue, Johnson, Bunk: Newberger, Eli

Morceau de Concerto (III, Allegro non troppo), Saint-Saëns, Camille: Piernik, Zdzislaw

The Morning Song, Kellaway, Roger: Arnsted, Jørgen Voight; Bobo, Roger

Moto Perpetuo, Paganini, Niccolo/Bell: Bell, William; Jacobs, Arnold; Phillips, Harvey

Move, Best, Denzil Decosta: Barber, John William (Bill)

Move, Best, Denzil Decosta/Buttery: Atlantic Tuba Quartet

Mummers (Dance Grotesque), Merle, John: Bell, William

Music for Tuba Ensemble, Rogers, Thomas: University of Miami Tuba Ensemble

Music 4 Tubas, Stevens, John: New York Tuba Quartet

Music Written for Monterey, Johnson, Howard: Johnson, Howard

Muskrat Ramble, Gilbert and Ory: Palmer, Singleton

Muzyka for Tuba Solo, Dobrowski, A.: Piernik, Zdzislaw

My Best Girl: Tarto, Joe

My Favorite Things, Rodgers, Richard/Cherry: Tennessee Technological University Tuba/Euphonium Ensemble

My Funny Valentine, Rodgers and Hart: Self, James

My Mother Is Here: Gay, Les

Nabucco Overture (excerpt), Verdi, Giuseppe: Jacobs, Arnold

Nancy with the Laughing Face, Van Heusen and Silvers/Smith, A.: Arwood, Jeffrey

Nature Boy, Ahbez, Eden/Cherry: Tennessee Technological University Tuba/Euphonium Ensemble

New England Reveries, Corwell, Neal: Nelson, Mark

New Orleans, Carmichael, Hoagy: Pilafian, Sam

New Stuff, Brown, Tom: Self, James

Nice Day, Collette, Buddy: Callender, Red

Night Lights, Brown, Tom: Self, James

A Nightingale Sang in Berkley Square, Sherwin, Manning/Mehlan: Monarch Tuba-Euphonium Quartet

A Nightingale Sang in Berkley Square, Sherwin, Manning/Smalley: British Tuba Quartet

Nocturnes, Powell, Morgan: Perantoni, Daniel

Non più Andrai from "Le Nozze di Figaro," Mozart, Wolfgang Amadeus: Fletcher, John

Nonet, Stewart, Bob: Stewart, Bob

Noreen's Nocturn, Peterson, Oscar/J. Petersen: Matteson-Phillips TubaJazz Consort

Nostalgia Medley, Sample, Steve: Tennessee Technological University Tuba/Euphonium Ensemble

Notater for three trombones and tuba, Holmboe, Vagn: Arnsted, Jørgen Voight

Notturno, Rimsky-Korsakov, Nicholas: British Tuba Quartet

Now Hear This, Dempsey, Raymond: Monarch Tuba-Euphonium Quartet

Nun komm der Heiden Heiland, Bach, Johann Sebastian: Hilgers, Walter

Nutty, Monk, Thelonius: Stewart, Bob

O Come, O Come, Emmanuel, Vaughan: Tubadours

O Come, O Come, Emmanuel, Wilder: Phillips, Harvey/TubaChristmas

O Come All Ye Faithful, Wilder: Phillips, Harvey/TubaChristmas

O Come Little Children, Schulz, Heinrich/Harclerode: Tubadours

O Du mein holder Abendstern from "Tannhäuser," Wagner, Richard: Fletcher, John

O Isis and Osiris, Mozart, Wolfgang Amadeus: Bell, William; Phillips, Harvey

O Little Town of Bethlehem, Wilder: Phillips, Harvey/TubaChristmas

O Mensch bewein' dein Sünde gross, BWV 622, Bach, Johann Sebastian/Hilgers: Hilgers, Walter

O Sanctissumus, Harclerode: Tubadours

O Tannenbaum, Harclerode: Tubadours

O Welt, ich muss dich lassen, Anonymous/Funderburk: United States Air Force Concert Band Tuba Section

October Sunshine, Botschinsky, Allan: Van Lier, Erik

Ode to Low Brass, Butts, Carrol: Megules, Karl

Oh, Daddy: Lehr, David "Red"

Oh Little Town of Bethlehem, Redner/Vaughan: Tubadours

Ol' Man River, Kern, Jerome: Pilafian, Sam

Ol' Rockin' Chair's Got Me, Carmichael, Hoagy: Gannett, Dave

Ola, O che bon eccho, Di Lasso, Orlando/Pilafian: Gerhard Meinl's Tuba Sextet

The Old Rugged Cross, Brennard, George/Arwood: Arwood, Jeffrey

Oleo, Rollins, Sonny: Draper, Ray

Oleo, Rollins, Sonny/Matteson: Matteson-Phillips TubaJazz Consort

Omaggi e Fantasie, Baker, Claude: Randolph, David

On a Slow Boat to China, Loesser, Frank: Gannett, Dave

On My Own from "Les Miserables," Schoenberg, C. M./Mead: British Tuba Quartet

On the Sunny Side of the Street, Fields and McHugh: Gannett, Dave

One Room Country Shack, Hooker, John Lee/ Clayton-Thomas: Bargeron, Dave

Onyx Club Review: Tarto, Joe

Original Rags: Lehr, David "Red"

Orpheus in the Underworld, Offenbach, Jacques/ Fletcher: Northern Tuba Lights

Out of the Depths, Dodson, John: Tennessee Technological University Tuba/Euphonium Ensemble

Overture Miniature from "Nutcracker," Tchaikovsky, Peter Ilyitch: Fletcher, John

Overture to Russlan and Ludmila, Glinka, Michael/ Smalley: British Tuba Quartet

Overture to the "Barber of Seville," Rossini, Gioacchino/Kile: United States Armed Forces Tuba-Euphonium Ensemble

Overture to the "Marriage of Figaro," Mozart, Wolfgang Amadeus/Fabrizio: Monarch Tuba-Euphonium Quartet

Overture to the "Marriage of Figaro," Mozart, Wolfgang Amadeus/Ferguson: British Tuba Quartet

Overture to the "Marriage of Figaro," Mozart, Wolfgang Amadeus/Gottschalk: University of Michigan Tuba and Euphonium Ensemble; United States Armed Forces Tuba-Euphonium Ensemble

Parable for Solo Tuba, Op. 147, Persichetti, Vincent: Nelson, Mark

Partita—Polacca, Rosler, J. J./D. Schmidt: Gerhard Meinl's Tuba Sextet

Partita in A minor for Flute Alone, Bach, Johann Sebastian: Pokorny, Gene

Pat-A-Pan, Bewley: Phillips, Harvey/TubaChristmas

Paul's Pal, Draper, Ray: Draper, Ray

Pavane pour une enfante défunte, Ravel, Maurice: Pokorny, Gene

Pavanne from the "Latin America Suite," Gould, Morton/Woo: University of Miami Tuba Ensemble

Peacherine Rag, Joplin, Scott: Pilafian, Sam

The Peacocks, Rowles, Jimmy: Self, James

Peggy's Blue Skylight, Mingus, Charlie: Self, James

Pennies from Heaven, Burke and Johnston: Gannett, Dave

Perpetual Motion, Cui, César: Bobo, Roger

Petit Caprice in the Style of Offenbach, Rossini, Gioacchino/Davis: Monarch Tuba-Euphonium Quartet

Piacer d'Amor, Martini, J. P. E./Yodo: Yasumoto, Hiroyuki

Picture of Dorian Blue, Gale, Jack: Self, James

Pièce en forme de habanera, Ravel, Maurice: Dowling, Eugene

Piernikiana for Solo Tuba, Szalonek, W.: Piernik, Zdizislaw

Pièta, Signora, Stradella, Alessandro: Megules, Karl

Piltdown Fragments for tuba and tape, Ross, Walter: Cummings, Barton

The Pink Panther, Mancini, Henry/Krush: British Tuba Quartet; Melton Tuba-Quartett; Northern Tuba Lights

Poème, Camphouse, Mark: Arwood, Jeffrey

Pompola, Martin, Carroll: Davis, Ronald

Poobah the Tuba, Wilder, Alec: Bell, William

Pop Suite, Frackenpohl, Arthur: British Tuba Quartet; Megules, Karl

Pop Suite (last movement), Frackenpohl, Arthur: British Tuba Quartet

Pop Suite for Barituba Ensemble, Frackenpohl, Arthur: University of Miami Tuba Ensemble

Power for four tubas, Stevens, John: Northern Tuba Lights; Stevens, John

Powerful: Gay, Les

Praeludium, Hilgers, Walter: Gerhard Meinl's Tuba Sextet

Prélude à l'après midi d'un faune, Debussy, Claude: Pokorny, Gene

Prelude in C # Minor, Gershwin, George: Newberger, Eli

Preludium, Bach, Johann Sebastian/Sabourin: Northern Tuba Lights

Priestess, Harper, Billy: Stewart, Bob

Primrose Lane, Boyle: Callender, Red

Projekt für Tuba und Tonband, Schäffer, Boguslaw: Piernik, Zdizislaw

Puttin' on the Ritz, Berlin, Irving/Gout: British Tuba Quartet

Quand le Tuba valse à Paris, Bologneisi, J.: Steckar, Marc

Quartet for Brass, Ramsoe, Emilio Wilhelm/Buttery: British Tuba Quartet; United States Coast Guard Tuba-Euphonium Quartet

Quartet for Brass (third movement), Ramsoe, Emilio Wilhelm/Buttery: United States Navy Band Tuba-Euphonium Quartet

Quartet for Low Brass, Bulla, Stephen: British Tuba Quartet; United States Navy Band Tuba-Euphonium Quartet

Quartet for Tubas, Holmes, Paul: University of Michigan Tuba and Euphonium Ensemble; British Tuba Quartet

Quartet for Tubas, Payne, Frank Lynn: Melton Tuba-Quartett; University of Miami Tuba Ensemble; University of Michigan Tuba and Euphonium Ensemble

Quartet No. 4 (Allegro molto), Ramsoe, Emilio Wilhelm/Buttery: Atlantic Tuba Quartet

Quatre Chansons, Dempsey: British Tuba Quartet; Monarch Tuba-Euphonium Quartet

A Question of Summer for harp and tuba, Childs, Barney: Hammond, Ivan

Quintet for Brass (Mvt. III, "Tuba Showpiece"), Wilder, Alec: Phillips, Harvey

Quintet for Tubas, Tarlow, Lawrence: Megules, Karl

Radiant Pathway, Condon, Leslie: Patterson, Graham, and Stokes, David

Ragtime Dance, Joplin, Scott/Werden: United States Navy Band Tuba-Euphonium Quartet

Ragtime Rosie: Lehr, David "Red"

Rakoczy (Hungarian) March from "Damnation of Faust" (excerpt), Berlioz, Hector: Jacobs, Arnold

The Raven and the First Men, Rollin, Robert: Turk, John

Ready & Able: Pilafian, Sam

Reciprocals II for Two Tubas, Birchall, Steven: Trice, Jerry

Reflections: Stewart, Bob

Reflections on a Park Bench, Beale, David: Tennessee Technological University Tuba/Euphonium Ensemble

Reincarnation of a Love Bird: Tafjord, Stein-Erik

Rhythm Futur, Rheinhart, Django: Pilafian, Sam

Ricercar for Solo Tuba, Gabrieli, Domenico/R. W. Morris: Davis, Ronald; McKee, Edward R.

Riverboat Shuffle: Matteson, Rich

Rock, Raph, Alan: McKee, Edward R.

Rocked in the Cradle of the Deep, Rollinson, T. H.: Lawhern, Tim

Romance, Elgar, Edward: Dowling, Eugene

Romanian Dance No. 2, Dumitru, Ionel: Bobo, Roger

Ronde and Saltarelle "Pour Quoy," Susato, Tielman/ Winter: Atlantic Tuba Quartet

Rondo, Bach, Johann Sebastian/Howard: British Tuba Quartet

Rondo, Hook, J./Garrett: British Tuba Quartet

Rondo, Mouret, Jean Joseph/Self: Tubadours

Rondo Allegro (tuba with brass quintet), Capuzzi, Antonio/Self: Self, James

Rondo in Eb Major, K371, Mozart, Wolfgang Amadeus: Piernik, Zdzislaw

Rouge, Lewis, John: Barber, John William (Bill)

Rouleaux de Printemps, Steckar, Franck: Steckar Elephant Tuba Horde

'Round Midnight, Monk, Williams, and Hanighen: Self, James

Roundarounds, Arbel, Chaya: Hershko, Adi

Row Row Rosie: Tarto, Joe

Royal Garden Blues, Williams and Williams: Lehr, David "Red"

Rumpole of the Bailey, Horovitz, Joseph: British Tuba Quartet

Saint Louis Blues, Handy, W. C./Holcombe: Melton Tuba-Quartett

Sakura Sakura, Traditional/Yamamoto: Yasumoto, Hiroyuki

Salty Sailor Tunes: Tarto, Joe

Samba Beach, Williams, Mason: Gannett, Dave

Samba Loco, Thingnäs, Frode: Scandinavian Tuba Jazz

Sambe Guitana, Mendez, Rafael: Sykes, Steven

Santa Claus Is Coming to Town, Gillespie/Vaughan: Tubadours

Santa Wants a Tuba for Christmas, Bewley, Norlan: Phillips, Harvey/TubaChristmas

Sareebar for Tuba and Percussion, Boyadjian, Hayg: Pilafian, Sam

Satin Doll, Ellington, Duke/Vaughan: Tubadours

Saturnalis, Kupferman, Meyer: Bobo, Roger

The Satyr, Nielsen, Hans Peter: Anonymous

Sax-Machine, Moschner, Pinguin: Moschner, Pinguin

Scenes from Childhood, Op. 15, Schumann, Robert/ Self: Self, James

Scherzando for Tubular Octet, Knox, Charles: Tennessee Technological University Tuba/Euphonium Ensemble

Scherzo, Golland, John: Sykes, Stephen

Science Fiction, Gasner, Moshe: Hershko, Adi

Sea Tubas, Minerd: Northern Tuba Lights

Second Horn Concerto, Strauss, Richard: Seward, Steven

Secrets, McDaniel, Ernie: Self, James

Selected Movements from Sonatas for Flute, Handel, George Friderik: Phillips, Harvey

Selections from 42nd Street, Durban and Warren/Minard: British Tuba Quartet

Semper Fidelis, Sousa, John Philip/Morris: British Tuba Quartet

Sentier de Nuit, Vigneron, Louis: Steckar Elephant Tuba Horde

Serenade, Schubert, Franz Peter: Bobo, Roger; Piernik, Zdzislaw

Serenade for Ten Wind Instruments, Persichetti, Vincent: United States Coast Guard Tuba-Euphonium Quartet

Serenade for tuba and piano, Schmidt, William: Conner, Rex; Johnson, John Thomas (Tommy)

Serenade for Tubas, Tchaikovsky, Peter Ilyitch/ O'Conner: Tennessee Technological University Tuba/Euphonium Ensemble

Serenade from Sonatine for Bass Saxhorn and Piano, Castérède, Jacques: Pokorny, Gene

Serenade No. 12 for Solo Tuba, Persichetti, Vincent: Phillips, Harvey

Sextet: Lewis, George

Shadowgraph 5: Lewis, George

Shake It Down, Williams and Urquhart: Newberger, Eli

A Short Suspense Story, Rufeisen, Arie: Hershko, Adi

Sieben Miniaturen für Vier Tuban, Kochan, Gunter: Self, James

Siegfried (excerpts), Wagner, Richard: Cooley, Floyd

Signals for trumpet, tuba, and brass choir, Reynolds, Verne: Bobo, Roger

S'il vous plait: Barber, John William

Silent Night, Gruber, Franz: Phillips, Harvey/Tuba-Christmas

Since You've Asked, Collins, Judy/Buttery: Atlantic Tuba Quartet

Sine Nomine, Kilon, Moshe: Hershko, Adi

Sinfonia III, Bach, Johann Sebastian/Self: Self, James

Six Studies in English Folksong, Vaughan Williams, Ralph: Dowling, Eugene; Pokorny, Gene

Sleeping Giants, Niehaus, Lennie: The Contraband

Sob Sister Sadie: Tarto, Joe

Sobbin' Blues, Kassel and Stitzel: Newberger, Eli

Social Studies: McIntyre, Earl

Soft Platonicism: Stewart, Bob

Solace, Joplin, Scott: Gannett, Dave

Somebody's Samba, Aldcroft, Randy: Self, James

Someone to Watch over Me, Gershwin, George: Pilafian, Sam

Sometimes I Feel Like a Motherless Child, Traditional: Stewart, Bob

Sonata, Hartley, Walter: LeBlanc, Robert

Sonata, Sibbing, Robert: Perantoni, Daniel

Sonata Capricciosa, Op. 81, Takács, Jenö: Randolph, David

Sonata Concertante for solo tuba and brass quintet, Gaathaug, Morten: Baadsvik, Øystein

Sonata for Bass Tuba and Piano, Beversdorf, Thomas: LeBlanc, Robert

Sonata for Bass Tuba and Piano, Hindemith, Paul: Augustin, Rudiger; Baadsvik, Øystein; Bobo, Roger; Fletcher, John; Georgie, Gerhard; Hoppert, Manfred; Lind, Michael; Perantoni, Daniel; Pokorny, Gene; Torchinsky, Abe; Turk, John

Sonata for French Horn, Tuba and Piano, Wilder, Alec: Phillips, Harvey

Sonata for Solo Tuba, Kranowski, A.: Piernik, Zdzislaw

Sonata for Tuba and Piano, George, Thom Ritter: Perantoni, Daniel; Randolph, David

Sonata for Tuba and Piano, Madsen, Trygve: Baadsvik, Øystein; Bobo, Roger

Sonata for Tuba and Piano, Sivelov, Niklas: Baadsvik, Øystein

Sonata for Tuba and Piano, White, Donald: Kaenzig, Fritz

Sonata for Tuba and String Quartet, Baker, David N.: Phillips, Harvey

Sonata in C Major, Op.1 No. 7 for tuba and organ, Handel, George Friderik/Hilgers: Hilgers, Walter

Sonata in E♭ Major, Bach, Johann Sebastian: Cooley, Floyd

Sonata in F Major for Tuba and Piano, Marcello, Benedetto: Lind, Michael

Sonata in F Minor, Telemann, Georg Philipp: Seward, Steven

Sonata in G Major, Handel, George Friderik: Pokorny, Gene

Sonata in G Major for tuba and piano (*Horn Sonata in F*), Beethoven, Ludwig/Proto: Thornton, Michael

Sonata in G Minor (I Prelude, II Courant), Eccles, Henry: Piernik, Zdzislaw

Sonata No. 1 for Tuba and Piano, Wilder, Alec: Phillips, Harvey

Sonata No. 4 in C, Bach, Johann Sebastian/Dowling/Norman: Dowling, Eugene

Sonata No. 5 in D Minor, Galliard, Johann Ernst: Bobo, Roger

Sonata-Fantasia, Calabro, Louis: Nelson, Mark

Sonate II, Bach, Johann Sebastian: Hilgers, Walter

Sonatina, Hartley, Walter: Popiel, Peter

Sonatina, Sear, Walter: Davis, Ronald; Megules, Karl

Sonatina for Trumpet and Tuba, Iannocone, Anthony: Smith, J. R.

Sonatina for Tuba and Piano, Op. 57, Koetsier, Jan: Duga, Jan Z; Hoppert, Manfred

Sonatina for tuba and piano, Stevens, Halsey: Perantoni, Daniel; Randolph, David; Self, James

Sonatine for Basstuba and Piano, Glass: Fletcher, John

Song and Dance for euphonium, tuba, and band, Frackenpohl, Arthur: Porter, William D. (David)

Song and Humoreske, Sinigaglia, Leone: Bobo, Roger

Song for Carol, Wilder, Alec: Phillips, Harvey

Song of the Flea, Mussorgsky, Modest: Fletcher, John

Song of the New World: Stewart, Bob

Song of the Wanderer, Moret, Neil: Tarto, Joe; Newberger, Eli

Sonority Study for Three Tubas, Butterfield, Don: United States Air Force Concert Band Tuba Section

Sonoro for horn, bass horn, and piano, Kellaway, Roger: Bobo, Roger

Sophisticated Lady, Ellington, Duke/Callender: Callender, Red

The Sound of the Wasp, Wilson, Phil: Matteson, Rich

Sousa Surrenders, Garbáge, Pierre: United States Armed Forces Tuba-Euphonium Ensemble

South, Charles, Moten, and Hayes: Matteson, Rich

Space Blossoms, Betti, Dino: Schiaffini, Giancarlo

Spain, Corea, Chick: Tennessee Technological University Tuba/Euphonium Ensemble

Speak Low, Weill, Kurt/Nash: Callender, Red

Sphinx: Tafjord, Stein-Erik

Spiralen: Unkrodt, Dietrich

Spiritual Jazz Suite, Niehaus: British Tuba Quartet

Splinters, Stevens, John: Stevens, John

Spoofy, Matteson, Rich: Matteson-Phillips TubaJazz Consort

St. Anne's Fugue, Bach, Johann Sebastian/Beckman: United States Armed Forces Tuba-Euphonium Ensemble

St. Louis Blues, Handy, W. C.: Lehr, David "Red"; Palmer, Singleton

Stabillo Steckardello, Steckar, Franck: Steckar Elephant Tuba Horde

Ständchen, Schubert, Franz Peter/LeClair: The Contraband

Stars and Stripes Forever, Sousa, John Philip/Weldon: University of Miami Tuba Ensemble

Stars and Stripes Forever, Sousa, John Philip/Werden: Atlantic Tuba Quartet; Northern Tuba Lights

Starts Same But Beautiful: Gay, Les

Steal Away, Traditional/Trippet and Howard: British Tuba Quartet

Steppin' in Society: Tarto, Joe

Stompin' at the Savoy, Sampson, Recaf, Foodman, and Webb: Matteson-Phillips TubaJazz Consort

Stravinsky: Gay, Les

Subi La Nas Alturas, Bell, Kelvyn: Stewart, Bob

Substructure, Taylor, Coleridge: Johnson, Howard

Substructures for ten tubas, Gottschalk, Arthur: University of Michigan Tuba Ensemble

Sugar, Young and Meyer: Gannett, Dave

Suite à suivre, Steckar: Steckar Tubapack

Suite Concertante, Russell, Armand: Cooley, Floyd

Suite for Flute and Tuba, Hartley, Walter: Phillips, Harvey

Suite for Low Brass, Lyon, Max J.: Atlantic Tuba Quartet

Suite for Tuba, Haddad, Don: Conner, Rex; Davis, Ronald

Suite for Tuba and Piano, Butts, Carrol: Cummings, Barton

Suite for II, Stevens, John: Stevens, John

Suite for Unaccompanied Tuba, Hartley, Walter: Conner, Rex; Fletcher, John; Popiel, Peter

Suite in Bb Minor for Flute, Bach, Johann Sebastian: Seward, Steven

Suite in Miniature (first and third movements), Catelinet, Philip: Megules, Karl

Suite No. 1 for Solo Tuba, Stevens, John: Stevens, John

Suite No. 1 for Tuba and Brass Quintet (Effie), Wilder, Alec/Hilgers: Hilgers, Walter

Suite No. 1 for Tuba and Piano (Effie), Wilder, Alec: Bobo, Roger; Lind, Michael; Phillips, Harvey

Suite No. 1 in G Major for Solo Cello (Minuet, Courante), Bach, Johann Sebastian: Fletcher, John

Suite No. 2 (Jessie), Wilder, Alec: Phillips, Harvey

Suite No. 2 for French Horn and Tuba, Wilder, Alec: Phillips, Harvey

Suite No. 3 (Little Harvey), Wilder, Alec: Phillips, Harvey

Suite No. 4 (Thomas), Wilder, Alec: Phillips, Harvey

Suite No. 5 (Ethan Ayer), Wilder, Alec: Phillips, Harvey

Summertime, Gershwin, George: Matteson-Phillips TubaJazz Consort

The Sun Has Got His Hat On, Butler, Gay, Sparke: Crowther, Shaun

Surinam, Traditional: Stewart, Bob

Swannee River, Foster, Stephen: Matteson, Rich

Sweet Disposition, Snow, Phoebe: Johnson, Howard

Sweet Georgia Brown, Bernie, Casey, and Pickard: Matteson, Rich; Palmer, Singleton; Pilafian, Sam

Sweet Georgia Brown, Bernie, Casey, and Pickard/Garrett: Tennessee Technological University Tuba/Euphonium Ensemble

Sweet Georgia Brown, Pinkard/Sellers: Perantoni, Daniel

Sweet Georgia Brown Sweet, Stewart, Bob: Stewart, Bob

Sweet Mama Janisse: Johnson, Howard

Swing Low, Kresin, Willibald: The Contraband

Swingin' Little Swiss Tuba . . . Cuckoo-clock, Janin, D.: Steckar, Marc

Swinging at the Palace: Stewart, Bob

Swiss Air, Newsome, Roy: Crowther, Shaun

Symphony No. 2 (fifth movement excerpt), Mahler, Gustav: Jacobs, Arnold

Symphony No. 3 (first movement excerpt), Mahler, Gustav: Jacobs, Arnold

Symphony No. 4 (first movement, excerpt), Bruckner, Anton: Jacobs, Arnold

Symphony No. 6 (fourth movement excerpt), Tchaikovsky, Peter Ilyitch: Jacobs, Arnold

Symphony No. 8 (fourth movement, excerpt), Bruckner, Anton: Jacobs, Arnold

Syrinx, Debussy, Claude: Self, James

Tabu for Tuba, Downey, John: Phillips, Harvey

Take the Stairs, Berg, Curt: Self, James

Tales of the Cultural Revolution, Holmes, Brian: Fritze, Gregory

Tangerine, Mercer, Johnny: Gannett, Dave

Tannhäuser Overture (excerpts), Wagner, Richard: Jacobs, Arnold

Tapestry III, De Mars, James: Perantoni, Daniel

Teddy Bears' Picnic, Bratton, John W./Roberts: Sibley, Graham

Tema Cantabile con Piernicazioni per tuba universale e pianoforte, Zajaczek, Roman: Piernik, Zdizislaw

That's A-Plenty, Gilbert and Pollack: Lehr, David "Red"

Them Basses, Huffine, G. H.: United States Armed Forces Tuba-Euphonium Ensemble

Them There Eyes, Pinkard, Casey, and Tauber: Pilafian, Sam

Theme and Variation on the "Blue Bells of Scotland," Pryor, Arthur: Pokorny, Gene; Seward, Steven

Theme and Variations, Paganini, Niccolo: Dumitru, Ionel

They Didn't Believe Me, Kern, Jerome/Holcomb: British Tuba Quartet

Things Ain't What They Used to Be, Ellington, Duke/Matteson: Matteson-Phillips TubaJazz Consort

Third: Gay, Les

Three Easy Pieces, Hindemith, Paul: Hanks, Toby

Three Essays for Solo Tuba, Penn, William: Turk, John

Three Folksongs for Four Brass, Denson, Frank: Gerhard Meinl's Tuba Sextet

Three for One, Wyatt, Scott: Perantoni, Daniel

Three Milongas, Crespo, Enrique: Gerhard Meinl's Tuba Sextet

Three Miniatures for tuba and piano, Plog, Anthony: Bobo, Roger; Perantoni, Daniel

Three Moods, Boone, Dan: University of Miami Tuba Ensemble

Three Mythical Sketches for Four Tubas, Iannaccone, Anthony: University of Michigan Tuba Ensemble

Three Pieces, Jae Eun Ha: Cummings, Barton

Three Romanzes, Schumann, Robert: Cooley, Floyd

Three Sixteenth Century Flemish Pieces, Singleton: Monarch Tuba-Euphonium Quartet

Three Songs, Rachmaninoff, Sergei: Pokorny, Gene

Thunder and Lightning, Stevens, John: Stevens, John

Tia Juanna Man, Jones-Dickerson: Newberger, Eli

Tico-Tico, Abreu, Zequinha/Smith, A.: Arwood, Jeffrey

Tiger Rag, La Roca, Nick: Lehr, David "Red"; Pilafian, Sam

Tin Roof Blues, Melrose, Walter: Palmer, Singleton

To Each His Own, Livingston and Evans/Inomata: Yasumoto, Hiroyuki

Toccata and Fugue in D Minor, Bach, Johann Sebastian/Morris: Tennessee Technological University Tuba/Euphonium Ensemble

Tom and Sally Drake, Mahal, Taj: Johnson, Howard

Too Fat Polka, Richardson and McLean/Whitcomb: Tubadours

Toot Your Roots, Botschinsky, Allan: Van Lier, Erik

A Touch of Tuba, Dedrick, Art: Popiel, Peter

Träumerei, Schumann, Robert: Piernik, Zdizislaw

Träumerei, Schumann, Robert/Seitz: Melton Tuba-Quartett

Treatments for Tuba, Stroud, Richard: Tennessee Technological University Tuba/Euphonium Ensemble

Tree Top Tall Papa, Brown, Sandy: Newberger, Eli

Trees, Rasbach: Cummings, Barton

Trepek, Tchaikovsky, Peter Ilyitch/Smalley: British Tuba Quartet

Tribute to Duke Ellington, Ellington, Duke/Sample: Tennessee Technological University Tuba/Euphonium Ensemble

Tricky Lix, Aldcroft, Randy: Self, James

Trigon, Zindars, Earl: Cooley, Floyd

Trilogy, Wood, Philip D.: Draper, Ray

Trio for Xylophone, Soprano and Tuba, Ziffrin, Marilyn J.: Cummings, Barton

Trio Sonata for Tuba, Batteries [percussion], *and Piano,* Toyama, Yuzo: Yasumoto, Hiroyuki

Triple Slow Mix: Lewis, George

Triptych, Weeks, Clifford: Megules, Karl

Triumph of the Demon Gods, Stevens, John: Stevens, John

Trombone Man Blues: Lehr, David "Red"

The Trouble with the Tuba Is, Relton, William: Crowther, Shaun

Trumpet Polka: Tarto, Joe

Tsiganochka (solo tuba, guitar, mandocello, accordian, and bazuki), Traditional/Buttery: Buttery, Gary

La Tuba, Traditional/Funderburk: United States Air Force Concert Band Tuba Section

Tuba Ballet for Tuba and Woodwind Quintet, Jacobsen, Julius: Lind, Michael

Tuba Banjo Dixie, Steckar and Colombo: Steckar, Marc

Tuba Blues, Wolking, Henry: British Tuba Quartet; Northern Tuba Lights

Tuba Bouchka, Quibel, R.: Steckar, Marc

Tuba Buffo, Jacobsen, Julius: Lind, Michael

Tuba Concerto, Ellerby, Martin: Harrild, Patrick; Sykes, Stephen

Tuba Concerto, Horowitz, Joseph: Gourlay, James

Tuba Concerto, Wuorinen, Charles: Brainard, David

Tuba Concerto with Band, Ross, Walter: Phillips, Harvey

Tuba Doina: Thornton, Donald

Tuba Encore Piece (A Tubist's Showcase), Wilder, Alec: Bobo, Roger

Tuba Juba Duba, Hutchinson, Terry: Melton Tuba-Quartett; Tennessee Technological University Tuba/Euphonium Ensemble

Tuba Magic, DiGiovanni, Rocco: Tennessee Technological University Tuba/Euphonium Ensemble; United States Armed Forces Tuba-Euphonium Ensemble

Tuba Man, Carr, S./Bell: Bell, William

Tuba Muckl, Schmidt, D.: The Contraband

Tuba Only, Solal: Steckar Tubapack

Tuba or Not Tuba, Busch, Sigi: Busch, Sigi

Tuba Quartet, Op.59, Gates, Crawford: Tennessee Technological University Tuba/Euphonium Ensemble

Tuba Rhapsody, Grundman, Clare: Varner, Lesley

Tuba Serenade (Eine kleine Nachtmusik), Mozart, Wolfgang Amadeus/Fletcher: Fletcher, John

Tuba Smarties, Traditional: Flowers, Herbie

Tuba Space, Coeuriot, M.: Steckar, Marc

Tuba Suite, Jacob, Gordon: Dowling, Eugene

Tuba Suite for tuba and three horns, Gould, Morton: Phillips, Harvey

Tuba Tapestry for Tuba and Brass Band, Brand, Michael: Anderson, Hans; Anonymous; Fletcher, John

Tuba Variations, Farkas, Antal: Szabo, Laszlo

Tubabando, Galliano, R.: Steckar, Marc

TubaChristmas Suite, Bewley: Phillips, Harvey/Tuba-Christmas

Tubacuba, Steckar and Galliano: Steckar, Marc

Tubafour, Heussenstamm, George: New York Tuba Quartet

A Tubalee Jubalee, Garrett, James: Tennessee Technological University Tuba/Euphonium Ensemble; United States Armed Forces Tuba-Euphonium Ensemble

Tubalied, Fredrickson, Thomas: Perantoni, Daniel

Tubas au Fujiyama, Steckar, Marc: Steckar Elephant Tuba Horde

Tubas in the Moonlight: Gannett, Dave

Tubas on Fujiyama, Steckar, Marc: Steckar, Marc

Tubasonatina, George, Thom Ritter: Tennessee Technological University Tuba/Euphonium Ensemble

Tubby at the Circus, Kleinsinger, George, and Tripp, Paul: Anonymous (Bell, William); Johnson, John Tommy

Tubby Meets a Jazz Band, Kleinsinger, George, and Tripp, Paul: Johnson, Tommy

Tubby the Tuba, Kleinsinger, George, and Tripp, Paul: Anonymous; Boujie, George; Bruno, Jerry; Call, R. Steven; Jenkel, Herbert; Johnson, John Thomas

(Tommy); Karella, Clarenge; Schmitz, Chester; Thorton, Michael

Tunk, Stewart, Bob: Stewart, Bob

Turkish Rondo, Mozart, Wolfgang Amadeus/Mehlan: Monarch Tuba-Euphonium Quartet

Two Moods for Tuba, Swann, Donald: Phillips, Harvey

Two Songs, Spillman, Robert: Bobo, Roger

Two Sons, Draper, Ray: Draper, Ray

Two Together (tuba and soprano), Amato, Bruno: Turk, John

Two Tunes (*You Stepped Out of a Dream; Temptation*), Brown, Nacio Herb/Sample: Tennessee Technological University Tuba/Euphonium Ensemble

Tyrolean Tuba, Clark, M.: Stern, Mary

Undecided Now, Robin and Shavers: Lehr, David "Red"

Under Paris Skies, Draper, Ray: Draper, Ray

The Unknown Soldier: Pilafian, Sam

Up a Lazy River, Carmichael, Hoagy: Pilafian, Sam

Valkyrie excerpts (*Magic Fire Music, Ride of the Valkyries*), Wagner, Richard: Jacobs, Arnold

Variationen for Tuba and Nine Horns, Heiden, Bernard: Phillips, Harvey

Variations for Tuba and Winds, Frackenpohl, Arthur: Popiel, Peter

Variations in Olden Style, Stevens, Thomas: Bobo, Roger

Variations on a Theme from "Judas Maccabeus," Beethoven, Ludwig/Bell: Bell, William

Variations on an Old Hymn Tune, Werle, Floyd: United States Armed Forces Tuba-Euphonium Ensemble; Tennessee Technological University Tuba/Euphonium Ensemble

Variations on the Cobbler's Bench, Frackenpohl, Arthur: Davis, Ronald

Verdurous Aubade for Tuba and Piano, Censhu, Jiro: Yasumoto, Hiroyuki

Vier ernste Gesänge, Brahms, Johannes: Cooley, Floyd

Vier ernste Gesänge (excerpts), Brahms, Johannes: Cooley, Floyd

The Village: Stewart, Bob

Vocalise, Rachmaninoff, Serge/Perantoni: Perantoni, Daniel

Vocalise, Rachmaninoff, Sergei: LeBlanc, Robert

The Volunteer, Rogers, Walter: Arwood, Jeffrey

Von Himmel Hoch, Bach, Johann Sebastian/Falconer: Tubadours

VOX per uno stromento ad ottone, Borkowski, Marian: Piernik, Zdizislaw

Wabash Blues, Reinken, Fred: Pilafian, Sam; Lehr, David "Red"

Wabash Cannonball, Traditional/Garrett: British Tuba Quartet

Walt's Samba, Eldsvoog, John: Self, James

Waltz from "Die Fledermaus," Strauss, Johann Jr./Berry: Tubadours

Waltz from "Sleeping Beauty," Tchaikovsky, Peter Ilyitch/Fletcher: Fletcher, John

Waltzing Matilda, Matteson: Matteson-Phillips Tuba-Jazz Consort

Waltzing with Bears, Marxsen, Dale: Davis, Ronald

Wann der Dudelsack kräht u. a., Well, Christoph: Well, Christoph

Warsaw Autumn: Piernik, Zdizislaw

Washington and Lee Swing, Robbins, Allen, and Sheafe: Matteson, Rich

Washington Post, Sousa, John Philip/Sabourin: British Tuba Quartet; Melton Tuba-Quartett

Washington Post, Sousa, John Philip/Werden: The Contraband

Waterloo, Moschner, Pinguin: Moschner, Pinguin

We Three Kings, Hopkins/Lycan: Tubadours

We Three Kings, Hopkins/Wilder: Phillips, Harvey/TubaChristmas

The Westwood Song, Kellaway, Roger: Bobo, Roger

What'll I Do? Berlin, Irving: Pilafian, Sam

What's Her Name? Wilson, Phil: Matteson, Rich

What's Up: Stewart, Bob

When She Cries, Novick, Billy: Newberger, Eli

When the Saints Go Marchin' In, Boyle: Callender, Red

When the Saints Go Marchin' In, Traditional: Palmer, Singleton

When Tubas Waltz, Bartles, Alfred: The Contraband; Tennessee Technological University Tuba/Euphonium Ensemble; Tubadours

When You See That Aunt of Mine: Tarto, Joe

When You Wish Upon a Star, Washington and Harline: Newberger, Eli

When You're Smiling, Fisher, Goodwin, and Shay: Pilafian, Sam

When Yuba Plays the Rhumba on the Tuba Down in Cuba, Hupfeld, Herman: Bell, William; Phillips, Harvey; Tarto, Joe; Washburn, Joe "Country"

Where Flamingos Fly: Johnson, Howard

Whirly Twirly: Pilafian, Sam

White Christmas, Berlin, Irving/Vaughan: Tubadours

Wiegenlied, Brahms, Johannes: Van Lier, Erik

Wild Man Blues, Armstrong and Morton: Newberger, Eli

William Tell Overture, Rossini, Gioacchino/Smalley: British Tuba Quartet

Willow, Willow (bass flute, tuba, percussion), Chihara, Paul: Price, Tony

Windsong, Morell, John: Self, James

Wind-up Landscape: Tafjord, Stein-Erik

Wolverine Blues, Morton, F. "Jelly Roll": Lehr, David "Red"

Won't You Come Home Bill Bailey, Garrett: Tennessee Technological University Tuba/Euphonium Ensemble

The World Is Waiting for the Sunrise, Lockhart and Seitz: Lehr, David "Red"; Newberger, Eli

Wot Shigona Dew, Wilson, Ted: Tennessee Technological University Tuba/Euphonium Ensemble

Der Wurst lebt, Moschner, Pinguin: Moschner, Ping

Y Luego, Hermann, Herman: Scandinavian Tuba Jazz

Yakkety Tuba: Gannett, Dave

The Yellow Bird, Tackett, Fred: Bobo, Roger

Yesterday, Lennon and McCartney/Ito: Yasumoto, Hiroyuki

Yesterdays, Harbach and Kern: Draper, Ray

You Ain't No Streetwalker, Mama Honey, But I Do Love the Way You Strut Your Stuff, Mahal, Taj: Johnson, Howard

You Are My Sunshine, Davis, Jimmie: Pilafian, Sam

You Made Me Love You, Monaco/Holcombe: British Tuba Quartet

You're Going to Need Somebody on Your Bond, Johnson, Blind Willie/Mahal: Johnson, Howard

Zing Went the Strings of My Heart: Lehr, David "Red"

Tuba Recordings by Composer

Abreu, Zequinha/Smith, A., *Tico-Tico:* Arwood, Jeffrey

Adamson/Lane, B., *Everything I Have Is Yours:* Barber, John William (Bill)

Adler, Samuel, *Canto VII for Solo Tuba:* Beauregard, Cherry

Ahbez, Eden/Cherry, *Nature Boy:* Tennessee Technological University Tuba/Euphonium Ensemble

Aldcroft, Randy, *Somebody's Samba:* Self, James

Aldcroft, Randy, *Tricky Lix:* Self, James

Amato, Bruno, *Two Together* (tuba and soprano): Turk, John

Anonymous/Baker, *Lute Dances:* British Tuba Quartet

Anonymous/Buttery, *Greensleeves:* Atlantic Tuba Quartet

Anonymous/Funderburk, *O Welt, ich muss dich lassen:* United States Air Force Concert Band Tuba Section

Anonymous/Lusher, *Come Dearest, the Daylight Is Gone:* Tubadours

Arban, J. B./Bell, *Carnival of Venice:* Bell, William

Arban, J. B./Berry, *Carnival of Venice:* Bobo, Roger

Arban, J. B./Domek, *Carnival of Venice:* Perantoni, Daniel

Arban, J. B./Bobo, *Fantaisie and Variations on the "Carnival of Venice":* Bobo, Roger

Arban, J. B., *Fantaisie and Variations on the "Carnival of Venice":* Lind, Michael

Arbel, Chaya: *Roundarounds:* Hershko, Adi

Arcadelt, Jacob/Self, *Ave Maria:* Melton Tuba-Quartett

Arlen and Harburg, *If I Only Had a Brain:* Pilafian, Sam

Armstrong and Morton, *Wild Man Blues:* Newberger, Eli

Arnold, Malcolm, *Fantasy for Solo Tuba:* Fletcher, John; Gourlay, James

Baader-Nobs, Heidi, *Bifurcation* for tuba and piano: Bjørn-Larsen, Jens

Bach, Johann Sebastian/Hilgers, *Adagio* from *Toccata, Adagio and Fugue in C Major,* BWV 564: Hilgers, Walter

Bach, Johann Sebastian/Bell, *Air and Bourrée:* Conner, Rex; Davis, Ronald; Phillips, Harvey; Popiel, Peter

Bach, Johann Sebastian, *Air for the G String:* Bobo, Roger

Bach, Johann Sebastian/Werden, *Air from Suite No. 3:* British Tuba Quartet; Atlantic Tuba Quartet

Bach, Johann Sebastian/Phillips, *Air from Suite No. 3 in D Major for Orchestra,* BWV 1068: Tennessee Technological University Tuba/Euphonium Ensemble

Bach, Johann Sebastian/Myers, *Allegro from Toccata in D Minor for Klavier,* BWV 913: Atlantic Tuba Quartet

Bach, Johann Sebastian, *Bandinerie:* Marshall, Oren

Bach, Johann Sebastian/Werden, *Bist du bei mir,* BWV 508: Atlantic Tuba Quartet; Melton Tuba-Quartett; United States Armed Forces Tuba-Euphonium Ensemble

Bach, Johann Sebastian, *Bourrée I and II from Suite for Unaccompanied Cello:* Bobo, Roger

Bach, Johann Sebastian/Morris, *Contrapunctus I:* Tennessee Tech Tuba-Euphonium Quintet

Bach, Johann Sebastian/Berry, *Fugue in G Minor:* Tubadours

Bach, Johann Sebastian/Gray, *Fugue in G Minor:* British Tuba Quartet

Bach, Johann Sebastian/Schmidt, D., *Fugue in G Minor:* Gerhard Meinl's Tuba Sextet

Bach, Johann Sebastian, *Invention No. 1* (flute and tuba); Phillips, Harvey

Bach, Johann Sebastian/Werden, *Jesu, Joy of Man's Desiring:* British Tuba Quartet

Bach, Johann Sebastian/Sauter, *Komm süsser Tod:* Megules, Karl; Phillips, Harvey/TubaChristmas; Tennessee Technological University Tuba/Euphonium Ensemble

Bach, Johann Sebastian, *Nun komm der Heiden Heiland:* Hilgers, Walter

Bach, Johann Sebastian/Hilgers, *O Mensch bewein' dein Sünde gross,* BWV 622: Hilgers, Walter

Bach, Johann Sebastian, *Partita in A Minor for Flute Alone:* Pokorny, Gene

Bach, Johann Sebastian/Sabourin, *Preludium:* Northern Tuba Lights

Bach, Johann Sebastian/Howard, *Rondo:* British Tuba Quartet

Bach, Johann Sebastian/Self, *Sinfonia III:* Self, James

Bach, Johann Sebastian, *Sonata in Eb Major:* Cooley, Floyd

Bach, Johann Sebastian/Dowling/Norman, *Sonata No. 4 in C:* Dowling, Eugene

Bach, Johann Sebastian, *Sonate II:* Hilgers, Walter

Bach, Johann Sebastian/Beckman, *St. Anne's Fugue:* United States Armed Forces Tuba-Euphonium Ensemble

Bach, Johann Sebastian, *Suite in Bb Minor for Flute:* Seward, Steven

Bach, Johann Sebastian, *Suite No. 1 in G Major for Solo Cello* (Minuet, Courante): Fletcher, John

Bach, Johann Sebastian/Morris, *Toccata and Fugue in D Minor*: Tennessee Technological University Tuba/Euphonium Ensemble

Bach, Johann Sebastian/Falconer, *Von Himmel Hoch*: Tubadours

Bach, P. D. Q., *Dutch Suite for Bassoon and Tuba*: Bishop, Ronald

Bach, Vincent, *Hungarian Melodies*: Seward, Steven

Baker, Claude, *Omaggi e Fantasie*: Randolph, David

Baker, David N., *Sonata for Tuba and String Quartet*: Phillips, Harvey

Barat, Joseph Eduoard, *Introduction and Dance*: Bobo, Roger

Barat, Joseph Eduoard/Phillips, *Introduction and Dance* (tuba and band): Bobo, Roger

Barboteu, George, *Divertissement* for tuba and brass quartet: Hilgers, Walter

Barham and Fuber, *Limehouse Blues*: Matteson, Rich; Pilafian, Sam

Barris and Cavanaugh, *Mississippi Mud*: Matteson, Rich

Barroso, Ary/Morris, *Brazil*: Tennessee Technological University Tuba/Euphonium Ensemble

Barry, Darrol, *Impromptu for Tuba*: Ferguson, Ken

Bartles, Alfred, *When Tubas Waltz*: The Contraband; Tennessee Technological University Tuba/Euphonium Ensemble; Tubadours

Beach, Bennie, *Dance Suite for Tuba and Triangle*: Cummings, Barton

Beach, Bennie, *Lamento*: Conner, Rex; LeBlanc, Robert

Beale, David, *Reflections on a Park Bench*: Tennessee Technological University Tuba/Euphonium Ensemble

Beethoven, Ludwig, *Minuet*: Conner, Rex

Beethoven, Ludwig/Proto, *Sonata in G Major for Tuba and Piano* (Horn Sonata in F): Thornton, Michael

Beethoven, Ludwig/Bell, *Variations on a Theme from "Judas Maccabeus"*: Bell, William

Bell, Kelvyn, *Subi La Nas Alturas*: Stewart, Bob

Bencriscutto, Frank, *Concertino for Tuba and Band*: Freese, Stanford

Benson, Warren, *Arioso*: Popiel, Peter

Benson, Warren, *Helix for Solo Tuba and Concert Band*: Phillips, Harvey; Robinson, Jack; Turk, John

Berg, Curt, *The Farewell Burn*: Self, James

Berg, Curt, *Take the Stairs*: Self, James

Berlin, Irving, *Alexander's Ragtime Band*: Pilafian, Sam

Berlin, Irving, *How Deep Is the Ocean*: Scandinavian Tuba Jazz

Berlin, Irving/Gout, *Puttin' on the Ritz*: British Tuba Quartet

Berlin, Irving, *What'll I Do?*: Pilafian, Sam

Berlin, Irving/Vaughan, *White Christmas*: Tubadours

Berlioz, Hector, *Rakoczy (Hungarian) March from "Damnation of Faust"* (excerpt): Jacobs, Arnold

Bernie, Casey, and Pickard, *Sweet Georgia Brown*: Matteson, Rich; Palmer, Singleton; Pilafian, Sam

Bernie, Casey, and Pickard/Garrett, *Sweet Georgia Brown*: Tennessee Technological University Tuba/Euphonium Ensemble

Bernie, Casey, and Pinkard/Sellers, *Sweet Georgia Brown*: Perantoni, Daniel

Best, Denzil Decosta, *Move*: Barber, John William (Bill)

Best, Denzil Decosta/Buttery, *Move*: Atlantic Tuba Quartet

Betti, Dino, *Space Blossoms*: Schiaffini, Giancarlo

Beversdorf, Thomas, *Sonata for Bass Tuba and Piano*: LeBlanc, Robert

Bewley, Norlan, *Santa Wants a Tuba for Christmas*: Phillips, Harvey/TubaChristmas

Bewley, Norlan, *TubaChristmas Suite*: Phillips, Harvey/TubaChristmas

Birchall, Steven, *Reciprocals II for Two Tubas*: Trice, Jerry

Blake, Eubie, *Goodnight, Angeline*: Newberger, Eli

Blake, Eubie, *Memories of You*: Pokorny, Gene

Blythe, Arthur, *Bush Baby*: Stewart, Bob

Blythe, Arthur, *Metamorphosis*: Stewart, Bob

Boccalari, E./Akers, *Fantasia di Concerto*: Conner, Rex

Boccherini, Luigi, *Minuet*: Piernik, Zdizislaw

Bologneisi, J., *Maria Alm*: Steckar Tubapack

Bologneisi, J., *Quand le Tuba valse à Paris*: Steckar, Marc

Boone, Dan, *Three Moods*: University of Miami Tuba Ensemble

Borkowski, Marian, *VOX per uno stromento ad ottone*: Piernik, Zdizislaw

Botschinsky, Allan, *Alster Promenade*: Van Lier, Erik

Botschinsky, Allan, *Chops a la Salsa*: Van Lier, Erik

Botschinsky, Allan, *Don't Shoot the Banjo Player ('Cause We've Done It Already)*: Van Lier, Erik

Botschinsky, Allan, *Interlude No. 4*: Van Lier, Erik

Botschinsky, Allan, *Kubismus 502*: Van Lier, Erik

Botschinsky, Allan, *The Lady in Blue*: Van Lier, Erik

Botschinsky, Allan, *Love Waltz*: Van Lier, Erik

Botschinsky, Allan, *October Sunshine*: Van Lier, Erik

Botschinsky, Allan, *Toot Your Roots*: Van Lier, Erik

Boyadjian, Hayg, *Sareebar for Tuba and Percussion*: Pilafian, Sam

Bozza, Eugene, *Allegro et Finale*: Georgie, Gerhard

Bozza, Eugene, *Concertino for Tuba and Piano*: Seward, Steven

Brahms, Johannes/Fote, *Chorale Prelude, Op. 122, No. 8, "Es ist ein Ros' entsprungen"*: Jacobs, Arnold

Brahms, Johannes, *Vier Ernste Gesänge*: Cooley, Floyd

Brahms, Johannes, *Vier Ernste Gesänge* (excerpts): Cooley, Floyd

Brahms, Johannes, *Wiegenlied*: Van Lier, Erik

Brand, Michael, *Tuba Tapestry for Tuba and Brass Band*: Anderson, Hans; Anonymous; Fletcher, John

Bratton, John W./Roberts, *Teddy Bears' Picnic*: Sibley, Graham

Brennard, George/Arwood, *The Old Rugged Cross*: Arwood, Jeffrey

Broadbent, Alan, *Another Time*: Self, James

Brown and Von Tilzer, *Dapper Dan*: Newberger, Eli

Brown, Nacio Herb/Sample, *Two Tunes* ("You Stepped Out of a Dream," "Temptation"): Tennessee Technological University Tuba/Euphonium Ensemble

Brown, Sandy, *Tree Top Tall Papa*: Newberger, Eli

Brown, Tom, *Kilo*: Self, James

Brown, Tom, *New Stuff*: Self, James

Brown, Tom, *Night Lights*: Self, James

Brubeck, Dave, *Blue Rondo alla Turk*: Tafjord, Stein-Erik

Brubeck, Dave/Esleck, *Blue Rondo alla Turk*: Tennessee Technological University Tuba/Euphonium Ensemble

Bruckner, Anton, *Symphony No. 4* (first movement, excerpt): Jacobs, Arnold

Bruckner, Anton, *Symphony No. 8* (fourth movement, excerpt): Jacobs, Arnold

Bull, John/Howard, *The King's Hunt*: British Tuba Quartet

Bulla, Stephen, *Celestial Suite*: British Tuba Quartet

Bulla, Stephen, *Quartet for Low Brass*: British Tuba Quartet; United States Navy Band Tuba-Euphonium Quartet

Burke and Johnston, *Pennies from Heaven*: Gannett, Dave

Burris and Smith, *Ballin' the Jack*: Palmer, Singleton

Busch, Sigi, *Tuba or Not Tuba*: Busch, Sigi

Butler, Gay, Sparke, *The Sun Has Got His Hat On*: Crowther, Shaun

Butterfield, Don, *Sonority Study for Three Tubas*: United States Air Force Concert Band Tuba Section

Buttery, Gary, *An English Folk Christmas*: United States Coast Guard Tuba-Euphonium Quartet

Butts, Carrol, *Ode to Low Brass*: Megules, Karl

Butts, Carrol, *Suite for Tuba and Piano*: Cummings, Barton

Byrd, William, *Agnus Dei*: University of Michigan Tuba and Euphonium Ensemble

Byrd, William/Winter, *Jhon, Come Kisse Me Now*: Atlantic Tuba Quartet; British Tuba Quartet

Calabro, Louis, *Sonata-Fantasia*: Nelson, Mark

Callender, Red, *Cris*: Callender, Red

Callender, Red, *Moon Mist Blues*: Callender, Red

Camphouse, Mark, *Ceremonial Sketch*: Tennessee Technological University Tuba/Euphonium Ensemble; United States Armed Forces Tuba-Euphonium Ensemble

Camphouse, Mark, *Poème*: Arwood, Jeffrey

Cannon, Hughie, *Bill Bailey Won't You Please Come Home*: Pilafian, Sam

Canter, James, *Appalachian Carol*: United States Armed Forces Tuba-Euphonium Ensemble

Capuzzi, Antonio/Self, *Rondo Allegro* (tuba with brass quintet): Self, James

Carmichael, Hoagy, *Georgia on My Mind*: Pilafian, Sam

Carmichael, Hoagy/LeClair, *Georgia on My Mind*: The Contraband

Carmichael, Hoagy/Matteson, *Georgia on My Mind*: Matteson-Phillips TubaJazz Consort

Carmichael, Hoagy, *New Orleans*: Pilafian, Sam

Carmichael, Hoagy, *Ol' Rockin' Chair's Got Me*: Gannett, Dave

Carmichael, Hoagy, *Up a Lazy River*: Pilafian, Sam

Carr, S./Bell, *Tuba Man*: Bell, William

Casas, Bartolomé Perez, *Concerto for Tuba*: Mas, Vicente Navarro

Castérède, Jacques, *Serenade from Sonatine for Bass Saxhorn and Piano*: Pokorny, Gene

Catelinet, Philip, *Suite in Miniature* (first and third movements): Megules, Karl

Censhu, Jiro, *Verdurous Aubade for Tuba and Piano*: Yasumoto, Hiroyuki

Charles, Moten, and Hayes, *South*: Matteson, Rich

Cheetham, John, *Consortium*: British Tuba Quartet; Tennessee Technological University Tuba/Euphonium Ensemble; United States Armed Forces Tuba-Euphonium Ensemble

Cherry, Don, *Art Deco*: Stewart, Bob

Chihara, Paul, *Willow, Willow* (bass flute, tuba, percussion): Price, Tony

Childs, Barney, *A Question of Summer* for harp and tuba: Hammond, Ivan

Chopin, Frederic/Abrams, *Mazurka No. 49 in A Minor, Op. 68, No. 2*: Hoffnung, Gerard; United States Air Force Concert Band Tuba Section

Chopin, Frederic/Mead, *Minute Waltz*: British Tuba Quartet

Christiansen, Henning, *Betrayal* for tuba, violin and vibraphone, Op. 144: Anderson, Hans

Christiansen, Henning, *Kirkeby and Edvard Munch* (in 12 movements): Anderson, Hans

Christiansen, Henning, *Maskemåned* for trumpet and tuba, Op. 148: Anderson, Hans

Clark, M., *Tyrolean Tuba*: Stern, Mary

Clarke, Herbert L., *Bride of the Waves*: Frazier, Richard

Clarke, Herbert L./LeClair, *Cousins*: The Contraband

Clarke, Herbert L., *From the Shores of the Mighty Pacific*: Hanks, Toby

Coeuriot, M., *Tuba Space*: Steckar, Marc

Cohen, Michael, *Diversita Continua*: Hershko, Adi

Coleman and Kay, *Come Follow the Band*: Stevens, John

Collette, Buddy, *Nice Day*: Callender, Red

Collins, Judy/Buttery, *Since You've Asked*: Atlantic Tuba Quartet

Condon, Leslie, *Celestial Morn*: Hornsberger, Albert

Condon, Leslie, *Radiant Pathway*: Patterson, Graham; Stokes, David

Corea, Chick, *Spain*: Tennessee Technological University Tuba/Euphonium Ensemble

Corelli, Archangelo, *Gigue*: Phillips, Harvey

Corwell, Neal, *New England Reveries*: Nelson, Mark

Couperin, F./Pilafian, *Les Barricades Mystérieuses*: Gerhard Meinl's Tuba Sextet

Crespo, Enrique, *Bruckner Etude*: Gerhard Meinl's Tuba Sextet

Crespo, Enrique, *Escenas Latinas*: Hilgers, Walter

Crespo, Enrique, *Three Milongas*: Gerhard Meinl's Tuba Sextet

Creuze, *Eria*: LeLong, Fernand

Croft, *Duet for Tenor Tuba and Bass Tuba*: Megules, Karl

Cugny, Laurent, *Molloy*: Steckar Elephant Tuba Horde

Cui, César, *Perpetual Motion*: Bobo, Roger

Cummings, Barton, *Fantasia Breve*: Nelson, Mark

Curnow, James, *Concertino for Tuba and Band*: McAdams, Charles; Perantoni, Daniel

Danielssohn, Christer, *Capriccio da Camera* for solo tuba and brass quintet: Hilgers, Walter; Lind, Michael

Danielssohn, Christer, *Concertante Suite for Tuba and Four Horns*: Hilgers, Walter; Lind, Michael

Dara, Olu, *Bell and Ponce*: Stewart, Bob

Davis, Akst/Woo, *Baby Face*: University of Miami Tuba Ensemble

Davis, Jimmie, *You Are My Sunshine*: Pilafian, Sam

Davis, Miles, *All Blues*: Scandinavian Tuba Jazz

De Mars, James, *Tapestry III*: Perantoni, Daniel

Debussy, Claude/Schaefer, *General Lavine—Eccentric*: Pokorny, Gene

Debussy, Claude, *Prelude à l'après midi d'un faune*: Pokorny, Gene

Debussy, Claude, *Syrinx*: Self, James

Dedrick, Art, *A Touch of Tuba*: Popiel, Peter

DeLange and Van Heusen, *Darn That Dream*: Callender, Red

Dempsey, Raymond, *Now Hear This*: Monarch Tuba-Euphonium Quartet

Dennis and Brent, *Angel Eyes*: Draper, Ray

Denson, Frank, *Three Folksongs for Four Brass*: Gerhard Meinl's Tuba Sextet

Di Lasso, Orlando/Robinson, *Mon Coeur se Recommende à Vous*: British Tuba Quartet

Di Lasso, Orlando/Pilafian, *Ola, O che bon eccho*: Gerhard Meinl's Tuba Sextet

Diero/Ferguson, *Il Ritorno*: British Tuba Quartet

DiGiovanni, Rocco, *Tuba Magic*: Tennessee Technological University Tuba/Euphonium Ensemble; United States Armed Forces Tuba-Euphonium Ensemble

Dobrowski, A., *Muzyka for Tuba Solo*: Piernik, Zdizislaw

Dodson, John, *Out of the Depths*: Tennessee Technological University Tuba/Euphonium Ensemble

Donaldson, W./Self, *Carolina in the Morning*: University of Miami Tuba Ensemble

Donalson and Kahn, *Makin' Whoopee*: Pilafian, Sam

Downey, John, *Tabu for Tuba*: Phillips, Harvey

Draper and Aplan, *Let My People Go*: Draper, Ray

Draper, Ray, *Clifford's Kappa*: Draper, Ray

Draper, Ray, *Empty Streets*: Draper, Ray

Draper, Ray, *Essii's Dance*: Draper, Ray

Draper, Ray, *Filidia*: Draper, Ray

Draper, Ray, *Happiness*: Draper, Ray

Draper, Ray, *I Hadn't Anyone Til You*: Draper, Ray

Draper, Ray, *Mess Around*: Draper, Ray

Draper, Ray, *Minor Dream*: Draper, Ray

Draper, Ray, *Paul's Pal*: Draper, Ray

Draper, Ray, *Two Sons*: Draper, Ray

Draper, Ray, *Under Paris Skies*: Draper, Ray

Dubensky, Arcady, *Concerto Grosso* for three trombones, tuba, and band: Anonymous

Dubin and Warren/Minard, *42nd Street Selections*: British Tuba Quartet

Dumitru, Ionel, *Fantezie Pentru Tuba si Pian*: Dumitru, Ionel

Dumitru, Ionel, *Romanian Dance No. 2*: Bobo, Roger

Dutton, Brent, *Carnival of Venice*: Dutton, Brent

Dvořák, Anton, *Humoresque*: Piernik, Zdizislaw

Eccles, Henry/Megules, *Adagio*: Megules, Karl

Eccles, Henry, *Sonata in G Minor* (I Prelude; II Courant): Piernik, Zdizislaw

Eldsvoog, John, *Walt's Samba*: Self, James

Elgar, Edward, *Chanson de Matin*: Fletcher, John

Elgar, Edward/Thornton, *Chanson de Matin*, Op. 15, No. 2: Thornton, Michael

Elgar, Edward, *Romance*: Dowling, Eugene

Ellerby, Martin, *Tuba Concerto*: Harrild, Patrick; Sykes, Stephen

Ellington, Duke, *Don't Get Around Much Anymore*: Pilafian, Sam

Ellington, Duke, *In a Sentimental Mood*: Callender, Red

Ellington, Duke/Vaughan, *Mood Indigo*: Tubadours

Ellington, Duke/Vaughan, *Satin Doll*: Tubadours

Ellington, Duke/Callender, *Sophisticated Lady*: Callender, Red

Ellington, Duke/Matteson, *Things Ain't What They Used to Be*: Matteson-Phillips TubaJazz Consort

Ellington, Duke/Sample, *Tribute to Duke Ellington*: Tennessee Technological University Tuba/Euphonium Ensemble

Emler, Andy, *Gicael Mibbs*: Steckar Elephant Tuba Horde

Escovez, Fermin Ruiz, *Dualismo* for tuba and flute: Mas, Vincente Navarro

Estes, Sleepy John/Mahal, *Diving Duck Blues*: Johnson, Howard

Farkas, Antal, *Tuba Variations*: Szabo, Laszlo

Felciano, Richard, *"and from the abyss"* for tuba and tape: Cooley, Floyd

Feldman, Morton, *Chorus and Instruments (II)*: Phillips, Harvey

Feldman, Morton, *Durations*: Butterfield, Don

Ferreira and Einhorn/Megules, *Batida Diferente*: Megules, Karl

Fields and McHugh, *I Can't Give You Anything But Love*: Lehr, David "Red"

Fields and McHugh, *On the Sunny Side of the Street*: Gannett, Dave

Fisher, Goodwin and Shay, *When You're Smiling*: Pilafian, Sam

Foster, Stephen, *Swannee River*: Matteson, Rich

Frackenpohl, Arthur, *Pop Suite*: British Tuba Quartet; Megules, Karl; University of Miami Tuba Ensemble

Frackenpohl, Arthur, *Pop Suite* (last movement): British Tuba Quartet

Frackenpohl, Arthur, *Song and Dance* for euphonium, tuba, and band: Porter, William D. (David)

Frackenpohl, Arthur, *Variations for Tuba and Winds*: Popiel, Peter

Frackenpohl, Arthur, *Variations on the Cobbler's Bench*: Davis, Ronald

Frank, Marcel G., *Lyric Poem*: United States Armed Forces Tuba-Euphonium Ensemble; University of Miami Tuba Ensemble

Fredrickson, Thomas, *Tubalied*: Perantoni, Daniel

Fritze, Gregory, *Basso Continuo*: Fritze, Gregory

Furber and Braham, *Limehouse Blues*: Matteson, Rich

Gaathaug, Morten, *Sonata Concertante* for solo tuba and brass quintet: Baadsvik, Øystein

Gabrieli, Domenico/Morris, R.W., *Ricercar for Solo Tuba*: Davis, Ronald; McKee, Edward R.

Gabrieli, Giovanni/Rauch, *Canzona, La Spiritata*: British Tuba Quartet

Gabrieli, Giovanni/Gray, *Canzona per Sonare No. 4*: Gerhard Meinl's Tuba Sextet

Gale, Jack, *Picture of Dorian Blue*: Self, James

Galliano, R., *French Tuba in Los Angeles*: Steckar, Marc

Galliano, R., *Tubabando*: Steckar, Marc

Galliard, Johann Ernst/Clemons, R., *Allegro* from *Sonata No. 3 in F Major*: Arwood, Jeffrey

Galliard, Johann Ernst, *Sonata No. 5 in D Minor*: Bobo, Roger

Garbáge, Pierre, *Sousa Surrenders*: United States Armed Forces Tuba-Euphonium Ensemble

Garrett, James, *Miniature Jazz Suite*: Tennessee Technological University Tuba/Euphonium Ensemble

Garrett, James, *A Tubalee Jubalee*: Tennessee Technological University Tuba/Euphonium Ensemble; United States Armed Forces Tuba-Euphonium Ensemble

Gasner, Moshe, *Science Fiction*: Hershko, Adi

Gates, Crawford, *Tuba Quartet*, Op. 59: Tennessee Technological University Tuba/Euphonium Ensemble

George, Thom Ritter, *Sonata for Tuba and Piano*: Perantoni, Daniel; Randolph, David

George, Thom Ritter, *Tubasonatina*: Tennessee Technological University Tuba/Euphonium Ensemble

Gershwin, George/Evans, *The Buzzard Song*: Barber, John William (Bill)

Gershwin, George/Ferguson, *Fascinatin' Gershwin*: British Tuba Quartet

Gershwin, George, *Fidgety Feet*: Matteson, Rich

Gershwin, George, *Foggy Day*: Callender, Red

Gershwin, George/Sample, *Gershwin Medley*: Tennessee Technological University Tuba/Euphonium Ensemble; United States Armed Forces Tuba-Euphonium Ensemble

Gershwin, George, *Prelude in C♯ Minor*: Newberger, Eli

Gershwin, George, *Someone to Watch Over Me*: Pilafian, Sam

Gershwin, George, *Summertime*: Matteson-Phillips TubaJazz Consort

Gilbert and Ory, *Muskrat Ramble*: Palmer, Singleton

Gilbert and Pollack, *That's A-Plenty*: Lehr, David "Red"

Gillespie/Vaughan, *Santa Claus Is Coming to Town*: Tubadours

Glass, *Sonatine for Basstuba and Piano*: Fletcher, John

Glinka, Michael/Smalley, *Overture to Russlan and Ludmila*: British Tuba Quartet

Godard and Steckar, *Et le Klaxon Retentit Derechef comme un Lézard Hongrois enrhumé*: Steckar Tubapack

Golland, John, *Scherzo*: Sykes, Stephen

Goret, Didier, *Detournement Mineur*: Steckar Elephant Tuba Horde

Gottschalk, Arthur, *Substructures* for ten tubas: University of Michigan Tuba Ensemble

Gould, Morton/Woo, *Pavanne from the "Latin America Suite"*: University of Miami Tuba Ensemble

Gould, Morton, *Tuba Suite* for tuba and three horns: Phillips, Harvey

Gounod, Charles/Berry, *Funeral March of a Marionette*: Tubadours

Graham and Williams, *I Ain't Got Nobody*: Newberger, Eli

Green, Freddie/Esleck, *Corner Pocket*: Tennessee Technological University Tuba/Euphonium Ensemble

Gregson, Edward, *Alarum* (solo tuba): Gourlay, James

Gregson, Edward, *Concerto for Tuba* (with brass band): Fletcher, John; Gourlay, James; Lind, Michael; Maierhofer, Josef; Wagner, Michael

Gregson, Edward, *Concerto for Tuba* (with concert band): Nord, Lennart

Grieg, Edvard, *In the Hall of the Mountain King*: Bell, William

Gruber, Franz, *Silent Night*: Phillips, Harvey/Tuba-Christmas

Grundman, Clare, *Tuba Rhapsody*: Varner, Lesley

Gruner, Joachim, *Konzert für Tuba und Orchester*: Unkrodt, Dietrich

Hackbarth, Glenn, *Double Concerto*: Perantoni, Daniel

Haddad, Don, *Suite for Tuba*: Conner, Rex; Davis, Ronald

Hancock, Herbie/Perry, *Cameleon*: Tennessee Technological University Tuba/Euphonium Ensemble

Handel, George Friderik, *Air and Bourrée*: Conner, Rex

Handel, George Friderik, *Andante*: Phillips, Harvey

Handel, George Friderik, *Air con Variazioni* from Suite No. 5 in E Major: Dowling, Eugene

Handel, George Friderik/Fitzgerald, *Aria con Variazioni*: Seward, Steven

Handel, George Friderik/Lafosse, *Concerto in G Minor for Oboe and Orchestra*: Popiel, Peter

Handel, George Friderik, *Joy to the World*: Phillips, Harvey/TubaChristmas

Handel, George Friderik, *Selected Movements from Sonatas for Flute*: Phillips, Harvey

Handel, George Friderik/Hilgers, *Sonata in C Major, Op. 1 No. 7, for tuba and organ*: Hilgers, Walter

Handel, George Friderik, *Sonata in G Major*: Pokorny, Gene

Handy, W. C., *Beale Street Blues*: Lehr, David "Red"

Handy, W. C., *St. Louis Blues*: Lehr, David "Red"; Palmer, Singleton

Handy, W. C./Holcombe, *Saint Louis Blues*: Melton Tuba-Quartett

Harbach and Kern, *Yesterdays*: Draper, Ray

Harlos, Steve, *Breakthrough*: Self, James

Harper, Billy, *Priestess*: Stewart, Bob

Harrison, Wayne, *Beneath the Surface*: Tennessee Technological University Tuba/Euphonium Ensemble

Hartley, Walter, *Bivalve Suite for Euphonium and Tuba*: LeBlanc, Robert

Hartley, Walter, *Concertino for Tuba and Wind Ensemble*: Turk, John

Hartley, Walter, *Double Concerto for Saxophone, Tuba and Winds*: Erickson, Martin

Hartley, Walter, *Miniatures for 4 Four Valve Instruments*: Atlantic Tuba Quartet

Hartley, Walter, *Sonata*: LeBlanc, Robert

Hartley, Walter, *Sonatina*: Popiel, Peter

Hartley, Walter, *Suite for Flute and Tuba*: Phillips, Harvey

Hartley, Walter, *Suite for Unaccompanied Tuba*: Conner, Rex; Fletcher, John; Popiel, Peter

Hastings, Ross, *Little Madrigal for Big Horns*: University of Miami Tuba Ensemble

Heiden, Bernard, *Variationen for Tuba and Nine Horns*: Phillips, Harvey

Henderson, Ray, *Alabamy Bound*: Lehr, David "Red"

Henley, James, *Indiana*: Pilafian, Sam

Henry, Cleo, *Boplicity*: Barber, John William (Bill)

Herbert, Victor/Vaughan, *March of the Toy Soldiers*: Tubadours

Hermann, Heinz, *Korn Blues*: Scandinavian Tuba Jazz

Hermann, Herman, *Y Luego*: Scandinavian Tuba Jazz

Heusen, Van/Barton, *Here's That Rainy Day*: British Tuba Quartet

Heussenstamm, George, *Tubafour*: New York Tuba Quartet

Hilgers, Walter, *Praeludium*: Gerhard Meinl's Tuba Sextet

Hiller, Lejaren, *Malta for Tuba and Tape*: Cummings, Barton

Hindemith, Paul, *Sonata for Bass Tuba and Piano*: Augustin, Rudiger; Baadsvik, Øystein; Bobo, Roger; Fletcher, John; Georgie, Gerhard; Hoppert, Manfred; Lind, Michael; Perantoni, Daniel; Pokorny, Gene; Torchinsky, Abe; Turk, John

Hindemith, Paul, *Three Easy Pieces*: Hanks, Toby

Holmboe, Vagn, *Notater* for three trombones and tuba: Arnsted, Jørgen Voight

Holmes, Brian, *Tales of the Cultural Revolution*: Fritze, Gregory

Holmes, Paul, *Lento*: Conner, Rex; Davis, Ronald; LeBlanc, Robert

Holmes, Paul, *Quartet for Tubas*: British Tuba Quartet; University of Michigan Tuba and Euphonium Ensemble

Holst, Gustav, *Mars from "The Planets"* (excerpts): Jacobs, Arnold

Hook, J./Garrett, *Rondo*: British Tuba Quartet

Hooker, John Lee/Clayton-Thomas, *One Room Country Shack*: Bargeron, Dave

Hopkins/Lycan, *We Three Kings*: Tubadours

Horovitz, Joseph, *Rumpole of the Bailey*: British Tuba Quartet

Horowitz, Joseph, *Tuba Concerto*: Gourlay, James

Howarth, Elgar, *Carnival of Venice*: Fletcher, John

Howe, Julia Ward, *Battle Hymn of the Republic*: Lehr, David "Red"

Huffine, G. H., *Them Basses*: United States Armed Forces Tuba-Euphonium Ensemble

Hupfeld, Herman, *When Yuba Plays the Rhumba on the Tuba Down in Cuba*: Bell, William; Phillips, Harvey: Tarto, Joe; Washburn, Joe "Country"

Hutchinson, Terry, *Tuba Juba Duba*: Melton Tuba-Quartett; Tennessee Technological University Tuba/Euphonium Ensemble

Iannaccone, Anthony, *Hades* for two euphoniums and two tubas: University of Michigan Tuba Ensemble

Iannacone, Anthony, *Sonatina for Trumpet and Tuba*: Smith, J. R.

Iannaccone, Anthony, *Three Mythical Sketches* for four tubas: University of Michigan Tuba Ensemble

Jacob, Gordon, *Tuba Suite*: Dowling, Eugene

Jacobsen, Julius, *Tuba Ballet for Tuba and Woodwind Quintet*: Lind, Michael

Jae Eun Ha, *Three Pieces*: Cummings, Barton

Jager, Robert, *Concerto for Bass Tuba*: Morris, R. Winston; Perantoni, Daniel

Jager, Robert, *Fantasy-Variations*: Daniel, Robert N.

Janin, D., *Swingin' Little Swiss Tuba . . . Cuckoo-clock*: Steckar, Marc

Jarreau, Al/Murphy, *Boogie Down*: Tennessee Technological University Tuba/Euphonium Ensemble

Jarrett, Keith/Matteson, *Lucky Southern*: Matteson-Phillips TubaJazz Consort

Johnson, Blind Willie/Mahal, *You're Going to Need Somebody on Your Bond*: Johnson, Howard

Johnson, Bunk, *Moose Blues*: Newberger, Eli

Johnson, Howard, *Album Album*: Johnson, Howard

Johnson, Howard, *Music Written for Monterey*: Johnson, Howard

Jones, Roger, *Duet No. 12 from "21 Distinctive Duets"*: University of Miami Tuba Ensemble

Jones and Dickerson, *Tia Juanna Man*: Newberger, Eli

Joplin, Scott, *The Cascades*: Pilafian, Sam

Joplin, Scott/Sabourin, *The Cascades*: British Tuba Quartet

Joplin, Scott/LeClair, *The Easy Winners*: The Contraband

Joplin, Scott/Picher, *Elite Syncopations*: British Tuba Quartet

Joplin, Scott/Self, *The Entertainer*: Tennessee Tech Tuba-Euphonium Quintet; United States Armed Forces Tuba-Euphonium Ensemble

Joplin, Scott/Werden, *Euphonic Sounds*: Atlantic Tuba Quartet; British Tuba Quartet

Joplin, Scott/Powell, *The Favorite Rag*: British Tuba Quartet

Joplin, Scott, *Peacherine Rag*: Pilafian, Sam

Joplin, Scott/Werden, *Ragtime Dance*: United States Navy Band Tuba-Euphonium Quartet

Joplin, Scott, *Solace*: Gannett, Dave

Kabalevski, Dmitri/Berry, *Comedian's Galop*: Tubadours

Kalina, Ron, *Children at Play*: Self, James

Kassel and Stitzel, *Sobbin' Blues*: Newberger, Eli

Kellaway, Roger, *Dance of the Ocean Breeze* for horn, bass horn, and piano: Bobo, Roger

Kellaway, Roger, *The Morning Song*: Arnsted, Jørgen Voight; Bobo, Roger

Kellaway, Roger, *Sonoro* for horn, bass horn, and piano: Bobo, Roger

Kellaway, Roger, *The Westwood Song*: Bobo, Roger

Kern, Jerome, *Ol' Man River*: Pilafian, Sam

Kern, Jerome/Holcomb, *They Didn't Believe Me*: British Tuba Quartet

Kilon, Moshe, *Sine Nomine*: Hershko, Adi

King, Karl L./Berry, *Barnum and Bailey's Favorite*: Tubadours

King, Karl L./Morris, *Barnum and Bailey's Favorite*: United States Armed Forces Tuba-Euphonium Ensemble

King, Karl L./Werden, *The Melody Shop*: United States Armed Forces Tuba-Euphonium Ensemble

Kingsbury/Harclerode, *Infant Holy*: Tubadours

Kleinsinger and Tripp: *The Further Adventures of Tubby the Tuba*: Johnson, John Thomas (Tommy); Phillips, Harvey

Kleinsinger and Tripp, *Tubby at the Circus*: Anonymous (Bell, William); Johnson, John Thomas (Tommy)

Kleinsinger and Tripp: *Tubby Meets a Jazz Band*: Johnson, John Thomas (Tommy)

Kleinsinger, George, and Tripp, Paul, *Tubby the Tuba*: Anonymous; Boujie, George; Bruno, Jerry; Call, R. Steven; Jenkel, Herbert; Johnson, John Thomas (Tommy); Karella, Clarange; Schmitz, Chester; Thornton, Michael

Kling, H.: *The Elephant and the Fly*: Phillips, Harvey

Knox, Charles, *Scherzando for Tubular Octet*: Tennessee Technological University Tuba/Euphonium Ensemble

Koch, Erland von, *Monolog No. 9 for Unaccompanied Tuba*: Lind, Michael

Kochan, Gunter, *Sieben Miniaturen für Vier Tuben*: Self, James

Koenig, Williams, and Handy, *Careless Love*: Palmer, Singleton

Koetsier, Jan, *Concertino* for tuba and string orchestra: Hoppert, Manfred

Koetsier, Jan, *Sonatina for Tuba and Piano*, Op. 57: Duga, Jan Z; Hoppert, Manfred

Konagaya, Soichi, *Fantasy for Tuba and Piano*: Yasumoto, Hiroyuki

Konagaya, Soichi, *Illusion*: Tennessee Technological University Tuba/Euphonium Ensemble

Kraft, William, *Encounters II for Solo Tuba*: Baadsvik, Øystein; Bobo, Roger

Kranowski, A., *Sonata for Solo Tuba*: Piernik, Zdizislaw

Kreines, *Chorale Variations, "Jesu meine Freude"*: Jacobs, Arnold

Kreisler, Fritz/Yasumoto, *Liebesfreud*: Yasumoto, Hiroyuki

Kresin, Willibald, *Chin Up!* The Contraband

Kresin, Willibald, *Swing Low*: The Contraband

Kupferman, Meyer, *Saturnalis* (tuba and amplified cello): Bobo, Roger

Kurnick, Jon, *Bosque De Manaus*: Self, James

La Roca, Nick, *Tiger Rag*: Lehr, David "Red"; Pilafian, Sam

Lachenmann, *Harmonica—Music for Large Orchestra with Solo Tuba*: Nahatzki, Richard

Lamb, Marvin, *Heavy Metal*: Tennessee Technological University Tuba/Euphonium Ensemble

Landes, B., *The Elephant Tango*: Bell, William

Langgaard, Rued, *Dies Irae* for tuba and piano: Arnsted, Jørgen Voight

Largent, Edward, *Four Shorts for Tuba and Piano*: Turk, John

Lazarof, Henri, *Cadence VI for Tuba and Tape*: Bobo, Roger

Lebedev, Alexander, *Concerto in One Movement*: Hoppert, Manfred

Lebedev, Alexander/Cohen, A., *Concerto in One Movement*: Arwood, Jeffrey

LeClair, David, *Carnival of Venice*: The Contraband; Monarch Tuba-Euphonium Quartet

LeClair, David, *Growing Up Together* (euphonium and tuba duet): The Contraband

LeClair, David, *Heidentüblein*: The Contraband

Lecuona, Ernesto/Morris, *Malagueña*: Tennessee Technological University Tuba/Euphonium Ensemble

Lennon and McCartney/Ito, *Yesterday*: Yasumoto, Hiroyuki

Lerner, Alan Jay/Belsha, *Get Me to the Church on Time*: British Tuba Quartet

Lerner, Alan Jay, *Heather on the Hill*: Self, James

Lerner, Alan Jay, *I Talk to the Trees*: Draper, Ray

Levy, Yehuda, *Mediterranean Rondo*: Hershko, Adi

Lewis, John, *Rouge*: Barber, John William (Bill)

Liptak, David, *Mixed Doubles* for trumpet, tuba, violin, and contrabass: Kaenzig, Fritz

Little, Donald, *Lazy Lullaby*: Davis, Ronald

Livingston and Evans/Inomata, *To Each His Own*: Yasumoto, Hiroyuki

Lockhart and Seitz, *The World Is Waiting for the Sunrise*: Lehr, David "Red"; Newberger, Eli

Loesser, Frank, *On a Slow Boat to China*: Gannett, Dave

Lohmann, Georg/D. Schmidt, *Bayerische Polka*: The Contraband; Gerhard Meinl's Tuba Sextet

Lundquist, Torbjørn Iwan, *Landscape for Tuba and Strings*: Lind, Michael

Lyon, Max J., *Suite for Low Brass*: Atlantic Tuba Quartet

Madsen, Trygve, *Sonata* for tuba and piano: Baadsvik, Øystein; Bobo, Roger

Mahal, Taj, *Big Kneed Gal*: Johnson, Howard

Mahal, Taj, *John, Ain't It Hard?* Johnson, Howard

Mahal, Taj, *Tom and Sally Drake*: Johnson, Howard

Mahal, Taj, *You Ain't No Streetwalker, Mama Honey, But I Do Love the Way You Strut Your Stuff*: Johnson, Howard

Mahler, Gustav/Perantoni and Yutzy, *Lieder eines Fahrenden Gessellen*: Perantoni, Daniel

Mahler, Gustav, *Symphony No. 2* (fifth movement excerpt): Jacobs, Arnold

Mahler, Gustav, *Symphony No. 3* (first movement excerpt): Jacobs, Arnold

Mancini, Henry/Luis, *Baby Elephant Walk*: Melton Tuba-Quartett

Mancini, Henry/Krush, *The Pink Panther*: British Tuba Quartet; Melton Tuba-Quartett; Northern Tuba Lights

Marcello, Benedetto, *Sonata in F Major for Tuba and Piano*: Lind, Michael

Martin, Blaine/Bewley, *Have Yourself a Merry Little Christmas*: Phillips, Harvey/TubaChristmas

Martin, Carroll, *Pompola*: Davis, Ronald

Martin, Glenn, *Bluesin' Tubas*: Tennessee Technological University Tuba/Euphonium Ensemble

Martin, Glenn, *Chops!* Tennessee Technological University Tuba/Euphonium Ensemble

Martini, J. P. E./Yodo, *Piacer d'Amor*: Yasumoto, Hiroyuki

Martino, Ralph, *Fantasy*: British Tuba Quartet; Monarch Tuba-Euphonium Quartet

Marxsen, Dale, *Waltzing with Bears*: Davis, Ronald

Massenet, Jules/Erickson, Margaret, *Aragonaise from "Le Cid"*: Monarch Tuba-Euphonium Quartet; United States Navy Band Tuba-Euphonium Quartet

Matteson, Rich, *Little Ole Softy*: Matteson-Phillips TubaJazz Consort

Matteson, Rich, *Spoofy*: Matteson-Phillips TubaJazz Consort

McBeth, Francis, *Daniel in the Lion's Den*: Perantoni, Daniel

McDaniel, Ernie, *Secrets*: Self, James

McDermot, *Dead End*: Scandinavian Tuba Jazz

McDonald and Hanley, *Indiana*: Lehr, David "Red"

McDonald, Goodwin, and Hanley, *Breeze*: Newberger, Eli

McLean, Jackie, *Beau Jack*: Draper, Ray

McLean, Priscilla, *Beneath the Horizon for Tuba and Taped Whale Songs*: Poore, Melvyn

Mehlan, Keith, *Bottoms Up Rag*: Monarch Tuba-Euphonium Quartet

Mehlan, Keith, *Eine kleine Schreckens Musik (A Little Fright Music)*: Monarch Tuba-Euphonium Quartet

Meier, Jost, *Eclipse finale?* for tuba and brass band: Baadsvik, Øystein

Melrose, Walter, *Tin Roof Blues*: Palmer, Singleton

Mendelssohn, Felix, *It Is Enough from "Elijah"*: Popiel, Peter

Mendez, Rafael, *Sambe Guitana*: Sykes, Steven

Mercer, Johnny, *Tangerine*: Gannett, Dave

Mercer and Arlen, *Blues in the Night*: Price, Tony

Merle, John, *Mummers (Dance Grotesque)*: Bell, William

Michel, Marc, *Le Jour ou Les Tubas*: Steckar Elephant Tuba Horde

Miller, Sy and Jackson, Jill, *Let There Be Peace on Earth*: Porter, William D.

Mingus, Charlie, *Peggy's Blue Skylight*: Self, James

Monaco/Holcombe, *You Made Me Love You*: British Tuba Quartet

Monk, Thelonius, *Blue Monk*: Steckar Tubapack

Monk, Thelonius, *Blues by Monk*: Johnson, Howard

Monk, Thelonius, *Coming on the Hudson*: Stewart, Bob

Monk, Thelonius, *Epistrophy*: Stewart, Bob

Monk, Thelonius, *Light Blue*: Stewart, Bob

Monk, Thelonius, *Nutty*: Stewart, Bob

Monk, Thelonius, *Off Minor*: Stewart, Bob

Monk, Williams, and Hanighen, *'Round Midnight*: Self, James

Monsborough, Abe, *Don't Monkey with It*: Newberger, Eli

Monti, V., *Czardas*: Hilgers, Walter

Morell, John, *Windsong*: Self, James

Moret, Neil, *Song of the Wanderer*: Newberger, Eli

Mori, Yoshiko, *Barcarolle for Tuba*: Yasumoto, Hiroyuki

Morrison, Van/Kile, *Moondance*: Tennessee Technological University Tuba/Euphonium Ensemble

Morton, F. "Jelly Roll," *Chicago Breakdown*: Newberger, Eli

Morton, F. "Jelly Roll," *Wolverine Blues*: Lehr, David "Red"

Moschner, Pinguin, *Antartic Love Song*: Moschner, Pinguin

Moschner, Pinguin, *Bouillabaisse (thanks, Maggie)*: Moschner, Pinguin

Moschner, Pinguin, *Deep Throb*: Moschner, Pinguin

Moschner, Pinguin, *Love Story (und dann ging's heiss hier)*: Moschner, Pinguin

Moschner, Pinguin, *Majobiwomo*: Moschner, Pinguin

Moschner, Pinguin, *Sax-Machine*: Moschner, Pinguin

Moschner, Pinguin, *Waterloo*: Moschner, Pinguin

Moschner, Pinguin, *Der Wurst lebt*: Moschner, Pinguin

Mouret, Jean Joseph/Mancini, *The Masterpiece*: Johnson, John Thomas (Tommy)

Mouret, Jean Joseph/Self, *Rondo*: Tubadours

Mozart, Wolfgang Amadeus/Self, *Allegro* from *Eine kleine Nachtmusik*: Tubadours

Mozart, Wolfgang Amadeus/Crespo, Hilgers, and Pilafian, *Divertimento No. 2 in B♭*: Gerhard Meinl's Tuba Sextet

Mozart, Wolfgang Amadeus/Fletcher, *Eine kleine Nachtmusik*: Melton Tuba-Quartett

Mozart, Wolfgang Amadeus, *Non più Andrai from "Le Nozze di Figaro"*: Fletcher, John

Mozart, Wolfgang Amadeus, *O Isis and Osiris*: Bell, William; Phillips, Harvey

Mozart, Wolfgang Amadeus/Fabrizio, *Overture to the "Marriage of Figaro"*: Monarch Tuba-Euphonium Quartet

Mozart, Wolfgang Amadeus/Ferguson, *Overture to the "Marriage of Figaro"*: British Tuba Quartet

Mozart, Wolfgang Amadeus/Gottschalk, *Overture to the "Marriage of Figaro"*: United States Armed Forces Tuba-Euphonium Ensemble; University of Michigan Tuba and Euphonium Ensemble

Mozart, Wolfgang Amadeus, *Rondo in E♭ Major*, K371: Piernik, Zdizislaw

Mozart, Wolfgang Amadeus/Fletcher, *Tuba Serenade (Eine kleine Nachtmusik)*: Fletcher, John

Mozart, Wolfgang Amadeus/Mehlan, *Turkish Rondo*: Monarch Tuba-Euphonium Quartet

Mueller, Florian, *Concert Music for Bass Tuba*: Conner, Rex

Mueller/Vaughan, *Away in a Manger*: Tubadours

Muscroft, Fred, *Carnival for Bass*: Baker, Fred

Mussorgsky, Modest, *Bydlo from "Pictures at an Exhibition"*: Piernik, Zdizislaw

Mussorgsky, Modest, *Song of the Flea*: Fletcher, John

Myers, Stanley, *Cavatina*: Self, James

Nelhybel, Vaclav, *Concerto Grosso for Tubas and Band*: Anonymous

Newsome, Roy, *The Bass in the Ballroom*: Sykes, Stephen

Newsome, Roy, *Swiss Air*: Crowther, Shaun

Newton, Rodney, *Capriccio for E♭ Bass*: Gourlay, James; Sykes, Steven

Niehaus, Lennie, *Brass Tacks*: Northern Tuba Lights

Niehaus, Lennie, *Grand Slam*: British Tuba Quartet

Niehaus, Lennie, *Miniature Jazz Suite*: Melton Tuba-Quartett

Niehaus, Lennie, *Sleeping Giants*: The Contraband

Nielsen, Hans Peter, *The Satyr*: Anonymous

Nilsson, Bo, *Bass* for solo tuba and buckle gongs: Lind, Michael

Novick, Billy, *When She Cries*: Newberger, Eli

Nyro, Laura/Cherry, *Eli's Coming*: Tennessee Technological University Tuba/Euphonium Ensemble

Offenbach, Jacques/Fletcher, *Orpheus in the Underworld*: Northern Tuba Lights

O'Hara, Betty, *Euphonics*: Tennessee Technological University Tuba/Euphonium Ensemble

Oliver, Joe, *Chimes Blues*: Newberger, Eli

Ott, Joseph, *Bart's Piece for Tuba and Electronic Tape*: Cummings, Barton

Paderewski, Ignacy Jan, *Minuet*: Piernik, Zdizislaw

Paganini, Niccolo/Bell, *Moto Perpetuo*: Bell, William; Jacobs, Arnold; Phillips, Harvey

Paganini, Niccolo, *Theme and Variations*: Dumitru, Ionel

Palmer and Williams, *I Found a New Baby*: Matteson, Rich; Pilafian, Sam

Parker, Charlie, *Au Privave*: New York Tuba Quartet

Parker, Charlie, *Little Suede Shoes*: Pilafian, Sam

Payne, Frank Lynn, *Quartet for Tubas*: Melton Tuba-Quartett; University of Miami Tuba Ensemble; University of Michigan Tuba and Euphonium Ensemble

Peasley, Richard, *The Devil's Herald*: Phillips, Harvey

Pegram, Wayne, *Howdy!* Tennessee Technological University Tuba/Euphonium Ensemble; United States Armed Forces Tuba-Euphonium Ensemble

Penderecki, Krystof, *Capriccio for Solo Tuba*: Bobo, Roger; Gourlay, James; Perantoni, Daniel; Piernik, Zdizislaw

Penn, William, *Three Essays for Solo Tuba*: Turk, John

Persichetti, Vincent, *Parable for Solo Tuba*, Op. 147: Nelson, Mark

Persichetti, Vincent, *Serenade for Ten Wind Instruments*: United States Coast Guard Tuba-Euphonium Quartet

Persichetti, Vincent, *Serenade No. 12 for Solo Tuba*: Phillips, Harvey

Peterson, Oscar/Petersen, J., *Noreen's Nocturn*: Matteson-Phillips TubaJazz Consort

Petrie, H. W., *Asleep in the Deep*: Bell, William

Petrie, H. W./Lamb, *Asleep in the Deep*: Mallon, Barney

Picchi, Ermanno/Mantia, *Fantasie Original*: Seward, Steven

Piernik, Zdizislaw, *Dialogue für Tuba und Tonband*: Piernik, Zdizislaw

Pinkard, Casey, and Tauber, *Them There Eyes*: Pilafian, Sam

Plog, Anthony, *Three Miniatures* for tuba and piano: Bobo, Roger; Perantoni, Daniel

Porter, Cole/Sample, *Cole Porter Medley*: Tennessee Technological University Tuba/Euphonium Ensemble

Porter, Cole, *I Love You*: Self, James

Powell, Baden/Buttery, *Bocoxe*: Atlantic Tuba Quartet; British Tuba Quartet

Powell, Morgan, *Midnight Realities*: Perantoni, Daniel

Powell, Morgan, *Nocturnes*: Perantoni, Daniel

Presser, William, *Capriccio for Tuba and Band*: Astwood, Michael

Proto, Frank, *The Four Seasons* for tuba, percussion, strings, and stereo tape: Thornton, Michael

Pryor, Arthur, *Theme and Variation on the "Blue Bells of Scotland"*: Pokorny, Gene; Seward, Steven

Purcell, Henry, *Allegro and Air*: New York Tuba Quartet

Quibel, R., *Tuba Bouchka*: Steckar, Marc

Rachmaninoff, Sergei, *Three Songs*: Pokorny, Gene

Rachmaninoff, Sergei, *Vocalise*: LeBlanc, Robert

Rachmaninoff, Serge/Perantoni, *Vocalise*: Perantoni, Daniel

Rainey and Arant, *Jelly Bean Blues*: Newberger, Eli

Ramsoe, Emilio Wilhelm, *Allegro Vivace from Quartet No. 5*, Op. 38: Fletcher, John

Ramsoe, Emilio Wilhelm/Buttery, *Andante Quasi Allegretto*: Melton Tuba-Quartett

Ramsoe, Emilio Wilhelm/Buttery, *Quartet for Brass*: British Tuba Quartet; United States Coast Guard Tuba-Euphonium Quartet

Ramsoe, Emilio Wilhelm/Buttery, *Quartet for Brass* (third movement): United States Navy Band Tuba-Euphonium Quartet

Ramsoe, Emilio Wilhelm/Buttery, *Quartet No. 4 (Allegro molto)*: Atlantic Tuba Quartet

Raph, Alan, *Rock*: McKee, Edward R.

Rasbach, *Trees*: Cummings, Barton

Ravel, Maurice, *Pavane pour une enfante défunte*: Pokorny, Gene

Ravel, Maurice, *Pièce en forme de habanera*: Dowling, Eugene

Razof, Johnson, *Louisiana*: Pilafian, Sam

Reck, David, *Five Studies for Tuba Alone*: Hanks, Toby

Redner/Vaughan, *Oh Little Town of Bethlehem*: Tubadours

Reed, Alfred, *Fantasia a due*: United States Air Force Concert Band Tuba Section

Reinhardt, Django, *Micro*: Pilafian, Sam

Reinken, Fred, *Wabash Blues*: Lehr, David "Red"; Pilafian, Sam

Relton, William, *The Trouble with the Tuba Is*: Crowther, Shaun

Reynolds, Verne, *Signals* for trumpet, tuba, and brass choir: Bobo, Roger

Rheinhart, Django, *Rhythm Futur*: Pilafian, Sam

Richardson and McLean/Whitcomb, *Too Fat Polka*: Tubadours

Rimsky-Korsakov, Nicholas/Fletcher, *Flight of the Bumblebee*: Fletcher, John

Rimsky-Korsakov, Nicholas/Gourlay, *Flight of the Bumblebee*: Gourlay, James

Rimsky-Korsakov, Nicholas/Wagner, *Flight of the Bumblebee*: Wagner, Michael

Rimsky-Korsakov, Nicholas, *Notturno*: British Tuba Quartet

Robbins, Allen, and Sheafe, *Washington and Lee Swing*: Matteson, Rich

Robin and Shavers, *Undecided Now*: Lehr, David "Red"

Rodgers, Richard/Cherry, *My Favorite Things*: Tennessee Technological University Tuba/Euphonium Ensemble

Rodgers and Hart, *My Funny Valentine*: Self, James

Rogers, Thomas, *Music for Tuba Ensemble*: University of Miami Tuba Ensemble

Rogers, Walter, *The Volunteer*: Arwood, Jeffrey

Rollin, Robert, *The Raven and the First Men* (tuba, horn, piano, electronics): Turk, John

Rollins, Sonny, *Doxy*: Draper, Ray

Rollins, Sonny, *Oleo*: Draper, Ray

Rollins, Sonny/Matteson, *Oleo*: Matteson-Phillips TubaJazz Consort

Rollinson, T. H., *Rocked in the Cradle of the Deep*: Lawhern, Tim

Rose, Jolson, and DeSylva, *Avalon*: Matteson, Rich; Pilafian, Sam

Rosler, J. J./D. Schmidt, *Partita—Polacca*: Gerhard Meinl's Tuba Sextet

Ross, Walter, *Concerto Basso*: Tennessee Technological University Tuba/Euphonium Ensemble

Ross, Walter, *Escher's Sketches*: Nelson, Mark

Ross, Walter, *Fancy Dances for Three Bass Tubas*: New York Tuba Quartet

Ross, Walter, *Midnight Variations* for tuba and tape: Cummings, Barton

Ross, Walter, *Piltdown Fragments* for tuba and tape: Cummings, Barton

Ross, Walter, *Tuba Concerto with Band*: Phillips, Harvey

Rossini, Gioacchino/Smalley, *La Danza*: British Tuba Quartet

Rossini, Gioacchino/Roberts, *Largo al Factotum*: Crowther, Shaun; Gourlay, James

Rossini, Gioacchino/Kile, *Overture to the "Barber of Seville"*: United States Armed Forces Tuba-Euphonium Ensemble

Rossini, Gioacchino/Davis, *Petit Caprice in the Style of Offenbach*: Monarch Tuba-Euphonium Quartet

Rossini, Gioacchino/Smalley, *William Tell Overture*: British Tuba Quartet

Rowles, Jimmy, *The Peacocks*: Self, James

Rubinstein, Arthur, *Bruegel—Dance Visions*: Self, James

Rufeisen, Arie, *A Short Suspense Story*: Hershko, Adi

Russell, Armand, *Suite Concertante*: Cooley, Floyd

Ruth, Matthew, *Exigencies*: Tennessee Technological University Tuba/Euphonium Ensemble

Saint-Saëns, Camille/Murley, *Adagio from Symphony No. 3*: British Tuba Quartet

Saint-Saëns, Camille/Yodo, *Carnival of the Animals (The Elephant)*: Yasumoto, Hiroyuki

Saint-Saëns, Camille, *Carnival of the Animals (The Elephant; The Swan)*: Piernik, Zdizislaw

Saint-Saëns, Camille/Cohen, *Marche Militaire Française*: United States Armed Forces Tuba-Euphonium Ensemble

Saint-Saëns, Camille, *Morceau de Concerto* (*III Allegro non troppo*): Piernik, Zdzislaw

Sample, Steve, *Nostalgia Medley*: Tennessee Technological University Tuba/Euphonium Ensemble

Sampson, Recaf, Foodman, and Webb, *Stompin' at the Savoy*: Matteson-Phillips TubaJazz Consort

Sass, Jonathon, *Meltdown*: Gerhard Meinl's Tuba Sextet

Sauter, Eddie, *Conjectures for Tuba and Band*: Phillips, Harvey

Schäffer, Boguslaw, *Projekt für Tuba und Tonband*: Piernik, Zdzislaw

Schiaffini, Giancarlo, *G. S.*: Schiaffini, Giancarlo

Schiaffini, Giancarlo, *Infernal Dream*: Schiaffini, Giancarlo

Schmidt, Ole, *Concerto for Tuba and Orchestra*: Lind, Michael

Schmidt, William, *Serenade* for tuba and piano: Conner, Rex; Johnson, John Thomas (Tommy)

Schoebel, Mares, and Rappolo, *Farewell Blues*: Lehr, David "Red"

Schoenberg, C. M./Mead, *On My Own from "Les Miserables"*: British Tuba Quartet

Schooley, John, *Cherokee* for tuba quartet: Northern Tuba Lights

Schop/Vaughan, *Break Forth O Beauteous Light*: Tubadours

Schubert, Franz Peter/LeClair, *Militärmarsch*: The Contraband

Schubert, Franz Peter, *Serenade*: Bobo, Roger; Piernik, Zdzislaw

Schubert, Franz Peter/LeClair, *Ständchen*: The Contraband

Schuller, Gunther, *Capriccio for Tuba and Orchestra*: Phillips, Harvey

Schuller, Gunther, *Five Moods for Tuba Quartet*: New York Tuba Quartet

Schulz, Heinrich/Harclerode, *O Come Little Children*: Tubadours

Schumann, Robert, *Adagio and Allegro in Ab*, Op. 70: Cooley, Floyd; Dowling, Eugene

Schumann, Robert, *Drei Romanzen*, Op. 94: Cooley, Floyd

Schumann, Robert, *Fantasiestücke*, Op. 73: Cooley, Floyd

Schumann, Robert/Bell, *The Jolly Farmer Goes to Town*: Bell, William

Schumann, Robert, *Märchenbilder* (Pictures of Fairyland), Op. 113: Cooley, Floyd

Schumann, Robert/Self, *Scenes from Childhood,* Op. 15: Self, James

Schumann, Robert, *Three Romanzes*: Cooley, Floyd

Schumann, Robert, *Träumerei*: Piernik, Zdzislaw

Schumann, Robert/Seitz, *Träumerei*: Melton Tuba-Quartett

Sear, Walter, *Sonatina*: Davis, Ronald; Megules, Karl

Self, James, *Courante*: Self, James

Semler-Collery, Jules, *Barcarolle et Chanson Bachique*: Popiel, Peter

Shearing, George/Perry, *Lullaby of Birdland*: Tennessee Technological University Tuba/Euphonium Ensemble

Sherwin, Manning/Mehlan, *A Nightingale Sang in Berkley Square*: Monarch Tuba-Euphonium Quartet

Sherwin, Manning/Smalley, *A Nightingale Sang in Berkley Square*: British Tuba Quartet

Shostakovich, Dimitri, *Adagio*: Bobo, Roger

Sibbing, Robert, *Sonata*: Perantoni, Daniel

Sikora, Elzbieta, *Il Viaggio 1 per tuba solo con pianoforte*: Piernik, Zdzislaw

Silver, Horace/Matteson, *Gregory Is Here*: Matteson-Phillips TubaJazz Consort

Sinigaglia, Leone, *Song and Humoreske*: Bobo, Roger

Sivelov, Niklas, *Sonata* for tuba and piano: Baadsvik, Øystein

Smith, Claude T., *Ballade and Presto Dance*: Daniel, Robert

Smith, Glenn, *Forowen 3* (tuba and piccolo): Turk, John

Smith, Jabbo, *Lina Blues*: Newberger, Eli

Smith, Warren, *Blues for E. L. C.*: Johnson, Howard

Smith, Warren, *Hello Julius*: Johnson, Howard

Smith, Warren, *Introduction to the Blues*: Johnson, Howard

Smith, Warren, *Lament*: Johnson, Howard

Snow, Phoebe, *Sweet Disposition*: Johnson, Howard

Solal, *Tuba Only*: Steckar Tubapack

Sousa, John Philip/Morris, *El Capitan*: British Tuba Quartet; Monarch Tuba-Euphonium Quartet

Sousa, John Philip/Werden, *Hands Across the Sea*: Northern Tuba Lights

Sousa, John Philip/Morris, *Semper Fidelis*: British Tuba Quartet

Sousa, John Philip/Werden, *Stars and Stripes Forever*: Atlantic Tuba Quartet; Northern Tuba Lights; University of Miami Tuba Ensemble

Sousa, John Philip/Sabourin, *Washington Post*: British Tuba Quartet; Melton Tuba-Quartett

Sousa, John Philip/Werden, *Washington Post*: The Contraband

Sowerby, Leo, *Chaconne*: Davis, Ronald

Spears, Jared, *Divertimento for Tuba Ensemble*: Tennessee Technological University Tuba/Euphonium Ensemble

Spillman, Robert, *Two Songs*: Bobo, Roger

Steckar, Franck, *Rouleaux de Printemps*: Steckar Elephant Tuba Horde

Steckar, Franck, *Stabillo Steckardello*: Steckar Elephant Tuba Horde

Steckar, Marc, *Danse pour un Kangourou*: Steckar Tubapack

Steckar, Marc, *Suite à suivre*: Steckar Tubapack

Steckar, Marc, *Tubas au Fujiyama*: Steckar Elephant Tuba Horde

Steckar and Colombo, *Butacudatuba*: Steckar, Marc

Steckar and Colombo, *Tuba Banjo Dixie*: Steckar, Marc

Steckar and Delaporte, *African Tuba Safari*: Steckar, Marc

Steckar and Galliano, *Bayerische Pop Tuba*: Steckar, Marc

Steckar and Galliano, *Tubacuba*: Steckar, Marc

Steele and Melrose, *High Society*: Lehr, David "Red"; Palmer, Singleton

Stevens, Halsey, *Sonatina* for tuba and piano: Perantoni, Daniel; Randolph, David; Self, James

Stevens, John, *Dances*: Hanks, Toby; Melton Tuba-Quartett; Northern Tuba Lights

Stevens, John, *The Liberation of Sisyphus*: Bobo, Roger

Stevens, John: *Manhattan Suite*: University of Michigan Tuba and Euphonium Ensemble

Stevens, John, *Moondance*: Summit Tubas; United Sates Air Force Concert Band Tuba Section

Stevens, John, *Music 4 Tubas*: New York Tuba Quartet

Stevens, John, *Power* for four tubas: Northern Tuba Lights; Stevens, John

Stevens, John, *Splinters*: Stevens, John

Stevens, John, *Suite for II*: Stevens, John

Stevens, John, *Suite No. 1 for Solo Tuba*: Stevens, John

Stevens, John, *Thunder and Lightning*: Stevens, John

Stevens, John, *Triumph of the Demon Gods*: Stevens, John

Stevens, Thomas, *Encore Boz*: Bobo, Roger

Stevens, Thomas, *Variations in Olden Style*: Bobo, Roger

Stewart, Bob, *CJ*: Stewart, Bob

Stewart, Bob, *First Line*: Stewart, Bob

Stewart, Bob, *Hambone*: Stewart, Bob

Stewart, Bob, *Nonet*: Stewart, Bob

Stewart, Bob, *Sweet Georgia Brown Sweet*: Stewart, Bob

Stewart, Bob, *Tunk*: Stewart, Bob

Stitzel, Mel, *The Chant*: Newberger, Eli

Stradella, Alessandro, *Pièta, Signora*: Megules, Karl

Strauss, Johann Jr./Smalley, *Chit Chat Polka*: British Tuba Quartet

Strauss, Johann Jr./Berry, *Waltz from "Die Fledermaus"*: Tubadours

Strauss, Richard, *Concerto No. 1 for Horn*: Jacobs, Arnold

Strauss, Richard, *Second Horn Concerto*: Seward, Steven

Stroud, Richard, *Treatments for Tuba*: Tennessee Technological University Tuba/Euphonium Ensemble

Strukov, Valery, *Concerto for Tuba and Orchestra*: Bjørn-Larsen, Jens

Subotnick, Morton: *First Dream of Light* (tuba, piano, electronic ghost score): Bobo, Roger

Susato, Tielman/Winter, *Ronde and Saltarelle "Pour Quoy"*: Atlantic Tuba Quartet

Swann, Donald, *Two Moods for Tuba*: Phillips, Harvey

Swanstone, McCarron, and Morgan, *The Blues My Naughty Sweetie Gave to Me*: Lehr, David "Red"

Szalonek, W., *Piernikiana for Solo Tuba*: Piernik, Zdzislaw

Tackett, Fred, *The Yellow Bird*: Bobo, Roger

Takács, Jenö, *Sonata Capricciosa*, Op. 81; Randolph, David

Tarlow, Lawrence, *Quintet for Tubas*: Megules, Karl

Taylor, Coleridge, *Substructure*: Johnson, Howard

Taylor, Jeffery, *Fanfare No. 1*: Monarch Tuba-Euphonium Quartet

Taylor, Mark, *Latin Fantasy*: Arwood, Jeffrey

Taylor, Tell/Vaughan, *Down by the Old Mill Stream*: Tubadours

Tchaikovsky, Peter Ilyitch/Self, *Dance of the Reedpipes*: Tubadours

Tchaikovsky, Peter Ilyitch, *1812 Overture* (excerpt): Jacobs, Arnold

Tchaikovsky, Peter Ilyitch/ Charlton, *March—Overture from "Nutcracker"*: Tubadours

Tchaikovsky, Peter Ilyitch, *Overture Miniature from "Nutcracker"*: Fletcher, John

Tchaikovsky, Peter Ilyitch/O'Conner, *Serenade for Tubas*: Tennessee Technological University Tuba/Euphonium Ensemble

Tchaikovsky, Peter Ilyitch, *Symphony No. 6* (fourth movement excerpt): Jacobs, Arnold

Tchaikovsky, Peter Ilyitch/Smalley, *Trepek*: British Tuba Quartet

Tchaikovsky, Peter Ilyitch/Fletcher, *Waltz from "Sleeping Beauty"*: Fletcher, John

Tcherepnin, Alexander, *Andante* for tuba and piano: Hoppert, Manfred

Telemann, Georg Philipp, *Fantasy in C Minor*: Hanks, Toby

Telemann, Georg Philipp, *Sonata in F Minor*: Seward, Steven

Thingnäs, Frode, *Fink Finster*: Scandinavian Tuba Jazz

Thingnäs, Frode, *Samba Loco*: Scandinavian Tuba Jazz

Thomas, Henry/Mahal, *Fishin' Blues*: Johnson, Howard

Tipei, Sever, *Cuniculi for Five Tubas*: University of Illinois Tuba Quintet

Tomasi, Henri, *Etre ou ne pas Etre* (monolog d'Hamlet) for tuba and three trombones: Hanks, Toby; Jacobs, Arnold

Torme and Wells/Bewley, *The Christmas Song*: Phillips, Harvey/TubaChristmas

Toyama, Yuzo, *Trio Sonata for Tuba, Batteries* [percussion], *and Piano*: Yasumoto, Hiroyuki

Traditional/Mancini, *Amazing Grace*: Johnson, John Thomas (Tommy)

Traditional/D. Schmidt, *Bayerische Zell*: Gerhard Meinl's Tuba Sextet

Traditional, *Dance of the Big Fairies*: Flowers, Herbie

Traditional, *Hey Mama*: Stewart, Bob

Traditional, *Just a Closer Walk with Thee*: Lehr, David "Red"

Traditional/Yamamoto, *Sakura Sakura*: Yasumoto, Hiroyuki

Traditional, *Sometimes I Feel Like a Motherless Child*: Stewart, Bob

Traditional/Trippet and Howard, *Steal Away*: British Tuba Quartet

Traditional, *Surinam*: Stewart, Bob

Traditional/Buttery, *Tsiganochka*: Buttery, Gary

Traditional/Funderburk, *La Tuba*: United States Air Force Concert Band Tuba Section

Traditional, *Tuba Smarties*: Flowers, Herbie

Traditional/Garrett, *Wabash Cannonball*: British Tuba Quartet

Traditional, *When the Saints Go Marchin' In*: Palmer, Singleton

Trujillo, Tommy, *If You Ever Wanna*: Draper, Ray

Uber, David, *Double Portraits (The City)* for trombone and tuba: Lind, Michael

Ustvolskaya, Galina, *Dona Nobis Pacem* for tuba, piccolo, and piano: LeClair, David

Van Heusen and Silvers/Smith, A., *Nancy with the Laughing Face*: Arwood, Jeffrey

Vaughan Williams, Ralph/Hare, *Concerto for Bass Tuba and Band*: Arwood, Jeffrey; Perantoni, Daniel

Vaughan Williams, Ralph, *Concerto for Bass Tuba and Orchestra*: Anonymous; Catelinet, Philip; Cooley, Floyd; Dowling, Eugene; Fletcher, John; Harrild, Patrick; Hoppert, Manfred; Jacobs, Arnold; King, Ian; Lind, Michael; Nahatzki, Richard; Phillips, Harvey; Strand, Donald

Vaughan Williams, Ralph, *Six Studies in English Folksong*: Dowling, Eugene; Pokorny, Gene

Vaughan, Rodger, *Concertpiece No.1*: Conner, Rex; Davis, Ronald

Vaughan, Rodger, *Jingle Bell Waltz*: Tubadours

Verdi, Giuseppe, *Nabucco Overture* (excerpt): Jacobs, Arnold

Vigneron, Louis, *Sentier de Nuit*: Steckar Elephant Tuba Horde

Vignola, Frank, *Chasin' the Antelope*: Pilafian, Sam

Vivaldi, Antonio, *Concerto in C Major for Two Trumpets*: Seward, Steven

Wagner, Richard, *Lohengrin* (Prelude Act III, excerpt): Jacobs, Arnold

Wagner, Richard, *O Du Mein Holder Abendstern from "Tannhäuser"*: Fletcher, John

Wagner, Richard, *Siegfried* (excerpts): Cooley, Floyd

Wagner, Richard, *Tannhäuser Overture* (excerpts): Jacobs, Arnold

Wagner, Richard, *Valkyrie* excerpts (*Magic Fire Music; Ride of the Valkyries*): Jacobs, Arnold

Waldron, Mal, *Flickers*: Draper, Ray

Waldron, Mal, *Mirage*: Draper, Ray

Waller, Thomas "Fats," *Black and Blue*: Pilafian, Sam

Waller, Thomas "Fats," *Jitterbug Waltz*: Self, James

Waller, Thomas "Fats," *Keepin' Out of Mischief Now*: Gannett, Dave

Wallington, George, *Godchild*: Barber, John William (Bill)

Washington and Harline, *When You Wish Upon a Star*: Newberger, Eli

Watkins, Doug, *Help*: Draper, Ray

Watz, F. Melton, *March*: Gerhard Meinl's Tuba Sextet

Weeks, Clifford, *Triptych*: Megules, Karl

Weill, Kurt, *Mack the Knife*: Pilafian, Sam

Weill, Kurt/Nash, *Speak Low*: Callender, Red

Well, Christoph, *Wann der Dudelsack kräht u. a.*: Well, Christoph

Werle, Floyd, *Concertino for Three Brass and Band*: Angerstein, Fred

Werle, Floyd, *Variations on an Old Hymn*: United States Armed Forces Tuba-Euphonium Ensemble

Werle, Floyd, *Variations on an Old Hymn Tune*: Tennessee Technological University Tuba/Euphonium Ensemble

White, Donald, *Sonata for Tuba and Piano*: Kaenzig, Fritz

Whitney, *Introduction and Samba*: Erickson, Martin

Wieniawski, *Mazurca*: Dumitru, Ionel

Wilder, Alec, *Carols for a Merry TubaChristmas*: Phillips, Harvey/TubaChristmas

Wilder, Alec, *Poobah the Tuba*: Bell, William

Wilder, Alec, *Quintet for Brass* (Mvt. III, Tuba Showpiece): Phillips, Harvey

Wilder, Alec, *Sonata for French Horn, Tuba and Piano*: Phillips, Harvey

Wilder, Alec, *Sonata No. 1 for Tuba and Piano*: Phillips, Harvey

Wilder, Alec, *Song for Carol*: Phillips, Harvey

Wilder, Alec/Hilgers, *Suite No. 1 for Tuba and Brass Quintet (Effie)*: Hilgers, Walter

Wilder, Alec, *Suite No. 1 for Tuba and Piano (Effie)*: Bobo, Roger; Lind, Michael; Phillips, Harvey

Wilder, Alec, *Suite No. 2 (Jessie)*: Phillips, Harvey

Wilder, Alec, *Suite No. 2 for French Horn and Tuba*: Phillips, Harvey

Wilder, Alec, *Suite No. 3 (Little Harvey)*: Phillips, Harvey

Wilder, Alec, *Suite No. 4 (Thomas)*: Phillips, Harvey

Wilder, Alec, *Suite No. 5 (Ethan Ayer)*: Phillips, Harvey

Wilder, Alec, *Tuba Encore Piece (A Tubist's Showcase)*: Bobo, Roger

Wilhelm, Rolf, *Concertino* for tuba and concert band: Bjørn-Larsen, Jens

Wilhelm, Rolf, *Concertino* for tuba and wind instruments: Bunn, Michael

Williams, Hank, *Jumbalaya*: Pilafian, Sam

Williams, Howard, *Concertino for Tuba, Percussion and Piano*: Cummings, Barton

Williams, John, *Jabba the Hutt from "Return of the Jedi"*: Pokorny, Gene; Schmitz, Chester

Williams, Mason, *Samba Beach*: Gannett, Dave

Williams, Spencer, *Basin Street Blues*: Lehr, David "Red"; Pilafian, Sam

Williams, Spencer/Mitchell, *Basin Street Blues*: Callender, Red

Williams and Urquhart, *Shake It Down*: Newberger, Eli

Williams and Williams, *Royal Garden Blues*: Lehr, David "Red"

Willis/Harclerode, *It Came Upon a Midnight Clear*: Tubadours

Wilson, Phil, *The Sound of the Wasp*: Matteson, Rich

Wilson, Phil, *What's Her Name?* Matteson, Rich

Wilson, Ted, *Wot Shigona Dew*: Tennessee Technological University Tuba/Euphonium Ensemble

Winfree, Dick, *China Boy*: Pilafian, Sam

Witkin, Beatrice, *Breath and Sounds for Tuba and Tape*: Hanks, Thompson

Wolf, Hugo, *Der Genesene an die Hoffnung*: Hilgers, Walter

Wolking, Henry, *Tuba Blues*: British Tuba Quartet; Northern Tuba Lights

Wood, Philip D., *Gentle Old Sea*: Draper, Ray

Wood, Philip D., *Home*: Draper, Ray

Wood, Philip D., *Trilogy*: Draper, Ray

Wozniak, Doug, *Fishy Song*: Davis, Ronald

Wrubel/Magidson, *Gone with the Wind*: Callender, Red

Wuorinen, Charles, *Tuba Concerto*: Brainard, David

Wyatt, Scott, *Three for One*: Perantoni, Daniel

Yoffe, Shlomo, *Andante and Rondo*: Hershko, Adi

Youmans, Vincent, *Carioca*: Arwood, Jeffrey; Pilafian, Sam

Youmans, Vincent/Norman, *Carioca*: Phillips, Harvey

Young and Meyer, *Sugar*: Gannett, Dave

Zajaczek, Roman, *Tema Cantabile con Piernicazioni per tuba universale e pianoforte*: Piernik, Zdizislaw

Zawinul, Josef/Arnold, *Birdland*: Tennessee Technological University Tuba/Euphonium Ensemble

Ziffrin, Marilyn J., *Four Pieces for Tuba*: Cummings, Barton

Ziffrin, Marilyn J., *Trio for Xylophone, Soprano and Tuba*: Cummings, Barton

Zindars, Earl, *Trigon*: Cooley, Floyd

Zinos, Frederick, *Elegy*: Cummings, Barton

Zonn, Paul, *Divertimento No. 1* (tuba, string bass, percussion): Perantoni, Daniel

Conference Recordings

Second International Brass Congress, Indiana University, Bloomington, Indiana, USA, June 3-8, 1984

June 3

#6 General Meeting and Gala Jazz Concert (Matteson-Phillips TubaJazz Consort) (two tapes)

June 4

#10 Tuba Session: Brian Bowman, Daniel Perantoni

#15 Tuba Session: Chester Schmitz "Orchestral Performance Technique"

#16 IBC2 Session: "Future and Careers in Pedagogy" Panel

#17a Rich Matteson: "Teaching Jazz Improvisation"

#17c T. U. B. A. Mock Orchestra Auditions

#19 The Scandinavian Brass Ensemble

June 5

#20 Tuba Session: Clinic with John Fletcher

#24 IBC2 Session: A Low Brass Presentation

#25 IBC2 Session: The Arban Concert

#28a Tuba Session: T. U. B. A. Competitions, Solo in Recital Competition, Euphonium

#28b Jazz Improv Competition, Tuba and Euphonium

#28c Solo in Recital Competition, Tuba

June 6

#33 Tuba Session: Unkrodt, Zerbe, Tokyo Barituba Ensemble

#36 IBC2 Session: Lecture by Arnold Jacobs

#38 Trombone/Tuba Session: "Doubling"

#40 IBC2 Session: "Writing for Brass, Assets and Liabilities" Panel

#41c T. U. B. A. Mock Band Auditions

44 IBC2 Session: The Modern Brass Ensemble, Budapest

June 7

#46 Tuba Session: Concert

#50 IBC2 Session: The Cleveland Orchestra Brass

#54 IBC2 Session/Tuba: Concert

#55 IBC2 Session: Concert

June 8

#57 Tuba Session: Concert

#60 IBC2 Session: Student Solo Competition Winners

#61 IBC2 Session: Brass Showcase

#62 IBC2 Session: The Massed Brass Concert

#63 Final Gala Concert (two tapes)

All tapes $7.00 each. Discount: $6.00 each for ten or more tapes.

Second Story Jazz Club Concerts at the Second International Brass Congress, June 4-8, 1984

June 4

J1 Slide Hampton, Matteson-Phillips TubaJazz Consort (two cassettes), $14

June 5

J2 Red Rodney, Matteson-Phillips TubaJazz Consort (two cassettes), $14

June 6

J3 Jim Self, Bill Watrous, Matteson-Phillips TubaJazz Consort (two cassettes), $14

June 7

J4 Jim Self, The Tennessee Tech Tuba Ensemble, Student Jazz Competition Winners, Matteson-Phillips TubaJazz Consort (two cassettes), $14

June 8

J5 Free-for-all Jam Session, Matteson-Phillips TubaJazz Consort (two cassettes), $14

Order from Audio Village, Box 291, Bloomington, IN 47402. Proceeds from tapes J1–J5 benefit musicians through grants administered by the Harvey Phillips Foundation.

International Tuba/Euphonium Conference, Sapporo, Japan, August 7-12, 1990

August 7
#1 Opening Concert
Euphonium Tuba Quartet—Shishiz: Rossini, Gioacchino, *Il Barbiere di Siviglia*; Telemann, Georg Philipp, *Tafelmusik*
Arizona State University Tuba Quartet: George, Thom Ritter, *Tubasonatine*; Saint-Saëns, Camille, *Adagio*; Shellans, Michael, *Funky Chunk*; Ramsoe, William, *Quartet for Brass*

August 8
#2 Panel Discussion: Composers and Players
#3 Solo Concert by Guest Artists
Brian Bowman, euphonium: Heim, Norman, *Sonnets for Euphonium and Piano*, Op. 103, "Legend of Delos"
Walter Hilgers, tuba: Handel, Georg Frideric/ Hilgers, *Sonate für Blockflöte in C Dur*
John Mueller, euphonium: Corwell, Neal, *Night Song*; Clarke, Herbert L., *From the Shores of the Mighty Pacific*
Koichi Matsushita, tuba: Ideta, Keizo, *Himatsuri for Tuba and Piano*
Melvin Culbertson, tuba: Goret, Didier, *Soufflés*; Emler, Andy, *Tubastone No. 1*
#4 Lecture on Orchestral Music
#5 Special Clinic and Performance on Contemporary Music
#6 Joint Concert
Tokyo Bari-Tuba Ensemble: Handel, Georg Frideric/Konagaya, *Royal Fireworks*; Respighi, Ottorino/Yodo, *Antiche Danza Atic*; Hoshina, Hiroshi, *Dialogue for the Tokyo Bari-Tuba Ensemble*; Stevens, John, *Higashi Nishi for the Tokyo Bari-Tuba Ensemble*; Ishii, Maki, *Bergklang für 12 Tuba-Euphonium*
United States Navy Band Tuba/Euphonium Quartet: Bulla, Stephen, *Celestial Suite*; Mehlen, Keith, *Tubalation*; Ramsoe, William, *Quartet for Brass*; Holst, Gustav/Erickson, *Two Songs*; Martino, Ralph, *Fantasy for Tuba Quartet*; Tchaikovsky, Peter/Fletcher, *Sleeping Tubas Waltz*; Foster, Stephen/McFayden, *Stephen Foster Medley*; Rossini, Gioacchino/ Davis, *Petit Caprice in the Style of Offenbach*

August 9
#7 Panel Discussion: "The Present State of Musical Education and the Future of Musicianship as a Career"

#8 Solo Concert by Guest Artists
Fritz Kaenzig, tuba: Telemann, Georg Philipp/ Kaenzig, *Sonata in Mi minore from "Essercizi Musici"*; Wyatt, Scott, *Three for One for Tuba and Tape*
Ikumitsu Tado, tuba: Strauss, Franz, *Variation*
Roger Behrend, euphonium: Barat, J. Ed., *Morceau de Concours*; Wiedrich, W., *Reverie*
Mogens Andersen, euphonium: Bach, J. S., *Suite No. 2 for Solo Cello*; Bartók, Béla/ Andersen, *Duet* (with Jørgen Arnsted, tuba)
Kenichi Osawa, tuba: Doi, Yoshiyuki, *Raum für Tuba und Klavier*
#9 Ensemble Concert by Guest Artists and Emerging Artists
Colonial Tuba Quartet: Frackenpohl, Arthur, *Suite for Tuba Quartet*; Fritze, Gregory, *Prelude and Dance*
The Danish Tuba Trio: Danish Traditional/ Anderson, *The Page's Masque*; Jager, Robert, *Variation on a Motive by Wagner*; Andersen, Mogens, *Scandinavian Suite*
Plainhearts: Sano, Satoshi, *Kokobunji Station*; Sano, Satoshi, *Road to Otaka*
The Childs Brothers: Graham, P., *Brilliante*; Bizet, Georges: *Deep Inside the Sacred Temple*; Golland, J., *Child's Play*; Paganini, Niccolo, *Moto Perpetuo*
The Summit Tuba Quartet: Stevens, John, *Moon Dance*

August 10
#10 Solo Concert by Emerging Artists
Isao Wantanabe, tuba: Bach, J. S., *Sonata for Flute in G minor*
Takashi Abo, tuba: Wilder, Alec, *Suite No. 3* (Little Harvey); Schumann, Robert, *Adagio and Allegro*, Op. 70
Gabor Adamik, tuba: Bach, J. S., *Sonata in G minor for Viola da Gamba* (first movement); Charpentier, J., *Prelude et Allegro*
Jerry Young, tuba: Ayers, Jesse, *The Dancing King* for tuba and tape
Jeffrey Funderburk, tuba: Broughton, Bruce, *Sonata for Tuba and Piano*
George Mazzarese, tuba: Mannino, Franko, *Tre Impressioni Seriali per Basso Tuba*
Miho Ofusa, euphonium: Asaka, Yuho, *Déja Vu*
Kiyoshi Sato, tuba: Madsen, Tyrgue, *Sonata for F Tuba*
Norhisa Yamamoto, euphonium: Kaneda, Choji, *Makyo II* for euphonium and percussion
Phil Sindar, tuba: Ruggiero, Charles, *Structured Marbles for Tuba and Digitally Synthesized Tape*
Finn Shumacker, tuba: Schmidt, Ole, *Concerto for Tuba*
Sotaro Fukaishi, euphonium: Miura, Mari, *Picturesque Sketches for Euphonium*

Koji Suzuki, tuba: Vaughan Williams, Ralph,
Concerto for Bass Tuba

Heiko Treibener, tuba: Bozza, Eugene,
Concertino for Tuba and Piano

#11 Solo Concert by Guest Artists

Shuzo Karakawa, tuba: Censhu, Jiro, *Bright and
Early Under the Silent Sky*

Martin Erickson, tuba: Wilder, Alec, *Convalescence Suite* (movements 1, 2, 3, 7, 8); Vivaldi,
Antonio, *Concerto in A minor*

Toru Miura, euphonium: Miyoshi, Akira,
Esquisses pour euphonium et marimba

Mark Evans, tuba: Handel, Georg Frideric/
Evans, *Concerto in G minor* for tuba and
klavier; Spohr, Ludwig/Evans, *Adagio*

Jim Gourlay, tuba: Steptoe, Roger, *Concerto*
(last movement); Bach, J. S., *Suite in Eb*;
Gregson, Edward, *Concerto* (last movement)

#12 Jazz Lecture and Performance

#13 Jazz Improvisation Competition

#14 Final Solo Competition

#15 Lecture in Tuba and Brass Ensemble

#16 Concert with Western and Japanese Musical
Instruments

Sotaro Fukaishi, euphonium: Tono, Tamami,
The link of notes

Hiroyuki Yasumoto, tuba: Nemoto, Takenori,
A Shadowless Tree for tuba, irregularly tuned
koto and Japanese multiple percussion;
Censhu, Jiro, *Vendurous Aubade*

Daniel Perantoni, tuba: Powell, Morgan,
Midnight Realities; Taki, Rentaro/Minami,
Kojo no Tsuki; Omura, Tetsuya, *Oh-Tou-Kab*;
Demars, James, *Tapestry VI—Great Streaked
Face with Beehives*

#17 Tuba-Euphonium and Sapporo Symphony
Orchestra Concert

Brian Bowman, euphonium: Vazzana, Anthony,
Concerto Sapporo

Warren Deck, tuba: Kellaway, Roger, *Songs of
Ascent*

August 11

#18 Solo and Ensemble Concert by Guest Artists
and Emerging Artists

John Mueller, euphonium: Bach, Jan, *Concert
Variations*

Martin Erickson, tuba: Cherubini, Luigi/
Tuckwell, *Sonata No. 2 for Horn*; Wilhelm,
Rolf, *Concerto for Tuba*; Traditional, *Just a
Closer Walk With Thee*

Hirohuki Yasumoto, tuba: Konagaya, Soichi,
Fantasy for tuba and piano

Larry Campbell, euphonium: Constantinides,
Dinos, *Fantasy* for solo euphonium; Arban, J.
B./Del Staigers, *The Carnival of Venice*

Koichi Matsushita and Shuzo Karakawa, tubas;
Vivaldi, Antonio/Matsushita, *Concerto for
two trumpets*

Skip Gray, tuba: Wyatt, Scott, *Lifepoints* for
tuba, percussion and electronic accompaniment

Mary Ann Craig, euphonium: Uber, David,
Sonata da Camera, Op. 238; Picchi,
Ermanno/Mantia, *Fantasie Original*

Harvey Phillips, tuba (with Colonial Tuba
Quartet): Baker, David, *Piece for solo tuba
and tuba quartet*

Jørgen Arnsted, tuba: Grieg, Edvard, *From the
Heart's Melodies*; Langgaard, Rued, *Dies Irae*;
Nielsen, Carl, *Three Songs*; Lennon, John,
and McCartney, Paul/Holmgaard, *Blackbird*

Osawa Ensemble: Kagiwada, Michio, *Funk
Music for a Hi Fi*

#19 Concert by Soloists and Sapporo Wind
Ensemble

Walter Hilgers, tuba: Crespo, Enrique, *Latin
Impressions* for tuba and wind ensemble

Toru Miura, euphonium: Ito, Yasuhide,
Variazioni di Concerto

James Self, tuba: Schmidt, William, *Tunes* for
tuba, winds, and percussion

Melvin Culbertson, tuba: Caens, Thierry, *Mister
M. C. with Brass Ensemble*

Roger Behrend, euphonium: Jacob, Gordon,
Fantasia for euphonium and band

August 12

#20 Solo Concert by Guest Artists

Fritz Kaenzig, tuba: White, Donald, *Sonata for
tuba and piano*

Mark Evans, tuba: Penderecki, Krzysztof,
Capriccio for solo tuba; Geier, Oscar:
Concertstuck

Brian Bowman, euphonium: Corwell, Neal,
Odyssey for euphonium

Ikumitsu Tado, tuba: Broughton, Bruce, *Sonata
for tuba and piano*

Jim Gourley, tuba: Vaughan Williams, Ralph,
Romanza from Concerto for Bass Tuba;
Horovitz, Joseph, *Concerto*

Dietrich Unkrodt, tuba: Kochan, Gunther,
Monolog; Katzenbeier, Hubert, *Drei Spiel-
stucke Nr. 1*; Bach, J. S., *Air in C*; Terzakis,
Dimitri, *Stixis iii*; Lincke, Paul, *Es war
Einmal*

John Stevens, tuba: Stevens, John, *Soliloquy—
Peace in Our Time* with tape; Stevens, John,
Dances for solo tuba and three tubas

Fumio Gato, euphonium: Tsuruhara, Isao,
Sonatine for euphonium and piano

Daniel Perantoni, tuba: Plog, Anthony, *Three
Miniatures* for tuba and piano

#21 Gala Concert

United States Navy Band Tuba-Euphonium
Quartet: Holst, Gustav/Schlesinger,
Intermezzo from First Suite for Military Band;
Mozart, W. A./Mehlan, *Rondo alla Turca*;
Corea, Chick/Mehlan, *Spain*

Roger Bobo, tuba, with Tokyo Bari-Tuba Ensemble: Stevens, John, *The Libertation of Sisyphus*

College All-Star Ensemble, R. Winston Morris, director: Kohl, Bernard, *Feiertagmusik*, Op. 107; Toyama, Yuzo, *Essay in Six Parts*; Mobberley, James, *A Bull in a China Shop*

Sapporo International Music Festival 1990 Tuba Quartet, James Self, conductor; Heussenstamm, George, *Tuba Quartet No. 3*

Childs Brothers, euphoniums: Sparke, P., *Two Part Invention*; Howarth, E., *Cantabile for John Fletcher*; Rimsky-Korsakov, N., *Flight of the Bumblebee*

Guests' Ensemble, Harvey Phillips, conductor: Bach, J. S./Phillips, *Air for the G String*

Conference Massed Tuba-Euphonium Ensemble: Saint-Saëns, Camille, *Adagio*; Mendelssohn, Felix/Smith, *Equali No. 3*; Sousa, John Philip, *Washington Post*; Hutchinson, Terry, *Tuba Juba Duba*; Mozart, W. A./Self, *Eine kleine Nachtmusik*; arr. Funderburk, *La Tuba*

Order from Steven Bryan, T.U.B.A. Treasurer; Dept. of Music; University of Texas at Austin; Austin, TX 78712-1208 USA. Make checks payable to T.U.B.A. Video tapes: one tape, $35.00; two tapes, $55.00; each additional tape, $20.00. Add $5.00 per order for shipping. Audio cassettes: one cassette, $14.00; two cassettes, $28.00; each additional cassette, $14.00. Add $2.00 per order for shipping.

United States Army Band Tuba-Euphonium Conferences

All of these conferences were recorded, and nearly everything since the 1987 conference has been released on cassette as a public service. For further information contact Tuba Conference, The United States Army Band, Ft. Myer, Arlington, VA 22211-5050 USA.

THE UNITED STATES ARMY BAND TUBA-EUPHONIUM CONFERENCE, OCTOBER 18-20, 1984

October 18

Concert: The United States Army Band "Pershing's Own," Colonel Eugene W. Allen, Leader and Commander, The Ceremonial Brass and Percussion, Captain David H. Dietrick, conductor

Robert Powers, euphonium: Gregson, Edward, *Symphonic Rhapsody* for euphonium and band

Michael Wagner, tuba: Gregson, Edward, *Concerto* for tuba and brass band

Harvey Phillips, tuba: Wilder, Alec, *Elegy*

Neal Corwell, euphonium: Bellstedt, Herman, *Napoli*

Jeffrey Arwood, tuba: Condon, Leslie, *Celestial Morn*

October 19

Artists Recital

U. S. Army Band Quartets: Kreisler, Fritz, *Schön Rosmarin* (Tom Waid, Otis Wilson, tubas); Bartles, Alfred, *When Tubas Waltz* (Charles Saik, Otis Wilson, tubas)

Gary Buttery, tuba: Kellaway, Roger, *Arcades* for tuba and piano; Heussenstamm, George, *Dialogue for Alto Saxophone and Tuba*

U. S. Marine Band Quartet (Eliot Evans, Jack Tilbury, tubas): Hovhaness, Alan/Loehr, *Sharagan and Fugue*; Bulla, Stephen, *Quartet for Low Brass*

David Werden, euphonium: Kellaway, Roger, *Morning Song*; Paganini, Niccolo/Werden, *Two Caprices*; Boda, John, *Sonatina*

Gary Buttery, tuba, and David Werden, euphonium: Luedeke, Raymond, *Wonderland Duets*

U. S. Army Quartet (Jeff Arwood, Jack Tilbury, Ross Morgan, tubas): Schuller, Gunther, *Five Moods for Tuba Quartet*

October 20

Artists Recital

John Mueller, euphonium: Handel, G. F., *Concerto in F minor*

Michael Gallo, tuba: Kraft, William, *Encounters II*

Robert Powers, euphonium: Barat, J. Ed., *Introduction and Dance*

Martin Erickson, tuba: Kellaway, Roger, *Morning Song*

October 20

Solo Recital

Gary Bird, tuba: Wilhelm, Rolf, *Concertino* for tuba and piano; Salerno, Chip, *New Work for Tuba*; Danielsson, Christer, *Concertant Suite* for tuba and brass instruments; Kellaway, Roger, *Dance of the Ocean Breeze* for horn, tuba and piano

Artists Recital

Jack Tilbury, tuba: Tilbury, Jack, *Sonata*

Neal Corwell, euphonium: Bellstedt, Herman, *Pièce de Concerte*

Michael Wagner, tuba: Koetsier, Jan, *Sonatina*

Brian Bowman, euphonium: Vivaldi, Antonio, *Sonata No. 6*

Matthew Simmons, tuba: Tomasi, Henri, *Etre ou ne pas Etre*

Solo Recital

David Lewis, tuba: Powell, David, *Sonate* for tuba and piano; Krzywicki, Jan, *Ballade*; Presser, William, *Minute Sketches* for tuba and piano; Broughton, Bruce, *Sonata* for tuba and piano; Wilder, Alec, *Suite No. 4* for tuba

and piano (Thomas Suite); Swann, Donald,
Two Moods

University of North Carolina-Greensboro
Tuba-Euphonium Ensemble, David Lewis,
director: Minerd, Doug, *Sea Tubas*; Bulla,
Stephen, *Quartet for Low Brass*; Niehaus,
Lennie, *Brass Tacks*

Grand Concert: The United States Army Band
"Pershing's Own," Colonel Eugene W. Allen,
Leader and Commander

Ross Morgan, tuba: Bencriscutto, Frank,
Concertino for tuba and band

Earle Louder, euphonium: Jacob, Gordon,
Fantasia for euphonium and band; arr. Ades,
Londonderry Air; Mantia, Simon, *Original
Fantasy*

Harvey Phillips, tuba: Vaughan Williams, Ralph,
Concerto for Bass Tuba

John Mueller, euphonium: Boccolari, Edoardo,
Fantasia Di Concerto; Corea, Chick/Brown,
Spain

THE UNITED STATES ARMY BAND TUBA EUPHONIUM
CONFERENCE, OCTOBER 1-5, 1985

October 1
Brass Quintet Night
United States Army Brass Quintet (Jack
Tilbury, tuba): Bolling, Claude/Tomaro,
Fugace; Berlioz, Hector/Tomaro, *Roman
Carnival Overture*; Edelbrocks, Dennis, *This
Five's for You*

The United States Naval Academy Brass
Quintet (Scott Tarabour, tuba): Bach, J. S./
Picher, *Prelude and Fugue in C minor*; Bach,
J. S./Rosenthal, *Air pour les Troumpetts*;
Hampton, Robert/Johnson, *Cataract Rag*;
Lamb, Joseph/Johnson, *Patricia Rag*;
Waller, Thomas "Fats"/Norris, *Ain't
Misbehavin'*; Renwick, Wilke, *Dance*

Madison Brass Quintet (Kevin Stees, tuba):
Calvert, Morley, *Three Dance Impressions*;
Riley, James, *Four Essays for Brass Quintet*;
Cohan, George M./West, *Over There*; arr.
West, *Gobbler in the Grass*; Glasel, John:
Saints Alive

United States Navy Brass Quintet (Martin
Erickson, tuba): Program announced

October 2
Artists Recital
Dan Vinson, euphonium: TBA
Robert Powers, euphonium, and Otis Wilson,
tuba: Frackenpohl, Arthur, *Brass Duo*; Gary
Buttery, tuba: Bach, J. S., *Sonata in G minor*;
Buttery, Gary, *Conversations with Grace* for
tuba and humpback whale

Jeff Arwood and Ross Morgan, tubas: Holmes,
Brian, *Tales of the Cultural Revolution*

Charles Saik, tuba: Purcell, Henry, *Arise ye
Subterranean Winds*

United States Army Band Tuba Quartet (Jeff
Arwood, Jack Tilbury, Ross Morgan, tubas):
Tchaikovsky, P. I./Fletcher, *Sleeping Tubas
Waltz*

October 3
Artists Recital
Michael Wagner, tuba: George, Thom Ritter,
Sonata for tuba and piano

Roger Behrend, euphonium: Uber, David,
Sonata for euphonium and piano

Michael Gallo, tuba: Kellaway, Roger, *Morning
Song*

Tom Waid, tuba: Dittersdorf, Carl Ditters von,
Symphonia Concertante for viola and tuba

Scott Tarabour, tuba, William Hunley and
Joseph Brown, euphoniums: Lind, Carlton,
Trio

Keith Mehlan, tuba: Arban, J. B., *The Carnival
of Venice*

United States Navy Tuba-Euphonium Quartet
(Martin Erickson, Keith Mehlan, tubas):
Ramsoe, William, *Quartet for Brass*;
Massenet, Jules/Margaret Erickson,
Argonaise from "Le Cid"; Bulla, Stephen,
Celestial Suite

The Armed Forces Tuba-Euphonium Ensemble, R. Winston Morris, conductor, TBA

October 4
Guest Recital
Daniel Perantoni, tuba: Bozza, Eugene:
Concertino; Capuzzi, Antonio, *Concerto*;
George, Thom Ritter, *Sonata for Tuba*;
Mahler, Gustav, *Songs of the Wayfarer*; arr.
Strange, *Ellington Medley*; Arban, J. B./
Damek, *Carnival of Venice*

October 5
Guest Recital
Skip Gray, tuba: Hindemith, Paul, *Sonata*;
Gould, Tony, *Duet for tuba and piano*; Bach,
J. S., *Sonata in Eb Major*; Johnson, Barry,
Sonata; Vaughan Williams, Ralph, *Concerto*

Artists Recital
Dan Vinson, euphonium: TBA
Martin Erickson, tuba: TBA
Neal Corwell, euphonium: Arban, J. B.,
Carnival of Venice

Artists Recital
Andrew Farnham, tuba: Villa-Lobos, Hector,
Cantilena from Bachinas Brasileiras No. 5

Robert Pallansch, ophicleide: Handel, G. F.,
Concerto in C Minor

Kevin Stees, tuba: Kellaway, Roger, *Morning
Song*; Broughton, Bruce, *Sonata*

Grand Concert
Armed Forces Tuba-Euphonium Ensemble:
King, K. L., *Barnum and Bailey's Favorite*;
Bach, J. S./Werden, *Bist du bei Mir* ; Mozart,

W. A./Peoples, *Eine kleine Nachtmusik*; arr.
Garrett, *Danny Boy*; Ager, Milton/Norton,
Ain't She Sweet; Bernie, Ben/Garrett, *Sweet
Georgia Brown*; Joplin, Scott/Sabourin, *The
Cascades*; Texidor, Jamie/Self, *Amparito
Roca*; Barroso, Ary/Morris, *Brazil*; Sousa,
John Philip/Morris, *The Stars and Stripes
Forever*
The United States Army Band "Pershing's
Own," Colonel Eugene W. Allen, Leader and
Commander
Jeff Arwood, tuba: Robinson, Willard/Smith,
Old Folks
Neal Corwell, euphonium: Clarke, Herbert L.,
Carnival of Venice
R. Winston Morris, tuba: George, Thom Ritter,
Concertino for tuba and winds
Arthur Lehman, euphonium: Mantia, Simon/
Brasch, *All Those Endearing Young Charms*
Arthur Lehman and Neal Corwell, euphoniums:
Foster, Stephen/Woitschach, *Gentle Annie*
Daniel Perantoni, tuba: Wilhelm, Rolf,
Concertino for tuba and wind instruments

UNITED STATES ARMY BAND TUBA-EUPHONIUM
CONFERENCE/REGION IV T. U. B. A. WORKSHOP,
FEBRUARY 4-7, 1987

February 4
Brass Quintet Night
U. S. Army Field Band Brass Quintet (Jerry
Beckman, tuba): Dukas, Paul, *Fanfare from
"La Péri"*; Frackenpohl, Arthur, *Brass Quintet*;
Cable, Howard, *Newfoundland Sketch*
Madison Brass (Kevin Stees, tuba): Albinoni,
Tomaso, *Sonata "St. Mark"*; Horovitz,
Joseph, *Music Hall Suite*; Waller, Thomas
"Fats"/Henderson, *Hand Full of Keys*
Air Force Band of the Midwest Lincolnland
Brass Quintet (Andy Bryan, tuba): Handel,
G. F./Grome, *For Unto Us a Child Is Born*;
Bozza, Eugene, *Allegro Vivo from Sonatine*;
Traditional, *Just a Closer Walk with Thee*
U. S. Air Force Brass Quintet (Edward McKee,
tuba): Bach, J. S./McKee, *Fugue No. 4 from
the Well-Tempered Klavier*; arr. Dosset, *My
Friend George—A Gershwin Medley*; Berlin,
Irving/Tarto, *Alexander's Ragtime Band*
U. S. Army Brass Quintet (Jack Tilbury, tuba):
Edelbrock, Dennis, *When Five's Company*;
Bach, Jan, *Carioca from Rounds and Dances*;
Herold, F./Tomaro, *Zampa Overture*
February 5
Artists Recital
David Miles, euphonium: Corwell, Neal, *Four
Short Narratives*
Robert Powers, euphonium: Boda, John,
Sonatina

Mike Wagner, tuba: Uber, David, *Sonata*
John Mueller, euphonium: Bach, Jan, *Concert
Variations*
U. S. Air Force Tubas (Gilbert Corella, Jan
Duga, Bruce Mosier, David Porter): Mozart,
W. A., *Eine kleine Nachtmusik*
Joe Brown, euphonium: Pokorny, F. X.,
Concerto
Mike Gallo, tuba: Marcello, Benedetto, *Sonata
No. 1 in F Major*
U. S. Naval Academy Tuba-Euphonium
Quartet (John White, Scott Tarabour, tubas):
Susato/Winter, *Ronde and Saltarello*; Bach,
J. S./ Pitts, *Contrapunctus IX*; Berlioz,
Hector/Werden, *Hungarian March*; arr.
Buttery, *Greensleeves*; Joplin, Scott/Werden,
The Easy Winners
February 6
Artists Recital
Jeff Funderburk, tuba: Marcello, Benedetto,
Sonata in E Minor; Kraft, William, *Encounters
II*; Wilhelm, Rolf, *Concertino*
Jeff Funderburk and Paul St. Pierre, tubas:
Devienne, F./Singleton, *Duet in F*
Brian Bowman, euphonium: Bach/Gounod/
Falcone, *Ave Maria*; Brahe, May, *Bless This
House—To the Memory of Harold Brasch*;
Brahms, Johannes, *O Tod*; Schumann,
Robert, *Ich grolle nicht*; Bizet, Georges, *La
fluer que tu m'avais*; Rossini, Gioacchino,
Una Voce M'ha Colpito; Scottish Traditional,
Ye Banks and Braes; Copland, Aaron/Quiller,
Simple Gifts; Copland, Aaron/Quiller, *Long
Time Ago*
Don Harry, Jeff Arwood, Jack Tilbury, tubas:
Corelli, Archangelo, *Trio Sonata*, Op. 1, No.
5
Don Harry, tuba: Bach, J. S., *Suite No. 5 in C
Minor*
Don Harry, Jeff Funderburk, tubas, Brian
Bowman, euphonium: Jager, Robert,
Variations on a Motive by Wagner
Don Harry, Jeff Arwood, Jack Tilbury, Ross
Morgan, Tim Loehr, Joseph Roccaro, tubas:
Wagner, Richard/Harry, *Prelude to Act III of
Die Meistersinger*
February 7
College Ensemble Recital
University of Maryland Tuba-Euphonium
Ensemble, Richard Sparks, director
James Madison University Tuba-Euphonium
Ensemble, Kevin Stees, director
Tuba Mirum, David Townsend, director
West Virginia Tuba-Euphonium Ensemble,
Richard Powell and Dave McCollum,
directors
Artists Recital
David Werden, euphonium: Schubert, Franz/
Werden, *Arpeggione Sonata*

Jan Duga, tuba: Castérède, Jacques, *Sonatine pour tuba ut*
Dan Vinson, euphonium: Horovitz, Joseph, *Concerto*
David Porter, tuba: Strauss, Richard, *Concerto No.1*, Op. 11
Dale Cheal, euphonium: Jazz Improvisations
February 7
Artists Recital
Charles Saik, Otis Wilson, tubas: Morley, Thomas/Saik, *Two Morley Fantasias*
Neal Corwell, euphonium: Arban, J. B., *Variations on Tyrolienne*
David Zerkel, tuba: Stevens, Halsey, *Sonatina*
Keith Mehlan, tuba: Bach, J. S., *Sonata*
Tom Waid, tuba: Rossini, Gioacchino/L. Waid, *Duet* for tuba and viola
Gilbert Corella, tuba: Danielsson, Christer, *Concertant Suite* for solo tuba and four horns
Grand Concert
U. S. Armed Forces Tuba-Euphonium Ensemble, R. Winston Morris, conductor: Rodgers, Thomas, *Air*; Forte, Aldo, *Adagio and Rondo*; George, Thom Ritter, *Two Interplays*; Bach, J. S./Garrett, *Passacaglia and Fugue in C minor*; Welcher, Dan, *Hauntings*
U. S. Armed Forces Tuba-Euphonium Massed Ensemble, R. Winston Morris, conductor: Parera, Antonio/Ishikawa, *El Capeo*; Saint-Saëns, Camille/Morris, *Adagio from Symphony No. 3*; Chopin, F./Morris, *Waltz* (Neal Corwell, euphonium soloist); Pachelbel, Johann/Cates, *Canon*; Canter, James, *Appalachian Carol*; Garrett, James, *Pop-Rock Medley*; Garrett, James, *A Tubalee Jubalee*; Fucik, Julius/Gray, *Thunder and Blazes*
The United States Army Band "Pershing's Own," Colonel Eugene W. Allen, Leader and Commander
Jeff Arwood, tuba: Camphouse, Mark, *Poème*
Don Harry, tuba: Clarke, Herbert L., *From the Shores of the Mighty Pacific*
Martin Erickson, tuba: Cherubini, Luigi, *Sonata No. 2*
Roger Behrend, euphonium: Boccalari, E., *Fantasia di Concerto*
Tommy Johnson, tuba: Broughton, Bruce, *Concerto for tuba and winds*

THE UNITED STATES ARMY BAND TUBA-EUPHONIUM CONFERENCE/REGION IV T. U. B. A. WORKSHOP, FEBRUARY 3-6, 1988

February 3
Brass Quintet Night
The U. S. Army Brass Quintet (Jack Tilbury, tuba): Bach, J. S./Seipp, *My Spirit Be Joyful*;

Boyce, William, *Centone No. 11*; Barnes, James, *Divertissment*
Brass Wind Quintet of the University of Tennessee (Sande MacMorran, tuba): Petrovics, Emil, *Quinteto per Ottoni*; Beveridge, Thomas, *Carmen Fantasy*; Delaney, Tom/Hough, *Jazz Me Blues*; Hough, Don, *Country Stough*
Highlands Brass Quintet from the U. S. Military Academy (Rick Gerard, tuba): Gabrieli, Giovanni/Page, *Canzona per sonare No. 4*; Grainger, Percy/Stanhope, *Shepherds' Hey*; Lavallee, Calixa/Cable, *La Rose Nuptiale*; Debussy, Claude/Kulesha, *The Girl with the Flaxen Hair*; Rossini, Gioacchino/Kulesha, *Largo al Factotum*; Pollack, Lew/Cooper, *That's A Plenty*
Combined Quintets: Gabrieli, Giovanni/King, *Canzona per sonare No. 2*
February 4
Artists Recital
U. S. Naval Academy Tuba-Euphonium Quartet (John White, Scott Tarabour, tubas): Holmes, Paul, *Quartet for Tubas*; Burrucker, Paul, *Nautical Medley*
Don Burleson, euphonium: Bellini/Arman, *Variations on a Theme from "Norma"*
Jerry Beckman, David Zerkel, tubas: Holmes, Brian, *Tales of the Cultural Revolution*
David Zerkel, tuba: Stevens, Halsey, *Sonatina*
Jan Duga, tuba: Spillman, Robert, *Four Greek Preludes*
Mark Williamson, euphonium: Boda, John, *Sonatina*
Mike Dunn, tuba, Michael Colburn, Dale Fredricks, Don Palmire, euphoniums: Sherwin, Manning/Colburn, *The Nightingale Sang in Berkley Square*; Shearing, George/Fredricks, *Lullaby of Birdland*; arr. Sample, *Ellington Medley*; Mozart, W. A./Colburn, *Overture to "The Marriage of Figaro"*
Robert Daniel, tuba: Jager, Robert, *Fantasy-Variations* for flute, tuba, and piano
Michael Colburn, euphonium: Nelhybel, Vaclav, *Concerto for Euphonium*
Air Force Band of the East Tuba Quartet (Hans Marlette, Doug Murphy, tubas): Hindemith, Paul, *Morgenmusik*; Ramsoe, William/Buttery, *Quartet for Brass*; Anonymous, *Angel Eyes*; Bartles, Alfred, *When Tubas Waltz*; King, K. L., *Barnum and Bailey's Favorite*
February 5
Concert
The U. S. Armed Forces Tuba-Euphonium Ensemble, R. Winston Morris, conductor: Bach, J. S./Morris, *Toccata and Fugue in D minor*; Rossini, Gioacchino/Kile, *Overture to*

"*The Barber of Seville*"; Ross, Walter, *Concerto Basso*; Clinard, Fred L. Jr., *Diversion*; Lamb, Marvin, *Heavy Metal*; Tomara, Mike, *Mr. Ed's Elephant Farm*

The U. S. Armed Forces Tuba-Euphonium Massed Ensemble, R. Winston Morris, conductor: Thinman/Gotcher, *She Is My Slender, Small Love*; Bach, J. S./Phillips, *Air from Suite No. 3 in D*; Glazunov, Alexander/Perry, *In Modo Religioso*, Op. 38; Holmes, Paul, *Quartet for Tubas*; Lecuona, Ernesto/Morris, *Malagueña*; Sherwin, Manning/Cochran, *A Nightingale Sang in Berkley Square*; Sousa, J./Morris, *Semper Fidelis*; DiGiovanni, Rocco, *TubaRhumba*; Huffine, G. H./Isabell, *Them Basses*

February 6
Artists Recital

Gilbert Corella, tuba: Barber, Clarence, *Theme and Variation* for tuba and percussion

Tom Waid, tuba: Marcello, Benedetto, *Sonata No. 1 in F*

John Mueller, euphonium: Bach, Jan, *Concert Variations*

Mike Dunn, tuba: Tomasi, Henri, *To Be or Not to Be*

William Porter, tuba: Persichetti, Vincent, *Serenade No. 12* for solo tuba

Carlyle Webber, euphonium: Bolling, Claud, *Suite* for cello and jazz piano trio

Guest Recital

Michael Bunn, tuba: Shostakovich, Dimitri, *Polka from the "Age of Gold"*; Danzi, Franz, *Concerto*; Bach, J. S., *Sonata*; Fauré, Gabriel, *Elegy*; Presser, William, *Minute Sketches*; Clarke, Herbert L., *From the Shores of the Mighty Pacific*

Grand Concert

The Army Blues Jazz Ensemble; guest artists: Ashley Alexander, Rich Matteson, Dale Cheal, Tim Northcut, Lew Chapman, Jim Self

ARMED FORCES TUBA-EUPHONIUM CONFERENCE, FEBRUARY 1-4, 1989

February 1
Brass Quintet Night

U. S. Army Brass Quintet (Jack Tilbury, tuba): Vivaldi, Antonio, *Concerto Grosso*; Beveridge, Thomas, *Five Pieces for Brass Quintet*; Renwick, Wilke, *Dance*

The Shenandoah Brass (Michael Bunn, tuba): Handel, G. F., *The Harmonious Blacksmith*; Stevens, John, *Triangles*; Bernstein, Leonard/Gale, *Selections from "West Side Story"*

Tennessee Technological University Brass Quintet (R. Winston Morris, tuba): Dukas,

Paul/Decker, *Fanfare from "La Peri"*; Liubovsky, Leonid, *Suite for Brass Quintet*; Brusick, William, *Contrasts for Brass Quintet*; Pollack, Lew/Cooper, *That's A Plenty*

Combined Quintets: Karg-Elert, Sigfred, *Motet*

February 2
Artists Recital

Michael Colburn, euphonium: Bach, Jan, *Concert Variations*

Jan Duga, tuba; Galliard, J. E., *Sonata No. 5*

Carlyle Webber, euphonium; Beethoven, Ludwig, *Sonata*, Op. 102, No.2

James Dunn, tuba; Vaughan Williams, Ralph/Vernon, *Concerto for Bass Tuba* (tuba and four trombones)

Neal Corwell, euphonium: Corwell, Neal, *Night Song*; Arban, J. B., *Carnival of Venice*

February 3
Artists Recital

Penn State All Star Diamond Anniversary Tuba-Euphonium Quartet (Keith Alexander, Dennis AsKew, tubas): arr. Quin, *Wondrous Love*; Payne, Frank Lynn, *Quartet for Tubas*; arr. Alexander, *Anthem* (Karin Quinn, euphonium soloist): Stevens, John, *Dances*; Bach, P. D. Q./Granger, *Presto, Hey Nonny Nonnio from the "Schleptet"*

Jerry Young, tuba: Lunde, Ivar, *Designs*, Op. 92; Chamberlain, Robert, *Elegy*; Young, Barbara, *The Carnival's Over*

Luis Maldonado, euphonium: Horovitz, Joseph, *Moderato from Concerto for euphonium*: Debussy, Claude, *"C'est l'extase" from Ariettes Oubliées*; Hutchinson, Warner, *Sonatina*; Bolling, Claude, *Suite* for cello and jazz piano

The West Point Tuba-Euphonium Quartet (Rick Gerard, Thomas Price, Joseph Roccaro, tubas): Susato, Tylman/Price, *Two Dances*; Lasso, Orlando/Robinson, *Mon coeur se recommende à vous*; Lyon, Max, *Suite for Four Bass Voices*; Joplin, Scott/Judd, *Peacherine Rag*; Cook, Kenneth, *Introduction and Rondino*

Concert

1989 Armed Forces Tuba-Euphonium Ensemble, R. Winston Morris, conductor: Bach, J. S./Beckman, *Saint Anne's Fugue*; Saint-Saëns, Camille/Cohen, *Marche Militaire Française*; Werle, Floyd, *Variations on an Old Hymn Tune*; Camphouse, Mark, *Ceremonial Sketch*; Garbáge, Pierre, *Sousa Surrenders*

1989 Armed Forces Tuba-Euphonium Massed Ensemble, R. Winston Morris, conductor: Bach, J. S./Werden, *Bist du bei Mir*; Frank, Marcel, *Lyric Poem*; Canter, James, *Appalachian Carol*; Cheetham, John, *Consortium*; DiGiovanni, Rocco, *Tuba Magic*; Joplin, Scott/Self, *The Entertainer*; Huffine, G. H., *Them Basses*

February 4
Grand Concert: The United States Army Band,
     "Pershing's Own," Colonel Eugene W. Allen,
     Leader and Commander
          Michael Bunn, tuba: Wilhelm, Rolf, *Concertino*
          for tuba and wind instruments
          John Mueller, euphonium: Curnow, James,
          Symphonic Variants
          Euphonium Section: Saint-Saëns, Camille, *The
          Swan*
          Robert Daniel, tuba: Smith, Claude T., *Ballade
          and Presto Dance*
          Brian Bowman, euphonium: Smith, Claude T.,
          Concertpiece for euphonium and band
          Roger Bobo, tuba: Barat, J, Ed., *Introduction
          and Dance*; Dumitru, Ionel, *Romanian
          Dance*; Arban, J. B./Berry, *Carnival of
          Venice*

THE UNITED STATES ARMY BAND EASTERN NATIONAL
TUBA-EUPHONIUM CONFERENCE, JANUARY 24-27,
1990

January 24
Brass Quintet Night
          U. S. Continental Army Band Brass Quintet
          (Joe Burton, tuba): Schein, Johann,
          Paudana: Frackenpohl, Arthur, *Brass
          Quintet*; Sullivan, Arthur/Battles and
          Holcombe, *Pirates of Penzance*; Bizet/
          Holcombe, *Habanera*
          U. S. Army Band Brass Quintet (Jack Tilbury,
          bass saxhorn): Fay, Conrad, *Wrecker's
          Daughter Quickstep*; Bela, Keler, *Lustspiel
          Overture*; Verdi, G./Muller, *Selections from
          "Rigoletto"*; Albert, R./Elrod, *Salutations to
          America Grand Polka*; arr. Downing and
          Porter, *Suite from 26th North Carolina
          Regiment Band*
          Bowie Brass Quintet (Martin Erickson, tuba):
          arr. Bulla, *All Creatures of Our God*; Bach,
          Jan, *Laudes*; Dempsey, Raymond, *Mouse, Pl.
          mice*; arr. Bulla, *Quintessential Gershwin*
          Combined Quintets: Marcello, Benedetto,
          Psalm XIX, The Heavens Declare
January 25
Concert: The U. S. Army Brass Band, Captain
     Thomas Palmatier, conductor
          Jeffrey Rideout, tuba: Gregson, Edward,
          Concerto for tuba and brass band
          The Childs Brothers: Sparke, Philip, *Two Part
          Invention*; Phillips, John, *Romance*; Rimsky-
          Korsakov, Nicolas, *Flight of the Bumblebee*;
          Graham, Peter, *Brilliante*; Golland, John,
          Childs Play; DeVita, A./Catherall, *Softly As I
          Leave Thee*
          Patrick Morris, euphonium: Redhead, Robert,
          Euphony

Michael Wagner, Otis Wilson, tubas: Condon,
     Leslie, *Radiant Pathway*
January 26
Artists Recital
          Yashio Abe, tuba: Barat, J. Ed., *Introduction
          and Dance*; Broughton, Bruce, *Sonata*;
          Spillman, Robert, *Two Songs*; Russell,
          Armand, *Suite Concertante*
          Patrick Sheridan and John Cradler, tubas:
          Stevens, John, *Duo*
          Mark Norman, tuba: Payne, Frank Lynn,
          Sonata for tuba and piano
          Ann Baldwin, euphonium: Schubert, Franz/
          Werden: *Arpeggione Sonata*
          Dan Sherlock, tuba: Wilder, Alec, *Suite No. 1*
          for tuba and piano (Effie)
          Edward McKee and Gilbert Corella, tubas:
          Butterfield, Don, *Duets*
January 27
Grand Concert: The United States Army Band,
     "Pershing's Own," Colonel Eugene W. Allen,
     Leader and Commander
          Michael Gallo, tuba: Curnow, James,
          Concertino for tuba and band
          Don Butterfield, tuba: Nagle, Paul, *Design for
          bass*
          Bob Powers, euphonium: Owen, Jerry,
          Variations
          Dave Cobb, John Mueller, Bob Powers,
          euphoniums: Leonard, Cuyler Hershey,
          Annie Laurie à la Moderne
          Tim Northcut, tuba: Jager, Robert, *Concerto*
          Frode Thingnaes, euphonium: Thingnaes, F.,
          Peace, Please
          Michael Lind, tuba: Thingnaes, F., *Concertino*;
          Thingnaes, F., *A Song for Michael*; Medberg,
          Gunnar, *Concerto* for tuba and band;
          Thingnaes, F., *Ballade and Samba from
          Second Jazz Suite*; Arban, J. B., *Carnival of
          Venice*
          Massed Euphoniums: King, K. L., *Melody Shop*
          Massed Tubas and Euphoniums: Huffine, G.
          H., *Them Basses*

THE EIGHTH ANNUAL UNITED STATES ARMY BAND
EASTERN NATIONAL TUBA-EUPHONIUM CONFERENCE,
JANUARY 9-12, 1991

January 9
Brass Quintet Night
          U. S. Army Field Band Brass Quintet (Daniel
          Sherlock, tuba): Handel, G., *Aria*; Cable,
          Howard, *A Newfoundland Sketch*; Gregson,
          Edward, *Quintet for Brass*; Shields, Larry and
          La Rocca, Nick, *At the Jazz Band Ball*
          U. S. Marine Band Brass Quintet (John
          Cradler, tuba): Walond, William/Reynolds,

Voluntary; Bach, J. S./Snedecor, *My Spirit Be Joyful*; Hellendael, Peter/Reynolds, *Centone*

U. S. Army Brass Quintet (Jack Tilbury, tuba): Beveridge, Thomas, *Fanfare of Happiness*; Barnes, James, *Classical Suite*

Combined Quintets: Gabrieli, Giovanni/Fromme, *Canzona Prima*

January 10
Artists Recital

John Mueller, Bob Powers, Patrick Morris, euphoniums: Haydn, F. J./Droste, *Divertimento No. 70*

Scott Watson, tuba: Mozart, W. A., *Concert Rondo*, K. 371; Rekhin, Igor, *Sonata* for tuba and piano; Copland, Aaron, *Old American Songs*; Brahms, Johannes, *Von Ewiger Liebe*; Crockett, Edgar, *Mystique*; Hartley, Walter, *Fantasia* for tuba and piano

Joe Dollard, euphonium: Redhead, Robert, *Euphony*

Jay Norris, tuba: Russell, Armand, *Suite Concertante*

January 11
Artists Recital

The Penn State Tuba-Euphonium Ensemble and TubaJazz Ensemble: Payne, Frank Lynn, *Quartet for tubas*; Petersen, Jack, *Hey Man*; Stravinsky, Igor/Gray, *Berceuse and Finale from "Firebird"*

Eastern Low Brass Quartet (Ann Baldwin and Laura Lineberger, euphoniums, Barbara Payne and Jan Duga, tubas): Reiche, Anton/Werden, *Quartet in B♭*; Debussy, Claude/Mattick, *La Fille*

Colonial Tuba Quartet (Mary Ann Craig and Jay Hildebrandt, euphoniums, Gary Bird and Gregory Fritze, tubas): Picchi, Ermanno/Craig, *Fantaisie Original*; Baker, David, *Piece for solo tuba and tuba quartet* (Harvey Phillips, soloist); Fritze, Gregory, *Prelude and Dance*

1991 Armed Forces Tuba-Euphonium Ensemble, R. Winston Morris, conductor: Bach, J. S./Morris, *Contrapunctus I*; Boone, Dan, *Three Moods*; Canter, James, *Circle VIII: Bowge IV*; Krol, Bernhard, *Feiertagmusik*; Konagaya, Soichi, *Celebration* (Jeff Arwood, soloist); Rose, David/Morris, *Holiday for Tubas*; King, K. L., *The Melody Shop*; Sousa, J. P./Rauchut, *The Liberty Bell*

January 12
Grand Concert: The United States Army Band, "Pershing's Own," Colonel L. Bryan Shelburne Jr., Leader and Commander

Patrick Sheridan, tuba: Schumann, Robert/Basta, *Adagio and Allegro*

Michael Colburn, euphonium: Curnow, James, *Symphonic Variants*

Daniel Perantoni, tuba: Wilhelm, Rolf, *Concertino* for tuba and wind instruments

Steven Mead, euphonium: Horovitz, Joseph, *Concerto* for euphonium

Massed Euphoniums: King, K. L., *The Melody Shop*

Massed Tubas and Euphoniums: Marquina, Pascual/Waid, *España Cani*; Huffine, G. H., *Them Basses*

THE UNITED STATES ARMY BAND EASTERN NATIONAL TUBA-EUPHONIUM CONFERENCE, JANUARY 29–FEBRUARY 1, 1992

January 29
Brass Quintet Night

The U. S. Army Brass Quintet (Jack Tilbury, tuba): Handel, G. F./Seippe, *The Rejoicing from Royal Fireworks*; Beveridge, Thomas, *Fantas*; Edelbrock, Dennis, *In the Park*

The U. S. Air Force Academy Brass (Paul Loucas, tuba): Bach, J. S., *My Spirit Be Joyful*; Bach, J. S., *Toccata and Fugue in D minor*; Danielsson, Christer, *Concertant Suite* for solo tuba; Prokofiev, Sergei, *March*, Op. 99; Bach, J. S., *Aria from Cantata No. 78*; Filmore, Henry, *The Klaxon*; Waller, Thomas "Fats," *Hand Full of Keys*; Sousa, J. P., *Stars and Stripes Forever*

Combined Quintets: Campra/Richard, *Rigaudon*

January 30
Guest Artist Recital

Wendy Picton, euphonium: Mendez, Rafael/Moore, *La Plegaria Taurina*; Goedicke, Alexander, *Concert Etude*; Ayoub, Nick/Picton, *Ballade for a Lady*; Liszt, Franz/Picton, *No. 5, "Le Grandes Etudes"*; Rimmer, William, *Grand Fantasia—Weber's Last Waltz*; James, Harry, *Concerto for Trumpet*

Melvin Culbertson, tuba: Goret, D., *Soufflés*; *International Suite*; Marais, *The Basque*; Noskovsky, *Polish Elegy*; Bach, *Badinerie*; Prokofiev, *Champ des Morts*; Dumitru, *Romanian Dance*; Emler, A., *Tuba Stone No. 1*

January 31
Concert

The 1992 U. S. Armed Forces Tuba-Euphonium Ensemble, R. Winston Morris, conductor: Scheidt, Samuel/Warren, *Canzona Bergamasca*; Pachelbel, Johann/Cates, *Kanon*; Forte, Aldo, *Adagio and Rondo*; Konagaya, Soichi, *Illusion*; Bernstein, Leonard/Butler, *Overture to "Candide"*; Texidor, Jamie/Self, *Amparito Roco*; King, K. L., *Barnum and Bailey's Favorite*; Garbáge, Pierre, *Sousa Surrenders*

Bob Stewart and the First Line Band

February 1
Artists Recital
  Mike Gallo, tuba: Kellaway, Roger, *The
    Morning Song*
  Neal Corwell, euphonium: Nagano, Mitsurhiro,
    Mandrix
  David Zerkel, tuba: Rachmaninoff, Sergei,
    Vocalise, Op. 34, No.1
  Gary Poffenbarger, euphonium; Marcello,
    Benedetto, *Sonata in A minor*
  Armed Forces Tuba-Euphonium Quartet
    (Michael Colburn and Ann Baldwin,
    euphoniums, Andrew Carlson and Daniel
    Sherlock, tubas): Buxtehude, Dietrich/
    Sherlock, *Prelude and Fugue No. 14*
Artists Recital
  Paul Loucas, tuba: Spillman, Robert, *Two Songs*
  Laura Lineberger and Ann Baldwin, euphoni-
    ums: Coulillaud, H., *Vocalise for Two Voices*
  U. S. Navy Tuba-Euphonium Quartet (Roger
    Behrend and David Miles, euphoniums,
    Martin Erickson and Keith Mehlan, tubas):
    arr. Dempsey, *Quatre Chansons* for tuba
    quartet; Sherwin, Manning/Mehlan, *A
    Nightingale Sang in Berkley Square*; arr.
    Mehlan, *Eine Kleine Schrecken Musik*
Grand Concert: The United States Army Band
  "Pershing's Own," Colonel L. Bryan Shelburne
  Jr., Leader and Commander
  David Werden, euphonium: Smith, Claude T.,
    Rondo; Levy, Jules, *Grand Russian Fantasia*
  Gary Buttery, tuba: Nelhybel, Vaclav, *Concerto
    for tuba*
  Luis Maldonado, euphonium: Gillingham,
    David, *Vintage*; Sparke, Philip/Maldonado,
    Pantomime
  Mel Culbertson, tuba: Broughton, Bruce,
    Concerto for Tuba and Wind Ensemble
  Wendy Picton, euphonium: Bourgeois, Derek,
    Concerto for euphonium for Wendy Picton,
    Op. 120
  Massed Euphoniums: King, K. L., *The Melody
    Shop*
  Massed Tubas and Euphoniums: Huffine, G.
    H., *Them Basses*

*Third International Tuba Euphonium Workshop
1978, University of Southern California, Los
Angeles*

Workshop Director Jim Self has reported that the
proceedings of this conference were recorded but that
the tapes were never duplicated, circulated, or made
available for purchase. Mr. Self expressed a desire to
donate the one set of coded tapes to the T. U. B. A.
Archives.

*Second National Tuba Euphonium Symposium
Workshop 1980, University of North Texas*

Symposium Director Donald Little has stated that
tape recordings were made at this workshop. The
recording technician was Mike Getzen, a member of
the United States Army Band at Fort Myer. All workshop programs were made available at that time. One
set of tapes is in the library at the University of North
Texas.

*International Tuba/Euphonium Conference
1983, University of Maryland*

Conference Director Brian Bowman has stated the
entire conference was recorded by Mike Getzen, a
member of the United States Army Band at Fort Myer.
Mr. Getzen is now retired, and his current address is
unknown. Mr. Bowman has one complete set of recordings but has no means for making it available.

*International Tuba Euphonium Conference
1986, University of Texas, Austin*

Conference Director Steve Bryant has stated that
recordings of this conference were made but that
University of Texas Recording Services rules made
duplicating and distribution impossible.

*International Tuba Euphonium Conference,
Lexington, Kentucky, May 12-16, 1992*

Conference Director Skip Gray has advised that the
events of this conference were recorded but that tapes
would not be available after November 1992.

Recorded Accompaniments

Alexander, Ashley. *Ashley's Big Band Play Alongs.* Dave
  Alexander Production/AJEM. Solo part with cassette. 1990. Vol. 1, *Alumni Band.* Cassette, #4001,
  $14.95. Vol. 2, *Alexander Plays Mantooth.* Cas-
  sette, #4002, $14.95. Vol. III, *Powerslide.* Cassette
  #4003, $14.95. Vol. IV, *Seems Like Old Times.*
  Cassette #4004, $14.95. Vols. I–IV, complete set
  of cassettes, save 10%, #4006, $53.82. Tuba Edi-
  tions (edited specifically for the jazz tubist), specify
  #4001/T–4006/T. Make check or money order
  payable to Dave Alexander Productions/AJEM,
  200 East Beltline, Building E, Suite 104, Coppell,
  TX 75019. Telephone: 214-393-1586.

Canadian Brass Book of Beginning Tuba Solos. Tuba solos (solo and accompaniment books) with a companion cassette. Side A: All selections recorded by Charles Daellenbach, tuba, and Bill Casey, piano. Side B: Piano accompaniments only. Hal Leonard Publishing Corporation, #50481629, 1992, $14.95. CONTENTS, Bill Boyd, *Canadian Brass Blues*; American traditional, *Yankee Doodle*; American folk song, *The Streets of Laredo*; adapted from Ludwig van Beethoven, *Ode to Joy*; Henry Carey, *America*; Julius Benedict, *Carnival of Venice*; English ballade, *The Riddle Song*; Jean Sibelius, *Finlandia*; American traditional, *Amazing Grace*; Emil Waldteufel, *The Skaters*; Jacques Offenbach, *Marine's Hymn*; Albert von Tilzer, *Take Me Out to the Ball Game*; Russian folk song, *Song of the Volga Boatman*; American folk song, *The Cruel War Is Raging*; Louis Bourgeois, *Doxology*; George M. Cohan, *Give My Regards to Broadway*; Red Foley, *Just a Closer Walk with Thee*. (Note: The piano is in the wrong key on the accompaniment side of tape.)

Canadian Brass Book of Easy Tuba Solos. Tuba solos (solo and accompaniment books) with a companion cassette. Side A: All selections recorded by Charles Daellenbach, tuba, and Patrick Hansen, piano. Side B: Piano accompaniments only. Hal Leonard Publishing Corporation, #50481625, 1992, $14.95. CONTENTS: Arthur Sullivan, *Miya Sama from "The Mikado"*; American folk song, *The Wayfaring Stranger*; Giuseppe Giordani, *Love Song* (Caro mio ben); Jean Schwartz, *Chinatown, My Chinatown*; American folk song, *The Erie Canal*; Scottish folk song, *Loch Lomond*; American hymn, *Come, Thou Font of Every Blessing*; George Fridrick Handel, *Lento*; George Fridrick Handel, *Repentance from "The Passion"*; Jean Baptiste Lully, *The Lonely Forest*; English folk song, *Hey, Ho! Nobody Home*.

Canadian Brass Book of Intermediate Tuba Solos. Tuba solos (solo and accompaniment books) with a companion cassette. Side A: All selections recorded by Charles Daellenbach, tuba, and Patrick Hansen, piano. Side B: Piano accompaniments only. Hal Leonard Publishing Corporation, #50481621, 1992, $14.95. CONTENTS: Franz Schubert, *An die Musik*; Giacomo Puccini, *Colline's Aria from "La Boheme"*; Franz Schubert, *Who Is Sylvia?*; Gabriel Fauré, *The Secret*; George Fridrick Handel, *Where E'er You Walk*; Arthur Sullivan, *The Pale Young Curate from "The Sorcerer"*; Giuseppe Verdi, *Il lacerato spirito from "Simon Boccanegra"*; Giovanni Bononcini, *Arietta "Non posso disperar"*; Scott Joplin/arr. Rick Walters, *Solace*.

Canadian Brass Solo Performing Editions. Tuba solos (solo and accompaniment books) with a companion cassette. Side A: All selections recorded by Charles Daellenbach, tuba, and Monica Gaylord, piano. Side B: Piano accompaniments only. Hal Leonard Publishing Corporation, 1989. Giordi-

ani/Henderson, *My Dearest Love*, #50488700, cassette/score package, $9.95. Mozart/Frackenpohl, *Suite No. 1 from "The Magic Flute"*, #50488698, cassette/score package, $10.95. Mozart/Frackenpohl, *Suite No. 2 from "The Magic Flute"*, #50488699, cassette/score package, $10.95.

Jacobs, Wesley. *Play Along Cassette Series from Encore Music.* Legato Etudes by Bordogni, Book 1 T–26. Encore Publications, $14.00. Bordogni Cassette 9005, $11.95. Bordogni Studies Nos. 1-15 clearly typeset and not over-edited. Each study begins with a click track introduction. The interpretations are musically correct.

Perantoni, Daniel. *Master Solos Intermediate Level.* Edited by Linda Rutherford. Hal Leonard Publishing Corporation, 8112 West Bluemound Road, Milwaukee WI 53213. Tuba with piano (cassette). 1976. Complete set with cassette tape (performance track and practice track), $9.95. CONTENTS: Dowland, *Dear If You Change* and *Now, O Now My Needs Must Part*; Dowland, *Come Again, Sweet Love Doth Now Invite*; Brahms, *Two Lieder*; Schumann, *Romance No. 3*; Bach, *Siciliano and Chorale*; Haydn, *Two Classical Themes*; Powell, *Introduction and Blues*; Lawrence, *Piece for Tuba and Piano*.

Vivace, A Complete Practice System. Coda Music Technology, 6210 Bury Drive, Eden Prairie, MN 55346-1718. Telephone: 612-937-9611 or 800-843-2066. FAX: 612-937-9760. Suggested retail price, $2,295. Study solo repertoire with the accompaniment orchestrated by the composer. With Vivace performers hear the complete orchestration. Vivace listens to and follows the soloist. The performer is free to be expressive. Accompaniments are available for every instrument at every grade level. Vivace allows players to tune with a 12-note digital strobe, have Vivace tune to them, cut passages as desired, loop sections for repeated practice, or play accompaniments in any key. Vivace includes Intelligent Accompaniment software from Macintosh, an internal professional synthesizer (32-voice, multi-timbral, sample playing), built-in computer interface and microphone. SOLOS PRESENTLY AVAILABLE: Bach/Swanson, *Gavotte*; Barnhouse/Buchtel, *Barbarossa*; Buchtel, *Song of the Sea*; Danburg, *Five Extemporizations*; Dedrick, *A Touch of Tuba*; Delameter, *Auld Lang Syne*; Denmark, *Scène de Concert*; Dowling, *His Majesty the Tuba*; Frackenpohl, *Variations*; Haddad, *Suite*; Handel/Bell, *Honor and Arms*; Handel/Little, *Larghetto and Allegro*; Handel/Swanson, *Bourrée*; Marteau/Barnes, *Morceau Vivant*; Mozart/Frackenpohl, *Suite No. 2 from "Magic Flute"*; Nelhybel, *Suite*; Sear, *Sonatina*; Senaillé/Catelinet, *Introduction and Allegro Spiritoso*; Vandercook, *Colossus*; Vaughan Williams, *Concerto for Bass Tuba*; Walters, *Forty Fathoms*; Walters, *Tarantella*. TUBA SOLO COLLECTIONS: Gershenfeld, *Masterworks Solos*

Volume 1; Voxman, *Concert Contest Collection*; Perantoni, *Master Solos Intermediate Book*.

Videos for the Tubist

The Canadian Brass Live. Canadian Brass Videos 50488559. Color, stereo, 50 minutes, $24.95. PAL Edition 50481396. Call for pricing.

The Canadian Brass Live at Wolf Trap. Canadian Brass Videos 50481394. $29.95.

The Canadian Brass Master Class. Canadian Brass Videos 50488557. Color, stereo, 55 minutes, $39.95. PAL Edition 50481397. Call for pricing.

The Canadian Brass Spectacular. Canadian Brass Videos 50488569. Color, stereo, 60 minutes, $29.95. PAL Edition 50481395. Call for pricing.

Canadian Brass Videos are distributed by Hal Leonard Publications, 7777 West Bluemound Road, P. O. Box 13819, Milwaukee, WI 53213.Telephone: 414-774-3630; FAX: 414-774-3259.

The Complete Band Instrument Series for the Beginning Student. Music Education Video, 1108 Ridgecrest, Bowling Green, KY 42104. Telephone: 502-782-5258. Regular price, $39.95 each; 20% school district discount, $31.99 each. Complete set, $454.00; 20% school district discount, $364.00. MEV introduces the Complete Band Instrument Series for the elementary and junior high entry level student. Concentrated 60-minute sessions are taught by college professors. Covers basics in tone production, breathing, care for the instrument, and more. Includes tuba, baritone, and euphonium.

Discovering the Orchestra. SIRS Music, P. O. Box 2348, Boca Raton, FL 33427-2348. Telephone: 800-374-7477. A series of five video tapes: strings, brass, woodwinds, percussion, orchestra.

Harvey Phillips on Tuba. Educational Video Series, Department of Continuing Education—Arts (Attn: Dick Wolf), 726 Lowell Hall, University of Wisconsin-Madison, 610 Langdon Street, Madison, WI 53703. Telephone: 608-263-6670. 95 minutes, $89.95. Harvey Phillips in an interview at the University of Wisconsin. CONTENTS: The Tuba and Its Relationship with the Musical Family, the Wind Family, the Brass Family; The Tuba Keyboard, Tone, Range, Resonating Chamber, Embouchure, Lower Range, Upper Range; Performance of *Andante* by G. F. Handel; The P's of the Tuba: Piano, Posture, Placement, Pronunciation, Projection, Practice, Performance, Pride, Personality, Potential, Performance, excerpt from *Sonata for Bass Tuba and Piano* by Paul Hindemith; Questions and Answers Regarding Tuba Performance and Pedagogy: The Prospective Student, When to Start and What Instrument to Play, What a Teacher Can Do, Mouthpiece, Listening Habits, The Tubist in the Large Ensemble, Balance, Literature, The Tubist After High School, The Tubist Beyond Technique; Performance of *Suite No. 1 for Tuba*

and Piano (Effie Suite) by Alec Wilder; Philosophical Remarks; Closing Remarks.

Tuba & Euphonium Care & Maintenance. UNITUBA, University of Northern Iowa, Cedar Falls, IA. 1989, $49.95. Jeffrey Funderburk demonstrates repairing and maintaining the rotary valve tuba. Since the counters differ on various video tape machines, a timing index is provided on-screen to make it easier for the viewer to find specific topics.

Tuba for Beginners—Maestro Music Instrument Instructional Video. Backstage Pass Productions, P. O. Box 90, Van Nuys, CA 91408-0090. BSPT25V, 1991. 56 minutes, $29.95. Distributed by Cambridge Career Products, 90 MacCorkle Avenue SW, South Charleston, WV 25303. Telephone: 800-468-4227; FAX 304-744-9351. Matthew Borger of Dayton, Ohio, is featured on this tape for the beginning tubist. Topics covered: unpacking, assembly, tuba nomenclature, posture, hand positions, breathing, notes, reading music. Includes a nine-page instructional booklet.

Tubby the Tuba. Family Home Entertainment, 15400 Sherman Way, Van Nuys, CA 91406. 1993, price not available. 60 minutes. Cartoon version (1977) of several Kleinsinger/Tripp stories. Begins and ends with *Tubby the Tuba*, and includes *Tubby at the Circus* and *The Story of Celeste.* Paul Tripp narrates. Features Dick Van Dyke as the voice of Tubby. The tuba soloist is not identified.

Tubby the Tuba and Friends. United American Video, P. O. Box 7647, Charlotte, N. C. 28241. 1989, $2.96. Reissue of the 1946 George Pal Puppetoon. Also includes puppetoon "Madcap Models" and two *Three Stooges* cartoons.

Tubby the Tuba and Other Cartoon Classics. Parents Approved Videos, P. O. Box 630662, Ojus, FL 33163. 1986, $3.00. Reissue of the 1946 George Pal Puppetoon. Also includes cartoons "A Waif's Welcome," "Balloon Land," and "Dover Boys at Pimento U."

Addresses of Recording Companies/ Distributors

A & R Records, Euphonium Concerts, 14274 Crystal Cove Drive South, Jacksonville, FL 32224

ACA Digital Recording, Department BR-T, P. O. Box 450727, Atlanta, GA 30345

Accura Music, P. O. Box 4260, Athens, OH 45701-4260

Accurate Records, 117 Columbia Street, Cambridge, MA 02139

Adelphi Records, Box 7688, Silver Spring, MD 20907

Adi Hershko, 123 Stern Street, Kiron 55.000, Israel

Al Opland Recording Service, 1006 5th Ave S. W., Pipestone, MN 56164

Al Teare Digital Recordings, 9076 Willoughby Road, Pittsburgh, PA 15237   412-367-1526 Amadeo, dist. by Polygram Group Distribution

AMIGA, Deutsche Schallplatten GmbH, Berlin, 1080, Reichstagsuger, Germany

Angel, CEMA Distribution, 21700 Oxnard St. #700, Woodland Hills, CA 91367

Ann Arbor Jazz, 1700 McMullen-Booth Road, Suite C-3, Clearwater, FL 34619

Argo, dist. by Polygram Group Distribution

Arista Records, Inc., 6 West 57th Street, New York, NY 10019

ASI Records, 711 West Broadway, Minneapolis, MN 55411

Atlantic Jazz, dist. by Warner-Electra-Atlantic Corp

Audicom Corporation, 4950 Nome Street, Unit C, Denver, CO 80239

Audio Fidelity, dist. by Leisure Audio

Audite, Koch International, 177 Cantiague Rock Road, Westbury, NY 11590

Avant, dist. by Western International Music

Barbirolli Society, 8 Tunnel Road, Retford Notts, Dn 22 7 TA, England

Basset Hound Music, 2139 Kress Street, Los Angeles, CA 90046

Bayrischen Rundfunk, Qualition Imports, 24-02 40th Ave., Long Island City, NY 11101

Bernel Music Ltd., P. O. Box 2438, Cullowhee, NC 28723

Black Saint, Sphere Marketing, P. O. Box 771, Manhasset, NY 11030

Blue Groove Records, Liebhartstal Strasse 15-5, A-1160 Vienna, Austria

Borgen Records, Henning Christiansen, Bakkehojgaard, 4792 Askeby, Denmark

Broadway, P. O. Box 100, Brighton, Michigan 48116

Cadence, dist. by North Country

Campro, IMPS Music, 70 Route 202 North, Peterborough, NH 03458

Capital Records, 1750 N. Vine Street, Hollywood, CA 90028

Caprice, Svenska Rikskonserter, Box 1225, 111 27 Stockholm, Sweden

CBS Masterworks, dist. by Sony Music Distribution

CBS Records, 51 W. 52nd Street, New York, NY 10019

Century Custom Recording Service. See Century Records

Century of Chicago. *See* Century Records

Century Records, 303 North Pine Street, Prospect Heights, IL

Chandos Records, LTD., 41 Charing Cross Road, London WC2HOAR, England

Circle Records, Collector's Record Club, GHB Jazz Foundation Building, 1206 Decatur St., New Orleans, LA 70116

College Presentation Series. *See* University of Illinois Band

Colosseum Records, Qualition Imports, 24-02 40th Ave., Long Island City, NY 11101

Columbia, dist. by Sony Music Distribution

Columbia Legacy, dist. by Sony Music Distribution

Composer's Recordings, Inc., 73 Spring Street, Room 506, New York, NY 10012

Concord Records, P. O. Box 845, Concord, CA 94522

Cornell University Wind Ensemble, Band Office, Lincoln Hall, Cornell University, Ithaca, NY 14850

Coronet Recording Co., 4971 N. High Street, Columbus, OH 43214

Crest Music, 33 Chambers Bridge Road, Lakewood, NJ 08901

Crest Records. *See* Golden Crest Records

Crown Records, reissued on Red Records, P. O. Box 750, Reseda, CA 91335

Crystal Records, 2235 Willida Lane, Sedro-Woolley, WA 98284

Dana Recording Project, Dana School of Music, Youngstown State University, Youngstown, OH 44555

Dave Gannett, 274 Pleasant Valley Road, Union Grove, AL 35175

Daybreak Express Records, P. O. Box 250, Van Brunt Station, Brooklyn, NY 11215

Deutsche Grammophon, Schlehecker Strasse 114, 5064 Roesrath-Durbusch, Germany

Diavolo Records, Schmid & Galke GbR, Kaiser Friedrich Strasse 4, Düsseldorf, Germany

Digitally Encoded Cassette Classics, dist. by Mr. Cassette, 360 Supertest Road, Ontario, Canada M3J 2M2

Disc BIM, dist. by North Country

Discophon, Calle Cardenal Tedeschini, 14-22, Esca: A - 2o, 4a, Barcelona - 27, Spain

Disneyland Records, Disneyland Productions, 350 S. Buena Vista, Burbank, CA 91521

Doyen Recordings, LTD., Doyen House, 17 Coupland Close, Moorside, Oldham, Lancs, England 0L4 2TQ

ECM, dist. by Polygram Group Distribution

Edition Wilhelm Hansen, Ole Schmidt, Brokbjergstrand 12, 4583 Sj. Odde, Denmark

Electrecord, Allegro Imports, 3434 S. E. Milwaukie Ave, Portland, OR 97202

Epic, dist. by Sony Music Distribution

Epic Soundtrax, dist. by Sony Music Distribution

Euphonia, Trinity Mews, Cambridge Gardens, London W10 6JA, England

Euphonium Concerts, 14274 Crystal Cove Drive South, Jacksonville, FL 32224

Excerpt Recording Company, P. O. Box 231 Kingsbridge Station, Bronx, NY 10463

Fanfare, Intersound International, P. O. Box 1724, Roswell, GA 30077

Flying Fish Records, 1304 W. Schubert, Chicago, IL 60614

Fonit-Cetra, Allegro Imports, 3434 S. E. Milwaukie Ave, Portland, OR 97202

Forces Command, Ft. McPherson, US Army Ground Forces Band, Fort McPherson, GA 30330

Four Leaf Records, Box 1231, 172 24 Sundbyberg, Sweden

Fresh Sound Records, a product of Jazz Workshop S. L. Barcelona, Spain

Gasparo Records, P. O. Box 600, Jaffrey, NH 03452

Geffin Records, dist. by UNI

GM Recordings, Gun Mar Music, 167 Dudley Road, Newton Centre, MA 02159

GNP Crescendo, 8400 Sunset Blvd., Los Angeles, CA 90069

Golden Crest Records, Inc., 220 Broadway, Huntington Station, NY 11746

Golden Records, 250 W. 57th Street, New York, NY 10019

Grammofonfirma BIS, Varingavagen 6, 182 63 Djursholm, Sweden

Harlequin Recording, Elgar House, Rufford, Tamworth, Staffordshire, England

Harvey Phillips Foundation, P. O. Box 933, Bloomington, IN 47402

Hat Art Records, Im Muhleboden 54, CH-4106 Therwil, Switzerland

Heavyweight Records, P. O. Box 57, Kettering, Northants NN15 5PL, England

Hemisphere Records, P. O. Box 3578, New York NY 10185

HPF Records and Tapes, P. O. Box 933, Bloomington, IN 47402

IDA Records, dist. by North Country

Impulse, dist. by MCA

Impulse Records, dist. by UNI

India Navigation, 177 Franklin St., New York, NY 10013, dist. by North Country

Innowo, Viale Verdi 1, 22037, Ponte Lambro, Italy

Jazz Heritage, 914 Lanyard Avenue, Kirkwood, MO 63122

JMT, dist. by Polygram

John Fletcher Trust Fund, 14 Hamilton Terrace, London NW8 UG

Kendor, P. O. Box 278, Delvan, NY 14042

Kibutz Movement League of Composers, Yashai Knoll, Kibutz Ramat Yochanan, 30035 Israel

Kitty Jazz, dist. by Polydor Japan

KM Educational Library, 2980 N. Ontario, Burbank, CA 91504

Koch International, 177 Cantiague Rock Road, Westbury, NY 11590

Kompost Rekords, Beat Blaser, Steinenstrasse 28, CH-5406 Baden-Rutihof, Switzerland

Kosei Publishing Co., ELF Music, Ludwig Music Publishing Co., 557 East 140th Street, Cleveland, OH 44110, USA

Legend Record Co., 12055 Burbank Blvd, N. Hollywood CA 91607

Leisure Audio, P. O. Box 56757, New Orleans, LA 70156-6757, (800) 321-1499

Leo Records, Box 193, 00101 Helsinki, Finland

Loft Records, Schlehecker Str. 114, 5064 Roesrath-Durbusch, Germany

London, dist. by Polygram Group Distribution

M-A Music, K-tel International, 15535 Medina Road, Plymouth, MN 55447

Macmillan–McGraw Hill Publishing, New York, NY

Mama Foundation, 555 E. Easy Street, Simi Valley, CA 93065

Marcophon, Im Schwantenmos 15, CH-8126 Zumikon, Switzerland

Mark College Jazz Series. See Mark Recordings

Mark Custom Recording Services. See Mark Recordings

Mark Educational Recordings. See Mark Recordings

Mark Recordings, 10815 Bodine Road, P. O. Box 406, Clarence, NY14031-0406

MCA Records International, 70 Universal City Plaza, Universal City, CA 91608

Mercury, dist. by Polygram Group Distribution

MGM, dist. by Polygram Group Distribution

MGM Children's Series, dist. by Polygram Group Distribution

Milestone, Fantasy, Inc., 10th & Parker, Berkeley, CA 94710

Mole Records, dist. by North Country

Mood Records, DA Music, USA, 362 Pinehurst Lane, Marietta, GA 30068

Morehead State University Book Store, 4950 Nome Street, Unit C, Denver, Colorado 80239

MPS Records, dist. by Polygram Group Distribution

Musica Helvetica, Swiss Broadcasting Coporation, Swiss Radio International, 3000 Berne 15 - Switzerland

Musical Heritage Society Orpheus, 1991 Broadway, New York, NY 10023

Navigation. See India Navigation

North Country, Cadence Building, Redwood, NY 13679

Northern Tuba Lights, Harri Lidsle, Lautamiehenkatu 10B13, 15100 Lahti, Finland

NOVA, Deutsche Schallplatten GmbH, Berlin, 1080, Reichstagsuger, Germany

Odyssey, dist. by Sony Music Distribution

Olufsen Records, Skt. Knudsvej 8, 1903 Frederiksberg C, Denmark

Opus One, 212 Lafayette Street, New York, NY 10012

Opus One, P. O. Box 604, Greenville, ME 04441

Peter Pan Records, Peter Pan Industries, 88 St. Francis Street, Newark, NJ 07105

Philips, dist. by Polygram Group Distribution

Polydor, dist. by Polygram Group Distribution

Polygram Group Distribution, Worldwide Plaza, 825 Eighth Avenue, New York, NY 10019

Polyphonic, 77-79 Dudden Hill Lane, London NW10 1BD, England

Prestige, Fantasy Records, Inc., 10th & Parker, Berkeley, CA 94710

Proviva, Deutsche Austrophon GMBH, D-2840 Diepholz, Bestell Nr.: ISPV 102, Germany

QCA Red Mark, Liben Records, Liben Music Publishers, 6265 Dawes Lane, Cincinnati, OH 45230

RCA, Bertelsman Music Group, 1133 Avenue of the Americas, New York, NY 10036

RCA Red Seal, Bertelsman Music Group, 1133 Avenue of the Americas, New York, NY 10036

RCA Victor, Bertelsman Music Group, 1133 Avenue of the Americas, New York, NY 10036

Recorded Publications Company, 1100 State Street, Camden, NJ 08105

Red Lehr, Rural Route 1, Box 90, New Athens, IL 62264

Ricordi, One World Records, 1250 W. Northwest Hwy., Suite 505, Palatine,IL 60067

Rondo Grammofon & Danish Brass Publishing, Indepent Music OH, P. O. Box 49, 2680 Sølrod Strand, Denmark

Rounder Records, 1 Camp Street, Cambridge, MA 02140

School of Music LP Records, University of Michigan, Ann Arbor, MI 48109

Sica-Sound-Music, Steinamangererstrasse 187, A-7400 Oberwart, Austria

Silver Cornet Productions, P. O. Box 681992, Franklin, TN 37068-1992

Silver Crest, 408 Carew Tower, Cincinnati, OH 45202 (see Golden Crest)

SIMAX-PSC, ProMusica AS, Boks 4379, Torshov, N-0402 Oslo, Norway

Simon Says, Record Guild of America, 144 Milbar Blvd., Farmingdale, NY 11735

Sony Music Distribution, P. O. Box 4450, New York NY 10101

Soul Notes, Sphere Marketing, P. O. Box 771, Manhasset, NY 11030

Sound Aspects, Cai Sound Aspects, Pedro R. de Freitas, Im Bluetengarten 14, 7150 Backnang, Germany

Sound Mark, 4950-C Nome Street, Denver, CO 80239

SPLASC(H), Via Roma 11 - P. O. Box 97, 21051 Arcisate, Italy

Stolat, Arista Records, Inc., 65 West 55th Street, New York, NY 19919

Stomp Off, Box 342, Dept. C, York, PA 17405

Strata-East Records, Box 36, G. C. S., New York, NY 10163

Studio für Angewandte Musik, dist. by Extraplatte

Summit Records, P. O. Box 26850, Tempe, AZ 85285

Swedish Society Discofil, Allegro Imports, 3434 S. E. Milwaukie Ave, Portland, OR 97202

T.A.P. Music Sales, R. R. 1, Box 186, Newton, IA 50208

Telarc, Telarc International Corporation, 23307 Commerce Park Road, Cleveland, OH 44122

Teldec, BMG Direct Marketing, 6550 East 30th Street, Indianapolis, IN 46219

Time Records, 2 West 45 Street, New York 36, NY

Tomato Records, , CEMA Distribution , 21700 Oxnard St. #700, Woodland Hills, CA 91367

Tomorrow River Music, P. O. Box 165, Madison, WI 53701

Trend Records–Discovery Records, P. O. Box 48081, Los Angeles, CA 90048

UNI Distribution Corp., 60 Universal City Plaza, Universal City, CA 91608

Unit Records, Beat Blaser, Steinenstrasse 28, CH-5406 Baden-Rutihof, Switzerland

United States Air Force Band, Director of Public Relations, Bolling Air Force Base, Washington,D.C. 20332-6458

United States Army Band, Commanding Officer, ATTN: Public Affairs, P. O. Box 70565, Washington DC 20024-1374

United States Coast Guard, Public Affairs Division, U. S. Coast Guard Band, U. S. Coast Guard Academy, New London, CT 06320

United States Navy Band, Public Relations, Washington Navy Yard, Washington, D. C. 20374-1052

University Brass Recording Series, P. O. Box 2374 Station A, Champaign, IL 61820

University of Illinois Band, 140 Harding Band Building, 1103 S. 6th Street, Champaign, IL 61820

Varese-Sarabande, 13006 Saticoy Street, North Hollywood, CA 91605

VDE-Gallo, Qualition Imports, 24-02 40th Ave., Long Island City, NY 11101

Warner Brothers, 3300 Warner Blvd, Burbank, CA 91510

Warner-Electra-Atlantic Corp., 111 N. Hollywood Way, Burbank, CA 91505

Watt Works, dist. by Polygram Group Distribution

Western International Music, 3707 65th Ave, Greeley, CO 80634-9626

Westmark Tapes, Opland Recordings, R. R. 10 Box 403, Sioux Falls, SD 57104

Wonderland, AA Wonderland Records, 12 Gelb Ave, Union, NJ 07083

13. Bibliography

Books

Michael A. Fischer

Every effort has been made to locate, review, and include all books that have references to the tuba. This project entailed national "on-line" computer and endless card catalogue searches, visits to Moody Library at Baylor University and to Willis Library at the University of North Texas, and communications from friends around the world. Many thanks go to Charles McAdams and R. Winston Morris. A special thank you goes to Kenyon D. Wilson and Jeremy Lane at Baylor University, and to the librarians at Moody Library, who provided patience and understanding assistance, especially Billie Peterson, Beth Tice, and Sha Towers. In addition, thanks go to David Burke of Willis Library.

Abbreviations: N.p.=no place, n.p.=no publisher, n.d.=no date.

Bibliography

Bell, William J., and R. Winston Morris. *Encyclopedia of Literature for the Tuba*. New York: Charles Colin, 1967.

Brown, Leon F. *Handbook of Selected Literature for the Study of Tuba at the University-College Level*. Denton: North Texas State University, 1966.

Bühler, Josef. *Tuba-Bibliographie*. Hofheim am Taunus, Germany: Freidrich Hofmeister, 1990.

Fasman, Mark J. *Brass Bibliography: Sources on the History, Literature, Pedagogy, Performance, and Acoustics of Brass Instruments*. Bloomington, Indiana: Indiana University Press, 1990.

Griffiths, John R. *The Low Brass Guide*. Hackensack, New Jersey: Jerona Music Corp., 1980.

Libal, Leopold. *Die Tuba Literaturliste*. Available from Leopold Libal, Bahnstrasse 1, A-2326, Maria Lanzendorf, Austria, 1992.

Marzan, Fred J. *20th Century Literature for Tuba*. Rev. ed. Lake Geneva, Wisconsin: DEG Music Products, Inc., 1972.

Mason, J. Kent. *The Tuba Handbook*. Toronto, Ontario: Sonante Publications, 1977.

Morris, R. Winston. *Tuba Music Guide*. Evanston, Illinois: Instrumentalist Co., 1973.

Rasmussen, Mary. *A Teacher's Guide to the Literature of Brass Instruments*. Durham, New Hampshire: Appleyard Publications, 1968.

Whitener, Scott. *A Complete Guide to Brass*. New York: Schirmer Books, 1990.

Biography

Bird, Gary, ed. *Program Notes for the Solo Tuba*. Bloomington: Indiana University Press, 1994.

Stewart, M. Dee, comp. *Arnold Jacobs: The Legacy of a Master*. Northfield, Illinois: The Instrumentalist Publishing Company, 1987.

Discography

Bell, William J., and R. Winston Morris. *Encyclopedia of Literature for the Tuba*. New York: Charles Colin, 1967.

Bühler, Josef. *Tuba-Bibliographie*. Hofheim am Taunus, Germany. Freidrich Hofmeister, 1990.

Griffiths, John R. *The Low Brass Guide*. Hackensack, New Jersey: Jerona Music Corp., 1980.

Morris, R. Winston. *Tuba Music Guide*. Evanston, Illinois: Instrumentalist Co., 1973.

Whitener, Scott. *A Complete Guide to Brass*. New York: Schirmer Books, 1990.

Equipment

Butterfield, Don. *It is Time to Modify the Bass Tuba*. Available from United Musical Instruments, P.O. Box 727, Elkhart, IN 46515, n.d.

Conner, Rex. *How to Care for a Rotary Valve Tuba*. Available from Getzen Co. Inc., P.O. Box 440, Elkhorn, WI 53121, n.d.

Little, Donald C. *Practical Hints on Playing the Tuba*. Practical Hints Series. Melville, New York: Belwin-Mills Publishing Corp., 1984.

Mason, J. Kent. *The Tuba Handbook*. Toronto, Ontario: Sonante Publications, 1977.

Whitener, Scott. *A Complete Guide to Brass*. New York: Schirmer Books, 1990.

General References

Baines, Anthony. *Brass Instruments: Their History and Development*. New York: Charles Scribner's Sons, 1981.

Cummings, Barton. *The Contemporary Tuba*. New London, Connecticut: Whaling Music Publishers, 1984.

Meucci, Renato. *Il Cimbasso e gli Strumenti affini nell' Ottocento Italiano*. Ed. Studi Verdiana Parma, 1988-1989.

Phillips, Harvey, and William Winkle. *The Art of Tuba and Euphonium*. N.p.: Summy-Birchard Music, 1992.

Stauffer, Donald W. *A Treatise on the Tuba*. Birmingham, Alabama: Stauffer Press, 1989.

Weckerlin, J. B. "Le serpent." In *Dernier musiciana*. Paris: Garnier Frères, 1899.

History

Baines, Anthony. *Brass Instruments: Their History and Development*. New York: Charles Scribner's Sons, 1981.

Bevan, Clifford. *The Tuba Family*. New York: Scribner, 1978

Eliason, Robert E. *Early American Brass Makers*. Brass Research Series No. 10. Nashville, Tennessee: Brass Press, 1979.

Mason, J. Kent. *The Tuba Handbook*. Toronto, Ontario: Sonante Publications, 1977.

Rutz, Roland Robert. *A Brief History and Curriculum for Tuba*. N.p.: n.p., 1975.

Whitener, Scott. *A Complete Guide to Brass*. New York: Schirmer Books, 1990.

Literature

Bell, William J., and R. Winston Morris. *Encyclopedia of Literature for the Tuba*. New York: Charles Colin, 1967.

Bird, Gary, ed. *Program Notes for the Solo Tuba*. Bloomington: Indiana University Press, 1994.

Bühler, Josef. *Tuba-Bibliographie*. Hofheim am Taunus, Germany: Freidrich Hofmeister, 1990.

King, Robert D. *Brass Player's Guide*. North Easton, Massachusetts: Robert King Music, 1993.

Libal, Leopold. *Die Tuba Literaturliste*. Available from author Leopold Libal, Bahnstrasse 1, A-2326, Maria Lanzendorf, Austria 1992.

Marzan, Fred J. *20th Century Literature for Tuba*. Rev. ed. Lake Geneva, Wisconsin: DEG Music Products, Inc., 1972.

Mason, J. Kent. *The Tuba Handbook*. Toronto, Ontario: Sonante Publications, 1977.

Morris, R. Winston. *Tuba Music Guide*. Evanston, Illinois: Instrumentalist Co., 1973.

Rasmussen, Mary. *A Teacher's Guide to the Literature of Brass Instruments*. Durham, New Hampshire: Appleyard Publications, 1968.

Thompson, Mark, and Jeffrey Jon Lemke. *French Music for Low Brass Instruments: An Annotated Bibliography*. Bloomington: Indiana University Press, 1994.

Whitener, Scott. *A Complete Guide to Brass*. New York: Schirmer Books, 1990.

Orchestration

Kunitz, Hans. *Die Instrumentation*. Teil 9: Tuba. Leipzig, Germany: Breitkopf & Härtel, 1968.

Pedagogy

Beaugeois. *Nouvelle méthode de plainchant, de musicque et de serpent*. Amiens, France: Caron-Vitet, 1827.

Bell, William. *Foundation to Tuba and Sousaphone Playing*. New York: Carl Fischer, 1931.

Bell, William J., and R. Winston Morris. *Encyclopedia of Literature for the Tuba*. New York: Charles Colin, 1967.

Brown, Merrill E. *Teaching the Successful High School Brass Section*. West Nyack, New York: Parker Publishing Company, 1981.

Caussinus, V. *Solfège-Méthode pour l'ophicléide-basse*. Paris: Meissonnier, ca. 1840.

Cornette, Victor. *Méthode d'ophicléide alto et basse*. Paris: Richault, ca. 1835.

Cummings, Barton. *The Contemporary Tuba*. New London, Connecticut: Whaling Music Publishers, 1984.

Garnier. *Méthode élémentaire et facile d'ophicléide à pistons ou à cylindres*. Paris: Schonenberger, ca. 1845-1850.

Griffiths, John R. *The Low Brass Guide*. Hackensack, New Jersey: Jerona Music Corp., 1980.

Hermenge, M. G. *Méthode élémentaire pour le serpent-forveille*. Paris: Forveille, ca. 1833.

Hunt, Norman J. *Brass Ensemble Method*. 3rd ed. Dubuque, Iowa: Wm. C. Brown Company Publisher, 1974.

———. *Guide to Teaching Brass*. 3rd ed. Dubuque, Iowa: Wm. C. Brown Company Publishers, 1984.

Kappey, J. *Bombardon and Contrabass Tutor*. London: n.p., ca. 1874.

Kastner, J. G. *Méthode élémentaire pour l'ophicléide*. Paris: Troupenas, ca. 1845.

Kietzer, *Robert. Schule für Tuba in B, od. C, Helikon, Bombardon, Sousaphon; für den Selbstunterricht ge-*

eignet. Op. 85. (School for Self-Instruction.) Zimmermann-Schule, no. 21. Frankfurt: W. Zimmermann, 1900.

Kuehn, David. *Toward Better Tuba Players.* Available from Getzen Co, Inc., P.O. Box 440, Elkhorn, WI 53121, n.d.

Little, Donald C. *Practical Hints on Playing the Tuba.* Practical Hints Series. Melville, New York: Belwin-Mills Publishing Corp., 1984.

Mason, J. Kent. *The Tuba Handbook.* Toronto, Ontario: Sonante Publications, 1977.

———. *Student's Guide to the Tuba.* Music Pamphlet Series. Agincourt, Ontario: GLC, 1980.

Mueller, Herbert C. *Learning to Teach Through Playing: A Brass Method.* Reading, Massachusetts: Addison-Wesley Publishing Company, 1968.

Reinhardt, Donald S. *The Encyclopedia of the Pivot System for All Cupped Mouthpiece Brass Instruments.* New York: Charles Colin, 1964.

Roxnoy, Richard T. *Trombone–Low Brass Techniques and Pedagogy.* Boulder, Colorado: n.p., 1978.

Rusch, Harold W. *Hal Leonard Advanced Band Method for Tuba.* Special Studies by Arnold Jacobs. Winona, Minnesota: Hal Leonard Music, Inc., 1963.

Rutz, Roland Robert. *A Brief History and Curriculum for Tuba.* N.p.: n.p., 1975.

Sax, Adolphe. *Méthode complète pour saxhorn et sax-tromba soprano, alto, ténor, baryton, basse et contrebasse à 3, 4 et 5 cylindres; suivie d'exercises pour l'emploi du compensateur.* Paris: Brandus & Dufour, n. d.

Teuchert, Emil. *Schule für die Basstuba in F oder ES und für Kontrabasstuba in C oder B.* Frankfurt am Main, Germany: Friedrich Hofmeister, n.d.

Whitener, Scott. *A Complete Guide to Brass.* New York: Schirmer Books, 1990.

Miscellaneous

Bobo, Roger. *Tuba: Word with a Dozen Meanings.* N.p.: Available from Mirafone Corporation. n.d.

Heyde, Herbert. *Trompeten, Posaunen, Tuben.* Wiesbaden, Germany: n.p., 1985.

Hunt, Norman J. *Brass Ensemble Method.* 3rd ed. Dubuque, Iowa: Wm. C. Brown Company Publishers, 1974.

———. *Guide to Teaching Brass.* 3rd ed. Dubuque, Iowa: Wm. C. Brown Company Publishers, 1984.

Kuehn, David. *Toward Better Tuba Players.* N.p.: Available from the Getzen Co, Inc., P.O. Box 440, Elkhorn, WI 53121, n.d.

Severson, Paul, and Mark McDunn. *Brass Wind Artistry: Master Your Mind, Master Your Instrument.* Athens, Ohio: Accura, 1983.

Dissertations, Theses, and Research Projects

Robert G. Brewer

The primary source for research in dissertations and theses is *Dissertations Abstracts International (DAI)* published by University Microfilms Inc. (UMI) of Ann Arbor, Michigan. Most university libraries and many public libraries are regular subscribers to this publication. UMI also publishes a sister to *DAI* known as *Masters Abstracts.* A search through the multitude of volumes of these publications was once necessary for a review of literature, particularly in doctoral research. Depending on the subject matter, one could spend days or even weeks searching volume after volume. Fortunately, UMI has made it easier with the advent of Dissertations Abstracts Online and Dissertations Abstracts Ondisk. Today one can go to the library, plug in one's own disk at the CD ROM terminal, and download to disk complete bibliographic references and abstracts of the searches specified in one afternoon. This vast improvement is heaven sent!

This is not to say, however, that the *DAI* CD ROM system does not have its limitations. As the system has evolved, the information given in the entries in *DAI* Online and *DAI* Ondisk has evolved as well. For instance, entries before 1980 are printed to disk as bibliographic references only; therefore, to obtain the abstract, one must still search in the correct volume. Fortunately, the volumes and page numbers are cited in the bibliographic reference. Entries between 1980 and 1990 contain complete bibliographic references, including the volume and page numbers in the printed version of *DAI* and the complete abstract. After 1990, *DAI* added the advisor's name to the bibliographic reference.

All the information given in the most recent entries is reproduced here, but time limitations make it impossible to search for extra information pertaining to the earlier entries, such as the advisor's name. When available, complete abstracts are included, essentially unedited at the request of UMI. When an entry was taken from a source other than UMI, that source is acknowledged.

The dissertation titles and abstracts contained here are published with permission of University Microfilms, Inc., publishers of *Dissertation Abstracts International* (copyright © 1965–1992 by University Microfilms Inc.), and may not be reproduced without their prior permission. Copies of the dissertations may be obtained from University Microfilms, Inc., 300 North Zeeb Road, Ann Arbor, MI 48106; telephone 1-800-521-3042.

The many research projects that were never published and are held in university libraries around the world could not have been listed without the assistance of tuba professors and enthusiasts with access to these libraries. Many thanks are due to Joan Acton, Robert M. Gifford, Philip Sinder, Richard Sorenson, Gary Buttery, Kenyon D. Wilson, Stephen Bryant, Ronald A. Davis, Gary Bird, Michael Easter, and L. Richmond Sparks, for invaluable help in locating and describing these documents.

Bibliography

Brewer, Robert Gary. "A Guide to the Use of Etudes and Exercises in Teaching the Tuba." D.M.A. diss., University of Illinois at Urbana-Champaign (0090), 1991, 150 pp. Advisor: Gray, R; Source: DAI 52/11A, p.3852; Publication No.: AAC9210752; Subject: Education, Music (0522); Music (0413).
Abstract: This project contains a thorough investigation of current pedagogical writings in tuba performance and training. Using Gordon Mathie's *Trumpet Teacher's Guide* as a model, the project then combines a list of performance and musical elements with a graded list of etudes and exercises for specific work on the individual elements. Cross-referencing to the discussion in pedagogical writings is provided. The study concludes that while there remain certain omissions from tuba training materials, such as contemporary special effects, there are sufficient tuba materials in the current repertory for the training of professional tuba performers.

Funderburk, Jeffrey Lee. "An Annotated Bibliography of the Unaccompanied Solo Repertoire for Tuba." D.M.A. diss., University of Illinois at Urbana-Champaign, 1992, 200 pp. Advisor Moore, M.; Source: Jeffrey Funderburk; unpublished. No abstract available.

Rabe, Arnold Fredrick. "Transcriptions of Graded Solos for Tuba, by Arnold Fredrick Rabe." M.A. thesis, State College of Iowa, 1965. No abstract available.

Sparks, L. Richmond. "An Annotated Bibliography of Tuba Solos with Band Accompaniment." D.M.A. diss., Arizona State University (0010), 1990, 262 pp. Source: DAI 52/01A, p. 17; Publication No.: AAC9116783; Subject: Music (0413); Education, Music (0522).
Abstract: Between Fred J. Marzan's, *20th Century Literature for Tuba* and Winston Morris's *The Tuba Music Guide*, there are only eighty tuba solos with band accompaniment listed. Both of these publications were printed within the years 1972 and 1973, and they remain the last catalogues of tuba literature published since that time. With the advent of the organization of the Tubists Universal Brotherhood Association, and especially the promotions by Mr. Harvey Phillips, a virtuoso tuba performer and tuba teacher at Indiana University, the literature for the tuba has expanded and developed into a repertoire comparable to the literature of the saxophone and percussion instruments.
There is a great need to keep track of the rapidly increasing works for the instrument. The works for tuba with band accompaniment have, alone, increased more than 150 percent. This paper presents an annotated bibliography of all those works written for tuba solo with band accompaniment. The annotation includes remarks about the solo and the band accompaniment in an effort to inform performers and conductors alike of the character and style of the composition, as well as the difficulty level of each, and the instrumentation needed to perform the work. Each entry (listed in alphabetical order by composer) includes the following information: composer; title, publisher or manuscript, date of copyright; catalog number; price; duration of the piece; difficulty level of solo part; difficulty level of band accompaniment; and the range of the tuba solo.
The scope of this project is limited to works that are published, works that are on rental, and works that are still in manuscript. A partial compilation has been made of out-of-print works since such compositions may be currently available through the fraternal "buddy system" of borrowing from personal libraries and/or fellow institutions. The tuba repertoire is comparatively smaller than those of other instruments, and every effort should be made to preserve any and all works available.

Thompson, John Mark. "An Annotated Bibliography of French Literature for Bass Trombone, Tuba, and Bass Saxhorn, Including Solos and Pedagogical Materials." D.M.A. diss., The University of Iowa, 1991. No abstract Available.

Performance

AsKew, Dennis Weston. "Three Programs of Tuba Music. (Performance)." A.Mus.D. diss., The University of Michigan (0127), 1991. Advisor: Kaenzig, Fritz; Source: DAI 52/ 03A, p.727; Publication No.: AAC0570057; Subject: Music (0413).
Abstract: One concerto performance with orchestra and two full-length recitals were given in lieu of a written dissertation. The first recital took place in Yountville, CA, on December 2, 1990, and consisted of a performance of John Williams' *Concerto for Tuba and Orchestra,* with Asher Raboy conducting the Napa Valley Symphony.

The second recital, which took place in Ann Arbor on January 13, 1991, opened with Georg Phillip Telemann's *Sonata in mi minore,* from his *Essercizi Musici.* Originally for viola da gamba, this work was transcribed for tuba by Fritz Kaenzig. *Three for One,* composed by Scott Wyatt in 1981, explores the timbral combinations that are possible when tuba and electronically produced sounds are combined. *Capriccio* (1980), a piece for solo tuba by Krzysztof Penderecki, exploits more recently developed techniques and effects on the tuba. Donald White's *Sonata for Tuba and Piano* is more traditional in its use of the instrument and is indicative of his writing for other brass instruments. The final work on the second recital was the *Sextet in Four Parts for Brass Instruments, Op. 30.* Although composed by Oskar Bohme in the first decade of this century, this work is stylistically a nineteenth-century piece.

The third recital, presented on February 17, 1991, opened with the *Sonata, Op. 17., for Horn and Piano,* by Ludwig van Beethoven, adapted for tuba by Dennis AsKew. The *Sonata for Tuba and Piano,* by Bruce Broughton, is one of several works for tuba written by Hollywood film score composers. *Three Songs for Soprano and Tuba* by Roger Vaughan, poetry by John Updike, provides the audience with an unusual timbral combination, as well as entertaining subject matter. Morgan Powell's *Midnight Realities* is typical of many advanced works written for tuba alone, experimenting with extended techniques such as multiphonics and non-traditional notation. The *Tuba Concerto* by Edward Gregson, originally scored for tuba and brass band, provides the tubist with a large scale work in the traditional twentieth-century British brass band idiom. The closing work on the third recital was Herbert L. Clarke's *The Maid of the Mist,* adapted for tuba by Dennis AsKew.

Bergee, Martin J. "An Application of the Facet-Factorial Approach to Scale Construction in the Development of a Rating Scale for Euphonium and Tuba Music Performance." See listing under "Pedagogy," below.

Berman, Eric M. "Performance Tasks Encountered in Selected Twentieth-Century Band Excerpts for Tuba: Their Identification, Categorization, and Analysis." Ph.D. diss., New York University (0146), 1981, 187 pp. Source: DAI 42/02A, p. 441; Publication No.: AAC8115474; Subject: Music (0413).
Abstract: The problem presented in this study was to identify, categorize, and analyze the performance tasks encountered in selected twentieth-century band excerpts for tuba. It was necessary to survey the tuba parts in twentieth-century band literature and select suitable excerpts, identify and categorize the performance tasks found in each excerpt, discuss the performance tasks, and offer suggestions for their execution.

Before the study was begun, a review of band music was conducted to determine which selections were suitable for inclusion in this study. Scores and literature dealing with band music were studied so that a twentieth-century band repertoire could be identified. Each composition had to be a major work for band and include an exceptional tuba part. A list of thirty-two selections was compiled and presented to a panel of three experts for the final selection process. The panel unanimously chose eleven compositions. One selection, *Stars and Stripes Forever,* predated the twentieth century but was considered to be of such importance that an exception was made for it. The others were composed between 1918 and 1970. They are *Emblems* by Aaron Copland, *Celebration Overture* by Paul Creston, *Irish Tune* from County Derry and *Shepherd's Hey* by Percy Grainger, *Lincolnshire Posy* also by Grainger, the *First* and *Second Suites for Military Band* by Gustav Holst, *Concerto for Band* by Gordon Jacob, *Symphony for Band* by Vincent Persichetti, and *Theme and Variations, Opus 43* by Arnold

Schoenberg. The panel reported that these pieces represent the range of the established band repertoire in the twentieth century.

It was then necessary to determine the nature and number of applicable performance tasks. Research in this area showed that well over one hundred different performance tasks had been identified by various scholars. Tasks that appeared in a minimum of four studies were used initially to identify the performance tasks found in the excerpts analyzed in this study. These thirty-one tasks were found to occur a total of 176 times in the excerpts. The performance tasks were then analyzed and discussed in reference to their use in each excerpt. Suggestions for their performance and discussions of tuba performance practices in general were also included.

Burdick, Daniel Henry III. "Three Programs of Tuba Music. (Performance)." A.Mus.D. diss., The University of Michigan (0127), 1993. Advisor: Kaenzig, Fritz A.; Source: DAI 54/02A, p.360; Subject: Music (0413).
Abstract: Hubert Katzenbeier, *Drei Spielstücke für Tuba Solo* (1983); Bernhard Krol, *Falstaff—Concerto for Tuba and Strings*, Op. 119 (1990); Armand Russell, *Suite Concertante for Tuba and Woodwind Quintet* (1963); Uwe Hilprecht, *Vier Haltungen zu einem alten Thema* (1981); Jan Koetsier, *Concertino für Tuba and Streichorchester*, Op. 77 (1978/ rev. 1982). Additional performers: Peter Collins, piano; Anne Fields, horn; Gina Hart-Kemper, flute; Jared Hauser, oboe; Patricia Holland, bassoon; Thomas Masse, clarinet.
Georg Philipp Telemann, "Solo No. 3" (TWV 41: a 6) from *Essercizii musici* (1739/40), arranged by Krzysztof Penderecki, *Capriccio für Tuba Solo* (1980); Scott A. Wyatt, *three for one* (1981); Jan Koetsier, *Sonatina per Tuba e Pianoforte*, Op. 57 (1970). Additional performers: Peter Collins, piano; Stacy Melles, tuba (continuo).
Donald H. White, *Sonato for Tuba and Piano* (1971); Leslie Hogan, *Radar Screen: Five etudes for solo tuba* (1993); Jan Bach, *Quintet for Solo Tuba and String Quartet* (1978). Additional performers: Peter Collins, piano; Andrew Wu and Heidi Senungetuk, violin; Jessica Nance, viola; Timothy Holley, cello. *Radar Screen* was commissioned by and dedicated to Daniel Burdick and received its premiere performance at this recital.
Mr. Burdick received a Dissertation Grant from the Rackham School of Graduate Studies, The University of Michigan. This grant funded the residency of Professor Jan Bach, who assisted in the preparation of his *Quintet for Solo Tuba and String Quartet* for the final recital. Mr. Bach presented a public master class on this work.

Easter, Stanley Eugene. "A Study Guide for the Performance of Twentieth-Century Music from Selected Ballet Repertoires for Trombones and Tuba." Ed.D. diss., Columbia University (0054), 1969, 139 pp. Source: DAI 31/06A, p.2953; Publication No.: AAC 7018135; Subject: Music (0413).
Abstract: The purpose of this study is to develop a body of educational materials which will provide the teacher of trombone and tuba with effective guidance in the study and performance of twentieth-century ballet music.
Chapter I includes a rationale supporting the need for a disciplined approach to the study of the performance of music for ballets. In recent years there has been an increased emphasis upon ballet in this country. Excellence in the live performance of often highly complex musical scores has a profound effect upon the ballet performance as a whole. The sources of information included performers and teachers of trombone and tuba who are authorities in the field of ballet music, ballet conductors, chronicles and libraries of certain ballet companies, and Lincoln Center, Columbia University, and Teachers College libraries. This is not a method for learning to play the trombone or tuba, nor is it an analysis of the musical compositions selected, but rather, it is a guide for studying problems in the performance of the music to the ballets here included.
Chapter III is a presentation of selected excerpts with appropriate commentary from twelve ballets including the following music: Charles Ives, *Central Park in the Dark*, and "In the Inn" and "In the Night" from *A Set of Theatre Pieces*. Anton Webern, *Pasacaglia, Opus 1*; *Six Pieces for Orchestra, Opus 6*; *Five Pieces for Orchestra, Opus 10*; *Konzert, Opus 24*; *Orchestra Variations, Opus 30*; *Fuga* (Ricercata) by Johann Sebastian Bach, orchestrated by Anton Webern. Sergei Prokofiev, *The Prodigal Son*. Igor Stravinsky, *Capriccio, Agon, Monumentum Pro Gesualdo, Movements for Piano and Orchestra, Variations (Aldous Huxley in Memoriam)*. Carlos Chavez, *Sinfonia India*. Aaron Copland, *Rodeo*. Leonard Bernstein, *Fancy Free*. Benjamin Britten, *The Young Person's Guide to the Orchestra*. Paul Creston, *Choric*

Dance II and *Invocation and Dance.*

Chapter IV summarizes the foregoing. The need for a more comprehensive and meaningful approach to the study of excerpts as represented by the format of this paper is stressed. Implications for investigation and development of similar materials for other instruments, employing some of the concepts evident in this dissertation, are suggested.

Holmes, William Dewey. "Style and Technique in Selected Works for Tuba and Electronic Prepared Tape: A Lecture Recital, Together with Three Recitals of Selected Works of V. Persichetti, A. Capuzzi, E. Gregson, W. Ross, N.K. Brown, and Others." See listing under "Literature," below.

Schulz, Charles August. "Two European Traditions of Tuba Playing as Evidenced in the Solo Tuba Compositions of Ralph Vaughan Williams and Paul Hindemith: A Lecture Recital, Together with Three Recitals of Selected Works of W. Ross, R. Beasley, A. Russell, V. Persichetti, W.S. Hartley, N.K. Brown, J.S. Bach, and Others." D.M.A. diss., University of North Texas (0518), 1980, 43 pp. Source: DAI 41/07A, p.2825; Publication No.: AAC 8029016; Subject: Music (0413).

Abstract: The lecture recital was given on June 16, 1980. The Ralph Vaughan Williams *Concerto for Bass Tuba* and the Paul Hindemith *Sonate for Tuba and Piano* were performed following a lecture on the historical evolution of the tuba in Europe. The lecture included a history of the predecessors of the tuba and their influence on the development of tuba playing traditions. Tuba performance practices in Europe developed around two playing traditions, one in France and England and a second in Germany. The ophicleide enjoyed tremendous popularity in France and England during the early nineteenth century. Because this instrument was a major competitor of the tuba in these countries, the tuba was viewed as an ophicleide replacement. Tubists in Europe and England had to develop facility and sound quality equivalent to that of the older instrument. In Germany the tuba's main competitor was the Russian bassoon, a form of upright serpent. At this same time, the serpent and its related forms were in decline. This lack of popularity with the older instruments provided an opportunity for the quick adoption of the tuba in Germany. In addition to the lecture recital,

three other recitals were performed incorporating solo and chamber works for tuba. The first recital was on July 7, 1976, and included works of Morton Gould, Walter S. Hartley, Ralph Vaughan Williams, and Newel Kay Brown.

The second recital was on June 9, 1978, and included works of Walter Ross, Vincent Persichetti, J. S. Bach, and Halsey Stevens.

The third recital was on October 22, 1979, and included works of Armand Russell, Roger Vogel, Walter Ross, and Rule Beasley.

All four programs were recorded on magnetic tape and are filed with the written version of the lecture material as a part of the dissertation.

Self, James Martin. "Performance (Tuba)." D.M.A. diss., University of Southern California (0208), 1976; Publication No.:AAC032 0425; Subject: Music (0413). No abstract available.

Young, Jerry Allen. "The Tuba in the Symphonic Works of Anton Bruckner and Gustav Mahler: A Performance Analysis." Ed.D. diss., University of Illinois at Urbana-Champaign (0090), 1980, 280 pp. Source: DAI 41/11A, p. 4641; Publication No.: AAC8108711; Subject: Education, Music (0522).

Abstract: This study was undertaken to determine characteristics of Bruckner's and Mahler's treatment of the tuba in their symphonies and to identify problems in the performance of the tuba parts in those symphonies. In order to accomplish these purposes, the following sub-problems were investigated: (1) What are the general performance problems of the tuba? (2) What characteristics of Bruckner's and Mahler's treatment of the tuba as an individual instrument within the orchestra can be identified? (3) What characteristics of Bruckner's and Mahler's treatment of the tuba as a member of the orchestral ensemble can be identified? (4) What performance problems for the tubist does each of the Bruckner and Mahler symphonies present? A review of related literature resulted in the identification of performance problems of the tuba in the areas of range, tone production, dynamics, and intonation. The investigator examined the tuba parts of each symphony to determine the existing performance problems and established possible solutions for the problems. The investigator analyzed the tuba part of each symphony to determine characteristic treatment of the tuba as an individual instrument within the orchestra. Special attention was given to pitch range, tessitura, dynamic range, articulation, rhythm, and special effects. He also identified the characteristic treatment of the tuba as a member of the orchestral ensemble. He examined the score of each symphony with special attention to the tuba's overall frequency of use, use as a solo instrument, and function as a member of the full orchestral ensemble and of the brass ensemble.

The analyses enabled the investigator to determine a number of specific characteristics peculiar to the tuba writing of each composer. Bruckner's style can best be described as highly problematic. Outstanding characteristics include the use of extreme high and low registers, extremely loud dynamics, and wide intervals. Bruckner most often used the tuba as a bass instrument in the orchestra and the brass ensemble, employing it only infrequently in solo or melodic roles. Mahler's tuba writing, in contrast, is challenging for the performer but is generally not problematic in nature. Characteristics include frequent use of changing dynamics, legato articulations, and strategic use of special effects. Mahler's tuba parts are definitely within the playing abilities of the average tubist. Mahler, like Bruckner, used the tuba most frequently as an orchestral bass instrument; unlike Bruckner, however, he often employed the tuba in melodic passages and as a solo instrument.

History

Bird, Gary. "A Musical Comparison of the Serpent and Ophicleide in Selected Compositions of the Nineteenth Century." D.Mus. diss., Indiana University, 1992. Advisor: Phillips, H.; Source: Gary Bird.
Abstract: This study compares the use of the serpent and ophicleide by composers in the first half of the nineteenth century, encompassing approximately thirty-five years, c. 1815-1850. It includes a brief history of the instruments followed by discussions of their use in the following works. Beethoven, *Military March in D*; Spontini, *Olympia*; Rossini, *"Overture" to The Siege of Corinth*; Mendelssohn, *A Midsummer Night's Dream Overture* and *Calm Sea and Prosperous Voyage Overture*, Berlioz, *Fantastic Symphony, Overture to King Lear*, and *Te Deum*; Wagner, *"Overture" to Rienzi, the Last of the Tribunes* and *"Overture" to The Flying Dutchman*, and Bennet, *The May Queen*.

There are eight primary considerations in evaluating the use of the serpent and/or ophicleide within these works: (1) soloistic treatment; (2) rhythmic treatment; (3) bass function; (4) single bass voice function; (5) instrument combination; (6) score position; (7) percentage of use; and (8) tessitura.

The final chapter makes verbal and visual comparisons and draws conclusions between the use of these instruments. The study includes instrumental illustrations, musical examples, and comparative graphs.

Keathley, Gilbert Harrell. "The Tuba Ensemble." D.M.A. diss., The University of Rochester, Eastman School of Music (0891), 1982, 145 pp. Source: DAI 43/08A, p. 2488; Publication No.: AAC8227841; Subject: Music (0413).
Abstract: This dissertation examines the tuba ensemble, an important experience in the training of tuba and euphonium students, and gives guidelines for composition in this medium. While the number of college tuba ensembles is rapidly increasing, the specific features of the literature and problems of composition are neither well understood nor properly documented. Composers need a resource when writing for the several members of the tuba family in ensemble, and this paper attempts to fill that void.

Background information includes the history of the tuba family from the serpent, through the Saxhorns, and to the modern orchestral tuba, with a description of the range and valve requirements of each of the differently pitched tubas now in use: BBb, CC, Eb, F, Bb, and C. Instrumentation possibilities and differing textural qualities are examined. Included is a survey of selected works of different styles from the literature, with 42 musical examples in the text, and sample programs. The last chapter addresses specific problems of composition, including range, orchestration, and acoustics. One contemporary work is analyzed briefly, and compositional features examined. The Appendix consists of statements of compositional practice from five important composers in the tuba ensemble field and comment by the author.

Solomonson, Glen Terrance. "The History of the Tuba to 1860: A Study of the Development of the Tuba through Its Ancestors." M.M.Ed. thesis, University of Louisville (0110), 1978, 54 pp. Source: MAI 17/01, p.30; Publication No.: AAC13111832; Subject: Educaton, Music (0522).

Abstract: The tuba has for some time been considered primarily a nineteenth-century invention, with no definite ancestral background. However, through research it is evident that there is a definite pattern through which the tuba has evolved starting back in history as early as biblical times. The Hebrews had their Keren, the Romans their Littus. During the Middle Ages, the various Businen of the period kept the concept of low brass wind instruments alive. With the Renaissance and Baroque, one can see that interest was arising once again, culminating in the development of first the bass cornett and then the serpent. As orchestras grew in size and volume, the demands for more powerful instruments led to the invention of the bass horn and then the ophicleide. Finally, with the invention of the valve, the tuba was invented to provide composers with the versatility which they needed.

Swain, John Joseph. "A Catalog of the E-Flat Tubas in the Arne B. Larson Collection at the Univesity of South Dakota (Instruments, Musical)." See listing under "Equipment," below.

Literature

AsKew, Dennis Weston. "Three Programs of Tuba Music. (Performance)." See listing under "Performance," above.

Benson, Mark Elling. "Chamber Concerto for Tuba. (Original Composition)." M.M. thesis, Michigan State University (0218), 1984, 29 pp. Source: MAI 23/02, p. 237; Publication No.: AAC132409; Subject: Music (0413).

Abstract: The melodic and harmonic material of this work is generated from a symmetrical all-interval twelve-tone set. Seconds and sevenths predominate the melodic material while thirds and sixths predominate the harmonic material. Perfect fourths, perfect fifths, and tritones are common to both parameters.

The solo tuba is supported by an ensemble consisting of two heterogeneous wind trios and a third trio of amplified double bass, timpani, and percussion. The three trios are used separately and in combinations to provide a variety of timbre-oriented sonorities. The form consists of alternating metered and unmetered sections, with the soloist dominating all unmetered sections. The writing for the tuba is characterized by a virtuosity which embraces glittering passage work as well as a variety of timbre modification techniques, e.g., unison tremolos and sung pitches.

Bowman, Brian Leslie. "The Bass Trumpet and Tenor Tuba in Orchestral and Operatic Literature." D.M.A. diss., The Catholic University of America (0043), 1975. No abstract available.

Brandon, Stephen Paul. "The Tuba: Its Use in Selected Orchestral Compositions of Stravinsky, Prokofiev, and Shostakovich." D.M.A. diss., The Catholic University of America (0043), 1974, 144 pp. Source: DAI 35/03A, p.1684; Publication No.: AAC7419498; Subject: Music (0413).

Abstract: The purpose of this study was to examine the use of the tuba in selected orchestral compositions of Stravinsky, Prokofiev, and Shostakovich in an effort (1) to discover the composer's musical understanding of the tuba as exhibited by his idiomatic treatment and compositional techniques; (2) to classify tuba music according to range and technical demands, thereby aiding the pedagogical repertoire of the instrument; and (3) to enhance the sparse amount of valid research concerning the tuba and its literature.

Predecessors of the tuba include the serpent and the ophicleide. The tuba came into existence in 1835 when the Prussian bandmaster Wilhelm Wieprecht suggested that Johann C. Moritz, a Berlin instrument maker, construct a bass brass instrument with valves. The use of the tuba in the nineteenth-century orchestra may be summarized as follows: adding solidity to the orchestral tuttis; doubling other bass instruments tutti or at the octave; as a solo melody, particularly on a leitmotif; the bass of a quartet with three trombones; the bass of the entire brass ensemble; and rhythmic punctuation.

Igor Stravinsky scored for the tuba in most of his major works. He began writing for the tuba in the tradition of Rimsky-Korsakov, but use of the instrument became more sophisticated during his career. The most independent parts are found in his serial compositions, which began with *Threni* (1957). He wrote idiomatically for the tuba with the exception of certain passages in *Le Sacre du Printemps*, in which the upper range is so extreme that some of the notes cannot be executed with certainty on a BB♭ or CC tuba.

Sergei Prokofiev utilized the tuba in the contrabass tuba tradition of Wagner. This tessitura of his parts is low, especially in his later compositions. Prokofiev scored the tuba primarily as the bass of the wind instruments, where it is usually found in conjunction with the trombones. He did not vary from the established use of the tuba but his parts are well crafted and interesting to perform. Of the three composers and their works examined in this study, Dimitri Shostakovich's use of the tuba is the most conservative. The parts are idiomatic, but not as individualistic as those of Stravinsky or Prokofiev. Like Prokofiev, Shostakovich casts the tuba in the contra-bass tuba tradition of Wagner.

All three composers used the tuba idiomatically. However, the parts that Stravinsky and Prokofiev composed are more creative than those of Shostakovich. Shostakovich primarily limits the use of the tuba to harmonic filler, rhythmic punctuation, doubling other bass instruments, and of course as the bass member of the trombone section. Stravinsky and Prokofiev, though, use the tuba as an independent instrument of the orchestra, often scoring the tuba with non-traditional combinations of instruments in order to create new colors.

Buttery, Gary. "The Tuba in Twentieth-Century Symphonic Literature." M.M. thesis, University of Northern Colorado, 1975. Source: Gary Buttery; unpublished.

Abstract: This study is designed to present the stylistic uses of the tuba by several of the twentieth century's more prolific composers. The diverse selection of composers used will not only show the difference in orchestrational use of the tuba, but also the nationalistic tendencies toward type of tuba written for.

The greatest differences in orchestrational scoring and tonal concepts between orchestras from Budapest, Vienna, Helsinki, Chicago, or Rio de Janeiro can be heard in the winds, particularly in the brass and specifically in the tuba. The tuba varies from the B♭ or C tenor found in French orchestras to the giant BB♭ contrabass Kaiser tuba specifically used in German orchestras for performances of Wagner's *Ring* operas. The choice of which tuba to use is usually a result of adapting to the needs of a particular musical environment.

The primary use of the F bass tuba in Germany and Austria is largely due to a combination of historical factors, tonal considerations, type of

literature, and practicality. A composer in the mid-nineteenth century, after the tuba came into general use, realized the need for a compact wind bass sound to blend with the brass in these comparatively smaller orchestras of the day. Even now in the twentieth century, the German concept of the tuba is of a brass instrument, not especially a bass instrument. Excluding the *Ring* operas, the application of the tuba by Wagner, Bruckner, Strauss, and Mahler assumes the role of a fourth voice to the trombones, the bottom voice in a horn choir (often in unison with the double basses or cellos to add color to a passage), or as a solo voice on a significant or exposed part. Even with later composers, the scores invariably call for a contrabass tuba, but the instrument chosen is usually the F tuba, letting the double basses (always excellent and heavy in sound in German orchestras) produce the fundamental necessary for orchestral balance.

An important difference should be discussed concerning the concept of homogeneity and tonal richness within the brass sections of German and American orchestras. The rotary-valve trumpets, with their widely tapered bells, have a more mellow sound in comparison to American instruments. The trombones are much darker in quality and are generally not capable of as immense a volume or carrying power of their American counterparts. With more tonal density in the upper voices, the compact and pointed tone of the F bass tuba is necessary for the German brass section to sound vibrant and exciting as opposed to the general use of the CC contrabass tuba, which adds power along with tonal richness to fill out the American orchestral brass section.

The French tuba is a tenor tuba which is very similar in size and sound to the euphonium but incorporates the necessary number of valves to enable production of the low notes. The literature is extensive at the Paris Conservatory for this tenor instrument in C or B♭ and provides difficult technical passages, with ranges of over three octaves being quite common. The choice of this instrument is adjusted to the preferred literature and other nationalistic considerations of France, but concerts of works involving different contexts no doubt suffer without the use of a larger instrument.

English orchestral brass playing has gone through great changes in recent years under an undeniable integration of American-made trumpets and trombones. Tubists have changed from the standard use of F tubas to large E♭ tubas and more recently to large CC contrabass tubas of domestic and foreign manufacture. The great variety of literature performed by English orchestras is quite demanding, and the larger instrument is augmented with an F tuba or tenor tuba for smaller orchestral work or for the performance of high parts. The very broad and expressive orchestral writing by composers of eastern Europe and Russia incorporates the tuba as an important voice of the brass section. The orchestral tuba utilized is usually a BB♭ or CC contrabass. Smaller orchestras such as the Komische Opera of East Berlin utilize the F tuba.

The rhythmic and nationalistic influences in the orchestral writing of Villa-Lobos and Revueltas can be seen even in the short tuba excerpts. The rhythmic intricacies common to the music of Brazil and Mexico are brought out in these compositions and demand strict control while executing the tuba passages. Composers of Central and South America utilize the tuba similar to the German, in that it can be an extension of the trombone and horn sections or can be a solo voice. One may see this effect in *Sensemaya*, where Revueltas introduces the main theme as a tuba solo in the first bars.

The analyses show specific examples of twentieth-century tuba orchestral excerpts and the various uses and colors strived for by composers of our own century. As mentioned earlier, the diverse examples used are meant to show the many interesting ways of scoring the tuba within the orchestra.

Holmes, William Dewey. "Style and Technique in Selected Works for Tuba and Electronic Prepared Tape: A Lecture Recital, Together with Three Recitals of Selected Works of V. Persichetti, A. Capuzzi, E. Gregson, W. Ross, N.K. Brown, and Others." D.M.A. diss., University of North Texas (0518), 1985, 58 pp. Source: DAI 47/01A, p. 14; Publication No.: AAC8604555; Subject: Music(0413).
Abstract: This study explores general stylistic characteristics of a sample of frequently performed works for solo tuba with prepared tape. Preliminary material includes a brief overview of the status of electronic music in the solo tuba repertoire as well as a short survey of the development of electronic music.

Four contrasting works for solo tuba with prepared tape are examined in chronological order. The use of musique concrète, timbral treatment, and synthesis of style are discussed in three works entitled *Midnight Variations* by Walter Ross, *Breath and Sounds for Tuba and Tape* by Beatrice Witkin, and *Three for One* by Scott Wyatt.

The fourth work, *Concerto for Tuba and Electronic Tape* by Joseph Ott, is explored in depth. Its compositional format and eclectic style form the basis for discussion. Treatment of sound and contemporary performance techniques are also examined.

Jarvis, Jeffery Wayne. "An Analysis of Two Works for Solo Tuba: *Serenade* No. 12 by Vincent Persichetti and *Encounters II* by William Kraft." D.M.A. diss., Michigan State University, 1992. Source: Philip Sinder (MSU); unpublished. No abstract available.

Kirk, Paul Judson, Jr. "The Orchestral Tuba Player: The Demands of His Literature Compared and Constrasted with Tuba Training Materials." See listing under "Pedagogy," below.

Kuehn, David Laurance. "The Use of the Tuba in the Operas and Music Dramas of Richard Wagner." D.M.A. diss., The University of Rochester, Eastman School of Music (0891), 1974. Source: ADD X1975; Publication No.: AAC0294770; Subject: Music (0413). No abstract available.

Lonnman, Gregory George. "The Tuba Ensemble: Its Organization and Literature." D.M.A. diss., University of Miami (0125), 1974, 63 pp. Source: DAI 35/12A, p. 7947; Publication No.: AAC7512870; Subject: Music (0413).
Abstract: The major purpose of this study is to develop a guideline for those individuals who are interested in organizing a tuba ensemble. The information included in the project was collected from a number of sources; however, the motivational force, as well as many of the ideas presented, was gained by the writer while attending the University of Miami School of Music and working as a graduate assistant with Constance Weldon, tuba instructor and founder and director of the University of Miami Tuba Ensemble.

The tuba ensemble is a relatively new addition to the ensemble offerings in many universities. Thus, this report reflects present-day practice at the University of Miami, as well as at a selected group of music schools with lower brass enrollments large enough to enable them to offer specialized tuba instruction. The information for this segment of the study was gained by means of a questionnaire sent to the forty-three largest schools of music as indicated by the 1972 directory of the National Association of Schools of Music.

Tuba ensemble activity in the United States colleges and universities began to flourish around 1970. Because of its infancy, few people are familiar with the sound, purpose, and literature of this medium. Only two brief articles have been published on the subject of tuba ensemble — one by Constance Weldon of the University of Miami and the other by Fred Marzan of Shenandoah Valley Conservatory at Winchester, Virginia. This study is intended to enlighten the reader on the organization and literature of the tuba ensemble and, furthermore, to demonstrate the need and performance facets for such a group in schools and colleges today.

The main types of discussion included in this project are as follows: historical background, objectives, literature and performance suggestions for the tuba ensemble, which have recently been included as standard ensembles offerings in many United States colleges and universities.

Although at first the tuba ensemble under William Bell was conceived as an enjoyable pastime for his tuba students at Indiana University, in only a decade, it has been transformed into a serious standardized ensemble, complete with its own literature. An informal survey included as part of this project indicated that twenty-six colleges and universities sponsored tuba ensembles. This number has, no doubt, grown in the past few years.

The objectives of the tuba ensemble presented by the writer are perhaps motivational in nature. They are as follows: intensified melodic playing, improved intonation, musical awareness, discussion of the tuba, teacher preparation, conducting experience, and individual responsibility to an organization. It is hoped that this information will stimulate the interest of brass teachers to form tuba ensembles at institutions where they currently do not exist. These objectives may also be helpful in providing new ideas and techniques for tuba ensembles already in existence.

The discussion of literature for the tuba ensemble should be of assistance to both composers and conductors. The suggested basic and advanced libraries represent some of the best-written works for tuba ensembles and should be most helpful to anyone in the process of forming an ensemble and selecting a basic repertoire.

Because the tuba plays in such a low register, it sets off a myriad of audible overtones when a note is sounded. While these overtones are necessary in the production of the tuba's true tone quality when more than one tuba is performing, a loss of clarity results. The discussion on performance and program suggestions should provide help in overcoming these acoustical problems encountered in performance. It is hoped that this study will furnish useful material for the further development and enhancement of the tuba ensemble movement.

McIrvine, Edward Charles. "Concerto for Tuba and Orchestra. (Original Composition)." D.Mus. diss., Indiana University (0093), 1984. Source: ADD S1977; Publication No.: AAC0373136; No abstract available.

Mowery, Carl Donald, Jr. "Two Sonatas for Solo Tuba and Piano. (Original Composition)." D.Mus.Ed. diss., The University of Oklahoma (0169), 1969, 101 pp. Source: DAI 30/08A, p. 3495; Publication No.: AAC7002328; Subject: Music (0413).
Abstract: Two sonatas for tuba and piano have been composed to serve a dual purpose: first, to enrich the literature for solo tuba and add to the materials for tuba instruction; and second, to develop the student's awareness of music and musical composition through an in-depth analysis of these sonatas.

These sonatas are composed in two different contemporary styles: the twelve-tone style and a free harmonic style. The first sonata uses the free harmonic style that, upon analysis, shows a consistent use of the projection of perfect fifths as its basis. The projections are clouded in all but a few instances by the use of added tones to the projections or by the use of two or more projections simultaneously.

The second sonata is built on a twelve-tone row. This row is used in a fairly strict manner. In the fourth movement, the waltz section makes use of a free interpretation of the twelve-tone technique. In this section, a permutation using even-numbered notes for the melodic line and freely mixed odd-numbered notes for the accompaniment is employed. There is generous use of sustained tones as pedal points and ostinato patterns, which create a stability of harmonic texture in various sections of this sonata.

From the viewpoint of educational literature, the full range of the tuba is exploited, both in tessitura and technical requirements. However, the extreme ranges of the tessitura of the tuba have been avoided to facilitate the use of these sonatas for a wider spectrum of students.

Nelson, Mark Allan. "The Brass Parables of Vincent Persichetti." D.M.A. diss., Arizona State University (0010), 1985, 120 pp. Source: DAI 46/05A, p. 1124; Publication No.: AAC 8514323; Subject: Music (0413).
Abstract: The series of compositions entitled "Parable" by Vincent Persichetti includes a number of unaccompanied solo pieces. This paper focuses on the compositions written for solo brass instruments: French horn, trumpet, trombone, and tuba.
The purpose of this paper is to provide an analysis of compositional techniques and a discussion of potential performance problems in the brass Parables in an effort to aid the performer's realization of more sensitive performance of the music. The analysis is provided through the categories of symbolism, melody, rhythm, dynamics, timbre, form, and effects. The performance problems are cited through the possible limitations of the performer's range, breath-control, slide/valve technique, articulation, endurance, and interpretive skills. A summary of the data and insights the writer found in the four compositions is presented in the concluding portion of the paper.

Potter, Carl David. "Concertino for Tuba, Winds, and Percussion. (Original Composition)." M.M. thesis, University of North Texas (0158), 1985, 107 pp. Source: MAI 24/02, p. 89; Publication No.: AAC1326459; Subject: Music (0413).
Abstract: *Concertino for Tuba, Winds, and Percussion* is a work for solo tuba and an ensemble consisting of two flutes, two oboes, two clarinets, bass clarinet, bassoon, four horns, two trumpets, two trombones, bass trombone, and three percussionists. The percussionists play small, medium, and large suspended cymbals, triangle, tam tam, metal wind chimes, five tom toms, snare drum, tenor drum, bass drum, two sets of two timbales, five temple blocks, maracas, glockenspiel, vibraphone, chimes, xylophone, marimba, and five timpani. The three movements of the work follow the arrangement of the standard concerto format (fast–slow–fast). The lengths of the movements are approximately four minutes and fifteen seconds, two minutes and twenty-five seconds, and four minutes and ten seconds respectively. The total duration of *Concertino* is about eleven minutes.

Randolph, David Mark. "New Techniques in the Avant-Garde Repertoire for Solo Tuba." D.M.A. diss., The University of Rochester, Eastman School of Music (0891), 1978, 161 pp. Source: DAI 39/01A, p. 18; Publication No.: AAC7811493; Subject: Music (0413).
Abstract: Since the decade of the 1960s, the solo repertoire for tuba has increased dramatically. The tubist now has literature available ranging from baroque transcriptions to compositions utilizing electronically produced sounds. Since a large segment of the avant-garde literature for tuba has been written for tuba alone, the writer has limited this study to only those compositions utilizing this medium.
These compositions make use of many new sounds produced by a wide variety of techniques. They utilize techniques for changing the timbre of a definite pitch sound, techniques for playing more than one pitch simultaneously, and techniques involving indefinite pitches.
In this study the writer has endeavored to examine these avant-garde techniques as they apply to nine selected compositions for solo tuba. The nine compositions are *Canto VII for Tuba Solo* by Samuel Adler (Boosey and Hawkes, 1974), *Six Likes for Solo Tuba* by Theodor Antoniou (Bärenreiter, 1968), *InconSequenza for One Tuba-Player* by Matthias Bamert (G. Schirmer, 1973), *Three for Barton for Solo Bass Tuba* by Allan Blank (Associated Music Publishers, 1974), *Patterns III for Solo Tuba* by James Fulkerson (Media Press, 1969), *Encounters II for Solo Tuba* by William Kraft (MCA Music, 1970), *Three Essays for Tuba* by William Penn (Seesaw Music Corporation, 1973), *Midnight Realities for Tuba Unaccompanied* by Morgan Powell (Brass Music, Ltd., 1974), and *Five Studies for Tuba Alone* by David Reck (C.F. Peters Corporation, 1968). The decision to include these compositions was based on the fact that each involves a tubist as the only performer, each is published and readily available, and each involves avant-garde techniques to some degree.
The avant-garde techniques included in these compositions have been examined from three perspectives: 1. Notation—How does the composer indicate the new sounds he desires? Is it an

effective, clear-cut symbol? 2. Method of production—How does the tubist produce the sound called for by the composer? 3. Context—How does the technique fit into the composition?

It is the hope of the writer that this manuscript will be of value to three varying groups of individuals: 1. The tuba student who is just beginning his study of the avant-garde literature for tuba, 2. the tuba instructor who is not familiar with this segment of the repertoire, 3. the composer who intends to write for tuba in this style and who would like to know what is possible, what is difficult, what works well, and what has been done by other composers.

Judgments of a subjective nature regarding the musical merits of the included compositions have been avoided. The criticisms offered have been limited to areas of clarity of notation or performance instructions and effectiveness of the new techniques. In several cases suggestions have been made as to how that effectiveness might be increased. It is the writer's opinion that, though they certainly are not of equal musical quality, each of the compositions included in this dissertation is at least worthy of study by the advanced student or professional tubist.

Smith, John Lee, Jr. "The Use of the Tuba in the Symphonic Poems of Richard Strauss." D.M.A. diss., University of Missouri-Kansas City, 1979, 206 pp. Source: DAI 40/02A, p. 534; Publication No.: AAC7918419; Subject: Music (0413).
Abstract: The purpose of this dissertation is to define the role of the tuba in the symphonic poems of Richard Strauss. In order to place this analysis within historical perspective, background information concerning the tuba, Strauss, and the symphonic poems was provided. Berlioz's *Treatise on Instrumentation*, as revised by Strauss, was examined to provide a comparative analysis between the tuba orchestration techniques as espoused in the text and the scoring techniques that were evident in the poems.

The tuba parts of the nine symphonic poems were examined in terms of the individual and ensemble characteristics. Individual characteristics were analyzed according to the following criteria: frequency of use, pitch range, tessitura, dynamic range, articulation, melodic characteristics, solo use, rhythmic treatment, special effects, and idiomatic problems. An examination of ensemble characteristics provided information concerning the relationships between the tuba and the orchestra. Criteria considered for this analysis

concerned heterogeneous instrumentation, multiple tubas, harmonic voicing, timbre effects, comparative dynamics, balance and blend, and special techniques. Where applicable, data comparisons were made between (1) the first four and last five symphonic poems, (2) the bass and tenor tuba parts, and (3) the tuba and trombone parts.

The conclusions found in this study attest to the superb orchestrational skills attributed to Strauss. He explored and employed many new concepts in orchestrating the tuba. Such orchestration techniques presented the tuba as an important and equal constituent of the orchestral resources.

Sorenson, Richard Allen. "Tuba Pedagogy: A Study of Selected Method Books, 1840–1911." See listing under "Pedagogy," below.

White, Joseph Pollard. "The Development of a Cosmopolitan Style in Early Twentieth-Century American Symphonies, and Concerto for Tuba and Orchestra. (Original Composition). (Symphonies)." D.M.A. diss., University of Washington (0250), 1991, 168 pp. Advisor: Eros, Peter; Source: DAI 52/05A, p. 1568; Publication No.: AAC9131723; Subject: Music (0413).
Abstract: Between 1900 and 1940, American music came to maturity. This paper discusses that development by examining different compositional approaches and their execution in the repertoire of symphonies written during those years. Early attempts to make a break from European tradition led to such transitional approaches as the use of American Indian or Negro music, ragtime, and jazz. There are some examples of these approaches being used in the repertoire of symphonies, but they are few and largely not successful. The music of Charles Ives suggested a different, more inclusive approach. That inclusivity, combined with potent new European influences and teachers after the First World War, helped to form a new cosmopolitan style: more worldly, more sophisticated, less provincial. In the 1920s and '30s, there was a flowering of American symphonies in this new style, many of which are currently being rediscovered as neglected masterpieces.

The *Concerto for Tuba and Orchestra* is in the traditional three-movement form. Instrumentation is double woodwinds, three horns, two trumpets, one trombone, xylophone, congas and chimes (one player), and strings.

Orchestration

Bowman, Brian Leslie. "The Bass Trumpet and Tenor Tuba in Orchestral and Operatic Literature." D.M.A. diss., The Catholic University of America (0043), 1975. Source: ADD X1976; Publication No.: AAC0316203; Subject: Music (0413). No Abstract available.

Brandon, Stephen Paul. "The Tuba: Its Use in Selected Orchestral Compositions of Stravinsky, Prokofiev, and Shostakovich." See listing under "Literature," above.

Kuehn, David Laurance. "The Use of the Tuba in the Operas and Music Dramas of Richard Wagner." See listing under "Literature," above.

Lindahl, Robert Gordon. "Brass Quintet Instrumentation: Tuba Versus Bass Trombone." D.M.A. diss., Arizona State University (0010), 1988, 139 pp. Source: DAI 50/01A, p. 18; Publication No.: AAC8907717; Subject: Music (0413).
Abstract: The brass quintet has become established as the standard brass chamber ensemble during the past forty years. Important to the standardization of the brass quintet has been the development of a repertoire and of instrumentation within the quintet. The two instrumentations of the brass quintet that are currently in use are the quintet of two trumpets, horn, trombone, and tuba; and the quintet of two trumpets, horn, trombone, and bass trombone.

The focus of the discussion is on the evolution of these two instrumentations, their literature, and the differences in the usage of the tuba and the bass trombone. A brief history of the brass quintet is given, and a review of literature for the two instrumentations as it pertains to performance practices is presented. The results of interviews with professional performers, composers, and pedagogues are provided.

The six works studied are Gunther Schuller's *Music for Brass Quintet*, Alvin Etler's *Quintet for Brass Instruments*, Jan Bach's *Laudes*, Charles Whittenberg's *Triptych*, Elliott Carter's *Brass Quintet*, and David Sampson's *Morning Music*. The discussion of these compositions concentrates on the lowest voice of the quintet and the differences that the use of a tuba or bass trombone has regarding ensemble timbre, technique, and balance.

Conclusions drawn from the study pertain to the use of "cross-over" literature and the use of a bass trombone or a tuba in a brass quintet.

Smith, John Lee, Jr. "The Use of the Tuba in the Symphonic Poems of Richard Strauss." See listing under "Literature," above.

Young, Jerry Allen. "The Tuba in the Symphonic Works of Anton Bruckner and Gustav Mahler: A Performance Analysis." See listing under "Performance," above.

Pedagogy

Beauregard, Cherry N. "The Tuba: A Description of the Five Orchestral Tubas and Guidelines for Orchestral Tuba Writing." Ph.D. diss., The University of Rochester, Eastman School of Music (0891), 1970. Source: ADD X1970; Publication No.: AAC0265351; Subject: Music (0413). No abstract available.

Bergee, Martin J. "An Application of the Facet-Factorial Approach to Scale Construction in the Development of a Rating Scale for Euphonium and Tuba Music Performance." Ph.D. diss., University of Kansas (0099), 1987, 232 pp. Advisor: Grashel, John W.; Source: DAI 49/05A, p. 1086; Publication No.: AAC 8813388; Subject: Education, Music (0522).
Abstract: The purpose of this study was to construct and validate a rating scale for the evaluation of euphonium and tuba performance. A facet-factorial approach to scale construction was employed in developing the rating scale.

In the preliminary phase, statements descriptive of euphonium/tuba performance were gathered from essays, adjudication sheets, and previous research. A content analysis of these materials yielded 112 statements, which were translated into items and paired with a five-option, Likert-type scale. The resulting item pool was used by five judges to evaluate one hundred euphonium and tuba performances. The obtained data were factor analyzed, initial orthogonal factors were extracted, and the structure was rotated to a terminal solution. Five factors were identified, and thirty items were chosen to define the subscales of a Euphonium/Tuba Performance Rating Scale (ETPRS).

To examine the stability of the ETPRS structure and to obtain data for interjudge reliability and criterion-related validity, three panels of judges rated three sets of ten different euphonium and tuba performances using the ETPRS. The data obtained were factor-analyzed and the ETPRS was revised to a four-factor structure. The four factors identified for the revised ETPRS were (a) Interpretation/Musical Effect, (b) Tone Quality/Intonation, (c) Technique, and (d) Rhythm/Tempo. Interjudge reliability estimates for the revised ETPRS total scores were .944, .985, and .975 for the three groups of judges respectively. Reliability estimates for subscales ranged from .894 to .992. Two studies examined criterion-related validity of the revised ETPRS. In the first, revised ETPRS evaluations were compared with global ratings obtained via a magnitude estimation procedure. Zero-order correlation coefficients between revised ETPRS total scores, subscale scores, and global criterion scores ranged from .502 to .992; most were above .850. To examine the contributions of the subscale scores in predicting the global criterion, a multiple regression analysis was performed. In the second criterion-related validity study, the MENC adjudicating ballot for wind instrument solo was used as the criterion. The same procedures used in the first study were applied; correlation coefficients ranged from .823 to .992.

Berman, Eric M. "Performance Tasks Encountered in Selected Twentieth-Century Band Excerpts for Tuba: Their Identification, Categorization, and Analysis." See listing under "Performance," above.

Brewer, Robert Gary. "A Guide to the Use of Etudes and Excercises in Teaching the Tuba." See listing under "Bibliography," above.

Kirk, Paul Judson, Jr. "The Orchestral Tuba Player: The Demands of His Literature Compared and Contrasted with Tuba Training Materials." Ph.D. diss., University of Colorado at Boulder (0051), 1976, 165 pp. Source: DAI 37/04A, p. 1865; Publication No.: AAC7623633; Subject: Music (0413).
Abstract: Tuba players are being trained in large numbers today, yet little research seems to have been directed at how well training materials relate to the professional needs of the tubist. The purpose of this study was to ascertain the adequacy of current pedagogical materials for preparing the student to perform the literature encountered in major symphony orchestras. Ques-

tions to be answered include the following: (1) What is the standard symphonic literature? (2) What is required of the tubist in performing this literature? (3) What are the strengths and weaknesses of the available tuba training materials in relation to symphonic demands? (4) What materials should be added to the existing tuba method books and etude collections in order to meet the needs of today's tuba players?
Programs of the concerts played by five major symphony orchestras over a period of five years were tabulated in order to determine the current standard symphonic repertoire. Works recorded by the same orchestras during the same time period were added to the list. Scores which did not contain tuba parts were omitted. The remaining works were assumed to be the tubist's orchestral repertoire.
A library of method books and etude collections for tuba was gathered.
The content of the symphonic tuba parts was analyzed to determine the technical demands and stylistic difficulties. These demands and difficulties were compared and contrasted with the selected training materials and strengths and weaknesses noted.
Few strengths and many weaknesses were found in the training materials. Perhaps the greatest need is for additional atonal exercises. Etudes are needed which imply harmony based on intervals other than the third. A collection of studies devoted to range extension is needed. Etudes are needed which give concentrated coverage to irregular note and rest patterns, and triplets and irregular syncopated patterns.
Suggestions were made for correcting the deficiencies by the addition of verbal explanation and musical exercises.

L'Hommedieu, Randi Louis. "The Management of Selected Educational Process Variables by Master Studio Teachers in Music Performance (Instructional Management)." Ph.D. diss., Northwestern University (0613), 1992, 343 pp. Advisor: Reimer, Bennett; Source: DAI 63/06A, p.1836; Subjects: Education, music (0522); Education, curriculum and instruction (0727).
Abstract: This dissertation reports the results of a qualitative study of master teachers in music performance. In order to identify the subjects of the study, a survey was conducted of musicians in 15 professional orchestras and applied faculty of 11 schools of music. Three master teachers (flute,

clarinet, and tuba) from among the teachers identified in the survey agreed to be interviewed and observed. An observational framework was developed that combined Benjamin Bloom's (1985) theory of talent development with his theory of school learning (Bloom, 1975). The observations focused on the master teacher's management of instructional cues, participation, reinforcement, and feedback/corrective strategies. Data were collected in three stages. First, preobservation interviews were conducted with the master teachers regarding preinstructional decisions and instructional context. Next, the teachers were observed and recorded in several studio lessons. Third, separate postobservation interviews were conducted with the teacher and student following each lesson. Analysis of the interview and observation data indicated that master teachers (1) provide instruction clearly and efficiently, (2) encourage high levels of task-engagement, (3) reinforce students effectively, and (4) carefully monitor the effects of instruction and make appropriate instructional correctives when necessary. In short, master teachers conform closely to Bloom's theory of how effective teachers manage instruction in one-to-one teaching/learning environments. However, the artist/teachers observed in this study exhibited a comparatively narrow repertoire of teaching strategies, and the pedagogical adaptability and accommodation associated with classroom teaching was largely absent. Nevertheless, the teachers were extraordinarily effective and revered by students. The apparent effectiveness of this seemingly static pedagogical style is partially explained by the teachers' extraordinary consistency and by careful auditioning that screens students for (1) technical and musical prerequisites, (2) ability to quickly respond to instruction, and (3) personal and pedagogical compatibility. Although many of the generic teaching skills exhibited by master studio teachers are worthy of emulation, other teachers should make adjustments for more common teaching environments, different levels of student aptitude, and divergent goals of instruction.

Robertson, James David. "The Low Brass Instrumental Techniques Course: A Method Book for College Level Class Instruction." D.M.A. diss., University of Northern Colorado (0161), 1983, 280 pp. Source: DAI 45/01A, p. 13; Publication No.:AAC8408154; Subject: Music (0413).

Abstract: The purpose of this study is to develop a method book of class instruction for low brass specifically for use at the college level. The instruments of the low brass homogeneous family groups are trombone, euphonium, baritone, bass trombone, and tuba. Typically the class is designed to help prepare students for careers in instrumental music teaching in the schools. The study is organized according to the following plan: (I) The Need for the Study, (II) The Construction of the Method, Appendix, and Bibliography.

The Appendix of the dissertation consists of the method book itself. This book is entitled *The Low Brass Book: A Method Book for College Level Class Instruction*. This book is organized according to the following plan: Preface; (I) A Brief History of the Low Brass Instruments; (II) The Breath Supply; (III) The Embouchure; (IV) Articulation; (V) Low Brass Acoustics; (VI) Tenor Trombone; (VII) Bass Trombone; (VIII) Euphonium and Baritone; (IX) Tuba; (X) Fundamental Studies; (XI) Melodies, Duets, Trios, and Quartets; Appendix.

The text and photographs of chapters I through IX are designed to give the student a clear presentation of the fundamentals of low brass playing. With a thorough understanding of these fundamentals and the ability to apply them as a player of at least one of the low brass instruments, the chances of success of the teacher-to-be should be greater.

The fundamental etudes and musical compositions of chapters X and XI were composed by the author specifically for the method book. Additionally, they are arranged to provide opportunity for performance regardless of the constituency of the class. Each etude and musical composition is given in two octaves so that any of the instruments of the class can participate at the appropriate level. A suggested routine for practice outlines a course of study suitable for either a college quarter or semester time period.

Sorenson, Richard Allen. "Tuba Pedagogy: A Study of Selected Method Books, 1840–1911." Ph.D. diss., University of Colorado at Boulder (0051), 1972, 367 pp. Source: DAI 33/08A, p.4462; Publication No.: AAC7301832; Subject: Music (0413).

Abstract: Recently there has been growing interest in studying the pedagogy of musical instruments. While several instruments have received considerable attention, the tuba has been largely neglected. There is now a need for further knowledge about tuba pedagogy. Excellent sources for this information are early tuba tutors. A study of these tutors showed basic pedagogical techniques and materials as they evolved, and a comparison of these books revealed a great deal about where tuba pedagogy is, why it is there, and where it may be going.

Twenty-five tuba tutors, from 1840–1911, were located, analyzed, compared and contrasted. Subquestions to the study were: 1) what are the basic pedagogical techniques and materials presented in selected tuba tutors from 1849–1911; 2) what are the similarities and differences in these techniques and materials; and 3) how do these similarities and differences relate to the development of tuba pedagogy?

A historical study of the development of the tuba and its predecessors was made to define the instrument and to show the relationships of its development to tuba pedagogy.

The modern tuba is not a direct descendant of any previously existing instrument. Several related instruments date back to ancient times, but the first true bass lip-reed instrument, the serpent, was not invented until about 1590. This instrument and improved models under various names were at first found only religious and military uses but were later used in the symphony orchestra. The invention of the valve in the second decade of the nineteenth century provided the means for developing the modern tuba. The first tuba, patented in 1835, was soon adopted for use in German military bands. However, until the last quarter of the nineteenth century there was little standardization of the bass lip-reed instrument. The serpent, ophicleide, saxhorn, bombardon, and tuba were used interchangeably until the superiority of the tuba was finally accepted. Even in the twentieth century, the key and size of tubas has not been completely standardized.

Few trends were noted in tutors from 1840–1911. Primary changes were a more rapid presentation of rudiments and technique paralleled with less written explanation and an increased need for teacher supervision and explanation.

Multi-purpose tutors, for whole families of instruments and/or instruments of various keys, were commonly used in earlier years. These were directly related to the lack of standardization of the bass lip-reed instrument of the era.

Most tutors followed the same unattractive format with little regard given to illustration or design. Treatment of rudiments was chiefly routine and uninspired; original music was mostly uninteresting and of little musical worth.

A few early tutors were arranged progressively with theory and practice combined, but the trend was to present material atomistically with emphasis placed upon gaining technique rapidly in several keys through methodical interval drills. Melodic studies, primarily of operatic or folksong origin, were often presented at the end of the tutors.

Some pedagogical techniques used in the nineteenth century have been discarded as ineffective and contradictory to our present philosophy of conceptual learning. However, other techniques are still applicable if brought up to date.

Much of the original music found in the tutors is of little musical worth, but some excerpts could enhance the known repertory of the tuba and wind ensemble. With editing and transcription, this literature could provide valuable additions to tuba study materials as well as nineteenth-century brass and wind ensemble literature of historical interest.

Walker, Ronald Dean. "A Survey of the Non-Traditional Performance Techniques Utilized in Solo Tuba Literature Published Since 1954 and the Techniques Required of the Performer." M.M.Ed. thesis, Southeast Missouri State University, 1986. Source: Robert M. Gifford; unpublished. No abstract available.

Equipment

Cattley, Gary Thomas. "Perception of Timbral Differences among Bass Tubas." M.M.thesis, University of North Texas (0158), 1987, 99 pp. Source: MAI 26/01, p. 7; Publication No.: AAC1331288; Subject: Music (0413).
Abstract: The present study explored whether musicians could (1) differentiate among the timbres of bass tubas of a single design, but constructed of different materials, (2) determine differences within certain ranges and articulations, and (3) possess different perceptual abilities depending on previous experience in low brass performance.

Findings indicated that (1) tubas made to the same specifications and constructed of the same material differed as much as those made to the same specifications, constructed of different materials; (2) significant differences in perceptibility which occurred among tubas were inconsistent across ranges and articulations, and differed due to phrase type and the specific tuba on which the phrase was played; (3) low brass players did not differ from other auditors in their perception of timbral differences.

Jones, George W. "A Study of Mutes for Tuba." M.M. thesis, University of North Texas (0158), 1973, 61 pp. Source: MAI 12/03, p. 282; Publication No.: AAC1305645; Subject: Music (0413).

Abstract: The purpose of this study was to determine what mutes are available for the tuba, how these mutes are constructed, how a tuba mute can be constructed, and how these mutes affect tuba performance.

Information giving the availability and specifications of mutes was included. To gain further insight into the problems of design and construction, a tuba mute was constructed.

Tests to determine intonation discrepancies and the acoustical structure of muted tuba tones were administered to selected mutes. All mutes tested were found to have intonation discrepancies, with certain mutes having fewer discrepancies than others. Photographs of tonal spectrums were included. Other than weakening the fundamental and strengthening the upper partials, no decisive pattern of the acoustical structure of tones tested could be determined.

Swain, John Joseph. "A Catalog of the E-Flat Tubas in the Arne B. Larson Collection at the University of South Dakota (Instruments, Musical)." Ph.D. diss., Michigan State University (0128), 1986, 395 pp. Source: DAI 47/04A, p.1111; Publication No.: AAC8613341; Subject: Music (0413).

Abstract: The Arne B. Larson Collection in the Shrine to Music Museum at the University of South Dakota contains approximately three thousand musical instruments plus assorted musical memorabilia. Approximately one hundred fifty E-flat tubas are part of this large collection, and these tubas represent a period of instrument manufacture from the middle of the nineteenth century to the middle of the twentieth century. Major European and American manufacturers are represented in the collection, and a number of smaller companies and individual craftsmen are represented as well.

The document outlines the development of the bass wind instrument from the sixteenth century to the twentieth century and presents a brief discussion of the use of the E-flat tuba in the United States. The major thrust of the paper is centered on a detailed study of the E-flat tubas in the Larson Collection. Measurements of bore diameter, valve slide lengths, bell diameter, weight, and height are given for individual instruments and compared to other like instruments. Valve slide arrangements, valve placement, and other details of construction are discussed and compared. Photographs of ten special instruments illustrate some of the unusual techniques of construction. Historical information about the manufacturers and agents represented in the collection is documented, and manufacturing information for York and some of the larger manufacturers is presented as well.

Conclusions drawn from the research support and amplify existing documents concerning the physical development of the tuba from about 1850 to the present. The poor quality of construction of many instruments and intonation problems caused by valve limitations and pitch modifications to existing instruments are cited as primary reasons for the decline in use of the E-flat tuba.

Miscellaneous

Cattley, Gary Thomas. "Perception of Timbral Differences among Bass Tubas." See listing under "Equipment."

McAdams, Charles Alan. "Investigation of Instrumental Music Teachers' Knowledge of the Tuba." Ed.D. diss., University of Illinois at Urbana-Champaign (0090), 1988, 145 pp. Source: DAI 49/09A, p.2575; Publication No.: AAC8823197; Subject: Education, Music (0522); Music (0413); Education, Tests and Measurements (0288).

Abstract: The purpose of this study was to investigate instrumental music teachers' knowledge of tuba pedagogy. The investigation sought to determine (1) the body of knowledge of tuba pedagogy is represented in pedagogical materials written for the instrumental music teacher, (2) what specific knowledge of tuba pedagogy do pedagogical experts believe is essential to elementary and secondary instrumental music teachers, and (3) to what extent do elementary and secondary instrumental music teachers differ in their knowledge of tuba pedagogy.

The investigator reviewed pedagogical materials written for the instrumental music education student, instrumental music teacher, college tubist, and professional tubist. This review determined the extent of the body of literature available and the categories of knowledge used in this investigation.

A panel of tuba pedagogy experts was mailed a rating scale and questionnaire. The experts rated specific categories of tuba knowledge important or unimportant (5-point scale) for elementary and secondary instrumental music teachers. A test was developed based on the pedagogical literature review and the ratings of the panel of experts. This criterion-referenced test was administered to a sample of elementary and secondary instrumental music teachers to determine their knowledge level. The investigation highlights which categories were answered correctly or incorrectly by each group. There were no significant differences in the scores of elementary teachers who were brass versus non-brass players. There was a significant difference in the mean scores of secondary teachers who were brass players versus the non-brass players. Recommendations include the need for teachers to learn specific cognitive knowledge about tuba pedagogy.

Shrum, Kenneth Earl. "An Analytical Commentary on the Euphonium and Tuba Music of Jan Bach." D.M.A. diss., Arizona State University (0010), 1989, 151 pp. Source: DAI 50/06A, p. 1479; Publication No.: AAC 8919653; Subject: Music (0413).
Abstract: This paper presents an analytical commentary on the euphonium and tuba music of Jan Bach. The rationale for this essay is that an understanding of the structural elements of a musical work is necessary for a convincing performance. The works represented are *Concert Variations* (1977, euphonium and piano) and *Quintet for Tuba and Strings* (1978, tuba and string quartet), and they are analyzed according to the criteria of form, melody, harmony, rhythm, dynamics, and performance problems.

The information in this study reveals that Bach utilizes basically simple formal structures which often closely model traditional formal structures, such as scherzo and fugue. Both works utilize a number of scale formations, but the *Concert Variations* features a synthetic variant of the Lydian mode known as the overtone scale as its major unifying concept; the *Quintet*, on the other hand, utilizes the chromatic scale as its structural basis. In addition, there is a strong tendency toward contrapuntal writing in both compositions.

Bach's concept of harmony features pervasive use of tertian, extended tertian, and compound structures in a non-traditional context. The interval of the tritone permeates the *Concert Variations*, while the *Quintet* features the third as an underlying harmonic concept. In terms of rhythm and dynamics, neither work strays far from the boundaries of convention, utilizing standard metric schemes and dynamic markings.

Both works present considerable performance challenges in the areas of range, endurance, valve technique, breath control, special effects, and ensemble relationships. Both are virtuosic, but in contrasting styles. The *Concert Variations* utilizes a number of contemporary effects, including: the bend, the alternate valve tremolo, the alternate valve scale in quartertones, multiphonic technique, and the fan valves glissando. The tuba solo, however, uses no special techniques except for one muted passage, and is virtuosic in a more traditional sense, with extreme range, valve technique, and endurance demands.

Articles

Kevin J. Stees

The compilation of the more than five hundred entries in this section of *The Tuba Source Book* would not have been possible without the help of two resources: *Brass Bibliography* by Mark Fasman, published by Indiana University Press, and the *T.U.B.A. Journal* index, courtesy of Karen Cotton, Publisher. Many thanks go to these two individuals.

Bibliography

Bryant, William. "Research for Tuba and Euphonium." *T.U.B.A. Journal* 13, no. 2 (Nov. 1985): 25.
Salmela, Juha. "Regulations of Examinations and Scales for Tuba." *Päijät-Hämeen Konservator* (1993).
"*T.U.B.A. Journal* Index, Volume 13 No. 1–Volume 18 No. 1." *T.U.B.A. Journal* 18, no. 2 (Winter 1990): 64–70.
Varner, J. L. "Anthology of Tuba Writings." *Brass and Percussion* 1, no. 5 (1973): 13–14.

Discography

Bishop, Ronald T. "Arnold Jacobs on Record: Its Influence on Me." *T.U.B.A. Journal* 15, no. 4 (May 1988): 27–29.

Bland, Vurl, and William Bryant. "A Catalog of Recordings for the Tuba." *T.U.B.A. Journal* 15, no. 1 (Aug. 1987): 13–16. Edited by Kenneth Kiesow and Joan Draxler.

Cummings, Barton. "Addenda for Tuba Record Guide." *T.U.B.A. Journal* 4, no. 1 (Fall 1976): 19.

Cummings, Barton. "Tuba Record Guide." *T.U.B.A. Newsletter* 3, no. 1 (Fall 1975): 18–20.

Cummings, Barton. "Tuba Record Guide." *T.U.B.A. Newsletter* 3, no. 3 (Spring/Summer 1976): 6.

Faulkner, Maurice. "Superb Brass Recordings: Tuba Solos and Ensembles." *The Instrumentalist* 36 (Nov. 1981): 79–82.

Hepola, Ralph. "The Jazz Niche: A Discography— Bob Stewart." *T.U.B.A. Journal* 17, no. 2 (Winter 1989): 12–13.

"Tuba Discography, Corrections." *T.U.B.A. Journal* 15, no. 3 (Feb. 1988): 33.

Performance

Bobo, Roger. "Symposium 78—Eyes Toward the Future." *T.U.B.A. Journal* 5, no. 1 (Fall 1977): 20–21.

Bobo, Roger. "Symposium 78: Looking Back." *Brass Bulletin-International Brass Chronicle,* no. 25 (1979): 19+.

Bobo, Roger. "Symposium 78—Looking Back." *T.U.B.A. Journal* 6, no. 1 (Fall 1978): 22–24.

Bowman, Brian. "Euphonium-Tuba Opportunities in Service Bands." *T.U.B.A. Newsletter* 1, no. 2 Winter 1974): 8.

Dempster, Stuart. "Tuba Time in Tacoma: A Thoroughly Biased Report on the First Northwest Annual Tuba-Euphonium Workshop." *T.U.B.A. Journal* 16, no. 1 (Fall 1988): 36–43.

Droste, Paul. "Brass Bands are Back: Performing Opportunities for Euphonium and Tuba Players." *T.U.B.A. Journal* 16, no. 3 (Spring 1989): 40–41.

Dutton, Brent. "Interchanges." *T.U.B.A. Journal* 7, no. 4 (Spring 1980): 19–21.

Dutton, Brent. "Interchanges: Tuba Recitals." *T.U.B.A. Journal* 8, no. 2 (Fall 1980): 8–9.

Eastep, Michael. "Authentic Performance of Verdi." *T.U.B.A. Journal* 4, no. 2 (Winter 1977): 18.

Fletcher, John. "The Tuba in Britain." *T.U.B.A. Journal* 5, no. 2 (Winter 1978): 22–23, 26–30.

Fritze, Greg. "The Basics of Playing a Bass Line." *T.U.B.A. Journal* 19, no. 3 (Spring 1992): 36–38.

Fritze, Gregory. "A Week of Jazz in Lexington." *T.U.B.A. Journal* 20, no. 1 (Fall 1992): 32–33.

Fry, Robert H. "Playing the Bach Suites for Unaccompanied Cello." *T.U.B.A. Journal* 17, no. 3 (Spring 1990): 17, 22.

Gay, Leslie C., Jr. "B. L. Lacerta—New Directions in Tuba Improvisation." *T.U.B.A. Journal* 7, no. 3 (Winter 1980): 23–25.

Gray, Skip. "Performance Considerations in the Vaughan Williams *Concerto for Bass Tuba.*" *T.U.B.A. Journal* 12, no. 2 (Nov. 1984): 4–9.

Johnson, T. "A Guide to Commercial Tuba Playing in the Los Angeles Area." *Brass Bulletin–International Brass Chronicle,* no. 25 (1979): 58–59.

Kaenzig, Fritz. "HETA Music Camp Report." *T.U.B.A. Journal* 19, no. 1 (Fall 1991): 14–16.

Keys, Stephen. "The University of Kentucky Regional Tuba-Euphonium Conference Review." *T.U.B.A. Journal* 15, no. 2 (Nov. 1987): 20–21.

Lancto, Peter C. "1988 New England Tuba-Euphonium Symposium/Workshop: Recital Reviews." *T.U.B.A. Journal* 16, no. 1 (Fall 1988): 53–54.

Mazzarese, Gregorio. "The Tuba in Italy." *T.U.B.A. Journal* 16, no. 3 (Spring 1989): 30.

"Mid-South Euphonium/Tuba Symposium." *T.U.B.A. Newsletter* 3, no. 3 (Spring/Summer 1976): 8.

"Midwest Regional Tuba-Euphonium Symposium— A Report." *T.U.B.A. Newsletter* 3, no. 2 (Winter 1976): 7.

Mueller, Frederick A. "Two Tubas for Symphony Orchestra and Chamber Music." *T.U.B.A. Newsletter* 1, no. 3 (Spring 1974): 8.

Nelson, Mark A. "Developing the College/Community Tuba-Euphonium Ensemble." *T.U.B.A. Journal* 16, no. 1 (Fall 1988): 34–35.

"1975 National T.U.B.A. Symposium-Workshop." *T.U.B.A. Newsletter* 1, no. 2 (Winter 1974): 12.

"1983 I.T.E.C.: A Wrap-Up—Part I." *T.U.B.A. Journal* 11, no. 2 (Fall 1983): 12–20.

"1986 International Tuba-Euphonium Conference Session Reviews." *T.U.B.A. Journal* 14, no. 1 (Aug. 1986): 11–34.

"1992 International Tuba-Euphonium Conference— Lexington, Kentucky, May 12–16, 1992: Concert and Clinic Reviews." *T.U.B.A. Journal* 20, no. 1 (Fall 1992): 52–78.

"1992 U.S. Army Band Tuba-Euphonium Conference Concert Reviews." *T.U.B.A. Journal* 19, no. 4 (Summer 1992): 8–13.

Northcut, Timothy, and Robert Daniel. "Region Four T.U.B.A. Regional Workshop: Review." *T.U.B.A. Journal* 12, no. 4 (May 1985): 14–15.

Perantoni, Daniel. "Contemporary Systems and Trends for the Tuba." *The Instrumentalist* 27 (Feb. 1973): 24–27.

Poore, Melvyn. "A Newsletter from England." *T.U.B.A. Journal* 6, no. 2 (Winter 1979): 3–8.

Popiel, Peter. "First National Tuba-Euphonium Symposium: A Report." *T.U.B.A. Newsletter* 3, no. 1 (Fall 1975): 2+.

Pröpper, K. "Tuba-Konferenz in Hammelburg." *Das Orchester* 36 (Jan. 1988): 41.

Randolph, David M. "Some Thoughts on Recital Programming." *T.U.B.A. Journal* 6, no. 3 (Spring 1979): 9.

Randolph, David M. "Avant-Garde Effects for Tuba: Music or Noise?" *T.U.B.A. Journal* 8, no. 3 (Winter 1981): 19–23.

Randolph, David M. "The Tuba in Korea, Taiwan, Hong Kong and China: A Report on the State of the Art." *T.U.B.A. Journal* 15, no. 3 (Feb. 1988): 17–19.

Reifsnyder, Bob. "T.U.B.A. Programs: What Are They Telling Us?" *T.U.B.A. Journal* 11, no. 2 (Fall 1983): 6–9.

Reimer, Mark U. "Brass Choir: A New Challenge for the Tubist." *T.U.B.A. Journal* 11, no. 4 (Spring 1984): 9–10.

Roberts, Chester. "Tuba Mock Orchestra Auditions." *T.U.B.A. Journal* 11, no. 2 (Fall 1983): 40–41.

"Second National Tuba-Euphonium Symposium-Workshop." *T.U.B.A. Journal* 7, no. 3 (Winter 1980): 16–22.

Self, James M. "Third International Tuba-Euphonium Symposium-Workshop—An Update." *T.U.B.A. Journal* 5, no. 3 (Spring/Summer 1978): 20.

Self, James. "The Studio Tubist." *The Instrumentalist* 43 (Dec. 1988): 25–26+.

Shoop, Stephen. "The Dixieland Band: A Meaningful Avenue of Performance for the Tuba Player." *T.U.B.A. Journal* 13, no. 1 (Aug. 1985): 13–14.

Shoop, Stephen. "Employment Opportunities Available to Tuba and Euphonium Players at America's Amusement-Theme Parks." *T.U.B.A. Journal* 15, no. 3 (Feb. 1988): 20–21.

Shoop, Stephen. "The Junior High and High School Tuba Ensemble." *T.U.B.A. Journal* 20, no. 1 (Fall 1992): 38–39.

"Third International Tuba-Euphonium Symposium-Workshop." *T.U.B.A. Journal* 5, no. 2 (Winter 1978): 33.

"Third International Tuba-Euphonium Symposium-Workshop." *T.U.B.A. Journal* 6, no. 1 (Fall 1978): 18–25.

Tilbury, Jack; David Porter; and Sally Wagner. "The United States Army Band Tuba-Euphonium Conference—February 4–7, 1987: A Summary." *T.U.B.A. Journal* 15, no. 2 (Nov. 1987): 14–19.

Vinson, Dan. "New England Artists Recital of the New England Tuba-Euphonium Symposium/Workshop—A Review." *T.U.B.A. Journal* 15, no. 4 (May 1988): 13.

Waldeck, L. "Symphonic Tuba Playing." *Brass Bulletin–International Brass Chronicle*, no. 23 (1978): 45–46.

History

Ahrens, C. "Dampfsirenen oder Musikinstrumente? Zur Auseinandersetzung um die Tiefen Blechblasininstrumente im 19. Jahrhundert." *Das Orchester* 38 (Apr. 1990): 362–365.

Altenburg, Wilhelm. "Zur Kenntnis des Serpents." *Deutsche Militär-Musiker Zeitung* 31 (1909): 577–578, 590.

Altenburg, Wilhelm. "Der Serpent und seine Umbildung in das Chromatische Basshorn und die Ophikleide." *Zeitschrift für Instrumentenbau* 31 (1910–1911): 668–671.

Bate, Philip. "A 'Serpent d'Eglise': Notes on Some Structural Details." *The Galpin Society Journal* 29 (May 1976): 47–50.

Bate, Philip. "Some Further Notes on Serpent Technology." *The Galpin Society Journal* 32 (May 1979): 124–129.

Bauer, P., comp. "A Complete Chronological Listing of the Trombone and Tuba Personnel of Stan Kenton's Orchestras." *Journal of the International Trombone Association* 11, no. 4 (1983): 24–25.

Beery, John. "The Sousaphones of the Greenleaf Collection." *T.U.B.A. Journal* 16, no. 3 (Spring 1989): 23–25.

Benson, Warren. "Serpentine Shadows." *T.U.B.A. Newsletter* 1, no. 2 (Winter 1974): 3.

Bevan, Clifford. "Background Brass." *Sounding Brass & the Conductor* 6, no. 3 (1977): 96–97.

Bevan, Clifford. "The Bass Tuba." *Sounding Brass & the Conductor* 8, no. 1 (1979): 23–24.

Bevan, Clifford. "The Saxtuba and Organological Vituperation." *The Galpin Society Journal* 43 (1990): 135–146.

Boulton, John. "Know Your Orchestra: The Tuba." *Hallé* (Sept. 1950): 14–17.

Brandon, S.P. "The French Tuba." *Woodwind World–Brass and Percussion* 15, no. 5 (1976): 38.

"Brass Tuba Directory." *Sounding Brass & the Conductor* 5, no. 3 (1976): 88–89.

Brüchle, Bernhard. "Eine Tuba der Superlative, von Historischer Bedeutung. . . ." *Brass Bulletin–International Brass Chronicle*, no. 9 (1974): 41–43.

Butler, John. "Tuba in Australia." *T.U.B.A. Journal* 4, no. 1 (Fall 1976): 8.

Catelinet, Phillip. "The Tuba in England." *T.U.B.A. Journal* 15, no. 2 (Nov. 1987): 29–31.

"Chicago Symphony Orchestra Low Brass Personnel 1891–1979." *International Trombone Association Newsletter* 7, no. 2 (1980): 14–15.

Chieffi, Brady. "The True (?) Roots of the Tuba Family Tree." *T.U.B.A. Journal* 9, no. 3 (Winter 1982): 41.

Chiemingo, Rich. "Playing Tuba with Guy Lombardo's Royal Canadians." *T.U.B.A. Journal* 7, no. 2 (Fall 1979): 8–10.

Cummings, Barton. "The Early Years." *T.U.B.A. Journal* 4, no. 3 (Spring/Summer 1977): 8–10.

Cummings, Barton. "Tuba Innovations [role in early jazz]." *Woodwind World–Brass and Percussion* 17, no. 5 (1978): 8–11.

Dahlstrom, J. F. "History and Development of the Tuba." *The School Musician* 41 (Apr. 1970): 60–61.

Dibley, Tom. "The Serpents of Beauchamp House." *Journal of the International Trumpet Guild* 12, no. 4 (May 1988): 46–47.

Eliason, Robert E. "A Pictorial History of the Tuba and Its Predecessors." *T.U.B.A. Newsletter* 2, no. 1 (Fall 1974): 6. Appears in subsequent issues through Summer 1976.

Eliason, Robert E. "A Pictorial History of the Tuba and Its Predecessors." *T.U.B.A. Journal* 4, no. 1 (Fall 1976): 14–15. Appears in subsequent issues through 13, no. 3 (Feb. 1986).

Eliason, Robert E. "Keyed Serpent." *T.U.B.A. Journal* 4, no. 1 (Fall 1976): 17–18.

Erb, R. H. "The Arnold Jacobs Legacy." *The Instrumentalist* 41 (Apr. 1987): 22–24+.

Evans, Eliot D. "All You Ever Wanted to Know about Washington D.C. Military Bands." *T.U.B.A. Journal* 8, no. 1 (Summer 1980): 2–12.

Fletcher, John. "Tuba Talk." *Sounding Brass & the Conductor* 2, no. 2 (1973): 59–61.

Fletcher, John. "More Tuba Talk." *Sounding Brass & the Conductor* 2, no. 3 (1973): 78–79+.

Fletcher, John. "Even More Tuba Talk." *Sounding Brass & the Conductor* 2, no. 4 (1973–1974): 110–112+.

Fletcher, John. "Yet Further Tuba Talk." *Sounding Brass & the Conductor* 3, no. 4 (1974–1975): 116–117.

Fletcher, John. "The Tuba in Britain." *T.U.B.A. Journal* 5, no. 2 (Winter 1978): 22–23.

Funderburk, Jeff. "The Man and His Horn." *T.U.B.A. Journal* 15, no. 4 (May 1988): 43.

Girschner, C. "Bemerkungen über Musik-Instrumenten-Bau." *Berliner allgemeine musikalische Zeitung* 6 (1829): 13–15.

Gottfried, K. H. "Die Ophikleide." *Das Orchester* 26 (Oct. 1978): 759–764.

Grace, Harvey. "A Note on the Serpent." *The Musical Times* 57 (1916): 500–501.

Griffith, Bobby. "Development of the Tuba in the Romantic Period." *T.U.B.A. Journal* 11, no. 4 (Spring 1984): 2–5.

Hadfield, J. M. "The Serpent." *The Musical Times* 58 (1917): 22, 264.

Halfpenny, Eric. "Playing the Serpent." *Symphony* (Apr. 1952): 9.

Heinkel, Peggy. "A Look at the Tokyo Bari-Tuba Ensemble." *T.U.B.A. Journal* 14, no. 2 (Nov. 1986): 18–19.

Heinroth. "Beschreibung und Empfehlung eines von G. Streitwolf in Göttingen Verfertigten Chromatischen Basshorns." *Allgemeine musikalische Zeitung* 22 (1820): 688–689.

Hepola, Ralph. "The Jazz Niche." *T.U.B.A. Journal* 17, no. 1 (Fall 1989): 15–17.

"Herkunft der Ophikleide." *Musik International-Instrumentenbau-Zeitschrift* 34 (Jan. 1980): 24.

Holmes, Brian. "The Tuba and Madame Mao: A Tale of the Cultural Revolution." *T.U.B.A. Journal* 13, no. 4 (May 1986): 23–26.

Homo. "The Ophicleide." *Musical World* 16 (1841): 215, 494.

Horwood, W. "Musical Musings: Grappling with the Past [ophicleide]." *Crescendo International* 22 (June–July 1984): 4.

Hunt, E. "Serpent in the Midst." *Recorder and Music* 9, no. 2 (1987): 35–36.

Kingdon-Ward, Martha. "In Defense of the Ophicleide." *Monthly Musical Record* 82 (1952): 199–205.

Kridel, C. "One Step for Intonation; One Giant Step for the Serpent." *Brass Bulletin–International Brass Chronicle*, no. 58 (1987): 36–39.

Leeka, Carter I. "History of the Tubists Universal Brotherhood Association." *T.U.B.A. Journal* 5, no. 1 (Fall 1977): 14–16.

Lelong, F., and R. Coutet. "Le Tuba en France." *Brass Bulletin–International Brass Chronicle*, no. 13 (1976): 26–35.

Lewis, David. "A Historical Perspective on Oc-T.U.B.A.fest and TubaChristmas: An Interview with Harvey Phillips." *T.U.B.A. Journal* 16, no. 4 (Summer 1989): 32–35.

Liagra, D. "Le Tuba." *Musique & Radio* 47 (1957): 213–114.

Lind, Michael. "The Tuba in Scandinavia." *T.U.B.A. Journal* 4, no. 2 (Winter 1977): 13–16.

"The London Serpent Trio." *Music and Musicians* 24 (Mar. 1976): 8+.

Lorenz, J. "Aus dem Leben der Tuba." *Das Orchester* 8 (1960): 1–5.

McCready, Matthew A. "Compensating Systems: An Historical Overview." *T.U.B.A. Journal* 10, no. 4 (Spring 1983): 5–6.

Megules, K. I. "Tuba Performance—Background & History." *Woodwind World–Brass and Percussion* 14, no. 4 (1975): 40+.

Meinl, Gerhard. "Effect of Valves on the Intonation of Brass Instruments." *T.U.B.A. Journal* 16, no. 4 (Summer 1989): 38–40.

Mende, Emily. "Die Tuba, Benjamin der Blechblasinstrumente." *Brass Bulletin–International Brass Chronicle*, no. 17 (1977): 11–14.

Miura, Toru. "The Euphonium and Tuba in Japan." *T.U.B.A. Journal* 8, no. 3 (Winter 1981): 10–12.

Monk, C. "The Serpent." *Woodwind World–Brass and Percussion* 20, no. 2 (1981): 6–8+.

Monk, C. "The London Serpent Trio." *Woodwind World–Brass and Percussion* 20, no. 5 (1981): 16–17.

Morley-Pegge, R. "The Evolution of the Large-Bore Bass Mouthpiece Instrument." *Musical Progress & Mail* (Mar.–July 1940).

Morley-Pegge, R. "The 'Anaconda.'" *The Galpin Society Journal* 12 (1959): 53–56.

Morris, R. Winston. "The Tuba Family." *The Instrumentalist* 27 (Feb. 1973): 33.

Morris, R. Winston. "The Evolution of the Tuba/Euphonium Ensemble." *The Instrumentalist* 43 (Dec. 1988): 15–17.

Myers, A. "A Slide Tuba?" *The Galpin Society Journal* 42 (1989): 127–128.

Nelson, Mark. "The Real Date of the Hindemith Tuba Sonata." *T.U.B.A. Journal* 9, no. 4 (Spring 1982): 18.

Nelson, Mark E. "The History and Development of the Serpent." *T.U.B.A. Journal* 10, no. 1 (Summer 1982): 10–14.

"1920 Tuba Ensemble." *T.U.B.A. Newsletter* 1, no. 2 (Winter 1974): 6.

Nowicke, C. Elizabeth. "A Pictorial History of the Tuba and Its Sordid Past (or What Does Robert Eliason Know?)" *T.U.B.A. Newsletter* 3, no. 2 (Winter 1976): 12–13.

Ohishi, Kiyoshi. "A History of Tuba and Euphonium in Japan." *T.U.B.A. Journal* 18, no. 2 (Winter 1990): 38–39, 42.

"One Step for Intonation: One Giant Step for the Serpent." *Journal of the International Trumpet Guild* 11, no. 2 (1986): 9.

"One Step for Intonation: One Giant Step for the Serpent." *T.U.B.A. Journal* 14, no. 2 (May 1987): 4–5.

"Die Ophicleide." *Caecilia* 9 (1828): 130.

"Ophicleide in Australien." *Instrumentenbau Musik International* 30, no. 6 (1976): 456.

"Overshoulder Tuba." *T.U.B.A. Newsletter* 2, no. 1 (Fall 1974): 7.

P., I. "On the Serpent, Bass-Horn and Trombone." *Harmonicon* (1834): 234.

Petersen, Mary. "The Arne B. Larson Collection." *T.U.B.A. Journal* 8, no. 2 (Fall 1980): 5–7.

Petersen, Mary. "The Arne B. Larson Collection: Part Two." *T.U.B.A. Journal* 8, no. 3 (Winter 1981): 15–18.

Phillips, Harvey. "About the Tuba." *T.U.B.A. Newsletter* 3, no. 2 (Winter 1975): 1.

Phillips, Harvey. "Tuba Recital Series." *T.U.B.A. Newsletter* 3, no. 2 (Winter 1976): 1.

Poncelet–Lecocq, P. "Du Basso Profondo." *L'Echo Musical* 1, no. 7 (15 Nov. 1869).

Reed, David. "Vaughan Williams' Tuba Concerto—A Retrospective Look Upon Its 25th Anniversary." *T.U.B.A. Journal* 8, no. 1 (Summer 1980): 13–14.

Rowe, Clement E. "The Tuba." *Etude* 52 (1934): 405+.

Rudoff, H. "Informal History of the Tuba." *Music Journal* 28 (May 1970): 56.

Saltzman, Joe. "How Tubby Was Born." *T.U.B.A. Journal* 9, no. 4 (Spring 1982): 2–3.

Schmidt, J. B. "Ueber die Chromatische Bass-Tuba und das Neu Erfundene Holz-Bass-Blas-Instrument, Genannt Bathyphon." *Allgemeine musikalische Zeitung* 42 (1980): 1041–1042.

Schulz, Charles A. "Ancestors of the Tuba." *T.U.B.A. Journal* 9, no. 2 (Fall 1981): 3–7.

Schulz, Charles A. "Ancestors of the Tuba: Part II." *T.U.B.A. Journal* 9, no. 3 (Winter 1982): 10–12.

Schweizer, G. "Ein Neues Instrument [Basstuba]." *Musica* 19, no. 3 (1965): 182.

Self, James. "Reclaiming our Heritage." *T.U.B.A. Journal* 5, no. 3 (Spring/Summer 1978): 12–14.

Skowronnek, K. "100 Jahre Basstuba." *Die Musik* 27 (1935): 515–516.

Starmer, W. W. "The Serpent." *The Musical Times* 57 (1916): 549–550.

Stewart, Bob. "Best of Series: New Roles and Dimensions for the Contemporary Jazz Tubist." *T.U.B.A. Journal* 18, no. 3 (Spring 1991): 62, 64–69.

Stewart, Gary M. "Clean That Old York on a Sunday Afternoon." *T.U.B.A. Journal* 14, no. 4 (May 1987): 28–30.

Stewart, Gary M., ed. "Tuba History." *T.U.B.A. Journal* 14, no. 1 (Aug. 1986): 40.

Stewart, Gary M., ed. "Tuba History." *T.U.B.A. Journal* 14, no. 2 (Nov. 1986): 34.

Stewart, Gary. "Sears & Roebuck Catalog Tubas." *T.U.B.A. Journal* 14, no. 3 (Feb. 1987): 81–82.

Stewart, Gary M., ed. "Tuba History." *T.U.B.A. Journal* 15, no. 1 (Aug 1987): 26–27.

Stewart, Gary. "C. G. Conn's Truth: Highlights of the September 1910 Issue." *T.U.B.A. Journal* 15, no. 3 (Feb. 1988): 26–27.

Stewart, Gary. "B-Flat Subcontrabass Tuba of the Harvard University Band." *T.U.B.A. Journal* 16, no. 1 (Fall 1988): 49–51.

Stewart, Gary. "Highlights from the 1924 C.G. Conn Bass Catalog." *T.U.B.A. Journal* 16, no. 3 (Spring 1989): 52–57.

Stewart, Gary. "Tin Tuba." *T.U.B.A. Journal* 16, no. 4 (Summer 1989): 31.

Stoddard, Hope. "The Tuba and Its Players in Our Bands and Orchestras." *International Musician* 48 (Jan. 1950): 20–22.

Swaim, John. "E–Flat Tubas in the Shrine to Music Museum." *T.U.B.A. Journal* 16, no. 2 (Winter 1988): 36–38, 17.

Swift, R. F. "Extinct Instruments [serpent]." *Woodwind World* 12, no. 2 (1973): 11+.

Torchinsky, Abe. "Tuba Trends." *The Instrumentalist* 18 (Apr. 1964): 86–87.

"Tuba Renaissance." *The Instrumentalist* 40 (Dec. 1985): 16–18.

"Tubas Once Struck a Low Note in China." *Variety* 288 (Oct. 19, 1977): 2.

Tucci, Robert. "The Tuba in Europe." *Brass Bulletin–International Brass Chronicle*, no. 11 (1975): 67–79.

Tucci, Robert. "The Tuba in Europe." *T.U.B.A. Journal* 4, no. 3 (Spring/Summer 1977): 2–3.

Vaillant, Joseph. "The Evolution of the Tuba in France." *T.U.B.A. Journal* 5, no. 3 (Spring/Summer 1978): 17–18.

Voigt, Alban. "Das Serpent." *Deutsche Instrumentenbau Zeitschrift* 38 (1937): 282.

W. St. "Was Wissen Sie von der Tuba? Des Basses Grundgewalt." *Neues Musikblatt* 15, no. 18 (1936): 5.

Weldon, Constance J. "The Tuba Ensemble." *The Instrumentalist* 27 (Feb. 1973): 35–36.

Weldon, Constance J., and Greg Lonnman. "The Evolution of the Tuba Ensemble." *T.U.B.A. Journal* 7, no. 1 (Summer 1979): 2–3.

Weston, Stephen J. "Improvements to the Nine-keyed Ophicleide." *The Galpin Society Journal* 36 (Mar. 1983): 109–114.

Weston, Stephen J. "The Untimely Demise of the Ophicleide." *Brass Bulletin–International Brass Chronicle*, no. 43 (1983): 10–17.

Westrup, J. A. "Sidelights on the Serpent." *The Musical Times* 68 (1927): 635–637.

Yarham, E. R. "Serpents in Church." *Music Journal* 21 (Jan. 1963): 76+.

Yeo, Douglas. "A Pictorial History of Low Brass Players in the Boston Symphony Orchestra, 1887–1986." *Journal of the International Trombone Association* 14, no. 4 (1986): 12–21.

Yeo, Douglas. "Tuba Players of the Boston Symphony Orchestra, 1913–1987." *T.U.B.A. Journal* 14, no. 4 (May 1987): 14–20.

Yi, Chong–il. "A Brief History of the Korea Tuba Association." *T.U.B.A. Journal* 18, no. 2 (Winter 1990): 13.

Zechmeister, G. "Die Entwicklung der Wiener Konzerttuba." *Brass Bulletin—International Brass Chronicle* no. 75 (1991): 44–47.

Literature

Badarak, Mary Lynn. "'Valse-to-Bass.'" *T.U.B.A. Newsletter* 3, no. 3 (Spring/Summer 1976): 7.

Bahr, Edward R. "Orchestral Literature Including Euphonium or Tenor Tuba." *T.U.B.A. Journal* 7, no. 2 (Fall 1979): 13–14.

Brown, Leon F. "Materials for Tuba." *The Instrumentalist* 10 (Nov. 1955): 37–40.

Catelinet, Philip. "The Truth About the Vaughan Williams Tuba Concerto." *T.U.B.A. Journal* 14, no. 2 (Nov. 1986): 30–33.

Chieffi, Brady. "Curios and Collectables: Music." *T.U.B.A. Journal* 13, no. 2 (Nov. 1985): 18–19.

Conner, Rex A. "Massed Ensemble Library." *T.U.B.A. Journal* 7, no. 2 (Fall 1979): 34.

Cummings, Barton. "New Material for Tuba and Euphonium." *T.U.B.A. Newsletter* 3, no. 2 (Winter 1976): 6.

Cummings, Barton. "New Music for Tuba." *T.U.B.A. Newsletter* 3, no. 3 (Spring/Summer 1976): 5.

Cummings, Barton. "New Materials." *T.U.B.A. Journal* 4, no. 1 (Fall 1976): 19.

Cummings, Barton. "Tuba and Percussion: Are They Compatible?" *Woodwind World–Brass and Percussion* 15, no. 6 (1976): 40–41+.

Cummings, Barton; Brian Bowman; and Larry Campbell. "New Materials—Tuba and Euphonium." *T.U.B.A. Journal* 5, no. 2 (Winter 1978): 34–37.

Cummings, Barton, ed. "New Materials—Tuba." *T.U.B.A. Journal* 5, no. 3 (Spring/Summer 1978): 21–23.

Cummings, Barton, ed. "New Materials—Tuba." *T.U.B.A. Journal* 6, no. 3 (Winter 1979): 9–12.

Cummings, Barton; Sandy Keathley; Gary Buttery; Gary Bird; and Jack Tilbury, eds. "New Materials." *T.U.B.A. Journal* 7, no. 1 (Summer 1979): 5–12.

"Dave Baker's *Sonata for Tuba and String Orchestra* for Harvey Phillips (second movement)." *Down Beat* 43 (Oct. 7, 1976): 43.

Davis, Ron. " 'F–E' Suite for Tuba (by A. Wildest)." *T.U.B.A. Newsletter* 2, no. 3 (Spring 1975): 8.

Dutton, Brent. "Interchanges: Composing Low Brass Music." *T.U.B.A. Journal* 7, no. 3 (Winter 1980): 5–6.

Dutton, Brent. "Interchanges—Merle Hogg." *T.U.B.A. Journal* 10, no. 2 (Fall 1982): 10–12.

Fletcher, John. "Thoughts on the Tuba." *Composer* [London], no. 44 (Summer 1972): 5–12.

Fletcher, John. "Is the Tuba Really a Solo Instrument." *Sounding Brass & the Conductor* 5, no. 1, 2 (1976): 13+, 54+.

George, Thom Ritter. "A Visit with Friends." *T.U.B.A. Journal* 12, no. 1 (Aug. 1984): 26.

Gray, Skip. "The Tuba Ensemble Today." *The Instrumentalist* 35 (Sept. 1980): 78+.

Greenstone, Paul. "Expanding the Tuba Repertoire." *T.U.B.A. Journal* 12, no. 3 (Feb. 1985): 9–10.

Hiller, Lejaren. "*Malta for Tuba and Tape 1975.*" *T.U.B.A. Newsletter* 3, no. 3 (Spring/Summer 1976): 7.

Ingalls, David M. "More Tuba Literature." *The Instrumentalist* 8 (Mar. 1954): 8+.

Klein, Stephen. "How to Obtain the Music You Heard at the Third International Tuba-Euphonium Symposium–Workshop." *T.U.B.A. Journal* 6, no. 3 (Spring 1979): 6–7.

Krenek, Beth. "A Survey of Solo Literature for Tuba." *T.U.B.A. Journal* 19, no. 1 (Fall 1991): 60–62.

Kuehn, David L. "A Selected List of Tuba Literature." *The Instrumentalist* 17, no. 4 (Dec. 1962): 48–49.

Laplace, Michel. "Les Tubas dans le Jazz et dans les Musiques populaires." *Brass Bulletin–International Brass Chronicle*, no. 56 (1987): 18–22.

Laplace, Michel. "Les Tubas dans le Jazz et dans les Musiques populaires." *Brass Bulletin–International Brass Chronicle*, no. 57 (1987): 84–88.

Levine, J. A. "Tuba Boom: Oom–pah–pah Fades." *The Christian Science Monitor* 68 (Jan. 29, 1976): 2.

Lind, Michael. "A Partial Listing of Scandinavian Tuba Music." *T.U.B.A. Journal* 19, no. 2 (Winter 1991): 10–11.

Maldonado, Luis. "Solo Music Literature for Junior High and High School Euphonium and Tuba Performers." *T.U.B.A. Journal* 14, no. 4 (May 1987): 39–41.

Maldonado, Luis. "Ensemble Literature for Junior High and High School Euphonium and Tuba Performers." *T.U.B.A. Journal* 15, no. 2 (Nov. 1987): 24.

Maldonado, Luis. "Addendum—Solo Music Literature for Junior High and High School Euphonium and Tuba Performers." *T.U.B.A. Journal* 15, no. 2 (Nov. 1987): 24–25.

"Manuscripts for Tuba." *T.U.B.A. Newsletter* 2, no. 1 (Fall 1974): 5.

Morris, R. Winston. "Music for Multiple Tubas." *The Instrumentalist* 24 (Apr. 1970): 57–58.

Morris, R. Winston. "A Basic Repertoire and Studies for the Serious Tubist." *The Instrumentalist* 27 (Feb. 1973): 33–34.

Morris, R. Winston. "New Materials—Euphonium–Tuba." *T.U.B.A. Newsletter* 1, no. 2 (Winter 1974): 10.

Morris, R. Winston. "New Materials—Euphonium–Tuba." *T.U.B.A. Newsletter* 1, no. 3 (Spring 1974): 6–7.

Morris, R. Winston. "New Materials—Euphonium–Tuba." *T.U.B.A. Newsletter* 2, no. 1 (Fall 1974): 4.

Morris, R. Winston. "New Solos and Studies for Tuba." *The Instrumentalist* 32 (Feb. 1978): 61.

Morris, R. Winston. "Tuba Solos and Studies." *The Instrumentalist* 33 (Jan. 1979): 80.

Morris, R. Winston. "Tuba [recent publications]." *The Instrumentalist* 36 (Dec. 1981): 68–70.

Morris, R. Winston. "New Literature for Tuba." *The Instrumentalist* 38 (Apr. 1984): 48+.

"Music for Tuba." Sounding Brass & the Conductor 8, no. 4 (1979): 153–154.

Payne, Barbara, and Jonathan D. Green. "A Critical Analysis of J. Ed. Barat's *Andante et Allegro*." *T.U.B.A. Journal* 19, no. 2 (Winter 1991): 36–39.

Popiel, P. "The Solo Tuba and Walter Hartley." *The Instrumentalist* 24 (1970): 63–68.

Popiel, Peter. "Tuba Solo Collections: A New Appraisal." *T.U.B.A. Journal* 18, no. 4 (Summer 1991): 42–43.

Pröpper, K. "Von Leidenschaftlicher Struktur: Anspruchsvolles Konzert für Tuba als Soloinstrument." *Neue Musikzeitung* 36 (Oct.–Nov. 1987): 51.

Randolph, David M. "A Tubist's Introduction to the Avant-Garde." *NACWPI Journal* 28, no. 2 (1980–81): 4–11.

Rasmussen, Mary. "Building a Repertoire for the Tuba Student." *The Instrumentalist* 8 (Jan. 1954): 36–37.

Rideout, Jeffrey J. "Annual Report of the T.U.B.A. Resource Library—1980." *T.U.B.A. Journal* 8, no. 4 (Spring 1981): 15–22.

Rideout, Jeffrey. "Resource Library Report." *T.U.B.A. Journal* 9, no. 3 (Winter 1982): 13.

Rideout, Jeffrey. "T.U.B.A. Resource Library August, 1983." *T.U.B.A. Journal* 11, no. 2 (Fall 1983): 44–56.

Ross, Walter. "Multiple Tuba Parts for the Orchestra." *T.U.B.A. Newsletter* 2, no. 1 (Fall 1974): 9.

Rozen, Jay. "The Virgil Thomson Commission." *T.U.B.A. Journal* 13, no. 2 (Nov. 1985): 17.

Schmidt, Paul. "Tuba & Euphonium Pedagogy: Potential Application of Bass Viol Literature." *T.U.B.A. Journal* 18, no. 4 (Summer 1991): 44–47.

Skillen, Joseph. "*Encounters II for Solo Tuba* by William Kraft: A Closer Look at the Compositional Techniques." *T.U.B.A. Journal* 19, no. 4 (Summer 1992): 38–40.

Thrall. R. S. "Reviews: Tuba Review." *Woodwind World–Brass and Percussion* 19, no. 3 (1980): 35.

Thrall, R. S. "Reviews: Tuba Solo." *Woodwind World–Brass and Percussion* 19, no. 4 (1980): 28.

Tilbury, Jack. "Annual Review of Solos and Studies: Tuba." *The Instrumentalist* 39 (Feb. 1985): 79–80+.

Troiano, William. "The New York State School Music Association Contest List for Tuba Solos and Tuba Ensembles." *T.U.B.A. Journal* 14, no. 2 (Nov. 1986): 20–24.

"T.U.B.A. Resource Library: List of Holdings." *T.U.B.A. Journal* 7, no. 2 (Fall 1979): 40–51.

"T.U.B.A. Resource Library Holdings 1980." *T.U.B.A. Journal* 8, no. 4 (Spring 1981): 15–22.

"Tuba." *Brass Bulletin–International Brass Chronicle*, no. 20 (1977): 14–15.

Varner, J. Lesley. "Annual Report of the T.U.B.A. Resource Library." *T.U.B.A. Journal* 6, no. 1 (Fall 1978): 8–16.

Varner, Lesley. "T.U.B.A. Resource Library." *T.U.B.A. Newsletter* 2, no. 3 (Spring 1975): 5.

Vaughan, Rodger. "Fiftieth Birthday Tuba Recital (2–2–82)." *T.U.B.A. Journal* 10, no. 2 (Fall 1982): 13.

Watson, Scott. "Walter Hartley: A Traditional Conservative." *T.U.B.A. Journal* 18, no. 2 (Winter 1990): 28–36.

Orchestration

Bobo, Roger. "Yes or No? Beware! [transcriptions]." *Brass Bulletin–International Brass Chronicle*, no. 21 (1978): 33–35.

Book, Brian. "Views of Berlioz on the Use of the Ophicleide and Tuba in His Orchestral Works." *T.U.B.A. Journal* 10, no. 4 (Spring 1983): 10–19.

Cummings, Barton. "New Techniques for Tuba." *The Composer* 6, no. 15 (1974–1975): 28–32.

McCready, Joan W. "Arranging Christmas Carols for the Tuba Ensemble." *T.U.B.A. Journal* 11, no. 2 (Fall 1983): 2–4.

Shoop, Stephen. "Arranging and Transcribing Music for the Junior High and High School Tuba Ensemble." *T.U.B.A. Journal* 20, no. 2 (Winter 1992): 36–37.

Biography

Aitken, T. "Tuba Britannica: John Fletcher." *Brass Bulletin–International Chronicle*, no. 47 (1984): 19–24.

Baker, William F. "T.U.B.A. Tuba Profile—George Black." *T.U.B.A. Journal* 7, no. 2 (Fall 1979): 2–5.

Beffaa, Chip. "Joe Tarto—Last of the Five Pennies." *Mississippi Rag* (Feb. 1985).

Bevan, Clifford. "Christopher Monk: 1921–1991. The Purest Serpentist." *T.U.B.A. Journal* 20, no. 2 (Winter 1992): 31–32.

Brubeck, David, and John Olah. "Connie's Final Toot!: An Interview with Constance Weldon." *T.U.B.A. Journal* 18, no. 4 (Summer 1991): 28–37.

Davis, Ron. "T.U.B.A. Tuba Profile—Tommy Johnson." *T.U.B.A. Journal* 9, no. 3 (Winter 1982): 2–6.

Dickman, Marcus. "Rich Matteson: Portrait of an Original." *T.U.B.A. Journal* 19, no. 2 (Winter 1991): 46–59.

Frazier, Richard and Elizabeth, eds. "William Rose: A Remarkable Career." *T.U.B.A. Journal* 18, no. 2 (Winter 1990): 50–61.

Gannett, David. "The Young Turk of the Tuba—Ain't Misbehavin'—Dave Zellinger." *West Coast Rag* (Dec./Jan. 1991/92): 18

Gannett, David. "Denna Swoboda: Tuba Goddess." *West Coast Rag* (Aug. 1992): 30

Gannett, David. "Le Jazz de toutes les Occasions! Gary Kiser—Tuba Vocals." *West Coast Rag* (June 1993): 13

Gannett, David. "Chuck Stewart." *West Coast Rag*.

Haugan, Paul W. "T.U.B.A. Tuba Profile—Arnold M. Jacobs, Tubist of the Chicago Symphony Orchestra." *T.U.B.A. Journal* 4, no. 2 (Winter 1977): 2–10.

Hauprich, Donna J. "T.U.B.A. Tuba Profile—Abe Torchinsky." *T.U.B.A. Journal* 6, no. 1 (Fall 1978): 2–5.

Hepola, Ralph. "The Jazz Niche [George S. 'Red' Callender]." *T.U.B.A. Journal* 15, no. 3 (Feb. 1988): 14–16.

Hepola, Ralph. "The Jazz Niche." *T.U.B.A. Journal* 16, no. 3 (Spring 1989): 19–20.

Hester, Steven. "Joe Tarto: Titan of the Tuba." *T.U.B.A. Journal* 15, no. 1 (Aug. 1987): 11–12.

Jones, Philip. "John Fletcher (1941–1987): An Appreciation." *T.U.B.A. Journal* 15, no. 3 (Feb. 1988): 7–9.

Klee, J. H. "Tuba Talk with Howard Johnson." *Down Beat* 39 (Feb. 3, 1972): 16+.

Kleinsteuber, Carl. "An Interview with Howard Johnson." *T.U.B.A. Journal* 11, no. 1 (Summer 1983): 6–11.

Leary, Bob. "Everything you wanted to know about Big Dog (Dave "Big Dog" Gannett)." *West Coast Rag* (Feb. 1993): 9.

Loucas, Paul. "T.U.B.A. Tuba Profile—Joe Tarto." *T.U.B.A. Journal* 5, no. 3 (Spring/Summer 1978): 2–3.

Maldonado, Luis. "Tribute to Abe Torchinsky." *T.U.B.A. Journal* 16, no. 4 (Summer 1989): 16–24.

Martin, J. A. "Gene Pokorny, Climbing New Peaks." *The Instrumentalist* 43 (Apr. 1989): 14–19+.

Mathez, Jean-Pierre. "Interview with John Fletcher." *Brass Bulletin–International Brass Chronicle*, no. 27 (1979): 41–44.

Meckna, Michael. "Roger Bobo and the Tuba Explosion." *T.U.B.A. Journal* 19, no. 4 (Summer 1992): 42–43.

Morris, R. Winston. "T.U.B.A. Tuba Profile—Allan Jaffe and Anthony 'Tuba Fats' Lacen." *T.U.B.A. Journal* 9, no. 2 (Fall 1981): 11–16.

Murrow, Richard. "August Helleberg, Sr. Part I." *T.U.B.A. Journal* 10, no. 1 (Summer 1982): 2–3.

Phillips, Harvey. "Tribute to Friends: Thomas Beversdorf, Edward Sauter and Alec Wilder." *T.U.B.A. Journal* 9, no. 4 (Spring 1982): 19–23.

"Professional Tubists in the Major U.S. Service Bands." *T.U.B.A. Journal* 6, no. 2 (Winter 1979): 18.

"Rex Connor and Friend." *T.U.B.A. Newsletter* 2, no. 1 (Fall 1974): 10.

Richardson, Lee. "T.U.B.A. Tuba Profile—Fred Pfaff." *T.U.B.A. Journal* 11, no. 1 (Summer 1983): 2–5.

Schulman, Michael. "T.U.B.A. Tuba Profile—Charles Daellenbach." *T.U.B.A. Journal* 6, no. 3 (Spring 1979): 2–4.

Solti, Georg, and others. "Who Is Arnold Jacobs?" *T.U.B.A. Journal* 15, no. 4 (May 1988): 30–34.

Stewart, Bob. "The Legitimate Jazz Artist: An Interview with Earl McIntyre." *T.U.B.A. Journal* 12, no. 1 (Aug. 1984): 5–8.

Stewart, Bob. "The Legitimate Jazz Artist—Part II: An Interview with Tony Price." *T.U.B.A. Journal* 12, no. 2 (Nov. 1984): 10–13.

Stewart, M. Dee. "An Arnold Jacobs Biography." *T.U.B.A. Journal* 15, no. 4 (May 1988): 14–17.

Taylor, John M. "Reminiscences of the Man and His Horn." *T.U.B.A. Journal* 9, no. 2 (Fall 1981): 2.

Thompson, Butch, and Charley DeVore. "Keeping the Faith—Allan Jaffe 1935–1987." *Mississippi Rag* (Apr. 1987).

"T.U.B.A. Tuba Profile—Ionel Dumitru." *T.U.B.A. Journal* 6, no. 2 (Winter 1979): 2–3.

"T.U.B.A. Tuba Profile—Ronald T. Bishop." *T.U.B.A. Journal* 7, no. 3 (Winter 1980): 2–4.

Wald, A. H. "Sumner Erickson, Tuba Prodigy." *The Instrumentalist* 37 (May 1983): 36+.

Whitfield, Edward J. "Remembrances and Recollections of Arnold M. Jacobs." *T.U.B.A. Journal* 12, no. 4 (May 1985): 7.

Wick, Denis. "John Fletcher: Some Reminiscences." *T.U.B.A. Journal* 15, no. 3 (Feb. 1988): 8–9.

Wilson, George C. "Harvey Phillips and Rex Conner—A Perspective from Their Teacher." *T.U.B.A. Journal* 15, no. 3 (Feb. 1988): 25.

Pedagogy

Anders, Volta Andy. "Ask the Experts: Embouchure." *T.U.B.A. Journal* 15, no. 4 (May 1988): 40.

Anderson, Eugene. "Fourteen Ways to Improve Intonation on Tuba and Euphonium." *T.U.B.A. Newsletter* 2, no. 2 (Winter 1974): 1.

Beauregard, Cherry. "Learning to Play Lip Slurs." *T.U.B.A. Journal* 7, no. 2 (Fall 1979): 6.

Beauregard, Cherry. "Clarity in Tuba Playing." *T.U.B.A. Journal* 7, no. 4 (Spring 1980): 2–3.

Beauregard, Cherry. "Trills." *T.U.B.A. Journal* 7, no. 3 (Winter 1980): 7–8.

Beauregard, Cherry. "Psychology in Pedagogy." *T.U.B.A. Journal* 9, no. 3 (Winter 1982): 18.

Beauregard, Cherry. "Diversity of Sound and Adaptability." *T.U.B.A. Journal* 9, no. 4 (Spring 1982): 9–10.

Bell, William. "The Tuba Triumphs!" *The International Musician* 58 (Sept. 1959): 16+.

Bishop, Ronald T. "Fundamentals of Tuba Playing." *T.U.B.A. Journal* 5, no. 2 (Winter 1978): 9–11.

Brandon, Dr. Sy. "Transferring Students to Tuba." *T.U.B.A. Journal* 17, no. 3 (Spring 1990): 16.

Brandon, S. P. "Improving the Low Register of the Tuba." *Woodwind World–Brass and Percussion* 15, no. 2 (1976): 50–51.

Brandon, S. P. "Tackling the Tuba." *Woodwind World–Brass and Percussion* 16, no. 1 (1977): 34–35.

Brandon, S. P. "Correcting Faulty Tuba Intonation." *Woodwind World–Brass and Percussion* 17, no. 3 (1978): 28–29+.

Brandon, S. P. "Improving the Band's Tuba Section." *The Instrumentalist* 39 (Dec. 1984): 55–60.

Brewer, Dr. Robert. "Tuba Pedagogy: Preparing New Etudes." *T.U.B.A. Journal* 19, no. 3 (Spring 1992): 42–43.

Brubeck, David W. "The Pedagogy of Arnold Jacobs." *T.U.B.A. Journal* 19, no. 1 (Fall 1991): 54–58.

Clements, T. "Why Buy a Tuba With Four (or Five) Valves?" *Woodwind World–Brass and Percussion* 23, no. 1 (1984): 20.

Conner, Rex A. "Employing the Tuba as a Solo Instrument." *The Instrumentalist* 8 (Feb. 1954): 26–27+.

Conner, Rex A. "The Tongue and the Tuba." *The Instrumentalist* 12 (May 1958): 55–57.

Conner, Rex A. "Tuba Talk." *The Instrumentalist* 16 (Oct. 1961): 49–50.

Conner, Rex A. "Discussing the Tuba." *The Instrumentalist* 19 (Dec. 1964): 80–83.

Conner, Rex A. "Fingering the Four and Five Valve Tubas." *The Instrumentalist* 24 (Apr. 1970): 59–62.

Conner, Rex. "Tuba Diphthongs." *T.U.B.A. Journal* 4, no. 3 (Spring/Summer 1977): 11.

Conner, Rex. "Fingering Tricks That Work." *T.U.B.A. Journal* 6, No. 3 (Spring 1979): 10–11.

Culbertson, Mel. "Mel Culbertson: On the Tuba in the Brass Quintet." *Brass Bulletin–International Brass Chronicle* no. 63 (1988): 28–29+.

Cummings, Barton. "A Brief Summary of New Techniques for Tuba." *Numus-West*, no. 5 (1974): 62–63.

Cummings, Barton. "Multiphonics and the Tuba." *T.U.B.A. Newsletter* 3, no. 3 (Spring/Summer 1976): 1–3.

Cummings, Barton. "Tuba Technique." *Woodwind World–Brass and Percussion* 22, no. 8 (1983); 8–11+.

Cummings, Barton. "The Tuba." *Woodwind World–Brass and Percussion* 24, no. 4 (1985): 22.

Edney, J. "Beginners' Page." *Sounding Brass & the Conductor* 4, no. 2 (1975): 64.

Engels, Hieronymus. "Tuba Pedagogy in Germany." *T.U.B.A. Journal* 4, no. 1 (Fall 1976): 5–7.

Fitzgerald, Bernard. "The Tuba—Foundation of the Band." *The Instrumentalist* 7 (Mar.–Apr. 1953): 40–41+.

Fletcher, John. "My Way [warm-up routine]." *Sounding Brass & the Conductor* 4, no. 1 (1975): 10–11.

Fritze, Gregory. "The Play-Along Method of Learning Jazz Improvisation." *T.U.B.A. Journal* 19, no. 1 (Fall 1991): 48–50.

Funderburk, Jeffrey L. "Proper Breath." *T.U.B.A. Journal* 14, no. 2 (Nov. 1986): 17.

Funderburk, Jeffrey L. "Audition Strategy." *T.U.B.A. Journal* 18, no. 3 (Spring 1991): 52.

Gray, Skip. "Organizing Your Practice: Structuring a System for Improvement." *T.U.B.A. Journal* 16, no. 2 (Winter 1988): 40–42.

Gray, Skip. "Problem Solving for Low Brass Students." *The Instrumentalist* 42 (Apr. 1988): 46+.

Gray, Skip. "Getting Ready for Advanced Study—Setting a Course for Success." *The Instrumentalist* 43 (Dec. 1988): 29+.

Harstine, E. L. "Are You Satisfied with the Bass Section in Your Band?" *The School Musician* 31 (Feb. 1960): 35+.

Heath, Fred. "Coping with Problems in Transferring to Low Brass from Trumpet." *T.U.B.A. Journal* 7, no. 2 (Fall 1979): 16–17.

Hepola, Ralph. "Roger Bobo Talks Tuba." *The Instrumentalist* 32 (Nov. 1977): 60–65.

Hepola, Ralph. "The Jazz Niche." *T.U.B.A. Journal* 15, no. 2 (Nov. 1987): 13, 22.

Hovey, H. "Low Sounds at an Early Age; or, How Do You Get the Young Students to Play Tuba." *Brass and Percussion* 2, no. 3 (1974): 13+.

Johnson, C. E. "Use That Fourth Valve." *The Instrumentalist* 14 (Apr. 1960): 56–58.

Kaenzig, Fritz. "Tuba Pedagogy: The Brief Practice Session." *T.U.B.A. Journal* 11, no. 4 (Spring 1984): 11–12.

Kaenzig, Fritz A. "Tuba Pedagogy: Building a Successful Low Register." *T.U.B.A. Journal* 13, no. 1 (Aug. 1985): 23–24.

Kaenzig, Fritz. "Improving Tone in the High Register." *T.U.B.A. Journal* 13, no. 2 (Nov. 1985): 20–21.

Kuehn, David L. "Helpful Hints for Tuba Players." The Instru*mentalist* 16, no. 9 (May 1962): 70–71.

Kuehn, David L. "Toward Better Tuba Players." *The Instrumentalist* 21 (Sept. 1966): 66–69.

Lhuillier, Alain. "A Newsletter from France." *T.U.B.A. Journal* 10, no. 1 (Summer 1982): 15–16.

Litman, Ross. "The Alaskan Tubist." *T.U.B.A. Journal* 7, no. 4 (Spring 1980): 4–5.

Little, Don. "An Arnold Jacobs Clinic." *T.U.B.A. Journal* 15, no. 4 (May 1988): 21–26.

Little, Donald C. "A Young Tubist's Guide to the Breath." *T.U.B.A. Journal* 8, no. 3 (Winter 1981): 2–7.

Maldonado, Luis. "Breathing Properly." *T.U.B.A. Journal* 16, no. 2 (Winter 1988): 24.

Maldonado, Luis. "Checking Up on Your Intonation: Part One." *T.U.B.A. Journal* 15, no. 3 (Feb. 1988): 31.

Maldonado, Luis. "Checking Up on Your Intonation: Part Two." *T.U.B.A. Journal* 15, no. 4 (May 1988): 39.

Maldonado, Luis. "Nervousness: What It Does and What We Can Do About It." *T.U.B.A. Journal* 13, no. 4 (May 1986): 39.

Maldonado, Luis. "Long Tones, Lip Slurs, and Scales—Do We Really Need Them?" *T.U.B.A. Journal* 14, no. 2 (Nov. 1986): 35.

Maldonado, Luis. "Response Problems. What Can I Do?" *T.U.B.A. Journal* 15, no. 1 (Aug. 1987): 18.

Maldonado, Luis. "Selecting and Developing Young Students." *T.U.B.A. Journal* 17, no. 2 (Winter 1989): 14–15.

Mazzaferro, T. "Master Classes: Tuba." *Accent* 7, no. 1 (1981): 25–27.

McAdams, Charles. "Let It Happen." *T.U.B.A. Journal* 12, no. 4 (May 1985): 9.

McAdams, Charles. "Performance Attitude: A Psychological Approach." *T.U.B.A. Journal* 13, no. 3 (Feb. 1986): 17–18.

McAdams, Charles. "Assessment of Select Instrumental Music Teachers' Knowledge of the Tuba." *Missouri Journal of Research in Music Education* no. 26 (1989): 92–108.

McAdams, Charles A. "What Do Instrumental Music Teachers 'Really' Need to Know About the Tuba?" *NACWPI Journal* 39, no. 1 (1990): 21–23+.

Megules, K. I. "The High School Tuba Ensemble." *Woodwind World–Brass and Percussion* 15, no. 5 (1976): 32–33+.

Meyer, G. C. "The Tuba Section." *The Instrumentalist* 15 (Dec. 1960): 57–59.

Moore, A. G. "Playing the Serpent." *Early Music* 3, no. 1 (1975): 21–24.

Morris, R. Winston. "Tuba Recordings Might Make the Difference." *The Instrumentalist* 25 (Feb. 1971): 45–46.

Morris, R. Winston. "A Tuba Clinic with Harvey Phillips." *The Instrumentalist* 29 (Jan. 1975): 51–55.

Nelson, Mark A. "Developing the Beginning Tuba/Euphonium Ensemble." *T.U.B.A. Journal* 9, no. 3 (Winter 1982): 14–16.

Nutaitis, Raymond. "Daily Routine—Do I Need It?" *T.U.B.A. Journal* 8, no. 4 (Spring 1981): 2–3.

Perantoni, Daniel. "Tuba Talk: Performance Tips." *The Instrumentalist* 38 (Jan. 1984): 40+.

Peruzzini, Andrew. "Auditioning as a Hobby, An Opinion." *T.U.B.A. Journal* 9, no.1 (Summer 1980): 2.

Pfaff, Fred E. "Nobody Knows the Tuba." *Metronome* 48 (Apr. 1932): 23–24.

Pfaff, Fred E. "Nobody Knows the Tuba." *T.U.B.A. Journal* 10, no. 3 (Winter 1983): 2–5.

Pitts, L. P. "Using the First Valve Slide to Adjust Tuba Intonation." *The Instrumentalist* 29 (Apr. 1975): 52.

Pokorny, Gene. "The Tuba and Brass Pedagogy in Israel." *T.U.B.A. Journal* 8, no. 2 (Fall 1980): 11–14.

Popiel, P. "The Tuba: Concepts in Low–Register Tone Production." *The Instrumentalist* 33 (Jan. 1979): 44+.

Popiel, P. J. "The Tuba and Transposition." *The School Musician* 38 (Aug.–Sept. 1966): 88–89.

Popiel, Peter. "A Direct Approach to Legato on the Low Brass Instruments." *T.U.B.A. Journal* 10, no. 3 (Winter 1983): 8–10.

"Potpourri." *The Instrumentalist* 23 (Nov. 1968): 10.

Pröpper, K. "Tuba–Kurs in Tirol." *Das Orchester* 35 (Oct. 1987): 1064.

Randolph, David M. "Toward Effective Performance of Multiphonics." *T.U.B.A. Journal* 8, no. 2 (Fall 1980): 2–4.

Randolph, David. "The Use of the F-Tuba in the College Teaching Studio." *T.U.B.A. Journal* 16, no. 3 (Spring 1989): 36–39.

Randolph, David. "The Use of the F-Tuba in the College Teaching Studio: Part II—Pedagogy." *T.U.B.A. Journal* 16, no. 4 (Summer 1989): 25–27, 35.

Reed, David F. "Primer on the Breathing Process." *T.U.B.A. Journal* 9, no. 1 (Summer 1981): 8–10.

Richardson, Jack. "The Double B-flat Bass." *T.U.B.A. Journal* 14, no. 4 (May 1987): 24–25.

Roberts, Chester. "Coping with the 'Extension Register'." *T.U.B.A. Newsletter* 1, no. 2 (Winter 1974): 1–2.

Roberts, Chester. "Some Marginal Notes on the F-Tuba." *T.U.B.A. Journal* 18, no. 4 (Summer 1991): 78–79.

Saverino, L. "Breathe into Your Tuba." *The School Musician* 23 (Feb. 1952): 12+.

Siener, M. "Thoughts about the Tuba." *The School Musician* 38 (Feb. 1967): 44–46+.

Siener, M. "Tuba Notes." *The School Musician* 41 (Feb. 1970): 8+.

Sinder, Phillip. "Thoughts on Tuba Vibrato." *T.U.B.A. Journal* 10, no. 2 (Fall 1982): 15–16.

Smith, Claude B. "1936 Bill Bell Interview." *T.U.B.A. Newsletter* 1, no. 3 (Spring 1974): 9.

Smith, Glenn P. "Tuba Forum." *Southwestern Brass Journal* (Fall 1957): 44–47.

Stancil, D. D. "Use of a Spectral Model in Developing Concepts of Tuba Timbre." *Brass Bulletin–International Brass Chronicle*, no. 19 (1977): 33+.

Stanley, D. "Teaching Concepts for Tuba." *The Instrumentalist* 21 (Feb. 1967): 66–69.

Stanley, D. "Legato Technique for Tuba." *The Instrumentalist* 24 (Dec. 1969): 59–61.

Stevens, John. "Practice for Performance." *T.U.B.A. Journal* 10, no. 1 (Summer 1982): 8–9.

Stevens, John. "Don't Neglect Alternate Fingerings." *T.U.B.A. Journal* 15, no. 1 (Aug. 1987): 17.

"The Truth About the Tones the Tuba Can't Toot." *Jacobs' Band Monthly* 10 (Dec. 1925): 16–17.

"Tuba Player Hits Wrong Note for Mom." *T.U.B.A. Newsletter* 1, no. 2 (Winter 1974): 5.

"Tuba Talent." *The Instrumentalist* 30 (Dec. 1975): 103.

"Two Tons of Tubas." *T.U.B.A. Newsletter* 1, no. 2 (Winter 1974): 5.

Vesely, Stanley J., Jr. "Tuba Forum." *Southwestern Brass Journal* 1 (Spring 1957): 33–36.

Watson, Scott. "Three Exercises for Correct Air Flow on the Tuba-Euphonium." *T.U.B.A. Journal* 10, no. 2 (Fall 1982): 8–9.

Whitehead, K. "Bob Stewart Interview." *Cadence, The Review of Jazz & Blues* 16 (Oct. 1990): 9–15.

Wick, S. "My Way." *Sounding Brass & The Conductor* 9, no. 1 (1980): 27.

Yeo, Douglas. "Everything You Always Wanted to Know about Tuba Auditions, but Didn't Know Who to Ask." *T.U.B.A. Journal* 11, no. 3 (Winter, 1984): 2–6.

Zonn, Paul. "Red Wiggler." *T.U.B.A. Newsletter* 2, no. 1 (Fall 1974): 3

Equipment

Altenburg, Wilhelm. "Die Neue Riesenbass (Subkontrabass-Tuba) der Firma Bohland & Fuchs in Graslitz." *Zeitschrift für Instrumentenbau* 32 (1911/12): 1285–1288.

Apperson, Ron. "Mutes or 'What Are We Putting Down Our Bells?'" *T.U.B.A. Journal* 6, no. 3 (Spring 1979): 12–13.

Apperson, Ron. "Ask the Experts: Tuba Mutes." *T.U.B.A. Journal* 16, no. 2 (Winter 1988): 39.

"BBBBBB Flat Tuba." *T.U.B.A. Newsletter* 1, no. 2 (Winter 1974): 6.

"Big Sound [World's Largest Tuba]." *The Instrumentalist* 28 (Nov. 1973): 35.

Bingham, S. "The Double C Versus the Double B-Flat Tuba: An Investigation of Tonal Differences." *Journal of Band Research* 15, no. 2 (1980): 45–49.

Bobo, Roger. "The Tuba Player Versus the Limitations of the Tuba." *T.U.B.A. Newsletter* 2, no. 3 (Spring 1975): 1.

Bobo, Roger. "And Approach the Realm of Making Beautiful Music." *Brass Bulletin–International Brass Chronicle*, no. 18 (1977): 27+.

Brandon, S. P. "The Tuba Mute." Woodwind *World–Brass and Percussion* 20, no. 7 (1981): 20–21.

Brüchle, Bernhard. "Zu mindest nach höhere." *Brass Bulletin–International Brass Chronicle*, no. 7 (1974): 112–113.

Brüchle, Bernhard. "Eine Tuba der Superlative, von Historischer Bedeutung...." *Brass Bulletin–International Brass Chronicle*, no. 9 (1974): 41–43.

"C. G. Conn Offers 15J 'Concertable' Tuba." *The Music Trades* 128 (June 1980): 86.

Capper, William. "Mutes—Fabricate Your Own." *T.U.B.A. Journal* 7, no. 3 (Winter 1980): 26–27.

Chieffi, Brady. "Curios and Collectables." *T.U.B.A. Journal* 11, no. 3 (Winter 1984): 23.

Conner, Rex A. "How to Care for a Rotary-Valved Tuba." *The Instrumentalist* 26 (Nov. 1971): 40+.

Conner, Rex. "Valve Clatter: Its Prevention and Cure." *T.U.B.A. Newsletter* 2, no. 3 (Spring 1975): 3.

Coss, B. "Tuba; Horn With Problems." *Down Beat* 29 (Feb. 1, 1962): 14.

Cummings, Barton. "You Need Four Valves." *Woodwind World–Brass and Percussion* 16, no. 2 (1977): 36–37.

Cummings, Barton. "Choosing a Tuba Mouthpiece." *Woodwind World–Brass and Percussion* 17, no. 2 (1978): 24.

Cummings, Barton. "The Future of the E-flat Tuba." *Woodwind World–Brass and Percussion* 18, no. 2 (1979): 38–39.

Cummings, Barton. "Further Thoughts on the Tuba in F." *Woodwind World–Brass and Percussion* 22, no. 5 (1983): 8–9.

Cummings, Barton. "Tuba Technique." *Woodwind World–Brass and Percussion* 22, no. 7 (1983): 8–9.

Cummings, Barton. "The Tuba and/or Sousaphone." *Woodwind World–Brass and Percussion* 23, no. 2 (1984): 13–15.

Cummings, Barton. "The E-Flat Tuba Revisited." *Woodwind World–Brass and Percussion* 23, no. 8 (1984): 21–22.

Cummings, Barton. "What Tuba is Best BB♭, CC, E♭ or F?" *The School Musician* 57 (Oct. 1985): 26–27.

Cummings, Barton. "Why the Fourth and Fifth Valves?" *Woodwind World–Brass and Percussion* 24, no. 3 (1985): 17–19.

"Czechs Display World's Largest Tuba—8 ft. High, 176 lbs." *Music Trades* 126 (Jan. 1978): 94.

DeVore, Ronald. "Repair Clinic: Reducing the Weight of the Rotor." *T.U.B.A. Newsletter* 3, no. 1 (Fall 1975): 24.

Flor, G. J. "Brass Workshop: Sousaphone or Convertible Tuba?" *The School Musician* 57 (Aug.–Sept. 1985): 22–23+.

Freeman, E. L. "The C Tuba? Si, Si!" *Woodwind World–Brass and Percussion* 19, no. 3 (1980): 24.

"Getzen Unveils 1/4-size Meinl BBb Tuba." *The Music Trades* 133 (Oct. 1985): 79.

Hammond, Ivan. "A Choice of One or Two or Both." *T.U.B.A. Newsletter* 1, no. 3 (Spring 1974): 1.

Hensel, Otto. "Die Basstuba in F mit 6 Ventilen." *Deutsche Musiker-Zeitung* 63 (1932): 285.

"Here's a Giant among Tubas." *The School Musician* 49 (Apr. 1978): 45.

Hirsbrunner, P. "Die Geschichte der Grossen York-Hirsbrunner Tuba aus der Sicht des Instrumentenbauers." *Brass Bulletin–International Brass Chronicle*, no. 40 (1982): 34–39.

Hovey, Arthur. "The Logic of the Tuba Valve System." *T.U.B.A. Journal* 8, no. 1 (Summer 1980): 18–25.

Keathley, Sandy. "Everyman's Guide to the Tuba Mouthpiece." *T.U.B.A. Journal* 5, no. 3 (Spring/Summer 1978): 10–11.

Krush, Jay. "Wingbolt Double-Bell Eight-Valve CC–BB Natural Deluxe Supertuba." *T.U.B.A. Newsletter* 2, no. 1 (Fall 1974): 8.

Kuehn, David L. "Care and Maintenance of the Tuba." *The School Musician* 40 (Apr. 1969): 72–73.

McCready, Matthew A. "Compensating Systems: A Mathematical Comparison." *T.U.B.A. Journal* 12, no. 3 (Feb. 1985): 11–13.

Meinl, Gerhard A. "The Tenor Tuba: Richard Strauss' Orchestration and the Revival of an Instrument." *T.U.B.A. Journal* 17, no. 4 (Summer 1990): 9–10.

"Mirafone Introduces Convertible Tuba." *Music Trades* 134 (May 1986): 116.

"Mobile Serpenphone Becomes Serpentine Pedalphone." *T.U.B.A. Newsletter* 2, no. 1 (Fall 1974): 9.

Pallansch, Robert. "Tuba Design—Improvements Are Needed." *The Instrumentalist* 27 (Feb. 1973): 31–32.

Pallansch, Robert. "Structural and Human-Engineering Factors in the Design and Manufacture of Conical-Bore Contrabass Cup-Mouthpiece Valve Instruments or The Tuba as She is Built." *T.U.B.A. Newsletter* 2, no. 1 (Fall 1974): 1.

Pallansch, Robert. "Venting of Tuba Valves." *T.U.B.A. Newsletter* 1, no. 2 (Winter 1974): 4.

Perantoni, Daniel. "Tuba Talk: Technical Information." *The Instrumentalist* 38 (Nov. 1983): 58+.

Randolph, David. "The Use of the F-Tuba in the College Teaching Studio: Part III—Equipment." *T.U.B.A. Journal* 17, no. 1 (Fall 1989): 18–20, 33.

Reynolds, G. E. "Tubas, Recording Basses and Sousaphones." *The School Musician* 33, no. 7 (Mar. 1962): 22+.

Roberts, Chester. "Tenor, Bass and Contrabass Tubas—Comparisons and Contrasts." *T.U.B.A. Newsletter* 1, no. 3 (Spring 1974): 3–4.

Roberts, F. Chester. "Some Otherwise Logic on Tuba Valve Systems." *T.U.B.A. Journal* 10, no. 1 (Summer 1982): 6–7.

Roberts, W. "New Addition to Brass: Soprano Tuba." *Music Journal* 22 (May 1964): 36+.

Rose, W. H. "The Birth of a New Mouthpiece." *The Instrumentalist* 26 (Jan. 1972): 69–70.

"Sam Pilafian Plays on World's Biggest Playable Tuba." *Brass Bulletin–International Brass Chronicle*, no. 5–6 (1973): 106–107.

Schooley, J. "Convertible Brasses, Sousaphones, or Tubas: Which to Choose." *Woodwind World–Brass and Percussion* 24, no. 1 (1985): 12–13.

"Schreiber Tuba." *T.U.B.A. Newsletter* 2, no. 3 (Spring 1975): 7.

Sellers, R. A. "Bell-Up or Bell-Front Tubas?" *The Instrumentalist* 28 (Feb. 1974): 32–33.

"Soprano Tuba." *Brass Bulletin–International Brass Chronicle*, no. 45 (1984): 6 News Suppl.

Stevens, John. "Modifying and Converting Tubas: An Interview with Robert Rusk." *T.U.B.A. Journal* 18, no. 3 (Spring 1991): 56–58.

"Stimmung und das Vierte Ventil." *Musik International-Instrumentenbau-Zeitschrift* 38 (Dec. 1984): 821.

Swain, J. J. "Basic Maintenance for the Rotary Valve Tuba." *The Instrumentalist* 41 (July 1987): 34+.

"A Tuba and Then Some." *T.U.B.A. Newsletter* 1, no. 2 (Winter 1974): 6.

Tucci, Robert. "The B&S Perantucci Model F Tuba." *T.U.B.A. Journal* 14, no. 4 (May 1987): 12, 30.

Tucci, Robert. "A Closer Look at the Hirsbrunner York Model CC-Tuba." *T.U.B.A. Journal* 17, no. 1 (Fall 1989): 34–37.

Weller, R. Otto. "Die Basstuba in F mit 6 Ventilen." *Deutsche Musiker-Zietung* 63 (1932): 832–833.

"Wenzel Meinl: Gebrauchsmusterschutz für Tuba-Modell Triebener." *Musik International-Instrumentenbau-Zeitschrift* 40 (Aug. 1986): 514.

Young, Dr. Frederick J. "A Complete Full Double Tuba." *T.U.B.A. Journal* 17, no. 4 (Summer 1990): 14–17.

Young, F. J. "The Full Double Tuba." *The Instrumentalist* 45 (Nov. 1990): 40+.

Young, Frederick J. "A New Sound for the Tuba." *The School Musician* 29 (Apr. 1958): 16–18+.

Miscellaneous

"Conn and Phillips Remake Calendar with 'Octubafest.'" *The Music Trades* 127 (Jan. 1979): 110.

"N.T.S.U.T.U.B.A." *T.U.B.A. Newsletter* 1, no. 2 (Winter 1974): 12.

"Octubafests 1975." *T.U.B.A. Newsletter* 3, no. 2 (Winter 1976): 4–5.

"T.U.B.A. at Mid-West Band and Orchestra Convention." *T.U.B.A. Newsletter* 2, no. 1 (Fall 1974): 2.

"Tuba ist in: Bericht Über das Tuba-Symposium in der Bundesakademie Trossingen." *Das Orchester* 27 (Sept. 1979): 661–662.

"Tuba Tuba in Walla Walla." *T.U.B.A. Newsletter* 1, no. 2 (Winter 1974): 12.

"Tubas Galore." *Brass Bulletin–International Brass Chronicle*, no. 25 (News Suppl. 1985): 6.

Bobo, Roger. "Tuba: A Word of Many Meanings." *The Instrumentalist* 15 (Apr. 1961): 65–67.

Bobo, Roger. "To The 94." *T.U.B.A. Journal* 6, no. 3 (Spring 1979): 8.

Bobo, Roger. "Tuba Humor." *T.U.B.A. Journal* 7, no. 2 (Fall 1979): 34.

Bowers, R.E. "Summer Heat and the Tuba—Reply to G. Fry." *Saturday Review of Literature* 24 (Aug. 9, 1941): 9.

Chieffi, Brady. "Infectious Tubitis: Is There a Cure?" *T.U.B.A. Journal* 10, no. 3 (Winter 1983): 13–14.

Cross, Steven B. "Practical Program to Make Your Next Octubafest a Complete Success." *T.U.B.A. Journal* 10, no. 4 (Spring 1983): 28–29.

Day, Joel. "International Tuba Day." *T.U.B.A. Journal* 11, no. 1 (Summer 1983): 14–15.

Dutton, Brent. "Interchanges: Interview with John Stevens." *T.U.B.A. Journal* 8, no. 4 (Spring 1981): 10–12.

Gannett, David. "Black Dog Gannetts' Tennessee Tryst. (An Adventure with some Old Southern Characters and a Naked Lady Tuba.)" *West Coast Rag* (May 1992): 1

Gannett, David. "The Old Tuba Roadhog." *West Coast Rag* (March 1992): 16

Gelfand, M. H. "Tuba Players Decide Now Is Time to Blow Their Own Horns." *The Wall Street Journal* 181 (May 23, 1973): 1+.

Heinkel-Wolfe, Peggy. "Marketing Your Ensemble for the Holidays." *T.U.B.A. Journal* 19, no. 1 (Fall 1991): 64–65.

Hepola, Ralph. "The Jazz Niche—'Roots.'" *T.U.B.A. Journal* 15, no. 1 (Aug. 1987): 19, 25.

Hoggard, Earle. "Viewpoint [Rex Conner]." *T.U.B.A. Journal* 19, no. 1 (Fall 1991): 88–90.

Keller, R. "Touting the Tuba." *The Instrumentalist* 45 (Aug. 1990): 38.

Kuehn, David L. "Tuba Symposium-Workshops." *T.U.-B.A. Newsletter* 3, no. 3 (Spring/Summer 1976): 8.

Maldonado, Luis. "Contests, Foundations and Awards for Tuba and Euphonium." *T.U.B.A. Journal* 18, no. 2 (Winter 1990): 24–27.

Mathez, J. P. "Le Tuba en Allemagne: Rencontre avec Dietrich Unkrodt." *Brass Bulletin–International Brass Chronicle* no. 71 (1990): 34–35+.

McAdams, Charles A. "Regional Chapters: Listing and Information." *T.U.B.A. Journal* 15, no. 2 (Nov. 1987): 34–35.

McAdams, Charles A. "Do Local Chapters Have a Place in T.U.B.A.?" *T.U.B.A. Journal* 18, no. 3 (Spring 1991): 54–55.

Morris, R. Winston. "'Harvey Phillips Day.'" *T.U.B.A. Journal* 4, no. 1 (Fall 1976): 16.

Pallansch, Robert. "How to Spot a Ponkt (Potentially Outstanding Natural Killer of Tubas)." *T.U.B.A. Journal* 8, no. 1 (Summer 1980): 15.

Passy, C. "Tuba Talk: The Trials and Tribulations of the Loneliest Brass." *Symphony* 41, no. 5 (1990): 26–29.

Phillips, Harvey, and Bill Lake. "Octubafest." *T.U.B.A. Newsletter* 1, no. 2 (Winter 1974): 12.

Pokorny, Gene. "Will the Gentleman in the Back Row Please Speak Up." *T.U.B.A. Journal* 17, no. 2 (Winter 1989): 17–23.

Poore, Melvin. "One Man's Perspective of the Tuba in Europe." *T.U.B.A. Journal* 11, no. 3 (Winter 1984): 40–42.

Rowe, Barton A., and Jerry A. Young. "The Tubist and the Banker, or You Want a Loan for WHAT?!!" *T.U.B.A. Journal* 10, no. 2 (Fall 1982): 2–3.

Shoop, Stephen. "Tax Deductions Available to Tuba and Euphonium Players and Teachers." *T.U.B.A. Journal* 13, no. 3 (Feb. 1986): 19.

Siener, M. "Why Not Be a Professional Tubaist?" *The School Musician* 40 (Feb. 1969): 12+.

Stanley, Donald. "The Regional Symposium: Where It All Begins." *T.U.B.A. Journal* 14, no. 3 (Feb. 1987): 18–19.

Troiano, William. "Tubafest in the Public Schools." *T.U.B.A. Journal* 16, no. 1 (Fall 1988): 59–60.

Weber, Carlyle. "Roster of U.S. Army Band Personnel." *T.U.B.A. Journal* 19, no. 2 (Winter 1991): 66–68.

Winteregg, Steven. "Across China with a Tuba." *T.U.B.A. Journal* 20, no. 1 (Fall 1992): 42–43.

Yeo, Douglas. "International Listing of Symphony, Opera and Ballet Orchestra Low Brass Personnel." *ITA Journal* 19, no. 1 (1991): 34–39.

Young, Jerry. "Duties of Low Brass Instructors." *T.U.B.A. Journal* 9, no. 4 (Spring 1982): 13–16.

Reference Works

Michael A. Fischer

Most of the books in this section mention the tuba only in a few sentences, while those listed above under "Books" refer to it throughout their length. The acknowledgments and gratitude expressed there are applicable to this section also.

Abbreviations: N.p. = no place, n.p. = no publisher, n.d. = no date.

Acoustics

Anfilov, Gleb. *Physics and Music.* Translated by Boris Kuznetsov. Moscow, USSR: Mir Publishers, 1966.

Askill, John. *Physics of Musical Sounds.* New York: D. Van Nostrand Company, n.d.

Backus, John. *The Acoustical Foundations of Music.* New York: W. W. Norton & Company, Inc., 1969.

Bahnert, Heinz; Theodore Herzberg; and Herbert Schramm. *Metallblasinstrumente.* Wilhelmshaven, Germany: Heinrichshofen, 1986.

Bartholomew, Wilmer T. *Acoustics of Music.* Englewood Cliffs, New Jersey: Prentice Hall, Inc., 1942.

Benade, Arthur H. *Horns, Strings, and Harmony.* Westport, Connecticut: Greenwood Press, 1960.

Briggs, Gilbert Arthur. *Musical Instruments and Audio.* Yorkshire, England: Wharfedale Wireless Works Limited, 1965.

Clappé, Arthur A. *The Wind-Band and Its Instruments: Their History, Construction, Acoustics, Technique, and Combination.* 1911. Reprint, Portland, Maine: Longwood, 1976.

Culver, Charles A. *Musical Acoustics.* 3rd ed. New York: The Blakiston Company, 1951.

Eickmann, Paul E., and Nancy L. Hamilton. *Basic Acoustics for Beginning Brass.* Syracuse, New York: Center for Instructional Development, Syracuse University, 1976.

Hamilton, Clarence G. *Sound and Its Relation to Music.* Philadelphia, Pennsylvania: Oliver Ditson Company, 1912.

Holcomb, Bruce. *Die Verbesserung der Stimmung an Ventilblasinstrumenten.* N.p.: Musikverlag Emil Katzbichler, 1981.

Kent, Earle L., ed. *Musical Acoustics.* Vol. 9. Benchmark Papers in Acoustics. Stroudsburg, Pennsylvania: Dowden, Hutchinson & Ross, Inc., 1977.

Levarie, Siegmund, and Ernst Levy. *Tone: A Study in Musical Acoustics.* Kent, Ohio: The Kent State University Press, 1968.

Lowery, Harry. *A Guide to Musical Acoustics.* New York: Dover Publications, Inc., 1966.

Mahillon, Victor Charles. *Elements d'accoustique.* Brussels, Belgium: Les Amies de la Musique, 1984.

Matzke, Hermann. *Unser Technisches Wissen von der Musik.* Lindau am Bodensee, Germany: Frisch und Preneder, 1949.

Meyer, Jürgen. *Akustik und Musikalische Aufführungspraxis.* Frankfurt am Main, Germany: Verlag Das Musikinstrument, 1972.

———. *Acoustics and the Performance of Music.* Translated by John Bowsher and Sibylle Westphal. Frankfurt am Main, Germany: Verlag Das Musikinstrument, 1978.

Olson, Harry F. *Music, Physics and Engineering.* 2nd ed. New York: Dover Publications, Inc., 1967.

Pierce, John R. *The Science of Musical Sound.* New York: Scientific American Library, 1983.

Rigden, John S. *Physics and the Sound of Music.* 2nd ed. New York: John Wiley & Sons, Inc., 1985.

Roederer, Juan G. *Introduction to the Physics and Psychophysics of Music.* Vol. 16. Heidelberg Science Library. New York: Springer-Verlag, 1973.

Schramm, Herbert. *Mein Metallblasinstrument.* Frankfurt am Main, Germany: Verlag Das Musikinstrument, 1981.

Scientific American. *The Physics of Music.* San Francisco, California: W. H. Freeman and Company, 1978.

Vogel, Martin. *Die Intonation der Blechbläser.* N.p.: Gesellschaft zur Förderung der Systematischen Musikwissenschaft, 1961.

Zahm, John Augustine. *Sound and Music.* 2nd ed. Chicago, Illinois: A. C. McClurg & Co., 1900.

Bibliography

Anderson, Paul G., and Larry Bruce Campbell. *Brass Music Guide: Solo and Study Material in Print.* 1985 ed. Vol. 4. Music Guide Series. Northfield, Illinois: Instrumentalist Co., 1984.

Anderson, Paul G., and Lisa Ormston Bontrager. *Brass Music Guide: Ensemble Music in Print.* Vol. 5. Music Guide Series. Northfield, Illinois: The Instrumentalist Company, 1987.

Bollinger, Donald E. *Band Director's Complete Handbook.* West Nyack, New York: Parker Publishing Company, Inc., 1979.

Brüchle, Bernhard. *Music Bibliographies for all Instruments (Musik-Bibliographien für alle Instrumente).* 1976. Available from the author: Munich 70 Germany, Box 700 308, D 8000.

Decker, Richard G. *Music for Three Brasses; a Bibliography of Music for Three Heterogeneous Brass Instruments Alone and in Chamber Ensembles.* Oneonta, New York: Swift-Dorr Publications, 1976.

Duckles, Vincent H., and Michael A. Keller. *Music Reference and Research Materials.* 4th ed. New York: Schirmer Books, 1988.

Helm, Sanford M. *Catalog of Chamber Music for Wind Instruments.* Ann Arbor, Michigan: Lithoprinted by Braun-Brumfield, 1952.

Instrumentalist. *Brass Anthology—A Compendium of Articles from* The Instrumentalist *on Playing the Brass Instruments.* Evanston, Illinois: The Instrumentalist Company, 1984.

Thompson, J. Mark, and Jeffrey Jon Lemke. *French Music for Low Brass Instruments: An Annotated Bibliography.* Bloomington, Indiana: Indiana University Press, 1994.

Yeats, Robert, ed. *University of Iowa School of Music Guide to Selected Wind and Percussion Materials.* Version 2.0. Iowa City, Iowa: University of Iowa and Eble Music, 1992.

Biography

Bridges, Glenn D. *Pioneers in Brass*. Rev. ed. Detroit, Michigan: Glenn D. Bridges, 1968.

Comettant, J. P. O. *Histoire d' un inventeur au XIXe siècle*. Paris, France: Pagnerre, 1860.

Gilson, P., and A. Remy. *Adolphe Sax*. Brussels, Belgium: Institut National Belge de Radiodiffusion, 1938–39.

Kalkbrenner, A. *Wilhelm Wieprecht, sein Leben und Wirken*. Berlin, Germany: n.p., 1882.

Musical Instruments and the Masters. Elkhart, Indiana: Conn Corporation, 1955.

Sousa, John Philip. *Marching Along*. Boston: Hale, Cushman & Flint, 1928.

Discography

Bollinger, Donald E. *Band Director's Complete Handbook*. West Nyack, New York: Parker Publishing Company, Inc., 1979.

Instrumentalist. *Brass Anthology—A Compendium of Articles from* The Instrumentalist *on Playing the Brass Instruments*. Evanston, Illinois: The Instrumentalist Company, 1984.

Poulton, Alan J., comp. *A Label Discography of Long-Playing Records*. Series 2. H. M. V. (Red Label) October 1952–December 1962. N.p.: The Oakwood Press, n.d.

Equipment

Ahrens, Christian. *Eine Erfindung und ihre Folgen: Blechblasinstrumente mit Ventilen*. Kassel, Germany: Bärenreiter, 1986.

Bach, Vincent. *Embouchure and Mouthpiece Manual*. Rev. ed. Elkhart, Indiana: Selmer Company, 1979.

Bahnert, Heinz; Theodore Herzberg; and Herbert Schramm. *Metallblasinstrumente*. Wilhelmshaven, Germany: Heinrichshofen, 1986.

Bollinger, Donald E. *Band Director's Complete Handbook*. West Nyack, New York: Parker Publishing Company, Inc., 1979.

Bowles, Benjamin Franklin. *Technics of the Brass Musical Instrument: A Condensed Instructive Treatise on the General Construction of Brass Musical Instruments and How to Choose Them; Care of the Instruments; and General Suggestions on Playing, Phrasing and Practicing*. New York: Carl Fischer, 1915.

Brand, Erick D. *Selmer Band Instrument Repairing Manual*. Elkhart, Indiana: H. & A. Selmer, 1959.

———. *Musical Instrument Repair Tools and Supplies*. Elkhart, Indiana: Erick D. Brand, n.d.

C. G. Conn Ltd. *How to Care for Your Instrument*. Elkhart, Indiana: C. G. Conn Ltd., 1942.

Clappé, Arthur A. *The Wind-Band and Its Instruments: Their History, Construction, Acoustics, Technique, and Combination*. 1911. Reprint, Portland, Maine: Longwood, 1976.

Colwell, Richard J., and Thomas Goolsby. *The Teaching of Instrumental Music*. 2nd ed. Englewood Cliffs, New Jersey: Prentice Hall, 1992.

Dullat, Günter. *Blasinstrumente und Deutsche Patentschriften*. 2 vols. Nanheun, Germany: 1985 (Vol. 1), 1986 (Vol. 2).

———. *Holz und Metallblasinstrumente*. Siegburg, Germany: Schmitt, 1986.

———. *Metallblasinstrumentenbau*. Frankfurt am Main, Germany: Bochinsky, 1989.

Duttenhöfer, Eva-Maria. *Gebrüder Alexander. 200 Jahre Musikinstrumentenbau*. Mainz, Germany: Schott, 1982.

Ferree, Cliff. *Ferree's Band Instrument Tools and Supplies*. Battle Creek, Michigan: Ferree's, P.O. Box 259, Battle Creek, MI 49016, n.d.

Franz, Oscar. *Die Musik-Instrumente der Gegenwart*. Dresden, Germany: J. G. Seeling, 1884.

Gregory, Robin. *The Horn: A Comprehensive Guide to the Modern Instrument and Its Music*. 2nd ed. New York: Frederick A. Praeger, 1969.

Hall, Jody C. *The Proper Selection of Cup Mouthpieces*. Elkhart, Indiana: Conn Corporation, 1963.

Heyde, Dr. Herbert. *Das Ventilblasinstrument*. Leipzig, Germany: VEB Verlag deutscher Musik, 1987.

Holcomb, Bruce. *Die Verbesserung der Stimmung an Ventilblasinstrumenten*. N.p.: Musikverlag Emil Katzbichler, 1981.

Instrumentalist. *Brass Anthology—A Compendium of Articles from* The Instrumentalist *on Playing the Brass Instruments*. Evanston, Illinois: The Instrumentalist Company, 1984.

Kent, Earle L. *The Inside Story of Brass Instruments*. Elkhart, Indiana: C. G. Conn, 1956.

Kirschner, Frederick. *Encyclopedia of Band Instrument Repair*. New York: Music Trade Review, 1962.

Krickeberg, Dieter, and Wolfgang Rauch. *Katalog der Blechblasinstrumente*. Berlin, Germany: Musikinstrumenten-Museum, 1976.

McGavin, E., comp. *A Guide to the Purchase and Care of Woodwind and Brass Instruments*. Bromley, England: Schools Music Association, 1966.

Meyer, R. F. "Peg." *The Band Director's Guide to Instrument Repair*. Edited by Willard I. Musser. Port Washington, New York: Alfred Publishing Co., Inc., 1973.

Møller, Dorthe Falcon. *Danske Instrumentbyggere 1770–1850 (Danish Instrument Factories and Builders 1770–1850)*. Copenhagen, Denmark: G. E. C. Gads., 1982.

Naur, Robert. *185 år blandt blæseinstrumenter. Skitser af et dansk instrumentmagerværksted gennem 7 slægtled* (185 Years among Wind Instruments. Sketches of a Danish Music Instrument Factory over Seven Generations). Copenhagen, Denmark: J. K. Gottfried, n.d.

Nödl, Karl. *Metallblasinstrumentenbau; ein Fach- und Lehrbuch über die handwerkliche Herstellung von Metallblasinstrumenten.* Frankfurt am Main, Germany: Das Musikinstrument, 1970.

Olson, R. Dale. *Sensory Evaluation of Brass Instruments.* Available from the author: R. Dale Olson, 1500 Sunny Crest Drive, Fullerton, California 92635, n.d.

Pontécoulant, Adolphe Le Doulcet. *Organographie.* Vol. 1. The Netherlands: Frits Knuf, 1971.

Ridley, Edwin Alexander Keane. *European Wind Instruments.* Foreword by David M. Boston. London, England: The Royal College of Music, 1982.

Schlesinger, Kathleen. *The Instruments of the Modern Orchestra.* 2 vols. London, England: William Reeves, 1969.

Schramm, Herbert. *Mein Metallblasinstrument.* Frankfurt am Main, Germany: Verlag Das Musikinstrument, 1981.

Seifers, Heinrich. *Katalog der Blasinstrumente.* N.p.: Deutsches Museum, 1980.

Springer, George H. *Maintenance and Repair of Band Instruments.* Boston, Massachusetts: Allyn and Bacon, Inc., 1970.

Tiede, Clayton H. *The Practical Band Instrument Repair Manual.* Dubuque, Iowa: Wm. C. Brown Company Publishers, 1962.

Weisshaar, Otto H. *Preventive Maintenance of Musical Instruments.* Rockville Center, New York: Belwin, 1966.

Weltausstellung 1873. *Mathematische und Physikalische Instrumente.* Group XIV, Sections 1 and 2. Vienna, Austria: K. K. Hof- und Staatsdruckerei, 1874.

Young, T. Campbell. *The Making of Musical Instruments.* London, England: Oxford University Press, 1939.

General Reference

Ammer, Christine. *The Harper Dictionary of Music.* 2nd ed. New York: Harper & Row Publishers, 1987.

Apel, Willi, and Ralph T. Daniel. *The Harvard Brief Dictionary of Music.* Cambridge, Massachusetts: Harvard University Press, 1960.

Arnold, Denis, ed. *The New Oxford Companion to Music.* New York: Oxford University Press, 1983.

Basso, Alberto, ed. *Dizionario Enciclopedico Universale della Musica e dei Musicisti.* Vol. 2. Torino, Italy: Unione Tipografico-Editrice Torinese, 1984.

Bennwitz, Hanspeter. *Kleines Musiklexikon.* Berne, Switzerland: A. Francke AG Verlag, 1963.

Blom, Eric. *The New Everyman Dictionary of Music.* Edited by David Cummings. 6th ed. London, England: J. M. Dent & Sons Ltd., 1988.

Brousse, Joseph. *Encyclopédie de la Musique et dictionnaire du Conservatoire.* Vol. 3. Paris, France: Belgrave, 1927.

Carlton, Joseph R. *Carlton's Complete Reference Book of Music.* Studio City, California: Carlton Publications, 1980.

Cook, Kenneth, comp. *The Bandsman's Everything Within.* London, England: Hinrichsen Edition Ltd., 1950.

Cooper, Martin, ed. *The Concise Encyclopedia of Music and Musicians.* New York: Hawthorn Books Inc., 1958.

Dufourcq, Norbert. *Larousse de la Musique.* 2 vols. Paris, France: Librairie Larousse, 1957.

Dunstan, Ralph. *A Cyclopaedic Dictionary of Music.* 4th ed. New York: Da Capo Press, 1973.

Encyclopaedia Britannica. 15th ed. Chicago, Illinois: Encyclopaedia Britannica, Inc., 1986.

Herzfeld, Friedrich. *Lexikon der Musik.* Berlin, Germany: Ullstein A. G., 1957.

Hughes, Rupert, comp. *Music Lovers' Encyclopedia.* Edited by Deems Taylor and Russell Kerr. 2nd ed. Garden City, New York: Garden City Publications Co., Inc., 1939.

Ingles, Elisabeth, ed. *Harrap's Illustrated Dictionary of Music and Musicians.* 2nd ed. Great Britain: Harrap Books Limited, 1990.

Isaacs, Alan, and Elizabeth Martin, eds. *Dictionary of Music.* New York: Facts on File, Inc., 1983.

Jacquot, A., ed. *Dictionnaire des instruments de musique.* Paris, France: n.p., 1886.

Kallmann, Helmut; Gilles Potvin; and Kenneth Winters, eds. *Encyclopedia of Music in Canada.* Toronto, Ontario: University of Toronto Press, 1981.

Kennedy, Michael, ed. *The Oxford Dictionary of Music.* 3rd ed. New York: Oxford University Press, 1985.

Lavignac, Albert, ed. *Encyclopédie de la musique.* Vol. 3. Paris, France: Librairie Delagrave, 1927.

Lexicon der Musik. N.p.: Druck und Buchbinderei-Werkstätten May & Co Nachf., 1976.

Macmillan Encyclopedia of Music and Musicans. New York: Macmillan Company, 1938.

Marcuse, Sibyl. *Musical Instruments.* 2nd ed. New York: W. W. Norton & Company, Inc., 1975.

Matzke, Hermann. *Unser Technisches Wissen von der Musik.* Lindau am Bodensee, Germany: Frisch und Preneder, 1949.

Mendel, Hermann. *Musikalisches Conversations-Lexikon.* Berlin, Germany: Verlag von Robert Oppenheim, 1878.

Michel, Francois. *Encyclopédie de la Musique.* Paris, France: Fasquelle, 1961.

Moore, John, W. *A Dictionary of Musical Information.* 1876. New York: Lenox Hill Pub. & Dist. Co., 1971.

———. *Complete Encyclopædia of Music.* 1880. Reprint, New York: AMS Press, Inc., 1973.

Morehead, Philip D., and Anne MacNeil. *The New American Dictionary of Music.* New York: Penguin Books USA Inc., 1991.

Morin, Gösta, ed. *Sohlmans Musik Lexikon.* Stockholm, Sweden: Sohlmans Förlag, 1952.

Moser, Hans Joachim. *Musik Lexikon.* Hamburg, Germany: Musikverlag Hans Sikorski, 1951.

Müller-Blattau, Joseph, ed. *Höhe Schule der Musik; Handbuch der gesamten Musikpraxis.* 4 vols. Potsdam, Germany: Athenaion, 1938.

New Lexicon Webster's Dictionary of the English Language. New York: Lexicon Publications, Inc., 1991.

Parkhurst, Winthrop, and L. J. de Bekker. *The Encyclopedia of Music and Musicians.* New York: Crown Publishers, 1937.

Pena, Joaquín. *Diccionario de la Música Labor.* Barcelona, Spain: Editorial Labor, S. A., 1954.

Plenckers, L. J. *Brass Instruments.* New York: Da Capo, 1970.

Posell, Elsa Z. *This Is an Orchestra.* Boston, Massachusetts: Houghton Mifflin Company, 1950.

Pratt, Waldo Selden, ed. *The New Encyclopedia of Music and Musicians.* 2nd ed. New York: The Macmillan Company, 1948.

Randel, Don Michael, ed. *The New Harvard Dictionary of Music.* 3rd ed. Cambridge, Massachusetts: The Belknap Press of Harvard University Press, 1986.

Riemann, Hugo. *Riemann Musik Lexikon.* Edited by Earl Dahlhaus. Mainz, Germany: B. Schott's Söhne, 1975.

Sachs, Curt. *Real-Lexicon der Musikinstrumente.* New York: Dover Publications, Inc., 1964.

———. *Handbuch der Musikinstrumente.* Wiesbaden, Germany: Breitkopf & Härtel, 1979.

Sadie, Stanley, ed. *The New Grove Dictionary of Music and Musicians.* London, England: Macmillan Publishers Limited, 1980.

———. *The New Grove Dictionary of Musical Instruments.* Vol. 3. London, England: Macmillan Press Limited, 1984.

———. *The Grove Concise Dictionary of Music.* London, England: Macmillan Press Ltd, 1988.

Sartori, Claudio, ed. *Dizionario Ricordi.* Milan, Italy: G. Ricordi & C., 1959.

Scholes, Percy. *The Oxford Junior Companion to Music.* London, England: Oxford University Press, 1963.

———. *Oxford Companion to Music.* Edited by John Owen Ward. 10th ed. London, England: Oxford University Press, 1977.

Schwartz, Harry Wayne. *Bands of America.* New York: Doubleday and Co. Inc., 1957.

Slonimsky, Nicolas. *Lectionary of Music.* New York: McGraw-Hill Publishing Company, 1989.

Thompson, Oscar, and Bruce Bohle, eds. *The International Cyclopedia of Music and Musicians.* 11th ed. New York: Dodd, Mead & Company, 1985.

Tonkunst. *Universal-Lexikon.* Edited by Eduard Bernsdorf. Offenbach, Germany: Verlag von Johann André, 1861.

University Musical Encyclopedia. New York: The University Society, 1912.

Webster's Third New International Dictionary of the English Language. Springfield, Massachusetts: G. & C. Merriam Co., 1971.

Westrup, J. A., and F. Ll. Harrison. *Collins Music Encyclopedia.* London: William Collins Sons & Co. Ltd., 1959.

———. *The New College Encyclopedia of Music.* Edited by Conrad Wilson. 2nd ed. New York: W. W. Norton & Company, Inc., 1976.

Wier, Albert E., ed. *The Macmillan Encyclopedia of Music and Musicians.* New York: The Macmillan Company, 1938.

History

Abraham, Gerald. *The Concise Oxford History of Music.* London, England: Oxford University Press, 1979.

Adler, Guido. *Handbuch der Musikgeschichte.* Frankfurt am Main, Germany: Frankfurter Verlags-Anstalt A. -G., 1924.

Andresen, Mogens. *Historiske Messingblæsinstrumenter* (Historic Brass Instruments). Copenhagen, Denmark: Engstrøm & Sødring Musikforlag A/S, 1988.

Andrews, George W., ed. *Musical Instruments.* The American History and Encyclopedia of Music. Toledo, Ohio: The Squire Cooley Co., 1910.

Bacharach, A. L., and J. R. Pearce, eds. *A Musical Companion.* Rev. ed. London, England: Victor Gollancz Ltd., 1977.

Baines, Anthony, ed. *Musical Instruments through the Ages.* Rev. ed. London, England: Faber and Faber Limited, 1966.

Boyden, David D. *An Introduction to Music.* 2nd ed. New York: Alfred A. Knopf, 1970.

Brand, Violet and Geoffrey, eds. *Brass Bands in the 20th Century.* Letchworth, Herts: Egon Publishers Ltd., 1979.

Britten, Benjamin, and Imogen Holst. *The Wonderful World of Music.* New York: Garden City Books, 1958.

Brown, Howard Mayer, and Stanley Sadie, eds. *Performance Practice: Music after 1600.* Vol. 2. New York: W. W. Norton & Company, 1990.

Buchner, Alexander. *Musical Instruments: An Illustrated History.* New York: Crown Publishers, Inc., 1973.

Burney, Charles. *The Present State of Music in France and Italy.* 2nd ed. Vol. 1. London, England: T. Becket and Co., 1773.

———. *The Present State of Music in Germany, the Netherlands, and United Provinces.* London, England: T. Becket and Co., 1773.

Carse, Adam. *Musical Wind Instruments. A History of the Wind Instruments Used in European Orchestras and Wind-Bands from the Middle Ages up to the*

Present Time. 1939. Reprint, New York: Da Capo, 1973.

Clappé, Arthur A. *The Wind-Band and Its Instruments: Their History, Construction, Acoustics, Technique, and Combination.* 1911. Reprint, Portland, Maine: Longwood, 1976.

Clendenin, William R. *History of Music.* Rev. ed. Totowa, New Jersey: Littlefield, Adams & Co., 1974.

Colwell, Richard J., and Thomas Goolsby. *The Teaching of Instrumental Music.* 2nd ed. Englewood Cliffs, New Jersey: Prentice Hall, 1992.

Cselenyi, Ladislav. *Musical Instruments in the Royal Ontario Museum.* N.p.: Royal Ontario Museum, 1971.

Diagram Group. *The Scribner Guide to Orchestral Instruments.* New York: Charles Scribner's Sons, 1983.

Dullat, Günter. *Holz und Metallblasinstrumente.* Siegburg, Germany: Schmitt, 1986.

Dundas, R. J. *Twentieth Century Brass Musical Instruments in the United States.* Cincinnati, Ohio: Queen City Brass Publications, 1986.

Duttenhöfer, Eva-Maria. *Gebrüder Alexander. 200 Jahre Musikinstrumentenbau.* Mainz, Germany: Schott, 1982.

Engel, Carl. *Musical Instruments in the South Kensington Museum.* 2nd ed. London, England: George E. Eyre and William Spottiswoode, 1874.

Farmer, Henry George. *A History of Music in Scotland.* London, England: Hinrichsen Edition Limited, 1947.

———. *Military Music.* New York: Chanticleer Press, 1950.

Ferguson, Donald N. *A History of Musical Thought.* 3rd ed. Westport, Connecticut: Greenwood Press Publishers, 1959.

Franz, Oscar. *Die Musik-Instrumente der Gegenwart.* Dresden, Germany: J. G. Seeling, 1884.

Gammond, Peter. *Musical Instruments in Color.* New York: Macmillan Publishing Co., Inc., 1975.

Gregory, Robin. *The Horn: A Comprehensive Guide to the Modern Instrument and Its Music.* 2nd ed. New York: Frederick A. Praeger, 1969.

Haas, Robert. *Aufführungspraxis der Musik.* Potsdam, Germany: Akademische Verlagsgesellschaft Athenaion, 1931.

Hadow, Sir W. H., ed. *The Oxford History of Music.* 2nd ed. New York: Cooper Square Publishers, Inc., 1973.

Haskell, Harry. *The Early Music Revival: A History.* London, England: Thames and Hudson, 1988.

Hawkins, Sir John, *A General History of the Science and Practise of Music.* 2nd ed. London, England: Novello, Ewer & Company, 1875.

Heinitz, Wilhelm. *Instrumentenkunde.* Wild Park-Potsdam, Germany: Akademische Verlagsgesellschaft Athenaion, 1929.

Henderson, William James. *The Story of Music.* New York: Longmans, Green and Co., 1889.

Hindley, Geoffrey, ed. *The Larousse Encyclopedia of Music.* New York: Crescent Books, 1989.

Instrumentalist. *Brass Anthology—A Compendium of Articles from* The Instrumentalist *on Playing the Brass Instruments.* Evanston, Illinois: The Instrumentalist Company, 1984.

Kinscella, Hazel Gertrude. *Music on the Air.* New York: The Viking Press, 1934.

Kirby, F. E. *An Introduction to Western Music.* New York: The Free Press, 1970.

Krickeberg, Dieter, and Wolfgang Rauch. *Katalog der Blechblasinstrumente.* Berlin, Germany: Musikinstrumenten-Museum, 1976.

Kunitz, Hans. *Instrumenten-Brevier.* Leipzig, Germany: n.p., 1961.

Lavoix, H. *Histoire de l'instrumentation.* Paris, France: n.p., 1878.

Lawrence, Ian. *Brass in Your School.* London, England: Oxford University Press, 1975.

Mahillon, V. C. *Catalogue descriptif et analytique du Musée instrumental du Conservatoire Royal de Musique de Bruxelles.* Vol. 2. Brussels, Belgium: n.p., 1893.

Mandel, C. *A Treatise on the Instrumentation of the Military Band.* London, England: n.p., 1859.

Mason, Daniel Gregory. *The Art of Music.* New York: The National Society of Music, 1915–1917.

Mende, Emily, and Jean-Pierre Mathez. *Pictorial Family Tree of Brass Instruments in Europe since the Early Middle Ages.* Moudon, Switzerland: Editions BIM, 1978.

Méndez, Rafael. *Prelude to Brass Playing.* New York: Carl Fischer, 1961.

Mersenne, Marin. *Harmonie universelle.* Translated by Roger E. Chapman. 2 pts. The Hague, Netherlands: Martinus Nijhoff, 1957.

Midgley, Ruth, ed. *Musical Instruments of the World.* N.p.: Paddington Press Ltd., 1976.

Moeck, Hermann, ed. *Fünf Jahrhunderte deutscher Musikinstrumenten.* Celle, Germany: Moeck, 1987.

Møller, Dorthe Falcon. *Danske Instrumentbyggere 1770–1850 (Danish Instrument Factories and Builders 1770–1850).* Copenhagen, Denmark: G. E. C. Gads, 1982.

Morse, Constance. *Music and Music-Makers.* London, England: George Allen & Unwin Ltd., 1926.

Müller-Blattau, Joseph, ed. *Höhe Schule der Musik; Handbuch der gesamten Musikpraxis.* 4 vols. Potsdam, Germany: Athenaion, 1938.

Musical Instruments and the Masters. Elkhart, Indiana: Conn Corporation, 1955.

Naur, Robert. *185 år blandt blæseinstrumenter. Skitser af et dansk instrumentmagerværksted gennem 7 slægtled* (185 Years among Wind Instruments. Sketches of a Danish Music Instrument Factory over 7 Generations). Copenhagen, Denmark: J. K. Gottfried, n.d.

Paine, John Knowles. The *History of Music to the Death of Schubert*. New York: Da Capo Press, 1971.

Pierre, Constant. *Les Facteurs d'Instruments de Musique*. Geneva, Switzerland: Minkoff Reprints, 1893.

Pratt, Waldo Selden. *The History of Music*. New York: G. Schirmer, 1907.

Remnant, Mary. *Musical Instruments of the West*. New York: St. Martin's Press, 1978.

Sachs, Curt. *Our Musical Heritage, a Short History of Music*. 2nd ed. Englewood Cliffs, New Jersey: Prentice-Hall, 1955.

———. *Handbuch der Musikinstrumente*. Wiesbaden, Germany: Breitkopf & Härtel, 1979.

Sadie, Stanley, ed., with Alison Latham. *The Cambridge Music Guide*. Cambridge, England: Cambridge University Press, 1985.

Sartori, Claudio, ed. *Enciclopedia della Musica*. 4 Vols. Milan, Italy: G. Ricordi & C., 1964.

Schlesinger, Kathleen. *The Instruments of the Modern Orchestra*. 2 vols. London, England: William Reeves, 1969.

Schwartz, Harry Wayne. *Bands of America*. New York: Doubleday and Co. Inc., 1957.

Siegmeister, Elie, ed. *The New Music Lover's Handbook*. New York: Harvey House, Inc., 1973.

Sousa, John Philip. *Marching Along*. Boston, Massachusetts: Hale, Cushman & Flint, 1928.

Stoddard, Hope. *From These Comes Music*. New York: Thomas Y. Crowell Company, 1952.

Ulrich, Homer. *Music: A Design for Listening*. New York: Harcourt, Brace and World, Inc., 1962.

Valentin, Erich. *Handbuch der Musik Instrumenten Kunde*. 2nd ed. Regensburg, Germany: Gustav Bosse Verlag, 1974.

Weltausstellung 1873. *Mathematische und Physikalische Instrumente. Group XIV, Sections 1 and 2*. Vienna, Austria: K. K. Hof- und Staatsdruckerei, 1874.

Widor, C. M. *Technique de l'orchestra moderne* (supplement to Berlioz, *Traité*). London, England: n.p., 1906.

Winternitz, Emanuel. *Musical Instruments of the Western World*. New York: McGraw-Hill Book Company, n.d.

Literature

Anderson, Paul G., and Larry Bruce Campbell. *Brass Music Guide: Solo and Study Material in Print*. 1985 ed. Vol. 4. Music Guide Series. Northfield, Illinois: Instrumentalist Co., 1984.

Anderson, Paul G., and Lisa Ormston Bontrager. *Brass Music Guide: Ensemble Music in Print*. Vol. 5. Music Guide Series. Northfield, Illinois: The Instrumentalist Company, 1987.

Bollinger, Donald E. *Band Director's Complete Handbook*. West Nyack, New York: Parker Publishing Company, Inc., 1979.

Brüchle, Bernhard. *Music Bibliographies for all Instruments (Musik-Bibliographien für alle Instrumente)*. 1976. Available from the author, Munich 70 Germany, Box 700 308, D 8000.

Decker, Richard G. *Music for Three Brasses; a Bibliography of Music for Three Heterogeneous Brass Instruments Alone and in Chamber Ensembles*. Oneonta, New York: Swift-Dorr Publications, 1976.

Del Mar, Norman. *Orchestral Variations*. London, England: Eulenburg Books, 1981.

Dvorak, Raymond Francis. *The Band on Parade*. New York: Carl Fischer, Inc., 1937.

Ensemble Publications Catalog. Ensemble Publications, Box 98, Bidwell Station, Buffalo, New York 14222, n.d.

Famera, K. M. *Chamber Music Catalogue*. New York: Pendragon Press, 1978.

Helm, Sanford M. *Catalog of Chamber Music for Wind Instruments*. Ann Arbor, Michigan: Lithoprinted by Braun-Brumfield, 1952.

Instrumentalist. *Brass Anthology—A Compendium of Articles from* The Instrumentalist *on Playing the Brass Instruments*. Evanston, Illinois: The Instrumentalist Company, 1984.

Louder, Earle L., and David R. Corbin, Jr. *Euphonium Music Guide*. Evanston, Illinois: The Instrumentalist Company, 1978.

Ode, James. *Brass Instruments in Church Services*. Minneapolis, Minnesota: Augsburg Pub. House, 1970.

Thompson, J. Mark, and Jeffrey Jon Lemke. *French Music for Low Brass Instruments: An Annotated Bibliography*. Bloomington, Indiana: Indiana University Press, 1994.

Uber, David. *New Catalogue of Unpublished Music*. Available from the author, Department of Music, Trenton State College, Trenton, New Jersey, n.d.

———. *New Catalog of Published Music*. Available from the author, Department of Music, Trenton State College, Trenton, New Jersey, n.d.

Orchestration

Adkins, Hector Ernest. *Treatise on the Military Band*. 2nd ed. New York: Boosey & Hawkes, 1958.

Adler, Samuel. *The Study of Orchestration*. New York: W. W. Norton and Company, 1982.

Anderson, A. O. *Practical Orchestration*. Boston, Massachusetts, 1929.

Bartenstein, Hans. *Hector Berlioz' Instrumentationskunst und ihre geschichtlichen Grundlagen*. Leipzig, Germany: Heitz & Co., 1939.

Bennett, Robert Russell. *Instrumentally Speaking*. Melville, New York: Belwin-Mills Publishing Corporation, 1975.

Berlioz, Hector. *Treatise on Instrumentation*. Edited by Richard Strauss. English translation by Theodore Frost. Rev. ed. New York: Edwin F. Kalmus Publishing, 1948.

Blatter, Alfred. *Instrumentation/Orchestration*. New York: Longman, Inc., 1980.

Burton, Stephen Douglas. *Orchestration*. Englewood Cliffs, New Jersey: Prentice-Hall, Inc., 1982.

Cacavas, John. *Music Arranging and Orchestration*. Melville, New York: Belwin-Mills Publishing Corporation, 1975.

Carse, Adam. *The History of Orchestration*. New York: E. P. Dutton & Co., 1925.

Clappé, Arthur A. *The Principles of Wind-Band Transcription*. New York: Carl Fischer, 1921.

Czerny, Carl. *School of Practical Composition*. Translated by John Bishop. New York: Da Capo Press, 1979.

Delamont, Gordon. *Modern Arranging Technique*. Delevan, New York: Kendor Music, 1965.

Dondeyne, D., and F. Robert. *Nouveau Traité d' Orchestration à l'usage des Harmonies, Fanfares et Musique Militaires*. Paris, France: H. Lemoine, 1969.

Erickson, Frank. *Arranging for the Concert Band*. Melville, New York: Belwin-Mills Publishing Corporation, 1983.

Evans, Edwin. *Method of Instrumentation*. Vol. 2. London, England: William Reeves Bookseller Limited, n.d.

Forsyth, Cecil. *Orchestration*. 2nd ed. New York: Macmillan and Co., 1946.

Gallo, Stanislao. *The Modern Band; a Treatise on Wind Instruments, Symphony Band and Military Band*. 2 vols. Boston, Massachusetts: C. C. Birchard, 1935.

Gardner, Maurice. *The Orchestrator's Handbook*. Great Neck, New York: The Staff Music Publishing Company, 1948.

Hansen, Brad. *The Essentials of Instrumentation*. Mountain View, California: Mayfield Publishing Company, 1991.

Hoby, Charles. *Military Band Instrumentation*. London, England: Oxford University Press, 1936.

Hofmann, Richard. *Practical Instrumentation*. Translated by Robin H. Legge. Leipzig, Germany: Doerffling & Franke, 1893.

Humperdinck, Engelbert. *Instrumentationslehre*. Edited by Hans-Josef Irmen. Vol. 128. Beiträge zur Rheinischen Musikgeschichte. Cologne, Germany: Verlag der Arbeitsgemeinschaft für rheinische Musikgeschichte, 1981.

Jacob, Gordon. *The Elements of Orchestration*. London, England: Herbert Jenkins, 1962.

———. *Orchestral Technique, A Manual for Students*. 3rd ed. London, England: Oxford University Press, 1982.

Jadassohn, S. *A Course of Instruction in Instrumentation*. Translated by Harry P. Wilkins. Leipzig, Germany: Breitkopf & Härtel, 1899.

Kennan, Kent Wheeler. *The Technique of Orchestration*. 4th ed. Englewood Cliffs, New Jersey: Prentice-Hall, 1990.

Kling, H. *Modern Orchestration*. Translated by Saenger. New York: n.p., 1902.

Koechlin, Charles, ed. *Traité de l'Orchestration*. 4 vols. Paris, France: Éditions Max Eschig, 1954.

Lang, Philip J. *Scoring for the Band*. New York: Mills, 1950.

Leibowitz, René, and Jan Maguire. *Thinking for Orchestra, Practical Exercises in Orchestration*. New York: G. Schirmer, Inc., 1960.

Leidzén, Erik. *An Invitation to Band Arranging*. Bryn Mawr, Pennsylvania: Theodore Presser Co., 1950.

Lockwood, Samuel Pierson. *Elementary Orchestration*. 2nd ed. Ann Arbor, Michigan: George Wahr, 1929.

Mandel, C. *A Treatise on the Instrumentation of the Military Band*. London, England: n.p., 1859.

Mason, Daniel Gregory. *The Orchestral Instruments and What They Do*. New York: H. W. Gray Co., 1937.

McKay, George Frederick. *Creative Orchestration*. Boston, Massachusetts: Allyn and Bacon, 1963.

Müller-Blattau, Joseph, ed. *Höhe Schule der Musik; Handbuch der gesamten Musikpraxis*. 4 vols. Potsdam, Germany: Athenaion, 1938.

Oboussier, Philippe. *Arranging Music for Young Players*. London, England: Oxford University Press, 1977.

Patterson, Frank. *Practical Instrumentation for School, Popular, and Symphony Orchestras*. 2nd ed. New York: G. Schirmer, Inc., 1923.

Piston, Walter. *Orchestration*. New York: W. W. Norton and Company, Inc., 1955.

Polansky, Larry. *New Instrumentation and Orchestration*. Oakland, California: Frog Peak Music, 1986.

Prout, Ebenezer. *The Orchestra*. Vol. 1. London, England: Augener and Co., 1897.

———. *Instrumentation*. Boston, Massachusetts: Oliver Ditson Company, 1900.

Rauscher, Donald J. *Orchestration, Scores and Scoring*. New York: Free Press of Glencoe, 1963.

Read, Gardner. *Thesaurus of Orchestral Devices*. New York: Pitman Publishing Corporation, 1953.

———. *Style and Orchestration*. New York: Schirmer Books, 1979.

Rimsky-Korsakov, Nikolas. *Principles of Orchestration*. Rev. ed. Newbury Park, California: P. L. Alexander, 1989.

Rogers, Bernard. *The Art of Orchestration*. New York: Appleton-Century-Crofts, Inc., 1951.

Shatzkin, Merton. *Writing for the Orchestra: An Introduction to Orchestration*. Englewood Cliffs, New Jersey: Prentice Hall, Inc., 1993.

Skeat, William James, and Harry F. Clarke. *The Fundamentals of Band Arranging*. Cleveland, Ohio: Sam Fox Publishing Co., 1938.

Skiles, Marlin. *Music Scoring for TV & Motion Pictures*. Blue Ridge Summit, Pennsylvania: Tab Books, 1976.

Stiller, Andrew. *Handbook of Instrumentation*. Berkeley, California: University of California Press, 1985.

Thomas, Eugène. *Die Instrumentation der Meistersinger von Nürnberg von Richard Wagner*. Mannheim, Germany: K. Ferd. Heckel, 1899.

Travis, F. L. *Verdi's Orchestration*. Zurich, Switzerland: n.p., 1956.

Voss, Egon. *Studien zur Instrumentation Richard Wagners*. Vol. 24. Studien zur Musikgeschichte des 19. Jahrhunderts. Regensburg, Germany: Gustav Bosse Verlag, 1970.

Wagner, Joseph Frederick. *Orchestration; A Practical Handbook*. New York: McGraw-Hill, 1959.

———. *Band Scoring*. New York: McGraw-Hill, 1960.

Walters, Harold L. *Arranging for the Modern Band*. New York: George F. Briegel, Inc., 1942.

White, Gary. *Instrumental Arranging*. Dubuque, Iowa: Wm. C. Brown Publishers, 1992.

White, William C. *Military Band Arranging*. New York: Carl Fischer, Inc., 1924.

Wright, Denis. *Scoring for Brass Band*. 4th ed. London, England: John Baker, 1967.

Yoder, Paul. *Arranging Method for School Bands*. New York: Robbins Music Corporation, 1946.

Pedagogy

Belfrage, Bengt. *Practice Methods for Brass Players*. Stockholm, Sweden: Ab Nordiska Musikförlaget, 1982.

———. *Uebungsmethodik für Blechbläser auf der Basis von physiologischen Faktoren*. Frankfurt am Main, Germany: Hansen, 1984.

Bell, William J. *A Handbook of Information on Intonation*. Elkhorn, Wisconsin: Getzen Co., 1968.

Bellamah, Joseph L. *A Survey of Modern Brass Teaching Philosophies*. San Antonio, Texas: Southern Music Company, 1976.

Bollinger, Donald E. *Band Director's Complete Handbook*. West Nyack, New York: Parker Publishing Company, Inc., 1979.

Bowles, Benjamin Franklin. *Technics of the Brass Musical Instrument: A Condensed Instructive Treatise on the General Construction of Brass Musical Instruments and How to Choose Them; Care of the Instruments; and General Suggestions on Playing, Phrasing and Practicing*. New York: Carl Fischer, 1915.

Clappé, Arthur A. *The Wind-Band and Its Instruments: Their History, Construction, Acoustics, Technique, and Combination*. 1911. Reprint, Portland, Maine: Longwood, 1976.

Colin, Charles. *Vital Brass Notes*. New York: Charles Colin, 1962.

———. *The Brass Player*. New York: Charles Colin, 1972.

Colwell, Richard J., and Thomas Goolsby. *The Teaching of Instrumental Music*. 2nd ed. Englewood Cliffs, New Jersey: Prentice-Hall, 1992.

Duvall, W. Clyde. *The High School Band Director's Handbook*. Englewood Cliffs, New Jersey: Prentice-Hall, Inc., 1960.

Farkas, Philip. *The Art of Musicianship*. Rochester, New York: Wind Music Inc., 1962.

———. *The Art of Brass Playing*. Bloomington, Indiana: The Author, 1962.

———. *L' art de jouer les cuivres. Traité sur la formation et l' utilisation de l' embouchure du musicien jouant un cuivre*. Translated by Alain Maillard. Paris, France: Leduc, 1981.

Fox, Fred. *Essentials of Brass Playing*. Pittsburgh, Pennsylvania: Volkwein, 1974.

Gordon, Claude. *Physical Approach to Elementary Brass Playing in Bass Clef*. New York: Carl Fischer, 1979.

Grupp, M. *In the Name of Wind-Instrument Playing*. New York: M. Grupp Studios, 1939.

Holck, Ingrid, and Mogens Andresen. *Breath Building*. Denmark: OH Music, P. O. Box 49, DK 2680 Solrød Strand, n.d.

Instrumentalist. *Brass Anthology—A Compendium of Articles from* The Instrumentalist *on Playing the Brass Instruments*. Evanston, Illinois: The Instrumentalist Company, 1984.

Kohut, Daniel L. *Musical Performance*. Englewood Cliffs, New Jersey: Prentice-Hall, Inc., 1985.

Lawrence, Ian. *Brass in Your School*. London, England: Oxford University Press, 1975.

Leidig, Vernon F. *Contemporary Brass Technique: Manual and Study Guide*. Norwalk, California: Highland Music Company, 1960.

Maddy, J. E., and T. P. Giddings. *Instrumental Technique for Orchestra and Band*. Cincinnati, Ohio: The Willis Music Company, 1926.

Porter, Maurice M. *The Embouchure*. London, England: Boosey & Hawkes, 1967.

Ridgeon, John. *Brass for Beginners*. London, England: Boosey & Hawkes, 1977.

Robinson, William C. *Tone Production and Use of the Breath for Brass Instrument Playing*. Waco, Texas: Baylor University, 1972.

Stevens, Roy. *Embouchure Self-Analysis and The Stevens-Costello Triple C Embouchure Technique (Complete)*. Edited by William Moriarity. New York: The Stevens-Costello Embouchure Clinic, 1971.

Sweeney, Leslie. *Teaching Techniques for the Brasses*. New York: Belwin Inc., 1953.

Thompson, J. Mark, and Jeffrey Jon Lemke. *French Music for Low Brass Instruments: An Annotated Bibliography*. Bloomington, Indiana: Indiana University Press, 1994.

Weast, Robert D. *Keys to Natural Performance for Brass Players*. Des Moines, Iowa: The Brass World, 1979.

Winslow, Robert W., and John E. Green. *Playing and Teaching Brass Instruments*. Englewood Cliffs, New Jersey: Prentice-Hall, Inc., 1961.

Winter, James H. *The Brass Instruments.* 2nd ed. Boston, Massachusetts: Allyn and Bacon, Inc., 1969.

Zorn, Jay D. *Brass Ensemble Method for Music Educators.* Belmont, California: Wadsworth Publishing Company, Inc., 1977.

Performance

Farkas, Philip. *The Art of Musicianship.* Rochester, New York: Wind Music Inc., 1962.

Gallwey, W. Timothy. *The Inner Game of Tennis.* New York: Random House, 1974.

Green, Barry, with W. Timothy Gallwey. *The Inner Game of Music.* New York: Doubleday, 1986.

Instrumentalist. *Brass Anthology—A Compendium of Articles from* The Instrumentalist *on Playing the Brass Instruments.* Evanston, Illinois: The Instrumentalist Company, 1984.

King, Robert D. *Proposals for Symphony Orchestra Brass.* N.p.: Robert D. King, 1985.

Kohut, Daniel L. *Musical Performance.* Englewood Cliffs, New Jersey: Prentice-Hall, Inc., 1985.

Olson, R. Dale. *Human Mechanisms of Brass Performance.* Available from author, 1500 Sunny Crest Drive, Fullerton, California 92635, n.d.

Ristad, Eloise. *A Soprano on Her Head.* Moab, Utah: Real People Press, 1982.

Stevens, Chris, with Dr. Ken Ravizza. *Head Control.* Available from author, Chris Stevens, 1848 Hackett Avenue, Long Beach, California, 90815, n.d.

Miscellaneous

Benade, Arthur H. *Acoustics of Musical Wind Instruments.* Abstract in Research at Case. Cleveland, Ohio: Case Institute of Technology, 1961.

Buchner, Alexander. *Musical Instruments: An Illustrated History.* New York: Crown Publishers, Inc., 1973.

———. *Musical Instruments through the Ages.* Translated by Iris Urwin. London, England: Spring Books, n.d.

Densmore, F. *Handbook of the Collection of Musical Instruments in the U. S. National Museum.* 1927. New York: n.p., 1971.

Donington, R. *The Instruments of Music.* 3rd ed. London, England: n.p., 1970.

Dullat, Günter. *Holz und Metallblasinstrumente.* Siegburg, Germany: Schmitt, 1986.

———. *Metallblasinstrumentenbau.* Frankfurt am Main, Germany: Bochinsky, 1989.

Gábry, György. *Old Musical Instruments.* 2nd ed. Budapest, Hungary: Corvina Press, 1969.

Heritage Music Press. *The Complete Encyclopedia of Fingering Charts.* Dayton, Ohio: HMP, 1992.

Hjelmervik, Kenneth, and Richard C. Berg. *Marching Bands: How to Organize and Develop Them.* New York: The Ronald Press Company, 1953.

King, Robert D. *Proposals for Symphony Orchestra Brass.* N.p.: Robert D. King, 1985.

Koch, Markus. *Abriss der Instrumentenkunde.* Kempten, Germany: Kösel, 1912.

Nickel, Ekkehart. *Der Holzblas-Instrumentenbau in der Freien Reichsstadt Nürnberg.* Munich, Germany: Katzbichler, 1971.

Plenckers, Leo J. *Catalogue of the Musical Instruments.* Vol. 1. New York: Da Capo Press, 1970.

Porter, Maurice M. *Dental Problems in Wind Instrument Playing.* London, England: British Dental Associaton, 1968.

Schlenger, Kurt. *Eignung zum Blasinstrumentenspiel. Schriften zur praktischen Psychologie.* Vol. 2. Dresden, Germany: F. Burgartz, 1935.

Schneider, Willy. *Handbuch der Blasmusik.* Mainz, Germany: Schott, 1986.

Stauffer, Donald W. *Intonation Deficiencies of Wind Instruments in Ensemble.* Washington D.C.: Catholic University of America Press, 1954.

Stewart, Gary M. *Keyed Brass Instruments in the Arne B. Larson Collection.* Edited by André P. Larson. Vol. 1. Shrine to Music Museum, Catalog of the Collections. Vermillion, South Dakota: Shrine to Music Museum, 1980.

Wiesner, Glenn R.; Daniel R. Balbach; and Merrill A. Wilson. *Orthodontics and Wind Instrument Performance.* Washington, D. C.: Music Educators National Conference, 1973.

Zimmermann, Julius Heinrich. *Musikinstrumente.* Frankfurt am Main, Germany: Zimmermann, 1984.

14. Biographical Sketches of Professional Tubists

Mark A. Nelson

The information in the following biographies of tubists, past and present, was gathered largely from questionnaires sent to professional tubists. Students, other than those who were holding concurrent professional positions, are not listed. Historic performers are listed only to the extent that information about them was readily accessible and relevant.

The overall philosophy of this chapter is to provide data concerning tuba performance and pedagogy only; thus, activities outside the guidelines in the questionnaire are not reported. In a number of cases, space does not permit a full listing of employment and contributions.

Some questionnaires were not returned or arrived too late for inclusion here. Those with incomplete information, illegible handwriting, or in a foreign language have been reconstructed to the extent possible. Some biographies have been culled from other published sources and edited to the established guidelines. Birth and death dates, when known, appear in the standardized order of month, day, and year.

Because the scope of the project sometimes precluded individual responses, the editor cannot assume responsibility for the accuracy of the information in every entry.

This chapter could never have been attempted without the contributions of the following people who not only developed performer lists but also created biographical databases for their respective areas: David Randolph, university and college personnel; Gregory Fritze, orchestra personnel; Robert Daniel and David Porter, military band personnel; Norlan Bewley, brass quintet and related personnel; and R. Steven Call, jazz and related personnel. Many thanks also go to the *TSB* International Consultants and their contributors. Finally, this editor wishes to thank his wife, Monica, whose patience and love made it possible for him to see this chapter through.

Adam, Eugene
    1881–1964
    Past Positions: Boston Symphony Orchestra (1918–47) (also Principal Trombone (1918–20), Assistant Principal Trombone (as needed) (1920–34).

Adamik, Gábor
    Born: 09/20/67
    Current Positions: University of Gyor 1991–, Academia Brass Quintet 1983–.
    Education: Franz Liszt University of Music (1991).
    Teachers: László Szabó, László Ujfalusi
Ahrens, Charles R.
    Born: 03/23/26
    Current Positions: Pussyfoot Stompers, The Roseburg Chamber Brass (founded in 1979 by C.R. Ahrens).
    Education: Naval Unit Band (1946) University of Wisconsin.
Aida, Yoshio
    Born: 08/21/37
    Current Positions: Osaka Municipal Symphonic Band 1958–.
    Past Positions: 3rd Ground Self Defence Force Band (1956–58).
    Teachers: Kiyoshi Yano.
Aikins, James M.
    Born: 06/15/56
    Current Positions: Columbus Symphony Orchestra 1981–, Professor, Ohio State University 1992–, Columbus Symphony Brass Quintet 1981–, Ohio Brass Quintet 1992–.
    Education: BM, MM Ohio State University (1978, 1982).
    Teachers: Robert LeBlanc, Ron Bishop, Fredrick Schaufele, Jr., Arnold Jacobs, Robert Ryker.
Alexander, Joe
    Born: 11/09/58
    Current Positions: Adjunct Professor, East Central University 1990–, Ada Community Band 1991–, Nanola Brass Quintet 1992–.
    Past Positions: Denton Community Orchestra (1987–90).
    Contributions: premieres of new tuba works.
    Education: BM East Carolina University (1981), MM James Madison University (1983), DMA University of North Texas (1991).
    Teachers: Gale Dilahay, Andrew Farnham, Bill Chamberlain, Bruce Mosier, Ken Meisinger.
Alvis, Hayes Julian
    5/1/07–12/29/72
    Contributions: Was a leading Chicago jazz tubist in 1920s. Played and recorded with Jelly Roll Morton, Earl Hines, Jimmie Noone. Played string bass with Duke

Ellington (1935–38). Starting in the early 1930s, played mostly string bass but returned to tuba in the 1950s to play with Wilbur de Paris. Considered by many to be one of the greatest early jazz tuba players.

Amiano, Troia
> Born: 05/16/67
> Current Positions: Banda Aeronautica Militare.
> Teachers: Edmondo Rossi.

Anders, Volta Andy
> Born: 11/03/44
> Current Positions: Professor, Arkansas Tech University 1968–, Arkansas Symphony Orchestra 1982–.
> Contributions: Advertising Coordinator, *TUBA Journal.*
> Education: BA Arkansas Polytechnic College (1967), MM Northwestern University (1968).
> Teachers: Don Owen, Robert Bright, Bruce Nelson, Arnold Jacobs, Frank Crisafulli, Skip Gray.

Anderson, Eugene D.
> Born: 01/28/44
> Past Positions: Instructor, Faculty Brass Quintet member, University of Toledo (1968–71); Instructor, Arizona State University (1971–75).
> Contributions: many original and arranged solo tuba and multiple publications.
> Education: BMEd University of Wisconsin–Madison (1968), MM Arizona State University (1974).
> Teachers: Donald Heeren, Arnold Jacobs, John Leissenring, Robert Gutter

Anderson, Hans F.
> Born: 07/26/45
> Current Positions: Århus Symphony Orchestra, Århus Brass Quintet, Teacher, Academy of Music Århus.
> Education: Pedagogical Diploma, Det Jydske Musikkonservatorium (1978).
> Teachers: Jørgen Arnsted, Roger Bobo, John Fletcher, Rex Martin, Arnold Jacobs.

Anjos, Marcos Dus
> Current Positions: Metalessencia Quintet, Banda Sinfonica do Estando de São Paulo, Sinfonica Jovem de Santo Andre, Filharmonica de São Caetano do Sul.
> Past Positions: Festival de Inverno de Campos do Jordao (1989), Orquestra do Festival de Verao de Pocos de Caldas.
> Education: Escola Municipal de Musical, Universidade Livre de Musica.
> Teachers: Drauzio Chagas, Donald Smith.

Annema, Dirk
> Born: 11/06/55
> Current Positions: Teacher, Conservatory of Enschede, Conservatory of Zwolle, Holland.

> Past Positions: Instructor, Leeuwarden, Heerenveen, Drachten schools, NCRV brass ensemble (Dutch Television), free-lance, Holland.
> Teachers: Guus Tomey, Sr., Donald Blakeslee, Roger Bobo.

Anthony, George
> Born: 10/27/66
> Current Positions: The Wallace Collection 1992–, London Jupiter Orchestra 1989–, Thames Brass 1986–, Royal National Theatre 1992–, The Campian School, St. Thomas Moore School 1993–.
> Contributions: Founder of the London Tuba Ensemble, Middlesex University Tuba Ensemble (arranging music for both), has premiered semi-improvisatory works for tuba and mixed ensemble.
> Education: AGSM (1989) Guildhall School of Music, ACPCS G SMD (1990), BEd Middlesex University (1994).
> Teachers: James Anderson, George Wall, Steve Wick.

Aoyagi, Tetsuo
> Born: 06/15/48
> Current Positions: Tokyo Bari-Tuba Ensemble, Japan Philharmonic Orchestra.
> Contributions: JETA committee member.
> Education: BA Tokyo University of the Arts (1946).
> Teachers: Motokichi Harada, Kiyoshi Ohishi.

Apone Olaya, Carlos Arturo
> Born: 11/21/53
> Current Positions: Banda Nacional de Bogatá.
> Education: Conservatory of Music of Tolima, Conservatory of Music University National.
> Teachers: Gaspar Richardone

Apostol, Vladimir P.
> Born: 07/26/51
> Current Positions: Associate Professor, Kiev State Conservatory 1987–, Smole Theatre Opera 1984–.
> Past Positions: State Band (orchestra) of Ukraine (1981).
> Education: Kiev Musical College (1976), Moscow State Conservatory (1981).
> Teachers: Victor Sinka, Alexej Lebedev.

Armandi, Richard Allan
> Born: 06/04/54
> Current Positions: Instructor, Concordia University 1987–, Triton College 1985–, Concordia University Faculty Brass Quintet 1987–, Triton Faculty Jazz Ensemble 1985–, Ethos Chamber Orchestra 1988–, North Shore Brass Quintet 1985–.
> Education: BM, MM Chicago Musical College of Roosevelt University (1983, 1985).
> Teachers: Arnold Jacobs, Ardash Marderosian, Frank Crisafulli, John Fletcher.

Arnold, Marcus Dale
    Born: 06/30/55
    Current Positions: Mr. Jack Daniel's Original
        Silver Cornet Band 1985–, utility tuba,
        Nashville Symphony 1984–.
    Past Positions: Nashville Chamber Brass (1980–
        84), adjunct faculty, Belmont College (1982–
        84).
    Contributions: numerous arrangements for
        multiple tubas.
    Education: attended Tennessee Tech University
        (1973–78).
    Teachers: R. Winston Morris.
Arnsted, Jørgen Voigt
    Born: 06/28/36
    Current Positions: Symphony Orchestra Odense
        1965–, teacher, Music Academy of Odense
        1966–.
    Past positions: Royal Danish Lifeguard (1959–
        65), Gothenburg Symphony Orchestra
        (1980–81), Music Academy Aarhus (1967–
        78), Royal Music Academy Copenhagen
        (1981–89), Music Academy of Gothenburg,
        Sweden (1980–82).
    Contributions: Arranged First Danish Tuba/
        Euph. Symposium (1977), founder, Danish
        Tuba Club (1974–83), premiered eleven
        Danish compositions for solo tuba or tuba
        quartet, Consultant for Rudolf Meinl Tuba
        Factory Germany (1976), member of Danish
        State Music Council (1990), many students
        placed in symphony orchestras.
    Education: Private education as tubist,
        Diploma, Music Academy of Odense (1970).
    Teachers: Ingbert Michelsen, Palmer Traulsen,
        Paul Bernard, Fernand Lelong.
Arwood, Jeffrey E.
    Born: 11/17/45
    Current Positions: The United States Army
        Band 1969–, Senior Soloist, The United
        States Army Band.
    Past Positions: Tuba Section Leader (1976–
        1992), The United States Army Band.
    Contributions: Founder/Chairman, The
        United States Army Band Tuba-Euphonium
        Conference (1983–), Editor of Military
        Bands, *TUBA Journal* (1985–1991),
        Programs Editor, *TUBA Journal* (1981–84).
    Education: BM Huron College (1967), MSE
        Northern State College (1969), MM
        Catholic University (1973).
    Teachers: Paul Christensen, Randall Lampe,
        William Winkle, Darwin Walker, David
        Bragunier.
Asbury, Joanna Ross
    Born: 03/23/71
    Current Position: The US Coast Guard Band
        1992–.

Education: Attended Arizona State University.
    Teachers: Daniel Perantoni, Jack Ingrahm.
AsKew, Dennis Weston
    Born: 07/18/64
    Current Positions: Assistant Professor, Univer-
        sity of North Carolina–Greensboro 1992–;
        Market Street Brass 1992–.
    Past Positions: Instructor, University of
        Michigan-Flint (1990–91); Bucknell
        University (1987–89).
    Contributions: New music reviewer *TUBA
        Journal.*
    Education: BMEd University of Georgia
        (1987), MM Pennsylvannia State University
        (1989), AMusD University of Michigan
        (1991).
    Teachers: Fritz Kaenzig, Mark Lusk, David
        Randolph.
Ausili, Pierluigi
    Born: 04/09/70
    Current Positions: Free-lance, Rome.
Baadsvik, Øystein
    Born: 08/14/66
    Current Positions: Free-lance, Sweden; Teacher,
        Norwegian Association of Wind Ensembles
        1985–.
    Past Positions: Trondheim Symphony Orchestra
        (1985–86), Nonköping Symphony Orchestra
        (1987–89), free-lance, Stockholm (1989–91).
    Contributions: 2nd prize tuba, Swiss prize
        (IEM–91), first Norwegian solo recording
        (1993).
    Education: Stockholm University of Music
        (1986–87).
    Teachers: Stein Erik Tafjord, Michael Lind,
        John Fletcher, Roger Bobo.
Back, Risto
    Born: 09/05/61
    Current Positions: Military Band Mikkeli 1981.
    Past Positions: Orchestra Mikkeli; free-lance
        (1981–1989).
    Education: Military School of Music (1981).
    Teachers: Raimo Pesonen, Eino Takalo-Eskola.
Bagoly, István
    Born: 07/02/49
    Current Positions: Hungarian Army Central
        Band.
    Past Positions: Hungarian Army Symphonic
        Orchestra.
    Education: Music School of the Hungarian
        Army.
    Teachers: Ferenc Steiner, László Szabó.
Baker, Jonathan
    Current Positions: Auckland Philharmonia
        Orchestra.
Baker, Neil Anthony
    Born: 01/07/59
    Current Positions: Göteborgs Musiken 1983–.

Education: LTCL, FTCL Trinity College of
Music, London (1979, 1980), LRAM Royal
Academy of Music, London (1980); ARCM
Royal College of Music, London (1980);
LWCMD Welsh College of Music and
Drama, Cardiff (1980).
Teachers: Deloi Jones, Nigel Seaman.

Baltz, Keith
Current Positions: Devil Mountain Jazz Band
1991–, free-lance, 1979–, Central Valley
Brass Quintet 1979–, Gustine City Band
1979–.
Past Positions: Headliners Jazz Band (1979–
82), Cell Block 7 (1982–84), B♯ and the
Accidentals (1984–85), Creole Jazz Kings
(1986–91).
Education: AA Modesto Jr. College (1970), BA
Cal State University, Stanislaus (1974), Tuba
Major Credential in Music Education (1985)
CSUS.
Teachers: Bert Stevenson, Gene Wisler, Jim
Klein.

Bambridge, John
1905–01/04/78
Past Positions: Saint Louis Symphony (1935–
46); free-lance, West Coast (1940s); staff
musician, Warner Brothers studios (1950–
58); L.A. productions of New York Opera,
Glendale (until 1978).
Contributions: considered by many to be one of
the great Dixieland style tubists of the earlier
part of the century.

Baranyó, Attila
Born: 09/20/63
Current Positions: North Hungary Symphonie
Orchestra, Miskolc.
Education: Bartók Béla Miskolc (1978–1982),
Music Academy "Liszt Ferenc" Miskolc
(1982–1985), Music Academy "Hanns
Eisler" Berlin (1987–1988).
Teachers: Nemes, Ferencé, Dietrich Unkrodt.

Barber, John William (Bill)
Born: 05/21/20
Current Positions: Goldman Band, Lincoln
Center, New York, NY 1962–.
Past Positions: Great Neck Symphony, Great
Neck, NY (1960–84); City Center Ballet and
Opera Company, New York, NY (1956–
1957); Sauter-Finegan Band (1952),
founding member, The New York Brass
Quintet (1950), Miles Davis Jazz Nonet,
Royal Roost, New York, NY; Claude
Thornhill Orchestra (1947–48); Kansas City
Symphony Orchestra (1945–47); Paul Rudoff
Training Orchestra, Nassau County, NY;
instrumental coach (1982–84), various
Broadway musicals (1948–54); 7th US Army
Band (1942–1945).

Contributions: listed in *International Who's
Who in Music*, and Leonard Feather,
Encyclopedia of Jazz, recorded with Miles
Davis, Sauter-Finegan, John Cole, and
others.
Education: BM, MMEd Manhattan School of
Music (1958); Juilliard School of Music,
Scholarship Student (1939–1942).

Bargeron, David W.
Born: 09/06/42
Current Positions: Free-lance, New York City
1978–, Gil Evans Orchestra 1972–, George
Gruntz Concert Jazz Band 1980–, Howard
Johnson's "Gravity" 1968–, Leader, Dave
Bargeron Quartet 1992–.
Past Positions: Doc Severinsen's "Now
Generation Brass" (1969–70); Blood, Sweat,
and Tears (1970–78); Jaco Pastorius "Word
of Mouth Band" (1980–82).
Contributions: Recorded tuba jazz solos with
Blood, Sweat, and Tears; Jaco Pastorius;
George Gruntz (euphonium); and Howard
Johnson.
Education: BM Boston University (1964), no
formal tuba instruction.

Barth, Richard
Past Positions: Cleveland Ballet Orchestra;
Metropolitan Brass Quintet; Erie Philhar-
monic; faculty, Naval Music School; Univer-
sity of Akron.
Contributions: soloist, Fifth Army Band,
arranger of tuba/euphonium ensembles,
recorded arrangements on commercial discs.
Education: BM Baldwin-Wallace College, MM
Northwestern University.

Barton, Mark J.
Born: 05/05/55
Current Positions: Affiliate Artist, University of
Houston; free-lance in Houston area 1981–;
Ambient Brass; extra, Houston Symphony.
Past Positions: Campanile Orchestra (1989–
91); Houston Symphony North (1988–90);
Cy-Five Brass Quintet (1981–88); Waco
Symphony (1973–76); Baylor Faculty Brass
Quintet (1973–76, 1979–81).
Education: BA University of St. Thomas
(1977), BM, BME Baylor University (1981).
Teachers: William Robinson, Thomas Stidham,
Andrew Russell, David Kirk.

Bautista, Juan Reverie Beltran
Born: 06/23/63
Current Positions: Professor, Conservatorio De
Gijon.
Past Positions: Professor, Conservatorio de
Cartagena Curso (1986–87); Conservatorio
de Corca Cursos (1989–92).
Education: Titulo de Professor de Tuba (1982).
Teachers: Wally Stormont, Miguel Navarro,
Miguel Moreno.

Bazsinka, József
  Born: 09/03/62
  Current Positions: Hungarian Opera House
    1983–, Anonymous Brass Quintet 1982–,
    Professor, Béla Bartók School of Music
    1989–, Hungarian Radio 1984–.
  Contributions: International Chamber Compe-
    titions: 1976 Concerto Praha, 1982 Barcs,
    1982 Ancona, 1986 Narbonne, Maurice
    André Quintet Competition, International
    Solo Tuba Competition: second prize
    (1984); third prize (1992); has premiered
    five new works for tuba 1984–; recording
    artist (1989).
  Education: Artist of Tuba, Teacher of Tuba,
    Franz Liszt Academy of Music (1985).
  Teachers: László Szody, László Ujfalusi, László
    Szabó.
Beauregard, Cherry N.
  Born: 10/06/33
  Current Positions: Rochester Philharmonic
    Orchestra 1962–; Professor, Eastman School
    of Music 1972–.
  Past Positions: Eastman Brass Quintet (1964–
    90), Bavarian State Opera Orchestra (1960–
    62).
  Education: BA Brigham Young University
    (1959), studied at the Stadt. Hochschule für
    Musik, Munich (1956–58), MM Eastman
    School of Music (1964), DMA Eastman
    School of Music (1969).
  Teachers: Norman J. Hunt, Friedrich Sertl,
    Donald L. Knaub.
Beery, John Wray
  Born: 04/30/39
  Current Positions: Associate Professor,
    Manchester College; summer staff, Inter-
    lochen Center for the Arts 1984–.
  Past Positions: Battle Creek Symphony
    Orchestra, West Shore Symphony Orchestra,
    West Michigan Wind Ensemble, Saginaw
    Symphony Orchestra.
  Contributions: articles in several periodicals.
  Education: BME, MA Central Michigan
    University (1961, 1962).
  Teachers: William H. Rivard, Norman C. Dietz,
    Leonard Falcone.
Bell, William J.
12/25/02–08/07/71
  Past Positions: Faculty Indiana University
    (1961–71), Faculty Columbia Teachers
    College, Juilliard School, Manhattan School
    of Music (1944–61), Faculty Cincinnati
    Conservatory of Music (1924–37), New York
    Philharmonic (1943–61), Asbury Park
    Municipal Band (1949–61), NBC Symphony
    Orchestra (1937–43), Goldman Band (1926–
    37), Cincinnati Symphony Orchestra (1924–
    37), Sousa Band (1921–24), Bachman's

Million Dollar Band (1920–21), North
    Dakota University (1918–20), W. W. Norton
    Band and Orchestra (1917–20).
Beniers, Bernard
  Born: 07/08/62
  Current Positions: Radio Filharmonisch Orkest
    1989–, Dutch Brass Sextet 1989–.
  Past Positions: Noord Hollands Philhaemonisch
    Orkest (1986–89).
  Education: Conservatoriem Silburg, Stockholm,
    Firenze.
  Teachers: Piet Joris, Michael Lind, Roger Bobo.
Bergstrom, Nils-Olaf
  Born: 10/29/65
  Current Positions: Malmo Theater Orchestra
    1992–.
  Past Positions: Free-lance (1990–92), Royal
    Swedish Army Band (1986–87).
  Education: Masters Degree, Malmo College of
    Music (1987–91).
  Teachers: Aldo Johansson, Christer Palm, Arne
    Svendsen, Robert Tucci.
Bertolet, Jay Paul
  Born: 12/12/60
  Current Positions: Florida Philharmonic
    Orchestra 1985–, Instructor, Broward
    Community College 1986–, Miami/Dade
    Community College 1986–, New World
    School for the Arts 1990–.
  Past Positions: Champaign/Urbana Symphony
    (1984–85), Detroit Civic Symphony
    (1983–84)
  Contributions: Co–Organizer and Soloist/
    Clinician for the Southern National Tuba/
    Euphonium Conference (1989).
  Education: BMus University of Michigan
    (1984), MMus University of Illinois (1988).
  Teachers: Fritz Kaenzig, Abe Torchinsky, Oscar
    LaGasse.
Bevan, Clifford James
  Born: 01/25/34
  Current Positions: Free-lance; UK/EC (tuba,
    ophicleide); serpent, London Serpent Trio.
  Past Positions: free-lance, London 1972–75;
    Royal Liverpool Philharmonic Orchestra
    1964–71.
  Contributions: author of articles on tuba in the
    *New Grove Dictionary of Music, Musical
    Instruments*, and *Jazz*, author of *The Tuba
    Family*, composer (mainly under pseudonym
    Josef Kronk).
  Education: BMus (Hons) London University,
    FLCM London College of Music, LRAM
    Royal Academy of Music, ARCM Royal
    College of Music.
  Teachers: Sidney Langston.
Bewley, Norlan
  Born: 12/05/59

Current Positions: Music Director, Top Brass
Quartet; Music Director, Harvey Phillips and
His TubaSantas.
Contributions: Contributor to *The Tuba Source
Book*, tuba/euphonium ensemble arranger.
Education: BM Indiana University (1982).
Teachers: Harvey Phillips, David Baker, Keith
Brown, Michael Lind, Mark Mordue, Albert
Buswell.

Bierley, Paul E.
Born: 02/03/26
Current Positions: Detroit Concert Band 1973–,
Hallelujah Brass/Ohio Village Brass 1982–,
Brass Band of Columbus 1984–, Columbus
Concert Band 1990–.
Past Positions: Columbus Symphony Orchestra
(1965–81), World Symphony Orchestra
(1971), Columbus Brass Quintet (1964–78),
Wheeling Steel Band (1942–44), North
American Aviation Concert Band (1961–76),
Instructor, Otterbein College (1990).
Education: BAeroEngr, Ohio State University
(1953).
Teachers: William J. Bell.

Bird, Gary
Born: 04/26/45
Current Positions: Professor, Indiana Univer-
sity of Pennsylvania 1971–, Johntown
Symphony Orchestra 1971–, Westmoreland
Symphony Orchestra and Brass Quintet
1978–.
Past Positions: Visiting Lecturer, Indiana
University School of Music (Spring 1991,
Summers 1989–91), Fort Worth Symphony
Orchestra (1970–71).
Contributions: Author of *Program Notes for the
Solo Tuba* (1994), record reviewer, *TUBA
Journal*
Education: BMEd Wisconsin State University
(1968), MM North Texas State University
(1971), DM Indiana University (1992).
Teachers: Harvey Phillips, David Kuehn, Ron
Bishop, Arnold Jacobs, Charles Dalkert,
Conrad DeJong.

Bishop, Ronald T.
Born: 12/21/34
Current Positions: The Cleveland Orchestra
1967–, Faculty, The Oberlin Conservatory of
Music, Oberlin College 1967–, The Cleve-
land Institute of Music 1967–.
Past Positions: The San Francisco Symphony
(1963–67), The San Francisco Opera
Orchestra (1963–67), The Buffalo Philhar-
monic (1960–63), The American Wind
Symphony (1960), The United States Army
Field Band (1956–59).
Contributions: Numerous recordings with the
Cleveland Orchestra, several recordings with
the Cleveland Symphonic Winds, recordings

of contemporary chamber music, articles
published in *The Brass Bulletin*, *Pedagogy
Editor*, *TUBA Journal* (1976–78).
Education: BM Eastman School of Music
(1956), MS University of Illinois (1960).
Teachers: Betty Hamilton Daboyaski, Roy S.
Thrall, Donald Knaub, Arnold Jacobs.

Bispo, Manuel Messias
Born: 07/22/34
Current Positions: Church orchestra tubist.
Teachers: Alvaro Cicarele.

Bjerregaard, Ole
Born: 12/11/22
Current Positions: Sjaellands Symfoniorkester,
Denmark, 1965–.
Past Positions: Copenhagen Summer Tivoli
(1950–65), Assistant, Royal Kapel, Danish
Broadcasting; Danish Symphony Orchestras.
Education: Det Kgl. Danske Musikkonserv-
atorium (1948–1952).
Teachers: Valdemar Christiansen, H. Kirstein
Christensen, Palmer Traulsen.

Bjørn-Larsen, Jens
Born: 09/14/65
Current Positions: Danish National Radio
Symphony Orchestra 1987–; Instructor,
Royal Danish Conservatory of Music 1987–.
Past Positions: free-lance Copenhagen
(1982–87).
Contributions: winner of several international
solo competitions; recipient of several Danish
prizes, including the Jacob Gade Prize, Music
Prize of Gladsaxe, and the Victor Borge
Prize; released several CD recordings; solo
concert tours; premieres of tuba composi-
tions.
Education: Royal Danish Conservatory of
Music.
Teachers: Asger Fredericia, JørgenVoight
Arnsted.

Black, George
1896–05/18/88
Past Positions: Tenth Regiment Band (1910–
1915); free-lance, Albany (1920–39); second
tuba, New York Philharmonic (1940s), New
York City Symphony, New York Broadway
shows; NBC Symphony; American Symphonic Band; Goldman Band; Golden Gate
Park Band; Los Angeles Light Opera;
teacher, Western Washington University
(1972–77); Bellingham Civic Band.
Education: self-taught.

Black, Phillip Conrad
Born: 05/25/55
Current Positions: Wichita Symphony 1986–,
Instructor, Wichita State University 1986–.
Past Positions: Galliard Brass Quintet (1980–
86), Flint Symphony Orchestra (1980–86),

New Mexico Brass Quintet (1977–80), New
Mexico Symphony (1977–80).
Contributions: two recordings with Galliard
Brass Quintet.
Education: BA Ball State University, MM
University of New Mexico.
Teachers: Abe Torchinsky, Karl Hinterbichler,
Lesley Varner, Sam Gnagy.

Bobo, Roger
Born: 06/08/38
Current Positions: International soloist and
presenter of masterclasses; Professor of Tuba,
Rotterdam Conservatorium; Professor of
Tuba and Brass Ensembles, Lausanne
Conservatoire; Professor of Tuba and Brass
Chamber Music, Fiesole Scuola di Musica
(Florence); Director of Brass, Italian National
Youth Orchestra.
Past Positions: Los Angeles Philharmonic
Orchestra (1964–89), Hollywood studio
musician (1964–89), Royal Concertgebouw
Orchestra (1962–62), Rochester Philhar-
monic Orchestra (1956–62).
Contributions: First tuba recital in Carnegie
Recital Hall (March 31, 1961); eight solo
recordings; author of numerous articles and
pedagogical materials for tuba; experimenta-
tion and development of instrument design;
guest artist on national television and
international brass conferences.
Education: BM Eastman School of Music
(1960), MM Eastman School of Music
(1961).
Teachers: Robert Marsteller, Donald Knaub,
William Bell, Emory Remington.

Boe, Morten
Born: 02/11/68
Current Positions: Teacher and Artist, Rana
Music School 1992–, Music Consultant,
Helgeland District of the Norwegian Band
Association 1992–.
Contributions: Initiator of the Rana "Tuba/
Euphonium Day," winner of the ITEC '92
quartet competition.
Education: BMEd University of Wisconsin-Eau
Claire (1992).
Teachers: Gerald Mattern, Bjorn E. Beverli,
Jerry A. Young.

Bouje, George
Past Positions: Free-lance studio musician, Los
Angeles.
Contributions: Recorded 1947 version of *Tubby
the Tuba* with Danny Kaye.

Bradley, Susan A.
Born: 07/14/54
Current Positions: Malvern Symphony Orchestra 1989–, free-lance jazz/chamber musician,
serpentist.

Education: BA Melborne University, Diploma
Education Melborne State College, Diploma
Arts Victoria College for the Arts, Licentiate
Trinity College, London.
Teachers: John Fletcher, John Jenkins, Stephen
Wick, John Woods, Simone de Haan, Peter
Sykes.

Brady, Angus J.
Born: 04/05/68
Current Positions: Halifax Militia Band 1985–,
Dalhousie Brass Quintet 1992–.
Education: BM Dalhousie University (1992).
Teachers: Ian Cowie, Herb Schoales.

Bragunier, David
Born: 03/11/39
Current Positions: National Symphony
Orchestra 1961–.
Past Positions: Faculty, Peabody Conservatory,
Catholic University, University of Maryland,
U.S. Army Field Band (1963–65).
Education: BM Peabody Conservatory (1961).
Teachers: Armand Sarro, William Bell,
Joseph Eger.

Brandon, Sy
Born: 06/24/45
Current Positions: Professor of Music, Millers-
ville University 1976–, York Symphony
Orchestra 1976–.
Past Positions: Instructor, Blue Mountain
Community College (1974–76); Visiting
Professor, Boise University (1973–74).
Contributions: Arranger and composer of works
for the tuba.
Education: BS, MS Ithaca College (1966,
1968); AMusD University of Arizona (1972).
Teachers: James Linn, Floyd Cooley.

Braunsdorf, Eugene
Past Positions: Detroit News Radio Orchestra,
station WWJ.

Brewer, Robert G.
Born: 10/25/57
Current Positions: Assistant Professor, Colo-
rado State University 1990–; CSU Faculty
Brass Quintet; Fort Collins Wind Symphony;
Fort Collins Symphony Orchestra.
Past Positions: South Arkansas Symphony
(1978–84), Henderson State University
Faculty Brass Quintet (1978–80).
Contributions: Contributor, *The Tuba
Source Book.*
Education: BME Henderson State University
(1980); MS, DMA University of Illinois
(1987, 1991).
Teachers: Fritz Kaenzig, Mark Moore, Robert
Gray, Dan Perantoni, Wesley Branstine, Volta
Anders.

Bridges, Andrew W.
Born: 05/07/61

Current Positions: Band of the Corps of Royal Engineers; Principal Tuba, Maidstone Symphony Orchestra.

Education: ARCM Royal College of Music (1979).

Teachers: John F. Smith, John Fletcher.

Brook, Cameron

Born: 05/15/61

Current Positions: West Australian Symphony Orchestra 1983–, Instructor, University of Western Australia 1985–.

Education: Dip. Arts (Mus) Victoria College of the Arts (1982).

Brown, E.L.

Past Positions: Noel Popping Orchestra, Buckingham Hotel Orchestra of Saint Louis, Roy Bargy and His Orchestra, Chicago (brother of Helen Brown).

Brown, Helen

Past Positions: Free-lance, St. Louis area (1920's) (sister of E.L. Brown).

Brun, Thomas

Born: 10/01/66

Current Positions:Copenhagen Radio Light Music Orchestra 1986–; Instructor, Frederikssund Jægerspris Guards and Youth Orchestra of Køge; free-lance, Copenhagen; Royal Danish Guard.

Education: Diploma Royal Danish Music Conservatory (1989).

Teachers: Arne Svendsen, Jørgen Voigt Arnsted, Jens Bjørn-Larsen.

Bryant, Steven

Born: 05/19/46

Current Positions: Associate Professor of Music, University of Texas at Austin 1976–; Austin Symphony Orchestra 1977–; Austin Lyric Opera 1989–.

Past Positions: Instructor, Central Methodist College (1971–72), Wichita Symphony Orchestra (1969–71).

Contributions: Treasurer (1992–), Publications Coordinator (1977–83) T.U.B.A.; Coordinator, 1976 International Tuba–Euphonium Conference; *TUBA Journal* Editor (1977–81).

Education: BM Ohio State University (1969), MM Wichita State University (1971), graduate study University of Iowa (1972–76).

Teachers: Robert LeBlanc, Donald Hummel, John Hill, Robert Yeats.

Bunn, Michael M.

Born: 09/03/54

Current Positions: Lecturer, University of Maryland 1979–; Howard University 1985–; Shenandoah University 1986–; George Mason University 1987–; St. Mary's College 1990–; Kennedy Center Opera House

Orchestra 1974–; Filene Center Orchestra 1974–; National Gallery Orchestra 1974–; Fairfax Symphony Orchestra 1985–; University of Maryland Brass Quintet 1979–; Shenandoah Brass Quintet 1986–; St. Mary's College Brass Quintet 1990–; Fairfax Symphony Brass Quintet 1985–; free-lance, Washington, D.C./Baltimore 1972–.

Education: BM, MM Peabody Institute (1977, 1979).

Teachers: Edward Whitfield, David Bragunier, Arnold Jacobs, Warren Deck.

Burger, Klaus

Born: 06/02/58

Current Positions: free-lance, RAI Torino; Ensemble 13; Ensemble Recherche, "Danses de Bouffons" jazz quartet.

Contributions: many tuba solos and chamber music pieces premiered, several recordings of ensembles, featured on German television.

Education: Diploma, Munich University

Teachers: Manfred Hoppert.

Burr, Paul A.

Born: 09/26/68

Current Positions: Band of the Corps of Royal Engineers.

Education: Royal Military School of Music, Kneller Hall.

Butte, William Carl

Born: 07/28/24

Current Positions: Free-lance, Oregon.

Past Positions: The Oregon Jazz Band, Capital City Jazz Band, Oregon Centennial Jazz Band, 70th Infantry Division Band.

Education: BA Williamette University (1953).

Teachers: Gordon Finlay, Vernon Wiscarson, "Cap" Beard, Maurice Brennan.

Butterfield, Don

Born: 06/15/22

Current Positions: Free-lance, New York; Tuba Instructor, Montclair State, Trenton State, Cean College, NYU, Columbia Teachers College, Mannes School.

Past Positions: American Symphony Orchestra (retired 1991), Radio City Music Hall, Studio Musician: New York, including CBS, NBC, ABC.

Contributions: Recorded with many great jazz artists, including Charles Mingus, Sonny Rollins, Cannonball Adderley, Teo Macero, Bill Evans, Dizzy Gillespie, Clark Terry, and the Thad Jones–Mel Lewis Orchestra. One of the most recorded tubists in history. By promoting the innovative sound of tuba to composers and arrangers in New York in the 1950s, he was largely responsible for the popularity of the instrument in commercial music. Recorded an award-winning jazz quintet album with Clark Terry in mid-

1950s. Composer and arranger of numerous works for tuba in ensembles.

Education: BM Juilliard School of Music (1952).

Teachers: Byron L. Miller (high school band director), William Bell.

Buttery, Gary A.

Born: 05/11/51

Current Positions: Principal tuba, US Coast Guard Band; Instructor of tuba, Connecticut College; Instructor of tuba, University of Rhode Island; A Different Village; Finest Kind; Whiskey Flats; Ireland's Eye; Griswold Inn Band.

Contributions: TUBA Regional Coordinator for New England, Coordinator for New England Tuba Symposium/Workshop (1984, 1988), Co-owner Whaling Music Publishers, first tuba soloist with NBC's Tonight Show Orchestra with Doc Sevrinsen, on Tonight Show (1979).

Education: BM, MM University of Northern Colorado (1974, 1975).

Teachers: Jack Robinson, Roger Bobo, Don Harry, Gale Dilehay, Ray Dusatko.

Call, R. Steven

Born: 6/29/49

Current Positions: Instructor of Tuba, Euphonium and Jazz Studies, Brigham Young University 1979–, Ballet West, Salt Lake City, Utah, free-lance, Utah.

Past Positions: Lecturer in Music, Utah State University (1971–72), Adjunct Instructor of Tuba, Euphonium and Jazz Piano, Weber State College (1981–85), Adjunct Instructor in Tuba and Music Education, University of Utah (1983–85), Alternate tubist, Utah Symphony (1973–90).

Contributions: Numerous recordings and tours with Mormon Tabernacle Choir and Utah Symphony, Contributor to the *The Tuba Source Book*, recorded *Tubby the Tuba* for Macmillan–McGraw Hill general music series (1993).

Education: BM, MM Utah State University (1971, 1975), post-graduate study, North Texas State University (1978), PhD University of Utah (in progress).

Teachers: Earl Swenson, Alvin Wardle, Charles Eckenrode, David Keuhn, Larry Zalkind, Michael Sanders.

Callender, George Sylvester "Red"

3/6/16–1990 (91?)

Former Positions: Free-lance, Los Angeles (1936–).

Contributions: Primarily a string bass player, performed and recorded with Louis Armstrong, Lester Young, Erroll Garner, Charlie Parker, Dexter Gordon, and Art Tatum. In the 1950s, became involved in commercial recording and recording for films and TV. One of the first modern jazz tuba soloists, recorded the first jazz tuba record, *Red Callender Speaks Low* (1957). Wrote autobiography *Unfinished Dream*, awarded Musician of the Year by the Los Angeles Jazz Society (1987).

Campbell-Wright, Stephen John

Born: 09/27/60

Current Positions: Deputy Music Director, Royal Australian Airforce Central Band 1989–.

Past Positions: Royal Australian Airforce Band Operational Command Band (1982–87).

Education: AM Australia (1983), AM Trinity College London (1989).

Teachers: Geoff Bailey, Arthur Hubbard.

Carlson, Andrew

Born: 09/13/56

Current Positions: The US Navy Band 1991–; Capital Brassworks 1991–; Brass Plus 1991–; Richmond Symphony 1992 (Interim).

Past Positions: Dallas Wind Symphony (1987–90); Instructor, Texas Christian University (1990); Chicago Civic Orchestra (1986); Orquesta Filarmonica de Santiago, Chile (1982–84).

Education: BME Illinois State University (1979), MM Indiana University (1985).

Teachers: Arnold Jacobs, Harvey Phillips, Ed Livingston, David Kirk, Ev Gilmore.

Carmona, Francisco Espejo

Born: 08/09/72

Current Positions: Quinteto de Metales de Montilla, Banda de Musica "Pascual Marquina."

Past Positions: Orquesta de Viento del Conservatorio de Cordoba (1992–93), Antigua Orquesta "Ciudad de Cordoba" (1991–92), Grupo de Metales del Conservatorio de Montilla (1990–91).

Education: Bachillerato Superior (1990).

Teachers: Juan Jose Amores Molero, Antonio Ureña Molina.

Carroll, Bill

Born: 01/24/34

Current Positions: Bob Schulz's Frisco Jazz Band (San Francisco), John Gill's Minstrels of Annie Street (New Orleans), Frisco Syncopators (San Diego), Eddie Bayard Classic New Orleans Jazz Orchestra (New Orleans).

Past Positions: Pat Yankee and the Sinners (1962–63); Red Garter Band (1963–65); Turk Murphy's Jazz Band (1965–87).

Contributions: One of the leading traditional jazz tubists in the U.S.; has performed extensively with Turk Murphy, including the historic 1987 Carnegie Hall recordings.

Education: Started playing tuba about 1960,
self-taught.

Carson, Cora Youngblood
Past Positions: owner, manager "Girls of the
Golden West," tuba and sousaphone soloist
worldwide, Cora Youngblood Carson Sextet.

Catelinet, Phillip Bramwell
Born: 12/03/10
Past Positions: BBC Military Band (1938–
1942), BBC Theatre Orchestra, London
Symphony, London Philharmonia, Faculty,
Carnegie-Mellon University (1956–76).
Contributions: premiered Vaughan Williams
tuba concerto with the London Symphony
Orchestra (1954); composer and arranger of
many works for tuba; honorary advisory
board, T.U.B.A.; contest adjudicator, Great
Britain and abroad.

Cates, Gerald L
Born: 03/01/63
Current Positions: The US Military Academy
Band 1989–, West Point Tuba Quartet
1989–.
Past Positions: Instructor of Tuba, Indiana
State University (1985–86).
Education: BME Tennessee Technological
University (1985), MME University of
Illinois (1986).
Teachers: R. Winston Morris, Fritz Kaenzig.

Cattley, Gary Thomas
Born: 11/2/55
Current Positions: Free-lance, New Jersey.
Education: BA Trenton State College (1979),
MM North Texas University (1987), PhD
University of North Texas (in progress).
Teachers: Don Little, Alex Cauthen, John
Stevens, David Uber.

Cazes, Alain
Born: 04/13/56
Current Positions: Professor, Montreal
Conservatory of Music 1983–, Instructor,
University of Montreal 1986–, Orchestre
Métropolitain 1983–, Société de Musique
Contemporaine du Québec, 1981–.
Past Positions: Instructor, University of
Quebec, Montreal (1981–89), McGill
University (1983–90), extra, Montreal
Symphony (1981–89), Paraiba State
Orchestra (Brazil) (1980–81).
Contributions: Founder and Editor of "Les
Editions Cazes-Cuivres" (1981–88), Summit
Brass Council (1987–88). Many arrange-
ments for tuba ensemble, brass choir,
premiered two works for tuba, featured on
radio education, Montreal Conservatory of
Music (1971–78).
Education: Conservatoire de Musique de
Montréal (1978).
Teachers: Joseph Zuskin, Joseph Novotny, Don
Harry, Ronald Bishop.

Cenciarini, Angelo
Born: 07/16/58
Current Positions: Banda Nazionale Dell'
Esercito.
Teachers: Carlo Ingrati.

Choi, Young Taek
Born: 01/09/1956
Current Positions: Academy Wind Orchestra
1985– .
Education: Seoul National University (1979).
Teachers: Lee Chong Il, Lee Cae Ok.

Chong Il Yi
Born: 02/20/44
Current Positions: KBS Symphony Orchestra
1967–; Korea Tuba Association Honorary
President 1988–; Korea Music Association
Board Member 1976–.
Past Positions: Korea Tuba Association
President (1978–88).
Education: BA College of Music, Seoul
National University (1961–65).
Teachers: Jae Ok Lee, Harvey Phillips.

Christensen, Goran K.
Born: 11/11/72
Current Positions: Swedish Army Life Dra-
goons, Stockholm; Instructor of Tuba in
Horse Riding.
Education: Conservatory of Music, Falun
(1991).
Teachers: Michael Lind, Svenolof Tuvas,
Roland Lindberg.

Cipriano, Antonio
Born: 09/04/46
Current Positions: Banda Nazionale Dell'
Esercito.
Teachers: Lacerenza.

Clark, William F.
Born: 01/24/42
Current Positions: Senior Instructor, University
of Colorado, Denver 1981–; leader, Queen
City Jazz Band 1985–.
Past Positions: Instructor, University of Denver
(1969–79).
Contributions: director, Rocky Mountain Low
Tuba Ensemble
Education: BMus University of Colorado
(1964), MM Northwestern University
(1966).
Teachers: Norman Beville, Don Herron, Arnold
Jacobs.

Clark, Willie E.
Born: 12/02/68
Current Positions: Walt Disney/MGM Studios
Tuba Quartet "The Tubafours."
Education: attended University of Illinois
(1986–89).
Teachers: Fritz Kaenzig, Richard Frazier, David
Pack, Roger Rocco, John P. Weber.

Clements, Tony
Born: 08/29/54

Current Positions: San José Symphony
Orchestra 1981–.
Education: California State University,
Northridge.
Teachers: Gary Tirey, Tommy Johnson, Jim
Self, Roger Bobo, Loren Marstellar.

Cole, June Lawrence (June Coles)
1903–10/10/60
Past Positions: McKinney's Cotton Pickers
(1923–26); Fletcher Henderson (1926–28).
After the 1920s, played string bass with
various jazz artists including Willie "The
Lion" Smith
Contributions: Was tubist on important
Fletcher Henderson recordings in the 1920s.

Cole-McCollough
Born: 05/22/46
Current Positions: Instructor, Maryhurst
College.
Education: BA Maryhurst College (1984), MM
University of Portland (1987).
Teachers: Charles Botton.

Connor, Rex Alton
Born: 03/15/15
Past Positions: US Army music positions
(1942–46); Faculty, Wayne State College
(NE) (1953–60); Instructor, National Music
Camp, Interlochen (1957–82); Professor,
University of Kentucky (1960–80).
Contributions: Many articles published in the
Instrumentalist magazine, first tuba specialist
hired by a major university, first tubist hired
by National Music Camp at Interlochen.
Education: BMEd Kansas University (1938),
MM University of Missouri (1953).
Teachers: George C. Wilson.

Conrad, Herman
Past Positions: Sousa Band, Pryor Band, Victor
Talking Machine Company Band, free-lance,
New York.

Conrad, Paul G.
Born: 06/29/56
Current Positions: State Orchestra of Mexico
1986–, Quinteto de Metales de Toluca
1982–
Past Positions: Professor, Escuela Superior de
Musica, Mexico City (1986–92), Conserva-
torio Nacional de Musica, Mexico City
(1986–92); Adjunct Professor, Faculty Brass
Quintet, Northern Kentucky University
(1983–86); Faculty Brass Quintet, Wright
State University (1983–84); Instructor,
Cincinnati Conservatory Preparatory
Department (1982–85).
Contributions: First Tuba soloist, State
Orchestra of Mexico; has premiered several
compositions.
Education: Bowling Green State University,
Cincinnati College Conservatory of Music.

Teachers: Jamie Halfter, Ivan Hammond, Sam
Green, Mike Thornton.

Corella, Gilbert C.
Born: 07/27/63
Current Position: The US Air Force Band 1985–.
Education: BM Catholic University (1989).
Teachers: David Fedderly, Milt Stevens,
Bernard Gucik, Steven Bryant, John Holland.

Cornacchia, Luciano
Born: 08/25/63
Current Positions: Banda Nazionale Dell'
Aeronautica.
Past Positions: Banda Esercito.
Education: Diploma Solfeggio.
Teachers: Carlo Ingrati.

Cotnoir, Jean-François
Born: 12/07/59
Current Positions: Foothills Brass Quintet,
1988–, Calgary Wind Quintet, 1992–,
Calgary Concert Band, 1991–.
Past Positions: Trois–Rivières Symphony
(1980–87); Mount Royal Orchestra,
Montreal (1986–88); Laurentian Brass
(1984–87); Brass Comarades (1981–87).
Education: Conservatoire de Musique au
Quebec (1987), BM, MM McGill University
(1982, 1986).
Teachers: Alain Cazes, Pierre Brandry, Gene
Pokorny, Joseph Zuskin, Harvey Phillips,
Dan Perantoni.

Cradler, John M.
Born: 12/01/65
Current Positions: The US Marine Band 1989–,
The US Marine Band Brass Quintet 1989–.
Education: BM University of Wisconsin–
Madison (1989), MM University of Akron
(1989).
Teachers: Tucker Jolly, John Stevens, Ronald
Davis, Daniel Perantoni, Dennis Miller, Ron
Bishop.

Cremer, Thomas G.
Born: 05/23/61
Current Positions: Free-lance, Bermuda 1990–.
Past Positions: National Symphony of Peru
(1985–87), Lima Brass Quintet (1985–87).
Education: BMus University of Massachusetts-
Amherst (1983), MM University of Kentucky
(1989).
Teachers: Skip Gray, Michael Thornton, Sam
Pilafian, George N. Parks.

Cresci, Andrew
Born: 01/25/59
Current Positions: Bournemouth Symphony
Orchestra 1986–.
Past Positions: Scottish Opera Orchestra
(1980–86), Scottish Ballet Orchestra
(1980–82).
Education: GRNCM PPRNCM Royal Northern
College of Music—Manchester (1977–80).

Teachers: Idris Rees, Nigel Seamen, Stuart
Roebuck.
Crump, Byron Leslie John
Born: 01/13/62
Current Positions: Brass Razoo Quintet, 1985–;
free-lance, Brisbane, 1985–.
Contributions: *Australian Trombone Education
Magazine* record reviews and articles 1986–.
Education: Diploma of Music, Qld Conserva-
torium (1986); Associate Diploma of Jazz (in
progress).
Teachers: Craig Cunningham, Arthur Middle-
ton, Ed Wilson.
Culbertson, Melvin
Born: 04/09/46
Current Positions: Orchestre National de
Bordeaux Aquitaine, France; Professor,
Superior Music Conservatory of Lyon;
Master Class Teacher, Conservatory of
Bordeaux and Perpignan.
Contributions: Instrument design consultant,
over 60 solo premieres.
Education: University of California-Long
Beach, Juilliard School of Music, New
England Conservatory.
Cummings, Barton
Born: 07/10/46
Current Positions: Vallejo Symphony 1985–,
Concord Pavillion Pops Orchestra 1986–,
Brass-Works of San Francisco 1985–, Solano
Dixie Jubilee 1987–.
Past Positions: Adjunct Instructor, Diablo
Valley College (1990–92), Instructor, Delta
State University (1979–82), Lecturer, San
Diego State University (1974–79), Lecturer,
Point Loma Nazarene College (1976–79).
Contributions: First Secretary for reorganized
TUBA (1972); Secretary-Coordinator, First
International Tuba-Euphonium Workshop
(1973); New Materials Editor, *TUBA
Journal*, commissioned and premiered several
dozen compositions, four solo albums,
published text, composed many published
tuba compositions.
Education: BSEd University of New Hampshire
(1968), MM Ball State University (1973),
post-graduate study Indiana University.
Teachers: Harvey Phillips, Mary Rasmussen,
Keith Polk, Paul Gay, J. Lesley Varner.
Cunningham, Craig W.
Born: 11/20/60
Current Positions: Queensland Symphony
Orchestra 1981–, Lecturer, Queensland
Conservatorium of Music 1982–, Queensland
Symphony Orchestra Brass Quintet.
Education: Music Diploma.
Teachers: Royston Whybird, Vin Fryer, Simone
de Haan, Harvey Phillips.
Da Silva, Fabio Jose
Born: 10/07/63

Current Positions: Banda Marcial Municipal de
Itaquaquece.
Past Positions: Ceramica Giotoku.
Education: Escola Municipal de Musica, São
Paulo.
Teachers: Drauzio Chagas.
Daellenbach, Charles
Born: 07/12/45
Current Positions: Canadian Brass 1970–.
Past Positions: Professor, University of Toronto
(1970–72), Hamilton Philharmonic, extra,
Rochester Philharmonic, free-lance, Toronto.
Contributions: published various arrangements
of music for tuba.
Education: BM, MM, PhD, Eastman School of
Music (1962–70).
Teachers: Conrad Daellenbach, Donald Knaub,
Arnold Jacobs, Ronald T. Bishop.
Damacena, Ulisses de Lima
Born: 12/11/68
Current Positions: Quinteto de Metail Nobre,
Banda Musical de Cubatão.
Contributions: Primeira Audição Mundial de
Recital de Tuba com Musica Popular
Brasileira; Recital Educativo de Tuba no
Centro Musical de Volta Redonda, Rio de
Janeiro; Audição com Solos de Tuba.
Education: Estudou na Escola Livre de Musica
da Banda Musical da Cosipa e Banda Musical
de Cubatão.
Teachers: Donald Smith, Eliezer Araujo.
Daniel, Robert N.
Born: 02/28/51
Current Positions: Principal Tuba, The US Air
Force Band 1974–, Camerata Brass Quintet
1975–.
Past Positions: Adjunct Professor of Music,
Virginia Commonwealth University
(1978–86).
Contributions: Consultant, *The Tuba Source
Book*, Past President TUBA (1989–91),
President TUBA (1987–89), Vice-President
TUBA (1985–87), TUBA Regional Coordi-
nator, Washington DC, Virginia, Maryland,
West Virginia (1978–84), Region IV
Workshop Coordinator, University of
Maryland (1979).
Education: BMEd Texas Tech University
(1973), MM Catholic University (1976).
Teachers: David Payne, David Bragunier.
Dapeer, David
Past Positions: Jack Denny's Orchestra,
Metropolitan Orchestra of New York.
Davis, Ronald Andrew
Born: 12/06/54
Current Positions: Associate Professor,
University of South Carolina; Augusta
Symphony Orchestra; Palmetto Brass.
Past Positions: Visiting Assistant Professor,
University of Wisconsin, Madison, Santa

Barbara Symphony Orchestra, Instructor, California State University, Fullerton, Instructor, California Lutheran College.

Contributions: Assistant Editor, *The Tuba Source Book*, cassette recording, contributing reviewer *TUBA Journal*.

Education: BM California State University, Fullerton (1977), MM Bowling Green State University (1979), DMA University of Southern California (1984).

Teachers: Jim Self, Tommy Johnson, Ivan Hammond, Roger Bobo, Ron Bishop.

De Freitas, Valdecir

Born: 09/08/66

Current Positions: Banda Sinfonica da ULM.

Past Positions: Banda Sinfonica de Itapecirica da Serra.

Education: Universidade Livre de Musica.

Teachers: Sebastiao Claudino de Freitas, Donald Smith.

Deck, Warren

Born: 02/20/54

Current Positions: New York Philharnomic 1979–, Instuctor, The Juilliard School 1988.

Past Positions: Houston Symphony (1977–79); Instructor, Rice University (1977–79).

Contributions: tuba manufacturer design consultant, premiered solo compositions.

Education: Attended University of Michigan (1972–75).

Teachers: Abe Torchinsky, Arnold Jacobs, Joseph Novotny.

Demchenko, Andrey V.

Born: 01/15/74

Current Positions: State Symphony Orchestra of Ukraine, trainee 1992–.

Education: Kiev Musical College (1993).

Teachers: Yuri Strelchuk.

Del Negro, Luke

Past Positions: Conway Band, Sousa Band, New York Symphony Orchestra, Capitol Theatre, New York. Victor Company recording artist.

Diamond, Kelly

Current Positions: US Navy Band 1993–.

Education: BM, BME University of Kentucky (1992).

Teachers: Skip Gray.

Donatelli, Phillip

Past Positions: Philadelphia Orchestra, Curtis Institute.

Contributions: One of the great teachers and players of the 1930s and 40s. Tubist on the soundtrack of Walt Disney's *Fantasia*. Arnold Jacobs was one of his many students.

Donley, Roger

Past Positions: Spike Jones Orchestra.

Dossadin, Vladimir

Born: 06/21/33

Current Positions: Professor, Russian Music Academy "Gnesin" 1973–.

Past Positions: Bolshoi Symphony Orchestra (1956–80)

Contributions: jury member for various competitions in Russia and in Geneva (1992); has recorded albums and radio recordings.

Douglas, Bruce E.

Born: 09/26/17

Past Positions: Rochester Symphony Orchestra; Rochester Brass Quintet.

Education: BA, MD University of Wisconsin.

Teachers: William Bell, Arnold Jacobs.

Dowling, Eugene A.

Born: 01/19/50

Current Positions: Adjunct Assistant Professor of Music, University of Victoria 1976–; Victoria Symphony 1976–; BrassWest 1976–.

Past Positions: Free-lance, Chicago (1972–76), substitute, Chicago Symphony Orchestra (1974–76).

Contributions: CD solo recording.

Education: BM Michigan State University (1972), MM Northwestern University (1974).

Teachers: Leonard Falcone, Arnold Jacobs.

Draper, Raymond Allen (Ray)

08/4/40–11/01/82

Past Positions: Played and recorded in and around New York with Jackie McLean (1956–57), Donald Byrd, John Coltrane (1956–58), Max Roach (1958–59), Don Cherry (1962). Moved to England in 1969, where he played with Archie Shepp and Dr. John. Move back to U.S. in 1971 and recorded with Brother Jack McDuff, taught for a short time at Wesleyan University, and played with Howard Johnson's tuba ensemble, "Gravity."

Contributions: One of the most recorded and promising jazz tubists of the 1960s, Draper had personal problems that kept him from achieving his potential. He served prison time in California in the 1960s and was killed in a robbery attempt in New York in 1982.

Drauzio, Chagas

Born: 07/09/36

Current Positions: Instructor, Municipal School of Music, São Paulo 1980–; Municipal Brass Quintet, 1981–.

Past Positions: Municipal Symphony Orchestra 1972, 1975, 1981.

Contributions: Brazilian popular music arranged for tubas and euphonium.

Education: attended Escola de Musica de São Paulo.

Teachers: Antonio Ceccato, Gilberto Gagliardi, Gasparo Pagliuso.

Duga, Jan Z

Born: 09/19/58

Current Positions: The US Air Force Band
1983–, Prince William Symphony Orchestra
1987–, Prince William Symphony Orchestra
Brass Quintet 1987–.
Contributions: Consultant, *The Tuba Source
Book*, New Materials Reviewer, *TUBA
Journal*
Education: BME Ohio State University (1980),
MM Arizona State University (1982).
Teachers: Robert LeBlanc, Raymond Nutaitis,
Michael Bunn, Paul Krzywicki.
Dumitru, Ionel
Born: 07/08/15
Past Positions: Faculty, Bucharest Military
School; Music High School in Bucharest;
Bucharest Music Academy; Tubist, The
George Enescu Philharmony; The Romanian
Army Orchestra; The Romanian Broadcasting
Company Orchestra; The Imperial Orchestra
of Teheran; free-lance tubist in concerts,
recordings, and radio broadcasts in Poland,
Yugoslavia, Bulgaria, France, Germany, Italy,
Greece, Turkey, Sweden, USSR, Belgium,
Czeckoslovakia, Hungary, and Switzerland.
Contributions: member of T.U.B.A. Advisory
Board, nomination in "Who's Who in Music,"
has arranged over 250 compositions for tuba,
has composed over 80 compositions for tuba.
Education: Music Gymnasium and Academy of
Music, Bucharest.
Duss, Hans
Born: 09/01/63
Current Positions: Teacher, Entlebucher
Musikschule 1986–; Tonhalle Orchester
1989–; Philharmonic Brass Quintet 1986–;
Schweizer Armeespiel 1991–.
Education: Teachers Diploma Konservatorium
Luzern (1991).
Teachers: Simon Styles, Rex Martin, Arnold
Jacobs, Roger Bobo.
Dutart, Thomas A.
Born: 07/04/35
Current Positions: Tuleburg Jazz Band 1980–.
Past Positions: Peat Dusters Jazz Band (1977–
80), "Music Makers" Stockton (1967–78).
Education: BA University of the Pacific (1961),
MS University of LaVerne (1992).
Teachers: Self-taught.
Dutton, Brenton Price
Born: 03/20/50
Current Positions: Professor, San Diego State
University 1981–, Brass coach, Jounesses
Musicales World Orchestra (Summers) 1986–,
San Diego Brass Consort 1983–.
Past Positions: Professor, California Institute of
the Arts (1982–85), Assistant Professor,
Central Michigan University (1976–81),
Instructor, Oberlin Conservatory (1975–76),
L'Orchestre Symphonique du Québec

(1971–74), LeGrande Ballet (1971–74),
Cleveland Brass Quintet (1974–76), Pacific
Tuba Quartet (1986–).
Contributions: Assistant Editor, *TUBA Journal*
(1976–80), over 30 original compositions
published, numerous recordings as performer
or composer.
Education: BM, MM (1975, 1976) Oberlin
Conservatory.
Teachers: Ron Bishop, Mel Carey, Tom
Toddington.
Earl, Brian R.
Born: 10/06/59
Current Positions: La Scala Opera House,
Milan 1983–.
Past Positions: Free-lance, Manchester, England
(1980–82), Hong Kong Philharmonic
(1978–79).
Education: ARCM Royal College of Music
(1980), BMus Royal Northern College of
Music (1982).
Teachers: Stuart Roebuck, John Jenkins,
Roger Bobo.
Eastep, Michael B.
Born: 10/20/50
Current Positions: Calgary Philharmonic
Orchestra, Bow Valley Brass Ensemble,
Beaver Fever Tuba Ensemble, Instructor,
University of Calgary.
Past Positions: Winnipeg Symphony Orchestra,
Instructor, Brandon University.
Education: Florida State University (1968–70),
BA North Texas State University (1973).
Teachers: William Cramer, David Kuehn,
Arnold Jacobs, Abe Torchinsky.
Easton Ewan, Kenneth
Born: 08/30/61
Current Positions: Ulster Orchestra 1983–,
Ulster Brass 1983–.
Past Positions: Brighouse and Rastrick (1979–
83), N.Y.O. (1975–78), E.C.Y.O.
(1979–83).
Contributions: British premiere of John
Williams' *Tuba Concerto* (May 1991).
Education: RNCM.
Teachers: Tom Atkinson, Stuart Roebuck.
Eklund, Steven K.
Born: 11/30/64
Current Positions: Air Mobility Command
Band, Scott AFB 1991–.
Past Positions: 590th Air Force Band, McCord
AFB (1990–91); Pacific Brass Quintet
(1984–90).
Education: BM Biola University (1986).
Teachers: David Pack, Norm Pearson, Tommy
Johnson, Sam Pilafian, Scott Mendoker,
Gene Pokorny.
Eliason, Robert E.
Born: 03/28/33

Current Positions: Dartmouth Symphony
Orchestra (1988–), Yankee Brass Festival
(1986–), Brass Works Quartet (1985–).
White Mountain Brass (1990–).
Past Positions: Kansas City Philharmonic
(1960–69), 7th Army Symphony Orchestra
(1956–57), Doug Jacobs Red Garter Banjo
Band (1972–85).
Contributions: TUBA International President
(1973–75), *TUBA Journal* Pictorial History
of the Tuba Series (1975–86).
Education: BM University of Michigan (1955),
MM Manhattan School of Music (1959),
DMA University of Missouri-Kansas City
(1969).
Teachers: Glen Smith, William Bell, Arnold
Jacobs.
Elliot, John D.
Born: 05/21/52
Current Positions: Free-lance, London 1974–,
Glyndebourne Opera 1990–.
Past Positions: Jerusalem Symphony Orchestra
(1973–74), "Barnum" (1981–86), Kent
Opera (1976–89), Scottish Opera Orchestra
(1987–88).
Contributions: Has several arrangements and
original compositions for tuba ensemble,
brass quintet, and solo tuba with various
combinations, including one commission.
Education: AGSM Guildhall School of Music,
London (1973).
Teachers: Michael Barnes, John Fletcher, Jim
Anderson.
Emilson, C. Rudolph
Born: 09/20/39
Current Positions: Associate Professor, SUNY-
Fredonia 1968–.
Past Positions: Niagara Falls Philharmonic
(1963–66), Binghamton Symphony (1967–
68), SUNY-Fredonia Faculty Brass Quintet
(1968–85).
Contributions: Numerous premieres of new
works for tuba.
Education: BSMusEd SUNY-Fredonia (1961),
MM Ithaca College (1967), doctoral work
Indiana University.
Teachers: Richard Meyers, James Linn, Keith
Brown, Harvey Phillips, Don Knaub.
Endrédi, Robert
Born: 01/08/66
Current Positions: Teacher, State Music Scolle
Kolcsei; Simfonic-Orcheste of Nyiregyháza;
Holborne Quintet of Nyiregyháza.
Education: Music Academy of Miskolc.
Teachers: Nemesné, Szabó Ilona.
Erhart, Werner
Born: 07/10/53
Current Positions: Philharmonischen Orchester
Freiburg.

Education: Musikhochschule Würzberg.
Teachers: Walter Daum.
Erickson, Martin D.
Born: 02/02/47
Current Positions: Bowie Brass Quintet 1987–,
Instrument design consultant 1993–.
Past Positions: Lansing Symphony 1966–67,
The US Navy Band 1967–93, Founding
Member of The US Navy Band Tuba–
Euphonium Quartet 1985–93, The US Navy
Band Brass Quintet 1969–93.
Contributions: President, TUBA (1991–
93), Vice-President, TUBA (1989–91),
Member, Executive Committee of
Leonard Falcone International Eupho-
nium Festival, consultant, *The Tuba
Source Book*, premiered over 25 composi-
tions for tuba–euphonium quartet and
brass quintet.
Education: Attended Michigan State University.
Teachers: Margaret Erickson, Rex A. Conner,
Gilbert Stansell, Edward Livingston, Leonard
Falcone.
Erickson, Sumner P.
Born: 04/01/62
Current Positions: Pittsburgh Symphony
Orchestra 1981–, Adjunct Professor,
Carnegie Mellon University 1983–.
Past Positions: Instructor, Duquesne University
(1984–87), Temple University Preparatory
Division (1980).
Education: attended Curtis Institute of Music
(1980–81).
Teachers: Richard Colvin, Steven Bryant, Paul
Krzywicki, Arnold Jacobs, Edward Klein-
hammer, Glenn Dodson.
Euler, Thomas
Born: 01/25/69
Current Positions: Ausbildungsmusikkorps der
Bundeswehr.
Education: Robert Schumann Hochschule
Düsseldorf.
Teachers: Hans Gelhar, Finn Schumacker.
Evans, Eliot D.
Born: 7/23/47
Current Positions: The US Marine Band 1977–.
Past Positions: The US Armed Forces Bicenten-
nial Band (1975–1976), The US Marine
Band (1970–1974).
Education: BM University of Michigan (1970).
Teachers: Howard Hovey, Don Butterfield,
Douglas Greer, David Peterson.
Evans, Mark
Born: 07/15/50
Current Positions: Deutsche Oper Berlin 1977–,
Berlin Chamber Brass 1993–.
Past Positions: Wichita Symphony Orchestra
(1973–75), Detroit Concert Band (1973–
76), Wichita Brass Quintet (1973–75),

Staatstheater Darmstadt (1976), Berlin Brass Quintet (1978–88), Brandenburg Quintet (1988–90), Bayreuth Festival Orchestra (1978).

Contributions: Design Consultant Yamaha Corporation, TUBA Board of Directors, juror for competition, music publisher.

Education: BM University of Michigan (1972), MM Wichita State University (1975).

Fabio da Silva, José
Born: 10/07/63
Current Positions: Banda Marcial Municipal de Itaquaquecetuba.
Past Positions: Cerâmica Giôtoku.
Education: Escola Municipal de Música, São Paulo.
Teachers: Drauzio Chagas.

Fedderly, David T.
Born: 11/04/53
Current Positions: Baltimore Symphony Orchestra (1983–), Instructor, The Peabody Institute Instructor of Tuba, Catholic University.
Past Positions: Instructor, DePaul University, Harper Junior College, St. Louis Symphony Orchestra (1982–83), extra tuba, Chicago Symphony (1976–82).
Education: BME Northwestern University (1976).
Teachers: Arnold Jacobs, Paul Walton.

Feldman, Enrique C. "Hank"
Born: 07/15/66
Current Positions: Associate Director of Bands/Professor of Tuba, University of Arizona 1992– .
Past Positions: University of Wisconsin (1990–92).
Contributions: Written and arranged for unaccompanied tuba and tuba in chamber music.
Education: BMEd University of Arizona (1988), MM, MS University of Illinois (1990).
Teachers: Dan Perantoni, Fritz Kaenzig, Mark Moore.

Fischer, Michael A.
Born: 07/23/57
Current Positions: Lecturer, Baylor University 1990–, Waco Symphony Orchestra 1990–.
Past Positions: Lincoln Symphony (1986–87), Great Plains Brass Quintet (1986–87), Midlands Brass Quintet (1984–87).
Contributions: Assistant to President of T.U.B.A. (1988–90).
Education: BME Pittsburgh State University (1980), MSME University of Illinois (1981), MM University of Nebraska-Omaha (1987).
Teachers: Alex Cauthen, Craig Fuller, Robert Kehle, Don Little, Daniel Perantoni, Gene Volleen.

Fletcher, John
05/19/41–10/06/87
Past Positions: BBC Symphony Orchestra, London (1964–68), London Symphony Orchestra (1958–87), Phillip Jones Brass Ensemble.
Contributions: one of England's greatest tubists, with solos featured in many radio broadcasts and recordings, published arrangements for tuba and piano, appeared as lecturer and recitalist in many international conventions.
Education: BA (Cantab.) Natural Sciences, Honorary RAM (Royal Academy of Music, London).

Foreman, Steve
Born: 01/04/62
Current Positions: free-lance, New York City; Cardinal Brass Quintet.
Past Positions: Ohio Chamber Orchestra.
Education: BM Oberlin College Conservatory (1984), MM Juilliard School of Music (1990).
Teachers: Ronald Bishop, Toby Hanks, Abe Torchinsky, Warren Deck.

Formeck, Michael Charles
Born: 12/11/52
Current Positions: Guest Lecturer, Grove City College 1979–, Musicians Concert Band 1985–.
Education: BSMusEd Clarion State College (1974), MMEd Duquesne University (1980).
Teachers: Paul Walker, Dean Franham, Stanley Michalski, Matty Shiner.

Fratia, Salvatore
Born: 06/19/59
Current Positions: Great Lakes Brass Quintet 1991–, Brassroots 1990–, Bottom Line Brass Tuba Quartet 1989–, Toronto free-lance 1987–.
Past Positions: Winnipeg Symphony Orchestra, Royal Winnipeg Ballet Orchestra, Manitoba Opera Orchestra, CBC Winnipeg Orchestra, Winnipeg Brass Ensemble, Northern Brass Quintet, tuba instructor at Universities of Brandon and Manitoba (all positions from 1982–87).
Education: BM Performance University of Toronto (1984).
Teachers: Don Harry, Claude Engli, Kent Mason, Don Johnson.

Frazier, Richard O.
Born: 07/07/47
Current Positions: Instructor, University of Oregon 1990–, Chicago Chamber Brass 1977–, Eugene Symphony Orchestra 1990–.
Past Positions: Adjunct Instructor, Lamar University (1989–90), Lake Charles Symphony (1989–90), Oak Park River Forest

Symphony (1977–81), Elmhurst Symphony (1977–80), Civic Orchestra of Chicago (1977–79), Instructor, Sam Houston State University (1973–77), Wharton County Junior College (1971–73), free-lance, Houston (1967– 77), Amarillo Symphony Orchestra (1965–67).

Contributions: Founder, Chicago Chamber Brass, former Texas-Louisiana Regional Chairman, T.U.B.A., organized Texas-Louisiana Tuba Euphonium Symposium (1976), founder and past-president, Metro-CATS (Chicago chapter of T.U.B.A.), presented Arnold Jacobs Workshop (1991), Pacific Northwest Regional T.U.B.A. Symposium (1992), published in *TUBA Journal*, many recordings with Chicago Chamber Brass, recipient of Ed Jablonsky Memorial Award for Distinguished Achievement in Tuba, University of Houston (1969).

Education: BMus MM University of Houston (1970, 1971).

Teachers: Arnold Jacobs, William Rose, Don Baird.

Frey, Michael
Born: 11/11/51
Current Positions: Jazz Sextet Interkantonale Blasabfuhr
Past Positions: Free-lance, Switzerland 1981–.
Education: Swiss Jazz School, Berklee College of Music.
Teachers: David LeClair.

Fritz, Eric Shawn
Born: 06/01/66
Current Positions: Orguesta Sinfonica de Xalapa, Veracruz.
Past Positions: Spoleto Festival Orchestra U.S.A. and Italy.
Education: BM University of Southern California (1989), MM Juilliard School of Music (1992).
Teachers: Warren Deck, Tommy Johnson, David Kirk, Doug Tornquist.

Fritze, Gregory P.
Born: 01/14/54
Current Positions: Rhode Island Philharmonic Orchestra 1983–, Instructor, Berklee College of Music 1979–, Cambridge Symphonic Brass Ensemble 1985–, Colonial Tuba Quartet 1989–.
Past Positions: Instructor, Brown University (1982–85), Rhode Island College (1984–1991), Thundermist Brass Quintet.
Contributions: Consultant, *The Tuba Source Book*, Contributing Editor, *TUBA Journal*, Coordinator, New England Tuba Festival (1981–83), Co-coordinator, New England Tuba Festival (1980, 1985, 1988), composer

of several pieces for tuba and tuba ensemble.
Education: BM Boston Conservatory of Music (1976), MM Indiana University (1979), Doctoral Studies, Indiana University (1978–81).
Teachers: F. Chester Roberts, Harvey Phillips.

Fulgenzio, Feliciano
Born: 04/25/63
Current Positions: Banda Nazionale Dell'Aeronautica.
Education: Diploma Solfeggio.
Teachers: Merolli Gemmaro.

Fuller, Craig L.
Born: 04/30/56
Current Positions: Omaha Symphony 1978–, Instructor, University of Nebraska, Lincoln 1989–, Odyssey Brass Quintet 1978–, Lincoln Symphony 1987–.
Past Positions: Adjunct Instructor, University of Nebraska, Omaha (1978–89).
Contributions: Contributor, *The Tuba Source Book*, Co-Director, TUBA Regional Symposium (1985), Sponsor, TubaChristmas and Octubafest, Omaha (1978–89).
Education: BM Indiana University (1978), Performer's Certificate (1977).
Teachers: Harvey Phillips, Ronald Bishop, Robert LeBlanc, Gary Tirey.

Funderburk, Jeffrey Lee
Born: 11/02/59
Current Positions: Associate Professor, University of Northern Iowa 1987–, Waterloo/Cedar Falls Symphony 1987–, Cedar Rapids Symphony 1989–, Northern Brass Quintet 1987–.
Past Positions: Artist-in-Residence, Custom Music Company.
Contributions: T.U.B.A. Board of Directors (1989–), Instrument Design Consultant for Meinl-Weston Tubas (1987–), Vice-President, T.U.B.A. 1993–, Chair, T.U.B.A. International Conference Committee (1987–91), video on tuba repair and maintenance.
Education: BM University of Southern Mississippi, MM, DMA University of Illinois.
Teachers: Scott MacMorran, Mark Moore, Dan Perantoni, Fritz Kaenzig, Arnold Jacobs.

Furgensen, Horst
Born: 09/14/37
Current Positions: Police Band Schleswig-Holstein, Kiel 1972–.
Past Positions: Police Band Essen (1968–72).
Education: Folkwang Conservatory Essen.

Gábor, Moldován
Born: 07/19/43
Current Positions: Hungarian Central Army Band.
Education: Budapest (1959–62).
Teachers: András Pehl.

Gagliano, Vincenzo
  Born: 07/23/66
  Current Positions: Opera di Roma.
  Past Positions: Teatro Massimo Palermo.
  Education: Scuola Musica Salerno.
  Teachers: Roddo Citro.
Gannett, David W. (Dave)
  Born: 05/13/51
  Current Positions: The Bok Tower Brass, The
    Barehanded Wolfchokers.
  Past Positions: Boston Symphony, Boston Pops,
    Don Ellis Band, Black Dogs, staff tubist, Walt
    Disney Productions, California and Florida;
    performed with Mel Torme, Peter Nero,
    Helen Reddy, Ray Charles, among others.
  Contributions: Composer, arranger, and
    director of tuba ensembles for jazz festivals,
    feature writer "Today's Tuba Masters" for
    West Coast Rag (1990–92), two solo albums.
  Education: New England Conservatory of
    Music (1969–71), Rockefeller Foundation
    Grant.
  Teachers: Bill Bell, Harvey Phillips, Robert
    Tucci.
Garamendi, Rocha Roberto
  Born: 05/03/64
  Current Positions: Sinfonica Nacional de
    Mexico.
  Past Positions: Orguesta Filharmonica del Bajio
    Guanajuato, Mexico.
  Education: Conservatorio Nacional de Musica,
    Escuela de Musica "Ollin Yolitzli."
  Teachers: Dwight Sullinger.
Gateau, Richard S.T.
  Born: 09/23/65
  Current Positions: Stockholms Spärvägsmäns
    Musikkår 1992–.
  Education: Malmö University of Music (1983–
    88), National Center for Orchestral Studies
    (London) (1987–88), Stockholm University
    of Music (1990–91).
  Teachers: Arne Svendsen, Robert Tucci, Jim
    Gourley, Michael Lind.
Gedeon, Jakab
  Born: 08/08/54
  Current Positions: Teacher, Musical School
    "Lajtha László" 1986–, "Gaudium" Wind
    Band
  Contributions: contributed to Fanfare Wind
    Band Magazine.
  Education: Liszt Ferenc Conservatory
    (1979–81).
  Teachers: László Szabó, András Pehl,
    György Zilc.
Geib, Fred
  Past Positions: Radio City Music Hall (1930s
    and 40s), New York Symphony Orchestra,
    free-lance recording artist, New York.

Contributions: author of several method books
    and solos.
Geiger, Loren D.
  Born: 01/23/46
  Current Positions: Orchard Park Symphony
    1970–; Buffalo Civic Orchestra 1973–;
    Clarence Summer Orchestra 1971–.
  Past Positions: 20th Century Symphonic Band
    (1968–83).
  Education: BM, MM Eastman School of Music
    (1968, 1970).
  Teachers: Donald Knaub, Peter Popiel, Robert
    Vehar, Ronald Bishop, William Kearney.
Geisler, Carsten
  Born: 03/21/50
  Current Positions: Den Kongelige Livgardes
    Musikkorps 1975–, Den Kongelige Livgardes
    Musikkorps Brass Quintet 1990–.
  Education: Det Fynske Musikkonservatorium
    (1970–76).
  Teachers: Jørgen Voigt Arnsted.
Geisler, K. Josef
  Born: 06/07/60
  Current Positions: Heeresmusikkorps 2, Kassel
    1993–, Symphony Orchester des Stadttheater
    Giessen 1988–.
  Past Positions: Heeremusikkorps 5, Giessen
    1985–1993.
  Education: Musikalische Fachprufung, Aus-
    bildungsmusikkorps der Bundeswehr in
    Hilden (1985), Künstlerische Abschluss-
    prüfung (Orchestermusiker), Robert
    Schumann-Institut Düsseldorf (1985).
  Teachers: Ulrich Wittke, Kralik, Inagawa.
Gerhard, Georgi
  Born: 04/17/39
  Current Positions: Südwest Funk Sinfonie
    Orchestra, Baden-Baden 1968–.
  Past Positions: Niedersächs Sinfonie Orchestra,
    Hanover (1966–68).
  Education: Musikhochschule, Frankfurt
    (1944–48).
  Teachers: G. Oltersdorf.
Gerhardt, Niels
  Born: 04/26/56
  Current Positions: Free-lance, Copenhagen
    (1984–), JazzGruppe 90 (1992–).
  Education: Diploma (Bass Trombone) Royal
    Danish Conservatory of Music (1991).
  Teachers: Jørgen V. Arnsted, Jens Bjørn-Larsen.
Gesl, Ludwig
  Born: 05/17/71
  Current Positions: Brass Band Jung-Ohing,
    Carnival Brass Band Waging/See.
  Teachers: Mase Pochner, Klaus Zahnbrecher,
    Gerhard Siltmann.
Gifford, Robert M.
  Born: 11/21/41

Current Positions: Professor, Southwest Missouri State University 1981–.

Past Positions: Associate Professor, Central Missouri State University (1973–81).

Contributions: Premieres of low brass ensemble music.

Education: BME University of Kansas (1964), MM University of Michigan (1971), MFA, DMA University of Iowa (1978).

Teachers: John D. Hill, Vernon Forbes, Glenn Smith, Frank Crisafulli, Arnold Jacobs, Dennis Smith.

Giordano, Vince
  Born: 03/11/52
  Current Positions: Vince Giordano's Nighthawks 1977–, free-lance: New York 1977–.
  Past Positions: Navy Show Band (1970–73), Clyde McCoy's Dixieland Band (1974–75), New York Jazz Repertory Co. (late 1970s).
  Contributions: Is a leading authority and arranger of 1920s and 1930s jazz and popular music and has performed on various soundtracks and films.
  Teachers: Joe Tarto.

Glidden, David Bruce
  Born: 06/02/59
  Current Positions: Radio Sinfonie Orchester Frankfurt (Hessischer Rundfunk) Germany 1988–.
  Past Positions: Teacher, Musikhochschulen in Karlsruhe and Frankfurt am Main, the R.S.O. Frankfurt, Radio Orchestra of Turin, Italy (RAI) (1983–88), Teacher, "Scuola di Alta Perfezonamente" Saluzzo, Italy.
  Education: BME University of Illinois (1982).
  Teachers: Daniel Perantoni, Arnold Jacobs, Robert Tucci.

Goldstein, Edward R.
  Born: 07/29/54
  Current Positions: Visiting Lecturer, Towson State University 1980–, Instructor, Essex Community College 1977–, Baltimore School for Arts 1982–, Peabody Preparatory Department of The Johns Hopkins University 1976–, Howard Community College 1983–, Annapolis Symphony Orchestra 1974–, Peabody Ragtime Ensemble 1974–, free-lance Baltimore (jazz and classical), Symphony Pops appearances with banjoist, Buddy Wachter.
  Past Positions: Instructor, University of Maryland, Baltimore County (1975–80), Community College of Baltimore.
  Contributions: Associate Editor: *The Tuba Source Book*, Concert reviews, *TUBA Journal*
  Education: BMEd Peabody Conservatory of Music (1976), MM Peabody Institute of the Johns Hopkins University (1978).

Teachers: David Bragunier, Charles Vernon, Arnold Jacobs, Ron Friedman, Vickie Perkins.

Good, Matthew J.
  Current Positions: Jacksonville Symphony Orchestra 1987–, Faculty, Brevard Music Center 1989–.
  Past Positions: Adjunct Faculty, University of Florida (1991).
  Education: BM Curtis Institute of Music (1985).
  Teachers: Donald Stanley, Donald Harry, Paul Krzywicki, Warren Deck.

Gorbyeiko, Vasily Alekseyevich
  Born: 08/18/48
  Current Positions: Russia State Symphony Choir.
  Past Positions: Moscow Television and Radio Symphony Orchestra (1972–81), USSR Ministry of Culture Symphony Orchestra (1981–92).
  Contributions: many solo radio broadcasts.
  Education: Kiev Music Academy (1965–68), Kiev Conservatory (1970–71), Moscow Conservatory (1971–75).
  Teachers: Prof. Garan, Prof. Lebedev.

Graham, B. Sibley
  Born: 04/04/69
  Current Positions: Northern Ballet Orchestra 1991–, Sheridan Brass Ensemble, Parnasus Brass Quintet.
  Education: GGSM Guildhall School of Music and Drama, London (1991).
  Teachers: James Anderson, Peter Ganve, Patrick Harrild.

Granger, William L.
  Born: 09/15/65
  Current Positions: Macon Brass Quintet 1989–, Cobb Symphony Orchestra 1990–, Sandy Springs Community Orchestra 1992–.
  Contributions: Arranger/composer of solo tuba, brass quintet, tuba-euphonium ensemble works.
  Education: BMus University of Georgia (1987), MMEd University of Georgia (1990).
  Teachers: David Randolph.

Gray, Skip
  Born: 09/09/55
  Current Positions: Professor of Music, University of Kentucky 1980–, Lexington Philharmonic 1980–.
  Past Positions: Orchestra Sinfonica di Torino de la RAI (1988–90).
  Contributions: Assistant Editor, *The Tuba Source Book*, Director, 1992 International Tuba-Euphonium Conference, Secretary, T.U.B.A. (1987–91), countless tuba-euphonium ensemble arrangements, solo CD recording (in progress).

Education: BM Baldwin-Wallace College
(1977), MM, DMA University of Illinois
(1979, 1994).
Teachers: Daniel Perantoni, Ronald Bishop.

Green, George
Past Positions: Free-lance and studio musician,
Los Angeles including MGM Studios.

Greigo, Thomas Damian
Born: 09/06/40
Current Positions: Teacher, Bundesreal-
gymnasium IX, Vienna 1992–.
Education: BA University of California, Los
Angeles (1963), MM University of Southern
California (1981), teaching credential,
Pepperdine University.
Teachers; Don Butterfield, Tommy Johnson.

Griffiths, John Roger
Born: 03/05/48
Current Positions: Regina Symphony Orchestra,
Wascana Brass Quintet.
Past Positions: R.C.M.P. Band (1967–73).
Contributions: Artist/Clinician, Yamaha-
Canada, author of popular low brass text.
Education: BMEd University of Regina (1974),
MM University of Michigan (1976).
Teachers: Abe Torchinsky, Robert Ryker, John
Upchurch.

Grose, Michael
Born: 04/05/60
Current Positions: Savannah Symphony
Orchestra 1986–, Faculty, Armstrong State
College 1987–.
Past Positions: Civic Orchestra of Chicago,
Chicago Philharmonic, Evanston (IL)
Symphony, Millar Brass Ensemble (1982–
86), Asbury Brass Quintet (1983–86).
Contributions: Organized the first BeeTUBAn
(à la Beethoven) Festival in Savannah, GA
(1989).
Education: Attended Portland State University,
Clark College (1978–81), BM, MM
Northwestern University (1984, 1985).
Teachers: Marc Wolters, John Richards, James
Sandberg, Robert Rusk, Arnold Jacobs,
Charles Vernon.

Gross, Clair E.
Born: 01/24/38
Current Positions: Reading Symphony Orchestra 1977–, Pottstown Symphony Orchestra
1980–, Reading Pops Orchestra 1969–.
Education: BS, MS West Chester University
(1962, 1969).
Teachers: L. Brunner Wallace, Tyrone Breun-
inger, Paul Krzywicki.

Gunn, Stuart Hall
Born: 01/10/44
Current Positions: Free-lance, Boston Area
1966–, Cape Cod Symphony 1991–, Boston
Brass Ensemble 1966–, Bob Connor's Early

Jazz Bands, Lee Child's Bourbon Street
Paraders, and Back Bay Ramblers (11
recordings).
Past Positions: Private teacher, (1972–80), Old
Jazz Ensemble of Boston (1974–82), Edaville
Roundhouse Ramblers Dixieland Band
(1976–89).
Contributions: Six recordings with Bob
Connors Yankee Rhythm Kings, two
recordings with Lee Childs Bourbon St.
Paraders, three recordings with Back Bay
Ramblers. Appeared prominently on the
sound track of several movies.
Education: BM, MM Boston Conservatory of
Music.
Teachers: Willis Traphagan, John Coffee, F.
Chester Roberts.

Gunning, Paul W.
Born: 06/06/61
Current Positions: Royal Australian Airforce
Central Band 1989–, Director: Melbourne
Tuba/Euphonium Ensemble.
Past Positions: Principal Study Teacher, Victoria
College of the Arts (1987–89), Band of the
Third Military District, Melbourne
(1987–88).
Contributions: Founding member, Solitaire
Tuba/Euphonium Ensemble, Co–founder,
Antipodes Tubas 1992–.
Teachers: Peter Sykes, Ian Perry, Frank Barzyk.

Gyula, Johann
Born: 04/15/67
Current Positions: Teacher, Lutheran Theologi-
cal Academy, Budapest 1989–, Brass-band
1990–.
Education: Pécs (1981–88).
Teachers: Stefan Sztankov.

Haas, Ulrich
Born: 03/07/59
Current Positions: Melton Tuba Quartet
(1987–), instructor at Folkwang Music
School of Duisburg (1988–), Duisburger
Sinfoniker (1983–).
Past Positions: State Opera at Kassel, Duisburg
Symphony/Deutsche Oper am Rhein (1983),
Rhein Brass Quintet (1984–90).
Contributions: Top national prize, Jugend
Musiziert competition.
Teachers: Hans Gelhar, Paul Heims.

Habersetzer, Martin
Born: 02/22/70
Current Positions: Ausbildungsmusikkorps der
Bundeswehr Hilden.
Education: Robert Schumann Hochschule
Düsseldorf.
Teachers: Hans Gelhar.

Hacken, Andreas
Born: 12/04/69

Current Positions: Ausbildungsmusikkorps der
Bundeswehr Hilden.
Education: Robert Schumann Hochschule.
Teachers: Hans Gelhar.

Hale, Edward L.
Born: 11/28/74
Contributions: International Consultant,
Austria: *The Tuba Source Book.*
Education: American Institute of Music, Vienna
(in progress).
Teachers: Davi Detwiler, Jan Duga, Sam
Pilafian, John Manning, Scott Mendoker,
Jonathan Sass.

Hall, Russell "Candy"
Past Positions: Spike Jones Orchestra.

Hallerståhl, Ingmar
Born: 06/26/53
Current Positions: Umeå Symphony Orchestra
1989–, Norrlands Operan 1989–, Umeå
Brass Ensemble 1989–.
Past Positions: Region Musiken Östersund
(1976–88), Lans Musiken Östersund
(1988–89).
Education: Musikhogskolan Malmö (1975).
Teachers: Jørgen Arnsted, Michael Lind.

Hammond, Ivan
Born: 02/25/41
Current Positions: Professor, Bowling Green
State University 1967–, Bowling Green Brass
Quintet 1967–, Great Lakes Brass Quintet
1977–.
Past Positions: L'Orchestre Symphonique du
Québec 1961–62, North Carolina Symphony
1963–65, American Symphony Orchestra
League's Shenendoah Festival Orchestra
1970–80.
Contributions: numerous premieres of solo
works and pieces for tuba and other
instruments.
Education: BM, MM, Performer's Certificate
Indiana University.
Teachers: Edwin "Buddy" Baker, William Bell,
Thomas Beversdorf, Abe Kniaz, Arnold
Jacobs, William Rose.

Haney, Ronald
Born: 01/17/50
Current Positions: The US Marine Band.
Education: BS George Washington University
(1976).
Teachers: Oscar LaCassey, Douglas Grier,
David Fedderly.

Hanks, Thompson (Toby)
Born: 07/03/41
Current Positions: New York City Ballet
Orchestra 1967–, Chautauqua Symphony
Orchestra 1972–, American Composers
Orchestra 1970–, Yale University, Manhattan
School of Music, New England Con-
servatory.

Past Positions: San Antonio Symphony (1964),
Minneapolis Symphony (1964–67), Puerto
Rico Symphony (1963), New York Brass
Quintet (1967–85).
Contributions: Premiere numerous works
with New York Brass Quintet, solo
recording (1977), several premieres and
commissions.
Education: Lamar University, Eastman School
of Music.
Teachers: Richard Burkart, Arnold Jacobs,
Donald Knaub.

Hansen, Carl Boye
Born: 11/24/65
Current Positions: free-lance, Copenhagen
1985–, Danish Tuba Quartet 1985–.
Past Positions: Diploma Royal Danish Academy
of Music (1991).
Teachers: Leo Sorensen, Jørgen Voight
Arnsted, Jens Bjørn-Larsen.

Harden, Viola
Born: 04/17/64
Current Positions: Hamburger Symphoniker
1982–.
Education: Diploma, Musikhochschule,
Hamburg (1979).
Teachers: Ronald Pisarkiewicz, Deiter Ciche-
wiecz, John Fletcher.

Harrild, Patrick
Born: 03/17/52
Current Positions: London Symphony Orches-
tra 1988–, Professor of Tuba, Royal Academy
1976–, Guildhall School 1989–, Royal
Military School of Music Kinglian Hall
1977–, National Youth Orchestra of Great
Britian 1987–, Member of London Sym-
phony Brass 1988–.
Past Positions: Royal Philharmonic Orchestra
(1974–88), Professor of Tuba, Royal College
of Music (1972–84).
Education: GGSM Guildhall School of Music
and Drama, Hon. ARAM (Asociate Royal
Academy).
Teachers: John Fletcher, James Anderson.

Harris, Charles W.
Past Positions: Rolfe's Colonial Sextette, Sousa
Band, free-lance, New York (1920s).

Hartman, Donald
Born: 04/29/29
Current Positions: Anchorage Civic Orchestra;
Anchorage Blaskapelle; Dixieland North Jazz
band.
Past Positions: Anchorage Symphony.
Education: BA, MA University of California,
Los Angeles (1954, 1957).
Teachers: Wendy Williamson, Larry Whitcomb,
Randall Holmes.

Harvey, Nigel
Born: 01/02/61

Current Positions: Stockholm Spårvagens
  Musickår.
Education: Dalaro Folkholskola; private study
  in London.
Teachers: John Fletcher, Carl-Otto Naessen.
Hegedüs, György
  Born: 04/27/65
  Current Positions: Concert Brass Band of the
    Hungarian Customs Police, Budapest 1988–
  Education: School of Music, Dunaujváros
    (1975–79), Conservatoire, Pecs (1979–83),
    Liszt College of Music, Szeged (1985–88)
  Teachers: Aattila Kovács, Stefán Stankov, Zsolt
    Nagy.
Hegels, Henning
  Born: 06/10/60
  Current Positions: Ausbildungsmusikkorps der
    Bundeswehr Hilden.
  Education: Robert Schumann Hochschule
    Düsseldorf.
  Teachers: Hans Gelhar.
Heil, Klaus
  Born: 07/09/58
  Current Positions: Slesvigske Fodregiment
    Musikkorps Haderslev 1986–, Haderslev
    Brass Quintet 1989–.
  Education: The Funen Academy of Music
    (1979).
  Teachers: Jørgen Voigt Arnsted, Hans An-
    dersen.
Heise, Martin
  Born: 08/19/70
  Current Positions: Ausbildungsmusikkorps der
    Bundeswehr Hilden.
  Teachers: Hans Gelhar.
Hellberg, John
  Past Positions: Sousa Band (son of August Sr.).
Helleberg, August Sr.
  Died: 1930s
  Past Positions: First tubist of Chicago Symphony
    Orchestra (1891–94), Philharmonic Society of
    Brooklyn Orchestra (1889–91), Theodore
    Thomas Orchestra (1889–91), Orchestra of
    Columbian Exposition (1893), Metropolitan
    Opera Orchestra, (1909–12), Sousa Band
    (1900, 1910), New York Military Band
    (1919), Goldman Concert Band (1920–21),
    Goldman's Metropolitan Sextette (1911).
Helleberg, August Jr.
  Past Positions: Sousa Band (son of August Sr.).
Henry, Eric L.
  Born: 06/08/54
  Current Positions: Harrisburg Symphony
    Orchestra 1984–, Hot House Early Jazz
    Band 1978–, Keystone Tuba Quartet 1986–,
    Lancaster Symphony Orchestra 1988–, free-
    lance, Pennsylvania.
  Past Positions: 19th Army Band, Fort Dix, New
    Jersey (1974–1976).

Contributions: Founder, Carlisle Octubafest,
  Keystone Chapter of TUBA, Co–founder,
  Winter Brass Project.
Education: BA Mansfield University
  (1980).
Teachers: Gary Bird, Don Stanley, David
  Fedderly.
Heo, Jae Young
  Born: 10/01/58
  Current Positions: Lecturer, University of Jung
    Ang 1985–, University of Kyung Hee 1986–,
    University of Han Yang 1992–, Seoul
    Philharmonic Orchestra 1982–, Seoul Brass
    Quintet 1986–.
  Past Positions: Korea Tuba Society President
    (1986–91).
  Contributions: Korea Festival Ensemble
    Member 1986–.
  Education: Jung-Ang University of Seoul,
    Korea (1977–82), Köln Musik Hochschule
    von Deutschland (Cologne University of
    Germany) (1983–1985).
  Teachers: Hans Gelhar, Ji-Chung Hi.
Herdman, Robert J.
  Born: 07/08/51
  Current Positions: Brucknerorchestra Linz
    1974–, Teacher of Tuba, Bruckner Conserva-
    tory 1977–.
  Education: Vienna Hochschule (Academy) of
    Music (1973), Institute of Advanced Musical
    Studies, Montreux, Switzerland (1974).
  Teachers: Leopold Kolar, Robert Tucci, Harvey
    Phillips, Mel Culbertson.
Hershko, Shmuel Adi
  Current Positions: Israel Philharmonic Orches-
    tra 1978–.
  Contributions: solo CD recording of Israeli
    composers, regular soloist with Israeli
    orchestras.
  Teachers: Roger Bobo, Arnold Jacobs.
Hess, Anton
  Born: 05/16/50
  Current Positions: Rheinische Philharmonie,
    Koblenz 1974–.
  Past Positions: Ernst Mosch Orchestra (1970–
    71); Munich Military Band (1971–73);
    Landestheatre Detmond (1973–74).
  Teachers: Bernhard Hesing, Manfred Graser.
Hildebrant, Donald Jay
  Born: 10/18/44
  Current Positions: Professor, University of
    Delaware 1978–, Bass Trombone, Delaware
    Symphony 1979–, Trombone/euphonium,
    Delaware Brass 1983–, euphonium, Colonial
    Tuba Quartet.
  Past Positions, Associate Professor of Music,
    University of Wisconsin-Stevens Point
    (1969–78), Associate Instructor, Indiana
    University (1971–73).

Contributions: Premiered numerous compositions with Colonial Tuba Quartet, arranger/transcriber, organizer of TUBACHRISTMAS and OCTUBAFEST events.
Education: BME, MM, DM Indiana University (1967, 1969, 1976).
Teachers: William Bell, Harvey Phillips, Henry C. Smith.

Hilgers, Walter
Born: 02/25/59
Current Positions: Professor, University of Music and Theatre, Hamburg; North German Broadcast Symphony Orchestra, Hamburg 1991–.
Past Positions: Philharmonic State Orchestra, Hamburg (1981–91); Symphony Orchestra, Dussaldorf (1978–81).
Contributions: Vice-President, Deutsches Tuba Forum, solo CD recording, appearances at international conventions, world premieres of tuba compositions.
Education: Examination of music artists, University of Music "Rheinland-Aachen."
Teachers: Fritz Huhn, Hans Gelhar.

Hiljanen, Jyrki
Born: 11/15/60
Current Positions: Satakunta Military Band 1981–.
Education: Niinisalo Garrison Band (1981), Warrant Officer School Phase I (1983), Warrant Officer School Phase II (1992).
Teachers: Taisto Nurum.

Hiljanen, Timo Antero
Born: 11/16/68
Current Positions: Satakunta Military Band, Artillery Brigade.
Past Positions: Finnish Defence Forces Military Music School Helsinki (1985–87), Lahti (1987–89).
Education: Conservatory Helsinki (1985–87), Lahti (1987–89, 92).
Teachers: Raimo Pesonen, Eino Takalo-Eskola, Juha Salmela.

Hindborg, Eigil
Born: 05/10/40
Current Positions: Prinsens Livregiment 1968–.
Teachers: Carl Cristensen, Kaj Kruse, Asger Fredericia.

Hinman, Paul R.
Born: 11/28/54
Current Positions: Assistant Professor, East Tennessee State University 1990–, Johnson City Symphony 1990–, East Tennessee Brass Quintet (1990–).
Education: BA, MA Western Illinois University (1977, 1982).
Teachers: Hugo Magliocco, Bob Rada.

Hipp, Lee
Born: 07/23/58

Current Positions: San Antonio Symphony 1989–, San Antonio Brass 1989–, Instructor, University of Texas at San Antonio 1989–, UTSA Faculty Brass Quintet 1985–.
Past Positions: Miami City Ballet Orchestra (1988–89), Southwest Florida Symphony (1987–89), Dallas Ballet Orchestra (1986–87), Dallas Wind Symphony (1985–87).
Education: BME Texas Tech University (1980), MM Southern Methodist University (1985).
Teachers: David Kirk, Everett Gilmore, David Payne, Don Little, Sandy Keathley.

Hoelzley, Paul D.
Born: 03/28/40
Current Positions: Associate Professor, Trinity Western University.
Past Positions: Instructor, University of Alberta (1984–86), University of Calgary (1978–81), Edmonton Symphony Orchestra (1983–84), Calgary Philharmonic Orchestra (1977–81), Israel Philharmonic Orchestra (1968–73), Tulsa Philharmonic Orchestra (1962–64), US Army Field Band (1959–61).
Education: BME University of Tulsa (1964), MM University of Michigan (1965), Certificate de Musique National Conservatoire de Paris (1968), PhD University of Alberta (1986).
Teachers: William Bell, Arnold Jacobs, Paul Bernard.

Högstedt, Anders
Born: 11/23/67
Current Positions: Free-lance, Stockholm.
Education: Musikhögskolan, Stockholm (1989).
Teachers: Michael Lind, Melvin Culbertson.

Hohmann, Hubert
Born: 03/03/59
Current Positions: Staadtstheater am Gärtnerplatz, Munich 1983–; Bavaria Brass Collection 1989–; "Pinguin's" Brass Ensemble 1990–.
Past Positions: Teacher, Leopold Mozart Konservatorium, Augsburg (1985–91).
Contributions: charter member, Deutsches Tuba Forum.
Education: Staatsexamen for tuba and music teacher, diploma Musikhochschule, Munich (1980, 1982).
Teachers: Manfred Hoppert.

Holmes, Ian Roy
Born: 08/07/62
Current Positions: Head of Brass, Clifton College Bristol, Sun Life Band, Bristol Philharmonia, Examiner, Guildhall School of Music.
Past Positions: Head of Brass, Hymers College Hull, Instructor, Musicale Holidays Ltd., University of Hull, London Brass Virtuosi.

Education: BA Yale University (1983), ARCM
Royal College of Music (1983), attended
Banff Centre of Fine Arts.

Teachers: Patrick Harrild, John Jenkins, John
Fletcher, Dan Perantoni, Dennis Miller.

Holmes, William D.
Born: 08/06/45
Current Positions: Associate Professor, Arkansas
State University 1977–, Northeast Arkansas
Symphony.
Past Positions: Instructor, Texas A & I
University (1971–75), U.S. Army Field Band
(1968–71), Corpus Christi Symphony
(1973–75).
Education: BME University of North Texas
(1966), MM Emporia State University
(1968), DMA University of North Texas
(1985).
Teachers: Leon Brown, Tom Wright, David
Kuehn, Donald Little.

Holmgaard, Lars
Born: 10/17/64
Current Positions: Royal Danish Orchestra
1989–, Royal Danish Brass 1989–.
Past Positions: Free-lance, Denmark, Sweden,
Norway, England.
Contributions: Arranger, brass ensemble, low
brass quintet, solo tuba.
Education: Academy of Music, Århus (1984–
86), National Centre for Orchestral Studies
(London) (1986–87), Academy of Music,
Århus (1987–88), Royal Acadamy of Music,
Copenhagen (1988–89).
Teachers: Hans Anderson, John Fletcher,
Patrick Harrild, Jørgen V. Arnsted.

Hommer, Lajos
Born: 09/20/51
Current Positions: Hungarian State Opera
Orchestra 1972–, Hungarian Philaharmonic
Society Symphony Orchestra, Music School
of the Hungarian Army 1983–.
Past Positions: Hungarian Army Band
(1970–72).
Education: Music School of the Hungarian
Army (1970).
Teachers: Márton Heltai, Rudolf Boda, Ferenc
Steiner, László Szabó.

Honma, Takashi
Born: 05/24/50
Current Positions: Japan Philharmonic
Orchestra, Tokyo Bari-Tuba Ensemble
Contributions: JETA committee member.
Education: BA Tokyo Music College (1975).
Teachers: Shinsuke Tanaka.

Hoppert, Manfred
Born: 11/24/34
Current Positions: Bavarian Radio Symphony
Orchestra; Professor, Music Conservatory,
Munich; Mozarteum, Salzburg.

Past Positions: Radiophilharmonic Orchestra,
Hannover.
Contributions: Vice-President and founding
member, Deutsche Tuba Forum; published
orchestral excerpts.
Education: State Conservatory, Weimar (1951–
56), private study with Paul Heims
(1959–60).
Teachers: Karl Arend, Paul Heims.

Hore, Phillip
Born: 07/27/42
Current Positions: Royal Scottish National
Orchestra 1968–.
Teachers: Paul Lawrence, Michael Barnes, John
Wilson.

Hovey, Arthur H.
Born: 10/06/42
Current Positions: Galvanized Jazz Band,
Connecticut Symphonic Band.
Past Positions: New Haven Symphony Orches-
tra, Elm City Brass Quintet.
Contributions: Contributor of articles to *TUBA
Journal*
Education: BA, MAT Yale University (1964,
1965).
Teachers: Howard Hovey.

Hovey, Karl M.
Born: 06/28/58
Current Positions: The US Navy Band 1992–,
Mt. Vernon Chamber Symphony 1992–.
Past Positions: Shreveport Symphony 1989–92,
Instructor, Stephen F. Austin University
(1990–92), Longview Symphony (1991–92),
San Antonio Symphony (1988), free-lance,
Dallas/Ft. Worth (1982–91), US Navy Band
(San Francisco 1980–82, Charleston 1978–
80), Charleston Symphony (1978–80).
Education: BM University of North Texas
(1987), MM University of North Texas
(1991).
Teachers: Donald C. Little, Abe Torchinsky,
Michael Sanders, Everett Gilmore.

Hull, Edward L.
Born: 05/12/54
Current Positions: Blue Street Jazz Band
1988–.
Past Positions: Free-lance, Los Angeles (1976–
80), Charleston Symphony Orchestra (1974–
76), 6th Naval District Band (1972–76).
Contributions: Arranger of feature numbers for
tuba with jazz band.
Education: Basic Course, Armed Forces School
of Music (Navy), Norfolk, VA (1973), BM
California State University Long Beach
(1979), MA California State University
Fresno (1988).
Teachers: Jeffrey Reynolds, Robert Simmer-
gren, Roger Rickson.

Hunsberger, Jay N.
  Born: 06/12/65
  Current Positions: Florida West Coast Symphony 1987–; Florida Brass Quintet 1987–; Professor, Manatee Community College 1990–.
  Education: BM Indiana University (1987).
  Teachers: Harvey Phillips, Sam Pilafian, James DeSano, Keith Brown, Ed Anderson, Donald J. Hildebrandt.
Hunt, Douglas
  Born: 08/17/44
  Current Positions: Visiting Lecturer, University of the Pacific 1989–, Stockton Symphony 1986–, Brassific Quintet 1989–.
  Past Positions: U.S. Naval Academy Band (1969–72), Annapolis Symphony (1969–73).
  Education: BM, MA University of the Pacific (1966, 1991).
Hupertz, Markus
  Born: 04/07/66
  Current Positions: Gebirgsmusikkorps 8 Garmisch-Partenkirchen.
  Contributions: Deutsches Tuba Forum EV.
  Education: Robert Schumann Hochschule Düsseldorf.
  Teachers: Hans Gelhar.
Hylander, Magnus
  Born: 12/04/67
  Current Positions: Brassa Nova brass quintet 1992–, Quintetto Enscendo 1990–.
  Past Positions: Malmö free-lance (1988–92).
  Contributions: Arranger of over 100 tuba/euphonium ensembles.
  Education: Malmö College of Music (1988–92).
  Teachers: Kjell Lindstrom, Arne Svendsen, Torbjorn Kuist.
Hyodo, Masahumi
  Born: 07/26/66
  Current Positions: Reoma World REM Band 1991–.
  Education: BA Kyoto College of Music (1990).
  Teachers: Kazuo Ishizaki, Hideo Sano, Eiichi Murayama.
Ingrati, Carlo
  Born: 01/25/47
  Current Positions: Orchestra Sinfonia Rai Roji.
  Past Positions: Bande Esercito.
  Education: Diploma Trombone.
  Teachers: Rocco Citro.
Irvine, J. Scott
  Born: 12/30/53
  Current Positions: Canadian Opera Company Orchestra 1984–, Hannaford Street Silver Band 1989–, Gabrieli Brass Quintet 1985–, Esprit Orchestra 1982–, New Music Concerts (Toronto) 1981–, Instructor of Tuba, York University (Toronto) 1982–.

Past Positions: Borgy's Banjo Reunion (1974–88), Professor Futz and his Band of Nutz (1977–82), Hogtown City Slickers (1974).
  Contributions: Has commissioned or influenced the composition of over a dozen new works featuring the tuba. Is active as a composer with a *Concertino* for euphonium and several works for brass band.
  Education: BM University of Toronto (1989).
  Teachers: Charles Daellenbach, J. Kent Mason.
Islas, Albert J.
  Born: 03/07/61
  Current Positions: The US Air Force Training Command Band 1990–, Air Training Command Band Brass Quintet 1992–.
  Past Positions: Naples Philharmonic, Naples, FL (1989–90).
  Education: BMEd Southwest Texas State University (1984), graduate work, Florida State University.
  Teachers: David Kirk, Michael Sanders, Paul Ebbers, J. Lesley Varner, Jesse Lotspeich.
Ito, Shinobu
  Born: 12/09/65
  Current Positions: Saitama Police Department Band 1989–.
  Contributions: Assistant Editor, *JETA Journal*.
  Education: BA Tokyo University of Arts (1989).
  Teachers: Kiyoshi Ohishi, Katsuhiro Nakanowatari.
Ivzhenko, Yuri G.
  Born: 12/27/57
  Current Positions: National Opera Theatre of Ukraine (1978).
  Education: Kiev Musical College (1978).
  Teachers: Victor Sinko.
Iwabuchi, Taisuki
  Born: 03/03/58
  Current Positions: Kanagawa Philharmonic Orchestra, Tokyo Bari-Tuba Ensemble.
  Contributions: JETA committee member.
  Education: BA Kunitachi Music College (1980).
  Teachers: Kiyoshi Ohishi, Ikumitsu Tado.
Jacobs, Arnold
  Born: 06/11/15
  Current Positions: worldwide lecturer, clinician, private instructor.
  Past Positions: Chicago Symphony Orchestra (1944–89), Philadelphia Orchestra (spring 1949), Pittsburgh Symphony (1939–44), Indianapolis Symphony (1936–38).
  Contributions: largely responsible for developing how human physiology and psychological aspects of respiration affect wind instrument and vocal performance, teacher to generations of professional tubists, first tubist to be invited to play at the Casals Festival (1962),

received highest award at the second
International Brass Congress (1984),
recorded Vaughan Williams's *Tuba Concerto*
with Chicago Symphony and has made
several other chamber recordings, hundreds
of Chicago Symphony recordings.
Education: Diploma Curtis Institute of Music
(1936), DM (hon) VanderCook College of
Music (1986).
Teachers: Philip A. Donatelli.

Jacobs, Wesley
Born: 11/30/46
Current Positions: Detroit Symphony Orchestra
1970–, Detroit Symphony Brass Quintet
1970–, Detroit Chamber Winds 1980–.
Past Positions: San Fransisco Opera (1968–70),
San Franscisco Brass Quintet, Los Angeles
Brass Society, Los Angeles Ballet, Los
Angeles Opera, studio musician, Los Angeles.
Education: Juilliard School of Music (1965–
68), University of California at Long Beach,
Music Academy of the West, Long Beach
City College.
Teachers: Tommy Johnson, Roger Bobo, Joe
Novotny.

Jaffe, Allan
1936–03/09/87
Past Positions: founder, Preservation Hall jazz
ensemble and club (1961–87).

Janka, László
Born: 07/27/54
Current Positions: Hungarian Army
Central Band.
Education: Béla Bartók Conservatory (1973).
Teachers: József Perlaki.

Jarvis, Jeffery
Born: 10/01/58
Current Positions: Assistant Professor, East
Carolina University 1987–, East Carolina
Brass Quintet 1989–.
Past Positions: North Carolina Symphony
(1991), Instructor, Central Missouri State
University (1987).
Contributions: Organizer, Mid-America Tuba-
Euphonium Symposium (1987), Southeast-
ern Tuba-Euphonium Symposium (1993),
solo premieres.
Education: BM, MM Baylor University (1981,
1983), DMA Michigan State University
(1992).
Teachers: Andrew Russell, Chris Matten, John
Meyer, Phillip Sinder, Sam Pilafian.

Jenkins, John
Born: 03/30/47
Current Positions: Philharmonia Orchestra
1969–, Professor, Royal College of Music
1973–, Equale Brass 1978–.
Past Positions: Royal Opera House, Covent
Garden (1966–69).

Contributions: Arranger of music for Equale
Brass Quintet and for "The Wallace Collec-
tion."
Education: Hon. ARCM Royal College of
Music (1965–66).
Teachers: Charles Brewer, Charles Luxon.

Johannsen, Torben
Born: 01/28/65
Current Positions: Prinsens Civregiments
Musikkorps, 1984–, Nordjyclands Brass
Quintet 1992–.
Past Positions: Vestjyosk Brass Quintet (1982–
84), Slesvigske Fodregiments Musikkorps
(1987–89).
Education: Music Academy of Esbjerg.
Teachers: Jørgen Arnsted.

Johansson, Aldo B.W.
Born: 02/14/37
Current Positions: Swedish Radio Symphony
Orchestra Stockholm 1963–, Radio Sym-
phony Brass Quintet 1970–.
Past Positions: Malmo Symphony Orchestra
(1957–63), Instuctor of Brass, Haminge
Music School (1968–73).
Education: Academy of Music, Stockholm
(1957).
Teachers: Carl-Johan Bergmarker, Eriik Ströberg,
Allan Olsson, Knut Gullbrandsson, Erik
Åkerwall, Miroslav Heijda, Helmut Hunger.

Johns, Stephen M.
Born: 07/27/46
Current Positions: Associate Tuba, Metropoli-
tan Opera 1969–, New York City Opera
1983–, New York Pops Orchestra 1983–,
Instructor, Mannes College of Music 1985–,
Little Orchestra Society 1988–, American
Symphony Orchestra 1991–.
Past Positions: Manhattan School of Music
Preparatory Division (1969–89).
Education: New England Conservatory of
Music (1964–66), Berkshire Music Center
(Tanglewood) (1965–67), BM Manhattan
School of Music (1969), MM The Juilliard
School (1976), MEd Teachers College,
Columbia University (1984).
Teachers: Kilton V. Smith, Herbert Wekselblatt,
Joseph Novotny.

Johnson, Howard Lewis
Born: 08/7/41
Current Positions: Baritone Sax/Bass Clarinet/
Clarinet, Norddeutscher Rundfunk (NDR)
Hamburg, Germany, free-lance, New York
1963–.
Past Positions: Free-lance, Los Angeles (1967,
1972), Musician, NBC Saturday Night Live
(1975–80) Band Leader (1979–80).
Contributions: Started the first jazz tuba
ensemble in March 1968.
Education: Self-taught player (all instruments).

Johnson, Kit
  Born: 08/20/60
  Current Positions: Black Swan Classic Jazz
    Band.
  Past Positions: 76th Army Band (West Ger-
    many) (1981–84), Misty Water Drifters
    (1986–88).
  Education: BA University of Oregon (1987).
  Teachers: Jesse Graham, David Grosvenor,
    Ira Lee.
Johnson, L. Keating
  Born: 01/05/51
  Current Positions: Associate Professor,
    Washington State University.
  Past Positions: Professor, California State
    University San Bernardino, Plymouth State
    College.
  Contributions: Original research on Wilhelm
    Wieprecht (designer of the tuba).
  Education: BM University of the Pacific, MM
    University of Wisconsin-Madison, DMA
    University of Southern California.
  Teachers: Don Heeren, Floyd Cooley, Arnold
    Jacobs, Tommy Johnson.
Johnson, Tommy
  Born: 01/07/35
  Current Positions: Adjunct Professor, Univer-
    sity of Southern California 1972–, Lecturer,
    UCLA 1972–, Glendale Symphony Orchestra
    1985–, Hollywood Recording Studios.
  Past Positions: Instructor, Cal State Northridge,
    Cal State Long Beach, Cal State Fullerton,
    California Institute of the Arts.
  Contributions: recorded over 2000 movie
    soundtracks, received National Academy of
    Recording Arts and Sciences Most Valuable
    Player Award for Tuba Player, 1974–80,
    awarded N.A.R.A.S "Emeritus Most Valuable
    Tuba Player" in 1981.
  Education: BM University of Southern
    California (1956).
  Teachers: Robert Marsteller.
Jolly, Tucker Ray
  Born: 12/30/46
  Current Positions: Associate Professor,
    University of Akron 1980–, Akron Symphony
    Orchestra 1986–, Blossom Festival Concert
    Band 1988–.
  Past Positions: Ohio Chamber Orchestra
    (1982–86), New Haven Symphony Orchestra
    (1974–80), U.S. Coast Guard Band (1970–
    74), Fort Worth Symphony Orchestra
    (1967–70), Eastern Brass Quintet (1970–
    80), Project Muse Brass Quintet and
    Orchestra (1966–69).
  Contributions: Performances at ITEC 1973 and
    1980, Sesson Chair at ITEC 1992.
  Education: BM University of North Texas, MA

University of Connecticut.
  Teachers: William Cramer, Leon Brown, David
    Kuehn, Ronald Apperson.
Jones, Edward William
  Born: 09/07/60
  Current Positions: Instructor, East Texas State
    University 1985–, ETSU Faculty Brass
    Quintet 1985–, East Texas Symphony
    Orchestra 1988–, Dallas Wind Symphony
    1991–.
  Education: BMEd Fort Hays State University
    (1983), MM East Texas State University
    (1985), DMA University of North Texas (in
    progress).
  Teachers: Lyle Dilley, Michael Morrow, Neil
    Humfield, Donald Little.
Jones, Timothy John
  Born: 06/9/69
  Current Positions: Free-lance, Melbourne
    including performing with Oxo Cubans
    (tuba, sax, trombone, percussion, vocal
    acoustic), Melbourne Symphony, Buckley's
    44 (band with newly constructed instruments
    including the curlaphone—an s-shaped
    baritone horn).
  Past Positions: State Orchestra of Victoria,
    Black Sorrows, Tibetan Dixie, Cairo Club
    Orchestra, various jazz ensembles.
  Education: Victoria College of the Arts School.
  Teachers: John Butler, John Woods, Frank
    Barzyk, Peter Sykes.
Kaenzig, Fritz
  Born: 01/30/52
  Current Positions: Professor, University of
    Michigan 1989–, Grant Park Symphony
    Orchestra 1984–.
  Past Positions: Professor, University of Illinois
    (1983–89), University of Northern Iowa
    (1976–83), Florida Symphony Orchestra
    (1975–76).
  Contributions: President T.U.B.A. 1993–,
    numerous other offices with T.U.B.A. and
    TUBA Journal, has premiered numerous
    compositions, many students placed in
    profession as performers and teachers.
  Education: BME The Ohio State University
    (1974), MM University of Wisconsin-
    Madison (1975).
  Teachers: Robert Woodbury, Robert LeBlanc,
    William Richardson, Arnold Jacobs.
Kagawa, Chitate
  Born: 03/20/44
  Current Positions: Sapporo Symphony Orches-
    tra 1969–, President of Hokkaido Eupho-
    nium/Tuba Association 1981–.
  Contributions: Chairman, T.U.B.A. Interna-
    tional Tuba/Euphonium Conference
    Sapporo, Japan (1990).

Education: Tokyo National University of Fine
  Arts and Music (1969).
Teachers: Genkichi Harada, Harvey Phillips.
Kaijima, Katsuhiko Jim
  Born: 05/22/43
  Current Positions: Associate Professor,
    Musashino Music College 1969–.
  Contributions: Committee of J.E.T.A.
  Education: BA Musashino Music College
    (1966), Indiana University (1969).
  Teachers: Kurahei Sato, William Bell.
Kang, Young Chel
  Born: 06/12/67
  Current Positions: Che Ju Philharmonic
    Orchestra 1985–.
  Education: BA Che Ju University Teachers
    College of Music (1988).
  Teachers: Yoo, Sung Joo, Jang Hong Yong.
Karlinski, Werner
  Born: 01/04/37
  Current Positions: Kiel Police Band 1970–.
Kazimierz, Jedlrusiak
  Born: 1941
  Current Positions: Polish Radio Symphony
    Orchestra 1961–, various brass quintets
    1983–.
  Past Positions: Vera Cruz Symphony Orchestra,
    Mexico (1980–83).
  Contributions: Recorded the Vaughan Williams
    tuba concerto on Compact Records (1987).
  Teachers: Feliks Kwiatkowski.
Keck, William Thomas
  Born: 11/14/43
  Current Positions: Constitution Brass Quintet
    1992–, New England Wind Symphony 1992–,
    New England Symphony Orchestra 1992–.
  Past Positions: Instructor, Cerritos Community
    College (1981–85), UConn Brass Quintet
    (1980–85), Instructor, University of
    Connecticut (1980–81), Mexico City
    Philharmonic (1978–80), National Conserva-
    tory of Music in Mexico City, Mexico (1978–
    80).
  Contributions: instrument design consultant.
  Education: BM Eastman School of Music
    (1965), MMEd Vandercook College of
    Music (1969).
Kelley, Timothy S.
  Born: 07/10/59
  Current Positions: Assistant Professor, Auburn
    University 1991–, Auburn Brass Quintet
    1991–.
  Past Positions: Instructor, University of Central
    Arkansas (1990).
  Contributions: New Materials reviewer, *TUBA
    Journal*, several arrangements for tuba-
    euphonium ensembles.
  Education: BM, BME University of Central

Arkansas (1982, 1983), MME North Texas
  State University.
  Teachers: Denis Winter, Donald C. Little, Don
    Lewis.
Keskitalo, Petri
  Born: 07/08/72
  Current Positions: Army Band, Hameenlinna
    1992–, Super Brass 1992–.
  Past Positions: Military School of Music Band
    (1988–1992), Lahti Symphony Orchestra,
    Lahti Brass Ensemble.
  Education: Military School of Music and
    Conservatory, Lahti (1992).
  Teachers: Kalevi Sarjanto, Raimo Maaranen,
    Eino Takalo-Eskola, Juha Salmela, William
    Stanton, Melvin Culbertson, Michael Lind.
Kezachenkov, Alexander Petrovich
  Born: 10/12/53
  Current Positions: Professor, Academy
    "Gwesinyh"; Russian National Symphony
    1991–.
  Past Positions: Bolshoi Theatre Brass Ensemble
    (1981–91); Bolshoi Theatre Orchestra
    (1976–91).
  Contributions: Appeared in several international
    festivals.
  Education: Diploma Moscow Conservatory
    (1978).
  Teachers: Alexi Lebedev.
Kidera, Satoshi
  Born: 08/11/38
  Current Positions: Osaka Municipal Symphonic
    Band 1958–.
  Teachers: Hiroshi Furukawa, Motoharu Kuzuo.
Kielniarz, Kenneth M.
  Born: 09/17/56
  Current Positions: Instructor, University of
    Nebraska, Omaha.
  Education: BME, MM Northwestern University
    (1979, 1983).
  Teachers: Philip Catelinet, Arnold Jacobs.
Kiilerich, Jens Ole
  Born: 02/12/46
  Current Positions: Aalborg Symphony Orches-
    tra 1974–, teacher, Northjutland Academy of
    Music 1975–.
  Past Positions: Free-lance, Copenhagen (1967–
    72), Aarhus (1972–74).
  Education: lessons (1954–62), private study
    (1962–74).
  Teachers: Erik Aakerwall, Jørgen Voigt Arnsted.
Kim, Sun Bo
  Born: 06/16/60
  Current Positions: Mok Won Brass Quintet
    l987–, Instructor, Mok Won University
    1984–, Tea Chon Philharmonic Orchestra
    1983–.
  Education: BA Mok Won University (1984).
  Teachers: Lee Chong Il.

Kingsley, Brian P.
> Born: 05/17/57
> Current Positions: Opera North, English
> Northern Philharmonia 1978–, Lecturer in
> Tuba, Royal Northern College of Music
> 1992– Tuba Tutor, Chethams School of
> Music 1990–, Yorkshire Classic Brass 1983–.
> Education: ARCM Royal College of Music
> (1978).
> Teachers: Patrick Harrild, John Jenkins.

Kirk, David E.
> Born: 02/20/60
> Current Positions: Houston Symphony 1982–,
> Lecturer, Rice University 1982–, Affiliate
> Artist, University of Houston School of
> Music 1988–, Symphonic Brass Quintet
> (University of Houston) 1988–.
> Past Positions: American Philharmonic
> Orchestra (1981–82)
> Education: BM Juilliard School (1982),
> Fellowship, Tanglewood Music Center
> (1981).
> Teachers: Donald Harry, Chester Schmitz, Neal
> Tidwell, Warren Deck, Paul Krzywicki.

Kita, Yoh
> Born: 01/04/31
> Current Positions: Professor, Osaka University
> of Arts.
> Past Positions: Kansai Symphony Orchestra
> (1950–60), Osaka Philharmonic Orchestra
> (1960–78).
> Contributions: Honorary Member of J.E.T.A.
> Teachers: Takeshi Ishikawa, Karl Sohadl,
> Heinrich Jürgens.

Kleinsteuber, Carl
> Born: 10/19/59
> Current Positions: Residentie Orchestra (Hague
> Philharmonic), Netherlands, free-lance with
> Rotterdam Philharmonic, Radio Philhar-
> monic, and Netherlands Philharmonic
> Orchestra.
> Past Positions: Free-lance, New York (1982–
> 84) including New York Philharmonic,
> Boston Symphony, Metropolitan Opera
> Orchestra, New York City Ballet Orchestra,
> Canadian Brass, Quincy Jones Orchestra,
> Lionel Hampton Band, and Gravity (jazz
> tuba sextet).
> Contributions: winner of Concert Artist Guild
> solo competition; awarded Carnegie Hall
> debut recital (1984), winner of T.U.B.A.
> International Jazz Competition (1983).
> Education: BM North Texas State University
> (1982), MM Manhattan School of Music
> (1984).
> Teachers: Warren Deck, Don Little, Toby
> Hanks, Dave Kuehn.

Klingler, Rolf
> Born: 12/06/56

Current Positions: Philharmonic Orchestra of
the State Theatre, Mainz.
> Education: private study.
> Teachers: Rüdiger Augustin.

Kmiec, Kazimierz
> Born: 10/31/54
> Current Positions: Philharmonic Orchestra
> 1977–, Teacher of Music in Jnowroclaw,
> Torun 1985–.
> Education: Panstwowa Wyzsia Szkola
> Muzyczna Lodzi (1976–80).
> Teachers: Ksawery Walaszek, Jan Pniak.

Kniffen, Anthony R.
> Born: 07/03/69
> Current Positions: Honolulu Symphony
> Orchestra 1989–, Honolulu Brass 1990–,
> Instructor, University of Hawaii 1991–.
> Education: attended Arizona State University.
> Teachers: Gene Pokorny, Daniel Perantoni,
> Bernard Schneider, Jerry Young.

Knox, Michael G.
> Born: 03/03/49
> Current Positions: Rogue Valley Symphony
> Orchestra 1977–; Bards Brass Quintet 1977–;
> Ashland City Band 1964–; Rogue Valley
> Wind Ensemble 1989–.
> Past Positions: Peter Britt Orchestra (1970–72).
> Contributions: Co-organizer of the Southern
> Oregon Heavy Metal Music Society,
> commissioned unaccompanied tuba work.
> Education: BS Southern Oregon State College
> (1972), MSW Michigan State University
> (1976).
> Teachers: Michael Sherline, Arnold Jacobs,
> William Bell.

Knurr, John
> Born: 12/23/41
> Current Positions: North Water St. Tavern
> Band 1981–, South Rampart St. Paraders
> 1992–.
> Past Positions: Holton-Elkhorn Concert Band
> (1976–80).
> Education: BS University of Wisconsin,
> Milwaukee (1966), MA California State
> University, Sacramento (1974).
> Teachers: J. Robert Manson.

Koller, Urs
> Born: 07/18/55
> Current Positions: Teacher, Music School
> Baar/CH, tubist with "Tangoo's."
> Past Positions: Interkantonale Blasabfuhr.
> Education: Jazz School Luzern,
> Konservatorium Zürich.
> Teachers: David LeClair.

Kornegay, Chris
> Born: 12/23/55
> Current Positions: South Arkansas Symphony
> 1972–; South Arkansas Brass 1987–;
> Immanuel Brass Quintet 1984–.

Past Positions: Adjunct Instructor, Henderson
State University (1988), Adjunct Instructor,
University of Arkansas, Little Rock (1981).
Education: BME Henderson State University
(1978), MME University of North Texas
(1980).
Teachers: Wesley Branstine, Don Little.

Kozeki, Yuji
Born: 06/14/59
Present Positions: Osaka Symphony 1989–;
Dämmern Brass Orchestra; jazz free-lance.
Contributions: Planning Manager (Director),
The Brass Association, Osaka.
Education: BA (with Grand Prix) Osaka
University of Arts (1983).
Teachers: Yo Kita.

Kramer, Karl
Born: 03/14/57
Current Positions: Associate Professor,
University of Bridgeport 1989–, New Haven
Symphony Orchestra 1982–, Brass Ring
1983–, Connecticut Grand Opera 1983–.
Contributions: Editor, Brass Ring Editions
1989–, several premieres and brass quintet
recordings.
Education: BMEd Temple University (1979),
MM Yale University (1983), DMA Manhat-
tan School of Music (1985).
Teachers: Thompson Hanks, Edmund E.
Moore.

Krauter, Alexander V.
Born: 01/27/65
Current Positions: Moscow State Symphony
Orchestra.
Past Positions: Moscow Radio Orchestra
(1989–90), Maliy Symphony Orchestra
(1985–87).
Education: Moscow Conservatory (1985–89).
Teachers: N.A. Assanov, A.K. Lebedev.

Krempl, Walter
Current Positions: Teacher, Oberösterreich-
ischen Landesmusik, Schulwerk.
Past Positions: Militärmusik Oberösterreich,
European-Festival Orchester, Jueness
Orchester Linz, Ensembles-Pro Brass.
Contributions: Recordings with ORF, Penta
Brass, Vokalmusikanten, instrument design
consultant.
Education: Bruchnerkonservatorium Linz,
Hochschule Mozartheum Salzburg.
Teachers: Robert Herdman, Bruce Holcomb,
Manfred Hoppert.

Krivorotenko, Stanislav
Current Positions: Moscow Brass Quintet,
Dokshitser Brass Quintet.
Contributions: First Place, Russian State Brass
Competition, Minsk Brass Competition.
Education: Russian Academy of Music.

Krupp, J. Paul Jr.
Born: 09/25/16
Current Positions: Instructor, Virginia Union
University, Richmond Philharmonic
Orchestra, Hanover Concert Band.
Past Positions: Richmond Symphony (1956–
67), Norfolk Symphony (1956–67), U.S.
Military Academy Band (1951–56).
Education: attended Cincinnati Conservatory of
Music.
Teachers: Fred Essex, Ernest Glover, Frank
Simon, John Clover.

Kruse, Kaj
Born: 07/19/36
Current Positions: Musikkorps Fyn, Odense
1968–.
Past Positions: Musikkorps, Viborg 1960–68.
Education: Private Teachers Course, Royal
Academy, Copenhagen (1963).
Teachers: Erik Åkerwall, Kirstein, Christensen,
Jørgen Arnsted.

Krysatis, Patrick
Born: 02/18/62
Current Positions: Teacher, Conservatory of the
City of Luxembourg.
Education: Diplome superieure Conservatory
Royale de Liège.
Teachers: Roger Dondelinger, Guillaume
Ackermanns.

Krzywicki, Paul M.
Born: 02/24/44
Current Positions: Philadelphia Orchestra
1972–, Instructor, Curtis Institute of Music
1972–.
Past Positions: Assistant Professor, Youngstown
State University (1971), Instructor, Aspen
Music Festival (1966–67,70–72), free-lance,
Boston, Portland (ME) Symphony, Buffalo
Philharmonic (1970), Instructor, Temple
University, Catholic University, University of
the Arts, Settlement School of Music.
Contributions: Participant, 1983 International
T.U.B.A. Conference, soloist with Philadel-
phia Orchestra on 4 occasions, several
students in professional symphony orchestras.
Education: Catholic University (1961–63), BM,
MM Performer's Certificate Indiana Univer-
sity (1963–67).
Teachers: Leo Romano, Abe Torchinsky, Lloyd
Geisler, Joseph Novotny, William Bell.

Kubo, Shuhei
Born: 08/14/49
Current Positions: Free-lance studio musician,
Tokyo Bari-Tuba Ensemble.
Past Positions: Tokyo Kosei Wind Orchestra.
Contributions: JETA committee member.
Education: BA Musashino Music College.
Teachers: Kurahei Sato, Ikumitsu Tado.

Kubota, Hiroaki
 Born: 10/28/64
 Current Positions: Ground Self Defence Force
  Band, Itami 1992–.
 Past Positions: 7th Ground Self Defence Force
  Band.
 Teachers: Yashio Abe.
Kuhn, John ("Red Cloud," "The Chief")
 Past Positions: Kryl Band, Harry Kogen
  Orchestra, first bass, Sousa Band.
 Contributions: mouthpiece designer, "the
  chief."
Ladd, Kevin D.
 Born: 10/20/50
 Current Positions: Syracuse Symphony
  Orchestra 1976–, Affiliate Artist, New
  England Music Camp 1992–.
 Past Positions: Adjunct Professor, Onondaga
  Community College (1976–86), Eastern
  Connecticut Symphony, Norwich Band,
  Greenwich Symphony.
 Education: BS SUNY Potsdam, BM MM
  Juilliard School.
 Teachers: Joseph Novotny, Cherry Beauregard,
  John Upchurch, Gordon Mathie.
Lancto, Peter C.
 Born: 11/09/53–07/93
 Past Positions: Free-lance, Boston 1973–93,
  Instructor, Eastern Nazarene College 1991–,
  Opera Company of Boston 1978–90,
  Professor, University of Lowell 1981–1989.
 Contributions: *TUBA Journal* New Materials
  reviews (1991–93), Co-founder New
  England Tuba Festival (1980), arranger of
  numerous tuba/euphonium ensembles and
  tuba and piano pieces.
 Education: BM Lowell State College (1975),
  MM University of Lowell (1980).
 Teachers: John Coffey, Donald S. Reinhardt,
  Willis Traphagan.
Landers, Michael D.
 Born: 06/22/67
 Current Positions: Mt. Hood Orchestra, free-
  lance, Vancouver.
 Past Positions: Substitute, Yakima Symphony
  Orchestra.
 Contributions: Published articles, composer and
  arranger for tuba ensemble, several solo
  premieres.
 Education: BM MM Central Washington
  University (1991).
 Teachers: J. Richard Jensen, Jeffery Snedeker,
  Larry Gookin, Robert M. Panerio, Sr., Russ
  Schultz.
Lange-Nelsen, Jakob
 Born: 03/28/68
 Current Positions: Golden Brass Quintet; free-
  lance, Copenhagen.

Past Positions: The Guard of Prince George.
 Education: Diploma Royal Danish Music
  Academy, Copenhagen (1993).
 Teachers: Jens Bjørn-Larsen.
Larsen, Aksel
 Born: 06/26/34
 Current Positions: Den Kongelige Livgardes
  Musikkorps 1961–.
 Past Positions: Fynske Livregimnets Musikkorps
  (1954–57), Slesviske Fodregiments Musik-
  korps (1957–59), Danske Livregiments
  Musikkorps (1959–61), Tivolis Harmoni-
  orkester (1969–70).
 Teachers: Asger Fredericia, Kirstein Christen-
  sen, Palmer Traulsen.
Larsson, Sven
 Born: 07/04/44
 Current Positions: Teacher, Sodra Latius
  Musikgymnasium, Stockholm Musik-
  pedagogiska Institute.
 Past Positions: Swedish Radios Jazz group
  (1969–88).
 Education: Musikhogskolan Stockholm,
  Stockholm's Musikpedagogiska Institute.
Layman, Stephen Richard
 Born: 10/12/53
 Current Positions: Instructor, University of
  Virginia 1984–, Charlottesville Community
  Orchestra 1977–.
 Contributions: Numerous workshops, clinics,
  solo appearances in Kentucky and Virginia.
 Education: BA Ohio Northern University
  (1975), MM University of Kentucky (1977).
 Teachers: Dale Laukhuf, Rex Connor.
Lebedev, Alexei K.
 1924–1993
 Past Positions: Professor, Moscow Conservatory
  1949–, Bolshoi Theatre (1950–66).
 Contributions: author, *School of Tuba Playing*,
  two books of transcriptions of Marcello,
  Boccherini, Handel, Ceusia.
 Education: Moscow Conservatory (1945–49).
 Teachers: Vladimir Schezbacov.
LeClair, David J.
 Born: 03/01/55
 Current Positions: Radio-Sinfonie-Orchester
  Basel, Switzerland 1982–, teacher, Conserva-
  tory of Music, Basel 1983–, founding
  member "Contraband" tuba quartet, Basel
  1987–.
 Past Positions: Bavarian State Opera, Gärtner-
  platz (1977–82).
 Contributions: International Consultant, *The
  Tuba Source Book*.
 Education: BM Indiana University.
 Teachers: Harvey Phillips, Robert Tucci.
Lee, Sun Young
 Born: 06/28/67

Current Positions: Yoido Full Gospel Church
Music Institute, Yoido Full Gospel Church
Hallelujah Orchestra 1991–.
Education: BA Seong Shin Womens College of
Music 1992–.
Teachers: Lee Choing Il, Heo Che Young.

Lehman, A.
Past Positions: Boston Symphony Orchestra
(1919–20).

Lehr, David "Red"
Born: 09/19/37
Current Positions: The Jazz Incredibles, St.
Louis Rivermen, Old St. Louis Levee Band,
the River City Ramblers.
Past Positions: Began playing professionally in
the early 1960s around St. Louis; first at Your
Father's Moustache, later at the Banjo Palace.
From 1977 to 1991 played at the Lt. Robert
E. Lee with the Jazz Incredibles and the Old
St. Louis Levee Band.
Contributions: Has played all the major
traditional jazz festivals worldwide with the
Jazz Incredibles and St. Louis Rivermen
including the Edinburgh, Scotland (1989,
1990, 1991), and the Breda, Holland,
festivals, performs numerous college concerts
with the River City Ramblers. In 1991 The
Jazz Incredibles were selected as the most
entertaining group at the Edinburgh Festival.
Has performed at International Tuba
Euphonium Conferences and has appeared as
guest soloist with the St. Louis and Honolulu
Symphonies.
Education: no formal musical training, took up
tuba at age eleven.

Lewis, David
Born: 05/31/35
Current Positions: Natural Gas Jazz Band
1971–, Santa Rosa Junior College Music
Department.
Past Positions: Santa Rosa Community
Orchestra (1988–91).
Education: AA College of Marin (1956).
Teachers: Floyd Cooley.

Lewis, David
Born: 03/22/49
Current Positions: Principal Tuba, North
Carolina Symphony 1975–, Tuba Instructor,
University of North Carolina-Chapel Hill
1993–, Crown Brass Quintet.
Past Positions: Tuba Instructor, University of
North Carolina–Greensboro, Tuba Instruc-
tor, East Carolina University 1981–1986,
Eastern Music Festival 1977–80.
Contributions: T.U.B.A. Treasurer (1987–92),
Publisher *T.U.B.A. Journal* (1990–1992)
Education: BM University of North Carolina-
Greensboro (1971), MM New England
Conservatory (1973).

Teachers: Thompson Hanks, Arnold Jacobs,
David Bragunier.

Lidsle, Harri
Born: 01/25/69
Current Positions: Sinfonia Lahti 1990–, Lahti
Brass Ensemble 1990–, Tammer Brass
Quintet 1987–.
Past Positions: Joensuu City Orchestra (1989–
90).
Education: Keski-Pohjanmaan Konservatorio
(1985–89).
Teachers: Sakari Lamberg, Eino Takalo-Eskola,
Michael Lind, Roger Bobo.

Lietzen, Jens Chr.
Born: 07/07/65
Current Positions: Århus free-lance 1987–;
Capriccio Brass Quintet 1990–.
Education: Diploma Det Jydske Musik-
konservatorium (1991).
Teachers: Hans Anderson, Jørgen Voigt
Arnsted, Arnold Jacobs.

Lilja, Satu
Born: 08/27/67
Current Positions: Free-lance, Gothenburg.
Education: Sibelius-Academy 1987–, University
of Music in Gothenburg 1989–.
Teachers: Morten Agerup, Raimo Pesonen.

Lind, Michael Erik
Born: 08/20/50
Current Positions: Royal Philharmonic
Orchestra, Stockholm 1975–, Teacher, Royal
Swedish Academy of Music 1980–, Interna-
tional Brass Soloists 1990–, Scandinavian
Tuba Jazz 1984–.
Past Positions: Prince Life Regimental Band
(1968–69), Sonderjyllands Symphony
Orchestra (1969–75), Stockholm Philhar-
monic Brass Ensemble (1975–87), Visiting
Professor, Indiana University (1980).
Contributions: Organizer, First Swedish Tuba-
Euphonium Workshop (1977), Second
Swedish Tuba-Euphonium Workshop
(1991), First Scandinavian Brass Symposium,
Stockholm (1978), Second Scandinavian
Brass Symposium, Helsinki (1989), Advisory
Board member T.U.B.A. (1978–), over 60
commissioned and dedicated solo and
ensemble compositions, solo recordings.
Education: Royal Conservatory, Copenhagen
(1966–68), Indiana University (1974).
Teachers: Asger Fredericia, Jørgen Arnsted,
Palmer Traulsen, Harvey Phillips, Arnold
Jacobs.

Litman, Ross
Past Positions: founder, Dorian Brass Consort;
University/Fairbanks Symphony Orchestra.
Contributions: articles in *T.U.B.A. Journal*,
regional coordinator for T.U.B.A.

Education: BFA Ohio University (1970).
Teachers: William Brophy, Ernst Bastin, Robert Smith, Duane Mikow.

Little, Donald C.
Born: 05/18/48
Current Positions: Professor, University of North Texas 1976–, Fort Worth Symphony Orchestra, Dallas Opera Orchestra 1989–, Texas Brass Ensemble 1980–.
Past Positions: Assistant Professor, University of Northern Iowa (1973–76), Chicago Civic Orchestra (1972–73).
Contributions: published over 30 transcriptions and arrangements for tuba or euphonium, President (1989–91), Secretary-Treasurer (1975–83), Chairman, Board of Directors (1991–93), Co–chair 1980 National Tuba-Euphonium Symposium Workshop T.U.B.A.
Education: BME Peabody Conservatory (1970), MM Northwestern University (1971), graduate studies Eastman School of Music.
Teachers: Cherry Beauregard, Arnold Jacobs, John Melick.

Llacer Sirerol, David
Born: 12/07/65
Current Positions: Orquesta Sinfonica de Tenerife, Professor, Conservatorio Superior de Musica de Tenerife, Quinteto de Metales Canarias.
Past Positions: Banda del Cuartel General del Ejercito (Madrid) (1984–86), Banda Municipal las Palmas de Gran Canaria (1986–87).
Teachers: Miguel Navarro Carbonell, Harvey Phillips, Walter Hilgers.

Loehr, Timothy Charles
Born: 04/04/47
Current Positions: Principal Tuba, The US Army Field Band 1978–.
Past Positions: The US Armed Forces Bicentennial Band (1975–76), free-lance, Dallas (1972–74), Dallas Civic Symphony (1970–74) Contributions: Coordinator, Washington DC TUBACHRISTMAS (1978–93).
Education: Attended University of North Texas (1970–74), Yale University.
Teachers: David Kuehn, Everett Gilmore, George Springer.

Long, Billy Jack
Born: 08/10/57
Current Positions: Free-lance, Riverside/San Bernardino CA , 1992–, Emmanuel Christian University of Indonesia (1994–).
Past Positions: Free-lance, Fort Worth (1989–92), US Army bands (1979–86).
Contributions: arrangements for tuba, brass quintet.

Education: Diploma US Army Element, School of Music (1979), BM Califormia Baptist College (1989), MM Southwestern Baptist Theological Seminary (1992).
Teachers: Gene Pokorny, Jim Jørgensen, Tommy Johnson, Jim Self, Winston Morris, Stephen Klein, David Jacobsen, Larry Johansen, Ev Gilmore.

Long, Gilbert Anderson
Born: 05/28/53
Current Positions: Nashville Symphony 1978–, Nashville Contemporary Brass Quintet 1979–, Nashville Chamber Brass Society 1979–, Kentuckiana Brass and Percussion Ensemble 1989–, Instructor, Belmont College 1980–, David Lipscomb College 1986–, Austin Peay State University 1991–.
Past Positions: Grand Rapids Symphony Orchestra (1976–78), Instructor, George Peabody College for Teachers (1978–79).
Contributions: brass quintet recording (1979).
Education: BMA University of Louisville (1975), Austin Peay State University (1975).
Teachers: Art Hicks, Arnold Jacobs, Abe Torchinsky.

Long, William
Born: 10/30/43
Current Positions: Assistant Professor, Newberry College 1992–; Casper Trooper Brum and Bugle Corps.
Past Positions: Montana Brass Quintet.
Contributions: arranger of brass quintet transcriptions.
Education: BSEd Black Hills State University (1965), MA Univerity of Northern Colorado (1969).
Teachers: Ben Henry.

Longstaff, Brent J.
Born: 01/02/71
Current Positions: Saskatoon Symphony Orchestra 1991–.
Education: BMus, MusEd University of Saskatchewan (in progress).
Teachers: D. Richard Lett, Michael McCawley, John R. Griffiths.

Lopez, José Luis Caballero
Born: 03/20/36
Current Positions: Orquesta de Radio Television Española
Past Positions: Musico Professor del Teatro de Opera de Barcelona (Teatroliceo) Musico de la Armada.
Education: Carrera de Tuba con Sobresalientes, Mencion de Honor Fin de Carrera Diploma 1st Clase de Solfeo/ Carrera de Violin con tres Matriculas de Honor.
Teachers: Lopez Calvo, Malato Ruiz, Celedonio, Pascual, Juon Canale D'Organ.

Ludwig, Gesl
    Born: 05/17/71
    Current Positions: Brass Band "Jung-OHing,"
        Carnival Brass Band
    Education: Music Teacher Association Traun-
        reut (1989–).
    Teachers: Klaus Zahnbrecher.
Luhn, Andreas
    Born: 03/05/63
    Current Positions: Norddeutsche Philharmonie
        Rostock 1985–, Blechbläserkonsort Rostock
        1991–.
    Contributions: Mitglied im "Deutsches
        Tubaforum."
    Teachers: Georgy Bolk.
Lukácsházi, Gyözö
    Born: 09/06/53
    Current Positions: Music Program Manager,
        Brass ad Libitum.
    Past Positions: Manager, Budapest Ragtime
        Band.
    Education: Liszt Ferenc Music Academy of
        Budapest (1973–78).
    Teachers: László Újfalussi.
Lyckberg, Thomas R.
    Born: 08/02/46
    Current Positions: The US Marine Band 1968–,
        Principal Tuba 1973–.
    Education: BM University of Illinois (1968).
    Teachers: Robert Gray, Ray Nutaitis, Arnold
        Jacobs.
Lynge, Carsten
    Born: 08/16/42
    Current Positions: Copenhagen Washboard
        Five 1988–, Orion New Orleans Brassband
        1992–.
    Past Positions: Copenhagen Railroad Band
        (1972–88).
Maciel, Jorge Luiz Lopes
    Born: 04/21/68
    Current Positions: BSGI Philharmonic
        Orchestra & Brass Quintet.
    Education: U.L.M.
    Teachers: Donald Smith.
MacMorran, William Sande
    Born: 06/05/48
    Current Positions: Associate Professor,
        University of Tennessee 1974–, Knoxville
        Symphony 1974–, Brasswind Quintet 1974–.
    Past Positions: The US Army Band (1971–74),
        The US Army Brass Quintet (1972–74).
    Education: BME Ball State University (1970),
        MM University of Wisconsin (1971), post-
        graduate work, Catholic University (1972).
    Teachers: Bernard Pressler, Arnold Jacobs.
Magee, Francis Joseph
    Born: 06/06/67
    Current Positions: Free-lance, Scotland 1987–,
        Scottish Chamber Orchestra Brass 1987–,

Athenaeum Brass 1985–, Lower Brass Tutor,
        Edinburgh Youth Orchestra 1991–.
    Past Positions: Tutor, Grampian Regional
        Youth Orchestra (1992).
    Education: BA Royal Scottish Academy of
        Music and Drama (1988).
    Teachers: Anthony Swainson, Stuart Roebuck.
Maierhofer, Josef
    Born: 1957
    Current Positions: free-lance, member of
        "Grazer Musical and Swing Orchester";
        substitute, Vienna Philharmonic Orchestra;
        guest professor, Hochschule für Musik und
        darstellende Kunst, Graz; guest professor,
        "Expositur Oberschützen."
Malody, Raymond Lee
    Born: 12/19/29
    Current Positions: Casper Metropolitan Brass
        Quintet; Casper Municipal Band.
    Past Positions: Casper Symphony Orchestra,
        Laramie Municipal Band.
    Contributions: author of tuba book.
    Education: BA, MEd University of Wyoming
        (1956, 1965), post-graduate work at
        Montana State University, University of
        South Florida, Kearney State College, Seattle
        Pacific College, and Casper College.
    Teachers: Edgar J. Lewis, Rex Tocum.
Marcos, Felix Da Silva
    Born: 12/26/56
    Current Positions: Congregation Church of
        Christ in Brazil, Orchestral Training of [the]
        University of Free Music in São Paulo.
    Teachers: Donald Smith, Severino.
Marinoni, Gustavo E.
    Born: 12/19/59
    Current Positions: Bahia Blanca Symphony
        Orchestra 1992–, Bahia Blanca Brass Quintet
        1990–, Memories Jazz Band 1993–.
    Contributions: arrangements of Argentine
        music for brass quintet, solo premieres.
    Teachers: Abel Larrosa.
Marshall, Carl A.
    Born: 09/21/71
    Current Positions: Band of the Corps of Royal
        Engineers.
    Education: Royal Military School of Music,
        Kneller Hall.
    Teachers: Paul Lawrence, Patrick Harrild.
Martin, Andrew J.
    Born: 10/16/51
    Current Positions: Royal Ballet Sinfonia 1972–,
        Professor of Tuba, Colchester Institute.
    Education: Royal Academy of Music, London.
    Teachers: John Fletcher.
Martin, "Chink" (Martin Abraham)
    06/10/1886–?
    Past Positions: New Orleans tubist who played
        and recorded in and around Chicago in 1923

and 1924. Recorded historic sessions with the augmented New Orleans Rhythm Kings and Jelly Roll Morton in Richmond, Indiana in 1923. Played string bass and tuba for most of his career in New Orleans.

Martin, Rex
Born: 07/12/60
Current Positions: Assistant Professor of Music, Northwestern University 1988–
Past Positions: free-lance, Chicago Symphony Orchestra (1982–89), St. Louis Symphony Orchestra (1989–91), Baltimore Symphony Orchestra (1983), Instructor, DePaul University (1983–89), University of Illinois–Chicago (1984–91), University of Notre Dame (1984–90), Illinois State University (1983–84).
Contributions: over 50 recordings with Chicago Symphony Orchestra, Saint Louis Symphony Orchestra, Chicago Pro Musica, Mannheim Steamroller and more, performed on over 1000 television and radio commercials.
Education: BM Illinois State University (1982), MM Northwestern University (1983).
Teachers: Arnold Jacobs, Edward Kleinhammer, Edward Livingston.

Martinson, Michael D.
Born: 06/16/59
Current Positions: Anchorage Symphony Orchestra 1987–.
Education: BMus Western Washington University (1982), MM Western Washington University (1988).
Teachers: Carla Rutschman.

Matchett, Steve Donivan
Born: 04/19/57
Current Positions: Lake Charles (LA) Symphony 1990–, Rapides (LA) Symphony 1990–, Houston Lyric Brass 1989–, free-lance.
Past Positions: Interim Tuba, Houston Symphony, Houston Grand Opera (1979–80), Houston Ballet (1978–80), Texas Chamber Orchestra (1982–84), Texas Chamber Brass (1982–84).
Contributions: composer, arranger, tuba ensembles.
Education: BM University of Houston (1985), MM Sam Houston State University (1993).
Teachers: Larry Campbell, William Rose.

Matsumoto, Daisuke
Born: 01/11/66
Current Positions: Free-lance, Osaka, Assistant Instructor, Osaka College of Music 1989–.
Education: BA Osaka College of Music (1988).
Teachers: Shuzo Karakawa, Tsutomu Morimoto.

Matsumoto, Kazushige
Born: 12/23/59

Current Positions: Ground Self Defence Force Band, Itami 1978–, Osaka Bari-Tuba Ensemble, Breeze Brass Band.
Teachers: Tsutomu Morimoto, Shuzo Karakawa.

Matsuoka, Shin
Born: 03/15/55
Current Positions: Kyoto Police Bands 1978–.

Mattersteig, P.
Past Positions: Boston Symphony Orchestra (1913–20).

Maurizio, Salvstri
Born: 10/23/54
Current Positions: Banda Esereito, Italy.
Education: self-taught.

May, Ernst
Born: 06/18/59
Current Positions: Teacher, Musikakademie, Basel 1991–, Concert Brass Basel (Brass Quintet), Contraband (Tuba Quartet).
Past Positions: Symphonisches Orchester Zurich (1983–87).
Contributions: brass quintet CD recording.
Education: Konservatorium und Musikhochschule Zurich (1987), Musikakademie Basel (1987–91).
Teachers: Franz Eger, David LeClair.

Mazura, János
Born: 01/16/70
Current Positions: Ernst Dohnanyi Symphonic Orchestra 1988–, Piston Brass 1989–, New Budapest Brass Ensemble 1992–.
Contributions: Arrangements for tuba, tuba ensembles, brass quintets.
Education: Conservatoire of Szeged (1988), Conservatoire Budapest (1989), Franz Liszt Academy of Music (1989–).
Teachers: Zsolt Nagy, László Szabó.

Mazurkowski, Artur
Born: 1944
Current Positions: Osnabrück Symphony Orchestra 1978–; Teacher, Osnabrück Conservatoire 1980–; Teacher, University of Osnabrück 1988–; "Osnabrücker Bleeh" brass quintet 1989–.
Past Positions: Cracow Philharmonic Orchestra (1964–71).
Education: Music-Liceum of Cracow (1958–63), Music-Academy of Cracow (1963–67).
Teachers: Sosim Tadeusz, Walther Willy.

Mazzaferro, Anthony P.
Born: 04/19/56
Current Positions: Assistant Professor, Fullerton College 1989–, Artisan Brass Quintet 1990–.
Education: BM California State University, San Francisco (1978), MM Northwestern University (1979), DMA Arizona State University (1986).

Teachers: Hank Niebott, Will Sudmeier, Daniel
   Perantoni.
Mazzarese, Gregorio
   Born: 02/08/63
   Current Positions: Accademia St. Cecilia Roma
      1983–.
   Past Positions: Teatro Fenice Venezia, Arena di
      Verona, Maggio Musicale, RAI Symphony
      1981–83.
   Education: Degree at Florence 1983.
   Teachers: Norino Righini, Tym Bryson, Roger
      Bobo.
McAdams, Charles A.
   Born: 06/03/58
   Current Positions: Associate Professor, Central
      Missouri State University 1983–, Central
      Brass Quintet 1983–.
   Contributions: Assistant Editor, *The Tuba
      Source Book*, Coordinator of Local Chapters,
      T.U.B.A. (1986–), published arrangements
      of tuba-euphonium ensembles, author of
      several articles on tuba/euphonium peda-
      gogy.
   Education: BS Tennessee Technological
      University (1980), MS EdD University of
      Illinois (1981, 1988).
   Teachers: R. Winston Morris, Daniel Perantoni,
      Robert Gray, Fritz Kaenzig.
McKee, Earl Alfred
   Born: 07/12/31
   Current Positions: High Sierra Jazz Band
      1976–.
   Past Positions: Jazzberry Jam Band (1973–76).
   Education: self–taught.
McKee, Edward R.
   Born: 10/03/46
   Current Positions: The US Air Force Band
      1980–, The US Air Force Brass Quintet
      1980–, leader of The US Air Force Dixieland
      Band 1980–, The Federal Jazz Commission
      1986–, The National Chamber Brass 1980–.
   Past Positions: Instructor of Tuba, Southern
      Illinois University-Edwardsville (1974–78),
      University of Missouri-St. Louis (1976–78),
      St. Louis Ragtimers (1974–78), St. Louis
      Municipal Opera (1974–78), Jim Cullum's
      Happy Jazz Band, San Antonio, TX (1978–
      79), Delta Queen Steamboat Jazz Band
      (1979–80).
   Contributions: Contributing Editor, *TUBA
      Journal* New Materials (1982–86).
   Education: BA Montclair State College (1968),
      Diploma Juilliard School of Music (1971),
      MM Washington University (1976).
   Teachers: Don Butterfield, Joe Novotny, John
      MacNulty, Harvey Phillips.
Mehlan, Keith E.
   09/16/61–1995

Current Positions: The US Navy Band 1984–
   95, McLean Orchestra 1992–95.
Contributions: Composer/arranger of tuba-
   euphonium quartet and ensemble.
Education: BM, BMEd Illinois State University
   (1983).
Teachers: Ed Livingston, David Fedderly.
Merz, Roland A.B.
   Born: 06/17/36
   Current Positions: Kammermusiker im
      Orchester des National-Theaters Mannheim,
      Lehrauftrag an der Musikhochschule
      Heidelberg-Mannheim.
   Past Positions: Kurorchester Cuxhaven (1957–
      1970), Städt. Orchester Heidelberg (1971),
      Nationaltheater Mannheim (1960), Wagner-
      festspiele Nice, France.
   Education: 7 Sem. Studium Hochschule fur
      Musik und Theater, Mannheim, Abschluss-
      diplom.
   Teachers: Karl Rinderspacher.
Metcalf, Owen W.
   Born: 05/17/37
   Current Positions: Associate Professor, Rowan
      College of New Jersey 1972–, Assistant
      Professor, West Chester University 1989–,
      Peter Nero/Philly Pops Orchestra, Concerto
      Soloists of Philadelphia Ensembles, Bridgeton
      Symphony, Rowan Brass Quintet, Ritten-
      house Brass Quintet.
   Education: BME, MME University of Colorado
      (1959, 1962), DM Indiana University 1978.
   Teachers: Hugh McMillen, William Bell,
      Harvey Phillips, Keith Brown.
Michalak, Andrzej
   Born: 11/21/60
   Current Positions: Orkiestra Teatru Wielkiego.
   Past Positions: Militar Orchester (1980–82);
      Teatr Muzyczny Szczecin (1982–85).
   Education: Akademia Muzyczna w Lodzi
      (1990).
   Teachers: Juliusz Pietrachowicz.
Mickelsen, William A.
   Born: 02/14/52
   Current Positions: The Florida Orchestra 1979–
      , The Florida Orchestra Brass Quartet 1979–,
      Professor of Tuba, University of South
      Florida 1988–.
   Past Positions: University of Rhode Island
      (1977–78), Southeastern Connecticut
      Symphony (1977–78), Contempra Brass
      Quintet (1977–82).
   Contributions: Co-founder of Tampa Bay Tuba
      & Euphonium Society, co-coordinator of
      Tampa Bay Tubachristmas 1989–.
   Education: BME, BM University of Northern
      Colorado (1976), MM Yale University
      (1980).

Teachers: Jack Robinson, Toby Hanks, Arnold Jacobs, Roger Bobo.

Mieger, Bernd
Born: 12/29/52
Current Positions: Staatsorchester Braunschweig; teacher, Stadt Musikschule Braunschweig.
Past Positions: Strabsmusikkorps Bundeswehr.
Education: Diplome Musikhochschule, Köln.
Teachers: Paul Heims, Hans Gelhar.

Miettinen, Jouni
Born: 09/08/59
Current Positions: Oulu Military Band 1980–, Oulu Philharmonic Orchestra 1980–, Northern Tuba Lights (Euphonium-Tuba Quartet) 1988–.
Past Positions: Instructor, Oulu Conservatoire (1984–90), Ylivieska College of Music 1986–87.
Education: Oulu Military School of Music (1979), Extension Course (1986).
Teachers: Eino Takalo-Eskola, Raimo Pesonen.

Miettunen, Harri
Born: 07/31/64
Current Positions: Tampere Philharmonic Orchestra 1989–, Teacher in Tampereen Konservatorio 1989–, Brassologia Quintet 1991–.
Past Positions: Joensuu City Orchestra (1986–89), The Guardian Military Band (1985–86).
Education: The Military School of Music, Helsinki (1981–85), Rotterdam Conservatory (1992–93).
Teachers: Raimo Pesonen, Roger Bobo, Michael Lind.

Miller, Dennis R.
Born: 05/04/44
Current Positions: Montreal Symphony Orchestra 1989–, Assistant Professor of Music, McGill University 1989–.
Past Positions: Vancouver Symphony Orchestra (1962–80, 1981–89), Houston Symphony Orchestra (1980–81), Music Faculty, University of Victoria (1970–74), Rice University (1980–81), University of British Columbia (1974–89), Banff Centre for the Arts (1982–88), Substitute, Winnipeg Symphony, Royal Liverpool Philharmonic, National Arts Centre orchestras.
Contributions: commissioned and premiered several solo works.
Teachers: Arnold Jacobs, William Bell, Abe Torchinsky.

Minana Juan, Jose Manuel
Born: 08/02/59
Current Positions: Conservatorio Superior de Musica de Valencia, Orquesta Sinfonica de Valencia, Valencia Brass Quintet.
Past Positions: Suboficial Musico (1979–84), Professor, Banda Municipal "Sevilla" (1984–87).
Contributions: founder, Asociacion de Tubas y Bombaronios de Valencia
Education: Titulu Profesor Tuba (1983), Titulo Profesor Superior Tuba (1986), Premio de Honor Fin Grado Superior de Tuba.
Teachers: Rafael Tortasada Dura, Daniel Alberola, Roger Bobo, Mel Culbertson

Moen, David
Born: 09/27/61
Past Positions: Springfield (IL) Orchestra (1989–91).
Current Positions: Principal tubist in the Orquesta Sinfonica del Principado de Asturias (1992).
Contributions: International Consultant, The *The Tuba Source Book*.
Education: BM University of North Texas (1984), MM Saint Louis Conservatory of Music (1989).
Teachers: Donald C. Little, Eugene Pokorny.

Móldovan, Gabor
Born: 07/19/43
Current Positions: Hungarian Army Central Band.
Education: Budapest (1962).
Teachers: Andras Pehl.

Moloney, Gregory James
Born: 08/06/62
Current Positions: Sutherlandsshire Symphony Orchestra 1989–.

Monch, George A.
Born: 10/17/55
Current Positions: Basel Symphony Orchestra, teacher, Freiburg Hochschule für Musik.
Past Positions: Caracas Filharmonic Orchestra, Maracibo Symphony Orchestra, Hong Kong Philharmonic.
Education: Attended Cleveland Institute of Music.
Teachers: Bob Tucci, Ron Bishop, Arnold Jacobs, Bob Pallanch.

Moore, Grant W. II
Born: 08/07/55
Current Positions: Philadelphia Brass 1985–, Adjunct Professor of Low Brass, Elizabethtown, Moravian and Muhlenberg Colleges 1989–.
Past Positions: River City Brass Band (1988–91), Harrisburg and Lancaster Symphonies (1980–84), free-lance: eastern Pennsylvania, New Jersey, and Maryland 1980–.
Education: BA Indiana University of Pennsylvania (1979).
Teachers: Gary Bird, Toby Hanks, Paul Krzywicki, Sam Pilafian, Dave McCollum.

Moore, Mark
Born: 04/25/52
Current Positions: Associate Professor,
University of Illinois 1989–, Champaign-
Urbana Symphony 1989–, Illinois Symphony
1991–, Illinois Brass Quintet 1989–, Sonus
Brass 1987–.
Past Positions: Associate Professor, University
of Southern Mississippi (1978–89), Shen-
andoah College and Conservatory
(1976–78).
Contributions: TUBA conference artist,
clinician, adjudicator, TUBA conference
planner.
Education: BSMusEd University of Illinois
(1974), MM Ohio State University (1976).
Teachers: Dan Perantoni, Robert LeBlanc,
Arnold Jacobs.
Moore, Michael
Born: 07/03/50
Current Positions: Atlanta Symphony Orchestra
1968–, Atlanta Symphony Brass Quintet
1968–, Faculty, Georgia State University,
Emory University.
Contributions: numerous brass quintet
arrangements, composer-performer of electric
tuba, founder of Atlanta Brass Society, Inc.,
founder of ABS Press.
Education: BMusLit Georgia State University.
Teachers: Arnold Jacobs, Ed Kleinhammer,
Ward Fern, William Hill, E.W. Moore.
Morgan, Richard S.
Born: 02/28/50
Current Positions: Instructor, Texas A&I
University 1990–, PentaBrass 1991–, Corpus
Christi Wind Symphony 1991–.
Past Positions: Dallas Wind Symphony (1985–
90), Richardson Symphony Orchestra (1980–
90), Adjunct Professor, Texas Christian
University (1983–90).
Education: BMEd Abilene Christian University
(1973), MA University of North Texas
(1981).
Teachers: Charles Trayler, Don Little.
Morgan, Ross N. Jr.
Born: 09/24/52
Current Positions: The US Army Band 1974–,
The Capital Band 1990–.
Past Positions: Utica Symphony (1972–74).
Contributions: Associate Editor of Programs,
TUBA Journal (1985–87), The US Army
Band Tuba-Euphonium Conference Execu-
tive Committee (1983–), Sec/Treas TUBA
National Capital Chapter (1986–).
Education: BMEd Ithaca College (1974), MM
Catholic University (1977).
Teachers: James Linn, Walter Beeler, David
Bragunier.

Morita, Masateru
Born: 04/17/53
Current Positions: Hiroshima Symphony
Orchestra 1977–, Tuba and Euphonium
Ensemble of Hiroshima, Iwakuni, Hiroshima
Brass Ensemble.
Education: BS Sakuyo University of Music
(1977).
Teachers: Yo Kita.
Morris, R. Winston
Born: 01/19/41
Current Positions: Professor, Tennessee
Technological University 1967–, Tennessee
Technological University Brass Quintet
1967–, Tech/Community Symphony
Orchestra 1967–, Matteson/Phillips
Tubajazz Consort 1976–.
Past Positions: Brass Instructor, Mansfield (PA)
State University (1966–67).
Contributions: Senior Editor, *The Tuba Source
Book*, author, *Tuba Music Guide*, Co-author
with William J. Bell, *Encyclopedia of
Literature for the Tuba*, Co-author, T.U.B.A.
Constitution, Past President and Publications
Coordinator of T.U.B.A., arranger/
transcriber/author of numerous materials for
tuba, premiered many compositions for
tuba/euphonium ensemble.
Education: BS East Carolina University (1962),
MM Indiana University (1965).
Teachers: William J. Bell.
Mosier, Bruce B.
Born: 05/10/55
Current Positions: The US Air Force Band, The
US Air Force Ceremonial Brass Quintet.
Past Positions: 5th US Army Band, 2nd
Infantry Division Band, 8th US Army Band.
Education: BS Ball State University (1978),
MM East Carolina University (1981).
Teachers: J. Lesley Varner, Daniel Perantoni.
Mulholland, Shane Michael
Born: 05/10/73
Current Positions: Movie World Marching
Band, Gold Coast Australia.
Education: Diploma of Instrumental Music (in
progress) Queensland Conservatorium of
Music.
Teachers: Craig Cunningham.
Müller, Hartmut
Current Positions: Melton Tuba Quartet,
Wuppertal Symphony 1988–, Remscheider
Brass Ensemble.
Past Positions: Saarbrucken Radio Symphony
Orchestra (1986–87).
Education: Aachen College of Music.
Teachers: Walter Hilgers, Ludwig Zoon.
Murányi, József
Born: 03/15/61

Current Positions: XVIII. ker. Zeneiskola, Uhrner zenekar.

Education: Györ (1980), Konzervatórium Budapest (1983), Tanárképzö.

Teachers: Nagy József, Szabó János, Pehl András.

Murphy, David John
  Born: 05/04/70
  Current Positions: Irish Army Band of the Southern Command, Cork Symphony Orchestra, University College Cork Orchestra.
  Contributions: Founder of Irish Low Brass Association, Ireland International Consultant for *The Tuba Source Book*.
  Education: Attending University College-Cork.
  Teachers: Härtmüt Pritzel.

Nagels, Lance Victor
  Born: 09/23/51
  Current Positions: Orchestra Symphony de Québec, Montreal Brass Quintet, Laval University Brass Quintet, Tuba Instructor, Université Laval.
  Past Positions: Canada Symphony Orchestra (1971–73), Tanglewood Festival Orchestra (1975), Vermont Symphony Orchestra (1976–79), Mexico City Opera (1978).
  Education: McGill University.
  Teachers: Robert Ryker, Ted Griffith, Ellis Wean.

Nagy, Zsolt
  Born: 03/29/61
  Current Positions: Szeged Symphonic Orchestra 1984–, Szeged Conservatory Brass Quintet 1984–, First assistant at Conservatory of Szeged 1984–.
  Past Positions: Hungarian State Opera House (1982–84), Purcell Brass Quintet (1982–84).
  Education: Liszt Ferenc Music Academy of Budapest (1979–84), scholarship at the Chicago Symphony Orchestra (1988).
  Teachers: Istvan Simor, László Ujfalusi, Arnold Jacobs.

Nahatzki, Richard
  Born: 01/15/49
  Current Positions: Radio Sinfonie Orchester Berlin.
  Past Positions: Staatstheater, Kassel; Saarländische Rundfunk.
  Contributions: solo appearances in Europe and the United States.
  Education: BM Peabody Conservatory, attended New England Conservatory.
  Teachers: John Melick, Chester Schmitz, Arnold Jacobs.

Nakanowatari, Katsuhiro
  Born: 07/12/47
  Current Positions: Faculty, Seikei Gakuen.
  Contributions: Editor, JETA Journal.

Education: BA Kunitachi Music College (1970), MM Tokyo University of Arts (1974), MME University of Michigan (1975).
  Teachers: Kiyoshi Ohishi, Abe Torchinsky.

Neesley, Daniel
  Born: 12/15/43
  Past Positions: Milwaukee Ballet Orchestra 1976–93, Newberry Brass 1974–93, Instructor, University of Wisconsin-Milwaukee, Instructor, Lawrence University.
  Contributions: Member of T.U.B.A. Board of Directors.
  Education: BFA University of Wisconsin-Milwaukee.
  Teachers: Arnold Jacobs, Val Hayworth.

Nelson, Mark A.
  Born: 05/20/57
  Current Positions: Associate Professor, Millikin University 1993–, Millikin Brass Quintet 1993–, Millikin-Decatur Symphony 1993–.
  Past Positions: Associate Professor, University of Vermont (1984–93), Vermont Symphony Orchestra (1984–93), Vermont Brass Quintet (1984–93), Vermont Town Brass (1986–93), Scottsdale Community College, AZ (1983–84), Arizona Brass Quintet (1982–84).
  Contributions: Assistant Editor, *The Tuba Source Book*, Editor, New Materials, 1990– Editor, Tuba News (1986–90) TUBA Journal, published many tuba/euphonium ensemble arrangements, several articles published, over a dozen solo compositions commissioned and premiered (1980–), solo CD recording (1991).
  Education: BA *magna cum laude* Point Loma Nazarene College (1980), LTCL Trinity College of Music, London (1980), MM, DMA Arizona State University (1982, 1985), MEd University of Vermont (1991).
  Teachers: Barton Cummings, Charles Hansen, Ray Nutaitis, Roger Bobo, Dan Perantoni.

Neto, Vicente Raiola
  Born: 03/13/62
  Current Positions: Banda Municipal de Apresentacão, Big Band, Orquestra a Consagração Cristã no Brasil, Pratica de Orquestra.
  Education: ULM
  Teachers: Armando Del Sole, Donald Smith.

Newberger, Eli
  Born: 12/26/40
  Current Positions: New Black Eagle Jazz Band 1971–, Mazzy and Newberger Duo 1985–.
  Past Positions: New Haven Symphony Orchestra (1958–66).
  Contributions: A leading traditional jazz tubist, was voted "Best Tuba Player" in 1983 *Jazzology* magazine readers' poll. Published

articles in *The Journal of Jazz Studies* and the *New England Journal of Medicine*.
Education: Studied music Juilliard, BM Theory Yale University (1962), MD Yale Medical School (1966).
Teachers: William Bell.

Nickel, Hans J.A.F.H.
Born: 10/19/58
Current Positions: Kolner Rundfunk Symphonie Orchester 1986–, Brassband Limburg 1990–, Brass Quintet K.R.S.O. 1988–, Assistant Professor, Cologne University of Music 1987–.
Past Positions: "Nordhollands Philharmonic Orkest" Haarlem (1982–86), Belgian Brass Soloists (1987–92), Professor, Summer School Javea, Spain (1981–82), Guest Professor, Moscow Conservatory (1990).
Contributions: many tuba recitals, solo CD recording with K.R.S. Orchestra, four major tuba solos with symphony orchestra, design consultant for yamaha.
Education: Teachers Certificate, Performers Diploma Maastricht Conservatoire (1985 1986).
Teachers: Piet Joris, John Fletcher, Mel Culbertson.

Nigel, Harvey
Born: 01/02/61
Current Positions: Stockholm Spruagens Musikker.
Education: Dalaro Folkhogskola.
Teachers: John Fletcher.

Nikaido, Mitsunori
Born: 09/25/66
Current Positions: Free-lance, Japan.
Education: BA Osaka College of Music (1990), Otani University (1992).
Teachers: Tsutomu Morimoto, Kazuo Ishizaki.

Nilsson, Wiktoria
Born: 08/19/66
Current Positions: Instructor, Orebro Community Music School 1993–, free-lance, Orebro 1993–.
Past Positions: Substitute, Malmö Symphony Orchestra (1992).
Education: Malmö Academy of Music.
Teachers: Morten Agerup, Torbjorn Kvist, Arne Svendsen.

Nishida, Kazuhisa
Born: 01/01/58
Current Positions: Assistant Instructor, Osaka University of Art 1984–, Osaka Quintet.
Past Positions: Nasu Symphonic Band (1980–81).
Education: BA Osaka University of Arts (1980), Tennessee Technological University (1987–88).

Teachers: Tsutomi Morimoto, Yo Kita, Ken-ichi Osawa, R. Winston Morris, Rex Martin.

Nishitani, Masão
Born: 08/21/64
Current Positions: Lecturer, Osaka College of Music 1992–, Osaka Brass Players 1990–, Osaka Bari-Tuba Ensemble.
Past Positions: Assistant Instructor, Osaka College of Music (1987–91).
Education: BA Osaka College of Music (1987).
Teachers: Tsutomu Morimoto, Kazuo Ishizaki.

Nishiura, Yoshiaki
Born: 01/18/58
Current Positions: Kyoto Police Bands 1985–, Kyoto British Brass.
Education: BA Kyoto City University of Arts (1983).
Teachers: Kiyoshi Oh-ishi, Kazuo Ishizaki, Shuzo Karakawa, Ei-ichi Murayama.

Nord, Lennart
Born: 12/08/62
Current Positions: Stockholm Symphonic Wind Band 1984–, Stockholm Chamber Brass 1985–.
Education: Royal Academy of Music, Stockholm (1983).
Teachers: Michael Lind, Morten Agerup.

Nordstrom, Yngre
Born: 02/28/61
Current Positions: Lansmusiken Brass Quintet 1985–, Symphony Orchestra 1985–.
Education: Gothenburg Conservatorium (1985).
Teachers: Morten Agerup, Jørgen Arnsted.

Northcut, Timothy J.
Born: 06/16/61
Current Positions: Instructor of Tuba, Cincinnati College-Conservatory of Music 1994–.
Past Positions: The United States Army Field Band (1984–87), free-lance, Atlanta, Georgia.
Education: BS Tennessee Tech University (1983), MM Catholic University of America (1987), DMA Arizona State University (in progress).
Teachers: James Garrett, R. Winston Morris, David Fedderly, Warren Deck, Daniel Perantoni, Harvey Phillips.

Noto, Samuel Gregory
Born: 11/02/56
Current Positions: Rosie O'Grady's Jazz Band 1984–; free-lance, Orlando and Tampa, Florida 1972–, including Walt Disney World, Circus World.
Education: BM University of Tampa.
Teachers: John Smith.

Nutaitis, Ray
Born: 07/19/40

Current Positions: Southwest Brass Quintet 1989–, free-lance, Phoenix Metro Area 1980–.

Past Positions: Assistant Professor, Arizona State University (1975–82), Assistant Professor, Wilkes College (1969–75), Buffalo Philharmonic (1968–69), Instructor, University of Illinois (1966–68), Instructor, Wilkes College (1964–66).

Education: BSMEd Wilkes College (1962), MM Eastman School of Music (1964), Performer's Certificate in Tuba, Eastman School of Music (1964).

Teachers: Bob Moran, Larry Weed, Abe Torchinsky, Donald Knaub, Arnold Jacobs, Joseph Novotny.

O'Dell, James Robert
Born: 11/29/56
Current Positions: Free-lance, Boston.

Past Positions: Served on the full-time faculties of Boston University, Mansfield University (PA), Phoenix College (AZ), part-time faculties of Massachusetts Institute of Technology, University of Oregon, Lane Community College, Ken Schaphorst Big Band, Jazz Composers Alliance Orchestra, Consortium Brass, Orange Then Blue, Shirim Klezmer Orchestra, Boston Globe Jazz Festival Repertory Orchestra, Boston Tuba Quartet, Continuum Jazz Brass Band.

Contributions: CD recordings with Ken Shaphorst Big Band, Jazz Composers Alliance Orchestra with Julius Hemphill and Sam Rivers.

Education: BS Southern Oregon State College (1978), MM University of Oregon (1984), DMA Arizona State University (in progress).

Teachers: Sam Pilafian, Dan Perantoni, Jeffrey Williams, Stuart Turner, David Caffey.

Ofenloch, Gary
Born: 03/31/51
Current Positions: Associate Professor, University of Utah 1984–, Utah Symphony 1983–, Boston "Pops" Esplanade Orchestra 1973–.

Past Positions: Boston Symphony Orchestra (1989–90), Boston Ballet Orchestra (1973–83), Portland (ME) Symphony Orchestra (1975–76), Assistant Professor, Northwestern University (1987–88), Adjunct Instructor, University of Connecticut (1981–83).

Education: BM MM New England Conservatory of Music (1973, 1975).

Teachers: Arnold Jacobs, Thompson Hanks, Harvey Phillips, Chester Schmitz.

Ogata, Fuminori
Born: 11/23/48
Current Positions: Century Orchestra Osaka

1989–, Lecturer, University of Soai, Faculty, Kyoto City University of Arts.

Past Positions: Osaka Prefecture Music Band (1972–89).

Education: BA Sakuyo University of Music.

Teachers: Tokuji Tagashire, Yo Kita, Hiroyuki Yasumoto.

Ogura, Sadayuki
Born: 03/14/57
Current Positions: Tokyo Kosei Wind Orchestra 1981–, Philharmonia Brass Quintet 1987–, Instructor, Kumamoto Music College, Tokyo Bari-Tuba Ensemble.

Past Positions: Oakland Symphony Orchestra (1981–86).

Contributions: International Consultant of the *The Tuba Source Book*, JETA committee member

Education: BA Tokyo University of the Arts (1979), MM California Institute of the Arts (1981).

Teachers: Kiyoshi Ohishi, Hiroyuki Yasumoto, Roger Bobo, Floyd Cooley.

Ohsawa, Kenichi
Born: 07/07/54
Current Positions: Instructor, Tamagawa University, Tokyo Bari-Tuba Ensemble.

Past Positions: Tokyo City Philharmonic Orchestra.

Contributions: JETA committee member.

Education: BA Kunitachi Music College.

Teachers: Kiyoshi Ohishi.

Olah, John Joseph Jr.
Born: 09/11/56
Current Positions: Associate Professor, University of Miami 1985–, Miami City Ballet Orchestra 1985–, Miami Brass Consort 1990–.

Past Positions: New Mexico Symphony, New Mexico Brass Quintet, Cleveland Ballet Orchestra, Cleveland Brass Consort.

Education: BM Baldwin Wallace College (1983), MM University of New Mexico (1985).

Teachers: Ron Bishop, Karl Hinterbichler.

Pack, David
Present Positions: Phoenix Symphony; Adjunct Instructor, Grand Canyon College.

Teachers: William Bell.

Pál, Kis
Born: 02/14/59
Current Positions: Hungarian Army Central Band 1984–.

Past Positions: Army Band TATA (1978–84).

Education: Music School of the Hungarian Army (1978).

Teachers: László Szabó.

Palmer, Singleton
1913–03/08/93

Contributions: In 1930s and 1940s played bass with territory bands, and with Count Basie for three years. Returned to St. Louis, his hometown, in 1949, where he led and played tuba in a jazz sextet until his death in 1993.

Park, Yun-Geun
  Born: 01/16/63
  Current Positions: Korean Symphony Orchestra.
  Education: University of Kyung-Hee (1988), Musik Hochschule für Köln.
  Teachers: Jong-il Lee, Hans Gelhar.

Parreott, Dorian L. II
  Born: 11/23/65
  Current Positions: Monmouth Symphony Orchestra 1989–; Garden State Philharmonic 1990–; Top Brass Quintet 1986–; Polished Brass Quintet 1988–; New Jersey free-lance 1980–.
  Education: BA Trenton State College (1988).
  Teachers: Bob Stuart, David Uber, Don Butterfield, Phil Birnbaum, Dorian Parreott Sr.

Pashetov, Sergey I.
  Born: 10/23/58
  Current Positions: Kiev Municipal Band 1992–.
  Past Positions: The State Band of Ukraine (1984).
  Education: Kiev Musical College (1980), Moscow State Conservatory (1985).
  Teachers: Victor Sinko, Alexei Lebedev.

Pászner, László
  Born: 12/29/57
  Current Positions: Debrecan Philharmonic Orchestra, Fönix Brass Quintet.
  Education: Györ (1972–76), Debrecen (1976–79).
  Teachers: Nagy József, Szabó Ilona.

Patterson, Gergory J.
  Born: 09/17/62
  Current Positions: US Navy Band San Francisco 1989–.
  Education: AA Columbia College (1991).
  Teachers: Ross Tolbert, Peter Wahrhaftig.

Patti, Giovanni
  Born: 12/05/60
  Current Positions: Banda Nazionale Dell' Aeronautica.
  Education: Diploma Solfeggio.
  Teachers: Antonio Solito, Carlo Ingrati.

Paulenz, Dirk
  Born: 05/03/63
  Current Positions: Police Band Kiel 1990–.
  Past Positions: Neubrandenburger Philharmonic 1987–89, Theater Stralsund 1984–87.
  Education: Hanns Eisler Conservatory.
  Teachers: Dietrich Unkrodt.

Pearson, Norman W.
  Born: 05/17/57
  Current Positions: Free-lance, Los Angeles including orchestra, ballet, opera, motion picture and television, instructor, California State University at Fullerton 1984–, Los Angeles Philharmonic 1994–.
  Past Positions: Los Angeles Philharmonic Orchestra (1989–92), Orquestra Filarmonica de Caracas (1981).
  Education: BM University of Southern California (1982).
  Teachers: Tommy Johnson, Roger Bobo, Jim Self.

Peck, Robert S.
  Born: 05/18/50
  Current Positions: Command Band of the US Air Force Reserve.
  Past Positions: 8th Air Force Band.
  Education: BMEd University Central Arkansas (1973).
  Teachers: Pat Hasty, Ron Fox, Bill Haskett, Don Kramer.

Perantoni, Daniel Thomas
  Born: 05/05/41
  Current Positions: Professor, Indiana University 1994–, Artist Faculty, Keystone Brass Institute 1986–, Summit Brass 1986–, St. Louis Brass Quintet 1980–, Del Sol Brass Quintet 1982–, Matteson-Phillips Tubajazz 1976–.
  Past Positions: Professor, Arizona State University (1982–94), Professor, University of Illinois (1968–82), Artist Faculty, Banff Centre (1982–88), San Antonio Symphony Orchestra (1963–64), U.S. Army Band (1964–67), Amsterdam Philharmonic Orchestra (1966–67), Champaign/Urbana Symphony (1968–82).
  Contributions: First President of T.U.B.A. (1971–74), Board of Directors, T.U.B.A. 1975–, several solo recordings, numerous other recordings, numerous published articles, design consultant, clinician, accessories developer.
  Education: BM Eastman School of Music (1963), MM Catholic University of America (1968).

Perez, Calleja Juan Carlos
  Born: 07/27/61
  Current Positions: Orquesta Sinfonica de Sevilla, Grupo de Metales de la O.S. de Sevilla.
  Past Positions: San Sebastian, Banda Municipal (1989–90).
  Education: Titulo Superior "Ecole de Musique" de Bayonne (France) (1984–85), Titulo Profes. "Cons. Sup de S. Sebastián (1986–87), "Prix Ville de Paris" Paris y Tit. Sup Conserv. de Aubervilliers–La Courneuve (Région de Paris, Fr.) (1987–88).

Teachers: Philippe Legris, Bernard Lienard, André Lassus, J. Antonio Rubio, Mel Culbertson.

Perez Martinez, Rafael Alberto
Born: 03/24/60
Current Positions: Sinfonie Orchestra of Cali, Colombia.
Past Positions: National Band of Bogotá.
Education: National Pedagogical University, Conservatory of Music.
Teachers: Juan Carlos Rodriguez, David Lloyd.

Perry, Stephen B.
Born: 11/29/53
Current Positions: Hartford Symphony Orchestra 1985–, Springfield (MA) Symphony Orchestra 1980–, Instructor, Hartt School of Music 1981–, Quiet City Brass Quintet 1982–.
Past Positions: Free-lance, New York City (1981–84).
Education: BS Central CT State University (1976), MA Yale School of Music (1981).
Teachers: Theodore Toupin, Thompson Hanks.

Pesonen, Raimo
Born: 07/08/37
Current Positions: Helsinki Philharmonic Orchestra 1956–, Teacher, Sibelius Academy 1974–.
Past Positions: The Orchestra of Saronlinna Opera Festival (1972–91), Joensuu Military Band (1955–56).
Teachers: John Fletcher, Aldo Johannson, Gosta Moller.

Pfaff, Fred
1889–?
Past Positions: Finland Band, Quakertown Band, Allentown Pioneer Band, Martin Klinger Band, Ringold Band (1910s), Arthur Pryor Band (1915–17), Conway Band (1918), Sousa Band (1920), free-lance, New York (radio) 1920–50s, Florida Symphony (1959–1974).
Teachers: Self-taught.

Phillips, Harvey G.
Born: 12/02/29
Past Positions: Distinguished Professor, Indiana University 1971–94, Faculty, Hartt College of Music, Mannes College of Music, New York College of Music, New England Conservatory of Music, Yale University, Northwestern University, Arts Consultant to many organizations, New York Brass Quintet, New York City Ballet, Metropolitan Opera Orchestra, U.S. Army Field Band.
Contributions: Consultant, *The Tuba Source Book*, Executive Editor, *Instrumentalist* magazine, Chairman, TUBA Board of Directors, instrument design consultant, clinician, President/Founder of Harvey

Phillips Foundation, Inc., Co-founder, Matteson-Phillips Tubajazz Consort, Past President, T.U.B.A., Organized first International Tuba Symposium, first and second International Brass Congresses, originated TUBACHRISTMAS and OC-TUBAFEST, numerous solo and ensemble recordings, instructional video, co–author of tuba text, over one hundred commissions and premieres of tuba music, international clinician, soloist.
Education: attended University of Missouri (1947–48), Juilliard School of Music (1950–54), Manhattan School of Music (1956–58), Honorary DM New England Conservatory of Music (1971), Honorary DH University of Missouri (1987).
Teachers: William Bell.

Pierluigi, Ausili
Born: 09/04/40
Current Positions: Free-lance, Rome.
Teachers: Gregorio Mazzarese.

Pilafian, Sam
Born: 10/25/49
Current Positions: Travelin' Light Jazz Ensemble 1990–, Associate Professor, Arizona State University 1994–.
Past Positions: Professor, Boston University 1974–94, Empire Brass Quintet (1972–93), Faculty, Berkelee College of Music (1971–74).
Contributions: record company arranger, producer (1980–), jazz tuba CD recording, many recordings with Empire Brass Quintet.
Education: BM *magna cum laude* University of Miami (1972).
Teachers: Constance Weldon, Rex Conner, Jerry Coker.

Pilloud, Pierre–Edmond
Born: 09/02/50
Current Positions: L'Orchestre de la Suisse Romande à Genève, 1975–, Professeur, Conservatoire de Genève.
Past Positions: Orchestre Mondial des Jeunes, Orchestre de Bienne, Orchestre du Festival de Lucerne, two seasons with the Orchestra of Biel-Bienne.
Education: Conservatory of Geneva.
Teachers: René Mermet, Michel Curit, Edouard Gros.

Pina, Jose Antonio Rublo
Born: 11/14/59
Current Positions: Orquesta Sinfonica de Euskadi, Txindoki Brass Quintet, Professor, Universidad Guipuzcoa.
Past Positions: Orquesta Mundial de Jovenes, Ensemble Contemporanne Paris, Stravinsky Brass Quintet (Paris), Hamburg Symphony

Orchestra, Jury Member, C.N.S.L. (Lyon
and Bordeaux, France).
Education: 1st Premio de Honor (Superior)
Conservatorio Superior de Barcelona.
Teachers: Miguel Navarro Carbonell, Mel
Culbertson.

Pniak, Jan
Born: 02/13/44
Current Positions: A. Rubinstein Philharmonic
Orchester 1969–.
Past Positions: Teacher, Lodz high school
music and Academy of Music 1970–80.
Contributions: performances on Polskie Radio,
TV, Film, school brass orchestras.
Education: P. Liceum Muzyczna, Katowice, P.
Wyzsza Szkola Muzyczna, Katowice (Acad-
emy of Music) 1969.
Teachers: Feliks Kwiatkowski.

Pokorny, John Eugene "Gene"
Born: 05/15/53
Current Positions: Chicago Symphony Orches-
tra 1989–, Summit Brass 1986–, Classic Brass
Quintet 1991–, Instructor, Rafael Mendez
Brass Institute 1986–.
Past Positions: Los Angeles Philharmonic
Orchestra (1992–93), St. Louis Symphony
Orchestra (1983–89), substitute, Teton
Music Festival (1986), Colorado Music
Festival (1982–87), Utah Symphony
Orchestra (1978–83), Israel Philharmonic
Orchestra (1975–78).
Contributions: Contributor, *The Tuba Source
Book*, several articles in *TUBA Journal*, solo
CD recording, several Summit Brass
recordings.
Education: University of Redlands (1971–73),
BM *cum laude* University of Southern
California (1973–75).
Teachers: Jeffrey Reynolds, Larry Johansen,
Tommy Johnson, Roger Bobo, Arnold
Jacobs.

Poore, Melvyn
Born: 10/09/51
Current Positions: Free-lance, Germany and
England, ETC Tuba Quartet, ETQ Tuba
Quartet, Georg Grawes's Grubenklang
Orchestra, Wolfgang Fuch's King Ubo
Orchestra, Radu Malfatti's Ohr Kiste,
Cambrian Brass Quintet.
Past Positions: Birmingham Arts Labratory
(1976–79), Rarry Guy's London Jazz
Composer's Orchestra (1980–83), Artist-in-
Residence, Victoria College of the Arts
(1984), Musician-in-Residence, City of
London (1986), Fine Arts Brass Ensemble
(1987), Instructor, Royal Northern College
of Music, Manchester (1989–91), Stipendiat,
Schloss Solituse, Stuttgart (1991).

Contributions: prominent avant-garde experi-
menter as performer and composer, many
commissions, compositions, recordings, use
of extended techniques, tuba as theatrical
device, as sculpture, with voice, with
electronics, as a meta-instrument.
Education: LRAM Royal Academy of Music
(1970), BMus (Hons) University of Birmingham (1974), MA University of Birmingham
(1975).

Porter, William Davidson II
Born: 05/15/58
Current Positions: The US Air Force Band
1983–, The US Air Force Tuba-Euphonium
Quartet 1992–, Christian Performing Artists
Fellowship 1984–, Private Instructor 1983–.
Past Positions: New Mexico Symphony (1980–
1982), New Mexico Tuba Quartet (1981–
82), University of New Mexico Brass Quintet
(1980–1982).
Contributions: Consultant, *The Tuba Source
Book*, TUBA Regional Coordinator (1985–
1989), Co–coordinator Eastern National
Tuba-Euphonium Conference (1989).
Education: BS Tennessee Technological
University (1980), MM University of New
Mexico (1982).
Teachers: R Winston Morris, Karl
Hinterbichler, David Fedderly.

Posch, August
Born: 12/30/57
Current Positions: Teacher, Landesmusikschule
Ried/1, Juvavum Brass Quintet.
Past Positions: Attended Militarmusik Linz.
Contributions: Brass quintet CD recording.
Education: Brucknerkonservatorium Linz,
Staatliche Reifeprufung.
Teachers: Robert Herdman.

Poulsen, Henrik Heick
Born: 10/23/63
Current Positions: Musikkorps Fyn 1988–,
Modern Brass Quintet 1989–, Odense Brass
Ensemble 1989–, Prinsens Livregiments
Musikkorps 1987–.
Past Positions: Atlanta Transit 1986–88.
Education: Royal Academy of Music Aarhus
(1989).
Teachers: Hans Andersen, Jørgen Voigt
Arnsted, Arnold Jacobs.

Powell, David
Born: 02/13/56
Current Positions: Docklands Sinfonietta
1990–, Generation Band 1993–, Dedication
Orchestra 1992–.
Past Positions: Loose Tubes (1982–90), Mike
Westbrook Orchestra (1980–1985).
Education: BMus London University (1977),
LRAM Royal Academy of Music, London
(1978).

Teachers: James Anderson, Patrick Harrild.

Pownall, Robert C. (Bob)
Born: 10/24/36
Current Positions: Adjunct Faculty, Nassau Community College 1971–; Associate Professor, Hofstra University 1972–; free-lance, New York 1955–.
Past Positions: Ernie Rudy Orchestra (1955–56); "Sing Man Sing" road show with Harry Belafonte (1956), Jerome Robbins "Ballet USA–New York Export Opus Jazz" (1957); "Flower Drum Song" (1958–60); Guy Lombardo Orchestra (1960–62).
Education: BA, MME Manhattan School of Music (1959, 1965).
Teachers: Phillip Donatelli, Abe Torchinsky, William Bell.

Price, Herbert Anthony Jr. (Tony)
Born: 06/28/41
Current Positions: Free-lance, New York, Orchestra of St. Lukes, Long Island Philharmonic Orchestra, L. I. P. Brass Quintet, Dave Matthew's Manhattan Jazz Orchestra, Harry Lip Jazz Band.
Past Positions: National Symphony Orchestra (1964–64), American Symphony Orchestra, Brass Arts Quintet, New York Tuba Quartet, David Matthews Big Band, Collins-Shepley Galaxy.
Contributions: has recorded with Freddie Hubbard, Art Farmer, Urbie Green, Yusef Lateef, John Tropea, Frank Sinatra, Mel Torme, Jon Faddis, Films and T.V. commercials. Has many arrangements and compositions for tuba.
Education: San Diego State College, Juilliard School of Music.
Teachers: Millard Biggs, Joseph Novotny, William Bell, Arnold Jacobs.

Price, Thomas W.
Born: 10/26/60
Current Positions: The US Military Academy Band 1986–, Heritage Brass Quintet 1986–, West Point Tuba-Euphonium Quartet 1987–.
Past Positions: Bedford Springs Festival Orchestra 1983–84.
Education: BMEd Southwest Texas State University (1983), MM University of Kansas (1986).
Teachers: J. Lesley Varner, Scott Watson.

Pröpper, Klemens
Born: 03/27/37
Current Positions: Professor, Music Conservatory Hannover and Detmold, State Opera Hannover.
Past Positions: Siegerland Orchestra, Niedersachsisches Sinfonie Orchester, Stadttheater Kassel.
Contributions: President, "Deutsches Tuba-forum," Editor, German *Tuba Journal* instrument design consultant, many students in professional orchestras, co-editor of orchestral excerpts text.
Teachers: Paul Heims, Hieronymus Engels.

Rabi, Gábor
Born: 04/30/68
Current Positions: Orchestra of Miskolc National Theatre 1990–, New Hungarian Brass 1990–, Brass teacher, Tiszaújváros 1991–, Gabrieli Quintett 1992–.
Education: Liszt Ferenc Academy of Music / Miskolc/ 1988–.
Teachers: Ilona Nemes, Roger Bobo.

Radoslaw, Rejewski
Born: 01/20/67
Current Positions: Muzyk Orkiestrewy, Polska Orkiestra Radiowa.
Education: Państwewa Szkola Muzczna 1987, Akademia Muzyczna im. F. Chopin w Warszawie 1991.
Teachers: Zdzislaw Piernik, Wlodzimierz Kukuc, Krzysztof Wejtyniak, Roman Siwek.

Randolph, David Mark
Born: 05/07/45
Current Positions: Associate Professor, University of Georgia 1973–, Georgia Brass Quintet 1973–.
Past Positions: US Army Band (1968–71), American Wind Symphony Orchestra (1966).
Contributions: Consultant, *The Tuba Source Book*; Editor, New Materials, *TUBA Journal* (1985–90), numerous articles and reviews in many journals, National Brass Chairman: M.T.N.A. (1981–85, 1991–93), two solo CD recordings.
Education: BMEd West Virginia University (1967); MM, Performer's Certificate, DMA, Eastman School of Music (1972, 1973, 1978).
Teachers: Reginald Fink, Donald Knaub, Cherry Beauregard.

Rankin, Donald
Born: 12/05/56
Current Positions: Instructor, University of South Maine, New England Conservatory Extension Division, Boston Ballet 1984–, Portland Symphony 1988–, Pro Arte Chamber Orchestra, Boston Philharmonic 1979–, Beacon Brass Quintet 1980–, Portland Brass Quintet 1983–.
Education: BM New England Conservatory (1978).
Teachers: Don Butterfield, Toby Hanks, Chester Schmitz.

Rath, Bernhard
Born: 10/21/38
Current Positions: Bodriruer Symphony 1985–; Teacher, Music School of Borium and Waltrop.

Past Positions: Oberhausener Orchestra (1962–65).

Education: Music-Academy of Lübeck.

Teachers: Horst North.

Rautianen, Helge

Born: 05/01/46

Current Positions: Turku Philharmonic Orchestra 1975–.

Past Positions: The Guardian Military Band (1966–75).

Education: The Military School of Music, Mikkeli (1961–66).

Teachers: Onni Virolainen.

Ray, Joe C.

Born: 08/21/48

Current Positions: Director of Insrumental Activities, Carson-Newman College 1976–, Knoxville Brass Quintet 1990–, Carson–Newman Faculty Brass Quintet 1981–.

Past Positions: Instructor of Music, Indiana State University (1974–76).

Contributions: contributor to *TUBA Journal* (1983–84).

Education: BMusEd University of Oklahoma (1970), MM Indiana University (1974).

Teachers: Harvey Phillips, Albert Buswell, Robert Tucci.

Redeczky, Tamás

Born: 12/05/63

Current Positions: Hungarian Army Central Band, Army Brass Quintet

Education: Music School of the Hungarian Army (1983)

Teachers: László Szabó, Miklós Wrhovszky.

Redondo Contreras, Jose Manuel

Born: 06/24/69

Current Positions: Orquesta Sinfonica de Castilla y Leon, Quinteto de Metales de le Orquesta Sinfonica de Castilla y Leon.

Past Positions: Quinteto de Metales Iberia (1990–91).

Education: Titulo Professional de Tuba (1989), Premio Extraordinario fin de Grado Professional de Tuba (1990), Titulo Elemental Viola (1990), Titulo Superior de Tuba (1991).

Teachers: Miguel Moreno, Harvey Phillips, Miguel Navarro, Mel Culbertson, Roger Bobo.

Reimund, John R.

Born: 09/07/64

Current Positions: The US Military Academy Band 1989–, Regimental Brass Quintet 1991–, Hudson Valley Opera Company 1993–.

Past Positions: Amarillo Symphony Orchestra (1983–89).

Education: BME, MM West Texas State University (1987, 1992).

Teachers: David Hawkins, Joseph Cox.

Renato, Pinto Costa

Born: 07/21/71

Current Positions: Brass Section Leader, Bahia Symphony Orchestra 1985–.

Education: attending University of Bahia.

Teachers: Zenio Alencar.

Renema, Sietze

Born: 08/05/65

Current Positions: Royal Military Band Netherlands Den Haag 1988–, Dutch Brass Ensemble, Arnhem 1991–, The Basemakers Tuba Quartet 1986–.

Education: Stedelyk Conservatorium Groningen (1989), Voninklyk Conservatorium Den Haag (1991).

Teachers: Donald Blakeslee, H. J. Renes.

Resta, Carlo

Born: 05/29/68

Current Positions: Banda Nazionale Dell' Esercito.

Teachers: Carmelo Tricsari.

Rhind, Kenneth A.

Born: 03/31/60

Current Positions: Orquestra Sinfonica de Bilbao; Brass Quintet of the O.S.B.; "Brassa-nova" brass ensemble.

Education: GRNCM, PPRNCM Royal Northern College of Music, England (1978–82), attended Richard Strauss Conservatory (1982–83).

Teachers: Anthony Swainson, Stuart Roebuck, Robert Tucci.

Ribeiro de Souza, Heber

Born: 07/21/65

Current Positions: Orquestra Filarmonica do Belm, Quinteto de Metals da Universidade Livre de Musica, Conjunto Juvenil de Metals de São Paulo.

Past Positions: Orquestra Assemblia de Deus, Lapa.

Teachers: Donald Smith, Drausio Chagas.

Richardson, Jack

Past Positions: Sousa Band.

Rideout, Jeffery

Born: 07/11/54

Current Positions: Artist-in-Residence, Custom Music Company 1987–; free-lance Detroit 1987–.

Past Positions: Instructor, Ball State University (1978–85).

Contributions: Instrument design and consulting, master classes and clinics.

Education: BSMEd Ball State University (1976), MM Ohio State University (1978), DMA Arizona State Univesity (in progress).

Teachers: J. Lesley Varner, Robert LeBlanc, Dan Perantoni, Ron Bishop.

Roberts, F. Chester
  Born: 06/29/21
  Current Positions: Instructor, Boston Conservatory 1972–, Gordon College 1982–.
  Past Positions: Chautauqua Symphony Orchestra (1951–71), San Francisco Symphony Orchestra (1967–69), Cleveland Orchestra (1950–67), Pittsburgh Symphony Orchestra (1946–50), Cleveland Brass Quintet (1955–66), Associate Teacher, Oberlin Conservatory (1954–67), Lecturer, Western Reserve University (1951–67).
  Contributions: T.U.B.A. Honorary Advisory Board, many published articles in several journals, published editor and arranger of tuba materials.
  Education: BM Cleveland Institute of Music.
Robertson, Eddie
  Past Positions: Spike Jones Orchestra.
Robinson, Jack C.
  Born: 06/06/37
  Current Positions: Associate Professor, University of Northern Colorada 1968–, Rocky Mountain Brass Quintet (1968–88), Greeley Philharmonic Orchestra 1968–.
  Past Positions: Instructor, Stetson University (1963–64).
  Contributions: T.U.B.A. Representative for Colorado and New Mexico, author of tuba text.
  Education: BM Stetson University (1963), MM Indiana University (1966).
  Teachers: William Bell, Don Harry, Thomas Beversdorf, Don Yaxley, Lewis Van Haney.
Roccaro, Joseph, J. Jr.
  Born: 11/30/57
  Current Positions: The US Military Academy Band 1981–, Section Leader 1989–, The Highlands Brass Quintet 1988–, The West Point Tuba–Euphonium Quartet 1987–.
  Education: BM, MM The Juilliard School of Music (1979, 1980).
  Teachers: Don Harry, Joseph Novotny, Paul Krzywicki.
Rocco, Roger
  Born: 03/17/49
  Current Positions: Free-lance tubist and teacher, Illinois, Editorial staff, *The Instrumentalist* magazine.
  Past Positions: Instructor, Vandercook College of Music, Northwestern University, Roosevelt University, Chicago State University, American Conservatory, Wheaton College, Northeastern Illinois University, Honolulu Symphony, Seattle Symphony.
  Contributions: Numerous articles and reviews on brass pedagogy in *The Instrumentalist*.
  Education: BM Roosevelt University, MM Northwestern University.

Teachers: Arnold Jacobs, Charles Guse, John Taylor.
Rochergin, Roman
  Born: 03/01/70
  Current Positions: Stravinsky Theatre; Nimesovich-Danchenko Theatre; "6" brass quintet.
  Education: Moscow Miltary Music School (1985–89), Moscow Conservatory (in progress).
  Teachers: Alexi Lebedev.
Rodgers, Andrew M.
  Born: 05/10/55
  Current Positions: Radio City Music Hall 1990–, Columbus Brass 1984–, Connecticut Orchestra 1986–, Instructor, Western CT State University 1989–.
  Education: BA Western CT State University (1980), MM Juilliard School (1984).
  Teachers: Harold Proudfoot, Sam Pilafian, Don Harry.
Rodriguez, Juan Carlos
  Born: 07/12/46
  Current Positions: Philharmonic Orchestra of Bogotá 1976–, Philharmonic Quintet.
  Education: Conservatory of Music, University National.
  Teachers: Marshall Steed, Edward Robert, Dwight Sullinger.
Roebuck, Stuart
  Current Positions: Professor, Royal Northern College of Music, Manchester 1964–; Head of Brass, Huddersfield Polytechnic, Yorkshire 1988–.
  Past Positions: Halle Orchestra (1963–84); Halle Brass Consort (1963–84).
  Teachers: Terence Nagel.
Rosa da Silva, Sidinei
  Born: 11/08/66
  Current Positions: Banda Sinfonica da Policia Militar do Estado de São Paulo 1987–.
  Education: Conservatorio Brooklin Paulista.
  Teachers: Drauzio Chagas.
Rose, William (Bill)
  Born: 07/08/26
  Past Positions: Associate Professor, University of Houston (1959–89), Symphonic Brass Quintet (1969–89), Houston Symphony and Houston Grand Opera (1949–77), Goldman Band, C.B.S. Symphony, New York Brass Quintet, free-lance, New York (1947–49), Mare Island Naval Shipyard Band (1944–46).
  Contributions: instrument and mouthpiece design consultant.
  Education: attended Juilliard School (1946–49).
  Teachers: William Bell.
Rozen, Jay
  Born: 05/16/55

Current Positions: Instructor, Southwest Texas
State University 1987–, Southwest
Brassworks 1987–, Creative Opportunity
Orchestra 1985–, European Tuba Quartet
1989–.
Past Positions: Jerusalem Symphony Orchestra
(1978–80).
Contributions: recorded artist, numerous
published compositions and arrangements.
Education: BM Ithaca College (1976), MM
Yale University (1980).
Teachers: Toby Hanks, Allen Ostrander, Sam
Pilafian, Don Little.

Rudolph, Ralf
Born: 08/12/62
Current Positions: Palatinian State Orchestra
1984–; "Rennquintett" member 1988–.
Education: Diploma Staat. Hochschule für
Musik, Mannheim (1987).
Teachers: Rüdiger Augustin, Robert Tucci,
Bernhard Hering.

Runyan, Paul T.
Born: 09/15/54
Current Positions: USAF Heartland of America
Band 1980–.
Education: BAMEd Augustana College, Sioux
Falls, SD (1976).
Teachers: Harold Krueger, Craig Fuller.

Russell, Fabian O.
Born: 05/14/68
Current Positions: State Orchestra of Victoria
1990–, Melbourne Brass Ensemble, Lecturer,
Victoria College of the Arts.
Past Positions: Sydney Symphony Orchestra
(1987–90), Melbourne Symphony Orchestra,
Adelaide Symphony Orchestra, Sydney Brass
Quintet (1987–90).
Teachers: Robert Johnston, Rex Martin.

Russell, Garry L.
Born: 09/01/47
Current Positions: Instructor, University of
Nevada at Las Vegas 1985–, Nevada School
of the Arts 1984–, Community College of
Southern Nevada 1987–, Nevada Symphony
Orchestra 1980–, Southern Nevada Wind
Ensemble 1987–.
Past Positions: Savannah Symphony Orchestra
(1964–65), Memphis Symphony Orchestra
(1965–70), U.S. Army Field Band (1970–
72), New World Brass Quintet (1977–91),
Rivera Hotel Orchestra (Las Vegas) (1976–
85), Flamingo Hilton Hotel Orchestra
(1986–89).
Education: BM Memphis State University.
Teachers: Jack Covert, Richard Dolph, Arnold
Jacobs, Daniel Perantoni, Charles Schultz,
Gail Wilson.

Rutschman, Carla J.
Born: 01/31/47

Current Positions: Associate Professor, Western
Washington University 1976–, Washington
Brass Ensemble 1977–, Peter Britt Festival
Orchestra 1977–.
Contributions: Premiered numerous works for
solo tuba, tuba and midi, tuba and piano,
tuba consultant.
Education: BA University of Northern Colo-
rado (1968), MM Arizona State University
(1971), PhD University of Washington
(1979).
Teachers: Buddy Baker, Don Heeren, John
Barrows, Chris Leuba.

Sabourin, David J.
Born: 01/31/57
Current Positions: Vancouver Opera.
Past Positions: Vancouver Symphony (1980–
81), Founder, Touch of Brass Quintet,
Founder, Vancouver Tuba Quartet.
Contributions: Founder, Touch of Brass
Publishers, providing music for tuba quartets
and brass quintets.
Education: BM University of British Columbia
(1979).
Teachers: Dennis Miller, Charles Daellenbach,
Arnold Jacobs.

Salmela, Juha
Born: 09/29/58
Current Positions: Professor, Paijat-Hameen
Konservatorio 1989–, Teacher, Orivesi
Summer Music Course 1990–, Lahti Brass
Ensemble 1989–, Lahti Brass Quintet 1989–.
Past Positions: Teacher, Ylivieskan Musiik-
kiopisti (1986–89).
Contributions: Regulations of Examinations
and Scales for tuba (1993).
Education: Ylivieskan Musiikkiopisto (1970–
80), Oulun Konservatorio (1980–83),
Sibelius Academy (1983–89).
Teachers: Sakari Lamberg, Raimo Pesonen,
Eino Takalo-Eskola, Michael Lind, John
Jenkins, Christian Delange, William Stanton,
Mel Culbertson.

Salotti, Harry Paul
Born: 04/01/60
Current Positions: Adjunct Faculty, Camden
County College 1989–, Seacoast Brass
Quintet 1985–, Midiri Brothers Jazz
Orchestra 1985–.
Contributions: arrangements of brass quintet
liturature.
Education: BA Glassboro State College (1982),
MM Indiana University (1984).
Teachers: Owen Metcalf, Harvey Phillips.

Salustri, Maurizio
Born: 10/23/54
Current Positions: Banda Nazionale Dell'
Esercito.
Education: Autodidatta.

Salzman, Michael J.
  Born: 09/29/61
  Current Positions: Cosmopolitan Brass Quintet, Concert Pops of Long Island 1983–, free-lance, New York 1983–.
  Past Positions: Long Island Philharmonic (1985–86).
  Education: BM Indiana University (1983), MM Mannes College of Music (1985).
  Teachers: Bill Barber, Harvey Phillips, Michael Lind, Sam Pilafian, Warren Deck.
Sanders, Michael
  Born: 04/08/51
  Current Positions: St. Louis Symphony Orchestra (1991–), Adjunct Faculty, Webster University, University of Missouri at St. Louis (1991–).
  Past Positions: San Antonio Symphony (1973–91), Utah Symphony Orchestra (1987–88, 1989–90), Adjunct Faculty, University of Texas at San Antonio (1978–91), Trinity University (1982–91), University of Utah (1987–88, 1989–90).
  Contributions: Soloist, I.T.E.C. (1986).
  Education: BM Eastman School of Music (1973).
  Teachers: Arnold Jacobs, Wayne Barrington, Donald Knaub, Cherry Beauregard, Robert Pallansch.
Sandmann, Harald
  Born: 04/06/68
  Current Positions: Marinemusikkorps Nordsee 1987–.
  Past Positions: Southwest German Television Orchestra, South German Television Orchestra, North German Radio Orchestra.
  Education: Robert Schumann Musik Hochschule, Düsseldorf (1988).
  Teachers: Paul Klose, Eiichi Inagawa, Hans Gelhar.
Sano, Hideo
  Born: 09/13/57
  Current Positions: Tokyo Brass Quintet 1979–, Instructor, Shobi Music College, Tokyo Bari–Tuba Ensemble.
  Contributions: JETA committee member.
  Education: BA Musashino Music College (1979).
  Teachers: Takao Ishikawa, Katsuhiko Kaijima, Ikumitsu Tado.
Santiago, Armando
  Born: 06/29/51
  Current Positions: Orquesta Sinfónica Nacional.
  Past Positions: Orquesta Sinfónica del Estado de Mexico.
  Education: Conservatorio Nacional de Musica.
  Teachers: William Keck, Edward Pearsall.
Sára, József
  Born: 12/24/64

Current Positions: Teacher, Bartók Béla Music School of Szolnok 1987–, Szolnok Symphony Orchestra 1989–, Szolnoki Olajbányász Wind Band 1989–, Abony Wind Band 1990–, Abony Brass Band 1992–.
  Education: Liszt Ferenc Music College of Debrecen (1984–87).
  Teachers: Volgyi Erno.
Sass, Jonathan McClain
  Born: 04/23/61
  Current Positions: Vienna Art Orchestra; Crack Jack Raido rock band; Hans Theessink and Blue Grove band; Hans Theessink and Jon Sass Duo.
  Past Positions: free-lance, New York (1978–82); free-lance Boston (1980–85); Cantabrigia Brass (1982–85).
  Contributions: premiered tuba and chamber music composition.
  Teachers: Howard Johnson, Sam Pilafian, Warren Deck.
Sato, Kiyoshi
  Born: 08/10/59
  Current Positions: Tokyo Metropolitan Symphony Orchestra 1991–, Tuba Quartet Shishiza
  Past Positions: Shinsei-Nihon Symphony Orchestra (1989–90)
  Contributions: JETA committee member
  Education: BA Tokyo University of the Arts (1983), University of Southern California (1985)
  Teachers: Ikumitsu Tado, Kiyoshi Ohishi, Tommy Johnson, Roger Bobo, Jim Self
Sato, Kurahei
  1900–07/09/86
  Past Positions: Japanese Navy Band (1917–27), free-lance, silent movies (1927–31), Shin-Tokyo-Philharmonic (NHK Philharmonic) (1931–58), teacher, Musashino College of Music (1956–74), Inspector, Nippon Philharmonic Orchestra (1958–?), many successful students in professional orchestras
  Education: Toku
  Contributions: one of the leading Japanese tubists of this century, first tuba concert in Japan (1965)
Saygers, David M.
  Born: 10/28/59
  Current Positions: Instructor, University of Toledo 1990–, Tower Brass Quintet 1981–, University of Toledo Brass Quintet 1990–.
  Past Positions: Instructor, Bowling Green State University, Galliard Brass Quintet (1989–90), American Waterways Wind Orchestra (1989).
  Contributions: arranger and composer of brass quintets, tuba solos, premiered over a dozen quintets and solos.

Education: BM University of Michigan (1981),
MM Bowling Green State University (1987).
Teachers: Abe Torchinsky, Ivan Hammond,
Fritz Kaenzig.

Schmidt, Paul Reinhardt
Born: 06/05/58
Current Positions: Founder, Heavy Metal Tuba
Quartet, free-lance, Chicago 1977–.
Contributions: many published tuba-eupho-
nium ensembles, pedagogical articles, owner
of Heavy Metal Music.
Education: Private instruction, Germany.

Schmieder, Peter
Born: 11/01/72
Current Positions: Ausbildungsmusikkorps der
Bundeswehr Hilden.
Teachers: Hans Gelhar.

Schmitt, Volker
Born: 01/19/69
Current Positions: Orchestermusiker.
Past Positions: Landesjugend & Bandes-
jugendorchester; Schleswig-Holstein
Festivalorchester.
Education: attended Hochschulen in Aachen
und Köln.
Teachers: Walter Hilgers, Hans Gelhar.

Schmitz, Chester
Current Positions: Boston Symphony Orchestra
1966–, New England Conservatory.
Past Positions: US Army Field Band (1963–66).
Contributions: premiered John William's *Tuba
Concerto*, 1985, soloist with Boston Sym-
phony and Boston Pops Orchestras, recorded
Tubby the Tuba with the Pops on video and
LP (1970), teacher, Boston Consevatory.
Education: BM University of Iowa.
Teachers: William Gower, Sr.

Schooley, John H.
Born: 02/08/43
Current Positions: Professor, Fairmont State
College 1970–, Fairmont Brass Quintet
1971–, Appalachian Brass Quintet 1991–,
music publisher 1984–
Past Positions: Instructor, Eastern Kentucky
University (1968–70), Corning NY Sym-
phony Orchestra (1963–65).
Contributions: composer of four published
works for tuba, author of articles in many
journals.
Education: BS Mansfield University (1965),
Certificate Royal Academy of Music, London
(1966), MM East Carolina University
(1968).
Teachers: John Baynes, William Bell, John
Fletcher.

Schuchat, Charles
Born: 08/23/61
Current Positions: Asbury Brass Quintet 1986–,
Associate Professor of Music, Northern

Illinois University, 1988–, free-lance,
Chicago 1983–.
Past Positions: Haifa Symphony Orchestra
(1981–82).
Education: BM Northwestern University
(1984).
Teachers: Arnold Jacobs.

Schultz, Charles A.
Born: 09/30/48
Current Positions: Memphis Symphony
Orchestra 1972–, Opera Memphis Orchestra,
Memphis Symphony Brass Quintet, Profes-
sor, Memphis State University 1974–,
Instructor, Tennessee Governor's School for
the Arts 1992–.
Contributions: arranger of tuba-euphonium
ensembles, New Materials contributor,
TUBA Journal (1980–82).
Education: BME The Ohio State University
(1970), MM Memphis State University
(1972), DMA North Texas State University
(1980).
Teachers: Robert LeBlanc, David Kuehn, Don
Little.

Schumacker, Finn
Born: 05/17/61
Current Positions: Bavarian State Opera,
Munich 1987–, Munich Brass Quintett
1988–.
Past Positions: Funen Life Regiment Band
(Military) (1983–87).
Education: Royal Conservatory of Music,
Copenhagen.
Teachers: Jørgen Arnsted.

Schweter, Klaus
Born: 01/06/40
Current Positions: Staatskapelle Dresden.
Contributions: Has premiered solo works.
Education: Hochshcule für Musik "Carl-Maria
von Weber," Dresden.
Teachers: Heinz Forlder.

Segress, Terry D.
Born: 07/06/39
Current Positions: Professor, Southwest
Oklahoma State University (1970–75,
1976–)
Education: BM Oklahoma City University
(1961), MM, PhD University of North Texas
(1965, 1979).
Teachers: James Neilson, Leon Brown, David
Kuehn, Irvin Wagner.

Seifert-Gram, Jesse C.
Born: 06/16/59
Current Positions: Instructor, Indiana State
University 1991–, Indiana State University
Faculty Brass Quintet 1991–.
Past Positions: Instructor, University of Oregon
(1984–90), Eugene Symphony Orchestra,
Eugene Opera, Eugene Ballet (1984–90),

Instructor, University of Tulsa (1982–83), University of Tulsa Faculty Brass Quintet (1982–84).
Education: BM Eastman School of Music (1982), MM Northwestern University (1989), DMA University of Illinois (in progress).
Teachers: Mark Moore, Rex Martin, Arnold Jacobs, Cherry Beauregard, Michael Bunn, Daniel Brown, David Bragunier.

Self, James
Born: 08/20/43
Current Positions: Free-lance and studio musician, Los Angeles 1974–, Pacific Symphony 1986–, Pasadena Symphony 1976–, Music Center Opera 1985–, Opera Pacific 1987–, Hollywood Bowl Orchestra 1991–, American Ballet Theater/Los Angeles, faculty, University of Southern California.
Past Positions: faculty, University of Tennessee Knoxville (1969–74), The US Army Band Washington D.C. (1965–67).
Contributions: Since 1974 has worked for all the major Hollywood studios performing for hundreds of motion pictures, television shows and records. Solos in major films include many by John Williams and James Horner; has recorded with Mel Torme, Frank Sinatra, Don Ellis, the L.A. Philharmonic, Pacific Symphony, Hollywood Bowl Orchestra, and many others; has one classical and three jazz recordings; Past President of T.U.B.A., a published composer and arranger, MUP Tuba four years, NARAS (Hollywood Studios), performs with the Steiner EVI (electronic valve instrument), Yamaha Performing Artist.
Education: BS Indiana University of Pennsylvania (1965) MM Catholic University (1967), DMA University of Southern California (1976).
Teachers: William Becken, Lloyd Geisler, Harvey Phillips, Tommy Johnson.

Senff, Les
Born: 11/21/56
Current Positions: Oregon Jazz Band 1989–, Bullmoose Project 1991–, Starlighters 1992–.
Past Positions: Central Oregon Symphony (1974–77, 1980–83), Cascade Brass Quintet (1980–1990), Central Oregon Wind Ensemble (1974–77, 1980–90), Wall Street Jazz Band (1980–90), Alpen Musiker (1982–90).
Education: BS University of Oregon (1979).
Teachers: Andrew Ehrenpfort, Jerry Yahna, Jesse Graham.

Seo, Jeong Bu
Born: 09/22/67

Current Positions: Po Hang Philharmonic Orchestra 1990–.
Past Positions: Po Hang Symphony Orchestra (1987–89).
Education: BA An Dong National University (1990).
Teachers: Park Sang Gon, Heo Jae Young.

Seob, Chun
Born: 09/17/59
Current Positions: Seoul Academy Symphony Orchestra 1990–.
Past Positions: Ars Nova Brass Quintet (1987–90).
Contributions: Seoul Academy Orchestra Sub Inspector.
Education: Seoul National University (1982–87).
Teachers: Lee Jae Ok, Lee Jong.

Serpa, Richard E.
Born: 02/19/62
Current Positions: Richmond Symphony 1993–, Richmond Symphony Brass Quintet 1993–, Instructor, Virginia Union University 1993–.
Past Positions: Acting Principal, Arkansas Symphony (1992–93).
Education: BM University of Kentucky (1992).
Teachers: Skip Gray, Don Harry.

Shearer, James Edward
Born: 04/05/64
Current Positions: Assistant Professor, New Mexico State University 1991–, Yamaha Performing Artist 1992–, El Paso Brass Quintet, World's Largest Horn Quartet.
Past Positions: Assistant Professor, Southern Arkansas University (1990–91), El Paso Symphony Orchestra (1987–88).
Contributions: Advertising Coordinator, *TUBA Journal* 1993–, commissioned and premiered several solo works.
Education: BM Delta State University (1986), MM New Mexico State University (1988), DMA, Performer's Certificate Eastman School of Music (1990).
Teachers: Cherry Beauregard, Edward R. Bahr, Barton Cummings, Rex Conner.

Sheridan, Patrick R.
Born: 07/09/68
Past Positions: The US Marine Band 1989–93, Alexandria Symphony 1992–93, Chicago Civic Orchestra 1986–88.
Education: Attended Northwestern University (1986–88), Arizona State University (1988–1989), BM George Mason University (1992).
Teachers: William Winkle, Harvey Phillips, Ross Tolbert, Roger Rocco, Gary Ofenloch, Arnold Jacobs, Jerry Young, Daniel Perantoni, James Self.

Sherlock, Daniel B.
  Born: 07/25/62
  Current Positions: The US Army Field Band
    1988–, The US Army Field Band Brass
    Quintet 1990–, Maryland Symphony
    Orchestra 1991–, Founding Member US
    Armed Forces Tuba/Euphonium Quartet
    1992–.
  Past Positions: New West Orchestra, Southwest
    Brass Quintet.
  Education: Attended Arizona State University.
  Teachers: Raymond Nutaitis, Daniel Perantoni.
Shoop, Stephen
  Born: 06/16/56
  Current Positions: Amazement Park Revue,
    Cedar Point Amusement Park.
  Contributions: Author of numerous articles for
    TUBA Journal, arranger of tuba/euphonium
    ensembles.
  Education: BME Texas Christian University
    (1978), MME Indiana University (1984),
    PhD University of North Texas (in progress).
  Teachers: Ronald Tasa, Harvey Phillips, Donald
    Little.
Short, Michael D.
  Born: 10/30/53
  Current Positions: Adjunct Instructor, Central
    College (Pella, IA) 1990–, Des Moines
    Symphony Brass Quintet 1992–, Red Sneaker
    Jazz Band 1991–, President, Dealers' Tuba
    Supply 1991–.
  Past Positions: Cedar Rapids Symphony and
    Brass Quintet (1992–93), Whirlwind Brass
    Quintet (1982–86), Northbrook Symphony
    (1980–86), Red Rose Ragtime Band (1980–
    86), West End Jazz Band (1978–86).
  Education: BA, MM University of Northern
    Iowa (1975, 1977).
  Teachers: Ron Munson, Don Little, Fritz
    Kaenzig, Arnold Jacobs.
Sibley, Graham B.
  Born: 04/04/69
  Current Positions: Northern Ballet Orchestra
    1991–; free-lance, London 1991–; Sheridan
    Brass Ensemble, Parnassus Brass Quintet.
  Education: GGSM Guildhall School of Music
    and Drama, London.
  Teachers: James Anderson, Peter Cane, Patrick
    Harrild.
Sidow, Paul
  Past Positions: Boston Symphony Orchestra
    1922–33, (Co–Principal 1928–33).
Siggstedt, Mats
  Current Positions: Gotlandsmusiken 1986–.
Simonetti, Vincent
  Born: 08/03/43
  Present Positions: president and owner, The
    Tuba Exchange, Inc. 1984–; Raleigh Concert
    Band 1988–; Basement Brass Quintet 1993–.

Past Positions: North Carolina Symphony
  (1967–75); substitute, Metropolitan Opera
  (1965).
Contributions: raising level and availability of
  instruments for students and professionals.
Education: BM, MMEd Manhattan School of
  Music (1965).
Teachers: Bill Bell, Joe Novotny, Harvey
  Phillips, Arnold Jacobs, Herb Wexelblatt.
Simonsen, Ole
  Born: 12/26/60
  Current Positions: Ensemble Hafniae Brass
    Quintet, Regiment Military Band.
  Past Positions: The Funen Regiment's Military
    Band (1987–88).
  Education: M, SC. (Econ).
  Teachers: Jens Bjørn Larsen, Jørgen Arnsted,
    Arne Svendsen.
Sinclair, Alan
  Born: 11/18/48
  Current Positions: City of Birmingham
    Symphony Orchestra 1980–.
  Past Positions: Bournemouth Symphony
    Orchestra (1970–73).
  Education: AGSM Performing and Teaching
    (1969), Post Graduate Studies (1969–70)
    Guildhall School of Music and Drama,
    London.
  Teachers: Denis Wick, John Fletcher.
Sinder, Philip N.
  Born: 07/22/57
  Current Positions: Professor, Michigan State
    University 1982–, Beaumont Brass Quintet
    1982–, Lansing Symphony Orchestra and
    Brass Quintet 1982–, Brass Band of Battle
    Creek 1990–.
  Past Positions: Colorado Music Festival (1991),
    Houston Symphony Orchestra (1981–82),
    Wichita Symphony Orchestra (1979–81),
    Colorado Philharmonic (1979), Wichita
    Brass Quintet (1979–81), Visiting Lecturer,
    Rice University (1981–82).
  Contributions: Coordinator, T.U.B.A.
    Composition Contest 1991–, author of
    articles and reviews for TUBA Journal,
    arranger of brass ensembles, Board of
    Advisors, Falcone International Euphoniun
    Festival.
  Education: BMEd Performer's Certificate
    Eastman School of Music (1979, 1978), MM
    Wichita State University (1981).
  Teachers: Bill Barber, Cherry Beauregard,
    Donald Hummel.
Sipes, Dan T.
  Current Positions: Artist-in-Residence, The
    Tuba Exchange.
  Past Positions: Instructor, University of North
    Carolina, Chapel Hill; Chapel Hill Brass
    Quintet; Western Carolina University;

Appalachian State University; Lenoir-Rhyne College; extra, Phoenix Symphony, North Carolina Symphony, Charleston Symphony.
Contributions: commercial cassette recording with Crossroads Consort chamber ensemble.
Education: attended DePaul University, BM Arizona State University (1982), MM Boone State University.
Teachers: Arnold Jacobs, Ray Nutaitis, Roger Bobo.

Siwek, Roman
Born: 03/05/41
Current Positions: Professor, F. Chopin Academy of Music.
Past Positions: Professor, Academy of Music, Katowice, Academy of Music, Krakow.
Education: MA State Higher School of Music in Katowice, Poland (1963).
Teachers: Feliks Kwiatkowski.

Sjöberg, Per Olov
Current Positions: Free-lance, Stockholm 1987–.
Education: Ingesunds Folkhogskola (1984), MFA Stockholm Royal College of Music (1989).
Teachers: Michael Lind.

Skagerfölt, Erik A.
Born: 07/02/60
Current Positions: Stockholm Sparuàgesmons Musikhar 1984–.
Education: Dalaro School of Music (1984).
Teachers: Michael Lind, Carl Jacobsson, Karl-Otto Wessen.

Smith, Jerry L.
Born: 08/21/63
Current Positions: US Air Force Band of Liberty.
Past Positions: US Air Force Band of Flight.
Teachers: Richard Byrnes.

Smith, John F.
Born: 02/25/50
Current Positions: English National Opera Company, Locke Brass Consort, London Concert Orchestra, Tutor, Goldsmith College.
Past Positions: London Gabrieli Brass Ensemble.
Education: LRAM Royal Academy of Music, London.
Teachers: John Fletcher.

Smith, Kilton Vinal
05/19/09–09/16/87
Past Positions: Boston Symphony Orchestra (1935–66) (also assistant principal trombone, euphonium 1935–47).

Smith, M. Daryl
Born: 01/29/55
Current Positions: Orchestra Sinfonia dell RAI di Milano 1983–, Ensemble Modern 1991–.

Past Positions: Orchestra del Teatro alla Scala (1980–92), Teatro Regio di Torino (1978–79).
Contributions: Tuba design technician and developer.
Education: BM Indiana University (1977).
Teachers: Rex Conner, Harvey Phillips, William Adam.

Smith, Paul
Born: 04/21/64
Current Positions: BBC Symphony Orchestra 1990–, Westminster Brass Ensemble 1984– Teacher, Pursell School (Harrow) 1991–, City University 1991–, Royal Holloway and Bedford College (Egham) 1992–.
Past Positions: Teacher, Herfordshire Education Authority (1987–90).
Education: GRSM Royal Academy of Music, London (1987).
Teachers: Patrick Harrild.

Smith, Robert D.
Born: 07/21/30
Current Positions: Professor Emeritus, Ohio University 1983–.
Past Positions: Professor, Ohio University (1954–83); US Army Bands (1951–54).
Contributions: brass music reviewer, NACWAPI state chair (1965–68).
Education: BFA Kearney State College (1954), MM Cincinnati Conservatory of Music (1955), attended Indiana University (1968–69).
Teachers: Ernest Glover, Lewis Van Haney, Jay Friedman, William Bell.

Sonntag, Rene
Born: 01/22/71
Current Positions: Ausbildungsmusikkorps der Bundeswehr Hilden.
Teachers: Hans Gelhar.

Spencer, Kevin R.
Born: 05/13/64
Current Positions: Band of the Corps of Royal Engineers, Britannic Symphony Orchestra, G.E.C. Avionics Brass Band.
Education: Royal Military School of Music, Kneller Hall.
Teachers: Patrick Harrild, Lesley Lake, Peter Wise.

Sprowl, Gregory B.
Born: 09/03/58
Current Positions: Air Force Band of Liberty 1991–, New England Philharmonic.
Past Positions: USAF Band of the Golden West (1981–91).
Education: BAMEd Lander College (1980).
Teachers: James Self, Keating Johnson, Larry Joe Cook.

St. Clair, Cyrus
1890–1955

Past Positions: New York City Tuba 1920s and 1930s, played with Wilbur De Paris and Charlie Johnson, Clarence Williams (1926–29), Cozy Cole's Hot Cinders (1930).

Contributions: Considered by some to be one of the greatest early jazz tubists.

Stamm, Ulrich
Born: 12/14/65
Current Positions: Extra, Niedersachenisches Staatsorchester, Hannover.
Contributions: German premiere of tuba composition (1992).
Education: Hochschule für Musik und Theatre, Hannover (in progress).
Teachers: Klemens Propper, Michael Lind.

Stanley, Donald A.
Born: 01/11/37
Current Positions: Williamsport (PA) Orchestra 1981–, Corning (NY) Philharmonic 1966–, Commonwealth Brass Quintet 1981–.
Past Positions: Professor, Mansfield University (1966–91), Mansfield University Faculty Brass Quintet (1972–91), Instructor, Kearney State College (1964–66).
Contributions: T.U.B.A. Region III Coordinator, Contributor to *The Tuba Source Book*, new music reviews, Pennsylvania Music Educators Association magazine.
Education: BS Ohio State University (1959), MFA Ohio University (1964).
Teachers: William Kearns, Robert Smith, William Richardson, Toby Hanks.

Start, Alan E.
Born: 02/28/38
Current Positions: Free-lance, Delaware 1961–, University of Delaware Brass Quintet 1981–, Kennett Square (PA) Symphony Orchestra 1986–, Renaissance Brass Quintet 1987–.
Past Positions: All-American Cornet Band (1982–84), 287th National Guard Band (1956–57), US Navy Bands (1958–61).
Contributions: Co-founder, Greater Newark Tuba Ensemble; Co-chair, OCTUBAFEST, TUBACHRISTMAS, University of Delaware.
Education: US Navy School of Music (1958).
Teachers: Jay Hildebrandt.

Stees, Kevin James
Born: 06/12/61
Current Positions: Assistant Professor, James Madison University 1985–, Madison Brass 1985–.
Past Positions: Instructor, Grand Canyon College (1984–85).
Contributions: Contributor, *The Tuba Source Book*, New Editor, *TUBA Journal* (1990–), premiered several solo works (1985–).
Education: BS University of Illinois (1983), MM Arizona State University (1985).
Teachers: Daniel Perantoni, Jack Tilbury.

Stefanelli, Elia
Born: 10/16/63
Current Positions: Banda Nazionale Dell' Aeronautica.
Education: Solfeggio.
Teachers: Tortora, Merolli, Carlo Ingrati.

Steinböck, Josef
Born: 06/23/67
Current Positions: Mozarteum Orchester, Salzburg, Klangforum,Vienna.
Past Positions: "Gustav Mahler" Jugend-orchesters, substitute, Vienna Symphoniker, Brucknerorchester Linz, Los Angeles Philharmonic.
Education: Musikhochschule Vienna, Jazz-konservatorium Vienna.
Teachers: Nikolaus Schafferer, Erich Klein-schuster.

Stenquist, Urban
Born: 08/24/59
Current Positions: Symphoniorkestern Norr-koping 1989–.
Past Positions: Regionmusiken Kristianstad (1978–88), Stor Teatern Goteborg (1989).
Education: Ingesnuds Musikhogskola.
Teachers: Michael Lind

Stern, Karl J.
Born: 08/21/33
Current Positions: Länsmusiker, Stockholms-musiken 1988–.
Past Positions: Regienmusikin Stockholm (1970–88), Musikfanjunkare, Kungel Svea Lingardermusikkar (1948–70), Solma Brass (1969–90).
Teachers: Erik Rundlölf, Allan Olsson.

Stevens, Hank
Past Positions: Spike Jones Orchestra (late 1930s early 40s).

Stevens, John D.
Born: 11/10/51
Current Positions: Professor, University of Wisconsin-Madison 1985–, Wisconsin Brass Quintet 1985–.
Past Positions: Professor, University of Miami (1981–85), Philharmonic Orchestra of Florida (1981–85), Greater Miami Opera (1981–85)
Contributions: T.U.B.A. Publications Coordinator, member of Executive Committee (1991–), composer of numerous published works for tuba, tuba-euphonium ensemble, brass quintet, etc.; recording of original compositions for tuba.
Education: BM Eastman School of Music (1973), MM Yale University (1975).
Teachers: William Kearney, Donald Knaub, Cherry Beauregard, Chester Roberts, Toby Hanks.

Stewart, Bob
  Born: 02/03/45
  Current Positions: Free-lance jazz tuba, New York.
  Past Positions: Moved to New York in 1968, began working with Carla Bley, Frank Foster's Loud Minority, Sam Rivers, Gil Evans, Arthur Blythe (from 1973 to late 1980s), Charles Mingus (1971), McCoy Tyner (1973), Henry Threadgill (1986).
  Contributions: Original member of the tuba ensemble "Gravity"; through work with Arthur Blythe, is largely responsible for bringing the tuba into the modern jazz rhythm section.
  Education: Philadelphia College of the Performing Arts (1962–66).
Stewart, Charles F. (Chuck)
  Born: 05/13/40
  Current Positions: Paramount Jazz Band of Boston 1985–, The Rent Party Revelers Jazz Band 1982–, The Concord Symphonic Band 1984–.
  Past Positions: East Bay City Jazz Band (1965–72), Your Father's Moustache banjo night club chain (1962–1971), Bobby Hackett (1971–72).
  Contributions: Recorded with Billy Butterfield, Johnny Mince, Banu Gibson, Paramount Jazz Band, Rent Party Revelers, East Bay City Jazz Band; appeared on the Ed Sullivan Show with Your Father's Moustache.
  Education: Northeastern University (no musical education).
  Teachers: Self-taught.
Stillion, Bradley J.
  Born: 04/24/63
  Current Positions: US Navy Band Newport 1991–.
  Past Positions: US Pacific Fleet Band (1986–91).
  Education: BMEd Bowling Green State University (1985).
  Teachers: Ivan Hammond.
Stockinjer, Eberhard
  Born: 07/05/59
  Current Positions: Orchestra Staatstheatre, Darmstadt 1979–; Schlossquintett (Darmstadt) 1986–; Symphonic Brass, Bayreuth 1991–; Teacher, Akademie für Tonkunst Darmstadt 1992–.
  Past Positions: Junge Deutsches Philharmonie (1978–79).
  Education: Richard Strauss Konservatorium, München (1975–80).
  Teachers: Robert Tucci.
Stofer, Lee A. Jr.
  Born: 03/03/57
  Current Positions: The US Army Europe Band,

Heidelberg 1992–, The US Army Europe Brass Quintet 1992–.
  Past Positions: The US Army Ground Forces Band (1989–92), US Army Band Europe (1985–89), 5th Army Band (1982–85), Mid-Texas Symphony (1984–85).
  Education: BM Western Kentucky University (1979).
  Teachers: F. Kent Campbell, Steven Bryant, Donald Strand.
Stormont, Walter Rand
  Born: 03/18/52
  Current Positions: Orquesta Sinfonica de Madrid 1986–.
  Past Positions: Orquesta Sinfonica de Las Palmas, G.C. (1978–79, 1982–86).
  Education: BA California State University, Northridge (1975).
  Teachers: Tommy Johnson, Roger Bobo, Mel Culbertson.
Strand, Donald L.
  Born: 9/7/56
  Current Positions: Assistant Professor, Coordinator of Brass Studies, Georgia State University 1986–, Atlanta Ballet Orchestra 1980–, Columbus (GA) Symphony Orchestra 1984–, Peachtree Brass 1979–, Atlanta Brass Works 1990–.
  Past Positions: Augusta (GA) Symphony Orchestra (1978–82), Instructor, West Georgia College (1985–92), Instructor, Columbus (GA) College (1985–93).
  Contributions: Coordinator, Atlanta TUBA-CHRISTMAS 1987–, arranger of tuba-euphonium ensembles.
  Education: BM University of Georgia (1982).
  Teachers: Arnold Jacobs, David Randolph, Abe Torchinsky, Michael Moore.
Strelchuk, Yuri F.
  Current Positions: Associate Professor, Musical College of Kiev 1983–, State Symphony Orchestra of Ukraine 1991–.
  Past Positions: Moscow State Symphony Orchestra (1978–79), Bolshoi Theatre of Moscow (1979–80), Big Symphony Orchestra of Radio and TV USSR (1979–81), State Band of Ukraine (1981–91).
  Education: Kiev Musical College (1975), Moscow State Conservatory (1980)
  Teachers: Victor Sinko, Alexej Lebedev.
Strohecker, Eric M.
  Born: 04/28/60
  Current Positions: USAF ACC Heartland of America Band.
  Education: BM Indiana University (1983).
  Teachers: Harvey Phillips, Gary Tirey.
Stroud, Richard Ernest
  Born: 01/26/29

Current Positions: Founder, The Sequoia Brass
Quintet, Co–founder, The Humboldt Bay
Brass Society, College of the Redwoods
Community Jazz Ensemble.
Contributions: Arranger of tuba/euphonium
ensembles.
Education: BA College of Idaho, MA University of Idaho.
Teachers: Ian Morton, William Billingsly, Gene
Whistler, Donn Mills, Jack Wheaton, Paul
Johnson.

Sugiyama, Jun
Born: 01/23/56
Current Positions: Tokyo Symphonic Band,
Uenonomori Brass Quintet, Instructor,
Tokoha University, Tokyo Bari-Tuba
Ensemble.
Contributions: JETA committee member.
Education: BA, MM Tokyo University of the
Arts (1980, 1987)
Teachers: Kiyoshi Ohishi, Ikumitsu Tado.

Sugiyama, Yasuhito
Born: 08/12/67
Current Positions: Free-lance, Japan.
Past Positions: Extra, Kyoto Symphony
Orchestra (1991).
Education: BA University of Soai (1990).
Teachers: Shuzo Karakawa, Fuminori Ogata,
Shigeo Takesada.

Sullinger, Dwight
Born: 12/10/45
Current Positions: Filarmonica de la Ciudad de
Mexico 1984–, Quinteto "Silvestre Revuel-
tas" 1985–.
Past Positions: Orquesta Sinfonica del Estado
de Mexico, Orcquesta Nacional de
Costa Rica.
Contributions: Consultant, *The Tuba Source
Book.*
Education: BM University of Oklahoma
(1968).
Teachers: Albert Buswell, Jr., John L. Smith,
William Bell, Don Harry, Yago Kong.

Surface, Edward
Born: 03/07/53
Current Positions: Instructor, Angelo State
University 1977–, San Angelo Symphony
Orchestra.
Past Positions: Assistant Instructor, Southwest-
ern Oklahoma State University (1975–76).
Education: BMEd Southwestern Oklahoma
State University (1975) MMEd Southwestern
Oklahoma University (1977).
Teachers: Albert Buswell, Terry Segress,
William Rose, Don Little.

Suzuki, Koji
Current Positions: Free-lance, Japan; Instructor,
Hokkaido Euphonium/Tuba Camp.

Education: BEd Hokkaido University of
Education (1988), Artist Diploma Indiana
University (1990), Meister diploma Hoch-
schule für Musik, München (1992–).
Teachers: Chitate Kagawa, Harvey Phillips,
Manfred Hoppert, Thomas Walsh, Robert
Tucci.

Swain, John J.
Born: 08/12/50
Current Positions: Music Department Chair,
California State University, Los Angeles.
Contributions: Several published articles,
composer of two works for solo tuba,
arranger/transcriber of works for tuba
ensemble, tuba and piano, tuba and band,
two CD-ROM Presentations.
Education: BFA, MM University of South
Dakota (1972, 1977), PhD Michigan State
University (1985).
Teachers: Philip Sinder, William Lake,
Lawrence Mitchell, Ray DeVilbiss.

Swainson, Tony
Born: 12/07/47
Current Positions: BBC Scottish Symphony
Orchestra 1971–, Tuba Professor, Royal
Scottish Academy of Music and Drama
1971–, Musical Director, Riverside Brass
(Glasgow) 1987–, Kopervik Musikkorps
(Norway) 1991–.
Education: Royal Manchester College of Music
(1966–70).
Teachers: Stuart Roebuck.

Swanson, David W.
Born: 06/07/63
Current Positions: 15th US Air Force Band of
the Golden West 1987–, California Brass
Company 1991–.
Past Positions: Free-lance, Cleveland
(1985–86).
Education: BSMEd Clarion University of
Pennsylvania (1985).
Teachers: Stanley Michalski, Ronald Bishop,
James Self.

Sykes, Peter Michael
Born: 09/26/55
Current Positions: Melbourne Symphony
Orchestra, Lecturer, Victoria College of the
Arts, Lecturer, Melbourne Institute of
Education.
Contributions: Founder, Director, Solitaire
Tuba-Euphonium Ensemble (1983–87), Co-
Founder, Director, Antipodes Tubas (1992–),
Twenty commissioned works for tuba-
euphonium ensemble and solo tuba, per-
formed and conducted premieres of over 25
tuba solos and works for tuba-euphonium
ensemble.
Teachers: Peter Walmsley, Baden McCarron,
Geoffrey Bailey, Dan Perantoni, Skip Gray.

Szabó, László
Born: 11/06/45
Current Positions: Hungarian State Symphony
Orchestra 1977–, Professor at the Ferenc
Liszt Music Academy of Budapest 1988–,
Budapest Brass Quintet 1977–.
Past Positions: Budapest Symphony Orchestra
part-time (1967–70), Hungarian State Opera
House (1970–77), Military Conservatory
(1966–81), Béla Bartók Conservatory (1982–
90).
Contributions: International Consultant of the
The Tuba Source Book, jury member of tuba
competitions, teacher of mastercourses.
Education: Diploma, summa cum laude, Ferenc
Liszt Academy of Music (1969).
Teachers: László Ujfalusi, György Zilc.
Szabó, Vilmos I.
Born: 05/26/40
Current Positions: Budapest (Radio) Symphony
1966–, Modern Brass Ensemble 1974–, PRO
BRASS Ensemble 1983–, Hungarian Brass
Ensemble (Modern Brass renamed) 1989–,
Brass Ad Libitum 1992–.
Past Positions: Professor, Schoolmaster of
Köszeg Music School (1964–66), conductor
of Köszeg Youth Brass Band (1964–66),
member of Koszeg Adult Brass Band (1964–
66), Szombathely Symphony Orchestra
(1964–66).
Contributions: Honorary member of T.U.B.A.
Education: Diploma summa cum laude,
Budapest Ferenc Liszt Academy of Music
(1964).
Teachers: János Hollai, László Ujfalusi.
Szalai, Csaba
Born: 07/21/67
Current Positions: Hungarian Symphony
Orchestra 1992–.
Education: Franz Liszt University of Music,
Budapest (1992).
Teachers: László Szabó, László Ujfalusi.
Székely, Zsolt
Born: 06/21/66
Current Positions: Budapest Concert Orchestra,
teacher at music school in Dunaharaszti,
Hungarian Brass Quintet.
Past Positions: Art Ensemble of the Hungarian
Army Symphony Orchestra.
Education: Béla Bartók Musical High School
(1986), Ferenc Liszt Music Academy of
Budapest (1986–91).
Teachers: László Szabó, László Ujfalusi.
Takács, Tibor
Born: 07/30/72
Current Positions: Teacher, Music School of
Biatorbágy 1992–, Abony Wind Band 1985–.
Contributions: International Tuba Competi-

tion, Markneukirchen 1992, Workshop,
Grieskirchen 1992.
Education: Liszt Ferenc Conservatory of Szeged
(1986–90), Liszt Ferenc Academy of Music
Budapest 1990–.
Teachers: Nagy Zsolt, László Szabó.
Takalo-Eskola, Eino H.
Born: 04/09/44
Current Positions: Radio Symphony Orchestra
1980–, Tanssiorkesteri Koivu 1985–.
Past Positions: Oulu Miltary Band (1964–79).
Education: The Military Music School, Oulu
(1959–64).
Teachers: Michael Lind, Gosta Moller, Raimo
Pesonen.
Takesada, Shigeo
Born: 05/10/60
Current Positions: Kyoto Symphony Orchestra
1985–, Osaka Brass Quintet 1985–, Lecturer,
Osaka College of Music 1990–, Lecturer,
Tokushima Burni University 1992–.
Education: BA Osaka College of Music (1982),
L.T. Munich (1990–91).
Teachers: Robert Tucci, Kazuo Ishizaki,
Tsutomu Morimoto, Shuzo Karakawa.
Tamminen, Ari
Born: 07/24/65
Current Positions: Instructor, Military School
of Music 1990–.
Past Positions: Lahti Military Band (1986–88),
Guardian Military Band (1988–90).
Education: Military School of Music (1983–
86), Paijat-Hameen Konservatorio (1990–).
Teachers: Raimo Pesonen, Juha Salmela, Eino
Takalo-Eskola.
Tarto, Joe
02/22/02–08/24/86
Past Positions: Joe Tarto's Dixieland Jazz band
(1919), Paul Spect Band (1922–24), Played
and recorded with Red Nichols (1920s and
1935–36), Miff Mole, the Dorsey Brothers,
Bix Beiderbecke, Joe Venuti, and others.
Played with Paul Whiteman intermittently for
25 years. CBS staff musician (1930–), New
Jersey Symphony, led the New Jersey
Dixieland Brass Quintet into the 1980s.
Contributions: Was a major free-lance recording
artist and arranger and was involved in all
kinds of commercial music as well as jazz,
solo recording, improvisation, text.
Tempas, Frederick William
Born: 09/11/53
Current Positions: Union Brass Company
1981–, Jewish Wedding Band 1990–.
Past Positions: Instructor, Humboldt State
University (1986–1990), Hall Street Honkers
(1982–89).
Education: BA Humboldt State University
(1978).

Teachers: Owen Fleming, Val Phillips, Floyd
    Cooley, Tony Clements.
Tene, Michael
    Born: 08/19/41
    Current Positions: Teacher, Jerusalem Munici-
        pal Band 1986–; Israeli Police Band 1980–;
        Jerusalem Tuba/Euphonium Quartet 1991–.
    Past Positions: Jerusalem Symphony Orchestra
        (1961–69); extra, Haifa Symphony Orchestra
        (1982–90); Jerusalem Brass Quartet (1979–
        86).
    Contributions: Israeli premiere of *Tubby the
        Tuba* with the JSO in 1961.
    Education: Dunia Weitzman Conservatory,
        Haifa (1959)
    Teachers: Wolfgang Levy, Arthur Hicks.
Theinert, Markus
    Born: 07/20/64
    Current Positions: Brandenburg Quintett
        Berlin, free-lance tuba player.
    Past Positions: Instructor of brass ensembles at
        College of Music, Berlin.
    Education: Royal College of Music, London
        (1986), Hochschule der Kunste, Berlin
        (1990), Johann-Gutenberg-Universität,
        Mainz (1991), Herbert von Karajan-Stiftung,
        Berlin (1992).
    Teachers: John Fletcher, Ulrich Wittke, Paul
        Hümpel.
Thibault, Thierry
    Current Positions: Epsilon Brass Quintet;
        Teacher, LeRaimey National Conservatory of
        Music, France.
    Contributions: composer and arranger of tuba
        pieces.
    Education: Paris Conservatory.
    Teachers: F. Lelong, Chester Schmitz, Sam
        Pilafian.
Thiessen, William Ernest
    Born: 09/17/34
    Current Positions: Oak Ridge Wind Ensemble
        1979–, Lower New York Avenue Har-
        monium (brass quintet) 1977–.
    Past Positions: Oak Ridge Symphony Orchestra
        (1978–90).
    Education: BS, PhD University of California at
        Berkeley.
    Teachers: R. Winston Morris, Sam Pilafian, W.
        Sande MacMorran.
Thomason, John C.
    Born: 11/21/58
    Current Positions: Nebraska Brass Quintet
        1988–, free-lance: Lincoln Symphony,
        Omaha Symphony, Nebraska Chamber
        Orchestra 1989–, Free-lance, Omaha 1992–.
    Past Positions: USAF Strategic Air Command
        Band/Brass Quintet (1980–92), Lincoln
        Symphony (1988–89), Nebraska Chamber
        Orchestra (1988–89), Nebraska Neoclassic

Jazz Orchestra (1976–77).
    Education: University of Nebraska (1976–
        80).
    Teachers: Gene Pokorny, Craig Fuller, Vernon
        Forbes.
Thornton, Michael D.
    Born: 01/10/52
    Current Positions: Lecturer in Tuba, Miami
        University 1987–, Instructor, Xavier
        University 1983–, Cincinnati Symphony
        Orchestra 1975–, Queen City Brass 1981–.
    Contributions: published arranger of tuba-
        euphonium ensembles, premiered two
        concertos.
    Education: BM University of Cincinnati
        Conservatory of Music (1974), MM Yale
        University (1976).
    Teachers: David Bragunier, Sam Green, Toby
        Hanks, Arnold Jacobs.
Tiede, Russell
    Born: 01/27/29
    Past Positions: Associate Professor, Millikin
        University (1968–93), Millikin Brass Quintet
        (1980–93), Millikin-Decatur Symphony
        (1968–1993).
    Contributions: Editor, *South Dakota Music
        Educator*, articles on tuba playing and
        teaching
    Education: BS South Dakota State University
        (1950), MS, EdD University of Illinois
        (1956, 1971).
    Teachers: Robert Gray, Fritz Kaenzig.
Tietz, Henrik
    Current Positions: Melton Tuba Quartet, State
        Opera Orchestra of Hamburg, Symphonic
        Brass Bayreuth, Beyreuth Festival Orchestra
        1991–.
    Past Positions: State Opera in Saarbrücken
        1989–92.
    Education: Cologne College of Music 1981–
        88.
    Teachers: Hans Gelhar, Robert Tucci.
Tirey, Gary R.
    Born: 12/20/40
    Current Positions: Associate Professor,
        Otterbein College 1968–.
    Past Positions: Columbus Symphony Orchestra,
        CSO Brass Quintet.
    Contributions: T.U.B.A. membership chair
        (1980s).
    Education: BME Capital University, MME
        Vandercook College of Music.
    Teachers: Harvey Phillips, Glenn Harriman.
Tolbert, Ross M.
    Born: 07/14/38
    Current Positions: Minnesota Orchestra 1967–,
        Faculty, University of Minnesota 1970–.
    Past Positions: North Carolina Symphony
        (1961), New Orleans Symphony (1959–67).

Education: Attended Manhattan School of
Music, Tulane University.
Teachers: William Bell, Arnold Jacobs.

Torchinsky, Abe
Born: 03/30/20
Past Positions: National Symphony (1942–43),
NBC Symphony (1946–49), Philadelphia
Orchestra (1949–72), Philadelphia Brass
Ensemble, Professor, University of Michigan
(1972–89).
Contributions: compiler and annotator of
thirteen published volumes of orchestral
excerpts for tuba, *20th Century Works for
Tuba*, published duets and arrangements,
featured on a solo recording, Philadelphia
Brass recordings, numerous recordings with
Philadelphia Orchestra.
Education: Curtis Institute (1940–42).
Teachers: Philip Donatelli, Arnold Jacobs, Fred
Geib, William Bell.

Torres, David J.
Born: 08/15/64
Current Positions: Orquesta Sinfonica de
Monterrey, Monterrey Brass Quintet.
Past Positions: Instructor, Banda Municipal,
Monterrey.
Education: Conservatory of Music "Vida y
Movimiento" Mexico City.
Teachers: Dwight Sullinger.

Torres Pantaleon, Jose
Born: 08/01/42
Current Positions: Orquesta Filamonica,
Universidad Nacional Autonama de Mexico
1974–.
Past Positions: Orquesta de la Universidad de
Morelia, Micheacan.
Education: Escuela Superior de Musica
Instituto Nacional de Bellas Artes.
Teachers: Rosendo Aguirre, Fernando Rivas,
William Keck.

Tosaka, Yasuki
Born: 04/07/43
Current Positions: Tokyo Philharmonic
Orchestra 1967–, Tokyo Bari-Tuba En-
semble.
Contributions: Executive Committee member,
President: JETA.
Education: BA Kunitachi Music College
(1967).
Teachers: Kikuo Sato, Kiyoshi Ohishi.

Traphagan, Willis
Born: 04/05/35
Current Positions: Professor, University of
Massachusetts, Lowell 1963–.
Past Positions: Free-lance, Boston (1960–80).
Contributions: Arranger of numerous works for
wind octet and various brass ensembles.
Education: BMus Ithaca College (1956), MM
Boston University (1965).

Teachers: Walter Beeler, William Whybrew.

Trievener, Heiko J. G.
Born: 11/24/64
Current Positions: Orchestra der Beethovenh-
alle, Bonn, Philharmonic Brass Ensemble,
Melton Tuba Quartet.
Past Positions: Radio Symphony Orchestra
Saarbrücken.
Contributions: Reviews and translations for
T.U.B.A. Journal, instrument developer.
Education: Music Science University of
Tübingen (1983–84).
Teachers: Hans Gruber, Rex Conner, Jerry
Young, Bob Tucci, Arnold Jacobs, Warren
Deck, Michael Lind, Roger Bobo.

Triscari, Carmelo
Born: 04/18/63
Current Positions: Banda Nazionale Dell'
Esercito.
Education: Diploma Conservatorio Di Salerno.
Teachers: Gregorio Mazzarese.

Troia, Adriano
Born: 05/16/67
Current Positions: Banda Nazionale Dell'
Aeronautica.
Education: Diploma Di Trombone.
Teachers: Edmondo Rossi.

Troiano, William
Born: 11/23/67
Current Positions: Nassau Symphony Orchestra
1980–, free-lance, New York 1980–.
Past Positions: Guy Lombardo Orchestra
(1976–78).
Contributions: Chairman, NYSSMA Manual
Tuba Section (1985–91), Suffolk County
Music Educator's Association Octubafest
1980–, Area Coordinator, Tuba Christmas,
Rockefeller Center, New York 1980–.
Education: BM State University College,
Fredonia, NY (1973), MM Eastman School
of Music, Rochester, NY (1974).
Teachers: C. Rudolph Emilson, Joe Novotny,
Cherry Beauregard, Harvey Phillips.

Tsukada, Akihiko
Born: 02/20/56
Current Positions: Ground Self Defence Force
Band, Itami 1978–.
Education: BA Sakuyo University of Music
(1978).
Teachers: Yo Kita.

Tucci, Robert
Born: 11/22/40
Current Positions: Bavarian State Opera 1972–.
Past Positions: Louisville Orchestra (1960–62),
Vienna State Opera (1964–65), U.S. Army
Field Band (1966–69), Buffalo Philharmonic
Orchestra (1969–70), State Theater, Kassel
(1970–71).

Contributions: Cooperation with manufacturers, development of instruments and accessories.

Education: Attended De Paul University (1958–60), BME University of Louisville (1960–62), Diploma State Academy of Music Vienna (1964).

Teachers: Harold McDonald, Arnold Jacobs.

Turk, John R.

Born: 11/04/45

Current Positions: Professor, Youngstown State University 1972–, Youngstown Symphony Orchestra 1972–, Dana Brass Quintet 1972– Director, Dana Recording Project 1989–.

Past Positions: United States Army Band (1967–70), Berkshire Music Festival Orchestra (1966–67), Blossom Music Festival Concert Band (1978–87).

Contributions: Premiered over 40 works for tuba, organizer of world's largest all-tuba marching band (Pro Football Hall of Fame Day Parade) (1977–78), solo recording

Education: BME Baldwin-Wallace College (1967), Performer's Certificate, MM Indiana University (1971 1972).

Teachers: William Bell, Harvey Phillips, Keith Brown, Ronald Bishop.

Turner, Daniel L.

Born: 04/26/50

Current Positions: Professor, Bob Jones University 1985–, Foundation Brass Quintet 1985–, Anderson (SC) Chamber Orchestra 1990–.

Contributions: Arranger of brass quintets and tuba-euphonium ensembles.

Education: BS Bob Jones University (1972), MM, EdD University of Illinois (1979 1988).

Teachers: Daniel Perantoni, Robert Gray, Fritz Kaenzig.

Turner, Kyle D.

Born: 04/21/62

Current Positions: Saturday Brass Quintet, Solid Brass, Concordia Chamber Symphony, free-lance, New York City area, New York City Ballet substitute, recording arrangements.

Past Positions: twelve years free-lance.

Education: Manhattan School of Music.

Teachers: Toby Hanks, Mike Sanders.

Uetz, Bruno

Born: 11/03/59

Current Positions: Nordharzer Städtebundtheater, Sachsen-Anhalt-Brass-Ensemble 1991–.

Past Positions: Würzburg Brass Quintett (1982–90).

Contributions: Free-lance musician with Ensemble Modern Frankfurt and many opera

and symphony orchestras in Germany, editor and author of music for tuba.

Education: Diplommusiker Musikhochschule Würzburg (1986), Musikhochschule Stuttgart (1990), PGRNCM Royal Northern College of Music Manchester (1987).

Teachers: Martin Goess, Berton Nordblom, Stuart Roebuck, John Fletcher, Thomas Walsh.

Ujfalusi, László

Born: 01/05/14

Past Positions: Hungarian Royal Opera House (1934–45), Hungarian State Opera (1945–72), Tuba Professor, Liszt Academy of Music in Budapest (1945–91).

Education: Hochschule für Musik, Vienna (1934).

Teachers: Professor Knapke.

Ulevičius, Leonardas Benediktas

Born: 03/21/43

Current Positions: Professor, Music Academy of Lithuania 1969–, National Symphony Orchestra of Lithuania 1967–, The Head, "Brass Quintet" 1977–.

Education: National Music Conservatory (1969), Conservatory Saint-Petersburg (1977), Music College, Berlin (1982).

Teachers: D. Svirskis, V. Bujanovsky, D. Unkrodt.

Unkrodt, Dietrich

Born: 08/25/34

Current Positions: Kammervirtuose, Orchester der Komischen Oper Berlin 1960–, Dozent, Hochschule für Musik "Hanns Eisler" Berlin 1979–, Tubaduo Unkrodt/Zerbe 1980–, Brassquintett Komische Oper Berlin 1991–.

Past Positions: Kammermusiker, Orchester des Meiniger Theaters (1955–60), "Dixieland Allstars Berlin" (1960–80), "Berlin Brassquintett" (1980–91).

Contributions: Founder, International Tuba Competition Markneukirchen 1980–, Founder, Suhler Blechbläserseminar 1986–, T.U.B.A. Vice President for International Relations 1991–.

Education: Hochschule für musik "Hanns Eisler" Berlin (1952–56).

Teachers: Richard Iser.

Ura, Hiroyuki

Born: 03/15/69

Current Positions: Osaka Police Bands 1989–.

Teachers: Shuzo Karakawa.

Uth, Lothar

Born: 04/29/53

Current Positions: Philharmonic Orchestra of Augsburg; Teacher, Leopold Mozart Conservatory, Augsburg.

Contributions: students have won competitions, premiered tuba composition.

Education: State Conservatory of Music, Saarbrücken.
Teachers: Joachim Lorek, Josef Heinrichs.

Vallee, Raymond J.
Born: 01/05/36
Current Positions: West Bay Brass Works, Slaughterhouse Six Dixieland Band, Showcase Concert and Parade Band, private instructor.
Education: BEd MEd Rhode Island College (1957, 1964).
Teachers: Abraham Schwadron.

Varpula, Ari
Born: 10/04/68
Current Positions: Joensu City Orchestra 1990–, Harald Brass Quintet 1987–.
Education: Military School of Music (1983–86), Sibelius Academy 1986–.
Teachers: Raimo Pesonen.

Vasquez Cruz, Erasto
Born: 07/25/53
Current Positions: Orquesta del Teatro de Bellas Artes.
Education: Escuela de Perfeccionamiento "Vida y Movimiento."
Teachers: William T. Keck, Morris Kainuma, Dwight Sullinger.

Veikkanen, Ari
Born: 09/17/62
Current Positions: Military Band Mikkeli 1983–.
Past Positions: Orchestra Mikkeli free-lance (1983–90).
Education: Military School of Music (1983).
Teachers: Rauno, Onni Virolainen, Risto Back.

Verway, Hugo
Born: 02/05/63
Current Positions: Amsterdam Wind Quartet 1988–, Dutch Tuba Quartet 1991–.
Education: DM Tuba, UM Tuba Brabants Conservatorium (1990, 1992).
Teachers: Piet Joris.

Vicente, Alexandre Cabral
Born: 12/30/69
Current Positions: Band Marcial, Big Band, Banda Sinf., private school of music.
Education: Universidade Livre de Musica.
Teachers: Donald Smith.

Vieira da Silva, Eduardo
Born: 08/22/61
Current Positions: Banda Sinfonica de São Bernardo 1978–.
Past Positions: Orquestra Sinfonica da Bahia (1980–84).
Education: Escola de Musica de São Paulo.
Teachers: Gasparo Pagliuso.

Vieira da Silva, Valmir
Born: 11/23/56
Current Positions: Professor, Universidade Federale da Paraiba; Orquestra Sinfònica da

Paraiba 1980–; Paraiba University Brass Quintet 1980–.
Past Positions: Banda Sinfonica de São Paulo (1974–80).
Teachers: Gasparo Pagliuso.

Vieira de Santana, Estevan Jr.
Born: 12/14/61
Current Positions: Orquestra Sinfonica do Recife, Quinteto de Metals de Recife, Professor da Escola de Musica da Cidude do Recife.
Past Positions: Orquestra Sinfonica Joven de Santos, Banda Musical de Cubatao
Education: Music School of Cubatão, São Paulo
Teachers: Donald Smith, Roberto Farias, Dimas Sedicias.

Volkman, Rudy
Born: 10/30/42
Current Positions: Chair, Paine College, Augusta, GA; founder, Savannah River Brass Works quintet.
Past Positions: Augusta Symphony Orchestra.
Contributions: written brass quintet and solo tuba compositions.
Education: attended Olympic Junior College (1959–62), BA Central Washington State College (1964), MM DePauw University (1968), DMA University of South Carolina (1987).
Teachers: Robert Cenocock.

Vuorinen, Jouko
Born: 08/25/42
Current Positions: The Orchestra of Finnish National Opera 1963–.
Past Positions: The Orchestra of Saronlinna Opera Festival (1970–90), The Guardian Military Band (1962–63).
Education: The Military School of Music, Helsinki (1957–62), Sibelius-Academy (1957–62).
Teachers: Raimo Pesonen, Oiva Lampinen, Pentti Mäkelä, Michael Lind.

Wagner, Michael D.
Born: 12/09/57
Current Positions: The US Army Band 1980–, The Commonwealth Brass 1981–.
Education: BM Michigan State University (1980), MM Catholic University (1982).
Teachers: Leonard Falcone, Paul Krzywicki.

Waid, Tom B.
Born: 08/26/48
Current Positions: The US Army Band 1980–.
Past Positions: Contemporary Brass Quintet (Philadelphia) (1978–79), Cambridge Brass Quintet (Boston) (1972), Portland Maine Symphony (1972), Florida Gulf Coast Symphony (1969–70).
Education: BA University of South Florida (1970).

Teachers: Don Owen, Don Kneeburg, Constance Weldon.

Wall, Ashley Grainger
    Born: 11/23/45
    Current Positions: Professor, Trinity College of Music, London 1976–, Orchestra of Royal Opera House Covent Garden, London 1974–.
    Past Positions: Tutor, Centre for Young Musicians, London (1973–91), Royal Philharmonic Orchestra (1969–74).
    Education: ARCM Royal College of Music, London.
    Teachers: Charles Luxon.

Walsh, Thomas Joseph
    Born: 11/12/53
    Current Positions: Munich Philharmonic 1979–; Richard Strauss Conservatory 1986–; Music Hochschule Stuttgart 1989–; Munich Gabrieli Ensemble 1980–.
    Past Positions: Opera Darmstadt (1977–79); Vienna Volksoper (1976), free-lance, Munich (1975–76).
    Contributions: premiered many brass quintet and ensemble pieces, first TUBA-CHRISTMAS in Germany (1989).
    Education: Performer's Certificate, BM Indiana University (1974, 1975), Kammermusiker of Munich (1989).
    Teachers: Harvey Phillips, Lewis Van Haney, Robert Tucci, Arthur Blatt, Tim Bryson, James Richter.

Washburne, Joe "Country"
    Past Positions: Spike Jones Orchestra 1942–?

Wassell, Steven John
    Born: 05/04/52
    Current Positions: Head of Brass, Saint Edmund's School, Canterbury, 1989–, Festival Brass Quintet 1988–, Festival Brass Ensemble 1990–.
    Past Positions: Professor, Royal College of Music Junior Dept. (1973–90), Guildhall School of Music (1987–89).
    Contributions: News contributor, BASBWE Journal.
    Education: LTCL Huddersfield School of Music (1969–72), ARCM Royal College of Music (1972–75), Certified Brookland Technical College (1988).
    Teachers: Tom Atkinson, Charles Luxon, John Jenkins, John Fletcher.

Watanabe, Iseo
    Born: 12/26/60
    Current Positions: Tokyo City Philharmonic Orchestra, Tuba Quartet Shishiza.
    Contributions: JETA committee member.
    Education: BA Tokyo University of the Arts (1984).

Teachers: Kiyoshi Ohishi, Ikumitsu Tado, Katsuhiro Nakanowatari.

Watson, Scott
    Born: 01/23/56
    Current Positions: Professor, University of Kansas 1979–, Kansas Brass Quintet 1979–, Lawrence Chamber Players 1986–, New American Tuba Quartet 1989–, Faculty, Midwestern Music Camp 1980–.
    Past Positions: Professor, Baker University (1982–83).
    Contributions: Editor, T.U.B.A. Press (1986–90), Coordinator of Composer Friends (1985–91), Acting Secretary (1988–89), Coordinator (1989–91), Chair, Commissions Committee (1989–91), Secretary 1991–, Etude Competitions, recital tour of Poland 1988, clinics on performance anxiety, instrument clinician.
    Education: BM Cincinnati Conservatory (1979), MM University of Kansas (1981).
    Teachers: Samuel Green, Stephen Anderson, Jamie Hafner.

Wean, Ellis
    Born: 09/30/49
    Current Positions: Vancouver Symphony Orchestra 1989–, CBC (Canadian Broadcasting Corp.), Vancouver Radio Orchestra 1989–, Instructor, University of British Columbia 1989–.
    Past Positions: Buffalo Philharmonic Orchestra (1970–73), Montreal Symphony Orchestra (1973–89), Instructor, McGill University (1973–89), Mount Royal Brass Quintet (1976–82).
    Contributions: Inventor and manufacturer of "Tru–VU Transparent Mouthpieces," Competition Winnner, CBC National Solo Competition for Winds (1979), winner First International Tuba Competition Markneukirchen, Germany (1980).
    Education: Boston University (1967–68), New England Conservatory of Music (1968–70), Berkshire Music Center (Tanglewood) Fellowship (1968–70).
    Teachers: John Coffey, Willis Traphagan, Chester Schmitz, Harvey Phillips.

Wedham, Ernst
    Born: 03/23/41
    Current Positions: Sønderjylland Symphonie 1975–; Instructor, the Guard of Sønderjylande brass band.
    Past Positions: Brass band instructor.
    Teachers: Erik Åkerwald, Jørgen Voigt Arnsted, Michael Lind, John Fletcher, Roger Bobo.

Weike, Paul Eugene Jr.
    Born: 05/27/63
    Current Positions: Instructor, Brevard Commu-

nity College 1992–, Universal Studios Florida Studio Brass 1992–.

Past Positions: Busch Brass at Busch Gardens–Tampa (1988–92), Community Music Division, University of South Florida (1990–91), Associate Instructor, Indiana University, Brass Menagerie Brass Quintet (1988–92).

Education: BA University of Central Florida (1986), MM Indiana University (1988).

Teachers: Harvey Phillips, Edwin Anderson, Roy Pickering, Mario Camamilli, Jamie Haffner.

Weldon, Constance "Connie"

Past Positions: Boston Pops Orchestra (1954–56), North Carolina Symphony, Netherlands Ballet Orkest, Amsterdam Concertgebouw, Kansas City Philharmonic, Miami Dolphins Band, Jackie Gleason Show Band, University of Miami (1960–85), Associate Dean (1985–91).

Contributions: Founder of the University of Miami tuba ensemble (the first college tuba ensemble) (1960), teacher of generations of now-professional tubists.

Education: BM, MEd University of Miami (1952, 1953).

Teachers: Bower Murphy, Arnold Jacobs, William Bell.

West, Keith R.

Born: 05/24/65

Current Positions: Lecturer, Sul Ross State University 1990–, free-lance, Texas 1990–.

Past Positions: Stillwater Brass Band (1983–87), Poca City Community Orchestra (1986).

Education: BS, MS Oklahoma State University (1987, 1991).

Teachers: Norlan Bewley.

Whetham, Scott P.

Born: 09/20/56

Current Positions: Edmonton Symphony Orchestra; Lecturer, The University of Alberta.

Education: Eastman School of Music (1977–78).

Which-Wilson, Peter J.

Born: 07/25/58

Current Positions: Adelaide Symphony Orchestra 1978–, Lecturer, Elder Conservatorium, Adelaide University 1979–.

Past Positions: State Orchestra of Victoria (1976–78), Lecturer, SA College of Advanced Education (1978–91), Canberra School of Music (1989–90), Adelaide Brass Quintet (1978–84).

Contributions: Active solo performer.

Teachers: John Woods, Ian King, Roger Bobo, Arnold Jacobs, Michael Lind.

Whitcomb, Larry E.

Born: 12/28/52

Current Positions: The Air Force Band of the Pacific 1989–, Southcentral Brass Quintet 1989–.

Past Positions: US Tactical Air Command Band (1982–89), Alaskan Air Command Band (1980–82), Alaska Brass (1980–82), Anchorage Symphony and Opera (1980–82), Air Force Band of the Gulf Coast (1976–80).

Education: BM Houghton College (1975), MM Ithaca College (1979).

Teachers: Harold McNeil, Ronald Bishop, Scott MacMorran, Mark Moore, James Linn, David Unland.

Wick, Stephen

Born: 12/15/53

Current Positions: Free-lance, London 1973–, London Gabrieli Brass Ensemble 1977–, London Classical Players 1988–, Professor, London College of Music 1988–.

Past Positions: Oslo Philharmonic Orchestra (1972–73).

Education: BMus (Hons.) University of Surrey (1976).

Teachers: John Fletcher.

Wiech, Axel

Born: 02/04/66

Current Positions: Berne Symphony Orchestra 1989–.

Past Positions: Radio-Symphonie Orchestra Saarbrücken (1988–89).

Contributions: Winner National Competition "Tagend Musiziert," Germany (1985).

Education: Conservatory Lübeck (1987), Conservatory of Music, Hamburg (1988/89).

Teachers: Walter Hilgers.

Wilhelm, Matthias

Born: 01/10/57

Current Positions: Orchestra of the Landestheatre, Detmold 1985–; Returnal Quartet 1990–; Trio in Aspik 1989–; Willi Bodde Big Band 1989–; Blue Moon Quartet 1991–; Blechjazz & Co. 1989–; Georg Rox Quartet 1987–.

Past Positions: Brassquintet Zurich (1980–82); Arta (1979–82); Aargaver Symphonieorchester (1975–82); Symphonisches Orchester, Berlin (1983–85).

Education: Konservatorium und Musikhochschule, Zurich (1976–82), Hochschule der Künste, Berlin (1982–85).

Teachers: Alfred Klaus, Dieter Studer, Franz Eger, Marc Evans, Paul Hümpel, John Tchicai, Ray Anderson.

Willett, James R.

Born: 01/08/63

Current Positions: Instructor, Eastern Kentucky University 1991–, Eastern Kentucky Brass Quintet 1991–.
Past Positions: Instructor, Indiana State University (1989–91).
Education: BM University of Iowa (1985), MM University of Akron (1987).
Teachers: Mark Moore, Fritz Kaenzig, Tucker Jolly, Robert Yeats.
Williams, Jack L.
Born: 02/08/50
Current Positions: Air Force Band of Liberty.
Past Positions: US Air Force Band of New England, Air Force Band of the Golden Gate, Air Force Band of the East.
Education: BM Hartt College.
Teachers: Ronald Apperson, Chester Schmidt.
Wilmoth, Barry D.
Born: 09/15/66
Current Positions: The US Air Force America's Band in Blue.
Education: BSMEd Tennessee Technological University.
Teachers: R. Winston Morris, Floyd Cooley.
Windfeld, Axel
Born: 04/09/39
Current Positions: Danish Radio Big Band 1969–; Concert band and Stage band, Tivoli Gardens, Copenhagen 1972–; free-lance 1963–.
Past Positions: Avangarden Party (1987–92); Erling Kroner Tentet (1975–88); Thad Jones Eclips (1979–81); Bent Ronak Big Band (1963–69).
Contributions: recordings with Danish Radio Big Band.
Education: University of Utah (1959–62), Royal Danish Conservatory of Music (1964–69).
Teacher: Palmer Traulsen.
Winkle, William Allan
Born: 10/01/40
Current Positions: Professor, Chadron State College 1971–, Faculty Brass Trio 1990–, Chadron Arts Trio 1978–, Yamaha Artist/Clinician 1977–, Tuba Instructor, Board of Directors, International Music Camp 1977–.
Past Positions: Extra, Omaha Symphony (1991), Casper Symphony (1990), Nebraska Panhandle Symphony and Symphonia (1971–89), Rapid City Symphony (1985).
Contributions: TUBA Regional ReCurrentative (1971–90), active forming massed tuba/euphonium ensembles, sponsored a regional tuba/euphonium symposium in upper Midwest United States.
Education: BM Huron College (1962), MA University of Vermont (1972), DA University of Northern Colorado (1976).

Teachers: Arnold Jacobs, Jack Robinson, Walt Seschin.
Winteregg, Steven L.
Born: 07/13/52
Current Positions: Assistant Professor, Wittenburg University 1979–, Dayton Philharmonic Orchestra 1987–, Carillon Brass Quintet 1979–, Dayton Opera Orchestra 1988–.
Past Positions: Adjunct Instructor, Cedarville College (1979–89), University of Dayton (1982–88), Central State University (1982–83).
Contributions: Composer of solo tuba and multiple tuba compositions.
Education: BME University of Cincinnati (1974), MM Wright State University (1979), DMA Ohio State University (1987).
Teachers: Robert LeBlanc, Samuel Green, Samuel Gnagy.
Wittke-Hussman, Ulrich
Born: 03/08/57
Current Positions: Berlin Brass 1983–, Teacher, Hochschule der Kunste (Hak) Berlin, Orchester der Deutschen Oper Berlin 1982–.
Past Positions: Staatstheater Kassel (1978), Mitglied des Orchesters der Deutschen Oper Berlin (1982), Lehrbeaufträger für Tuba an der Hochschule der Kunste in Berlin (1985).
Education: Stadtischen Konservatorium Osnabruck, Hochschule für Musik und Theater Hannover.
Teachers: Klemens Pröpper.
Woo, Hong Jae
Born: 10/25/65
Current Positions: Tae Ku Philharmonic Orchestra 1991–, Tae Ku Philharmonic Brass Quintet 1991–.
Education: BA Young Nam University of Music (1991).
Teachers: Sang Gon Park, Sung Huen Kim.
Woodruff, Frank N. (Bud)
Born: 01/07/35
Current Positions: Adjunct Professor, University of Southern California 1972–, Lecturer, U.C.L.A. 1972–, Glendale Symphony Orchestra 1985–, Hollywood Recording Studios.
Past Positions: Instructor, Sam Houston State University (1978–83), Houston Ballet Orchestra (1975–84), Houston Pops Orchestra (1981–90).
Contributions: Arranger of tuba studies.
Education: BM, MM Teacher's Certification University of Houston (1972, 1975).
Teachers: William H. Rose, Albert C. Buswell, Dennis Miller.
Woods, Ilsa V.
Born: 09/10/69

Current Positions: Australian Royal Army Air Force Band 1992–.

Education: Diploma of Arts in Music, Victoria College of the Arts (1990).

Teachers: John Woods, Frank Barzyk, Peter Sykes, Paul Gunning.

Woods, John C.

Born: 04/15/44

Current Positions: Director, St. Leo's College, Melbourne.

Past Positions: Queensland Symphony Orchestra, Melbourne Symphony Orchestra.

Contributions: premiere of tuba concerto.

Teachers: Arnold Jacobs.

Wright, Dave

Born: 08/14/48

Current Positions: Hot Frogs Jumping Jazz Band 1989–, free-lance, Los Angeles, San Bernardino, Riverside areas.

Past Positions: Fullertown Strutters (1983–85).

Contributions: Numerous festival appearances and recordings with the Hot Frogs Jumping Jazz Band.

Education: Mostly self-taught (had one lesson with Jim Self!).

Yahata, Kunikiko

Born: 03/19/57

Current Positions: Ground Self Defence Force, 3rd Division Band, Japan.

Yeats, Robert E.

Born: 03/28/44

Current Positions: Associate Professor, University of Iowa 1970–; Iowa Brass Quintet; Cedar Rapids Chamber Brass; Iowa Chamber Players.

Past Positions: Instructor, University of Northern Iowa (1971–72); Cedar Rapids Symphony (1970–89).

Contributions: editor, *University of Iowa Guide to Selected Wind and Percussion Materials.*

Education: BS Ithaca College (1966), MA, MSA University of Iowa (1972, 1978).

Teachers: Willis Traphagen, Walter Becher, Marvin Howe, James Linn, John Hill.

Yi, Chong Il

Born: 02/20/44

Current Positions: Inspector General and Tuba, Korea Broadcast Orchestra.

Contributions: past-president of Korea Tuba Association.

Education: BA College of Music, Seoul National University (1965).

Teachers: Jae Ok Lee, Harvey Phillips.

Yoo, Kyoung Ae

Born: 04/07/60

Current Positions: Chon City Orchestra 1983–.

Education: BA Seoul National University (1982).

Teachers: Lee Jae Ok, Lee Jong Il.

Yoo, Sung Joo

Born: 04/26/57

Current Positions: Chung Nam Symphony Orchestra 1991–, Instructor, Dan Kook University 1991–, Vice President, Korea Tuba Ensemble 1992–, Seoul Brass Quintet 1990–, Chung Nam Symphony Brass Quintet 1991–.

Past Positions: Instructor, Han Yang University (1991–1992), Extra, Waterloo Symphony Orchestra (1988–90), Extra, Cedar Rapids Symphony Orchestra (1989–90), Danville Symphony Orchestra (1986–87), Palm Springs Community Orchestra (1983–88), Spokane River Front Park Band (1981–82), Seoul Philharmonic Orchestra (1979–80), Korea Brass Quintet (1979–80), Seoul Wind Symphony (1975–80, 1990–).

Education: BA Dan Kook University (1979), MM University of Nothern Iowa (1990).

Teachers: Arnold Jacobs, Fritz Kaenzig, Jeffrey Funderburk, Jon Bak Kim, Chong Chul, Ok Yun Hung.

Yoshida, Shinji

Born: 02/05/59

Current Positions: Osaka Police Bands 1985–, Breeze Brass Band.

Education: BA Osaka University of Arts (1981).

Teachers: Yo Kita, Shuzo Karakawa.

Yoshilda, Koichi

Born: 01/23/48

Current Positions: Ground Self Defence Force, 3rd Division Band.

Yoshimura, Jinske

Born: 05/22/43

Current Positions: Ground Self Defence Force, 3rd Division Band.

Young, Jerry A.

Born: 08/25/52

Current Positions: Professor, University of Wisconsin-Eau Claire 1983–, Instructor, Interlochen Arts Camp 1983–.

Past Positions: Assistant Professor, Central Missouri State University (1980–83).

Contributions: Publications Coordinator (1985–91), Journal Editor (1985–90) *TUBA Journal*, Coordinator of Composer Friends (1981–85), T.U.B.A., premiered six new works (1983–92).

Education: BSE University of Arkansas–Fayetteville (1974), MS, EdD University of Illinois (1978, 1980).

Teachers: Gerald Sloan, Daniel Perantoni.

Zeilinger, Daniel Eugene

Born: 02/14/54

Current Positions: Free-lance, Southern California 1974–, The Misbehavin' Jazz Band 1985–, Knotts Berry Farm 1988–.

Past Positions: National Association of Jazz
Educators National Collegiate Dixieland
Band Champions 1981, Head Brass Instruc-
tor, Velvet Knights Drum and Bugle Corps
(1981–83).
Education: Orange Coast College (1975),
Golden West College (1981).

Zelinka, Douglas A.
Born: 04/07/65
Current Positions: New Philharmonic Orchestra
1990–; Prism Music Festival Orchestra
1989–; Chamber Brass Players 1990–;
Bensenville Symphonic Wind Ensemble
1988–; Wheaton Symphony Orchestra
1989–.
Past Positions: Cornerstone Choral & Brass
(1988–89); Cathedral Brass (1988–90); Civic
Orchestra of Chicago (1989–90); Instructor,
Trinity College (1988–90).
Education: BA Taylor University (1987),
MMus Northwestern University (1988).
Teachers: Arnold Jacobs, Rex Martin, Gary
Ofenloch, Gene Pokorny, Albert Harrison.

Zerkel, David H.
Born: 09/21/63
Current Positions: The US Army Band 1989–,
Adjunct Professor of Music, Virginia
Commonwealth University 1990–.
Past Positions: Richmond Symphony (1991–
92), The US Army Field Band (1986–1989).
Contributions: First brass performer to win first
prize in the Peabody Conservatory Concours.

Education: BM Peabody Institute, MM
University of Maryland.
Teachers: David Fedderly, David Bragunier, Ed
Livingston, Michael Bunn.

Zervopoulos, Nicholas
Born: 12/21/57
Current Positions: Teacher of the P. Nacas
Conservatory 1989–, Athens State Symphony
Orchestra 1992–, Melos Brass Quintet
1990–, Greek Contemporary Ensemble
1992–.
Past Positions: Athens Municipal Brass Band
(1989), Colour's Symphony Orchestra
(1989).
Education: Pindarion Conservatory (1989).
Teachers: I. Wauner, D. Nick, F. Orval, Stefos
Panagiotis.

Zngrati, Carlo
Born: 01/25/47
Current Positions: RAI Symphony Orchestra,
Rome.
Past Positions: Bande Esercito.
Education: Diploma Trombone.
Teachers: Romeo Citro.

Zook, Alan
Born: 04/25/58
Current Positions: North Iowa Concert band.
Education: BA Buena Vista College, AA North
Iowa Area Community College, attended
University of Northern Iowa and Cal Poly
University.
Teachers: Fritz Kaenzig.

15. Doubling for Tubists

James Self

Doubling is a timely topic. At some time in their performing life, nearly all tubists will deal with changing instruments. For some, the switch will be as minor as playing an instrument with a different bore. For others, the change will be from CC to F tuba, or necessity might require a change to an unrelated instrument such as the electric bass or the bass trombone. The school music director, who must create a meaningful musical program and present concerts and shows with limited personnel and restricted budgets, has to find ways to make the program more viable. Teaching doubles is one solution. Students who aspire to become professional performers and teachers should learn as many skills as possible in order to prosper in a very competitive marketplace. College instructors, besides needing advanced degrees, must now demonstrate broad knowledge of several disciplines, including the performing and teaching of secondary instruments. All these situations can be improved by doubling. The purpose of doubling is not just to play two or more instruments in the same ensemble but to make the player more versatile, so that he or she can play a variety of instruments in different ensembles: tuba in the band, bass trombone in the big band, string bass in the orchestra, or electric bass in the rock band. It makes sense that the vast majority prepare themselves for a career that requires diversity in playing and teaching. Doubling is presented here in its broadest sense.

The economic benefits of doubling are very important. It allows an employer to get two or more instruments for less than the cost of two or more musicians, and the doubler receives a certain percentage increase for his or her versatility. For engagements covered under the American Federation of Musicians, doubles pay significant premiums. In film recording the rate is 50 percent for the first double, 25 percent for the second, and 10 percent for subsequent doubles. Records pay 25 percent for the first double. Percussionists, woodwind players, and synthesists often have three to five doubles and earn double scale or more. For tubists it is often one and sometimes two doubles. But even 50 percent is a strong incentive for being prepared on a second instrument. Doubles in casual and orchestral work vary from (union) local to local and contract to contract. In the United States 25 percent is the most common rate for the first double. Outside the United States, doubling rates vary from a rare 50 percent to zero.

The cost of owning and maintaining additional instruments (especially tubas and other large instruments) can be a strong deterrent. The musician should keep in mind that brass instruments (particularly tubas), if properly cared for, are good investments. In periods of low interest, putting money in instruments may be a better investment than putting it in a bank. Justifying the cost of a second tuba may be difficult, but an electric bass or bass trombone will pay for itself many times over. Compare the cost of a violin or a cello—those instruments often cost more than ten tubas.

Even tubists who focus entirely on preparing themselves for that rare symphony job (that pays a professional wage) need to play doubles. The days when a symphony tubist could play an entire career on one BB♭ or CC tuba are over. The young tubist must have the right equipment when auditioning for a professional symphony position: a CC tuba, an F tuba, and possibly a tenor tuba and a cimbasso to play the excerpts accurately. Often hundreds of qualified tubists apply for these coveted positions. Each player is looking for an edge in order to be a little more attractive to the audition committee; versatility may provide that edge. Once the job has been won, the need for doubling is often by choice of the player or conductor.

The symphony tubist should master the instruments called for in the literature. Most tuba parts do not specify which instrument to play. The range demands are quite daunting, and a professional tubist must have a range of more than four octaves. The majority of orchestral work can be played on the contrabass tuba, but often range, timbre, acoustics of the hall, and knowledge of the composer's intentions will lead the tubist to choose another instrument to suit these conditions. The conductor and other brass colleagues may also make suggestions. (The tubist should be careful when submitting to the wishes of the bass trombonist when choosing an instrument. While his opinion is usually well intended, it is prejudiced by his position on stage, and he cannot hear from the tubist's, conductor's or audience's perspectives.)

Orchestral tubists are expected to play all the bass brass parts in the repertoire, and they often choose the higher bass and tenor instruments to achieve accuracy. The earliest pre-tubas were serpents. This S-shaped wooden instrument had open hole fingerings and was played with a cup-shaped mouthpiece. In the orchestra these very ancient instruments are seen in the operas and oratorios of Handel through some of the works of early nineteenth-century composers, Mendelssohn, among others. Essentially they were baritone in range and mouthpiece size. While a few tubists may double on serpent (usually in period ensembles), most use an F bass tuba or tenor tuba for those parts. Much more common is the ophicleide. This bass member of the key-bugle family was the standard bass brass instrument in orchestras of the late eighteenth and early nineteenth centuries. The works of Berlioz and his (particularly French) contemporaries specified ophicleide. This too is really a baritone instrument in tessitura with a small mouthpiece. Contemporary tubists usually choose an F tuba to play ophicleide parts. *Symphonie Fantastique* calls for two ophicleides (tubas) and is a standard audition piece. When valves were invented (circa 1835 in Germany), a true bass tuba followed. The early works of Wagner were among the first to specify tuba. F bass tubas were probably the first true tubas, and the deeper contrabass instruments in BB♭ and CC quickly followed.

For many years terminology was as varied as national boundaries. France, Italy, and Germany each developed families of brass instruments, and their respective composers specified them. Tubists will see parts for bombardon, cimbasso, saxhorn, tenor tuba, flicorno, ophicleide, serpent, and many others. The word *tuba* in itself does not necessarily mean a certain instrument. Only recently have there been attempts to use standard nomenclature. Twentieth-century music is much more international, and tubists can usually use the terms *contra-bass*, *bass*, and *tenor* for classification. To cope with a range of more than four octaves, players often choose to switch tubas within a piece—to double. In some works, like Stravinsky's *Rite of Spring* or *Petrushka*, the tubist will generally choose the F tuba. In others, Schoenberg's *Gurrelieder* and Strauss's *Salome*,

for example, the part will specify contra-bass tuba switching to bass tuba.

Occasionally the tubist will be asked to play tenor tuba or euphonium, but these parts, like those in the works of Strauss and Holst, are usually played by trombonists or euphonium specialists. When playing tenor tuba or euphonium, tubists will often use a special mouthpiece with a small cup and a large rim. Some of these mouthpieces are available commercially, but most tubists will prefer to have them built to their specifications. One of the most difficult excerpts for the orchestral tubist is the "Bydlo" solo from Mussorgsky's *Pictures at an Exhibition*. Most tubists will switch instruments when playing this solo, which was written for the French tuba in C—using a contrabass for the other movements and an F tuba, tenor tuba, or euphonium for "Bydlo." Even the greatest tubists miss notes in this solo. It is so difficult that many orchestras have a trombonist play it on euphonium. There are still some misguided tuba players who insist on playing it even if they "miss more than they play." Other orchestra members and listeners do not tolerate wrong notes, and tubists suffer a lot of criticism for that.

A very common instrument name that the orchestral tubist will encounter is the *cimbasso*. It was the standard bass brass instrument in the Italian orchestras of the nineteenth and early twentieth centuries. It is an extension to the valve trombones in the section and is really a valve contra-bass trombone in F or BB♭. The works of Verdi and Puccini, which are standard literature for both symphony and opera orchestras, call for cimbasso. Depending on the edition, one may see bass trombone, cimbasso, bombardon, or tuba; but the correct instrument is the cimbasso. Tuba players usually use a small tuba for these parts, but for some of the more aggressive Verdi operas, such as *Don Carlo* and *Aida*, a true cimbasso would be the ideal. Since the part may be called "bass trombone," tubists should be careful that trombonists do not "get the job."

One other double often played by the orchestral tubist is the contrabass trombone. Standard contrabass trombones are pitched in F, E♭, or BB♭. This instrument is trombone-like in technique but tuba-like in range, mouthpiece, and wind production. It is amusing to watch bass trombonists try to fill up a large BB♭ contrabass trombone. The contrabass trombone is called for in Wagner's *Ring* and in Schoenberg's *Gurrelieder*; however, if a tubist plays the part, another will be required for the real tuba part. Some contemporary works by Varese and others call for the contrabass trombone with no tuba. The tubist learning this instrument will do well to follow the suggestions presented later for learning bass trombone. It is obvious that the orchestral tubist must be an accomplished doubler.

With the exception of those few who get the major orchestra jobs, most tubists will have careers that are a mosaic of jobs. Most will combine part-time symphony/opera/ballet work with a combination of studio work, Dixieland gigs, brass quintets, dance bands, concert/marching bands, and road shows; and many will devote much of their time to teaching. They may also play in drum and bugle corps, brass bands, tuba ensembles, period instrument ensembles, polka bands, rock and roll bands, new music ensembles, and every other conceivable group. Some may also have solo careers or be composers, conductors, arrangers, librarians, copyists, music editors, sound engineers, contractors, orchestra managers, or union officials. Others may work in instrument repair, retail sales, record production, promotion, or other related fields. Finally, many tubists are accomplished amateurs who satisfy their need to perform in any number of ways. The possibilities for doubling are endless.

The history of doubling for tubists is interesting. In the early days of recording, microphones were so poor that louder instruments, such as the recording tuba and sousaphone, played an important role. The tuba was the predominant bass voice in all the early motion pictures and records, and the first recordings of Mozart, Haydn, and Beethoven symphonies were made with a sousaphone doubling the string basses. Bands like those of John Phillip Sousa were the popular music of their era, and tubas were the solid bass instrument of those ensembles. They were also important instruments in the bands of the Dixieland era, and hundreds of tuba players worked in dance halls and on radio broadcasts. Popular culture, as always, was reflected in the Hollywood studios. Styles changed in the 1930s and 1940s. Common time replaced two-beat. The string bass, which could "walk" more easily, took over the primary bass role, and tuba players became bass doublers. With few exceptions they were better bass players than tuba players. Shows of that era, like *South Pacific* and *Hello Dolly*, require a string bass double. From the beginnings of sound motion pictures until the late 1950s, the major film studios had free-lance and contract orchestras that gave employment to many tuba/bass players. When television came of age (circa 1960), the studios disbanded their orchestras, and all film work went on a free-lance basis with generally smaller orchestras and a net loss of work for tubists. About this time the nature of the music changed drastically. Rock and roll was in, and the electric bass became the primary bass voice. In recording, the tuba became more of a specialized instrument. It was used for dramatic effect, comedy, and for source music (Dixieland, band music, etc.). The role of the tuba further changed in the early sixties, when Tommy Johnson "broke into the business." He was the first "modern" tubist to play in the studios. He played CC tuba and was a virtuoso soloist. The composers wrote for his talents, firmly establishing the tuba as an important solo instrument. Johnson set the standard for technical ability and solo playing. Don Waldrop, Johnson, and others also established the bass trombone as the standard double for tuba players. Today it would be very difficult for a tuba player to make a good living in the studios without that double. Contemporary rhythm sections rarely call for a tuba double, but writers frequently ask for a bass trombone/tuba double in the low brass section, and this combination is quite common in Broadway shows, big bands, and accompaniments for commercial singers.

The free-lance scene, particularly recording, offers the most possibilities for doubling for tuba players. Only a few large cities offer the economic base for free-lancing. In the United States, New York and Los Angeles are the only ones where a large amount of recording is done. All kinds of recording sessions are done in both places, but Los Angeles is the center for motion pictures and television, and New York is the center for "jingles" (ads for radio and television) and jazz and classical records. Pop records are produced in both cities. Nashville, Chicago, Dallas, and Toronto also have some recording work but very little for tubists. The major cities in Europe and Japan have recording industries, and radio orchestras in London, Paris, Berlin, Tokyo, and many other cities do a significant amount of recording. These are usually contract jobs.

Much has been said about the electronic revolution and its effect on work for acoustic instruments. The horror stories are true, and they are especially true in the studios where synthesizers have replaced standard orchestral instruments. Producers and audiences are always looking for the latest sounds, regardless of quality, to the point where some estimates say that 75 percent of all film and television and almost all rock recordings are done with computers and synthesizers. This, of course, means less work for tubists. A generation of people have the notion that our instruments, and indeed all strings, woodwinds, and brass, are old-fashioned. That is the down side but there is some hope for a better future. Recently there seems to be a small backlash to the electronic bombardment and with it a desire on the part of composers to use larger orchestras and to use synthesizers and acoustic instruments in creative combinations. The same quest for new sounds allows room for new instruments. In Los Angeles some unusual low brass doubles have been built and used in recording. Contrabass horn, contrabass trumpet, tubone, valve bass trombone, double-bell tuba, cimbasso, super bass trombone, contrabass trombone, bass saxophone, didgeridoo, and bass kazoo are some of the unique doubles played in the studios and other free-lancing. Creative tubists and instrument makers everywhere continue to put together unusual instruments.

Finally, two electronic doubles have found limited use in recent years. Some projects have asked for amplified tuba or an electronically altered tuba. This is commonly a standard tuba with an effective pick-up or direct microphone. Amplifiers, octave dividers, delay lines, and tone processors were common fare in the 1970s and 1980s, but today virtually any electronic or midi source can alter the tuba at the whim of the composer. The other electronic double is the Steiner electronic valve instrument (EVI). This fascinating synthesizer uses wind generation and brasslike technique to create a myriad of sounds in a uniquely expressive manner. The range goes from below to above the human ear. The EVI is played with three valves in the right hand while the left hand operates a fourth valve that splits the octave into fourths and fifths. The left hand also turns a rotor that changes octaves. Tubists and other brass players can find many similarities to their regular instrument, but mastering the EVI is quite difficult. The left hand is awkward for most. Tuba players have experimented with the EVI in recording and jazz, but most of the work is being done by specialists on the EVI and its sister instrument for woodwind players, the electronic woodwind instrument (EWI). Those players have invested thousands of dollars in mixers, samplers, and outboard synthesizers.

There is and always will be some work for tuba players in recording. But it does mean that they and prospective studio tubists must be exceptional and versatile musicians. In Los Angeles, only three or four professional tubists make a living in the studios. All double on bass trombone and other instruments, and all do a variety of other jobs: in symphony, opera, and ballet orchestras; and in jazz and dance bands. Also, there are some teaching positions in area colleges. Most of the studio bass trombonists double on tuba, and there are also several fine young tubists who occasionally get studio jobs. Doubling is a necessary resource for all.

Another useful skill for the free-lance tubists is the ability to read chord changes and to improvise jazz. This does not mean playing only the root and fifth of the chord. It means creating a solo or bass line with a good "feel" based on the correct scales and in the style of the masters. To do so requires hard work. Occasionally a musician is asked to play something in another key, or be asked to play someone else's part by rote. Jazz, transpositions, and all ensemble playing require a mature "ear." The tubist who has played Dixieland, who has the doubling experience of playing bass in a jazz band, or who has piano or guitar experience will have skills which will serve well in playing those special jobs.

The best instruments for recording are tubas that have a clear tone. Big orchestral tubas often dominate the room and leak into other mikes. They also respond more slowly and do not record as well because of the preponderance of low frequencies. Standard instruments for a recording date in Los Angeles would be a medium-bore CC tuba, an F tuba, and a bass trombone, with all the appropriate mutes, of course.

Learning to play secondary instruments is not a monumental task. Once the basics are learned, it is easy to transfer them to other disciplines. Keep in mind that total musicianship should be the goal of all musicians. The adult student may even have more resources than the child. Sometimes the ear and self-confidence to learn other instruments are not sufficiently developed at an early age. The following steps suggested for teachers may also be applied to the self-taught adult.

As most successful directors have discovered, choosing the best possible musicians to become their tuba players pays big dividends for their bands and other ensembles. Too often the most talented beginners choose and are encouraged to play the "solo" instruments (trumpet, flute, clarinet, etc.) while tubists are often chosen from those who have failed at other instruments. Many difficult circumstances conspire to bring this about. The glamour is in playing the melody instruments: the parts are more technical. Students (usually because of their body size) often start on higher brass instruments and switch to tuba later. A director would be wise to encourage the student with the better ear, sense of rhythm, and self-confidence to become a tubist. The long-term benefit for both the director and the student will be significant. The entire band will play better, rhythm will be more solid, and ensemble intonation (which finds its foundation in the low instruments that play the fundamental) will greatly improve. Even if the school director can develop only one tuba player with these special musical skills, the entire instrumental program will improve. The director will have someone who can easily learn to double on other instruments and provide the same solid musicianship to other ensembles, particularly the orchestra and the jazz band. The player will be challenged and educated by playing in a wide variety of ensembles, acquiring skills to succeed in college and as a professional and possibly earning some income, even as early as high school. If a talented musician is chosen to be a tubist in junior high, the school will have the makings of a string and/or electric bass player or bass trombone/tuba player for the jazz ensemble; a bass player, bass trombonist, euphoniumist, and/or tubist for the orchestra; as well as a tubist for the concert and marching bands.

Any suggestions for learning to double will be much easier to teach and learn if the students have musical talent. A good "ear" is essential. "Music is music" and the associations between instruments are best learned by ear and with visual associations. Traditional method books and reading should be used as a supplement but only after aural and visual techniques have been introduced and understood. All brass instruments are similar: all are based on the overtone series. All low instruments are similar: they share the bass clef and emphasize support roles in the ensemble.

With the possible exception of the kazoo, the electric bass is the easiest instrument to learn. Thousands of amateurs play them. Electric basses are inexpensive, plentiful, and nearly indestructible; and the frets make intonation easy. It makes an ideal double for tubists and has no negative

effects on tuba playing. The work possibilities for this double are by far the most lucrative. Instructors should begin teaching the electric bass strictly by ear and visual references, starting with teaching proper hand and finger position and playing on the open strings. (Yes, the fingers will hurt but that will soon pass.) Written notes are only a form of shorthand (and usually get in the way). As in all practice, playing along with recordings, copying the music of great musicians (by ear), and using a tape recorder for instant analysis are useful habits. Many young electric bass players become interested in jazz and want to add the string bass to their skills. Bowing is the major obstacle, but once the basics are learned, the player can become a member of a symphony orchestra. But keep in mind that the string bass is a complex instrument, and mastering orchestral style and technique requires serious study and practice.

The other important double for tuba is the bass trombone. As mentioned earlier, this is the standard double in modern big bands, show bands, and studio work. The bass trombone parts in stage bands often ask for a tuba double. Two major problems confront the student making the switch: mouthpiece size and slide technique. Some tuba players have had special mouthpieces made to solve the former problem. These mouthpieces are a hybrid standard bass trombone cup, backbore, and stem with a regular tuba rim. To the tubist it feels like a tuba (i.e., an A♭ feels like an A♭). The advantages are a big sound, great low notes, accuracy, and comfort in switching back to tuba. (Sometimes on a cartoon recording session the doubler may have to play a shouting big band bass trombone part, have four bars rest, and then play a sensitive tuba solo.) The large rim mouthpiece may make that easier. The main disadvantages are that the high register will be more difficult and the sound may be too "spread." The doubler can learn to use a standard size mouthpiece and just switch with the instrument—in effect having two embouchures. Young musicians have the flexibility to do this more easily than mature musicians; they don't know how hard it really is! In Los Angeles it seems that the tuba players who double on bass trombone prefer the large rim, and the bass trombonists who double on tuba prefer to switch. Some tubists have had valve sections made that replace the slide. Used with the F and D (E♭) attachments on the bell section of the bass trombone, the player has complete chromatic capability. This is a very useful adaptation and can get the tubist (who may have weak slide technique) through some difficult parts. Tuba players are generally better at "thinking" valves.

The best way to teach the switch from tuba to bass trombone is to follow the same ear and visual approach as recommended for electric bass. All brass instruments are the same—built on the overtone system. Open notes and valve combination are the same on all, and trombone slide positions directly correspond to valve combinations. It helps to draw this association when teaching slide technique. Start with open/first position notes, comparing the bass trombone with tuba while observing the octave change. The trigger directly corresponds to the tuba's fourth valve. As with the bass, start slowly by ear and gradually add more notes, scales, and melodies. Return frequently to the tuba for reference, and use a metronome.

Most school band directors are faced with switching students from one instrument to another: trumpet to baritone, baritone to tuba, E♭ tuba to BB♭ tuba, and sousaphone to tuba. Use of the aural and visual associations will make those switches much easier. Finally, teachers can help by encouraging study of piano at an early age. The keyboard teaches harmony, theory, and overall good ear training; and it opens the door for acquiring skills in arranging and composition. Tubists, like all musicians, should expand their knowledge by learning piano.

The first instrument that most students play is a BB♭ tuba or sousaphone, and their first challenge is in making the switch to tubas of other pitches. To the college-bound student, this is usually to a CC tuba with F and/or E♭ tubas later added to master the solo and orchestral literature. Again, the same aural and visual references mentioned above are effective here. Do not use music at first. Anyone who has switched from CC to F tuba will recognize the following: at first the F will be frustrating (with lots of errors); then, for a while, the CC and F will both seem impossible; then the F might become the stronger; and finally the doubler will feel comfortable with both. The ear takes over, the mind switches gears, and two separate but equal thought processes occur. By following this procedure, each succeeding double will be progressively easier.

The free-lancer can expect to be called for a great variety of work with special kinds of music calling for special instruments: sousaphone for Dixieland, cimbasso for opera, E♭ tuba for brass band, electric bass for rock and roll, or CC tuba for the symphony. The same ear and visual references can be used to switch thought processes. One must still emphasize that one is a tubist first and one's reputation rests on continued expertise on that instrument. All other instruments are doubles, which should be maintained well enough to do the job, but rarely as well as specialists on those instruments. It is important to do one thing well. The real pitfall is to place too much importance on doubling and be a master of none.

16. The Tuba in Jazz: A Historical View
R. Steven Call

Although the tuba had an important role in the origin and development of jazz, it is yet to be universally accepted as a solo instrument in that idiom. The tuba was part of the Negro brass bands in the American South around 1900. It was frequently used in dance bands and recorded jazz bands in the 1920s and early 1930s. The tuba virtually disappeared from jazz during the swing/big band era of the 1930s and 1940s. In the mid to late 1940s it reappeared in a few innovative big bands, in the new sounds of "cool jazz" and in traditional jazz revival bands. Starting around 1950, innovations in jazz orchestration established the tuba as a unique voice in various jazz ensembles. Since the 1960s, a small number of jazz tuba ensembles and a handful of pioneering jazz tuba soloists have prepared the way for the emergence of a new generation of jazz tubists.

Early Jazz

In New Orleans and other areas of the American South, Negro brass bands played for many kinds of social functions, from funerals to picnics. They played written arrangements of marches and popular songs and created extemporaneous versions of hymns and blues. The same musicians who played for funeral processions and parades during the day could be found playing the same style of music in dance halls, saloons, and bordellos at night.

The first jazz was created by bringing together components of ragtime, brass band music, blues, and black church music. The instrumentation and formal structure had their origins in brass band music, while much of the improvised melodic content, harmony, and rhythm came from the blues and church music. In both brass band music and early jazz, the tuba had the same role: It defined the tempo and style by playing on the strong beats, framing the harmonic function by playing primarily the roots and fifths of the chords.

The first jazz recordings used no tuba or string bass. The functional bass part was provided by the striding left hand of the pianist and often by the trombone. This was true for the recordings of the Original Dixieland Jazz Band, New Orleans

Rhythm Kings (early recordings), King Oliver's Creole Jazz Band, and Louis Armstrong's Hot Five. The earliest known jazz recordings using tuba were made in 1923 by the New Orleans Rhythm Kings with Jelly Roll Morton playing piano. Recorded in Richmond, Indiana, they featured New Orleans tubist Chink Martin (Martin Abraham).

By 1927 the tuba was widely used in jazz recording by Louis Armstrong, Jelly Roll Morton, and others. Armstrong's Hot Seven recordings made in Chicago that year included Pete Briggs on tuba. Between 1926 and 1930 Jelly Roll Morton recorded many masterpieces with some of the great jazz players in Chicago and New York. These well-rehearsed studio sessions were released as records by Jelly Roll Morton's Red Hot Peppers. Although the 1926 recordings used string bass, most of the sessions from 1927 to 1930 employed tuba. Tubists who recorded with Morton during this period included Quinn Wilson, Hayes Alvis, Bill Benford, Bass Moore, Harry Prather, Billy Taylor, and Pete Briggs. Tubist, string bassist, and arranger Joe Tarto performed and recorded with virtually every jazz and popular musician in New York in the 1920s, including Bix Beiderbecke, Red Nichols, Joe Venuti, and the Dorsey Brothers. He also had a long, but intermittent, association with the Paul Whiteman Orchestra.

Recording technology had an important impact on the inclusion of tuba in many early recordings of jazz and other styles of music. The earliest acoustical recording equipment was not particularly sensitive to certain instruments. The sound of the tuba, especially those instruments with forward-facing bells (including sousaphones), could be picked up by a stylus imprinting an acoustical signal on a wax cylinder or disk much more easily than the sound of the string bass or the low notes of the piano. As electronic recording technology developed in the late 1920s and 1930s, the tuba's role in the rhythm section began to be replaced by the string bass. Since most of the early jazz bass players were expected to play both string bass and brass bass (tuba), this trend did not put many tuba players out of work. They just started playing string bass more often than tuba.

The Swing Era

In the transition to the Swing Era (late 1920s and early 1930s), there were two types of large dance bands: "sweet" and "hot." Sweet bands played a more commercial style and were less likely to make use of improvised solos. In the hot bands, improvised solos were an essential component, and the ensembles played with a more hard-driving approach to swing. Although this dichotomy did not necessarily break down along racial lines, the black bands, like Fletcher Henderson's, played generally hotter than the white bands. The Paul Whiteman Orchestra, the most popular of the white bands of this period, played with a sweet ensemble approach, but at times it employed hot soloists like Bix Beiderbecke and Jack Teagarden.

The tuba was a standard part of nearly every dance band in the 1920s and early 1930s, both sweet and hot. The Paul Whiteman Orchestra employed the tuba in symphonic settings as well as in a two-beat dance style, and it even used two tuba players at times. Fletcher Henderson's band, as a result of Louis Armstrong's short tenure in the trumpet section, had developed a highly stylized ensemble sound with hard-driving riffs and chase choruses. Tubist June Cole's bouncing bass lines can be heard in Henderson's vintage 1926 and 1927 New York sessions. Fletcher Henderson's style and arrangements (with a preference for string bass rather than tuba) were soon to be adopted by the Benny Goodman band, whose popularity launched the "swing era." By the time swing became the popular music of the day, propelling the big band movement into full gear, the tuba had been replaced by the string bass in all the hot bands. A few sweet bands like Guy Lombardo's continued to use tuba in a two-beat traditional rhythm section role throughout the 1930s, 1940s, and beyond.

The decision to supplant the tuba with the string bass may have been made largely by the tubists themselves. Many of the prominent string bass players of the day, including Pops Foster, John Kirby, Milt Hinton, and Red Callender, either started on tuba or learned tuba as a double. Perhaps the musicians and band leaders thought the tuba sound to be old-fashioned or too difficult for playing modern bass lines. Had there been musicians who played tuba as well as Oscar Pettiford, Jimmy Blanton, or Milt Hinton played string bass, perhaps the tuba would not have disappeared from the scene.

The changing roles of the rhythm-section instruments in the new swing style may also have led to the decline of the tuba in jazz in the 1930s and 1940s. In Kansas City, the Benny Moten Orchestra (which was later taken over by Count Basie) was playing a more hard-driving rhythmic style. Bassist and former tubist Walter Page was playing straight 4/4 walking bass lines, while pianist Basie started to abandon the striding left hand. The role of the drums also changed as the style evolved with the rhythm of the hi-hat cymbals taking the place of the alternate stride (counts two and four) in the piano. Guitar, rather than banjo, played straight 4/4 rhythm strummed on each beat. The inclusion of string bass in this lighter-textured, yet harder-driving, Kansas City style secured its future role in jazz.

Late in the swing era, the tuba was reintroduced as an orchestral color instrument. Claude Thornhill, an alumnus of Artie Shaw's orchestra, organized his own band in 1946, which used French horns and tuba. His sidemen included tubist John "Bill" Barber and arranger Gil Evans. Both became important contributors to the Miles Davis Nonet a few years later. In 1952 Eddie Sauter and Bill Finegan joined forces to create the Sauter-Finegan Orchestra. These two prominent composer-arrangers orchestrated for the tuba in unique ways: with the saxophone section, the brass section, or as a unique independent voice. Harvey Phillips, Bill Barber, and Jay McCallister were among the tubists who played with Sauter-Finegan.

Modern Jazz of the 1950s and 1960s

The tuba was absent from the innovations leading to bebop in the mid 1940s but made an amazing reappearance in "cool jazz," which was a reaction to bebop. Trumpeter Miles Davis organized a nonet which included tuba not as part of the rhythm section but as a means of expressing color and texture in the ensemble. Arrangements by Gerry Mulligan, Tadd Damaron, Gil Evans, and others made excellent use of tubist Bill Barber's talents. This music can be heard in the classic recordings released as *The Birth of the Cool* on Capitol Records in 1949. A recent CD release, *The Miles Davis Tuba Band* (Natasha Imports NI-4015), features this innovative ensemble in the only live broadcast recordings from the famous Royal Roost appearance in September 1948.

At about the same time, also in New York, the "third stream" movement attempted to merge modern "serious" composition and jazz. Many of the musicians involved with "cool jazz" were principal musicians and composers in the third stream. They included Gunther Schuller, John Lewis, J. J. Johnson, and Gil Evans. Tuba was an important part of the color palette of these composers. Although third stream music never gained much acceptance by either classical or jazz audiences, the use of orchestral color involving tuba continued, especially in the collaborations of Gil Evans and Miles Davis.

In the 1950s and 1960s several important recordings were made by Evans and Davis. These Columbia Records releases with Bill Barber on tuba included *Miles Ahead, Porgy and Bess*, and *Sketches of Spain*. The use of tuba, French horn, flute, bassoon, and other instruments in these recordings had a lasting impact on jazz. Stan Kenton started using tuba and mellophoniums (French horn–like instruments with forward bells) in his orchestra. In New York Johnny Richards began performing and recording with a band which used Jay McCallister on tuba. On the West Coast, the innovative trumpeter and composer Don Ellis used tuba, played by Doug Bixby, and French horn in his band.

The Traditional Jazz Revival

By the end of the 1930s and beginning of the 1940s, swing music had become a major part of popular culture. Many jazz musicians of the day were forward-thinking and striving to be "modern." New Orleans jazz and 1920s two-beat dance music were thought to be old-fashioned and undesirable. A revival movement originating in San Francisco brought the tuba back into the jazz rhythm section. The principal musicians in this movement were devotees and record collectors of early New Orleans jazz. (The San Francisco style incorporates tuba and banjo in the rhythm sections and usually, but not always, is played in a two-beat style.)

Lu Watters organized the Yerba Buena Jazz Band in San Francisco. It recreated the spirit, sounds, and improvisational styles of the great jazz recordings of the 1920s by King Oliver, Louis Armstrong, Jelly Roll Morton, and others. Dick Lammi was tubist with the band, and several other original members went on to start other popular traditional jazz bands on the West Coast. Trombonist Turk Murphy led a traditional band in San Francisco into the 1980s, and cornetist Bob Scobey's Frisco Jazz Band recorded a number of albums in the 1950s and 1960s featuring Rich Matteson playing tuba and bass trumpet.

By 1950 dozens of these traditional jazz and Dixieland bands had sprung up all over the United States, especially on the West Coast. Although they do not usually consist of full-time professional players, these revival bands continue to produce genuinely original music, reflecting the New Orleans style of improvisation and polyphony. It is within this genre that many fine jazz tubists, including David "Red" Lehr, Eli Newberger, and Dave Gannett, have emerged. The traditional jazz revival is still flourishing by way of numerous traditional jazz festivals and recordings released by specialty labels such as Stomp Off and Good Time Jazz.

The Emergence of the Jazz Tuba Soloist and Jazz Tuba Ensembles

In the late 1950s a young New York tubist, Ray Draper, played and recorded with Max Roach, John Coltrane, and Jackie McLean. His phrasing and style showed the influence of trumpeter Clifford Brown, and his improvisations were outstanding in rhythmic and motivic development. Beset with personal problems, he was unable to realize his potential. After serving prison time in California in the 1960s, he moved to England for a while, then moved back to New York and played briefly with Howard Johnson's group, Gravity. Draper was killed in a robbery attempt in 1982.

New York studio musician Don Butterfield was associated with many great jazz performers. Known for his fluid technical skill, he played and recorded with Charles Mingus, Sonny Rollins, and Cannonball Adderley. In the mid-1950s he recorded an award-winning album, *Top and Bottom Brass,* with Clark Terry on Riverside Records; it was recently reissued as Riverside CD OJCCD-764-2 (RLP-1137).

In 1968, self-taught multi-instrumentalist Howard Johnson organized a tuba quintet called Substructure, which included himself, Jack Jeffers, Morris Edwards, Dave Bargeron (of Blood, Sweat, and Tears fame), and Bob Stewart. They played around New York and recorded with blues/folk singer Taj Mahal. Later Johnson added two more tubists, Earl McIntyre and Joe Daley. Johnson performs more frequently on baritone saxophone and was leader of the NBC Saturday Night Live Band for a time. Although Johnson has played tuba extensively with Gil Evans and his own tuba ensembles and is considered by many to be the leading jazz tubist, he has no solo tuba recordings under his leadership.

Tubist Harvey Phillips and the late euphoniumist Rich Matteson organized the Matteson-Phillips TubaJazz Consort, which gave its first performance at the First International Brass Congress in Montreux, Switzerland, in 1976. It consists of three euphoniums, three tubas, piano, guitar, bass, and drums, with R. Winston Morris and Daniel Perantoni on tuba, and Ashley Alexander (replaced by John Allred after Alexander's death) and Buddy Baker on euphonium. The group has produced two albums, and it continues to perform at jazz and brass conventions and symposia. It is known for its innovative arrangements, tight ensemble playing, and exciting soloists. The vast majority of the improvised solos are handled by the rhythm section and the euphonium players.

Rich Matteson, whose primary instrument was euphonium, played tuba in traditional jazz groups, including the Dukes of Dixieland and Bob Scobey's Frisco Jazz Band. He was an exceptional educator and an exciting bebop-oriented soloist, and he played euphonium and tuba in his numerous guest appearances with college and high school jazz bands.

The concept of a large group of tubas playing jazz caught on in Europe as well as the United States. Tubapack, which preceded the TubaJazz Consort, was founded by Marc Steckar in France and included Daniel Landreat, Michel Godard, and Christian Jous. In 1984 Swedish tubist Michael Lind organized Scandinavian Tuba Jazz, which released a recording in 1986. Other members of the group include Norwegian tubist Stein-Erik Tafjod, Norwegian euphonium player Frode Thingnaes, and Danish euphonium player Torolf Molgard. Peter Kowald, Larry Fishkind, and Pinguin Moschner are some other notable European jazz tubists. The 1980s saw a substantial increase in the number of jazz tuba recordings. Bob Stewart, Jim Self, and Sam Pilafian have each released jazz CDs. Known for his inventive and energetic bass lines, Bob Stewart has recorded extensively with saxophonist Arthur Blythe and pianist Carla Bley. He was an original member of the jazz tuba ensemble Gravity. His CD, *First Line Band: Goin' Home,* was released on the German record label JMT. Los Angeles studio musician and jazz tubist Jim Self has three jazz CDs to his credit. These recordings make use of creative arrangements by some of the leading West Coast jazz writers and showcase Self's lyrical phrasing and beautiful tone. Former Empire Brass Quintet tubist Sam Pilafian is no stranger to the tuba world. He burst onto the jazz scene in

1988 with the release of *Travlin' Light,* a collection of traditional jazz and swing tunes presented in a happy-go-lucky, off-the-cuff manner which shows off his wonderful sense of swing and incredible command of the instrument. This CD was enormously popular and received much radio air play nationwide. Pilafian released a second CD, *Travlin' Light: Makin' Whoopee,* in 1993. In these recordings the tuba functions as a solo instrument at times and as the bass at other times.

Given its role in the origin of jazz and its unique voice within many styles, the tuba is yet to be universally accepted as a solo jazz instrument. Although no jazz tubist's contribution has been on a level with the major jazz stylist of the clarinet, saxophone, trumpet, trombone, piano, guitar, bass, or drums, each tubist mentioned in this chapter has added a unique voice to the eclectic sound of the tuba in jazz. The fact that the tuba is thought of as an unusual instrument in jazz should not preclude it from having its own truly great artists. Though the harmonica has its Toots Thielemans, the violin its Stephane Grappelly, and the euphonium its Rich Matteson, no tubist has reached that level of artistry. Perhaps the twenty-first century will reveal a jazz tubist who will take his or her place of honor in the company of Charlie Parker, Louis Armstrong, J. J. Johnson, Bill Evans, Wes Montgomery, Ray Brown, Art Blakey, and Ella Fitzgerald.

Bibliography

Berendt, Joachim E. *The Jazz Book: From Ragtime to Fusion and Beyond.* New York: Lawrence Hill Books, 1989.
Chilton, John. *Who's Who of Jazz: Storyville to Swing Street.* Philadelphia: Chilton, 1972.
Dickman, Marc. "Rich Matteson: Portrait of an Original." *T.U.B.A. Journal,* Vol. 19, no. 2., 1991.
Feather, Leonard. *The Encyclopedia of Jazz.* New York: Horizon, 1960.
Kernfeld, Barry, ed. *The New Grove Dictionary of Jazz.* New York: Grove's Dictionaries of Music, Inc.
Laplace, Michel. "Les tubas dans le jazz et dans les musiques populaires." *Brass Bulletin,* no. 56, 1986, 18; no. 57, 1987, 84.
Morris, R. Winston. TUBA Tuba Profile: "Allan Jaffe and Anthony 'Tuba Fats' Lacen." *T.U.B.A. Journal,* Vol. IX, no. 2, 1981.
Nelson, Mark. "TubaNews" *T.U.B.A. Journal,* Vol. 14, no. 4, 1987.
Pilafian, Sam. *Travlin' Light.* Telarc CD-80281 liner notes.
Stewart, Bob. "New Roles and Dimensions for the Contemporary Jazz Tubist." *T.U.B.A. Journal.* Vol. 18, no. 3, 1991.

17. The Free-Lance Tubist

R. Steven Call

Professional opportunities for free-lance tubists include playing with part-time orchestras, bands, small ensembles, and jazz groups. Free-lance performance also includes playing as an extra, substituting with a full-time orchestra, and recording. Teaching is also an important part of most free-lance musicians' careers.

The Free-Lance Tuba Scene

Prominent free-lance tubists created their careers by developing the ability to play many kinds of music, by involving themselves in new and innovative settings for their instrument, and by promoting the tuba and their own talents. By examining the careers of some of the great free-lance tubists, a model for success can be drawn which may help young tubists achieve their goals. Along with being involved in innovative musical activities and teaching, most of these tubists also play or have played in part-time orchestras, bands, and chamber groups, and they also double on other instruments. They are highly motivated "self-starters," who, by carving a successful career for themselves, have expanded the possibilities for all tubists.

Don Butterfield, an accomplished arranger/composer as well as tubist, aggressively sold his tuba sound to music producers in New York in the 1950s and 1960s, thus contributing to the popularity of the instrument in commercial music. Along with playing numerous Broadway shows, Bill Barber recorded with Claude Thornhill, Sauter-Finigen, Miles Davis, and Gil Evans, thus helping to reestablish the tuba as an important voice in jazz. On the West Coast, the beautiful soloistic playing of Tommy Johnson and Jim Self helped to secure the tuba as an essential voice in motion picture and television sound tracks. Each of these great performers has simultaneously been involved in teaching. Don Butterfield is on the faculty of six colleges and universities in New York and New Jersey. Before retiring from education in 1982, Bill Barber taught public school music for a number of years on Long Island. Tommy Johnson was a junior high school band director for many years and is still on the faculty at the University of Southern California and U.C.L.A. Jim Self is active as a guest soloist/clinician and teaches applied music at the University of Southern California.

Most past and many present free-lance tubists double on other instruments. Nearly all of the early free-lance tubists also play string bass. In the 1950s, Red Callender performed on string bass with Erroll Garner, Charlie Parker, and other jazz greats at night while playing studio sessions on tuba during the day. A look at the current scene reveals many free-lance tubists doubling on other instruments. Jim Self also plays bass trombone, cimbasso, electric valve instrument (EVI), acoustic bass, electric bass, and harmonica. New York studio tubists Tony Price and Dave Bargeron also play trombone, and it is reported that much of the tuba studio work there is being played by musicians whose major instrument is trombone.

Opportunities for the Free-Lance Tubist

One might expect that a free-lance tubist could make a living only in a very large metropolitan area like New York or Los Angeles. More and more tubists, however, are proving that successful free-lancing can take place in medium-sized cities, especially if teaching is part of the plan. The limited number of full-time orchestras, military bands, and performance organizations employing tuba players can be discouraging to someone who wants a career in music. As a young man, this writer was told that his chances of landing a position with a full-time orchestra in the United States were the same as becoming governor of a state (still not an inaccurate statement). For a tubist with a high level of musicianship, but without a full-time playing or teaching position, there are many musical activities which can add up to a financially and musically satisfying career. However, a tubist must either have or develop the ability to sell his or her musical services. A free-lance tubist must also meet and make favorable impressions on the people who can help.

Part-Time Orchestras and Bands

Many excellent orchestras are made up of free-lance musicians, university teachers, and accomplished players who are community members.

These orchestras are often led by excellent professional conductors and play the great orchestral literature. They usually have relatively short seasons of ten to twenty weeks, with perhaps three to five rehearsals per concert. Many large and medium-sized cities also have local ballet, musical theater, and/or opera companies which hire free-lance musicians. These can be an excellent source of income and musical satisfaction. Most large and many medium-sized communities have summer concert bands, often financed in part by the Music Performance Trust Fund (MPTF) and administered by a local musicians' union. These kinds of orchestras and bands can provide great opportunities to meet other free-lance musicians with whom to collaborate in organizing small, commercially viable ensembles like brass quintets, tuba quartets, and Dixieland bands.

Small Ensembles

Since the founding and subsequent success of Canadian Brass and the Empire Brass, hiring a brass ensemble for concerts and community events has become appealing to many clients. Fine arts grants are available for concert performances and tours. Brass quintets frequently play for weddings and private parties. Often businesses hire brass quintets for meetings or commercial grand openings. Young Audiences, Inc., and other school arts associations contract with brass quintets for educational programs in schools. A tubist/entrepreneur can organize a brass quintet concert series at a library or other community location, then solicit funds from local businesses to pay the musicians. These are just a few ways that a motivated musician can create opportunities. Although it may be a little harder to sell, a tuba-euphonium quartet can also be organized and marketed the way a brass quintet is.

Dixieland Bands

The traditional jazz revival, which started in the 1940s in San Francisco, is alive and still thriving. Many Dixieland bands use tuba in the rhythm section. Learning to improvise bass lines from a lead sheet is not as difficult as some might expect. Any competent tubist with an interest in playing Dixieland jazz can pick up the techniques and style rather quickly by listening to appropriate recordings and practicing from a "fake book" with the standard tunes.

Dixieland bands play for all kinds of occasions, from sports events to political rallies. Although these groups can command good fees, many of the musicians playing in these bands are amateurs who are usually impressed with a "real tuba player."

Playing as an Extra and Substituting with an Orchestra

A good working relationship with a principal tuba player of a full-time professional orchestra can be helpful. The best way to get acquainted with such a person is to take some lessons from him or her. The lessons will not only help the free-lancer's playing but will provide a means for establishing a friendly relationship and letting his or her expertise and availability be known. This can lead to referrals for other playing engagements and calls to substitute or be an extra with the orchestra.

A number of standard orchestral works require an extra tuba: Berlioz's *Symphonie Fantastique* and *Requiem*, Strauss's *Ein Heldenleben* and *Also Sprach Zarathustra*, and Stravinsky's *Rite of Spring*, among others. When these works are programmed, the free-lance tubist should be sure to be available. Often orchestra personnel managers do not plan ahead, and give extra players little notice. By looking at orchestra concert schedules in advance and practicing the appropriate excerpts, the free-lancer can be prepared when called to substitute or be an extra.

Recording

Although New York and Los Angeles are still the major centers for music recording for motion pictures, television, and popular music, state-of-the-art recording studios are starting to appear in more medium-sized cities. With them come opportunities to record for films, television programs, commercials, and other media. Many such recordings are for low-budget movies, cable TV, or commercials for local markets. Because some recording situations do not have the sanctioning of a local or national musicians' union, a free-lance musician needs to resolve union questions and issues before accepting recording jobs.

In local advertising, the tubist can also make his or her own opportunities. This author has written jingles for, recorded, and appeared in a number of local television commercials for an automobile dealership group. Not only was it financially rewarding but it also gave the tuba exposure in the community and opened the door to more paid tuba quartet performances.

Teaching

Teaching can be an important component of a free-lance career because the income generated can see a musician through lean times. Most colleges and universities do not have full-time tuba teachers. Tuba students are often taught by full-time faculty who would gladly turn them over to an adjunct tuba instructor. Affiliation with a college or university can open many doors and provide performance opportunities for the free-lancer's other projects. This writer once taught at three different universities on three different days of the week while holding down a part-time public school teaching position, in addition to other freelancing. As is sometimes the case, one of the university positions eventually turned into a full-time teaching post.

Junior high and high school tuba students can be recruited by contacting local band directors and volunteering to present clinics or teach sectional rehearsals. Once a studio of tuba students is established, it is important that the teacher be aware of student auditions for honor groups like all-district or all-state bands as well as upcoming solo and ensemble festivals. When a free-lance tubist's students begin to win first chair in all-state band (better if it is first, second, and third) and earn recognition at solo festivals, the teacher can command higher lesson fees and begin to have the luxury of a student waiting list.

Conclusion

It is not necessary to be a member of a full-time professional orchestra or military band to make a living as a tubist. What is needed is excellent musicianship, motivation, creativity, dependability, a confident personality, and an appropriate location.

18. Guidelines for Composers, Orchestrators, and Arrangers
Harvey G. Phillips

The primary goal of this chapter is to provide a definitive source for those who would write music of any genre for the tuba. A representative cross section of individuals who have been successful in composing and arranging for the tuba were requested to participate in this project. Included in this group are a number of tubists who have also been recognized for their arranging/compositional talents. These individuals have a very special understanding of all parameters of writing for the tuba.

Each participant was asked to outline his attitude and approach to composing or arranging for the tuba and to recommend range and technical considerations. As can be seen by the following contributions, each individual responded to this request in his own unique manner, with everything from simple statements of "attitude" to definitive documentation on the specifics of writing for tuba(s).

The editors are extremely grateful to all the respondents for their participation and for their significant contributions to the body of musical literature available for the tuba.

David N. Baker

Indiana University

Through the years, as I have matured as a composer, I have fallen in love with the tuba in its many and varied roles. I have found it to be perhaps the most versatile of all the brass instruments. It has all of the technical capabilities and agility of the smaller valved instruments (trumpet, horn, euphonium) but a much wider range. Because of its wonderful sound, character, and ability to make all of the other instruments in an ensemble sound better, it is completely at home as a member of an orchestra, band, jazz band, brass choir, French horn section, trombone choir, and trumpet ensemble, or with woodwind or string groups.

In the jazz ensemble I find myself using the tuba much as Duke Ellington used Harry Carney's baritone saxophone in the Ellington band, that is, for its wonderful and distinctive color as much as for its ability to anchor the other sec-

tions. I cannot imagine writing for my jazz bands without a tuba. In my brass writing the two most important voices are the lead trumpet and the tuba.

As a solo instrument, I think that the tuba has been inexplicably and unjustifiably neglected until very recently. However, most composers, myself included, have begun to take advantage of the tremendous technical, sonorous, and expressive potential of this often magical instrument.

James Barnes

The University of Kansas

My comments concern writing for tubas in the ensemble where the instrument is *king*: the wind band. Even today, the tuba is often an afterthought among most orchestral composers, but in the wind band, tubas are the starting point for the creation of blend, balance, and good intonation in the ensemble. To this day, many of my conducting colleagues talk only of balance when discussing the lowest octave of the wind band. They do not appreciate the importance of having the rich, sonorous sound of the tubas in their ensemble. Good tuba sections grab the whole band by the nose and drag them around the rehearsal room. The sound and drive of a great tuba section is what gives the wind band the great propulsion that makes it such an exciting medium to compose for and listen to. It is possible to have a good wind band without strong double reeds. It is even possible to have a good wind band without extremely strong middle and high brass. But I have never heard a great band that did not have great tubas. The tuba sound is as essential to the overall makeup of the wind band as are the cellos and basses to the symphony orchestra. Neither ensemble can exist without these sections, which must constantly provide the powerful fundamental pitch beneath the rest of the ensemble.

The roles of the tuba in the orchestra and in the wind band are quite different, but unfortunately, many teachers of the instrument do not seem to understand this concept, nor do they get this point over to their students, probably because they remain so infatuated with the nineteenth-century orchestral tradition. In the orchestra, the tuba takes on the role of the *reinforcer*. It reinforces the tutti orchestra; it reinforces the brass section by providing the lowest octave of the bass sound; it reinforces the strings and woodwinds at various times. Once in a great while, it is given a solo, usually in an awkward register (either sky-high or extremely low, since most orchestral composers are pianists and have little experience with the tuba). In the symphonic band or wind ensemble, tubas should be the *enforcers*. Tubas are the bass sound of the ensemble. All the other instruments, like bass and contra-alto clarinets, bassoons, baritone saxophone, and double bass should be subservient to the tubas, because in any tutti passage, the tubas should dominate the bass sound of the wind band. If you hear a wind band that does not sound this way, it has weak tubas.

Because the tubas are written for as a section (anywhere from two to six, depending on the philosophy of the conductor and the availability of players), they must be scored quite differently than the "lonely artiste" buried in the back of the orchestra, and since their function in the ensemble is so different, the demands on the players vary appreciably. To address some of these aspects, I shall divide the discussion into the following areas of interest: practical ranges for wind band tuba sections; scoring possibilities for the tuba section (including the use of their euphonium cousins.); and scoring possibilities for the tuba section with other sections of the wind band.

Practical Ranges for Wind Band Tuba Sections

Ex. 1. *Young Bands*
(*Elementary and Junior High*)

Ex. 2. *Intermediate*
Bands (*High School*)

Ex. 3. *College Bands*

Ex. 4. *Professional Bands*

The ranges in Exx. 1–4 are extremely practical. The "safe zones" are indicated by white notes, and the possible but not always advisable extended ranges are the black notes. It is important to remember that it is a lot easier to play high

on the tuba than it is to play in its lowest register. Do not keep players "in the basement" all the time; it will make your music sound heavy and muddy, and, sooner or later, it will definitely impact the endurance of the tuba section.

Pedal Tones

When writing music for younger wind bands, we do not normally write pedal tones because most kids cannot play them and because there is the distinct possibility that, because you have written a pedal note, one of the tuba players will attempt to play it anyway, thus destroying any hope of intonation for that moment in the work. Pedal tones are best saved for collegiate or professional players in a situation where one knows who will be playing the part. In this case they can be extremely effective. Good practical ranges are shown in Exx. 5–7.

Ex. 5. *F Tuba**

*Tubists normally use the pedal tones on the F tuba when playing standard passages, because its much shorter pedal range is the same as the lower regular notes of the CC and BBb Tubas.

Ex. 6. *CC Tuba*   Ex. 7. *BB♭ Tuba*

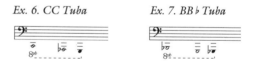

A tried-and-true method for writing pedal notes in a wind band tuba part is to write a "practical range" part; then indicate in the score and part the particular passages that you think might sound good with pedal notes below the normal octave by adding the indication *optional 8va Bassa*. Normally, only one player provides these pedal notes under the rest of the section. The pitches are so low that two or more players might be hard-pressed to match intonation in this register. The best uses of this sort of writing are as follows:

1. Pedal notes on last chords, especially on final chords. It is really a waste of time to write pedal notes underneath chords louder than *forte*. Tubas do not have the power in their pedal registers for this. It may look good on the score paper, but it seldom works, unless you have a

professional playing the part. Even then it is usually not worth the effort.

2. Notes under extended pedal points, especially in soft passages.

3. Slow-moving melodies or bass lines. Avoid writing anything fast in the pedal register, and make sure that you give the tubist many opportunities to grab breaths. Tubists use about a liter of air every second they play in the pedal register. Also, it would be very humane of you not to write exposed solo entrances or long-sustained tones on pedal notes. Do not emulate Prokofiev, who, in his *Seventh Symphony,* asks the tubist to enter on a pedal C♯ solo, *pianissimo,* and hold it until the cavalry shows up.

Scoring Possibilities for the Tuba Section

Unless the composer or arranger indicates "solo," "one player," or perhaps "two players" on the tuba line of the score, the part will be played in unison by the entire section, just like cellos or basses. It is often important to make such indications to ensure proper balance in a softer or more delicate passage. Many wind ensembles use only two tubas, but sections can be as large as four to six. Three or four tubas are the best balance for the larger symphonic band setup. Depending on the quality of the players, six tubas can be quite heavy. If they are all very good players, this will not be a problem; but if their ability drops off considerably toward the end of the section, they will sound extremely sluggish and tend to produce intonational nightmares. In most wind band music, the parts are not very challenging. This is really boring for good players. Do not be afraid to write more difficult lines and a broader range for advanced groups. Exx. 8 and 9 show instances of more difficult passages in some of my works for wind band:

Ex. 8. Barnes, Pagan Dances, Mvt. II, Mystics.

Used with the permission of Southern Music Co., San Antonio, TX. Copyright 1991.

Ex. 9. Barnes, Symphonic Overture.

Copyright 1992 by Southern Music Co.

Divisi Writing

The most common *divisi* for tubas is at the octave. They really sound terrific this way. This traditional scoring goes back to the days when wind bands used both E♭ and BB♭ tubas in their sections. Bass-line passages were often divided into octaves to accommodate the E♭ tubas, which could not play as low as the BB♭ instrument. This concept is similar to the orchestral device of splitting the cellos and basses into octaves to accommodate the cello's range restrictions, and the results are just as wonderful. There is great power and sweep with octave tubas. It is a good idea to indicate that one player play the upper octave while the rest of the tubists perform the lower octave because it is easier to play the upper octave and it is often more difficult to get enough volume in the lowest register of the instrument. Contrary to popular opinion, it is really difficult to play the tuba loudly in its lower register, especially below A♭$_2$ or G$_1$. Special care should be taken by the conductor to make certain that the upper octave tubist does not play louder than the lower octave players (this is very easy to do). The lower octave should, of course, always be stronger to ensure richness and good overall balance. It might not be a bad idea to ask that the best tubist always play the lower octave on *divisis,* while the upper-octave assignments might go to the second or third player, who usually does not have as effective a low range as does the principal.

Ex. 10. Fantasy Variations *on a Theme by Niccolo Paganini*

Copyright 1989.by Southern Music Co.

Exx. 10 and 11 show effective use of tubas in octaves. Please note that I am quoting my own works because I know why each passage is scored the way it is written and so that I will not have to spend six months getting copyright clearances.

In music for younger bands, we divide the tubas into octaves to accommodate the students with limited lower range (Ex. 11).

There are instances in many works of diminished fifths, but one of the most commonly used intervals in the wind band is the perfect fifth. In this instance, it is important that the upper note does not sound stronger than the lower one.

Ex. 11. Century Tower, *Overture for Band*

Copyright 1984 by Southern Music Co.

The composer/arranger can ask for one player on the upper part and the rest on the lower note (see Ex. 12). (The Italian terms for these indications are *solo* and *gli altri*.)

Ex. 12. Riverfest

Copyright 1986 by Southern Music Co.

Fifths under a major or minor chord give the bottom octave great power and help bring out more overtones in the upper octaves. Parallel fifths in a melodic passage give music an ominous dignity or a sort of primeval, barbarous power. Exx. 13–15 show the use of tubas in fifths.

Ex.13. Impressions of Japan *(perfect fifths in a short melodic passage)*

Copyright 1993 by Southern Music Co.

Ex. 14. Centennial Celebration Overture *(last chord, fifths under whole brass section)*

Copyright 1986 by Southern Music Co.

Ex. 15. Pagan Dances, Mvt. III: The Master of the Sword *(parallel diminished fifths)*

Copyright 1991 by Southern Music Co.

Of course, tubas can be scored in any interval, but major and minor seconds would be only for the effect. In the lower octaves of the tuba range, this interval would sound particularly "cluttered." Major thirds and minor thirds would be more suitably scored in tenths (see Exx. 16 and 17).

Ex. 16. Possible

Ex. 17. Better

In general, unless you intend a very dissonant effect, it is not advisable to score tubas closer than perfect fourths in the lower register (Ex. 18) and no closer than minor thirds extending up from G (Ex. 19).

There is a very effective passage for tubas in major sixths in the first movement of Hindemith's *Symphony in Bb for Concert Band*. Tubas in major or minor sevenths or major or minor ninths are certainly possible; it is really up to the imagination of the composer/arranger. The above comments are merely made as suggestions for scoring clarity.

Ex. 18.   Ex. 19.

SCORING CHORDS

Ex. 20. Pagan Dances, Mvt. III, The Master of the Sword

Copyright 1991 by Southern Music Co.

Ex. 21. Torch Dance

Copyright 1985 by Southern Music Co.

Scoring chords for tubas assumes that the wind band will have at least three tubas in the section. This will present problems for wind ensembles, who would not be able to play this passage with the desired color because they do not normally use three tubas. Cue the top voice of the chord in the euphonium to accommodate these groups. If there are four or more players for a three-note chord, put one player on the top part, one on the middle, and the rest on the bottom note. This will not guarantee that the chord will be balanced, but it will certainly go a long way toward doing so. Of course, there is no rule against writing four or more notes in a chord just for tubas, so long as there are enough players to play all the notes.

The possibilities for scoring whole passages for tubas alone multiply greatly with the addition of the tuba's little cousin, the euphonium. The blend between the euphonium and the tuba is superb (since they are both originally members of the saxhorn family), and the beautiful middle and high range of the euphoniums give this tuba

choir a practical range of about three and one-half octaves. Until now, tuba choir passages in the wind band have normally been written in four voices (two euphoniums, two tubas), but there is no reason why they cannot be scored in more ways than this. I have always stayed at four voices to make sure that there were enough players to cover the parts. Most wind bands carry only two euphoniums. If the standard number were three, then the composer/arranger could safely score for a quintet of three euphoniums and two tubas. Dividing CC or BB♭ tubas three ways gets rather thick and heavy, but if the highest tuba part were played on an F or E♭ tuba, it would sound marvelous. If you are writing for a specific wind band and you do not care whether your music gets into print, then by all means score for as many as you would like. Just remember to keep the intervals larger and larger as you write lower for the tuba choir. Exx. 22–24 contain tuba choir passages using only euphoniums and tubas.

Ex. 22. Fantasy Variations *on a Theme by Niccolo Paganini (Variation V)*

Copyright 1989 by Southern Music Co.

This discussion is merely a brief account of the possibilities of scoring for tubas (and euphoniums) as a section. Scoring possibilities in such a

Ex. 23. Lonely Beach

Copyright 1993 by Southern Music Co.

Ex. 24. Brave Sailors, Valiant Ships

Copyright 1985 by Southern Music Co.

format are limited only by one's own creativity and the playing abilities of any particular wind band. Adding two or three flugelhorns to the tuba and euphonium choir would make it possible to score entire sections of a work in this gorgeous, round, homogeneous sound. The addition of flugelhorns gives the wind band a true saxhorn choir, a color combination that would be a most welcome permanent addition to the wind band.

Scoring Possibilities of the Tuba Section with Other Sections of the Wind Band

The tuba section can generally be scored together with any major choir of the wind band: the double-reed choir, the flute and clarinet choir, the saxophone choir, the entire woodwind choir, and, of course, just about any combination of brasses. The beauty of the tuba section is that it can put a warm, full sound under any of these combinations at practically any dynamic level. The danger in scoring for the wind band is that the tubas are used so much that they lose their effect as an independent color, much as the double basses do in a large portion of the nineteenth-century orchestral repertoire. Constant use of either makes the music sound "gray" and "over-stuffed." After a while, too much "bottom" actually gets to be a bad thing.

A sensible solution to this problem would be to score some passages with only woodwinds (and the double bass—a most necessary addition to any good wind band) on the bass line. This works well in good wind bands, but in younger ensembles, these passages should always be cued in the tuba part (preferably *solo*) to make certain that the bass line is safely covered in any situation. All independent double bass passages should also be cued in the tuba part, since unfortunately, many fine wind bands do not have a double bass.

In most wind band music, the problem lies more in doubling all the low woodwinds with the tubas than the other way around. (Please note the word *doubled* as opposed to *cued*.) All this constant doubling makes the bass line sound rather clumsy and too full, and brings out the "grayness" that I mentioned before. Doubling is understandable in music for very young, inexperienced wind bands because so many of them have few or no tubas, so the bass line must be played all the time by the entire low woodwind section. However, constant doubling in wind bands of better ability is boring and noncreative. A good solution is to score a passage with the exact bass line you desire (for example, bassoons in octaves). Then, if you feel it necessary to cross-cue it in other players, do so. In this instance, perhaps tenor and baritone saxophones in octaves, with euphonium and tuba as a second choice. This gives one the exact sound desired, but the passage is safely cued in the second and, in this particular instance, third choices.

Some composers/arrangers do not believe in cueing at all, which is fine as long as one is working with high quality wind bands with full instrumentation. To write publishable music for wind band, one would be advised to add sensible, tasteful cueing to ensure more (and better) performances of one's works. Cross-cueing is a fact of life in wind band writing; there is no standard instrumentation in the world of school bands. The composer/arranger has no idea what the instrumentation of any particular wind band will be, thus, it is better that the composer or arranger supply the second choice for the bass line than to leave it with the band director, who may have no idea of what color is desired, and, more than likely, will just leave the whole bass line out of the passage.

In most wind band music, the tubas play too much. Constant use of the tuba section makes the music less interesting. The following are some useful combinations of tubas with other sections of the wind band:

1. Tubas with bassoons and low saxophones (written in four-part choir fashion: two or three voices in tubas, plus tenor and baritone saxophones interlocked in the voicing; add a solo euphonium on the top voice to get a fantastic sound).

2. Tubas with saxophone choir (put a soprano saxophone on top and add the euphoniums in the mix to get a very expressive sound).

3. Tubas with horns (used almost like Wagnertuben). Add euphoniums and flugelhorns to this to produce the roundest sound in the world.

4. One tuba scored underneath the clarinet choir (usually doubling the contra-alto clarinet and double bass at the unison). Adds solidity to the sound and gets rid of the fuzziness that sometimes plagues this choir because of bad pitch and immature tone in the lower clarinets.

5. In softer passages, one tuba an octave above the double bass and contra-alto or contrabass clarinet. This is a very "creepy" sound. It is much more interesting and colorful than the standard bass clarinet or bassoon octave doubling. Mark the tuba at least one dynamic softer than the contra-alto or contrabass clarinet to make certain that the tubist does not overpower the other players.

(Tubas with trombones and/or euphoniums and other more standard combinations are not discussed here because of the numerous effective examples of these standard voicings.)

These are but a few examples. Here again, the scoring possibilities are limited only by one's imagination and the abilities of a particular group. It should be added that in all of these combinations, the lowest notes of the passage should be played by at least a portion of the tuba section. Tubas are too powerful to be scored only on inside voices, leaving the low clarinets and/or double bass to play the bottom note. It will not work; it will not sound good. No matter how

"cute" it looks on paper, put at least one tuba on the bottom note (except in combination 5).

SEATING ARRANGEMENTS

IN THE SECTION

The traditional practice of seating tubas by ability from one end to the other is quickly becoming antiquated. There are more effective ways of arranging a section and positioning it onstage so that the players can hear themselves better, both within the section and within the entire ensemble, and can sound and blend better with the rest of the group. The following examples show three and four tubas, the most common numbers of tubas in wind bands.

D C B A or C B A

Figure 1. Standard Seating

Although Fig. 1 is still the most commonly used setup in wind bands, it puts the first player (A) a long distance from the third and fourth players, making it more difficult for them to match pitch, length of notes, and style with the principal. It also makes it more difficult for the principal to communicate verbally with the section during rehearsals. In the seating arrangement in Fig. 2, the principal player has a better chance of hearing the bottom of the section, where most of the playing problems occur. It also gives the second player a real earful of the first tubist's playing, making it all the easier to match pitch, length, and style with the section leader. This setup does not work well with egomaniacs who have to be seen playing first chair, but for the rest of us, this system is far superior to the old "down-the-line" standard seating.

D C A B or C A B

Figure 2. Middle Seating

Fig. 3 shows four players because there is no need for such a setup for three. It places the four tubists in two rows (usually along the outside stage left of the band). The principal sits on the outside of the front row (usually right behind the euphoniums). The United States Air Force Band uses this setup, and it is very effective. It allows all the players to hear better, and it concentrates the pitch and power in a very small space. Note that the third and fourth tubas are seated in the back row between the first and second chairs so that they can see the conductor. This box setup has been used for years by orchestral horn sections.

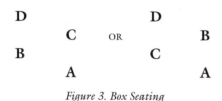

D   D
   C   OR   B
B   C
A   A

Figure 3. Box Seating

Bass Dr. "New Guy" S. Watson J. Barnes
(principal)

Figure 4. Lawrence Community Band Seating

Fig. 4 is a totally illogical setup, by seniority. It is not based on talent, ability, or musicianship. Essentially, the rule is: whoever has been a member of the town band tuba section for longest gets to sit the farthest away from the bass drum!

WITHIN THE WIND BAND

Effective section seating is a combination of musical, logical, and aesthetic decisions. The conductor should seat the tubas close to the instruments they play with most, so as to improve the blend, pitch, and rhythm within the overall ensemble. It does not make much sense to place them far from the rest of the brass section, even if they do play with the woodwinds a considerable amount of the time. Last, but certainly not least, whether consciously or subconsciously, conductors like to set up the wind band so that it has aesthetic symmetry and balance. While these last factors are important, they are not as crucial as the more musically oriented considerations. Most wind bands are seated in one of the following ways: by choirs (woodwind choir in front, brass choir in the back); by layers of octaves (highs in the front, lows in the back); by standard voicing procedures (groupings by voicing); by particular acoustical considerations (setups to fit small or acoustically problematic rehearsal halls and concert venues; this arrangement would differ so much from one room to another that it is not possible to discuss it here).

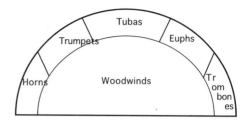

Figure 5. By Choirs. Here the tuba section is placed in the back row.

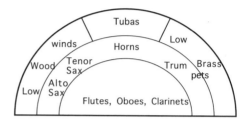

Figure 6. By Layers of Octaves. Here the tubas are placed in the back row with all the other bass instruments.

The setup in Fig. 7 groups instruments who normally play together in close proximity. It takes

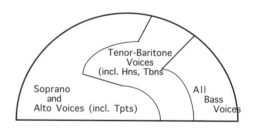

Figure 7. By Standard Voicing Procedures.

a few days for players to get used to such a configuration, primarily because they have never had the opportunity to hear the other instruments playing the same part. Actually, this setup is not far from the arrangement of the symphony orchestra string section, which starts with the highs stage right and goes to the lows stage left. Notice that the tubas are seated on far stage left, much like the double basses in the standard orchestral setup. This setup works fine except when the tubas find themselves in front of the proscenium arch. They will sound too bright and will overbalance the efforts of the rest of the ensemble, because their bells normally point out toward the hall. In this situation it might be best to put the euphoniums on the outside of the row, since their bells normally point in toward the ensemble, and place the tubas farther in the back row to get them behind the proscenium wall. In recent years, the ongoing philosophical differences about wind band seating has been strained to the point where some conductors actually change seating for each piece. That seems a bit excessive, and it makes for some unbearably long concerts (featuring more furniture moving than music). However, the primary concept is sound. There is no reason why a wind band cannot reseat at the intermission, for example, while the audience is out of the hall. If there are three logical seatings for the pieces to be performed on a concert, then why not have two intermissions to allow for the third setup? Logical seating mixed with some common sense render the most effective solutions in this matter.

Team Discipline and Esprit de Corps

The tuba section of the wind band is quite like the offensive line on a football team: the players seldom handle the ball, fans seldom know the linemen's names, but nobody can win without these guys. When professional football Hall of Famer John Riggins was having his best years as a running back with the Washington Redskins, he constantly credited his offensive line (affectionately nicknamed "The Hogs" by Riggins) for every yard he gained. In fact, he took the whole line out to dinner every week because he realized how important their *esprit de corps* and self-esteem were to the success of the entire team. Developing these same traits in a tuba section can be a very fundamental and productive step in building a fine wind band. Here are some practical suggestions for developing a good rapport in the tuba section:

1. Treat them with the same respect you would give to flutists, clarinetists, or trumpeters. Avoid insulting or mocking them and avoid making any sarcastic remarks about "oom-pah-pah," "Tubby the tuba," and all the other hackneyed innuendo used by musical ignoramuses. When the section plays well, the conductor should make a point of complimenting them. Most tuba sections would be astounded if anyone ever said anything nice to them.

2. Pay more attention to them in rehearsal. Tell them what you want to hear, to whom they should listen, and how they can attain the points for which you ask. Do not let them "off the

hook" just because they are tuba players. Conductors give up on the tubas too quickly. Insist that they play just as musically and accurately as any other members of the ensemble. Challenge them, but be specific and encouraging with your suggestions.

3. Insist that the tubas have sectionals. It is difficult to get all the tubas to match pitch, control the length and color of tone, and agree on style in the many unison passages of wind band scoring just by showing up to full-band rehearsals. The conductor can run these sectionals if he or she believes that the individual players need tutoring, but it is usually better to consult with the principal, then let that person run the sectional. It is more time-efficient, and it establishes the section leader as the principal authority figure in the section, rather like a platoon sergeant. Regular sectionals are best but are not always possible.

4. Not all the musical decisions should be made from the podium during rehearsals. Most musical decisions about cut-offs, breath spots in phrasing, intonation problems, line doubling, selection of solo passages, and octave doubling assignments should be made by the section leader, in consultation with the conductor.

5. When a conductor stops to correct the tuba section or to make any sort of musical suggestion, those comments should be directed to the section leader. This reinforces the leader's authority in the section.

6. Encourage the members of the section to be socially active outside of rehearsals and performances. Friendship and pride in what they do is what this is really all about.

For teachers of younger wind bands, the following are some useful suggestions for improving your tuba sections:

1. Do not start students with limited musical ability on the tuba. Look for bright, aggressive youngsters, the ones with some spunk. Do not forget about girls. They make great tubists.

2. Try to furnish your tuba players with good equipment. Supply them with good mouthpieces and decent instruments. Do not expect first-class results on a second-class budget.

3. Teach the students how to maintain and tune their instruments. Insist that they keep the valves oiled and the slides greased. Spend the same amount of time on this as you do on trumpet and clarinet tuning and maintenance and you will see excellent results.

4. Furnish tuba students with recordings of good players. Even better, give them the chance to hear good tubists and good tuba sections by bringing in tuba clinicians or taking the students to hear good college bands or the major service bands. If the kids do not have a model, it is more difficult for them to understand what you are asking for in rehearsal. In tuba playing, concept is everything.

5. Buy the tuba students method books, assign them etudes to prepare, and grade them on their progress. No one ever became a good tubist from playing half notes and whole notes in band parts.

6. If at all possible, try to give students lessons or arrange for them to study privately with a good teacher. Nothing beats personal instruction on the tuba. It is a very specialized instrument, so much so that one can see rapid progress from a bright student under the tutelage of a good private teacher.

7. Have your tuba students play in small ensembles, like brass quintets and brass ensembles. It is good for them to have the opportunity to be the only person responsible for playing a passage in a piece. Tubists who never play in anything but band sections seldom develop rhythmic independence and usually have less confidence and a smaller sound.

8. If you have enough tuba and euphonium players, start a tuba ensemble, even if it is only a trio or quartet. This sort of hands-on, one-on-a-part instruction will pay dividends in your larger ensembles.

9. Above all, remember to encourage them, brag about them, pamper them as if they were oboists or bassoonists. The success of your ensemble depends much more on the quality of your tubists than it does on your double reeds, so nurture them.

Summary

The use of tubas in the wind band is a very complex subject. Most of the suggestions that I have made here do not appear in any textbook of which I am aware. Of course, they are merely my opinions, but being a composer, a conductor, and a broken-down old tuba player myself, I feel comfortable discussing these matters with some authority. My love for the tuba is surpassed only by my appreciation of the usefulness of this instrument en masse in the modern wind band. The tuba has marvelous potential as a solo instrument; it is the unifying element of the modern

brass quintet; it is a crucial factor in the overall sound of the symphony orchestra; but it will always remain most at home where it began: in the wind band.

Norlan Bewley

Top Brass Quartet

Tuba Solo with Band

When writing for solo tuba and band, the primary challenge is to make sure that the solo tuba voice clearly stands out from the band. The tuba will blend in with the band too easily unless care is taken to provide textures and colors that contrast or complement the sonorous tuba sound. The tuba range is the same one that most core accompaniment patterns occupy. In this range it is important to use either instrumental colors that complement the tuba or accompaniment activity that directly contrasts with the solo part and does not compete with it. For example, use saxophones to play sustained chords rather than low brass; use short punctuated and spacious rhythmic accompaniments during technical runs in the solo part; double a lyrical solo passage with the flutes an octave or two higher than the solo tuba. When the other brass instruments are used in an accompanimental role, they compete the most with the tuba in a solo context. Use them with care.

Complement:	Compete:
Saxophones	Trombones
Flutes	
	Trumpets
Other woodwinds	French horns
Percussion	Euphoniums
Harp	Tubas
Silence	Timpani

Tuba Solo with Orchestra

The combination of solo tuba and orchestra allows the solo tuba voice to stand out. The strings are very complementary to the tuba sound. They can be used in a more flexible manner to contrast and complement the solo tuba. Harp and tuba is one of the best combinations possible, whether used in conjunction with the string instruments or not. It is more complementary to the tuba sound than piano. The brass instruments, although fewer in number, will still compete in an accompanimental role unless used

Tuba with Jazz Band

When the tuba is used with jazz band, it is most effective as a color instrument in a melodic or harmonic context. Using it to double the bass or bass trombone part is less desirable. The tuba is very effective at bringing out melodic lines by itself or when doubling the trumpet, saxophone, or flute an octave or two lower. This also works well with piano and guitar. Use it for counterpoint and obbligato lines that move inside the texture.

When writing for tuba and trombone section, use it as a middle voice rather than the bottom voice unless a symphonic effect is desired. Give it the harmonic color tones in chordal figures. In a jazz band, it will do more for the section sound when used in this way than it will as a bottom voice.

The tuba is also effective as a sixth voice in the saxophone section. It will fill out the sax sound when used during harmonized solo sections or backgrounds and works well as the bottom voice. A good tuba player will have the technique required to play this type of passage. The tuba and saxophone sounds are very complementary.

The amplified bass will generally overwhelm the tuba sound if it is doubled with the bass line. If a solo tuba performs with a jazz band, it will need to be amplified. The brass will not compete with the solo tuba in this context, as long as they are not used in a lead capacity while the tuba is being featured.

Tuba Solo with Voices

The tuba has a much lower range than the bass vocalist. To have a bass line under the solo part, the solo tuba has to stay in the bass clef or a piano needs to be used with the voice. Voices are very flexible and will complement or contrast with the solo tuba quite nicely. Use of text and vowel sounds are a major consideration toward this end.

Tuba Euphonium Ensemble

When writing for tuba/euphonium ensemble, it is very easy to score too thickly. A chord voicing normally used in another context will sound twice as thick in a tuba/euphonium ensemble. Octaves and open fifths will sound very full and rich. Keep thirds and any extended harmonies above C_2. Four-, five-, and six-part writing works best.

To give the tubas a clear lead line, either rest the euphoniums or give them spacious rhythmic patterns. If sustained harmony is required, either minimize the rhythmic activity in all of the accompaniment parts or use simpler rhythmic patterns in the bass line. A tuba melody with an active tuba bass line and nothing else will sound much more complete than might be expected. This also helps to break up the texture and provide effective contrast.

Give the euphoniums more rest than the tubas. Playing the upper parts in a tuba/euphonium ensemble is more physically taxing than in other ensemble situations.

Save tuba pedal tones for key points such as climaxes and final chords. This is one of the ensemble's most powerful effects, and it is easily wasted by constantly doubling the bottom part down an octave.

Bruce Broughton

Hollywood Film Composer

When writing for solo tuba, I try to be specific as to whether the instrument should be in C or F. Except for reasons of effect, extreme ranges on the tuba generally are not of much interest to me. I like as much clarity of tone and precise articulation as possible and, for the most part, am not too fond of the pale notes in the upper nether regions (which, to me, always sound like a struggle) nor for the flatulent-sounding ones in the extreme lower. In general, for solo passages I find that the notes in the staff for an F tuba are clear and sonorous, the best "singing" range is approximately F_1 to c'. For the C tuba the equivalent range is a fourth lower.

For lyrical passages that need to move quickly, I prefer the tuba in F, the clarity of which I love, particularly mid-range in the staff. I try to use the C tuba for pieces or passages that call for an overall darker or richer sound, or for anything that needs mass. Agility is not an important consideration, since I find that both instruments are able to perform nimbly all over the staff.

In orchestral writing, unless the tuba is being used to augment the bass line for reasons of mass and weight or unless the specific color of an extremely low note is desired or intended, I normally find it most useful and effective as a bass instrument placed in the lower staff, with a range extended downward from the range indicated above to approximately Ab_1.

Used with the bass trombone in *forte*, a unison note in the lower staff will generally produce greater power and clarity than placing the instruments in octaves, a combination which results in a much more massive sound. In order to free the cellos and support the bass line, like Wagner, I often use the tuba in place of cellos an octave above the basses, particularly in sustained passages.

As far as orchestral color combinations are concerned, the tuba blends remarkably well with everything (tuba and horns in unison, for instance), but the tuba player must understand that he is now a section player and not an independent. Except for instruments of similar aural weight (the bass trombone, for example), I do not, as a rule, feel there is much to be gained by doubling the tuba with any single instrument, such as a bassoon or bass clarinet, Strauss's *Don Quixote* notwithstanding.

Occasionally for a television or motion picture score I have used tubas in groups of three or four as a brass section and have found that, though the sound can be immensely powerful, the greatest problem is that of achieving a uniform performance ensemble so that the tubas will sound like a section rather than like individual players.

Another element of orchestral writing that I have noticed to be effective is to relieve the tuba as often as possible of playing only the bass. Since it is quite agile and has an enormous playing and dynamic range, it literally lightens the orchestration to have the tuba become a melodic rather than a harmonic instrument. In other words, a pianist who is a composer/arranger, should regard the tuba as being a great deal more than the instrument which plays only the notes of the left hand's little finger.

Gary Buttery

The United States Coast Guard Band

My concern with composing or arranging for the tuba rests with the final product—what music is conveyed to the audience and how the vehicle, the tuba, conveys it. There is a wealth of material, old and new, that arrangers and composers have used and can use in writing for the tuba. However, major works for other instruments, i.e., Mozart's *Concerto in B♭* (K.191) for bassoon and orchestra, should be off limits in public performances to tubists and all other instruments besides bassoonists, out of professional courtesy.

The tuba has such a wide variety of range, dynamics, tonal qualities, special effects, and expressiveness that discretion in dealing with transcriptions should be only a minor problem. In my experience, the range of styles possible on the instrument is extensive, and I have enjoyed writing for the tuba from the folk idiom to avant-garde; and, of course, technical as well as lyrical compositions are all at home on the tuba. As a restatement of my initial sentence, if a work is enjoyable for the performer to perform, most likely, it will be enjoyable for the audience to hear as well.

Arthur Frackenpohl

Potsdam College of SUNY *(Professor Emeritus)*

Background: In high school I started on trumpet, but was soon switched to low brass (in order: E♭ sousaphone, BB♭ tuba, euphonium and trombone). At Eastman I wrote a brass quartet but nothing for tuba other than in orchestral writing. While teaching at the Crane School, I transcribed some music for quintets, but it was with the writing of *Brass Quartet* and the *Concertino for Tuba and Strings* that I became interested in further low brass writing.

Range and Technique: The tuba has a large range, from CC to c' (as well as lower and higher). It has excellent agility in the upper register (on the staff)—the instrument speaks more slowly in the lower register, where sustained and slower moving passages are effective—and wonderful lyrical capabilities throughout its range.

Muting: This lowers the sound level considerably and should be used with discretion. In quintet writing, muting should be used with the other instruments muted, although it is possible to use open tuba with the others muted.

Unaccompanied Solos: The best way to avoid balance problems! Baroque music is an excellent source for transcriptions. Much contemporary music is written for unaccompanied tuba.

Solo Instrument: The tuba is an excellent solo instrument with piano, orchestra, and band. It is easily covered, and scoring should be light, preferably in the upper register (pizzicato strings, upper woodwinds, muted brass, upper register of piano). Antiphonal writing works well. When the tuba is in upper register it is possible to have supporting notes below it.

Quintet Writing: The tuba is a good solo

instrument with light support. Doubling with trumpet at two or three octaves with harmonies in between works well. The tuba is a very good foundation instrument and works well in octaves with trombone and in one and two octaves with trombone and horn. A trio of horn, trombone, and tuba is a nice lower choir in the quintet.

Quartet Writing: Writing for two euphoniums and two tubas is more difficult than quintet writing because of the smaller range and fewer tonal colors. Because of muddy textures, octaves and fifths below the staff work better than other intervals.

Band and Orchestra Thoughts: In band writing, a choir of horns, euphoniums and tubas works well. In orchestral writing, the tuba doubles well with cellos and/or bassoons.

I am grateful for the encouragement shown by many tuba and euphonium performers and conductors, as well as by several publishers, especially TUBA Press.

Gregory Fritze

Berklee College of Music

Solo tuba and euphonium/tuba ensembles have become more popular media for composers and arrangers recently. One reason is willingness of the performers to play new works. It is interesting that when I attend a composers' convention the most discussed topic among the participants is the problem of getting performers to play "our music." It is also interesting that a common topic at tuba and euphonium conventions is "how to get composers to write for our instrument." Obviously there are places in the world where factions of these two contingents are bumping into each other and addressing each other's needs. It is very common, however, that a composer will write a piece for a tuba or euphonium/tuba ensemble with less knowledge than he or she has for other instruments. The composer may have written for piano, violin, trumpet, string quartets, full orchestra, even brass quintets; but when it comes to tuba or euphonium/tuba quartet, that is a different situation.

I am happy to receive recognition for having composed many pieces for tuba and euphonium/tuba quartet and ensemble. Over the past twenty years I have placed the double-bar at the end of over thirty compositions and arrangements for this medium. I have also tutored many student composers and arrangers at Berklee College of

Music and elsewhere so they won't have to "learn the hard way," as I often did. With this in mind I am very happy to write this statement on my attitude and approach to composing and arranging for solo tuba and euphonium/tuba ensembles.

When a composer first learns his/her craft in an orchestration class, a common exercise is to arrange a piano piece for different combinations of instruments. Thousands of composers over the last few hundred years have followed this process in their compositional activities. As a rule many (if not most) composers jot down their ideas in a piano-like format (a short score of two or three staves). Many of them test out their ideas on the piano and then orchestrate to larger scores of many staves. I feel that teachers should demonstrate this procedure (I do so in my orchestration classes). There is a problem in choosing examples to show the students how to do this. Everybody knows that Ravel's orchestration of Mussorgsky's *Pictures at an Exhibition* is the most popular transcription of a piano piece. Everybody knows it, and everybody uses it in orchestration class. There are even editions of *Pictures at an Exhibition* that show the piano part below the orchestra score for comparison. An orchestration teacher often says, "This is perfect for my classes—a built-in textbook! It even has a tuba solo—the *Bydlo* movement to learn how to write for tuba!" As all tubists know, Ravel did not write it for the tuba, but for the euphonium! This causes the young composer to think that it is perfectly normal to write a high g#' for the tuba. "If Ravel did it, I can do it."

I suggest that every composer consider this practical range for the tuba: from the second partial to the sixth partial. On a CC tuba this would be from CC to G. Let me reiterate that this is the *practical* range of the tuba. This can also be called the "safe range," or as professional tubists call it the "cash register," where most tuba parts lie. A composer who writes in this range will have the benefit of having the tuba convey the music most easily.

There is an *extended range*, which lies a perfect fourth both below and above the practical range. A good tubist would have little difficulty with these few extra notes of the register, but they can become orchestration problems in some situations. If a composer writes in the extended range upwards, the tuba may project more than the composer wants. It is also more difficult to perform rapid passages in conjunction with other instruments of the orchestra. It is more difficult to play very softly in the upper extended register, hence it could cause a problem of blending with other instruments. The tuba can blend very well acting as a fifth French horn (see Bartók's *Concerto for Orchestra*, second movement), but if it is in the upper extended register, it can overpower the horns if there is only one horn on a part. It is usually undesirable to have the tuba play unison with the trombones when the tuba is in the upper extended range. It is more common to have the tuba an octave lower. This adds support to the melody, especially in louder passages. If a softer unison passage with trombone in the upper extended range is desired, I suggest that it be much less technical. The reason for this doubling would obviously be for timbre. I always suggest that when timbre is the element that the composer wants the listener to be attracted to, the composer must "let the listener be aware of the timbre by letting it settle in." If a passage is too active melodically or rhythmically, then the effect of timbre will not be apparent anyway.

The extended range below the practical range also can have many difficulties. These lower notes often do not project well. They are more difficult to attack with the tongue, hence it is more difficult to play staccato notes, especially at a louder dynamic. It is very desirable for the composer to have the tuba double the bass trombone down an octave. Many tuba parts have been written this way. This is one of the many facets of tuba playing where well-trained tubists have mastered inappropriate demands of the composer. Actually this type of orchestration can be performed very well (see Stravinsky, *Petrushka* mm. 1–2). All orchestral tubists work very hard on the *Petrushka* excerpt, as it is on most orchestra auditions. It should still be noted that this kind of writing is very difficult and awkward to project and should be avoided if possible. The notes below the practical range also take more air to play. A *cantabile* melody can sound very beautiful in this lower register, but it should be at a lower dynamic and have many spaces for breathing (see Prokofiev, *Symphony No. 5*, first movement).

There is also a register that should be followed when a tubist is asked to project a solo. This solo projection range lies between the fourth partial and the eighth partial. It is only one octave but it is the place where a tubist playing a solo will be most comfortable. Since the tuba can be a very expressive instrument, many composers write melodies *espressivo* that should fit well within this

range. A good example is the beginning of the second movement of Mahler's *Symphony No. 1*. The solo projection range is also the area in which tubists find it most comfortable to play vibrato. Playing vibrato above the eighth partial is much more difficult because the upper partials are so close together. Playing vibrato below the fourth partial is often an undesirable effect on a BB♭ or CC tuba. Playing on an E♭ or F tuba allows one to have an effective vibrato down to the second partial (these are corresponding notes to the BB♭ and CC tuba). For this reason, as well as others, many performers choose the F or E♭ tuba for performing a solo. When composing for a particular individual, it is wise to find out on which tuba he/she would like to perform. For an orchestral composition, one must assume that a CC tuba will be used. However, in different countries, different tubas are used in the orchestra. In Germany the F tuba is the most common tuba whereas in England the E♭ tuba is very common. In Russia the BB♭ tuba is very often used as an orchestral staple. The trend during the last part of the twentieth century has been a move toward the CC as the most common orchestral instrument, while the BB♭ is still used most extensively in military bands.

The above ranges are a bit conservative, but are good guidelines for composers writing a tuba part when they do not know who will be playing it. If the performer is known, I strongly suggest that the composer talk with the tubist about more personal practical, extended, and solo projection ranges. William Kraft certainly was in close contact when he composed his *Encounters II* for Roger Bobo. This certainly provided an opportunity for Kraft to write a very difficult, but very idiomatic composition. *Encounters II* goes an octave higher than my suggested extended range. I suggest that composers look at *Encounters II* in order to see how the tuba can play. Many tubists consider it the best solo tuba piece ever written. Even with all the success of *Encounters II*, I would not consider it the standard way of writing for the tuba. An orchestral tubist might be very angry if such writing were put before him/her in an ensemble situation.

A very common problem is not having enough air to play a segment of music. Composers should realize that the tuba is four times as long as a trumpet. This does not necessarily mean that a trumpet can play four times as long without breathing—perhaps twice as long is more appropriate. Tubists compensate for composers not giving them enough breath. Most of us can "cheat" a breath and make it sound smooth, but the composer should still be considerate of this problem.

The tuba is a very agile instrument and should not be compared to the trombone in this aspect. The trombone is much less agile because of its slide. The tuba has the ability to play fast chromatic and scale passages. A good example is the end of the first movement of *Symphony for Band* by Paul Hindemith, where the tuba supports the fast woodwind theme. This theme is very playable on the tuba, although it is very difficult for breathing. I suggest that when rapid scale and chromatic passages are used, that there are adequate spaces for breathing.

Tonguing on the tuba is most easily performed in the practical range. This also goes for double and triple tonguing. Articulations above this range tend to get too "heavy," thus delicate articulations at softer dynamics should be avoided. Articulations below the practical range become more difficult to produce.

The euphonium/tuba ensemble falls into two categories: the large ensemble, with two, three, or more players on each part; and the chamber ensemble, will only have one on a part. A melodic line will sound very different when played by one tuba than by two or more tubas playing the same line. Writing unison tuba lines is the exact opposite of writing unison bassoon lines. Both the bassoon and the tuba blend timbre very well, but where two, three, or more bassoons can blend very easily on a technical passage, two, three, or more tubas will have a lot of difficulty, even with the best players. The tuba can be a very agile instrument, but it lacks definition when compared with the bassoon. A slow melodic line played in unison by several tubas can sound beautiful if it is a slow *cantabile* melody. A composer who keeps this ideal orchestration in mind will be very successful. When the composer moves away from this ideal by increasing the tempo and adding faster articulation (thus causing differences in tonguing), the piece will deteriorate in clarity. The tuba lacks definition more than does the double bass in the orchestra. Many orchestration books caution composers about writing for many double basses in unison. This caution should be amplified for a section of tubas.

Making a distinction between one on a part and several on a part also requires addressing a difficulty factor. If one composes or arranges a piece with the idea that it will be played by a massed ensemble (such as at a TubaChristmas), the composer must undertand that the level of technical ability expected will be very low. There may be professional-level performers in the ensemble, but there are more likely to be many amateur players who have difficulty with intonation, blend, and technical facility. A composer who knows that his/her piece will be played by a massed ensemble should write the piece with these conditions in mind. Most large euphonium/tuba ensembles are not like large string ensembles, which rehearse on a regular basis. I have heard (and have had the privilege to play in) ensembles made up of the world's best euphonium and tuba players, and even these ensembles have difficulty in intonation, blend, and technical facility when everybody gets together in one ensemble. The big euphonium/tuba ensembles at the larger universities sound wonderful, but one will find that their directors choose pieces that make the ensemble sound good. When a composer writes a piece that is above a certain level of difficulty, it is usually played only once and then put in the back of the book, never to be played again.

The chamber ensemble, usually a euphonium/tuba quartet or quintet, is a different story. Many euphonium/tuba quartets rehearse on a regular basis. It is quite common that difficult technical passages are very successful in performance. The most common quartet instrumentation is two euphoniums, an F tuba, and a CC tuba. For the laymen who ask me what a euphonium/tuba quartet (often called the tuba quartet, since the euphonium is thought of as a tenor tuba) sounds like, I always say that it sounds like a men's chorus. The voices of tenor I, tenor II, baritone, and bass actually relate very well to the ranges of the tuba (euphonium/tuba) quartet.

Several common problems come up when a composer writes for the tuba quartet for the first time:

1. No variance in texture. Most composers write for all four instruments to play at the same time. I believe this comes from writing for string quartets, where it is more the norm. Young composers also feel uncomfortable with anything besides four-part harmony. I suggest that harmony in two and three parts be utilized so that not more than 50 percent of the composition is scored for all parts. In the better (and more often performed) brass quintets, this 50 percent rule is usually followed.

2. Taxing the first euphonium. Very often the composer writes the melody in the first euphonium. This is again from the string quartet experience (such as in the early pieces of Mozart and Haydn), where the first violin may have the melody throughout most of the piece. I suggest that the second euphonium also be used to play the upper part. In chamber music of this kind the two euphoniums should be used almost as equals.

3. Writing the F and CC tubas too low. Writing the third and fourth parts below "low interval limits" always creates an undesirable muddy sound. "Low interval limits" is a term for guidelines in jazz (big band) arranging and can be found in any good jazz arranging book. This chart, which was originally meant for saxophones and trombones, is also a good guideline for tubas.

4. Inadequate chord voicings. Muddy sounds often come from open chord voicings. It is usually more desirable to use closed voicings for tuba quartets.

5. Dynamics not used. The tuba quartet can make very effective crescendos and diminuendos. It is very surprising that few tuba quartet compo

I cannot suggest too strongly that composers who have not yet written for this medium talk to performers and also look at scores. From the many compositions that I have composed, I would suggest *Twenty Characteristic Etudes for Tuba* (T.U.B.A. Press) for solo tuba writing and *Prelude and Dance* (T.U.B.A. Press) for euphonium/tuba quartet.

James Garrett

Free Lance Composer/Arranger, Tennessee

My approach to arranging is two-fold: aesthetic and technical. As to the aesthetic aspect, whenever possible, I like to have a "good tone" to work with, one that I like. Having studied Palestrinian counterpoint while at college, I grew to appreciate good voice leading. This applies in instrumental music as well. I try to avoid awkward, 'unsingable' skips when I write an arrangement. Of course, this is not always possible. If the individual parts are well written, the players will enjoy playing them. I try to write parts that I myself would enjoy playing. I feel that if the players enjoy playing the arrangement, then the audience will enjoy listening to it.

As a composer and arranger, I have come to realize that composing and arranging are very similar. Decisions must be made on a regular basis (chord alterations, muted tuba and euphonium effects, etc.) requiring the arranger to be a "composer" of sorts.

In writing for four-part tuba ensemble, I like to keep the voices as far apart as possible, no closer than a perfect fifth between the two lower voices. Anything closer tends to muddy the sound. In the upper instruments, however, the notes can be closer together. Naturally, there are times when a muddy effect is desirable, so then, anything goes.

In some of my earlier works, I tried so hard to avoid muddiness that I was writing the first euphonium part so high that it made everything sound frantic and strained, not to mention putting euphonium players in the hospital with hernias and brain damage. If all parts are in the "meaty" range of the instrument most of the time, the results are usually more sonorous and satisfying. See the example below.

very sonorous   not so good   good   thick, muddy

Finally, I try to be as economical as possible within the context of the effect I am trying to convey. I try to avoid excessive "noteyness." If one note will do, there is no point in using two, although, there are times when a "notey" effect is needed. Writing for tuba ensemble can be largely a matter of trial and error, sometimes requiring extensive revision. So, if you are a young arranger, remember that the notes you write are not set in stone and unchangeable. Be ready and willing to make whatever might be wrong into something right.

Thom Ritter George

Idaho State University

A starting point for considering the practical range of the instrument is the listing found in any good orchestration book. However, composers will discover that the usable range is governed by the size of the instrument and the ability of the player. Large tubas generally have a more sonorous quality on low notes. These instruments are very good for orchestral music; they provide a solid bass note upon which a harmonic structure can be built. On the other hand, I have found the F tuba best for solo writing. It is more agile than the lower tubas. It is able to perform quick and intricate passages with good response. This instrument also has a good lyric solo range, which is strikingly similar to that of a baritone singer. In fact, lyrical musical lines should be designed for F tuba and for the voice in the same way.

Performers should be consulted when the composer is considering unusually high ranges, technical passages, or special effects. The possibilities and results will vary greatly from one artist to the next. As it is with all brass instruments, it is best to conceive musical ideas so that the player is led up to high notes, rather than having to leap for them. Leading improves accuracy in performance and is artistically sound in a purely musical sense. Many players have problems jumping to low tones, particularly extreme pedal tones. For this reason, it is best to lead into the lower range also, especially when there is no rest in the music during which the player can prepare the note.

Tuba performers generally have significantly better endurance than other brass players. Nevertheless, solos are most comfortable when short rests are embedded in the tuba part. This is helpful to the player and will result in a better performance.

Creating changes of color in a longer work (such as a sonata) is a challenge for both the performer and the composer. One of the few limitations of the instrument is its naturally diffuse tonal quality, which can make the music sound the same in every passage. The use of the mute in slow movements, or in other places for that matter, is an effective method of providing a new tone color. A composer is lucky when a player thinks deeply enough about a passage to provide an appropriate tone color for it. The process of constantly searching for new tone colors is one of the most vital attributes of a fine artist.

Tubas are perfectly capable of playing fast music of a virtuosic character, and composers should not hesitate to assign such music to them when it suits the artistic purposes of the work. Many composers are surprised by the beautiful soft notes and passages the tuba can produce. In many contexts, such a note is the perfect textural solution. Prokofiev's many uses of soft tuba notes in orchestral compositions demonstrates how dramatic the instrument can be in quiet settings.

Walter S. Hartley

Fredonia College of SUNY
(Professor Emeritus)

For 35 years I have been writing music featuring the tuba family, and for low brass in general even longer, although I play no wind instrument. I have done so for two reasons: my attraction to the sounds of these instruments; and the persuasiveness of my many low brass playing friends (the late Emory Remington, Byron McCulloh, Richard Myers, Reginald Fink, Rex Conner, Henry C. Smith, Harvey Phillips, C. Rudolph Emilson, Michael Lind, Barry Kilpatrick, and Scott Watson come most immediately to mind, but by no means do these exhaust the list). I have learned an incalculable amount from these individuals, although it would not be easy to specify just what in each case. I would advise those who intend to compose and/or arrange for low brass to cultivate the acquaintance of as many such accomplished musicians as possible.

In general, the technical capacities and limitations of all brass instruments, low or high, is more analogous to those of the human voice than could be said of any other instrumental family. This is particularly true in regard to range (tessitura) and dynamics. Dynamic and tonal control are easiest in the middle of the range, and (mostly) it is hardest to play (or sing) soft high notes and loud low ones. The relation between embouchure and harmonic series presents similar problems in all brass instruments, as does the necessity of sufficient breathing space and resting time.

Anyone who writes for the tuba should be aware that there are several sizes of that instrument; the tonal differences among them are very subtle, but generally, the larger the instrument, the lower (however slightly) the tessitura most appropriate to it. Some solo works work better on the F tuba, and some on the lower ones; I understand that the CC tuba is most favored for orchestral performance, and the BB♭ for band, at least in North America. The "helicon" and "Sousaphone" used in marching bands and sometimes (less fortunately) in concert bands can present some lower-register problems, because they usually have only three valves. The conical bore of tubas results in a tone quality less intense in its higher partials than is the case with cylindrical instruments; thus they are more easily blended with horns and euphoniums than with trumpets and trombones, unless particular care is taken with spacing.

Robert Jager

Tennessee Technological University

Even though the tuba is in the bottom-most range of the musical instrument family, I do not consider it to be solely a "bass" instrument. In fact, much of its beauty and color lie in its middle to upper register, from F to bb. As with any instrument, when taken as a solo, range is not much of a consideration, especially when the tuba possesses a spread of three and a half to four octaves. In an ensemble situation, such as band or tuba ensemble, more care must be given, but even then, the tuba should not be relegated solely to bass or "oom-pah" parts.

I tend to avoid extremely rapid passages in the range below F (F a twelfth below middle c'). Even though these passages are possible by a few outstanding players, rapidity in this low range is not a grateful experience, either for the player or the audience. Exceptions would be acceptable if you wish to have a particular effect. Aside from that, I have little or no concern about range or technical passages.

I also feel that the muted tuba has a lot to offer in the way of color, especially in ensemble situations, and here again, I have used it frequently and freely.

In short, the only limitations that the tuba has is that of the performer, and that of the uninformed, or uninspired, composer or arranger!

Roger Kellaway

Composer and Pianist

After playing double bass for ten years, it has always been easy for me to hear "melody" in the bass register. Because of this advantage I am not afraid of composing a theme in the bottom of the "harmonic register."

When you realize that extended themes can be sung in any register, then the challenge of the tuba becomes more inviting. After all, the tuba says, "Hey—I can sing too!!!"

Regarding range and technical limitations, I have little to say—as most of my writing has been for Roger Bobo or Warren Deck!!

Keith Mehlan

The United States Navy Band

Introduction

The tuba-euphonium quartet has a short history as a serious ensemble for the performance of chamber music (Morris, 1988). Consequently, there is a paucity of literature written for this combination of instruments, and much of it is not reliable, partially because there are no accepted criteria for writing good compositions or arrangements for tuba-euphonium quartet.

The composer or arranger faces several technical problems in writing for this ensemble: Melody lines are often handled with too narrow an approach; there is confusion as to what kind of literature transcribes well for the tuba-euphonium quartet; selecting an appropriate key is important; and one must be familiar with suitable ranges for players of different ages or levels of talent.

This essay examines ways of writing a successful arrangement or composition for tuba-euphonium quartet. Specifically, it will include basic information about the instruments; possible instrumentations for tuba-euphonium quartet or ensemble and the advantages and disadvantages of each; acoustics and ideas on scoring in order to avoid a thick, muddy sound; and ranges for high school, college, and professional euphonium and tuba players. It will discuss the differences between the baritone horn and the euphonium, some literature choices for arrangements, how to select a key signature, melody distribution, and scoring.

Instrumental Ranges

Familiarity with basic instrumental ranges for euphonium and tuba players for different age or talent levels is necessary to ensure the most logical choices for scoring. Table I lists potential ranges for high school, college, and professional euphonium (Behrend and Miles, 1992) and tuba players. *Potential* is the key word, for while it is true that the pitches listed are possibile on these instruments, using pitches in the extended portions of the range can cause problems for inexperienced players. Players trying to force high pitches out of their instruments could cause physical damage to their lips (Bowman, 1983), and players trying to play in the extended low register can produce most unpleasant sounds.

When writing for euphonium, the low portions of the register (shown in Example 1; Miles, 1992) should be avoided.

Ex.1

Although these pitches are well within the range of all tuba ranges given in Table I, they can be played much more comfortably and with a better sound on tuba than on euphonium. However, there are occasions when the euphonium could play pitches in the low register—to add

TABLE 1

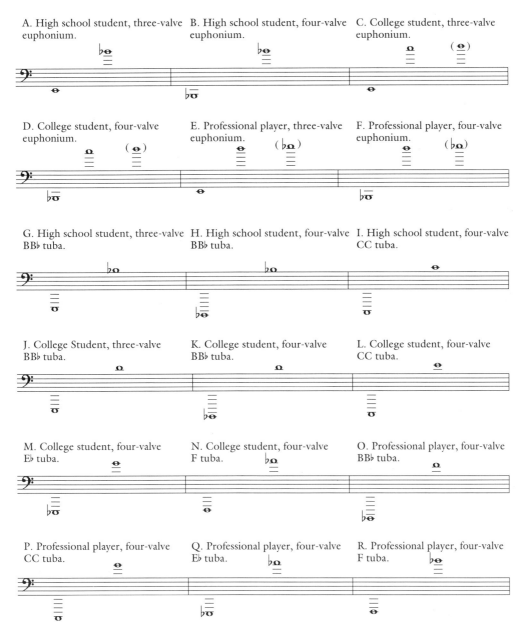

A. High school student, three-valve euphonium.

B. High school student, four-valve euphonium.

C. College student, three-valve euphonium.

D. College student, four-valve euphonium.

E. Professional player, three-valve euphonium.

F. Professional player, four-valve euphonium.

G. High school student, three-valve BB♭ tuba.

H. High school student, four-valve BB♭ tuba.

I. High school student, four-valve CC tuba.

J. College Student, three-valve BB♭ tuba.

K. College student, four-valve BB♭ tuba.

L. College student, four-valve CC tuba.

M. College student, four-valve E♭ tuba.

N. College student, four-valve F tuba.

O. Professional player, four-valve BB♭ tuba.

P. Professional player, four-valve CC tuba.

Q. Professional player, four-valve E♭ tuba.

R. Professional player, four-valve F tuba.

more brightness to the sound (see Example 2) or when scoring a tone cluster to get a percussive sound (see Example 3).

Ex. 2

The Fs in parentheses in the euphonium 2 part are the important notes in this example. With this kind of writing, the expectation is that a thicker sound (the tuba 2 part is a fifth lower than the euphonium part in question) with some brightness will be produced by the ensemble.

Arrangement by Keith Mehlan, "Angels We Have Heard On High." Copyright 1992.

Ex. 3

In this example, the two euphonium parts together will produce a percussive sound that is made more effective by the use of the sixteenth-note rhythm in measure two. The proximity of the tuba 2 part to the euphonium parts highlights this percussive effect.

Ex. 4

Ex. 5

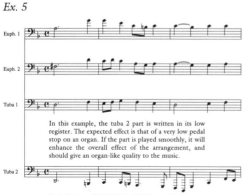

In this example, the tuba 2 part is written in its low register. The expected effect is that of a very low pedal stop on an organ. If the part is played smoothly, it will enhance the overall effect of the arrangement, and should give an organ-like quality to the music.

Bach, J. S. arr. Keith Mehlan, "O Haupt voll Blunt und Wunden." Copyright 1992 Horizon Press, PO Box 483, Newington, VA 22122. Used with permission.

Overuse of the extended high register (see Example 4) can cause fatigue for both inexperienced and experienced players, which can result in intonation and tone quality problems. In those instances when the high register is appropriate, it should be used sparingly or alternated between the euphoniums for lengthy passages.

The extended low register of the tuba can be used very effectively in chorales and in passages from other pieces where the music moves slowly (see Example 5). However, there are two problems with extended low register in quick moving music: in the hands of an unskilled player, the tone quality can be very thick and heavy; and this register is not as facile as the middle register of the instrument, and thus tempos can be unintentionally slowed (see Example 6). As with the euphonium, the low register of the tuba can be used effectively for percussive effects (see Example 7).

Ex. 6

The second and third measures of the tuba 2 part are difficult. Notes in this register can be less responsive than notes a fourth or fifth higher for inexperienced players. If this part were written a fourth or fifth higher, it would be easier for the tuba 2 player.

Ex. 7

This example is similar to example 3. The two tuba parts produce the percussive sound, which is heightened by the rhythm used and the proximity of the euphonium 2 part to the tuba parts.

The tuba's extended high register poses the same challenges as the euphonium's. Fatigue can cause problems of intonation and tone quality, but unlike euphoniums, for tubas trading parts is not always an option. Care must be used in scoring because of the differences in tone quality between F or E♭ and CC or BB♭ tubas. When trading off parts the goal is to match tone qualities so that the listener is not aware that it has been done. If parts are traded between the small and large tubas, and the tone quality difference is great, the purpose will be defeated. Use care in scoring for the tuba in the extended high register (see Example 8).

Ex. 8

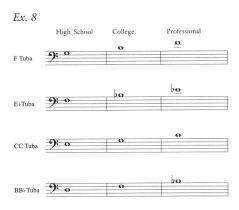

The Timbres of the Baritone Horn and the Euphonium

The baritone horn is a three-valve instrument with the same range as the three-valve euphonium. Generally, its tone is lighter than that of the euphonium, and in the low register it is thinner (Bowman, 1983). The composer or arranger intending to use the baritone horn in the tuba-euphonium quartet will be faced with several challenges. First, the overall homogeneity of sound will be affected by the light, bright tone quality of the baritone horn. When one baritone horn and one euphonium are used the baritone horn may sound out of place. In an ensemble consisting of one baritone horn, one euphonium, one F or E♭ tuba, and one CC or BB♭ tuba, there will be four distinctly different voices with which to work, from the lightest to the heaviest sound of the low brass. The standard tuba-euphonium quartet consists of two euphoniums, one F or E♭ tuba, and one CC or BB♭ tuba. Here the F or E♭ tuba, whose tone quality lies between those of the euphonium and the CC or BB♭, acts as a bridge between them. But this situation makes it

awkward to score the F or E♭ tuba below the CC or BB♭ instrument for an extended period of time. In an ensemble consisting of one baritone horn, one euphonium, one F or E♭ tuba, and one CC or BB♭ tuba, there is no single bridge to join the instrumental tone qualities. In this case, the euphonium serves as a bridge between the baritone horn and the F or E♭ tuba because the baritone's sound is brighter than the euphonium's (Bowman, 1983), but because of this, it would be awkward to score the baritone under the euphonium for an extended period of time. This means that the baritone should be in a prominent role, and it limits the options of the composer/arranger. The sound of the baritone horn can be an advantage if it is a featured instrument, a disadvantage if it is not. For this reason, the baritone horn may be better used in a large tuba ensemble, where overall homogeneity of sound is less critical and scoring may be done differently.

Clef Considerations

Baritone, euphonium, and tuba parts are not always written in bass clef. Baritone parts should be written in treble clef and euphonium parts in bass clef. Tenor clef can be used, but it is not standard. British baritone players read treble clef, and many military band compositions that distinguish between baritone and euphonium parts print the baritone parts in treble clef and the euphonium parts in bass clef. Also, brass band baritone players read treble clef.

When writing for players who normally play in brass bands, use transposing treble clef for all the parts, including the tuba parts. The baritone and euphonium will be written in B♭ treble clef, a major ninth higher than the part sounds (see Example 9). The E♭ tuba will be written in treble clef in E♭, an octave and a major sixth higher than the part sounds (see Example 10). The BB♭ tuba

Ex. 9. Baritone or euphonium transposition from bass to treble clef.

Ex. 10. E♭ tuba transposition from bass to treble clef.

will be written in B♭ treble clef, an octave and a major ninth higher than the part sounds (see Example 11).

Ex. 11. BB♭ tuba transposition from bass to treble clef.

Sounds   Written

The Tuba-Euphonium Quartet

There are several possible combinations of instruments that can be called a tuba-euphonium quartet.

ONE EUPHONIUM AND THREE TUBAS

Advantages:

A good way to feature the euphonium. A good example is John Stevens' *Dances* (1978).

Disadvantages:

Final product may unintentionally sound like a euphonium solo with tuba accompaniment.

Hinders ability to trade melodic lines between like instruments.

May present range difficulties in scoring the high tuba part (see Examples 12 and 13).

Ex. 12. An excerpt of a typical tuba 1 part.

Joplin, Scott, arr. David Werden. *Rag-Time Dance.* Copyright 1979 Whaling Music, PO Box 1212, New London, CT 06320. Used with permission.

Ex. 13. This part, originally for euphonium, is obviously in an uncomfortable register for tuba.

Joplin, Scott, arr. David Werden. *Rag-Time Dance.* Copyright 1979 Whaling Music, PO Box 1212, New London, CT 06320. Used with permission.

Sound Quality:

Homogeneous with three F or E♭ tubas; lowest part may not be prominent enough.

Homogeneous with two F or E♭ tubas and one CC or BB♭ tuba.

Heavy with one F or E♭ and two CC or BB♭ tubas.

Heavy with three CC or BB♭ tubas.

ONE BARITONE HORN, ONE EUPHONIUM, TWO TUBAS

Advantages:

A good way to feature the baritone horn.

Disadvantages:

Using two CC or BB♭ tubas will cause range problems for the high tuba part (see Example 14).

Scoring can be difficult because some options for trading lines are limited.

Tone quality differences between baritone horn and euphonium detract from the general homogeneity.

Sound Quality:

Light with two F or E♭ tubas.

Acceptable in some instances with one F or E♭ tuba and one CC or BB♭ tuba.

Heavy with two CC or BB♭ tubas.

Ex.14. This tuba part lies on the upper limit of the register of the F or B♭ tuba, and is too high for CC or BB♭ tuba.

Ramsoe, Wilhelm, arr. Gary Buttery. *Quartet for Brass.* Copyright 1978 Whaling Music, PO Box 1212, New London, CT 06320. Used with permission.

TWO EUPHONIUMS AND TWO TUBAS

Advantages:

Many opportunities for duet writing between like instruments, and combinations of like and unlike instruments.

Can give one instrument a melody the first time through a strain and the accompaniment the second.

Can split long phrases in the middle between like instruments (see Example 15).

Ex. 15. In this example, the original melody line, which is too long to be comfortably played by one instrument, is split between two like instruments.

Mozart, Wolfgang Amadeus, arr. Keith Mehlan. *Piano Sonata in A Major,* K. 331. Copyright 1987 PP Music, PO Box 10550 Portland, ME 04104. Used with permission.

Melody can be split between instruments note-to-note (see Example 16).

Ex. 16

In the above grouping of the euphoniums, the intervallic leaps may be difficult for both players. The bottom grouping is another idea that results in the same effect.

Bach, J. S. excerpt arr. by Keith Mehlan. *Toccata and Fugue in D Minor.*

Disadvantages:
None
Sound Quality:
Most homogeneous sound with one F or E♭ tuba and one CC or BB♭ tuba.
Light with two F or E♭ tubas; good for vocal jazz arrangements.
Heavy with two CC or BB♭ tubas.

THREE EUPHONIUMS AND ONE TUBA

Advantages:
Good way to feature tuba soloist in an ensemble.
Good way to feature euphonium trio with tuba accompaniment.
Disadvantages:
May present difficulties in scoring the low euphonium part (see Example 17).

Ex. 17

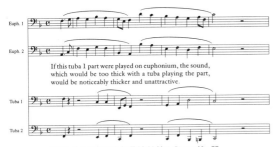

If this tuba 1 part were played on euphonium, the sound, which would be too thick with a tuba playing the part, would be noticeably thicker and unattractive.

Haydn, F. J. excerpt arr. by Keith Mehlan. Quartet No. 77.

Homogeneity of ensemble sound may be a problem.
Sound Quality:
Homogeneous with one F or E♭ tuba.
Contrast in instruments prominent with one CC or BB♭ tuba.

FOUR TUBAS

Advantages:
Many opportunities for duet writing between like instruments, and combinations of like and unlike instruments.
Can give one instrument a melody the first time through a strain and the accompaniment the second.
Can split long phrases in the middle between like instruments.
Melody can be split between instruments note-to-note.
Disadvantages:
Limited effective upper register, especially depending on ability of players and the combination of instruments used (see Table I for range information).
Sound Quality:
Homogeneous, but heavy.

LARGE ENSEMBLES—MORE THAN FOUR PLAYERS

Advantages:
Good for younger players; advantage of safety in numbers.
Overall sound can be tremendously exciting.
Disadvantages:
Composer's flexibility is limited because of the need to write for a choir as opposed to individual instrumentalists.
Sound Quality:
Homogeneous, depending on balance of instruments and parts.

Choosing Literature

In literature selected for arrangements the music must be able to be expanded or reduced to four parts, and it must it be idiomatically logical or present logical solutions to idiomatic problems. Some arpeggio techniques can be performed by a pianist or an organist but not by a tubist. For example, the famous celeste solo in Tchaikovsky's *Nutcracker Suite* is not idiomatically logical for a tuba or euphonium because it is too technically difficult. However, it could be rescored by either altering the rhythm or presenting the arpeggios in block chord form. That is a logical solution to an idiomatic problem. Stevens (1992) says that if the music is singable, it can be arranged.

The following are some styles of music to consider. Scoring is the key to success with all these sources, because they can be scored more thickly than tuba-euphonium quartet literature.

Barbershop quartets are a good idea for arrangements using the baritone horn. They are popular tunes that make good program pieces. Score with care, particularly in the first and second euphonium parts and the first tuba part, because of the potential for thickness. The arrangement does not necessarily have to use original voicings, and depending on how closely they are scored, probably should not.

Chorales and hymns are a good tool for working out ensemble intonation and blend problems, and they can be effective performance pieces, too. Care should be taken in scoring the second euphonium and first tuba parts so they are not too thick.

Folk songs or folk music work well. Arrangements of music by Stephen Foster can be enlivened with alternate chords and rhythms to give a fresh approach to the music.

Patriotic music and children's songs are always popular in concerts for younger audiences, and are easy to arrange.

Jazz works well for the quartet, and especially well for the large ensemble, as anyone who is familiar with the Matteson-Phillips TUBAJAZZ CONSORT will attest. Use tunes from any source. From a marketability standpoint, it is a good idea to include written-out solos for those who do not read chord changes.

Marches are always popular with audiences. While Sousa is usually chosen to be arranged, there are other march composers such as King, Alford, Blankenburg, and Teike, who should not be ignored.

Movie and television themes work well on programs for younger audiences. These familiar tunes are a good way to increase the popularity of the tuba-euphonium quartet as a performing ensemble.

Other kinds of popular music, such as Christmas carols and tunes from musicals and Broadway shows, work well. As an example, Kern's music would be suitable for tuba-euphonium quartet, particularly music from *Showboat*.

Renaissance, Baroque, Classical, Romantic, or contemporary music should be carefully consid-

ered. Singleton's (1984) arrangement of *Three Flemish Dances* is an example of Renaissance music that works well. Bach chorales are quite effective for performance and for ensemble development. Music of Mozart can be favorably transcribed. An example of Romantic music that works well is the Ramsoe *Quartet for Brass* (Buttery, 1978), and in the contemporary period, consider art songs of Strauss, Barber, Wolf, and others.

Rock and roll tunes are fun both to play and to hear. Performers should be encouraged to play the tunes with a rock band. The average listener does not realize that the tuba-euphonium quartet can be used successfully with this kind of ensemble, and given the right arrangement, it will work very effectively.

Band or orchestral music can work well. The music of Holst (the *Suites for Military Band*) is quite effective.

Organ, piano, and string quartet music would be appropriate, depending on the thickness and idiomatic challenges in the music.

Consider vocal or choral music, either classical or popular.

Selecting a Key

Consider the following four factors in selecting a key for an arrangement or an original composition.

1. For whom is the music being written—high school players, college players, professional players, or an ensemble that is known to the writer? A certain level of familiarity with different keys should be expected with each different age and experience group. This does not mean it is a good idea to use all keys, though, because of fingering problems inherent with some keys. If there is a target ensemble in mind, a determination of what will be appropriate can be made.

2. What is the overall range of the piece? Specifically consider the highest note for the euphonium and the lowest note for the tuba. The lowest note for the euphonium and the highest note for the tuba are not crucial because they can be rewritten in scoring and voicing the chords later.

3. Where in the overall range does a particular key put the melody? The tessitura of the key will help to determine the most logical way to divide the melody between instruments and will help to determine where potential scoring problems will occur. These problems include determining

whether a melody will cross below an accompaniment line, whether it will consistently lie below an accompaniment line, or whether it will be so close to an accompaniment line that it will thicken the sound.

4. Consider what kind of fingering problems will a particular key present? Sharp keys are not the only ones that cause problems. Some flat keys work very well for Bb instruments, but not so well for CC, Eb or F instruments (see Example 18).

Ex. 18. While this key should be comfortable for brass instruments, this passage contains fingering difficulties, particularly for the Eb tuba.

Mozart, Wolfgang Amadeus, arr. Keith Mehlan. *Piano Sonata in A Major*, K. 331. Copyright 1987 PP Music, PO Box 10550 Portland, ME 04104. Used with permission.

If the music is technically difficult, making sure it is not too demanding will give it a better chance of being performed.

Handling the Melody

Before scoring the piece, decide how to handle the melody. The following are some some possibilities:

1. Write a feature piece for a particular instrument or individual. This does not mean that one instrument will have the melody throughout the piece. It can be split up and still result in an effective feature piece. A good example is Fletcher's (1983) arrangement of the *Sleeping Tuba Waltz*, which prominently features the first euphonium part.
2. Find interesting ways to split up the melody among all parts. If the melody line is long, divide it in half between two like instruments (see Example 15). This way lines can be kept flowing smoothly rather than being interrupted by breaths.
3. Trade the melody between instruments by phrases. In ascending lines, one possibility is to start the melody in the second tuba and move it up to the first tuba. This effectively gets everyone in the ensemble involved.
4. Move the melody around note-by-note (see Example 16). This will challenge the quartet to develop their listening, balancing, and blending skills, and if it is done effectively, the audience

may not be aware that it is happening. It can also present the arranger with the challenge of writing smooth lines.

After the deciding how to handle the melody, make an outline of the score. This will help keep track of who has the melody and will also help to anticipate scoring and voicing decisions so that changes in the melody can be handled gracefully.

Scoring

Write the score for each instrument several measures or a phrase at a time. Score the melody first, then the bass line, and then the accompaniment lines. The advantage to this is that the parts to be filled in will become obvious and easier to score.

Crossing voices in order to avoid a thick chord is acceptable, but keep the melody line obvious when crossing like voices. This can be accomplished by indicating a lower dynamic for the accompaniment line than for the melody line; or by giving the accompaniment line a significant leap over the melody line so that it is obvious which way the melody is going.

Be aware of thickness, muddiness, or murkiness. Because of the nature of the instruments, thickness is inevitable in tuba-euphonium quartet compositions and arrangements, and that itself is not bad. Use the ear as the guide to determining when thickness becomes excessive, and consider re-scoring or re-voicing the arrangement if necessary.

ACOUSTICAL CONSIDERATIONS

It is helpful to look at the acoustical causes of thickness, its origins, and ways of avoiding it. Thickness is caused by scoring two or more voices of the quartet too close together within the first five pitches of the harmonic series. Generally speaking, below a certain point in the register, scoring tuba parts in thirds will cause thickness (see Example 19), and if there are two stacked thirds below a certain point in the register in the same chord, thickness will result (see Example 20).

Ex. 19. Do not score thirds for tubas below this point.

Ex. 20. The stacked thirds in this example will always result in thickness.

John Stevens lecture. "Composing and Arranging for Tuba Ensemble." May 13, 1992.

I believe that thickness in tuba quartet compositions and arrangements is a result of tones which exist in the sounding chords but are absent from the score. When two tones are sounded together, a third one, called the *difference tone*, will result (Asmus, 1978). This is a simplistic statement and not entirely accurate. Actually, a wide range of tones, called *combination tones*, will be present (Olson, 1969). I am particularly concerned with the *first-order difference tone* (Asmus, 1978) because of all the combination tones, it is the one heard most frequently (Plomp, 1965) and easily (Benade, 1960; Greenfield, 1990). Asmus (1978) states that difference tones may have an effect on perceived tone quality. I believe that the first-order difference tone is what causes thickness in tuba-euphonium quartet music.

If there is a note of frequency f_1, and it is sounded with a lower note of frequency f_2, the first-order difference tone, or more simply the difference tone, can be determined by subtracting f_2 from f_1 (Asmus, 1978) (see Example 21). If three tones are sounded simultaneously, three difference tones will result (Leuba, 1980) (see Example 22). To carry this one step further, if four tones are sounded together, six difference tones will result (see Example 23).

Ex. 21

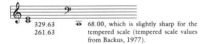

329.63
261.63
68.00, which is slightly sharp for the tempered scale (tempered scale values from Backus, 1977).

Ex. 22. When sounded together, the three notes in measure one will produce the difference tones in measure two. There are two occurrences of the difference tone in parentheses.

Ex. 23. The four notes in measure one will produce the six difference tones in measure two. There are two occurrences of the difference tone in parentheses.

My hypothesis is based on the spacing of pitches within the voicing chosen: 1. If two or more occurrences of the same difference tone are lower than the fundamental of the harmonic series of a chord when the top three voices are in a closed position, the chord will have a thick,

muddy quality. 2. If two or more occurrences of the same difference tone are lower than the fundamental of the harmonic series of a chord, or if there is one difference tone that is lower than the fundamental of the harmonic series of a chord and that difference tone is caused by the two lowest pitches of the voicing in an *open* position, the chord will have a thick, muddy quality. Three rules can be drawn from this hypothesis, and will be used in the examination of chords in both closed and open spacings. The key of F major will be used, and chords will be examined in root position, first inversion and second inversion.

Rule 1. If a voicing produces two or more difference tones below the fundamental of the chord, the voicing will sound thick and muddy.

Rule 2. If a voicing produces one difference tone below the fundamental of the chord, and that difference tone is produced by the two lowest voices of the chord, the voicing will sound thick and muddy.

Rule 3. Any voicing that does not fall into the above rules will have an acceptable sound.

In Table II, the voicings in Letters A, B, D, E, and F are impractical because they are scored so low for the top two instrumental parts. The ear would reveal that these voicings will be thick and muddy, but there is a definite, identifiable problem with each voicing. Specifically, there are either two or three occurrences of the "C" difference tone below the fundamental of the chords. The "C" difference tones are produced by each group of pitches—the two bottom, the two middle, and the two top—being stacked within the first five pitches of the harmonic series. Any time this happens, the voicing will be thick and muddy. The voicing in Letter C is also too thick to be practical even though all the pitches of the voicing are well within the instrumental ranges of the instruments of the tuba-euphonium quartet. The problem with this voicing is the two "C" difference tones below the fundamental, which are caused by the bottom three pitches of the voicing being stacked in thirds within the first five pitches of the harmonic series. Any time this voicing is used, the sound will be unacceptably thick and muddy.

All the voicings in Table III have a single "C" difference tone below the fundamental that is produced by the bottom two pitches of the chord. Even though the spacings of all these voicings are fairly open, I maintain that because of the presence of the difference tone below the fundamental these voicings will be thick and muddy. In Rule 3 voicings, it will be shown that some voicings have a difference tone below the fundamental and are considered acceptable. I believe that this is a result of the combination of instrumental timbres in different registers. The combination of the lowest like voices in close spacing will produce a thicker sound than will the combination of unlike voices in the middle of a chord.

Table IV shows a representative sample of Rule 3 voicings. The voicings in Letters A, B, and C have one difference tone below the fundamental, which is produced by the two middle voices and is acceptable. The voicing in Letter D has one difference tone below the fundamental, which is produced by the bottom two voices, but because the chord is in a closed position, this difference tone is acceptable.

The voicings in Letters E, F, and G produce three fundamental difference tones. The voicing in Letter E is significant because it reveals that it is not possible to produce a difference tone below the fundamental in an open spacing with the bottom two pitches an octave apart. This is so because of the position the pitches occupy on the harmonic series. Intervals within a perfect fifth or less, which are used within the first five steps of the harmonic series with chordal pitches added between the steps of the series, can produce difference tones below the fundamental. One must be careful in scoring chords in this area. The voicing in Letter G is interesting because of its lowest written note. This second inversion spacing produces three fundamental "F" pitches in the difference tone because of the way it is stacked. Notice that the voicings of Letters E, F, and G are based strictly on the steps of the harmonic series. This is significant because pitches included in the voicings that are not in the steps of the harmonic series can create difference tones that are below the fundamental, causing thickness. Also notice that the difference tones produced by each voicing are the same.

The voicings in Letters H through R all produce two fundamental difference tones and produce a full, rich sound. Notice the similarities in the difference tones produced between Letters H and O, I and P, J and R, and L and N. It may be that these voicings produce similar sounds.

TABLE II

Rule 1 voicings. They have multiple difference tones below the fundamental of the harmonic series of the voicing. Difference tones are in parentheses.*

A. Closed position. B. Closed position. C. Closed position. D. Closed position. E. Closed position. F. Open position.

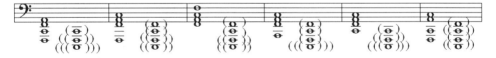

*Calculations of the difference tones were made either using the harmonic series based on steps of 100 CPS (cycles per second, or Hertz) following Leuba's (1980) example, or were made using frequencies of the tempered scale (Backus, 1977) when reasonable approximations could not be made.

TABLE III

These voicings all have one difference tone below the fundamental that is produced by the bottom two pitches of the chord. Difference tones are enclosed in parentheses.

A. Open position. B. Open position. C. Open position. D. Open position. E. Open position.

TABLE IV

These voicings, listed from heaviest to lightest in sound, are all acceptable.
Difference tones are enclosed in parentheses.

A. Closed position. B. Closed position. C. Closed position. D. Closed position. E. Open position. F. Closed position.

G. Closed position. H. Open position. I. Closed position. J. Closed position. K. Closed position. L. Closed position.

M. Closed position. N. Closed position. O. Open position. P. Closed position. Q. Closed position. R. Open position.

S. Open position. T. Closed position. U. Open position. V. Open position. W. Open position. X. Closed position.

Y. Open position. Z. Open position. AA. Closed position. BB. Closed position. CC. Open position. DD. Closed position.

EE. Open position. FF. Open position. GG. Open position. HH. Open position. II. Open position. JJ. Open position.

KK. Open Position.

The voicings in Letters S through DD all result in one fundamental difference tone and produce a good sound. There are similarities in difference tones produced between Letters U and W, and Letters Y, Z, and AA.

Letters EE and FF are unique because no fundamental difference tone is produced. The reason is that there is an octave between the two lowest pitches of these voicings, and the octave will produce its lowest pitch as its difference tone.

The voicing in Letter GG produces three difference tones that are the lowest pitch of the voicing.

The voicings in Letters HH through JJ produce two difference tones that are the lowest pitch of the voicing, and the voicing in Letter KK produces one difference tone that is the lowest pitch of the voicing. This will be the lightest sound in terms of difference tone production.

While calculating the difference tones can tell a lot about whether the chosen voicing will be muddy, I believe that the final guide has to be the discriminating ear of the musician. Thickness is acceptable if it is not excessive.

The Audibility Issue

Much study has been done on the perception of difference tones. According to Helmholtz (1954), they are most easily heard when they are less than an octave apart. Campbell and Greated (1987) and Greenfield (1990) quantify this by placing a limit of about a perfect fifth on the original tones. Olson (1969) states that the difference tone must be between 20 and 20,000 Hz and 0-130 dB. Plomp (1965) states that the difference tone becomes audible when the primary tones are about 51–57 dB (Asmus [1978] requires 70 dB or greater), and since lower frequency tones more easily cover higher frequency tones, the difference tone is the combination tone most easily heard. Greenfield (1990) notes that the difference tone is most obvious when the two original tones are high in pitch. Lundin (1953) believes perception is best when the original tones are between 500 and 2,000 cps.

Hearing difference tones in a tuba-euphonium quartet composition or arrangement may be a challenge, according to the studies of Greenfield and Lundin (1953). Our inability to hear them does not mean they do not exist. Asmus (1978) believes difference tones occur often in performance, and both he and Olson (1969) believe that difference tones affect the perception of tone quality. Winckel (1968) states

that difference tones are important to the overall sound in that they can reinforce the fundamental. These statements support the belief that difference tones have a great deal to do with the issue of thickness and muddiness in tuba-euphonium quartet music.

There are several ways to avoid thickness and muddiness. Try to voice chords according to the harmonic series of the fundamental of the chord. This will force space into the potential voicings of the chords. When voicing according to the harmonic series is not possible, determine which difference tones will result from the voicing chosen, and try to use a voicing that does not result in multiple difference tones below the fundamental of the root of the chord. Use caution in the first five notes of the harmonic series (see Example 24).

Ex. 24. There are two ways to look at this series of pitches. The first is to recognize that it is a harmonic series starting on the second harmonic. The fundamental is essentially unusable. The second is to view this series as a harmonic series with added, functional notes. Regardless of how it is viewed, this is the area in which to be careful.

Recommendations for Future Researchers

There is a need for more commentary on composing and arranging for tuba-euphonium quartet, in such areas as writing for specific combinations of instruments, writing for players of specific age and/or ability levels, and comparisons of different styles or genres to see how suitable they are for this ensemble. Because the tuba-euphonium ensemble is relatively new, the field is wide open for study, and if proponents want to see an improvement in the quality of literature being written, study should be encouraged.

There is also a need for further study of difference tones and their relation to music performance. According to White and Grieshaber (1980), most earlier research used sine tones as the stimuli. In order to determine if there really is a relationship between difference tones and tone quality, musical instruments should be used. It has already been stated that perception of difference tones is best when the original tones are between 500 and 2,000 cps (Lundin, 1953). The upper region of the tuba register starts at about 261 cps, or c (the piano's middle "C"), and is well below this range of best perception, but that does not mean that difference tones have no effect on tuba performance. Scientific study is necessary in order to determine this, and to provide a definitive explanation of thickness and muddiness and how it can be avoided in tuba-euphonium quartet literature.

Bibliography

Asmus, E. P. "Perception and Analysis of the Difference Tone Phenomenon as an Environmental Event." *Journal of Research in Music Education* 26 (1978): 82–89.

Baker, Mickey. *Complete Handbook for the Music Arranger.* New York: Amsco Music Pub., 1972.

Behrend, Roger, and David Miles. Personal interview, 18 Sept. 1992.

Benade, Arthur H. *Horns, Strings and Harmony.* Garden City: Anchor Books, Doubleday & Co., 1960.

Bowman, Brian. *Practical Hints on Playing the Baritone.* New York: Belwin Mills Publishing Corporation, 1983.

Campbell, M., and C. Greated. *The Musician's Guide to Acoustics.* London: Dent, 1987.

Greenfield, Jack. "Tones Created by the Ear." *Piano Technicians Journal* (August 1990).

Helmholtz, Hermann. *On the Sensations of Tone.* New York: Dover Publications, 1954.

LaBarbera, John. "Turn Ho-Hum Tunes Into Show Stoppers: Basic Tools For Better Arranging." *Jazz Educators Journal* 23 (Summer 1991)

Leuba, Christopher. "A Study of Musical Intonation." *Brass Bulletin* 32 (1980).

Lundin, Robert W. *An Objective Psychology of Music.* New York: Ronald Press, 1953.

Miles, David. Personal interview, 24 Nov. 1992.

Morris, R. Winston, "The Evolution of the Tuba/Euphonium Ensemble." *The Instrumentalist* 43 (1988): 15–17.

Olson, Don. "Musical Combination Tones and Oscillations of the Ear Mechanism." *American Journal of Physics* 37 (1969).

Plomp, R. "Detectability Threshold for Combination Tones." *The Journal of the Acoustical Society of America* 37 (1965).

Rimsky-Korsakov, Nikolay. *Principles of Orchestration.* New York: Dover Publications, 1964.

Stevens, John. "Composing and Arranging for Tuba-Euphonium Quartet." Paper presented at the International Tuba-Euphonium Conference at the University of Kentucky, 13 May 1992.

Turkel, Eric. "Arranging: Checklist for Strong Arrangements." *Keyboard Magazine* 17 (April 1991).

Wenner, Claude H. "Intensities of Aural Difference Tones." *The Journal of the Acoustical Society of America* 43 (1968).

White, G., and K. Grieshaber. "On the Existence of Combination Tones as Physical Entities." *Journal of Research in Music Education* 28 (1980).

Winckel, Fritz. "Optimierungsprozesse in musikalischen Strukturen." In *Aspekte der Neuen Musik,* p. 112. Kassel, 1968.

Alfred Reed

University of Miami

Writing effectively for the tuba, whether as a solo instrument or a member of an ensemble, large or small, seems to me no different, basically, than writing effectively for any other instrument; the writer's main concern is with two factors: *technique* and, for want of a better word, *style.*

Technique is relatively easy to define and talk about in specific terms. Such matters as range (both overall possible range and most effective playing range), articulation, valve mechanisms and their effect on articulation, fingerings, breath control in slurred phrases, colors and effects obtainable in the different registers of the instrument, the different models of tubas currently available. All of these have been explored in some depth during the past 40 years, with meaningful results. A glance at the section dealing with tubas in Cecil Forsyth's *Orchestration,* one of the standard works on the subject, last revised in 1935, will show just how far we have come in our thinking and practice concerning the tuba.

The second factor, however, which I have termed *style,* is a more difficult concept to grasp, i.e., much more elusive to pin down in specific terms. Yet, once we have gone past the technical matters, it is probably the most important of all.

I can best demonstrate what this word *style* means for me by recalling one of the most telling points made by my teacher Paul Yartin, with whom I was studying when I was still a teenager! We were analyzing Debussy's *Afternoon of a Faun* from the point of view of the instrumental scoring. After we played through the famous opening of the piece by the unaccompanied solo flute, up to the point where other instruments first join in, Yartin asked, "Now just how do you think Debussy conceived this single line? Did he just hear the pitches and the rhythm, wrote them down, and then wondered about which instrument was to play them? After all, that line could be played by several instruments most effectively; it lies well within their normal and therefore most effective playing registers. It could be played by an oboe, English horn, clarinet, muted trumpet, solo violin or viola—even by a saxophone. Do you think that Debussy, having jotted down the pitches and rhythms, then proceeded to imagine all of the above possibilities, one by one, imagining the line in each of those tone colors and finally coming to the conclusion that, well, it had better be a flute? Is that the way it happened? No, no, not at all! Debussy heard that melody, those pitches and rhythms, in the flute color from the very beginning; he conceived the musical line in terms of that specific color from the first. He did not write the line first and then color it in by the numbers!"

This left an indelible impression on me. I can still hear his voice after more than 50 years, making this point, trying to get me to see that the secret of successful instrumental writing went beyond the purely technical aspects of playing the written (or improvised) sounds well; that colors imparted to the basic pitches and sounds by the individual instruments for which they are written is as much a part, an original part, of the total musical structure as its melodic, rhythmic, and harmonic components and not something later as a sort of embellishment.

Looked at in this way, instrumentation, for whatever combination of instruments, or even solo instruments, becomes a truly creative part of composition itself, sometimes even more so than the pitches, rhythms, and harmonies making up the music. Consider that more than half of the 90 themes that have been identified by analysts and commentators over the years as being the building blocks of Wagner's *Ring of the Nibelungen*, sixteen and a half hours of music, are nothing but out-and-out bugle calls or simple variants of them. Think of the Fafner motif itself, which twists and winds like the dragon it is meant to portray, in the sounds and color of the tuba and Wagner tuben, even though it is also heard, at times, in other instruments. And for sheer powerfully dramatic effect, take the entrance of Hunding in the first act of *Die Walküre*. The four Wagner tuben and contrabass tuba thunder out the three bars of his motif in five-part writing with a sinister force and brutality of expression impossible to achieve with any other tone color, even though this same motif is heard in several other sections of the orchestra during the first two acts.

Think of the second section of Respighi's *Fountains of Rome*, where one can almost *see* the glistening water spray, mist, and droplets of the Neptune Fountain cascading in the bright noonday sun through the colors of the music, not just in its melodic lines, rhythms, or harmonic underpinnings. And the virtual kaleidoscope of constantly shifting colors in Rimsky-Korsakoff's "oriental" works, such as *Scheherazade* and *Le Coq d'Or*, where the traditional diatonic melodic lines and chords seem to have been dipped in a rainbow of exotic colors that make them appear as though coming from another world. This is creative instrumental writing at its finest and this is what is almost impossible to teach or pass on, no matter how hard one may try.

For the aspiring writer for the tuba, as for any other instrument or groups of instruments, one can only suggest the constant listening to works of all kinds, all types, both with and without score in hand. Strangely, I would advise first listening to the music without the score, trying to picture what the sounds would have to look like on the manuscript or printed page; what the composer/arranger had to write down to obtain the sound being heard. And then, after repeating this procedure several times if necessary, listen to the music once again, with score in hand, to see whether what you imagined corresponds to what was actually written at each point. If it does not, ask yourself why.

If, in listening to any performance, live or recorded, you hear a sound, an effect, an instrumental combination, anything that captures your attention and makes you ask, "What is that? How did the composer get this?" You should get hold of the score, as soon as possible—while the sound is still fresh in your ear—and see just what was done to obtain it. In my own experience, such an occurrence is a crucial learning opportunity if only because whatever it was that produced this effect in the music affected me as strongly as it did.

No composer, arranger, or orchestrator can experience any and all possible sounds resulting from choices and combinations of various instruments in the writing and scoring of every conceivable type of musical texture; there is always something to be learned in the work of others, some little quirk or unusual sound, some individualistic approach to the combining of differing tone colors that you have never thought of, some trick in the handling of lines and chords that produces an arresting and artistic sound that just reaches out, "grabs you," and fairly forces you to inquire further about it. My advice is to do just that, immediately and fully.

I believe that all writers build up a sort of musical glossary, or index, of instrumental sounds, singly and in combination, in their minds as they go along, and that this kind of vocabulary enrichment continues throughout one's career, just as with a novelist or a poet. After all, music is nothing but another language: a language of non-verbalized sound (except, perhaps, for the singing of a text), and it, too, experiences a constantly expanding vocabulary and grammar.

As to technique, the saying goes that every writer develops his or her own as time, experiment, error, and success are experienced in actual work. It is sometimes difficult to separate technique from style; one is bound up with the other, and the more successful the writer's music, the more this duality of technique and style, working together, will be seen to account for it.

My own instrumental technique is based on adherence to a principle first brought to my attention, again by Paul Yartin when we were looking at the orchestral writing of the Haydn-Mozart period, the so-called Classic style. Yartin pointed out how much of the time the parts these two masters wrote lie in the middle registers of the various instruments. Consequently, they are relatively easy to play, and sound well as a result. Extreme ranges were to be avoided except for special effects, and the fewer times such effects were heard, the greater their effect would be. Yartin's expression was that all the instrumental parts and lines written on this basis would be "happy" with one another and would sound like a "big, happy family where everyone gets along and goes along with everyone else." Is there a better way to describe the overall effect of Mozart's instrumental music, with its perfect balance between means and ends? I doubt it.

To my ears, the range between the G_1 and b♭ is the most effective for all four of the tubas I find myself writing for; the double BB♭, double CC, F, and E♭, in sectional work in orchestra and band. In my *Fantasia a Due*, the only solo work I have written so far for the tuba, I expanded this range upward to the e', thereby giving the advanced or professional player an opportunity to demonstrate dexterity in this area.

As a brass player (trumpet was my principal instrument), I am very concerned with the contrasting effects of tonguing articulations on the one hand and *sostenuto* on the other, and especially in the case of the large-bore lower brasses, the effect of tempo on each. I am a firm believer that no performer in any group, large or small,

can really hear what the overall effect of the music produced onstage is out in the audience, no matter how keen their ear or how hard they listen while the group is performing. The reason is that the acoustical conditions obtained in the hall, room, or whatever space it may be (including the outdoors) add a dimensional quality to the sound of each performer and to the overall sound of the group. No matter how many performers there are onstage, there is always one more performer in the group, and that is the room itself.

Under such inescapable conditions (the laws of physics do not recognize even the greatest writing or performing talent; alas, it is the talent that must recognize and work with them if anything of value is to be accomplished), we realize that clarity is indispensable for successful performance. The audience must hear it, literally every second of the time, without the slightest effort on its part. Must hear what? The musical texture that the writer has created, with each component in place and perfectly balanced with every other element. And it is the three interrelated factors of articulation, *sostenuto*, and tempo that, working together in perfect balance, make this possible.

Writers of music for wind instruments who have never studied or played one themselves should be aware that what the bow arm is to the string player, the tongue is to the wind player. Especially in faster tongued passages, such as staccato eighth- and sixteenth-note figures, but also in passages where the notes are not slurred or connected in any way, the writer should literally tongue the notes he is writing as he is writing them, in order to see how the tones will be produced on the instrument for which he is writing. Nowhere is this more true than in the case of the tuba. All wind players, woodwind or brass, have at their command three basic tonguing attacks: the so-called "ordinary," or normal attack; the hard, "marcato" attack; and the soft, legato-tongue attack. These attacks must echo in the writer's ear as he conceives and notates each passage. Only then can he correlate the clarity of the texture he wishes with the proper tempo in which to achieve it, first, for the successful realization of the music in the ears and minds of the audience, not just in those of the performer onstage, and second, for the style, that feeling of inevitable "rightness" when the listener feels that the music and the instrument producing it are perfectly matched. The opening flute theme of *Afternoon of a Faun* could not have been conceived in any other way. In other words, do we accept an example or passage as a piece of real tuba music, or is it just music played, even if superbly, by a tubist of great technical achievement?

No easy answers here, I am afraid. The overwhelming success of our modern methods of instruction, the production of first-class instruments on a scale never before seen, and the present large pool of skilled students lead one to believe that almost anything can be played on the tuba today, even what as recently as 25 years ago would have been declared "impossible." It is tempting, therefore, to say that anything that can be performed on the instrument is ipso facto "good" tuba music, just because it can be accomplished. But beyond the technical achievement must also come the musical, the artistic achievement, without which all of the purely technical virtuosity will leave us a bit cool, even depressed. It is like fireworks: a dazzling display for a few wonderful moments and then just darkness once again, nothing of the lasting comfort and pure joy that the performance of a fine piece of music brings us regardless of how difficult the technical performance may be for the player. With the technical frontiers seemingly being pushed back with each passing week, the audience is no longer as dazzled by the virtuosity as in former times, when it responded instinctively to the technical challenges the performer was overcoming onstage. Today, with each new soloist able to play a little louder, faster, and higher than the last one, the average audience, cannot recognize the next step in technical virtuosity. The net result is very much that of watching highly trained animals at a circus or aquarium perform dazzling feats of no real or lasting value; we are entertained while watching them "do their thing," but once the show is over, we quickly forget the whole experience.

Even though I was trained as a brass player myself, I have learned the danger of imagining long, lyrical, sustained melodic lines, and writing them down with slurs of impossible length. Speaking of the bassoon, Forsyth says in his *Orchestration*, "Wagner's terrific slurs that stretch so magnificently across his pages like the Rainbow-Bridge of his own imagining are a sheer impossibility except to a race of giants." If this be true of the double reed instruments, which have always been able to sustain a slur longer than any other wind instrument, how much more does it apply to the tuba? No matter how long a slur is written, the player will have to break it up according to his capacity to sustain the notes, their intonation, and the required dynamics of the passage. Skilled tubists, like string players, whose bows must change direction at some point, are adept at disguising such breaks in *legato-sostenuto* passages, so that the listener barely notices them. The more a writer is aware of such matters, and accepts the limitations they impose on his unbridled, fiery, heat-of-the-moment creative imagination, the better his music will sound, both technically and stylistically; the less time it will take in rehearsal; and the greater his respect from both conductor and performer. Correct phrasing, to me, is a matter of life and death as far as style is concerned; and because of this it should not be left by the writer to mere chance and the individual taste of the performer—although I must also admit that many performers are more likely to make better decisions than several writers I know!

Finally, a word about keys, where tonal music is predominantly concerned. This is a matter of great and almost continual disputation. Just as with fingerprints, no two human beings have exactly the same physical/mental hearing/comprehension systems, and therefore no two people hear or comprehend the same sound in exactly the same way. So I can only offer here what I myself hear in actual performance, or in my mind's ear when I am creating something. In tonally oriented musical textures, the brasses, almost all of which are built in the so-called flat keys, tend to sound extremely brilliant to me when playing in the sharp keys. I once took a relatively simple piece of music and scored it for the same combination of instruments, with the musical texture untouched and only the keys changed from one version to the next. Was it only my own imagination that the brasses sounded more brilliant in the versions written in the sharp keys than in the flat keys, even though one or two of the flat-key versions were actually higher in pitch? Was I only trying to convince myself of something I already believed? I cannot tell today, but I do know that since then, whenever I have written a piece in the sharp keys, especially D major and A major, I have enjoyed a feeling of sparkling brilliance from the sound of the brasses and the woodwinds, even though the technical problems caused by the use of these keys were sometimes more demanding.

And so, after studying all the fingering charts, the overtone series, the manufacturers' manuals and, most of all, the works of the great masters of instrumentation, the contemporary student, and even the professional writer, must maintain an open ear, an open mind, and be willing to keep learning his craft, with the hope that his music will be stylistically and artistically held up as a model for the next generation.

Verne Reynolds

Eastman School of Music

We live and work in a remarkable time. At the close of the twentieth century, tuba playing, musically and technically, is at a very high level. More people play the tuba, instruments are better, instruction is widely available, tuba recordings are abundant, and information about the instrument and its literature is obtainable through the *TUBA Journal* and other publications. The tuba is no longer confined to the narrow path of the bass voice in the orchestra or band but is a vital member of the chamber music community, and on college campuses it is often heard in full-length recitals. Is it possible that this rosy picture indicates that we are near the beginning of a true golden age of tuba playing? Will its arrival depend upon a large and continuous flow of new works of the highest quality?

There is no escape from the fact that tuba literature has no Mozart concerto, Beethoven sonata, Liszt rhapsody, or Brahms intermezzo. While pianists can train on a diet of Bach inventions, Haydn sonatas, and Chopin etudes, there are no equivalents in the tuba world. Eighteenth- and nineteenth-century pianists who composed wrote for their own instrument. Nineteenth- and twentieth-century tuba players have not done so. Therefore, since tuba literature has very little past, we must provide for the present and future. New works of excellent quality are needed in method books, etudes, solo recital pieces, chamber music, concerti, and works with voice or voices, strings, woodwinds, piano or pianos, percussion, tape, tuba ensemble, and whatever else human creativity can bring into existence. There are no limitations except those occasioned by lack of imagination, skill, industry, and intelligence.

Tuba players must shoulder a good share of the burden by their willingness to become producers and not merely consumers of the music they play. While no tuba player has ever suffered any permanent damage from applying pencil to staff paper, there are other ways of enriching the literature. As students, tuba players can encour-age fellow students to write for them. Brass players and composers should know each other's work, for each has much to offer the other. Composers must learn, invent, and store a vast treasury of sounds, colors, combinations, and balances; what better way to do so than by consulting fine players? Performers, likewise, must constantly expand their knowledge of new notation and contemporary composition techniques so that their vision is always forward; symbiosis is defined as an association which is advantageous, necessary, and not harmful to either party. Later, during one's professional years, it is even more necessary for this partnership to thrive, since the mature player is more likely to be in a position to commission or otherwise encourage the creation of new masterpieces. The giants of the tuba have done so, and we are all grateful for their efforts.

For the composer there are some hazards. Now that fine tuba players can deliver an astonishingly wide range from high to low and from soft to loud, one is tempted to place the technical cart before the musical horse. Outer ranges and dynamics are legitimate and valuable parts of tuba playing, but they must emerge as inevitable musical necessities. Horn players prize the singing voice of their instrument and work very hard to achieve a smooth warmth and line. There is an obvious kinship between the horn and the tuba, and the wise composer does not sacrifice noble cantabile in the pursuit of stunning virtuosity or meretricious novelty.

The tuba and the horn share other characteristics. Both are long instruments compared with the trumpet, and both play over a much wider range as measured in distance from their fundamental. Both, because of their predominantly conical tubing and, in the case of the tuba, wide bore size, have tone qualities that blend well but project less well. This blending ability accounts for much of the success of the tuba as the bass voice in the standard brass quintet and in the symphony orchestra. Its sound does not separate from the other lower- and middle-register brass instruments. The lower trio of tuba, horn, and trombone forms an integrated tone quality unit in the brass quintet at any but the extreme levels of volume or range. The richness of the three lower voices contrasted with the brightness of the trumpets forms the familiar and appropriate sound of the best brass quintet transcriptions of sixteenth- and early seventeenth-century vocal and instrumental music. The tuba is the natural bass voice of this type of music. If the arranger has to do much manipulation of the outer voices that is an indication that the particular piece is not suitable for brass transcription.

The blending asset can be a projecting liability when the tuba is encircled by other sounds. Paul Hindemith, in his *Sonata for Bass Tuba and Piano*, solved this by having the least possible piano sound in the general vicinity of the tuba. Because the tuba operates most often from middle C downward, most of the competing sound is above the tuba. This is natural when the tuba supplies the bass as a harmonic voice; it offers some interesting possibilities when the tuba is the leading melodic voice. As a worst case, one can imagine a setting in which the tuba is asked to play a gentle, middle register melodic line while surrounded by a thick entanglement of sound in the same register. The tuba is either buried or is forced to elevate the volume to a degree inconsistent with the nature of the music.

Balance, in the generally accepted sense of a reasonable equality of volume, can also be achieved through the adjustment of dynamic markings. There is no law that requires all participants to attain balance through a dogged consistency of dynamic levels. Imagine the magic resulting from the tuba playing very loudly while the piano plays very softly, or the tuba playing very softly during loud, thick, but short piano chords. These balance and texture patterns can spring from the composer's mental treasury of aural images, from the composer's examination of how others have handled similar events, and from consultation with fine players.

Speedy technique can present other hazards which can be linked to balance, dynamics, and register. Rules of thumb often stifle imagination but composers should seek guiding principles by a consideration of the following:

1. The effect of articulation patterns on projection. Two of the most common articulation patterns consist of two notes slurred, two notes tongued in groups of four notes, or two notes slurred, one note tongued in groups of three notes. In both patterns the second of the slurred notes is the only non-tongued note and is least likely to maintain the general level of volume and projection. At a moderate tempo this presents little difficulty but as the speed increases there is less time for the second note to sound and it falls below the prevailing volume level.

2. Multiple tonguing patterns always contain notes that are not begun by a sharp tongue stroke. These notes also lose projection as the speed increases. Horn players and tuba players, because of the tube length of their instruments, are therefore well advised to develop the fastest possible single tongue. For horn players the single tongue can be considered fast if it can produce four strokes for each beat at a metronome setting of 138–144 over an extended period. This varies somewhat among horn players and, one suspects, among tuba players. A single tonguing speed results in more clearly defined pitches, whereas multiple tonguing speed results in velocity but often at the expense of clarity. Speed and its effect on projection should be discussed and understood by players and composers.

3. Register is always a consideration in the clear projection of technique. Most brass players feel that the vast "middle register" yields better clarity than the outer registers. The lowest notes tend to respond slowly and the highest notes are often thin in volume and quality. The trumpet can create an exciting moment by a fast, rising articulated line ending on a very loud sustained note. This scenario works considerably less well on the tuba.

4. Clarity and projection are affected by competing sounds. It is logical that as the ensemble texture becomes concentrated, technical clarity becomes diluted. Listening to tuba recordings is not especially helpful in this matter since volume and balance can be altered electronically. Composers are often startled to discover how different a work can sound on tape as compared with a live performance.

5. Listening to the tuba at close range can be deceiving, since projection is affected by space. It is interesting to compare the effect of space and distance on various instruments. It is generally true that the shorter the instrument the less the sound changes as it travels. The oboe, for example, tends to sound very much the same in the last row of the balcony as on the stage. The horn sound changes noticeably as it reflects off the back wall to the conductor's podium. This seems to confirm that the conductor does not have the best seat in the house. A "dead" hall helps clarity but hinders volume and tone quality. A "live" hall can work in exactly the opposite way. Struggling with these variables can lead to establishing a general set of principles covering clarity and balance. The risk is that composers will fall too easily into patterns that are interesting but safe, colorful but predictable, and fashionable but not pertinent.

The most recent *College Music Society Directory* lists over 500 teachers of low brass instruments. One assumes that a good percentage of these teach the tuba. The same directory lists over 1,600 teachers of composition. Granted that most of them also teach in other areas, but these two figures offer strong evidence that the academy, not the professional world, is the fertile soil in which tuba playing and composition for the tuba can grow and prosper. Practically every "big name" in composition and tuba is found in this directory. Let us put to rest the misunderstanding that "academic" means formalism, conventionality, and conservatism, and return to the original meaning of academy, a place where there is a constant questioning of assumptions, and where learned individuals unite for the advancement of the arts, sciences, and literature. In such an environment composers and performers can unite to pave the road to a golden age.

Kjell Roikjer

Composer, Sweden

Many years ago one of my colleagues (a tuba player) in the Royal Danish Orchestra asked if I could write a quartet. This led to my first attempt to compose for brass instruments, my Op. 50, for two trumpets, trombone, and tuba. My colleagues were so pleased with the result, that they asked me to produce some more. This materialized as Op. 52, *Variations and Fugue on a Danish Folksong.*

Until a few years ago, chamber music for brass has been a scarcity in my country and because my first attempts were a success, I felt like proceeding. I have written twenty-four works, of which thirteen are in print.

During my many years as an orchestral musician (bassoon), I studied the timbre and mobility of the different instruments in solo as well as groups. I have always looked upon the tuba as a somewhat heavy instrument with which one should be a little careful, especially when it came to volume and sound in connection with orchestration. However, as I composed and listened to my works, I gradually became aware of the flexibility of the tuba when it is put in the right hands.

My knowledge of its technical possibilities and the reason my works have proliferated is most of all thanks to my acquaintance with Michael Lind. Since 1974, when Michael did the original performance of my *Tuba Concerto,* he has been a keen advocate for my works, especially the duets, the trios, the quartets, and the educational pieces, Op. 75. That's why I have dedicated most of my works to Michael Lind.

Walter Ross

University of Virginia

As a horn player for many years in orchestras and wind and brass ensembles of all kinds, I have learned a great deal about writing for brass instruments directly from performance experience. I particularly enjoy writing for brass and wind instruments, and I like to write music that people will like to play as well as hear. Traditionally tuba parts in ensemble music have been fairly conservative, and composers have not realized how very agile an instrument it can be—far beyond what most books on instrumentation indicate. I, myself, was not aware of the full extent of the possibilities of the instrument until I attended the first international T.U.B.A. Conference. I was especially impressed by the outstanding quality of modern performers and became excited about writing music which would treat the tuba seriously as a recital instrument. My more recent work reflects this change in my awareness.

For the most part I use the pitches shown in Example 1 as a good working range for the tuba and reserve the lower notes, shown in Example 2, for special effects. I don't feel that it is necessary to extend the range higher. I know that many tubists can play higher, but I see no reason to give a performer nightmares. The usual admonitions for writing for brass instruments (rapid articulations on the lowest notes, rapid wide intervals, rapid downward slurs over wide intervals) are all awkward, and the musical effect is not worth the effort required of the performer. I always write with the CC tuba fingerings in mind. The result is that the tuba performer sounds good without Herculean effort. I try to make the music pleasing and accessible to the audience while showing off the performer and the instrument, and so much of my recent music is modal/pandiatonic and rhythmically exciting

I have a very positive feeling about writing for tuba, and this is beause of the attitude of tubists themselves. Without exception I have found them eager to perform and sympathetic to recent music of all kinds.

Ex. 1 *Ex. 2*

William Schmidt

Composer and Publisher

My approach to the tuba has been determined more by demands from tuba players than from any other influence. These demands were mostly technical in nature, so I usually selected the content and form.

The *Serenade for Tuba and Piano* was written in 1958 for Tommy Johnson when we were fellow graduate students at the University of Southern California. It was one of the first published compositions for tuba utilizing twelve-tone technique. Although it was considered a difficult work at that time (and I heard many bad performances of it in the 50s) it is now placed on most of the state high school contest lists in the United States.

Another approach to my writing for the tuba was through the several brass ensembles functioning in the Los Angeles area during the 1960s, especially the Los Angeles Brass Quintet and the Los Angeles Brass Society. Part-writing for the tuba became quite complex, resulting in a somewhat difficult part in *Suite No. 3 for Brass Quintet* (1956).

Many changes in my approach to solo writing were influenced over the last 35 years by the several soloists who commissioned works from me. One of the more important pieces was *Tuba Mirum for Tuba and Symphonic Winds*, commissioned by Michael Lind of Sweden. This full-length, nineteen-minute concerto employs longer lines, more extensive ranges, and some jazz techniques that I had not used before. *Sonata for Tuba and Piano,* commissioned by Mel Culbertson of France, was my next step in virtuoso writing. Mel has a phenomenal, aggressive style of playing and understands contemporary music, so the opportunity to write a difficult composition presented itself. When Jim Self and Tony Plog asked for a duo based on jazz for a recording project, I was intrigued because of my experience as a jazz arranger during the 40s and 50s. *Tony and The Elephant or Jim and the Road Runner* is a five-movement suite that uses matching cup, straight and bucket mutes. *Latin Rhythms for Tuba and Percussion* was another departure, since the use of only Latin percussion

instruments and rhythms gives the tuba a chance to execute these rhythms along with some false fingering techniques. *"Tunes" for Tuba, Winds and Percussion,* in collaboration with Jim Self, was commissioned by the Sapporo International Music Festival '90. The first movement is especially complicated rhythmically and uses false fingering throughout. This was an outgrowth of *Latin Rhythms.*

Probably the most satisfying instrumental accompaniment for tuba is the chamber orchestra. My *Concerto for Tuba and Chamber Orchestra* is scored for flute, oboe, clarinet, bassoon, trumpet, two horns, trombone, percussion and strings (6, 6, 4, 4, 2). The tuba can be matched with any combination of the four sections and still enjoy the full orchestral sound without the heaviness associated with a large orchestra.

Composing for the tuba has been interesting and enlightening. The progress made during the last 40 years by contemporary composers writing for the tuba has been phenomenal. The tuba has a repertoire that did not exist a few decades ago; the challenge now is to perform these works so they become established and familiar to the listening public.

Gunther Schuller

Composer

Writing for the tuba is in essence no different from writing for any other instrument, which is to say one must know the instrument well and write for it idiomatically. By idiomatically, I mean that the writing must be uniquely suited to that instrument and not interchangeable with any other. Writing idiomatically for the tuba does not mean writing easy music; indeed, it can mean writing something very challenging and complex. There is technically easy music that is unidiomatic and technically difficult music that is truly idiomatic.

I love the tuba and writing for it, as I love composing for all the low register "underdog" instruments. In the hands of a fine player the tuba can express anything any other instrument can.

John Stevens

University of Wisconsin-Madison

In most ways, writing for the tuba is no different from writing for any other instrument. The composer/arranger must understand the capabilities of the instrument (in terms of both "characteristic" writing and extended techniques) and then be able to make intelligent decisions regarding the most appropriate manner of writing for a particular piece or style. The tuba does not pose limitations, only a wide variety of possibilities. However, there are three considerations that I keep in mind at all times when writing for tuba: clarity, dynamics, and range.

Because of its large size and omni-directional sound-generating design, clarity is always a concern when the tuba is used in an ensemble (particularly a tuba or tuba/euphonium ensemble!). Articulation and range (or voicing, in the case of music for multiple tubas) are key factors. Excessive use of slurs (especially in rapid passages), writing "busy" passages in the low register (below C, two ledger lines below the bass clef staff), and voicing multiple tubas in intervals smaller than perfect fourths (from the middle of the staff down) all can contribute to lack of clarity, or "muddiness."

The tuba is capable of an extremely wide range of dynamics, which allows it to be orchestrated with virtually any instrument or group of instruments without fear of the tuba overpowering them. The stereotypical "cartoon" concept of the tuba is that of a very loud instrument, but because it is a low-pitched, conical-bore instrument, it produces a mass of supportive sound (even in loud dynamics) rather than a penetrating, "up-front" sound. One should not shy away from pairing the tuba with what we usually think of as more delicate instruments, such as oboe, flute, or violin. If the complete dynamic range of the tuba is employed, anything is possible!

Knowing the proper register in which to write a particular tuba passage is important. The color, or sound quality, and "feel" of the articulation vary throughout the range. Upwards from d (middle of the bass clef staff) is the most singing, lyrical register. It is the most "present" solo register of the instrument and also the one that allows the tuba to blend with (as opposed to standing out from) other instruments. From C down to G_1 is the most characteristic, or "classic," tuba register. When the tuba is being used as the bass voice in a chord and/or as a rhythmic foundation instrument (like the string/electric bass in a jazz or popular idiom), 90 percent of the notes should be in this register. This is also the register that allows for the loudest, most powerful tuba sound. A common mistake made by composers, who want a loud, powerful tuba sound, is to write the part too low. For example, for most players, an $f\!f$ F (one space below the staff) will produce a more powerful, present sound than the same pitch one octave lower.

The notes below G_1 are the least melodious on the instrument but are extremely important in a supportive musical role. Like the lowest notes on an organ, tuba sonorities in this register provide a bass "feel" as well as sound, along with a sense of musical strength and solidity. In recent years, many composers have emphasized the upper register of the tuba but, after all, the instrument was invented to provide sonorous tones in the low registers. Prokofiev used the lower register beautifully, and almost exclusively, in his compositions. I recommend his music as an excellent study for orchestrating for the tuba. Rather than employing only the usual techniques of grouping the tuba with the trombones or the string basses, Prokofiev used it as a fifth horn or in a wide variety of groupings with woodwinds or high strings. I mention this because despite the increased role of the tuba as a solo instrument, I still feel that its greatest strength lies in its many outstanding qualities as an ensemble, or "social," instrument.

Because a great deal of my work as a composer and arranger has been for tuba or tuba/euphonium ensembles, I would like to list a few guidelines that will lead to successful arrangements or compositions for that type of ensemble:

Write for a balanced group. For example, for a tuba/euphonium quartet, I recommend using two of each instrument, rather than one and three, or three and one. A balanced group allows for more orchestrational possibilities and avoids having one type of instrument always standing out from the rest, regardless of the nature of the part that it is playing at any given time.

If all the voices are playing at a particular section of a piece, write for the highest and lowest voices first, then fill in the inner parts. Top voice (euphonium): up to $b\flat^1$, occasionally, but rarely, to c" above that. Lowest voice (tuba): down to $A\flat_2$, rarely lower.

Closed voicing may be used in the upper registers, but a more open voicing (larger intervals) must be used from the middle of the bass staff on down. Except for final, or other unavoidable low chords, don't write a major or minor third interval lower than B♭ to D♭ in the staff.

If one note must be omitted from a chord, the fifth is usually the best. Retaining the root, third, seventh and other added chord tones.

A march is an excellent type of piece to begin with when learning how to arrange for tuba ensembles. I recommend working from a condensed band score if possible, and writing for five voices; either two euphoniums and three tubas, or three and two. Voice 1: Melody most of the time, except when the melody in the band version is in lower voices (Trio, for example). Then the upper two parts would play counterlines or rhythmic figures. Voices 2, 3, and 4: These three voices must cover the countermelody (or double the melody an octave lower for a strong sound in certain passages) and the rhythmic/ harmonic figures. Voice 5: Bass line.

Indicate tempos on the fast side to build energy and vitality into the piece. For example, mark a march at 126 rather than the usual 120.

When considering types of pieces to arrange, it is helpful to have some idea of whether the arrangement will be successful. The following are some very general recommendations: Music that works: Marches, madrigals, chorales, jazz/rock tunes. Music that does not: Contrapuntal music (much of Bach's music, for example); works that are very "pianistic"; trumpet, horn, or trombone ensemble music (the voicing rarely works when transposed into a reasonable tuba range).

Finally, I want to encourage all of you who are tuba performers to try your hand at writing for your instrument. Begin with arranging or transcribing if you are unsure about your creative ideas for new music. You know much more about the capabilities and subtleties of your instrument than many composers. Why not use that knowledge to create new literature? Do not be afraid to fail. Write something, get it played, and use the experience as a learning tool to help you improve on your next writing project. Composing or arranging for the tuba is extremely rewarding and could add a new dimension to your musical life and career.

David Uber

Trenton State College

The tuba is a unique musical instrument—an indispensable part of the band, wind ensemble, orchestra, and chamber groups and invaluable in the performance of jazz. The instrument is relatively easy to play, but extremely difficult to master as regards technique, pure legato, rapid articulation, and range. Composers and arrangers must bear this in mind and give it the utmost consideration. Because of the rich, deep, and resonant tone the tuba can produce, voicings in tuba ensemble music must not be too close together. Such scoring frequently results in harmonic muddiness, since the slow vibrations of the overtone series intertwine and overlap. Except when a "primitive" dissonance is desired, it is well to avoid voicing multiple intervals of chromatic half tones, major seconds, or even thirds in the extreme low register.

Tubas placed in chamber music combinations—duets, trios, quartets, quintets, or larger groupings—sound best when spaced in intervals of fourths, fifths, sixths, and, best of all, tenths. Thirds are excellent in the middle upper range. When writing chorale-type passages, proper spacing in the parts is most essential. In four-voice writing, the ideal combination of low brass instruments has traditionally been two euphoniums on the upper parts and two bass tubas on the lower parts. This grouping provides a great flexibility in both range and sonority. Composing or arranging music for four or more tubas without the euphoniums demands great skill and a thorough familiarity with the tuba range and overtone series.

With the addition of the fourth valve, the composer of solos, etudes, and studies must meet the challenge of writing colorful melodies and exercises within a far greater compass. In addition, the advanced skills of the modern-day tubist allow for a liberal use of the upper register. In the past twenty-five years the player engaged in solo performance has encountered notes far above those formerly used by composers in more traditional passages. At the same time, melodic and rhythmic patterns demand a technique that was unheard of in the early and middle years of the twentieth century. The challenge to both player and listener has become awesome and yet very musical and interesting. In short, the tuba has risen to a position of importance equal to that of any other instrument in the musical environment of the late twentieth century.

Along with the modernization of the tuba repertoire, composers must consider the great intake of breath and the importance of breath control in both solo and ensemble performance. Most important is the study of the overtone series, alternate fingerings using the fourth valve, and length of phrasing.

There is no question that the emergence of the bass tuba as a vital force in the music of the world has brought about a dramatic change in the entire approach to scoring for this instrument. Young composers should diligently listen to the recordings of such artists as Harvey Phillips, Roger Bobo, R. Winston Morris, Barton Cummings, Arnold Jacobs, Toby Hanks, and Daniel Perantoni, to mention a few, in order to understand the brilliant capabilities of present-day performers. Listening to these outstanding players will seriously affect future solo, chamber music, jazz, concert band, and orchestral writing by the talented young composers and arrangers of the next generation.

Rodger Vaughan

California State University-Fullerton

My attitude toward composing for the tuba is the same as composing for anything else. It is, as Paul Hindemith says, an outgrowth of one's musical experience. I always try to include a challenging part for the instrumentalists, an intriguing experience for the listeners, and a valid musical form which facilitates that experience. There are many times when a quote and/or musical joke can be included. Finally, I try to write a piece which will offer rich rewards to the musicological student who is willing to delve into the analysis. If you cannot have a bit of fun while trying to produce a piece of music, what's the use?

I also feel that composing is a natural activity of being a musician. I listen (to a large collection of tapes and records); I teach (36 years of college-university instruction); I practice (every morning), and perform (every so often), and I try to be an example for my students. Certainly music is an all-encompassing art and one must participate if one wishes to enjoy its incredible spectrum.

19. Equipment

Tuba Manufacturers and Distributors and Their Products

Lee Hipp

The tuba manufacturers listed here have instruments available directly through their factories or through their distributors. Prices are given as a general guide so that one may compare the various manufacturers' suggested retail prices, but readers should be aware that by the time this book is published, most of them will be out of date. Model numbers are those given in the manufacturers' catalog and may not coincide with the model numbers used by all distributors. Unless otherwise indicated, valve configurations are front action. The options listed are those indicated in manufacturers' brochures and do not indicate all the options available to the buyer. Thanks are extended to Bob Baier of Orpheus Music; Allan Jensen, tubist with the Kiel Philharmonic; and all the manufacturers and distributors that provided help and information. Sincere apologies are extended to anyone inadvertently missed in this endeavor. Finally, I want to thank my wife, Melinda, for putting up with endless hours on the computer and the telephone and, most importantly, for proofreading and finding all my mistakes.

Manufacturers and Authorized Distributors

Musik-Alexander. Gebr. Alexander. Rhein. Musikinstrumentenfabrik GmbH. D-6500 Mainz, Bahnhofstr. 9, Postfach 1166, Germany. Tel. 0 61 31/ 23 29 44. Fax 0 61 31/22 42 48.

Amati. Kraslice, Czechoslovakia. Further information available through Geneva International Corp., 29 E. Hintz Rd., Wheeling, IL 60090. Tel. (708) 520-9970. (800) 533-2388; Fax (708) 520-9593.

B&S. Vogtlandische Musikinstrumentenfabrik GmbH. Markneukirchen. Bismarckstrasse 11, 0-9659 Markneukirchen, Germany. For further information on Perantucci models contact Custom Music Co., 1930 Hilton, Ferndale, MI 48220. Tel. (810) 546-4135, (800) 521-6380; Fax (810) 546-8296.

Bach/Bundy. The Selmer Co. L.P., P.O. Box 310, Elkhart, IN 46515-0310.(219) 522-1675.

Besson. Boosey & Hawkes, P.O. Box 130, Libertyville, IL 60048. Tel. (708) 816-2500; Fax (708) 816-2514.

E. K. Blessing Co., Inc., 1301 W. Beardsley Ave., Elkhart, IN 46514. Tel. (219) 293-0833, (800) 348-7409; Fax (219) 293-8398.

Böhm & Meinl, GmbH. D-8192 Geretsried 1, Postfach 1627, Isardamm 133, Germany. Tel. 0 81 71/ 600 07.

Canadian Brass Musical Instruments. N. 56 W., 13585 Silver Spring Dr., Menomonee Falls, WI 53051. Tel. (800) 488-2378.

Cervney. Hradec Kralove, Czechoslovakia. Further information available through Geneva International Corp., 29 E. Hintz Rd., Wheeling, IL 60090. Tel. (708) 520-9970, (800) 533-2388; Fax (708) 520-9593.

Conn. United Musical Instruments U.S.A., Inc., P.O. Box 727, Elkhart, IN 46515. Tel. (219) 295-0079, Fax (219) 295-8613.

Courtois. P. Gaudet, et Cie, S.A. 8, Rue de Nancy, 75010 Paris, France. Tel. (1) 42 40 3132.

Mel Culbertson. For further information see VMI.

Gronitz, H. Haydnstr. 10, D-22761 Hamburg, Germany. Tel. (040)-89 16 49.

Hanstone. For further information contact The Tuba Exchange, 1825 Chapel Hill Rd., Durham, NC 27707. Tel. (919) 493-5196, (800) 869-TUBA; Fax (919) 493-8822.

Hirsbrunner & Co. AG. Musikinstrumentenfabrik, CH-3454 Sumiswald, Switzerland. Tel. 034 / 71 15 54. For further information contact Custom Music Co. 1930 Hilton, Ferndale, MI 48220. Tel. (810) 546-4135, (800) 521-6380; Fax (810) 546-8296.

Holton. Leblanc Corp. 7001 Leblanc Blvd., Kenosha, WI 53141-1415. Tel. (800) 558-9421.

Jupiter. Jupiter Band Instruments, Inc., P.O. Box 90249, Austin, TX 78709-02249. Tel. (512) 288-7400, Fax (512) 288-6445.

Kalison, Di A. Benicchio, Via Pellegrino Rossi, 96 Milan, Italy. Tel.(02) 6453060, Fax (02) 6465927. For further information contact The Tuba Exchange, 1825 Chapel Hill Rd., Durham, NC 27707. Tel. (919) 493-5196, (800) 869-TUBA; Fax (919) 493-8822.

King. United Musical Instruments U.S.A., Inc., P.O. Box 727, Elkhart, IN 46515. Tel. (219) 295-0079, Fax (219) 295-8613.

Kurath-Perantucci. Willson Music Co., W. Kurath, CH-8890 Flums, Switzerland. Tel. 085 / 31478, Fax 085 / 31906. For further information contact

Custom Music Co. 1930 Hilton, Ferndale, MI 48220. Tel. (810) 546-4135, (800) 521-6380; Fax (810) 546-8296.

Rudolf Meinl. Musikinstrument-Herstellung. Blumenstrasse 21, D-8531, Diespeck/Aisch, Germany. Tel. 0 91 61 / 23 57.

Meinl-Weston (Melton). Melton Musikinstrumentenmanufaktur GmbH. D-8192 Geretsried 2, Seniweg 4, Postfach, 710 Germany. Tel. 08171 / 31642 or 51018, Fax 08171 / 80288. For further information contact Orpheus Music, 13814 Lookout Rd., San Antonio, TX 78233. Tel. (210) 637-0414, (800) 821-9448; Fax (210) 637-0232.

Meister Walter Nirschl. For further information contact Orpheus Music, 13814 Lookout Rd., San Antonio, TX 78233. Tel. (210) 637-0414, (800) 821-9448; Fax (210) 637-0232.

Miraphone, e.G. Metall-Blasinstrumente, 8264 Waldkraiburg, Germany. Tel. 86 38 / 40 56.

Sanders. For further information contact Custom Music Co., 1930 Hilton, Ferndale, MI 48220. Tel. (810) 546-4135, (800) 521-6380; Fax (810) 546-8296.

Vespro. For further information contact Orpheus Music, 13814 Lookout Rd., San Antonio, TX 78233. Tel. (210) 637-0414, (800) 821-9448; Fax (210) 637-0232.

VMI (Vogtland Musical Instruments). Vogtlandische Musikinstrumantenfabrik, GmbH Markneukirchen. Bismarckstrasse 11, 0-9593 Markneukirchen, Germany. For further information contact Orpheus Music, 13814 Lookout Rd., San Antonio, TX 78233. Tel. (210) 637-0414, (800) 821-9448; Fax (210) 637-0232.

Willson. Willson Music Co., W. Kurath, CH-8890 Flums, Switzerland. Tel. 085 / 31478, Fax 085 / 31906. For further information contact DEG Music Products, P.O. Box 968, Lake Geneva, WI 53147. Tel. (414) 248-8314, (800) 558-9416; Fax (414) 248-7953.

Yamaha. 3445 E. Paris Ave., SE, P.O. Box 899, Grand Rapids, MI 49512-0899. Tel. (616) 940-4900.

Product Information

Information on instruments is presented under the manufacturer's name in the following order:

Key of instrument (F, E♭ [EE♭], CC or BB♭ [B♭]) and Size (1/2, 3/4, 4/4, 5/4, or 6/4)
Model number
Bore size in hundredths of an inch
Bell diameter in inches (")
Number and type of valves and any particular configuration
Finish
Price manufacturer's suggested retail price
Options available

"n/a" indicates that in a given category information is not available.

ALEXANDER

F 4/4. 157. .728. 15". Six rotary, four right and two left. Brass lacquer. $n/a. Also available in red brass and silver plate.

F/C double tuba 4/4. 166. .728–.768. 15". Five rotary. Brass lacquer. $n/a. Also available in red brass and silver plate.

F 4/4. 156. .728. 15". Six rotary, three right and three left. Brass lacquer. $n/a. Also available in red brass and silver plate.

F 4/4. 155. .728. 15". Five rotary, four right and one left. Brass lacquer. $n/a. Also available in red brass and silver plate.

CC 4/4. 173. .768. 16 1/2". Five rotary, with second valve trigger. Brass lacquer. Also available in red brass and silver plate.

CC 5/4. 163. .807. 16 1/3". Four rotary. Brass lacquer. $n/a. Also available in red brass and silver plate.

BB♭ 5/4. 163. .807. 16 1/3". Four rotary. Brass lacquer. $n/a. Also available in red brass and silver plate.

BB♭ 6/4. 164, kaiser. .846. 17 3/4". Four rotary. Brass lacquer. $n/a. Also available in red brass and silver plate.

AMATI

BB♭ 4/4. ABB 221. .638. 15 1/2". Three piston. Brass lacquer. $2,420.00. Case, $350.00.

BB♭ 4/4. ABB 221C, convertible leadpipe. .638. 15 1/2". Three piston. Brass lacquer. $2,476.00. Case, $350.00.

BB♭ 4/4. ABB 321. .640. 15 1/2". Four piston. Brass lacquer. $2,770.00. Case, $350.00.

BB♭. ASH 260, sousaphone. .640. 25 1/4". Three piston. Brass lacquer. $3,000.00. Also available in E♭ and F/E♭. Case, $446.00.

B♭ 3/4. ABB 223, baby bass. .638. 13 3/4". Three piston. Brass lacquer. $2,420.00. n/a.

B♭ 3/4. ABB 223C, convertible leadpipe. .638. 13 3/4". Three piston. Brass lacquer. $2,476.00. n/a.

B&S

F 4/4. 3094. .668. 15". Four rotary. Brass lacquer. $n/a. Available in red brass and silver plate; second valve slide trigger available.

F 4/4. 3099. .668–.825, 4th or .748–.825, 4th. 16 1/2". Five rotary. Brass lacquer. $n/a. Available in red brass and silver plate; fifth valve thumb trigger, and second valve slide trigger available.

F 4/4. 3100. .668–.825, 4th or .748–.825, 4th. 16 1/2". Six rotary. Brass lacquer. $n/a. Available in red brass and silver plate; fifth valve thumb trigger, and second valve slide trigger available.

E♭ 4/4. 3091. .748. 14 1/2". Three rotary. Brass lacquer. $n/a. Available in red brass and silver plate; second valve slide trigger available.

EE♭ 4/4. 3092. .748. 14 1/2". Four rotary. Brass lacquer. $n/a. Available in red brass and silver plate; second valve slide trigger available.

CC 4/4. 3096. .748. 16 1/2". Four rotary. Brass lacquer. $n/a. Available in red brass and silver plate; second valve slide trigger available.

CC 4/4. 3097, short model. .748–.825. 16 1/2". Five rotary. Brass lacquer. $n/a. Available in red brass and silver plate; fifth valve thumb trigger, and second valve slide trigger available.

CC 4/4. 3097, long model. .748–.825. 16 1/2". Five rotary. Brass lacquer. $n/a. Available in red brass and silver plate; fifth valve thumb trigger, and second valve slide trigger available.

B♭ 4/4. 3102. .748. 16 1/2". Three rotary. Brass lacquer. $n/a. Available in red brass and silver plate; second valve slide trigger available.

BB♭ 4/4. 3103. .748. 16 1/2" or 19". Four rotary. Brass lacquer. $n/a. Available in red brass and silver plate; second valve slide trigger available.

BB♭ 4/4. 3105. .748. 16 1/2". Five rotary. Brass lacquer. $n/a. Available in red brass and silver plate; fifth valve thumb trigger, and second valve slide trigger available.

B&S PERANTUCCI

F, standard or orchestral. PT-11. .668–.825 or .745–.825. 16 5/8". Six rotary. Brass lacquer. $8,795.00. Silver plate, $1400.00; uni-ball linkage, $450.00; first and second valve trigger, $495.00.

F, standard or orchestral. PT-11GB. Same as above with gold brass. $9,095.00. Silver plate, $1400.00; uni-ball linkage, $450.00; first and second valve trigger, $495.00.

F, standard. PT-8. .668–.825. 16 5/8". Five rotary. Brass lacquer. $7,495.00. Silver plate, $1400.00; uni-ball linkage, $450.00; first and second valve trigger, $495.00.

F, solo. PT-9. .709–.825. 16 5/8". Five rotary. Brass lacquer. $7,495.00. Silver plate, $1400.00; uni-ball linkage, $450.00; first and second valve trigger, $495.00.

F, orchestral. PT-10. .745–.825. 16 5/8". Five rotary. Brass lacquer. $7,895.00. Silver plate, $1400.00; uni-ball linkage, $450.00; first and second valve trigger, $495.00.

F, orchestral. PT-10GB. Same as above with gold brass. $8,795.00. Silver plate, $1400.00; uni-ball linkage, $450.00; first and second valve trigger, $495.00.

CC, York. PT-5. .748–.825. 19 1/2". Five rotary. Brass lacquer. $9,350.00. Silver plate, $1400.00; uni-ball linkage, $450.00; first and second valve trigger, $495.00.

CC 4/4. PT-3. .748–.825. 16 1/2". Five rotary. Brass lacquer. $8,350.00. Silver plate, $1400.00; uni-ball linkage, $450.00; first and second valve trigger, $495.00.

CC 4/4. PT-3P. .748–.825. 16 1/2". Four piston and one rotary. Brass lacquer. $9,150.00. Silver plate, $1,400.00.

CC 4/4. PT-4. .750. 19 1/2". Five rotary. Brass lacquer. $8,195.00. Silver plate, $1,400.00.

BB♭ 4/4. PT-1. .750. 19 1/2". Four rotary. Brass lacquer. $7,460.00.

Silver plate, $1400.00; uni-ball linkage, $450.00; first and second valve trigger, $495.00.

BACH

BB♭ 3/4. 879. .656. 16 1/4". Four piston. Brass lacquer. $4,010.00. n/a.

BB♭ 3/4. 869. .656. 16 1/4". Three piston. Brass lacquer. $3,360.00. n/a.

BESSON

E♭ 3/4. 777-1. .650. 12 1/4". Three piston. Brass lacquer. $3,150.00. Case, $650.00.

E♭ 3/4. 777-2. Same as above with silver plate. $3,600.00. Case, $650.00.

EE♭ 4/4. 981-1. .689. 19". Four piston, compensating. Brass lacquer. $5,120.00. Case, $695.00.

EE♭ 4/4. 981-2. Same as above with silver plate. $5,825.00. Case, $695.00.

EE♭ 4/4. 982-1, parade model with narrower mouthpipe. .689. 19". Four piston, compensating. Brass lacquer. $5,115.00. Case, $695.00.

EE♭ 4/4. 982-2. Same as above with silver plate. $5,825.00. Case, $695.00.

B♭ 3/4. 787-1. .689. 13". Three piston. Brass lacquer. $3,150.00. Case, $650.00.

B♭ 3/4. 787-2. Same as above with silver plate. $3,600.00. Case, $650.00.

B♭ 3/4. 788-1, marching conversion with interchangeable mouthpipe. .689. 13". Three piston. Brass lacquer. $3,170.00. Case, $650.00.

B♭ 3/4. 788-2. Same as above with silver plate. $3,620.00. Case, $650.00.

BB♭ 4/4. 794-1. .730. 19". Four piston. Brass lacquer. $4,145.00. Case, $695.00.

BB♭ 4/4. 794-2. Same as above with silver plate. $3,620.00. Case, $695.00.

BB♭ 4/4. 994-1. .730. 19". Four piston, compensating. Brass lacquer. $6,970.00. Case, $695.00.

BB♭ 4/4. 994-2. Same as above with silver plate. $7,680.00. Case, $695.00.

BB♭. 798-1, sousaphone. .730. n/a. Three piston. Brass lacquer. $6,455.00. Case, $695.00.

BB♭. 798-2. Same as above with silver plate. $7,065.00. Case, $695.00.

BLESSING

BB♭ 3/4. B-450, marching conversion. .670. 15". Three piston. Brass lacquer. $2,795.00. Case, $350.00; silver plate, $500.00.

BÖHM & MEINL

F 4/4. 282. n/a. 15". Three rotary. Brass lacquer. $n/a. Available in silver plate.

F 4/4. 282-4. n/a. 15". Four rotary. Brass lacquer. $n/a. Available in silver plate.

F 4/4. 282-5. n/a. 15". Five rotary. Brass lacquer. $n/a. Available in silver plate.

E♭ 4/4. 283. n/a. 15". Three rotary. Brass lacquer. $n/a. Available in silver plate.

EE♭ 4/4. 283-4. n/a. 15". Four rotary. Brass lacquer. $n/a. Available in silver plate.

E♭ 4/4. 52. n/a. 15". Three piston. Brass lacquer. $n/a. Available in silver plate.

EE♭ 4/4. 52-4. n/a. 15". Four piston. Brass lacquer. $n/a. Available in silver plate.

E♭. 61, sousaphone. n/a. 24 1/2". Three piston. Brass lacquer. $n/a. Available in silver plate.

CC 4/4. 5520. .750. 20". Four piston. Brass lacquer. $6,800.00. Available in silver plate; fifth rotary valve, $1000.00.

B♭ 1/2. 284. n/a. 14 1/4". Three rotary. Brass lacquer. $n/a. Available in silver plate.

BB♭ 1/2. 284-4. n/a. 14 1/4". Four rotary. Brass lacquer. $n/a. Available in silver plate.

B♭ 3/4. 285. n/a. 15 3/4". Three rotary. Brass lacquer. $n/a. Available in silver plate.

BB♭ 3/4. 285-4. n/a. 15 3/4". Four rotary. Brass lacquer. $n/a. Available in silver plate.

B♭ 4/4. 286. n/a. 16 1/2". Three rotary. Brass lacquer. $n/a. Available in silver plate.

BB♭ 4/4. 286-4. n/a. 16 1/2". Four rotary. Brass lacquer. $n/a. Available in silver plate.

B♭ 5/4. 290, kaiser. n/a. 19 1/2". Three rotary. Brass lacquer. $n/a. Available in silver plate.

BB♭ 5/4. 290-4, kaiser. n/a. 19 1/2". Four rotary. Brass lacquer. $n/a. Available in silver plate.

B♭. 54. n/a. 15". Three piston. Brass lacquer. $n/a. Available in silver plate.

BB♭. 54-4. n/a. 15". Four piston. Brass lacquer. $n/a. Available in silver plate.

B♭. 55. n/a. 15". Three piston. Brass lacquer. $n/a. Available in silver plate.

BB♭. 55-4. n/a. 15". Four piston. Brass lacquer. $n/a. Available in silver plate.

B♭. 63, sousaphone. n/a. 26". Three piston. Brass lacquer. $n/a. Available in silver plate.

BB♭. 63-4, sousaphone. n/a. 26". Four piston. Brass lacquer. $n/a. Available in silver plate.

B♭. 66, helicon. n/a. 17 3/4". Three piston. Brass lacquer. $n/a. Available in silver plate.

BB♭. 66-4, helicon. n/a. 17 3/4". Four piston. Brass lacquer. $n/a. Available in silver plate.

BUNDY II

BB♭. 1529, sousaphone. n/a. n/a. Three piston. Fiberglass. $2,660.00. n/a.

CANADIAN BRASS

CC 4/4. CB-50. .689. 19". Four piston, one rotary. Brass lacquer. $9,000.00, with case. Available in silver plate.

BB♭ 4/4. Available in 1994.

CERVENY

F 4/4. AFB 654-6. .717. 14 1/4". Six rotary. Brass lacquer. $n/a. Case, $400.00; available with nickel silver mouthpipe and bell rim; also in red brass.

F 5/4. AFB 661-6, kaiser. .795. 15 3/4". Six rotary. Brass lacquer. $n/a. Case, $400.00; available with nickel silver mouthpipe and bell rim; also in red brass.

F 4/4. AFB 641-3. .717. 14 1/4". Three rotary. Brass lacquer. $n/a. Case, $400.00; available with nickel silver mouthpipe and bell rim; also in red brass.

F 4/4. AFB 641-4. .717. 14 1/4'. Four rotary. Brass lacquer. $3,483.00. Case, $400.00; available with nickel silver mouthpipe and bell rim; also in red brass.

EE♭ 4/4. AEB 641-3. .717. 14 1/4". Three rotary. Brass lacquer. $n/a. Case, $400.00; available with nickel silver mouthpipe and bell rim; also in red brass.

EE♭ 4/4. AEB 641-4. .717. 14 1/4". Four rotary. Brass lacquer. $3,415.00. Case, $400.00; available with nickel silver mouthpipe and bell rim; also in red brass.

CC 4/4. ACB 681-5. .795. 15 3/4". Five rotary. Brass lacquer. $5,460.00. Case, $350.00; available with nickel silver mouthpipe and bell rim; also in red brass.

CC 5/4. ACB 601-4. .835. 19 5/8". Four rotary. Brass lacquer. $5,880.00. Case, $350.00; available with nickel silver mouthpipe and bell rim; also in red brass; also available with fifth valve.

CC 5/4. ACB 603-4, compact model. .835. 15 3/4". Four rotary. Brass lacquer. $6,510.00. Case, $350.00; available with nickel silver mouthpipe and bell rim; also in red brass; also available with fifth valve.

CC 4/4. ACB 683-5, compact opera. .795. 14 1/4". Five rotary. $n/a. Case, $350.00; available with nickel silver mouthpipe and bell rim; also in red brass.

BB♭ 4/4. ABB 681-4. .795. 15 3/4". Four rotary. Brass lacquer. $4,112.00. Case, $350.00; available with nickel silver mouthpipe and bell rim; also in red brass.

BB♭ 4/4. ABB 781-4. .795. 15 3/4". Four rotary. Red brass. $5,370.00. Case, $350.00; available with nickel silver mouthpipe and bell rim; also in red brass.

BB♭ 5/4. ABB 601-4. .835. 19 5/8". Four rotary. Brass lacquer. $n/a. Case, $350.00; available with nickel silver mouthpipe and bell rim; also in red brass.

BB♭ 4/4. ABB 683-4, compact model. .795. 14 1/4". Four rotary. Brass lacquer. $4,830.00. Case, $350.00; available with nickel silver mouthpipe and bell rim; also in red brass.

BB♭. AHL 631-4, helicon. .795. 19 5/8". Four rotary. Brass lacquer. $5,250.00. Also available in E♭ and F; cover, $92.00.

CONN

BB♭ 3/4. 15J. .640. 15". Three piston, upright. Brass lacquer. $3,735.00, with case. Bright silver plate or satin silver with bright interior bell, $520.00.

BB♭ 3/4. 15JM. Same as above with convertible mouthpipe. $3,920.00, with case. Bright silver plate or satin silver with bright interior bell, $520.00.

BB♭ 3/4. 12J. .658. 18". Three piston, front. Brass lacquer. $3,980.00, with case. Bright silver plate or satin silver with bright interior bell, $520.00.

BB♭ 3/4. 5J. Same as above with four piston valves. $4,600.00, with case. Bright silver plate or satin silver with bright interior bell, $520.00.

BB♭. 36K, sousaphone. .687. 26". Three piston. Fiberglass. $3,100.00, with case. n/a.

BB♭. 14K, sousaphone. .687. 26". Three piston. Brass lacquer. $4,700.00, with case. Bright silver plate or satin silver with bright interior bell, $845.00.

BB♭. 20K, sousaphone. .734. 26". Three piston, short action. Brass, lacquer. $5,200.00, with case. Bright silver plate or satin silver with bright interior bell, $1,200.00.

COURTOIS

BB♭ 4/4. 174. .700. 17 1/2". Three piston. Brass lacquer. $4,950.00. n/a.

BB♭ 4/4. 175. .700. 17 1/2". Four piston. Brass lacquer. $n/a. n/a.

BB♭ 4/4. 176. .700. 17 1/2". Five valve. Brass lacquer. $n/a. n/a.

MEL CULBERTSON

F 7/4. MC-Apollo. .768 in fifth and sixth valves. 18 3/4". Six rotary. Gold lacquer. $n/a. Supplied with two leadpipes. Case, $500.00

CC 6/4. MC-Neptune. .745–.846. 20". Five rotary. Gold lacquer.

H. GRONITZ

F. Bore n/a. Bell 17 1/2". Four piston, one rotary. Brass lacquer. $n/a. Available in silver plate. n/a.

EE♭. Bore n/a. Bell 18". Four piston, one rotary. Brass lacquer. $n/a. Available in silver plate. n/a.

HANSTONE

BB♭ 4/4. 101L. .748. 16 1/2". Four rotary. Brass lacquer. $5,400.00. n/a.

HIRSBRUNNER

F 3/4. HB-8. .690. 14 1/2". Five rotary. Silver plate. $10,650.00. Case, $995.00; first slide trigger, $400.00.

F 4/4. HB-9. .770. 14 1/2". Five rotary. Silver plate. $10,950.00. Case, $995.00; first slide trigger, $400.00.

F 4/4. HB-10. .750. 14 1/2". Four piston, one rotary. Silver plate. $10,950.00. Case, $995.00; first slide trigger, $500.00.

CC 4/4. HB-1. .770. 18". Four rotary. Silver plate. $10,995.00. Case, $995.00; first slide trigger, $400.00.

CC 4/4. HB-1P. .750. 18". Four piston. Silver plate. $10,995.00. Case, $995.00; first slide trigger, $500.00.

CC 4/4. HB-2. .770. 18". Five rotary. Silver plate. $11,995.00. Case, $995.00; first slide trigger, $400.00.

CC 4/4. HB-2P. .750. 18". Four piston, one rotary. Silver plate. $10,995.00. Case, $995.00; first slide trigger, $500.00.

CC 4/4. HB-20, with York style straight-in leadpipe, main tuning slide after the fifth valve. .750. 18". Four piston, one rotary. Silver plate. $10,995.00. Case, $995.00; first slide trigger, $500.00.

CC 4/4. HB-21, with York style straight-in leadpipe, main tuning slide after the fifth valve. .770. 18". Four piston, one rotary. Silver plate. $10,995.00. Case, $995.00; first slide trigger, $500.00.

CC 5/4. HB-6. .810. 18". Five rotary. Silver plate. $Request. Case, $995.00; first slide trigger, $400.00.

CC 6/4. HBS-500, York. .750. 20 1/2". Four piston, one rotary. Silver plate. $Request. Case, $995.00; first slide trigger, $500.00.

BB♭ 4/4. HB-4. .770. 18". Four rotary. Silver plate. $10,995.00. Case, $995.00; first slide trigger, $400.00.

BB♭ 4/4. HB-5. .770. 18". Five rotary. Silver plate. $11,945.00. Case, $995.00; first slide trigger, $400.00.

BB♭ 5/4. HB-7. .810. 18". Four rotary. Silver plate. $Request. Case, $995.00; first slide trigger, $400.00.

HOLTON

BB♭ 4/4. BB346R. .730. n/a. Four piston. Brass lacquer. $3,975.00. Silver plate, $400.00.

BB♭ 3/4. BB661R. .610. 13 3/8". Three piston, top action. Brass lacquer. $3,350.00. Marching conversion kit available; silver plate, $400.00.

BB♭ 3/4. BB662R. .610. 13 3/8". Three piston. Brass lacquer. $3,050.00. Silver plate, $400.00.

BB♭. BB300, sousaphone. .687. n/a. Three piston. Fiberglass. $2,875.00. n/a.

BB♭. BB310, sousaphone. .687. 26". Three piston. Brass lacquer. $4,350.00. Silver plate, $800.00.

JUPITER

BB♭ 3/4. 382L. .709. 15". Three piston. Brass lacquer. $2,495.00, with case. Silver plate, $400.00.

BB♭ 3/4. 384L, marching conversion. .709. 15". Three piston. Brass lacquer. $2,495.00, with case. Left shoulder; comes with convertable mouthpipe.

BB♭. 594L, sousaphone. .669. 24". Three piston. Brass lacquer. $3,495.00, with case. Silver plate, $800.00.

BB♭. 596L. .669. 24". Three piston. Fiberglass. $2,795.00, with case. n/a.

KALISON

F 4/4. Daryl Smith Soloist. .703. 15". Four piston, one rotary. Brass lacquer. $n/a. Available in silver plate; also in E♭.

F 5/4. Pro 2000. n/a. n/a. Six rotary. Brass lacquer. $n/a. Available in silver plate.

CC 4/4. Daryl Smith Symphonic Model. .750. 18 3/4". Four piston, one rotary. Brass lacquer. $9,254.00. Available in silver plate; also available in all rotary.

CC 5/4. Pro 2000. .750. 18 3/4". Four piston, one rotary. Brass lacquer. $10,512.00. Available in silver plate; also in B♭; available in all rotary.

BB♭ 4/4. Daryl Smith Model. .750. 18 3/4". Four piston. Brass lacquer. $9,350.00. Available in silver plate; also available in all rotary.

KING

BB♭ 3/4. 1140W. .640. 15". Three piston, top action. Brass lacquer. $3,735.00, with case. n/a.

BB♭ 3/4. 1140MW, marching conversion .640. 15". Three piston. Brass lacquer. $3,920.00. Comes with conversion mouthpipe; silver plate or satin silver with bright interior bell, $520.00.

BB♭ 4/4. 2340UBW, detachable upright bell. .687. 19". Three piston. Brass lacquer. $4,525.00, with cases. Silver plate or satin silver with bright interior bell, $820.00.

BB♭ 4/4. 2340BFW, detachable bell front. Same as above. Silver plate or satin silver with bright interior bell, $820.00.

BB♭ 4/4. 2341UBW, detachable upright bell. .687. 22". Four piston. Brass lacquer. $4,925.00, with cases. Silver plate or satin silver with bright interior bell, $820.00.

BB♭ 4/4. 2341BFW, detachable bell front. Same as above. Silver plate or satin silver with bright interior bell, $820.00.

TU2343, bell front section only for 2340 or 2341, $1,040.00. Silver plate or satin silver with bright interior, $400.00.

TU2343, upright bell section only for 2340 or 2341, $1,040.00. Silver plate or satin silver with bright interior, $400.00.

BB♭. 2350W, sousaphone. .687. 26". Three piston. Brass lacquer. $4,700.00, with case. Silver plate or satin silver with bright interior, $845.00.

BB♭. 2370W, sousaphone. .687. 26". Three piston. Fiberglass. $3,100.00, with case. n/a.

KURATH-PERANTUCCI

F 4/4. KP-15. .710–.750. 18". Four stainless steel piston, one rotary. Brass lacquer. $10,250.00. Available in silver plate.

CC 5/4. KP-16. .750–.820. 20". Four stainless steel piston, one rotary. Brass lacquer. $10,950.00. Available in silver plate.

BB♭ 5/4. KP-17. .770. 20". Four rotary. Brass lacquer. $9,950.00. Available in silver plate.

RUDOLF MEINL

F. Cimbasso 5S. n/a. 11". Five rotary. Brass lacquer. $n/a. Available with nickel silver bell ring; second and fifth valve slide triggers; also with drum or spiral valve springs.

C. Cimbasso. n/a. n/a. Five rotary. Brass lacquer. $n/a. Available with nickel silver bell ring; second and fifth valve slide triggers; also with drum or spiral valve springs.

F 4/4. RM 1F41, export. .770–.825. 16". Six rotary. Brass lacquer. $10,150.00. Available with nickel silver bell ring; also with drum or spiral valve springs.

F 5/4. RM1F43, export II. .725–.825. 17". Six rotary. Brass lacquer. $11,875.00. Available with nickel silver bell ring; also with drum or spiral valve springs.

EE♭ 1/2. RM 1S33. n/a. 13". Four rotary. Brass lacquer. $n/a. Available with nickel silver bell ring; also with drum or spiral valve springs.

EE♭ 3/4. RM 1S35. n/a. 14". Four rotary. Brass lacquer. $n/a. Available with nickel silver bell ring; also with drum or spiral valve springs.

EE♭ 4/4. RM 1S38. n/a. 15". Four rotary. Brass lacquer. $n/a. Available with nickel silver bell ring; also with drum or spiral valve springs.

CC 1/2. RM 1C39. n/a. 15". Four or five rotary. Brass lacquer. $n/a. Available with nickel silver bell ring; also with drum or spiral valve springs.

CC 3/4. RM 1C43. .765. 17". Four or five rotary. Brass lacquer. $10,505.00. Available with nickel silver bell ring; also with drum or spiral valve springs.

CC 4/4. RM 1C45. .770. 18". Four or five rotary. Brass lacquer. $11,835.00. Available with nickel silver bell ring; also with drum or spiral valve springs.

CC 5/4. RM 1C50. .900. 20". Four or five rotary. Brass lacquer. $13,065.00. Available with nickel silver bell ring; also with drum or spiral valve springs.

BB♭ 1/8. RM 1B33. n/a. 13". Four rotary. Brass lacquer. $n/a. Available with nickel silver bell ring; also with drum or spiral valve springs.

BB♭ 1/4. RM 1B36. n/a. 14". Four rotary. Brass lacquer. $n/a. Available with nickel silver bell ring; also with drum or spiral valve springs.

BB♭ 1/2. RM 1B39. n/a. 15". Four rotary. Brass lacquer. $n/a. Available with nickel silver bell ring; also with drum or spiral valve springs.

BB♭ 3/4. RM 1B43. .765. 17". Four rotary. Brass lacquer. $9,350.00. Available with nickel silver bell ring; also with drum or spiral valve springs.

BB♭ 4/4. RM 1B45. .820. 18". Four rotary. Brass lacquer. $10,095.00. Available with nickel silver bell ring; also with drum or spiral valve springs.

BB♭ 5/4. RM 1B50. .900. 20". Four rotary. Brass lacquer. $11,270.00. Available with nickel silver bell ring; also with drum or spiral valve springs.

BB♭ 6/4. RM 1B56, kaiser. n/a. 22". Four rotary. Brass lacquer. $n/a. Available with nickel silver bell ring; also with drum or spiral valve springs.

MEINL-WESTON (MELTON)

F. 1144H, kaiser baritone. .630. 13 1/2". Four rotary. $n/a. Available with nickel silver bell ring; red brass or silver plate; and first and fourth valve triggers.

F. 1145H, kaiser baritone. Same as above with five rotary valves.

F. Cimbasso. n/a. n/a. Five rotary, with first valve slide trigger and fifth valve thumb trigger. $n/a. Available with nickel silver bell ring; red brass or silver plate.

F 4/4. 191. .630. 15". Three rotary. Brass lacquer. $n/a. Available with nickel silver bell ring; red brass or silver plate; and first valve trigger.

F 4/4. 192. .630. 15". Four rotary. Brass lacquer. $n/a. Available with five rotary valves; nickel silver bell ring; red brass or silver plate; first and fourth valve triggers; and fifth valve thumb trigger.

F 6/4. 43. .728. 15". Three rotary. Brass lacquer. $n/a. Available with nickel silver bell ring; red brass or silver plate; and first valve trigger.

F 6/4. 44. .728 to .768. 15". Four rotary. Brass lacquer. $n/a. Available with five rotary valves; nickel silver bell ring; red brass or silver plate; first and fourth valve triggers; and fifth valve thumb trigger.

F 6/4. 45K. .728,4th to .768, 5th. 15". Five rotary. Brass lacquer. $n/a. Available with nickel silver bell ring; red brass or silver plate; first and fourth valve triggers; and fifth valve thumb trigger.

F 6/4. 45S. .728 to .846. 16 1/2". Five rotary. Brass lacquer. $8,800.00. Available with nickel silver bell ring; red brass or silver plate; first and fourth valve triggers; and fifth valve thumb trigger; case, $695.00.

F 6/4. 45S/G. .768, 3rd to .807, 4th to .846, 5th. 16 1/2". Five rotary. Brass lacquer. $11,100.00. Available with nickel silver bell ring; red brass or silver plate; first and fourth valve triggers; and fifth valve thumb trigger; case, $695.00.

F 6/4. 45H-ML. .728, 4th to .768, 5th. 15". Five rotary. Brass lacquer. $n/a. Available with nickel silver bell ring; red brass or silver plate; first and fourth valve triggers; and fifth valve thumb trigger.

F 6/4. 46. .728,3rd to .768. 15 1/2". Six rotary. Brass lacquer. $n/a. Available with nickel silver bell ring; red brass or silver plate; first and fourth valve triggers; also with Vienna style valves.

F 6/4. 46S. .728–.846. 16 1/2". Six rotary. Brass lacquer. $n/a. Available with nickel silver bell ring; red brass or silver plate; first and fourth valve triggers.

F 6/4. 46QH. .768–.807, 5th. 16 1/2". Six rotary. Brass lacquer. $n/a. Available with nickel silver bell ring; red brass or silver plate; first and fourth valve triggers; also with Vienna style valves.

F 6/4. 46H-ML. .728,4th to .768. 15". Six rotary. Brass lacquer. $11,100.00. Available with nickel silver bell ring; red brass or silver plate; first and fourth valve triggers; also with Vienna style valves; case, $695.00.

F/C double tuba. .748. 16 1/2". Four stainless steel pistons, compensating, one rotary changing valve. Brass lacquer. $15,900.00. Available with nickel silver bell ring; red brass or silver plate. Case, $795.00.

E♭ 3/4. 39. .728. 15". Three rotary. Brass lacquer. $n/a. Available with nickel silver bell ring; red brass or silver plate; and first valve trigger.

EE♭ 3/4. 39. .728. 15". Four rotary. Brass lacquer. $n/a. Available with nickel silver bell ring; red brass or silver plate; and first and fourth valve triggers.

CC 4/4. 30. .768. 17 3/4". Four rotary. Brass lacquer. $n/a. Available with nickel silver bell ring; red brass or silver plate; and first and fourth valve triggers.

CC 4/4. 32. .768. 17 3/4". Five rotary, with thumb trigger. Brass lacquer. $n/a. Available with nickel silver bell ring; red brass or silver plate; and first and fourth valve triggers.

CC 4/4. 35, W. Bell. .689. 16 1/2". Four rotary. Brass lacquer. $n/a. Available with nickel silver bell ring; red brass or silver plate; and first and fourth valve triggers.

CC 4/4. Special Edition 37, W. Bell. .689. 16 1/2". Five rotary, with thumb trigger. Gold lacquer. $n/a. Available with nickel silver bell ring; red brass or silver plate; and first and fourth valve triggers. Comes with separate travel cases for body and bell.

CC 4/4. 2144. .748–.778. 16 1/2". Four stainless steel pistons. Brass lacquer. $n/a. Available with nickel silver bell ring; red brass or silver plate; case, $695.00.

CC 4/4. 2145. .748 to .846, 5th. 16 1/2". Four stainless steel pistons, one rotary. Brass lacquer. $9,900.00. Available with nickel silver bell ring; red brass or silver plate; case, $695.00.

CC 4/4. 2145A. .748 to .846, 5th. 17 1/2". Four stainless steel pistons, one rotary. Brass lacquer. $9,900.00. Available with nickel silver bell ring; red brass or silver plate; case, $795.00.

CC 5/4. 2154. .807–.846. 17 3/4". Four rotary. Brass lacquer. $n/a. Available with nickel silver bell ring; red brass or silver plate; case, $695.00.

CC 5/4. 2155. .807 to .846, 5th. 17 3/4". Five rotary. Brass lacquer. $n/a. Available with nickel silver bell ring; red brass or silver plate; case, $695.00.

CC 6/4. 2164, W. Deck. .748–.787. 19 3/4". Four stainless steel pistons. Brass lacquer. $n/a. Available with nickel silver bell ring; red brass or silver plate; case, $795.00.

CC 6/4. 2165, W. Deck. .748 to .846, 5th. 19 3/4". Four stainless steel pistons, one rotary. Brass lacquer. $15,900.00. Available with nickel silver bell ring; red brass or silver plate; case, $795.00.

CC 6/4. 2165R, W. Deck. Same as above in rotary valves.

Bb 1/4. 185. .630. 15". Three rotary. Brass lacquer. $n/a. Available with nickel silver bell ring; red brass or silver plate; and first valve trigger.

BBb 1/4. 185. .630. 15". Four rotary. Brass lacquer. $n/a. Available with nickel silver bell ring; red brass or silver plate; and first and fourth valve triggers.

Bb 1/2. 15. .689. 15". Three rotary. Brass lacquer. $n/a. Available with nickel silver bell ring; red brass or silver plate; and first valve trigger.

BBb 1/2. 16. .689. 15". Four rotary. Brass lacquer. $n/a. Available with nickel silver bell ring; red brass or silver plate; and first and fourth valve triggers.

Bb 3/4. 19. .768. 16 1/2". Three rotary. Brass lacquer. $n/a. Available with nickel silver bell ring; red brass or silver plate; and first valve trigger.

BBb 3/4. 20. .768. 16 1/2". Four rotary. Brass lacquer. $n/a. Available with nickel silver bell ring; red brass or silver plate; and first and fourth valve triggers.

Bb 4/4. 24. .768. 17 3/4". Three rotary. Brass lacquer. $n/a. Available with nickel silver bell ring; red brass or silver plate; and first valve trigger.

BBb 4/4. 25. .768. 17 3/4". Four rotary. Brass lacquer. $n/a. Available with nickel silver bell ring; red brass or silver plate; and first and fourth valve triggers.

BBb 4/4. 25E. .768. 17 3/4". Five rotary. Brass lacquer. $n/a. Available with nickel silver bell ring; red brass or silver plate; fifth valve thumb trigger and first and fourth valve triggers.

BBb 4/4. 26S. .807. 16 1/2". Four rotary. Brass lacquer. $n/a. Available with nickel silver bell ring; red brass or silver plate; and first and fourth valve triggers.

BBb 5/4. 197. .846. 16 1/2". Four rotary. Brass lacquer. $n/a. Available with nickel silver bell ring; red brass or silver plate; and first and fourth valve triggers.

BBb 5/4. 198. .807–.846. 17 3/4". Five rotary. Brass lacquer. $n/a. Available with nickel silver bell ring; red brass or silver plate; fifth valve thumb trigger; and first and fourth valve triggers.

Bb 6/4. 199. .846. 19 3/4". Three rotary. Brass lacquer. $n/a. Available with nickel silver bell ring; red brass or silver plate; and first valve trigger.

BBb 6/4. 200. .846. 19 3/4". Four rotary. Brass lacquer. $n/a. Available with nickel silver bell ring; red brass or silver plate; and first and fourth valve triggers.

MEISTER WALTER NIRSCHL

CC 5/4. 54C. .748. 19". Four stainless steel pistons, one rotary. Silver plate. $7,900.00. Available in clear lacquer.

MIRAPHONE

F 4/4. 180. .770. 15". Three, four, five, or six rotary. Brass lacquer. $n/a. Available in red brass, silver, or nickel plate; also with various valve configurations.

F 4/4. 181. .770–.830. 16 1/2". Four, five, or six rotary. Brass lacquer. $n/a. Available in red brass, silver, or nickel plate; exchangeable leadpipe; also with various valve configurations.

EEb 4/4. 183. .700. 15". Three, four, or five rotary. Brass lacquer. $n/a. Available in red brass, silver, or nickel plate; also with various valve configurations.

EEb. 200. .610. 13". Three or four piston. Brass lacquer. $n/a. Available in red brass, silver, or nickel plate; also with various valve configurations.

EEb. 1261. .740. 19". Four piston, compensating, three top and one side. Brass lacquer. $n/a. Available in silver or nickel plate.

BBb or CC 1/2. 184. .700. 14 1/4". Three, four, or five rotary. Brass lacquer. $n/a. Available in red brass, silver, or nickel plate; also with various valve configurations.

BBb or CC 3/4. 185. .740. 14 3/4". Three, four, or five rotary. Brass lacquer. $n/a. Available in red brass, silver, or nickel plate; also with various valve configurations.

BBb or CC 4/4. 186. .770. 17 3/4". Three, four, or five rotary. Brass lacquer. $n/a. Available in red brass, silver, or nickel plate; bell front; also with various valve configurations.

BBb 5/4. 187. .770. 17 3/4". Three, four, or five rotary. Brass lacquer. $n/a. Available in red brass, silver, or nickel plate; also with various valve configurations.

CC 4/4. 188. .770. 17 3/4". Five rotary. Brass lacquer. $n/a. Available in red brass, silver, or nickel plate; also with various valve configurations.

BBb or CC 5/4. 190. .840. 19 1/2". Three, four, or five rotary. Brass lacquer. $n/a. Available in red brass, silver, or nickel plate; also with various valve mechanisms.

BBb 3/4. 200. .670. 15 3/4". Three or four piston. Brass lacquer. $n/a. Available in red brass, silver, or nickel plate; also with various valve mechanisms.

CC 4/4. 1290. .770. 19 1/2". Four piston and one rotary. Brass lacquer. $n/a. Available in red brass, silver, or nickel plate; also with various valve configurations.

BBb 4/4. 1280. .770. 19 1/2". Four piston, compensating. Brass lacquer. $n/a. Available in red brass, silver, or nickel plate; also with exchangeable mouthpipe.

BBb 3/4. 1255A. .610–.640. 11 1/2". Four piston, compensating, three top and one side. $n/a. Available in red brass, silver, or nickel plate; also with slide trigger.

BBb, CC or EEb. 300, sousaphone. .740. 26 1/2". Three or four piston valves. Brass lacquer. $n/a. Available in silver plate.

SANDERS

CC 4/4. SM-1324U. .795. 15 3/4". Five rotary. Brass lacquer. $5,295.00. n/a.

CC 4/4. SM-1325U, compact. .795. 14". Five rotary. Brass lacquer. $4,650.00. n/a.

CC 4/4. SM-1374U, compact. .835. 15 3/4". Four rotary. Brass lacquer. $6,000.00. n/a.

CC 5/4. SM-1344U. .835. 19 2/3". Four rotary. Brass lacquer. $4, 650.00. n/a.

CC 4/4. MT-2. .795. 17 3/4". Four rotary. Brass lacquer. $5,650.00. n/a.

CC 4/4. MT-5, compact. .835. 15 3/4". Four rotary. Brass lacquer. $6,050.00. n/a.

CC 4/4. MT-6, compact. .795. 14". Five rotary. Brass lacquer. $7,650.00. n/a.

CC 4/4. MT-7. .795. 15 3/4". Five rotary. Brass lacquer. $6,050.00. n/a.

CC 5/4. MT-4, kaiser. .835. 19 3/4". Four rotary. Brass lacquer. $5,850.00. n/a.

BB♭ 3/4. SM-1384U. .638. 13 3/4". Three piston. Brass lacquer. $2,875.00. n/a.

BB♭ 4/4. SM-1385U. .638. 15 3/4". Three piston. Brass lacquer. $2,875.00. n/a.

BB♭ 4/4. SM-1394U. .638. 15 3/4". Four piston. Brass lacquer. $3,095.00. n/a.

BB♭ 4/4. SM-1314U. .795. 15 3/4". Four rotary. Brass lacquer. $4,265.00. n/a.

BB♭ 4/4. SM-1315U, compact. .795. 14". Four rotary. Brass lacquer. $4,650.00. n/a.

BB♭ 5/4. SM-1334U, kaiser. .835. 19 2/3". Four rotary. Brass lacquer. $5,595.00. n/a.

BB♭ 3/4. MT-1S, compact. .795. 14". Four rotary. Brass lacquer. $5,550.00. n/a.

BB♭ 4/4. MT-1. .795. 17 3/4". Four rotary. Brass lacquer. $5,650.00. n/a.

BB♭ 5/4. MT-3. .835. 19 3/4". Four rotary. Brass lacquer. $5,850.00. n/a.

VESPRO

BB♭ 4/4. VE-901. .750. 16 1/2". Four rotary. Brass lacquer. $4,995.00. Case, $695.00; silver plate, $1,500.00.

VMI (VOGTLAND MUSICAL INSTRUMENTS)

CC 4/4. VO-130. .748. 17 3/4". Four rotary. Brass lacquer. $6,100.00. Case, $695.00; silver plate, $1,500.00.

CC 4/4. VO-132. .748. 17 3/4". Five rotary. Brass lacquer. $6,995.00. Case, $695.00; silver plate, $1,500.00.

BB♭ 3/4. VO-200. .630. 15". Three piston. Brass lacquer. $3,550.00. Case, $695.00; silver plate, $1,500.00.

BB♭ 3/4. VO-201. .630. 15". Four piston. Brass lacquer. $4,100.00. Case, $695.00; silver plate, $1,500.00.

BB♭ 3/4. VO-101. .630. 15". Four rotary. Brass lacquer. $5,300.00. Case, $695.00; silver plate, $1,500.00.

BB♭ 4/4. VO-103. .748. 16 1/2". Four rotary. Brass lacquer. $6,100.00. Case, $695.00; silver plate, $1,500.00.

WILLSON

F 4/4. 3200. .710. 17". Four piston, one rotary. Brass lacquer. $7,975.00. Case, $300.00; available in silver plate.

EE♭ 4/4. 3400. .710. 17". Four piston, one rotary. Brass lacquer. $5,950.00. Case, $300.00; available in silver plate.

EE♭ 4/4. 2729. .710–.750. 15". Four piston, compensating, three top and one side. Brass lacquer. $4,770.00, with case. Available in silver plate.

EE♭ 4/4. 2829. .710–.750. 17". Four piston, compensating, three top and one side. Brass lacquer. $7,540.00, with case. Available in silver plate.

EE♭ 4/4. 2830. .750–.787. 19". Four piston, compensating, three top and one side. Brass lacquer. $8,610.00, with case. Available in silver plate.

CC♭ 4/4. 3000. .710. 18". Four piston, one rotary. Brass lacquer. $7,875.00. Case, $300.00; available in silver plate.

CC 5/4. 3100. .750. 20". Four piston, one rotary. Brass lacquer. $7,875.00. Case, $370.00; available in silver plate.

BB 5/4. 2930. .750–.787. 19". Four piston, compensating, three top and one side. Brass lacquer. $8,610.00, with case. Available in silver plate.

YAMAHA

F 3/4. YFB-621. .689. 14 1/8". Four piston, one rotary. Brass lacquer. $7,070.00, with case. Available in silver plate.

F 4/4. YFB-822. .768. 17 1/2". Four piston, one rotary. Brass lacquer. $8,030.00, with case. Available in silver plate.

EE♭ 3/4. YEB-321S. .689. 15 1/8". Four piston. Silver plate. $4,695.00, with case. n/a.

EE♭ 3/4. YEB-381S. .689. 15 1/8". Four piston, one rotary. Silver plate. $n/a. n/a.

EE♭ 4/4. YEB-631S. .689–.768. 17 1/2". Four piston, compensating, three top and one side. Silver plate. $7,120.00, with case. n/a.

CC 3/4. YCB-621. .689. 14 3/8". Four piston. Brass lacquer. $6,460.00, with case. Available in silver plate.

CC 4/4. YCB-822. .768. 19 1/2". Four piston, one rotary. Brass lacquer. $8,935.00, with case. Available in silver plate.

CC 4/4. YCB-861. .815. 17 6/8". Five rotary. Brass lacquer. $9,500.00, with case. Available with red brass bell.

B♭ 3/4. YBB-103. .661. 14 3/8". Three piston. Brass lacquer. $3,525.00, with case. n/a.

B♭ 4/4. YBB-201. .728. 17 1/2". Three piston. Brass lacquer. $4.310.00, with case. Available in silver plate.

BB♭ 4/4. YBB-321. .728. 17 1/2". Four piston. Brass lacquer. $4,900.00, with case. Available in silver plate.

BB♭ 3/4. YBB-621. .689. 14 3/8". Four piston. Brass lacquer. $6,460.00, with case. Available in silver plate.

BB♭ 4/4. YBB-631S. .689–.768.. 17 1/2". Four piston, compensating, three top and one side. Silver plate. $7,120.00, with case. n/a.

BB♭ 4/4. YBB-641. .812. 16 1/2". Four rotary. Brass lacquer. $6,565.00, with case. n/a.

BB♭ 4/4. YBB-841. .815. 17 1/8". Four rotary. Brass lacquer. $n/a. Available with red brass bell.

BB♭ 3/4. YBB-104, marching conversion. .610. 14 3/8". Three piston. Brass lacquer. $4,065.00, with case. Available in silver plate.

BB♭ 4/4. YBB-201M, marching conversion. .728. 17 1/2". Three piston. Brass lacquer. $4,565.00, with case. Available in silver plate.

BB♭. YBB-301B, sousaphone. .728. 26 1/8". Three piston. Fiberglass. $2,870.00, with bag. n/a.

BB♭. YBB-411, sousaphone. .728. 26". Three piston. Brass lacquer. $4,945.00, with case. Available in silver plate.

Tuba Mouthpieces and Accessories

Volta Andy Anders and Denis Winter

The preparation of this list of tuba-specific products currently available has included perusal of numerous catalogues, publications, and advertisements available in the U.S.A. Additional information has been obtained from international sources and manufacturers. Sincere appreciation is extended to those whose contributions allowed this listing to achieve international scope: Edward Hale, Austria; Thomas G. Cremer, Bermuda; Markus Haeller, Denmark; Harri Lidsle, Finland; Heiko Triebener, Robert Tucci, and Gerhard A. Meinl, Germany; Nicholas Zervopoulos, Greece; David J. Murphy, Ireland; Kazuhisa Nishida and Sadayuki Ogura, Japan; Dirk K. Annema, The Netherlands; Jan Pniak, Poland; Bernard Ebbinghouse, Sultanate of Oman; David LeClair, Switzerland; and R. Winston Morris. If indeed the future of the tuba depends upon such labors of love, it can be assured a secure future.

Many manufacturers responded, but some did not. In an attempt to make the listing as complete as possible, virtually every firm/product suggested, even if by word-of-mouth, has been included. This has resulted in some incomplete entries. The addresses listed indicate the manufacturer or dealer for the product. In the interest of consistency, prices quoted attempt to reflect suggested retail price. Many products are regularly available at a discounted price, and individu-als should inquire about products they are interested in purchasing.

Mouthpieces

Alexander, Gebr. D-6500 Mainz, Bahnhofstrasse 9, Postfach 1166, Germany. (0 61 31) 23 29 44. Fax (0 61 31) 22 42 48. F tuba, E♭ Sousaphone, DM 100,00. B tuba, B sousaphone, DM 111.00.

Alterna Brasswind Mouthpieces. DEG Music Products, Inc. P.O. Box 968. Lake Geneva. WI. 53147. USA. 800-558-9416. Models: A02-24AW, A02-TU25.

Amati. Geneva International Corp. 29 E. Hintz Rd., Wheeling, IL 60090. USA. 708-520-9970. Fax 708-520-9593. Replacement.

Bach. The Selmer Company, L.P., P.O. Box 310., Elkhart, IN 46414-0310. USA. 219-522-1675. Fax 219-522-1334. Models: 7 (33.25mm), 12 (33.75mm), 18 (32.1mm), 22 (31.6mm), 24W (31.25mm), 24AW (31.25mm), 25 (30.6mm), 30E (30mm), 32E (29.5mm), silver $52.00, gold $110.00.

Benge. United Musical Instruments USA, Inc. 1000 Industrial Pkwy., Elkhart, IN 46516. USA. 219-295-0079. Fax 219-295-8613. Models: 7, 18, 24AW, 25, $45.00.

Black Hill. Giardinelli Band Instrument Co., 7845 Maltage Drive, Liverpool, NY 13090. USA. 315-652-4792. Fax 315-652-4355. Custom one-piece, $125.00; custom two-piece, $165.00.

E.K. Blessing. 1301 Beardsley Ave., Elkhart, IN 46514. USA. Models: 18, 24AW, $51.00.

Boosey & Hawkes. Boosey & Hawkes Buffet Crampton, Inc., P.O. Box 130, Libertyville, IL 60048. USA. 708-816-2500. Fax 708-816-2514. Models: 1L (32.5mm), 2L (31.26mm), 3L (31.25mm), 3SL (31.25mm), 4L (30.5mm), 5L (30mm), No. 4886 gold, No. 5886 silver.

The Brasswind. 19889 State Line Rd., South Bend, IN 46637. USA. 800-348-5003. Fax 219-227-2542. Analyzation rim, $22.00.

Cerveny. Geneva International Corp. 29 E. Hintz Rd. Wheeling. IL. 60090. USA. 708-520-9970. Fax 708-520-9593. Replacement.

Conn. United Musical Instruments USA, Inc., 1000 Industrial Pkwy., Elkhart, IN 46516. USA. 219-295-0079. Fax 219-295-8613. Models: 7, 18, 24AW, 25, 2, Helleberg S, Helleberg 7B, silver $52.00, gold $106.00.

Antione Courtois. P. Gaudet et Cie, rue de Nancy, 75010 Paris, France. 1 42 40 3132. Model: 32 (32.5mm).

DEG Music Products, Inc. P.O. Box 968, Lake Geneva, WI 53147. USA. 800-558-9416. Model: Astro-AW14, $45.00.

Denis Wick. Giardinelli Band Instrument Co., 7845 Maltage Drive, Liverpool, NY 13090. USA. 315-652-4792. Fax 315-652-4355. Silver $85.00, gold $110.00.

Discount Music, Inc. P.O. Box 148027, Chicago, IL 60614. USA. 800-829-4713. Fax 312-663-3857. Analyzation rim, $30.00.

Doug Elliott Mouthpieces. 13619 Layhill Road, Silver Spring, MD 20906. USA. 301-871-3535. Models: CB 118 (30mm), CB 120 (30.5mm), CB 122 (31mm), CB 124 (31.5mm), TU 126 (32mm), TU 128 (32.5mm), TU 130 (33mm), TU 132 (33.5mm), Rims: N, 2N, 4N. Polycarbonate Cups: L, N, P, R, G, J. Shanks: S, M, B, C, H, W, A, At. Backbores: 2, 3, 4, 5, 6, 8. $110 and up.

E-Z Tone. United Musical Instruments USA, Inc., 1000 Industrial Pkwy., Elkhart, IN 46516. USA. 219-295-0079. Fax 219-295-8613. Models: 25, 24AW

Faxx. The Brasswind, 19880 State Line Rd., South Bend, IN 46637. USA. 800-348-5003. Fax 219-227-2542. Models: 18, 24AW, $45.00.

Giardinelli Artist Series. Giardinelli Band Instrument Co., 7845 Maltage Drive, Liverpool, NY 13090. USA. 315-652-4792. Fax 315-652-4355. Models: Butterfield (31mm), F-21 (31.5mm), WD-24 (31 mm), 18 (32mm), 24W (31mm), 24AW (31mm), 25 (30.5mm), Helleberg (33mm).

Instrumentenbau Egger. Turnerstrasse 32, CH-4058 Basel, Switzerland. 061 6814233. Models: H1 (32.5mm), F2 (32.6mm), sfr 120.

Hanstone. The Tuba Exchange, 1825 Chapel Hill Rd., Durham, NC 27707. USA. 800-441-9160. Replacement.

JK. Josef Klier, D-8531 Diespeck über Neustadt/ Aisch, Schleifmuhlstr. 6, Germany. 0 91 61/26 71. Fax 0 91 61/46 90. Also Wenzel Meinl GmbH., D-8192 Geretsried 2, Seniweg 4, Postfach 710, Germany. 08171/31642. Fax 80171/80288. Five cup depths, five throat bores, variety of rim widths. Models: Nr. 216 (29-29.8mm), DM 86, plexiglas DM128. Nr. 217 (30.2-31mm), DM 74, plexiglas DM128. Nr. 218 (31.2-32mm), DM 86, plexiglas DM128. Nr. 236 (29.2-29.8mm), DM 82, plexiglas DM 128. Nr. 237 (30.4-31mm), DM 86, plexiglas DM 128. Nr. 238 (31.4-32mm), DM 86, plexiglas DM 128. "Exklusive": T1 (34mm), T2 (33.5mm), T3 (33mm), T4 (32.5mm), T5 (32 mm), T6 (31.5mm), T7 (31mm), T8 (30.5mm), T9 (30mm), silver DM 110. Mouthpiece analyzation rim Nr. 225, DM 70, plastic rim available.

Jupiter Band Instruments. P.O. Box 90249, Austin, TX 78709-0249. USA. 800-283-4676. Model: 24AW, $40.00.

Kalison. Kalison Fabrica Strumenti Musicali, Via Pelligrino Rossi 96, Milan, Italy. 39 2 645 3060. Also The Tuba Exchange, 1825 Chapel Hill Rd., Durham, NC 27707. USA. 800-441-9160. Replacement.

Marcinkiewicz. P.O. Box 7, Sunland, CA 91041. USA. 818-834-1952. Models: N, 2N, 3N, 4N, 1W, 2W, 3W, 4W, H1, H2, H3, H4, $75.00.

George McCracken. 19230 Tabernacle Rd., Barhamsville, VA 23011. 804-566-0564. One model plus custom.

Melton. Wenzel Meinl GmbH., D-8192 Geretsried 2, Seniweg 4, Postfach 710, Germany. 08171/ 31642. Fax 80171/80288. Models: 130-3, 130-7, 150-4, 150-8, DM 78. Meinl-Weston #22, #80, #81, Modell Wm Bell (King), Modell Hoppert. "Walter Hilgers": Nr. 1 (31.5mm), Nr. 2 (31.8mm), Nr. 3 (31.8mm), Nr. 4 (31.8mm), Nr. 5 (31.8mm), Nr. 6 (32.), Nr. 7 (32.), Nr. 8 (32mm), Nr. 9 (32mm), DM 118.

Miraphone. Metall-Blasinstrumente, Traunreuter Strasse 8, 844 78 Waldkraiburg, BRD. Models (measurements converted to mm): C2 (30.2mm), C3 (32.5mm), C4 (32.9mm), C5 (31.0mm), C6 (33.0mm), C7 (32.8mm), C8 (Morris) (32.00 mm), Rose Solo (33.3mm), Rose Orchestra (33.3 mm). $160.00.

Neill Sanders Mouthpieces. 186 Podunk Lake Rd., Hastings, MI 49058-9282. USA. 616-948-8329. Fax 616-948-4399. Models: 6 (30mm), 4 (32mm), 3 (33mm), 2 (35mm), silver $57.00, gold $78.00.

Perantucci. The Tuba Center, Hauptstr. 17-19, D-8031 Eichenau, Germany. (0049) 0 81 41/8 20 45. Fax (0049) 0 81 41/7 18 85. Also Custom Music Co., 1930 Hilton, Ferndale, MI 48220. USA. 800-521-6380. Fax 810-546-8296. Models: American-style: PT-30 (32mm), PT-31 (32.5mm), PT-32 (32.5mm), PT-34 (32.5mm), PT-36 (33 mm), PT-38 (34mm), PT 42 (33mm), PT-44 (33 mm), PT-48 (33.5mm), PT-50 (33mm). German-style: PT-60 (32mm), PT-62 (32mm), PT-64 (32 mm), PT-66 (32.5mm), PT-68 (32.5mm), PT-70 (33mm), PT-72 (32.5mm), PT-80 (32.5mm), PT-82 (32.5mm), PT-83 (33mm), PT-84 (32mm), PT-86 (33.7mm), PT-88 (33.5mm), $98.00. Plastic rim $188.50, gold $162.50.

Schilke Music Products, Inc. 4520 James Place, Melrose Park, IL. 60160-1007. USA. 708-343-8858. Fax 708-343-8912. Models: 62 (31.85mm), 66 (31.52mm), 67 (32.41mm), 69C4 (32.76), S-H (31.84mm), silver $65.00, gold $105.00. Analyzation rim, $30.00. Custom/duplicating services.

Stromvi. Calle Antonio Molle 8, Valencia, Spain.

Bruno Tilz Kunstlerserie. Wenzel Meinl GmbH., D-8192 Geretsried 2, Seniweg 4, Postfach 710, Germany. 08171/31642. Fax 80171/80288. Models: 2H, 3H, 24S for Melton, "2" for Meinl-Weston. DM 118.

TRU-VU Transparent Mouthpieces. Ellis Weam, L-S Music Innovations, 250 H St., Suite 8110, Dept. 718, Blaine, WA 98230. USA. 800-661-7797. Fax 604-682-5618. Models: small, medium, $60.00. Custom available.

Yamaha Corporation of America. Band and Orchestra Division, P.O. Box 899, Grand Rapids, MI 49512-0899. USA. 616-940-4900. Models (diameters estimated from comparison charts): YAC-BB65

(30.6mm), YAC-BB66 (31.84mm), YAC-BB66B (31.52mm), YAC-BB6D4 (31.25mm), YAC-BB67B4, YAC-BB67 (31.6mm), YAC-67C4, YAC-BB68B (32.76mm). Five cup depths, five rim shapes, five rim thicknesses, five backbores. $50.00.

Zottola. The Brasswind, 19880 State Line Rd., South Bend, IN 46637. USA. 800-348-5003. Fax 219-227-2542.

ACCESSORIES

BREATHING DEVICES

Discount Music Inc. Breath Builder (available in tall and short models). Develops relaxed breathing techniques. $18.00. Incentive Spirometer. Increases lung capacity, visual device. $20.00. Rubber Re-breather Bag (available in four, five, and six liter capacities). Builds and maintains excellent breath control. $24.00, $27.00, and $35.00 respectively. P.O. Box 148027, Chicago, IL 60614. USA. 800-829-4713. Fax 312-663-3857.

RJN Marketing, Inc. The Breath Builder. Develops relaxed breathing techniques. 1278 Glenneyre #144, Laguna Beach, CA 92651. USA.

CASES, HARD

Alexander, Gebr. D-6500 Mainz, Bahnhofstrasse 9, Postfach 1166, Germany. (0 61 31) 23 29 44. Fax (0 61 31) 22 42 48. Four sizes. DM 985,00–1,235,00.

E.K. Blessing Co., Inc. Tuba case. Wood shell. C-450. $350.00. 1301 Beardsley Ave., Elkhart, IN 46514. USA. 800-348-7409. Fax 219-293-8398.

Boosey & Hawkes. Tuba and sousaphone cases. More than ten configurations of tuba and sousaphone cases available. $450.00–$690.00. 1925 Enterprise Court, P.O. Box 130, Libertyville, IL. 60048. USA. 708-816-2500. Fax 708-816-2514.

DEG Music Products, Inc. Tuba and sousaphone cases. More than 60 configurations of wood shell tuba and sousaphone cases. $381.00–$706.00. P.O. Box 968, Lake Geneva, WI 53147. USA. 800-558-9416. Fax 414-248-7953.

GEWA GmbH. Tuba case. Postfach 220, W-8102 Mittenwald, Germany. 08823-310. Fax 08823-3165.

Jakob Winter GmbH. Tuba case. Graslitzer Str. 10, Postfach 1462, W-6085 Nauheim, Germany. 06152-60112. Fax 06152-64266.

Kolberg Percussion GmbH. Tuba case. Stuttgarten Str. 157, W-7336 Uhingen, Germany. 07161-37696.

Meili Co. Tuba case. Kappelistrasse, CH-6281 Aesch, Switzerland. 041-85-31-41. Fax 041-85-29-44.

National Music Supply of Florida. Tuba and sousaphone cases. More than fifteen configurations of tuba and sousaphone cases available. $159.00–$454.00. P.O. Box 14421, St. Petersburg, FL 33733. USA. 800-383-6006. Fax 813-822-4836.

Riedl Variso Etuimanufaktur. Tuba case. Gutengerstr. 3, W-3549 Wolfhagen, Germany. 05692-5862.

United Musical Instruments, U.S.A., Inc. Tuba and sousaphone cases. Eight configurations available for tubas and sousaphones. $360.00–$380.00. 1000 Industrial Pkwy., Elkhart, IN 46516. USA. 219-295-0079. Fax 219-295-8613.

Van der Glas B.V. Tuba hard case. f 850,00. Postbus 85, 8440 AB Heerenveen, The Netherlands. 05130-2 26 52. Fax 05130-2 64 50.

Wenzel Meinl GmbH. Melton Tuba/Sousaphone hard cases. ABS plastic and plywood cases, available in several configurations for various tubas and sousaphones. DM 857–1,177. D-8192 Geretsried 2, Seniweg 4, Postfach 710, Germany. 08171-31642. Fax 08171-80288.

Yamaha Corporation of America. Tuba case for YBB-103. BBC-25. $500.00. Tuba case for YBB-201/321. BBC-32. $620.00. 3445 East Paris Avenue, SE., P.O. Box 899, Grand Rapids, MI 49512-0899. USA.

CASES, SOFT

Alexander, Gebr. D-6500 Mainz, Bahnhofstrasse 9, Postfach 1166, Germany. (0 61 31) 23 29 44. Fax (0 61 31) 22 42 48. Upholstered, soft bags, leather trim, two sizes. DM 312.00–360.00.

Altieri BrassPacs. Tuba backpacks and shoulder totes, padded, waterproof, and comfortable. 5 South Fox, Denver, CO 80223. USA. 303-744-7415.

Bari-Tuba Club. Grand Gakki Co., Ltd. Bari-Tuba Club Gig Bag. Available as backpack and shoulder or just as shoulder. ¥ 55000, ¥ 59000. 658 1-7-1. Vozaki-nakamachi, Higashi-nada-ku, Kobe-shi, Hyogo pref., Japan. 078-412.

BarrLines. Leather gig bags. Available for Hirsbrunner CC and BB♭, B&S F and CC, B&H EE♭ and BB♭, Miraphone 88, and custom. $490.00. P.O. Box 430, High Wycombe, Bucks HP13 5QT, England. 0494-437265. Fax 0494-437619.

Chukan (Chubu-Kangakki) Mfgr. Tuba gig bag for EE♭, BB♭, or compact tubas. ¥ 25000, ¥ 28000, ¥ 24000. 460 2-22-14, Shin-sakae, Naka-ku, Nagoya-shi, Aichi pref., Japan. 052-262-7878.

DEG Music Products, Inc. Tuba gig bags. Black cordura, four configurations available. C30-SP100, C30-SP200, C30-SP300, C30-SP400. $244.00, $263.00, $284.00, $308.00. P.O. Box 968, Lake Geneva, WI 53147. USA. 800-558-9416. Fax 414-248-7953.

GEWA GmbH. Tuba flight bag. Postfach 220, W-8102 Mittenwald, Germany. 08823-310. Fax 08823-3165.

Götz, Josef & Söhne. Gig bags. Rodenbachstrasse 7, W-6409, Dipperz 1, Germany.

S. Hayashi. Hayashi Gakki-Shokai Co., Ltd. Tuba gig bag. Available as backpack and shoulder or just as shoulder. ¥ 59000, ¥ 55000. 166 2-45-7, Wada Suginami-ku ,Tokyo pref., Japan.

Hayashi Soft Case Co., Ltd. Nero Music. Tuba gig bag. 2-9-10 Shibuya, Shibuya-Ku, Tokyo, Japan. 3-3400-5766. Fax 3-3406-6090.

Humes & Berg Mfg. Co., Inc. Tuxedo tuba bags. Two configurations: small and large, can be hand carried or used as a back pack. TX8245, TX8250. $153.00, $161.00. 4801 Railroad Ave, East Chicago, IN 46312. USA. 219-397-1980. Fax 219-397-4534.

Klangfarbe. Tuba flight bag. Einsiedlerplatz 4, A-1050 Vienna, Austria. 0222-545-17-17.

Meili Co. Tuba gig bag. Kappelistrasse. CH-6281 Aesch, Switzerland. 041-85-31-41. Fax 041-85-29-44.

National Music Supply of Florida. Sousaphone carrying case. Made of rugged Naugahyde, fits all Conn BB♭ sousaphones. Model 8770. $67.75. P.O. Box 14421, St. Petersburg, FL 33733. USA. 800-383-6006. Fax 813-822-4836.

Reunion Blues. Tuba gig bags. Available in five configurations, each in leather or cordura. 3-TF-4, C3-TF-4, 3-TB-6, C3-TB-6, 3-TC-8, C3-TC-8, 3-TE-9, C3-TE-9, 3-TS-3, C3-TS-3. $298.00–$718.00. 2525 16th St., San Francisco, CA 94103. USA. 415-861-7220. Fax 415-861-7298.

United Musical Instruments, U.S.A., Inc. Sousaphone carrying bag. Durable vinyl construction to fit all Conn and King sousaphones. 7129. Tuba carrying bags. One-piece vinyl bags for 18-inch and 15-inch upright bell models. 7131 (fits Conn 5J and 12J) and 7132 (fits Conn 15J and King 1140 and 1140M). Tuba carrying bags. Two-piece vinyl bags for bell and body sections for King 2340 and 2341 tubas. 7133. 1000 Industrial Pkwy. Elkhart. IN. 46516. USA. 219-295-0079. Fax 219-295-8613.

Van der Glas B.V. Sousaphone gig bag. f 375,00. Tuba gig gag. Available in 3 configurations. f 350,00, f 125,00, f 150,00. Postbus 85, 8440 AB Heerenveen, The Netherlands. 05130-2 26 52. Fax 05130-2 64 50.

Wenzel Meinl GmbH. Melton tuba/sousaphone gig bags. Available in several configurations for various tubas and sousaphones. R21U, R22U, R23U, R24U, R25U, R26U, R45U, R55U. DM 230–555. D-8192 Geretsried 2, Seniweg 4, Postfach 710, Germany. 08171-31642. Fax 08171-80288.

Franz Wussler Feintäschner. Gig bags for F or BB♭ tuba, leather. DM 910.00, DM 1,044.00. Beethovenstrasse 1, 5632 Wermelskirchen, Germany. 02196-4243.

Yamaha Corporation of America. Sousaphone gig bag. Cordura nylon, no-scratch lining, with exterior pocket. YAC SHC-31 (for YSH-301). $220.00. Tuba gig bag. Cordura nylon, no-scratch lining, with exterior pocket. YAC 1371 (for YBB-103/104), YAC 1370 (for YBB-201/321). $185.00 and $195.00. 3445 East Paris Avenue, SE., P.O. Box 899, Grand Rapids, MI 49512-0899. USA.

LUBRICANTS

Aerospace Lubricants. ALiSYN® Cork and Slide Grease. Non-petroleum, non-silicone synthetic products. No. 2190. $4.95. ALiSYN® Solvent/Cleaner. For cleaning deposits of grime both inside and outside of instrument. No. 2390. $4.95. ALiSYN® Valve Slide Key Oil. Non-petroleum, non-silicone synthetic products. No. 2090. $3.50. 1505 Delashmut Ave, Columbus, OH, 43212. USA. 800-441-9160. Fax 800-441-2521.

Holton Oil. Leblanc Corp. 7001 Leblanc Blvd, Kenosha, WI 53141-1415. USA. 800-558-9421.

Products of MAMCO. Spacefiller TS. Non-toxic lubricant for tuning slides. Ultimate I Spacefiller. Non-toxic valve lubricant. Ultimate II Spacefiller. Non-toxic valve lubricant for new or recently plated valves. P.O. Box 1417, Decatur, GA 30030. USA. 404-373-1050.

Pro-Oil. MusiChem Inc., San Diego, CA. USA. Various oil products in different sizes.

Roché-Thomas. San Bernadino. CA. 92402. USA. Premium valve oil.

Selmer Company. Bach Rotor Oil. No. 1886. Bach Tuning Slide Grease. No. 1887. Bach Valve Oil. No. 1885. Selmer Rotary Valve Oil. No. 2938. Selmer Tuning Slide and Cork Grease. No. 2942. Selmer Valve Oil. No. 2932. P.O. Box 310, Elkhart, IN. 46515-0310. USA. 219-521-1675. Fax 219-522-0334.

United Musical Instruments, U.S.A., Inc. Al Cass "Fast" Oil. Combination valve, slide, and key lubricant. 341. Benge Tuning Slide Grease. Assures long-lasting, smooth-acting slides. 336. Benge Valve Oil. For all piston valve instruments, contains no silicones. 331. Conn Rotor Oil. Formulated for close-tolerance rotary valves. 3103. Conn Tuning Slide Grease. Formulated to keep slide working hours longer. 3106. Conn Valve Oil. Formulated for close-tolerance valves. 3101. King Rotor Oil. Thin viscosity formula for rotary valves. 323. King Tuning Slide Grease. Easy to apply grease. 326. King Valve Oil. Highly refined to minimize valve wear. 321. 1000 Industrial Pkwy., Elkhart, IN 46516. USA. 219-295-0079. Fax 219-295-8613.

Yamaha Corporation of America. Lever oil. YAC 1014. $4.50. Premium rotor oil. YAC 1012. $6.25. Premium valve oil. YAC 0900. $3.00. Rotor oil. YAC 1002. $1.75. Rotor spindle oil. YAC 1013. $4.50. Slide grease. YAC 1011. $1.00. Valve oil. YAC 1000. $1.75. 3445 East Paris Avenue, SE., P.O. Box 899, Grand Rapids, MI 49512-0899. USA.

MOUTHPIECE POUCHES

DEG Music Products, Inc. Tuba molded pouch. AO6-SR400. $5.00. P.O. Box 968, Lake Geneva, WI 53147. USA. 800-558-9416. Fax 414-248-7953.

Josef Klier. Mouthpiece bag. Nr. 242. DM 19. D-8531, Diespeck, Über Neustadt/Aisch, Schleifmühlstr. 6. Germany. 09161-2671. Fax 09161-4690.

Reunion Blues. Mouthpiece boot. Leather pouch for tuba mouthpieces. 2-MOB. $10.00. 2525 16th St., San Francisco, CA 94103. USA. 415-861-7220. Fax 415-861-7298.

Schilke Music Products, Inc. Tuba mouthpiece pouch. Naugahyde, $8.00, leather, $13.00. 4520 James Place, Melrose Park, IL 60160-1007. USA. 708-343-8858. Fax 708-343-8912.

Selmer Company. Flexible plastic mouthpiece enclosure. No. 1804. Padded black nylon pouch. No. 1893. P.O. Box 310, Elkhart, IN 46515-0310. USA. 219-522-1675. Fax 219-522-0334.

United Musical Instruments, U. S. A., Inc. Conn tuba pouch. Black vinyl with zipper. 171L. $4.75. UMI Kleargard mouthpiece pouches. Molded from flexible, heavy gauge "see thru" vinyl. 173L. UMI Precision Vinyl™ mouthpiece pouches. Black vinyl pouches with zipper closures. 171L. 1000 Industrial Pkwy., Elkhart, IN 46516. USA. 219-295-0079. Fax 219-295-8613.

Yamaha Corporation of America. Tuba mouthpiece pouch. Vinyl with zippered closures. YAC 1351. $5.00. 3445 East Paris Avenue, SE., P.O. Box 899, Grand Rapids, MI 49512-0899. USA.

MUTES

Alexander, Gebr. D-6500 Mainz, Bahnhofstrasse 9, Postfach 1166, Germany. (0 61 31) 23 29 44. Fax (0 61 31) 22 42 48. Wood straight mute, 8 sizes. DM 710.00–820.00.

Apperson Mutes. Aluminum with redwood ends. $85. 3008 Riva Ridge Way, Boise, ID 83709. USA. 208-362-6353.

NP Griffith Co. Tuba mute. Aluminum body with redwood ends, available in large and small sizes. $75.00. 1436 S. 11th Street, Omaha, NE 68108. USA. 402-345-2466.

Humes & Berg Mfg. Co., Inc. BB♭ recording bass mute. No. 195. $75.20. BB♭ tuba straight mute. Stone-lined tuba upright 14"–18" bell. No. 193. $57.70. BB♭ tuba straight mute. For Meinl Weston. No. 197. $57.20. EE♭ tuba straight mute. For EE♭ tuba. No. 194. $44.20. Sousaphone practice mute. No. 192B. $97.00. Sousaphone straight mute. No. 196. $70.90. Stone-lined tuba upright 20"–25" bell. No. 190. $59.90. Straight mute. Symphonic all-metal tuba (case for mute is available). Mute No. 206, $130.70. Case No. 206C, $75.70. Symphonic all-metal tuba—large bore. Metal mute No. 208, $173.20. Case No. 208C, $81.70 for case. Tuba cup mute No. 209. $119.90. Tuba (large bore) fiber mute No. 207, $83.50. Case No. 207C, $81.70. Tuba practice mute. No. 192. $97.00. Velvet-Tone Mute. For bell sizes 16", 18", 20", and 22". No. 191A, 191B, 191C, and 191D respectively. $53.50, $54.20, $56.70, and $63.00. Velvet-Tone Sousa Mute—25B. No. 191E. $65.20. Velvet-Tone Sousaphone Mute 22"–28".

No. 181E. $57.20. 4801 Railroad Ave., East Chicago, IN 46312. USA. 219-397-1980. Fax 219-397-4534.

Marcandella Co. Tuba mutes. Available for CC, BB♭, EE♭, and F tubas. P.O. Box 492, 8201 Schaffhausen, Switzerland.

Joachim Pöltl. Tuba mute. Fexmühle 37, W-5204 Lohmar 21, Germany. 02206-80867.

Prima Gakki. Yupon Tuba Mute. ¥ 35000. 1-1-8, Higashi-Nihonbashi chuo-ku, Tokyo pref., Japan. 03-3866-2210.

Tenn Tech-T.U.B.A. Tech Tuba Mutes. Large, $50.00, small $45.00. P.O. Box 5045, Cookeville, TN 38505. USA.

Wenzel Meinl GmbH. Tuba mute. Available for F, CC, and BB♭ tuba. DM 410, DM 420, DM 420, respectively. D-8192 Geretsried 2, Seniweg 4, Postfach 710, Germany. 08171-31642. Fax 08171-80288.

OTHER ACCESSORIES

Air Acoustics. The Acousticoil. A state-of-the-art removable acoustic insert. 1234 S. Quince Way, Denver, CO 80231. USA. 303-751-0673.

Chukan (Chubu-Kangakki) Mfgr. Chukan (Chubu-Kangakki) Tuba Strap. ¥ 2400. 460 2-22-14. Sinsakae Naka-ku, Nagoya-shi, Aichi pref., Japan. 052-262-7878.

Conn Band Instruments. Music-stand size fingering charts. Colorful fingering chart for BB♭ three-valve tuba. E14. $.20. Poster-size fingering charts. 22" x 30" format, ideal for group instruction. E4. $2.00. P.O. Box 727, Elkhart, IN 46515. USA.

DEG Music Products, Inc. Brass short cut for tuba. Made of copper. AO9-BSC-6. $43.00. Sousaphone mouthpipe. Conn upper mouthpipe. A23-A210, A23-A210S. $57.70 (brass), $69.80 (silver). Sousaphone mouthpipe. King upper mouthpipe. A23-K191, A23-K191S. $48.10 (brass), $60.20 (silver). Sousaphone mouthpipe. Olds and Reynolds upper mouthpipe. A23-O150, A23-O150S. $52.90 (brass), $65.00 (silver). Sousaphone tuning bits. Conn tuning bit set. A23-A211, A23-A211S. $43.30 (brass), $52.90 (silver). Sousaphone tuning bits. King tuning bit set. A23-K190, A23-K190S. $24.10 (brass), $33.10 (silver). Sousaphone tuning bits. Olds and Reynolds tuning bit set. A23-O151, A23-O151S. $24.10 (brass), $33.70 (silver). P. O. Box 968, Lake Geneva, WI 53147. USA. 800-558-9416. Fax 414-248-7953.

Endsley Brass Instrument Mouthpieces. Tuba mouthpiece rounder. $15.00. 2253 Bellaire Street, Denver, CO 80207. USA. P.O. Box 968, Lake Geneva, WI 53147. USA. 800-558-9416. Fax 414-248-7953.

Ferree's Tools, Inc. Ferree Polygon Spring. Unique shape gives an especially smooth and fast action to this piston valve spring. S79. $9.00. Rotary valve action smoothers and springs. When installed, provides a lighter, smoother and faster depression.

S94C (set of two smoothers), S95C (set of six smoother springs). $9.00 and $4.70. 1477 E. Michigan Ave., Battle Creek, MI 49017. USA. 616-965-0511. Fax 616-965-7719.

King Musical Instruments. Poster-size fingering charts. 22" x 30" format, ideal for group instruction. K76. $2.00. P.O. Box 727, Elkhart, IN 46515. USA.

Josef Klier. Mouthpiece adapter, F-EE♭-BB♭. Nr. 250. DM 32. Mouthpiece bag. Nr. 242. DM 19. Mouthpiece brush. Nr. 244. DM 1.40. D-8531, Diespeck, Über Neustadt/Aisch, Schleifmühlstr. 6. Germany. 09161-2671. Fax 09161-4690.

Lorenz Corporation. Tuba fingering chart. PP 269. $1.95. Box 802, Dayton, OH. 45401-802. USA.

Marcandella Co. Tuba straps. 2.5 x 83 cm., 2.5 x 113 cm., and 4 x 115 cm. P.O. Box 492, 8201 Schaffhausen, Switzerland.

George McCracken. Tuba bells. Made of special carbon fiber. $800.00. Tuba mouthpipe. Made of special carbon fiber. $300.00. 19230 Tabernacle Road, Barhamsville, VA 23011. USA. 804-566-0564.

Musical Enterprises. Tuba BERP (Buzz Extension & Resistance Piece). Center your sound, build strength, and add resonance by buzzing with this device. $23.96. P.O. Box 1041, Larkspur, CA 94977-1041. USA.

Prima Gakki. Yupon Tuba Strap. ¥3900. 1-1-8, Higashi-Nihonbashi chuo-ku, Tokyo pref., Japan. 03-3866-2210.

Schilke Co. Mouthpiece visualizer. 4520 James Place, Melrose Park, IL 60160-1007. USA. 708-343-8858. Fax 708-343-8912.

Selmer Company. Care kit for tuba/sousaphone. Complete set of accessories to care for and maintain your instrument. No. 2969. Grime gutters. Attaches at bottom of valve casings to absorb oil. No. 628. Mouthpiece brushes. No. 815. P.O. Box 310, Elkhart, IN 46515-0310. USA. 219-522-1675. Fax 219-522-0334.

United Musical Instruments, U.S.A., Inc. Sousaphone accessory pouch. Pouch for mouthpipe, tuning bits, mouthpiece, etc. 550. Sousaphone Econo Pads. Compact and comfortable shoulder pad. 549B, 549W. Sousaphone mouthpipes. Replacement mouthpipes for all Conn and King Sousaphones. AC1352, AC1353, AC1354, SU30130. Sousaphone Protecto-Pads. Shoulder pad provides maximum comfort, and undercarriage pad protects the bottom bow from scratches. 546B, 546W (shoulder pads) and 547B, 547W, 548B, 548W (undercarriage pads). $95.00, $95.00, $40.00, $40.00, $55.00, and $55.00 respectively. Sousaphone tuning bits. Replacement tuning bits for all Conn and King Sousaphones. AC1349, AC1350, AC1351, SU30140. 1000 Industrial Pkwy., Elkhart, IN 46516. USA. 219-295-0079. Fax 219-295-8613.

Van der Glas B.V. Sousaphone shoulder pad. f 55,00. Postbus 85, 8440 AB Heerenveen, The Netherlands. 05130-2 26 52. Fax 05130-2 64 50.

Western Music Co. Tuba or sousaphone storage hang-ups. P.O. Box 1389, Grand Junction, CO 81502. USA. 303-242-3272

Yamaha Corporation of America. Marching tuba lyre. YAC 1512. $11.00. 3445 East Paris Avenue, SE., P.O. Box 899, Grand Rapids, MI 49512-0899. USA.

TUBA SPECIALISTS

Custom Music Company. Tuba World™ (Division of Custom Music Company). Offers various accessories for tuba including cases. 1930 Hilton, Ferndale, MI 48220. USA. 800-521-6380. Fax 810-546-8296.

Geneva International Corp. Offers various accessories for the tuba, including hard cases by Amati. 200 Larkin Dr., Wheeling, IL 60090. USA. 800-533-2388. Fax 708-520-9593.

Giardinelli Band Instrument Co. Offers various accessories for tuba, including cases. 7845 Maltlage Dr., Liverpool, NY 13090. USA. 800-288-2334. Fax 315-652-4534.

HEER Co., P.O. Box 616, 8010 Zurich, Switzerland. 01-730-4103. Fax 01-730-9833.

International Musical Suppliers, Inc. Offers various accessories for tuba, including cases. P.O. Box 357, Mount Prospect, IL 60056. USA. 800-762-1116. Fax 708-870-1767.

Interstate Music Supply. Offers various accessories for tuba, including cases. P.O. Box 315, New Berlin, WI 53151. USA. 800-837-2263. Fax 414-786-6840.

National Music Supply of Florida. Offers various accessories for tuba, including cases. P.O. Box 14421, St. Petersburg, FL 33733. USA. 800-383-6006. Fax 813-822-4836.

Orpheus Music. Offers various accessories for tuba. 13814 Lookout Rd., San Antonio, TX 78233-4528. USA. 800-821-9448.

Osmun Brass Instruments. Offers various accessories for tuba. 438 Common St., Belmont, MA 02178. USA. 800-223-7846. Fax 617-489-0421.

Rayburn Musical Instruments. Offers various accessories for tuba. 263 Huntington Ave., Boston, MA 02115. USA. 617-266-4727.

The Brasswind. The Woodwind & The Brasswind. Offers various accessories for tuba, including cases; exclusive agent of the Stewart Stand for Tuba. 19880 State Line Road, South Bend, IN 46637. USA. 800-348-5003. Fax 219-272-8266.

The Tuba Center. Offers various accessories for tuba. Hauptstrasse 17–19, D-8031 Eichenau bei München, Germany. 08141-82045. Fax 08141-71885.

The Tuba Exchange. Offers various accessories for tuba. 1825 Chapel Hill Road, Durham, NC 27707. USA. 800-869-TUBA. Fax 919-493-8822.

Wichita Band Instruments. Offers various accessories for tuba, including cases. 2525 E. Douglas, Wichita, KS 67211. USA. 800-835-3006. Fax 316-684-6858.

TUBA STANDS

DEG Music Products, Inc. DEG Handy Tuba Rest. Folding tripod-type stand to support the instrument. A18-KA100. $89.50. P.O. Box 968, Lake Geneva, WI 53147. USA. 800-558-9416. Fax 414-248-7953.

Kolberg Percussion GmbH. Tuba stand. Stuttgarten Str. 157, W-7336 Uhingen, Germany. 07161-37696.

König & Meyer. Tuba stand. Kiesweg 2, W-6980 Wertheim, Germany. 09342-8060. Fax 09342-80639.

Robert James Products. Weight Lifter Tuba Stand. $75. P.O. Box 2514, San Marcos, CA 92079-2514. USA. 800-345-8923. Fax 619-744-4620.

The Woodwind & The Brasswind. Stewart Tuba Stand. Attaches directly to instrument. No. SWTU. $89.00. 19880 State Line Rd, South Bend, IN. 46637. USA. 800-348-5003. Fax 219-277-2542.

United Musical Instruments, U.S.A., Inc. UMI Precision Sousaphone Stand. Adjustable, chrome-plated steel. 488. UMI Precision Tuba Stand. Adjustable, chrome-plated steel. 487. 1000 Industrial Pkwy., Elkhart, IN 46516. USA. 219-295-0079. Fax 219-295-8613.

Wenzel Meinl GmbH. Tuba Stand. Available in two models: M 149-5, M 149-40. DM 270, DM 155. D-8192 Geretsried 2, Seniweg 4, Postfach 710, Germany. 08171-31642. Fax 08171-80288.

Specialized Repair Sources

Craig L. Fuller

Information on repairs was compiled from a questionnaire sent to all T.U.B.A. members in the United States listed in the 1992 roster as "professional." The respondents were asked "to identify a significant number of the repair persons and shops throughout the world who are doing outstanding work on brass instruments. Instead of listing every repair shop or repair person, those responsible for the outstanding work in their region or country should be identified." Information on repair services overseas came from the *TSB* international consultants. Apologies are extended to any repair persons who have been missed.

Contributors were asked to list the types of repair services available from each repair source. In some cases they listed only the repairs they have seen the shops accomplish, although other services may be offered. Most of the European brass instrument manufacturers will also do overhauls on the instruments they have made. Some will repair other brands of instruments as well. They are listed above under "Tuba Manufacturers and Distributors and Their Products."

Thanks to the following contributors who have helped to make this section of *The Tuba Source Book* a reality: Jim Akins, Jerry Beckman, Jay Bertolet, Gary Bird, Ronald Bishop, Phillip C. Black, Dr. Sy Brandon, Gary Buttery, Leonard Byrne, Steve Call, Rex Conner, Barton Cummings, Robert Daniel, Jack Denniston, Judith Fuller, Matthew Good, Nate Griffith, Markus Haeller, Edward Hale, Keating Johnson, Charles Kelley, Peter J. Krill, Igor Krivokapic, David LeClair, Don Little, Bill Long, William Mickelsen, David Moen, R. Winston Morris, Kazuhisa Nishida, Mark Nelson, Timothy Northcut, Kelly George Okamoto, Stephen Perry, Sam Pilafian, Jan Pniak, Gene Pokorny, Jack Robinson, Robert Rusk, Michael Sanders, Jim Self, William Sprague, John Stevens, Ron Tasa, Dwight Thomas, W. E. Thiessen, Gary Tirey, Ross Tolbert, Jan Tracy, Heiko Triebener, Bob Tucker, John Turk, Michael Short, Michael Wagner, Scott Watson, Steve Winteregg, Curt Wood, and Jerry Young.

The trade association in the United States for professional repair persons is National Association of Professional Band Instrument Repair Technicians (NAPBIRT), Chuck Hagler, Executive Director, P.O. Box 51, Normal, IL 61761. Tel. (309) 452-4257, Fax (309) 452-4825. NAPBIRT holds an annual conference with workshop and clinic sessions for technicians. It has a certification program.

A few schools in the United States teach instrument repair, and many technicians have learned the trade through informal apprenticeships with the masters of the trade. The following organizations offer formal training in instrument repair: Allied Music, Elkhorn, Wisconsin; Eastern School of Musical Instrument Repair; Red Wing, Minnesota, Vocational-Technical; Western Iowa Technical College, Sioux City, Iowa

Supplies, parts, and tools for the repair trade can be purchased from the following companies:

Allied Supply Corporation, P.O. Box 288, Elkhorn, WI 53121. Tel. (800) 558-3226. Fax (414) 723-2051.

Ferree's Tools, Inc., 1477 E. Michigan Ave., Battle Creek, MI 49017. Tel. (800) 253-2261. Fax (616) 965-7719.

Ed Myers, Co., 1622 Webster St., Omaha, NE 68102. Tel. (800) 228-9188.

Strege-Wattke Tool & Supply Corp., Rt. 3, Box 252A, Elkhorn, WI 53121. Tel. (800) 654-4369. Fax (414) 723-2587

Repair Services in the United States by Region and State

Key toTypes of Services Provided

a. Cleaning, minor repairs
b. Dent removal
c. Slide repairs
d. Valve adjustment
e. Valve replating
f. Complete overhaul
g. Custom tuning, slide adjustment mechanisms
h. Mouthpiece replating
i. Custom mouthpiece design, alterations
j. Addition of fifth valve to instruments
k. BB♭ to CC conversions

NORTHEAST

CONNECTICUT

Sturm Brassworks (Brian Sturm), 38 Highland Dr., Ledyard, CT 06339. (203)572-8275. Services: a–d.

MARYLAND

Brass Arts Limited (Randy Harrison), 545 Fuselage Avenue, Baltimore, Maryland 21221. (410) 686-6108. "From dent work to complete overhauls."

Mizzel Music (Larry Mizzel), 835 S. Potomac Street, Hagerstown, Maryland 21740. (301) 791-1305. "Set up for complete overhauls—very reasonable."

MASSACHUSETTS

Osmun Brass (Jim Becker/Chuck Sheppard), 438 Common St., Boston, MA 02178. (617) 489-0810. Fax (617) 489-0421. Services: a–j. Comments: "extremely thorough, most impressive valve work, emergency work."

PENNSYLVANIA

The Band Shop (Bernie Pitkin), 11687 Church Drive, Shippensburg, PA 17257. (717) 532-3336. Services: a–h, j–k. Comments: "Tubist and excellent repairman."

Brass & Woodwind Shop (Ted Woehr), 519 Carothers Ave., Carnegie, PA 15106. (412) 276-6899. Services: a–i, k. Comments: "A Master Craftsman." "Excellent craftsmanship. Is willing to try new ideas."

Horn Hospital (Jim Haunstein), 3796 Valley Rd., Marysville, PA 17053. (717) 957-2775. Services: a–e, g–h. Comments: "Very fast, dependable, rea-sonable rates. A fellow tubist, knows the instruments."

Zapf's (Leonard F. Zapf), 5429 N. 5th, Philadelphia, PA 19120. (215) 924-8736. Services: a–d, f–h. Comments: "Excellent dent removal and valve adjustment."

VERMONT

Vermont Musical Instrument Repair (Jeffrey Vovakes), RD 3, Box 3230, Montpelier, VT 05602. (802) 229-4416. Services: a–e, g–h. Comments: "Good for all-around general repair. Complete dent-removal and valve adjustment."

NEW YORK

Brass Lab (Chuck McAlexander), 525 W. 25th St., New York, NY 10001. (212) 243-7180. Services: a–h, j. Comments: "Makes custom leadpipes. Can also turn the rotor of rotary valves so the valve doesn't cut the air flow." "Great leadpipe work!"

Wendall Harrison Music (Bob Kelly), 106 Luther Ave.,Liverpool, NY. (315) 475-0001. Services: a–h, j–k. Comments: "Excellent work. Will do immediate repairs for emergencies."

SOUTHEAST

VIRGINIA

Kratz Custom Service (David Kratz), 709 S. Adams St., Arlington, VA 22204-2114. (703) 521-4588. Services: a–g, j. Comments: "Designs and engineers custom solutions to mechanical problems." "A meticulous craftsman!" "Also manufactures custom lightweight rigid cases."

George McCracken Horns (George McCracken), SR Box 5C, Barhamsville, VA 23011. (804) 564-3564. Services: a–d, g. Comments: Made the self-centering device on Ron Bishop's Alexander tuba. "An excellent craftsman."

Robert Pallansch (Robert Pallansch), 2808 Woodlawn, Falls Church, VA 22042. (703) 532-0137. Services: a–h, j. Comments: "Excellent work, very creative." Copies of mouthpieces (in plastic and wood) and custom mouthpiece work.

FLORIDA

The Brass and Woodwind Shop (Ed Kennedy), 1517-C E. Fowler Ave.,Tampa, FL 33612. (813) 971-2120. Services: a–d, f, g. Comments: "Excellent."

Florida Brass (Roy Lawler), 1958 County Rd. 427, Suite 120, Longwood, FL 32750. (407) 331-2884. Services: a–d, f–g, i–k. Comments: "Roy is the only repairman that I trust with my equipment." "A consummate perfectionist," "any custom modification," "a rotary valve specialist."

Vollers Band Instrument Repair (Berndt Voller), Cacciatore Plaza, 5522 Hanley Rd., Suite 111, Tampa, FL 33634. (813) 884-2201. Services: a–d, f, g. Comments: "Excellent."

SOUTH

KENTUCKY

Alex Cory, 194 Swigert Ave., Lexington, KY 40505. (606) 299-6652. Services: a–d, f–g. Comments: "Consummate repairman for all instruments."

TENNESSEE

Mid-South Music (Joe Sellmansberger), 3699 Summer,Memphis, TN 38122 (901) 458-8791. Fax (901) 327-9520. Services: a–k. Comments: "Custom work; work has always been excellent."

Rush's Musical Services, Inc. (Greg Welton), 2868 Alcoa Hwy, Knoxville, TN 37920-3799. (615) 573-4138. Services: a–d, g. Comments: "First quality work."

The Band Room, Inc. (Harley Tatarsky), 600 West Main, Hendersonville, TN 37075. (615) 822-0202. Services: a–d, g, j.

TEXAS

Alternative Valve Designs (Curtis L. Wood), 4206 Pineville, Spring, TX 77388. (713) 288-6151. Services: a–k. Comments: "Top flight repairman."

P & H Music Services (Arnold Preist), 6412 Bandera Rd., San Antonio, TX 78238. (210) 520-7948, (800) 344-6174. Fax (210) 657-0046. Services: a–h. Comments: "Good clean work, high quality workmanship, emergencies."

Swanson Band Instrument Repair (Eric Swanson), 1609 Holt St., Fort Worth, TX 76103. (817) 654-4225. Fax: (817) 654-4460. Services: a–d, g, j. Comments: "Complete work on trombones, which is his specialty, but he also does quite a bit of work on tubas as well."

MIDWEST

ILLINOIS

The Brass Bow (Wayne Tanabe, Dana Hofer), 702-E. Northwest Hwy., Arlington Heights, IL 60004. (708) 253-7552. Services: a–d, g. Comments: "Whenever the CSO's York is in trouble, I take it to Wayne."

Quinlan and Fabish Music Company (Ron Collier and staff), 2563 West 79th Street, Chicago, IL 60652. (312) 737-4789. Services: a–k. Comments: "Good on the design/imagination end of things."

IOWA

Grady Instrument Repair (Merlin Grady), 5605 Ansborough Way, Des Moines, IA 50701. (800) 373-6297. Services: a–e, h. Comments: "Excellent repairman."

Rieman's Music (John Salak), 4420 E. Broadway Ave., Des Moines, IA 50317. (515) 262-0365. Fax (515) 262-0365. Services: a–d, g. Comments: "Very easy person to work with."

OHIO

Central Instrument Company (Peter La Victorie), 739 Portage Trail, Cuyahoga Falls, OH 44221. (216) 928-6000. Services: a–d, f, g, j. Comments: "A good craftsman. Works very hard to please."

Daybreak Instrument and Repair (Tim and Gordon Cleal), 116 North High St., Cortland, OH 44410. (800) 878-2163. Services: a–i. Comments: "Super craftsmanship, know and play tubas."

Kincaid's (Loren Gladson), 1325 W. First St., Springfield, OH. (513) 325-7071. Services: a–e., g. Comments: "Good for basic repair."

Spillman Musical Instrument Repair (Ray Spillman), 7887 Concord Rd., Delaware, OH 43015. (614) 292-1526. Services: a–d, g–h.

MINNESOTA

Peterson Brass Repair (Eric Peterson), 2801 Irving Av. N., Minneapolis, MN 55411. (612) 722-1989. Services: a–h, j. Comments: "Excellent workmanship. One of the very best in the U.S."

MISSOURI

St. Louis Woodwind and Brass (Bill Meyers), 737 N Highway 67, Florissant, MO 63031. (314) 921-0012. Services: a–k. Comments: "Very good, clean work."

WISCONSIN

Allied Music Corp. (Ed Getzen), 530 S. Hwy. H, Elkhorn, WI 53121. (800) 562-6838 or (414) 723-5455. Fax (414) 723-4245. Services: a–h, j. Comments: "Largest band instrument repair shop around; parts, fabrication. They have seen and done it all."

Robert Rusk, 2524 E. Strattford, Shorewood, WI 53066. (414) 962-7174. Services: j–k. Comments: "Adjustments and modifications on old instruments to bring them back to life. Bob Rusk is the world's leading expert on York tubas and converting BB♭ tubas to CC." "I strongly recommend."

Schmitt Music Repair Shop (Raymond Hurst), 2953 London Square, Eau Claire, WI 54701. (715) 832-8915. Fax (715) 832-5576. Services: a–d, g–h. Comments: "Bearing work done here; chemical flush available."

Ward-Brodt Music Mall (Alton "Corky" Cain), 2200 W. Beltline Highway, Madison, WI 53713. (608) 271-1460. Fax (608) 271-8519. Services: a–d, g. Comments: "A terrific guy who does very high quality work."

MOUNTAIN AND PLAINS STATES

NEBRASKA

The Horn Works (Bill Sprague, Nate Griffith), 7328 Harrison, Omaha, NE 68128. (402) 592-5655. Services: a–j. Comments: "Very capable, creative and easy to work with."

John Gill, 4812 Ginny Ave., Lincoln, NE 68516. (402) 486-1334. Services: a–d. Comments: "Great for minor repairs, emergencies. Staff repair technician at University of Nebraska-Lincoln."

COLORADO

Graner School Music (Larry Mynette), 4448 Barnes Rd., Colorado Springs, CO 80917. (719) 574-2001. Services: a–d, f. Comments: "Always does extraordinary work."

The Repair Shop (Dave Chandler), 2321 E. Mulberry, #4, Ft. Collins, CO 80524. (303) 493-2806. Services: a–d, f–g, i–j. Comments: "Highly skilled person. Standard and custom work. Innovative. Fair prices."

KANSAS

Emde Music Shop (Kenneth Emde), 1800 Kansas, Topeka, KS 66612. (913) 235-8171. Services: a–d, f–g. Comments: "Good, solid repair shop. Very good at adapting and tuning. Custom slide adjustment mechanism to various horns."

Jim Starkey Music Center (Steve Slater), 1318 W. 18th St., Wichita, KS 67214. (316) 262-2351. Services: a–d, f–g. Comments: "Known for his first-rate workmanship, works wonders."

IDAHO

Keeney Bros. Band Instrument Center (Lyle Keeney), 123 Third, Moscow, ID 83843. (208) 882-1751. Services: a–g, j. Comments: "Created valve and tuning slide mechanisms for euphoniums and tubas. Have converted tubas to ball and socket systems."

MONTANA

Pascoe Music Services (Art Pascoe), Industrial Park, Butte, MT 59701. (406) 494-2486. Services: a–f, h. Comments: "Superior band repair shop."

UTAH

Dobson Instrument Repair (Robert C. Dobson), 1419 Vintry Lane, Salt Lake City, UT 84121. (801) 277-3001. Services: a–d, g, h, j. Comments: "A unique talent for designing and constructing tuning mechanisms for installation on tuning slicks. Vents valves."

SOUTHWEST

ARIZONA

Desert Winds Music Inc. (Gerry Evoniuk), 1889 E. Broadway, Tempe, AZ 85282. (602) 966-1180. Services: a–d, g. Comments: "Repair technician for Arizona State University. Staff technician for Rafael Mendez Brass Institute."

WESTERN

CALIFORNIA

Randy Anglin. 12692 Fletcher Dr., Garden Grove, CA 92640. (714) 537-8086. Services: a–f, g, h, j.

Best Instrument Repair (Dick Ackright), 564 14th St., Oakland, CA. (510) 832-2452. Services: a–k. Comments: The "best in North California."

The Brass Shop (Alan Baer), 2717 E. 15th St., Long Beach, CA 90804. (310) 987-4432. Services: a, b, d, f–h, j. Comments: "Good at custom modifications, also dent work, valve work."

M M. P. (Joe Marcinkiewicz), 11400 Skyland Rd., Sealand, CA 91040. (818) 352-0129. Fax (818) 845-7833. Services: h, i. Comments: "Well-known mouthpiece maker for all brass."

Bob Malone's Brass Technology, 7625 Havenhurst Ave. #47, Van Nuys, CA 91406. (818) 988-8341. Fax (818) 988-7407. Services: a–f, g, h, j. Comments: "Very skilled repair person, real artist—creative. Yamaha specialist."

Larry Minick, 2435 C&D Village Lane, Cambria, CA 93428. (805) 927-1626. Services: a–h, j–k. Comments: "Artist, makes many original instruments, great at problem solving."

Robb Stewart, 140 E Santa Clara St. #1, Arcadia, CA 91006. (818) 447-1904. Services: f–h, j, k. Comments: "Specialist in replicas; perfectionist, artist, very creative."

Repair Services outside the United States

AUSTRIA

MUSICA GmbH., A-4400 Steyr, Wolfernstrasse 20b, Tel. 0 72 52-6 2378. Fax 0 72 52/6 23 70.

Musik Engel, 1160 Wien, Koppstr. 94, Tel. 0222/92 52 10.

Musikhaus Ernst Ankerl, 1160 Wien, Haberlgasse 11, Tel. 0222/92 32 89.

Votruba Musik, Lerchenfelder Guertel 4, A-1070 Wien. Tel. 0222/93 74 73; Herzog-Leopold Strasse 28, 2700 Wiener Neustadt. Tel. 02622/229 27; Beethovengasse 1, 2700 Wiener Neustadt. Tel. 02622/229 27-13.

Wilhelm Dreisinger, 1020 Wien, Taborstr. 14. Tel. 0222/24 91 07.

CANADA

Joe De Bruycker Music Instrument Repair, 70–7788 132nd St., Surrey, B.C. Tel. (604) 596-7616.

Ron Partch, 14 Kingsmount Park, Toronto, Ontario. Tel. (416) 690-3988.

St. John's Music (Fred Saurrer), 1330 Portage Ave.,Winnipeg R3C OV6.

Ward Music Ltd., 412 W. Hastings, Vancouver V6B 1L3.

GERMANY

Jurgen Metzger, Hannover.
Rudolf, Hannover.

ITALY

Onerati Strumenti Musicali Via Prato, Via Il Prato 69r,
50123 Firenze. Tel. 055/2398170.

JAPAN

Hitoshi Nakajima, Grand Gakki Co. Ltd., 1-7-1,
Uozaki-nakamachi, Higashinada-ku, Kobe-shi,
Hydago Pref., 658. Tel. 078-412-3100.

POLAND

Zakiad Naprawy Instrumention Dztych (Wojciech
Praybylski), Sprawiedliwa 15, Lodz. Tel. 52 44 69.
Zakiad Naprawy Instrumention Dztych (Wieslaw Bu-
kowski), Obr. Stalingrad 23, Lodz. Tel. 33 27 07.

SLOVENIA

Mirko Mach-Popravila Pihal In Trobil, 62000 Mari-
bor, Pod Gradiscem 8. Tel. (062) 29829.

SPAIN

Honiba S. A., Buen Pastor, 19, 46920 Mislata, Valen-
cia. Tel. 96-3790657.
Manuel Parra Rubinos, Ave Maria, 12, 28012 Madrid.
Tel. 92-2302933.
Real Musical (Sr. Arias), Carlos III, 28013 Madrid.
Tel. 91-5413009.

SWITZERLAND

Atelier Inderbinen, Aarauerstrasse, 5030 Buchs AG,
Gallen, Neuchatel, and Winterthur.
A. Egger, Turnerstr. 32, 4058 Basel (mouthpiece
specialist). Tel. 0616814233.
Hirsbrunner and Co., CH-3454 Sumiswald, Tel. 034-
71 15 54. Fax 034-71 32 05.
Jurg Lohri, Alpenquai, 6000 Luzern.
Musik Haag, 8280 Kreuzlingen.
Musik Rettenmund,8630 Ruti ZH. Tel. 0616817220.
Musik Siegenthaler, Mittelstrasse 15, 4900 Langenthal.
Rene Spada, Scheunenstrasse,3400 Burgdorf.
Marcandella Musikhaus, Stadthausgasse 21,8201
Schaffhausen.
Musik HUG (Markus Haeller, repairman), Basel, Zu-
rich, Lucerne, Lausanne, Solothurn.
Musik Oesch, Spaalenvorstadt 27, 4051 Basel.
Musikhaus Burri, Morillonstr. 11, 3007 Bern.
Servette-Music (Rene Hagman), rue Edouard-Racine
1, 1202 Geneva.

Instrument Collections

Robert E. Eliason

This writer thanks those who submitted information that identified tuba collections in their

areas. Information about private collections
could not be included here without explicit permission from the owners, nor did the time frame
of this project allow time to acquire permission
for the many geographically diverse collections.
However, this information was passed on to the
editors of instrument collection reference works
soon to be published for possible inclusion in
their forthcoming editions.

The tuba and the euphonium are late arrivals
in the history of musical instruments and are
included in collections, in many cases, only to
show local production or use, to complete the
brass family, or to illustrate some important facet
of brass instrument history as a whole. Larger
brass family instruments that preceded the tuba
and euphonium (the Scandinavian lur, the alphorn, the serpent and its various improvements,
and the ophicleide) are often of greater interest to
historians and the public and are more likely to be
collected and displayed.

Among the many facets of brass instrument
history that are of interest to the tubist are the
advance from signaling instruments to more musical uses; the materials and techniques used by
instrument makers; different means for changing
the sounding length, shape, or physical arrangement of the tubing; instruments produced in specific areas that contributed to brass instrument
development; and instruments used by a performer
or called for by composers of a particular period.

Of these, the history of methods for changing
the sounding length is probably of primary importance to the tuba historian in that these techniques and inventions made it possible to have
larger brass instruments. Much imagination and
genius were applied to this problem, beginning
with finger holes, crooks, and slides; then keys
and the many varieties of valves. Additional
thought, experimentation, and invention went
into correcting the problem of valve combinations. Low notes were important to tubas, and it
is precisely these notes that were most affected by
valve combinations. Providing a more continuous uninterrupted cone shape was a formidable
challenge on larger instruments and remains a
subject of experimentation to this day. Tubas also
presented problems of configuration, strength,
bracing, protection, water removal, and tuning
that were addressed in many different ways.

Public displays of tubas are rare. Even if museums or collectors have a number of tubas, they
are likely to be kept in storage rooms. This may
sound like a disadvantage at first, and it is, for the

casual, spur-of-the-minute visitor. But, if one is interested in examining the instruments closely, it is far better to have access to them in storage. To see them there requires more input, perhaps a letter or phone call in advance, and more importantly, some knowledge of tuba and brass instrument history and a good idea of what one wants to see. The instruments will not be in lighted cases, with identification, maker, place and date of manufacture, previous owners, performance history, important features, and historical context on display. The interested person will have to know some of this and know how to look for the information.

It is not likely that one will be allowed to play the older instruments in a collection. The wear on fragile and unlubricated parts and the moisture introduced by playing are often too great a risk for the owner or curator to allow. Plan to get the data by examination and photograph. Nonmetallic measuring devices and a light source are essential.

Museum curators and collectors are interested in any information or discoveries about the instruments in their collections. They are very appreciative if a visitor can provide some facts about their instruments, refer them to new sources of information, or tell them of other similar instruments of importance.

Why examine older instruments? It is possible to learn about the sound, agility, and expressiveness composers expected at the time they wrote particular compositions. It is also instructive to see earlier attempts at solving various problems, both as ideas for new solutions and as a catalog of past mistakes not to be repeated. Enthusiastic tuba players often want to find period instruments on which to perform a particular work: saxhorns for Saint-Saëns, ophicleides for Berlioz, and serpents for Mendelssohn, for example. However, there is no point in the tubist playing an instrument of the period unless the rest of the orchestra does the same. It is highly unlikely that a modern orchestra will take up period instruments in the strings, woodwinds, brass, and percussion for a single composition. Even if the tuba player had spent the necessary time and effort to become proficient on an early instrument and had acquired a reasonably good horn in the right pitch, the results are not likely to be effective.

The following list indicates where one might find the more common types of large brass instruments important in the historic development of the tuba.

The earliest large brass instruments, the Scandinavian lurs, can be seen in Copenhagen and Stockholm; and there are reproductions at the Museum of Fine Arts in Boston.

Large alphorns, a nineteenth-century development of the traditional herdsman's instrument, are now the Swiss national instrument and are found everywhere. Early smaller examples exist in Swiss collections as well as in eastern Europe, Russia, Scandinavia, and the United States.

Serpents abound in Holland, France, Belgium, and England; improved upright serpents, such as bass horns, Russian bassoons, ophimonicleides, and the serpent Forveille can be found in those countries and in Germany as well. A few of both types can also be found in most major American collections, but a particularly good collection of all types of serpents is at the Shrine to Music Museum in Vermillion, South Dakota. Examples of the hibernicon, as well as a recently made double-sized serpent, can be seen in Edinburgh, Scotland.

Ophicleides are found throughout Europe and the United States, but the greatest variety of design is seen in Belgium, France, and England. Some German collections have another type of ophicleide, which is narrow in bore and has a completely different key system. Examples of this type of ophicleide are also found at the Central Missouri State University in Warrensburg, Missouri.

Brass instrument valve history, upon which development of the modern tuba depended, can be seen in detail at the Shrine to Music Museum and at the Henry Ford Museum in Dearborn, Michigan, as well as in the European countries where much of the development occurred. Nuremberg, Berlin, Leipzig, and Munich collections all have important examples. Basel, Paris, Brussels, The Hague, London, Oxford, and Edinburgh also have many excellent early valved instruments.

A few bombardons, bass tubas, cimbassi, bass saxhorns, tubas, sousaphones, tenor horns, baritones, euphoniums, and other large-valved instruments from the nineteenth and twentieth centuries are found in most large collections throughout Europe and America.

In the United States, the Shrine to Music Museum offers the most comprehensive and accessible collection of low brass and brass instrument history. Collections at the Fine Arts Museum, Boston; Metropolitan Museum of Art, New York City; and Smithsonian Institution,

Washington, D.C., also have examples. Some other examples are the Trumpet Museum, Pottstown, Pennsylvania; The Henry Ford Museum, Dearborn, Michigan; the Stearns Collection, University of Michigan, Ann Arbor; the Essig Collection, Central Missouri State University, Warrensburg; the Fiske Collection, Claremont University Center, Claremont, California; and the Conn Collection at Interlochen, Michigan.

Many local historical societies own tubas or euphoniums. Private collectors also have examples of interesting instruments, but they must be identified through the collection directories or by reference from other researchers and curators.

No definitive collection of large brasses only has yet been assembled. It remains for some dedicated, tenacious tuba fanatic with a large house to identify the representative and important historical milestones and search the world for the finest examples.

The following reference works will direct the reader to collections of brass instruments throughout the world. One can also consult the articles on collections in *The New Grove Dictionary of Music and Musicians* or *The New Grove*

Dictionary of Musical Instruments. Collections and museums in the area where the development occurred are most likely to have examples of that development. Major early brass-making centers can be determined by reading other articles in these and other reference works on the trumpet, horn, trombone, and tuba.

International Directory of Musical Instrument Collections, edited by Jean Jenkins, and Fritz Knuf for International Council of Museums (ICOM) 1977.

International Directory of Musical Instrument Collections, 2nd ed., edited by Barbara Lambert, to be published under the auspices of the International Council of Museums (ICOM) Committee on Musical Instruments (CIM CIM), (1994?). Will include the United States and Canada.

A Survey of Musical Instrument Collections in the United States and Canada, conducted by a committee of the Music Library Association; William Lichtenwanger, chairman and compiler. Music Library Association, 1974.

Music Instrument Collections in the British Isles, by Clifford Bevan. Winchester, Hampshire: Piccolo Press, 1990.

APPENDIX A. MUSIC DISTRIBUTORS

Mark Moore

The following businesses are generally good sources of tuba publications representing many different publishing concerns. Prices are generally retail, and the availability of a given publication should be established before placing an order.

U. S. A. Distributors

A-Z Music Center, 343 W. Bridge Streeet, Morrisville, PA 19067.

Bernel Music Ltd., P.O.Box 2438, Cullowhee, NC 28723. Tel: 704-293-9312. Fax: 704-293-9312.

Brook Mays Music Co., 652 W. Mockingbird Lane, Dallas, TX 75247. Tel: 800-442-7680.

Carl Fischer, 312 S. Wabash, Chicago, IL 60604. Tel: 312-427-6652. Fax: 312-427-9545.

Eble Music Co., Box 2570, Iowa City, IA 52244. Tel: 319-338-0313. Fax: 319-338-0108.

Rettig Music, Inc., 510 Clinton St., Defiance, OH 43512.

Robert King Music Sales, Inc., 140 Main Street, North Easton, MA 02356. Fax: 508-238-2571.

Stanton's Sheet Music, 330 South Fourth St., Columbus, OH 43215. Tel: 614-224-4257. Fax: 614-224-5929.

Distributors Outside the U. S. A.

The Brass Music Specialists, 90 Appel Street, Graceville 4075, Queensland, Australia. Tel: 07 278 1311. Fax: 07 379 5146.

Musikhaus Doblinger, Dorotheergasse 10, A-1010 Vienna, Austria.

Danish Brass Publishing, Rytterkaer 21, 3670 Vekso Sj., Denmark.

Danish Brass Publishing Independent Music OH, P.O. Box 49, DK 2680 Solrod Strand, Denmark. Tel: 5311146644.

Edition Egtved, Box 20, 6040 Egtved, Denmark.

Edition Wilhelm Hanson, Bornholmsgade 1, 1.sal, 1266 Copenhagen K, Denmark.

Engström og Södring A/S, Palaegade 6, 1261 Copenhagen K, Denmark.

The Society for Publishing Danish Music, Grabrodre Plads 16, 1154 Copenhagen K, Denmark.

June Emerson Wind Music, Ampleforth, North Yorks, England. Tel: 01 44 4393 324.

Horn & Tuba Center, Haupstrasse 17–19, D-82223 Eichenau bei München, Germany. Tel: 0049 8141 82045. Fax: 0049 8141 71885

Ulrich Kobl, Ubostrasse 21, W-8000 Munchen 60, Germany. Tel: 089 871 4753 or 089 863 3553. Fax: 089 863 3159.

R.I.M., Drift 23, 3512 Br Utrecht, Holland.

Ado Gakki Co., Ltd., 1-3-17 Namba-naka, Naniwa-ku, Osaka-shi Osaka Pref. 556, Japan. Tel: 06 641 1327.

Dolce Gakki Co., Ltd., Morishita Build. 5F, 2-5-20 Do Shin, Kita-ku, Osaka-shi Osaka Pref. 530, Japan. Tel: 06 356 9119. Fax: 06 356 9687.

Grand Gakki Co., Ltd., Bari-Tuba Club, 1-7-1 Uozaki-nakamachi, Higashinada-ku Kobe-shi, Hyogo Pref. 658, Japan. Tel: 078 412 3100.

Japan Tuba Center, Chitate Kagawa, Shinoro 6-jo 5 Chome 5-6, Kita-ku, Sapporo, Japan 002. Tel: 771 0559.

Nero Music, 2-9-10 Shibuya Shibuya-ku, Tokyo, 150, Japan. Tel: 3 3400 5766. Fax: 3 3383 6090.

Real Musical, Ctra. Alcorcon a San Martin de Valdeiglesias km. 9300, 28670 Madrid, Spain. Tel: 616 02 08 or 616 05 61. Fax: 91/616 28 17.

APPENDIX B. RECORDING THE TUBA

Shawn Murphy

The following information has been provided via James Self. Shawn Murphy is a recording engineer for major motion pictures. His list of clients includes John Williams, James Horner, James Newton Howard, Maurice Jarre, and John Barry. *Hook, Home Alone II, Rocketeer, Jurassic Park,* and Academy Award winner *Dances with Wolves* are among the many scores he has recorded. Murphy graduated with a minor in music (tuba) from San Francisco State University and has a special ear for recording tuba.

Acoustic Environment

One does not always have access to the best acoustical environment for a recording effort, but a wise choice of the facilities available will often aid in making a good recording. The main item to note is the primary frequency response (and overtones) of the instrument versus the size of the room. Second, the acoustic power (which can be measured in watts, just like an amplifier) of the instrument is a major concern. This is quite high in the case of the tuba. The ideal studio would be a large room with a lively character (though not too live) and one with no low or mid-frequency resonances to cloud the response of the instrument. Normally this will preclude living rooms, which will amplify through standing waves the frequencies in the 400–600Hz area and which will overwhelm the overtone series of the instrument. Assembly halls, churches, and auditoria are usually more satisfactory, with a desired reverberation time of about 2.0 seconds. As noted below, a higher reverberation time is acceptable, but the microphonerophone technique will be compromised by moving in too closely (with attendant mechanical and wind noise). The usual recording environment of a band or orchestral rehearsal room is normally not acceptable because of resonances in the 125–250Hz range (parallel walls and untreated ceiling), which will cloud the fundamentals and sound boomy and uneven.

Professional recording engineers and producers choose rooms for their ambient character, lack of intrusive noise, technical facilities, and cost. For low brass, most commercial studios are too small and not live enough. In Los Angeles, a few of the larger studios and scoring stages are satisfactory. However, for most local recording venues, the best recommendations are churches, assembly halls, and auditoria.

Recording Techniques

This is truly a case where simple is better. For ensemble work, an orchestral recording using three to seven microphonerophones will always balance and sound better than one using twenty to thirty microphonerophones. The placement of the primary pickup is very important in recording solo or accompanied brass. One should be aware of the directional character of the instrument as well as the best balance points for a pickup. For tuba the directly over-the-bell approach is one of most definition, but this position lacks warmth, is usually noisy and bright, and will accentuate imbalances within the room or instrument. A pickup slightly off the bell (toward the player) will smooth out the response and reduce the noise. A distance of two to four meters is optimal, with the room acoustics determining the exact distance. If the tuba is accompanied, a pair of microphones on the piano will work well, with a single solo microphone on the tuba. The players should be facing each other and slightly farther apart than in recital. Normally the main pickup should be placed (for both solo and piano) about eight to ten feet above the floor and two to three meters from the players. If only two microphones (or one stereo) are used for solo and piano, some experimentation in placement of players and microphones will be in order for best balance and direct-to-reverb character.

The substantive impression of the recording should be slightly distant, with good definition and harmonic character. Moving microphones closer will provide definition, but at the expense of ambience. Moving farther away will provide less detail and more ambience. In many tuba and brass recordings made in a poor room acoustic, the microphones are placed very close to the players to minimize room resonances. For in-room recording, the higher the elevation of the microphones, the brighter the sound; conversely, the lower the elevation, the warmer or fuller the sound. The combination of distance from the players and elevation of the main microphones will determine the best placement and recording balance.

Start with two microphones only in an ORTF or closely spaced array—approximately ten inches spacing, with the microphones at an outward angle of 110°. Other minimal techniques are the XY/MS and Blumlein techniques, which can be more fully investigated in Bruce Bartlett's *Stereo Microphone Techniques* or John Eargle's *Microphone Techniques*.

Equipment

In this day of inexpensive recording media, a wise choice is a DAT recorder as the primary two-track medium.

Suggested Microphones

For overall best solo (large diaphragm, multi-patterned): Neuman TLM-170i.

For warmth (ribbon): Coles 4038; Beyer M-160; RCA 44BX; Beyer M-360.

For brightness, definition (large diaphragm): AKG C414EB/ULS; Sanken CU-41.

For good price / quality (ribbon): Beyer M-500.

For isolation from other sounds: Electro-Voice RE20; Sennheiser MD-421/422.

For ensemble (ORTF / XY): Schoeps CMC-34; Neumann KM-140; Sennheiser MKH-40.

Stereo microphones (Blumlein / MS / XY): Schoeps CMTS-501; Neumann SM-69; AKG C-422 / C-426.

Suggested Electronics

Microphone preamps: Avalon M2; John Hardy; George Massenburg.

Mixers: Ramsa; Soundcraft; DDA.

Recorders: Sony; Panasonic.

Donald A. Stanley

Professional organizations provide musicians with important sources of information and a means of sharing ideas and news of interest, which is necessary if one is to be informed of current events and the most recent development in his or her area of expertise. Many of these groups publish periodicals and journals that contain information not accessible by other means. Membership in professional organizations also permits members to contribute findings from their research or other studies. Reviews of new literature, recordings, or pedagogical investigations are reported, enabling one to be aware of the most recent materials and trends. Information concerning the meetings and workshops sponsored by the organization is usually given in these journals as well. Musicians of all ages will find that professional organizations provide a useful and important form of networking with others who share similar interests. Employment opportunities are frequently publicized and made available to the membership. Finally, membership in the appropriate professional organization indicates to others a commitment to one's profession. It speaks of one's interest in and concern for his or her area of expertise. It is a part of being a professional.

This writer gratefully acknowledges the *TSB* International Consultants and *The Instrumentalist* magazine for their help and cooperation in providing information regarding American and Canadian associations.

BRAZIL

Brazilian Young Concert Artists. This organization attempts to stimulate new talent. Sula Jaffe, Dir. Gen., Rua Hilario de Gouvea 30-Ap. 1004, Copacabana-Rio de Janeiro-RJ, 22040.

Artist Society of Culture. Invites international artists and organizations to perform in Brazil. Helena A. Oliveira, Pres., Av. Franklin Roosevelt 23, Rm 310, 10021, Rio de Janeiro-RJ.

Youth Talent of Brazil. Encourages young composers and instrumentalists. Marlos Nobre, Gen. Mgr., Rua Pres. Carlos de Campos, 115-B1.2 Ap. 902, 22231 Rio de Janeiro-RJ.

Musicians Syndicate of the State of São Paolo. The office of musicians' wages and their professional needs. Largo Paissandu, São Paolo-SP.

Brazilian Society of Contemporary Music. Promotes Brazilian music and Brazilian arts in general. Paulo Affonso de Moura Ferreira, Pres., SQS 105, Bloco B, Ap. 506, 70344 Brazilia-DF.

Brazilian Society of Playwrights and Authors. Sponsors and presents seminars and symposiums. Daniel Rochs, Pres., Av. Almirante Barroso, 97-3rd ff, P.O. Box 1503, 20031, Rio de Janeiro-RJ.

Society of Composers and Authors. Recognizes earned royalties. Jose Raimundo, Coucil Adim. Pres., Largo Paissandu, 51-10th, 11th, & 16th Flrs., 01034 São Paolo-SP.

Brazilian Federal Musicians' Union. Advocates respect among all artists and professional organizations and protects artists in any state. Av. Rio Branco 185, Rio de Janeiro-RJ. Dues are $10 U.S. currency.

Brazilian Composers Union. Recognizes earned royalties. Vanisa Santiago, Pres., Rua Visconde de Inhauma 107, 20091 Rio de Janeiro-RJ.

CANADA

The Canadian Band Association. Promotes and develops the musical and educational values of bands. Publishes *Canadian Band Journal*. Keith Mann, Box 5005, Red Deer, Alberta, Canada. Dues $25 U.S. currency.

Canadian Music Centre. Promotes Canadian Music. Can provide read-outs of music by instrument. The current chamber music listing includes 216 works by Canadian composers utilizing the tuba. John Reid, Prairie Region, 2500 University Drive NW, Calgary, Alberta.

DENMARK

Den Danske Jazzkreds. The purpose is to provide an organization for Danish jazz musicians and Danish jazz music. Kjeld Langesgade 4-A, 1367 Copenhagen K.

Dansk Komponist Forening. An association of Danish composers. Can serve as a contact to Danish composers. Grabreodre Plads 16, 1154 Copenhagen K.

DanskMusiker Forbund. The Danish musicians' union. Vendersgade 25, 1363 Copenhagen K.

Dansk Rock Samrad (ROSA). An organization for

Danish rock music and rock musicians. Sjellands-gade 51, 1367 8000 Arhus C.

Samfundet til Udgivelse af Dansk Musik. A society for the publication of new Danish music. Grabrodre-straede 18-1, DK 1156 Copenhagen K.

Statens Musicrad (Danish State Music Council). Serves as the advisor for the Minister of Culture. Takes care of the Danish law pertaining to music. Each year it donates about one hundred million Dkr. to Danish musical life. Vesterbrogade 24, 1620 Copenhagen V.

FINLAND

Suomen Pasuuna-ja Tuubaseura ry (SuPaTuS). The Finnish Trombone and Tuba Association. Petri Aaarnio, Hakaniemenranta 12 D 91, 00530 Helsinki.

GERMANY

Deutsches Tuba Forum. Organizes yearly workshops and meetings. Has been successful in making it possible for tubists to participate in the German Music Academy competitions. Their efforts are also directed at getting the tuba accepted as a solo instrument in professional German orchestras. Pro-fessor Klemens Propper, Saarbruckener Str. 26, D-W-3000 Hannover 71. Dues DM 75.

HOLLAND

Ministerie van Welzijn, Volksgezondheid en Cultuur. The Ministry of Welfare, Public Health, and Cul-ture, from which one may obtain general informa-tion on the arts. Within the ministry there is a department of music. Sponsors a Dutch music award for participants with a high level of performance ability. The award includes lessons abroad. Request to participate must be made before March 15 each year. Postbus 5406, NL-2280 HK, Rijswijk. The address of the advisory board to the minister is R.J. Schimmelpennicklaan 3, NL-2517 JN Den Haag.

Koninklijke Nederlandse Toonkunstenaarsvereniging. A trade union. Keizersgracht 480, 1017 EG, Amsterdam. Membership fee depends on income.

Kunstenbond FNV. A trade union. Arie Biemondstraat 11, 1054 PD, Amsterdam. Membership fee de-pends on income.

Nederlandse Toonkunstenaarsbond. A trade union. Herengracht 272, 1016 BW, Amsterdam. Mem-bership fee depends on income.

IRELAND

Irish Low Brass Association. Organizes workshops, recitals, and seminars and encourages composition and performance of material for the tuba and eu-phonium. A quarterly *Newsletter* supplies informa-tion on everything from playing techniques to ac-cessories. J. Buflin and David Murphey, The Verger's House, 30 St. FinnBarr's Place, Cork City, Rep. Ireland. 110 per year.

JAPAN

Japan Euphonium Tuba Association. Develops and expands the environment for tuba and euphonium players in Japan and promotes friendship among the players of these instruments. Yasuki Tosaka (Head Official), 1-8-1116 Kugayama Suginami, Tokyo 168, Japan. Dues 10,000 yen per year for professionals/6,000 yen per year for amateurs.

Hokkaido Euphonium Tuba Association. Encourages growth and friendship in the tuba-euphonium soci-ety in Hokkaido. Chitate Kagawa, President, Shinoro 6-jo 5-5-6 Kita-ku, Sapporo 002 Japan. Dues 3000 yen per year.

KOREA

The Korea Tuba Ensemble. Develops all areas of tuba activity in Korea and provides a forum for the exchange of information and the development of friendship among the members. Dues $25.00 per quarter or $100.00 per year.

NORWAY

Norwegian Musicians Union. Deals with ordinary union matters, such as wages, working conditions, and conflicts. Tore Nordvik, Leader, Youngsgt. 11, 0181, Oslo. Dues 1.8% of income per year.

Norwegian Tuba Association. Arranges concerts and maintains a center of information to spread knowl-edge about tuba literature and tuba players. Stein Erik Tafjord, Fossviein 23, 0551, Oslo. Dues ap-proximately NK 200 per year.

Norwegian Jazzmusician Union. Takes care of jazz mu-sicians' interests, such as economic conditions, amount of work, obtaining money from the ministry of Norway, and publicizing news of the membership. Toftesgt. 69, 0552 Oslo. Dues NK 300 per year.

SPAIN

Asociacio Amigos de la Tuba. Composed of profes-sional and student tubists from the entire country. It provides a monthly newsletter, with information about competitions, master classes, and anything else of interest to tubists. It also maintains a library of tuba works. Luis Pablo Mestre, President, Calle Maudes 11-4 F, Madrid, 28003.

SWEDEN

The World Association of Symphonic Bands and En-sembles. Concerned with greater understanding be-tween countries. Has a source library of tapes and scores, international scholarship, members' register, and regular bulletins to its members. Presidentgatan, 24-552, 65 Jankoping. 036-1600980. 300 active members; annual dues $20 individuals, $75 associ-ate/industrial.

UNITED KINGDOM

International Society for Music Education. Stimulates music education throughout the world as an integral part of general education and community life. Yasuharu Takahagi, president; Elizabeth Smith, administrator, I.S.M.E. Music Education Centre, University of Reading, Bulmershe Court, Reading, England RG6 1HY. 1,700 members.

Musicians' Union. Recognized as the authoritative voice of musicians in Great Britain. The union sets basic rates of pay, and helps to recover unpaid fees, gives advice on contracts, and provides legal assistance and aid. National Office, 60-62 Clapham Road, London SW9 OJJ. Membership fee is determined by salary earned from music.

UNITED STATES

Amateur Chamber Music Players, Inc. Composed of people who like to play or sing chamber music, list and grade themselves, and use the *North and Central American Directory of Members* (which alternates with the *International Directory*) to find new players. The directories are helpful when traveling. The organization also publishes *Annual Newsletters*. 545 Eighth Avenue, New York, NY. 3,500 members in the United States, 1,000 overseas; $15 contribution suggested.

American Bandmasters Association. Honors distinguished bandmasters, composers, and arrangers of band music. Membership in the association is by invitation. Maintains a research center at the University of Maryland and publishes the *Journal of Band Research* at Troy State University. Richard E. Thurston, secretary-treasurer, 110 Wyanoke Drive, San Antonio, Texas. 264 members, 70 associate members.

American Federation of Musicians. The bargaining representative of professional musicians in all phases of the music industry, including recording, television, theater, motion pictures, and symphony orchestras. Publishes *International Musician*. Mark Tully Massagli, president, Suite 600 Paramount Building, 1501 Broadway, New York, NY. 212-869-1330. 180,000 members; dues vary.

American Music Center. The official United States information center for music. The membership consists of composers, performers, music students, professionals, institutions, and publishers, all dedicated to promoting the creation, performance, and appreciation of contemporary American serious music. The center publishes a monthly opportunity update, and its circulating library houses some 39,000 scores and recordings. Nancy S. Clarke, executive director, 30 West 26th Street, Suite 1001, New York, NY, 212-366-5260. 2,100 active members; annual dues $45.

American Music Conference. Encourages music education and amateur music making for people of all ages. For information about publications, membership, and research on music participation in the U.S. contact Karl Bruhn, executive director, 5140

Avenida Encinas, Carlsbad, CA. 619-431-9124. Membership dues vary.

American Musical Instrument Society. An international organization to promote study of the history, design, and use of musical instruments in all cultures from all historical periods. It publishes three newsletters and an annual journal. Margaret Downie Banks, membership registrar, c/o The Shrine to Music Museum, 414 East Clark, Vermillion, SD. 605-677-5306. 850 active members; annual dues $35, $20 for students.

American Musicological Society, Inc.. Publications include the *Journal of the American Musicological Society, AMS Newsletter,* and the *Directory.* Alvin H. Johnson, executive director, 201 South 34th Street, Philadelphia, PA. 215-898-8698. 3,500 active members; annual dues $36.

American School Band Directors Association. Dedicated to the advancement and improvement of instrumental music instruction in elementary and secondary schools. Provides a common meeting ground for research in methods, materials, procedures, facilities, and attitudes. It is particularly interested in the promotion of the concert band. Membership by invitation. Gayle Stalheim, president; James Hewitt, office manager, P.O. Box 146, Otsego, MI. 616-694-2092. 1,220 members.

American Society of Composers, Authors and Publishers. (A.S.C.A.P.). A nonprofit membership organization that licenses on a non-exclusive basis the non-dramatic right of public performance of its members' musical compositions. Licensees include symphony orchestras, chamber ensembles, colleges, universities, local television and radio stations, television networks, Muzak and similar wired music services, clubs, restaurants, concert halls, discos, non-commercial radio and television stations, cable systems, airlines, and so on. All monies received from these media are distributed to the society's members, after deduction of operating expenses, on the basis of a scientifically designed survey of performances. To become a full member, all that is needed is one "regularly published" work (a commercially recorded musical composition or a commercially available copy of the sheet music for such a composition) or the program of an event at which a musical composition has been performed at a licensable venue. Associate membership is open to anyone with at least one work copyrighted (as evidenced by an appropriate U.S. Copyright Office registration). Frances Richard, director, Symphony and Concert Department, A.S.C.A.P., 1 Lincoln Plaza, New York, NY. 212-621-6327. Annual dues $10 for writers, $50 for publishers; 49,696 active members, 1,756 associate members.

American Symphony Orchestra League. The national service organization for symphony and chamber orchestras. Through workshops, seminars, research activities, in-field training programs, a national conference, and publications, the League works to promote artistic, financial, and organizational strength in American orchestras. Membership is open to orchestras, businesses, and individuals. The League also has a professional affiliate membership, which provides career information to conductors and administrators. Publications include *Symphony* magazine, statistical reports and surveys, *Managing a Youth Orchestra, Orchestra Education Programs, Facing the Maestro, A Musician's Guide to Orchestral Audition Repertoire, Selecting a Music Director: A Handbook for Trustees and Management,* and the *Gold Book.* Carole Birkhead, chairman; Catherine French, chief executive officer, 777 14th Street, N.W., Suite 500, Washington, D.C. 202-628-0099. 850 orchestra members, 4,500 individual members; annual dues $35–75 for individuals.

Association of Concert Bands. A professional organization for adult band musicians, directors, music educators, music industry, bands, and band enthusiasts that promotes and assists community/municipal and concert bands worldwide. It publishes the quarterly magazine *Advance,* the *National Band Directory,* books, and articles to assist in the funding, organization, and promotion of bands and band music. Its official magazine is *The Instrumentalist,* which includes the A.C.B. news and articles. Toni Ryon, executive director, 2533 S. Maple Ave. #102, Tempe, AZ. 800-726-8720. 850 active members; annual dues are $40 individual, $20 associate, $50 organizational (bands), $75 corporate, $300 life.

Association of Performing Arts Presenters (formerly the Association of College, University, and Community Arts Administrators, Inc.). An association of organizations that present professional performances on tour. Members include 1,600 nonprofit presenters plus business affiliate members consisting of 350 artists, artist management firms, arts consultants, and suppliers. Dues range from $225 to $675, depending on budget. Publications include the *Bulletin* (published ten times a year), *Inside Arts* (a quarterly magazine), and books on management and touring. Susan Farr, executive director, 1112 16th Street N.W., Suite 400, Washington, D.C. 202-833-2787.

Broadcast Music, Inc. (B.M.I.). Acquires performing rights from over 125,000 songwriters, composers, and publishers, and, in turn, grants licenses for the public performance of its repertory of over two million compositions. Publishes the quarterly magazine *Music World.* Frances W. Preston, president and chief executive officer, 320 W. 57th Street, New York, NY. 212-586-2000. One-time fee of $50 for publishers, none required for writers.

Chamber Music America. A national service organization to advance the interests of chamber music in all its forms. Its programs and services are designed to promote professional chamber music and to make

chamber music a vital part of American cultural life. Membership services include *Chamber Music* (a quarterly magazine), grant programs for residencies, commissioning, and consulting; conferences and seminars; *C.M.A. Matters,* a technical assistance bulletin; awards for adventuresome programming and excellence in chamber music teaching; discount long-distance service; instrument insurance; and health, life, and disability insurance. Paul Katz, president; Dean Stein, executive director, 545 Eight Avenue, New York, NY. 212-244-2772. 580 professional chamber ensemble members, 200 chamber music presenters, 3,000 associate members; annual dues $65–$300 voting, $35 associate. Annual conference in January, regional meetings and seminars.

Christian Instrumental Directors Association. A professional association for church-related private school instrumental music directors and church musicians who use instrumental music in worship. It provides four newsletters with updates of current happenings in this area, the *Listing of Published Sacred Instrumental Music,* a program exchange, and other services. David E. Smith, membership chairman, 4826 Shabbona Road, Deckerville, MI. 313-376-4552. 350 active members; annual dues $20, retired $10, students majoring in instrumental music $7.

College Band Directors National Association. Assists its members in seeking individual and collective growth as musicians, educators, conductors, and administrators. Membership categories exist for Active, Retired Active, Professional Associate, Music Industry, Student, and Institutions. Ray Cramer, president; Richard L. Floyd, secretary-treasurer, University of Texas at Austin, Box 8028, Austin, TX. 512-471-5883. 1,050 members; annual dues $40 active.

The College Music Society. Publications include *College Music Symposium, CMS Reports,* and the *CMS Newsletter.* Robby Gunstream, executive director, 202 W. Spruce Street, Missoula, MT. 406-721-9616. Annual dues $30, students $20.

Conductors' Guild, Inc.. An international organization open to all conductors of symphony orchestras, opera, ballet, choral ensembles, music theatre, wind ensembles, bands, and similar groups. Publications include an annual directory, quarterly journal and newsletter, and monthly job announcements. Judy Ann Voois, executive secretary, P.O. Box 3361, West Chester, PA. 215-430-6010. 1,250 active members, 100 associate members; annual dues $50, students $25, institutions $60.

Delta Omicron International Music Fraternity. An organization to create and foster fellowship among musicians. Publications include *The Wheel of Delta Omicron* and *The Whistle.* Jane Wiley Kuckuk, executive secretary, 1352 Redwood Court, Columbus, OH. 614-888-2640. 23,100 members.

The Historic Brass Society. Provides a forum for the latest research and performance practice information in the early brass field. It publishes an annual newsletter and an annual *Historic Brass Society Journal.* Jeffrey Nussbaum, president, 148 West 23rd Street #2A, New York, NY. 10011. Dues $15 for US and Canada residents, $20 for residents of other countries.

The International Association of Jazz Educators. A nonprofit volunteer organization dedicated to fostering and promoting the understanding, appreciation, and artistic performance of jazz music in the schools; disseminating educational and professional news of interest to music educators; and cooperating with all organizations in furthering the development of musical culture in America. Publishes *Jazz Educators Journal.* Dennis Tini, president, Bill McFarlin, executive director, Box 724, Manhattan, KS. 913-776-8744. 4,000 active members; annual dues $35 active, $50 foreign active, $15 student, $22 foreign student, $140 associate dues, $900 patron dues.

International Horn Society. Establishes contact among horn players of the world for the exchange and publication of ideas and research in all fields pertaining to the horn. Publishes *Horn Call, Horn Call Annual,* and newsletters. Ellen Powley, executive secretary, 2220 North 14 East, Provo, UT. 801-377-3026. Approximately 2,750 members; annual dues $25, $60 for three years, $350 for life.

The International Society of Bassists. Dedicated to stimulating public interest, improving performance standards, and providing an organization for musicians specializing in the teaching, learning, performing, repairing, making, research, and enjoyment of the double bass. John Clayton, Jr., president; Madeleine Crouch, general manager, 4020 McEwen #105, Dallas, TX. 214-233-2141. 2,000 active members.

International Trombone Association. Dedicated to the advancement of trombone teaching, performance, and literature. Publications include a quarterly journal and an annual membership directory. Vern Kagarice, College of Music, University of North Texas, Denton, TX. Membership dues vary.

International Trumpet Guild. Promotes communication among trumpet players around the world and works to improve the artistic level of performance, teaching, and literature associated with the trumpet. Members represent forty-three countries and include professional and amateur performers, teachers, students, manufacturers, publishers, and others. A journal published quarterly includes special music supplements; a membership directory is published annually. Bryan Goff, treasurer, School of Music, Florida State University, Tallahassee, FL. Fax 904-386-8613. 5,200 active members; annual dues $26, students $18.

Kappa Kappa Psi National Honorary Band Fraternity. Supports collegiate band programs through service, scholarships, clinics, and the commissioning of new works. Publishes *The Podium.* David E. Solomon, executive director, P.O. Box 849, Stillwater, OK. 405-372-2333. 3,000 active members.

Mu Phi Epsilon. An international professional music fraternity for men and women in collegiate and alumni chapters. This organization publishes *The Triangle* and offers grants, scholarships, and artist concerts. Mimi Altman, international executive secretary-treasurer, 730 Waukegan Road, Deerfield, IL. 708-940-1222. 10,000 active members; dues $12 alumni, $10 collegiate.

Music Critics Association, Inc. Acts as an educational medium for the promotion of high standards of music criticism in the press. Albert H. Cohen and Doris La Mar, managers, 7 Pine Court, Westfield, NJ. 240 active members; annual dues $50.

Music Distributors Association. Association of companies that manufacture, wholesale, or distribute musical merchandise to retail stores and manufacturers, as well as importers who distribute through wholesalers. Jerome Hershman, executive vice president, 40 West 21 St., 5th Floor, New York, NY. 212-924-9175. 145 members; annual dues $650 for distributors, $325 for foreign distributors.

Music Educators National Conference. The largest nonprofit association dedicated to the advancement of music education. Its varied membership includes educators from pre-school to university level teaching all disciplines of music, including general classroom, instrumental, and vocal. M.E.N.C.'s stated objective is to assure that children will receive a sequential, high quality program of music instruction. It publishes the *Music Educator's Journal, Journal of Music Teacher Education, Journal of Research in Music Education, Soundpost, General Music Today, Update,* 70 books, and audio-visual materials. Valerie Stansbury, M.E.N.C., 1902 Association Drive, Reston, VA. 703-860-4000. 62,000 members; annual dues $46-$73.

Music Industry Conference. An auxiliary of the Music Educators National Conference composed of suppliers of goods and services to the music education community. Publishes *MIC Guide for Music Educators.* Leroy Esau, president, c/o M.E.N.C., 1902 Association Drive, Reston, VA. 703-860-4000. 350 members.

The Music Publishers' Association of the United States. A trade association organized in 1895 and primarily concerned with the publication of standard and educational music. Its publications *A Guide to the U.S. Copyright Law* and *Music Publishers' Sales Agency List* are available upon request. 205 East 42 St., New York, NY.

Music Teachers National Association. Serves music educators at all levels of instruction. The association's purpose is to enhance the professional caliber of music teachers and to provide opportunities for growth and enrichment through student competitions, a national certificate program, conventions, conferences, workshops, and festivals. The association publishes the *American Music Teacher.* Ronald L. Molen, executive director, Susan Conner, editorial director, 617 Vine Street, Suite 1432, Cincinnati, OH. 513-421-1420. 25,000 active members.

National Association of Band Instrument Manufacturers. Promotes the growth of instrumental music throughout the world. Twenty-five member firms. For additional information contact executive vice president, Jerome Hershman, 40 West 21 St., 5th Floor, New York, NY. 212-924-9175.

The National Association of College Wind and Percussion Instructors. Provides a forum for communication within the profession of applied music on college and university campuses. Projects include a placement service, a research library, a composition project, and a quarterly publication, the *N.A.C.W.P.I. Journal.* Richard Weerts, executive secretary-treasurer, Division of Fine Arts, Northeast Missouri State University, Kirksville, MO. 816-785-4442. Annual dues $25.

The National Association of Composers/USA. Performs, publishes, broadcasts, and houses contemporary music by American composers and sponsors a composition contest and a contest for performers of new music. Publishes *Composer/USA* quarterly. Marshall Bialosky, president, 84 Cresta Verde Drive, Rolling Hills Estate, CA. 500 active members.

National Association of Music Merchants. Provides a variety of services to retail and commercial members of the music products industry, including trade shows, membership services, and market development. N.A.M.M. is a co-sponsor of the National Coalition for Music Education. Larry R. Linkin, president, 5140 Avenida Encinas, Carlsbad, CA. 2,500 retail and 1,400 commercial members.

The National Association of Professional Band Instrument Repair Technicians (N.A.P.B.I.R.T.). Provides a central agency for the exchange of information and implements a code of ethics that exemplifies the dignity and credibility of the profession. Publishes *Techni-Com* bi-monthly. Chuck Hagler, executive director, P.O. Box 51, Normal, IL. 309-452-4257. 1,000 active members, 100 associate members; annual dues $70.

National Association of School Music Dealers. Serves the musical needs of schools at all levels. Publications include newsletters. Joe Hume, president, 5801 W. 21 St., Topeka, KS. 913-272-3948. 200 dealer members, 60 associate members; annual dues $150.

National Association of Schools of Music. The accrediting agency for educational programs in music. Publications include a handbook of standards, a directory, and the proceedings of each annual meeting. Frederic Miller, president; Samuel Hope, executive director; Karen P. Moynahan, associate director; Betty Weir, constituent services representative, 11250 Roger Bacon Drive, Suite 21, Reston, VA. 703-437-0700. 551 member schools, 275 individual members; annual dues $45 individual, $575–$1,505 institutions.

National Band Association. Promotes the musical and educational significance of bands and is dedicated to achieving excellence in bands and band music. Membership is open to anyone interested in bands. Members receive a subscription to *The Instrumentalist,* the *N.B.A. Journal,* the *N.B.A. Selected Music List for Bands,* and the *Annual Directory.* Various awards recognizing outstanding professional performance and contributions include the sponsorship of the N.B.A./Band Mans Company Composition Contest and the N.B.A. Hall of Fame of Distinguished Band Conductors. Annual meetings are held in conjunction with the Mid-West International Band and Orchestra Clinic each December. Robert E. Foster, president, Director of Bands, University of Kansas; L. Howard Nicar, secretary-treasurer, P.O. Box 121292, Nashville, TN. 615-343-4775. Over 3,000 active members; dues $30.

National Catholic Bandmasters' Association. Publications include a newsletter, annual proceedings, reports, and official information. Rev. George Wiskirchen, executive secretary, Box 1023, Notre Dame, IN. 219-239-7136, 219-239-5054. 220 members; annual dues $30 active and associate, $50 commercial.

National Council of Music Importers and Exporters. Purposes include the mutual protection and promotion of members' trade interests with special reference to governmental problems arising in connection with importing and exporting musical merchandise. Fosters and encourages international trade in musical products. Periodic newsletters are published for its members. Jerome Hershman, executive vice president, 40 West 21 St., 5th Floor, New York, NY. 212-924-9175. 55 members; annual dues $250.

National Federation of Music Clubs. Seeks to bring together music clubs, organizations, and individuals directly associated with music. Encourages music education and the development of high musical standards, as well as the promotion of American composers and artists. Publications include *Music Clubs Magazine* and *Junior Keynotes.* Virginia F. Allison (Mrs. D.Clifford), 2340 Richmond, Wichita, KS. 500,000 active members.

National Jazz Service Organization. Provides advocacy, technical assistance, regranting programs, and publications for and a national database of the jazz field. Technical assistance program consists of a series of symposia held in various sites throughout the country and individualized consultations. Publications include the quarterly *N.J.S.O. Journal.* Dues $25 artists, $50 patrons, $100 jazz organization, $125 other organization. John Murph, membership director, P.O. Box 50152, Washington, D.C. 202-347-2604.

National Music Publishers' Association. Publishes the quarterly *News & Views.* Edward P. Murphy, president; Margaret A. O'Keeffe, 205 East 42nd St., New York, NY. 212-922-3266. 440 members; annual dues $50.

National School Orchestra Association. Founded in 1958 to support instrumental music teachers dedicated to the development of school orchestra programs. *N.S.O.A. Bulletin* is a forum for sharing ideas and influencing the course of orchestral music education at the national level. The N.S.O.A. has a unique role in providing a common forum for wind, brass, percussion, and string educators in their unified purpose to promote school orchestras. The N.S.O.A. serves as the "national voice for school orchestra directors," as it works closely with related professional music organizations, collaborating at state, regional, and national levels to promote school orchestras. N.S.O.A. and M.E.N.C. co-sponsor the national High School Honors Orchestra at the biennial M.E.N.C. National Conference. N.S.O.A. membership offers access to N.S.O.A. publications, awards, job listing service, exchange concert service, summer conferences, and the opportunity to become professionally involved in state and national clinics. Subscriptions included with membership are *N.S.O.A. Bulletin* quarterly and *The Instrumentalist* monthly. 1,600 active members; annual dues are $30. For more information contact Norman Mellin, Starkville High School, 801 Louisville Road, Starkville, MS. 601-324-7569.

North American Brass Band Association, Inc. A nonprofit corporation to encourage the establishment, growth, and development of adult amateur British-style brass bands throughout the United States and Canada. With British-style brass bands flourishing around the globe, N.A.B.B.A. feels that the time is right to revive and expand brass band tradition. Publications are *The Brass Band Bridge,* "How to Start a British Brass Band," and "The Care and Feeding of a Community British Brass Band." Also available is "Strike up the British Brass Band," a 13-minute tape/slide show for rental at $10. Don W. Kneeburg, president, 17304 Lynnette Drive, Lutz, FL. 813-949-1022. 600 active members, 100 associate members; annual dues $10 student, $20 regular, $50 member band, $100 corporate/institutional, $250 sustaining, $500 patron, $1,000 leadership.

Phi Mu Alpha Sinfonia Fraternity. Encourages and actively promotes the highest standards of creativity, performance, education, and research in music in America. Publishes *The Sinfonian* and *The Gold.* Barry W. Magee, director of fraternal activities, 10600 Old State Road, Evansville, IN. 812-867-2433. 115,000 members; annual dues $90.

Pi Kappa Lambda, National Honor Society of Music. More than 170 chapters in colleges and universities throughout the United States. Publishes a semi-annual newsletter and a handbook. Membership requires a high grade-point average and high musicianship standards. Pin and certificate are included with one-time dues. Lilias Circle, secretary-treasurer, School of Music, Northwestern University, 711 Elgin Road, Evanston, IL. 708-491-5737. 43,000 members; dues $35.

Sigma Alpha Iota International Music Fraternity. Founded at the University of Michigan in 1903. Membership is based on scholarship, musicianship, and character; it is open to college music students of undergraduate and graduate level schools where the fraternity has chapters and to music faculty members. College, alumnae, patroness, honorary, and Friends of the Arts and National Arts Associates members; the last three categories include concert artists, composers, and arts patrons of exceptional musical standing. Publishes *Pan Pipes.* Mrs. James Whinery, national executive secretary, 4119 Rollins Avenue, Des Moines, IA. 176 college chapters, 78,138 initiated members.

Society for Ethnomusicology. Publishes *Ethnomusicology* and the *SEM Newsletter.* Anthony Seeger, president; Shelly Kennedy, administrative secretary, Morrison Hall 005, Indiana University, Bloomington, IN. 812-855-6672. 2,000 active members.

The Suzuki Association of the Americas, Inc. Publishes *American Suzuki Journal.* Pamela Brasch, P.O. Box 17310, Boulder, CO. 303-444-0948. 4,600 active members, 1,400 associate members; active dues $35, subscription only $17.50.

Tau Beta Sigma National Honorary Band Sorority. Supports collegiate band activities through service, scholarships, clinics, and the commissioning of new works. Publishes *The Podium.* David E. Solomon, executive director, National Office, P.O. Box 849, Stillwater, OK. 405-372-2333. 3,000 active members.

Tri-M Music Honor Society. A program of Music Educators National Conference. It is the international music honor society for junior and senior high school music students. Members are selected by their music faculty on the basis of excellence in academic and music subjects, performance, character, leadership, cooperation, and service. *Tri-M News* is published semi-annually by M.E.N.C. More than 2,000 chapters chartered. Annual chapter registration $10/$20 for U.S. and domestic/ foreign addressed chapters; Charter fee $20/$30 for U.S. and domestic/foreign addressed chapters. Sandra Fridy, program manager, 1902 Association Drive, Reston, VA. 703-860-4000.

Tubists Universal Brotherhood Association. A worldwide organization whose purpose is to maintain a liaison among those who take a significant interest in the development, literature, pedagogy, and performance of instruments of the tuba and euphonium family. Publishes *T.U.B.A. Journal.* Steven Bryant, treasurer, Department of Music, University of Texas at Austin, Austin, TX. 512-471-0504. 2,500 active members; annual dues $35, student and retired $20.

Women Band Directors National Association. Represents every woman band director at the national level. 400 active members, 25 student members. Meets at Midwest International Band Clinic, December, Chicago, IL. Catherine Heard, 6954 Garland Avenue, Baker, LA. 504-774-7842.

APPENDIX D. CONTINUING SYMPOSIA, COMPETITIONS, EVENTS, FESTIVALS, AND SUMMER STUDY

Jan Z Duga

Many thanks go to Frank and Sharon Pappa-john for their support and the use of their computer.

Continuing Symposia

Arkansas Low Brass Symposium. Volta Andy Anders, 202 S. Fairbanks Avenue. Russellville. AR 72801. USA. 501-967-5484 or 501-968-0476. Encompasses all college-level low brass students and faculty. Hosted by various universities in Arkansas, depending on availability, includes performances by faculty members, student master classes, small ensembles, and instrument clinics. Past clinicians include Jerry Young, Mark Moore, Volta Andy Anders, and Jim Shearer.

Curso. Amigos de la Tuba. Espejo, 4. 28013 Madrid, Spain. 91-5349050. This seminar takes place in the Conservatory of the Community of Madrid. It first featured Heiko Triebener, tubist with the Beethoven Symphony, Bonn, Germany.

Curso de Instrumentos de Viento. Junto de Comunidades de Castilla-La Mancha. Trinidad, 8. 45002 Toledo, Spain. 952-223450. A course held in July at the Residencia María Molin.

Curso de Música Instrumental-Ciudad de El Ferrol. Ayuntamiento de El Ferrol, Pz. de Armas, s/n. 15402 El Ferrol, La Coruna, Spain. 981-320211 and 355435. Held each December.

Hokkaido Tuba Camp. Chitate Kagawa, President. Hokkaido Euphonium-Tuba Association. Sapporo 002, Japan. 011-771-0559. This annual event for tuba and euphonium players features clinics, master classes, coaching ensembles and students. Guest artists have included Dr. Brian Bowman, euphonium, and Mark Nelson, tuba.

International Tuba-Euphonium Conference. Conference Coordinator, T.U.B.A. Presents recitals, lectures, master classes, and competitions by the world's foremost tubists and euphoniumists. Exhibits by manufacturers and publishers in the low brass field offer the latest in instrument designs and music publications.

New England Tuba-Euphonium Symposium/Workshop. No information available.

New York Brass Conference. 315 W. 53rd St., New York, NY 10019. USA. 212-581-1480. An annual conference showcasing all realms of brass performance, including lectures, workshops, exhibits, and recitals. Held annually at the Roosevelt Hotel, Madison Avenue at 48th St., New York, NY 10017.

Northwest Annual Tuba-Euphonium Workshop. Ron Munson, Director. University of Puget Sound, Tacoma, WA. 98416. USA.

Tennessee Technological University Tuba/Euphonium Symposium. R. Winston Morris, Director. Department of Music, Tennessee Technological University, Cookeville, TN 38501. USA. 615-372-3168. An annual event since 1968, probably the original tuba symposium. Held the Friday before Thanksgiving, this one-day event is intended for the advanced high school tubist and euphoniumist. Participation is by invitation only through the director of the symposium.

The United States Army Band Tuba-Euphonium Conference. Jack Tilbury, Conference Chairman. The U.S. Army Band, Ft. Myer, Arlington, VA 22211-5050. USA. 703-696-3643. Offers an intensive, yet supportive performance and learning environment for people of all ages. This international conference has grown throughout the years, providing a broad spectrum of professional artists' performances, master classes, and exhibits. All performances are provided at no charge and are held annually at Brucker Hall, Ft. Myer, VA, in late January.

Competitions

Artists International's Young Musicians Audition. Leo B. Ruiz, Founder-Director. 521 Fifth Avenue, Suite 1700, New York, NY 10017. USA. 212-757-6454. Open to instrumentalists, ensembles, and singers to age thirty-five who have not given a New York recital debut or have not received a New York review for a solo recital performance. The prize is a New York recital debut in Carnegie Recital Hall. Fee $50.

Baltimore Symphony Orchestra Soloist Competition. Hilde Vocelka, 1212 Cathedral Street, Baltimore, MD 21201. USA. Legal residents of or current students in Maryland under twenty-six years of age are eligible. Cash prizes are awarded, and the grand prize winner may have the opportunity to perform with the Baltimore Symphony. Entrance fee $25.

BBC Television Young Musician of the Year. BBC - TV. Kensington House, Richmond Way. London, W14 0AX, England. 81-895-6189 Fax 81-749-9259. This biennial, televised, competition for piano, strings, winds, and brass is open to British residents under nineteen years of age as of the competition year. No entrance fee required; cash prizes total £32,000.

Brevard Music Center. Kristin Olsen, P.O. Box 592, Brevard, NC 28712. USA. 704-884-2011. Offers three divisions of study: The Transylvania Music Camp, ages thirteen through high school; The Advanced Division; and The Division of Special Studies, as arranged on an individual basis with the director. A Concerto Competition is available, and interested students should contact the center for an appropriate concerto list. Session runs from the end of June through the first week of August.

Coleman Chamber Ensemble Competition. Kathy Freedland, Executive Director, 202 S. Lake Avenue, No. 201, Pasadena, CA 91101. USA. 818-793-4191. Fax 818-787-1293. For string, wind and brass chamber ensembles, to encourage excellence in chamber music performance. Non-professional chamber ensembles under the direction of a coach are eligible. Individual members must be under twenty-seven years of age. There are cash prizes; entrance fee $25 per player.

Composition Contest, sponsored by T.U.B.A. Phillip Sinder, Contest Coordinator, School of Music, Michigan State University, East Lansing, MI 48824. USA. 517-336-1220. Annual composition competition for works pertaining to solo and/or ensemble tuba/euphonium performance. Winning compositions are published by TUBA Press, and all worthy entries will also be given consideration for publication.

Concert Artists Guild International New York Competition. Ellen Highstein, Executive Director, 850 Seventh Avenue, Suite 1205, New York, NY 10019. USA. 212-333-5200. Fax 212-977-7149. Emerging soloists and chamber ensembles who are seeking an active performing career are eligible. Applicants should have advanced musical training and performance experience. Prizes include a fully sponsored New York recital, recitals in four other major U.S. cities, a cash award of $2,500, free management services leading to appearances on recital series and as soloist with orchestras throughout the United States and overseas, and an exclusive recording contract with Amsterdam's Channel Classics Recordings. Entrance fee $40.

Concerto Competition. June McCoy, Concerto Competition, Chm. Auditions Committee, P.O. Box 18321, Oklahoma City, OK 73154. USA. 405-751-3300. Fax 405-755-3231. A biennial competition for piano and other recognized orchestral instruments playing standard concerto repertoire. Eligibility is limited to residents of or students in Arkansas, Kansas, Missouri, New Mexico, Colorado, Louisiana, Oklahoma, or Texas, up to and including twenty-six years of age. Prizes up to $4,000 and performance opportunities. Competition is held in March; $25 entrance fee.

Concerts Atlantique Foundation. Travis Gering, Director, 54 W. 21st Street, Suite 1206, New York, NY 10010. USA. 212-633-1128. Fax 212-633-1129. Offers programs for serious musicians who wish to further their careers through performing, especially internationally. Anyone demonstrating the ability to perform is eligible, and prizes consist of subsidized international performance production and management assistance. Auditions are arranged individually throughout the year; send a self-addressed stamped envelope along with a $60 entrance fee.

Disney All-American Instrumentalists Auditions. Robert Raddock, Manager, P.O. Box 10000, Lake Buena Vista, FL 32830-1000. USA. 407-345-5701 (FL), 714-490-3126 (CA). A summer opportunity to perform in an orchestra, marching band, or show band for a weekly stipend. All auditions are done on a walk-in basis. Summer housing and transportation to work provided. Auditionees must be at least eighteen years of age and a current college undergraduate.

East & West Artists Prize for New York Debut. Ms. Adolovni Acosta, Exec. Director, 310 Riverside Dr. #313, New York, NY 10025. USA. 212-222-2433. Fax 212-222-2433. Instrumentalists, ensembles and singers who have not given a New York debut recital are eligible; age limit thirty-six (also average age for ensemble). Prizes include a fully sponsored debut at Weill Recital Hall at Carnegie Hall, cash awards, and radio and concert engagements as they become available. Audition by cassette tape with an entrance fee of $60.

Fort Collins Symphony Association Young Artists Competition. Michael Klesert, General Manager, P.O. Box 1963, Fort Collins, CO 80522. USA. 303-482-4823. Fax 303-482-4858. Promote students' interest in music. For the Senior Level, students must not be more than twenty-five, for the Junior Level eighteen years of age by the final round. Senior Level, piano/instruments (alternate years), prizes include cash and chances for the three finalists to perform with orchestra in the final round. For the Junior Level, piano/instruments, there are cash prizes for first and second place. Entrance fee $25 (S) and $15 (J).

Fort Smith Symphony Association Young Artist Competition. Carol Sue Wooten, Exec. Director, P.O. Box 3151, Fort Smith, AK 72913. USA. 501-452-7575. Fax 501-452-8985. Open to anyone eighteen years of age or younger whose nineteenth birthday does not occur before April 1 of the contest year. Previous prize winners are ineligible. First prize is $1,000 plus a concert appearance with the Fort Smith Symphony, second and third are cash prizes. The first, second, and third prize winners are eligible for a full tuition and fees scholarship to the University of Arkansas. Entrance fees $15.

Frank Huntington Beebe Fund for Musicians. c/o Beebe Fund Secretary, 290 Huntington Avenue, Boston, MA 02115. USA. 617-262-1120/ Ext. 267. Several scholarships are awarded to American post-graduate students for study abroad. The deadline is mid-December, and no fee is required.

Friday Woodmere Music Club Young Artists Competition. Louise Masi, Chief Officer, 976 Newbridge Road, North Bellmore, NY 11710. USA. 516-221-4680. A biennial competition for persons fourteen to eighteen years of age. Entrance fee $20; cash prizes are awarded.

Ima Hogg National Young Artist Audition. Charlotte A. Rothwell, Chm., c/o The Houston Symphony (Attn: Ellen Happe), 615 Louisiana St, Houston, TX 77002. USA. 713-224-4240. Fax 713-222-7024. An annual event for instrumentalists and pianists nineteen to twenty-seven years of age. Top prizes include $5,000 plus performance with the Houston Symphony during the Summer Concert Series; $2,500 plus performance with the Houston Symphony during the Summer Concert Series; and $1,000. Entrance fee $25.

Institute of International Education/Fulbright and Other Graduate Study Scholarships. Theresa Granza, U.S. Student Programs Division Director, 809 United Nations Plaza, New York, NY 10017. USA. 212-984-5330. Fax 212-984-5325. For U.S. citizens with B.A. or equivalent for graduate study abroad. Deadline October 31 for the following academic year, competition date May 1.

Kingsville International Young Performers' Competition (Presented by The Music Club of Kingsville). Mr. and Mrs. J.D. Tyler, Co-Directors, P.O. Box 2873, Kingsville, TX 78363. USA. 512-592-2374. For young pianists and orchestral instrumentalists under 26 years of age. Pre-College and College levels, each with their own cash awards. The top winner receives a minimum of $5,000 and a performance with the Corpus Christi Symphony Orchestra and Winter Festival at San Miguel de Allende, Mexico. Entrance fee $20.

Louise D. McMahon International Music Competition. Dr. Earl Logan, Director, 2800 W. Gore Blvd., School of Fine Arts, Cameron University, Lawton, OK 73505. USA. 405-581-2440. For instrumental (woodwind, brass, and keyboard percussionist) (1993), voice (1994), and piano (1995), rotating annually. Contestants must be twenty-five years of age or older on January 15 of the competition year. Cash prizes totaling $10,000 plus a return solo performance with orchestra for the first place winner. Applications must be postmarked by December 1 of the year preceding; entrance fee $60.

Masterplayers International Music and Conductors Competition (Masterplayers Prize). Richard Schumacher, President, Cable: Masterplayers Lugano. Via Losanna 12, c/o Masterplayers International Music Academy, CH-6900 Lugano, Switzerland. (91) 23-30-63. Fax (91) 23-30-63. Held annually to give international support to artists of great talent. No age limit. Prizes include cash and engagements in Europe and America.

Meadows Foundation Young Artists Auditions Competition. Miriam Lynn Nelson, Artistic Director, 8

Drake Rd., Somerset, NJ, 08873 USA. 908-828-1812. For piano, voice, all chamber ensembles, and all orchestral string, woodwind and brass instruments. Three divisions; Junior (grades 6-8), High school (grades 9-12), and Senior (any young artist, through 35 years of age). Prizes include monetary awards and numerous recital, concert, and chamber music opportunities. Entrance fee $25 (individual), $35 (ensemble).

Midland-Odessa Symphony and Chorale, Inc. National Young Artist Competition. Don T. Jaeger, Music Dir./Con., P.O. Box 60658, Midland, TX 79711. USA. 915-563-0921. A biennial competition for strings, piano, voice, winds, and percussion. For secondary school to age twenty-six and enrollment in secondary school, college, or conservatory. Cash prizes and two performances with the Midland-Odessa Symphony and Chorale in March for the top three winners. Entrance fee $25.

Music Academy of Gdansk and Ministry of Art. Akademia Muzyczna. Roman Suchecki, Head, Music Dept., ul Lagiewniki 3, 80-847 Gdansk, Poland. 31-77-23. A competition for brass instruments, including tuba, is held every four years.

National Federation of Music Clubs. Chairman, Scholarship Department and Scholarship Board, 1336 North Delaware Street, Indianapolis, IN 46202. USA. 317-638-4003. This biennial competition with over a dozen categories includes orchestral brass (trumpet, horn, trombone, and tuba). For application forms, repertoire lists, and state audition chairmen's names contact the above address. Entrance fee $30.

New Jersey Symphony Orchestra Young Artists Auditions. Judith Nachison, Auditions Coordinator, Robert Treat Center, 50 Park Place, 11th Floor, Newark, NJ 07102. USA. 201-624-3713. Fax 201-624-2115. For piano, strings, and orchestral instruments. Restricted to New Jersey residents under age twenty. Cash prizes range from $500 to $3,000, and the top prize includes an appearance with the orchestra. No entrance fee.

Olga Koussevitzky Young Artist Awards Competition (sponsored by the Musicians Club of New York). Constance Mensch, Young Artists' Committee Chm., 165 W. 66 St., New York, NY 10023. USA. 212-877-2127. For voice (1993), strings (1994), winds (1995), piano (1996), rotating annually. Entrants must be sixteen to twenty-six as of April 1 of the year of competition. Prizes include cash totaling $3,500, concert performances, and auditions arranged for career opportunities. Apply before March 1; entrance fee $30.

Richardson Symphony Orchestra Lennox Young Artists Competition. P.O. Box 8351675, Richardson, TX, 75083-1675 USA. 214-234-4195. For serious brass and woodwind students, ages eleven through nineteen as of the concert date. College students are ineligible. First place prize is $500 and an appearance with the Richardson Symphony Orchestra. Second and third place prizes are $300 and $100 respectively. Entrance fee $20.

Rotary Young Artists Awards. Irene Klug Nielsen, General Manager, c/o Fresno Philharmonic Orchestra, 1300 N. Fresno St., Suite 201-B, Fresno, CA 93703. USA. 209-485-3020. For instrumental (1994), piano(1995), and voice (1996), rotating annually. Restricted to residents or students in Alaska, Arizona, California, Colorado, Hawaii, Idaho, Montana, Nevada, New Mexico, Oregon, Utah, Washington, and Wyoming. Applicants must be eighteen years of age by July 1 of the year prior to the competition and not older than thirty by January 1 of the competition year. Cash prizes and an appearance with the Fresno Philharmonic Orchestra are for top winners. Entrance fee $20.

San Angelo Symphony Hemphill-Wells Sorantin Young Artists Award. Gene C. Smith, Managing Director, P.O. Box 5922, San Angelo, TX 76902. USA. 915-658-5877 or 915-949-0464. For instrumentalists under age twenty-eight. Cash prizes totaling $3,750 and a performance with the San Angelo Symphony and Big Spring Symphony. Entrance fee $20.

Scheveningen International Music Competition. Anton de Beer, Manager, Gevers Deynootweg 970 Z, 2586 BW, Scheveningen, Holland. 70-352-51-00. Fax 70-352-21-97. Open to young professional musicians up to age twenty-eight. The instruments of the competition rotate annually, and the jury is composed of well-known international artists.

Summit Brass International Brass Ensemble Competition. David Hickman, Chief Officer, c/o Summit Brass, Box 26850, Tempe, AZ 85282. USA. 602-496-9486. Fax 602-965-8233. No age or level restrictions. Ensembles must have at least three brass instrumentalists; groups with non-brass instrumentalists must be composed of at least half brass players. Cash prizes totaling $10,000 are awarded. Entrance fees $50 per musician.

United Musical Instruments International Solo Competition. Summit Brass, Box 26850, Tempe, AZ 85285. USA. 602-965-6239. Open to anyone born on or after June 19, 1961, who is not currently a recognized soloist with a full-time military band, or under the auspices of major management as a concert soloist. Cash prizes are awarded for trumpet, horn, trombone, euphonium, and tuba. Applicants must register for both weeks of the competition.

The United States Air Force Band Young Artist Competition. MSgt. Lucille J. Snell, The USAF Band, 23 Mill Street, Bolling Air Force Base, Washington, DC 20332. USA. 202-767-4224. An annual competition open to woodwind, brass, and percussion soloists in grades ten through twelve. Entrants must provide their own accompanist for both rounds. Repertoire lists are provided, and the winner will perform with The USAF Band at a Guest Artist Series Concert.

Women's Association of the Minnesota Orchestra Young Artist Competition. Susan Armstrong, Eleanor Dulebohn, Co-Chairs, 1111 Nicollet Mall, Minneapolis, MN 55403. USA. 612-371-5654. Restricted to pianists and players of orchestral instruments under the age of twenty-six who are residents or students registered in Iowa, Minnesota, Missouri, Nebraska, North Dakota, South Dakota, Wisconsin, Manitoba, or Ontario.

Yamaha International Brass Ensemble Competition. Summit Brass, Box 26850, Tempe, AZ 85285. USA. 602-965-6239. Student, amateur, faculty, and professional ensembles may enter provided that the ensemble is not under a signed agreement with a major artists' management at the time of the competition, or a full-time military brass ensemble. Previous First Place winner not eligible. Each ensemble must have at least three brass instrumentalists in any like or mixed combination. A cash prize will be awarded for first, second, and third places.

Events

International Tuba Day. Joel Day, Founder, 347 Oak Terrace, Saint Davids, PA 19087. USA. Founded in 1979, International Tuba Day has been celebrated annually on the first Friday in May in various cities in Pennsylvania. It was created to recognize tubists in musical organizations around the world who go through the hassle of handling a tuba.

Festivals/Summer Study

Boston University Tanglewood Institute. 855 Commonwealth Avenue, Boston, MA 02115. USA. 617-353-3386. An eight-week program open to grades nine through twelve. Programs include a brass quintet workshop (Sam Pilafian, tuba instructor), orchestral and solo performance, and private instruction. Participants can attend concerts by the Boston Symphony Orchestra. Auditions for the Fellowship Orchestra are held around the country.

Breckenridge Music Festival. Breckenridge Music Camp, Karen Turtscher, P.O. Box 1254, Breckenridge, CO 80424. USA. 303-453-9142. Festival runs from the end of June to the beginning of August and is home to the National Repertory Orchestra. The camp is open to grades seven through twelve, and the tuba instructor is Mark Mordue.

Coups de Vents International Festival for the Creation of Wind Music. Coups de Vents, BP 5045, F76071, Le Havre, France. Fax (33) 35 45 58 07. Past festivals have featured solo tuba artists Roger Bobo, Mel Culbertson, the Melton Tuba Quartet, and Klemenz Pröpper. The festival offers over 400 concerts by musicians from 25 countries and composition and performance competitions.

Drake University Summer Music Festival. James Cox, Drake University, Music Department, Des Moines,

IA 50311. USA. 515-271-2823. This one-week festival, held in June, offers band, brass ensemble, jazz, and orchestra performance opportunities. Cathy Light is the low brass instructor.

Fairbanks Summer Arts Festival. Jo Scott, P.O. Box 80845, Fairbanks, AK 99708. USA. 907-479-6778. Fax 907-479-4329. A study/performance program starting in late July. Participants must be eighteen years of age and older; college credit is available. Includes performance opportunities in chamber ensembles, jazz, and orchestra. Jim Self is the tuba instructor.

Harmony Ridge Brass Center Summer Festival. Ginger Culpepper, Founder, Harmony Ridge Brass Center, Inc., Box 573, East Poultney, VT 05741. USA. Newly established festival held in August for developing the art of solo performance on brass instruments. For college age and professional players. Master classes, recitals, and brass ensemble performances are the emphasis. Guest artists include Warren Deck, tuba, as well as other respected brass soloists.

International Serpent Festival. United Serpents, P.O. Box 8915, Columbia, SC 29202. USA. This festival, first held in 1989, features performances, composition premieres, and appearances by various North American serpent soloists, ensembles, and wind bands.

Internationale Blechbläsertage (Brass Days). Kristel Potocnik, arts projects, Getreidemarkt 13/16, A-1060 Vienna, Austria. The first Internationale Brass Days took place in Grieskirchen, Austria in July 1992. Dietrich Unkrodt and Howard Johnson gave classical and jazz tuba master classes and concerts. This festival promises to be a great success in years to come.

Lieksa Brass Week. Erkki Eskelinen, Director, Koski-Jaakonkatu 4, Lieksa SF-81700, Finland. (75) 23133 Fax (75) 23133. Brass courses and concerts held in late July.

Marrowstone Music Festival and Institute, Port Townsend, WA. Lisa Lederer, Seattle Youth Symphony Orchestras, 11065 Fifth Avenue, Seattle, WA 98125. USA. 206-362-2300. A three-week program held in August for grades seven through college. Emphasis is on orchestral performance, and visiting guest artists give recitals, master classes, and clinics. John Helmer is the low brass instructor.

Music Festival of Arkansas. North Arkansas Symphony, P.O. Box 1243, Fayetteville, AR 72702. USA. 501-521-4166. This three-week festival held in June offers chamber music and orchestral experience for grades eleven through adult. The tuba instructor is Keith Yarbrough.

Sewanee Summer Music Center and Festival. Director, Sewanee Music Center, The University of the South, 735 University Avenue, Sewanee, TN 37375-1000. USA. 615-598-1225. Fax 615-598-1145. This festival, held late June to August, is open to grades seven through adult. Chamber

music and orchestra are emphasized, along with private instruction. Winner of the concerto competition has an opportunity to play with the festival orchestra. Gilbert Long is the tuba instructor.

Southern Illinois University Music Festival. Robert Weiss, School of Music, Southern Illinois University, Carbondale, IL 62901. USA. 618-536-7505. Offers two weeks of intensive study for junior and senior high students respectively. Robert Weiss is the tuba instructor.

Summer Conservatory Music Festival, Fort Burgwin, Ranchos de Taos, New Mexico. Summer Conservatory Music Festival, Patrick Moulds, Meadows School of the Arts, Southern Methodist University, Dallas, TX 75275. USA. 214-768-3680. Fax 214-768-3272. This three-week festival offers comprehensive study in chamber music, orchestra, and private instruction. Open to college students and post-graduates. A high school level wind ensemble program is also available. John Kitzman teaches low brass, and Everett Gilmore gives master classes on tuba.

Trobada d'Agrupacions de Metals (Festival of Brass Ensembles). Sociedad Unión Musical de Benimodo, Pz. Machi, 1, 46291 Benimodo, Valencia, Spain. 96-2530081. An annual brass ensemble festival held in August at the Auditorio San Felipe.

Vaskimusiikin Talvitapahtuma (The Winter Happening of Brass Music). Reima Jaatinen, Mannerheimintie 86 A5, Helsinki 00250, Finland. An annual event held in March.

Summer Study

Aspen Music Festival. Aspen Music School, 250 54th Street, 10th Floor East, New York, NY 10019. USA. 212-581-2196. This comprehensive music program offers chamber music and orchestral performance experience. The eight-week program is open to students and adults, with college credit available. Participants can sign up for full or half sessions. Abe Torchinsky is the tuba instructor.

Baldwin-Wallace College Summer Music Clinic. William Carlson, Director, Conservatory of Music, Baldwin-Wallace College, 275 Eastland Road, Berea, OH 44017-2088. USA. 216-826-2362. A concentrated two-week program that offers wind ensemble, orchestra, and private instruction.

Blue Lake Fine Arts Camp. Registrar, Blue Lake Fine Arts Camp, Route 2, Crystal Lake Road, Twin Lake, MI 49457. USA. 616-894-1966 or 800-221-3796. The Leonard Falcone International Euphonium/Baritone Horn Festival sponsors an annual Euphonium-Tuba Day to include master classes with guest artists, solo recitals, and massed ensemble performances. For more information write to: 5200 Parkway Ct., Bay City, MI 48706, tel. 517-684-0462.

Central Missouri State University Summer Music Camp. Neal Seipp, Department of Music, Central

Missouri State University, Warrensburg, MO 64093. USA. 816-543-4530. Held in June. Offers a variety of music performance opportunities. Charles McAdams is the tuba instructor.

Chautauqua Institute. Chautauqua School of Music, Richard Redington, P.O. Box 1098, Department IA, Chautauqua, NY 14722. USA. 716-357-6233. Open to grades nine through graduate school. From late June through mid-August. Performance opportunities are available in brass ensembles and orchestra. Toby Hanks is the tuba instructor.

Courtenay Youth Music Centre. Registrar, Courtenay Youth Music Centre, P.O. Box 3056, Courtenay, BC, V9N 5N3 Canada. 604-338-7463. A four-week program open to all students ages eight and up. Band, orchestra, and chamber music, including brass ensembles, are offered. Eugene Dowling is the tuba instructor.

Crane Youth Music. Roy Schaberg, Graduate and Continuing Education Office, Room 206, Raymond Hall, Potsdam College, Potsdam, NY 13676. USA. 315-267-2167 or 800-458-1142. A two-week program open to grades six through twelve with concentration on chamber music and orchestra. Peter Popiel is the tuba instructor and provides master classes in brass ensembles.

Curso International de Música Instrumental. Conservatorio Profesional de Música de Cuenca, Palafox, 1, 16001 Cuenca, Spain. 966-226911/12.

Disney All-American Instrumentalists Auditions. See above under "Competitions."

Dixie Band Camp. Russell Langston, University of Central Arkansas, 201 South Donaghey Ave., UCA Box 4966, Conway, AR 72032. USA. 501-450-5764. Open to students grades seven through twelve, this one-week camp in June offers opportunities in brass ensemble and band performance. Lowell Cavender is the low brass instructor.

Domaine Forget Music and Dance Academy, St. Irenée, Québec. Francoys Bernier, Le Domaine Forget De Charlevoix Inc., 398 chemin les Bains, St. Irenée, Québec, Canada. 418-452-8111 Fax 418-452-3503. An eight-week program is for serious students and adults to participate in band, chamber music, orchestra and private instruction.

Eastern Music Festival. Charles Evans, Director, Eastern Music Festival, P.O. Box 22026, Greensboro, NC 27420. USA. 919-272-9575. This internationally acclaimed summer festival offers a wide variety of professional orchestra and chamber music concerts, recitals, and educational opportunities for talented young musicians.

Eastern U.S. Music Camp at Colgate University. Thomas A. Brown, Eastern U.S. Music Camp, 7 Brook Hollow Road, Ballston Lake, NY 12019. USA. 518-877-5121. Offers the gamut of music performance opportunities. Two-week sessions for grades six through twelve from the end of June to late July. Brass ensemble recitals are given weekly. Ed Carroll is the tuba instructor.

Edinboro Band Camp for Adults. John Fleming. Institute for Research and Community Services, University of Pennsylvania 139 Meadville St., Edinboro, PA 16444. USA. 814-732-2672. A one-week camp for adult concert band musicians who play woodwind, brass, and percussion instruments. Other master classes, clinics, and ensembles are offered.

The Encore Music Camp of Pennsylvania. Nancy Sanderson Campbell, Wilkes University, Dept. of Music, Theater, and Dance, P.O. Box 111, Wilkes-Barre, PA 18766. USA. 800-945-5378/4426. A five-week camp open to grades five through twelve. Weekly recitals and concerts are given by a variety of ensembles, including bands, orchestras, and jazz and brass ensembles. Jerome Campbell is the low brass instructor.

Endless Mountains Music Camps. Joseph Murphy. Mansfield University, Butler Center, Mansfield, PA 16933. USA. 717-662-4710. This one-week camp for grades nine through twelve offers band and chamber music opportunities. Brass ensembles are formed within the camp. Stephen McEuen is the tuba instructor.

Florida State University Summer Music Camps. George Riordan, Summer Music Camps, Florida State University, School of Music R-71, Tallahassee FL 32306-2098. USA. 904-644-2508. Two sessions beginning at the end of June for grades seven through twelve. Master classes, band, chamber music, and orchestral opportunities are available. Acceptance into the Honors ChamberWinds is tuition-free.

Hartt Summer Music Youth Festival. Neal Smith, Hartt School of Music, 200 Bloomfield Ave, West Hartford, CT 06107. USA. 203-768-5020. Summer term is offered to adults and college students for credit. The Youth Music program meets for three weeks in July and is divided into junior and senior high school camps.

Hong Kong Youth Music Camp. Music Administrator, Music Office, RCB Hong Kong Government, Wanchai Tower, 12 Harbour Road, Hong Kong. 852-417-6431. Fax 852-802-8440. Participants must play Western or Chinese orchestral instruments and be under age twenty-five. Orchestral experience is an advantage. Guest artists are invited to give lectures, chamber music training, orchestral training, and workshops. The two-week program is divided into intermediate and senior levels.

Idaho State University Summer Music Camp. Alan Stanek, Idaho State University Music Dept., Box 8099, Pocatello, ID 83209. USA. 208-236-3636. A one-week camp open to grades eight through twelve. Band, chamber music, and private instruction are available. Patrick Brooks is the low brass instructor.

Idyllwild School of Music and the Arts. I.S.O.M.A.T.A. Summer Program, P.O. Box 38, Idyllwild, CA 92549. USA. 909-659-2171/365.

A six-week program open to grades seven through college. Band, chamber music, orchestra, and private instruction are available. The low brass instructor is Scott Smith.

Indiana University Summer Music Clinic. Ray Cramer, Summer Music Clinics, Indiana University, School of Music, Merrill Hall, Bloomington, IN 47405. USA. 812-855-1372. Open to grades nine through twelve, including graduating seniors, this one-week clinic offers opportunities in solo performance as well as band, jazz, and orchestral experience. Master classes are given by Indiana University faculty and graduates of I.U.

Indianhead Arts Center. Darrell Aderman, University of Wisconsin, Box 315, Shell Lake, WI 54871. USA. 715-468-2414. A one-week seminar in August geared toward advanced high school students and adults. John Tuinstra is the tuba instructor.

Instrumental Institute for 7th, 8th, and 9th Grades. Office of Extended Education, Texas Christian University, Box 32927, Fort Worth TX. 76129. USA. 800-TCU-7134. This one-week camp for grades seven through nine offers band performance and private instruction. Steve Weger is the low brass instructor and provides brass sectionals.

Interlochen Arts Camp. Interlochen Center for the Arts, Director of Admissions, P.O. Box 199, Interlochen, MI. 49643-9989. USA. 616-276-9221. This eight-week session offers a variety of musical experiences for talented students ages nine through eighteeen. Guest artists, master classes, clinics, and private applied instruction are available. David Randolph is the tuba instructor.

International Music Camp, International Peace Garden near Dunseith. John Alme, International Music Camp, 1725 11th Street S.W. Minot, ND, 58701 USA. 701-838-8472. A seven and one-half week program open to grades five through adult. Offerings include band, orchestra, jazz, and chamber music participation. Brass ensembles and master classes are available. William Winkle is the tuba instructor.

Luther College Dorian Music Camp. Katie Lawless, Luther College, Music Department, Decorah, IA 52101. USA. 319-387-1389. Two weeks of music camp for grades seven through nine and ten through twelve respectively. Fred Nyline is the low brass instructor.

Maine Summer Youth Music Junior and Senior Camps. Maine Summer Youth Music, Curvin Farnham, University of Maine, 5743 Lord Hall, Orono ME. 04469-5743. USA. 207-581-1242. Two sessions in July for grades seven through eight and nine through twelve respectively.

Mid-America Music Camp, Grand Island. Jeff James or Dan Ehly, 1402 M Street, Aurora, NE 68818. USA. 402-694-6763. This one- to two-week camp offers daily low brass classes as well as band performance opportunities for grades seven through nine. Matt Sheppard is the tuba/euphonium instructor.

Midwestern Music Camp. David Bushouse, 218 Murphy Hall, Lawrence, KS 66045. USA. 913-864-4730. Junior Division (grades six through eight) and Senior Division (grades eight through twelve). Held mid- to late June into July, with a variety of music performance opportunities. Scott Watson is the tuba instructor.

Mountaineer Music Camp. Dave Satterfield, P.O. Box 6111, Morgantown, WV 26506. USA. 304-293-5330/156. This one-week camp in July offers participation in band, orchestra, and private instruction.

National High School Music Institute. Don Owens, 711 Elgin Road, Room I Evanston, IL 60208. USA. 708-491-3141. A five-week program open to grades nine through twelve. Opportunities for band, jazz, chamber music, wind ensemble, orchestra, and private instruction. Rex Martin is the tuba instructor.

The National Orchestral Institute. Office of Summer and Special Programs, Donald Reinhold, University of Maryland, College Park, MD 20742. USA. 301-405-6540, Ext. 6548. Held at the University of Maryland, College Park campus.A full scholarship training program for advanced orchestral musicians aged eighteen through thirty held in June. Auditions are held in major cities from January to March. David Fedderly of the Baltimore Symphony is the tuba instructor.

New England Conservatory Music Day Camp, Natick. Susan Kent, New England Conservatory, 290 Huntington Avenue, Boston, MA 02115. USA. 617-262-1120/350. This four-week camp is open to students age nine through thirteen who have had at least one year of private instruction on their applied instrument. James Freemont Smith is the brass instructor.

New England Music Camp, Oakland. New England Music, Davis Wiggin, 549 I Spring Street, Manchester, CT 06040. USA. 203-646-1642.

New York State Music Camp and Institute. Steven Zvengrowski, Hartwick College, Oneonta, NY 13820. USA. 607-431-4801 or 800-388-0337. Two-, four-, and six-week sessions with performance opportunities in band, chamber music, and orchestra. Faculty from the Philadelphia Orchestra and Metropolitan Opera Orchestra provide instruction.

Northern Arizona University Summer Music Camp. Joe Lloyd, Northern Arizona University, P.O. Box 6041, Flagstaff, AZ 86011. USA. 602-523-2323. This four-week program is divided into junior (grades seven through nine) and senior (grades nine through twelve) camps. Opportunities for solo performance recitals, band, jazz, and orchestra are offered. Randy Wright is the tuba instructor.

Oklahoma Summer Arts Institute. Linda DeBerry, Oklahoma Arts Institute, P.O. Box 18154, Oklahoma City, OK 73154. USA. 405-842-0890. A two-week program for Oklahoma residents, grades 7–12. Emphasis is on orchestral performance; however, brass ensembles opportunities are available. Pat Crumpley is the tuba instructor.

Orpheus Festival for High School Musicians. Robert Larsen, Simpson College Music Department, 701 North C Street, Indianola IA. 50125. USA. 515-961-1637. A two-week camp for grades nine through twelve. Taped auditions are required for scholarship funds. Opportunities for brass quintets and ensemble performance are available. Jack Denniston is the tuba instructor.

Rafael Mendez Brass Institute. Gail Wilson, Summit Brass, Box 26850, Tempe, AZ 85285. USA. 602-496-9486. Open to anyone interested in brass instruction, repertoire, and career development. Attendance may be for one or two weeks and participants range from interested amateurs to professional performers. Held on the campus of Arizona State University, Tempe, in June.

Redlands Summer Music Camp. Irm Jennings. University of Redlands, School of Music, 1200 East Colton Ave., Redlands, CA 92373-0999. USA. 909-793-2121/3264. Loren Martsteller is the low brass instructor. Open to grades seven through twelve.

Rocky Ridge Music Center. P.O. Box 81727, Lincoln, NE 68501-1727 or 465 Longs Peak Rd., Estes Park, CO 80517. USA. 402-486-4363; 303-586-4031 after June 1. A seven-week program of intensive individual study and solo performance opportunities. Master classes, chamber music and symphony orchestra performances round out the curriculum.

Seminar. Carl Doubleday School Of Music, Western Michigan University, Kalamazoo, MI 49008-3831. USA. 616-387-4667. This two-week program offers a variety of music performance opportunities, including wind ensemble, brass quintet, and brass choir. Steve Wolfinbarger is the tuba instructor.

Shenandoah Conservatory Arts Camp for Music and Dance. David Cottrell, Shenandoah Performing Arts Camp, 1460 University Drive, Winchester, VA 22601. USA. 703-665-4598. This comprehensive program is open to grades seven through twelve. Combining music, dance, and theater, students audition for placement in band and orchestra programs. Michael Bunn is the tuba instructor.

Southeast Summer Music Camps. Barry Bernhardt, One University Plaza, Southeast Missouri State University, Cape Girardeau, MO 63701. USA. 314-651-2335. Open to grades 5–12, this camp offers various music performance opportunities at the elementary, junior, and senior high school level.

Southern Illinois University Music Festival. See above under "Festivals/Summer Study."

Texas Tech Band/Orchestra Camp. James Sudduth, Box 42033 School of Music, Texas Tech University, Lubbock, TX 79409. USA. 806-742-2225. This one-week camp offers a full spectrum of musical activities for grades six through twelve. Guest artists, clinics, brass ensemble, and private instruction are included. David Payne is the tuba instructor. Former guest artists have included Robert N. Daniel, principal tuba, The United States Air Force Concert Band.

Thousand Hills Summer Youth Music Camps. Dan Peterson, Northeast Missouri State University, Kirksville, MO 63501. USA. 816-785-4439. Open to grades six through twelve, this one- to four-week camp provides ample opportunity for brass ensemble experience, band, jazz, and private instruction.

United Musical Instruments International Solo Competition. See above under "Competitions."

University of Southern Mississippi Summer Camps. Tom Fraschillo, Director, University Bands, Southern Station Box 5032, Hattiesburg, MS 39406. USA. 601-266-4990. A one-week camp open to grades eight through twelve. Band and private instruction are available. Tom Stein is the tuba instructor.

University of Southwestern Louisiana Woodwind and Brass Chamber Music Camp. Andrea Loewy, University of Southwestern Louisiana, School of Music, Drawer 41207, Lafayette, LA 70504-1207. USA. 318-231-5214. Open to grades seven through twelve, this chamber music camp offers performance opportunities in brass quintets, choirs, and master classes.

University of West Florida Symphonic Band Camp. Dr. Grier Williams, University of West Florida, 11000 University Parkway, Pensacola, FL 32514-5751. USA. 904-474-2147. This one-week camp for students in grades seven through twelve offers band, jazz, and private instruction. Brass demonstrations and lessons are provided by Grier Williams.

Yamaha International Brass Ensemble Competition. See above under "Competitions."

Yellowstone Summer Music Camp. Neil Hansen, Northwest College, 231 W. Sixth Street, Powell, WY 82435. USA. 307-754-6307. This one-week music camp is open to grades 7–12. Band and chamber music performance are available. Low brass instruction is handled by Randy Cohlenberg, and Todd Rosenberger teaches tuba.

The editors have made every attempt to present a complete and accurate listing of publishers and composers who sell their own works. Undoubtably there are errors, as publishers (and composers) tend to move from time to time. In some instances, the last known address is given in order to provide at least a lead for locating the person or business.

A. A. Kalmus Limited. 38 Eldon Way. Paddock Wood. Tonbridge, Kent. England.

A M Percussion Publications. PO Box 436. Lancaster. NY. 14086. USA. 716-937-3705.

A R Publishing Company. Box 292. Candlewood Isle. CT. 06810. USA.

A. Squire. Out of business.

AB Carl Gehrmans Musikforlag. Box 6005. S-102 31 Stockholm. Sweden. 46 8 16 52 00. FAX: 08 31 42 44.

Abingdon Press. 201 Eighth Avenue S. Nashville. TN. 37203. USA. 615-749-6158. FAX: 615-749-6512.

Accentuate Music. 4524 14th Street W. Bradenton. FL. 34207-1428. USA.

Accolade Press. PO Box 28547. Atlanta. GA. 30358. USA.

Accura Music. Box 4260. Athens. OH. 45701-4260. USA. 614-594-3547. FAX: 614-592-1609.

Adler Musikverlag. Postfach 9. 8990 Bad Aussee. Germany.

Advance Music. Maierackerstr. 18/Induskriegebiet. D7407 Rottenburg am Neckar. Germany.

Albam, Manny. 7 Glengary Road. Croton. NJ. 10520. USA.

Albert. See: J. Albert & Son Pty, Limited.

Albian, Franco. W298N6971 Ridgeview Lane. Hartland. WI. 53029. USA. 414-538-1477.

Aldo Bruzzichelli, Eds. US Rep: Margun Music. Borgo S. Frediano 8. Florence 1-50124. Italy.

Alessi Music Studio. 15 Anchorage Court. San Rafael. CA. 94903. USA.

Alfred Publishing Company Incorporated. 16380 Roscoe Blvd. PO Box 10003. Van Nuys. CA. 91410-0003. USA. 818-891-5999. FAX: 818-893-5560.

Allaire Music Publications. 93 Gooseneck Point Road. Oceanport. NJ. 07757. USA. 908-229-6156.

Allans Publishing Pty. Limited. US Rep: E.C. Schirmer. 165 Gladstone Street. South Melbourne, Victoria. 3205. Australia. 03 696 0588. FAX: 03 696 1181.

Allen Music Limited. 8168 Benton Way. Arvada. CO. 80003-1810. USA.

Almita Music Company. See: Kendor Music, Incorporated.

Almqvist & Wiksell Publishing Limited. Box 6411. S-113 82 Stockholm. Sweden. 46 8 690 92 00. FAX: 46 8 690 93 00.

Alphonse Leduc Editions Paris. US: See Robert King Music Sales. 175 rue St. Honoré. Paris. F-75040. France.

American Composers Alliance. American Composers Edition, Incorporated. 170 W. 74 Street. New York. NY. 10023. USA. 212-362-8900.

American Composers Edition, Incorporated. See: American Composers Alliance.

American Music Center. 30 West 26th Street. Suite 1001. New York. NY. 10010-2011. USA. 212-366-5263. FAX: 212-366-5265.

AMSI. 2710 Nicollet Avenue South. Minneapolis. MN. 55408-1630. USA. 612-872-8831. FAX: 612-729-4487.

Anderson, Møgens. Peter Rordamsvej 7, 2800 Lyngby. Denmark.

Anderson's Arizona Originals. 524 E. 26th Avenue. Apache Junction. AZ. 85219. USA. 602-982-2045. 602-983-2350.

Andrieu Frères. See: Theodore Presser Company.

Anglo-American Music Publishers. 4 Kendall Avenue. Sanderstead, Surrey. CR2 0NH. England.

Anton Boehm & Sohn. Augsburg. Germany.

Anton J. Benjamin. Hamburg. Germany.

Argee Music Press. 720 Terrace Lane. Greencastle. IN. 46135. USA.

Arizona University Music Press. School of Music. University of Arizona. Tucson. AZ. 85721. USA.

Arpèges. 24 rue Etex. 75018 Paris. France.

Ars Nova. See: Theodore Presser Company.

Ars Polana. Karkowskie Przedmiexcie #7. 00-068 Warsaw. Poland.

Artia, Foreign Trade Corp. Prague. Czechoslovakia.

Arts Lab. Holt Street. Birmingham. B7 4BA. England.

Ashley Dealers Incorporated. 133 Industrial Avenue. Hasbrouck Heights. NJ. 07604. USA. 201-288-8080. FAX: 201-288-0389.

Associated Board of the Royal School of Music. US Rep: Theodore Presser Company. 14 Bedford Square. London. WCIB 3JG. England.

Associated Music Publishers. 225 Park Avenue S. New York. NY. 10003. USA. 212-254-2100. FAX: 212-254-2013.

Astoria Verlag. Berlin. Germany.

Atlanta Brass Society Press. 953 Rosedale Road NE. Atlanta. GA. 30306. USA.

Atlantic Music Supply Corp. 6124 Selma Avenue. Hollywood. CA. 90029. USA.

Atlantis Publications. 406 E. 31st Street. Baltimore. MD. 21218. USA. 410-235-4636.

Augsburg Fortress Publishers. PO Box 1209. Minneapolis. MN. 55440. USA. 612-330-3300. FAX: 612-330-3455.

Augsburg Publishing Company. 426 S. 5th Avenue. Box 1209. Minneapolis. MN. 55440-1209. USA. 800-328-4648 or 612-330-3344. FAX: 612-330-3455.

Aulos Music Publishers. PO Box 54. Montgomery. NY. 12549. USA. 914-344-3959.

Australian Music Centre. PO Box N690. Grosvenor Place. Sydney, NSW 2000. Australia.

Australian Trombone Education Magazine. c/o Canberra School of Music. PO Box 804. Canberra City Act 2601. Australia.

Autograph Editions: See: Philharmusica Corporation.

Avant Music. See: Western International Music.

Avvakoumov, Valentin. Str. Schotman 9-1-232. St. Petersburg. 193232. Russia.

Award Music Company. Oliveri Dist. Corp. PO Box 591. Oakdale. NY. 11769. USA.

Axelrod Music. 251 Weybosset Street. Providence. RI. 02903. USA.

B. Schott's Söhne Mainz. US Rep: European American Music. Weihergarten 5, Postfach 3640. D-6500 Mainz 1. Germany. 49 6131 505123, 49 6131 505115.

Baltimore Horn Club Publication. 7 Chapel Court. Lutherville. MD. 21093. USA. 410-561-9465.

Banks Music Publications. 139 Holgate Road. York. England.

Bärenreiter Verlag. Postfach 100329. D-3500 Kassel. Germany.

Barnhouse. See: C. L. Barnhouse Company.

Baron. See: M. Baron Company, Incorporated.

Barry Ed. Com e Ind. SrL. Lavalle 1145-4 A. 1048 Buenos Aires. Argentina. 1-35-7132.

Bartlesville Publishing Company. Box 265. Bartlesville. OK. 74005. USA. 918-333-1502.

Basset Hound Music. 2139 Kress Street. Los Angeles. CA. 90046. USA. 213-656-6510.

Beasley, Rule. Santa Monica College. 1815 Pearl. Santa Monica. CA. 90405. USA.

Belaieff. See: M. P. Belaieff.

Belden, George. 1211 LeLande. Anchorage. AK. 99504. USA.

Belmont Music Publishers. PO Box 231. Pacific Palisades. CA. 90272. USA. 310-454-1867. FAX: 310-573-1925.

Belwin. See: CPP/Belwin Incorporated.

Belwin Mills Incorporated. See: CPP/Belwin Incorporated.

Benedetti, Donald. Trenton State College. Trenton. NJ. 08625. USA.

Benjamin. See: Anton J. Benjamin.

Berklee Press. See: Hal Leonard.

Bernel Music LTD. PO Box 2438. Cullowhee. NC. 28723. USA. 704-293-9312. FAX: 704-293-9312.

Bewley Music Incorporated. PO Box 9328. Dayton. OH. 45409. USA. 513-253-5812.

Bizet (Editions) Belgium. 13 Rue de la Madeleine. Brussels 1. Belgium.

BKJ Publications. Box 377. Newton. MA. 02161. USA.

Blasmusikverlag Fritz Schultz GmbH. Am Marzengraben 6. W-7800 Freiburg-Tiengen. Germany. 07664 1431. 07664 5123.

Blatter, Alfred. 153 Latches Lane. Media. PA. 19063. USA.

Bliss, Marilyn. 34-40 79th Street. Apartment 5E. Jackson Heights. NY. 11372. USA.

Boccaccini & Spada Editori Rome. US Rep: Theodore Presser Company. Via Francesco Duodo 10. Rome. 1-00136. Italy.

Boehm: See: Anton Boehm & Sohn.

Bold Brass Studios. PO Box 77101. Vancouver, BC. V5R 5T4. Canada.

Bonesteel Music Company. PO Box 50862. Denton. TX. 76206. USA.

Boosey & Company. See: Boosey & Hawkes, Incorporated.

Boosey & Hawkes, Incorporated. 52 Cooper Square. New York. NY. 10003-7102. USA. 212-979-1090. FAX: 212-979-7056.

Bornemann (Editions) Paris. US Rep: Theodore Presser Company. 15 Rue de Tournon. Paris F-75006. France.

Bosse Edition. Regensburg. Germany.

Boston Music Company. 172 Tremont Street. Boston. MA. 02111. USA. 617-426-5100. 617-695-9142.

Boston Public Library. Copley Square. Boston. MA. 02117. USA.

Bosworth & Company, Limited. US Rep: Brodt Music. 14/18 Heddon Street Regent Street. London W1. England.

Bote and Bock K.G. Hardenbergstrasse 9a. D-1000 Berlin 12. Germany. 0 30 31 10 03 0. FAX: 0 30 3 12 42 81.

Bourne Company. 5 W. 37 Street. New York. NY. 10018. USA. 212-391-4300. FAX: 212-391-4306.

Bowdoin College Music Press. Bowdoin College Music Dept. Gibson Hall. Brunswick. ME. 04011. USA. 207-725-3747. FAX: 207-725-3123.

Brass Lion. Box 331. Southboro. MA. 01772. USA.

Brass Music Limited. c/o Robert King Music Sales, Incorporated. 140 Main Street. North Easton. MA. 02356. USA. FAX: 508-238-2571.

Brass Press, The. c/o Robert King Music Sales, Incorporated. 140 Main Street. North Easton. MA. 02356. USA. FAX: 508-238-2571.

Brass Wind Publications. 4 St. Mary's Road. Manton. Leicester. LE15 8SU. England. 057 285 409 210.

Brassworks. 225 Regency Court. Waukesha. WI. 53186. USA.

Breitkopf & Härtel. Walkmuhlstrasse 52. D-6200 Wiesbaden 1. Germany. 6 11 4 50 08 0. FAX: 6 11 4 50 08 59. Telex: 4 182 647.

Brelmat Music. 241 Kohlers Hill Road. Kutztown. PA. 19530-9181. USA. 215-756-6324.

Brixton Publications. 4311 Braemar Avenue. Lakeland. FL. 33813. USA. 813-646-0961.

Broad River Press. Box 50329. Columbia. SC. 29250. USA.

Brodt Music Company. PO Box 9345. 1409 East Independence Blvd. Charlotte. NC. 28299. USA. 1-800-438-4129 or 704-332-2177. FAX: 800-446-0812.

Broude Brothers Limited. 141 White Oaks Road. Williamstown. MA. 01267-2257. USA. 800-225-3197 or 413-458-8131.

BTQ Publications. Meadow View 10. Old Forge Road. Fenny Draton, Warwickshire. CV13 6BD. England.

C. F. Peters Corporation. 373 Park Avenue S. New York. NY. 10016. USA. 212-686-4147. FAX: 212-689-9412.

C. L. Barnhouse Company. PO Box 680. 250 Cowan Avenue. Oskaloosa. IA. 52577. USA. 515-673-8397. FAX: 515-673-4718.

C & R Publishing Company, Incorporated. PO Box 53513. Fayetteville. NC. 28305. USA.

Camara Music Publishers. 23 LaFond Lane. Orinda. CA. 94563. USA.

Camden House. Columbia. SC. 29201. USA.

Camphouse, Mark D. Department of Music. Radford University. Radford. VA. 24142. USA.

Canadian Music Centre. 911 Library Tower. 2500 University Drive N.W. Calgary, Alberta. T2N 1N4. Canada. 403-284-7403.

Canadian Musical Heritage Society. PO Box 262 Sta. A. Ottawa, Ontario. K1N 8V2. Canada. 613-232-3406. FAX: 613-232-3406.

Canzona Publications. 2253 Downing Street. Denver. CO. 80205. USA.

Carl Fischer Incorporated. 62 Cooper Square. New York. NY. 10003. USA. 212-777-0900. FAX: 212-477-4129.

Carlin Music Publishing Company. PO Box 2289. Oakhurst. CA. 93644. USA. 209-683-7613.

Carp Music, Incorporated. See: Theodore Presser Company.

Carpe-Diem Musikverlag Claudia Wolpper. D-97953 Konigheim. Germany.

Carus-Verlag GmbH. US Rep: Mark Foster. Wannenstr. 45 D-7000. Stuttgart 1. Germany. FAX: 700 60 20 91.

Cautious Music. PO Box 32493. Kansas City. MO. 64111.

Cavata Music Publishers. See: Theodore Presser Company.

Cazes Cuivres. Canada.

Cellar Press. 322 Swain Avenue. Bloomington. IN. 47401. USA.

Censhu, Jiro. 1-2-25-301 Terauchi. Toyonaka, Osaka 560. Japan. 06 864 2834.

Ceskeho hudebniho fondu. 110 00 Prague 1. Parizska 3. Czechoslovakia.

Chamber Brass Library. See: Mentor Music.

Chamber Music Library. 168 Serpentine Road. Tenafly. NJ. 07670. USA.

Chantry Music Press Incorporated. PO Box 1101. 32-34 N. Center Street. Springfield. OH. 45501. USA. 513-325-9992.

Chappell & Company, LTD. 50 New Bond Street. London W1. England. 71-491 2777. 71-491 0133.

Charles Colin. 315 W. 53rd Street. New York. NY. 10019. USA. 212-581-1480. FAX: 212-489-5186.

Cherry Lane Music Company, Incorporated. 10 Midland Avenue. Port Chester. NY. 10573. USA. 914-937-8601. FAX: 914-937-0614.

Chester Music Limited. London. 89 Frith Street. London. W1V 5TZ. England. 71 434-0066. FAX: 71 439-2848.

Childs, Barney. School of Music. University of Redlands. Redlands. CA. 92373. USA.

Choristers Guild. 2834 W. Kingsley Road. Garland. TX. 75041. USA. 214 271-1521.

Cimarron Music & Productions. 8585 N. Stemmons Freeway, M17. Dallas. TX. USA. 214-634-3403. FAX: 214-634-3407.

Cirone Publications. Box 612. Menlo Park. CA. 94025. USA.

Clark-Baxley Publications. PO Box 417694. Sacramento. CA. 95481. USA.

Claude Benny Press. c/o Joseph Ott. Department of Music. Emporia State University. Emporia. KS. 66801. USA. 816-931-8606.

Cleveland Chamber Music Publishers: See: Philharmusica Corporation.

Co-Op Press. Sy Brandon. RD 2 Box 150A. Wrightsville. PA. 17368. USA. 717-252-3385 or 717-872-3439.

Coburn Press. See: Theodore Presser Company.

Colding-Jorgensen, Henrik. Hjulbakvej 5, Tolstrup. 4174 Jystrup. Denmark.

Colin. See: Charles Colin.

Collected Editions Limited. 750 Ralph McGill Blvd NE. Atlanta. GA. 30312. USA. 404-525-4444. FAX: 404-525-4545.

Columbia Pictures Publications. 15800 N.W. 48th Avenue. Miami. FL. 33014. USA.

Compello, Joseph. See: Joseph Compello Publications.

Composer's Manuscript Edition. 33 Springfield Gardens. London, NW9. England.

Composers Library Editions. See: Theodore Presser Company.

Concert Music Publications: See: Columbia Pictures Publications.

Concordia Publishing House. 3558 Jefferson Avenue.

St. Louis. MO. 63118. USA. 314-664-7000. FAX: 314-664-1492

Conservatory Publications. 18 Van Wyck. Croton-on-Hudson. NY. 10520. USA.

Consort Press. Box 50413. Santa Barbara. CA. 93150. USA. 800-995-7333 or 805-969-1138.

Consortium Musical. See: Theodore Presser Company.

Constantinides, Dinos. School of Music. Louisiana State University. Baton Rouge. LA. 70803. USA.

Cor Publishing Company. 67 Bell Place. Massapequa. NY. 11758. USA.

CPP/Belwin Incorporated. 15800 NW 48 Avenue. Miami. FL. 33014. USA. 305-620-1500. FAX: 305-621-4869.

Criterion Music Corp. 6124 Selma Avenue. Hollywood. CA. 90028. USA. 213-469-2296. FAX: 213-962-5751.

Crown Music Press. 4119 N. Pittsburgh. Chicago. IL. 60634. USA.

Cumberland Press. 917 8th Avenue S. Nashville. TN. 37203. USA.

Cundy-Bettoney. See: Carl Fischer Incorporated.

Czech Music Fund. 118 00 Prague 1. Besedni 3. Czechoslovakia. 539-720.

Dako Publishers. 4225 Osage Avenue. Philadelphia. PA. 19104. USA. 215-386-7247.

Danish Brass Publishing. PO Box 49. DK-2680. Solrød Strand. Denmark. 03 14 66 44.

Danish Music Information Center. Vimmelskaftet 28. DK 1161. Copenhagen K. Denmark. 45 33 11 20 66. FAX: 45 33 32 20 16.

Dankwart, Schmidt. Seuerberger Str. 6. D-W-8196. Beuerberg/Achmule. Germany.

Dantallan Incorporated. 11 Pembroke Street. Newton. MA. 02158. USA. 617-244-7230.

David E. Smith Publications. 4826 Shabbona Road. Deckerville. MI. 48427-9988. USA. 313-376-4552. FAX: 313-376-8429.

DB Publishing Company. 64 Saint Philip Drive. Clifton. NJ. 07013. USA. 201-471-9384.

de haske muziekuitgave bv. Windas 2. 8441 RC. Heerenveen. Holland. 05139-493. 05139-515.

Delrieu & Cie. US Rep: E.C. Schirmer. Palais Belle-cour B. 14 Rue Trachel. Nice F-06000. France. 93 82 23 69. FAX: 93 82 11 00.

Deutscher Verlag für Musik. See: Breitkopf & Härtel.

DID Publishing. 123 Steinmann Avenue. Middlebury. CT. 06762. USA.

DiGiovanni, Rocco. 10907 Camarillo Street. North Hollywood. CA. 91602. USA.

Dilia. Vysehradska 288, Nove Mesto. Prague 2. Czechoslovakia. 2-966-515.

Dolmetsch Musical Instruments England. US Rep: Theodore Presser Company. 107 Blackdown Rural Inds. Haste Hill. Haslemere, Surrey. GU273AY. England.

Domek, Richard. School of Music. University of Kentucky. Lexington. KY. 40506-0022. USA. 606-257-1966.

Doms. See: Johann Doms.

Donemus Publishing House. US Rep: Theodore Presser Company. Paulus Potterstr. 14. Amsterdam. 1071 C2. Netherlands.

Dorn Publications, Incorporated. PO Box 206. Medfield. MA. 02052. USA.

Dover Publications Incorporated. 31 E. Second Street. Mineola. NY. 11501. USA. 516-294-7000. FAX: 516-742-5049.

Dramatic Publishing Company. PO Box 109. 311 Washington Street. Woodstock. IL. 60098. USA. 815-338-7170. FAX: 815-338-8981.

Dunster Music. 22 Woodcote Avenue. Wallington, Surrey. England.

Dunvagen Music Publishers Incorporated. 853 Broadway, Room 1105. New York. NY. 10003. USA. 212-979-2080. FAX: 212-473-2842.

Durand SA Editions Musicales. US Rep: Theodore Presser Company. 215 rue du Faubourg St. Honoré. Paris F-75008. France.

Dutton, Brent. Department of Music. San Diego State University. San Diego. CA. 92182. USA.

E. C. Schirmer Music Company, Incorporated. 138 Ipswich Street. Boston. MA. 02215. USA. 617-236-1935. FAX: 617- 236-0261.

Earlham Press Limited. London. US Rep: Theodore Presser Company. Fleming Road Earlstrees. Corby, Northants. NN17 2SN. England.

ECS Publishing. 138 Ipswich Street. Boston. MA. 02215. USA. 800-777-1919 or 617-236-1935. FAX: 617-236-0261.

Editio Musica Budapest. Hungary.

Editio Supraphon. Vodickova 27. 110 00. Prague 1. Czechoslovakia.

Editions Andel Uitgave. Madeliefjeslann 26. B-8400 Oostende. Belgium. 059-703222. 059-708350.

Edition Elvis. Saveltajat ja Sanoittajat Elvis. Runeberg-inkatu 15A 6. SF 00100 Helsinki. Finland. 358 0 40 79 91.

Edition Eulenburg. See: European American Music.

Edition Fazer. Lansituulentie 1A PL169. 02101 Espoo. Finland.

Edition Foetisch. 6, rue de Bourg. Lausanne. Switzerland. FAX: 41 21 311 50 11.

Edition Hans Pizka. Weidenweg, 12. D-8011 Kirchheim. Germany.

Edition Helbling. Pfaeffikerstr. 6. 8604 Volketswil-Zurich. Switzerland. FAX: 41 1 945 69 28.

Edition Helios. Kirkeveg 26B. 5690 Tommerup. Denmark.

Edition Ka We. Brederodestraat, 90. 1054 VE Amsterdam. Holland.

Edition Marbot. Hamburg. Germany.

Edition Wilhelm Hansen. US Rep: G. Schirmer. Bornholmsgade 1 1.sal. Copenhagen K. DK-1266. Denmark.

Editions Billaudot. 14 rue de l'Echiquier. 75010 Paris. France. 47 70 14 46.

Editions Bim. CH-1630 Bulle. Switzerland.

Editions Choudens. 38, rue Jean-Mermoz. Paris 75008. France.

Editions de L'Oiseau Lyre. 122, rue de Grenelle. 75007 Paris. France.

Editions Durand & Cie. See Durand SA Editions Musicales.

Editions Françaises de Musique. 12, rue Magellan. 75008 Paris. France.

Editions Henn. 8, rue de Hesse. 1211 Geneva. Switzerland.

Editions M. Combre. 24, BD Poissonière. 75009 Paris. France. 1 48 24 89 24. FAX: 1 42 46 98 82.

Editions Max Eschig. 215, rue du Faubourg St. Honoré. 75008 Paris. France. 42 89 17 13.

Editions Metropolis. Van Ertbornstr. 5. 2018, Antwerp. Belgium. 404-902-249.

Editions Musicales Brogneaux. 73 avenue Paul Janson. Brussels. Belgium.

Editions Musicus. Box 1341. Stamford. CT. 06904. USA.

Editions Ricordi. 22 Rue Chauchat. F-75009 Paris. France. 1 47 70 37 28.

Editions Rideau Rouge. 24, rue de Longchamp. Paris 16. France.

Editions Robert Martin. B. P. 502. F 71009-Macon. Germany.

Editions Salabert. US Reps: G. Schirmer and Hal Leonard. 22 Rue Chauchat. Paris. F-75009. France. 1 48 24 55 66.

Editions Selmer. 18, rue la Fontaine au Roi. 75011 Paris. France.

Edizioni Curci. Galleria del Corso 4. 20122 Milan. Italy.

Edizioni Melodi. Via Quintiliano. 40 Milano. Italy.

Edizioni Musical Bèrben. Via Redipuglia 65. 1-60100 Ancona. Italy.

Edizioni Suvini Zerboni. Via Quintilano 40. 20138 Milan. Italy.

Edward B. Marks Music Company. c/o Freddy Bienstock Enterprises. 1619 Broadway. New York. NY. 10019. USA.

Edwin Ashdown Limited. 19 Hanover Street. London W1. England.

Edwin F. Kalmus & Company. Incorporated. See: CPP Belwin, Incorporated.

Egtved ApS (Edition). US Rep: Mark Foster. Box 20. Egtved DK-6040. Denmark.

Elite Music Company. 1314 W. Mountain Avenue. Fort Collins. CO. 80521. USA.

Elizabeth Thomi-Berg Verlag. Postfach 12 68. Bahnhofstr. 94 A. D-8032 Grafelfing bei Munich. Germany. 89-85 32 79. FAX: 89-854-1857.

Elkan. See: Henri Elkan Music Publishing Company. Incorporated.

Elkan-Vogel. See: Theodore Presser Company.

Ellerby, Martin. 1, St. Hilda's Close. College Gardens. London. SW17 7UL. England.

Emberson, Steve. 1387 Ambridge Way. Ottawa, Ontario. K2C 3T3. Canada. 613-727-3595.

Emerson Edition Limited. Windmill Farm, High Street. Ampleforth, Yorkshire. YO6 4HF. England. 04393 324.

EMI Music Publishing Limited. 138-149 Charing Cross Road. London. WC2H OLD. England.

Encore Music Publishers. PO Box 786. Troy. MI. 48099-9990. USA. FAX: 313-643-6425.

Engström & Södring Musikforlag A/S. Palaegade 6. DK 1261. Copenhagen K. Denmark. 45 33 14 32 28. FAX: 45 33 14 32 37.

Ensemble Publications. c/o Lyceum Music Press. PO Box 747. Ithaca. NY. 14850-0747. USA. 800-442-5397 or 607-272-8262. FAX: 607-272-2203.

Eschig. See: Editions May Eschig.

Euromusic GmbH. Neulerchenfelder Strasse 3-7. A-1160 Vienna. Austria.

European American Music Distributors Corp. 2480 Industrial Blvd. Paoli. PA. 19301. USA. 215-648-0506. FAX: 215-889-0242.

Ewoton Musikverlag. Kirschstrasse 22. 6791 Queldersbach. Germany.

Excelsior Music Publishing Company. See: Theodore Presser Company.

F.E.C. Leuckart Germany. See: Thomi-Berg. Nibelungenstr. 48. Munich 19. D-8000. Germany.

F M I, Finnish Music Information. Runebergsgatan 15 A 6. 00100 Helsinki. Finland.

FTW Publishing. 415 Allyn St. #1, Akron, Ohio 44304. 216-569-2816. 216-434-1615.

Faber Music Incorporated. Boston. 50 Cross Street. Winchester. MA. 01890. USA. 617-756-0323. FAX: 617-729-2783.

Facsimile Editions. See: Carl Fischer Incorporated.

Faimo Edition. Gronkullavagen 2 F. S 871 60. Harnosand. Sweden. 46 611 1 07 79. FAX: 46 611 1 94 32.

Fazer Music Finland. PO Box 169. SF-02101 Espoo. Finland.

Fema Music Publications. Box 419878. 2026 Broadway. Kansas City. MO. 64141. USA. 800-258-9566 or 816-221-6688.

Fenette Music. 8, Horse & Dolphin Yard. London. W1V 7LG. England.

Fentone Publications England. US Rep: Theodore Presser Company. Fleming Road Earlstrees. Corby, Northants. NN17 2SN. England.

Fetter, David. 3413 Oakenshaw Place. Baltimore. MD. 21218. USA. 410-889-2277.

Fidelio Music Publishing Company. 39 Danbury Avenue. Westport. CT. 06880. USA. 203-227-5709. FAX: 203-227-5715.

Fiegel, E. Todd. 203 Artemos Drive. Missoula. MT. 59803. USA. 406-543-0841.

Fillmore. See: Carl Fischer Incorporated.

Fillmore Bros. See: Carl Fischer Incorporated.

Fillmore Bros. Company. See: Carl Fischer Incorporated.

Fillmore Music House. See: Carl Fischer Incorporated.

Finnish Music Information Centre. Runeberginkatu 15 A. SF-00100. Helsinki 10. Finland. 358 0-409134. FAX: 358 0-409634.

Fischer, Carl. See: Carl Fischer, Incorporated.

Fleischer Music Collection. Free Library of Philadelphia. Logan Square. Philadelphia. PA. 19103. USA.

Folklore Productions Incorporated. 1671 Appian Way. Santa Monica. CA. 90401. USA. 213-451-0767. FAX: 213-458-6005.

Foreign Music Distributors. 13 Elkay Drive. Chester. NY. 10918. USA. 914-469-5790. FAX: 914-469-5817.

Frank E. Warren Music Service. 26 Wiswall Street. West Newton. MA. 02165. USA. 617-332-5394.

Frederick Music Publications. 120 N. Charles. McPherson. KS. 67460. USA.

Fredonia Press. 3947 Fredonia Drive. Hollywood. CA. 90068. USA.

Fredrickson, Thomas. School of Music, University of Illinois. 1111 W. Nevada. Urbana. IL. 61801. USA. 210-333-2620

Friederich Hofmeister. Ubierstrasse, 20. Hofheim/Taunus. Germany.

Fritze, Gregory. 15 Falcon Road. Sharon. MA. 02067. USA. 617-784-2561.

Frost Music A/S. PO Box 38, Refstad. N 0513. Oslo 5. Norway. 147 2 11 50 73. FAX: 47 2 41 89 90.

Frost Noter. A/S P.B. 79 Ankertorget 0133. Oslo. Norway.

G. Henle USA Incorporated. St. Louis. PO Box 1753, 2446 Centerline Industrial Drive. Maryland Heights. MO. 63043. USA. 314-991-0487. FAX: 304-991-3807.

G. LeBlanc Company. 7001 Leblanc Blvd. Kenosha. WI. 53141-1415. USA.

G. Ricordi & Company. Via Berchet 2. 1-20121 Milan. Italy.

G. Ricordi & Company, Limited. See: Boosey & Hawkes.

G. Schirmer (Australia) Pty. Limited. 4th Floor, 72 Bathurst Street. Sydney N.S.W. 2000. Australia. 2 267 7433. FAX: 2 267 1328

G. Schirmer Incorporated. 225 Park Avenue S. New York. NY. 10003. USA. 914-469-2271. FAX: 914-469-7544.

G. Zanibon. Piazza dei Signori, 24. Padua. Italy.

Galaxy Music Corporation. c/o ECS Publishing. 138 Ipswich Street. Boston. MA. 02215. USA. 800-777-1919 or 617-236-1935. FAX: 617-236-0261.

Galliard Limited. Great Yarmouth. Norfolk. England.

Gamble Hinged Music Company. See: Gamble Music Company.

Gamble Music Company. 312 South Wabash. Chicago. IL. 60604. 800-621-4290.

Garland Publishing. 717 5th Avenue #2500. New York. NY. 10022-8101. USA. 212-686-7492. FAX: 212-889-9399.

Garrett, James. 5611 Forrester Ridge Road. Lyles. TN. 37098. USA.

General Music Publishing Company. See: Boston Music Company.

Georg Bauer Musikverlag. 47/49 Luisenstrasse. D-7500 Karlsruhe/Rhein. Germany.

George, Thom Ritter. Department of Music. Idaho State University. Pocatelo. ID. 83209. USA.

Georges Delrieu & Cie. Nice. France.

Gerard Billaudot. See: Theodore Presser Company.

Gia Publications. 7404 South Mason Avenue. Chicago. IL. 60638. USA. 708-496-3800. FAX: 708-496-2130.

Gipps, Ruth. Allfarthings. Hermitage Road. Kenley, Surrey. CR2 5EB. England.

Glouchester Press. c/o Heilman Music. Box 1044. Fairmont. WV. 26554. USA. 304-366-3758.

Glover, Jim. 898 Lawnsberry Drive. Orleans, Ontario. K1E IX9. Canada. 613-824-4294.

Gordon Music Company. PO Box 2250. Canoga Park. CA. 91306. USA.

Gordon V. Thompson Limited. 29 Birch Avenue. Toronto, Ontario. M4V 1E2. Canada.

Gottschalk, Arthur. Shepard School of Music. Rice University. Houston. TX. 75251-1892. USA. 713-527-4854. FAX: 713-285-5317.

Grantwood Music Press. c/o James Grant. 7001 Charles Ridge Road. Baltimore. MD. 21204. USA. 410-825-1390.

Great Works Publishing, Incorporated. 15788 Mennell Road. Grafton. OH. 44044. USA. 216-926-1100.

Green Bay Music. 26 Dolbear Street. Green Bay. Auckland 7. New Zealand. 64 09 817 3295.

Grosch-Musikverlag. Postfach 1268. Bahnhofstrasse 94A. D-8032 Grafelfing bei Munich. Germany. 89 85 32 79. FAX: 89 854 18 57.

GunMar Music, Incorporated. 167 Dudley Road. Newton Centre. MA. 02159. USA. 617-332-6398. FAX: 617-969-1079.

H.L. Grahl. Frankfurt am Main. Germany.

Haenssler Verlag. PO Box 50. Bismarckstrasse 4 . 7303 Neuhausen, Stuttgart. Germany.

Hal Leonard Publishing Corp. PO Box 13819. 7777 W. Bluemound Road. Milwaukee. WI. 53213. USA. 414-774-3630.

Hallwag Verlag. Nordring 4. 3001 Bern. Switzerland. FAX: 41 31 41 41 33.

Hamelle & Cie France. US Rep: Theodore Presser Company. 175 Rue St. Honoré. Paris. F-75040. France.

Hans Busch Musikforlag. Stubbstigen 3. Lidingo S-181 46. Sweden.

Hans Schneider. Musikantiquariat U. Musikwiss. Verlag. D 8132 Tutzing-Obb. Germany.

Harald Lyche Musikforlag. 3003 Drammen. PO Box 2171 Stromso. Oslo 1. Norway.

Hargail Music Incorporated. See: CPP Belwin, Incorporated.

Harmonia Uitgave. Nieuw-Loodsdrechtsedijk 105. Postbus 210. 1230 AE Loosdrecht. Netherlands. 02158-27595. 02158-27675.

Harold Gore Publishing Company. 314 South Elm. Denton. TX. 76201. USA. 800-772-5918.

Hartley, Walter S. 27 Lowell Place. Fredonia. NY. 14063.

Harvey Phillips Foundation. PO Box 933. Bloomington. IN. 47402. USA. 812-824-8833. FAX: 812-824-4462.

Heavy Metal Music. PO Box 954. Mundelein. IL. 60060. USA.

Heilman Music. PO Box 1044. Fairmont. WV. 26554. USA. 304-366-3758.

Heinrichshofen Verlag. Postfach 620. Liebigstrasse 16. Wilhelmshaven. Germany. 44 21 20 20 04. FAX: 44 21 20 20 07.

Helicon Music Corporation. See: European American Music Distributors Corp.

Henle. See: G. Henle USA Incorporated.

Henmar Press Incorporated. See C.F. Peters.

Henri Elkan Music Publishing Company, Incorporated. PO Box 7720, FDR Station. New York. NY. 10150. USA. 212-362-9357.

Henry Lemoine et Cie. US Rep: Theodore Presser Company. 17 Rue Pigalle. Paris. F-75009. France.

Heritage Music Press. c/o Lorenz Corporation. Box 802, 501 E. Third Street. Dayton. OH. 45401-0802. USA. 513-228-6118. FAX: 513-223-2042.

Hermann Moeck Verlag. See: European American Music. Postfach 143. D 3100 Celle. Germany.

Heugel & Cie. US Rep: Theodore Presser. 175 Rue St. Honoré. Paris. F-75040. France.

Heussenstamm, George. 5013 Lowell Avenue. La Crescenta. CA. 91214. USA.

Heuwekemeljer (Editions) Netherlands. US Rep: Theodore Presser Company. c/o Poeltuyn BV, PO Box 105. Hilversum. 2180 AC. Netherlands.

Hewitt, Harry. 345 S. 19th Street. Philadelphia. PA. 19103. USA.

Hidalgo Music. 88 Tanner Hill Road. New Preston. CT. 06777. USA. 800-497-8609.

Highland Music Company. 1344 Newport. Long Beach. CA. 90804.

Hildegard Publishing Company. Box 332. Bryn Mawr. PA. 19010. USA. 215-649-8649. FAX: 215-649-8649.

Hinrichsen Edition, Limited. See: C. F. Peters Corporation. 10-12 Baches Street. London. N1 6DN. England.

Hinshaw Music Incorporated. PO Box 470. Chapel Hill. NC. 27514. USA. 919-933-1691. FAX: 919-967-3399.

HOA Music Publishers. 756 S. 3rd Street. DeKalb. IL. 60115. USA. 815-756-9730.

Hofmeister. See: Friederich Hofmeister.

Hope Publishing Company. 380 S. Main Pl. Carol Stream. IL. 60188. USA. 708-665-3200. FAX: 708-665-2552.

Horizon Press. See TUBA Press.

Hornists' Nest, The. Box 253. Buffalo. NY. 14226-0253. USA.

Hornseth Music Company. 4318 Hamilton Street #10. Hyattsville. MD. 20781. USA.

Hoyt Editions. 706 W. Halladay. Seattle. WA. 98119. USA. 206-283-3148.

Howe, Marvin C. 5105 Bush Road. Interlochen. MI. 49643. USA.

Hug & Company Musikverlage. Fusslistrasse 4. CH-8022 Zurich. Switzerland.

Huhn/Nobile Verlag. Aixhelmer Str. 25. 7000 Stuttgart 75. Germany.

Iceland Music Information Center. 34 Sidumuli. IS-108 Reykjavik. Iceland. 354 1 683122. FAX: 354 1683124.

Impero Verlag. US Rep: Theodore Presser Company. Postfach 620. Wilhelmshaven. Germany.

Imudico Musikforlaget. Gladesaxeveg 135. 2850 Soborg. Denmark.

Indiana Music Center. 322 S. Swain. Bloomington. IN. 47401. USA.

Instrumentalist, The. 200 Northfield Road. Northfield. IL. 60093. USA.

International Music Company. 5 W. 37th Street. New York. NY. 10018. USA. 212-391-4200. FAX: 212-391-4306.

Intrada Music Group. PO Box 1240. Anderson. IN. 46015. USA.

Iowa State University Press. South State Street. Ames. IA. 50010. USA.

Israel Brass Woodwind Publications. PO Box 2811. Holon 58128. Israel.

Israel Music Institute. Box 3004. Tel-Aviv. 61030. Israel. 03 246475 .

Israeli Music Center. 73 Nordau Blvd . Tel Aviv. Israel.

Israeli Music Publications Limited. PO Box 7681. Jerusalem. Israel.

Italian Book Corporation. 1119 Shore Pkwy. Brooklyn. NY. 11214. USA. 718-236-5803.

ITC Editions Marc Reift. Case Postale 308. CH-3963 Crans-Montana. Switzerland. FAX: 011-41-27-434243.

J. Albert & Son Pty, Limited. 139 King Street. Sydney. Australia.

J. E. Agnew. See: CPP/Belwin Incorporated.

J. Maurer Editions Musicales. 7, avenue du Verseau. Woluwe St. Lambert. Brussels 1200. Belgium.

J. R. Lafleur & Son & Harry Coleman. Out of business.

Jack Spratt Music Company. c/o Plymouth Music Company, Incorporated. 170 N.E. 33rd Street. Fort Lauderdale. FL. 33334. USA.

Jalni Publications. See: Boosey & Hawkes & Company.

Jamey Aebersold. 1211 Aebersold Drive. New Albany. IN. 47150. USA. 812-945-3142. FAX: 812-949-2006.

Jasemusiikki. PKL 136. 13101 Hameenlinna 10. Finland. 358 17 532 102. FAX: 917 532 102.

Jensen Publications. See: Hal Leonard Publications.

Jerona Music Corporation. 81 Trinity Place. Hackensack. NJ. 07601.

Johann Doms. Hubertusallee 24b. D-1000, Berlin 33. Germany.

Jones, Roger. 303 Kenilworth Drive #29. Monroe. LA. 71203. USA.

Josef Weinberger. 10-16 Rathbone Street. London. W1P 2BJ. England.

Josef Weinberger Musikverlag GmbH. Neulerchenfelder Strasse 3-7. A-1160 Vienna. Austria.

Joseph Boonin. See: Jerona Music Corporation.

Joseph Compello Publications. 11132 Old Carriage Road. Glen Arm. MD. 21057. USA. 668-1806.

Joseph Wood Music Company. 148 East Main Street. Norton. MA. 02766. USA.

JPM Publishers. 64459 Dulin Creed Rd. House Springs. MO. 63051. USA. 314-285-7003.

JTL Publications. 14505 Fox Knoll Drive. Colonial Heights. VA. 23834. USA.

Jubilate Verlag. Postfach 8078. Eichstatt. Germany.

Julio Tancredi. 78 Oakwood Avenue. Providence. RI. 02909. USA.

Kallisti Music Press. 810 S. Saint Bernard Street. Philadelphia. PA. 19143. USA. 215-724-6511.

Kalmus. See: A. A. Kalmus Limited.

Karamar Publications. 255 Oser Avenue. Hauppauge. NY. 11788. USA. 516-273-7500.

Kendor Music, Incorporated. PO Box 278. Main & Grove Streets. Delevan. NY. 14042. USA. 716-492-1254. FAX: 716-492-5124.

Kibutz Movement League of Composers. 10 Dubnov Street. Tel-Aviv. Israel.

Kirklee Music. Brighouse, West Yorks. England.

Kistner & Siegel. Cologne. Germany.

KIWI Music Press. Box 1151. Groton. CT. 06340. USA. 203-536-7229.

Kjos. See: Neil A. Kjos Music Company.

Kleppinger-Pfaff Music Company. c/o Dr. Paul Dorsam, Music Dept. Box 163, Wm. Carey College. Hattiesburg. MS. 39401. USA.

Knox, Charles. 482 Page Avenue, N.E. Atlanta. GA. 30307-1730. USA.

Ko Ko Enterprises. 1515 Chickees Street. Johnson City. TN. 37601. USA.

Koff Music Company. Box 1442. Studio City. CA. 91604. USA. 213-656-2264.

KSM Publishing Company. Box 3819. Dallas. TX. 75208. USA.

L'Edition le Grand Orgue. Box 48. Syosset. NY. 11791. USA.

Lackey, Jerry. 18050 Chipstead Drive. South Bend. IN. 46637. USA. 219-277-1938.

Laissez-Faire Music. See: T.U.B.A. Press.

Larrick, Geary. 2337 Jersey Street. Stevens Point. WI. 54481. USA. 715-341-4367.

Larsen, Libby. 2205 Kenwood Avenue. Minneapolis. MN. 55405. USA.

Lawson-Gould Music Publishers Incorporated. 250 W. 57 Street, Suite 932. New York. NY. 10107. USA. 212-247-3920.

Lea Pocket Scores. PO Box 138, Audubon Station. New York. NY. 10032. USA. 212-866-4026.

LeBlanc. See: G. LeBlanc Company.

Leduc. See: Alphonse Leduc Editions Paris.

Lema Musikforlag. Vetevagen 24. S 691 48. Karlskoga. Sweden. 46 586 3 57 17.

Lemirre, Florent. 17 rue Roger Salengro. 59139 Wattignies. France. 20.95.05.81.

Lemoine. See: Henry Lemoine et Cie. France.

Les Editions Ouvrières. 12, Avenue Soeur-Roselie. Paris 13. France.

Leslie Music Supply Canada. Box 471. Oakville Ont. L6J 5A8. Canada.

Liben Music Publishers. 1191 Eversole Road. Cincinnati. OH. 45230. USA. 513-232-6920.

Lillenas Publishing Company. Box 419527. Kansas City. MO. 64141. USA. 800-877-0700. FAX: 816-753-4071.

Lindenfeld, Harris. Department of Music. Hamilton College. Clinton. NY. 03323. USA.

Lindsay Music England. 23 Hitchin Street. Biggleswade Beds. SG18 8AX. England. 767 316521 or 767 317221.

Lino Florenzo. 121 rue Barthelmy Delespaul. 59000, Lille. France.

Litolff Verlag. Frankfurt am Main. Germany.

London Pro Musica Edition. 155 Ferndale Road. London. SW4 7RR. England.

Long Island Brass Workshop. PO Box 85. Halesite. NY. 11743. USA.

Lorenz Corporation. Box 802. 501 E. Third Street. Dayton. OH. 45401-0802. USA. 513-228-6118. FAX: 513- 223-2042.

Lorge, John. 4450 48th Street. San Diego. CA. 92115. USA. 619-286-9141.

Loux Music Publishing Company. 2 Hawley Ln. PO Box 34. Hannacroix. NY. 12087-0034. USA. 518-756-2273.

Luck's Music Library Incorporated. PO Box 71397. Madison Heights. MI. 48017. USA. 810-583-1820. FAX: 810-583-1114.

Ludwig Doblinger K.G. Dorotheergasse 10. A-1010 Vienna. Austria.

Ludwig Music Publishing Company. 557 E. 140 Street. Cleveland. OH. 44110-1999. USA. 800-851-1150. 216 851-1150. FAX: 216-851-1958.

Lyceum Music Press. PO Box 747. Ithaca. NY. 14850-0747. USA. 800-442-5397 or 607-272-8262. FAX: 607-272-2203.

Lyra Music Company. 133 W. 69 Street. New York. NY. 10023. USA. 212-874-3360. FAX: 212-580-9829.

M. Baron Company, Incorporated. Box 149, South Road. Oyster Bay. NY. 11771. USA.

M. Brass Musikforlag. Sweden.

M J Q Music Incorporated. 1697 Broadway. New York. NY. 10019. USA. 212-582-6667.

M. P. Belaieff. Frankfurt. Germany.

M. Witmark and Sons. 619 West 54th St. New York. NY. USA.

Maecenas Music Ltd. 5 Bushey Close. Old Barn Lane. Kenley. Surrey. CR2 5AU. Great Britain.

Magnolia Press. 133 N. Ashland Avenue. Lexington. KY. 40502. USA. 606-266-7260.

Malama Arts Incorporated. PO Box 1761. Honolulu. HI. 96806. USA. 808-329-5828.

Malterer, Edward. Box 763. Morehead State University. Morehead. KY. 40351. USA.

Manhattan Beach Music. 1595 E. 46 Street. Brooklyn. NY. 11234. USA. 718-338-4137.

Manncy Music. 7 Glengray Road. Crofton. NY. 10520. USA.

Manny Gold Music Publisher. 895 McDonald Avenue. Brooklyn. NY. 11218. USA. 718-435-1910.

Manuscript Publications. Rt 2, Box 150A. Wrightville. PA. 17368. USA.

Mapa Mundl London. US Rep: E. C. Schirmer. 61 Torriano Avenue. London. NW5. England.

Mapleson Music Rental Library. 208 N. Broadway. Lindenhurst. NY. 11757. USA. 516-226-2244.

Margun Music, Incorporated. 167 Dudley Road. Newton Centre. MA. 02159. USA. 617-332-6398. FAX: 617-969-1079.

Mark Foster Music Company. PO Box 4012. 28 E. Springfield. Champaign. IL. 61824. USA. 217-398-2760. FAX: 217-398-2791.

Mark Herman and Ronnie Apter. 5748 W. Brooks Road. Shepherd. MI. 48883-9202. USA. 517-773-5141.

Mark Tezak. Postfach 101360. 5090 Leverkusen 1. Germany.

Marks Music. See: Edward B. Marks Music Company.

Marseg Limited. 18 Farmstead Road. Willowdale, Ontario. ML 2G2. Canada.

Masters Music Publications, Incorporated. PO Box 810157. Boca Raton. FL. 33481-0157. USA. 407-241-6169. FAX: 407-241-6347.

Max Hieber GmbH. Am Dom, Liebfauenstrasse 1. 8000 Munich 2. Germany. 22 70 45 46 47.

MCA Music Corp. 1755 Broadway, 8th Floor. New York. NY. 10019. USA. FAX: 306-172-1958.

McCoy Horn Library. 3204 West 44th Street. Minneapolis. MN. 55410. USA.

McGinnis & Marx Music Publishers. 236 W. 26 Street, No. 11-S. New York. NY. 10001-6736. USA. 212-675-1630.

McKimm, Barry. PO Box 30. Warrandyle 3113 Victoria. Australia.

Media Press. Box 250. Elwyn. PA. 19063. USA.

Medici Music Press. 5017 Veach Road. Owensboro. KY. 42303. USA. 502-684-9233.

Mel Bay Publications Incorporated. PO Box 66. #4 Industrial Drive. Pacific. MO. 63069. USA. 314-257-3970. FAX: 314-257-5062.

Mentor Music Incorporated. 13205 Indian School Road. Albuquerque. NM. 87112. USA. 505-275-8176.

Metropolitan Museum. c/o Henry Fischer. RR #1, Box 389. Sherman. CT. 06784. USA.

Mexicanas de Musica SA Ediciones Mexico. Avda Juarez 18 Despacho 206. Mexico. 06050. Mexico, D.F.

MGP. 10 Clifton Terrace. Winchester, Hants. England.

Michigan State University Press. Box 550. East Lansing. MI. 48823. USA.

Middle Branch Music. PO Box 265. East Randolph. VT. 05401. USA.

Mills Music. See: CPP/Belwin Incorporated.

Mitre Music. 680 Anniesland Road. Glasgow. G14 OXR. Scotland. 041-954-8757.

M.M. Cole Publishing Company. Out of business.

MMB Music, Incorporated. 10370 Page Industrial Blvd. St. Louis. MO. 63132. USA. 800-543-3771 or 314-427-5660. FAX: 314-426-3590.

Modern Editions. PO Box 653. Taylor. TX. 76574. USA.

Modrana. 6 Summerdale. Shotley Bridge. Consett, Company. Durham. England.

Molenaar N.V. See: Uitgave Molenaar.

Morning Star Music Publishers. 2117 59th Street. St. Louis. MO. 63110-2800. USA.

Moseler Verlag. Postfach 1661. D-3340 Wolfenbüttel. Germany. 05331 4976. 05331-43348.

MS Publications. 1045 Garfield. Oak Park. IL. 60304. USA.

Mueller, Frederick A. Music Department. Morehead State University. Morehead. KY. 40351. USA.

Muradian, Vazgen. 269 W. 72nd Street. Apt. 11A. New York. NY. 10023-2713. USA. 212-724-7452.

Music Arts Company. PO Box 327. Ripon. WI. 54971-0327. USA.

Music Box Dancer Publications Limited. Canada. US Rep: Theodore Presser Company. 2600 John Street. Markham, Ontario. L3R 2W4. Canada. 416-475-1848.

Music Express. PO Box 331. Lambertville. NJ. 08530. USA. 800-841-1432. FAX: 609-882-3182.

Music for Percussion. c/o Plymouth Music Company, Incorporated. 170 N.E. 33rd Street. Fort Lauderdale. FL. 33334. USA.

Music Graphics Press. 117 Washington Street. San Diego. CA. 92103. USA.

Music in Action. 15 Clearwater Lane. Hilton Head Island. SC. 29926. USA.

Music Sales Corp. 225 Park Avenue S. New York. NY. 10003. USA. 212-254-2100. FAX: 212-254-2013.

Music 70 Music Publishers. 170 NE 33 Street. Fort Lauderdale. FL. 33334. USA. 305-563-1844. FAX: 305-563-9006.

Music Theatre International. 545 Eighth Avenue. New York. NY. 10018. USA. 212-868-6668. FAX: 212-643-8465.

Music Treasure Publications. 620 Fort Washington Ave., No. 1-F. New York. NY. 10040. USA.

Musica Budapest (Edition). US Rep: Theodore Presser Company. Vorosmarty ter 1. Budapest. H-1051. Hungary.

Musica Islandica. Rejkjavik. Iceland.

Musica Rara. Le Traversier. Chemin de la Buire. 84170 Monteux. France.

Musical Evergreen, The. See: Philharmusica Corporation.

Musicians Publications. Box 7160. West Trenton. NJ. 08628. USA.

Musik Verlage Hans Sikorski. Hamburg. Germany.

Musikk-Huset A/S. Postboks 1459. Vika, Oslo. Norway.

Musikk-Huset Forlag. Postboks 822, Sentrum. N 0104. Oslo 1. Norway. 47 2 42 50 90. FAX: 47 2 42 55 41.

Musikverlage Hans Gerig, Drususgasse 7-11. Cologne. Germany.

Musikverlag Barbara Evans. Sybelstrasse 24. 1000 Berlin 12. Germany. 30 323 55 98. FAX: 30 323 55 98.

Musikverlag Johann Kliment KG. A-1090 Vienna. Kolingasse 15. Austria. 43 0222 34 51 47. FAX: 43 0222 310 08 27.

Musikverlag Martin Scherbacher. Just.-Kemer-Strasse 15-7450. Hechingen. Germany.

Musikverlag Robert Lienau. Postfach 450 528. Ferdinandstrasse 33. D-1000 Berlin 45. Germany. 030 7 72 5127. FAX: 030 7 73 82 30.

Musikverlag Rundel GmbH. Untere Gewendhalde 27. 7956 Rot an der Rot. Germany.

Musikverlag Stafan Reischl. A4181 Oberneukirchen 162. Germany.

Musikverlag Wilhelm Halter. Gablonzer Strasse 24. Postfach 2106 62. D-7500 Karlsruhe 21. Germany. 721 55 09 16 55 33 34. FAX: 721 56 26 74.

Muziekuitgeverij Saul B. Groen. Ferdinand Bolstraat 6. Amsterdam. Holland.

Nazarene Publishing House. c/o Lillenas Publishing Company. Box 419527. Kansas City. MO. 64141. USA. 800-877-0700. FAX: 816-753-4071.

Neil A. Kjos Music Company. PO Box 178270. 4382 Jutland Drive. San Diego. CA. 92117-0894. USA. 800-854-1592. FAX: 619-270-3507.

Neilsen, Erik. See: Middle Branch Music.

New Music West. PO Box 7434. Van Nuys. CA. 91409-7434. USA. 818-363-6913.

New Valley Music Press of Smith College. Smith College Music Dept. Sage Hall. Northampton. MA. 01063. USA. 413-585-3150. FAX: 413-585-3180.

New World Enterprises of Montrose Incorporated. 2 Marisa Court. Montrose. NY. 10548. USA. 914-737-2232. FAX: 914-737-2232.

New York Women Composers Incorporated. 114 Kelburne Avenue. North Tarrytown. NY. 10591. USA. 914-631-6444.

Nichols Music Company. 10 Oxford Street. Winchester. MA. 01890. USA.

Nick Stamon Press. 4380 Middlesex Drive. San Diego. CA. 92116. USA. 619-284-1679.

Nicolai Music. c/o Neal Corwell. PO Box 253. Clear Spring. MD. 21722. USA. 301-842-3307.

Noga Music. c/o Lyceum Music Press. PO Box 747. Ithaca. NY. 14850-0747. USA. 800-442-5397 or 607-272-8262. FAX: 607-272-2203.

Noga Music. PO Box 4025. Jerusalem. 91040. Isreal. 02 341333.

Nordiska Musikforlaget Stockholm. US Rep: G. Schirmer. Nybrogaten 3. S 114 34 Stockholm. Sweden. 46 8 679 82 40. FAX: 46 8 611 21 67.

Norman Lee Publishing Company. See: C. L Barnhouse, Company.

Norsk Musikforlag Oslo. US Rep: MMB Music. Toftesgt. 69.N-0552 Oslo. Norway. 47 2370909. FAX: 47 2356938.

Nova Music Limited. England. US Rep: E. Schirmer. Goldsmid Mews, 15a Farm Road. Hove, Sussex. BN3 1FB. England. 273-773-547.

Novello & Company. US Rep: Theodore Presser Company. Univ 3 Vestry Estate. Sevenoaks, Kent. TN14 5EL. England. 71 287 5061 or 71 287 0816.

O. Pagani & Brother Incorporated. c/o PD Mus. Headquarters. PO Box 252, Village Station. New York. NY. 10014. USA. 212-242-5322.

Obrasso Verlag AG. Baselstr. 23c. CH-4537. Wiedlisbach. Switzerland. 065 76 37 27. FAX: 065 76 26 44.

Ohio Valley Tuba Quartet Press. 1870 S. Springcrest Court. Beavercreek. OH. 45432. USA.

Ongaku No Tomo Sha Corp. US Rep: Theodore Presser Company. Kagurazaka 6-30 Shinjuku-ku. Tokyo. Japan. 3 268 6151.

Opus Music Publishers. 1315 Sherman Place. Evanston. IL. 60201. USA.

Ott, Joseph. See Claude Benny Press.

Otto Heinrich Noetzel Verlag. Liebigstrasse 16. Postfach 620. D 2940 Wilhelmshaven. Germany. 0 44 21/20 20 04.

Oxford University Press Incorporated. 200 Madison Avenue. New York. NY. 10016. USA. 212-679-7300, ext. 7164. FAX: 212- 725-2972.

Paganiniana Publications Incorporated. PO Box 427, 1 TFH Plaza. Third & Union. Neptune City. NJ. 07753. USA. 908-988-8400. FAX: 908-988-5466.

Panton. Radlicka 99. 150 00. Prague 5. Czechoslavakia.

Paolo Baratto. Rumelbachstr. 39. CH 8153 Rumlang. Switzerland.

Parga Music. 113 Magnolia Lane. Princeton. NJ. 08540. USA. 609-921-6374.

PAS Music. 2808 Jefferson Dr. Alexandria. VA. 22303. USA.

Pasquina Publishing Company. 5600 Snake Road. Oakland. CA. 94611. USA.

Paterson's Publications. Dist. by Peters Edition. 10-12 Baches Street. London. N1 6DN. England. 71 251 1638.

Paumanok Press. 974 Hardscrabble Road. Chappaqua. NY. 10514. USA.

Paxman of Covent Garden. 116 Long Acre. London. WC3E 9PA. England. 71 240 3642. 71 836 0859.

Payne, Frank Lynn. PO Box 60806. Oklahoma City. OK. 73146.

Peer International Corporation. See: Theodore Presser Company.

Peer Musikverlag GmbH. Muehlenkamp 43. Postfach 60 21 29. Hamburg 60. D-2000. Germany. 040 271 33 71. FAX: 040 270 62 59.

Peer-Southern Organization. 810 Seventh Avenue. New York. NY. 10019. USA. 212-265-3910. FAX: 212-489-2465.

Peermusic (UK) LTD. 8 Denmark Street. London. WC2 8LT. England. 71 836 4524.

Pelikan Musikverlag. Zurich. Switzerland.

Pembroke Music Company, Incorporated. 62 Cooper Square. New York, NY. 10003.

Pepper, J.W., & Son, Inc. PO Box 850. Valley Forge. PA. 19482.

Peters. See: C. F. Peters Corp.

Peters Editions Limited. 10-12 Baches Street. London. N1 6DN. England. 71 251 1638.

PF Music Company. PO Box 8625. Woodcliff Lake. NJ. 07675. USA.

Philharmusica Corporation. 234 Fifth Avenue. New York. NY. 10101. USA.

Piedmont Music Company. c/o Freddy Bienstock Enterprises. 1619 Broadway. New York. NY. 10019. USA. 212-489-8170. FAX: 212-956-3039.

Pierre Noel, Editeur. 24, boulevard Poissonière. 75009 Paris. France.

Piston Reed Stick & Bow Publisher. PO Box 107, Convent Station. Morristown. NJ. 07961-0107. USA.

Plymouth Music Company, Incorporated. 170 N.E. 33rd Street. Fort Lauderdale. FL. 33334. USA. 305-563-1844. FAX: 305-563-9006.

Polskie Wydawnictwo Muzyczne. PWM-Edition. Al. Krasinskiego 11a. 31-111 Krakow. Poland. 12 220174. FAX: 12 220174.

PolyGram International Publishing Incorporated. 1416 N. La Brea Avenue. Los Angeles. CA. 90028-7563. USA. 818-843-4046. FAX: 818-840-0409.

PP Music. PO Box 10550. Portland. ME. 04104. USA. 207-282-4604.

PRB Productions. 963 Peralta Avenue. Albany. CA. 94706-2144. USA. 510-526-0722.

Presser: See: Theodore Presser Company.

Prima Musica. 6670 Country Field. San Antonio. TX. 78240. USA.

Pro Art Publications: See: CCP/Belwin Incorporated.

Pro Musica Verlag. Leipzig. Germany.

Providence Music Press. See: Hope Publishing Company.

Przedstawicielstwo Wydawnictw Polskich. Krakowskie Przedmiescie 7. Warsaw. Poland.

Queen City Brass Publications. See: PP Music.

Quiroga (Ediciones). US Rep: Theodore Presser Company. Alcala 70. Madrid 9. Spain.

RBC Publications. PO Box 29128. San Antonio. TX. 78229. USA. 800-548-0917. FAX: 512-736-2919.

R B P Music Publishers. 2615 Waugh Drive Suite 198. Houston. TX. 77006. USA. 713-520-6039.

R G O, Orchestral Hire Library. Fuggerstr. 1, PO Box 27. W-8019 Glonn. Germany. 8093-44-93. FAX: 8093-23-19.

R. Smith and Company Limited. PO Box 367. Aylesbury. Bucks. HP22 4LJ. England. 296 682220. 296 681989.

Raphael Valerio. Box 16045. Asheville. NC. 28816. USA.

Real Musical. Ctra. Alcorcon a San Martin de Valdeiglesias km.9300. 28670 Madrid. Spain. 616 02 08. FAX: 91/616 48 17.

Rebu Music Publications. Box 504, RD 1. Wallingford. VT. 05773. USA.

Rebus Music. 10 E. 16th Street, No. 5. New York. NY. 10003. USA.

Regina Verlag. POB 6148. 6200 Wiesbaden 1. Germany.

Regus Publisher. 10 Birchwood Lane. White Bear Lake. MN. 55110. USA. 612-426-4867.

Reimers (Edition) Stockholm. US Rep: Theodore Presser Company. Box 15030, 161. Bromma 15. S-161 15. Sweden.

Richard Schauer Music Publishing. US Rep: Theodore Presser Company. 67 Belsize Lane, Hampstead. London. NW3 5AX. England.

Ricordi. See: G. Ricordi & Company.

Robbins Music. See: CPP/Belwin Incorporated.

Robert Fairfax Birch Publications. See: Theodore Presser Company.

Robert King Music Sales, Incorporated. 140 Main Street. North Easton. MA. 02356. USA. FAX: 508-238-2571.

Robert Martin Editions. US Rep: Theodore Presser Company. 106, Grande Rue de la Coupée. 71850 Charnay-lès-Macon. France. 85 34 46 81. FAX: 85 29 96 16.

Roberton Publications England. US Rep: Theodore Presser Company. The Windmill Wendover. Aylesbury, Bucks. HP22 6JJ. England.

Roder Bernd. Presse und Verlagsservice. Baumweg 6. 5206 Neunkirchen-Seelscheid. Germany.

Rodgers & Hammerstein Concert Library. 21-03 41st Avenue. 2nd Floor. New York. NY. 11101. USA. 718-786-0900. FAX: 718-361-6753.

Roger Dean Publishing Company. See: Lorenz Corporation.

Roger Rhodes Music Limited. Box 855. Radio City Station. New York. NY. 10019. USA.

Roikjer, Kjell. Kogevej 8 B. Frejerslev, 4690 Haslev. Denmark.

Rondo-Independent Music Dist. of Scandinavia. PO Box 49. Solod Strand. Denmark.

Rosehill Music Publishing Company, Limited. The Old House. 64 London End. Beaconsfield, Bucks. HP9 2JD. England. 494 674411. FAX: 494 670932.

Rottler, Werner. Schmledberg 19. 8011 Buch am Buchsberg. Germany.

Royal Danish Brass Pub. Box 49. Jersie Strandvej 5. DK-2680 Solrod Strand. Denmark. 03 14 66 44.

Rubank, Incorporated. See: Hal Leonard.

Rufer Verlag. Postfach 11 43. Hauptstrasse 23 u. 27. D-6946 Gorxheimertal. Germany. 0 362 01 29 47-0. FAX: 0 62 01 29 47-20.

Russell, Armand. University of Hawaii, Music. 2411 Dole Street. Honolulu. HI. 96822. USA.

Saga Music Press. 12550 9th Avenue NW. Seattle. WA. 98177. USA.

Salvationist Publishing & Supplies, Limited. 117-121 Judd Street. King's Cross. London. WC1H 9NN. England.

Sam Fox Music Sales. 170 NE 32nd Street. Fort Lauderdale. FL. 33334. USA.

Sam Fox Publishing Company. Incorporated. 5276 Hollister Street. Suite 251. Santa Barbara. CA. 93111. USA. 805-683-9003.

Samfundet til udgivelse af Dansk Musik. Valkendorfsgade 3. DK-1151 Copenhagen K. Denmark. 33 13 54 45. FAX: 33 93 30 44.

Sanjo Music Company. Box 7000-104. Palos Verdes. CA. 90274. USA.

Schaffner Publishing Company. 224 Penn Avenue. Westmont. NJ. 08108-1839. USA. 609-854-3760. FAX: 609-854-5584.

Scherzando Editions Musicales. 14, rue Auguste Orts. Brussels. Belgium.

Schirmer. See: E. C. Schirmer Music Company, Incorporated; G. Schirmer.

Schmidt, Dankwart. Beujerberger Str. 6, D-W-8196 Beuerberg/Achmuhle. Germany.

Schmitt Publications. Schmitt Music Centers. 110 North Fifth Street. Minneapolis. MN. 55403. USA.

Schola Cantorum. 76, rue des Saints-Peres. 75007 Paris. France.

Schott. See: B. Schott's Söhne Mainz.

Schott & Company, Limited. US Rep: European American Music. 48 Great Marlborough Street. London. W1V 2BN. England.

Schott Frères. 30, rue Saint Jean. Brussels. Belgium.

Scottish Music Information Centre. 1 Bowmont Gardens. Glasgow. G12 9LR. Scotland. 041 334 6393.

Seesaw Music Corporation Publishers. 2067 Broadway. New York. NY. 10023. USA. 212-874-1200.

Sengstack Group Limited. 180 Alexander Street. Princeton. NJ. 08540. USA. 609-497-3900. FAX: 609- 924-1618.

Shawnee Press, Incorporated. Delaware Water Gap. PA. 18327. USA. 800-962-8584 or 717-476-0550. FAX: 717- 476-5247.

Simton Musikproduktion und Verlag. Berweg 2. 8170 Bad Tolz. Germany.

Sloan, Gerald. 1735 Overcrest. Fayetteville. AR. 72703. USA. 501-443-4587.

Smith, Jason R. 2303 Ohio Avenue. Apt. 37. Cincinnati. OH. 45219. USA. 513-784-9655.

Smith Publications/Sonic Art Editions. 2617 Gwynndale Avenue. Baltimore. MD. 21207. USA. 410-298-6509.

Snoek's Muziekhandel. Hoogstraat 156. Rotterdam 3001. Holland.

Snow, David. 21 Bishop Street. New Haven. CT. 06511. USA.

Societe d'Editions Musicales Internationales. US Rep: Peer-Southern Organization. 5 Rue Lincoln. Paris. F-75008. France.

Sohgaku-Sha. Tokyo Bldg. 3F; Kami-Ochiai, Shinjuku. Tokyo 161. Japan.

Solid Brass Music Company. 71 Mt. Rainier Drive. San Rafael. CA. 94903. USA.

Sonante Publications. Box 25001, Hi Way Market PO Kitchener, Ontario. N2A 4A5. Canada.

Sonic Arts, Incorporated. Room 302. 3-3-14 Azabudai. Minato-ku pref 106. Japan.

SOS Music Services. 1817 29th Avenue E. Tuscaloosa. AL. 35405. USA.

Sound Ideas Publications. PO Box 7612. Colorado Springs. CO. 80933. USA.

Soundspells Productions. 86 Livingston Street. Rhinebeck. NY. 12572.

Southern Music Company. PO Box 329. 1100 Broadway. San Antonio. TX. 78292. USA. 512-226-8167. FAX: 512-223-4537.

Southern Music Publishing Company. (Also see Theodore Presser Company.) 1740 Broadway. New York. NY. 10019. USA.

Southern Music Publishing Company, Limited. London. US Rep: Peer-Southern Organization. 8 Denmark Street. London. WC2 BLT. England.

Spears, Jared. Box 2259. State University. AR. 72467. USA.

Spectrum Music Publishers. Box 5187. Greensboro. NC. 27435. USA.

Stadt und Universitätbibliothek. Bockenheimer Landstrasse 134-138. 6 Frankfurt am Main 1. Germany.

Stainer & Bell Limited. US Rep: Galaxy Music Corp. PO Box 110. Victoria House, 23 Gruneisen Road. London. N3 1DZ. England. 81 343 3303. FAX: 81 343 3024.

Stansfeld Music Company. 9709 Roosevelt Way NE. Seattle. WA. 98115. USA.

Stauffer Press. Box 101082. Birmingham. AL. 35210. USA. 205-951-3881.

Stegmann, Richard. 87 Wurzburg. Waldkugelweg 5a. Germany.

Step Two Musikverlag. Neulerchenfelder Strasse 3-7. A-1160 Vienna. Austria.

Stevens, John D. 1606 Baker Avenue. Madison. WI. 53705. USA. 608-233-6199.

STIM. See: Swedish Music Information Center.

Stockhausen-Verlag. c/o Ione H. Stephens. 2832 Maple Lane. Fairfax. VA. 22031. USA. 703-560-3039.

Stroud, Richard. 131 Huntoon. Eureka. CA. 95501. USA.

Studio Music Company. 77-79 Dudden Hill Lane. London. NW10 1BD. England.

Studio 224. See: CPP/Belwin Incorporated.

Summy-Birchard Publishing Company. 265 Secaucus Road. Secaucus. NJ. 07096-2037. USA. 201-348-0700.

Svarda, William. 4532 Creek View Drive. Middletown. OH. 45042. USA.

Swand Publications. 3133 W. 231 Street. North Olmsted. OH. 44070-1459. USA.

Sweden Music AB. Mariehallsvagen 35. PO Box 20504. S-161 02 Bromma. Sweden. 46 8 14 30 20. FAX: 46 8 21 53 33.

Swedish Music Information Center-STIM. Sandhamnsgatan 79. Box 27327. S-102 54 Stockholm. Sweden.

Symphony Land. 4 Rue P. Dupont. 75010 Paris. France.

TAP Music Sales. R.R. #1, Box 186. Newton. IA. 50208. USA. 800-554-7628 or 515-792-0352. FAX: 515-792-1361.

T. I. S. Publications. PO Box 669. Bloomington. IN. 47402. USA.

T R N Music Publishers. PO Box 1076. Ruidoso. NM. 88345. USA. 505-258-4325.

T.U.B.A. Journal. c/o Karen Cotton. 133 Stagecrest Drive. Raleigh. NC. 27603. USA. 919-779-5178. FAX: 919-779-5178.

Taiga Press. PO Box 81382. Fairbanks. AK. 99709. USA. 907-455-6235. FAX: 907-456-1942.

Taurus Press. 17 The Common, Troston. Bury St. Edmunds, Suffolk. England.

Tempo Music Publications. PO Box 392. Chicago. IL 60690.

Tenuto Publications. See: Theodore Presser Company.

Tezak. See: Mark Tezak.

Themes & Variations. 39 Danbury Avenue. Westport. CT. 06880. USA. 203-227-5709. FAX: 203-227-5715.

Theodore Presser Company. Presser Place. Bryn Mawr. PA. 19010. USA. 215-525-3636. FAX: 215-527-7841.

Thomi-Berg. See: Elizabeth Thomi-Berg Verlag.

Thompson Edition. 231 Plantation Road. Rock Hill. SC. 29732-9441. USA. 803-366-4446. FAX: 803-366-4446.

Thore Ehrling Musik AB. Box 21133. 10031 Stockholm. Sweden.

Tierolff Muziekcentrale. PO Box 18. Markt 90-92. 4700 AA Roosendaal. Holland. 01650 4 12 55. FAX: 01650 5 83 39.

Tillander Enterprises. 260 West End Avenue, Suite 7A. New York. NY. 10023. USA. 212-874-4892.

TMC Publications. Out of business.

Toa Music International Company. Japan.

Tokyo Bari Tuba Ensemble. c/o Toru Miura, 2-112, Shih Tamagawa Hgim. 1048-1 Nakanoshima, Kama-Ku. Kamasaki City, Kanagawa Prefecture. 214. Japan.

Touch of Brass Music Corporation. c/o Ward Music Ltd. 412 W. Hastings Street. Vancouver, BC. V6B 1L3. Canada. 604-682-5288.

Toyama, Yuzo. c/o Kaijimoto Concert Management Company, Limited. attn: Junichi Isogai. 8-6-25. Chuo-ku, Tokuo 104. Japan.

Transatlantiques (Editions Musicales). US Rep: Theodore Presser Company. 50 Rue Joseph de Maistre. Paris. F-75018. France.

Transcontinental Music Publications. 838 Fifth Avenue. New York. NY. 10021-7064. USA. 212-249-0100. FAX: 212-734-2857.

Trigram Music, Incorporated. 1888 Century Park East. Suite 1900. Century City. CA. 90067-1702. USA. 310-284-6890.

Triple Letter Brand. PO Box 396. Tenafly. NJ. 07670. USA.

Tritone Press. See: Theodore Presser Company.

Tromba Publications. 2253 Bellaire Street. Denver. CO. 80207. USA.

Trombacor Music. 240 Benson Ave. Toronto, Ontario. Canada. ON M6G 2J.

Trombone Association Publishing. See: TAP Music Sales.

TUBA Press. 3811 Ridge Road. Annandale. VA. 22003. USA. 703-256-1998.

Tuba/Euphonium Music Publications. Out of business.

Tuba Materials Center. Out of business.

Uitgave Molenaar. Postbus 19. N.V. Wormerveer. 1520AA. Holland.

Unicorn Music Company. See: Boston Music Company.

UNITUBA Press. Out of business.

Universal Edition. US Rep: European American Music. Vienna. Austria.

Universal Songs BV. US Rep: Theodore Presser Company. Oude Enghweg 24, Postbus 305. Hilversum. 1200 AH. Netherlands.

Universe Publishing. 733 E. 840 North Circle. Orem. UT. 84057. USA.

University Microfilm. 300 N. Zeeb Road. Ann Arbor. MI. 48106. USA.

University of Massachusetts Press. Box 429. Amherst. MA. 01004. USA.

University of Miami Press. See: Sam Fox Music Sales.

University of Tennessee Series. Out of business.

Vaughan, Rodger D. 226 W. Borromeo. Placentia. CA. 92670. USA.

VEB Deutscher Verlag für Musik Leipzig.

Veb Friedrich Hofmeister. Karlstrasse 10. 0-7010 Leipzig. Germany. 341 20 99 08. 341 29 51 14.

Verlag Merseberger. Buero Kassel Motzstrasse 13. 35 Kassel. Germany.

Verlag Neue Musik. Berlin. Germany.

Verlag von Paul Zschocher. Hamburg. Germany.

Viola World Publications. 14 Fenwood Road. Huntington Station. NY. 11746. USA. 516-271-4399. FAX: 516- 271-4399.

Virgo Music Publishers. 9018 Walden Road. Silver Spring. MD. 20901. USA. 301-588-0836.

Virgo Music Publishers. PO Box 1068. Knowle, Solihull. West Midlands. B94 6DT. England. 21 778 5569. 21 702 2493.

Visible Music. 276 Massachusetts Avenue, No. 411. Arlington. MA. 02174. USA. 617-641-4741.

Vivace Press. NW 310 Wawawai Road. Pullman. WA. 99163-2959. USA. 509-334-4660. FAX: 509-334-3551.

Volkwein Bros. See: CPP/Belwin Incorporated.

Vydavatelstvi Chf-Praha. 150 00 Praha 5-Smichov. Radlicka 99. Czechoslovakia. 53 41 37-8. FAX: 54 86 27.

W.W. Norton and Company, Incorporated. 500 Fifth Avenue. New York. NY. 10110. USA. 212-354-5500. FAX: 212-869-0856.

Wallan Music Company. 170 NE 33rd Street. Fort Lauderdale. FL. 33334. USA.

Wandle Music Limited. 26 Chiltern Street. London. W1M 1PH. England.

Warner Brothers Music. 265 Secaucus Road. Secaucus. NJ. 07094. USA.

Warner Chappel Music Scandinavia AB. Box 2004. S 194 02 Upplands. Vasby. Sweden. 760-880 85. FAX: 760-875 61.

Warner Chappell Musikverlag GmbH. Diefenbachgasse 35. A-1150 Vienna. Austria.

Warner/Chappell Music Incorporated. 9000 Sunset Boulevard, Penthouse. Los Angeles. CA. 90069. USA. 310-273-3323. FAX: 310-271-4843.

Warren, Frank. See: Frank E. Warren Music Service.

Watts, Charles. 1503 Sherrill Boulevard. Murfreesboro. TN. 37130. USA.

Weinberger. See: Josef Weinberger.

Weintraub Music Company. See: G. Schirmer.

Welcher, Dan. Department of Music. University of Texas. Austin. TX. 78712. USA.

Wenström-Lekare, Lennart. Ynglävagen 20. 182 62 Djursholm. Sweden.

Werle, Floyd. 504 Aldrich Lane. Springfield. VA. 22151. USA.

Wessner, John. 822 E. Joppa Road. Baltimore. MD. 21204. USA.

West Wind Music Company. 2729 S. Marshall Street. Denver. CO. 80227. USA.

Western International Music. 3707 65th Avenue. Greeley. CA. 80634-9626. USA. 303-330-6901. FAX: 303-330-7738.

Westleaf Edition. RD #2, Box 2770. Cox Brook Road. Northfield. VT. 05663. USA. 802-485-8019.

Whaling Music Publishers. PO Box 1212. New London. CT. 06320. USA.

Wilfredo Cardoso. Esmeraldo 1075. Buenos Aires 1007. Argentina.

Wilhelm Hansen Musikforlag. Gothersgade 9-11. 1123 Copenhagen K. Denmark.

Wilhelm Zimmermann. Frankfurt am Main. Germany.

William A. Pfund. 36529 Weld Cty Road #41. Eaton. CO. 80615. USA.

William Elkin Music Services. Station Road Industrial Estate. Salhouse. Norwich. NR13 6NY. England. 603 721302. FAX: 603 721801.

William Grant Still Music. 22 S. San Francisco Street, Suite 422. Flagstaff. AZ. 86001. USA. 602-526-9355.

Williams Music Publishing Company. 300 Fallen Leaf Lane. Roswell. GA. 30075. USA.

Willis Music Company. 7380 Industrial Road. Florence. KY. 41042. USA. 800-354-9799 or 606-283-2050. FAX: 606-283-1784.

Wimbledon Music Incorporated. 1888 Century Park East. Century City. CA. 90067. USA. 310-284-6890.

Wind Music Incorporated. 153 Highland Parkway. Rochester. NY. 14620. USA.

Wingert-Jones Music, Incorporated. Box 419878. 2026 Broadway. Kansas City. MO. 64141. USA. 800-258-9566 or 816-221-6688.

Winteregg, Steven L. 419 Westview Place. Englewood. OH. 45332. USA. 513-836-8593.

Wiscasset Music Publishing Company. Box 810. Cambridge. MA. 02138. USA. 617-492-5720. FAX: 617-492-4031.

Witmark. See: M. Witmark and Sons.

Wolfgang Haas Musikverlag. 5000 Koln. Germany.

Woodsum Music Limited. RFD 2, Box 244. Harrison. MA. 04040. USA. 207-583-4875.

World Library Publications. 3815 N. Willow Road. PO Box 2701. Schiller Park. IL. 60176. USA.

Yamaha Kyohan Company Limited. Koshin Building 3F. 6-12-13 Ginza Chuo-ku. Tokyo pref. 104. Japan.

Yamaha Music Foundation. 3-24-22 Shimo-meguro-ku. Tokyo pref. 153. Japan.

Yarra Yarra Music Services.

Ybarra Music. PO Box 665. Lemon Grove. CA. 91946. USA.

Zanibon. See: G. Zanibon.

Zonn, Paul Martin. 122 Bay View Drive. Hendersonville. TN. 37075. USA. 615-264-6392.

Zurfluh. 73 Boulevard Raspail. 75006 Paris. France. 45 48 68 60. FAX: 42 22 21 15.

INDEX